The Mammoth Encyclopedia of
MODERN CRIME FICTION

Also available

The Mammoth Book of Awesome Comic Fantasy
The Mammoth Book of Best New Erotica
The Mammoth Book of Best New Horror 2000
The Mammoth Book of Best New Science Fiction 14
The Mammoth Book of Bridge
The Mammoth Book of British Kings & Queens
The Mammoth Book of Chess
The Mammoth Book of Comic Fantasy
The Mammoth Book of Endurance and Adventure
The Mammoth Book of Erotica (New Edition)
The Mammoth Book of Erotic Photography
The Mammoth Book of Fantasy
The Mammoth Book of Gay Erotica
The Mammoth Book of Great Detective Stories
The Mammoth Book of Gay Short Stories
The Mammoth Book of Haunted House Stories
The Mammoth Book of Hearts of Oak
The Mammoth Book of Historical Erotica
The Mammoth Book of Historical Whodunnits
The Mammoth Book of How It Happened
The Mammoth Book of How It Happened in Britain
The Mammoth Book of International Erotica
The Mammoth Book of Jack the Ripper
The Mammoth Book of Jokes
The Mammoth Book of Legal Thrillers
The Mammoth Book of Lesbian Erotica
The Mammoth Book of Lesbian Short Stories
The Mammoth Book of Life Before the Mast
The Mammoth Book of Locked-Room Mysteries and Impossible Crimes
The Mammoth Book of Men O'War
The Mammoth Book of Murder
The Mammoth Book of Murder and Science
The Mammoth Book of New Erotica
The Mammoth Book of New Sherlock Holmes Adventures
The Mammoth Book of Private Lives
The Mammoth Book of Pulp Action
The Mammoth Book of Puzzles
The Mammoth Book of SAS & Elite Forces
The Mammoth Book of Seriously Comic Fantasy
The Mammoth Book of Sex, Drugs & Rock 'n' Roll
The Mammoth Book of Short Erotic Novels
The Mammoth Book of Soldiers at War
The Mammoth Book of Sword & Honour
The Mammoth Book of the Edge
The Mammoth Book of The West
The Mammoth Book of True Crime (New Edition)
The Mammoth Book of True War Stories
The Mammoth Book of UFOs
The Mammoth Book of Unsolved Crimes
The Mammoth Book of Vampire Stories by Women
The Mammoth Book of War Correspondents
The Mammoth Book of Women Who Kill
The Mammoth Book of the World's Greatest Chess Games
The Mammoth Encyclopedia of Science Fiction
The Mammoth Encyclopedia of Unsolved Mysteries

The Mammoth Encyclopedia of
MODERN CRIME FICTION

Compiled by
Mike Ashley

ROBINSON
London

Constable & Robinson Ltd
3 The Lanchesters
162 Fulham Palace Road
London W6 9ER
www.constablerobinson.com

First published in the UK by Robinson,
an imprint of Constable & Robinson Ltd, 2002

A copy of the British Library Cataloguing in Publication Data is available from the British Library.

ISBN 1–84119–287–2

Printed and bound in the EU

10 9 8 7 6 5 4 3 2 1

To Sue

For her love, patience and fortitude.

It's a mystery how she puts up with me

and it's a crime when my writing keeps us apart.

Contents

Acknowledgments

Undertaking a project of this size can be a daunting and lonely task and I am therefore grateful to all those who have helped me through the process. I must first thank my editor at Constable and Robinson, Krystyna Green, for her guidance, advice and remarkable patience. I must also thank all of the many authors whom I contacted to ensure the accuracy of their entry and pestering them for "final facts". I am also grateful to so many more for providing such useful websites of their work without which I would have had to pester them even more. I must thank both Martin Edwards and Mike Ripley for their advice on authors and entries; Stephen Holland, whom I would frequently pester at a moment's notice to double check pseudonym and bibliographical data; and Dennis Lien who searched through on-line catalogues looking for obscure citations. A huge thank you goes to Allen J. Hubin, whose *Crime Fiction III* was my main source for bibliographical data and who always responded promptly to my queries. My thanks also to all of those who helped me with translations of non-English titles and helped me identify non-English award winners. These include William Adamson, René Beaulieu, Pierre-Paul Durastanti, Anders Hammarqvist and Takashi Amano. Also thanks to Hugh Lamb, not only a master proofreader but a fund of information. To these and all the others who found themselves on the other end of a letter, phone call or e-mail at a moment's notice, my sincere thanks. At the end of the day, however, any mistakes or omissions are all down to me.

Preface

This encyclopedia has been compiled for you, the reader, who enjoys crime fiction and wants to know more about the field, especially your favourite writers, books, detectives, films and TV series.

If you're anything like me then you want to know the ins and outs of crime fiction. So, without going into too much detail, this book provides a wide range of information about authors, series and their characters, different types of crime fiction (from cozies to noir), films, TV, magazines, awards and what's on the Web.

Crime fiction, as a genre, generally outsells every other field. Hardly a week goes past without some new crime drama on TV, a new blockbuster film, or the latest bestseller from a major writer. There are more people actively writing crime fiction today than there has ever been.

Even limiting it to "modern" crime fiction – and I explain what I mean by that in the introduction – there are still two or three times as many authors that I could have included, and this book already covers nearly 500 and close to 10,000 books. It also covers over 300 films and TV series, and I could easily have covered twice that many. So there will be some entries missing, but I think you'll find that most of the people and films you'd expect are included. I've tried to cover as much variety as possible and have selected authors and films as much for their originality and creativity as for their popularity and influence.

This book concentrates on *crime* fiction. So, if the books are about the breaking and enforcement of the law, that's crime fiction, and the chances are it's here. I have not looked at authors whose primary output is espionage or spy fiction as that is large enough to constitute a field in its own right, though certainly if those authors also produced a considerable amount of straight crime fiction then they are included. Likewise I have not covered books where the crime or the detection involve the supernatural, so psychic detectives are out. There are also those nebulous categories so beloved of publishers or film-makers called the "thriller" or "suspense" or "mystery". These describe the mood of the story, not its content, so whilst some crime fiction may also be classified as a thriller, not all thrillers are crime fiction. The same applies to mystery, suspense or horror fiction. All of these may feature a crime, but not necessarily. For example, a fine mixture of suspense, mystery and thriller can be achieved in a story of coded messages and a hunt for lost treasure, but it's not crime fiction. But if someone is murdered during the quest, or if the treasure is found and then stolen ... then we're into home territory.

Hopefully reading an entry on your favourite author will lead you to discover others, or alert you to films based on their books. If an author mentioned in one entry has an entry of their own then their surname appears in SMALL CAPITALS. Every author entry has a "similar stuff" signpost at the end to point you to other writers whose works you may like.

Crime fiction is a huge field and hopefully this book will help you find your way about and provide further enjoyment and appreciation of your favourite authors and films.

Mike Ashley
February 2002

Introduction

A Guide to Modern Crime Fiction

What is it?

When designing this book it was evident that the field of crime fiction is too huge to try and cover sufficiently in just one volume. There have been other encyclopedias and reference books over the years (many are listed in the bibliography at the back of this book) but all too many of these concentrate on the well-known authors of yesteryear and give little if any coverage to present-day writers. It was decided therefore that the field had to be sub-divided.

In the simplest terms the phrase "modern crime fiction" means anything produced since the Second World War. However, anyone acquainted with the field knows that it is not quite that simple. In Britain, the War certainly affected the way that authors perceived their characters and events, but for many years (and still today for that matter) there were those writers who still enjoyed producing the traditional detective story as published before the War, from the Golden Age of crime and mystery. Crime fiction, particularly in Britain, took a while to change and adapt and it was not really until the sixties that "modern" crime fiction could be said to have arrived.

The lead, inevitably, was established in America, even before the War. Writers such as Carroll John Daly, Dashiell Hammett, James M. Cain and Raymond Chandler rebelled against the traditional British form of fiction (the most common form of which is dubbed the "cozy" or "country house" murder), which had no relevance in the years of the Depression and the rise of gangsterism in American cities. These writers preferred to tell it like it was on the streets – the "mean streets" as they became known – and wrote a more hard-edged, violent, realistic form of fiction which became dubbed "hard-boiled". The hard-boiled school was applied almost wholly at the outset to the private detective field. The private detective or private eye (P.I.) was usually a loner and, after Chandler, something of a knight errant, and steadily became the modern day representative of the wild-west lawman or gunman striving to keep order in a generally lawless world. This is what made the P.I. peculiarly American and continues so to this day, with the real template established after the War by Ross Macdonald with his champion of the underdog, Lew Archer. At the other extreme were the works of Mickey Spillane, whose crime fighter Mike Hammer had no compunction when it came to killing thugs and villains and operating like a vigilante.

Hard-boiled fiction was not suited to the British milieu of the thirties or even forties, and though many British writers wrote in imitation of the Americans, most notably Peter Cheyney and James Hadley Chase, their works remained the exception. Novels about gangsters in Britain were avoided by "respectable" publishers and it was not until the growth in realistic fiction from the "angry young men" of the late fifties, such as John Osborne and Alan Sillitoe, that some publishers dipped their toe in the water. Even then Britain was cautious and it was not until 1970 that the real sea change came with *Jack's Return Home* by Ted Lewis, better known by its film title, *Get Carter*. This was the first book to accurately portray gang life in Britain.

In short true "modern" crime fiction is a more realistic treatment of crime, recognizing the real roots of crime in society and the human factors involved, both on the side of the criminal and the law enforcer. G.F. Newman admirably told the story of his corrupt policeman Terry Sneed in *Sir, You Bastard*, also published in 1970. The true "modern" crime story is less a puzzle and more a social drama, edging closer to the main-stream of fiction.

However, to focus purely on "modern" crime fiction by that definition alone would exclude a large amount of other crime fiction being produced today. The "cozy" form of traditional crime fiction is still with us in strength and highly popular and it has been amplified by the humorous crime story which can range from the caper novels of Donald E. Westlake to the outright farce of Douglas Lindsay or Peter Guttridge. The police detective series is arguably more popular than ever with TV favourites such as Inspectors Morse, Frost, Dalziel and Pascoe or Taggart and there has also been a growth in the popularity of the police procedural novel. Since the advent of Ellis Peters's Brother Cadfael, the historical mystery has become a ripe area for plunder. Forensic science has brought with it new detectives like Patricia Cornwell's Kay Scarpetta or TV's Samantha Ryan in *Secret Witness*. TV's *Cracker* showed us the psychological profiler and these now feature heavily in novels, such as Jonathan Kellerman's Alex Delaware or Val McDermid's Tony Hill. Let us also not forget that true crime and murder is violent and at the real core of modern crime fiction is the study of crime in the raw, such as in the works of James Crumley, James Ellroy, Victor Headley or Mark Timlin. And the consequence of crime will affect us all and lead to completely altered lives, depression and that bleak world of "noir", so effectively portrayed in the works of Jim Thompson, James Lee Burke or Charles Willeford.

Women have always been major writers in crime fiction, and have often paved the way. Just as Agatha Christie was the queen of crime fiction for most of her long career, with close claimants Dorothy L. Sayers, Margery Allingham and Ngaio Marsh, so today we have P.D. James and Ruth Rendell with such new claimants to the throne as Minette Walters or Mary Higgins Clark. Likewise Sue Grafton and Sara Paretsky were amongst the prime movers in the growth of the female P.I. Janet Evanovich and Sparkle Hayter have shown how to inject humour into crime. Lynda La Plante revolutionized the portrayal of crime and women detectives on TV, and writers like Stella Duffy, Jan Burke, Karen Kijewski and Liza Cody show that they pull no punches in portraying the dark and violent criminal world.

All of this means that in becoming "modern", crime fiction has grown and evolved and matured and mutated. It is now a multi-headed beast. It is no longer simply stories of detectives nabbing villains. Indeed Russell James would call those "anti-crime" stories and true crime fiction is about the lives of criminals. Stories told from the viewpoint of psychotics had also grown out of the hard-boiled school particularly in the hands of Jim Thompson. This took a major step forwards with *Psycho* by Robert Bloch which, when transferred to screen by Alfred Hitchcock in 1960, was another revolution in the portrayal of criminals, which we are still seeing in the works of Bret Easton Ellis and Thomas Harris.

As a consequence defining the entries in this encyclopedia has not been simple. As a general rule of thumb authors are included only if their major contributions to the field have been since 1960. Some exceptions are made for authors who either had a profound influence in the fifties in establishing the roots of modern crime fiction, such as Stanley Ellin or Ed McBain, or for writers, like Michael Gilbert or Michael Underwood, whose careers are so long and so productive that they have created work of merit ever since the immediate post-war years. The emphasis has always been placed on work that has moved the field forwards, but I have tried not to ignore enjoyable writing along the way, no matter how traditional.

In order to provide a guide to all of the facets of modern crime fiction the following section is broken down by key themes. For each theme there is a brief history and list of authors covered in this volume who contributed to that theme. That should set you up for your tour of the encyclopedia.

Private eyes

You won't go far in crime fiction without stumbling over a private detective, and it seems the best place to start. Strictly speaking a true private eye should hold a licence and the following covers only those who hold a licence (or come pretty close!). They're called by lots of names, from the more respectable private investigator to private dick or the colloquial "gumshoe", so-called because of the soft-soled stealthy shoes they wear.

The most famous early private detective was, of course, Conan Doyle's Sherlock Holmes and he spawned a hundred imitators in the Classic Age of crime fiction, such as Arthur Morrison's Martin Hewitt and R. Austin Freeman's Dr John Thorndyke. Into the Golden Age and private detectives dominate the scene not only in Britain – Agatha Christie's Hercule Poirot, Dorothy Sayers's Lord Peter Wimsey, John Rhode's Dr Lancelot Priestley – but in America, where Rex Stout's Nero Wolfe was also in the traditional mould. The new breed of private detective, better known as private eyes or P.I.s in the States, emerged from the pulp magazine as "hard-boiled dicks". These include Carroll John Daly's Race Williams, Dashiell Hammett's Continental Op and Sam Spade and Raymond Chandler's legendary Philip Marlowe. Chandler remains the most influential – in fact in American crime fiction he's even more influential than Doyle or Christie. He established the P.I. as the loner, the knight errant, the gumshoe with a soul! Most P.I.s created since Chandler, like Brett Halliday's Mike Shayne or Ross Macdonald's Lew Archer, model themselves on Marlowe and his world. Only a few follow the Daly route, the most obvious being Mickey Spillane with Mike Hammer. The odd one out that doesn't really fit any model is Richard S. Prather's Shell Scott who acts more like some of the commercialized TV P.I.s and is perhaps the precursor for *Magnum*.

Chandler's most influential disciple who firmly established the post-war P.I. was Ross Macdonald with Lew Archer. Archer has a conscience and is determined to root out the truth, especially in the world of corporate crime where the individual is the victim. Archer also explores the psychological and social aspects of crime. It was Macdonald, through Archer, who took the hard edge off the hard-boiled P.I. and put him into a modern social context, closer to the literary mainstream. His influence has been profound and not just on male writers. Sara Paretsky owes much to Macdonald in her creation V.I. Warshawski.

Since Macdonald the P.I. field has proliferated. Although the fifties in the US still saw many P.I.s in the pulp mode – like Ed McBain's Curt Cannon or Dan Marlowe's Johnny Killain – a more sophisticated P.I. started to emerge, both in films and TV and in books. On the Chandler side is Robert Parker's Spenser, whilst on the darker side is Lawrence Block's Mat Scudder. These are at the pinnacle of modern-day P.I. novels, with Bill Pronzini's Nameless Detective and Michael Collins's Dan Fortune in close pursuit. Some writers, especially Max Allan Collins and Stuart Kaminsky have chosen to set their P.I.s in the thirties and forties recapturing the spirit of the past but with the vantage of the present.

The first post-feminist female P.I. (if we side-step Honey West – see under *Burke's Law* for details) emerged in Britain, not the US and was Cordelia Gray, created by P.D. James in 1972. She was soon followed in the US by Maxine O'Callaghan's Delilah West in 1974 and Marcia Muller's Sharon McCone in 1977. They paved the way for the two best known female P.I.s, Sara Paretsky's V.I. Warshawski and Sue Grafton's Kinsey Millhone, who appeared within months of each other in 1982.

Some critics maintain that P.I. novels are unrealistic and that they do not reflect the true world of the private detective. Some writers are or have been P.I.s and have used their experiences in their fiction. These include Joe Gores, Parnell Hall, Jerry Kennealy, Nancy Baker Jacobs, Julie Smith and Don Winslow.

The following lists all those authors who have entries in this encyclopedia and where an important part of their work includes P.I.s. The majority, not surprisingly, are US. I've listed the non-US separately.

US: Michael Allegretto, Michael Avallone, Linda Barnes, Richard Barre, Larry Beinhart, Lawrence Block, Robert Campbell, Thomas Chastain, Carol Higgins Clark, Max Allan Collins, Michael Collins, K.C. Constantine, Bruce Cook, Robert Crais, Bill Crider, James Crumley, Janet Dawson, Stephen Dobyns, Stanley Ellin, Earl W. Emerson, Loren D. Estleman, Joe Gores, Sue Grafton, Stephen Greenleaf, Parnell Hall, Steve Hamilton, Gar Anthony Haywood, Jeremiah Healy, Robert Irvine, Nancy Baker Jacobs, Jerry Kennealy, Karen Kijewski, Dennis Lehane, Michael Z. Lewin, Dick Lochte, John Lutz, Arthur Lyons, Ed McBain, Taylor McCafferty, John D. MacDonald, Ross Macdonald, Dan Marlowe, Martin Meyers, Walter Mosley, Marcia Muller, Warren Murphy, Reggie Nadelson, Maxine O'Callaghan, Sara Paretsky, Robert B. Parker, George Pelecanos, Richard S. Prather, Bill Pronzini, Robert J. Randisi, Sam Reaves, Rick Riordan, Gillian Roberts, Les Roberts, S.J. Rozan, James Sallis, Walter Satterthwait, Benjamin Schutz, Sandra Scoppettone, Roger L. Simon, Julie Smith, Walter Sorrells, Mickey Spillane, Ernest Tidyman, Jonathan Valin, Mary Wings, Don Winslow, Steven Womack, Eve Zaremba, Sharon Zukowski.

Non-US: Jakob Arjouni, Liza Cody, Peter Corris, Philip Daniels (but set in US), Marele Day, Stella Duffy, Sarah Dunant, Howard Engel, Dick Francis, Lesley Grant-Adamson, P.D. James, Dan Kavanagh, Lynda La Plante (but set in US), Val McDermid, James Mitchell, Manuel Vázquez Montalbán, Roger Ormerod, Gillian Slovo, Mark Timlin, Miles Tripp, Gordon M. Williams, Robert Wilson.

The Police Detective

The police detective was where real "modern" crime fiction began – modern, that is, to the middle of the 19th century. Most of the crime fiction published then, especially that appearing in the notorious "penny dreadfuls", were taken straight from the pages of the *Police Gazette*. Both Dickens and Wilkie Collins introduced police detectives in their novels

Bleak House and *The Moonstone*, whilst in France Émil Gaboriau's Monsieur Lecoq was all the rage. However, by the end of the 19th century the police detective gave way to the private and the police force were frequently shown to be amateurish in the light of the brilliant minds of Holmes, Poirot or S.F.X. Van Dusen, "the Thinking Machine". Only A.E.W. Mason's Inspector Hanaud of the Paris Sûreté had any significant standing and it was again in France that the investigations of Simenon's Jules Maigret emerged in the thirties followed in England by Ngaio Marsh's Roderick Alleyn. The police inspector became a major part of crime fiction thereafter in Britain and Europe, especially in the 1940s and 1950s, whereas in the US the private eye predominated. Lawrence Treat is generally recognized as the first to introduce the police procedural novel in America with *V as in Victim* (1945), which introduced his police detective Mitch Taylor. Soon after Hillary Waugh's *Last Seen Wearing* (1952) took the police procedural out of the city and into small-town America. By then the 1948 film *The Naked City* and Jack Webb's radio series, *Dragnet*, were popularizing the realism of the police procedural and when it transferred to TV in 1952 the police procedural became the vogue. In 1956 Ed McBain began his long running 87th Precinct series which placed the police procedural firmly on the map.

The police procedural is really a specific sub-set of the police detective novel. Strictly speaking it is an ensemble piece which brings in all of the skills and demands at a local police station or precinct rather than focusing on any one detective. In Britain the best examples will be found in the work of Jonathan Ross and John Wainwright. TV series such as Britain's *The Bill* and US's *N.Y.P.D. Blue* are sound examples. This is distinct from those novels where the police detective is a loner and acts more like a private detective. You hardly ever see P.D. James' Adam Dalgliesh in a police station and he seldom has a partner. Michael Connelly's Harry Bosch is an extreme loner. This allows scope for the development of the maverick cop who frequently breaks procedures even if he stays narrowly within the law in order to achieve justice. Clint Eastwood's portrayal of Harry Callahan in *Dirty Harry* is a prime example.

There was a danger, especially in British fiction, that the police detective remained rooted in tradition, becoming a dinosaur of the forties or fifties rather like the TV *Dixon of Dock Green*. It took such bombastic characters as Inspector Barlow in *Z-Cars* to rattle the cage, and during the sixties and early seventies the change gathered pace. Some may say it went too far. G.F. Newman's corrupt cop, Terry Sneed, in *Sir, You Bastard* (1970), was probably more realistic than most wanted to accept at that time.

There are, inevitably and most welcomingly, police detectives who do not fit into any category. There are the outright parodies, of which Peter Sellers's creation of Inspector Clouseau in Blake Edwards's *The Pink*

Panther (1964) is the most extreme. Anyone who likes that will enjoy Peter Dickinson's Inspector Pibble or Colin Watson's Flaxborough series.

As with P.I.s, women had to fight to make their presence known. One of the first women writers of police procedurals was Elizabeth Linington, though she had to write under various male pseudonyms. Long before Jane Tennison struggled to maintain respect and authority in Lynda La Plante's *Prime Suspect* (1991) or even before Maggie Forbes established herself in *The Gentle Touch* (1980), Gwendoline Butler (writing as Jennie Melville) created the first senior woman police officer in the character of Charmian Daniels in *Come Home and Be Killed* (1962). Dorothy Uhnak, herself a former policewoman, revealed the scale of prejudice in the force in *The Bait* in 1968. The first TV female police officer was D.S. Vicky Hicks in *Fraud Squad* in 1969 whilst in the States it was *Amy Prentiss* (1974). Lillian O'Donnell's Norah Mulcahaney series, which began with *The Phone Calls* (1972), is the longest-running police procedural series featuring a woman officer. It was not till Eleanor Taylor Bland created Marti MacAlister in *Dead Time* (1992) that a black woman police officer appeared as a lead in a series.

The following lists the key authors of police detective or police procedural novels. This time it is the reverse of the P.I., with the majority of novels being non-US.

UK: Jane Adams, Catherine Aird, James Anderson, Robert Barnard, M.C. Beaton, Pauline Bell, Jo Bannister, W.J. Burley, Roger Busby, Gwendoline Butler, Douglas Clark, Clare Curzon, Colin Dexter, Michael Dibdin (set in Italy), Peter Dickinson, Kate Ellis, Anthea Fraser, Nicolas Freeling, Michael Gilbert, B.M. Gill, Caroline Graham, Bill Granger, Christine Green, John Harvey, S.T. Haymon, Mark Hebden (set in France), Reginald Hill, John Buxton Hilton, Bill James, P.D. James, Quintin Jardine, Roderic Jeffries, H.R.F. Keating, Michael Kenyon, Bill Knox, Lynda La Plante, Peter Lovesey, Jill McGown, William McIlvanney, Sarah J. Mason, James Melville (set in Japan), Kay Mitchell, Patricia Moyes, Magdalen Nabb (set in Italy), G.F. Newman, Emma Page, Ellis Peters, Sheila Radley, Ian Rankin, Derek Raymond, Ruth Rendell, Nicholas Rhea, Jonathan Ross, David Serafin (set in Spain), Dorothy Simpson, June Thomson, Peter Turnbull, John Wainwright, David Williams, R.D. Wingfield.

US: Thomas Adcock, Doug Allyn, George Baxt, William Bayer, Paul Bishop, Eleanor Taylor Bland, Rex Burns, Jerome Charyn, Michael Connelly, K.C. Constantine, Thomas H. Cook, Deborah Crombie (set in UK), Barbara D'Amato, Jeffrey Deaver, Susan Dunlap, Katherine V. Forrest, Elizabeth George (set in UK), Bartholomew Gill (set in Eire), Leslie Glass, Paula Gosling, Martha Grimes (set in UK), Tony Hillerman, Chester Himes, Eugene Izzi, Michael Jahn, Stuart

Kaminsky, Faye Kellerman, Laurie R. King, Donna Leon (set in Italy), Elizabeth Linington, Ed McBain, Michael Malone, Margaret Maron, Carol O'Connell, Lillian O'Donnell, James Patterson, Richard Martin Stern, Dorothy Uhnak, Marilyn Wallace, Joseph Wambaugh, Teri White, Collin Wilcox, Charles Willeford.

Other: A.C. Baantjer, John Brady, Jon Cleary, John Connolly (set in US), Laurence Gough, Batya Gur, James McClure, Donald MacKenzie, Barry Maitland, William Marshall, Peter Robinson (set in UK), Jennifer Rowe, Carsten Stroud, Paul Thomas, Janwillem van de Wetering, Per Wahlöö, Timothy Williams, Eric Wright, L.R. Wright.

The Other Professionals

The third big category of detective is usually referred to as the "amateur", but that's not strictly true. Right from the earliest days of crime fiction there has been a category of other professionals who are heavily involved in detection. The most common was the medical sleuth – the doctor. Holmes' one fixed point, Dr Watson, immediately springs to mind as well as Dr John Thorndyke. Today the field has become more specialized and the doctor has given way to the forensic pathologist. This is a rapidly growing category, with Patricia Cornwell's Kay Scarpetta in the vanguard. The territory has been well mined for television, starting with *The Expert* as far back as 1968 and including the US series *Quincy, M.E.* and the British *Silent Witness*. There is also the medical sleuth Dr Mark Sloane in *Diagnosis: Murder*.

Alongside the pathologist is the forensic anthropologist, when bones are discovered at archaeological sites, and forensic archaeology is another growing specialism in crime fiction. Readers interested in both forensic pathology and forensic anthropology or medical research may want to check out the following authors:

Douglas Clark, Beverly Connor, Patricia Cornwell, Clare Curzon, Susan Dunlap, Aaron J. Elkins, Ridley Pearson, Kathy Reichs.

When not considering the body, the detective has to consider the mind, and what makes the criminal "tick". The world of the criminal psychologist and profiler has grown rapidly in the last twenty years. Caleb Carr's *The Alienist* explored its origins in the 1890s, whilst Jody Shields' *The Fig Eater* (2001), set in 1901, uses Sigmund Freud's recently published principles in a murder case. In addition to the books based on the TV series *Cracker*, are some by the following:

Caleb Carr, Patricia Cornwell, Ed Gorman, Jonathan Kellerman, Lynda La Plante, Val McDermid, Benjamin Schutz.

Others interested in the wider world of archaeology and antiquarianism may like to try:

Margot Arnold, Kate Ellis, Roy Lewis, Jessica Mann, Elizabeth Peters.

This category leads us into the world of the academic sleuth and the halls of academe. It is inevitable that an academic on any subject would be consulted by the police and that expert may become lured into detection. But it's even more fascinating when crimes are committed within the halls of learning. The classic volume is Dorothy L. Sayers's *Gaudy Night* (1935). In more recent years the number of detectives centred in Oxford, not least Inspector Morse, have caused the University to became a favourite site for murder.

Those interested specifically in academic mysteries may want to check out the following:

Gail Bowen, Amanda Cross, Batya Gur, M.D. Lake, Jane Langton, Jessica Mann, Francis M. Nevins, Joan Smith, Veronica Stallwood, M.J. Trow.

Closely associated with the academic mystery is the literary mystery or bibliomystery. This can involve authors as sleuths or mysteries involving books themselves – books are the ideal medium for codes and ciphers. Libraries are atmospheric settings for mysteries, as Marion Boyd admirably discovered in *Murder in the Stacks* (1934), whilst bookstores are just the right place for mystery fans to gather together and solve crimes. Most of these mysteries are temptingly cozy. Devotees of the bibliomystery need look no further than the following:

Jeff Abbott, J.S. Borthwick, Jon L. Breen, Anna Clarke, Amanda Cross, Charlotte MacLeod, Orania Papzoglou, Robert Richardson, Gillian Roberts.

As with the academic mystery, there are many devotees of the clerical or ecclesiastical mystery. These can range from crimes committed within the cloisters of cathedrals or other religious building, a setting which Charles Dickens used for *The Mystery of Edwin Drood* (1870), or the clerical sleuth, of which the first popular character was G.K. Chesterton's Father Brown, starting in 1911. Thanks to TV the best known clerical sleuth today is probably Ralph McInenry's Father Dowling, though one could count Ellis Peters's 12th-century Brother Cadfael. Many of these books fall into the cozy category. Some ecclesiastical mysteries turn on a question of faith, as in the books by Terrance Faherty or the consequences of a faith on a community, as with the Mormons in the books by Robert Irvine. The film *Messenger of Death* is also built around an interpretation of faith. Authors whose books fall into this category include:

Kate Charles, Terrance Faherty, D.M. Greenwood, Robert Irvine, Harry Kemelman, William X. Kienzle, Ralph McInerny, Sister Carol Anne O'Marie. Also Jean M. Dams and Andrew M. Greeley (not covered in this volume).

The less cozy aspect of religion is when individuals become involved with religious or fanatical cults, a theme which has increased recently since such horrific incidents as Waco. Authors who have written one or more books involving religious cults include:

A.C. Baantjer, Rex Burns, John Connolly, William Deverell, Peter Dickinson, Bartholomew Gill, Jeremiah Healy, Harry Kemelman, Laurie R. King, Arthur Lyons, Margaret Millar, Daniel Odier, Gillian Roberts, Peter Turnbull, Mary Willis Walker, Mary Wings, Steven J. Womack.

Amongst the other amateur/professional sleuths the biggest category is that of the investigative journalist, whether for newspapers, magazines, or TV. It has some link to the bibliomystery – the reporter may be conducting research for a book, as in the case of Nancy Pickard's Marie Lightfoot – but more often it is trying to get a news scoop. Journalist sleuths appear in books by these authors:

Lillian Jackson Braun, Christopher Brookmyre, Edna Buchanan, Jan Burke, Barbara D'Amato, William L. DeAndrea, Jeffrey Deaver, Anabel Donald, Antonia Fraser, Lesley Grant-Adamson, Patricia Hall, Carolyn G. Hart, Sparkle Hayter, Karen Kijewski, Michael Kurland, Laura Lippman, Nancy Pickard, Elizabeth D. Squire, Mary Willis Walker, Penny Warner.

Another area of crime is art theft and the specialist knowledge of the art connoisseur, such as Derek Wilson's Tim Lacy, is invaluable. On the other side of the coin you have those with the skills to forge antiques. They may be connoisseurs, such as the professor forging Etruscan relics in Michael Gilbert's *The Family Tomb*, or a wheeler-dealer, such as the irrepressible Lovejoy. Arts and antique crimes will be found under the following authors:

Kyril Bonfiglioli, Jonathan Gash, Michael Gilbert, Lauren Henderson, John Spencer Hill, Charlotte MacLeod, John Malcolm, Edward Marston, Sujata Massey, John Mortimer, Marcia Muller, Iain Pears, Neville Steed, Derek Wilson.

Another area of expertise is that of corporate business and finance, ranging from major investments to fraud and tax loopholes. The detective skills of a former tax inspector are put to good use in the character of G.D.H. Pringle created by Nancy Livingstone, whilst the books by Emma Lathen have a Wall street banker as a sleuth. Many of the major corporate crimes are treated separately under "thrillers". Authors whose books take place in business, political or financial circles include:

Robert Campbell, Ruth Dudley Edwards, Emma Lathen, Nancy Livingston, Shane Maloney, Annette Meyers, Kay Mitchell, Janet Neel, David Williams.

A new area for writers is that of the ecological crime. It was never raised as an issue in fiction until the sixties but now crimes against nature and the environment are major concerns. The TV series *Badger* raised awareness to crimes against wildlife. The following authors place a particular emphasis on eco-crime.

Nevada Barr, Ann Cleeves, Sandy Dengler, James W. Hall, Carl Hiaasen, Roger Longrigg, Gwen Moffat, Julian Rathbone, Dana Stabenow.

Sport has also featured in crime fiction. In the Golden Age it was more gentlemanly pursuits such as cricket or golf or skiing or perhaps rowing that provided a means for a crime, but more recently the big money in sport has given rise to a different approach. Dick Francis was one of the main factors in this development, an ex-jockey who wrote excellent thrillers in the world of horseracing, and to other sports, including the Olympics. The Olympics also feature in books by Julian Rathbone, and by Peter Lovesey who is himself an official statistician for athletics. Authors whose books feature crimes involving sports or sporting sleuths include:

Jon L. Breen, Jon Cleary, Harlan Coben, Dick Francis, John Francome, Emma Lathen, Peter Lovesey, Shane Maloney, Edward Marston [as Keith Miles], Julian Rathbone, Peter Temple.

The final major area for the specialist amateur/professional sleuth is that of stage and screen. Thespians have a remarkable death rate in books but also their propensity for disguise allows them to be excellent sleuths – or murderers. There seems to be much emnity and rivalry in the world of film and the theatre. Hollywood in particular has attracted many private detectives, working in the film business. George Baxt has written a number of celebrity murder cases whilst Ron Goulart has made a remarkable detective out of Groucho Marx. Probably the best known of the actor sleuths is Simon Brett's Charles Paris. Excluding the historical theatre, authors whose novels have a theatrical or movie background include:

Linda Barnes, George Baxt, Simon Brett, P.M. Carlson, Peter Corris, Jane Dentinger, Terence Faherty, Ron Goulart, Parnell Hall, Wendy Hornsby, Stuart Kaminsky, Annette Meyers, Barbara Paul, Simon Shaw, Collin Wilcox.

Legal Thrillers

Although the lawyer detective is strictly another professional sleuth, the world of the courts and the true dispensation of justice is a separate category. The author who made this category his own was Erle Stanley Gardner and, even thirty years or more after his death, we are all still well acquainted with his attorney, Perry Mason, thanks primarily to the long-running television series starring Raymond Burr. Gardner wasn't the first to use lawyers, though he did establish the courtroom drama as a category in its own right, and the Mason formula has been used successfully today by Robert L. Fish, Thomas Chastain and Parnell Hall, as well as the TV series *Matlock*. Amongst the earliest was Melville Davisson Post's lawyer, Randolph Mason, who was something of a rogue, always looking for loopholes in the law for his clients. In Britain the equivalent of Gardner was Cyril Hare whose barrister detective was Francis Pettigrew.

Whereas Americans tend to use the courtroom to explore major issues and develop dramatic tension, such as in the works of John Grisham or Scott Turow, the British are as likely to demonstrate that old adage that "the law is an ass", and highlight the idiosyncracies and eccentricities of judges and barristers. The supreme artist in this field is John Mortimer, but Michael Gilbert has also shown the law in a multitude of hues.

The drama of the courtroom lends itself superbly to the big and small screen. Some of the classic films have included Agatha Christie's *Witness for the Prosecution* (1957), James Stewart in *Anatomy of a Murder* and the definitive jury-room drama *Twelve Angry Men*. More recent TV series have included *Kavanagh, Q.C.* in Britain and *L.A. Law* in the States the latter, like *The Practice*, looking beyond individual court cases to the tensions and rivalries within a legal practice itself.

Authors whose books revolve around major legal issues, legal thrillers, courtroom dramas or lawyer-sleuths include:

Rosemary Aubert, William Bernhardt, Jay Brandon, James Lee Burke, Sarah Caudwell, William Coughlin, William Deverell, Martin Edwards, Robert L. Fish, Frances Fyfield, Michael Gilbert, E.X. Giroux, Stephen Greenleaf, John Grisham, Parnell Hall, William Harrington, Joe L. Hensley, George V. Higgins, Paul Levine, Ed McBain, Margaret Maron, Lia Matera, M.R.D. Meek, John Mortimer, Michael Nava, Richard North Patterson, Nancy Taylor Rosenberg, Lisa Scottoline, Walter Sorrells, Robert K. Tanenbaum, William G. Tapply, Scott Turow, Michael Underwood, Carolyn Wheat, Kate Wilhelm, Stuart Woods, Sharon Zukowski.

Historical Mysteries

It seems almost a contradiction in terms to say that one of the biggest growth areas in "modern" crime fiction is that of the historical mystery. Just when history begins (or ends) has been defined by the CWA which sets a date of anything before 1964 for its Historical Dagger, so we have the situation that books written in the fifties may still be considered contemporary whilst those written today but set in the fifties are historical. Another potential line is before the Second World War, when the nuclear age ushered in modern times. As to how far back you can go, there seems no limit. Sandy Dengler has a Neanderthal sleuth in her books, set nearly 40,000 years ago.

The historical mystery as a publishing niche was spawned with the success of the Brother Cadfael books by Ellis Peters, but examples had been around long before. Melville Davisson Post created the character of Uncle Abner set in the days of the young United States in *Uncle Abner,*

Master of Mysteries (1918). Agatha Christie wrote the first ancient Egyptian whodunnit in *Death Comes at the End* (1941) and Josephine Tey produced a classic in her re-assessment of the death of the Princes in the Tower in *The Daughter of Time* (1951). Ancient Rome has become a favourite period amongst modern writers, not least the best-selling works of Lindsey Davis and Steven Saylor, whilst Lynda Robinson and Lauren Haney have selected Ancient Egypt for their sleuths. Paul C. Doherty is undoubtedly the most prolific writer of historical mysteries with books ranging from Ancient Egypt and Alexander the Great to the Napoleonic period. Recently it has become fun to select a well-known historical character and turn him into a sleuth at a major event. Max Allan Collins thus has Edgar Rice Burroughs as investigator in *The Pearl Harbor Murders* whilst Howard Engel pits together Dr Joseph Bell and Arthur Conan Doyle as the original Holmes and Watson in *Mr Doyle and Dr Bell*.

The following lists key authors of historical mysteries rated by period.

Pre-history: Sandy Dengler.

Ancient Egypt: Paul C. Doherty (also Anton Gill, Lauren Haney, Lynda Robinson not covered in this volume).

Ancient Greece and Rome: Lindsey Davis, Paul C. Doherty, Steven Saylor, Marilyn Todd.

7th century: Peter Tremayne, Robert Van Gulik.

11th and 12th centuries: Edward Marston, Sharan Newman, Ellis Peters.

Middle Ages: Paul C. Doherty, Umberto Eco, Elizabeth Eyre, Margaret Frazer, Susanna Gregory, Michael Jecks, Ian Morson, Candace Robb, Caroline Roe, Kate Sedley, Derek Wilson.

Age of Discovery: Judith Cook, Patricia Finney, Dale Furutani, Edward Marston, Maan Meyers, Iain Pears, Jeremy Potter, Laura Joh Rowland.

18th century / Regency: Bruce Cook, Janet Laurence, Deryn Lake, Kate Ross.

Victorian / Edwardian: Caleb Carr, Clare Curzon, William L. DeAndrea, Michael Dibdin, Carole Nelson Douglas, Howard Engel, John Buxton Hilton, H.R.F. Keating, Alanna Knight, Gillian Linscott, Peter Lovesey, William Marshall, Miriam Grace Monfredo, Amy Myers, Michael Pearce, Anne Perry, Elizabeth Peters, Robert J. Randisi, Walter Satterthwait, Julian Symons, Donald Thomas, June Thomson, M.J. Trow.

Between the Wars: Harold Adams, Rennie Airth, K.K. Beck, Max Allan Collins, James Ellroy, Loren D. Estleman, Stuart Kaminsky, Laurie R. King, Michael Kurland, Charles Todd.

Social Factors

All crime is rooted in society. Our environment and where and how we live affects how we develop and can make the difference between a life of crime or making good. Environment, ethnic, social and family backgrounds all have their part to play, and all feature in modern crime fiction.

The social background, particularly the impact of inner city degradation, is probably the most significant. Inner cities and the related problems of gangs, drugs and juvenile delinquency were first explored by Evan Hunter [Ed McBain] in *The Blackboard Jungle* in 1954 and gave rise to a sub-genre of "juvie" novels throughout the fifties in America. These settings are the complete opposite of the cozy crime of the traditional English village setting, dubbed "Mayhem Parva" by Colin Watson and against which he created his own chaotic Flaxborough. The perils of inner city life are drawn in vivid detail in the books of William McIlvanney (Glasgow), John Harvey (Manchester) and Mark Timlin (London), whilst in the US Michael Connelly and Gar Anthony Haywood (Los Angeles), Eugene Izzi (Chicago) and Lawrence Block or Donald E. Westlake (New York). Here is a list of authors covered whose work is set in difficult social environments:

🗡 Nicholas Blincoe, Lawrence Block, Liza Cody, Michael Connelly, Loren Estleman, John Harvey, Gar Anthony Haywood, Victor Headley, George V. Higgins, Chester Himes, Russell James, Quintin Jardine, Bill Knox, Lynda La Plante, William McIlvanney, Carol O'Connell, Ian Rankin, Derek Raymond, Mark Timlin, Peter Turnbull, Jonathan Valin, Donald E. Westlake, Gordon M. Williams.

The ethnic element has been developed considerably in recent fiction. I do not include here books that use stereotypical images of various cultures as either detective or villain, nor those that simply feature a sleuth from a particular ethnic background. The author must use the ethnic background as a key part of the character and plot. Perhaps the best examples today are Tony Hillerman's novels featuring Navajo detectives Joe Leaphorn and Jim Chee. Although Native Americans had appeared as sleuths as long ago as Judson R. Taylor's *Phil Scott, the Indian Detective* (1882) the first modern treatment of the American Indian appeared in books by Richard Martin Stern and Brian Garfield. This came within less than a generation of African Americans receiving serious consideration in crime fiction, due primarily to the work of Chester Himes. Today ethnic elements feature in many novels, but the following authors have utilized them to good effect:

🗡 Doug Allyn, John Ball, Gail Bowen, Bruce Cook, Leslie Glass, Jean Hager, Victor Headley, Tony Hillerman, Chester Himes, Faye Kellerman, Rochelle Majer Krich, Walter Mosley, Marcia Muller, Barbara Neely, Abigail Padgett, Orania Papazoglou, George Pelecanos, Thomas Perry, Mike Phillips, Les Roberts, S.J. Rozan, Richard Martin Stern, Ernest Tidyman, Robert Wilson.

The other key element is the family background and upbringing.

Dysfunctional families, child abuse and social disintegration are common elements in many modern crime novels, and is especially key in the work by the following included in this encyclopedia.

Eleanor Taylor Bland, Natasha Cooper, Janet Dawson, Susan Dunlap, Patricia Hall, Gar Anthony Haywood, Nancy Baker Jacobs, J.A. Jance, Michael Z. Lewin, Denise Mina, Gwen Moffat, Marcia Muller, Abigail Padgett, Nancy Pickard, Peter Turnbull, Andrew Vachss, Jonathan Valin.

Gangsters and Villains – the Real "Crime" Novel

One of the most evident facts about modern crime fiction is its portrayal of gangster life. Although Charles Dickens wrote about the street life of villains in *Oliver Twist*, when crime fiction became established the villain was glamourized and often made a hero in his own right. E.W. Hornung's Raffles in England, Maurice LeBlanc's Arsène Lupin in France and Frederick Irving Anderson's Godahl in the US were all master criminals and gentlemen. Their crimes were always against the unscrupulous or mega-rich and so seen as harmless. The gentleman thief continues to this day – Lawrence Block's Bernie Rhodenbarr is a direct descendant, Daniel Odier's Gorodish or Robert L. Fish's master smuggler Kek Huuygens. We can all enjoy the adventures of villain against villain if it's harmless, such as Jonathan Gash's Lovejoy or Donald E. Westlake's John Dortmunder, or losers like Peter Doyle's Billie Glasheen. Much of today's fiction about criminals, however, best exemplified by Quentin Tarantino's film *Pulp Fiction*, is a more realistic and humanized look at organized crime and violent gangs.

Some authors wrote from direct experience having served prison sentences. In the case of E. Richard Johnson, his entire writing career was while he was in gaol. His life fell apart when he was released. The following writers have all produced fiction based on their own prison experiences and life on the streets:

Edward Bunker, Clarence Cooper Jr., Chester Himes, E. Richard Johnson, Donald Mackenzie.

The growth in organized crime and Mob rule in America in the 1920s, primarily as a result of Prohibition, led to a profusion of gangster fiction, of which W.R. Burnett's *Little Caesar* (1929) was the seminal novel. This development was less prevalent in Britain until the late sixties and seventies with the rise and downfall of such London gangsters as the Krays and depicted in novels like *Jack's Return Home* (1970) by Ted Lewis. At the same time American films, such as *Point Blank* (1967), based on the character of Parker created by Donald E. Westlake and *The Godfather* (1972), from the books by Mario Puzo, gave a more realistic view of gangsters, both loners and organized crime. Since then the volume of novels concentrating on the criminals themselves and usually told from their viewpoint has proliferated. The following lists those authors covered in this book whose work brings the underworld or corruption to the surface.

- US: Edward Bunker, James Ellroy, George V. Higgins, Chester Himes, Eugene Izzi, E. Richard Johnson, Elmore Leonard, Mario Puzo, Iceberg Slim, Charles Willeford.
- UK: Jake Arnott, Nicholas Blincoe, Victor Headley, Bill James, Russell James, Ted Lewis, William McIlvanney, G.F. Newman, Derek Raymond, Mark Timlin.
- Other: James McClure, Leonard Sciascia, Josef Skvorecky, Gillian Solovo, Robert Wilson.

There is also the unsettling fiction that takes us into the minds of the villain so that we see life through their eyes and almost understand their actions. The legendary filmmaker Michael Powell achieved this at the cost of his career in *Peeping Tom*, and we've all reacted to the great psychopaths on the screen such as Robert Bloch's Norman Bates or Thomas Harris's Hannibal Lecter. The following authors have taken us into the mind of the murderer:

- Robert Bloch, James Lee Burke, Bret Easton Ellis, James Ellroy, Thomas Harris, Patricia Highsmith, Phil Lovesey, Andrew Taylor, Jim Thompson, Charles Willeford.

With the rise in crime there are moments when the victims want to take the law into their own hands. The idea of vigilantes gained new prominence with Michael Winner's film version of Brian Garfield's *Death Wish*, but the revenge novel in the form of the one-man crusade against crime had been around for a long time and had become notorious in the fifties through Mickey Spillane's Mike Hammer. It took on new proportions after the Vietnam War when soldiers continued their war against the enemy at home, with one-man battles against organized crime or communism. These became typified in such films as *Rambo*, based on the novel *First Blood* by David Morrell, and reached their nadir in the long-running *Executioner* series by Don Pendleton. These books are closer to war novels than crime novels, though Andrew Vachss has attempted to reunite the fields in his dark and brooding Burke series of a crusader against child abuse. It's almost an accepted norm in crime fiction that certain P.I.s take on this rôle, like knights errant, but sometimes this can go to an extreme. In addition to the Harry Callahan spin-off books listed under *Dirty Harry*, authors whose characters become vigilantes or take the law into their own hands in a big way include:

- Lawrence Block, James Crumley, Brian Garfield, John Godey, Joe Gores, Eugene Izzi, John D. MacDonald, Dan J. Marlowe, Warren Murphy, Don Pendleton, Mario Puzo, Mickey Spillane, Andrew Vachss, Donald E. Westlake.

Thrillers, Suspense and Noir

There are two categories beloved by publishers and movie-makers that are not exclusive to crime fiction. Both are descriptive of the mood the story creates, and that mood may be created by a crime story, but not necessarily. Thrillers, these days, tend to be thick books or multi-million-dollar films which are high on action and intense on plot. Many spy and espionage novels fall into the thriller category and indeed such early books as Erskine Childers' *The Riddle of the Sands* (1903), Edgar Wallace's *The Four Just Men* (1905) and John Buchan's *The 39 Steps* (1915) were formative crime thrillers. Major writers of spy and espionage thrillers who are not covered in this volume include Eric Ambler, Len Deighton, Ian Fleming, Frederick Forsythe, Jack Higgins and John Le Carré. Other thriller writers whose work falls into the crime field who are included are:

Peter Abrahams, Warren Adler, Stephen J. Cannell, Lionel Davidson, Clare Francis, Bartholomew Gill, John Godey, William Goldman, Bill Granger, William Harrington, William Heffernan, E. Howard Hunt, Elizabeth Ironside, Jerry Kennealy, Ingrid Noll, James Patterson, Julian Rathbone, Sam Reaves, Lawrence Sanders, Ross Thomas.

Sometimes books are labelled "psychological thriller", but this phrase is almost indistinguishable from "suspense". Suspense is actually a technique most novels contain to heighten tension in the reader and keep them turning the page. It is always about the expectation of something to happen, which the reader may only partially guess at. In crime fiction it is typical in the "Had-I-But-Known" school of fiction of the individual who visits a house only to find themselves trapped, or captured, or that feeling of being watched. Stalker novels are full of suspense. The suspense novel has a long history going right back to the gothic novels of the 18th century, through the sensation novels of the Victorian period, epitomized by Wilkie Collins and Mary E. Braddon, to the early 20th-century masters such as Daphne du Maurier and Charlotte Armstrong. The undisputed present-day masters of mystery suspense are Mary Higgins Clark in the US and Ruth Rendell, in her Barbara Vine persona, in the UK, though the past master, Dorothy Salisbury Davis can still lay claim to the crown. Writers primarily known for their suspense fiction included in this volume are:

Marian Babson, Hilary Bonner, Mary Higgins Clark, Dorothy Salisbury Davis, Stanley Ellin, Howard Fast, Nicci French, Frances Fyfield (as Frances Hegarty), B.M. Gill, Lesley Grant-Adamson, Patricia Highsmith, Tami Hoag, Judith Kelman, Ira Levin, Jill McGown, Margaret Millar, Natsuki Shizuko, Joyce Carol Oates, Elizabeth Peters (as Barbara Michaels), Bill Pronzini, Ruth Rendell (as Barbara Vine), Robert Richardson, Anthony Shaffer, Julian Symons, Masako Togawa, Miles Tripp, Minette Walters, Margaret Yorke.

The more psychological and frightening the suspense, the more you tip into noir. Noir fiction is that bleak and nightmarish world where all hope has gone. It is a dark, cynical world of brooding pessimism. It has long been associated with hard-boiled fiction, but the only real elements in common may be the utter relentlessness of the circumstances with which the nightmare began, or the nature of the criminals who inflicted it. The two writers whose work helped establish the noir mood in American fiction were James M. Cain and Cornell Woolrich and their combined mantle was taken up by Jim Thompson in the fifties. Writers whose work is dark, bleak and unremitting include:

Christopher Brookmyre, James Lee Burke, John Connolly, Thomas H. Cook, James Crumley, James Ellroy, Ed Gorman, John Harvey, William Hoffman, Joe Lansdale, Dennis Lehane, Derek Raymond, Jim Thompson, Daniel Woodrell.

Fun and Games

Not all crime fiction has to be harsh, bleak and unremitting. Crime fiction can be entertaining in several ways. The field is big enough to look after itself and thus is open to parody. Also the story itself can become a challenge to unravel the mystery before the author reveals all. Crime fiction still has its devotees of the pure puzzle story.

Crime fiction took itself too seriously for too long although even early in its history there were parodies of Sherlock Holmes and other well-known characters. Holmes parodies continue to this day and one of the past masters, with his Schlock Homes stories, was Robert L. Fish. Black humour emerged early in such books as Anthony Berkeley's *Malice Aforethought* (1931) and Richard Hull's *Murder of My Aunt* (1934), both of which were regarded as "modern" in their day. Hull's book, about an individual's rather inept efforts to kill his aunt, is a fine example of the clumsy criminal which became a stock part of British comedy films in the fifties, particularly the classic *The Lavender Hill Mob* (1951). This in turn gave rise to the comic caper movie, soon to be firmly established by *Topkapi*, *The Pink Panther* and *The Italian Job*. The comic caper is where some grand scheme falls apart due either to the stupidity of the thieves or other humorous circumstances beyond their control.

Today humorous and comic crime takes on all forms, from the sophisticated parodies of Emma Lathen and Janet Evanovich to the near Goonish escapades of Douglas Lindsay and Peter Guttridge to the wicked lampoons of Joyce Porter, whose Inspector Dover was without doubt the most revolting detective in all fiction.

Authors, some of whose books may amuse you or make you laugh out loud or bring a wry smile include:

James Anderson, Simon Brett, Sarah Caudwell, Natasha Cooper, Ruth Dudley Edwards, Janet Evanovich, William Goldman, Ron Goulart, Peter Guttridge, Sparkle Hayter, Carl Hiaasen, Douglas

Lindsay, Gillian Linscott, Nancy Livingston, Gregory McDonald, Charlotte MacLeod, John Mortimer, Barbara Paul, Thomas Perry, Mike Ripley, Laurence Shames, Simon Shaw.

In addition to the above are the comic capers. The king of these is Donald E. Westlake, in particular with his adventures of John Dortmunder. There are great caper novels by:

Margot Arnold, Lawrence Block, Thomas Chastain, Joe Gores, James W. Hall, Mark Hebden, Carl Hiaasen, Susan Moody, Thomas Perry, Richard S. Prather, Lawrence Sanders, Laurence Shames, Donald E. Westlake.

If you take the humour to extremes then the fiction can become eccentric, quirky and even surreal. That's what Colin Watson did with his Flaxborough novels, Peter Dickinson with Inspector Pibble and Tim Heald with Simon Bognor. When Martha Grimes began her Richard Jury series she emphasized the eccentricities and oddities of the British. The following authors have pushed their parodies and observations towards the eccentric:

Paul Auster, K.K. Beck, Jerome Charyn, Peter Dickinson, Stephen Dobyns, Kinky Friedman, Ron Goulart, Martha Grimes, Tim Heald, Michael Kenyon, Jonathan Lethem, Mark McShane, William Marshall, Daniel Pennac, Colin Watson.

The impossible crime may also belong to the realms of the surreal. A true impossible crime, though, is baffling in its presentation but often simple in its revelation. The standard impossible crime is the locked-room mystery, where a murder may have been committed in a room where there was no way that the murderer could have got in or out. Other impossible crimes include people being in two places at once, or cars vanishing along an open stretch of road, or trains vanishing in a tunnel. The master of this craft was John Dickson Carr goaded on at times by Clayton Rawson, and the present day master is Edward D. Hoch, though Paul Doherty, who provides all his impossible crimes in a historical setting, is rapidly establishing his own reputation. On TV, Jonathan Creek currently investigates impossible crimes, and in the past it was the domain of *Department S* or *Banacek*. The following authors have produced one or more impossible crime novels or stories.

Catherine Aird, Douglas Clark, Barbara D'Amato, Paul C. Doherty, Elizabeth George, Michael Gilbert, Edward D. Hoch, H.R.F. Keating, Peter Lovesey, Warren Murphy, Roger Ormerod, Bill Pronzini, Donald Thomas.

Not all puzzles are "impossibles" but they can still seem baffling. The following authors are experts at the puzzle story:

Thomas Chastain, Parnell Hall, Edward D. Hoch, Sebastien Japrisot, Sarah J. Mason, Henry Slesar.

The Traditional Cozy

We have already encountered some "cozies" but not all, so let's end our tour with a soft landing. The cozy mystery – a term coined in a review in 1958 – refers to the traditional mystery where even though a violent murder has been committed, no one seems materially affected by it. Everything is handled with good humour, the world goes on much the same, life remains comfortable and ordered, with nothing else sordid intervening. It's typical of the country house or small English village mysteries and Agatha Christie's Miss Marple is the quintessential example. It was this type of mystery that Raymond Chandler rebelled against and criticized in an essay "The Simple Art of Murder" (1950). Nevertheless it still has its supporters many of whom enjoy the escapism and pleasure of a seemingly harmless mystery where everything returns to normal afterwards and all's right with the world. Hence the success of such TV series as *Murder She Wrote* and *Diagnosis: Murder* and even *Columbo*, which is a more sophisticated form. Cozies are written predominantly, but not exclusively, by women. The Agatha award, which is given to the best traditional mystery each year, has been won almost exclusively by women, though somehow Robert Barnard and Jeff Abbott were allowed into the inner sanctum. The male version of the cozy has been covered elsewhere and is often disguised as an academic, literary, ecclesiastical or locked-room mystery. The following represents the main authors covered for the traditional cozy.

Deborah Adams, M.C. Beaton, J.S. Borthwick, Simon Brett, Dorothy Cannell, Heron Carvic, Jill Churchill, Ann George, Caroline Graham, Ann Granger, Joan Hess, Harry Kemelman, Taylor McCafferty, Charlotte MacLeod, Sarah J. Mason, Kay Mitchell, Patricia Moyes, Mary Monica Pulver, Sheila Radley, Dorothy Simpson, Jill Staynes & Margaret Storey, June Thompson.

There are two other categories that fit within the cozy but which are big enough to warrant a separate mention. The first is the animal mystery – and that's exclusively cats and dogs. It's a large area of fiction and only the surface is tapped in this encyclopedia and will be found under the following entries.

Lydia Adamson, Marian Babson, Carole Lea Benjamin, Lilian Jackson Braun, Susan Conant, Carole Nelson Douglas.

Then there is the culinary mystery – cooks, master chefs, restaurateurs – all with ample opportunity to poison or unravel other poisoners. Authors include:

Dorothy Cannell, Diane Mott Davidson, Ellen Hart, Janet Laurence, Amy Myers, Barbara Neely.

All of which seems to suggest further food for thought.

With the paths mapped out, it is only left for me to say that I hope you find this encyclopedia useful and that it opens many more doors for you and increases your enjoyment of modern crime fiction.

Abbreviations

Abbreviations are kept to a minimum but occasionally, to save space, some frequently used words or phrases are abbreviated. In each entry the author's name is reduced to their initials so that Lawrence Block becomes LB, Bret Easton Ellis becomes BEE and so on. In addition the following have been used:

AHMM – *Alfred Hitchcock's Mystery Magazine*
CWA – Crime Writers Association
CWC – Crime Writers of Canada
ed – editor or edited by
EQMM – *Ellery Queen's Mystery Magazine*
IACW – International Association of Crime Writers
MSMM – *Mike Shayne Mystery Magazine*
MWA – Mystery Writers of America
P.I. – Private Investigator or Private Eye
PWA – Private Eye Writers of America
rev'd – revised
WW1 and WW2 – World War I and II

Books and Authors

This section provides entries on nearly 500 authors. They are organized alphabetically by the author's most common form of name, with cross-references to pen-names or other variants. Each entry gives, where possible, a birth (and death) date, and nationality in the header, followed by a brief biography and survey of that author's major books and series.

Every author entry is followed by a bibliography. This is broken down into novels, short story collections, non-fiction books and books edited or compiled by the author. These listings are complete for all relevant crime-fiction books and some associational items, but they do not include anything outside the genre. Books are listed in chronological order of publication with the date of first publication. Title changes are noted in brackets. It is usually assumed that the book is published in the country of nationality of that author but if variant titles are published elsewhere, they are indicated by either UK or US for British or American, or similar abbreviations for other countries.

In addition to the bibliography there are various key notes at the end of each author entry providing further data where applicable. Not every entry necessarily has all these data, but it will have some or all of the following:

Full/Real name. Entries are listed under the author's most common form of name, which may sometimes be a pen-name or an abbreviated use of their name. If a real name is significantly different it is listed here.

Pen-names. This lists all pen-names used by that writer in the crime fiction field, or on some associational works. In some cases these pen-names may be on stories in magazines rather than on books. It also notes if they have written under house names (that is a name used by a publishing house and shared between several writers) or they have ghosted for other writers.

Where to start. Usually with a small number of books or a single short series it makes sense to start at the beginning and work through. If authors have written many books though it can be bewildering knowing which to try first and this suggests some of the more representative (but not necessarily the best) titles. If there's no "where to start", start at the beginning.

Awards. This notes all literary awards received by each author and some other interesting non-literary awards. Full details of all crime-fiction awards will be found starting on page 689.

Books about. This lists any biographies or interesting studies of the authors. Authors' own autobiographies are listed under the bibliography above.

Website. This lists the author's official website plus any significant unofficial site or a site developed around a series character.

Similar stuff. This alerts you to other writers whose work may resemble the author's or may be of similar interest. It does not necessarily mean they write in the same style.

Final fact. Wherever possible I have included some other intriguing, amusing or unusual fact about the author. Quite often these have been provided directly by the author themselves and may not have been revealed in print before.

Jeff Abbott (b. 1963) US

In just four novels and one story, JA has established a strong following for his mysteries featuring Jordan Poteet, a small-town librarian in Mirabeau, Texas. In the first novel, *Do Unto Others*, Poteet returns home to look after his mother, who is suffering from Alzheimer's, and becomes involved with the murder of a local religious fanatic. Although in traditional style, the books explore current social issues, especially those bubbling under the surface in small-town America. In *Distant Blood* Poteet has to come to terms with the knowledge that his father is not who he thought he was. The first book won JA both the Agatha and Macavity awards for Best First Novel. *A Kiss Gone Bad*, about the death of a porn star investigating his brother's disappearance, is a change of direction and bodes a new series. JA worked for some years designing computer software.

Novels

Jordan Poteet series: *Do Unto Others* (1994), *The Only Good Yankee* (1995), *Promises of Home* (1996), *Distant Blood* (1996).
Non-series: *A Kiss Gone Bad* (2001).

Awards: Agatha, best novel (1995), Macavity, best novel (1995).
Similar stuff: Deborah ADAMS, Bill CRIDER.
Final fact: JA was the first and, so far, only male author to win the Agatha award for a novel.

Peter Abrahams (b. 1947) Canada

PA is usually classified as a thriller writer. His first book, *The Fury of Rachel Monette*, is about a prolonged search for a killer as the eponymous Rachel digs deep into her inner strength when she finds her husband murdered, her house burned down and her child kidnapped. *Red Message* is similar when a young woman refuses to believe her fiancé has defected to

Communist China. PA's plots explore the theme of obsession in a life falling apart. In *The Fan* (filmed 1996) it is the obsession and subsequent destroyed illusion of a fan for an ageing baseball player. In *Tongues of Fire* it is an overwhelming hatred of an Israeli against the Arabs. In *Lights Out*, which was nominated for an Edgar Award, it is the vengeful quest by Eddie Nye, after serving fifteen years in prison, to discover who set him up. In *A Perfect Crime*, an ego-maniac with a near genius IQ seeks the perfect way to dispose of his adulterous wife. In *Last of the Dixie Heroes* a man's fascination for the Civil War begins to take over from his present life. PA's books are taut, powerful and intense. Born and raised in Canada, PA now lives in the USA.

Novels. *The Fury of Rachel Monette* (1980), *Tongues of Fire* (1982), *The Red Message* (1986), *Hard Rain* (1988), *Pressure Drop* (1989), *Revolution #9* (1992), *Lights Out* (1994), *The Fan* (1995), *A Perfect Crime* (1998), *Crying Wolf* (2000), *Last of the Dixie Heroes* (2001).

Where to start: *Lights Out* or *The Perfect Crime*.
Website: <www.peterabrahams.com>
Similar stuff: Nicci FRENCH, Ingrid NOLL for other books about obsessional behaviour.
Final fact: PA is Stephen King's favourite American suspense novelist.

Deborah Adams (b. 1956) US

Whatever the subject – be it endurance horse riding, tap dancing or genealogy – DA throws herself into it with full dedication and her enthusiasms flow over into her writing. All of her books are set in Jesus Creek, Tennessee, a town as beset by murders and mysteries as anything in Stephen King's Castle Rock, Maine. The town is sprinkled with eccentrics and almost everyone has a skeleton in their closet. There are even serial killers and apparent alien abductions. The first book, *All the Great Pretenders*, where a little rich girl goes missing and a purported psychic is brought in to find her, was nominated for the Agatha Award. DA brings wit, satire and a keen perception to this series of small-town mysteries. DA is involved with a domestic violence prevention organization and her experiences fed into *All the Hungry Mothers*, perhaps the most powerful of the series. DA has written several short stories, of which "Cast Your Fate to the Wind" (1994) won the Macavity Award.

Novels
Jesus Creek series: *All the Great Pretenders* (1992), *All the Crazy Winters* (1992), *All the Dark Disguises* (1993), *All the Hungry Mothers* (1994), *All the Deadly Beloved* (1995), *All the Blood Relations* (1997), *All the Dirty Cowards* (2000).

Awards: Macavity best short story (1995).
Website: <www.jesuscreek.com>
Similar stuff: Joan HESS, Jeff ABBOTT.
Final fact: In 1995 DA competed in the 25-mile Natchez Trace horseback endurance race during a hurricane.

Harold Adams (b. 1923) US

HA is best known for his long-running series of novels about Carl Wilcox, an itinerant sign painter in Dakota during the years of the Depression. A former cowboy, WW1 veteran and convict (arrested for alleged cattle rustling), Wilcox steadily earns a reputation as a trustworthy sleuth and is called upon by small town mayors when things get a little sensitive. In the early novels Wilcox is an echo of the hard-boiled detectives of the pulps, a drinker, womanizer and tramp, more likely to solve his crimes by violence. But the character matures, using his instincts and knowledge of human nature. He even ends up married in the most recent books. The strength of the series is in its depiction of the Dakota Badlands during the Depression. *The Man Who Was Taller than God* won HA the Shamus Award. HA has also started a series about modern-day investigative reporter Kyle Champion.

Novels

Carl Wilcox series: *Murder* (1981), *Paint the Town Red* (1983), *The Missing Moon* (1983), *The Naked Liar* (1985), *The Fourth Widow* (1986), *The Barbed Wire Noose* (1987), *The Man Who Met the Train* (1988), *The Man Who Missed the Party* (1989), *The Man Who Was Taller Than God* (1992), *A Perfectly Proper Murder* (1993), *A Way With Widows* (1994), *The Ditched Blonde* (1995), *Hatchet Job* (1996), *The Ice Pick Artist* (1997), *No Badge, No Gun* (1998), *Lead, So I Can Follow* (1999).
Kyle Champion series: *When Rich Men Die* (1987).

Awards: Shamus Best novel (1993).
Similar stuff: Michael KURLAND's Alexander Brass books.
Final fact: Carl Wilcox is based on Adams's uncle.

Jane Adams (b. 1960) UK

JA's first novel, *The Greenway*, was nominated for the CWA John Creasey Award and the Author's Club Best First Novel Award. It introduced her character D.I. Mike Croft in his frantic search for a missing child and its connections to when another child went missing twenty years before. It instantly established her as an author to watch and demonstrated her ability in handling complex, highly emotional situations. The second book involved child abuse and pornography, *Fade to Grey* a serial rapist, whilst *Final Frame* involves a national hunt for a violent killer. *Bird* is more like JA's recent novels with a hint of the supernatural as a girl tries to uncover a mystery in her grandfather's past. With *The Angel Gateway*, JA introduced the supernatural more firmly as ex-policeman Ray Flowers, invalided out after a bomb blast, finds his life becoming intermeshed with that of a woman accused of witch-craft 350 years before. JA's writing is both sensitive and assured.

Novels

Mike Croft series: *The Greenway* (1995), *Cast the First Stone* (1996), *Bird* (1997), *Fade to Grey* (1998), *Final Frame* (1999).
Ray Flowers series, *The Angel Gateway* (2000), *Like Angels Falling* (2001).

Where to start: *The Greenway.*
Website: <www.twbooks.co.uk/authors/janeadams.html>
Similar stuff: Ruth RENDELL, S.T. HAYMON.
Final fact: JA was once lead vocalist in a folk rock band and is an expert in Aikido and Tae Kwon Do.

Lydia Adamson (b. 1936) US

Under his real name of Frank King, LA, a former New York copywriter, started his career writing strong hard-boiled thrillers. *Down and Dirty* was about homosexual police officer John Mekkler who is forced to resign because of his reliance on drink and drugs but sobers up when he finds an old friend hanged. King shifted into suspense fiction with a psychological thriller about dreams and obsession, *Night Vision*, and then a wartime novel, *Raya*, attempting to transplant *Casablanca* to Cairo. After a horror novel, *Southpaw* (1988), he switched tack completely. Under his own name he began a light-hearted series about part-time actress and waitress Sally Tepper who takes in stray dogs. In *Sleeping Dogs Die*, Sally uses her dogs to help her track down the killer of a homeless friend while *Take the D Train* has Sally on the trail of a stolen dog. Having found his niche King changed his identity entirely and adopted the LA persona for the Alice Nestleton series. Alice looks after cats rather than dogs but otherwise the premise is the same. The series has proved immensely popular appearing at the rate of two a year, with over a million copies in print. In 1994 LA started a new series about young vet Dr Deidre Nightingale, who becomes embroiled in murders and mysteries. This series is more soft-boiled than cozy and arguably has a wider appeal, but LA wound it up after twelve books. A third series, featuring the eccentric bird-watching librarian Lucy Wayles has so far reached only three volumes. All of the books are set in New York and are light and undemanding.

Novels

Alice Nestleton series: *A Cat in the Manger* (1990), *A Cat of a Different Color* (1991), *A Cat in Wolf's Clothing* (1991), *A Cat in the Wings* (1992), *A Cat by any Other Name* (1992), *A Cat With a Fiddle* (1993), *A Cat in a Glass House* (1993), *A Cat with No Regrets* (1994), *A Cat on the Cutting Edge* (1994), *A Cat on a Winning Streak* (1995), *A Cat in Fine Style* (1995), *A Cat Under the Mistletoe* (1996), *A Cat in a Chorus Line* (1996), *A Cat on a Beach Blanket* (1997), *A Cat on Jingle Bell Rock* (1997), *A Cat on Stage Left* (1998), *A Cat of One's Own* (1999), *A Cat With the Blues* (2000), *A Cat With No Clue* (2001), *A Cat Named Brat* (2002).

Dr Nightingale series: *Dr Nightingale Comes Home* (1994), *Dr Nightingale Rides the Elephant* (1994), *Dr Nightingale Goes to the Dogs* (1995), *Dr Nightingale Goes the Distance* (1995), *Dr Nightingale Enters the Bear Cave* (1996), *Dr Nightingale Chases Three Little Pigs* (1996), *Dr Nightingale Rides to the Hounds* (1997), *Dr Nightingale Meets Puss in Boots* (1997), *Dr Nightingale Races the Outlaw Colt* (1998), *Dr Nightingale Traps the Missing Lynx* (1999), *Dr Nightingale Seeks Greener Pastures* (2000), *Dr Nightingale Follows a Canine Clue* (2001).

Lucy Wayles series: *Beware the Tufted Duck* (1996), *Beware the Butcher Bird* (1997), *Beware the Laughing Gull* (1998).
Sally Tepper series as Frank King: *Sleeping Dogs Die* (1988), *Takes the D Train* (1990).
Non-series as Frank King: *Down and Dirty* (1978), *Night Vision* (1979), *Raya* (1980).

Real name: Franklin King.
Pen-name: Lydia Adamson.
Where to start: *Sleeping Dogs Die*.
Similar stuff: for cats Marian BABSON, Lilian Jackson BRAUN or Carole Nelson DOUGLAS; for dogs Carole Lea BENJAMIN; for bird-watching Ann CLEEVES.
Final fact: King was inspired into his animal mysteries following a meeting with a homeless bag-lady who told King that her dog had been kidnapped by the Mayor.

Thomas Adcock (b. 1947) US

TA is best known for his novels featuring NYPD Detective Neil "Hock" Hockaday of the Manhattan Street Crimes Unit – S.C.U.M. for short. He first appeared in a series of stories in *EQMM* starting with "Christmas Cop" (1986), which was shortlisted for the Edgar award. In the first novel, *Sea of Green*, Hock tries to protect the life of a powerful radio preacher while he is himself menaced by a homicidal maniac. The second novel, *Dark Maze*, won the Edgar Award. With the third novel, *Drown All the Dogs*, which is set partly in Ireland, Hock's character develops as we learn about his past. The series powerfully evokes the seamy side of Manhattan, where TA lives, with gripping plots and strong characters. TA learned about the police force first hand. Not only did he spend many years as a reporter, covering the police beat, starting in his native Detroit, but he also spent a year with the officers on Manhattan's Upper East side, which formed the basis for his first semi-factual novel, *Precinct 19*. Previous to this he claims to have written at least a dozen books under three pen-names, all with the initials B.S. One of these was Buck Sanders, a house name used on the thriller series featuring T-Man Ben Slayton who, in the first novel, *A Clear and Present Danger*, tries to save the life of the American President when a serial killer works his way through Congress.

Novels

Neil Hockaday series: *Sea of Green* (1989), *Dark Maze* (1991), *Drown All the Dogs* (1994), *Devil's Heaven* (1995), *Thrown Away Child* (1996), *Grief Street* (1997).
Non-series: *Precinct 19* (1984).
as Buck Sanders: *A Clear and Present Danger* (1981), *Trail of the Twisted Cross* (1982).

Full name: Thomas Larry Adcock
Pen-name: Buck Sanders (house name shared with Jeffrey Frentzen).
Where to start: *Sea of Green*.
Awards: Edgar, best original paperback (1992).

Website: <www.uni.edu/kollasch/darmaze>
Similar stuff: Jeffery DEAVER.
Final fact: TA is married to actress Kim Sykes.

Warren Adler (b. 1927) US

WA was a successful business man, with four radio stations and a TV station, his own advertising agency and a public relations agency, before the publication of his first novel, *Banquet Before Dawn* in 1974. Further success came with *The Sunset Gang* (1977), a lively sequence of stories about the goings-on in a retirement village, which was made into a TV mini-series (1991), and *War of the Roses* (filmed 1989), about the violent break-up of a marriage. Before then he had been a newspaper columnist and reporter and was the Washington Correspondent for the Armed Forces Press Service during the Korean War. Amongst his 25 or so books are several suspense thrillers and a series featuring Fiona Fitzgerald, a rich, well-connected society girl who has become a detective-sergeant in Washington D.C. in order to fight injustice. The daughter of a senator, she understands the higher echelons of the power structure and is often called upon by its members for help. In *American Quartet* a serial killer is replicating the assassination of past American Presidents. In *American Sextet* a young woman who is blackmailing key people is found murdered. The novels are filled with intrigue, sex and power struggles and the inevitable deceit, manipulation and foul play that arises. Other novels of interest include *We Are Holding the President Hostage*, in which an aging Mafia Don takes the President hostage in order to gain the release of his daughter and grandson who have been kidnapped by terrorists, and *Madeline's Miracles*, a study of an alleged psychic who manipulates a family to her own ends. His romantic suspense novel, *Random Hearts* (1984), was filmed in 1999 with Harrison Ford.

Novels

Fiona Fitzgerald series: *American Quartet* (1981), *American Sextet* (1983), *Immaculate Deception* (1991), *Senator Love* (1991), *The Witch of Watergate* (1992), *The Ties That Bind* (1994).

Non-series (selected): *Trans-Siberian Express* (1976), *The Henderson Equation* (1976), *Blood Ties* (1978), *The Casanova Embrace* (1978), *We Are Holding the President Hostage* (1986), *Madeline's Miracles* (1989).

Where to start: *American Quartet* and *The Sunset Gang*.
Website: <www.warrenadler.com>
Similar stuff: James PATTERSON.
Final fact: WA attended writing classes with fellow student Mario Puzo.

Catherine Aird (b. 1930) UK

CA's novels are police detection in the classic mould, with ingenious plots and a cast of disreputable characters. All but one of them feature Inspector C.D. Sloan – "Seedy" to his colleagues – the well educated and long-suffering detective in the fictitious English county of Calleshire. Sloan solves his cases despite his bad-tempered and stupid boss, Superintendent Leeyes, and his incompetent Detective Constable Crosby – known as the "Defective Constable". Sloan finds solace with his beloved wife and his rose garden. Sloan's Berebury is the traditional English village, which seems set aside from the world's real problems apart from a regular flow of murders and other crimes. What CA brings to the genre is a sense of humour and a charming eccentricity where she takes liberties with the field she knows so well. The result is a refreshing if at times unbelievable series of wonderful puzzles and labyrinthine solutions. *The Religious Body* has a nun murdered in a convent. *Henrietta Who?* reveals that the victim of a hit-and-run isn't who everyone thought she was. *A Late Phoenix* involves the discovery of two bodies on an archaeological site. *His Burial Too* is an "impossible" crime set in a locked church. In *Harm's Way* members of a footpath society discover a piece of a human body, but where's the rest? Perhaps the most delightful is *The Complete Steel*, about murder in a stately home, with a fascinating puzzle and an audacious solution. CA has also written several short stories featuring Sloan, collected in *Injury Time*. This also includes stories involving Henry Tyler of the Foreign Office. CA's one non-series novel, *A Most Contagious Game*, is a fascinating story of a man who retires to the country only to find a 200-year-old skeleton walled up in his house. CA was awarded the M.B.E. in 1988 for her services to the Girl Guide Association.

Novels
Inspector Sloan series: *The Religious Body* (1966), *Henrietta Who?* (1968), *The Complete Steel* (1969; US *The Stately Home Murder,* 1970); *A Late Phoenix* (1971), *His Burial Too* (1973), *Slight Mourning* (1975), *Parting Breath* (1977), *Some Die Eloquent* (1979), *Passing Strange* (1980), *Last Respects* (1982), *Harm's Way* (1984), *A Dead Liberty* (1986), *The Body Politic* (1990), *A Going Concern* (1993), *After Effects* (1996), *Stiff News* (1998), *Little Knell* (2000), *Amendment of Life* (2002).
Non-series: *A Most Contagious Crime* (1967).
Short Stories: *Injury Time* (1995).

Real name: Kinn Hamilton McIntosh.
Pen-name: Catherine Aird.
Where to start: *The Complete Steel.*
Awards: CWA Golden Handcuffs (1992).
Similar stuff: E.X. Ferrars, Caroline GRAHAM, Ann GRANGER, Martha GRIMES, Roger ORMEROD, Susannah STACEY.
Final fact: CA has passed into the quotation books with Inspector Sloan's admonition in *His Burial Too*: "If you can't be a good example, then you'll just have to be a horrible warning."

Rennie Airth (b. 1935) S. Africa

RA's first novel about Inspector John Madden of Scotland Yard, *River of Darkness*, was published to considerable acclaim and went on not only to win the French Grand Prix de Littérature Policière but to be shortlisted for five other major crime fiction awards. Set in 1921, we meet Madden, a quiet, reflective man, harrowed by his service in the Great War and by the death of his wife and child in the flu epidemic, who is sent to investigate the apparent motiveless slaughter of a family in a small Surrey village. The novel is a skilful blend of the Golden Age detective novel with modern psychological profiling. RA has chosen not to write an open-ended series abour Madden but a closed trilogy. The second book is set in 1932, with Madden established as a farmer. The discovery of a girl's body draws Madden into the investigation against the backdrop of the growing threat of Nazism. RA is a South-African born journalist who came to England in 1957, working for Reuters as a foreign correspondent. He is now settled in Italy. He wrote two earlier books of which *Snatch!* is a comic thriller about a bungled kidnapping.

Novels
John Madden series: *River of Darkness* (1999), *The Blood-Dimmed Tide* (2002).
Non-series: *Snatch* (1969), *Once a Spy* (1981).

Where to start: *River of Darkness*
Awards: Grand Prix de Littérature Policière Best Foreign (2000).
Similar stuff: Charles TODD.
Final fact: *Snatch!* was mooted to be filmed as the new *Lavender Hill Mob*, but nothing came of it

Peter Alding *pseudonym, see* Roderic Jeffries

Bruce Alexander *pseudonym, see* Bruce Cook

Michael Allegretto (b. 1944) US

MA won the Shamus Award and was shortlisted for the Anthony for his first novel featuring Denver, Colorado P.I. Jacob Lomax, *Death on the Rocks*. We first see Lomax in typical P.I. mode, something of a loner, embittered after the tragic death of his wife, and untrusting. But as the series develops he emerges from his shell and though tough becomes more sensitive. He is an updated Philip Marlowe in a Western setting. The stories are witty and believable. MA has written several non-series psychological suspense stories including *Night of Reunion*, where a psychotic woman wreaks her revenge upon a family and *The Suitor*, where a woman is constantly plagued by the unwanted attentions of another. Perhaps the best of these, and certainly the most bizarre, is *Shadow House*, where a woman, investigating the death of her sister, uncovers all manner of strangeness in an old mansion.

Novels

Jacob Lomax series: *Death on the Rocks* (1987), *Blood Stone* (1988), *The Dead of WInter* (1989), *Blood Relative* (1992), *Grave Doubts* (1995).
Non-series: *Night of Reunion* (1990), *The Watchmen* (1991), *The Suitor* (1993), *Shadow House* (1994).

Where to start: *Death on the Rocks*
Awards: Shamus, best first novel (1988).
Similar stuff: Rex BURNS.
Final fact: Allegretto's father was a detective in the Denver Police Department.

Conrad Allen *pseudonym, see* Edward Marston

Doug Allyn (b. 1942) US

Despite having written several novels DA is still best known for his short stories. He is perennially popular in the pages of both *AHMM* (where he debuted in 1985) and *EQMM* (where he first appeared in 1988). His first story, "Final Rites", won the Robert L. Fish Award in 1986 and his stories have also won the Macavity, Edgar and Derringer awards, plus many more nominations. "Final Rites" also introduced DA's tough Latino homicide detective, Lupe Garcia, who went on to appear in DA's first two books, the squeamishly violent *The Cheerio Killings*, about a serial killer, and *Motown Underground*. Some stories have been expanded into novels. "Icewater Mansions"(*EQMM*, 1992) became the first of the Michelle Mitchell books. Mitch is a single mother and underwater welder who returns to Michigan – DA's home state – when her father dies mysteriously. Curiously in the original short story she was a he – Brian Mitchell! The stories are full of tension, emotion, drama and action, particularly *A Dance in Deep Water* which explores an entanglement of parent/child relationships. DA's stories are always inventive and suspenseful. He has created several memorable characters. These include Detroit P.I. "Ax" Axton (starting in "Mojo Man", *AHMM*, 1990), Tony Delacroix, an Ojibwa reservation policeman in "Candles in the Rain" (*EQMM*, 1992 – voted the most popular story of the year), Tallifer, a wandering minstrel from Shrewsbury, England, at the time of the Crusades (whose story "Dancing Bear" (*AHMM*, 1994) won DA his Edgar award) and veterinary doctor David Westbrook, starting in the highly acclaimed "Franken Kat' (*EQMM*, 1995). At present only the Westbrook stories have been collected in book form as *All Creatures Dark and Dangerous*, but DA is working on further collections and novelizations of his stories, as well as possible television adaptations. The Axton stories best reflect DA's alternate career as a musician, singer and songwriter with his wife Eve in the rock group Devil's Triangle.

Novels

Lupe Garcia series: *The Cheerio Killings* (1989), *Motown Underground* (1993).

"Mitch" Mitchell series: *Icewater Mansions* (1995), *Black Water* (1996), *Dance in Deep Water* (1997).
Non-series: *Welcome to Wolf Country* (2001).
Short Stories. Dr Westbrook series: *All Creatures Dark and Dangerous* (1999).

Full name: Douglas Allyn
Where to start: *Icewater Mansions, All Creatures Great and Small.*
Awards: Robert L. Fish, best first story (1986), Macavity, best story (1989), American Mystery Award, best short story (1993), Edgar, best story (1995), Derringer, best novella (1999).
Similar stuff: Edward D. HOCH for versatility.
Final fact: DA is fluent in Chinese.

James Anderson (b. 1936) UK

JA secured himself a small piece of literary immortality when, with tongue planted firmly in cheek, he wrote a parody of the classic English country house murder mystery, *The Affair of the Blood-stained Egg Cosy.* Everything goes wrong at a large house party held by the earl of Burford. With a cast of eccentrics and a Detective Inspector (Wilkins) who'd rather everyone kept their little secrets to themselves, the result is huge fun. He almost repeated the triumph in the sequel *The Affair of the Mutilated Mink Coat*. Similar is *Assault and Matrimony*, where a husband and wife independently decide to kill each other but their plans are thrown into disarray with the arrival of new neighbours. The light-hearted touch also led to JA writing three novelizations of the TV series, *Murder, She Wrote* featuring Jessica Fletcher – *The Murder of Sherlock Holmes*, *Hooray for Homicide* and *Lovers and Other Killers* – the last title, for instance, concerns the death of a family pet which was set to inherit a fortune. Flipping the coin we find the serious side of JA, whose fiction writing career began with *Assassin*, the first of two books featuring crook Mikael Petros, set in a fictitious mid-European country. Petros is condemned to death for murder but is given a chance to live if he will assassinate the President of a neighbouring country. Petros returns in *The Abolition of Death* in which he is sent to stop a scientist who has found how to retard the aging process handing the secret over to a dictator. Of his non-series books the most intriguing is *The Alpha List* in which the blackmailer has established a form of round-robin blackmail. *Additional Evidence* is a more conventional story about a woman who teams up with a detective inspector to prove her husband's innocence of the murder of his mistress.

Novels

Mikael Petros series: *Assassin* (1969), *The Abolition of Death* (1974).
Inspector Wilkins series: *The Affair of the Blood-Stained Egg Cosy* (1975), *The Affair of the Mutilated Mink Coat* (1982).
Jessica Fletcher series: *The Murder of Sherlock Holmes* (1985), *Hooray for Homicide* (1985), *Lovers and Other Killers* (1986).

Non-series: *The Alpha List* (1972), *Appearance of Evil* (1977), *Angel of Death* (1978), *Assault and Matrimony* (1980), *Auriol* (1982), *Additional Evidence* (1988).

Where to start: *The Affair of the Blood-stained Egg Cosy*
Similar stuff: Peter DICKINSON or Tim HEALD for eccentricity.

Peter Antony *pseudonym, see under* Anthony Shaffer

Anna Apostolou *pseudonym, see* Paul C. Doherty

William Arden *pseudonym, see* Michael Collins

Jakob Arjouni (b. 1964) Germany

Hailed as having produced the "greatest German mystery novel since World War Two", JA, who is of Turkish descent, hit the ground running with *Happy Birthday, Turk*, the first of his series featuring Frankfurt P.I. Kemal Kayankaya. Kayankaya is cut from the same cloth as Philip Marlowe and Sam Spade except that he is of Turkish origin and thus up against ethnic hatred in Germany. This provides an added edge, since Kayankaya already makes himself unpopular unearthing corruption and cover-ups resulting in him frequently being attacked and beaten. In the first novel he looks into the murder of a migrant Turkish worker who is also in the drug trade. The second book involves a radical green group's attempt to blow up a chemical plant that results in murder. In the third he unearths a slave trade when a young Thai girl goes missing. Only one of JA's non-series novels has been translated so far, *Magic Hoffmann*, a fascinating study in revenge as a man, who alone was imprisoned following a bungled bank robbery, seeks out his former partners in crime. Although JA's basic material is routine he brings to it a sharp contemporary edge that shocks it back into life.

Novels

Kemal Kayankaya series: *Happy Birthday, Turk* (1987; trans. 1993), *More Beer* (1987; as *And Still Drink More*, US 1994), *One Man, One Murder* (1991; as *One Death to Die*, US 1997), *Kismet* (2001).
Non-series: *Magic Hoffman* (1996; trans. 1998), *Edelmann's Daughter* (1996), *The Story of a Friend* (1998).

Where to start: *Happy Birthday, Turk*.
Similar stuff: Ingrid NOLL.

Andrew Arncliffe *pseudonym, see under* Nicholas Rhea

Margot Arnold (b. 1925) US

For lovers of mysteries involving archaeology, the books by MA are a light-hearted diversion. Petronelle Cook, the identity behind MA, is an anthropologist and historian, and much of herself is imbued in the character of

Penny Smith, who teams up with her son's father-in-law, archaeologist Toby Glendower, on a series of investigations. In the first, *Exit Actors, Dying*, a body found in an ancient amphitheatre in Turkey soon disappears. Matters get more personal in *Zadok's Treasure*, set in Israel, where one of Toby's old friends is tortured and murdered. The series is truly international. *Death of a Voodoo Doll* is set in New Orleans where an ancient Creole family is receiving threatening letters. *Death on the Dragon's Tongue* takes place at a prehistorical monument in Brittany where a pagan murder occurs. *Toby's Folly* involves not only a cave in Wales but a murder at the Brighton Pavilion. And there are other cases in Hawaii, Scotland, Rome and Greece. MA has also written two non-series thrillers, including *Sinister Purposes*, describing a race to rescue an heiress kidnapped by terrorists, and a book on the queen consorts of England.

Novels
Smith & Glendower series: *Exit Actors, Dying* (1979), *Zadok's Treasure* (1980), *The Cape Cod Caper* (1980), *Death of a Voodoo Doll* (1982), *Death on the Dragon's Tongue* (1982), *The Menehune Murders* (1989), *Lament for a Lady Laird* (1990), *Toby's Folly* (1990), *The Catacomb Conspiracy* (1991), *The Cape Cod Conundrum* (1992), *Dirge for a Forest Druid* (1994), *The Midas Murders* (1995).
Non-series: *Desperate Measures* (1986), *Sinister Purposes* (1988).

Real name: Petronelle Marguerite Mary Cook.
Pen-name: Margot Arnold.
Where to start: *Exit Actors, Dying*.
Similar stuff: Beverly CONNOR, Roy LEWIS, Jessica MANN.

Jake Arnott (b. 1961) UK

Although it took JA seven years to sell his first novel, during which time he had an array of odd jobs and was living in a squat, he was thrust on top of the literary tree as being in the vanguard of British gangland nostalgia. His first book, *The Long Firm*, gained popular acclaim for its unveiling of the murkier side of the swinging sixties, revealed with all the gusto of the nineties. More a series of episodes than a novel the book takes different snapshots of the homosexual (not "gay"!) racketeer, porn merchant and club owner Harry Starks, an image of Ronnie Kray, charting his rise and fall and attempt to rise again. It was filmed as a TV mini-series. *He Kills Coppers* is a more potent evocation of the sixties as a fictional reconstruction of the notorious Harry Roberts murder of three policemen in 1966, set against the backdrop of a police operation during the World Cup.

Novels. *The Long Firm* (1999), *He Kills Coppers* (2001).

Similar stuff: Nicholas BLINCOE, Ian RANKIN.
Final fact: JA was purportedly the actor inside the bandages as "the Mummy" in the Universal blockbuster film.

Jeffrey Ashford *pseudonym, see* Roderic Jeffries

Rosemary Aubert (b. 1942) US

An in-house publisher's editor since 1974, and author of romance books since 1983 (with *Song of Eden),* RA's interest turned to the crime world when she helped retired police superintendent Jack Webster write his autobiography, *Copperjack,* in 1990. She was also at that time dealing with women in conflict with the law as Director of Community Relations for the Elizabeth Fry Society in her native Toronto. Her first crime story, "The Midnight Boat to Palermo" (1994) won the Canadian Arthur Ellis award. Soon after she began her critically acclaimed series about Ellis Portal, a former lawyer and judge who, convicted of a crime, ends up in prison and a mental institution and is later homeless. The first book, *Free Reign*, plots his downfall and struggle to regain a place in society. He discovers a dismembered hand wearing a ring that he recognizes and this causes him to contact former friends to help solve the crime but as a vagrant he is shunned by the world he once knew. A slightly rushed ending spoils the book's overall impact but there was no such mistake in the award-winning sequel, *The Feast of Stephen*, where Portal goes after a serial killer. In *The Ferryman Will be There*, Portal is trying to find a missing girl and a murderer. All three novels brilliantly portray the world of the outcast.

Novels

Ellis Portal series: *Free Reign* (1997), *The Feast of Stephen* (1999), *The Ferryman Will be There* (2001).

Awards: Arthur Ellis, short story (1995), novel (2000).
Website: <www.doortosummer.com/aubert>
Similar stuff: Walter SORRELLS.
Final fact: RA was born on the US side of Niagara Falls but has lived in Canada since 1970.

Paul Auster (b. 1947) US

Although PA's incursion into crime fiction comprises only four books, they are of such individuality that they cannot be ignored. The pseudonymous *Squeeze Play*, which was shortlisted for the Shamus Award in 1983, is about the stereotypical down-on-his-luck P.I. who gets drawn into the ambitious life of a former baseball star. Of greater import are the three separate novels encased in *The New York Trilogy*. In *City of Glass* (shortlisted for the Edgar award in 1985), the author receives a strange phone call that leads him into a labyrinthine world that totally changes his life. In *Ghosts*, there is another helix of who is spying on whom. Whilst in *The Locked Room*, the narrator is trying to find a missing novelist and ends up taking over his life, a conclusion that takes us back to the start of *City of Glass*. The stories are surreal and nightmarish and yet frighteningly lifelike. PA was hitherto better known as a poet and formerly taught creative writing at Princeton University.

Novels. *City of Glass* (1985), *Ghosts* (1986), *The Locked Room* (1987).
as Paul Benjamin: *Squeeze Play* (1982).

Pen-name: Paul Benjamin.
Similar stuff: Jonathan LETHEM.
Final fact: In 1979 PA was awarded the National Endowment for the Arts Fellowship for Poetry.

Michael Avallone (1924–99) US

The works of MA, only a portion of which are listed below, are for a dedicated readership. The man enjoyed his writing too much to take it seriously. He never plotted a book in advance and his stories often take about-turns or employ absurd *deus ex machina* devices to resolve increasingly improbable situations. The most bizarre of these occur in his long running Spillane-esque series featuring New York P.I. Ed Noon, whose mind exists somewhere in the films of the forties, but who is famous enough to undertake special assignments for the President of the USA. The delight in reading his material is to look for the mangled prose and creative word pictures such as "Dolores came around the bed with the speed of a big ape. She descended on me like a tree full of the same apes she looked like." Or, "We are a long time dead, when we're dead." In this MA was in a class of his own. The Ed Noon novel *High Noon at Midnight* was even nominated for an Anthony Award even though it's the start of a bizarre sequence in which Noon fights off aliens from space, and includes many of MA's favourite film icons, such as Gary Cooper. MA could write more serious material when he chose, such as his original novel based on the TV series *The Felony Squad*, where Detective Sergeant Sam Stone tries to track down a serial killer, or his thriller *Missing!* when the President elect is kidnapped. He wrote over 200 books. In addition to those listed below are 25 gothic suspense novels as Edwina Noone, Priscilla Dalton, Dorothea Nile and Jean-Anne de Pre, several further film novelizations, including *Beneath the Planet of the Apes* (1970), TV tie-ins and a dozen or more erotic novels. He wrote eleven novels under the Troy Conway house-name for the series about sex-mad super-spy Rod Damon. MA regarded the Conway novel, *I'd Rather Fight Than Swish*, as "one of the best detective puzzles" he had created. He also contributed nine novels (under the house name Stuart Jason) to the long-running series about The Butcher, an all-action avenger, like PENDLETON's The Executioner or Morrell's Rambo.

Novels

Ed Noon series: *The Tall Dolores* (1953), *The Spitting Image* (1953), *Dead Game* (1954), *Violence in Velvet* (1956), *The Case of the Bouncing Betty* (1957), *The Case of the Violent Virgin* (1957), *The Crazy Mixed-Up Corpse* (1957), *The Voodoo Murders* (1957), *Meanwhile Back at the Morgue* (1960), *The Alarming Clock* (1961),

The Living Bomb (1963), *The Bedroom Bolero* (1963; as *The Bolero Murders*, UK 1972), *There is Something About a Dame* (1965), *Lust is No Lady* (1965; as *The Brutal Kook*, UK 1965), *The Fat Death* (1966), *The February Doll Murders* (1967), *Assassins Don't Die in Bed* (1968), *The Horrible Man* (1968), *The Flower-Covered Corpse* (1968), *The Doomsday Bag* (1969; as *Killer's Highway*, UK 1970), *Death Dives Deep* (1970), *Little Miss Murder* (1971; as *The Ultimate Client*, UK 1971), *Shoot it Again, Sam* (1972; as *The Moving Graveyard*, UK 1973), *London, Bloody London* (1973; as *Ed Noon in London*, UK 1974), *The Girl in the Cockpit* (1973), *Kill Her – You'll Like It!* (1973), *Killer on the Keys* (1973), *The X-Rated Corpse* (1973), *The Hot Body* (1973), *The Big Stiffs* (1977), *Dark on Monday* (1977), *High Noon at Midnight* (1988), *Open Season on Cops/Arabella Nude* (1992).

U.N.C.L.E. series: *The Thousand Coffins Affair* (1965), *The Birds of a Feather Affair* (1966), *The Blazing Affair* (1966).

Felony Squad series: *The Felony Squad* (1967).

Hawaii Five-O series: *Hawaii Five-O* (1968), *Terror in the Sun* (1969).

Mannix series: *Mannix* (1968).

Satan Sleuth series: *Fallen Angel* (1974), *The Werewolf Walks Tonight* (1974), *Devil, Devil* (1975).

Non-series: *The Little Black Book* (1961), *The Doctor's Wife* (1963), *The Man from AVON* (1967), *The Coffin Things* (1968), *The Killing Star* (1969), *Missing!* (1969), *When Were You Born?* (France, 1971), *The Night Before Chaos* (France, 1971), *Carquake* (1977).

Film novelizations: *Shock Corridor* (1963), *Kaleidoscope* (1966), *Madame X* (1966), *The Incident* (1968), *A Bullet for Pretty Boy* (1970), *One More Time* (1970), *Charlie Chan and the Curse of the Dragon Queen* (1981), *The Cannonball Run* (1981), *Friday the 13th Part Three* (1982).

Nick Carter series as Nick Carter: (with Valerie Moolman): *The China Doll* (1964), *Run, Spy, Run* (1964), *Saigon* (1964).

Coxeman series as Troy Conway: *Come One, Come All* (1968), *The Man-Eater* (1968), *Had Any Lately* (1969), *A Good Peace* (1969), *I'd Rather Fight That Switch* (1969), *The Big Broad Jump* (1969), *The Blow-Your Mind Job* (1970), *The Cunning Linguist* (1970), *All Screwed Up* (1971), *The Penetrator* (1971), *A Stiff Proposition* (1971).

as Mark Dane (film novelization): *Felicia* (1964).

as Dora Highland: *153 Oakland Street* (1973), *Death is a Dark Man* (1974).

as Steve Michaels (film novelization): *The Main Attraction* (1963).

as Vance Stanton, Partridge Family series: *Keith Partridge, Master Spy* (1972), *The Fat and Skinny Murder Mystery* (1972), *The Walking Fingers* (1972), *Who's That Laughing in the Grave?* (1972).

as Sidney Stuart: *The Beast With the Red Hands* (1973); film novelizations: *The Night Walker* (1964), *Young Dillinger* (1965).

as Max Walker (film novelization): *The Last Escape* (1970).

Short Stories

Ed Noon series: *Ed Noon's Five Minute Mysteries* (1978).

Non-series: *Tales of the Frightened* (1963), *Where Monsters Walk* (1978), *CB Logbook of the White Knight* (1977).

Editor. *Edwina Noone's Gothic Sampler* (1966).

Full name: Michael Angelo Avallone, Jr.

Pen-name: Michele Alden, James Blaine, Nick Carter (house), Troy Conway, Priscilla Dalton, Mark Dane, Jean-Anne de Pré, Fred Frazer, Dora Highland, Amanda Jean Jarrett, Stuart Jason (house), Steve Michaels, Memo Morgan, Dorothea Nile, Ed Noon, Edwina Noone, Vance Stanton, Sidney Stuart, Max Walker (ghosting), Lee Davis Willoughby.
Where to start: If you tackle Ed Noone then start at the beginning with *The Tall Dolores*, but you might try *The Felony Squad* first.
Similar stuff: No one really, but for deliberate humour try Ron GOULART.
Final fact: MA once wrote a novel in a day-and-a-half and a 1,500-word short story in twenty minutes – almost a world record!

A. C. Baantjer (b. 1923) Netherlands

Although his first book was published in Holland in 1959 and his popular series about the police detective inspector Jurrian De Cock has been running since 1963, the first of them was not translated into English until 1992, so it is only in the last few years that ACB's work has been discovered beyond continental Europe where his books have been selling in the millions. A TV series was made in Holland in 2001 and at last De Cock – whose name was rather unnecessarily translated as DeKok for the American readership – is becoming better known. ACB served in the Amsterdam Municipal Police for 38 years, 25 of those as a homicide detective, so he brings considerable experience to his novels. They are true to life, focusing on the misfortunes of the victims – frequently prostitutes – and their constant struggle to exist in a corrupt world. He also highlights the difficulty and lacklustre life of police work. De Cock is human – sympathetic but world weary and often short-tempered with his impulsive assistant Vledder. In this respect he is more like Inspector Morse than Maigret, with whom he is often compared. Although many of the novels are routine, the investigation is always fascinating and occasionally the plots are unusual. In *DeKok and the Brothers of the Easy Death*, a series of drownings leads DeKok to investigate a religious cult; in *DeKok and the Begging Death*, the kidnapping of a rich banker's grandson opens up a can of worms, whilst in *DeKok and the Naked Lady*, the death of a young professor sets DeKok on the trail of a serial killer. The English translations of these books are a little stilted, but sufficient to do justice to ACB's methodical detection. ACB (whose name usually appears solely as "Baantjer") has written at least ten other non-series books, none of which has been translated.

Novels (Translations only)
DeKok series as translated (all titles start *DeKok and ...*): *DeKok and Murder on the Menu* (1990; US 1992), ... *the Sombre Nude* (1967; US 1992), *Murder in Amsterdam* (contains ... *the Sunday Strangler* (1965) and ... *the Corpse on Christmas Eve* (1965; US 1993), ... *the Sorrowing Tomcat* (1969; US 1993), ... *the Dead Harlequin* (1968; US 1993), ... *the Disillusioned Corpse* (1970; US 1993), ... *the Careful Killer* (1971; US 1993), ... *the Romantic Murder* (1972; US 1994), ... *the Naked Lady* (1978; US

1994), ... *the Corpse at the Church Wall* (1973; US 1994), ... *the Dying Stroller* (1972; US 1994), ... *the Dancing Death* (1974; US 1994), ... *the Brothers of Easy Death* (1979; US 1995), ... *the Deadly Accord* (1980; US 1997), ... *Murder in Séance* (1981; US 1997), ... *Murder in Ecstasy* (1982; US 1998), ... *the Begging Death* (1982; US 1999), ... *the Deadly Warning* (1988; US 1999), ... *the Murder First Class* (1989; US 1999), ... *the Murder in Bronze* (1988; US 1999), ... *and Murder on Blood Mountain* (1985; US 2000), ... *and the Mask of Death* (1987; US 2000), ... *Murder by Instalments* (1985; US 2000), ... *Murder Depicted* (1990; US 2000).

Full name: Albert Cornelius Baantjer.
Where to start: *DeKok and the Sombre Nude.*
Books about: *Baantjer en de Cock* (1990) by John Bakkenhoven.
Website: <Baantjer.net>
Similar stuff: Jan Willem VAN DE WETERING; Nicolas FREELING.

Marian Babson (b. 1929) US

Born in Salem, Massachusetts, MB settled in England in her childhood in 1960 and stayed there. Many of her books may be seen as traditionally English, but they are more a satisfying blend of English atmosphere and American flair. MB can produce both dark suspense – as in *The Stalking Lamb*, where an American school-girl visiting England is stalked and victimized – or humour – as in *Queue Here for Murder*, where all manner of problems arise while an unruly queue of shoppers wait for the start of a department store sale. Generally, MB's series stories are humorous. Her early books featured Douglas Perkins and Gloria Tate, partners in a public relations firm, who become involved in crimes in the most unlikely of circumstances, such as a cat show. When these books were first published in the US, 17 years after their UK appearance, MB revived the series, this time with Perkins's cat, Pandora, as a more important character. MB has a passion for cats and has written a sequence of generally unconnected novels in all of which cats play a significant rôle. These include *Miss Petunia's Last Case*, a delightful literary romp in *Murder, She Wrote* style, featuring writer Lorinda Lucas and her cats Had-I and But-Known, and the mayhem that follows when she tries to kill off her favourite character. MB has also lampooned the country house murder mystery in *Weekend for Murder*, whilst her series featuring ageing actors Trixie Dolan and Evangeline Sinclair, trying to stage a comeback, allows MB golden opportunities to find fun and mystery in the world of films and the theatre. When not opening the valves of humour, MB is tightening the screw of suspense. *Deadly Deceit* finds a girl suspected of murdering her twin sister. *Tightrope for Three* has a family isolated on fog-bound Dartmoor with an escaped murderer on the loose. *There Must be Some Mistake* has a woman on the edge of a nervous breakdown trying to prove her husband's innocence from fraud and murder. In *The Lord Mayor of Death* a child goes missing and the novel switches between many viewpoints to heighten the suspense over the child's safety. MB enjoys pursuing different perspectives. In her most unusual book, *Nine Lives to Murder*, a cat and a human switch consciousness and both have to cope with their circumstances and use them to solve a crime. In a pair of novels, *Death Swap* and *A Trail of Ashes*, MB traces the problems that settle on two families who exchange homes for holidays, one in England and one in New England. MB's books are always original and creative.

Novels
Douglas Perkins series: *Cover-Up Story* (1971), *Murder on Show* (1972; as *Murder at the Cat Show*, US 1989), *Tourists are for Trapping* (1989), *In the Teeth of Adversity* (1990).
Dolan & Sinclair series: *Reel Murder* (1986), *Encore Murder* (1989), *Shadows in Their Blood* (1991), *Even Yuppies Die* (1993), *Break a Leg, Darlings* (1995).
Non-series: *Pretty Lady* (1973), *The Stalking Lamb* (1974), *Unfair Exchange* (1974), *Murder Sails at Midnight* (1975), *There Must be Some Mistake* (1975), *Untimely Guest* (1976), *The Lord Mayor of Death* (1977), *Murder, Murder, Little Star* (1977), *Tightrope for Three* (1978), *So Soon Done For* (1979), *The Twelve Deaths of Christmas* (1979), *Dangerous to know* (1980), *Queue Here for Murder* (1980; as *Line Up for Murder*, US 1981), *Bejewelled Death* (1981), *Death Warmed Up* (1982), *Death Beside the Seaside* (1982; as *Death Beside the Sea*, US 1983), *A Fool for Murder* (1983), *The Cruise of a Deathtime* (1983), *A Trail of Ashes* (1984; as *Whiskers and Smoke*, US 1997), *Death Swap* (1984; as *Paws for Alarm*, US 1998), *Death in Fashion* (1985), *Weekend for Murder* (1985; as *Murder on a Mystery Tour*, US 1987), *Fatal Fortune* (1987), *Guilty Party* (1988), *Past Regret* (1990), *Nine Lives to Murder* (1992), *The Diamond Cat* (1994), *Miss Petunia's Last Case* (1996; as *Canapés for the Kitties*, US 1997), *The Multiple Cat* (1999; as *The Company of Cats*, US 1999), *A Tealeaf in the Mouse* (2000; as *To Catch a Cat*, US), *Deadly Deceit* (2001), *The Cat Next Door* (2002).

Real name: Ruth Stenstreem.
Pen-name: Marian Babson.
Where to start: *The Stalking Lamb* for suspense or *Weekend for Murder* for humour.
Awards: CWA Special Award (1985), CWA Dagger in the Library (1996).
Website: <www.twbooks.co.uk/authors/mbabson.html>
Similar stuff: For suspense, Charlotte Armstrong, Margaret YORKE; for cats, Lilian Jackson BRAUN.
Final fact: MB accumulated over 500 rejection slips before she stopped counting.

John Ball (1911–88) US

Occasionally a book will prick the conscience of the public and one such was JB's first novel, *In the Heat of the Night*. This introduced his black homicide detective Virgil Tibbs, based in Pasadena, but sent to a small town in the American South to investigate a murder. The mystery takes second place to the wonderful characterization of Tibbs as he comes up against small-town bigotry in the form of the town's chief of police Bill Gillespie and officer Sam Wood, who at first arrests Tibbs but later comes to admire him. JB's forceful depiction of racial and other prejudices makes this one of the most powerful crime novels of the sixties. Not only did it win both the Edgar and CWA awards but the movie based on the book (1967), starring Sidney Poitier and Rod Steiger, won the Edgar and five Academy Awards. Tibbs was not the first prominent black police detective (he was preceded by Ed LACY's Toussaint Moore) but this was the first crime novel to hit racial prejudice head on. JB wrote five further novels featuring Tibbs, plus several short stories, but none has the power of the first. Via Tibbs, JB highlighted other social issues, especially the American gun laws with an innocent but vengeful child loose with a gun in *Johnny Get Your Gun*. Also of interest are *Five Pieces of Jade*, involving the drug trade, and *Then Came Violence*, where Tibbs is forced into another life. JB also explored small town troubles in his series featuring Jack Tallon, chief of the Whitewater police department in Washington State, who left behind the big city. As with the Tibbs series these books are plotted with painstaking detail, peopled with meaningful characters and not afraid to explore challenging ideas. *Chief Tallon and the S.O.R.* takes on quasi-religions and the New Age movement. JB's non-series books are less successful. *The First Team* is about a secret organization that is the last hope in defending the USA after a Soviet take-over. *Mark One – The Dummy* is about an espionage writer who starts to act out his chief super-spy character. Perhaps the best is *The Killing in the Market*, the only book on which JB collaborated, which weaves a fine mystery around fraud and murder on the New York Stock Exchange.

JB was turned 50 before he wrote his first novel. He served in the US Army Air Corps in the Second World War and was a former Command Pilot in the Civil Air Patrol. He later became a director of public relations at the Institute of the Aerospace Sciences before he turned to full-time writing. His interest in flying is evident in three thrillers, *Rescue Mission* (1966), where two unqualified pilots have to fly a plane out of a hurricane zone, *Last Plane Out* (1970), a war-time adventure, and *Phase Three Alert* (1977) about an attempt to recover a B-17 bomber and its secret cargo thirty years after it crashed in Greenland. JB was also interested in music and from 1946–51 was music editor of the *Brooklyn Eagle*. This led to his first two books, the informative *The Phonograph Record Industry* and *Records for Pleasure* (both 1947).

Novels

Virgil Tibbs series: *In the Heat of the Night* (1965), *The Cool Cottontail* (1966), *Five Pieces of Jade* (1972), *The Eyes of Buddha* (1976), *Then Came Violence* (1980), *Singapore* (1986).

Jack Tallon series: *Police Chief* (1977), *Trouble for Tallon* (1981), *Chief Tallon and the S.O.R.* (1984).

Non-series: *Johnny Get Your Gun* (1969; rev'd as *Death for a Playmate*, 1972), *The First Team* (1971), *Mark One – The Dummy* (1974), *The Killing in the Market*, with Bevan Smith (1978), *The Murder Children* (1979), *The Kiwi Target* (1988), *The Van* (1989).

Short Story (Virgil Tibbs): *The Upright Corpse* (1979).
Editor: *The Mystery Story* (1976), *Cop Cade* (1978), *Murder, California Style*, with Jon L. Breen (1987).

Full name: John Dudley Ball, Jr.
Where to start: *In the Heat of the Night.*
Awards: Edgar, best first novel (1966), CWA, best foreign novel (1966).
Similar stuff: Howard FAST, Brian GARFIELD, Ed LACY.
Final fact: JB was an expert in martial arts and held a black belt in aikido.

Jo Bannister (b. 1951) UK

While working her way from office junior to editor of the *County Down Spectator* over a span of fifteen years, JB – Rochdale born, Birmingham raised, North Ireland resident – was also establishing her writing career. She began with three science fiction novels, *The Matrix* (1981), *The Winter Plain* (1982) and *A Cactus Garden* (1983), but then found her true vocation with the crime and thriller novel. Her first, *Striving With Gods*, introduces ex-doctor turned mystery writer Clio Rees who becomes entangled with Chief Inspector Harry Marsh when her friend is murdered. By the time JB returned to the characters, in *Gilgamesh*, they had married and are involved in another murder and intrigue at a horse-eventing competition. The Rees and Marsh series falls into the fairly traditional English cozy, but not so the two thrillers JB wrote during the 1980s, *Mosaic* and *The Mason Codex*, both novels of individuals imperilled by international intrigue, and this spilled over into *Shards*, the first of the Mickey Flynn series. Flynn is an American photographer sent to photograph a PLA terrorist training camp, who rapidly becomes a victim of the political situation. The Flynn books are hard-hitting action novels. JB then started her third, and most popular, series with *A Bleeding of Innocents.* This introduced Inspector Liz Graham who is transferred to the Castlemere force to help an old friend, D.C.I. Frank Shapiro, when another detective is killed. Also on the force is the difficult and unpredictable Sergeant Cal Donovan, determined to solve the problem of his partner's death. The characters are well rounded and develop through the series which is tightly written and intelligently plotted. More recently JB has started a fourth series, less powerful than the Castlemere books, but equally as intriguing. Rosie Holland is a former pathologist who turns agony aunt who always has unorthodox answers to people's problems. In *The Primrose Convention* she goes searching for a correspondent's missing brother while in *The Primrose Switchback* she tried to prove the innocence of one of her fellow reporters who, under hypnosis, confesses to a murder. Of JB's non-series books the most enjoyable is *The Lazarus Hotel*, in the tradition of Christie's *Ten Little Indians*, where an assortment of ill-matched individuals find themselves trapped in a new hotel, where one by one they meet with nasty "accidents". JB has also written several neat twist-in-the-tail stories for *EQMM* of which "Howler" (1992) was shortlisted for an Edgar award.

Novels

Rees & Marsh series: *Striving With Gods* (1984; as *An Uncertain Death*, 1997), *Gilgamesh* (1989), *The Going Down of the Sun* (1989).

Mickey Flynn series: *Shards* (1990; as *Critical Angle*, 2000), *Death and Other Lovers* (1991).

Castlemere series: *A Bleeding of Innocents* (1993), *Sins of the Heart* (1994; as *Charisma*, US 1994), *Burning Desires* (1995; as *A Taste for Burning*, US 1995); *No Birds Sing* (1996), *Broken Lines* (1998), *The Hireling's Tale* (1999), *Changelings* (2000), *True Witness* (2002).

Rosie Holland series: *The Primrose Convention* (1998), *The Primrose Switchback* (1999).

Non-series: *Mosaic* (1986), *The Mason Codex* (1988; as *Unlawful Entry*, 1998), *The Lazarus Hotel* (1997), *Echoes of Lies* (2001).

Where to start: *A Bleeding of Innocents.*
Similar stuff: Jill McGown, Sheila Radley.

Jack Barnao *pseudonym, see* Ted Wood

Robert Barnard (b. 1936) UK

RB has been called the "Jane Austen of mystery writers" and to the extent that he is a meticulous craftsman and is able to caricature and satirize society, this is an admirable compliment. Although RB's work is firmly in the traditional British mystery – he even calls them "old-fashioned" – this is really a clever ploy. RB uses this background to explore a variety of themes, not least the pretentiousness of certain classes of society and the hypocrisy prevalent in all walks of life, and he does this with a biting wit and wry humour. Add to this the fact that all of RB's books contain solid and very pleasing puzzles, wonderful characterization and masterly storytelling and it is not surprising that RB has garnered a shelf-full of awards and is ranked amongst the leading exponents of the detective story. An Essex man (brought up in Brightlingsea) he was a lecturer (later Professor) in English Literature at universities in New South Wales and Norway between 1961 and 1984 before returning to England. He has written *A Short History of English Literature* (1984) for students as well as a biography of Emily Brontë (he was vice-chairman and then chairman of the Brontë Society for a total of six years). He has also written a study of Agatha Christie's work in *A Talent to Deceive*. The world of academia was the subject of his first novel, *Death of an Old Goat*, which unravels the fate of a professor on a lecture tour of Australia (speaking, coincidentally, about Jane Austen). Literary plots appear in several books – *Unruly Son*, *Posthumous Papers* and *The Missing Brontë*. The church bears the brunt of RB's wit in *Blood Brotherhood* and *Disposal of the Living*, whilst it is village busybodies who meet their fate in *A Little Local Murder* and *Mother's*

Boys. After these early works RB's books, while retaining their incisive humour, also became more sinister and multi-layered. Families, especially the rôle of the children, feature strongly and rather chillingly in *Little Victims* (set in a private school), *Corpse in a Gilded Cage* (which also satirizes the class system), *No Place of Safety* (which explores the world of the homeless), *The Masters of the House* (in which children take over their house when their mother dies and their father has a breakdown) and the compelling *A City of Strangers* (where a teacher tries to help a young child from a disreputable local family). RB unpeels the layers of society even further in *Out of the Blackout*, where a child evacuated from wartime London finds himself abandoned and over the next 40 years has to discover who he really is, and in *A Fatal Attachment*, where a biographer succeeds in infiltrating a family and taking over the children. In *The Bones in the Attic* a young man discovers the skeleton of a small child, which causes him to explore his own childhood. These books are not only excellent mysteries but first-class novels that explore and dissect people and their rôle in society.

Politics has also been the butt of RB's cynicism. It is the background to his thirties' mystery *The Skeleton in the Grass*, and the modern-day *Political Suicide*. It has also provided RB with a new series, starting with the overtly Holmesian *A Scandal in Belgravia*. Finally, under the alias Bernard Bastable, RB has been writing historical mysteries. These include two books set in an alternate history where Mozart survives and lives to an old age in Regency London where he turns his skills to detection, and two books which, like *The Skeleton in the Grass*, explore power struggles and tragedies within dynastic houses.

Much of RB's work is unrelated, but recently he has developed several series of which the longest running began with the bizarre *Sheer Torture*, a favourite amongst many readers. This introduces D.I. Perry Trethowan of Scotland Yard who has to investigate the death of his own father. The Trethowan books are all solid mysteries, if slightly eccentric. His constable, a black detective called Charlie Peace, who first appeared in *Bodies*, is promoted and moves up north to Leeds (RB's home town) where he works with Superintendent Mike Oddie, who had featured in *A City of Strangers*. This series has taken on a more sympathetic and less cynical view of society and it is these novels that have taken RB deeper into the psychological aspects of crime. RB's subject matter is always diverse, but is always treated with a controlled but powerful command.

Novels

Trethowan [T], Peace [P] & Oddie [O] series: *Sheer Torture* [T] (1981; as *Death by Sheer Torture*, US 1982), *Death and the Princess* [T] (1982), *The Missing Brontë* [T] (1983; as *The Case of the Missing Brontë*, US 1983), *Bodies* [T/P] (1986), *Death in Purple Prose* [T/P] (1987; as *The Cherry Blossom Corpse*, US 1987), *Death and the Chaste Apprentice* [P] (1989), *A City of Strangers* [O] (1990), *A Fatal Attachment*

[P/O] (1992), *A Hovering of Vultures* [P/O] (1993), *The Bad Samaritan* [P/O] (1995), *No Place of Safety* [P/O] (1998), *The Corpse at the Haworth Tandoori* [P/O] (1999), *Unholy Dying* [O/P] (2001), *The Bones in the Attic* [P] (2001).
Non-series: *Death of an Old Goat* (1974), *A Little Local Murder* (1976), *Death on the High C's* (1977), *Blood Brotherhood* (1977), *Unruly Son* (1978; as *Death of a Mystery Writer*, US 1979), *Posthumous Papers* (1979; as *Death of a Literary Widow*, US 1980), *Death in a Cold Climate* (1980), *Mother's Boys* (1981; as *Death of a Perfect Mother*, US 1982), *Little Victims* (1983; as *School for Murder*, US 1984), *A Corpse in a Gilded Cage* (1984), *Out of the Blackout* (1985), *The Disposal of the Living* (1985; as *Fète Fatale*, US 1985), *Political Suicide* (1986), *The Skeleton in the Grass* (1987), *At Death's Door* (1988), *A Scandal in Belgravia* (1991), *The Masters of the House* (1994), *Touched by the Dead* (1999; as *A Murder in Mayfair*, US 2000).
as Bernard Bastable, Mozart series: *Dead, Mr. Mozart* (1995), *Too Many Notes, Mr. Mozart* (1993); non-series: *To Die Like a Gentleman* (1993), *A Mansion and Its Murder* (1998).
Short Stories. *Death of a Salesperson* (1989), *The Habit of Widowhood* (1996).
Non-fiction. *A Talent to Deceive: An Appreciation of Agatha Christie* (1980), *Emily Brontë* (2000).

Pen-name: Bernard Bastable.
Where to start: *Sheer Torture* or *Out of the Blackout.*
Awards: Agatha, best short story (1989), Anthony, best short story (1988), Macavity, best short story (1988), Nero Wolfe, best novel (1991), CWA Golden Handcuffs (1994).
Website: <www.poisonedpenpress.com/robertbarnard/>
Similar stuff: Ruth RENDELL.
Final fact: RB was himself subject to a police investigation when a girl disappeared and had last been seen near his house. He was twice interviewed, his house and garden searched and his photograph taken with his dog. Entirely innocent, of course, but he found the experience "extremely useful".

Julian Barnes, *see pseudonym* Dan Kavanagh

Linda Barnes (b. 1949) US

A former drama teacher and award-winning playwright, LB's first four books featured Michael Spraggue, a P.I.-turned-actor, who is reluctantly dragged back to investigate cases amongst his friends. The series was popular but LB regarded them as "apprentice work". She felt there was a fundamental flaw in the amateur-detective story in that there are only so many crimes that an everyday individual can encounter and the accumulation of these is likely to be depressing. Spraggue becomes more depressed with each book to the point where the reader ceases to engage with him. LB also wanted out. From the start she had wanted to write about a female detective from the first-person perspective. She tested out the character Carlotta Carlyle in the story "Lucky Penny" (1988), which took three years to get published and then won the Anthony award as well as being nominated for both the Shamus and the American Mystery

Awards. The first Carlyle novel, *A Trouble of Fools*, also won the American Mystery Award and was nominated for the Edgar, Anthony and Shamus awards. Since then LB has written nine Carlyle novels. The books are set in Boston where Carlyle, an ex-cop (fired for reprimanding a senior officer) turned P.I., also works as a taxi-driver. She is a formidable character, just over six feet tall (LB is five-eleven), red-haired, short-tempered and a good fighter if pushed. The strength of the series is the sensitivity and believability that LB brings to the characters and the plot. Carlyle does not do the rash things so many fictional detectives seem to do. She is surrounded by good friends who care for her and help, including her punk roommate Roz, her police contact, Lieutenant Mooney, and her lover, Sam Gianelli, who is related to a Mafia family. The books take on major issues, not only murders but gun-running (*A Trouble of Fools*), illegal immigrants (*Coyote*), property developers (*Flashpoint*), hospital maladministration and drug-dealing (*Snapshot*) and extortion (*Hardware*). Carlyle is also a blues guitarist (as is LB) which serves as the background to *Steel Guitar*, but perhaps the most interesting case so far is *Cold Case*, about a literary starlet who disappeared over twenty years before (and a maniac was charged with her murder) but now a new manuscript has emerged undoubtedly by the lost author. LB began the book because of her fascination with memory and how we all remember the same events differently. In Carlyle LB has created a believable character with memorable plots.

Novels

Michael Spraggue series: *Blood Will Have Blood* (1982), *Bitter Finish* (1983), *Dead Heat* (1984), *Cities of the Dead* (1986).

Carlotta Carlyle series: *A Trouble of Fools* (1987), *The Snake Tattoo* (1989), *Coyote* (1990), *Steel Guitar* (1991), *Snapshot* (1993), *Hardware* (1995), *Cold Case* (1997), *Flashpoint* (1999), *The Big Dig* (2002).

Full name: Linda Joyce Barnes (née Appelblatt).
Where to start: *A Trouble of Fools*.
Awards: Anthony, best short story (1986), American Mystery Award, best PI novel (1988).
Website: <www.lindabarnes.com>
Similar stuff: Jan Burke, Sue Grafton, Sara Paretsky.
Final fact: When a child LB saw a youth shot outside her house by the policeman next door.

Nevada Barr (b. 1952) US

A former National Park Service ranger, NB has created an absorbing series featuring law-enforcement park ranger Anna Pigeon. Pigeon is a loner, withdrawn from life following the tragic death of her husband, and devoted to her work as a park ranger and environmentalist. A chronic drinker, Anna relies on her sister, Molly, who is a New York psychiatrist and, from the second book in the series, Frederick Stanton, an FBI agent. NB's love of nature fills the books with atmosphere within which are fascinatingly original crimes, each one set in a different national park or locale. The first, *The Track of the Cat*, was nominated as the best first mystery of the year. Set in the Guadalupe Mountains of Texas a fellow ranger is found dead with all the signs of being killed by a mountain lion, but Anna decides to look further. Surprisingly for their wide-open spaces, NB's books show a penchant for the fear of enclosure. *A Superior Death* takes us into the chill waters of the Great Lakes in the Isle Royale National Park. *Firestorm*, perhaps the most intense novel to date, takes on the form of a locked-room mystery with the fire-fighting rangers enclosed by the forest fire and a murder victim in their midst. *Blind Descent* is set in the extensive cave system of the New Mexico Carlsbad Caverns. The series, which is outspoken about environmental issues, has received national attention and *Blood Lure* hit the *New York Times* bestseller list.

NB's parents operated a small mountain airport but she began her career as an actress in New York, where she also wrote some plays. One of these she later adapted into the short ghost story "The Crimson Moccasins" (*Mary Higgins Clark Mystery Magazine*, 1997). She wrote four historical novels before she began the Anna Pigeon series but only one of these was published, *Bittersweet* (1984), about two women trying to survive in the primitive settler days in Nevada.

Novels
Anna Pigeon series: *Track of the Cat* (1993), *A Superior Death* (1994), *Ill Wind* (1995), *Firestorm* (1996), *Endangered Species* (1997), *Blind Descent* (1998), *Liberty Falling* (1999), *Deep South* (2000), *Blood Lure* (2001), *Hunting Season* (2002).
Editor. *Malice Domestic 10* (2001).

Where to start: *Track of the Cat.*
Awards: Agatha, best first novel (1994), Anthony, best first novel (1994), Barry, best novel (2001).
Website: <www.nevadabarr.com>
Similar stuff: Jane LANGTON, Sandy DENGLER.
Final fact: Although born in Nevada, NB's first name actually came from the character in one of her father's favourite novels.

Richard Barre (b. 1943) US

RB, a travel writer and editor, who formerly owned and ran his own advertising agency in California from 1975–90, hit the bullseye with his first novel, *The Innocents.* A devotee of Raymond Chandler, RB wanted to produce a series that echoed the strengths and atmosphere of the hard-boiled P.I. story but which had more sensitivity – both heart and soul. His character, Wil Hardesty, is a Vietnam vet who lost his son in a surfing accident some years before. Though hardened by his period in Vietnam, Hardesty is haunted by the guilt of his son's death, which led to his own breakdown, and looks for opportunities to redeem himself. The cases in which he is involved are all soul-searching and frequently involve guilt and redemption. This is no better exemplified than in *The Innocents*, where a storm exposes the remains of seven children, one of whom had been sold by a Mexican peasant (now a rich restaurateur) years before. *Bearing Secrets* also unearths the past when the 17-year-old wreckage of a plane is discovered, whilst *The Ghosts of Morning* brings alive again the horror and legacy of Vietnam and *Blackheart Highway* re-opens a 20-year-old crime when the man imprisoned for the murder of his wife and children is released on parole. In all of these books the characterization is strong and the plots and motives well developed.

Novels

Wil Hardesty series: *The Innocents* (1995), *Bearing Secrets* (1996), *The Ghosts of Morning* (1998), *Blackheart Highway* (1999).

Awards: Shamus, best first P.I. novel (1996)
Similar stuff: Michael CONNELLY, Dennis LEHANE.

Bernard Bastable *pseudonym, see* Robert Barnard

George Baxt (b. 1923) US

GB established an instant reputation when he wrote *A Queer Kind of Death* which introduced Pharaoh Love, a black, gay detective in the NYPD. In this, and its immediate sequel, *Swing Low, Sweet Harriet* (a title GB demanded stayed on the book), Baxt took the lid off the homosexual underground in New York (and this when the swinging sixties were only just becoming liberated). Although GB treated the subject matter seriously, he seasoned it with his wry, laconic humour. The remaining books in the series, including two that he wrote nearly thirty years later, are less successful. For much of his life Brooklyn born-and-educated Baxt has been involved with films. He has scripted at least a dozen, starting with his work on the uncredited *The Revenge of Frankenstein* (1958) and including *Circus of Horrors* (1960), *Night of the Eagle* (aka *Burn, Witch, Burn!*, 1962) and *Vampire Circus* (1972) as well as writing for the TV series *The Defenders* in 1961. He drew on this background for the novel *The Neon Graveyard* and the wicked short story "What Have You Been Up to Lately?" (*EQMM*, 1981) before launching into a delightful series where Hollywood personalities become involved in murder cases. Because of their personalities and GB's own inventive wit, the best in the series are those featuring Dorothy Parker, Alfred Hitchcock, Tallulah Bankhead and Bette Davis. Bette Davis even teams up with Agatha Christie to solve the murder of an Egyptologist. GB also wrote a completely wacky series featuring NY police detective Max Van Larsen and author/teacher Sylvia Plotkin. The books are filled with way-out characters and bizarre situations, verging on the Michael Avallone, and though the first, *A Parade of Cockeyed Creatures*, was shortlisted for an Edgar Award, they are not on the same level as the early Pharaoh Love or Celebrity Murder books. In his non-series books GB often draws upon standard plots in which he injects his own humour. Indeed both *Process of Elimination* and *Who's Next?*, where a group of rich and famous are killed off one by one, are really spoofs of Christie's *Ten Little Indians*. GB's humour, though, is refreshing and his delight for puns, which crop up throughout his books, is also evident in such story titles as "Adamant Eve", "In the Time of Nick" and the excruciating "Veal Meat Again". A collection of his short stories is long overdue.

Novels
Pharaoh Love series: *A Queer Kind of Death* (1966), *Swing Low, Sweet Harriett* (1967), *Topsy and Evil* (1968), *A Queer Kind of Love* (1994), *A Queer Kind of Umbrella* (1995).
Plotkin & Van Larsen: *A Parade of Cockeyed Creatures* (1967), *"I!" Said the Demon* (1969), *Satan is a Woman* (1987).
Celebrity Murder series: *The Dorothy Parker Murder Case* (1984), *The Alfred Hitchock Murder Case* (1986), *The Tallulah Bankhead Murder Case* (1987), *The Talking Pictures Murder Case* (1990), *The Greta Garbo Murder Case* (1992), *The Noel Coward Murder Case* (1992), *The Marlene Dietrich Murder Case* (1993), *The Mae West Murder Case* (1993), *The Bette Davis Murder Case* (1994), *The Humphrey Bogart Murder Case* (1995), *The William Powell and Myrna Loy Murder Case* (1996), *The Fred Astaire and Ginger Rogers Murder Case* (1997), *The Clark Gable and Carole Lombard Murder Case* (1997).
Non-series: *The Affair at Royalties* (1971), *Burning Sappho* (1972), *The Neon Graveyard* (1979), *Process of Elimination* (1984), *Who's Next?* (1988).
Short Story. *Scheme and Variations* (chapbook, 1994).

Where to start: *A Queer Kind of Death* or *The Dorothy Parker Murder Case*
Similar stuff: for celebrity murder series Stuart KAMINSKY; for Pharaoh Love Roger L. SIMON.
Final fact: When working in Britain in the late fifties GB had no work permit and so instead of banking his money he kept it in the fridge wrapped up as cheese.

William Bayer (b. 1939) US

WB is a mainstream novelist who came to crime fiction as the ideal medium for his ideas. It must also have been in the blood – his parents had collaborated on four mystery novels in the 1940s under the name Oliver Weld Bayer (pronounced "buyer"), and his mother was also a screenwriter as Eleanor Perry (1914–81). WB entered the film industry, working for the US Information Agency as a staff filmmaker, which took him to Vietnam, before he became a freelance writer and filmmaker in 1968. He has also written two books about the cinema. His first novel was published pseudonymously soon after he graduated from Harvard (*Love With a Harvard Accent* as by Leonie St. John, 1962) and three other novels followed (*In Search of a Hero*, 1966; *Stardust*, 1974; *Visions of Isabelle*,

1976) before his first crime novel, *Tangier*. At that time WB was living in Morocco and the book tells of a young Moroccan police inspector trying to understand and unravel the complexities of expatriate life in Tangier. The book was clearly not designed as a crime novel, but the theme lured WB into the genre. Next came *Punish Me With Kisses*, labelled a "psycho-sexual thriller" in which a promiscuous young girl is murdered and her sister starts to discover the truth. *Peregrine*, which dealt with a psychotic killer who uses a trained falcon for his crimes, introduced NYPD detective Frank Janek. It won the Edgar Award for best novel. Three further Janek novels followed, all of them deeply psychological. WB's fascination is with the motive and method of the crimes and how Janek works his way into the criminal's psyche. The popularity of the books led to seven TV movies starring Richard Crenna as Janek. The first, *Doubletake* (1985), was adapted from the second novel, *Switch*, where Janek has to solve the problem of two decapitated women. The third novel, *Wallflower*, was also adapted for the series as *The Forget-Me-Not Murders* (1994). WB wrote the teleplay for another episode, *Internal Affairs* (1988), plus the original story for two more, *Murder Times Seven* (1990) and *A Silent Betrayal* (1994). Janek is a thoroughly believable detective who becomes psychologically bruised through the pain of his cases. WB's other non-series books include *Pattern Crimes*, set in Israel, where a police detective investigating serial killings becomes ensnared within the wider politics of the region, and *Blind Side*, in which murderer uses the camera as his weapon. Photography is also the basis for his two novels written as David Hunt, which feature colour-blind photographer Kay Farrow who literally sees the world in black and white, and thus approaches her murder investigations from a different perspective. WB's books are always thoroughly researched and sustain a level of dark intensity.

Novels

Frank Janek series: *Peregrine* (1981), *Switch* (1984), *Wallflower* (1991), *Mirror Maze* (1994).

Non-series: *Tangier* (1978), *Punish Me With Kisses* (1980), *Pattern Crimes* (1987), *Blind Side* (1989), *The Dream of Broken Horses* (2002).

as David Hunt (Kay Farrow series): *The Magician's Tale* (1997), *Trick of Light* (1998).

Pen-names: David Hunt, Leonie St. John (with Nancy Hermon).
Where to start: *Peregrine*.
Awards: Edgar, best novel (1982).
Website: <www.williambayer.com>
Similar stuff: Thomas ADCOCK, Michael CONNELLY.
Final fact: Two of WB's documentaries won Cine Golden Eagle awards and his first feature film, *Mississippi Summer* (1971), won a Best First Feature award at the Chicago International Film Festival.

M. C. Beaton (b. 1936) UK

Scottish author, MCB has written around a hundred romance novels (mostly regencies) under her own name and various pseudonyms, but has also found time to write two series of detective novels. The first features Scottish constable Hamish Macbeth in the small village of Lochdubh in the Scottish Highlands. The second is about local village busybody, Agatha Raisin, retired from her public relations firm but just as active. The Macbeth series, which was adapted for BBC Television with Robert Carlyle in the rôle, is a quiet, easy-going series, where Macbeth feigns ignorance and indifference, but who cannily investigates the many deaths that are dotted around his otherwise quiet home town. Agatha Raisin, by comparison, is a brash, ruthless individual who spares nothing to push her way into the society ranks in the Cotswold village she has made her home. She is a Miss Marple of the 21st century. In both series MCB has a deft observation of village life, and an assurety of plotting that takes the reader along for a pleasant and enjoyable ride. Perhaps not too surprisingly, the Macbeth books are more popular in Britain and the Agatha Raisin books seem to be preferred in the USA.

Novels

Hamish Macbeth series: *Death of a Gossip* (1985), *Death of a Cad* (1987), *Death of an Outsider* (1988), *Death of a Perfect Wife* (1989), *Death of a Hussy* (1990), *Death of a Snob* (1991), *Death of a Prankster* (1992), *Death of a Glutton* (1993), *Death of a Travelling Man* (1993), *Death of a Charming Man* (1994), *Death of a Nag* (1995), *Death of a Macho Man* (1996), *Death of a Dentist* (1997), *Death of a Scriptwriter* (1998), *Death of an Addict* (1999), *A Highland Christmas* (1999), *Death of a Dustman* (2001), *Death of a Celebrity* (2002).

Agatha Raisin series: all begin *Agatha Raisin and* … … *the Quiche of Death* (1992), … *the Vicious Vet* (1993), … *the Potted Gardener* (1994), … *the Walkers of Dembley* (1995), … *the Murderous Marriage* (1996), … *the Terrible Tourist* (1997), … *the Wellspring of Death* (1998), … *the Witch of Wyckhadden* (1999), … *the Wizard of Evesham* (1999), … *the Fairies of Fryfam* (2000), … *the Love from Hell* (2001).

Full name: Marion Chesney Beaton.

Pen-names: M.C. Beaton (for crime fiction); Marion Chesney, Sarah Chester, Helen Crampton, Ann Fairfax, Jennie Tremaine, Charlotte Ward (all for romances).

Where to start: *Death of a Gossip.*

Similar stuff: Marian BABSON, Susannah STACEY.

Simon Beaufort *pseudonym, see* Susanna Gregory

K. K. Beck (b. 1950) US

Most of KKB's books are light-hearted and rather loving parodies of Golden Age mysteries. Her work falls into two series and several stand-alone books. The first features student Iris Cooper, a "flapper" in the "smart set" society of the 1920s, who teams up with reporter Jack Clancy in a trio of eccentric but well-plotted murder mysteries. The second series has a contemporary setting. Jane da Silva is recently widowed and lacks money but has access to her deceased uncle's money provided she works for his Foundation for Righting Wrongs in Seattle, Washington (KKB's home town). This requires Jane seeking out and helping "hopeless cases" who can't afford a P.I. It's an engaging premise but the plots are generally too lightweight, though they all have fine characterizations. KKB is perhaps at her best in her one-off mysteries where she can lighten or darken the mood as necessary. These include *Young Mrs Cavendish and the Kaiser's Men,* set in 1916, featuring a newspaper society columnist in San Francisco who undergoes a variety of adventures in her efforts to establish herself. There is much humour in *The Body in the Cornflakes*, about skullduggery in the grocery business, and her most eccentric book to date, *The Revenge of Kali-Ra*, set in the film world. At the other extreme, KKB has produced a dark suspense novel in *Unwanted Attentions* about a stalker. A former copy-writer, trade magazine editor and public relations officer, KKB is now a full-time writer and is married to author Michael DIBDIN.

Novels

Iris Cooper series: *Death in a Deckchair* (1984), *Murder in a Mummy Case* (1986), *Peril Under the Palms* (1989).

Jane da Silva series: *A Hopeless Case* (1992), *Amateur Night* (1993), *Electric City* (1994), *Cold Smoked* (1995).

Non-series: *The Body in the Volvo* (1987), *Young Mrs. Cavendish and the Kaiser's Men* (1987), *Without a Trace* (1988), *Unwanted Attentions* (1988), *A Body in the Cornflakes* (1992), *We Interrupt this Broadcast* (1997), *The Revenge of Kali-Ra* (1999).

as Marie Oliver: *Death of a Prom Queen* (1984).

Full name: Kathrine Kristine Beck (name changed legally from Kathrine Marris).

Pen-names: K.K. Beck, Marie Oliver.

Where to start: *Young Mrs. Cavendish and the Kaiser's Men*

Similar stuff: Marian BABSON, Janet L. Smith.

Final fact: KKB was once a contestant on the TV show *Jeopardy*.

Larry Beinhart (b. 1947) US

LB is probably best known for his outrageous political satire *American Hero*, where Operation Desert Storm turns out to have been staged by Hollywood as a major film propaganda for President Bush. Presented with copious footnotes as if it was factual reporting, *American Hero* has a conspiracy-theorist appeal and formed the basis for the film *Wag the Dog* (1997). Previously LB had written a short series about New York P.I. Tony Casella. The first, *No One Rides for Free*, won the Edgar award and was shortlisted for the Shamus. Like all of LB's books the plotting is devious, the characterization strong and the writing assured. LB has written few short stories and yet "Death in a Small Town" (1992) was nominated for an Edgar and "Funny Story" (1995) won the CWA short story dagger. Clearly LB was well qualified to write *How To Write a Mystery Story*, an engaging if none too serious guide. LB is married to author and actress Gillian Farrell.

Novels

Tony Casella series: *No One Rides for Free* (1986), *You Get What You Pay For* (1988), *Foreign Exchange* (1991).
Non-series: *American Hero* (1993).
Non-fiction. *How to Write a Mystery* (1996).

Full name: Lawrence Beinhart.
Where to start: *No One Rides for Free.*
Awards: Edgar, best first novel (1987), CWA, short story dagger (1995).
Similar stuff: Martin MEYERS, Lawrence SANDERS.
Final fact: LB loves to ski so set his third Tony Casella novel in Austria in order that he could ski and research at the same time.

Pauline Bell (b. 1938) UK

A retired schoolteacher from Halifax, Yorkshire, PB has created a rewarding police procedural series featuring Detective Constable Benedict Mitchell. Mitchell is frequently at odds with his DCI, Thomas Browne, not helped by the fact that Mitchell becomes interested in Browne's daughter, Virginia. Their relationship is a theme throughout the books – they are married in the fifth volume. The crimes are all set around the town of Cloughton in Yorkshire, a fictionalized Halifax. Although the books all carry their quota of murders, methodically investigated by Cloughton's finest, the strength of the books is in the interplay between the characters and in the original twists and turns of the plots. Church politics rear their head in *Feast Into Mourning*, antiquarian books in *The Way of a Serpent*, drugs in *Downhill to Death*, the threat of AIDS in *Stalker*, and the consequences of wartime misdemeanours in *Blood Ties.*

Novels.

Benny Mitchell series: *The Dead Do Not Praise* (1990), *Feast Into Mourning* (1991; as *Murder at St. Oswald's*, US 1993), *No Pleasure in Death* (1992), *The Way of a Serpent* (1993), *Downhill to Death* (1994), *Sleeping Partners* (1995), *A Multitude of Sins* (1997), *Blood Ties* (1998), *Stalker* (2000), *Reasonable Death* (2001).

Similar stuff: Ann CLEEVES, Anthea FRASER.
Final fact: PB has three children, one of whom is a police constable married to a detective.

Carole Lea Benjamin (b. 1937) US

Since CLB was a former detective and has written several books on canine behaviour and dog training it seems inevitable that when she turned to fiction she would produce a series about a female P.I. (Rachel Alexander) and her dog, a pit bull terrier called Dashiell. The cases always involve dogs, either missing ones (in *This Dog for Hire* and *Lady Vanishes*), or as a witness to a death (in *The Dog Who Knew Too Much*), or the need to provide security for them (in *A Hell of a Dog*). Although contrived, the books are more serious than their plots may suggest, and are a treasure for dog lovers.

Novels
Rachel & Dash series: *This Dog for Hire* (1996), *The Dog Who Knew Too Much* (1997), *A Hell of a Dog* (1998), *Lady Vanishes* (1999), *The Wrong Dog* (2000), *The Long Good Boy* (2001).

Awards: Shamus, best first P.I. novel (1997).
Website: <www.carolleabenjamin.com>
Similar stuff: Susan CONANT.
Final fact: CLB's dog-training manual was used successfully by mystery writer Harlan COBEN with his bearded collie, Chloe.

William Bernhardt (b. 1960) US

WB has established a reputation for his series featuring lawyer Ben Kincaid. These fast-action, suspenseful but also humorous novels explore major social, legal and political issues. Kincaid soon discovers that lawyers have to face many dilemmas in their work and this was no better exemplified than in *Perfect Justice*, the book that really established the series. Here Kincaid finds that he has to represent a white supremacist even though it is abhorrent to Kincaid's principles. Elsewhere Kincaid faces corruption (*Deadly Justice*), pollution (*Silent Justice*), eco-terrorism (*Dark Justice*) as well as a host of none-too-straightforward murders. WB has written two non-series legal thrillers: *Double Jeopardy*, where the defence attorney and prosecution find themselves working together in a case with Mafia connections, and *The Midnight Before Christmas*, a highly emotional story of a female lawyer who becomes entangled in a broken family. WB was himself a practising trial lawyer for nine years, noted for his work for the underprivileged and with teenagers. For his overall body of work he was presented with the H. Louise Cobb Distinguished Author award for having "profoundly influenced the way in which we understand ourselves and American society at large." He was also presented with a special award by the Oklahoma Bar Association for Outstanding Service to the Public.

Novels
Ben Kincaid series: *Primary Justice* (1991), *Blind Justice* (1992), *Deadly Justice* (1993), *Perfect Justice* (1994), *Cruel Justice* (1996), *Naked Justice* (1997), *Extreme Justice* (1998), *Dark Justice* (1999), *Silent Justice* (2000), *Murder One* (2001).
Non-series: *Double Jeopardy* (1995), *The Midnight Before Christmas* (1998), *Final Round* (2002).
Editor. *Legal Briefs* (1998).

Where to start: *Primary Justice* or *Perfect Justice.*
Awards: Oklahoma Book Award for Best Fiction (1995, 1999), H. Louise Cobb Distinguished Author Award (2000), Booklovers Career Achievement Award (2000).
Website: <www.williambernhardt.com> and <www.hawkpub.com/bernhardt.htm>
Similar stuff: Jay BRANDON, John GRISHAM, Scott TUROW.
Final fact: WB is the founder and owner of Hawl Publishing, an independent trade publisher based in Tulsa.

Paul Bishop (b. 1954) UK

Although born in Britain, PB emigrated with his family to the US in 1962 and has worked for the LAPD since 1977. From 1992–2000 he headed the Sex Crimes and Major Assault Crimes units, taking over a Robbery Unit in 2001. He has twice been honoured as "Detective of the Year". This has provided him with more than enough material for his novels and stories. After writing several pseudonymous westerns, including *Shroud of Vengeance* in the Diamondback series (which is virtually a cops-and-robbers western), he sold his first Calico Jack Walker novel, *Citadel Run.* Walker is coming up for retirement and accepts a challenge to undertake the unauthorized and, in this case, ill-fated "Citadel Run" (a police car race between LA and Vegas). His partner is a Japanese woman police officer, Tina Tamiko. In the later novels Walker is retired and running a fishing boat business but remains in contact with Tina. These stories are standard hard-boiled police procedurals but with plenty of humour and original twists. His series featuring Fey Croaker, a supervisor on the LAPD Homicide Unit (one of PB's former posts) is more character-driven, less action-orientated, with more plot development. In her forties, Fey is hardened and embittered by life's knocks, but her resolution to overcome these problems makes her determined and painstaking. Her problems include her father, who had been a bent cop. Neither of these series prepares the reader for PB's other novel featuring Ian Chapel, a former footballer turned reporter who becomes a sports investigator. US readers may not necessarily appreciate how much the title of *Chapel of the Ravens* is a spoof on English comic-book hero Roy of the Rovers. PB has also written for the TV series *Diagnosis: Murder*, *The New Detectives* and *Navy Seals.*

Novels

Calico Jack Walker series: *Citadel Run* (1988), *Sand Against the Tide* (1990).
Fey Croaker series: *Kill Me Again* (1994; as *Sins of the Dead*, UK 1994), *Twice Dead* (1996), *Tequila Mockingbird* (1997), *Chalk Whispers* (2000).
Non- series: *Chapel of the Ravens* (1991).
as Pike Bishop: *Shroud of Vengeance: Diamondback #6* (1985).
Short Stories. *Pattern of Behavior* (2000).

Pen-name: Pike Bishop (house name).

Where to start: *Kill Me Again.*
Website: <www/bookradio.com/Bishop/>
Similar stuff: Joseph WAMBAUGH, Michael CONNELLY's Harry Bosch.
Final fact: PB admits that he has "ridden the bench (i.e. played with the reserves) for obscure football teams in both England and America as an enthusiastic if slow midfielder."

Laura Black *pseudonym, see* Roger Longrigg

Anne Blaisdell *pseudonym, see* Elizabeth Linington

Margaret Blake *pseudonym, see* B. M. Gill

Eleanor Taylor Bland (b. 1944) US

ETB created the first black woman homicide detective in Marti MacAlister, a former Chicago cop, who moves out of the city to the Lincoln Prairie police force after her husband's death (purportedly by suicide). Although ETB is herself black, she does not regard herself as any one nationality or race – her mother was a white German. As a consequence racial issues do not predominate the MacAlister series. You have a tough, hard-working cop going about her business. She develops as each book progresses, especially by *Done Wrong*, where she returns to Chicago to unravel the truth about her husband's death. ETB is involved in several social support programmes including a shelter for homeless mothers and their children and a treatment centre for sexually abused children, and these issues reoccur throughout the series. Two children are witnesses to a serial killer in *Dead Time*, a child dies in a fire in *Slow Burn*, there's child abuse in *Keep Still* and there's a young drug addict and a homeless man in *Tell No Tales*. Mental illness appears in *Dead Time* and *Tell No Tales*. ETB is an expert at building up a story from the little details and developing strong characters, real situations and harrowing plots.

Novels

Marti MacAlister series: *Dead Time* (1992), *Slow Burn* (1993), *Gone Quiet* (1994), *Done Wrong* (1995), *Keep Still* (1996), *See No Evil* (1998), *Tell No Tales* (1999), *Scream in Silence* (2001), *Whispers in the Dark* (2001).

Where to start: *Dead Time.*
Awards: Chester Himes (2000).
Website: <home.earthlink.net/~etbland>
Similar stuff: Barbara NEELY.
Final fact: Surprisingly ETB achieves all the above and is a full-time auditor.

Oliver Bleeck *pseudonym, see* Ross Thomas

Nicholas Blincoe UK

Though he now lives in London, where he is a journalist and broadcaster, NB was born in Rochdale, Lancashire and raised in Manchester, and it is Manchester that is the setting for his first, highly acclaimed novel, *Acid Casuals*. With the club and record scene as background, it is the story of trans-sexual Estela (formerly Paul) who returns to Manchester to kill her ex-boss, a seedy club owner and money launderer. Bleak, perverse but laced with dark humour, it was a needle-in-the-brain debut. The gang show move to London in *Jello Salad*, where a gangster's wife has used his proceeds (unbeknown to him) to open a restaurant. Further Manchester dropouts appear in *Manchester Slingback*, where the police home in on a dried-up casino owner to help solve a past murder. With *The Dope Priest* NB moved to even greater conflict in Palestine and drug smuggling. After his eyeballs-out debut NB has cemented his reputation as one of the most creative crime fiction writers of the new century.

Novels. *Acid Casuals* (1995), *Jello Salad* (1997), *Manchester Slingback* (1998), *The Dope Priest* (2000), White Mice (2002).
Short Stories. *My Mother Was a Bank Robber* (1998).
Editor (with Matt Thorne). *All Hail the New Puritans* (2000).

Where to start: *Acid Casuals*.
Awards: CWA Silver Dagger (1998).
Website: <www.twbooks.co.uk/authors/nicholasblincoe.html>
Similar stuff: Jake ARNOTT, Steve Aylett.
Final fact: NB wrote *Acid Casuals* in six weeks at a steady rate of a chapter a day. Each book since took a while longer.

Robert Bloch (1917–94) US

RB has been immortalized as the "author of *Psycho*" and, though this became something of a millstone around his neck in later years, it demonstrates the impact of the novel – or more accurately of the film (1960) that Alfred Hitchcock made from it. Chicago-born, RB sold his first stories to *Weird Tales* in the mid-thirties and for a while was a disciple of H.P. Lovecraft. Although RB drew upon the supernatural in these early stories, and also branched into science fiction, the majority of these stories can easily be shed of their veneer of the outré and be seen as studies in madness and terror. He put this to good effect in thirty-nine scripts that he wrote for the radio series *Stay Tuned for Terror* (1944–5). RB's talent was to allow the reader to see the action through the mind of the maniac. This was used in the short story "Yours Truly, Jack the Ripper" (*Weird Tales*, 1943), where Jack the Ripper is still alive and roams the streets of present-day Chicago, and in his first novel, *The Scarf*, a powerful first-person narrative of a psychopathic strangler. The working of a deranged mind and the control exerted by such individuals became RB's trademark. *The Kidnapper* is a repeat of *The Scarf*, but equally chilling and effective.

The Will to Kill features a Korean War veteran trying to piece together his life between mental blackouts. Then came *Psycho*, a study of a mother-dominated psychopath. RB eventually returned to the Bates Motel 23 years later (in the decade that engendered sequelitis) with *Psycho II* and *Psycho House*, both studies of how violence is perceived. These books were not related to the sequence of films that kept the memory of Norman Bates alive. In the intervening years RB continued to make studies of aberrant minds. In *The Dead Beat* it was a con-man who works his way into a friendly family. In *Firebug* it is a pyromaniac and in *The Couch* (based on RB's own screenplay for the 1962 film), it is a serial killer. *Night World* relates the search for an escaped maniac. *American Gothic* is based on the 1890s Chicago mass-murderer Herman Mudgett. RB rounded out his reworkings of vicious killers in *The Night of the Ripper* and *The Jekyll Legacy* (with Andre Norton). In all of these books RB does not seek to excuse the actions of these individuals but he does seek to understand them and explain them in terms that may be horrifying yet compelling.

With the success of *Psycho* RB was in demand in Hollywood and a number of films were made from RB's stories. He also wrote several original scripts. These include *The Cabinet of Caligari* (1962), *Strait-Jacket* (1964), *The Night Walker* (1964, based on a story by Elizabeth Kata), *The Psychopath* (1966), *Torture Garden* (1967), *The Deadly Bees* (1967, with Anthony Marriott based on *A Taste for Honey* by H.F. Heard), *The House That Dripped Blood* (1970), *Asylum* (1972), *The Cat Creature* (TV 1973), *The Dead Don't Die* (TV 1974) and *The Amazing Captain Nemo* (1979). He also wrote many screenplays (or had stories adapted) for the TV series *Alfred Hitchcock Presents, Lock-Up, Thriller, Darkroom, Night Gallery, Tales from the Darkside* and *Star Trek.*

Novels

Bates Motel series: *Psycho* (1959), *Psycho II* (1982), *Psycho House* (1990).

Non-series (selective, crime only): *The Scarf* (1947; as *The Scarf of Passion*, 1948; rev'd 1966), *Spiderweb* (1954), *The Kidnapper* (1954), *The Will to Kill* (1954), *Shooting Star* (1958), *The Dead Beat* (1960), *Firebug* (1961), *The Couch* (1962), *Terror* (1962), *Night-World* (1972), *American Gothic* (1974), *There is a Serpent in Eden* (1979; as *The Cunning Serpent*, 1981), *The Night of the Ripper* (1984), *Lori* (1989), *The Jekyll Legacy*, with Andre Norton (1990).

as Collier Young (ghost-written): *The Todd Dossier* (1969).

Short Stories (selective, those with mostly crime stories). *Terror in the Night* (1958), *Blood Runs Cold* (1961; abr UK 1962), *Bogey Men* (1963), *Tales in a Jugular Vein* (1965), *Chamber of Horrors* (1966), *Cold Chills* (1977), *The King of Terrors* (1977), *Out of the Mouths of Graves* (1979), *Such Stuff as Dreams Are Made of* (1979) *Bitter Ends* (1987), *Final Reckonings* (1987), *Last Rites* (1987), *Fear and Trembling* (1989).

Autobiography. *Once Around the Bloch* (1993).

Full name: Robert Albert Bloch.

Pen-names: Tarleton Fiske, Will Folke, E.K. Jarvis, Wilson Kane, Sherry

Malone, John Sheldon (all used on short fiction, mostly fantasy, sf and horror); Collier Young (ghost-written).
Where to start: *The Scarf.*
Awards: Hugo award, best sf short story (1959), Ann Radcliffe award (1960, 1966), Count Dracula Society Award for Literature (1969), World Fantasy Award, lifetime achievement (1975), Hugo Special Award (1984), Bram Stoker Award, lifetime achievement (1990), World Horror Grand Master (1991).
Books about: *Robert Bloch*, Randall Larson (1986), *The Robert Bloch Companion: Collected Interviews 1969-86*, Randall Larson, 1989.
Website: (unofficial) <mgpfeff.home.sprynet.com/bloch.html>
Similar stuff: Thomas HARRIS.
Final fact: The character of Norman Bates was based on the murderer Ed Gein who was arrested in 1957 when remains of 15 bodies were found on his isolated farm. Gein would dress in the skin of his female victims and pretend he was his mother.

Lawrence Block (b. 1938) US

Multi-award winner and Mystery Writer Grand Master, LB is one of the most prolific and best-selling of all crime-fiction writers. He sold his first story to *Manhunt* in 1957 and since then has published over 50 crime novels and over 70 sex/erotic novels, the last under a variety of unrevealed pen-names. An omnibus of his short stories is available as *Collected Short Stories*, subsequently augmented as *Enough Rope*. Most of his novels fall into one of five series, of which the most popular feature alcoholic ex-cop Matthew Scudder or good-natured bookstore-owner and gentleman burglar Bernie Rhodenbarr. The early Scudder novels are dark and unrelenting. Originally a good police detective, Scudder tries to stop a hold-up but a little girl is killed and his world is never the same. Soon he's slipping down the slope into alcoholism, he loses his job, his wife leaves him and he struggles to sustain himself as an unlicensed P.I. Yet LB draws Scudder's character so finely against the harsh backdrop of New York that you care for him. The series appeared to come to a climax in *Eight Million Ways to Die* (filmed 1986), one of the most powerful P.I. novels ever written, where Scudder faces the beast that is killing him. But two years later LB brought him back in the story "By the Dawn's Early Light" (*Playboy*, 1984) which was expanded into *When the Sacred Ginmill Closes*. Now he's sober and trying to pull his life back together again and, though the world owes him no favours, we see Scudder returning to the light, along with a wonderful cast of characters,. This series is the most highly honoured in all crime fiction. Five of the novels at present have won awards and a further three were shortlisted. The Rhodenbarr stories are a light-hearted antidote to Scudder. Firmly in the Raffles tradition (a cat called Raffles turns up in *The Burglar Who Traded Ted Williams)*, the series follows Bernie's often highly amusing adventures as his burgling gets him into trouble and he has to solve the crime to get out of it. The books are ingenious and always well crafted, though have not yet garnered the same volume of awards. *The Burglar in the Closet* formed the basis of the film *Burglar* (1987) with Whoopi Goldberg as a somewhat transformed Rhodenbarr.

LB's earliest series featured Evan Tanner who, as a result of a wound received in Korea, cannot sleep and spends that extra time as part-academic, part-spy. It was yet another twist on the larger-than-life spy adventures of the mid-sixties and not to be taken too seriously. Under the alias Chip Harrison LB wrote two non-crime sex-romps featuring Harrison himself. He then reintroduced Harrison as an assistant to private detective Leo Haig acting like a slightly wilder Archie Goodwin to Haig's Nero Wolfe. These two later books, which were collected in a single volume as *A/K/A Chip Harrison*, remain mildly erotic but are clever puzzles and you can almost see the genesis of Rhodenbarr in the "reformed" character of Harrison. More recently LB has started two new series, both of which grew out of short stories. Keller is a lone assassin, and it's to LB's credit that he makes the reader come to terms with and even understand this cool, lethal but increasingly questioning killer. *Hit Man* is a collection of the first series of stories but *Hit List* is a full-length novel which allows Keller's character to develop and provides a mystery of its own when Keller discovers he's on someone else's hit list. Martin Ehrengraf is a defence lawyer prepared to use any trick to help his client, regardless of their guilt or innocence.

Of LB's non-series books several are worth a brief mention. Under the alias Paul Kavanagh he wrote three books. The first two are violent but realistic special agent adventures but the third, *Not Comin' Home to You*, is a powerful reworking of the Starkweather murders in Nebraska in 1958 – the same murders that inspired the films *Badlands* (1973) and *Natural Born Killers* (1994). In *Deadly Honeymoon* (filmed *Nightmare Honeymoon* 1972) a bride is raped on her wedding night and she and her husband pursue the rapist. *After the First Death* is a Woolrichian-style novel about a recently freed jailbird, imprisoned for murder, who finds himself framed for the death of another woman. *Random Walk* is LB's strangest but arguably most profound book. A bartender walks away from his job and keeps on walking. Others join him and the power of this group is put to the test when it comes up against a maniac who has gone on a killing binge. LB has also written two posthumous collaborations. He completed a Lou Largo P.I. novel, *Babe in the Woods*, by William Ard (1922–60) and Cornell Woolrich's last novel, *Into the Night*.

LB is arguably the best writer of hard-boiled P.I. fiction currently active, but his talent extends way beyond that as one of the most versatile, entertaining and rewarding writers in the field.

Novels

Evan Tanner series: *The Thief Who Couldn't Sleep* (1966), *The Canceled Czech* (1966), *Tanner's Twelve Swingers* (1967), *Two for Tanner* (1968), *Tanner's Tiger* (1968), *Here Comes a Hero* (1968), *Me Tanner, You Jane* (1970), *Tanner on Ice* (1998).

Matthew Scudder series: *Sins of the Fathers* (1976), *Time to Murder and Create* (1977), *In the Midst of Death* (1976), *A Stab in the Dark* (1981), *Eight Million Ways to Die* (1982), *When the Sacred Ginmill Closes* (1986), *Out on the Cutting Edge* (1989), *A Ticket to the Boneyard* (1990), *A Dance at the Slaughterhouse* (1991), *A Walk Among the Tombstones* (1992), *The Devil Knows Your Dead* (1993), *A Long Line of Dead Men* (1994), *Even the Wicked* (UK 1996), *Everybody Dies* (1998), *Hope to Die* (2001).

Bernie Rhodenbarr series: *Burglars Can't be Choosers* (1977), *The Burglar in the Closet* (1978), *The Burglar Who Liked to Quote Kipling* (1979), *The Burglar Who Studied Spinoza* (1981), *The Burglar Who Painted Like Mondrian* (1983), *The Burglar Who Traded Ted Williams* (1994), *The Burglar Who Thought He Was Bogart* (1995), *The Burglar in the Library* (1997), *The Burglar in the Rye* (1999).

Markham series (TV tie-in): *The Case of the Pornographic Photos* (1961; as *You Could Call It Murder*, 1987).

Leo Haig series (originally published as by Chip Harrison; reprinted as by LB): *Make Out With Murder* (1974; as *Five Little Rich Girls*, UK 1986), *The Topless Tulip Caper* (1975; as by LB, UK 1984).

Keller series: *Hit Man* (1998), *Hit List* (2000).

Non-series (selective, crime only): *Mona* (1961; as *Sweet Slow Death*, 1986), *Death Pulls a Double Cross* (1961; as *Coward's Kiss*, 1987), *The Girl With the Long Green Heart* (1965), *Deadly Honeymoon* (1967), *After the First Death* (1969), *The Specialists* (1969), *Ronald Rabbit is a Dirty Old Man* (1971), *Ariel* (1981), *Random Walk* (1988).

Collaborations: *Babe in the Woods* completion of novel by William Ard (1960), *Code of Arms*, with Harold King (1981), *Into the Night*, completion of novel by Cornell Woolrich (1987).

as Paul Kavanagh: *Such Men are Dangerous* (1969), *The Triumph of Evil* (1971), *Not Coming Home to You* (1974).

Short Stories. *Sometimes They Bite* (1983), *Like a Lamb to Slaughter* (1984), *Some Days You Get the Bear* (1993), *Ehrengraf for the Defense* (1994), *One-Night Stands* (1999), *Collected Mystery Stories* (1999), *The Lost Cases of Ed London* (2001), *Enough Rope* (2002).

Non-fiction. *Writing the Novel from Plot to Print* (1979), *Telling Lies for Fun & Profit* (1981), *Write for Your Life* (1986), *Spider, Spin Me a Web* (1987).

Editor. *Death Cruise* (1999), *Master's Choice* (1999), *Master's Choice 2* (2000), *Opening Shots* (2000), *Speaking of Lust* (2001), *Speaking of Greed* (2001), *Opening Shots 2* (2001).

Pen-names: Jill Emerson, Chip Harrison, Paul Kavanagh. Also ghost-wrote under the name William Ard.

Where to start: Scudder, *When the Sacred Ginmill Closes*; Rhodenbarr, *The Burglar Who Painted Like Mondrian.*

Awards: Edgar, best short story (1985, 1994, 1998), best novel (1992); Nero Wolfe Award (1979); Shamus, best hardcover novel (1983), best story (1985,

1994), best novel (1994); Japanese Maltese Falcon (1987, 1992), German Marlowe (1995), French Societe 813 Trophy (1985, 1994), MWA Grand Master (1994), Anthony, best anthology (2001).
Books about: *After Hours: Conversations with Lawrence Block* (1995) by Ernie Bulow & Lawrence Block.
Website: <www.lawrenceblock.com>
Similar stuff: Donald E. WESTLAKE.
Final fact: The idea for the Scudder book *A Long Line of Dead Men* came to LB while he was in agony riding a Bactrian camel across the Takla Makan desert in China – so almost but not quite Lawrence of Arabia.

Kyril Bonfiglioli (1928–85) UK

A Master of Arts from Balliol College, Oxford, KB was, for the first half of his adult life, a director of two art galleries, a bookshop and an antique shop. He also edited the magazine *Science Fantasy* from 1964–6 and launched its short-lived successor *Impulse*. In 1966, however, KB made his money through a special art deal and retired. Eventually, KB overcame his natural slothfulness and wrote *Don't Point that Thing at Me*. This introduced the character of Charlie Mortdecai, a rather unpleasant art dealer (modelled unglamorously on KB himself) who, similar to Jonathan GASH's Lovejoy, which appeared at about the same time, is drawn into unsavoury situations as a result of his rather dubious connections. Mortdecai is a coward and a cheat but has his own code of honour when up against other cowards and cheats and ends up having to investigate crimes before the dirty gets done on him. The first book won the John Creasey Memorial Award. The series has been alikened to Ronald Firbank writing Raymond Chandler or P.G. Wodehouse writing Edgar Wallace. KB wrote only the three books. A fourth, based on his notes, was completed by Craig Brown as *The Great Mortdecai Moustache Mystery*, where Mortdecai is called back to solve a murder at an Oxford college. KB also wrote a picaresque historical adventure, *All the Tea in China*, in which a Dutchman trying to earn his fortune ends up in the tea and opium trade.

Novels

Mortdecai series: *Don't Point That Thing at Me* (1972; as *Mortdecai's Endgame*, US 1972), *Something Nasty in the Woodshed* (1976), *After You with the Pistol* (1979) – these 3 assembled as *The Mortdecai Trilogy* (1991). Completed by Craig Brown, *The Great Mortdecai Moustache Mystery* (1996).
Non-series: *All the Tea in China* (1978).

Where to start: *Don't Point That Thing at Me.*
Awards: John Creasey Memorial Award (1973).
Similar stuff: Jonath GASH's Lovejoy books.
Final fact: KB was at one time a sabre champion.

Hilary Bonner (b. 1949) UK

Former showbusiness editor of the *Mail on Sunday* and *Daily Mirror*, HB turned freelance in 1989 but continues to cover film, television and theatre. She worked with actor Gordon Kaye on his autobiography and with Dennis Kirkland on his book about Benny Hill as well as writing the official companion to the TV series *Heartbeat: The Real Life Story* (1994; see Nicholas RHEA). In 1994 she completed her first novel, *The Cruelty of Morning*, which she had started 20 years earlier. It deals with a reporter who, in her younger days, discovered a woman's body in the sea at the same time as a girl disappears, and 20 years later finds herself investigating the deaths. HB's novels have become noted for their sexual content – they've been likened to Ruth Rendell with a dash of Jackie Collins. But this does not detract from the fascination or horror of the crimes. HB's books are psychological thrillers with intriguing murder puzzles and revealing investigations. Two of the books feature DCI Rose Piper of which *For Death Comes Softly*, where she finds her life falling apart and seeks solace on a remote North Devon island, is the closest HB comes to the gothic suspense novel in true Daphne du Maurier style.

Novels

Rose Piper series: *A Passion So Deadly* (1998), *For Death Comes Softly* (1999).
Non-series: *The Cruelty of Morning* (1995), *A Fancy to Kill For* (1997), *A Deep Deceit* (2000), *A Kind of Wild Justice* (2001), *A Moment of Madness* (2002).

Where to start: *A Passion so Deadly*.
Similar stuff: Nicci FRENCH.
Final fact: HB reached her present height of 1.8m (5ft 11in) when she was 13.

J.S. Borthwick (b. 1923) US

JSB, a former volunteer teacher, lives in Maine, where most of her books are set. She has written a series featuring a young graduate student turned teacher, Sarah Deane, and a doctor and fellow bird-watcher Alex Mackenzie. In the first book Deane's lover is killed, and over the course of the next few books Deane and Mackenzie draw closer till they marry in *The Bridled Groom*. The books are all solid traditional mysteries, with a leisurely pace and a light touch but also a slight biting edge to make them just a cut above simple cozies. In fact JSB calls them "medium egg cozies – yolk runny, white firm." They handle topical subjects, such as a cure for cancer in the first book, and involve some fascinating puzzles, such as a victim entombed in an ice sculpture in *The Student Body*. The books are replete with maps and plans, drawn by JSB's daughter, alerting the reader to the need to follow the plot carefully.

Novels

Deane & McKenzie series: *The Case of the Hook-Billed Kites* (1982), *The Down East Murders* (1985), *The Student Body* (1986), *Bodies of Water* (1990), *Dude on*

Arrival (1992), *The Bridled Groom* (1994), *Dolly is Dead* (1995), *The Garden Plot* (1997), *My Body Lies Over the Ocean* (1999), *Coup de Grace* (2000), *Murder in the Rough* (2002).

Full name: Joan Scott Creighton-Borthwick.
Similar stuff: Jane LANGTON, Ann CLEEVES.
Final fact: JSB's first book came about when she noticed that bird-watchers were so intent on looking out for the latest avian appearance that a murder could happen right under their binoculars and they wouldn't notice.

Gail Bowen (b. 1942) Canada

GB is one of Canada's foremost crime-fiction writers. Born in Toronto, she lives and works in Saskatchewan, where she is Assistant Professor and Department Head of English at the Saskatchewan Indian Federated College of the University of Regina. Her continuing character is Joanne Kilbourn, a professor of and commentator on political science. GB uses this as a means of exploring political issues and her books are flavoured with native Canadian art and culture. There are perhaps a few too many murders for a college professor to stumble across – her husband, a cabinet minister, has already been murdered before the first book starts, and this makes her determined to have a strong home-life for her children. Kilbourn's friends, acquaintances and enemies die at the rate of one or two a book, making her a dangerous person to know. Nevertheless the crimes are deftly handled, the writing is tight, and the characters well drawn. The fourth in the series, *A Colder Kind of Death*, won the Canadian Albert Ellis Award, and it is the most profound book of the series so far. Kilbourn has to reappraise her life and family as she digs deeper into her husband's murder and becomes the suspect in another murder. All of the books have been adapted as movies for Canadian television.

Novels

Joanne Kilbourn series: *Deadly Appearances* (1990), *Murder at the Mendel* (1991; as *Love and Murder*, US 1993), *The Wandering of Soul Murders* (1992), *A Colder Kind of Death* (1994), *A Killing Spring* (1996), *Verdict in Blood* (1998), *Burying Ariel* (2000).

Full name: Gail Bowen (*née* Bartholomew).
Awards: Arthur Ellis, best novel, 1995, YWCA Woman of the Year (1995).
Similar stuff: Caroline ROE (as Medora Sale), L.R. WRIGHT.
Final fact: Together with Ron Marken, GB has written a play, *Dancing in the Poppies* (1993), adapted from her first novel *1919*, which is based on the private letters between a soldier in the War and his love back home.

John Brady (b. 1955) Eire/Canada

The work of the police force in Ireland is brought home in JB's series about Sergeant (later Inspector) Matt Minogue of the Dublin C.I.D. JB was born in Dublin but emigrated to Canada in 1975, after he graduated from Trinity College. He was an elementary school teacher before turning full-time writer. The first of the series, *Stone of the Heart*, starts at Trinity College, where a student is found murdered. Minogue has only just come back to duty after being nearly killed in an IRA bombing, and his superiors are concerned as to whether he can cope. Minogue has to tread carefully, even when the case takes on sinister political overtones. All of the books in the series reflect the tensions in Northern Ireland where Minogue has to watch his back at every turn. But he is tenacious and, despite the bleakness of many of the situations – such as his partner's attempted suicide in *All Souls* – the grimness of the locale, and the constant lurking menace, he remains sensitive and even witty. Excellent characterization and complex plots are the hallmark of this series. The first book won the Arthur Ellis award whilst *The Good Life*, where he investigates the death of a woman dragged from the Grand Canal and has to outwit Dublin's underworld, was shortlisted for the award.

Novels

Inspector Minogue series: *Stone of the Heart* (1988), *Unholy Ground* (1989), *Kaddish in Dublin* (1990), *All Souls* (1993), *The Good Life* (1994), *A Carra King* (2000).

Full name: John Mary Brady.
Awards: Arthur Ellis, best first novel (1989).
Similar stuff: Bartholomew GILL.

Jay Brandon (b. 1953) US

JB runs his own law firm in San Antonio, Texas, the setting of most of his books. He previously served with the District Attorney's office and has a Master's Degree in writing (from John Hopkins University) so is amply qualified for his second career as a writer of legal thrillers. Although none of his books is connected (except for occasional common characters), because several revolve around the DA's function in Texas there is a feeling of unity between them. They are not courtroom dramas in the traditional sense but explore the tensions and dangers that surround the lawyer's work. In *Deadbolt* a lawyer is haunted by a dangerous former client whose case he lost. *Fade the Heat* (shortlisted for an Edgar) and *Loose Among the Lambs* feature D.A. Mark Blackwell who finds his son is being framed for rape in the first, and becomes involved with a child molester in the second. In *Local Rules*, an assistant DA finds the whole town against him when he tries to defend a boy charged with attempted murder. In *Defiance County* a young female prosecutor has to take on small town anger and pressure when the parents of a young girl are murdered and the girl kidnapped. DA Chris Sinclair appears in *Angel of Death*, where he has to pit his wits against a dangerous community leader, and in *After Image* where he finds skeletons in his own closet. JB sometimes spreads his net wider. In *Tripwire* the police try to protect a witness against a possible hit-man who claims he's the witness's long lost son. In *Predator's Waltz* a small shopkeeper finds himself in the midst of an Asian gang war. In all of his books there is tension, drama and intensity. *Executive Privilege* involves a lawyer having to serve papers on the President of the United States.

Novels. *Deadbolt* (1985), *Tripwire* (1987), *Predator's Waltz* (1989), *Fade the Heat* (1990), *Rules of Evidence* (1992), *Loose Among the Lambs* (1993), *Local Rules* (1995), *Defiance County* (1996), *Angel of Death* (1998), *After Image* (2000), *Executive Privilege* (2001).

Full name: Jay Robert Brandon
Website: <www.jaybrandon.com>
Similar stuff: William BERNHARDT, John GRISHAM.
Final fact: JB still works as a lawyer, doing mostly family law and criminal appeals. Family law includes divorce work and JB grimly notes that "more divorce lawyers get shot each year than any other kind."

Lilian Jackson Braun (b. 1919?) US

A true ailurophile, LJB, who was for many years a feature writer for the *Detroit Free Press* and before that a copywriter and a Public Relations Director, has done more than anyone to popularize the cat detective story. LBJ was spurred into writing about cats following the death of her own Siamese after a fall from a tenth-storey balcony. She sold a few unconnected stories to *EQMM* in the early sixties before beginning her noted series featuring Jim Qwilleran (known as Qwill), a middle-aged and rather untidy divorcé, and his two Siamese feline sleuths, Koko and Yum Yum. Qwill, like LJB, was a newspaper feature writer and his assignments always took him to new and interesting places where crimes and mysteries were not hard to find. The cats themselves do not solve the crimes, Qwill is the detective, but they help with their sniffs and scratching, their mannerisms and attitudes. Nevertheless Koko acts like he is psychic whilst Yum Yum is quiet and intuitive. LBJ has a real kinship with cats and anyone, cat-lover or no, cannot help but appreciate her wonderfully descriptive writing and perceptive observation. She completed three books in the mid-sixties, and though they attracted the interest of cat lovers, they created no great ripples. After eighteen years she returned to the series and suddenly the books caught the public's imagination. *The Cat Who Saw Red*, which will also appeal to those with an interest in *haute cuisine*, was nominated for an Edgar, and the next book, *The Cat Who Played Brahms*, was an Anthony nominee. In these later books Qwill has inherited a fortune and moved to a remote town in upstate Michigan, but that doesn't stop him and the cats travelling to interesting assignments. The books have the atmosphere of cozies, but the crimes can be violent and the mood may shift suddenly, yet there remains a special attachment between Qwill and the reader as he takes us into his confidence in understanding his cats. LJB's deft handling of what could otherwise seem an absurd set-up is what makes these books so special. Despite the title, *The Cat Who Had 14 Tales*, is not part of the series, but is an assortment of ailuromysteries.

Novels

Jim Qwilleran series (all begin *The Cat Who …*): … *Could Read Backwards* (1966), … *Ate Danish Modern* (1967), … *Turned On and Off* (1968), … *Saw Red* (1986), … *Played Brahms* (1987), … *Played Post Office* (1987), … *Knew Shakespeare* (1988), … *Sniffed Glue* (1988), … *Went Underground* (1989), … *Talked to Ghosts* (1990), … *Lived High* (1990), … *Knew a Cardinal* (1991), … *Moved a Mountain* (1992), … *Wasn't There* (1992), … *Went into the Closet* (1993), … *Came to Breakfast* (1994), …*Blew the Whistle* (1994), … *Said Cheese* (1996), … *Tailed a Thief* (1997), … *Sang for the Birds* (1998), … *Saw Stars* (1999), … *Robbed a Bank* (2000), … *Smelled a Rat* (2001), …*Went Up the Creek* (2002).

Short Stories. *The Cat Who Had 14 Tales* (1988).

Books about: *The Cat Who … Companion* by Sharon A. Feaster (1998).

Website: No official site, but the Unofficial Fan Club is at
<www.geocities.com/Heartland/Estates/6371/lillian.html>
and there are other detailed sites at
<members.tripod.com/~KaTeRiNaB69/catwho/catwho.html>
and <home.att.net/~RACapowki/lilian.htm>

Similar stuff: Lydia ADAMSON, Marian BABSON, Rita Mae Brown.

Final fact: LBJ was encouraged to write by her mother but all of her early attempts were sad stories with unhappy endings. Her mother suggested she should write something funny but she couldn't do that until she started writing about cats.

Jon L. Breen (b. 1943) US

Mystery afficianado JLB, who is Professor of English at Rio Hondo College, Whittier, California, has been reviewing books for *EQMM* since 1977 and the *Wilson Library Bulletin* since 1972, and has written extensively about the field garnering five awards in the process. His love for the field is only too apparent in his endearing parodies of classic detectives collected as *Hair of the Sleuthhound*. Further stories and parodies appear in *Drowning Ice Cube*. His love of books comes through in his stories about Rachel Hennings, who inherits a bookshop in Los Angeles. *The Gathering Place* is really a homage to mystery fiction and literary icons. In *Touch of the Past*, which was shortlisted for the CWA Dagger Award, Rachel finds herself investigating the murder of a long-dead writer. JLB also has a passion for sport and this fuelled his short series of stories about baseball umpire Ed Gordon in *EQMM* (1971-2) and his novels featuring Jerry Brogan, an announcer at a horse racetrack. Because JLB knows the field so well he knows how to avoid standard plots and devices, yet his books have a simplicity and an ease that belie their intricate construction.

Novels
Jerry Brogan series: *Listen for the Click* (1983; as *Vicar's Roses*, UK 1984), *Triple Crown* (1985), *Loose Lips* (1990), *Hot Air* (1991).
Rachel Hennings series: *The Gathering Place* (1984), *Touch of the Past* (1988).
Short Stories. *Hair of the Sleuthhound* (1982), *Drowning Ice Cube and Other Stories* (1999).
Non-fiction. (selective) *What About Murder?* (1981) and *What About Murder (1981-1991)?* (1993), *Novel Verdicts* (1984).
Editor. anthologies: *American Murders,* with Rita A. Breen 1986); *Murder California Style*, with John Ball (1987); *Sleuths of the Century*, with Ed Gorman (2000). Essays: *Murder Off the Rack: Critical Studies of Ten Paperbacks*, with Martin H. Greenberg (1989); *Synod of Sleuths: Essays on Judeo-Christian Detective Fiction*, with Ed Gorman & others (1990).

Full name: Jon Linn Breen.
Where to start: *The Gathering Place.*
Awards: Edgar, best critical work (1982, 1985), Anthony, best critical work (1991, 1994), Macavity, best critical work (1994), Ellen Nehr award, criticism (2000).
Similar stuff: sport, Dick FRANCIS, John FRANCOMBE; bookshop owners, John Dunning, Joan HESS.
Final fact: JLB's first job was as a radio sports announcer.

[John] Michael Brett *pseudonym, see* Miles Tripp

Simon Brett (b. 1945) UK

SB has been a full-time writer since 1980. Prior to that he was a programme producer for BBC Radio (1967–77) and at London Weekend Television (1977–9). He worked primarily in light entertainment producing many notable comedy programmes, and was instrumental in getting Douglas Adams's *The Hitchhiker's Guide to the Galaxy* on radio. He still writes for radio, recently contributing scripts to Barry Devlin's series about academic Franciscan priest and philosophy lecturer Paolo Baldi (first series, January 2000) whose study of semiotics gives him a new perspective on crime. SB is best known for his long-running series of novels featuring Charles Paris, a middle-aged actor who is frequently not acting, and who has grown too fond of the bottle. Through Paris we get a cynical but light-hearted view of the world of television, radio and the theatre. Paris is easily bored and, though the bottle provides solace, he likes to test himself as an amateur detective, though he's not very good at it, and his solutions are quite often wrong until some last-minute revelation. The value of the "Old Boy network" is strong in these books, not only in providing Paris with work but in helping him resolve crimes. Paris is often helped by his old college friend and rich solicitor, Gerald Venables. The plots are often light but the characterization is strong and the acting world fascinating. The Mrs Pargeter books are similarly light-hearted and turn the typical "cozy" on its head. She is a widow and though she never fully understood what her husband did it was clearly nefarious and shady. Mrs P. has inherited the business "empire" but now uses the criminal skills of her husband's loyal band of "employees" to right wrongs. Recently SB has started a new series, inspired by the location of his home in Sussex, where he and his family moved in the 1980s. Set in the retirement village of Fethering, it features Carole Seddon and her new-found friend Jude. In the first book they find a body on the beach but it disappears by the time the police arrive. Of his non-series mysteries, two are "cozies", but the others show a different side to SB's work. *A Shock to the System* (filmed 1990, starring Michael Caine) depicts a spoiled and arrogant business executive who finds he can get away with murder. *Singled Out* steadily reveals a story of child abuse and serial murder. SB has also written many short stories, three of which have been shortlisted for various awards. They will be found in his two collections, listed below. SB's other books include a novelization of his popular radio series, *After Henry* (later adapted for TV), and the bestselling *How to be a Little Sod* (1992), which with its sequels, *Look Who's Walking* (1994) and *Not Another Little Sod* (1997), are about the perils of raising children.

Novels
Charles Paris series: *Cast in Order of Disappearance* (1975), *So Much Blood* (1976), *Star Trap* (1977), *An Amateur Corpse* (1978), *A Comedian Dies* (1979), *The Dead Side of the Mike* (1980), *Situation Tragedy* (1981), *Murder Unprompted* (1982), *Murder in the Title* (1983), *Not Dead, Only Resting* (1984), *Dead Giveaway* (1985), *What Bloody Man is That?* (1987), *A Series of Murders* (1989), *Corporate Bodies* (1991), *A Reconstructed Corpse* (1993), *Sicken and So Die* (1995), *Dead Room Farce* (1998).
Mrs Pargeter series: *A Nice Class of Corpse* (1986), *Mrs, Presumed Dead* (1988), *Mrs Pargeter's Package* (1990), *Mrs Pargeter's Pound of Flesh* (1992), *Mrs Pargeter's Plot* (1996), *Mrs Pargeter's Point of Honour* (1998).
Fethering series: *The Body on the Beach* (2000), *Death on the Downs* (2001), *The Torso in the Town* (2002).
Non-series: *A Shock to the System* (1984), *Dead Romantic* (1985), *The Christmas Crimes at Puzzel Manor* (1991), *Singled Out* (1995).
Children's books: *The Three Detectives and the Missing Superstar* (1986), *The Three Detectives and the Knight in Armour* (1987).
Short Stories. *A Box of Tricks* (1985; as *Tickled to Death*, US 1985), *Crime Writers and Other Animals* (1998).
Plays (published). *Murder in Play* (1994), *Mr. Quigley's Revenge* (1995), *Silhouette* (1998).
Other. *Crime in Rhyme and Other Mysterious Fragments* (1999)

Full name: Simon Anthony Lee Brett.
Where to start: *Cast in Order of Disappearance* or *Singled Out*.
Awards: Writers Guild of Great Britain, radio award (1973), Broadcasting Press Guild award (1987).

Similar stuff: TV or theatrical sleuths: Linda BARNES, Jane DENTINGER, Simon SHAW.
Final fact: SB once dressed up as Father Christmas for a London department store.

Christopher Brookmyre (b. 1968) UK

CB is a Scottish journalist and former film critic. Although his first published book was the fourth he had written it seems he hit the ground running and was instantly hailed a new literary genius. His books are undoubtedly distinctive. Three of them feature investigative journalist Jack Parlabane who, although unscrupulous and morally ambiguous, does have a strong sense of right and wrong and a particular dislike of political corruption. The stories are violent, fast-paced and witty, the writing assured and heavily into Scot's argot, and the whole package, dubbed "Tartan noir" by *The Independent*, is keenly observed and highly contemporary. Of his non-series books, *Not the End of the World*, is set in the USA in the hysteria of the Millenium celebrations, and *One Fine Day in the Middle of the Night* is a darkly humorous thriller where terrorists take over an oil rig and take a school reunion party hostage. CB has also written short fiction of which "Bampot Central" (1997) was shortlisted by the CWA.

Novels

Jack Parlabane series: *Quite Ugly One Morning* (1996), *Country of the Blind* (1997), *Boiling a Frog* (2000).
Non-series: *Not the End of the World* (1998), *One Fine Day in the Middle of the Night* (1999), *A Big Boy Did it and Ran Away* (2001).

Where to start: *Quite Ugly One Morning*.
Awards: Critics' First Blood award, best first crime novel (1997), Sherlock, Best Comic Detective (2001).
Website: <www.brookmyre.clara.net>
Similar stuff: Carl HIAASEN, Mark TIMLIN, Iceberg SLIM.
Final fact: At school CB was hauled up in front of the Head of the English Department for writing stories about necrophilia.

Edna Buchanan (b. 1939) US

Born in New Jersey, EB had a tough childhood when her father abandoned his family. She dropped out of school at 10th grade in order to work full time, having already spent evenings and holidays doing factory work. She moved to Florida in the late sixties where she became a reporter, inaugurating the police beat assignment on the *Miami Herald* in 1973. She became nationally famous for her hard-edged, gritty but very personal reporting for which she was awarded a Pulitzer Prize in 1986. Two collections of her reporting memoirs were assembled as *The Corpse Had a Familiar Face* and *Never Let Them See You Cry*. The first was made into a TV film (1994) starring Elizabeth Montgomery as EB. EB took a year's sabbatical in 1988 to write her first novel, and has never looked back. *Nobody Lives Forever* explores the dark side of Miami and shows how various police officers are affected by the crimes of a serial killer. It was shortlisted for the Edgar Award for best first novel. *Contents Under Pressure* introduced her main character, Britt Montero who, like EB, is a police-beat reporter for a Miami newspaper. There, EB insists, the similarity ends as Montero is everything EB wants to be – tough, determined, fearless, though EB was equally determined as a reporter. Once reporting a plane crash in Miami she nearly fell from a second-floor balcony but was saved by a detective – yet she still went on asking questions. That relentless drive is what fuels EB's books and puts Montero in danger. In the first book she tries to uncover racism in the police force following the death of a black football star in a car chase. In *Miami, It's Murder*, which was also nominated for an Edgar, a serial rapist is terrorizing Miami. In *Suitable for Framing* a teenage gang is stealing cars and shooting the drivers. The one big difference from real life is that in EB's stories the villains get their just deserts. EB finds writing fiction therapeutic because she can ensure that justice is done.

Novels
Britt Montero series: *Contents Under Pressure* (1992), *Miami, It's Murder* (1994), *Suitable for Framing* (1995), *Act of Betrayal* (1996), *Margin of Error* (1997), *Garden of Evil* (1999), *You Only Die Twice* (2001).
Non-series: *Nobody Lives Forever* (1990), *Pulse* (1998).
Non-fiction. *The Corpse Had a Familiar Face* (1987), *Never Let Them See You Cry* (1992).

Full name: Edna Rydzik Buchanan.
Where to start: *Nobody Lives Forever*.
Awards: Society of Professional Journalists, Green Eyeshade award (1982), Pulitzer Prize for general reporting (1986).
Similar stuff: Jan BURKE, Faye KELLERMAN.
Final fact: When EB was a reporter someone tried to mug her but she just pushed him aside saying that there wasn't time as she had a deadline to meet.

Marie Buchanan *pseudonym, see* Clare Curzon

Edward Bunker (b. 1933) US

No one can write crime fiction like EB, because few have that combination of experience and talent. Between 1951 and 1976, EB spent 18 years in and out of various state penitentiaries. He learned how to survive amongst the most hardened criminals. Whenever he was released he was unable to fight the system and before long was back in prison. At one time a parole violation turned him into a fugitive on the FBI's most-wanted list. But his delight in reading, his innate intelligence (an IQ of 152), and his discovery that fellow prisoner Caryl Chessman had sold books, focused his mind on becoming a writer. EB acquired a typewriter and the support he needed. He wrote 6 books and 100 short stories spread over 17 years before he sold his first book, *No Beast So Fierce*. It is a highly autobiographical account of an ex-con's efforts to go straight but the system drags him down. It was filmed as *Straight Time* (1978), starring Dustin Hoffman, and earned the accolade from Quentin Tarantino as the "best first-person crime novel ever written". EB, recently paroled from gaol, was given a small part in the film, the first of what would be 19 film appearances. His next book, *The Animal Factory*, was a realistic view of life inside a prison. It was followed by *Little Boy Blue*, where EB dug into his childhood memories and showed how an early life in institutions dragged a boy into a life of crime. This book sold poorly and EB concentrated on writing or adapting screenplays. His big success came with the Jon Voight film *Runaway Train* (1985), when EB was brought in to incorporate realistic dialogue and ended up making the script his own. It received an Oscar nomination. After 15 years EB wrote a fourth novel, less autobiographical but still drawn from life. *Dog Eat Dog* concerns three ex-cons who try to cope under California's three strikes law but are drawn to commit the perfect crime.

Novels. *No Beast So Fierce* (1973; as *Straight Time*, 1978), *The Animal Factory* (1977), *Little Boy Blue* (1981), *Dog Eat Dog* (1996).
Autobiography. *Mr Blue: Memoirs of a Renegade* (1999; as *Education of a Felon*, US 2000).

Where to start: *No Beast So Fierce*.
Awards: CWA, Non-fiction Gold Dagger (2000).
Similar stuff: Clarence COOPER, Jr., James ELLROY.
Final fact: EB's mother was a chorus girl in the Busby Berkeley musicals and through her EB knew Louise Wallis (wife of Hal Wallis) who bought him his first typewriter and introduced him to Ayn Rand, Aldous Huxley and William Randolph Hearst.

James Lee Burke (b. 1936) US

JLB is best known for his series featuring Louisiana Cajun detective Dave Robicheaux. They are amongst the darkest, most intense novels in the genre spiking the traditional hard-boiled novel with gothic noir. In the first, *The Neon Rain*, Robicheaux, a Vietnam veteran, gradually overcoming his drink problem, has worked fourteen years for the New Orleans Police Department. By the end of the book, with a complicated and violent plot involving drugs and arms-smuggling and a corrupt cop (his partner), we find him resigning from the police force. By the end of the second book, *Heaven's Prisoners* (filmed 1996), he is newly married, they have adopted a daughter (actually an illegal immigrant) but his wife is murdered. In subsequent novels Robicheaux wrestles with his grief and the demons and ghosts that both torture and guide him, and moves continually into ever more dangerous territory. JLB pulls no punches. His books are violent, the torment experienced by Robicheaux and others is tangible, the writing vivid and the characters, which include some of the most evil and vicious in crime fiction, haunting. The result is passionate and unforgettable.

JLB began his literary career as a writer of complex character-driven regional novels, in the vein of William Faulkner but his first three books, starting with *Half of Paradise* (1965), stirred little interest at the time. After his third book it was twelve years before his next appeared, *Two for Texas* (1983), the closest JLB has come to a western, based on his mother's family history – the Hollands. He returned to this family for a new series featuring Texas small-town defence lawyer Billy Bob Holland. Racked with guilt from his own past, Holland uncovers corruption and deceit in his own town when trying to defend a local boy accused of rape and murder. Though not as dark as the Robicheaux series, the Holland books are just as complex and almost as intense.

It took JLB nine years to sell his one other crime novel, *The Lost Get-Back Boogie*, which is a straight non-mystery about a man coming to terms with having committed a murder. Another deep psychological character study it earned JLB a Pulitzer Prize nomination.

Novels

Dave Robicheaux series: *The Neon Rain* (1987), *Heaven's Prisoners* (1988), *Black Cherry Blues* (1989), *A Morning for Flamingoes* (1990), *A Stained White Radiance* (1992), *In the Electric Mist with Confederate Dead* (1993), *Dixie City Jam* (1994), *Burning Angel* (1995), *Cadillac Jukebox* (1996), *Sunset Limited* (1998), *Purple Cane Road* (2000), *Jolie Blon's Bounce* (2002).

Billy Bob Holland series: *Cimarron Rose* (1997), *Heartwood* (1999), *Bitterroot* (2001).

Non-series: *The Lost Get-Back Boogie* (1986).

Short Stories. *The Convict* (1985).

Where to start: *The Neon Rain.*

Awards: Edgar, best novel (1990, 1998), Grand Prix de Littérature Policière, best foreign (1992), Hammett, best novel (1995), French Trophée 813 (1998), CWA Golden Dagger (1998), Guggenheim Fellowship, 1989.

Similar stuff: James ELLROY, Jim THOMPSON.

Final fact: JLB received 111 rejection slips before he sold *The Lost Get-Back Boogie*, which he claims is the most rejected book in the history of New York publishing.

Jan Burke (b. 1953) US

Born in Texas, JB moved to southern California when she was seven. She graduated from California State University with a degree in history and her capacity for research is only too evident in the background of her books. These feature Irene Kelly, an investigative reporter in the fictional Californian coastal city of Las Piernas, south of Los Angeles. She meets up with and later marries Frank Harriman, a local homicide detective. The first book, *Goodnight Irene*, in which Kelly is drawn into a 30-year-old murder case, was shortlisted as the best first novel for both the Agatha and Anthony Awards. These books aren't cozies but strong and often violent hard-boiled thrillers. JB's strength is in exploring the effects of crime upon Kelly and on the victims or their relatives. In *Sweet Dreams, Irene*, she suffers extreme emotional trauma after her confrontation with three violent men and this is still reverberating through *Dear Irene*, when she starts to receive threats from a serial killer. *Hocus*, in which her husband is kidnapped, earned an Agatha and a Macavity nomination and *Bones*, where a vicious murderer plea-bargains in order to reveal the location of a body of someone who disappeared four years ago, won the Edgar award. JB's work is powerful and memorable. Her short story "Unharmed" (*EQMM*, 1994) not only won the Macavity Award but was also voted best story of the year by the readers of *EQMM*, the first time a story by a woman had ever topped the annual poll.

Novels
Irene Kelly series: *Goodnight, Irene* (1993), *Sweet Dreams, Irene* (1994), *Dear Irene* (1995), *Remember Me, Irene* (1996), *Hocus* (1997), *Liar* (1998), *Bones* (1999), *Flight* (2001).
Short Stories. Special limited editions of *Unharmed* (1996) and *A Fine Set of Teeth* (1997).

Awards: Macavity, best short story (1995), *Romantic Times*, Lifetime Achievement Award for Contemporary Suspense (1995), Edgar, best novel (2000), Agatha, best short story (2001).
Website: <www.janburke.com>
Similar stuff: Sue GRAFTON, Faye KELLERMAN, Sara PARETSKY.
Final fact: JB's research for her books has allowed her to crawl around inside a huge Sikorsky helicopter, follow cadaver dogs to where a body has lain in a field, examine a drawer full of US Civil War soldiers' skulls, and visit a factory where artificial limbs are designed. All in a day's work.

W. J. Burley (b. 1914) UK

WJB worked as a gas engineer until 1950 but then studied at Balliol College, Oxford, obtained a degree in Zoology, and became Head of Biology, first at a school in Richmond (Surrey) and then in his native Cornwall, where he now lives. He became a full-time writer when he retired at 60. Soon after he wrote a non-series book called *The Schoolmaster*, in which a relatively timid, guilt-racked teacher is the main suspect for the murder of his wife's lover. WJB had started writing only a few years earlier when attracted to the genre by the books of Georges Simenon. Two of his early books feature Henry Pym, a zoologist at a grammar school, who uses his knowledge to analyse the behaviour of humans. WJB soon dropped Pym in favour of Charles Wycliffe, a

Superintendent in the Cornish C.I.D. Cornwall is an excellent area for mystery stories, not only because of its dramatic scenery and coastline but because the county attracts intellectuals, artists and "new-agers", and thus allows ample scope for unusual story-lines, all of which are admirably exploited in the series. WJB enjoys exploring the tensions between various groups of locals or visitors, and the psychological consequences that arise. Wycliffe is more of an intuitive detective than a detail man. He likes to study the people who knew the victim (who is usually a young woman) and deduce motives and solutions from their behaviour. Over the 30 years of the series WJB has shifted increasingly towards psychological character studies. In *Wycliffe and the Beales* a once-respected villager becomes a tramp, whilst in *Wycliffe and the Redhead,* the apparent suicide of a recently released prisoner leads Wycliffe into a complicated family relationship. The series was adapted for television in 1993 with Jack Shepherd as Wycliffe.

Novels

Pym series: *A Taste of Power* (1966), *Death in Willow Pattern* (1970).

Wycliffe series: *Three-Toed Pussy* (1966), *To Kill a Cat* (1970; as *Wycliffe and How to Kill a Cat*, 1993), *Guilt Edged* (1971; as *Wycliffe and the Guilt-Edged Alibi*, 1994), *Death in a Salubrious Place* (1973), *Death in Stanley Street* (1974), *Wycliffe and the Pea-Green Boat* (1975), *Wycliffe and the Schoolgirls* (1976), *Wycliffe and the Scapegoat* (1978), *Wycliffe in Paul's Court* (1980), *Wycliffe's Wild-Goose Chase* (1982), *Wycliffe and the Beales* (1983), *Wycliffe and the Four Jacks* (1985), *Wycliffe and the Quiet Virgin* (1986), *Wycliffe and the Winsor Blue* (1987), *Wycliffe and the Tangled Web* (1988), *Wycliffe and the Cycle of Death* (1990), *Wycliffe and the Dead Flautist* (1991), *Wycliffe and the Last Rites* (1992), *Wycliffe and the Dunes Mystery* (1993), *Wycliffe and the House of Fear* (1995), *Wycliffe and the Redhead* (1997), *Wycliffe and the Guild of Nine* (2000).

Non-series: *The Schoolmaster* (1977), *Charles and Elizabeth* (1979), *The House of Care* (1981).

Full name: William John Burley.
Where to start: *Wycliffe and How to Kill a Cat.*
Similar stuff: Roger BUSBY's Riley series.

Rex Burns (b. 1935) US

Under his real name of Raoul Sehler, RB was a Professor of American literature at the University of Colorado until he retired in 2000. Born in San Diego he earned his degree in English and Creative Writing at Stanford University and went on to get his PhD in American Studies at the University of Minnesota, his studies interrupted by a term in the US Marines, rising to the rank of Captain. He was forty before he wrote his first crime novel but experience told and *The Alvarez Journal* won an Edgar award. It introduced Gabriel Wager, a detective in the Denver Police Department, who is half Hispanic, and is troubled by a failed marriage, a tendency to drink, and his mixed heritage – ethnic issues feature strongly in the series. Wager seeks redemption in proving he is a good cop and overcoming his problems. The result is a solid and realistic police procedural series that incorporates an astute understanding of modern police methods and mentality. There is a strong sequence in *Angle of Attack*, where Wager endeavours to entrap a murderer who is eluding the law, and *The Avenging Angel* (filmed 1988 as *Messenger of Death*), where Wager deals with his guilt over his past actions whilst dealing with a fanatical group of Mormon renegades. RB's other series features Devlin Kirk, an ex-secret service agent who runs a security company and becomes involved in big business crime, such as the trade in human organs in *Parts Unknown*. As Tom Sehler, RB wrote one novel, *Where Reason Sleeps*, about an ex-Marine looking for a runaway girl amongst a satanist cult. RB is also known as an authority on the crime fiction field and has written many scholarly articles and reviews.

Novels

Gabe Wager series: *The Alvarez Journal* (1975), *The Farnsworth Score* (1977), *Speak for the Dead* (1978), *Angle of Attack* (1979), *The Avenging Angel* (1983), *Strip Search* (1984), *Ground Money* (1986), *The Killing Zone* (1988), *Endangered Species* (1993), *Bloodline* (1995), *The Leaning Land* (1997).

Devlin Kirk series: *Suicide Season* (1987), *Parts Unknown* (1990), *Body Guard* (1991), *Body Slam* (1997).

as Tom Sehler: *When Reason Sleeps* (1991).

Editor. *Crime Classics*, with Mary Rose Sullivan (1990).

Real name: Raoul Stephen Sehler.

Pen-names: Rex Burns, Tom Sehler.

Where to start: *The Alvarez Journal.*

Awards: Edgar, best first novel (1976).

Similar stuff: Michael ALLEGRETTO, Bruce COOK.

Final fact: Tom Sehler was the name of RB's father, who always wanted to be a writer but was killed when the USS *Aaron Ward* sank at Guadalcanal in WW2.

Roger Busby (b. 1941) UK

As a crime reporter in Birmingham for many years and an information officer with the Devon and Cornwall Constabulary since 1973, RB was ideally placed to ensure authenticity in his crime novels. H.R.F. KEATING rates them as "among the best informed and most effective police procedurals of the British school." Apart from a few standalone books his output falls distinctly into two groups. While working in Birmingham he wrote the series featuring Detective Inspector Leric, which are set in and around the Midlands and depict an efficient if rather rough-and-ready D.I. who does not always engender loyalty from his colleagues despite, or sometimes because of, his sole-minded determination. The story-lines are fascinating such as *A Reasonable Man* where a body is found in the case for a double bass. After a gap of some years, once settled in Devon, RB began a new series featuring D.I. Riley, this time set in the southwest. Riley is a more up-to-date version of Leric, and the cases more fast-paced. *Snow Man*, a complicated story of three tenacious police detectives up against an international drug-smuggling cartel, won the *Police Review* Award for the year's most authentic police procedural. *Fading Blue* is a collection of stories in anecdotal form, mostly humorous. "The Arrow Bridge Jumper" formed the basis for RB's last novel, *High Jump*, about a maverick policeman who twists the law.

Novels

D.I. Leric series: *Robbery Blue* (1969), *The Frighteners* (1970), *Deadlock* (1971), *A Reasonable Man* (1972), *Pattern of Violence* (1973).
D.I. Rowley series: *The Hunter* (1985), *Snow Man* (1987), *Crackshot* (1990).
Non-series: *Main Line Kill*, with Gerald Holtham (1968), *New Face in Hell* (1976), *Garvey's Code* (1978), *High Jump* (1992).
Short Stories. *Fading Blue* (1984).

Full name: Roger Charles Busby.
Where to start: *The Hunter*.
Awards: CWA/*Police Review* award (1988).
Similar stuff: W.J. BURLEY, Bill KNOX, Jonathan ROSS, R.D. WINGFIELD.

Gwendoline Butler (b. 1922) UK

Under her own name and that of Jennie Melville, GB has written over seventy novels. A few of these are romance (such as *Butterfly* and *Let There be Love*), and a few others are gothic suspense (such as *Ironwood* and *Nun's Castle*) but the majority are crime fiction and these fall into two main groups. First there is the series featuring Inspector John Coffin (who rises through the ranks over the forty years of the series and is now a Chief Commissioner). He operates in the Second City of London, the area south of the Thames, based on Blackheath where GB was born and raised. He is a self-educated man always pushing and proving himself, so he is tough, determined and becomes involved in the more complicated and bizarre crimes, many of them involving elderly women. He lurks in the wings in GB's early books, where Inspector Winter took centre stage, starting with the multiple murder case *Receipt for Murder*. But Coffin soon takes over and the books step up a gear. *Death Lives Next Door* is set in Oxford (where GB earned her degree in modern history, which she then taught for eight years) where Coffin goes on the trail of a missing person. *Coffin on the Water* takes us back to Coffin's very first case after he is demob'd in 1946. *A Coffin from the Past* involves the murder of an MP in a house where a family had been massacred a century before. In *Coffin in Fashion*, set in the swinging sixties, Coffin moves into a new house only to find bodies under the floorboards. GB seldom pulls any punches. Cases involve the murder of children (*A Grave Coffin*), dismemberment (*Coffin's Ghost*) and terrorists (who kidnap Coffin's wife in *Coffin's Game*). Several stories have shock endings, especially *A Coffin for the Canary* and

Coffin Underground, and all of them have a tangible atmosphere of suspense and fear. Readers should note that *A Coffin for Pandora*, for which GB received the CWA Silver Dagger, is not part of the series but is set in Oxford in the 1880s. GB has written several non-series novels with historical settings (*The Vesey Inheritance, The Brides of Friedberg*) and her new series featuring William Pitt's special agents Mearns and Denny, charged with keeping an eye on the increasingly unpredictable George III, which began with *The King Cried Murder!*

As Jennie Melville GB is arguably more famous, as she created the women's police procedural with *Come Home and Be Killed*, featuring Charmian Daniels of Deerham Hill (a fictionalized Oxford and Thames Valley). This series is every bit as powerful as the Coffin novels with the bonus that involving a female detective (who also rises through the ranks to Chief Superintendent) the stories tend to be more sensitive, bringing a pleasing mix of pseudo-coziness and potent atmosphere. The eighth book in the series, *Death Has a Pretty Face*, was shortlisted for a CWA Golden Dagger.

Novels

Inspector Winter series: *Receipt for Murder* (1956), *Dead in a Row* (1957), *The Murdering Kind* (1958), *The Dull Dead* (1958).

Inspector Coffin series: *The Interloper* (1959), *Death Lives Next Door* (1960; as *Dine and be Dead*, US 1960), *Make Me a Murderer* (1961), *Coffin in Oxford* (1962), *Coffin for Baby* (1963), *Coffin Waiting* (1964), *Coffin in Malta* (1964), *A Nameless Coffin* (1966), *Coffin Following* (1968), *Coffin's Dark Number* (1969), *A Coffin from the Past* (1970), *A Coffin for the Canary* (1974; as *Olivia*, US 1974), *Coffin on the Water* (1986), *Coffin in Fashion* (1987), *Coffin Underground* (1988), *Coffin in the Black Museum* (1989; as *Coffin in the Museum of Crime*, US 1990), *Coffin and the Paper Man* (1990), *Coffin on Murder Street* (1991), *Cracking Open a Coffin* (1992), *A Coffin for Charley* (1993), *The Coffin Tree* (1994), *A Dark Coffin* (1995), *A Double Coffin* (1996), *Coffin's Game* (1997; as *Coffin's Games*, US 1998), *A Grave Coffin* (1998), *Coffin's Ghost* (1999), *A Cold Coffin* (2000), *Coffin Knows the Answer* (2002).

Mearns & Denny series: *The King Cried Murder!* (2000).

Non-series: *A Coffin for Pandora* (1973; as *Sarsen Place*, US 1974), *The Vesey Inheritance* (US 1975), *The Brides of Friedberg* (1977; as *Meadowsweet*, US 1977).

as Jennie Melville:

Charmian Daniels series: *Come Home and Be Killed* (1962), *Burning is a Substitute for Loving* (1963), *Murderer's Houses* (1964), *There Lies Your Love* (1965), *A Different Kind of Summer* (1967), *A New Kind of Killer, An Old Kind of Death* (1970; as *A New Kind of Killer*, 1971), *Murder Has a Pretty Face* (1981), *Windsor Red* (1988), *A Cure for Dying* (1989; as *Making Good Blood*, 1990), *Witching Murder* (1990), *Footsteps in the Blood* (1991), *Dead Set* (1992), *Whoever Has the Heart* (1993), *Baby Drop* (1994; as *A Death in the Family*, US 1995), *The Morbid Kitchen* (1995), *The Woman Who Was Not There* (1996), *Revengeful Death* (1997), *Stone Dead* (1998), *Dead Again* (2000), *Loving Murder* (2001).

Non-series: *Nell Alone* (1966), *The Hunter in the Shadows* (1969), *The Summer*

Assassin (1971), *Ironwood* (1972), *Nun's Castle* (1973), *Raven's Forge* (1975), *Dragon's Eye* (1976), *Axwater* (1978; as *Tarot's Tower*, US 1978), *The Painted Castle* (1982), *The Hand of Glass* (1983), *Listen to the Children* (1986), *Death in the Garden* (1987; as *Murder in the Garden*, US 1990), *Complicity* (2000).

Full name: Gwendoline Butler (née Williams).
Pen-names: Jennie Melville.
Where to start: Butler, *Death Lives Next Door*; Melville, *Come Home and Be Killed*.
Awards: CWA Silver Dagger (1973), Romantic Novelists Association, Silver Rose Bowl (1981).
Books about: *Gwendoline Butler: The Inventor of the Women's Police Procedural*, John Kennedy Melling (chapbook, 1993).
Similar stuff: Ruth RENDELL, S.T. HAYMON.
Final fact: When GB created her alter ego of Jennie Melville she would often write two novels at a time, one in the morning the other in the afternoon.

Robert Campbell (1927–2000) US

Born in Newark, New Jersey of Irish descent, RC trained as an artist but after his military service and a few years as a freelance illustrator and fledgling disc-jockey, he turned to the cinema. He wrote and appeared in *Five Guns West* (1955) and several other westerns, which led him to script episodes for the TV series *Maverick* and *Cheyenne*. He scripted many B-movies, including *Man of a Thousand Faces* (1957), the bio-pic of Lon Chaney, for which he was nominated for an Academy Award, and *The Masque of the Red Death* (1964). His best work in TV was for the P.I. series *Harry-O* (1974–6) but he also scripted episodes of *Marcus Welby M.D.* and had *Wondersmith*, his first stage play, produced (1977). During a scriptwriters' strike in Hollywood RC turned to writing novels. The first, *The Spy Who Sat and Waited*, was a thriller about German spies planted as sleepers in Scotland after the First World War. It was shortlisted for the American Book Award. *Circus Couronne* also has a WW1 setting whilst *Where Pigeons Go to Die* (filmed 1990) is a non-crime, touching coming-of-age novel. *Killer of Kings* was his first contemporary crime novel, a dark, intense story of a deranged obsessive who develops a hatred for a film star. Most of RC's stand-alone novels, and his La-La stories featuring the laconic Hollywood P.I. Whistler (the first of which was nominated for a Shamus award), explore themes of obsession, deviousness, power and the inevitable decline into moral and physical decay. This might suggest that RC is a saddened, cynical author, but these are the work of a man who cares about his world and is active, vocal and encouraging. This other side of RC appears in his Jimmy Flannery series. These idiosyncratic novels about a Chicago politician (who somewhat resembles Jimmy Cagney, whom RC knew well) have a lighter, Runyonesque touch and though they remain cynical of the political world, portray a man determined to do his best to ensure justice wins. The first in the series,

The Junkyard Dog, where Flannery's ire is inflamed when a young girl is killed during the bombing of an abortion clinic, won both the Anthony and Edgar awards that year. RC also wrote two novels about womanizing railroad detective Jake Hatch.

Novels

Jimmy Flannery series: *The Junkyard Dog* (1986), *The 600-Pound Gorilla* (1987), *Hip-Deep in Alligators* (1987), *Thinning the Turkey Herd* (1988), *The Cat's Meow* (1988), *Nibbled to Death by Ducks* (1989), *The Gift Horse's Mouth* (1990), *In a Pig's Eye* (1991), *Sauce for the Goose* (1994), *The Lion's Share* (1996), *Pigeon Pie* (1998). First 3 vols available as *A Flannery Trilogy* (1999).
Whistler series: *In La-La Land We Trust* (1986), *Alice in La-La Land* (1987), *Sweet La-La Land* (1990), *The Wizard of La-La Land* (1995).
Jake Hatch series: *Plugged Nickle* (1988), *Red Cent* (1989).
Non-series (first six as R. Wright Campbell): *The Spy Who Sat and Waited* (1975), *Circus Couronne* (1977), *Killer of Kings* (1979), *Malloy's Subway* (1981), *Fat Tuesday* (1983), *Honor* (1987), *Juice* (1988), *Boneyards* (1992).
as F.G. Clinton: *The Tin Cop* (1983).

Full name: Robert Wright Campbell.
Pen-names: F. G. Clinton.
Where to start: *Killer of Kings* or *The Junkyard Dog*.
Awards: Anthony, best paperback original (1987), Edgar, best paperback original (1987).
Similar stuff: Robert CRAIS and Ron GOULART for variants on the Hollywood detective.
Final facts: RC was the inventor of the term "La-la land" for Los Angeles and Hollywood. He was the brother of actor William Campbell who, in the late sixties became notorious as the alleged "impostor" who was supposed to have replaced Paul McCartney in the Beatles after McCartney's rumoured death.

Dorothy Cannell (b. 1943) UK

DC found a receptive readership, especially amongst women, when she made the heroine of her first book overweight and depressed. Ellie Simon, an interior designer, hires an escort when she has to visit an uncle. The escort, Ben Haskell, is a chef who writes erotic novels. When the uncle dies she can only inherit his estate on condition that she loses weight, Haskell writes a clean book and they find some hidden treasure. It's not a crime novel but a delightfully charming cozy mystery – in fact DC is credited with having brought the cozy back into fashion. *Down the Garden Path* does not feature Ellie but introduces two elderly and eccentric spinster sisters, Hyacinth and Primrose Tramwell, who run a detective agency. With *The Widow's Club*, which was nominated for both the Agatha and Anthony awards, DC reintroduced Ellie, now married to Ben, and united them with the Tramwell sisters in an investigation into how the widows became widows. Subsequent books are all rather dotty and amusing mysteries, sometimes also with the Tramwells. DC pokes fun at society's attitudes and conventions. Ellie is always worrying whether she looks overweight and the whole concept of glamour is turned on its head in *How to Murder the Man of Your Dreams*. DC was born and raised in Nottingham but after a holiday in the USA in 1963, she met her future husband and decided to stay. They live in Illinois, the setting for *Mum's the Word*, where Ellie is expecting her first baby but still investigates the deaths of members of a gourmet society. The books are fun if you like your mysteries light and your characters eccentric.

Novels

Ellie Haskell series: *The Thin Woman* (1984), *The Widow's Club* (1988), *Mum's the Word* (1990), *Femmes Fatal* (1992), *How to Murder Your Mother-in-Law* (1994), *How the Murder the Man of Your Dreams* (1995), *The Spring-Cleaning Murders* (1998), *The Trouble With Harriet* (1999), *Bridesmaid Revisited* (2000), *The Importance of Being Earnestine* (2002).
Non-series: *Down the Garden Path* (1985), *God Save the Queen!* (1997).

Full name: Dorothy Reddish Cannell.
Where to start: *The Thin Woman.*
Awards: Romance Writers of America, best paperback novel (1985), Agatha, best short story (1995).
Similar stuff: Joan HESS, Charlotte MACLEOD.
Final fact: DC discovered she had a knack for writing when she wrote an article about socks, which appeared in a college magazine.

Stephen J. Cannell (b. 1941) US

Until recently SJC was better known for his writing and production of some of television's best-loved crime and thriller programmes. He produced or co-created such series as *The Rockford Files*, *The A-Team*, *Hardcastle and McCormick*, *Renegade* (in which he also starred as the corrupt cop) and *Silk Stalkings*. Since 1967 he has scripted over 350 and produced over 1,500 episodes of over 40 different series, which is remarkable for someone who grew up with dyslexia. His break came with *Adam 12*, when he had to deliver a script over a weekend. He became head writer and soon had his own office at Paramount Studios. In 1979 he formed his own independent production company followed in 1986 by the highly successful Cannell Studios. For this tremendous body of TV work SJC received a Shamus lifetime achievement award in 1994. In 1995 the Studios were sold and, though SJC is still heavily into TV and movies, he has also turned to writing thrillers. Both *The Plan* and *Riding the Snake* are political thrillers – the first about a Mafia project to install a puppet President of the USA, the second about a Triad plot to rig Hong Kong's first democratic elections. *Final Victim* sees a bunch of losers trying to regain their credibility in tracking down a serial killer. *King Con*, arguably his most accessible book, sees a con-man wreak revenge by creating the ultimate scam. *The Devil's Workshop* has the development of biological weapons as its background and a woman's efforts to investigate the death of her husband and stop a gang of white supremacists from letting the weapon loose. *The Tin Collectors* is about police corruption and a framed cop. As might be expected from SJC's background these books are fast on action and excitement, but have given him a chance to develop characters. Sometimes, as in *Final Victim*, the plots seem less credible, but when it all comes together, as in *King Con*, the result is a delight.

Novels. *The Plan* (1995), *Final Victim* (1996), *King Con* (1997), *Riding the Snake* (1998), *The Devil's Workshop* (1999), *The Tin Collectors* (2001), *The Viking Funeral* (2002).

Full name: Stephen Joseph Cannell.
Where to start: *King Con*.
Awards: Shamus, lifetime achievement (1994).
Website: <www.cannell.com>
Similar stuff: Warren ADLER.
Final fact: When SJC began writing he would frequently start at 4.00 or 5.00 in the morning and work through to the afternoon, every day including weekends.

Curt Cannon, *see pseudonym* Ed McBain

P. M. Carlson (b. 1940) US

PMC is a qualified psychologist and statistician and has written books on child development and behavioural statistics. Her first series of mystery novels is set in the late sixties and early seventies. It features Maggie Ryan, a college undergraduate in the first book, studying statistics, who becomes involved with a group of actors. Maggie meets her future husband, actor Nick O'Connor, when the life of Nick's then wife, Lisette, is in danger from drug abuse. The series follows Ryan and O'Connor's relationship. They are married by *Murder Unrenovated* and in later books Ryan, now a qualified statistician, uses her skills to unravel puzzles whilst trying to raise her children. The series builds upon its historical background and particularly the effects of the Vietnam War upon the characters. This is most evident in *Murder in the Dog Days* (shortlisted for an Edgar Award) where a Vietnam vet and an ex-nurse turned police detective, both suffer from post-traumatic shock syndrome. All of the stories have an acting theme, which is also the background to PMC's sprightly short stories featuring roguish Bridget Mooney, a scheming actress and sleuth at the turn of the last century who becomes involved with just about every famous person possible. The stories, two of which were nominated for Agatha awards, are collected as *Renowned be thy Grave*. PMC's other series, featuring Marty Hopkins, a working mother and sheriff's deputy in Indiana, is more contemporary. The two novels tackle strong issues including child abuse and racism with considerable skill.

Novels
Ryan & O'Connor series: *Audition for Murder* (1985), *Murder is Academic* (1985), *Murder is Pathological* (1986), *Murder Unrenovated* (1988), *Rehearsal for Murder* (1988), *Murder Misread* (1990), *Murder in the Dog Days* (1991), *Bad Blood* (1991). Marty Hopkins series: *Gravestone* (1993), *Bloodstream* (1995).
Short Stories. Bridget Mooney series: *Renowned be thy Grave* (1998).

Full name: Patricia Carlson (née McEvoy).
Where to start: *Gravestone*.
Similar stuff: Jane DENTINGER, Nancy PICKARD.
Final fact: PMC was born in Guatemala where her father, a radio engineer, and her mother had fled to escape the Depression and find work.

Caleb Carr (b. 1955) US

The Alienist caused a stir when it hit the *NYT* bestseller list for 24 weeks and sold well over a million copies. Set in New York in 1896 it studies the approach of an "alienist", the name then applied to a psychologist, to analysing and detecting a serial killer. The book is intended as the first of an occasional series featuring the alienist, Dr Kreizler, but told by different people within his ensemble. The second book, *The Angel of Darkness*, may lack the shock impact of the first, which had uncovered the seamy side of 1890s New York, but it was more powerful in its portrayal of infanticide. Though a child of the Beat generation – his father was close friends with Allen Ginsburg and Jack Kerouac – CC reacted against that. He was fascinated with military history from an early age, obtained a degree in history, and has written books about the American Civil War. His first book, *Casing the Promised Land* (1980) was a coming-of-age novel. He has also written a science-fiction novel, *Killing Time* (2000) set in the year 2023 when the Internet is destroying the fabric of society. CC intends to return to the world of the alienist and to other historical thrillers.

Novels
Dr Kreizler series: *The Alienist* (1994), *The Angel of Darkness* (1997).

Awards: Anthony, best first novel (1995), Grand Prix de Littérature Policière Best Foreign (1996).
Similar stuff: William MARSHALL's Virgil Tillman books for 1890s New York.
Final fact: CC's father, Lucien, was imprisoned in 1944 for murder but was released after two years, having convinced the court it was self-defence.

Jolyon Carr *pseudonym, see* Ellis Peters

Heron Carvic (1913–80) UK

HC was an established actor, noted for his radio performances because of his mellifluous voice. Moving into semi-retirement, he created the character of Miss Emily Seeton, a retired art teacher who settles in a village in

Kent, not unlike HC's own near Maidstone. Miss Seeton is rather like a cross between Miss Marple and Hiram Holliday. Innocent, sweet, naïve, she treats adults and children alike, but appears to have an almost preternatural psychic vision of evil. In the first book, *Picture Miss Seeton*, which was shortlisted for an Edgar award, Miss Seeton disturbs a murderer, but can only recall a shadowy figure. However when she draws a sketch it becomes a perfect portrait of the killer. Her ability to produce these "psychic" sketches and her amazing knack at getting out of difficulties with her knowledge of yoga and her trusty umbrella makes her invaluable to Scotland Yard. This ultra-cozy series is a delight. Tragically HC was killed in a car accident on his return home from a BBC recording, but the series failed to die. Its continued popularity caused the publisher to resurrect it with books written first by James MELVILLE and then Sarah J. MASON.

Novels
Emily Seeton series: *Picture Miss Seeton* (1968), *Miss Seeton Draws the Line* (1969), *Miss Seeton, Bewitched* (1971; as *Witch Miss Seeton*, US 1971), *Miss Seeton Sings* (1974), *Odds on Miss Seeton* (1975).

Real name: Geoffrey Richard William Harris.
Pen-name: Heron Carvic.
Similar stuff: Dorothy Gilman, Simon BRETT.
Final fact: HC played the part of Gandalf in the 1967 BBC radio adaptation of *The Hobbit*.

Sarah Caudwell (1939–2000) UK

SC's death of cancer at the age of 60 robbed the field of one of its rare gems. Although she was not prolific, SC's books were worth the wait. They were meticulously researched, finely crafted and ingeniously plotted. Her last book had been promised since 1997, but SC continued to work on it until her final illness overtook her. All four books feature Professor Hilary Tamar, an Oxford don and occasional sleuth of deliberately undefined sex. SC had read law at St Anne's College, Oxford and had worked hard to break down the barriers to women's admission to the Oxford Union. Tamar lectures on legal history. He has an intricate knowledge of the minutiae of medieval English law, and becomes involved in cases – or more aptly "experiences" – arising amongst the barristers in chambers at Lincoln's Inn, known as the "nursery". These are a wonderful bunch of the exotic, eccentric, erotic and elaborate, and their adventures and investigations are equally engaging. Usually one or more of the barristers will venture to foreign climes only to need the help of the others in resolving a complicated problem, often by correspondence. The third book, *The Sirens Sang of Murder*, a complex case involving international tax law, murder and witchcraft, won an Anthony Award. SC wrote only one short story, "An Acquaintance with Mr

Collins" (*A Suit of Diamonds*, 1990) in which Tamar ponders the complexities of inheritance law. SC was herself a practising barrister for many years.

Novels
Hilary Tamar series: *Thus Was Adonis Murdered* (1981), *The Shortest Way to Hades* (1985), *The Sirens Sang of Murder* (1989), *The Sibyl in Her Grave* (2000).

Real name: Sarah Cockburn.
Pen-name: Sarah Caudwell.
Awards: Anthony, best novel (1990).
Similar stuff: Edmund Crispin, John MORTIMER.
Final fact: SC's father was the author Claud Cockburn and her mother the actress Jean Ross, believed to be the model for Christopher Isherwood's Sally Bowles.

Simon Challis, *see under pseudonym* Philip Daniels

Peter Chambers, *see under pseudonym* Philip Daniels

Hampton Charles *pseudonym, see* James Melville.

Kate Charles (b. 1950) US

Born and raised in Cincinatti, with a degree from Illinois State University, JC came to England in 1986 and has stayed. Her transplantation was so thorough that many believed that she was an English author and US publishers have regarded her recent books as "too English". Her series featuring solicitor David Middleton-Brown and artist Lucy Kingsley are firmly in the classic English tradition. They all have a church background – KC has worked as a church administrator and she has made Middleton-Brown interested in church architecture. In the first book, which involves the blackmailing of a local priest, Middleton-Brown meets Lucy Kingsley and their relationship is part of the thread through the series. The plots are rich in church politics, and there is a cast full of fascinating characters with enough ecclesiastical lore to please the afficianado. *The Snares of Death* looks at the conflict between high and low church, and *A Dead Man Out of Mind* involves the ordination of women. In 1996, after undergoing open-heart surgery, KC wrote a one-off suspense novel, still with an ecclesiastical background, and has not returned to the Book of Psalms series, although a sixth novel, *Free Among the Dead*, is completed. *Unruly Passions* was followed by two further non-series books, of which *Cruel Habitations* only has a church element, but all three are explorations of the deep and dangerous relationships that can develop between people – love and hatred, sinned against and sinner. These are far more intense than her Middleton-Brown books and show a growing fascination for the psychological thriller.

Novels
Book of Psalms series: *A Drink of Deadly Wine* (1991), *The Snares of Death* (1992), *Appointed to Die* (1993), *A Dead Man Out of Mind* (1994), *Evil Angels Among Them* (1995).
Non-series: *Unruly Passions* (1998), *Strange Children* (1999), *Cruel Habitations* (2000).

Real name: Carol A. Chase.
Pen-name: Kate Charles.
Where to start: *A Drink of Deadly Wine*.
Website: <www.twbooks.co.uk/authors/katecharles.html>
Similar stuff: D.M. GREENWOOD, Susan Howatch.
Final fact: When KC's boss, the local vicar, discovered she was writing mystery novels involving the church he was most upset and KC was forced to leave her job. She later felt redeemed however when she met the former Archbishop of Canterbury who admitted he enjoyed all her books.

Jerome Charyn (b. 1937) US

Less than half of JC's 40 or so books could be classified as crime fiction, and even these are not crime in the conventional sense, which makes them amongst the more refreshingly unusual works in the field. JC, born and raised in the Bronx, a teacher and later Professor of English, founding editor of the *Dutton Review* (1970–2) and executive editor of *Fiction* (1970–5), looks at the world with childlike wonder and finds no answers. His early works, starting with *Once Upon a Droshky* (1964) and including the story collection *The Man Who Grew Younger* (1967), are surreal fables of an imagined New York, in the tradition of Isaac Bashevis Singer. Much of his work is an interweaving of the real and imagined, a confusion which extends even to the two volumes of reminiscences of his youth, *The Dark Lady of Belorusse* (1997) and *The Black Swan* (2000). JC's early efforts at pushing life towards the irrational had limited appeal so, inspired by Ross Macdonald's *The Galton Case* (itself a psychological quest for the past), JC turned to detective fiction. His brother was a detective with the NYPD and JC spent time with him while writing *Blue Eyes*. The title character is Manfred Coen, a New York detective who, during a series of vivid and rather grotesque investigations, ends up at odds with his mentor, the deputy chief inspector, Isaac Sidel. In the shock finish, Coen is killed. JC then stepped back to view the events leading up to this in *Marilyn the Wild*, whilst *The Education of Patrick Silver* brings Sidel centre stage, a haunted man obsessed by his hatred of the New York crime world. In *Secret Isaac*, the last of the original sequence, we still find Sidel struggling to come to terms with Coen's death and discovering that no matter how moral he tries to be it is through immoral actions that he has risen to be Commissioner of Police. That sequence, collected as *The Isaac Quartet*, stands alone and JC contrasted it with two books about hit-man Sidney Holden. Holden is the antithesis of Sidel. In *The Paradise Man* he has no scruples but in *Elsinore* (which was shortlisted for a Hammett prize) develops a morality and tries to stop killing people but finds it unavoidable to save himself. The result, for good or for evil, is the same. After twelve years JC returned to Sidel in *The Good Policeman* and has since written five more novels following Sidel's looking-glass adventures as he leaves the police force and rises to New York mayor and the candidacy for Vice President, attempting to clean-up New York crime en route. JC's non-series crime novels are equally surreal, especially *Hurricane Lady*, a roller-coaster nightmare which reads like Woolrich out of Hemingway. His book about Wild Bill Hickock, *Darlin' Bill* (1980) won the Rosenthal Foundation Award.

Novels
Isaac Sidel series: *Blue Eyes* (1975), *Marilyn the Wild* (1976), *The Education of Patrick Silver* (1976), *Secret Isaac* (1978) – these four collected as *The Isaac Quartet* (UK 1984); *The Good Policeman* (1990), *Maria's Girls* (1992), *Montezuma's Man* (1993), *Little Angel Street* (1994), *El Bronx* (1996), *Citizen Sidel* (France 1996, US 1999).
Sidney Holden series: *Paradise Man* (1987), *Elsinore* (1991).
Non-series: *The Franklin Scare* (1977), *War Cries Over Avenue C* (1985), *Billy Budd, KGB* (1991), *Death of a Tango King* (1998), *Hurricane Lady* (2001).
Editor. *The New Mystery* (1993).

Where to start: *Blue Eyes*.
Awards: Rosenthal Foundation Award (1981), Deauville Film Festival, Fiction Award (1995), Chevalier, Order of Arts and Letters (1989).
Books about: *The Review of Contemporary Fiction*, Summer 1992 special "Jerome Charyn" issue.
Similar stuff: Paul AUSTER, Jonathan LETHEM.
Final fact: In his youth JC was a weightlifter and claims that by the age of 14 he was the youngest weightlifter in the *Guinness Book of Records*.

Thomas Chastain (1921–94) US

TC was the master of the puzzle mystery although it was a while before he found the right medium. His early books include *Death Stalk* (TV film 1974), about a violent struggle for survival along the Salmon River as three vacationing couples are menaced, *Deliverance*-style, by escaped convicts, and *Nightscape*, where a mother searching for her lost child encounters feral children in Central Park, New York. He also wrote a series featuring private investigator J.T. Spanner and New York's Deputy Chief Inspector Max Kauffman. The first, *Pandora's Box*, in which Spanner learns of a major heist and informs the police, is an example of TC's delight for intricate plotting. Spanner takes centre stage in *Vital Statistics*, where he tries to solve the death of a young girl. Kauffman is the main character in the rest of the series where he has to pit his wits against master criminals with major plans. TC's fame, though came when agent and book packager Bill Adler came up with the idea of a competition. TC wrote *Who Killed the Robins Family?*, in which eight members of a family are killed in all manner of ingenious ways all over the world and the publisher offered $10,000 to whoever proposed the best solution. The book captured the imagination and topped the *NYT* best-seller list at the start of 1984. The paperback edition contains the winning answer. Adler came up with several more such books until interest waned, but they established TC's knack for creating complicated and seemingly insoluble crimes. This led to the estate of Erle Stanley Gardner authorizing TC to write two new Perry Mason novels, the first in twenty years. Both books are considered excellent imitations. TC also wrote an ingenious murder mystery at the Oscars in *Where the Truth Lies* whilst, in *The Prosecutor*, he looks at the trials and tribulations in the career of New York's first female District Attorney.

Novels

Kauffman/Spanner series: *Pandora's Box* (1974), *911* (1976; as *The Christmas Bomber*, UK 1976), *Spanner* (1977), *Vital Statistics* (1977), *High Voltage* (1979), *The Diamond Exchange* (1981).
Robins Family series: *Who Killed the Robins Family?* (1983), *The Revenge of the Robins Family* (1984).
Perry Mason series: *The Case of Too Many Murders* (1989), *The Case of the Burning Bequest* (1989).
Non-series: *Judgement Day* (1962), *Death Stalk* (1971), *Nightscape* (1982), *The Picture-Perfect Murders* with Bill Adler (1987), *Where the Truth Lies* with Helen Hayes (1988), *The Prosecutor* (1992).
as Nick Carter: *Assassination Brigade* (1973).

Pen-names: Nick Carter (house name).
Where to start: *Pandora's Box* or *The Case of Too Many Murders.*
Similar stuff: Henry SLESAR, Parnell HALL and Edward D. HOCH also produce puzzle stories.
Final fact: TC used to contribute a "Brain Bogglers" column to *Discover* magazine.

Peter Chester, *see under pseudonym* Philip Daniels

Lee Child (b. 1954) UK

LC was born in Coventry but grew up in Birmingham. He took a degree in law, but his fascination for the theatre led him to work as a director for Granada Television in Manchester for 18 years. His ambition, though, ever since a child of four, was to live in America. He married a New Yorker and, following the success of his first book, was able to settle in America in 1998. His books all feature Jack Reacher, a former military policeman but now a drifter across the States. In the award-winning *Killing Floor*, the people of a small town in Georgia are horrified by two brutal murders and Reacher becomes their prime suspect. Even after he proves his innocence he still finds himself personally linked to the crimes.

Later novels find Reacher drifting from town to town, sometimes the victim of crime (he is kidnapped and held to ransom in *Die Trying*) or needing to solve the crime (in *Tripwire* a stranger who is searching for Reacher is found dead and Reacher has to work out who the man is and why he wanted him). The character of Reacher is deep – you learn more about him with each book. A loner with no roots, he has to use his innate cunning to keep out of trouble.

Novels

Jack Reacher series: *Killing Floor* (1997), *Die Trying* (1998), *Tripwire* (1999), *Running Blind* (2000; as *The Visitor*, UK 2000), *Echo Burning* (2001), *Without Fail* (2002).

Where to start: *Killing Floor.*
Awards: Anthony, best first novel (1998), Barry, best first novel (1998), W.H. Smith Thumping Good Read award (1999).
Website: <www.leechild.com>
Similar stuff: Michael CONNELLY's Harry Bosch series.
Final fact: While working for commercial television LC worked on such series as *Prime Suspect* and *Cracker*.

P.F. Chisholm *pseudonym, see* Patricia Finney

Jill Churchill (b. 1943) US

JC's Jane Jeffry books are amongst the ultimate in cozies. Jane is a young widow with three children who lives in a small neighbourhood where everyone knows everyone else. She and her friends, especially Shelley Nowack, do volunteer and charity work and get involved in all kinds of murders. They are light-hearted and, as the excruciating title puns demonstrate, unpretentious, but there is much clever detective work done based on common sense and the everyday observation of the little things. Jane Jeffry is a young Miss Marple. The first book, *Grime and Punishment*, won both the Agatha and Macavity awards for best first novel and was shortlisted for the Anthony. JC's other series features a brother and sister, Robert and Lily Brewster, who lost their finances in the Wall Street Crash of 1929 but who inherit a rambling mansion called Grace and Favor from their great uncle. They will also inherit his wealth, but have to wait ten years for that and, in the meantime they have to work. They come up with various schemes to avoid work and thereby encounter crimes and murders galore. The series is light-hearted but less frivolous than the Jeffry books, with a good period feel and clever set pieces. Under her real name of Janice Young Brooks, she is the author of many serious historical novels, mostly set in the fledgling USA, but including one on the fate of the Princes in the Tower, *Forbidden Fires* (1977).

Novels

Jane Jeffry series: *Grime and Punishment* (1989), *A Farewell to Yarns* (1991), *A Quiche Before Dying* (1993), *The Class Menagerie* (1993), *A Knife to Remember* (1994), *From Here to Paternity* (1995), *Silence of the Hams* (1996), *War and Peas* (1996), *Fear of Frying* (1997), *The Merchant of Menace* (1998), *A Groom with a View* (1999), *Mulch Ado About Nothing* (2000), *The House of Seven Nobles* (2002).
Grace and Favor series: *Anything Goes* (1999), *In the Still of the Night* (2000), *Someone to Watch Over Me* (2001).

Real name: Janice Young Brooks.
Pen-names: Jill Churchill, Valerie Vayle.
Where to start: *Grime and Punishment.*
Awards: Agatha, best first novel (1990), Macavity, best first novel (1990).
Website: <www.jillchurchill.com>
Similar stuff: Dorothy CANNELL, Charlotte MACLEOD.
Final fact: JC says that she likes to write exactly the kind of books she likes to read: "Books that have a light touch and a sense of community."

Carol Higgins Clark (b. 1956) US

The actress daughter of author Mary Higgins CLARK, CHC turned to writing when someone suggested that she write a part she could easily play. She created Los-Angeles-based private detective Regan Reilly, of Irish descent, whose mother is a famous mystery novelist. CHC hardly knew her own father but Reilly's father is a funeral director so death is never far away. Like CHC, Reilly has a good sense of humour and the books move along at a breezy light-hearted pace, with clever wit amongst the suspense and some ingenious plotting. Each book takes place at a trendy setting. *Decked* (which was nominated for the Agatha and Anthony awards) is on board a luxury Atlantic liner, *Snagged* at a plush Miami hotel (at, of all things, a panty-hose convention), *Iced* at an Aspen ski resort, *Twanged* at a fashionable beach home in the Hamptons, and *Fleeced* at an exclusive club. CHC doesn't take herself too seriously and that makes the books more enjoyable. Reilly also turns up in *Deck the Halls*, written with her mother. Reilly is an enjoyable character – someone you'd like to know.

Novels

Regan Reilly series: *Decked* (1992), *Snagged* (1993), *Iced* (1995), *Twanged* (1998), *Fleeced* (2001).
with Mary Higgins Clark: *Deck the Halls* (2000), *He Sees You When You're Sleeping* (2001).

Similar stuff: Antonia FRASER.
Final fact: CHC appeared in the TV movie adaptation of her mother's novel *A Cry in the Night* (1992).

Douglas Clark (1919–93) UK

DC's series featuring the distinguished, handsome and wealthy Chief Inspector (later Chief Superintendent) Masters and his older plain-speaking often resentful Chief Inspector, Bill Green, includes some of the most methodical and ingenious detective work. The relationship between the two officers, which grows with the series, almost presages that of Morse and Lewis in Colin DEXTER's books, and the cases are equally complex. The majority rely on a detailed knowledge of medical and pharmaceutical matters, especially poisons, and DC's career as a copywriter and executive in a pharmaceutical company provided the expertise. Occasionally his enthusiasm gets the better of him and dominates the plot, but when everything comes together, as in *Nobody's Perfect*, *Shelf Life* and *Table d'Hote*, the plotting is excellent, the murder method ingenious and the clues to the final revelation are handled masterly. DC writes in the classic mode, with a seasoned eye. At least two of his books fall into the impossible crime category. In *Shelf Life* a drunk dies in his locked cell, and in *Death After Evensong* a vicar is shot through the heart but with no evidence of a bullet or a gun. DC's books deserve to be better known. He wrote four other mysteries as James Ditton. He served in the British Army from 1939-56 and wrote about some of his experiences in *Suez Touchdown* (1964). He also wrote plays for BBC Radio.

Novels

Masters & Green series: *Nobody's Perfect* (1969), *Death After Evensong* (1969), *Deadly Pattern* (1970), *Sweet Poison* (1970), *Sick to Death* (1971), *Premedicated Murder* (1975), *Dread and Water* (1976), *Table d'Hote* (1977), *The Gimmel Flask* (1977), *The Libertines* (1978), *Heberden's Seat* (1979), *Poacher's Bag* (1980), *Golden Rain* (1980), *Roast Eggs* (1981), *The Longest Pleasure* (1981), *Shelf Life* (1982), *Doone Walk* (1982), *Vicious Circle* (1983), *The Monday Theory* (1983), *Bouquet Garni* (1984), *Dead Letter* (1984), *Jewelled Eye* (1985), *Performance* (1985), *Storm Centre* (1986), *The Big Grouse* (1986), *Plain Sailing* (1987), *Bitter Water* (1990).
as James Ditton: *You're Fairly Welcome* (1973), *The Bigger They Are* (1973), *Escapemanship* (1975), *Copley's Hunch* (1980).

Full name: Douglas Malcolm Jackson Clark.
Pen-names: James Ditton, Peter Hosier.
Where to start: *Nobody's Perfect*.
Similar stuff: Colin DEXTER, Ruth RENDELL'S Inspector Wexford.

Mary Higgins Clark (b. 1929) US

MHC become internationally known with the bestseller status of her first novel, *Where Are the Children?*. This taut, complex novel about a mother, previously found guilty of murdering her first two children and who becomes the prime suspect when the children of her new family go missing, earned MHC the soubriquet of "Queen of Suspense", and she has worn that crown proudly for nearly 30 years. It was not an overnight success. Her father had died when she was 10 so immediately after graduating from high school MHC became a secretary for three years (1946–9) then an air stewardess (1949–50). She married in 1949 raising a family of five children, including actress and writer Carol Higgins CLARK. She turned to writing, selling her first story in 1956, but these were only occasional sales. After her husband died in 1964 she became a radio scriptwriter and in 1969 sold her first book, *Aspire to the Heavens*, a biography of George Washington. Fascinated with mystery fiction, she looked at items in the news and picked on the case of Alice Crimmins, accused of the murder of her two children. Rather than follow the police investigation, MHC concentrated on the emotional and psychological drama unfolding with the victims and their family with which readers could more readily identify and which heightened the suspense. Add to this a focus on children and she had a gold-plated formula for success. Her next few books all featured children, or isolated and vulnerable women linked to an issue topical in the news. With *A Stranger is Watching* it was capital punishment. A family is in turmoil when the mother is murdered and a man convicted of the murder awaits his execution, but only the mother's young son knows the identity of the real killer. With *The Cradle Will Fall*, a taut medical thriller, it was the subject of test-tube babies and medical ethics. *A Cry in the Night* was a rather more traditional neo-gothic thriller of a woman in love with the man of her dreams who takes her to his isolated home where she discovers the dark secrets of his past. *Stillwatch* was a more contemporary political thriller. The process has continued with MHC injecting potent topical themes into vulnerable lives. Kidnapping remains a popular theme, emerging again in *All Around the Town* and *Silent Night*, whilst *Let Me Call You Sweetheart* is another medical thriller. *Remember Me* is an especially atmospheric neo-gothic and the closest MHC has come to a haunted house story, whilst *Before I Say Goodbye* explores the world of psychics.

MHC occasionally lets her hair down and has rather more fun. The comparatively less successful *Weep No More My Lady* (which MHC revised for subsequent reprintings to make the solution less obvious) introduced the character of Alvirah Meehan, a former cleaning lady who won the biggest ever lottery prize, and her husband Willy. With more money than she needs Alvirah becomes first an investigative reporter and then, in a series of stories collected as *The Lottery Winner*, something of an amateur sleuth. These stories are more light-hearted without losing the elements of tension and surprise. Alivirah and Willy have returned in two further books including *Deck the Halls*, written with her daughter Carol, and including her detective Regan Reilly. With over 50 million copies of her books in print world wide, MHC is amongst the best selling of all mystery and suspense writers, but she has never forgotten her roots or her family. She married again in 1996 to a widower thereby inheriting his large family alongside hers, and is currently writing her autobiography. In 1996 Family Circle issued the *Mary Higgins Clark Mystery Magazine* in the US published twice a year, but full of stories and features by the major writers. In 2001 MHC's publisher, Simon and Schuster sponsored the

Mary Higgins Clark Award for the writer producing material that best reflects the MHC tradition. The first recipient was Barbara D'AMATO.

Novels

Non-series: *Where Are the Children?* (1975), *A Stranger is Watching* (1977), *The Cradle Will Fall* (1980), *A Cry in the Night* (1982), *Still Watch* (1984), *While My Pretty One Sleeps* (1989), *Loves Music, Loves to Dance* (1991), *All Around the Town* (1992), *I'll Be Seeing You* (1993), *Remember Me* (1994), *Let Me Call You Sweetheart* (1995), *Silent Night* (1995), *Moonlight Becomes You* (1996), *Pretend You Don't See Her* (1997), *You Belong to Me* (1998), *Before I Say Goodbye* (2000), *On the Street Where You Live* (2001), *He Sees You When You're Sleeping*, with Carol Higgins Clark (2001), *Daddy's Little Girl* (2002).

Alvirah Meehan series: *Weep No More, My Lady* (1987), *The Lottery Winner* (1994), *All Through the Night* (1998), *Deck the Halls*, with Carol Higgins Clark (2000).

Short Stories. *The Anastasia Syndrome and Other Stories* (1989), *Death on the Cape* (1993), *My Gal Sunday* (1996).

Editor. *Murder on the Aisle* for MWA (1987), *Bad Behavior* (1995), *The Plot Thickens* (1997), *The Night Awakens* (2000). [MHC is sometimes credited with compiling *Malice Domestic 2* (1993) but this was ghost-edited by Martin H. Greenberg.]

Where to start: *Where Are the Children?*

Awards: Grand Prix de Littérature Policière Best Foreign Mystery (1980), Irish-American Historical Society Gold Medal of Honor (1993), American Mystery Award, best romantic suspense (1993), Anthony, best short story anthology (1994), Albert Einstein College of Medicine Spirit of Achievement Award (1994), Horatio Alger Award for Distinguished Americans (1997), MWA Grand Master (2000).

Website: <www.simonsays.com/subs/>

Similar stuff: Judith KELMAN, Ruth RENDELL as Barbara Vine.

Final fact: During her year as an air stewardess MHC was caught in a revolution in Syria and was on the last flight into Czechoslovakia before the Iron Curtain came down.

Anna Clarke (b. 1919) UK

AC's work includes some of the most intriguing and satisfying literary mysteries in the field, yet by her own admission she has never taken her writing seriously and has a greater interest in mathematics than fiction. It was when a serious illness curtailed her career as a secretary that AC turned to writing and with a background of several years at two publishing houses it was to the literary world that she turned. Several of her books are deep psychological quests for truth, either involving a search into the past, as in *My Search for Ruth*, or the past coming back to reveal hidden truths, as in *Letter from the Dead*, *We the Bereaved* or *The Deathless and the Dead*. In the latter a scholar's study into the life of a 19th-century poet reveals the truth about her death. Similar is *The Lady in Black*, set in Victorian England and revealing a murder story that may be more fact than fiction. Others are more contemporary, such as *The End of the Shadow*, where questions hang over the death of a publisher's wife, or *Plot Counter-Plot*, a wonderfully spiral story where a plot by one author to steal the plot of another author's book becomes entwined and convoluted. It was nearly 20 years before AC settled on a series character and even then Paula Glenning, a Professor of English Literature and a biographer, only emerged steadily, having a minor rôle in *Last Judgement*, where two professors clash over the ownership of an author's rights. Over the next two books in the series Glenning moves to centre stage and the series grows in strength. In all of the novels, but especially *The Mystery Lady*, AC merges fact and fiction in a maze of maybes to create challenging and rewarding mysteries.

Novels

Non-series: *The Darkened Room* (1968), *A Mind to Murder* (1971), *The End of a Shadow* (1972), *Plot Counter-Plot* (1974), *My Search for Ruth* (1975), *Legacy of Evil* (1976), *The Deathless and the Dead* (1976; as *This Downhill Path*, US 1977), *The Lady in Black* (1977), *Letter from the Dead* (1977), *One of Us Must Die* (1977), *The Poisoned Web* (1979), *Poison Parsley* (1979), *Last Voyage* (1980), *Game, Set and Danger* (1981), *Desire to Kill* (1982), *We the Bereaved* (1982), *Soon She Must Die* (1984).

Paula Glenning series: *Last Judgement* (1985), *Cabin 3033* (1986), *The Mystery Lady* (1986), *Last Seen in London* (1987), *Murder in Writing* (1988), *The Whitelands Affair* (1989), *The Case of the Paranoid Patient* (1991), *The Case of the Ludicrous Letters* (1996), *The Case of the Anxious Aunt* (1996).

Where to start: They are all good but *Plot Counter-Plot*, *The Deathless and the Dead* and *The Mystery Lady* are representative of the best.

Similar stuff: Amanda CROSS.

Final fact: AC had a fairly cosmopolitan upbringing. She was born in South Africa and educated in Montreal and Oxford.

Jon Cleary (b. 1917) Australia

JC's writing career extends over nearly 60 years. He began during his wartime military service, selling stories to magazines and a radio play, *Safe Horizon*, for which he received a broadcasting award. Before the war he had held a variety of jobs, including a commercial traveller, and you know from his books that JC has a grass-roots understanding of what makes Australia tick. It was an outlook that made *The Sundowners* (1952; filmed 1960), his best-known book, so successful. Through his books you can chart changes in Australia's society, from his first novel, *You Can't See Around Corners* (filmed 1968), about how a deserter is treated when he returns home, to *Bear Trap*, which looks at the attitudes to the Olympics being held in Sydney in 2000 and a plot to assassinate the Premier. This novel parallels *City of Fading Light*, set in Berlin during the 1936 Olympics and a plot to assassinate Hitler. Several of JC's books are historical novels or have wartime settings, whilst others are contemporary, such as the award-winning *Peter's Pence*, about an IRA conspiracy to kidnap the Pope. JC's reputation as a crime novelist rests primarily on his series featuring Sydney police inspector Scobie Malone, which has appeared through five decades. Malone is a family man with rigid principles and a dogged determination. Through Malone, Cleary confronts contemporary issues in Australia such as racism in *Pride's Harvest* and *Dragons at the Party*, homosexuality in *Different Turf* and crime cartels in *Five-Ring Circus*. An interesting four-book sequence looks at the changing face of Sydney and also considers changing family practices – *Dark Summer, Bleak Spring, Autumn Maze* and *Winter Chill*. Throughout all this Malone remains steadfast even when he becomes a potential victim, in *Murder Song*. Two of the books have been filmed: *The High Commissioner* (1968, aka *Nobody Runs Forever*) and *Helga's Web* as *Scobie Malone* (1975).

Novels
Non-series: *You Can't See Round Corners* (1947), *The Long Shadow* (1949), *Just Let Me Be* (1950; as *You the Jury*, Aus 1990), *The Climate of Courage* (1954; as *Naked in the Night*, US 1955), *Justin Bayard* (1955; as *Dust in the Sun*, US 1957), *North from Thursday* (1960), *Forests of the Night* (1963), *A Flight for Chariots* (1963), *The Fall of an Eagle* (1964), *The Pulse of Danger* (1966), *The Long Pursuit* (1967), *Season of Doubt* (1968), *The Liberators* (1971; as *Mask of the Andes*, UK 1971), *Peter's Pence* (1974), *The Safe House* (1975), *A Sound of Lightning* (1976), *High Road to China* (1977), *Vortex* (1977), *The City of Fading Light* (1985).
Scobie Malone series: *The High Commissioner* (1966), *Helga's Web* (1970), *Ransom* (1973), *Dragons at the Party* (1987), *Now and Then, Amen* (1988), *Babylon South* (1989), *Murder Song* (1990), *Pride's Harvest* (1991), *Dark Summer* (1992), *Bleak Spring* (1993), *Autumn Maze* (1994), *Winter Chill* (1995), *Endpeace* (1996), *Different Turf* (1997), *Five-Ring Circus* (1999), *Dilemma* (2000), *The Bear Pit* (2000), *Yesterday's Shadow* (2001).
Short Stories. *These Small Glories* (1946), *Pillar of Salt* (1963).

Full name: Jon Stephen Cleary.
Where to start: *Peter's Pence* or *Now and Then, Amen*.
Awards: Australian Broadcasting Commission prize for radio drama (1944), Australian Literary Society's Crouch Medal, best Australian novel (1950), Edgar, best novel (1975), Ned Kelly, lifetime contribution (1996).
Similar stuff: Peter CORRIS, Peter DOYLE.
Final fact: JC met his wife in 1946 on board ship bound for England along with many Australians hoping to find work there, including actors Leo McKern and Dick Bentley.

Ann Cleeves (b. 1954) UK

One would not automatically think that a background in social work and ornithology could come together in an enjoyable detective series but AC achieves that in her books featuring the Palmer-Joneses. George is a retired civil servant whose work at the Home Office included producing a manual on interviewing techniques for the police. He is also a dedicated bird-watcher. His wife, Molly, is a retired social worker with an eye for human nature. AC's own background was in social work and probation but she was also a cook at a remote bird observatory on Fair Isle and an auxiliary coastguard on the isle of Hilbre in the Wirral, Cheshire. Her husband, whom she married in 1977, is a warden for the RSPB. All this comes together in an enjoyable series of semi-cozy mysteries where George and Molly pursue their bird-watching interests encountering crimes en route. AC incorporates such environmental issues as stealing eggs from the nests of rare birds (in *A Prey for Murder*) and the use of illegal poisons and pesticides (in *Another Man's Poison*). You don't need to be an aviphile to enjoy the books, which have original settings and clever plots. AC's other series, featuring Inspector Stephen Ramsay of the Northumbrian police, is more traditional. Ramsay is a loner but methodical and persistent and the series brings out the remoteness and at times cliqueness of the villages in Northumbria – in fact remoteness is an element in most of AC's books.

Novels
George Palmer-Jones series: *A Bird in the Hand* (1986), *Come Death and High Water* (1987), *Murder in Paradise* (1988), *A Prey to Murder* (1989), *Sea Fever* (1991), *Another Man's Poison* (1992), *The Mill on the Shore* (1994), *High Island Blues* (1996),
Stephen Ramsay series: *A Lesson in Dying* (1990), *Murder in My Back Yard* (1991), *A Day in the Death of Dorothea Cassidy* (1992), *Killjoy* (1993), *The Healers* (1995), *The Baby Snatcher* (1997).
Non-series: *The Crow Trap* (1999), *The Sleeping and the Dead* (2001).

Full name: Ann Cleeves (née Richardson).
Where to start: *Murder in Paradise* and *Murder in My Backyard.*
Website: <www.twbooks.co.uk/authors/anncleeves.html>
Similar stuff: Nevada BARR, J.S. BORTHWICK, Susan CONANT.
Final fact: In 1999 AC was Reader in Residence to libraries in Cumbria, Northumberland, Gateshead and North Tyneside, a huge area, and to encourage people to use libraries she put on a special murder evening.

Michael Clynes *pseudonym, see* Paul C. Doherty

Harlan Coben (b. 1962) US

HC hit the big time with *Tell No One*, a page-turner about a man whose wife had been murdered eight years before and then he suddenly receives an e-mail from her. Crime fiction fans though had already known HC as one of their secret weapons for a decade. He had long struck a responsive chord with his books featuring Myron Bolitar, a former basketball player who, when injured, studied law and became a sport agent in New York. He is surrounded by an interesting group of characters, especially Win

Lockwood, who runs a security firm, rents space to Bolitar and handles the financial side. Like many good investigators, Bolitar is wise-cracking and canny and the stories have many light moments, but he is also intensely human and neurotic. This has developed through the series up to the tear-jerking *Darkest Fear*, where he learns of a son he never knew who is dying from cancer. HC is able to juxtapose humour and pathos in the right quantities to make the plots compulsive and bring the characters alive. HC is surprisingly not a great sports fan, but regardless of whether it's basketball (*Fade Away)*, tennis *(Drop Shot)* or golf *(Back Spin)*, he has done his research. Major sports are big business, and where there's money there's crime. The success of HC's books, which have creamed awards and nominations throughout the crime-fiction field, has revived interest in his first two books, now highly collectible. *Play Dead* had another sports theme when a Boston Celtics player is found drowned. There's also a basketball player in *Miracle Cure*, but this is primarily a medical thriller where patients in a centre for research into AIDS are being murdered. HC was born and raised in New Jersey and graduated from Amherst College with a degree in political science. After several years working in the travel industry he turned to writing. He lives in New Jersey with his wife, a paediatrician, and children.

Novels
Non-series: *Play Dead* (1990), *Miracle Cure* (1991), *Tell No One* (2001), *Gone For Good* (2002).
Myron Bolitar series: *Deal Breaker* (1995), *Drop Shot* (1996), *Fade Away* (1996), *Back Spin* (1997), *One False Move* (1998), *The Final Detail* (1999), *Darkest Fear* (2000).

Where to start: *Deal Breaker.*
Awards: Anthony, best paperback original (1996), Barry, best paperback original, (1998), Edgar, best paperback original (1997), Shamus, best paperback original (1997).
Website: <www.harlancoben.com>
Similar stuff: David Alexander's Bart Harbin, Paul BISHOP's Ian Chapel, Bill GRANGER's Jimmy Drover.
Final fact: HC believes he was a born writer and at the age of four used to regale his chums with pirate stories.

Liza Cody (b. 1944) UK

In Anna Lee, LC has created a believable hard-boiled female English private detective – something rare in mystery fiction. A former policewoman, Anna joined a small detective agency as their only female investigator, Anna is shrewd and determined and pragmatic enough to cope with the inevitable pathetic macho comments from the men who surround her and the bitchiness from the women in the organization. But Anna proves her worth in a series of difficult and dangerous cases – she is even kidnapped in *Bad Company*. Anna is usually employed to either find someone, such as a missing daughter in *Headcase* or a lost furniture dealer in *Stalker,* or to protect someone, such as a rock star in *Under Contract*, but the assignments rapidly take dark and unexpected turns. Tense and unnerving, LC nevertheless rations the violence in the books and achieves a solid air of believability. The quality of the series is attested by two Edgar nominations, a CWA Gold Dagger nomination and the John Creasey Memorial Award. *Head Case* was made into a TV film in 1993 as a pilot for a series of five two-hour episodes. *Dupe* and *Stalker* were also adapted along with new scripts by others. LC felt she had lost her character, which had been adapted too freely for TV, and so created a new series featuring disbarred professional woman wrestler and security guard Eva Wylie. This is set in the same world as Anna Lee, who is Eva's employer, but Anna takes a back seat. Wylie works on both sides of the law and is the ideal character to penetrate the underworld. She is a survivor, despite what life has thrown at her. The first book *Bucket Nut* was awarded the CWA Silver Dagger. In *Gimme More*, LC has created a new character, Birdie, con-artist and widow of a rock musician who was killed in a fire. The book penetrates the glamour of the rock world to show the sleaze and exploitation beneath. LC's earlier book, *Rift*, is set in Ethiopia in the turmoil of war and famine. LC is a qualified artist and designer, trained at the Royal Academy School of Art and the books reflect her strong visual images. Her novels are powerful with strong characters and show a determination to succeed whatever life throws at you..

Novels

Anna Lee series: *Dupe* (1980), *Bad Company* (1982), *Stalker* (1984), *Headcase* (1985), *Under Contract* (1986), *Backhand* (1991).

Eva Wylie series: *Bucket Nut* (1992), *Monkey Wrench* (1994), *Musclebound* (1997).

Non-series: *Rift* (1988), *Gimme More* (2000).

Editor (with others). *1st Culprit* (1992), *2nd Culprit* (1993), *3rd Culprit* (1994)

Real name: Liza Nassim.

Pen-name: Liza Cody.

Where to start: *Dupe*.

Awards: CWA John Creasey Memorial Award, best first novel (1980), Anthony, best short story (1992), CWA Silver Dagger (1992), German Marlowe (1998).

Website: <www.twbooks.co.uk/authors/lcody.html>

Similar stuff: Sarah DUNANT, Sue GRAFTON, Val MCDERMID.

Final fact: LC once worked at Madame Tussaud's making fingers for the waxworks.

Tucker Coe *pseudonym, see* Donald E. Westlake

Max Allan Collins (b. 1948) US

MAC is a dedicated enthusiast of the crime fiction genre and especially of hard-boiled crime and with an amazing amount of energy has involved himself in all aspects of it, from novels to films to reference studies to comic books, and all points in between – he'll even provide the music! His work is typically American, emerging via descent from Hammett, Chandler, SPILLANE and WESTLAKE, but he has imbued it with his own humour, his own sense of time and place and, above all, a sense of humanity. His characters must live the life they lead, not go through the motions. As a consequence at the outset he avoided the traditional hard-boiled P.I. field for characters more suited to their period. Frank Nolan was a relic of a bygone age, a former thief who, slowly, but with increasing determination, is trying to go straight. Quarry was a Vietnam veteran who turns hit-man. He has no compunctions about killing people since he's assigned to take out those whom he regards as the scum of society and have already bought their ticket – such as murderers and drug dealers. Due to the skill of MAC's writing Quarry takes on redeeming qualities. Mallory is an amateur sleuth and mystery writer modelled on MAC himself. This series is more traditional, though still with a hard edge, and building on the author's love of crime fiction – *Kill Your Darlings* is even set at the world mystery convention. It became clear that excellent though these series were, they were MAC's apprenticeship for his chief desire to produce a P.I. series. Believing this to be anachronistic in the eighties, he set his Nate Heller series in the Chicago of the thirties and recreated the Golden Age of gangsters. Heller is an ex-cop turned P.I., not averse to a little corruption whose conscience is pricked by his father's suicide. MAC fits Heller into the real world. *True Detective* features Al Capone, *True Crime* John Dillinger, *The Million-Dollar Wound* Frank Nitti, *Neon Mirage* Bugsy Siegel and the creation of Las Vegas, *Stolen Away* the Lindbergh child kidnapping, *Carnal Hours* the murder of Sir Harry Oakes, *Blood and Thunder* Huey Long, *Damned in Paradise* Clarence Darrow, *Flying Blind* the disappearance of Amelia Earhart and *Majic Man* the Roswell incident. All of the books are extensively researched with detailed notes as an appendix. Their overwhelming acceptance by readers as being amongst the premier P.I. series is demonstrated by seven of the first eight books being nominated for the Shamus award, with two of them winning. MAC developed this territory with first a spin-off series featuring Eliot Ness of *The Untouchables* fame, and then his 'Disaster' series. This selects key historical disasters and links them to a literary sleuth – the *Titanic* and Jacques Futrelle, the *Hindenburg* and Leslie Charteris, Pearl Harbor and Edgar Rice Burroughs.

In what remains of his spare time, MAC has written many film novelizations, including a key linking novel in the *NYPD Blue* TV series, and has scripted many comic strips. He took over the *Dick Tracy* strip when its creator, Chester Gould, retired in 1977, and created the *Ms Tree* series in 1981, the first female P.I. in a comic strip series. Both of these series have been issued in book form. He has also scripted six films, and produced, directed and composed the music for one of them, *Mommy* (1995), a reversal of Stephen King's *Carrie*, in which a young girl discovers that her mother is pure evil. If MAC had written nothing other than the Nate Heller series, he would be held in high regard, yet there is a consistency about all his work, demonstrating that you don't have to sacrifice quality for quantity when your heart and mind are dedicated to your work.

Novels

Frank Nolan series: *Bait Money* (1973; rev'd 1981), *Blood Money* (1973; rev'd 1981), *Fly Paper* (1981), *Hush Money* (1981), *Hard Cash* (1981), *Scratch Fever* (1982), *Spree* (1987), *Mourn the Living* (1999).

Quarry series: *The Broker* (1976; as *Quarry*, 1985), *The Broker's Wife* (1976; as *Quarry's List*, 1986), *The Dealer* (1976; as *Quarry's Deal*, 1986), *The Slasher* (1977; as *Quarry's Cut*, 1986), *Primary Target* (1987).

Mallory series: *The Baby Blue Rip-Off* (1983), *No Cure for Death* (1983), *Kill Your Darlings* (1984), *A Shroud for Aquarius* (1985), *Nice Weekend for a Murder* (1986).

Nathan Heller series: *True Detective* (1983), *True Crime* (1984), *The Million-Dollar Wound* (1986), *Neon Mirage* (1988), *Stolen Away* (1991), *Carnal Hours* (1994) *Blood and Thunder* (1995), *Damned in Paradise* (1996), *Flying Blind* (1998), *Majic Man* (1999), *Angel in Black* (2001).

Eliot Ness series: *The Dark City* (1987), *Butcher's Dozen* (1988), *Bullet Proof* (1989), *Murder by the Numbers* (1993).

Dick Tracy series (also see below): film novelization, *Dick Tracy* (1990), *Dick Tracy Goes to War* (1991), *Dick Tracy Meets His Match* (1992).

Mommy series (based on his own films): *Mommy* (1997), *Mommy's Day* (1998).

"Disaster" series: *The Titanic Murders* (1999), *The Hindenburg Murders* (2000), *The Pearl Harbor Murders* (2001).

Non-series: *Midnight Haul* (1986), *Regeneration*, with Barbara Collins (1999).

Film/TV novelizations and tie-ins: *In the Line of Fire* (1993), *Maverick* (1994), *Waterworld* (1995), *NYPD Blue: Blue Beginning* (1995), *Daylight* (1996), *Air Force One* (1997), *NYPD Blue: Blue Blood* (1997), *U.S. Marshals* (1998), *Saving Private Ryan* (1998), *The Mummy* (1999), *U-571* (2000), *The Mummy Returns* (2001), *CSI: Double Dealer* (2001), *The Scorpion King* (2002).

Film/TV tie-in (as Peter Brackett): *I Love Trouble* (1994).

Comic-strip collections/Graphic novels

Dick Tracy series: *Dick Tracy meets Angeltop* (1979), *Dick Tracy meets the Punks* (1980), *Tracy's War-Time Memories* (1986), *Dick Tracy and the Nightmare Machine* (1991),.

Ms. Tree series: *The Files of Ms. Tree, Volume One* (1984), *Volume Two: The Cold Dish* (1985), *Volume Three* (1986). *Ms. Tree* (1988).

Batman/Eliot Ness series: *Batman: Scar of the Bat* (1996).

Non-series: *Road to Perdition* (1998).

Short Stories

Nate Heller series: *Dying in the Post-War World* (1991), *Kisses of Death* (2001).

Philip Marlowe: booklet, *The Perfect Crime* (1992).

General: *Murder His and Hers*, with Barbara Collins (2001), *Blue Christmas and Other Holiday Homicides* (2001).

Non-fiction. *Jim Thompson: The Killers Inside Him*, with Ed Gorman (1983), *One Lonely Knight: Mickey Spillane's Mike Hammer*, with James L. Traylor (1984), *The Best of Crime and Detective TV*, with John Javna (1988), *The Mystery Scene Movie Guide* (1995), *For the Boys: The Racy Pin-Ups of World War II* (2000), *The History of Mystery* (2001).

Editor

with Martin H. Greenberg: *Dick Tracy: The Secret Files* (1990).

with Dick Locher: *The Dick Tracy Casebook* (1990), *Dick Tracy's Fiendish Foes* (1991).

with Mickey Spillane: *Murder is My Business* (1994), *Vengeance is Hers* (1997), *Private Eyes* (1998), *A Century of Noir* (2002).

with Jeff Gelb: *Flesh and Blood: Erotic Tales of Crime and Passion* (2001).

Full name: Max Allan Collins, Jr.

Pen-names: Peter Brackett.

Where to start: *True Detective*.

Awards: Inkpot Award, Outstanding Achievement in Comic Arts (1982), Shamus, best P.I. hardcover novel (1984, 1992).

Website: <www.muscanet.com/~phoenix/main.html>

Similar stuff: Michael KURLAND's Alexander Brass, William F. Nolan's Black Mask Boys.

Final fact: MAC appears with his jazz band playing at the dance in the film *Mommy*.

Michael Collins (b. 1924) US

MC is today the best-known and sole remaining pen-name of Dennis Lynds. He took the name from the Irish revolutionary. A chemist by training, Lynds was, from 1951–66, an editor of various chemical industry technical and trade journals. He sold a few stories to literary magazines during the fifties but did not turn to writing crime fiction till 1962, soon after he had sold his first novel, *Combat Soldier* (1962), which drew upon Lynds's wartime experiences in the US Infantry for which he received a Purple Heart, Bronze Star and Combat Infantry Badge. Lynds wrote one other mainstream novel, *Uptown Downtown*, about the double life of a New York executive and, much later, a short novel, *Talking to the World* (1995). By 1962 he was writing regularly for the crime-fiction magazines starting with "It's Whisky or Dames" (*MSMM*, 1962), the first of 13 short stories featuring one-armed sleuth Slot-Machine Kelly. These were an early version of Lynds' better-known character Dan Fortune, and at the start were tongue in cheek. Fortune, all of whose books appear under the MC name, had been a rebel in his youth until he lost an arm trying to loot a freighter and thereafter turned to the right side of the law. Because of his incapacity Fortune cannot resort to violence, though his strength should not be underestimated. So he uses his brain, and his ability to talk and listen. Fortune is persistent. Even when told a crime has been solved, or when warned off in rather more violent ways, he will not give up. The keynote of the Fortune series is the pyramid factor. The crime may start at the bottom, fairly insignificant and minor, but as Fortune explores the connections between the many individuals with whom he comes into contact he rises up the pyramid to the real perpetrator at the pinnacle, most often in corporate business. All of the Fortune cases are complicated and all the more rewarding for that. Fortune has to know why the crime had been committed, Lynds bringing to the series his scientific training. Fortune also followed his creator from New York to California (where Lynds moved in 1964). MC received an Edgar award for the first book, *Act of Fear*, and some 20 years later was presented with a PWA Lifetime Achievement award primarily on the strength of the Fortune novels. The most prominent aspect of the Fortune novels and stories is their strong social consciousness and use of mainstream literary techniques.

Early in his career Lynds produced a quantity of novels for hire including new books in the Nick Carter and Charlie Chan series. These began with eight new Shadow novels as Maxwell Grant. He also took over the Three Investigators juvenile series started by Robert Arthur, in the Hardy Boys tradition. These were written under the William Arden alias. Of his own creation, three other series are worth highlighting. As Arden he wrote the Kane Jackson books about industrial espionage, drawing upon his experiences in the chemical industry. As Mark Sadler he created Paul Shaw, a Vietnam veteran turned P.I., who operates out of a posh New York office with his partner John Thayer. He only does work for major corporate clients with money and class. The series is more medium-rare than hard-boiled. As John Crowe he created a series set in Buena Costa county, California. This series features several different P.I.s and cops, though the main continuing character is Lee Beckett, a county investigator.

Lynds has been married four times. He used the name of his third wife, Sheila McErlean, on one book (and as Sheila Lynds on a story). He has been married to best-selling novelist Gayle Stone since 1986 and, early in her career they collaborated on two novels in the Mack Bolan "Executioner" series. Like MC, Gayle has been a magazine editor, written five Nick Carter books and three in the Three Investigators series. She worked for the government as a "think-tank" editor and has since turned her skills to writing espionage thrillers, including *Masquerade* (1996), *Mosaic* (1998) and *Mesmerized* (2001), plus two thriller collaborations: *The Hades Factor* (2000) and *The Paris Option* (2002) with Robert Ludlum.

Novels

Dan Fortune series: *Act of Fear* (1967), *The Brass Rainbow* (1969), *Night of the Toads* (1970), *Walk a Black Wind* (1971), *Shadow of a Tiger* (1972), *The Silent Scream* (1973), *Blue Death* (1975), *The Blood-Red Dream* (1976), *The Nightrunners* (1978), *The Slasher* (1980), *Freak* (1983), *Minnesota Strip* (1987), *Red Rosa* (1988),

Castrato (1989), *Chasing Eights* (1990), *The Irishman's Horse* (1991), *Cassandra in Red* (1992), *The Cadillac Cowboy* (1995).

Kane Jackson series as William Arden: *A Dark Power* (1968), *Deal in Violence* (1969), *The Goliath Scheme* (1970), *Die to a Distant Drum* (1972; as *Murder Underground*, UK 1974), *Deadly Legacy* (1973).

Three Investigators series as William Arden: *The Mystery of the Moaning Cave* (1968), *The Mystery of the Laughing Shadow* (1969), *The Secret of the Crooked Cat* (1970), *The Mystery of the Shrinking House* (1972), *The Secret of Phantom Lake* (1973), *The Mystery of the Dead Man's Riddle* (1974), *The Mystery of the Dancing Devil* (1976), *The Mystery of the Headless Horse* (1977), *The Mystery of the Deadly Double* (1978), *The Secret of Shark Reef* (1979), *The Mystery of the Purple Pirate* (1982), *The Mystery of the Smashing Glass* (1984), *The Secret of Wrecker's Rock* (1986), *Hot Wheels* (1989).

Paul Shaw series as Mark Sadler: *The Falling Man* (1970), *Here to Die* (1972), *Mirror Image* (1972), *Circle of Fire* (1973), *Touch of Death* (1981), *Deadly Innocents* (1986).

Lee Beckett series as John Crowe: *Another Way to Die* (1972), *A Touch of Darkness* (1972), *Bloodwater* (1974), *Crooked Shadows* (1975), *When They Kill Your Wife* (1977), *Close to Death* (1979).

as William Arden (non-series): *The Mystery of the Blue Condor* (1973).

as Nick Carter (all in Nick Carter series): *The N3 Conspiracy* (1974), *The Green Wolf Connection* (1976), *Triple Cross* (1976), *The Master Assassin* (1986), *Mercenary Mountain* (1986), *The Samurai Kill* (1986), *Blood of the Falcon* (1987).

as Carl Dekker: *Woman in Marble* (1973).

as Maxwell Grant (all in The Shadow series): *The Shadow Strikes* (1964), *Shadow Beware* (1965), *Cry Shadow!* (1965), *The Shadow's Revenge* (1965), *Mark of the Shadow* (1966), *Shadow – Go Mad!* (1966), *The Night of the Shadow* (1966), *The Shadow – Destination Moon* (1967).

as Dennis Lynds: *Uptown Downtown* (1963), *Charlie Chan Returns* (1974), *Crossfire* (1975)

as Sheila McErlean: *Mask of Silence* (1968).

as Mark Sadler with Gayle Lynd writing as Don Pendleton (both Executioner series): *Blood Fever* (1989), *Moving Target* (1989).

Short Stories

Non-series: *Why Girls Ride Sidesaddle* (1980), *Talking to the World* (1995).

Dan Fortune series: *Crime, Punishment and Resurrection* (1992), *Fortune's World* (2000), *Spies and Thieves, Cops and Killers, Etc.* (2002).

Full name: Dennis Lynds.

Pen-names: William Arden, John Crowe, Carl Dekker, John Douglas, Sheila Lynds, Sheila McErlean, Mark Sadler, plus house names Nick Carter, Walter Dallas, Robert Hart Davis, Maxwell Grant, Don Pendleton.

Where to start: *Act of Fear*.

Awards: Edgar, best first novel (1968), Shamus, lifetime achievement (1988).

Website: None but he features on his wife's site <www.gaylelynds.com>

Similar stuff: Ross MACDONALD, Bill PRONZINI.

Final fact: When MC's first Slot-Machine Kelly story sold to *MSMM*, editor Leo Margulies invited MC to write the lead Mike Shayne novelette. As they paid by the word, MC delivered 30,000 words, which gave Margulies a fit (the lead novelettes were usually half that length). Nevertheless, writing at slightly shorter length, MC went on to write the lead novelette for every issue for over 6 years, 88 stories in all.

Susan Conant (b. 1946) US

Bringing together her own expertise in human development and her family's passion for raising and training dogs, SC has produced a popular series about Holly Winter, a dog trainer and magazine columnist, and her dogs Rowdy and Kim, both Alaskan Malamute. Though dogs or dog events are usually central to the plot it is Holly who does the detecting, though often with canine help. The cases are all canine cozies though the animal welfare issues confronted may unsettle some. The books are littered with eccentric characters and equally eccentric dogs – there's even a psychic dog in *The Barker Street Regulars.* The books are not always solidly constructed mysteries (SC sometimes introduces new facts rather late in the day, or takes too long to get round to the crime) but they are extremely amusing and cast a wonderfully skewed perspective on human activity. When not writing her novels or serving as the Massachusetts state co-ordinator of the Alaskan Malamute Protection League SC has written personal and psychological guidance books such as *Living with Chronic Fatigue* (1990).

Novels

Holly Winter series: *A New Leash on Death* (1989), *Dead and Doggone* (1990), *A Bite of Death* (1991), *Paws Before Dying* (1991), *Gone to the Dogs* (1992), *Bloodlines* (1992), *Ruffly Speaking* (1993), *Black Ribbon* (1995), *Stud Rites* (1996), *Animal Appetite* (1997), *The Barker Street Regulars* (1998), *Evil Breeding* (1999), *Creature Discomforts* (2000), *The Wicked Flea* (2002).

Awards: Maxwell Award for fiction writing (1990, 1991).
Similar stuff: Carole Lea BENJAMIN, Joan HESS.
Final fact: SC's father's pointer, Lexington Millington Jock, was the New England Field Trial Champion in the late 1930s.

Michael Connelly (b. 1956) US

No other author in the history of crime fiction has won so many awards in so short a time. And if he didn't win, almost every book has been shortlisted. MC has been fascinated with the crime world since his teens and at college became immersed in the works of Raymond Chandler. He studied journalism and creative writing and set his sights on becoming a police reporter, which he achieved in 1981 on the *Fort Lauderdale News and Sun Sentinel.* In 1986 he and two fellow reporters were shortlisted for the Pulitzer Prize for their coverage of a major airline disaster and this high profile gained him the post as crime reporter for the *Los Angeles Time*. The experience gained has fuelled his work ever since and the success of *The Black Echo* allowed him to write full time. This book introduced his character Hieronymous "'Harry" Bosch, named by his mother, a prostitute, after the painter of the only painting she liked. Bosch never knew his father. His mother is murdered when he is eleven and he is brought up in an orphanage and fostered out. He becomes institutionalized, serving in the army (in Vietnam) and joining the police force. He is a loner, hostile to authority, and dedicated to righting wrongs. A complicated and fascinating character, it is no surprise that in *The Black Echo* Bosch is determined to solve the murder of a fellow Vietnam vet despite the torment it causes him. Bosch's cases are always turbulent. In *The Black Ice* it's drugs, in *The Concrete Blonde* it's whether Bosch shot the wrong man during the arrest of a serial killer, while in *The Last Coyote*, suspended and turning to drink, Bosch looks back into the murder of his mother, decades before. In addition to the Bosch books MC has introduced two other investigators. In *The Poet* it's Jack McEvoy, a crime reporter whose brother, a homicide detective, dies an apparent suicide. In *Blood Work* it's Terry McCaleb, a former FBI agent retired because of his heart condition who is asked to look into the death of the woman whose heart he received in a transplant operation. In *A Darkness More Than Night* both Bosch and McCaleb clash when their separate cases overlap. For television MC and Josh Meyer developed and helped script the series *Level-9* about a task force chosen to fight cyber crime. MC is one of the most exciting talents to hit crime fiction in the last ten years.

Novels

Harry Bosch series: *The Black Echo* (1992), *The Black Ice* (1993), *The Concrete Blonde* (1994), *The Last Coyote* (1995), *Trunk Music* (1997), *Angel's Flight* (1999), *A Darkness More than Night* (2001), *City of Bones* (2002).
Terry McCaleb series: *Blood Work* (1997); also appears in Bosch novel *A Darkness More than Night*.
Non-series: *The Poet* (1996), *Void Moon* (1999).

Full name: Michael Joseph Connelly.
Where to start: *The Black Echo*.
Awards: Edgar, best first novel (1993), 38 Calibre award (France), best novel (1993), Japanese Maltese Falcon (1995), Dilys (1996, 1997), Anthony, best novel (1997, 1999), Nero Wolfe (1997), German Marlowe (1997), Barry, best novel (1998), Grand Prix de Littérature Policière, best foreign (1999), Macavity, best novel (1999), Sherlock, Best Detective Created by an American (2001).
Website: <www.michaelconnelly.com>
Similar stuff: James ELLROY, James PATTERSON.
Final fact: MC's fascination with the world of crime began when he was 16 and witnessed a man throw a gun over a hedge. The man had just robbed and shot someone. MC retrieved the gun and was interviewed by police.

John Connolly (b. 1968) Eire

Although born and raised in Ireland, journalist JC spends almost as much of his time now in the US where his series featuring former NY detective

Charlie 'Bird' Parker is set. Treading the same dark territory as Stephen King and Joe R. LANSDALE, JC's books hover in that territory between dark suspense and the supernatural with an overriding atmosphere of menace. In *Every Dead Thing* Parker has to cope with the brutal and unsolved murders of his wife and daughter and that he had not been there to save them. His quest for reparation and a search for a missing girl bring him up against a vicious serial killer who collects faces. In the subsequent Parker novels the menace is as much from the past as the present. *Dark Hollow* sees Parker on the trail of a murderer but facing a shadowy figure from the past, whilst *The Killing Kind* concerns the secrets of a bizarre religious cult that led one woman to her death. Although developed as a trilogy JC has in fact written a fourth novel where the supernatural element intrudes further. JC combines fear and detection with the power of a tidal wave.

Novels

Charlie Parker series: *Every Dead Thing* (1999), *Dark Hollow* (2000), *The Killing Kind* (2001), *The White Road* (2002).

Website: www.twbooks.co.uk/authors/johnconnolly.html
Awards: Shamus, Best First P.I. Novel (2000)
Similar stuff: Joe R. LANSDALE, Ed GORMAN, James Lee BURKE.
Final fact: The publishing deal for JC's first two books (£350,000) was the highest ever for an Irish writer.

Beverly Connor (b. 1948) US

BC's books are for all lovers of archaeological mysteries and those steeped in forensic identification. BC is a forensic archaeologist and a bone specialist, working as a Professor at the University of Georgia. Her books feature her alter ego Lindsay Chamberlain whose knowledge is in much demand when, in the first book in the sequence, rather more recent remains turn up on an archaeological dig. Not all of the books delve into ancient burials but perhaps her most challenging case is *Skeleton Crew*, where Lindsay is involved not only in a recent murder but trying to solve a 450-year-old murder that happened on a Spanish galleon which has at last been uncovered. The series has perhaps too many recent murders, always a problem with amateur detectives, but the detail and delving into the past is fascinating.

Novels

Lindsay Chamberlain series: *A Rumor of Bones* (1996), *Questionable Remains* (1997), *Dressed to Die* (1998), *Skeleton Crew* (1999), *Airtight Case* (2000).

Website: <www.atens.net/~bconnor/>
Similar stuff: Margot ARNOLD, Jessica MANN.
Final fact: The idea for Lindsay came to BC when she was working at excavations and producing burial drawings. After studying the bone structure of so many skulls she could almost visualize the face the person once had and it felt like she was starting to know them.

K.C. Constantine (b. 1934) US

All of KCC's police procedurals are set in the fictional small town of Rocksburg, Pennsylvania. The series originally featured police chief Mario Balzic, reaching a climax in *Cranks and Shadows*. Thereafter Balzic retires, handing the responsibility on to new acting police chief Ruggiero "Rugs" Carlucci, but since then Balzic has returned as a private investigator and the recent novels have alternated between him and Carlucci. The series, which *Booklist* has called "one of the best mystery series ever published" has two great strengths – the characters and the sense of place. As KCC maintains, he is not writing mysteries or whodunnits but stories about people and the problems that they face. KCC also has a keen ear for natural dialogue which brings people alive. Balzic, who is overweight, irritable, foul-mouthed and hits the bottle too much, nevertheless empathizes with other people which allows him to open up his investigations. Moreover, despite not being a lovable character, KCC's development of Balzic allows us to sympathize with his life and troubles and, through him, with the plight of the small town which has lost its glamour and, with failing local industry, is becoming a backwater. The *Washington Post* recognized that Constantine was writing "some of the best American regional fiction appearing today." Surprisingly for such a popular series none of the books has won an award although *Joey's Case* was shortlisted for the Edgar.

Novels

Mario Balzic series: *The Rocksburg Railroad Murders* (1972), *The Man Who Liked to Look at Himself* (1973), *The Blank Page* (1974), *A Fix Like This* (1975), *The Man Who Liked Slow Tomatoes* (1982), *Always a Body to Trade* (1983), *Upon Some Midnights Clear* (1985), *Joey's Case* (1988), *Sunshine Enemies* (1990), *Bottom Liner Blues* (1993), *Cranks and Shadows* (1995), *Family Values* (1998), *Blood Mud* (1999).

Rugs Carlucci series: *Good Sons* (1996), *Brushback* (1998), *Grievance* (2000).

Real name: Carl Constantine Kosak.
Pen-name: K. C. Constantine.
Where to start: *The Rocksburg Railroad Murders.*
Similar stuff: Hillary Waugh's Fred Fellows, Paula GOSLING.
Final fact: KCC used to play professional baseball but has always shunned publicity and intrusion upon his private life.

Bruce Cook (b. 1932) US

It's easy to imagine that BC's alter ego, Bruce Alexander, is English, because his books about 18th-century blind magistrate Sir John Fielding, founder of the Bow Street Runners, the first police force, are steeped in English history and character. Fielding was half-brother to Henry Fielding, dubbed the "Father of the English novel" so, since the novel and the police force came together in the same period and family, it seems more than appropriate to commemmorate it in a series of novels. In the first, *Blind Justice*, Sir John rescues a young orphan boy, Jeremy Proctor, from hanging for a crime he did not commit and thereafter Proctor becomes Sir John's eyes. BC may have made Sir John more human and less irrascible than his historical counterpart, but the series is a strong evocation of this important period when not just the police force came into existence but new laws ushered in the dawn of criminal justice. Under his real name, BC, a former journalist and newspaper editor, has written a variety of books, including a study *The Beat Generation* (1971) and a book about Berthold Brecht, *Brecht in Exile* (1983). BC is fluent in German and worked for some years in Intelligence as a translator. His first crime novel was *Sex Life*, about a possible homosexual double murder in Chicago. Soon after this BC set about developing his Fielding books but put them in stasis for ten years because he could not secure a good publishing deal. In the interim he wrote a four-book sequence featuring the Mexican-American ex-Los Angeles cop-turned P.I. Antonio "Chico" Cervantes. This explored the ethnic tensions on the Mexican/Californian border and Chico was well rounded in his desires to right wrongs. BC also wrote the final book in William COUGHLIN's Charley Sloan series, *The Judgment*, based on Coughlin's notes.

Novels

Chico Cervantes series: *Mexican Standoff* (1988), *Rough Cut* (1990), *Death as a Career Move* (1992), *The Sidewalk Hilton* (1994).

Non-series: *Sex Life* (1978).

Sir John Fielding series as Bruce Alexander: *Blind Justice* (1994), *Murder in Grub Street* (1995), *Watery Grave* (1996), *Person or Person's Unknown* (1997), *Jack, Knave and Fool* (1997), *Death of a Colonial* (1999), *The Color of Death* (2000), *Smuggler's Moon* (2001).

as William Coughlin (ghost-written): *The Judgment* (1997).

Pen-name: Bruce Alexander.

Where to start: *Mexican Standoff* for contemporary crime; *Blind Justice* for historical.

Website: <www.angelfire.com/ct/tortuga/bruce.html>

Similar stuff: Rex BURNS (for modern ethnic detective), Deryn LAKE (for 18th-century historicals).

Final fact: BC knew he wanted to be a writer when at school he had to write an essay and read it to the class. He wrote it on how you can't tickle yourself.

Judith Cook (b. 1933) UK

Born and raised in Manchester JC became a journalist for the *Guardian* and later turned freelance, winning awards for her investigative journalism. She has written several non-fiction books including *To Brave Every Danger* (1993) about highwaywoman Mary Bryant and *Unlawful Killing* (1994) which looked into the apparent cover-up over the death of Hilda Murrell in 1984. Her first foray into crime fiction was with *The*

Waste Remains, a contemporary mystery, though it drew upon wartime and post-war experimentation with chemical warfare. It was nearly ten years before she returned, this time to the Elizabethan period for which she is well known, with *The Slicing Edge of Death*, which reconstructed the death of Christopher Marlowe. Since then she has been working on the series featuring Elizabethan physician and astrologer Simon Forman whose investigations bring him in touch with many of the powerful individuals of that period. In addition she has written a biography of the real man, *Dr Simon Forman* (2001). JC is currently a part-time lecturer in Elizabeth and Jacobean theatre at Exeter University.

Novels
Non-series: *The Waste Remains* (1984), *The Slicing Edge of Death* (1993).
Simon Forman series: *Death of a Lady's Maid* (1997), *Murder at the Rose* (1998), *Blood on the Borders* (1999), *Kill the Witch* (1999), *School of the Night* (2000).

Full name: Judith Anne Cook.
Where to start: *Death of a Lady's Maid* or *The Slicing Edge of Death*.
Similar stuff: Patricia FINNEY, Lillian de la Torre (for reconstructing historical crimes), Edward MARSTON (for Elizabethan theatre).
Final fact: JC has written *The Golden Age of the English Theatre* (1995), an ideal companion for those interested in mysteries set during that period (1580–1642).

Robin Cook, *see pseudonym* Derek Raymond

Thomas H. Cook (b. 1947) US

THC's work contains some of the most powerful and sombre crime fiction to appear in the last twenty years. They explore the dark and sinister connections and influences in families or small communities over generations – hence the use of "blood" in several titles. This approach appeared in his trilogy about Atlanta cop, Frank Clemons, who, in the Edgar-nominated *Sacrificial Ground*, is haunted by the suicide of his teenage daughter. He becomes obsessed with tracking down the murderer of a young woman but the torment drives him to drink and eventually loses him his job. In the companion books Clemons becomes a P.I. in New York but the past continues to haunt him. The trilogy as a whole is profound and despairing and almost drained THC dry. He has not written any further continuing series. Nevertheless his books, from *Evidence of Blood* on, show his growing fascination with a guilty past and family secrets. In *Mortal Memory* a father kills his wife and children and then disappears. Thirty years later the sole surviving son tries to understand the crime and looks for his father. In *Breakheart Hill*, considered by Otto Penzler to be the best crime novel of the 1990s, there is the death of a young girl amongst a party of college kids and thirty years later one of those kids, now the town doctor, unearths the past. *The Chatham School Affair*, which won Cook his first Edgar, goes back further in time, to a series of nightmare events at a school in 1926 and now the son of the then headmaster reopens the matter. THC was born in Alabama and educated in Georgia and many of his books are set in the south. *Streets of Fire* is a striking study of bigotry and small-town relationships in Alabama, where a detective tries to solve the murder of a young girl against a background of civil rights demonstrations. *The City When it Rains* is one of his few non-series novels with a wholly contemporary setting, though this investigation by a photographer into a girl's apparent suicide is as dark and despairing as they come. THC's first book, *Blood Innocents*, was nominated for an Edgar, and he was also shortlisted for *Blood Echoes*, a study of the slaughter of the Alday family in Georgia in 1973. *Early Graves* is the true story of Judith Neelley, aged 18, the youngest woman sentenced to Death Row.

Novels
Non-series: *Blood Innocents* (1980), *The Orchids* (1982), *Tabernacle* (1983), *Streets of Fire* (1989), *The City When it Rains* (1991), *Evidence of Blood* (1991), *Mortal Memory* (1993), *Breakheart Hill* (1995), *The Chatham School Affair* (1996), *Instruments of Night* (1998), *Places in the Dark* (2000), *The Interrogation* (2002).
Frank Clemons series: *Sacrificial Ground* (1988), *Flesh and Blood* (1989), *Night Secrets* (1990).
Non-fiction. *Early Graves* (1990), *Blood Echoes* (1992).

Where to start: almost anywhere but perhaps *Breakheart Hill*.
Awards: Edgar, best novel (1997), Herodotus, best short story (1999), Swedish Martin Beck (2000).
Similar stuff: James Lee BURKE, William HOFFMAN.

Clarence Cooper, Jr. (1934–78) US

CC was a black American from Detroit who became a drug addict in his youth and spent years in and out of prison. During the fifties he worked for a time as an editor on the *Chicago Messenger*. He spent his time in prison writing and apparently sold other stories and novels under unidentified pen-names. His first book *The Scene* had been written in 1954 and Bennet Cerf showed interest in publishing it if CC rewrote it from the viewpoint of the police rather than the criminals. CC refused and the book remained unpublished until 1960 when it appeared to considerable critical acclaim, *The New Yorker* comparing CC to William Burroughs. It is a harrowing book about the drug scene and the investigation by a young black narcotics detective into the death of a rich white boy from an overdose of near pure heroin. Publishers remained wary of Cooper's books because of his no-holds-barred openness about drugs. *The Syndicate*, about a hit-man's search for those responsible for a bank heist, had to be published under a pseudonym. CC's eventual champion was Harlan Ellison at Regency Books, which published CC's next three books. *Weed* is a stark portrayal of the lives of those who have succumbed to drugs; *The Dark Messenger* draws on CC's experiences as a reporter for a black newspaper; *Black* was a collection of novelettes exploring the dark side of life amongst young blacks. CC continued to be in and out of prison and grew disillusioned at the hostile response to his work. *The Farm*, his last novel, is an unrelenting look at life in prison and rehabilitation centres. CC had been married with three children but he alienated himself from his friends and died penniless and alone in New York, aged 44. His friends thought he had died years before.

Novels. *The Scene* (1960), *Weed* (1961), *The Dark Messenger* (1962), *The Farm* (1967).
as Robert Chestnut: *The Syndicate* (1960).
Short Stories. *Black* (1963)

Full name: Clarence Lavaugn Cooper, Jr.
Pen-names: Robert Chestnut.
Where to start: *The Scene.*
Similar stuff: Chester HIMES, Walter MOSLEY.
Final fact: CC once ran out of a barber's, complete with apron around him, to catch Willard Motley, author of *Knock on Any Door* (1947) and *Let No Man Write My Epitaph* (1958), who had just had his hair cut there.

Natasha Cooper (b. 1951) UK

NC is the best known pseudonym of author Daphne Wright. A Londoner born and bred, NC worked for an art gallery, an architect, and an interior designer, before she entered publishing. She began as a secretary/ editorial assistant at Chatto & Windus and worked her way up to an editorial director at Quartet. In between she spent six years at Hutchinson's, during which, in 1980, she received the Tony Godwin Memorial Trust Award (to encourage the talents of young publishers), which took her to New York for six weeks. With the publication of *The Distant Kingdom* (1987), an historical novel set during the Afghan War in 1842, she was able to leave publishing and write full-time. Alongside four further romance books Wright created her Cooper persona for a series of light-hearted romantic mysteries. These feature Willow King who, for part of the week, is a civil servant in the Department of Old Age Pensions living in a drab flat in Clapham but thereafter she becomes romance novelist Cressida Woodruffe, living in a luxury apartment near Sloane Square. This unlikely premise works due to NC's skills as a writer and the wonderful characterization of Willow King, who has to make this double life work. During the series Willow's defences gradually fall. She has a romance with and later marries detective Tom Worth. They have their first child in *Fruiting Bodies* where Willow (now 44) investigates the death of her obstetrician from her hospital bed. Despite the deliberate frivolous nature of the series at the outset the crimes are ingenious and the books well plotted. For her next series NC turned to something considerably darker. Trish Maguire is a barrister specializing in cases involving children and, in *Creeping Ivy*, becomes a suspect in the disappearance of her cousin's young daughter. In *Fault Lines*, a social worker and key witness in a case of alleged child abuse is murdered. The Trish Maguire series tackles major social issues head on and pulls no punches. Intrigued by the effects of such crimes upon the victim's friends and relatives, NC created a new persona, Clare Layton, for a series of psychological thrillers. Both *Clutch of Phantoms* and *Kill Fee* explore the long-term consequences, twenty or more years downline, of violent crimes.

Novels
Willow King series: *Festering Lilies* (1990; as *A Common Death*, US 1991), *Poison Flowers* (1991), *Bloody Roses* (1992), *Bitter Herbs* (1993), *Rotten Apples* (1995), *Fruiting Bodies* (1996; as *The Drowning Pool*, US 1997), *Sour Grapes* (1997).
Trish Maguire series: *Creeping Ivy* (1998), *Fault Lines* (1999), *Prey to All* (2000).
as Clare Layton: *Clutch of Phantoms* (2000), *Those Whom the Gods Love* (2001).

Real name: Daphne Wright.
Pen-names: Natasha Cooper, Clare Layton.
Where to start: for fun, *Festering Lilies*, otherwise *Creeping Ivy*.
Website: <www.twbooks.co.uk/authors/ncooper.html>
Similar stuff: Patricia HALL, Denise MINA, Abigail PADGETT.
Final fact: The idea for *Prey to All* came to NC as she lay in a locked cell on A-wing in Brixton Prison during a fund-raising sleepover.

Christopher Coram, *see under* Nicholas Rhea

Patricia D. Cornwell (b. 1956) US

The only time all of the major awards have ever agreed upon an author's best first novel was with PDC's *Post-Mortem.* This introduced Dr. Kay Scarpetta, the Chief Medical Examiner for Virginia. PDC had worked for six years (1985–91) as a computer analyst in the Office of the Chief Medical Examiner and before that had been a police reporter in Charlotte, North Carolina for nearly three years, winning an award for her investigative work. When she combined her knowledge of police procedures and forensic pathology she brought a sharp, grim but compelling realism to crime fiction. Scarpetta is determined, forceful, independent but human. The reader hits the ground running with her and follows her through every agonizing move as she searches for evidence to resolve the crime – usually that of a serial killer – before others are murdered. The pace and steady unveiling of the clues is masterfully handled to bring the right amount of tension and suspense. There is a regular cast of characters, including homicide detective Peter Marino, FBI profiler Benton Wesley (who provides the love interest and also has a tragic fate later in the series) and Scarpetta's niece, Lucy, a computer whizz-kid. Lucy is the only character who seems to age through the series, being ten at the start but into her twenties by the later books, when she joins the police force. *Cruel and Unusual*, which won the CWA Golden Dagger, has Scarpetta re-opening an old case in order to resolve a new one. This began a short sequence including *The Body Farm* and *From Potter's Field* involving the serial killer Temple Gault. Keeping a series about set characters fresh is always a challenge and PDC has been accused of stagnating in recent books despite the increasing plot intricacies and emotional turbulence. As an alternative PDC has started a new series featuring Police Chief Judy Hammer, her deputy Virginia West and reporter-turned-cop Andy Brazil. The series began in Charlotte, North Carolina, involving a serial killer, but moved to Richmond, Virginia in *Southern Cross*, to allow them to fight the gang problem. The series lacks the intensity of the Scarpetta books and is slightly more light-hearted, allowing PDC to satirize political and social attitudes. In her light-hearted moments PDC has also created two Dr Scarpetta cook-books and a story for young children, *Life's Little Fable* (1999).

Novels

Kay Scarpetta series: *Post-Mortem* (1990), *Body of Evidence* (1991), *All That Remains* (1992), *Cruel and Unusual* (1993), *The Body Farm* (1994), *From Potter's Field* (1995), *Cause of Death* (1996), *Unnatural Exposure* (1997), *Point of Origin* (1998), *Black Notice* (1999), *The Last Precinct* (2000).

Hammer & Brazil series: *Hornet's Nest* (1997), *Southern Cross* (1999), *Isle of Dogs* (2001).

Non-fiction. *A Time for Remembering* (1983; rev'd as *Ruth, a Portrait*, 1997).

Full name: Patricia Daniels Cornwell.

Where to start: *Post-Mortem.*

Awards: North Carolina Press Association Investigative Reporting award (1980), Gold Medallion Book award (1985), CWA John Creasey Memorial Award (1990), Anthony, best first novel (1991), Edgar, best first novel (1991), Macavity, best first novel (1991), French Prix du Roman d'Aventure (1990), CWA Gold Dagger (1993), French Trophée 813 (1996), Sherlock Award, best detective by a US writer (2000).

Books about: *The Unofficial Patricia Cornwell Companion* by George Beahm (2001).

Website: <www.patriciacornwell.com>

Similar stuff: Susan DUNLAP's O'Shaugnessy series, Kathy REICHS.

Final fact: PDC was raised by Ruth Bell Graham, wife of the evangelist Billy Graham, when PDC's own mother had a nervous breakdown. When PDC published a biography of Ruth, *A Time for Remembering*, Ruth did not talk to PDC for seven years.

Peter Corris (b. 1942) Australia

With Cliff Hardy, PC succeeded in transferring the traditional moody, independent, loner P.I. from the mean streets of Chandler's and MACDONALD's Los Angeles – which was becoming anachronistic in the

1980s – to Sydney, Australia where, intriguingly, it still seems to work. Hardy is, of course, his own man and not an imitation of Marlowe or Archer, but he fits neatly into the general P.I. mould, with his own idiosyncracies and relationships. A former boxer, who can thus look after himself, and a one time insurance investigator, Hardy operates out of the rundown Glebe neighbourhood of Sydney. He undertakes the usual range of duties, looking for missing persons, serving as bodyguard and solving shady deaths, and most cases lead him into trouble. A few cases are especially strange as in *Aftershock*, when a man, whose body has just been dug out of the rubble after an earthquake, had been seen alive five minutes after the quake. In *The Other Side of Sorrow*, Hardy confronts his past and discovers he has a daughter that his ex-wife, whom he hasn't seen for 20 years, is trying to trace. Only one of the books, *The Empty Beach*, has been filmed (1985) although others, including the rather over-the-top *O'Fear*, have been adapted for radio. PC is an Adjunct Professor in the School of Humanities, Media and Cultural Studies at Southern Cross University. He started his career as an academic historian and has many non-fiction books to his credit and several historical novels and he is also interested in boxing, having written a study defiantly titled *Lords of the Ring*. He has written other crime novel series. *Pokerface* introduced Ray Crawley, a Federal Security Agent who finds himself in a dangerous game of bluff and counterbluff. "*Box Office*" *Browning* introduced a light-hearted series about Australian rogue Richard Browning who heads off to Hollywood in the forties and becomes a part-time actor and part-time P.I. The series is a chance to meet all the Hollywood greats. Finally in *Set Up*, we meet Luke Dunlop, an ex-cop who is assigned to the dangerous job of witness protection.

Novels

Cliff Hardy series: *The Dying Trade* (1980), *White Meat* (1981), *The Marvellous Boy* (1982), *The Empty Beach* (1983), *Make Me Rich* (1985), *Deal Me Out* (1986), *The Greenwich Apartments* (1986), *The January Zone* (1987), *O'Fear* (1989), *Wet Graves* (1991), *Aftershock* (1991), *Beware of the Dog* (1992), *Matrimonial Causes* (1993), *Casino* (1994), *The Reward* (1997), *The Washington Club* (1997), *Forget Me If You Can* (1997), *The Black Prince* (1999), *The Other Side of Sorrow* (1999).

Ray Crawley series: *Pokerface* (1985), *The Baltic Business* (1988), *The Kimberley Killing* (1988), *The Cargo Club* (1990), *The Azanian Action* (1991), *The Japanese Job* (1992), *The Time Trap* (1994), *The Vietnam Volunteer* (2000).

Richard Browning series: *"Box Office" Browning* (1987), *Beverly Hills Browning* (1987), *Browning Takes Off* (1989), *Browning in Buckskin* (1991), *Browning P.I.* (1992), *Browning Battles On* (1993), *Browning Sahib* (1994), *Browning Without a Cause* (1995).

Luke Dunlop series: *Set Up* (1992), *Cross Off* (1993), *Get Even* (1994).

Non-series: *The Winning Side* (1984), *The Gulliver Fortune* (1989), *Naismith's Dominion* (1990), *The Brothers Craft* (1992), *Wimmera Gold* (1994).

Short Stories
Cliff Hardy series: *Heroin Annie* (1984), *The Big Drop* (1985), *Man in the Shadows* (1988), *Burn and Other Stories* (1993).
Autobiography. *Sweet and Sour* (2000).

Full name: Peter Robert Corris.
Where to start: *The Dying Trade* for the original P.I. slant or *"Box Office" Browning* for a new look at Hollywood.
Awards: Ned Kelly, lifelong contribution (1999).
Books about: *Peter Corris: a Biography* by Stuart Coupe (1998).
Similar stuff: Shane MALONEY, Peter TEMPLE.
Final fact: When his book *The Empty Beach* was filmed, PC lent actor Bryan Brown his leather jacket and faded jeans for the rôle.

William J. Coughlin (1929–92) US

WJC was a defence attorney and a federal judge in Detroit for twenty years. He used his expertise to write a string of mostly unconnected legal thrillers that were noted for their exploration of the intricacies of court life and politics, as best shown in *Day of Wrath*, and the dilemmas judges face. This was brought out most strongly in *The Heart of Justice*, where a judge has to decide between his marriage and upholding the rule of law. WJC's books are stronger for their legal background than for their characters though he portrayed some highly effective women attorneys in *The Twelve Apostles*, *Her Father's Daughter* and *Her Honor*. Not all of his books are about the courts. *The Stalking Man* is a powerful story of the failure of the legal system where a serial killer is released from prison only to resume his crimes. At the time of his death WJC was developing an interesting series featuring attorney Charlie Sloan, who had been reinstated after losing his licence through alcoholism and who struggles to regain his reputation. The third book in the series was completed by Bruce COOK from WJC's notes whilst a further book, *Proof of Intent*, has been ghost-written by Walter SORRELLS.

Novels
Non-series: *The Destruction Committee* (1971), *The Grinding Mill* (1973), *The Stalking Man* (1979), *Day of Wrath* (1980), *No More Dreams* (1982; rev'd as *The Court*, 1999), *The Twelve Apostles* (1984), *Her Father's Daughter* (1986), *Her Honor* (1987), *In the Presence of Enemies* (1989), *The Heart of Justice* (1995).
Stoney Walsh series: *The Widow Wondered Why* (1968), *The Dividend Was Death* (1969).
Charlie Sloan series: *Shadow of a Doubt* (1991), *Death Penalty* (1992), *The Judgement* completed by Bruce Cook (1997).
as Sean A. Key, Cain series: *Cain's Chinese Adventure* (1974; as *Cain's Chinese Puzzle*, 1981), *The Mark of Cain* (1975).

Full name: William Jeremiah Coughlin.
Pen-name: Sean A. Key.
Where to start: *The Twelve Apostles*.

Similar stuff: William BERNHARDT, John GRISHAM, Paul LEVINE, Lisa SCOTTOLINE.

Ailsa Craig *pseudonym, see* Charlotte MacLeod

David Craig *pseudonym, see under* Bill James

Robert Crais (b. 1953) US

In *The Monkey's Raincoat* RC introduced the characters of Elvis Cole, a Los Angeles P.I., and his sidekick ex-LAPD officer and gunshop owner, Joe Pike. Both are Vietnam vets, but Pike is more battle scarred and embittered and in many ways the deeper character. Cole's investigations, usually into missing persons, are often influenced by Pike's reactions. However, as the series develops so Cole's character deepens and in *Voodoo River*, where he helps a girl seek out her birth mother, RC is writing from the heart. That novel is set mostly in Louisiana, where RC was born. His father, and several other close relatives, were all in the police force, and it was expected RC would follow, but he went to college, dropped out and moved west. His first story was sold as a result of the science-fiction writers' Clarion workshop in 1976 ("With Crooked Hands") and he was soon writing for television. He worked on *Baretta*, *Quincy*, *Hill Street Blues*, *The Equalizer*, and *Miami Vice*, but his favourite show was *Cagney & Lacey*, which he helped develop in the first season. He grew dissatisfied with scriptwriting because he lacked total control. When his father died and RC found he had to step into his shoes to look after his mother, RC developed the plotline of his first Elvis Cole book where Elvis finds himself helping a woman whose husband and son have disappeared. The book won both the Anthony and Macavity awards and was nominated for a Shamus. Four others in the series were nominated for awards, with *Sunset Express* taking the Shamus. The next book, *Indigo Slam*, hit the *L.A. Times* bestseller lists. Yet RC became aware of the constraints of the traditional first-person P.I. format. *L.A. Requiem* saw a more multi-perspective viewpoint and a deeper exploration of characters, especially Pike, whom Cole now suspects in a murder case. RC has recently developed a new series. *Demolition Angel* introduced Carol Starkey, a former bomb-squad operator whose lover was killed in an explosion. Now, popping pills and drink, she is trying to function as an LAPD detective when she has to face a serial bomber. This series has taken RC to new heights and a wider readership.

Novels

Elvis Cole series: *The Monkey's Raincoat* (1987), *Stalking the Angel* (1989), *Lullaby Town* (1992), *Free Fall* (1993), *Voodoo River* (1995), *Sunset Express* (1996), *Indigo Slam* (1997), *L.A. Requiem* (1999), *The Last Detective* (2002).
Carol Starkey series: *Demolition Angel* (2000), *Hostage* (2001).

Full name: Robert Kyle Crais.
Pen-names: Elvis Cole, Jerry Gret Samouche (both used on his TV writing).
Where to start: *The Monkey's Raincoat.*
Awards: Anthony, best paperback original (1988), Macavity, best first novel (1988), Shamus, best P.I. novel (1997), Dilys (2000).
Website: <www.robertcrais.com>
Similar stuff: Harlan COBEN, Dennis LEHANE.
Final fact: RC is a good cook and has even taken classes, and his favourite food is Cajun.

Hamilton Crane *pseudonym, see* Sarah J. Mason

Bill Crider (b. 1941) US

BC has long been a fan of the crime and mystery field; even his PhD thesis in 1972 was on private eye fiction. Texas born and bred, he is devoted to the small-town life of his home state and all of his books are set in Texas. His longest-running series features Sheriff Dan Rhodes of Clearview in Blacklin County. Rhodes is laid-back and crime generally bypasses Clearview – a highlight of the day may be the search for someone's lost false teeth. But occasionally bigger problems come along. Motorbike gangs, or a riot at a local nursing home, or the disappearance of the local dentist. Rhodes takes his time, strolling and yarning and thinking, but he always gets there in the end. The series is light-hearted but subtle and has a greater depth than at first seems. The first book *Too Late to Die*, where Rhodes has to investigate a murder while he is up for re-election, won the Anthony Award for best first novel. BC has written plenty of other series. Carl Burns is a Professor of English literature at a local college, mirroring BC's own academic career. (BC is currently Chair of the Department of English and Fine Arts at Alvin Community College, Texas.) The crimes that Burns investigates are more sinister – the murder of the college dean, or the death of a visiting lecturer. BC has returned to the campus for a new series featuring Dr Sally Good, his female alter ego, in rather more cozy, period-feel whodunnits. A further series features Truman Smith, a reluctant P.I. operating out of Galveston Island, near BC's hometown. The first in the series, the Shamus-nominated *Dead Man on the Island*, has Smith almost giving up his agency when he can't find his own sister, but he is soon galvanized into a search for a friend's missing daughter. All these books are light, easy-going and fun, with a modicum of tension. BC has written much darker material. In addition to several horror suspense novels under the alias Jack MacLane, there are *Blood Marks*, a violent work about a serial killer, and *The Texas Capitol Murders*, which shows that BC is capable of dealing with wider political and social concerns. He has written several mysteries disguised as westerns. *Ryan Rides Back* is about a gunman who returns to his hometown to investigate his sister's murder. *Colorado*

Special, under the name William Grant, was part of a series featuring a detective agency involved in investigating railroad crimes. BC has also written several books for children including the humorous Mike Gonzo adventure series of which *Mike Gonzo and the UFO Terror* (1997) won him the Golden Duck Award for the best juvenile sf novel. BC's fiction obviously has wide appeal.

Novels

Dan Rhodes series: *Too Late to Die* (1986), *Shotgun Saturday Night* (1987), *Cursed to Death* (1988), *Death on the Move* (1989), *Evil at the Root* (1990), *Booked for a Hanging* (1992), *Murder Most Fowl* (1994), *Winning Can be Murder* (1996), *Death by Accident* (1998), *A Ghost of a Chance* (2000), *A Romantic Way to Die* (2001).
Carl Burns series: *One Dead Dean* (1988), *Dying Voices* (1989), *...A Dangerous Thing* (1994).
Truman Smith series: *Dead on the Island* (1991), *Gator Kill* (1992), *When Old Men Die* (1994), *The Prairie Chicken Kill* (1996), *Murder Takes a Break* (1997).
Sally Good series: *Murder is an Art* (1999), *A Knife in the Back* (2001).
Stanley Waters series, written with Willard Scott: *Murder Under Blue Skies* (1998), *Murder in the Mist* (1999).
Western Crime/Mysteries: *Ryan Rides Back* (1988), *Galveston Guman* (1989), *A Time for Hanging* (1989), *The Colorado Special* as William Grant (1989), *Medicine Show* (1990), *Outrage at Blanco* (1999), *Texas Vigilante* (1999).
Mark Stone series with Stephen Mertz under house name Jack Buchanan: *Miami War Zone* (1988), *Desert Death Raid* (1989), *Back to 'Nam* (1990).
Nick Carter series with Jack Davis under house name Nick Carter: *The Coyote Connection* (1981).
Non-series: *Blood Marks* (1991), *The Texas Capitol Murders* (1992).
as Jack MacLane: *Keepers of the Beast* (1988), *Goodnight, Moon* (1989), *Blood Dreams* (1989), *Rest in Peace* (1990), *Just before Dark* (1990).
Short Stories. *My Heart Cries Out for You*, single story (booklet 1992), *The Nighttime is the Right Time* (2001).

Full name: Allen Billy Crider
Pen-names: Jack MacLane; also writes under house names Cliff Banks, Jack Buchanan, Nick Carter, William Grant.
Where to start: *Too Late to Die*.
Awards: Anthony, best first novel (1987).
Website: <www.readthewest.com/billcrider.htm>
Similar stuff: Jeff ABBOTT, M. D. LAKE.
Final fact: BC collects old paperbacks and recalls an occasion, years ago, after he published an interview with the writer Harry Whittington in the magazine *Paperback Quarterly*. "I also placed an ad in the magazine for some of his books that I couldn't find. A few days later the postman left several big boxes at our door. I discovered that Harry had sent me all the books I'd mentioned and some I hadn't even known about. That's when I decided that writers (some of them, anyway) were the best people around."

Deborah Crombie (b. 1952) US

It is not easy for a writer of one country to set their crime fiction in another but DC has done just that to considerable effect. Though born and educated in Texas, where she still lives, DC is an inveterate traveller. She lived for several years in England and Scotland and still visits regularly. Her series features Scotland Yard partners Superintendent Duncan Kincaid and Detective Sergeant Gemma James. Kincaid is in his late thirties, divorced, intelligent, sensitive and with an upper class background. James is late twenties, also divorced with a young child, bright, determined and impulsive. She is of a somewhat lower social class than Kincaid, but they make a strong team and, over the course of the series, are drawn together, though there is always friction and uncertainty. The stories are thoroughly researched with detailed police procedural background, intelligently plotted cases and considerable emotional tension amongst the main characters. The first title, *A Share in Death*, was shortlisted for both the Agatha and Macavity awards. The fifth, *Dreaming of the Bones*, which starts out with Kincaid's ex-wife researching the life and death of a poet for a biography, and ends in tragedy, was not only shortlisted for the Agatha and Edgar awards but won the Macavity. It was also selected by the Independent Mystery Booksellers of America as one of the hundred best crime novels of the century. DC's work is fiction to savour.

Novels

Duncan Kincaid/Gemma James series: *A Share in Death* (1993), *All Shall Be Well* (1994), *Leave the Grave Green* (1995), *Mourn Not Your Dead* (1996), *Dreaming of the Bones* (1997), *Kissed a Sad Goodbye* (1999), *A Finer End* (2001).

Full name: Deborah Darden Crombie.
Where to start: *A Share in Death.*
Awards: Macavity, best novel (1998).
Website: <www.deborahcrombie.com>
Similar stuff: Clare CURZON, Anthea FRASER, Elizabeth GEORGE.

Amanda Cross (b. 1926) US

AC is the pen-name of Carolyn Heilbrun, Professor of English and of Humanities at Columbia University. AC was a noted feminist in the days when it was not fashionable. She is the author of *Towards a Recognition of Androgyny* (1973), *Reinventing Womanhood* (1979) and *Writing a Woman's Life* (1988), the last regarded as a feminist classic. She has also written studies of David Garnett and Christopher Isherwood. She believed that detective fiction had lost its literary appeal since the days of Sayers and that it was being tailored to its readership. She wanted fiction that was erudite, intelligent and literary and which featured strong, independent women. So she created Kate Fansler, a Professor of English Literature in New York and an ardent feminist. Fansler has been accused of being snobbish and elitist, and this is true only in so far as she has principles and standards and sticks to them. She uses a keen understanding of literature and psychology in her investigations into murders as in the first book, *In the Last Analysis*, which was an Edgar nominee, where a psychoanalyst becomes a murder suspect and Fansler uses Freud's theories – in effect profiling – to identify the murderer. In *The Theban Mysteries* she is able to find parallels in Greek literature to help a Vietnam draft dodger. Fansler is not infallible. In *A Question of Max* her outlook on life initially blinkers her to the solution, but in the award-winning *Death in a Tenured Position*, it is her understanding of human nature that leads her to the murderer. Written over a span of nearly forty years, the quality of the books is variable and Fansler's attitudes have grown with AC's, but overall the series is remarkable for its originality and style.

Novels

Kate Fansler series: *In the Last Analysis* (1964), *The James Joyce Murder* (1967), *Poetic Justice* (1970), *The Theban Mysteries* (1971), *The Question of Max* (1976), *Death in a Tenured Position* (1981; as *A Death in the Faculty*, UK 1981), *Sweet Death, Kind Death* (1984), *No Word from Winifred* (1986), *A Trap for Fools* (1989), *The Players Come Again* (1990), *An Imperfect Spy* (1995), *The Puzzled Heart* (1998), *Honest Doubt* (2000).

Short Stories. *The Collected Stories* (1997).

Real name: Carolyn Gold Heilbrun.
Pen-name: Amanda Cross.
Where to start: *In the Last Analysis.*
Awards: Nero Wolfe (1981).
Similar stuff: Anna CLARKE (for female investigative professor), Sara PARETSKY (for strong feminist views).
Final fact: AC was forced to adopt her alias in order to keep her writing secret and thus retain her post. Her identity was not revealed until 1972.

John Crowe *pseudonym, see* Michael Collins

James Crumley (b. 1939) US

Born in Texas and now living in Montana, JC served in the US Army for three years before earning his degree in history and becoming a professor of English. His first book, *One to Count Cadence* (1969); was a stark account of the dawn of the Vietnam War. Many new fictional P.I.s have fallen out of the aftermath of that war, but none so violently as JC's C.W. Sughrue. An army spy and war criminal Sughrue has set himself up as a P.I. in western Montana. Down the road is Milo Milodragovitch, struggling to be human but washed up by drink and cocaine. His parents both committed suicide and he lives only to inherit a family fortune. In two novels apiece the two carry out their tawdry investigations separately. JC's world is violent, nasty, bleak and despairing. The books are like modern westerns. There are no real heroes and villains, just victims – of society, of war and, above all, of themselves. Hunting for missing persons and becoming involved with merciless killers, both P.I.s head towards tragedy. Sughrue is left for dead at the end of the award-winning *The Mexican Tree Duck*, after his hunt for a gang of Mexican thugs. In *Dancing Bear* (nominated for a Shamus), Milo has to come to terms with his anticipated fortune having been plundered by a con-artist. *Bordersnakes* unites the two in an orgy of revenge. Although the book is even more bleak and despairing, written with a profound pessimism, JC also writes with a wry humour which helps the reader survive the book. JC is not for the meek and mild, but you won't find a more violent antidote to the cozy mystery.

Novels
Sughrue series: *The Last Good Kiss* (1978), *The Mexican Tree Duck* (1993).
Milo Milodragovitch: *The Wrong Case* (1975), *Dancing Bear* (1983), *The Final Country* (2001).
Both characters feature in *Bordersnakes* (1996).
Short Stories. *Whores* (1988), *The Muddy Fork and Other Things* (1991).

Where to start: *The Last Good Kiss.*
Awards: Japanese Maltese Falcon (1985), Hammett (1994).
Similar stuff: James Lee BURKE, James ELLROY.
Final fact: JC admits to being restless, and has been known to drive 1000 miles to play a game of Black Jack or 1500 miles to see a woman.

E. V. Cunningham *pseudonym, see* Howard Fast

Clare Curzon (b. 1922) UK

CC is the third incarnation of author and former interpreter, teacher and probation officer, Eileen-Marie Duell Buchanan. She began writing in the early sixties under the alias Rhona Petrie. *Death in Deakins Wood*, a tale of murder and arson, introduced Inspector Marcus MacLurg in a series of traditional methodical whodunnits, yet the series failed to make a mark. Mrs Duell next experimented briefly with an Anglo-Sudanese forensic scientist, Dr Nassim Pride, who applied inscrutable logic to his problems and brought everything together in a final analysis. More could have been made of him but CC moved into her second incarnation as Marie Buchanan, producing a series of novels dealing with the paranormal, a mood which leached over into her first book as CC, *A Leaven of Malice*, which is about voodoo and psychic possession. In *I Give you Five Days* she introduced her characters Superintendent Mike Yeadings and Sergeant (later Inspector) Angus Mott of Thames Valley Police. It took several books before these characters took shape. They hardly appear in *Masks and Faces*, which is a hangover from the Buchanan period about a young teenager who believes he has been made to kill his father by an evil force. However, by *The Blue-Eyed Boy*, which introduced WPC Rosemary Zyczynski (known as 'Z'), the series was settling down and through the nineties has produced some of the more satisfying police procedurals of the period. The series deals with contemporary issues but CC never feels wholly comfortable with this and it is not surprising she has started a new series, set in the early 1900s, which explores the tragedies that beset an aristocractic family, the Stakerleys. The first of these, *Guilty Knowledge*, won the Herodotus award.

Novels

Mike Yeadings series: *I Give You Five Days* (1983), *Masks and Faces* (1984), *The Trojan Hearse* (1985), *The Quest for K* (1986), *Three-Core Lead* (1988), *The Blue-Eyed Boy* (1990), *Cat's Cradle* (1991), *First Wife, Twice Removed* (1992), *Death Prone* (1992), *Nice People* (1993), *Past Mischief* (1994), *Close Quarters* (1996), *All Unwary* (1997), *Cold Hands* (1999), *Don't Leave Me* (2001), *Body of a Woman* (2002).

Sian Westbury series: *Trail of Fire* (1987), *Shot Bolt* (1988).

Stakerley series: *Guilty Knowledge* (1999), *The Colour of Blood* (2000).

Non-series: *A Leaven of Malice* (1979), *Special Occasions* (1981), *The Face in the Stone* (1989).

as Rhona Petrie:

Inspector MacLurg series: *Death in Deakins Wood* (1963), *Murder by Precedent* (1964), *Running Deep* (1965), *Dead Loss* (1966), *MacLurg Goes West* (1968).

Nassim Pride series: *Foreign Bodies* (1967), *Despatch of a Dove* (1969).

Non-series: *Thorne in the Flesh* (1971).

as Marie Buchanan: *Greenshards* (1972; as *Anima*, US 1972), *An Unofficial Death* (1973), *The Dark Backward* (1975), *Morgana* (1977).

as Marie Duell: *The Countess of Sedgwick* (1990).

Short Stories

as Rhona Petrie: *Come Hell and High Water* (1970).

Full name: Eileen-Marie Duell Buchanan (née Belderson).
Pen-names: Marie Buchanan, Clare Curzon, Rhona Petrie.
Where to start: *The Blue-Eyed Boy*.
Awards: Herodotus, best first international historical mystery (2000).
Similar stuff: Anthea FRASER.

Barbara D'Amato (b. 1938) US

BD is best known for her series featuring Cat Marsala, a freelance investigative journalist in Chicago. Cat had turned freelance because she wanted to be able to explore complex social issues in more detail and all of the books in the series follow that framework. In the first, *Hardball*, Cat is checking out a group promoting the legalisation of drugs when the head of that group is killed in an explosion. In *Hard Women* it's prostitution, in *Hard Case* it's about specialized trauma centres, whilst *Hard Luck* is about lotteries and gambling. Cat's clearly a dangerous person to be near as her investigations always attract murders, sometimes aimed at her, but she is determined and street-wise and frequently probes where the police can't follow. The books seldom answer the social issues raised but they provide considerable material of interest besides the intrigue of the murder mystery. Both *Hard Women* and *Hard Christmas* were shortlisted for various mystery awards. BD developed the character of Cat following her own work investigating the case of Chicago doctor John Branion who had been falsely convicted of murder in 1968. BD's research unearthed new facts and helped provide the data leading to Branion's release. She wrote the case up in *The Doctor, the Murder, the Mystery*, which won the Anthony and Agatha awards. Her research also featured in the TV series *Unsolved Mysteries*. Before she took up the Branion case BD had written two novels featuring a Chicago forensic pathologist, Gerritt DeGraaf, the first of which, *The Hands of Healing Murder*, is a classic locked-room mystery. Her next two books, *The Eyes of Utopia Murders* and the stand-alone *On My Honor* (which was shortlisted for an Anthony), both explore the potential for children as murderers. Most recently BD has started a new police procedural series, also set in Chicago (where BD lives with her husband), which is less traditional and more high-impact. *Good Cop, Bad Cop* earned BD the Carl Sandburg Award for excellence in fiction. She also won a cache of awards for her poisonously light-hearted story "Of Course You Know that Chocolate is a Vegetable" (*EQMM*, 1998) and was the first recipient of the Mary Higgins Clark Award for *Authorized Personnel Only*.

Novels

Gerritt DeGraaf series: *The Hands of Healing Murder* (1980), *The Eyes of Utopia Murders* (1981).

Cat Marsala series: *Hardball* (1990), *Hard Tack* (1991), *Hard Luck* (1992), *Hard Women* (1993), *Hard Case* (1994), *Hard Christmas* (1995), *Hard Bargain* (1997), *Hard Evidence* (1999), *Hard Road* (2001).

Chicago Police series: *Killer.app* (1996), *Good Cop, Bad Cop* (1998), *Help Me Please* (1999), *Authorized Personnel Only* (2000).

as Malacai Black: *On My Honor* (1989).

Non-Series: *White Male Infant* (2002).

Non-fiction. *The Doctor, the Murder, the Mystery* (1992).

Pen-name: Malacai Black.

Where to start: Almost anywhere but *Hard Case* and *Killer.app* are very representative.

Awards: Agatha, best non-fiction (1994), best short story (1999), Anthony, best non-fiction (1993), best short story (1999); Carl Sandburg Award for Excellence in Fiction (1998), Macavity, best short story (1999), Mary Higgins Clark Award (2001).

Website: <www.barbaradamato.com>

Similar stuff: Jan BURKE, Mickey Friedman, Nancy PICKARD.

Final fact: BD started her literary career as a playwright, but between raising a family and returning to college to earn her degree, she worked as a carpenter for stage magic illusions and as an assistant tiger handler.

Philip Daniels (b. 1924) UK

Dennis Phillips, who writes under four pen-names (only one book has appeared under his own name) is an extremely versatile writer. He is best known for his 36-book Mark Preston series published under the alias Peter Chambers. Set in Monkton City, California, it features a stereotypical Chandleresque laconic, wise-cracking loner private eye. Yet although the formula is there, the writing is assured, the plotting creative and the pace fast. The books were well received in America showing that Phillips was thorough in his research. Phillips had first appeared under the pen-name Peter Chester with a short series featuring P.I. Johnny Preston, a precursor of Mark Preston, but under his alter ego Philip Daniels the author demonstrated his versatility with a rich and varied set of mysteries with an English setting. These books may yet be Phillips's lasting testament. They range from government intrigue in *Nice Knight for Murder* to insider trading in *Foolproof*, to ritual murder at a horror party in *The Dracula Murders* to a traditional English cozy in *A Genteel Little Murder*.

Novels

Mark Preston series as Peter Chambers: *Murder is for Keeps* (1961), *Wreath for a Redhead* (1962), *The Big Goodbye* (1962), *Dames Can be Deadly* (1963), *Down-Beat Kill* (1963), *Lady, This is Murder* (1963), *This'll Kill You* (1964), *Nobody Lives for Ever* (1964), *You're Better Off Dead* (1965), *Always Take the Big Ones* (1965), *No Gold When You Go* (1966), *Don't Bother to Knock* (1966), *The Bad Die Young* (1967), *The Blonde Wore Black* (1968), *No Peace for the Wicked* (1968), *Speak Ill of the Dead* (1968), *They Call it Murder* (1973), *Somebody Has to Lose* (1975), *The Deader They Fall* (1979), *Lady, You're Killing Me* (1979), *The Day of the Big Dollar* (1979), *The Beautiful Golden Frame* (1980), *Nothing Personal* (1980), *The Deep Blue Cradle* (1980), *A Long Time Dead* (1981), *The Lady Who Never Was* (1981), *Female – Handle With Care* (1981), *Murder is its Own Reward* (1982), *The Highly Explosive Case* (1982), *A Miniature Murder Mystery* (1982), *Jail Bait* (1983), *Dragons Can be Dangerous* (1983), *Bomb Scare: Flight 147* (1984), *The Moving Picture Writes* (1984), *The Vanishing Holes Murders* (1985), *The Hot Money Caper* (1992).

Non-series as Peter Chambers: *The Day the Thames Caught Fire* (1989).

Johnny Preston series as Peter Chester: *Killing Comes Easy* (1958), *Murder Forestalled* (1960), *The Pay-Grab Murders* (1962).

Non-series as Peter Chester: *Blueprint for Larceny* (1963), *The Traitors* (1964).

as Simon Challis: *Death on a Quiet Beach* (1968).

as Philip Daniels: *Goldmine – London W.1* (1979), *The Scarred Man* (1980), *The Nice Quiet Girl* (1980), *Alibi of Guilt* (1980), *Foolproof* (1981), *Suspicious* (1981), *The Inconvenient Corpse* (1982), *A Genteel Little Murder* (1982), *Nice Knight for Murder* (1982), *The Dracula Murders* (1983), *Cinderella Spy* (1984), *Enquiries Are Proceeding* (1986), *The Hunting of Mr. Gloves* (1986).

as Dennis Phillips: *Revenge Incorporated* (1970).

Full name: Dennis John Andrew Phillips.

Pen-names: Simon Challis, Peter Chambers, Peter Chester, Philip Daniels.

Where to start: *The Scarred Man.*
Similar stuff: Basil Copper's Mike Faraday books; Roger ORMEROD.

Diane Mott Davidson US

On first consideration it may be hard to see the reason for the success of DMD's Goldy Bear series. They are generally cozy mysteries where the amateur sleuth is a caterer who encounters murders almost every month. *Publisher's Weekly* at the time the first book appeared called it "embarrassing" and yet that same volume was shortlisted for the Agatha, Anthony and Macavity awards and, nine years later, *Tough Cookie*, hit the *New York Times* bestseller lists. Part of the appeal may lie in the fact that each book contains several enticing recipes – there's even a recipe index. But the real strength lies in Goldy herself. She is a single parent, the victim of domestic abuse and now divorced but not free from her violent husband, and trying to raise an 11-year-old son. Her courage, determination and fortitude carry her through and provide the driving force to the series. In the first book she becomes romantically involved with police detective Tom Schulz and by the end of *The Last Suppers* they are married. The books gain in complexity and confidence as the series progresses and now each volume is eagerly awaited. DMD was born in Honolulu but raised in Virginia. She has been a schoolteacher, counsellor and is a licensed lay preacher. She did start a second series featuring police detective Toni Underwood, described as "the soft-hearted copy with the hard-boiled attitude", but that series has gone on ice. *Deadly Rendezvous*, set in Palm Springs, California, is a dark psychological chiller with a series of mindless murders, while *Deadly Gambit* takes on the Mob in Las Vegas.

Novels

Goldy Bear series: *Catering to Nobody* (1990), *Dying for Chocolate* (1992), *Cereal Murders* (1993), *The Last Suppers* (1994), *Killer Pancake* (1995), *The Main Corpse* (1996), *The Grilling Season* (1997), *Prime Cut* (1998), *Tough Cookie* (2000), *Sticks and Stones* (2001), *Chopping Spree* (2002).
Toni Underwood series: *Deadly Rendezvous* (1994), *Deadly Gamble* (1996).

Where to start: *Catering to Nobody.*
Awards: Anthony, best short story (1993).
Website: <mysterybooks.about.com/library/mad/blmad_davidsonm.htm>
Similar stuff: Ellen HART, Janet LAURENCE; Amy MYERS's August Didier series.
Final fact: DMD undertakes research by joining a team of caterers for each book. The first time she did it she felt dead within a week because it was such hard work.

Lionel Davidson (b. 1922) UK

LD, who for over 50 years has been a freelance journalist and editor, is one of those individuals whom the word "unique" aptly describes. He has written just eight novels for adults in forty years, and though all of them can be classified as "thrillers" and three were awarded the CWA Gold Dagger as that year's best novel, only one of them, *The Chelsea Murders*, comes close to being a conventional crime novel. It is about a vicious murderer who plays games with the police about his next victim. Two of the books, *The Night of Wenceslas* (filmed 1964 as *Hot Enough for June*) and *The Sun Chemist*, fall into the category of espionage. Three of the books consider the post-war issues facing Israel and the Jews. In *Making Good Again* a lawyer tries to settle reparation over a Jewish banker who disappeared during WW2. In *A Long Way to Shiloh* the state of Israel is a tangible background to an absorbing quest for a golden menorah stolen from Solomon's Temple in AD 70. In *Smith's Gazelle* it is the confrontation between an individual Jew and Arab over what each believes is a God-given quest. Finally *The Rose of Tibet*, many people's choice as the best of LD's books, is a twist on the Shangri-La theme when Charles Whittington's quest for his missing brother takes him to a remote monastery run by an evil abbess. All these books contain elements of crime, mystery, adventure, romance even humour, but beyond all that they are books about the human desire for justice.

Novels. *The Night of Wenceslas* (1960), *The Rose of Tibet* (1962), *A Long Way to Shiloh* (1966; as *The Menorah Men*, US 1966), *Making Good Again* (1968), *Smith's Gazelle* (1971), *The Sun Chemist* (1976), *The Chelsea Murders* (1978; as *Murder Games*, US 1978), *Kolymsky Heights* (1994).

Pen-names: David Line (for children's books).
Where to start: For pure crime go for *The Chelsea Murders* otherwise they are all equally excellent.
Awards: CWA Gold Dagger (1960, 1966, 1978), Israeli President's Prize for Literature (1971), Diamond Dagger (2001).
Similar stuff: Eric Ambler.

Dorothy Salisbury Davis (b. 1916) US

A MWA Grand Master, DSD has been around for so long that it's easier to think of her as a classic-period writer rather than modern, but her first book was not published until 1949, after several years working in advertising and as a librarian. Her work helped lay the groundwork for a new attitude in crime fiction, concentrating on the psychological views of the villain and victim rather than the detection. DSD deplored violence and through her books explored the causes of crime. Her early books take place in small midwest towns where people keep themselves to themselves – the title of *A Town of Masks* neatly describes it – and where the seething anger and resentment of people often bubbles just under the surface, as in *The Judas Cat* and *The Clay Hand*. That last book explored the growing poverty in the coal-mining areas in the Appalachians. Later books moved this approach to the big cities. *Black Sheep, White Lamb* is a powerful portrayal of a teenager who turned murderer when a robbery goes wrong. *The Little Brothers* extends this to explore the fraternity within a gang of youths and their reaction to a murder. It is perhaps best exemplified in *Where the Dark Streets Go* (filmed TV 1987 as *Broken Vows*), set amongst the slums of New York where a parish priest struggles with his own conscience whilst investigating a murder. A priest was also the key figure in DSD's early novel, *A Gentle Murderer*, still regarded by many as one of her best. A killer confesses to a local priest of a murder and the priest tries to find the killer before the police do and before he kills again.

Most of DSD's books are standalones, but she developed two interesting series characters. In *Death of an Old Sinner* we are introduced to the retired General Jarvis who is murdered because of his blackmailing schemes. His observant housekeeper, Mrs Norris, investigates, along with DA Jasper Tully. DSD brought Mrs Norris and Tully back in two further novels and a short story. Her other main character is Julie Hayes, a footloose character who, in *A Death in the Life*, sets up a fortune-telling shop in New York's red light district. She gets to know the pimps and prostitutes well, so that when a friend of hers is killed and a prostitute goes missing Julie is able to help the police. This was one of five novels for which DSD was shortlisted for the Edgar Award, the others being *A Gentleman Called*, *The Pale Betrayer*, *God Speed the Night* and *Where the Dark Streets Go*. Julie Hayes returned in three other novels. In the last, *The Habit of Fear*, she has become a newspaper columnist and goes in search of the father she never knew. DSD is also an accomplished writer of short stories, two of which have received Edgar nominations, though the best is probably "Born Killer" (*EQMM*, 1953), a psychological study of a young farmboy. "By the Scruff of the Soul" (*EQMM*, 1963) saw the start of a very occasional series related by a smalltown lawyer, to which DSD is still adding.

Novels

Non-series: *The Judas Cat* (1949), *The Clay Hand* (1950), *A Gentle Murderer* (1951), *A Town of Masks* (1952), *Black Sheep, White Lamb* (1963), *Enemy and Brother* (1967), *Where the Dark Streets Go* (1969), *Shock Wave* (1972).

Mrs Norris series: *Death of an Old Sinner* (1957), *A Gentleman Called* (1958), *Old Sinners Never Die* (1959).

Lieutenant Marks series: *The Pale Betrayer* (1965), *The Little Brothers* (1973).

Julie Hayes series: *A Death in the Life* (1976), *Scarlet Night* (1980), *Lullaby of Murder* (1984), *The Habit of Fear* (1987).

with Jerome Ross: *God Speed the Night* (1968).

Short Stories. *Tales for a Stormy Night* (1984), *In the Still of the Night* (2001).

Editor. *A Choice of Murders* (1958), *Crime Without Murder* (1970).

Where to start: *A Gentle Murderer* (1951).
Awards: MWA Grand Master (1985), Anthony, lifetime achievement (1989).
Similar stuff: Celia Fremlin, B.M. GILL, Patricia HIGHSMITH, Ruth RENDELL.
Final fact: The deep secrets in DSD's fiction may in part be inspired by the fact that when she was 17 she discovered she had been adopted when one year old. It took her a year before she could confront her adoptive parents about it and another 50 years before she checked out the original documents and found that she had been one of twins, but that her twin sister had died before they were registered.

Val Davis *pseudonym, see* Robert R. Irvine

Lindsey Davis (b. 1949) UK

Since the death of Ellis Peters, LD seems to have inherited the mantle of Britain's Queen of the Historical Mystery, with her masterful series featuring informer and imperial agent, Marcus Didius Falco, at the time of the Roman Emperor Vespasian. LD did not start out with that in mind. Birmingham born and bred, and with a B.A. at Oxford in English language and literature, LD set out to write the great English Civil War novel but no one was interested. While she worked for the Department of the Environment, LD began writing romances for *Woman's Realm*, and saw the potential in a Roman romance about Vespasian and his mistress. It was ten years before that book, *The Course of Honour* (1998), found a publisher, but in the meantime LD, fascinated with the period (AD 70s), developed the character of Falco, a somewhat disreputable, streetwise informer. Through his lover and later wife, Helena, he has connections with the upper levels of society, right up to the Emperor. Narrated in the first person we come to know and love Falco for his all-too-human characteristics and sense of fun. Like Chandler's Marlowe, he is quick-witted and amusing, and has rather more scruples than some of his fellows, though not enough to spoil his conscience. Unlike Marlowe, Falco is not a loner, though he has few people he wants to call friends. The series is light-hearted, drawing as much from the perspective of Douglas Adams as crime fiction, but it also contains much fascinating detail about Roman life and culture. LD is often audacious with her treatment of plot and characters, and occasionally has Falco speak to the reader, all of which endears him and makes the stories human and believable. LD has brought ancient Rome to life and imported it right into our homes.

Novels

Falco series: *The Silver Pigs* (1989), *Shadows in Bronze* (1990), *Venus in Copper* (1991), *The Iron Hand of Mars* (1992), *Poseidon's Gold* (1993), *Last Act in Palmyra* (1994), *Time to Depart* (1995), *A Dying Light in Corduba* (1996), *Three Hands in the Fountain* (1997), *Two for the Lions* (1998), *One Virgin Too Many* (1999), *Ode to a Banker* (2000), *A Body in the Bath House* (2001), *The Jupiter Myth* (2002).

Awards: Authors' Club Best First Novel (1989), CWA Dagger in the Library (1995), CWA Ellis Peters Historical Dagger (1999), Sherlock Award, best comic detective (2000), Herodotus, Lifetime Achievement (2001).
Website: <www.lindseydavis.co.uk>
Similar stuff: John Maddox Roberts, Rosemary Rowe, Steven SAYLOR have all written series set in ancient Rome.
Final fact: LD used to visit archaeological sites in Britain for her research, but it rained too much, so she changed to visiting Rome instead.

Janet Dawson (b. 1949) US

JD was an enlisted journalist and officer in the US Navy from 1975–83, rising to the rank of lieutenant. She then became a legal secretary until the success of her books allowed her to write full-time in 1995. Her first book, *Kindred Crimes*, which introduced Oakland female P.I. Jeri Howard, won the St Martin's Press/PWA contest for best first unpublished novel in 1989. Jeri is hired by a husband to find his vanished wife, but it transpires the woman is not who she said she was. The book went on to be nominated for the Shamus, Anthony and Macavity Awards, and JD developed a series. We don't learn much about Jeri throughout the novels, other than that she is perfectly normal, unlike most private detectives. Instead the books concentrate on key social issues such as battered wives in *Take a Number*, abandoned children in *Nobody's Child* and the state of ethnic minorities in the US in *Till the Old Men Die*. In most cases Jeri discovers the origins of the mystery are set deep in the past and the delight of the series is in the gradual removal of the layers of history to get at the truth. JD was born in Oklahoma but educated in Colorado and California, where she now lives. She currently works in a small research unit at the University of California.

Novels

Jeri Howard series: *Kindred Crimes* (1990), *Till the Old Men Die* (1993), *Take a Number* (1993), *Don't Turn Your Back on the Ocean* (1994), *Nobody's Child* (1995; as *The Missing Child*, UK 1995), *A Credible Threat* (1996), *Witness to Evil* (1997), *Where the Bodies are Buried* (1998), *A Killing at the Track* (2000).

Where to start: *Kindred Crimes.*
Awards: St. Martin's Press/PWA best first (unpublished) novel (1989).
Website: <www.janetdawson.com>
Similar stuff: Marcia MULLER, Abigail PADGETT.
Final fact: After JD graduated from the University of Colorado and before she joined the navy, she had her first encounter with a murderer. She recalls: "I was a newspaper reporter and editor for a small daily paper in southeastern Colorado. Part of my job was to visit the courthouse each day. One morning I'd heard that the sheriff had been called out to the nearby town of Holly. I went to the courthouse and got into an elevator with two men, one of them a deputy, the other an ordinary-looking man who didn't seem worth a second glance. I asked the deputy what had happened in Holly. The man next to him said, quite calmly, 'I killed a

woman.' I don't remember anything else about the case, just that ordinary-looking man and his calm voice, a killer admitting his crime. Perhaps it's because he looked so normal, but that encounter has stayed with me for nearly 30 years."

Marele Day (b. 1947) Australia

MD created Australia's first fictional female P.I. in the shape of Claudia Valentine in *The Life and Crimes of Harry Lavender*. Though the series uses all the trappings of the hard-boiled detective it's really more sophisticated than that. Claudia does rent an office in a seedy part of Sydney, she does drink too much, and she likes blonds (men that is), but she is not excessively violent (though she is karate trained), she is not a loner (quite the opposite) and she is not riven by depression or angst. Her cases are innovative and complicated. The first involves an investigation into a man who apparently died of cardiac arrest, but the victim's sister thinks differently. Claudia believes the answer lies in what the victim had been writing on his computer. *The Case of the Chinese Boxes* is a frustrating case for Claudia as she has to find a lost key but no one will tell her why this key is so important. *The Last Tango of Delores Delgado* won the Shamus award and it is the most accomplished of the series. Claudia impersonates the victim to find out why an exotic dancer died. *The Disappearance of Madalena Grimaldi* finds Claudia investigating not only a missing school-girl but also the death of her father whom she has not seen for 30 years. This is an excellent gritty series, written with flair and style. Despite its success MD felt constrained by the format and, after compiling a book on crime writing, she wrote a mainstream novel, *Lambs of God*, about what happens to an isolated community of nuns when the church decides to sell the monastery. This book proved highly successful and placed MD's name on the map. She has since written a spoof on amateur detectives in *Mavis Levack PI*, featuring 60-something nosey parker Mavis who gets involved in all manner of bizarre crimes, such as the mysterious disappearance of many of Sydney's P.I.s, including Peter CORRIS's Cliff Hardy. Played for laughs it demonstrates the all round skills and abilities of MD. A graduate of Sydney University, MD trained as a teacher but has travelled extensively and held a variety of jobs, most recently as a freelance editor, until she turned to full-time writing. Her first novel, *Shirley's Song*, was a comedy set in Ireland.

Novels

Claudia Valentine series: *The Life and Crimes of Harry Lavender* (1988), *The Case of the Chinese Boxes* (1990), *The Last Tango of Delores Delgado* (1992), *The Disappearance of Madalena Grimaldi* (1994).

Non-series: *Lambs of God* (1998).

Short stories. *Mavis Levack PI* (2000).

Non-fiction. *The Art of Self-Promotion: successful promotion by writers* (1993); as Editor, *How to Write Crime* (1996).

Full name: Marele Lorraine Day.
Where to start: *The Life and Crimes of Harry Lavender* (1988).
Awards: Shamus, best P.I. novel (1993), Ned Kelly, best non-fiction (1997).
Website: <www.twbooks.co.uk/authors/mareled.html>
Similar stuff: Claire McNab, Peter CORRIS.
Final fact: While on a journey from Cairns in Australia to Singapore, MD was shipwrecked on a catamaran in the Java Sea.

William L. DeAndrea (1952–96) US

WLD became attracted to crime fiction when he first read the work of Ellery Queen, and the classic Queen touch of solving the crime in the final scenes with the least-suspected person is a technique WLD loves to employ when he can. His longest-running series featured Matt Cobb, an investigator employed by a TV network who narrates his own adventures. Cobb is likeable enough, though there is a tendency for WLD's humour to get the better of the story and minimize the ingenious plots he's developing. The earlier books are the best – indeed the first, *Killed in the Ratings*, won an Edgar Award as the year's best first novel. WLD was better when he took things seriously, though his humour always seeps through somewhere. His best series features the eccentric Professor Niccolo Benedetti, a renowned criminologist who, in *The HOG Murders* turns his mind to the problem of a serial killer who signs himself "the Hog". It has one of the most audacious solutions in all crime fiction, and it won WLD his second Edgar. It was twelve years before he resurrected Benedetti in two further delightfully complicated and cunning crimes. With *Cronus* he introduced a spy with no name. He is called Clifford Driscoll in this first outing but takes on other personas in the later books. Though a more serious series, WLD does not feel at home in the spy arena. Much more fun is *The Lunatic Fringe*, set in New York in 1896 when Theodore Roosevelt was the Police Commissioner. WLD experimented again with historical mysteries in a western crossover series featuring former federal marshall Lobo Blacke and his dime novelist biographer Quinn Booker. This has some delightfully quirky moments and the humour is well placed. Of WLD's other novels, *Five O'Clock Lightning* is a baseball murder set in 1953 and *Unholy Moses* is an art-world mystery. WLD was a regular reviewer and columnist in the mystery magazines and his knowledge of the field allowed him to compile the immensely readable *Encyclopedia Mysteriosa*, which won him his third Edgar. Tragically WLD died in 1996 aged only 44.

Novels

Matt Cobb series: *Killed in the Ratings* (1978), *Killed in the Act* (1981), *Killed With a Passion* (1983), *Killed on the Ice* (1984), *Killed in Paradise* (1988), *Killed on the Rocks* (1990), *Killed in Fringe Time* (1995), *Killed in the Fog* (1996).

Niccolo Benedetti series: *The HOG Murders* (1979), *The Werewolf Murders* (1992), *The Manx Murders* (1994).
"Clifford Driscoll" series: *Cronus* (1984), *Snark* (1985), *Azrael* (1987), *Atropos* (1990).
Blacke & Booker series: *Written in Fire* (1995), *The Fatal Elixir* (1997).
Non-series: *The Lunatic Fringe* (1980), *Five O'Clock Lightning* (1982).
as Philip DeGrave: *Unholy Moses* (1985), *Keep the Baby, Faith* (1986).
Non-fiction. *Encyclopedia Mysteriosa* (1994).

Full name: William Louis DeAndrea
Pen-names: Philip DeGrave, Lee Davis Willoughby.
Where to start: *The HOG Murders.*
Awards: Edgar, best first novel (1979), best paperback original (1980), best non-fiction (1995).
Similar stuff: Max Allan COLLINS, Loren D. ESTLEMAN (for crossover westerns).
Final fact: WLD met his future wife, the writer Orania PAPAZOGLOU [Jane Haddam] at the Murder Ink bookstore in Manhattan. They married in 1984.

Jeffery Deaver (b. 1950) US

Born in Chicago, JD earned his journalism degree from the University of Missouri, spent a few years struggling to work as a poet and songwriter and then studied law at Fordham University before becoming a Wall Street corporate attorney during the 1980s. After a couple of routine early novels, one of which was the horror thriller *Voodoo*, JD became noticed with *Manhattan is my Beat*. This introduced the character of Rune, whom JD describes as "a modern Holly Golightly". In this first Edgar-nominated novel, Rune is working in a video store when one of her regular customers is murdered and she believes the motive lies in a video that he frequently borrowed. In *Death of a Blue Movie Star* Rune is in the film business and finds herself on the wrong end of a terrorist group. *Hard News* finds Rune at a TV news station investigating a man she believes was wrongly imprisoned. Though the plots were exciting, full of JD's usual twists and turns, the framework had its built-in limitations. Under the alias of William Jefferies, JD began a new series featuring John Pellam, a former Hollywood director who had served a prison sentence and now works as a location scout for a film studio. The series is more intense than the Rune books. Pellam frequently finds himself as much the hunted as the hunter, especially in *Bloody River Blues*, where the police believe Pellam witnessed a gangland killing and Pellam finds himself pursued by just about everyone while he tries to find the real killer. The first book in the series, *Shallow Graves*, which was shortlisted for the Edgar, finds Pellam in a small town in upstate New York where a murder causes the town to close in on itself and Pellam becomes the outsider. The book was JD's homage to the film *Shane*. In 1997 JD completed *The Bone Collector* (filmed 1999), which introduced Lincoln Rhyme, a former scene-of-crime officer who, following an accident, is left bed-ridden as a paraplegic and can move only his head and one finger (by which he operates an amazing range of computer equipment). With a young female cop, Amelia Sachs, doing his legwork, they set about identifying a warped serial killer who buries his victims alive. Despite what may seem a restricted plot format the chemistry between Rhyme and Sachs is vibrant and allows for considerable tension that is developed in the later books in the series, particularly *The Empty Chair*, where Rhyme and Sachs disagree over the guilt of the villain. JD has written several standalone books, all of which have strong unpredictable plots and unusual features. *A Maiden's Grave* (filmed 1996 as *Dead Silence*) uses sign language to help rescue a group of deaf students taken hostage by escaped convicts. *Lesson of Her Death* involves a detective's learning-impaired daughter as the key to identifying a murderer who kills every full moon whilst *The Blue Nowhere* takes us into the world of cybercrime. JD has also written several short stories, two of which received Edgar nominations, "The Kneeling Soldier" (*EQMM*, 1997) and "Triangle" (*EQMM*, 1999). JD's sister is Julie Reece Deaver who writes taut suspense and dramatic stories for young adults.

Novels

Rune series: *Manhattan is my Beat* (1989), *Death of a Blue Movie Star* (1990), *Hard News* (1991).

Lincoln Rhyme series: *The Bone Collector* (1997), *The Coffin Dancer* (1998), *The Empty Chair* (2000), *The Stone Monkey* (2002).

John Pellam series (as William Jeffries): *Shallow Graves* (1992), *Bloody River Blues* (1993), *Hell's Kitchen* (2001).

Non-series: *Voodoo* (1988), *Always a Thief* (1989), *Mistress of Justice* (1992), *Lesson of Her Death* (1993), *Praying for Sleep* (1995), *A Maiden's Grave* (1996), *The Devil's Teardrop* (1999), *The Blue Nowhere* (2001).

Editor. *A Century of Great Suspense Stories* (2001).

Full name: Jeffery Wilds Deaver.
Pen-name: William Jefferies.
Where to start: *Shallow Graves* or *The Bone Collector*.
Awards: Nero Wolfe (1999).
Website: <www.jefferydeaver.com>
Similar stuff: Thomas ADCOCK, Thomas HARRIS.
Final fact: JD completed several unpublished novels before his first sale and was so disgusted with one that he put it through the office shredder.

Philip DeGrave *pseudonym, see* William L. DeAndrea

Delacorta *pseudonym, see* Daniel Odier

Sandy Dengler (b. 1939) US

SD writes mostly books for children and young adults which are grouped under such headings as "Inspirational Fiction" or "Christian Fiction".

Her series for adult readers are also strong on Christian values but without being overly moralizing. She has produced three series. Two of them are interesting enough but it is the third that stands out. *Hyaenas* features what must be the most historical detective of all: Gar, a Neanderthal Shaman in France, 35,000 years ago. Set during a period when the Neanderthals are under threat from the Cro-Magnon, Gar not only has to solve a murder but find out why the Neanderthals and Cro-Magnons hate each other. Although the story does not have the depth of Jean Auel's books, SD must be congratulated for pulling off a very difficult task and establishing the pioneer detective. She has two other series. One features Jack Prester, a National Parks ranger who teams up with Evelyn Brant in solving crimes within the Parks (SD's husband was a park ranger for 33 years). The other features Joe Rodriguez, a police sergeant in Phoenix, Arizona, who has to dig deep into his faith to resolve the dangerous crimes he encounters. Not to everyone's taste, but different.

Novels

Jack Prester series: *Death Valley* (1993), *A Model Murder* (1993), *Murder on the Mount* (1994), *The Quick and the Dead* (1995).
Joe Rodriguez series: *Cat Killer* (1993), *Mouse Trapped* (1993), *The Last Dinosaur* (1994), *Gila Monster* (1994), *Fatal Fishes* (1994).
Gar the Neanderthal series: *Hyaenas* (1998), *Wolves* (2000).

Where to start: *Death Valley*.
Similar stuff: Nevada BARR for park ranger series.
Final fact: SD is pursuing a PhD in palaeontology and has, for the last several years, been building dinosaurs for a natural history museum.

Jane Dentinger (b. 1951) US

JD studied acting and directing at Ithaca College and has worked in regional and off-Broadway theatres in both capacities. Like so many in the theatre world there are times when JD was between engagements and having been inspired by seeing an actress at a party that she would so love to have killed, JD had a go at writing mysteries. She developed the character of Jocelyn O'Roarke, or Josh, who is very thespian in her wit and manners, and has a bright and incisive mind. The theatrical world is full of wonderfully eccentric characters which adds to the delight of this cozy series, though JD keeps the edge sharp with Josh's uneasy relationship with police detective Philip Gerard, and with the pressures upon actors and directors today. The series is set mostly in New York, though *Dead Pan* takes Josh to Hollywood. The delight of the series is in the background details JD paints and the tidbits of lore and gossip about the theatre. The series has lain fallow for a while whilst JD has worked on her first stage play and while she works as Editor for Doubleday's Mystery Book Club.

Novels

Jocelyn O'Roarke series: *Murder on Cue* (1983), *First Hit of the Season* (1984), *Death Mask* (1988), *Dead Pan* (1992), *The Queen is Dead* (1994), *Who Dropped Peter Pan?* (1995).

Where to start: *Murder on Cue.*
Similar stuff: Simon BRETT, Susan Isaacs.
Final fact: From 1980–88 JD ran the Murder Ink bookstore in New York.

William Deverell (b. 1937) Canada

WD started out as a journalist while he was studying for his law degree and subsequently established his own law practice in British Columbia in 1964. He was a strong civil rights activist and former President of the B.C. Civil Liberties Association. He turned to writing fiction in 1978 and his first book, *Needles*, won the $50,000 Seal First Novel Award. It is a tense drama where a lawyer, with a heavy drug habit, is assigned to prosecute a drug dealer. WD's next two novels were slightly off-centre – *High Crimes* was about a major drugs haul and *Mecca* was an espionage thriller – but *Dance of Shiva* brought him firmly back to base. It introduced the characters at the Vancouver law firm of Pomeroy & Partners, who feature in several novels. In *Dance of Shiva* they find themselves defending the head of a cult accused of murdering his followers. In *Kill All the Lawyers* they find themselves on an executioner's list, while in the award-winning *Trial of Passion*, one of the attorneys, hoping to retire and overcome his alcoholism, has to defend a respected law professor accused of rape. Of WD's other novels, *Platinum Blues* deals with problems that escalate to murder in the rock music industry and *Mindfield* (filmed 1989) deals with a case of drug experimentation on a police officer many years ago. In 1985 WD scripted the TV movie *Shellgame* about a firm of Toronto lawyers. This became the pilot for the long-running TV series *Street Legal* (1986–94), and WD reworked the original pilot and some of the early series episodes into the book *Street Legal: The Betrayal*. WD has also written an account of a bizarre murder case that he defended as an attorney in *Fatal Cruise*.

Novels

Pomeroy & Partners series: *The Dance of Shiva* (1984), *Kill All the Lawyers* (1993), *Trial of Passion* (1997),
Non-series: *Needles* (1979), *High Crimes* (1981), *Mecca* (1983), *Platinum Blues* (1987), *Mindfield* (1989), *Street Legal: The Betrayal* (1995), *Slander* (1999).
Non-fiction. *Fatal Cruise* (1990).

Full name: William Herbert Deverell.
Where to start: *The Dance of Shiva.*
Awards: Seal First Novel Award (1979), Periodical Distributors of Canada, Book of the Year (1981), Arthur Ellis, best novel (1998), Hammett Prize (1998).
Website: <www.deverell.com>

Similar stuff: William BERNHARDT, Jay BRANDON, John GRISHAM.
Final fact: WD's daughter Tamara is an art director and production designer and has worked on several films including David Cronenberg's controversial adaptation of J.G. Ballard's *Crash*.

Colin Dexter (b. 1930) UK

UK author and former classics master, best-known for his character Inspector Morse. Dexter earned both a B.A. (1953) and M.A. (1958) in classics at Christ's College, Cambridge, but it was Oxford, where he lives, which he chose as the setting for his first detective novel. *Last Bus to Woodstock* (1975) introduced the irascible but determined Inspector Morse and his partner, the equally dogged but more affable Sergeant Lewis. Key to each of the novels is a complex puzzle, with many false paths and dead ends that Morse and Lewis must overcome, each pursuing their own solutions which may sometimes cause friction between them. Dexter is a noted compiler of crossword puzzles and a former national champion of the British cryptic crossword-puzzle championships. The series achieved international fame through its adaptation to television, starring John Thaw in 1987. Dexter committed the near unforgivable sin of killing off his detective in *The Remorseful Day* (1999).

Novels
Inspector Morse series: *Last Bus to Woodstock* (1975), *Last Seen Wearing* (1976), *The Silent World of Nicholas Quinn* (1977), *Service of all the Dead* (1980), *The Dead of Jericho* (1981), *The Riddle of the Third Mile* (1983), *The Secret of Annexe 3* (1986), *The Wench is Dead* (1989), *The Jewel That Was Ours* (1991), *The Way Through the Woods* (1992), *The Daughters of Cain* (1994), *Death is Now My Neighbour* (1997), *The Remorseful Day* (1999).
Short Stories. *Morse's Greatest Mystery* (1993, rev'd 1995).

Full name: Norman Colin Dexter
Where to start: Any of the early novels such as *Last Bus to Woodstock* or *Last Seen Wearing*.
Awards: CWA Gold Dagger (1989, 1992), CWA Silver Dagger (1979, 1981), CWA Diamond Dagger (1997), Macavity, Best Short Story (1996); Sherlock, Best British Detective (2000), Swedish Academy of Detection, Grand Master (2000).
Website: No personal one but a Morse site is at <www.inspectormorse.co.uk>
Similar stuff: W.J. BURLEY, Douglas CLARK.
Final fact: Like Alfred Hitchcock, Dexter has a cameo walk-on role in each TV episode of *Inspector Morse*.

Michael Dibdin (b. 1947) UK

MD has established a sound reputation for his novels about Italian Police Commissioner Aurelio Zen – the first three books each won major international awards that demonstrated the cosmopolitan nature of his work. For readers in Britain or the US, Zen's world may be part of a different culture but the politics, bureaucracy, corruption and human attitudes and foibles all resonate, and the setting allows MD to experiment and develop ideas less applicable elsewhere. Life in Venice, Florence, Rome, Sardinia and Sicily is not the same as in Britain or the US and this brings a richness and diversity to the series. MD is a disciplined writer with a strict control of the English language and as a result the reader never has a chance to get bogged down in what are often complicated and (for Zen) frustrating investigations. MD had not intended Zen to become a series character and thus he was not fully developed in the first book, *Ratking*, where MD saw him as a "facilitator". He has grown with the series, although there is much still hidden about him, which grows even shadowier in the near-tragic *Blood Rain* and *And Then You Die*. The series is amongst the most polished in crime fiction.

MD wrote *Ratking* after he had spent four years in Italy (1980–84) as an English teacher. Born in Wolverhampton, he was raised in Northern Ireland, took his B.A. in English literature in England and his M.A. in Canada, where he held a variety of jobs until he returned to England in 1975. He completed four books before his first was published, *The Last Sherlock Holmes Story*, which sets Holmes and Moriarty in the world of the Jack the Ripper murders. *A Rich Full Death* was another historical mystery featuring Robert Browning in Victorian Venice. But after *Ratking* there was a complete change of pace and his non-series books have, by and large, been deep psychological character studies exploring hatred and violence. *The Tryst* is about the dangerous relationship between a psychiatrist and her client. *Dirty Tricks* (filmed TV 2000) is set in the world of academe but where relationships again spiral out of control. *The Dying of the Light* takes a conventional, almost Christie-like setting and a complex plot but weaves a totally unconventional story. In *Dark Spectre* a series of brutal but seemingly random murders is the start of a study of obsession and cultism. *Thanksgiving* is a disturbing story of apparent motiveless revenge. With each novel MD is broadening the boundaries of conventional crime into the territory of the mainstream. MD currently lives in Seattle and is married to writer K.K. BECK.

Novels

Aurelio Zen series: *Ratking* (1988), *Vendetta* (1990), *Cabal* (1992), *The Dead Lagoon* (1994), *Cosi Fan Tutti* (1996), *A Long Finish* (1998), *Blood Rain* (2000), *And Then You Die* (2002).

Non-series: *The Last Sherlock Holmes Story* (1978), *A Rich, Full Death* (1986), *The Tryst* (1989), *Dirty Tricks* (1991), *The Dying of Light* (1993), *Dark Spectre* (1995), *Thanksgiving* (2000).

Editor. *The Picador Book of Crime Writing* (1993).

Where to start: *Ratking*.

Awards: CWA Gold Dagger (1988), CWA '92 Award (1990), Grand Prix de Littérature Policière Best Foreign (1994).

Similar stuff: Donna LEON, Magdalen NABB, Timothy WILLIAMS for other Italian police procedurals.
Final fact: An American publisher once returned one of MD's Zen books asking for several seemingly pointless revisions. MD just held on to the manuscript for a few weeks and then returned it unchanged thanking the editor for the suggestions and hoping this was an improvement. The book was published with no changes.

Peter Dickinson (b. 1927) UK

PD's mystery fiction is in a class of its own – in fact it's unclassifiable. It is as if PD plots a conventional English mystery and then turns everything inside out making it as surreal and fantastic as possible and then, through the skill of his writing, takes us back through the mirror to make it all believable. His originality has brought him a cabinet full of awards and though he is perhaps better known for his books for young adults, most of which are fantasy or science fiction, he has written a substantial body of mystery fiction which has its own cadre of followers. Early in his career PD wrote a series featuring Superintendent James Pibble of Scotland Yard, who is the one element of normality around which a cast of eccentrics revolve. In *Skin Deep* the chief of a New Guinea tribe is murdered in London. In *A Pride of Heroes* it's not so much that the butler did it but that the butler's done in – by a lion. *The Seals* finds Pibble on a remote Hebridean island where an aging scientist is held captive by a bizarre religious cult. PD restrained from killing-off Pibble but in *One Foot in the Grave* Pibble is contemplating suicide in a nursing home when a murder gives him something to do. PD's humour may come in part from the fact that he was assistant editor of *Punch* for 17 years (1952–69) during which time he also reviewed crime fiction for the magazine. PD continues the bizarreness in other novels, most notably *The Poison Oracle*, set in an Arab emirate in a palace that was built upside down and where the only witness to the murder was a chimpanzee that is being taught to communicate. Occasionally PD's mysteries do step over into the borders of fantasy. *King and Joker* and its sequel are set in an alternate England where the Romanovs are the ruling royal family, but both involve conventional crimes. *Walking Dead* involves voodoo and the powers of the mind on Haiti. More recently PD's quirkiness has mellowed but his story structure has mutated as he explores his crimes across time. *The Last Houseparty*, in many ways his most satisfying book, starts in the present but leaps about between now, 1937 and 1940 and gradually reveals the decline and fall of an aristocratic family and their dark secret. *Perfect Gallows* switches between 1944 and 1984 to explore the effect upon a young boy of finding a man hanging in an old country house and how he resolves the mystery. In *The Yellow Room Conspiracy* a couple look back over 30 years to a strange death in the family, whilst in *Some Deaths Before Dying* a paralysed 90-year old tries to discover how a pistol that she gave her husband many years ago, has turned up on a television show. With PD's mysteries you always expect the unexpected but he still surprises you. He is the 20th century's Lewis Carroll of mystery. PD is married to fantasy writer Robin McKinley.

Novels

Superintendent Pibble series: *Skin Deep* (1968; as *The Glass-Sided Ants' Nest*, US 1968), *A Pride of Heroes* (1969; as *The Old English Peep Show*, US 1969), *The Seals* (1970; as *The Sinful Stones*, US 1970), *Sleep and his Brother* (1971), *The Lizard in the Cup* (1972), *One Foot in the Grave* (1979).
Princess Louise series: *King and Joker* (1976), *Skeleton-in-Waiting* (1989).
Non-series: *The Poison Oracle* (1974), *The Lively Dead* (1975), *Walking Dead* (1977), *A Summer in the Twenties* (1981), *The Last Houseparty* (1982), *Hindsight* (1983), *Death of a Unicorn* (1984), *Tefuga* (1986), *Perfect Gallows* (1988), *Play Dead* (1990), *The Yellow Room Conspiracy* (1994), *Some Deaths Before Dying* (1999).

Full name: Peter Malcolm de Brissac Dickinson.
Where to start: Either plunge in with *Skin Deep* or *The Poison Oracle* or ease in gently with *The Last Houseparty*.
Awards: CWA Gold Dagger (1968, 1969), *Guardian* Award (1977), *Boston Globe* Horn Book award for non-fiction (1977), Whitbread Children's award (1979, 1990), Library Association Carnegie Medal (1980, 1981).
Similar stuff: James ANDERSON, Dorothy CANNELL, Mark MCSHANE.
Final fact: PD was born in Northern Rhodesia (now Zambia) within the sound of Victoria Falls and did not come to England until he was seven.

Robert Dietrich *pseudonym, see* E. Howard Hunt

James Ditton *pseudonym, see* Douglas Clark.

Stephen Dobyns (b. 1941) US

SD is a poet and writer of high repute. Since 1987 he has been the Director of Creative Writing at Syracuse University but was for three years (1969–71) a reporter for the *Detroit News*. His crime fiction happily co-exists alongside his poetry and his more existential literary novels. His primary crime fiction consists of a series about loser Charlie Bradshaw. An ex-cop and ex-security guard – in fact ex-everything – Bradshaw is passing through a mid-life crisis and getting nowhere. Charlie had quit the force to operate as a private detective, but with little success, and he has a poor relationship with his former police colleagues. He spends more time helping out in a hotel and doing a milk round. He has no method to his detection and usually bumbles in and out of crimes or strikes them head on. Yet the cases have a force and direction of their own, leading almost inevitably to some bizarre climax, like the chase in the milk float in *Saratoga Headhunter*. Charlie usually operates with his friend Victor Plotz, an engaging character who is sometimes the victim, as in *Saratoga*

Snapper, when he is run down and his camera stolen, or sometimes the sleuth, when he helps Charlie out in *Saratoga Backtalk*. The series is quirky and unconventional. Not all of SD's non-series books are crime fiction, though all consider the instabilities of life and the untoward actions that may arise. However some are firmly in the tradition. His first book, *A Man of Little Evils*, is about an investigative journalist following up a murder in London. *Dancer With One Leg* is about an arsonist whilst *A Boat off the Coast* explores how a boatowner might profit from informing on local drug smuggling. His major crime novel, however, is *The Church of Dead Girls* in which a series of disappearances of young girls in a small upstate New York town brings out vigilantism and the mob instinct in the townsfolk.

Novels
Charlie Bradshaw series: *Saratoga Longshot* (1976), *Saratoga Swimmer* (1981), *Saratoga Headhunter* (1985), *Saratoga Snapper* (1986), *Saratoga Bestiary* (1988), *Saratoga Hexameter* (1990), *Saratoga Haunting* (1993), *Saratoga Backtalk* (1994), *Saratoga Fleshpot* (1995), *Saratoga Strongbox* (1998).
Non-series: *A Man of Little Evils* (1973), *Dancer With One Leg* (1983), *Cold Dog Soup* (1985), *A Boat off the Coast* (1987), *The Two Deaths of Señora Puccini* (1988), *The House on Alexandrine* (1990), *After Shocks/Near Escapes* (1991), *The Wrestler's Cruel Study* (1993), *The Church of Dead Girls* (1997), *Boy in the Water* (1999), *Angel Zone* (2001).
Short Stories. *Eating Naked* (2000).

Full name: Stephen Dobyns.
Where to start: *Saratoga Headhunter* for the Bradshaw series, but overall *The Church of Dead Girls.*
Awards: Numerous awards for his poetry, including the Poetry Society of America's Melville Cane Award (1987), Guggenheim fellowship (1983).
Similar stuff: Paul AUSTER, Jerome CHARYN.

Paul C. Doherty (b. 1946) UK

PCD is currently the most prolific writer of historical mysteries, having published around 60 novels in 16 years whilst still holding a full-time post as headmaster of a Catholic school in Essex (PCD studied for three years for the priesthood). He maintains this output by dictating rather than typing, and for the most part the books maintain a high standard in terms of historical background and the manner of the mystery, with the emphasis on puzzle and plot. PCD has a penchant for the impossible crime, especially the locked-room mystery. Examples include the first Hugh Corbett novel, *Satan in St. Mary's*, where a man is found murdered inside a locked church, and the first Roger Shallot mystery, *The White Rose Murders*, where a murder is committed in a locked room in the Tower of London. PCD obtained his doctorate at Oxford University with a thesis on the wife of Edward II, and the fate of that king was the focus of his first novel, *The Death of a King*. He also tackled one of the most famous of all historical mysteries about the princes in the Tower in *The Fate of Princes*. Most of PCD's books fall into a number of series. His earliest period is ancient Egypt around 1479BC with the investigations of Amerotke the Judge. Under the alias Anna Apostolou he began a series about Alexander the Great, starting with the murder of Alexander's father, and that series has now transmuted into a new one under his own name. Most of his mysteries take place between the late 13th and mid-16th centuries with the longest-running featuring Hugh Corbett, a clerk of the King's Bench in the Court of Chancery. *The Nightingale Gallery* introduced Brother Athelstan, clerk to Sir John Cranston, Coroner of the City of London in the 1370s/80s. One of PCD's most popular series began with *An Ancient Evil*, featuring mysteries related by the pilgrims on the road to Canterbury. Canterbury is also the setting for a lesser-known series featuring Kathryn Swinbrooke, a physician during the time of Edward IV. Some of the most challenging mysteries, and most light-hearted, are those featuring Sir Roger Shallot, a rogue and self-appointed agent to Cardinal Wolsey at the time of Henry VIII. His widest-ranging series appeared under the pen-name Ann Dukthas and featured a time-travelling investigator, Nicholas Segalla, whose trips have taken him to Mary, Queen of Scots, Bloody Mary, the Napoleonic era and the Hapsburgs.

Novels

Hugh Corbett series: *Satan in St. Mary's* (1986), *Crown in Darkness* (1988), *Spy in Chancery* (1988), *The Angel of Death* (1989), *The Prince of Darkness* (1992), *Murder Wears a Cowl* (1992), *The Assassin in the Greenwood* (1993), *The Song of a Dark Angel* (1994), *Satan's Fire* (1995), *The Devil's Hunt* (1996), *The Demon Archer* (1999), *The Treason of the Ghosts* (2000), *Corpse Candle* (2001).

Matthew Jankyn series: *The Whyte Hart* (1988), *The Serpent Among the Lilies* (1990).

Canterbury Tales series: *An Ancient Evil* (1993), *A Tapestry of Murders* (1994), *A Tournament of Murders* (1996), *Ghostly Murders* (1997), *The Hangman's Hymn* (1998), *A Haunt of Murder* (2002).

Brother Athelstan series (as Paul Harding for first 8 titles): *The Nightingale Gallery* (1991), *The House of the Red Slayer* (1992; as *Red Slayer*, US 1994), *Murder Most Holy* (1992), *The Anger of God* (1993), *By Murder's Bright Light* (1994), *The House of Crows* (1995), *An Assassin's Riddle* (1996), *The Devil's Domain* (1998), *The Field of Blood* (1999).

Sir Roger Shallot series (as Michael Clynes): *The White Rose Murders* (1991), *The Poisoned Chalice* (1992), *The Grail Murders* (1993), *A Brood of Vipers* (1994), *The Gallows Murders* (1995), *The Relic Murders* (1995).

Kathryn Swinbrooke series (as C.L. Grace): *A Shrine of Murders* (1993), *The Eye of God* (1994), *The Merchant of Death* (1995), *The Book of Shadows* (1996).

Nicholas Segalla series (as Ann Dukthas): *A Time for the Death of a King* (1994), *The Prince Lost to Time* (1995), *The Time of Murder at Mayerling* (1996), *In the Time of the Poisoned Queen* (1998).

Alexander the Great series (first two as Anna Apostolou): *A Murder in Macedon*

(US 1997), *A Murder in Thebes* (US 1998), *The House of Death* (2001), *The Godless Man*.
Amerotke series: *The Mask of Ra* (1998), *The Horus Killings* (1999), *The Anubis Slayings* (2000), *The Slayers of Seth* (2001).
Non-series: *The Death of a King* (1985), *The Fate of Princes* (1990), *Dove Amongst the Hawks* (1990), *The Masked Man* (1991), *The Rose Demon* (1997), *The Soul Slayer* (1997), *The Haunting* (1997), *Domina* (2002).

Full name: Paul Charles Doherty.
Pen-names: Anna Apostolou, Michael Clynes, Ann Dukthas, C.L. Grace, Paul Harding.
Where to start: Pick your period. However *Satan in St. Mary's* and *The White Rose Murders* set the tone.
Awards: Herodotus, lifetime achievement (2000).
Similar stuff: Edward MARSTON, Jeremy POTTER, Josephine Tey (for Princes in the Tower).
Final fact: Early in his career PCD wrote two Dracula books, *The Prince Drakulya* and *The Lord Count Drakulya*. They had limited sales at the time and now those first editions are highly collectable and sell for up to £400.

R.B. Dominic, *see pseudonym* Emma Lathen

Anabel Donald (b. 1944) UK

AD established a reputation with her first novel, *Hannah at Thirty-Five*, about a woman regaining her life after a difficult marriage. AD was born in India, educated at Oxford, taught English literature at the University of Texas and became headmistress of a school in Doncaster. Her one detective series features Alex Tanner, a freelance TV researcher who also operates as a part-time private investigator. Tanner is independent, strong-willed and self-reliant, having had to depend on her own resources from her childhood when she passed around many foster homes. Tanner's patch is the Notting Hill area of London, though *The Loop* finds her travelling back and forth across the Atlantic on the trail of a missing person. In the first book, *An Uncommon Murder*, Tanner reopens a 40-year-old society murder. The latest, *Destroy Unopened*, introduces a welcome new angle on the serial killer plot. The books are inventive, tough without excessive violence, leavened by keen observation and wit – what the *Sunday Telegraph* called "sparkling writing".

Novels

Alex Tanner series: *An Uncommon Murder* (1992), *In at the Deep End* (1993), *The Glass Ceiling* (1994), *The Loop* (1996), *Destroy Unopened* (1999).

Pen-names: Serena Galt, Kate Rhys (neither used on crime fiction).
Where to start: *An Uncommon Murder*.
Similar stuff: Marele DAY, Sarah DUNANT, Val MCDERMID.
Final fact: AD's long-held ambition was to ride across America on a Harley-Davidson, which she eventually fulfilled in 2000.

P.S. Donoghue *pseudonym, see* E. Howard Hunt

Carole Nelson Douglas (b. 1944) US

Although her first book, *Amberleigh*, was a post-feminist historical gothic in the mould of Daphne du Maurier, CND's reputation was first established in the fantasy field with a series of popular novels in the early 1980s, starting with *Six of Swords* (1982). An element of fantasy has leached over into her mystery novels, especially the series featuring Midnight Louie, a black cat and midnight prowler, whose first-person narratives guide us through the darker parts of the otherwise third-person recounted investigations of Temple Barr. Barr is a publicist in the dazzle and glitter of Las Vegas, probably the closest you get to fantasy in the US yet remain in the "real" world. Louie usually stumbles across the bodies and helps Barr discover further clues, rather like Koko and Yum-Yum help Jim Qwilleram in BRAUN's feline sleuth series. CND's world though is gutsier, more active, with Midnight Louie being the eyes into the hard-boiled sinister side of life. As the series developed, the books became multi-viewpoint involving all four key human characters. CND regards the books as "cozy-noir" and has planned the series out to 27 books, plus the revisions to the early savagely edited romance books, *Crystal Days* and *Crystal Nights*, that introduced Midnight Louie in 1990. Far removed from Las Vegas but equally tinged with the imagination is Victorian London at the time of Sherlock Holmes. CND has taken Irene Adler, the one person who outwitted Holmes and recreated her world. Until she became a full-time writer in 1984, CND had been a feature writer for the *St Paul Dispatch* in her then hometown in Minnesota. She earned her degree in English, speech and drama and in 1997 wrote and staged a one-woman show, *Sunset Strip*, in which CND played Marilyn Monroe on the eve of her posthumous comeback.

Novels

Irene Adler series: *Good Night, Mr Holmes* (1990), *Good Morning, Irene* (1991), *Irene at Large* (1992), *Irene's Last Waltz* (1994), *Chapel Noir* (2001).

Midnight Louie series: *Catnap* (1992), *Pussyfoot* (1993), *Cat on a Blue Monday* (1995), *Cat in a Crimson Haze* (1995), *Cat in Diamond Dazzle* (1996), *Cat With an Emerald Eye* (1996), *Cat in a Flamingo Fedora* (1997), *Cat in a Golden Garland* (1997), *Cat on a Hyacinth Hunt* (1998), *Cat in an Indigo Mood* (1999), *Cat in a Jewelled Jumpsuit* (2000), *Cat in a Kiwi Con* (2000), *Cat in a Leopard Spot* (2001), *Cat in a Midnight Choir* (2002). Note: the original pre-series Louie books have since been revised, restored and expanded as follows: *Crystal Days* (1990) as *The Cat and the King of Clubs* (1999) and *The Cat and the Queen of Hearts* (1999); and *Crystal Nights* (1990) as *The Cat and the Jill of Diamonds* (2000) and *The Cat and the Jack of Spades* (2000).

Non-series: *Amberleigh* (1980).

Editor. *Marilyn on Mount Rushmore* (1996), *Marilyn: Shades of Blonde* (1997), *Midnight Louie's Pet Detectives* (1998).

Where to start: *Catnap* or *Good Night, Mr Holmes.*
Awards: American Mystery Award (1990), Cat Writers' Association Muse Medallion (1995), Jonny Cat Literary Award (1995).
Website: <www.catwriter.com>
Similar stuff: Lilian Jackson BRAUN for cat detectives; L.B. Greenwood and Laurie R. KING for female viewpoints on Sherlock Holmes.
Final fact: CND has been interested in finding homes for stray and unwanted cats since she was four years old and now operates an Adopt-a-Cat program tied in with her book signing sessions.

Peter Doyle (b. 1951) Australia

PD is a musician and lecturer based in Sydney who has rapidly established himself as a writer with his series of books about petty criminal and no-hoper, Billy Glasheen. The first two won the Australian Ned Kelly award. They take place in the late 1950s where Glasheen keeps looking for that chance to come up trumps and "get rich quick", as he ducks and dives his way through and around other criminals and the bent police. The third novel takes us back to the start of Glasheen's criminal career just after WW2. The books are heavily Australian, full of slang, and depicting a way of life to make even the most hardened reader ponder anew.

Novels

Billy Glasheen series: *Get Rich Quick* (1996), *Amaze Your Friends* (1998), *The Devil's Jump* (2001).

Awards: Ned Kelly Award, best first novel (1997), best novel (1999).
Similar stuff: Peter CORRIS, Marele DAY, for similar Australian writers.
Final fact: PD conducts masses of research for his books, far more than he can use, so he also writes essays and cultural histories so that the research isn't lost.

Hastings Draper *pseudonym, see* Roderic Jeffries

Ivor Drummond *pseudonym, see* Roger Longrigg

Marie Duell *pseudonym, see* Clare Curzon

Stella Duffy (b. 1963) UK

SD is a theatre and radio performer who teaches improvization to actors and writers. She has written a play, *The Hand*, a one-woman show, *The Tedious Predictability of Falling in Love*, and two novels exploring complicated relationships, *Singling Out the Couples* (1998), and *Eating Cake* (1999), but she has become best known for her series about lesbian P.I. Saz Martin. Aside from the highly charged erotic content, what makes this series interesting is the dark and shady world in which Martin operates, where masked individuals like "September" and "the Wavewalker" hide their real identities and yet control and influence events. The series oozes the contemporary London scene, not just through its emphasis on sex, drugs and music, but in its portrayal of the falseness, deception and corruption of the nineties designer lifestyle. Although born in the UK, SD was raised in New Zealand and she writes from the viewpoint of a detached but informed observer.

Novels

Saz Martin series: *Calendar Girl* (1994), *Wavewalker* (1996), *Beneath the Blonde* (1997), *Fresh Flesh* (1999).

Where to start: *Calendar Girl*.
Website: <www.twbooks.co.uk/authors/sduffy.html>
Similar stuff: Liza Cody.

Anne Dukthas *pseudonym, see* Paul C. Doherty

Sarah Dunant (b. 1950) UK

TV and radio presenter SD, best known as the one-time host of the nightly cultural magazine programme *The Late Show*, is also the author of several thought-provoking and intelligently written novels, including the series featuring P.I. Hannah Wolfe. SD knows her field and gets great fun out of reworking and subverting clichés. Although her patch is London, Wolfe is rather too Americanized to feel quite genuine, but she is fun and though laid back she takes her work seriously. In *Birthmarks* she tries to find a missing ballet dancer. In the highly acclaimed *Fat Lands* she has to safeguard a young girl from a radical animal rights group while in *Under My Skin* she is in the world of the health farm. SD's first two books had been written with her husband Peter Busby under the alias Peter Dunant. *Exterminating Angels* was about terrorism and *Intensive Care* was a political thriller. Both these and her first solo novel, *Snowstorms in a Hot Climate*, which plots the relationship between two former schoolfriends as they are sucked into the world of drug smuggling, are written against a broad canvas. Her later novels are more personal and intense. *Transgressions* brings to life the terrifying world of the stalker victim. *Mapping the Edge* is a cleverly constructed novel which tells two variant stories about a young mother who disappears. Both these books take the reader deep into the victim's psyche.

Novels

Hannah Wolfe series: *Birth Marks* (1992), *Fat Lands* (1993), *Under My Skin* (1995).

Non-series: *Snow Storms in a Hot Climate* (1988), *Transgressions* (1998), *Mapping the Edge* (1999).

as Peter Dunant (with Peter Busby): *Exterminating Angels* (1983), *Intensive Care* (1986).

Pen-name: Peter Dunant (with Peter Busby).
Where to start: *Birth Marks*.
Awards: CWA Silver Dagger (1993).

Similar stuff: Natasha COOPER, Clare FRANCIS, Ruth RENDELL.
Final fact: SD appears as herself in John HARVEY's Resnick novel *Living Proof*.

Susan Dunlap (b. 1943) US

SD's primary series is a police procedural set in Berkeley, California. It features Jill Smith, a homicide detective, and a cast of interactive characters who help bring Berkeley alive. SD's background was in social work, indeed her early unpublished novels featured a social worker as the main character, but the series did not gel until she converted her to a detective. Even then her relationship with less fortunate people comes through strongly in the early novels, especially *As a Favor* and *Not Exactly a Brahmin*. SD undertakes regular research with the Berkeley Police Department and one of the strengths of the series is its feeling of authenticity. *Cop Out* ended with Smith being suspended and the series is currently in hiatus. Alongside Jill Smith, SD began a new and less conventional series featuring VeJay Haskell, a meter reader in the fictional Californian town along Russian River. In the first book Vejay is suspected of a murder because of her ready and easy access to homes, and thereafter she is regarded as something of an expert and is employed by other suspects to help clear them. The series did not have the selling power of the police series so was dropped, but SD began a third about a former medical examiner, Kiernan O'Shaughnessy, who had been fired from her job and so uses her skills as a private investigator. The first two books in this series were both nominated for Anthony awards and have strong character development. Again SD undertakes detailed research but the strength of this series is in the psychological anguish that O'Shaughnessy encounters in her work and is a suitable reminder of the closeness and tragedy of death. SD has also won awards for her short fiction, which is usually more light-hearted and imaginative, often to the point of stepping into fantasy.

Novels

Jill Smith series: *Karma* (1981), *As a Favor* (1984), *Not Exactly a Brahmin* (1985), *Too Close to the Edge* (1987), *A Dinner to Die For* (1987), *Diamond in the Buff* (1990), *Death and Taxes* (1991), *Time Expired* (1993), *Sudden Exposure* (1996), *Cop Out* (1997).

Vejay Haskell series: *An Equal Opportunity Death* (1984), *The Bohemian Connection* (1985), *The Last Annual Slugfest* (1986).

Kiernan O'Shaughnessy series: *Pious Deception* (1989), *Rogue Wave* (1991), *High Fall* (1994), *No Immunity* (1998).

Short Stories. *The Celestial Buffet and Other Morsels of Murder* (2001).
Editor. *Deadly Allies II*, with Robert Randisi (1994).

Full name: Susan D. Sullivan Dunlap.
Where to start: *Karma* or *Pious Deception*.
Awards: Anthony, best short story (1991, 1994), Macavity, best short story (1994).
Similar stuff: Patricia CORNWELL, Margaret MARON.

Final fact: SD used to teach a very gymnastic form of yoga and from that learned a lot about how the body works, information which she feeds into her O'Shaughnessy novels.

Jack Early *pseudonym, see* Sandra Scoppettone

Umberto Eco (b. 1932) Italy

UE is not a writer of crime fiction. He is a professor of semiotics, the study of communication through signs and symbols, at the University of Bologna. But he is also a philosopher, a historian and a literary critic and with *The Name of the Rose* (filmed 1986) wrote one of the most talked about books of the 1980s. Set in a remote 14th century monastery in Italy, it is the account of how William Baskerville solves a series of bizarre murders. The account is written years later by a young man who accompanies him. Wonderfully cryptic with clear homage to Poe and Doyle and others in the context of the book, it was one of the spurs, along with the works of Ellis Peters, that encouraged the seedling genre of historical whodunnits to flourish. Those anticipating further Baskerville stories have been disappointed. UE wrote an explanatory *Postscript* (1983) but otherwise his few subsequent novels (merely a fraction of his considerable academic and literary output since 1956) are philosophical games, such as the enigmatic *Foucault's Pendulum*, where three editors perpetrate a hoax by creating hitherto lost books. Like many non-English writers whose works are rarely translated, UE serves us to remind us that masterpieces continue to appear outside the English-speaking world.

Novels. *The Name of the Rose* (1983; orig. *Il nome della rosa*, 1980), *Foucault's Pendulum* (1989; orig. *Il pendolo di Foucault*, 1988), *The Island of the Day Before* (1995; orig. *L'isola del giorna prima*, 1994).
Editor, with T.A. Sebeok. *The Sign of Three: Peirce, Holmes, Dupin* (US 1983)

Where to start: *The Name of the Rose*.
Awards: Many literary awards and decorations including Commander de l'Ordre des Arts et des Lettre (1985), Marshall McLuhan Award from UNESCO (1985), World Economic Forum Crystal Award (1999).
Website: <www.dsc.unibo.it/dipartimento/people/eco>
Similar stuff: Caroline Roe and Ellis Peters for period.
Final fact: UE has a personal library in excess of 30,000 books.

Martin Edwards (b. 1955) UK

ME's character, Harry Devlin, is a solicitor in Liverpool who, in *All the Lonely People*, is tragically hurled into the amateur detective business when his estranged wife is found dead and he becomes the prime suspect. The book was shortlisted for the CWA John Creasey Award. ME's knowledge of the law – he is a partner in a firm of solicitors, has a first class honours degree in law (Balliol, Oxford, 1977) and has written several hundred articles and seven books on the subject – provides a solid reliability to the Devlin books, but their strength lies in the evocation of Liverpool both past and present. Although set in the nineties the series recognizes Liverpool's past, especially in the music business – all the titles come from sixties records. These themes come together strongly in *Yesterday's Papers*, when an amateur criminologist employs Devlin to look into a 30-year old crime. ME has written many short stories, including several Devlin stories, all of which will be found in *Where Do You Find Your Ideas?* He has also edited the annual CWA anthology series since 1996, with *Perfectly Criminal*, plus several regional anthologies. In 1999 he took on the daunting but ultimately satisfying job of completing Bill KNOX's final book, *The Lazarus Widow*.

Novels
Harry Devlin series: *All the Lonely People* (1991), *Suspicious Minds* (1992), *I Remember You* (1993), *Yesterday's Papers* (1994), *Eve of Destruction* (1996), *The Devil in Disguise* (1998), *The First Cut is the Deepest* (1999).
Non-series: *Take My Breath Away* (2002).
completed for Bill Knox: *The Lazarus Widow* (1999).
Short Stories. *Where Do You Find Your Ideas?* (2001).
Editor. *Northern Blood* (1992), *Northern Blood 2* (1995), *Anglian Blood*, with Robert Church (1995), *Perfectly Criminal* (1996), *Whydunit* (1997; as *Perfectly Criminal 2*, 1998), *Past Crimes* (1998, as *Perfectly Criminal 3*, 1999), *Northern Blood 3* (1998), *Missing Persons* (1999), *Scenes of Crime* (2000), *Murder Squad* (2001).

Full name: Kenneth Martin Edwards.
Where to start: *All the Lonely People*.
Website: <www.twbooks.co.uk/authors/medwards.html>
Similar stuff: Michael GILBERT, Roy LEWIS, M.R.D. MEEK.
Final fact: ME the solicitor counts Liverpool FC amongst his clients.

Ruth Dudley Edwards (b. 1944) Eire

A prize-winning biographer and historian, RDE, who regards herself as "intellectually English and temperamentally Irish", is also the author of a series of extremely funny and mischievous satires of the English establishment. Although born and raised in Dublin, RDE has lived in England since she graduated and her work as a lecturer, marketing executive, civil servant (Department of Industry) and journalist all provide background to her novels. They feature Robert Amiss who, in the first two books, is a civil servant, but thereafter takes on a variety of jobs which almost always lead him into trouble. The first, *Corridors of Power*, in which a top-level civil servant is found murdered, was short-listed for the John Creasey Award. The series involves Detective Chief Superintendent James Milton and his detective sergeant Ellis Pooley, but it's Amiss who ends up doing most of the investigating. From *Matricide at St Martha's*, which involves murder at a women's college, we are introduced to Ida "Jack" Troutbeck who, in *Ten Lords A-Leaping*, is elevated to the peerage. Amiss becomes the Baroness's unofficial snoop and troubleshooter. RDE has a sharp eye for the absurd and succeeds in intertwining clever burlesques with ingenious puzzles. Both *Clubbed to Death* and *Ten Lords A-Leaping* were shortlisted for the CWA Last Laugh award.

Novels

Amiss & Milton series (with Troutbeck from book 5): *Corridors of Death* (1981), *The St Valentine's Day Murders* (1984), *The School of English Murder* (1990; as *The English School of Murder* US 1990), *Clubbed to Death* (1992), *Matricide at St Martha's* (1994), *Ten Lords A-Leaping* (1995), *Murder in a Cathedral* (1996), *Publish and be Murdered* (1997), *The Anglo-Irish Murders* (2000), *Carnage on the Committee* (2000).

Where to start: *Corridors of Death* or *Matricide at St Martha's.*
Awards: James Tait Black Memorial Prize (1987).
Website: <www.twbooks.co.uk/authors/rdedwards.html> and <www.ruthdudleyedwards.co.uk>
Similar stuff: Amanda CROSS, Tim HEALD.
Final fact: RDE's brother is scholar and Conan Doyle expert Owen Dudley Edwards.

Lesley Egan *pseudonym, see* Elizabeth Linington

Aaron J. Elkins (b. 1935) US

AJE is best known for his series featuring forensic anthropologist Gideon Oliver, known as "the Skeleton Detective". Oliver tours the world lecturing or researching and his expertise is inevitably required in resolving some ancient or not so ancient mystery. It may be the combination of an ancient skeleton, a modern murder and a Mayan curse (*Curses!*) or victims killed in an avalanche 30 years before (*Icy Clutches*) or a recent body in a Bronze Age dig (*Murder in the Queen's Armes*). *Old Bones*, set on the romantic island of Mont St. Michel in Brittany, involving a 50-year-old wartime crime, won AJE an Edgar Award. *Twenty Blue Devils* took Oliver even further afield, to Tahiti. All of the books are meticulously researched, based on AJE's years of experience as a professor and lecturer in anthropology, and involve intriguing logical deductions in the spirit of the traditional crime novel. There are also anthropological mysteries in their own right, such as the fate of the Neanderthals, considered in *Skeleton Dance*, or the last days of the American Indian tribe, the Yahi, in *The Dark Place*, AJE's favourite amongst his books. The TV series *Gideon Oliver* (1988–9) was drawn from AJE's character but otherwise bore no relationship.

AJE produced a short series featuring art museum creator Chris Norgren, which is just as meticulous in its knowledge of art history. *Old Scores* won AJE the Nero Wolfe award and was nominated for an Agatha. *Loot* introduced a new, though similar, character, Boston art expert Ben

Revere, in a more thriller-orientated series drawing upon the Nazi wartime looting of art. AJE has also worked with his wife Charlotte on a rather more lightweight and light-hearted series featuring pro woman golfer Lee Ofsted and her cop friend Graham Sheldon.

Novels

Gideon Oliver series: *Fellowship of Fear* (1982), *The Dark Place* (1983), *Murder in the Queen's Armes* (1985), *Old Bones* (1987), *Curses!* (1989), *Icy Clutches* (1990), *Make No Bones* (1991), *Dead Men's Hearts* (1994), *Twenty Blue Devils* (1997), *Skeleton Dance* (2000).
Chris Norgren series: *A Deceptive Clarity* (1987), *A Glancing Light* (1991), *Old Scores* (1993).
Ben Revere series: *Loot* (1999), *Turncoat* (2002).
Lee Ofsted series, with Charlotte Elkins: *A Wicked Slice* (1989), *Rotten Lies* (1995), *Nasty Breaks* (1997).

Where to start: *Fellowship of Fear*.
Awards: Edgar, best novel (1988), Agatha, best short story [with Charlotte] (1993), Nero Wolfe (1994).
Similar stuff: Beverly CONNOR (for anthropology), Marcia MULLER and Iain PEARS (for art/museum crimes).

Stanley Ellin (1916–86) US

SE was one of the most meticulous craftsmen in the field. He would agonise for days over the opening sentence for a story and revise everything painstakingly. Not surprisingly, he seldom completed more than a couple of stories a year but they are almost all classics. He had held several jobs, including a teacher, steelworker and dairy farmer, before his wartime military service. Thanks to the faith and support of his wife, when SE was discharged from the army he became a full-time writer and was "discovered" by Ellery Queen (or at least the Frederick Dannay half) with his now near-legendary story of the ultimate delicacy, "The Specialty of the House" (*EQMM*, 1948). Most of his stories fit into the field of macabre suspense and were ideally suited for the TV series *Alfred Hitchcock Presents*. Many have twist endings and SE was not afraid to explore and push the boundaries of acceptability, thus making him one of the pioneers of modern crime fiction. Two of his stories, "The House Party" (*EQMM*, 1954) and "The Blessington Method" (*EQMM*, 1956) won Edgar awards and Julian Symons called his first collection, *Mystery Stories*, "the finest collection of stories in the crime form published in the past half century." His short fiction achievements have perhaps overshadowed his novels which were equally painstakingly plotted and usually took a year or more to complete. The first, *Dreadful Summit* (filmed 1951 as *The Big Night*), is a powerful story of a boy's revenge for his father's abuse. *The Key to Nicholas Street* (filmed 1959 as *Web of Passion* [aka *A Double Tour* and *Leda*]), is an ingenious investigation into a murder told from the varying viewpoints of the five main characters. His third novel, the Edgar-winning *The Eighth Circle*, is a detailed ethical study of a private detective, who works on behalf of his client even though he believes he is guilty. SE tested the boundaries again in his most original novel *Mirror, Mirror on the Wall*, which explored the theme of schizophrenia and self-loathing. Its significance was first recognized in Europe where it won the French Grand Prix de Littérature Policière and where H.R.F. KEATING listed it as one of the top hundred best crime novels. SE never stopped pushing the boundaries. His two novels featuring New York P.I. Johnny Milano are both challenging. In *Star Light, Star Bright* Milano is hired to protect a religious zealot who actually wants to be killed. *The Dark Fantastic* features a violently insane racist whose views caused the book to be rejected by SE's regular publisher. Even two decades after his death SE's work remains amongst the most original and accomplished in the field.

Novels
Non-series: *Dreadful Summit* (1948; as *The Big Night*, 1950), *The Key to Nicholas Street* (1952), *The Eighth Circle* (1958), *The Winter After This Summer* (1960), *The Panama Portrait* (1962), *House of Cards* (1967), *The Valentine Estate* (1968), *The Bind* (1970; as *The Man from Nowhere*, UK 1970); *Mirror, Mirror on the Wall* (1972), *Stronghold* (1975), *The Luxembourg Run* (1977), *Very Old Money* (1985).
Johnny Milano series: *Star Light, Star Bright* (1979), *The Dark Fantastic* (1983).
Short Stories. *Mystery Stories* (1956; as *Quiet Horror*, 1959; as *The Speciality of the House*, UK 1967), *The Blessington Method* (1964), *Kindly Dig Your Grave* (1975), *The Specialty of the House* (1979).

Full name: Stanley Bernard Ellin.
Where to start: *The Specialty of the House* (1979) for his stories or *The Eighth Circle.*
Awards: Edgar, best short story (1954, 1957), novel (1959), Grand Prix de Littérature Policière Best Foreign (1974), MWA Grand Master (1981).
Similar stuff: Gerald Kersh, Roald Dahl.

Bret Easton Ellis (b. 1964) US

BEE's *American Psycho* (filmed 2000) has been called the most violent novel ever written. About a serial killer, who is otherwise suave, humorous and good company, the book explored in graphic, self-indulgent detail the killer's delectation for torture and perversity. BEE's original publisher refused to publish it; there were moves to ban the book and BEE received death threats. BEE was exploring territory that had long been covered in horror and crime fiction, and his emphasis on violence was not necessarily any more graphic or gratuitous. The shock comes more from the difficulty to believe that such a likeable individual could be so depraved. In this respect *American Psycho* was a natural outgrowth from BEE's first two novels and the stories that make up *The*

Informers, all of which explore the twisted, obsessional and depraved world of the privileged, the get-rich-quick and the brat packs of mega-city life. The theme continues in *Glamorama*, where sex and drugs vie with violence for expression, and where the lives of the rich and glamorous are shaken by mass murder and terrorism. BEE may not have been exploring new territory, but his approach opened the eyes of many to a violent, vicious and depressing world that was all too real.

Novels. *Less Than Zero* (1985), *The Rules of Attraction* (1987), *American Psycho* (1991), *Glamorama* (1999).
Short Stories. *The Informers* (1994).

Similar stuff: Thomas HARRIS.
Final fact: BEE's maternal grandmother, Suzanne Easton Dennis, was the author of children's stories.

Kate Ellis (b. 1953) UK

Born and raised in Liverpool (she went to the same primary school as writer Clive Barker), KE studied drama in Manchester and then spent several years as a teacher and raising her own family. She also wrote several plays of which *Clearing Out* won the North-West Playwrights' competition in 1990. She turned to writing in the mid-nineties and developed the police procedural series featuring Detective Sergeant Wesley Peterson set in South Devon (around a thinly disguised Dartmouth). Peterson is also an archeology graduate and remains in touch with his former fellow student (now archeologist) Neil Watson. The series makes intriguing links between the past and present. In *The Merchant's House* it's a parallel between the murder of a woman on a Devon cliff top and the discovery of a pair of 400-year-old skeletons in a cellar. In *The Armada Boy* it's two suspicious deaths, one from the Second World War, the other from the days of the Spanish Armada. KE's books are the perfect proof that "what goes around comes around".

Novels
Wesley Peterson series: *The Merchant's House* (1998), *The Armada Boy* (1999), *An Unhallowed Grave* (1999), *The Funeral Boat* (2000), *The Bone Garden* (2001), *A Painted Doom* (2002).

Full name: Kate Ellis-Bullock.
Where to start: *The Merchant's House.*
Website: <www.kateellis.co.uk>
Similar stuff: Nancy PICKARD and Rick RIORDAN for links with the past.
Final fact: KE was the first New Year's Day baby born in Liverpool in 1953.

James Ellroy (b. 1948) US

JE's turbulent and near self-destructive youth was eventually channelled into something creative through his fiction after he had spent time in prison for breaking-and-entering, had become nearly schizophrenic through his reliance on drugs and drink and developed "post alcohol brain syndrome". The most traumatic episode of his childhood was the murder of his mother, a crime that remains unsolved. It still haunts JE. He used it as the basis for his second novel, *Clandestine*, and his attempt to solve the murder was told in *My Dark Places* (filmed 2001). JE was working as a golf caddy while he wrote his first book, *Brown's Requiem*, his only traditional P.I. novel. He found that world unreal and his fascination was for the underbelly of crime that pervaded his native Los Angeles. JE's fascination with murders, especially unsolved ones, resulted not only in a non-fiction study, *Murder and Mayhem*, but also in his great novel, *The Black Dahlia*, which used as its starting point a notorious murder in Hollywood in 1947. Almost all of JE's novels are set in Los Angeles and his L.A. Quartet traces the city's crime and corruption from 1947 through the fifties. JE's books are noted for their violence and dark moods – he is one of the kings of modern noir fiction, but has used noir to depict social history. It was not until *L.A. Confidential* that JE had mastered his techniques and written through most of his angst to allow his humour to emerge. The early books, especially the Lloyd Hopkins trilogy, set in present day Los Angeles, are almost excessively violent and bleak. Hopkins is an unsympathetic, near deranged but intellectually brilliant homicide detective in the LAPD, but his fight against crime blurs the distinctions between hero and villain. These books owe much to the influence of Hammett but JE's expression is uncontrolled, just as in his own violent youth when he provoked fights at school through his extreme views. His recent fiction has toned down a notch to what may be an acceptable level to some but which seems tame to others. *The Cold Six Thousand* gained a fairly cool reception compared to its predecessor, *American Tabloid*, hailed by some as JE's best book. These two form part of JE's Underworld trilogy, which continues the exploration of crime and corruption from the L.A. Quartet, but across the entire USA, starting with the assassination of President Kennedy. The projected third volume, *Police Gazette*, will bring the saga to 1972. JE says he will stop short of Watergate because it bores him. The scope and increasing complexity of JE's work have seen him hailed as a 20th-century American Balzac. He is, in fact, recreating the hidden history of America through its crime and violence on a Tolstoyan scale. In addition to the film of *L.A. Confidential* (1997), which cemented JE's reputation world wide, both *Brown's Requiem* (1998) and *Blood on the Moon* (1987 as *Cop*) have been filmed.

Novels

Non-series: *Brown's Requiem* (1981), *Clandestine* (1982), *Silent Terror* (1986; as *Killer on the Road*, 1990).

Lloyd Hopkins series: *Blood on the Moon* (1984), *Because the Night* (1985), *Suicide Hill* (1986). Reissued as omnibus *L.A. Noir* (1998).

L.A. Quartet: *The Black Dahlia* (1987), *The Big Nowhere* (1988), *L.A. Confidential* (1990), *White Jazz* (1992).

Underworld USA series: *American Tabloid* (1995), *The Cold Six Thousand* (2001), *Police Gazette* (forthcoming).
Short Stories. *Hollywood Nocturnes* (1994; as *Dick Contino's Blues*, UK 1994), *Crime Wave* [includes non-fiction] (1999).
Non-fiction. *Murder and Mayhem* (1992), *My Dark Places* (1996), *Crime Wave* (includes fiction) (1999), *Breakneck Pace* (includes fiction) (e-book, 2000).

Full name: Lee Earle Ellroy
Where to start: *The Black Dahlia.*
Awards: French Trophée 813 (1988, 2001), Japanese Maltese Falcon (1997).
Website: <www.ellroy.com>
Similar stuff: James Lee BURKE, Jim THOMPSON
Final fact: JE was expelled from school for ranting about Nazism and received a dishonourable discharge from the US Army by faking mental instability.

Earl W. Emerson (b. 1948) US

EWE's twenty years as a lieutenant in the Seattle Fire Department has provided plenty of experience for his series featuring small-town Washington fire chief and arson investigator Mac Fontana. Although EWE draws upon his expertise the detection and analysis is not overly technical but the mysteries are seldom straightforward. Despite the constant danger of firefighters' lives Fontana's characterization is not as deep as that of EWE's other series character, Thomas Black. Black is an ex-cop turned P.I. in Seattle. He is a fairly normal character free from most of the neuroses that trouble so many P.I.s, but he has one problem. He retired from the force after killing a hoodlum in self-defence and thereafter cannot use a gun. Black's fear of using his gun means he ends up in more fights than is good for him and both series have a degree of violence, allowing EWE to explore whether it serves a purpose. This comes to a head in *The Portland Laugher*, where Black kills an innocent man. Four of the Black novels were short-listed for the Shamus award with *Poverty Bay*, also nominated for an Edgar, taking the prize. The Fontana novel, *Morons and Madmen*, was nominated for an Anthony. Common to both series are problems deep in the past that have repercussions in the present, particularly their impact upon families and children, and EWE is adept at gradually reconstructing the picture.

Novels
Thomas Black series: *The Rainy City* (1985), *Poverty Bay* (1985), *Nervous Laughter* (1986), *Fat Tuesday* (1987), *Deviant Behaviour* (1988), *Yellow Dog Party* (1991), *The Portland Laugher* (1994), *The Vanishing Smile* (1995), *The Million-Dollar Tattoo* (1996), *Deception Pass* (1997), *Catfish Café* (1999).
Mac Fontana series: *Black Hearts and Slow Dancing* (1988), *Help Wanted: Orphans Preferred* (1990), *Morons and Madmen* (1993), *Going Crazy in Public* (1996), *The Dead Horse Paint Company* (1997).
Non-series: *Vertical Burn* (2002).

Where to start: *The Rainy City*.
Awards: Shamus, best novel (1986).
Similar stuff: Kate WILHELM and Don WINSLOW for other arson investigators.
Final fact: EWE was included amongst six other writers on President Bill Clinton's list of favourite authors.

Howard Engel (b. 1931) Canada

HE was one of the founders of the Crime Writers of Canada in 1982. At that time he was scarcely a published author, though he had a long career in radio behind him as both a producer and broadcaster. HE did not feel that Canada was properly represented in detective fiction so he created his own small-town (Grantham, Ontario) detective, Benny Cooperman. Aside from the fact that he is Jewish, everything else about him is flawlessly Canadian and every inch the normal guy. Cooperman is almost the atypical P.I., and that's his appeal. He goes about his investigations in a matter-of-fact way with no flashes of intuition, no rough stuff, no drink or personal angst. That doesn't stop the cases being complicated or dangerous – the award-winning *Murder Sees the Light* even involves satanism – but Cooperman's calm, collected and persistent doggedness always gets there in the end. Cooperman's strength is his dependability and the books' charm is their reassuredness despite the twists, turns and convolutions of the plots. TV movies were made of *The Suicide Murders* (1985) and *Murder Sees the Light* (1987), both scripted by HE. Apart from the novelization of the TV script *Murder in Space*, which HE wrote with his wife, Janet Hamilton, HE has written two historical mysteries. *Murder in Montparnasse* is a fascinating insight into the artistic expatriate communities in Paris in the 1920s, including Gertrude Stein, Alice B. Toklas and a thinly disguised Ernest Hemingway and F. Scott Fitzgerald. *Mr Doyle and Dr Bell* takes us back to Edinburgh University in the 1870s and Dr Joseph Bell, the inspiration for Sherlock Holmes. In both books HE weaves literary icons with real historical cases to produce fascinating glimpses on possible pasts.

Novels
Benny Cooperman series: *The Suicide Murders* (1980; as *The Suicide Notice*, US/UK 1980), *The Ransom Game* (1981), *Murder on Location* (1982), *Murder Sees the Light* (1984), *A City Called July* (1986), *A Victim Must Be Found* (1988), *Dead and Buried* (1990), *There Was an Old Woman* (1993), *Getting Away with Murder* (1995), *The Cooperman Variations* (2001).
Non-series: *Murder in Montparnasse* (1992), *Mr Doyle and Dr Bell* (1997).
as F.X. Woolf (with Janet Hamilton): *Murder in Space* (1985).
Short stories. Special edition single story booklets: *The Whole Megillah* a Cooperman novella (1991), *A Child's Christmas in Scarborough* (1997).
Non-fiction. *Behold the Lord High Executioner* (1996), *Crimes of Passion* (2002).
Editor. *Criminal Shorts* with Eric Wright (1992).

Pen-name: F.X Woolf (with Janet Hamilton)

Where to start: *The Suicide Murders.*
Awards: Arthur Ellis, best novel (1985), Academy of Canadian Film and Television award, best film script (1988), Derrick Murdoch Award (1998).
Similar stuff: Walter SATTERTHWAIT's *Masquerade* has much in common with *Murder in Montparnasse.*
Final fact: HE had a walk-on part in the film of *The Suicide Murders.*

Walter Ericson *pseudonym, see* Howard Fast

Loren D. Estleman (b. 1952) US

It took LDE eight years, with around 160 rejection slips, before he sold his first book, *The Oklahoma Punk*, an historical crime novel based on 1930s Public Enemy No.1, Wilbur Underhill. Nearly 50 books later, LDE is the most critically acclaimed of all US writers of crime fiction. He has been nominated for more Shamus awards than any other writer, and has won three times. His work has also been shortlisted for the Edgar, the National Book Award, the CWA Golden Dagger and was twice nominated for the Pulitzer prize for his historical work. He is as highly recognized in the field of western fiction where he has won four Golden Spurs, two Stirrups and a Western Heritage Award. It might seem strange in the light of all this to say that LDE's much praised Amos Walker series is not especially original. It is a traditional P.I. series firmly in the Chandler mould but transplanted to modern day Detroit, with all the modern day problems besetting the city. Against this, Walker, although a Vietnam veteran, seems almost an anachronism and whilst the books are solidly written with a strong pace, good characterization, many twists and turns and intriguing plots, LDE is not breaking new ground. LDE has written a spoof on the P.I. genre with *Peeper*, featuring Ralph Poteet, a scumbag way down in the food chain, but it's LDE's other work, often overlooked in the shadow of Walker, where he is more original. *Kill Zone* introduced the character of Peter Macklin, an average guy who is also a hired assassin, a hit-man for the Mob. But in the first book he had to free a boatload of hostages held by terrorists and thereafter the Mob are after him. *Whiskey River* began what may prove to be LDE's most proclaimed series. These novels are set at different periods of Detroit's history, exploring aspects of the city's crime and pain. *Whiskey City* takes place during the prohibition days, *Jitterbug* places corruption and racial tension centre stage during WW2, and race riots also feature in *Motown* and *Stress*. It's a powerful series that exposes the dark side of Detroit.

Perhaps LDE's most original work is in the field of western fiction, all too easily overlooked by mystery fans. His Page Murdock series features a rather lawless US Marshal working for the federal court. These are genuine historical mysteries set against the western frontier. Other western novels are fictionalized biographies of notable western heroes or villains: *Aces & Eights* (1981) recounts the life of Wild Bill Hickok as outlined during the trial of his murderer. *This Old Bill* (1984) is about Buffalo Bill. *Gun Man* (1985) explores the violent life of outlaw turned lawman John Miller and *Bloody Season* (1988) recreates the gunfight at the OK Corral. LDE has also written a critical assessment of western fiction in *The Wister Trace* (1987).

Novels

Amos Walker series: *Motor City Blue* (1980), *Angel Eyes* (1981), *The Midnight Man* (1982), *The Glass Highway* (1983), *Sugartown* (1984), *Every Brilliant Eye* (1986), *Lady Yesterday* (1987), *Downriver* (1988), *Silent Thunder* (1989), *Sweet Women Lie* (1990), *Never Street* (1997), *The Witchfinder* (1998), *The Hours of the Virgin* (1999), *A Smile on the Face of the Tiger* (2000), *Sinister Heights* (2002).
Peter Macklin series: *Kill Zone* (1984), *Roses Are Dead* (1985), *Any Man's Death* (1986), *Something Borrowed, Something Black* (2002)
Page Murdock series: *The High Rocks* (1979), *Stamping Ground* (1980), *Murdock's Law* (1982), *The Stranglers* (1984), *City of Widows* (1994), *White Desert* (2000).
Detroit series: *Whiskey River* (1990), *Motown* (1991), *King of the Corner* (1992), *Edsel* (1995), *Stress* (1996), *Jitterbug* (1998), *Thunder City* (1999).
Sherlock Holmes series: *Sherlock Holmes vs Dracula* (1978), *Dr Jekyll and Mr Holmes* (1979).
Non-series: *The Oklahoma Punk* (1976; as *Red Highway*, 1987), *Peeper* (1989).

Short Stories

Amos Walker series: *General Murders* (1988), *Eight Mile and Dequindre*, single story (1991)
Non-series: *The Best Western Stories of Loren D. Estleman* (1989), *People Who Kill* (1993).

Where to start: *Kill Zone* or *The High Rocks*
Awards: Shamus, best hardcover (1985), best short story (1986, 1989), American Mystery Award, best P.I. novel (1989), best crime novel (1991).
Website: <www.lorenestleman.com>
Similar stuff: Lawrence BLOCK, James ELLROY.
Final fact: All of LDE's 50 or so books and several hundred stories and articles are written on an old manual typewriter.

Janet Evanovich (b. 1943) US

It's not difficult to keep track of JE's series about Stephanie Plum as all the titles are neatly enumerated. JE studied as an artist but developed a rash from pigment and turned to writing. After ten years of rejection slips, JE then wrote a dozen humorous romance novels, three of them pseudonymously, until, as she says, she 'ran out of sexual positions'. She turned to the mystery field and rapidly became a bestseller. Although her books are set in New Jersey, the books have a strong British feel, especially in their humour, and they have been enthusiastically received in Britain where she has won three awards from the CWA. The first book, *One for the Money*, was also nominated for the CWA Last Laugh award as well as for the Agatha, Edgar and Shamus. Plum works as a bounty hunter for her Cousin Vinnie's Bail Bonds agency. Her assignments are often dangerous and usually violent but JE has a delightfully skewed view on life and peppers the novels with an array of oddball characters and bizarre situations. In fact the series has everything – sex, drugs, violence, heroes, villains and Rex the hamster.

Novels
Stephanie Plum series: *One for the Money* (1994), *Two for the Dough* (1996), *Three to Get Deadly* (1997), *Four to Score* (1998), *High Five* (1999), *Hot Six* (2000), *Seven Up* (2001), *Hard Eight* (2002).

Pen-name: Steffie Hall (on romances).
Awards: CWA John Creasey Memorial Award (1995), Dilys (1995, 1998), CWA Last Laugh (1996), CWA Silver Dagger (1997), Lefty Award (1998, 1999).
Website: <www.evanovich.com>
Similar stuff: Sparkle HAYTER, D.M. GREENWOOD.
Final fact: JE's first attempt at a story, which remained unsold, was about the pornographic adventures of a fairy who lived in a second-rate forest.

Elizabeth Eyre *pseudonym, see* Jill Staynes & Margaret Storey

Terence Faherty US

A technical writer in Indianapolis, TF is the author of two crime series, both out of the usual run of things. The first features Owen Keane, a former student at a seminary who left because he questioned his faith and thereafter his quest for the "Truth" and his compulsive fascination for solving puzzles leads him into all kinds of mysteries. *Deadstick*, which was nominated for an Edgar best first novel award, involves an assignment to find the truth behind a 40-year-old plane crash. *The Lost Keats* takes us back to Keane's days at the seminary and the search for a missing seminarian and a lost Keats sonnet. *Die Dreaming* also takes us back into Keane's past when Keane believes an investigation he carried out in 1978 may somehow have led to the death of a fellow classmate ten years later. His other series features Scott Elliott, an actor whose career was terminated by WW2 and who now works for a Hollywood security firm, dealing in the movie's dirty business. The first book, *Kill Me Again*, is set in 1947 whilst *Come Back Dead*, which won the Shamus award, moves on to 1955 and the problems arising from the sale of the RKO studio assets. The Keane books are fascinating soul-searching puzzles that are a refreshing change, whilst the Elliott books are full of detail for the delight of film buffs.

Novels
Owen Keane series: *Deadstick* (1991), *Live to Regret* (1992), *The Lost Keats* (1993), *Die Dreaming* (1994), *Prove the Nameless* (1996), *The Ordained* (1998), *Orion Rising* (1999).

Scott Elliott series: *Kill Me Again* (1996), *Come Back Dead* (1997), *Passage to Lisbon* (1998), *Raise the Devil* (2000).

Where to start: *Deadstick.*
Awards: Shamus, best .P.I novel (1998).
Website: <www.terencefaherty.com>
Similar stuff: Stuart KAMINSKY and Max Allan COLLINS for Hollywood; Ralph MCINERNY.

Howard Fast (b. 1914) US

HF's career has spread over nearly 70 years. He sold his first story to a science-fiction magazine in 1932 and his first book, *Two Valleys*, appeared a year later. He is best known for his historical novels, many of which deal with the American Revolution, such as *The Unvanquished* (1942) and *The Crossing* (1971), but which also include *Spartacus* (1952) and *Moses, Prince of Egypt* (1958). HF was an open and defiant member of the Communist party from 1943–56 and this led to his being blacklisted during the McCarthy era. As a result he turned to publishing his own books, including *The Story of Lola Gregg*, where the FBI pursue a Communist activist. His agent sold other titles under pen-names. All of this pseudonymous work, mostly as E.V. Cunningham, was mystery, crime and suspense fiction. He began a series of one-off novels connected only by their titles, the name of that book's heroine. The first was *Sylvia*, where a millionaire hires an investigator to check out his wife-to-be, just days before the wedding. The most suspenseful is *Sally* (filmed TV 1971 as *The Face of Fear*) in which a woman who believes she has leukemia hires a gunman to kill her at any unexpected moment. She later learns she does not have leukemia but by then has severed contact with the assassin. *Samantha*, about a woman who is systematically killing the men who, years before, destroyed her film career, introduced his Japanese detective Masao Masuto. Masuto has a sharp wit and likes to catch others off guard by slipping into an imitation of Charlie Chan. Masuto's cases are usually amongst the rich of Beverly Hills, who never quite understand this highly philosophical detective. Like Masuto, HF is a Zen Buddhist. He regarded these suspense novels as fun and light relief from his more serious work, and sometimes the plots stretch credulity. For example, in *Fallen Angel* (filmed 1965 as *Mirage*) a man unaccountably loses his memory and discovers men are out to kill him. In *Shirley* (filmed TV 1971 as *What's a Nice Girl Like You. . .?*) a working girl is kidnapped and forced to impersonate a rich socialite. Nevertheless there is a zest and flair about the books that make them a delight.

Novels

as Fast: *The Story of Lola Gregg* (1956), *The Winston Affair* (1959), *The Confession of Joe Cullen* (1989), *Greenwich* (2000).

as E.V. Cunningham:
Non-series: *Sylvia* (1960), *Phyllis* (1962), *Alice* (1963), *Shirley* (1964), *Helen* (1966), *Sally* (1967), *The Wabash Factor* (1986).
Harvey Krim series: *Lydia* (1964), *Cynthia* (1968), *The Assassin Who Gave Up His Gun* (1969).
Comaday & Cohen series: *Penelope* (1965), *Margie* (1966).
Masao Masuto series: *Samantha* (1967; as *The Case of the Angry Actress*, 1984), *The Case of the One Penny Orange* (1977), *The Case of the Russian Diplomat* (1978), *The Case of the Poisoned Eclairs* (1979), *The Case of the Sliding Pool* (1981), *The Case of the Kidnapped Angel* (1982), *The Case of the Murdered Mackenzie* (1984).
as Walter Ericson: *Fallen Angel* (1952; as *The Darkness Within*, 1953; as *Mirage* by Fast, 1965).

Full name: Howard Melvin Fast.
Pen-names: E.V. Cunningham, Walter Ericson.
Where to start: *Sally* or *The Case of the One Penny Orange*.
Awards: Newspaper Guild award (1947), Jewish Book Council of America award (1948), Screenwriters award (1960), Emmy, television play (1976), Grand Prix de Littérature Policière (1973).
Website: <www.trussel.com/f_how.htm>
Similar stuff: Kenneth Fearing, Cornell Woolrich, Robert RICHARDSON, Lawrence SANDERS.
Final fact: HF was imprisoned in 1950 for his contempt of Congress when he refused to name names to the House Committee on Un-American Activities.

James Ferguson, *see under pseudonym* Nicholas Rhea

Monica Ferris *pseudonym, see* Mary Monica Pulver

Tom Ferris, *see under pseudonym* Nicholas Rhea

Patricia Finney (b. 1958) UK

PF's first book, written when she was seventeen, was a Celtic historical fantasy, *A Shadow of Gulls* (1977) followed by *The Crow Goddess* (1978). The daughter of two barristers and subsequently married to a barrister, PF nevertheless studied modern history at Wadham College, Oxford and then launched into a career as a freelance journalist and editor. During this time she became fascinated with the Elizabethan period and after five years' research completed *Firedrake's Eye*. It's about loyal courtier Simon Ames and his rather dubious friend David Becket who stumble across a plan to assassinate Queen Elizabeth. A complex plot involving Elizabethan spies and counter-espionage and narrated in the first person, complete with Elizabethan vocabulary, the book was sufficiently rewarding for Ruth RENDELL to dub PF "the Le Carré of the 16th century". It was six years before PF completed the second Ames and Becket book, *Unicorn's Blood*, another complicated adventure involving the search for a rare book and the fight to save Mary Queen of Scots. In between these books PF started a new series, writing as P.F. Chisholm. Set a decade later, this involves Sir Robert Carey, Elizabeth I's cousin and Deputy Warden of the Scottish borders. Caught in the constant turmoil between the English and the Scots and always in trouble, Carey endeavours to uphold the rule of law and solve murders whilst all about him is chaos. *A Plague of Angels* finds Carey summoned to London, deep in debt, and fighting for his own survival. An enthralling series, full of period atmosphere.

Novels

Simon Ames series: *Firedrake's Eye* (1992), *Unicorn's Blood* (1998).
Robert Carey series as P.F. Chisholm: *A Famine of Horses* (1994), *A Season of Knives* (1995), *A Surfeit of Guns* (1996), *A Plague of Angels* (1998).

Pen-name: P.F. Chisholm.
Where to start: *Firedrake's Eye*.
Awards: David Higham award, best first novel (1978), *Radio Times* Drama award, best radio play (1988).
Website: <www.patricia-finney.co.uk>
Similar stuff: Judith COOK, Keith MILES, Iain PEARS.
Final fact: PF has also written a children's book from the viewpoint of a dog, *I, Jack*.

Robert L. Fish (1912–81) US

Even those who do not know the name of RLF will remember the film *Bullitt* (1968) if for no other reason than the amazing car chase. It was adapted from RLF's *Mute Witness*, the first of his police procedurals about Lieutenant Clancy of Manhattan's 52nd Precinct, who attempts to save a powerful underworld gangster from Mob execution. RLF wrote three Clancy novels but, after the success of the film, RLF changed Clancy's name to Reardon and transferred him to San Francisco and wrote four more solid, action-packed police procedurals. RLF was 56 with the success of that film, but had only been writing for three years. For most of his career he had been a consulting engineer in the plastics industry that took him all over the world, but mostly South America. Brazil is the setting for RLF's long-running series featuring Captain Jose da Silva, liaison officer to Interpol. In *The Fugitive*, which won RLF the best first novel Edgar award, Da Silva, and his sidekick Wilson from the American embassy, are involved in a search for a Nazi war criminal. Da Silva is an engaging character, unhurried and often ill equipped but always determined. RLF's other main series features Kek Huuygens, the world's greatest smuggler. Originally written as a series of short stories, RLF developed them into a sequence of ingenious novels showing a super-thief at work. RLF first appeared in print in *EQMM* with a series of irrevent parodies of Sherlock Holmes featuring the Jewish equivalent, Schlock Homes who lives as 221B Bagel Street. The stories are full of outrageous puns and Homes is always rushing to the wrong inept conclusion. RLF's humour is also apparent in the Murder League trilogy in which three English mystery writers, Carruthers, Simpson and Briggs, no longer able to sell their work decide to carry out the plots they had created. RLF also completed an unfinished novel by Jack London, *The Assassination Bureau, Ltd.* (filmed 1969).

Novels
Jose da Silva series: *The Fugitive* (1962), *Isle of the Snakes* (1963), *The Shrunked Head* (1963), *Brazilian Sleigh Ride* (1965), *The Diamond Bubble* (1965), *Always Kill a Stranger* (1967), *The Bridge That Went Nowhere* (1968), *The Xavier Affair* (1969), *The Green Hell Treasure* (1971), *Trouble in Paradise* (1975).
Kek Huuygens series: *The Hochmann Miniatures* (1967), *Whirligig* (1970), *The Tricks of the Trade* (1972), *The Wager* (1974).
Murder League trilogy: *The Murder League* (1968), *Rub-a-Dub-Dub* (1971; as *Death Cuts the Deck*, US 1972), *A Gross Carriage of Justice* (1979).
completed for Jack London: *The Assassination Bureau, Ltd.* (1963).
Non-series: *The Trials of O'Brien* (1965), *A Handy Death* with Henry Rothblatt (1973), *Pursuit* (1978), *The Gold of Troy* (1980), *Rough Diamond* (1981).
as Robert L. Pike:
Lieut. Clancy series: *Mute Witness* (1963; as *Bullitt*, 1968), *The Quarry* (1964), *Police Blotter* (1965).
Lieut. Reardon series: *Reardon* (1970), *The Gremlin's Grampa* (1972), *Bank Job* (1974), *Deadline 2 A.M.* (1976)
Short Stories
Schlock Homes series: *The Incredible Schlock Homes* (1966), *The Memoirs of Schlock Homes* (1974), *Schlock Homes: The Complete Bagel Street Saga* (1990).
Kek Huuygens series: *Kek Huuygens, Smuggler* (1976).
Editor. *With Malice Toward All* (1968), *Every Crime in the Book* (1975).

Full name: Robert Lloyd Fish.
Pen-names: Robert L. Pike, Lawrence Roberts, A.C. Lamprey.
Where to start: *The Fugitive*.
Awards: Edgar, first novel (1963), short story (1972).
Similar stuff: Ron GOULART.
Final fact: RLF was always the champion of new writers and in 1984 the MWA instigated the Robert L. Fish Award for the best short story arising from the MWA's new writers' training programme.

Katherine V. Forrest (b. 1939) Canada (US resident)

KVF is an editor at Naiad Press, which has published all her books, including several romance titles of which *Curious Wine* is amongst the best-selling of all lesbian novels. Amongst her output is a series of novels featuring ex-Marine, LAPD homicide detective Kate Delafield. All of the novels have a lesbian theme or background. Delafield is a tough and demanding officer in an unrelenting and prejudicial world. She has kept her sexual orientation a secret but this increasingly becomes a problem in her work. The cases are difficult and KVF pulls no punches. *Murder at the Nightwood Bar*, which has been optioned for the cinema, shows hostility by lesbians to Delafield when she investigates a murder at a lesbian bar. Delafield had served in Vietnam and *Liberty Square* involves a murder at a Vietnam reunion. Though these books emphasize lesbian sexual attraction, they remain at the core solid police procedurals.

Novels
Kate Delafield series: *Amateur City* (1984), *Murder at the Nightwood Bar* (1986), *The Beverly Malibu* (1989), *Murder by Tradition* (1991), *Liberty Square* (1996), *Apparition Alley* (1997), *Sleeping Bones* (1999).

Full name: Katherine Virginia Forrest.
Awards: Lambda, best lesbian fiction (1990, 1992).
Website: <www.art-with-attitude.com/forrest> and <www.geocities.com/WestHollywood/Heights/9558/KVForrest.htm>
Similar stuff: Claire McNab, Sandra SCOPPETTONE.

Jack Foxx *pseudonym, see* Bill Pronzini

Clare Francis (b. 1946) UK

CF shot into the headlines in 1973 when she became the fastest woman to sail solo across the Atlantic. Over the next four years she became something of a national hero with her sailing achievements, which seemed all the more remarkable for a lady who had spent six years working in marketing and had originally trained to be a ballet dancer. Besides the books about her adventures, starting with *Come Hell or High Water* (1977), she turned to writing fiction. Her first four books are thrillers, more in the vein of Ken Follett or Frederick Forsyth than pure crime novels. *Night Sky* is a complex and rewarding novel set amongst the French Resistance in WW2. *Red Crystal* is about an international terrorist group intent on provoking war. *Wolf Winter* is a tense novel of the Cold War set in Norway. *Requiem* is an environmental novel about dangerous chemicals let loose in Britain. Her more recent books, written since she was cruelly struck down with ME, are more personalized novels in the crime and suspense tradition. Both *Deceit* and *A Dark Devotion* are about searches for missing people (a husband in the first and a wife in the second) and the discovery of the hidden lives they had led. *A Death Divided* also starts with a search, this time for a missing childhood friend, but her discovery sets off a dangerous train of events. *Betrayal* concerns a man accused of murdering a former lover. *Keep Me Close*, perhaps the most personal of CF's books, is about a woman injured in a vicious attack and the attempts to find out who did it and why. All of CF's books are complex with a multitude of characters and a strong personal viewpoint.

Novels. *Night Sky* (1983), *Red Crystal* (1985), *Wolf Winter* (1987), *Requiem* (1991;

as *The Killing Winds*, US 1992), *Deceit* (1993), *Betrayal* (1995), *A Dark Devotion* (1997), *Keep Me Close* (1999), *A Death Divided* (2001).

Full name: Clare Mary Francis
Where to start: *Betrayal*.
Similar stuff: Ken Follett, Nicci FRENCH.
Final fact: CF was awarded the MBE in 1978.

Dick Francis (b. 1920) UK

DF is one of those rare examples of someone who has moved between two challenging professions and achieved top status in both. He was a successful steeplechase jockey from 1946 to 1957, being National Hunt champion in 1953 and 1954. When he turned to writing crime novels he proved he was no flash-in-the-pan and has been honoured with a CWA Diamond Dagger and made an MWA Grand Master. He was also made an OBE in 1984. DF's books never fail to entertain. At his best he is a masterful and highly respected author. Inevitably when he turned to writing, his books were going to focus on the Sport of Kings and, although he has occasionally distanced himself from that field, he always returns, because that's what readers expect. His first book, *Dead Cert*, was a rather routine novel of a jockey turned P.I. to solve the murder of a fellow jockey, but DF soon had the bit between his teeth. *Nerve* is a much stronger book about a jockey who appears to have lost his nerve. DF has generally eschewed a regular series character. He comes closest with Sid Halley, a former champion jockey who turns P.I. when an accident forces him to retire. Even then he has written only three Halley books of which *Whip Hand*, where Halley investigates a doping scandal, is amongst his best books and received both an Edgar award and a Gold Dagger. *Come to Grief*, dealing with violence to horses, also won an Edgar. DF does not confine his novels to the UK. *Blood Sport* involves a search for stolen horses across the US; *Smokescreen* is set in South Africa. In *Slay Ride* a jockey disappears in Norway whilst in *Trial Run*, DF took on the matter of the controversial Moscow Olympics. *The Edge* is a wonderful throw-back to the classic age with a murder on the Canadian Pacific Railway. DF places emphasis on personal relationships and the psychological aspects of crime making his books more suspense thrillers than conventional whodunits. This was most evident in *Forfeit*, his first award-winning novel, where a racing correspondent, who is planning to expose a racing fraud, finds his disabled wife under threat. DF's own wife of 53 years, Mary, died suddenly of a heart attack in September 2000 aged 76. This sad occasion caused DF to state that he might not write another book.

Novels

Non-series: *Dead Cert* (1962), *Nerve* (1964), *For Kicks* (1965), *Flying Finish* (1966), *Blood Sport* (1967), *Forfeit* (1969), *Enquiry* (1970), *Rat Race* (1970), *Bonecrack* (1971), *Smokescreen* (1972), *Slay Ride* (1973), *Knock-Down* (1974),

High Stakes (1975), *In the Frame* (1976), *Trial Run* (1978), *Reflex* (1980), *Twice Shy* (1981), *Banker* (1982), *The Danger* (1983), *Proof* (1984), *Hot Money* (1987), *The Edge* (1988), *Straight* (1989), *Longshot* (1990), *Comeback* (1991), *Driving Force* (1992), *Decider* (1993), *Wild Horses* (1994), *To the Hilt* (1996), *10-lb Penalty* (1997), *Second Wind* (1999), *Shattered* (2000).
Sid Halley series: *Odds Against* (1965), *Whip Hand* (1979), *Come to Grief* (1995).
Kit Fielding series: *Break In* (1985), *Bolt* (1986).
Short Stories. *Racing Classics*, booklet (1995), *Field of Thirteen* (1998).
Autobiography. *The Sport of Queens* (1957; 4th rev. 1988).

Full name: Richard Stanley Francis
Where to start: *Nerve* or *Odds Against.*
Awards: Edgar, best novel (1970, 1981, 1996), CWA Gold Dagger (1979), CWA Diamond Dagger (1989), MWA Grand Master (1996), Agatha, lifetime achievement (2000).
Books about: *Dick Francis* by Melvyn Barnes (1986), *Dick Francis* by J. Madison Davis (1989).
Similar stuff: John FRANCOME.
Final fact: DF's wife helped him extensively with his research, even to the point of learning to fly a light aircraft.

John Francome (b. 1952) UK

Like Dick FRANCIS, JF was a champion National Hunt jockey (for seven seasons) and retired in 1985 after riding his 1,038th winner. He was awarded the MBE in 1986. He became a trainer and a racing commentator but also, like Francis, turned to writing mysteries. Unlike Francis, all of JF's books are set in the UK and he concentrates more directly on the world of horse racing. He was assisted on his first five books by professional writers and went it alone from *Stud Poker*, which pursued the idea that an accident that ended a jockey's career may not have been an accident at all. JF's novels look at all the possible angles of corruption in the sport, though inevitably the plots hinge around a murder. JF has avoided continuing characters but has created some interesting ones. This includes insurance investigator Jack Hendred who, in *Blood Stock*, looks into the death of a stud stallion. JF's books generally lack the broader scope of Francis' but are competent and readable mysteries for those fascinated by the world of horse racing.

Novels

(first four with James MacGregor and fifth with Terence Blacker). *Eavesdropper* (1986), *Riding High* (1987), *Declared Dead* (1988), *Blood Stock* (1989), *Stone Cold* (1990), *Stud Poker* (1991), *Rough Ride* (1992), *Outside* (1993), *Break Neck* (1994), *Dead Ringer* (1995), *False Start* (1996), *High Flyer* (1997), *Safe Bet* (1998), *Tip Off* (1999), *Lifeline* (2000), *Dead Weight* (2001).
Autobiography. *Born Lucky* (1985).

Where to start: *Eavesdropper* or *Stud Poker*
Similar stuff: Dick FRANCIS.

Final fact: JF won his first public race as a jockey in 1969 but his second race ended with a broken wrist.

Anthea Fraser (b. 1930) UK

AF turned to writing in the early sixties, though it had always been in her blood as her mother, Adelaide Q. Roby, had been a writer. AF wrote short stories for magazines before she sold her first book in 1971, a Mills & Boon romance, *Designs of Annabelle*. Two more Mills & Boon books followed before she switched first to romantic suspense, with *Motive for Murder*, *Dangerous Deception* ands *Home Through the Dark*, and then to a string of supernatural mysteries, from *Laura Possessed* to *The Macbeth Prophecy*. With *A Shroud for Delilah*, AF made another change. This book introduced Detective Chief Inspector David Webb and his detective sergeant Ken Jackson who operate in the town of Shillingham in fictional Broadshire, roughly equating to northern Wiltshire. These are highly methodical police procedurals with a small cast of characters, in which Webb applies due process and occasional leaps of faith in resolving the crimes. During the course of each book AF gives a very rounded picture of the individuals and their lives and allows you to follow Webb through his investigation. Recently AF has turned to writing occasional non-series crime novels, such as *Dangerous Deception*, about a case of mistaken identity in a remote Welsh hotel.

Novels. Non-series: *Laura Possessed* (1974), *Home Through the Dark* (1974), *Whistler's Lane* (1975), *Breath of Brimstone* (1978), *Presence of Mind* (1978), *Island-in-Waiting* (1979), *The Stone* (1980), *The Macbeth Prophecy* (1995), *Motive for Murder* (1996), *Dangerous Deception* (1998), *Past Shadows* (2001), *Fathers and Daughters* (2002).
Webb & Jackson series: *A Shroud for Delilah* (1984), *A Necessary End* (1985), *Pretty Maids All in a Row* (1986), *Death Speaks Softly* (1987), *The Nine Bright Shiners* (1987), *Six Proud Walkers* (1988), *The April Rainers* (1989), *Symbols at your Door* (1990), *The Lily-White Boys* (1991; as *I'll Sing You Two-O*, US 1996), *Three, Three the Rivals* (1992), *The Gospel Makers* (1994), *The Seven Stars* (1995), *One is One and All Alone* (1996), *The Ten Commandments* (1997), *Eleven That Went Up to Heaven* (1999), *The Twelve Apostles* (1999).

Full name: Anthea Mary Fraser.
Pen-names: Lorna Cameron, Vanessa Graham.
Where to start: *A Shroud for Delilah*
Similar stuff: Jane ADAMS, Dorothy SIMPSON.
Final fact: AF enjoys receiving fan mail but had a disconcerting moment at the time she was writing mostly supernatural fiction. A fan wrote to tell her that he had been guided to her book in the bookshop by the spirit of Emanuel Swedenborg. She was intrigued to know she had such a distinguished ghost as a publicity agent.

Antonia Fraser (b. 1932) UK

AF is one of Britain's most renowned historians. She comes from a highly literary family. Her parents, Lord Longford and Elizabeth Longford, her brother Thomas Pakenham and sister Rachel Billington and now her daughter Flora Fraser are all acclaimed writers. After her first marriage to Hugh Fraser, AF is now married to playwright Harold Pinter. AF's first two books were for children, *King Arthur and the Knights of the Round Table* (1954) and *Robin Hood* (1955). She was general editor of Weidenfeld and Nicolson's Kings and Queens of England series and she has since written such definitive volumes as *Mary Queen of Scots* (1969), for which she was awarded the James Tait Black Memorial Prize, *Cromwell Our Chief of Men* (1973), *The Six Wives of Henry VIII* (1992) and *The Gunpowder Plot* (1996), for which she received the CWA Gold Dagger for best non-fiction. With her profound knowledge of history it would seem natural for AF to produce historical fiction but quite the contrary. Her only foray into fiction, is crime fiction, and features the very modern, highly independent, strongly feminist Jemima Shore, an investigative journalist with her own TV series. Shore's upbringing and her society connections, as well as her taste for mischief, allow her an access to and insight of a life beyond the understanding of everyday police detectives. The first book, for instance, *Quiet as a Nun* (TV serial, 1978), takes her back to her old school, the Convent of the Blessed Eleanor, to help solve a sudden death and mysterious apparitions. *The Wild Island* is also set in a closed world, that of a remote Scottish island, whilst *Oxford Blood* takes us into the Halls of Academe. The character, who was adapted for television in *Jemima Shore Investigates* (1983), with Shore portrayed superbly by Patricia Hodge, was ideally suited to the growing affluence, feminism and social climbing of the 1970s and 80s. Pressure of work on her historical books has prevented AF continuing the series though she plans to return.

Novels

Jemima Shore series: *Quiet as a Nun* (1977), *The Wild Island* (1978), *A Splash of Red* (1981), *Cool Repentance* (1982), *Oxford Blood* (1985), *Your Royal Heritage* (1987), *The Cavalier Case* (1990), *Political Death* (1994).

Short Stories. *Jemima Shore's First Case* (1986), *Jemima Shore at the Sunny Grave* (1991). Note: *Jemima Shore Investigates* (1983) is an anthology of stories from the TV series adapted by John Burke and Frances Heasman from stories by Simon BRETT, Anthony Skene, Tim Aspinall and others.

Full name: (Lady) Antonia Pakenham Fraser.

Where to start: *Jemima Shore's First Case*.

Awards: James Tait Black Memorial Prize for biography (1970), Wolfson Prize for history (1984), Prix Caumont-La-Force (1985), CWA Non-fiction Gold Dagger (1996), St Louis Literary Award (1996), Schlossbauverein Prize (1997).

Similar stuff: Lesley GRANT-ADAMSON's Rain Morgan and Lesley Flynn, P.D. JAMES's Cordelia Gray.

Final fact: To catch future plagiarists or copyists, and on the advice of a friend, AF shrewdly included an unconfirmable detail in her biography of Mary Queen of Scots when she wrote that at the Queen's execution Lord Shrewsbury wept, though she knows of no evidence for this.

Margaret Frazer US

MF began as the pseudonym of two writers, Gail Frazer (b. 1946), and Mary Monica PULVER (*see separate entry*). They met at the Society for Creative Anachronism. Mary had developed a plot for a novel set in a Benedictine priory in Oxfordshire in 15th century England, but she needed someone to help her with the historical detail. In the end Gail did more than that and it became a true collaboration. The series features Dame Frevisse who has skills in detection and deduction. In *The Novice's Tale*, set in 1431, she solves a crime of unholy passions within the priory, but later books take her beyond the priory's walls into the wider world. *The Servant's Tale*, which was shortlisted for an Edgar, even has Dame Frevisse seeking out a serial killer. In *The Bishop's Tale*, nominated for a Minnesota Book award, a man dares God to strike him down. When he dies Frevisse has to find out if death was by the hand of God or the hand of man. After six books Mary wanted to work on more contemporary mysteries and the Margaret Frazer alias passed wholly to Gail. Her first solo book, *The Prioress' Tale*, was also nominated for an Edgar. Gail has continued the series at one book a year and has also written several short stories. "Neither Pity, Love nor Fear", a poignant tale about the death of Henry VI, was awarded the Herodotus award as the year's best historical mystery short story.

Novels

Dame Frevisse series: *The Novice's Tale* (1992), *The Servant's Tale* (1993), *The Outlaw's Tale* (1994), *The Bishop's Tale* (1994), *The Boy's Tale* (1995), *The Murderer's Tale* (1996), *The Prioress' Tale* (1997), *The Maiden's Tale* (1998), *The Reeve's Tale* (1999), *The Squire's Tale* (2000), *The Clerk's Tale* (2002).

Awards: Herodotus, best historical short story (2000).
Website: <www.soncom.com/fenyx/index.htm>
Similar stuff: Ellis PETERS, Paul DOHERTY.
Final fact: Gail Frazer thinks she may have become a bit too immersed in the 1400s. Once, one of her sons, when he was small, started to ask a question, but then stopped, saying "Oh, never mind. That's after your time," and walked away.

Nicolas Freeling (b. 1927) UK

NF is a suitably cosmopolitan writer. Born in London, raised mostly in France, educated in England, Ireland and France, for the twelve years (1948–60) after serving in the RAF he worked in the hotel business throughout Europe. NF has become the master of the *roman policier*, somewhat in the style of Georges Simenon. He has created two police detectives. The best known is Piet Van der Valk who operates out of Amsterdam. Irascible and sceptical about bureaucracy and officialdom, Van der Valk is sympathetic to the victims of crime and has a degree of compassion for the young who find themselves in trouble. His years of experience and cynical views of the human condition help him in his dogged persistence to solve a crime. NF's own cynicism about the law is often vocalized through Van der Valk and the reader is taken deep into the inspector's philosophy and world-view. The first Van der Valk book was filmed as *Amsterdam Affair* (1968) but more people will remember the detective as portrayed by Barry Foster in three separate TV series (1972/3, 1977 and 1991/2). Key to the series is Van der Valk's French wife, Arlette, who is a gourmet cook and brings her own intuitive and logical views to his cases. NF felt he had taken the character far enough and in *A Long Silence* Van der Valk was killed. Arlette took up and solved the case. NF wrote two further books featuring Arlette, and brought Van der Valk back in a case early in his career in *Sand Castles*. Arlette also featured in a later novel, *Lady MacBeth*, with NF's new series character, Henri Castang. Castang is a French police detective who operates from Brussels. Like Van der Valk he has a foreign wife, Vera, who is Czech and has a strongly independent outlook on life. He is less bombastic and argumentative than Van der Valk but otherwise the cases are as detailed and distinctive, with a tangible European flavour. NF retired Castang in *A Dwarf Kingdom*, though as you'd expect, nothing ends simply. NF's non-series books should not be overlooked. They are deep psychological studies. *The Dresden Green* is about a compulsive murderer. Both *This is the Castle* and *Some Day Tomorrow* are explorations of the minds of criminals, whilst in *One More River* NF takes us deep into the past of the main character to find out why someone wants to kill him. NF's work is always original and challenging and makes the reader question the very nature of crime and of law and order.

Novels

Van der Valk series: *Love in Amsterdam* (1962; as *Death in Amsterdam*, US 1964), *Because of the Cats* (1963), *Gun Before Butter* (1963; as *Question of Loyalty*, US 1963), *Double-Barrel* (1964), *Criminal Conversation* (1965), *The King of the Rainy Country* (1966), *Strike Out Where Not Applicable* (1967), *Tsing-Boum!* (1969; as *Tsing-Boom!*, US 1969), *Over the High Side* (1971; as *The Lovely Ladies*, US 1971), *A Long Silence* (1972; as *Auprès de ma Blonde*, US 1972), *The Widow* (1979), *One Damn Thing After Another* (1981; as *Arlette*, 1981), *Sand Castles* (1989).

Henri Castang series: *A Dressing of Diamond* (1974), *What are the Bugles Blowing For?* (1975; as *The Bugles Blowing*, US 1976), *Lake Isle* (1976; as *Sabine*, US 1978), *The Night Lords* (1978), *Castang's City* (1980). *Wolfnight* (1982), *The Back of the North Wind* (1983), *No Part in Your Death* (1984), *A City Solitary* (1985), *Cold Iron* (1986), *Lady MacBeth* (1988), *Not as Far as Velma* (1989), *Those in Peril* (1990), *The Pretty How Town* (1992; as *Flanders Sky*, US 1992), *You Who Know*

(1993), *The Seacoast of Bohemia* (1995), *A Dwarf Kingdom* (1996).
Non-series: *Valparaiso* (1964, as by F.R.E. Nicolas but reprinted (1965) as Freeling), *The Dresden Green* (1966), *This is the Castle* (1968), *Gadget* (1977), *One More River* (1998), *Some Day Tomorrow* (2000), *The Janeites* (2002).
Non-fiction. *Criminal Convictions* (1994).

Pen-name: F.R.E. Nicolas.
Where to start: *Love in Amsterdam.*
Awards: Grand Prix de Littérature Policière Best Foreign (1965), Edgar, best novel (1967).
Similar stuff: A.C. BAANTJER, Georges Simenon, Jan WILLEM VAN DE WETERING.
Final fact: NF has written books about his days as a chef in *Kitchen Book* (1970).

Nicci French UK

NF is the pen-name of Nicci Gerrard (b. 1958) and her second husband Sean French (b. 1959). Both studied English at Oxford University and both are journalists, though they did not meet until 1990. Gerrard had taught English in the UK and US and edited her own short-lived magazine on art and literature, *Women's Review*, before taking on editorial roles at the *New Statesman* (where she met Sean) and later *The Observer*. Sean French was already a published author of biographies and non-crime novels before they combined their talents on a series of highly acclaimed psychological suspense novels. To some extent they are all books about hidden secrets and obsessions. *The Memory Game* explores the skeletons in the closet of the Martello family when the body of one of the daughters who vanished 25 years ago is found. In *Killing Me Softly* a young woman falls under the spell of a charismatic man and only begins to discover his past when it's too late. *Beneath the Skin* concerns three women, unknown to each other until they all receive threats from the same psychotic killer and struggle to understand the common link between them. Powerful though these books are the other two stand out. *The Safe House* concerns a female psychiatrist who opens a clinic for those suffering from post-traumatic disorders only to find her refuge threatened when the police bring her a girl who has survived a vicious attack and witnessed the murder of her parents. Likewise *The Red Room* deals with a police consultant psychologist facing her own fears and convictions during the investigation of a series of murders. Both are powerful studies of dilemma and psychological disintegration.

Novels. *The Memory Game* (1997), *The Safe House* (1998). *Killing Me Softly* (1999), *Beneath the Skin* (2000), *The Red Room* (2001).

Where to start: *The Memory Game* or *The Safe House*.
Website: <www.niccifrench.com>
Similar stuff: Clare FRANCIS, Tami HOAG, Ruth RENDELL as Barbara Vine.
Final fact: *The Safe House* owes some inspiration to Nicci's first job working with

emotionally disturbed children in a children's home in Sheffield. She found the work deeply distressing because she "loved the children too much".

Kinky Friedman (b. 1944) US

KF is a chip off the new block, writing like someone who didn't know he was breaking all the rules and creating a whole new set instead. Although he hails from Texas, where throughout the seventies he headed a country-music band called The Texas Jewboys, he bases his novels in New York. Friedman himself is the lead character in the books, a musician turned detective who lives with his cat in a loft in Greenwich Village. He has created an almost Holmesian atmosphere around modern-day New York and even has a gang of guys, the Village Irregulars. Friedman brings real friends and characters into his books and frequently real incidents from his life. With KF it's the journey that's the fun not the destination and in all his books you are off on a wild adventure with no real concern where you will arrive. The books have basic plots but reel and weave all over the place as KF follows his anarchic muse. They read like Frank Zappa out of Alexei Sayle. Occasionally KF leaves New York. In *Frequent Flyer* the death of an old friend takes KF on a rampage through the jungles of Borneo, where he operated with the Peace Corps from 1966–68. *Armadillos and Old Lace* finds KF in small-town Texas looking into the deaths of several old ladies. In *Steppin' on a Rainbow* KF is in Hawaii in search of a missing friend. Wherever you encounter KF you will delight in his homespun philosophies, his fun with the language and his goonish imagery, and somewhere en route you may even solve a mystery.

Novels

Kinky Friedman series: *Greenwich Killing Time* (1986), *A Case of Lone Star* (1987), *When the Cat's Away* (1988), *Frequent Flyer* (1989), *Musical Chairs* (1991), *Elvis, Jesus and Coca Cola* (1993), *Armadillos and Old Lace* (1994), *God Bless John Wayne* (1995), *The Love Song of J. Edgar Hoover* (1996), *Road Kill* (1997), *Blast from the Past* (1998), *Spanking Watson* (1999), *Mile High Club* (2000), *Steppin' on a Rainbow* (2001).

The first three books were issued in the UK in one volume as *The Kinky Friedman Crime Club* (1992; as *Three Complete Mysteries*, US 1993) and the next three books as *More Kinky Friedman* (1993).

Full name: Richard Friedman.
Pen-name: Kinky Friedman
Website: <www.kinkyfriedman.com>
Similar stuff: Sandra SCOPPETTONE for another Greenwich Village detective; Mike RIPLEY for the music and humour.
Final fact: KF became interested in writing after he became a 15-minute hero by rescuing a young woman from a mugger with a knife in Greenwich Village.

Dale Furutani (b. 1946) US/Japanese

For someone who has been writing mysteries for little more than five years DF has made a significant impact. His first book won the Anthony and Macavity awards — he was the first Asian-American to win such awards and to write about an Asian-American detective. He has also been invited to speak at the Library of Congress and the Japanese American National Museum. Born on Hawaii to Japanese parents, DF was raised in Los Angeles amongst adoptee parents and has worked in marketing and IT in the car industry. *Death in Little Tokyo* is about unemployed computer programmer Ken Tanaka who is mistaken as a real PI when he poses as one at a mystery club gathering. He goes along with it only to find himself a suspect in a Japanese Mafia killing. DF wrote a second Tanaka mystery but has since concentrated on a trilogy set in 17th-century Japan. This features Matsuyama Kaze, an unaffiliated samurai who is searching for the missing daughter of his Lord. The quest spans over three books but in each volume Kaze becomes involved in a specific mystery. The books are both intriguing action-packed mysteries and authentic recreations of a turbulent time in Japanese history.

Novels

Ken Tanaka series: *Death in Little Tokyo* (1996), *The Toyotomi Blades* (1997).
Samurai trilogy: *Death at the Crossroads* (1998), *Jade Place Vendetta* (1999), *Kill the Shogun* (2000).

Where to start: Either *Death in Little Tokyo* or *Death at the Crossroads.*
Awards: Anthony and Macavity, best first novel (1997).
Website: <members.aol.com/Dfurutani/>
Similar stuff: Laura Joh ROWLAND.
Final fact: DF's mother was in Pearl Harbor during the Japanese attack in December 1941 and witnessed it from across the bay.

Frances Fyfield (b. 1948) UK

FF is a practising criminal lawyer who has worked as a prosecutor with the Metropolitan Police and Crime Prosecution Service. The success of her writing means she now puts in less hours as a criminal prosecutor, but still keeps a finger on the pulse. Her first book, *A Question of Guilt* (filmed TV 1993) introduced Crown Prosecutor Helen West and Detective Superintendent Geoffrey Bailey of New Scotland Yard. It's an inverted mystery in that the guilty party is known early on but the problem is finding the evidence to convict her. This brings West and Bailey together and starts a relationship that is tested by the pressures and conflicts of their work. FF is more interested in why a crime is committed and the books, all except *Trial by Fire*, usually identify the criminal at the outset and concentrate on the motive. The first book was nominated for the Edgar, Anthony and Agatha awards, the second won the CWA Rumpole award, whilst the third, *Deep Sleep*, a fascinating study in method and deduction, received the CWA Silver Dagger. The West books have been developed for TV (2002) with Amanda Burton in the title rôle. FF has also written an occasional series about lawyer Sarah Fortune, a deeply complex individual, still troubled after the death of her unfaithful husband. Sarah's often too carefree and amoral actions lead her into dangerous territory and this series is at times truly harrowing and more suspenseful than the West novels. It is closer to the psychological suspense novels FF has written under her own name, Frances Hegarty. Almost all of FF's books revolve around relationships, particularly women in danger from obsessive men. In the Hegarty books these relationships may be more poignant or subtle. It may be between two people with a similar interest as in *Half Light*, the volatility between a woman and her ageing mother in *Let's Dance*, or the fractured trust between a married couple when the husband suspects one of their children is not his, in *The Playroom*. FF's books are powerful, even disturbing, but always realistic. A.N. Wilson called her "much the best crime writer alive in Britain."

Novels
Helen West series: *A Question of Guilt* (1988), *Trial by Fire* (1990; as *Not That Kind of Place*, US 1990), *Deep Sleep* (1991), *Shadow Play* (1993), *A Clear Conscience* (1994), *Without Consent* (1996).
Sarah Fortune series: *Shadows on the Mirror* (1989), *Perfectly Pure and Good* (1994), *Staring at the Light* (1999).
Non-series: *Blind Date* (1998), *Undercurrents* (2000), *The Nature of the Beast* (2001).
as Frances Hegarty: *The Playroom* (1991), *Half Light* (1992), *Let's Dance* (1995).

Real name: Frances Hegarty.
Pen-name: Frances Fyfield.
Where to start: *A Question of Guilt.*
Awards: CWA Rumpole Award (1990), CWA Silver Dagger (1991), Grand Prix de Littérature Policière Best Foreign (1998).
Similar stuff: Ruth RENDELL (as Barbara Vine), Minette WALTERS.
Final fact: FF has also presented a short radio series, *Footprints* (2002), which looks at real life investigations and research, such as tracing missing people.

Nick Gaitano *pseudonym, see* Eugene Izzi

Brian Garfield (b. 1939) US

Just as Robert BLOCH could never escape being remembered as "the author of *Psycho*", so BG's name is immortalized as "the author of *Death Wish*". In fact more people remember the film (1974), directed by Michael Winner and starring Charles Bronson as Paul Kersey (renamed from Paul

Benjamin in the book), whose wife and daughter have been attacked by three hoodlums and subsequently die. He goes after the gang and thereafter becomes a self-appointed vigilante and local hero, taking on muggers and thugs. BG disowned the film for glorifying violence and had nothing to do with its four sequels. He wrote his own sequel, *Death Sentence*, which showed Benjamin's fall from "grace" into his own personal hell. Dismayed at the misinterpretation of his book, he subsequently wrote an unconnected novel, *Recoil*, in which, when a witness protection programme fails, its hero defeats a Mafia don without any violence (aside from blackmail and kidnapping). A pseudonymous novel, *Fear in a Handful of Dust* (filmed 1984 as *Fleshburn*), also shows how four people can survive the vengeance of a psychotic by their own wits without violence. BG has been a prolific writer. He sold his first novel, *Range Justice*, in 1960 and that and the next 20 or so were all westerns, mostly written under pen-names. He was in danger of becoming a hack writer until he branched out in the mid-sixties, and thereafter he never thought of himself as a genre writer, other than under the broad head of "thrillers". His output included gangster novels like *The Hit*, modern-day westerns such as *Relentless* (filmed TV 1977) and its sequel, featuring part Navajo State Trooper Sam Watchman, wartime adventures such as *The Paladin*, and political thrillers such as *Deep Cover*, *Line of Succession* and *The Romanov Succession*. Several of these books fall into the espionage category, of which the best is *Hopscotch*, which won the Edgar award. The book is about an ex-CIA agent who is forcibly retired and decides to take his revenge by writing his autobiography whilst the CIA do their best to stop him. When Garfield adapted it into the film *Hopscotch* (1981) with Bryan Forbes, they converted it into a more lighthearted spy spoof. BG also wrote a series of stories about agent Charlie Dark collected as *Checkpoint Charlie*.

Novels

Non-series: *The Last Bridge* (1966), *The Villiers Touch* (1970), *The Hit* (1970), *What of Terry Coniston?* (1971), *Deep Cover* (1971), *Line of Succession* (1972), *Tripwire* (1973), *Kolchak's Gold* (1974), *The Romanov Succession* (1974), *Hopscotch* (1975), *Recoil* (1977), *The Paladin* (1980), *Necessity* (1984), *Manifest Destiny* (1989).

Sam Watchman series: *Relentless* (1972), *The Threepersons Hunt* (1974).

Paul Benjamin series: *Death Wish* (1972), *Death Sentence* (1975).

as John Ives: *Fear in a Handful of Dust* (1977; as *Fear*, UK 1978), *The Marchand Woman* (1979).

as Drew Mallory: *Target Manhattan* (1975).

as Frank O'Brian: *The Rimfire Murders* (1962).

with Donald E. Westlake: *Gangway!* (1973).

Short Stories. *Checkpoint Charlie* (1981), *Suspended Sentences* (1993).

Editor. *I, Witness: True Personal Encounters with Crime by Members of the Mystery Writers of America* (1978), *The Crime of My Life: Favorite Stories by Presidents of the Mystery Writers of America* (1984).

Full name: Brian Francis Wynne Garfield.
Pen-names: Bennett Garland, Alex Hawk, John Ives, Drew Mallory, Frank O'Brian, Jonas Ward, Brian Wynne.
Where to start: *Hopscotch* or *Recoil.*
Awards: Edgar, best novel (1976), Swedish Academy of Detection, Best Foreign (1979).
Similar stuff: Tony HILLERMAN and Alanna KNIGHT for other Navajo detectives, Andrew VACHSS, Joe GORES *A Time of Predators* for revenge.
Final fact: BG was driven to write *Death Wish* when he was surprised at the violence of his own reaction when vandals slashed the cloth top of his car.

Joe Gash *pseudonym, see* Bill Granger

Jonathan Gash (b. 1933) UK

One of the more delightful characters to emerge in modern crime fiction is the shady antiques dealer Lovejoy. Lovejoy and his cronies operate in East Anglia and don't mind which side of the law they are on. Lovejoy has his own code of honour but it's mostly related to his desire for women and his genuine love of antiques. He is a "divvie", someone who can "divine" genuine antiques, though he can also create his own "antiques" and both skills are often in demand by others. Each book follows a fairly standard plot, a formula that works and which readers anticipate. Lovejoy is usually in search of something rare and precious (duelling pistols in *The Judas Pair*, Roman gold coins in *Gold by Gemini*, even the Holy Grail in *The Grail Tree*), either for himself or on behalf of a woman, and encounters opposition, either the law or someone more dangerous. Lovejoy often has to fight his way out of difficult corners, though never at the cost of an antique. He is one of those rogues we can despise for his lifestyle but admire for his passions. He was admirably portrayed by Ian McShane in the long-running TV series *Lovejoy*. One can be forgiven for assuming that JG is himself an antiques dealer, so profound is his expertise in the novels. In fact he is a qualified physician and worked for many years as a pathologist and microbiologist until his semi-retirement in 1988. He has put his professional background to use in his new series featuring Dr Clare Burtonall. Though married, in *Different Women Dancing* she becomes suspicious of her husband's business practices when she witnesses a hit-and-run accident. Combining forces with another witness, Bonn, who turns out to be a male escort, Burtonall and Bonn investigate the matter themselves. JG has written one suspense novel, *The Incomer*, as Graham Gaunt, which studies the effect in an East Anglian village when a murderer, whose conviction is overturned through a technicality, returns home. JG has also written an historical family saga with some element of mystery as Jonathan Grant.

Novels

Lovejoy series: *The Judas Pair* (1977), *Gold from Gemini* (1978; as *Gold by Gemini*, US 1979), *The Grail Tree* (1979), *Spend Game* (1980), *The Vatican Rip* (1981), *Firefly Gadroon* (1982), *The Sleepers of Erin* (1983), *The Gondola Scam* (1983), *Pearlhanger* (1985), *The Tartan Ringers* (1986; as *The Tartan Shell*, US 1986), *Moonspender* (1986), *Jade Woman* (1988), *The Very Last Gambado* (1989), *The Great California Game* (1990), *The Lies of Fair Ladies* (1992), *Paid and Loving Eyes* (1993), *The Sin Within Her Smile* (1993), *The Grace in Older Women* (1995), *The Possessions of a Lady* (1996), *The Rich and the Profane* (1998), *A Rag, a Bone and a Hank of Hair* (1999), *Every Last Cent* (2001).
Dr Clare Burtonall series: *Different Women Dancing* (1997), *Prey Dancing* (1998), *Die Dancing* (2000), *Bone Dancing* (2002).
as Graham Gaunt: *The Incomer* (1981).
as Jonathan Grant: *The Shores of Sealandings* (1991), *Storms at Sealandings* (1992), *Mehala, Lady of Sealandings* (1993).

Real name: John Grant.
Pen-names: Jonathan Gash, Graham Gaunt.
Where to start: *The Judas Pair*.
Awards: CWA John Creasey Memorial Award (1977).
Website: (unofficial) <www.frii.com/~saunders/gash.htm>
Similar stuff: Kyril BONFIGLIOLI's Mortdecai series.
Final fact: JG devised his penname from the Cockney or Romany slang word "gash", which means worthless.

Graham Gaunt *pseudonym, see* Jonathan Gash

Anne George (1928–2001) US

AG was a former schoolteacher who lived in Birmingham, Alabama, and had never lived anywhere other than Alabama. Hence it's the setting for her light-hearted murderous romps featuring two 60-something sisters, who are otherwise totally dissimilar. The elder, Mary Alice, is tall, overweight, and a three-times rich widow. Patricia is half Mary's weight, short, and still happily married after 40 years. She tries to be the eloquent Southern lady, but both act outrageously to outdo each other. In their first adventure, *Murder on a Girls' Night Out*, which won an Agatha award, Mary decides to buy the local bar but Patricia disagrees and both have second thoughts when they find a body in the bar's wishing well. Each novel pits the two sisters against each other as they try and solve increasingly bizarre murders. In the eighth novel, where Mary is about to marry a fourth time, they investigate the death of an Elvis impersonator at a contest. All good-humoured Southern comfort. AG has also written a saga spanning five decades of an Alabaman family with its own elements of sinister suspense, *This One and Magic Life* (1999).

Novels

Southern Sisters series: *Murder on a Girls' Night Out* (1996), *Murder on a Bad Hair*

Day (1996), *Murder Runs in the Family* (1997), *Murder Makes Waves* (1997), *Murder Gets a Life* (1998), *Murder Shoots the Bull* (1999), *Murder Carries a Torch* (2000), *Murder Boogies With Elvis* (2001).

Full name: Anne Carroll George
Where to start: *Murder on a Girl's Night Out*
Awards: Agatha, best first novel (1997).
Similar stuff: Dorothy CANNELL and Barbara Taylor MCCAFFERTY for other investigative sisters.
Final fact: AG was Alabama's State Poet and her collection, *Some of It is True* (1993) was nominated for a Pulitzer prize.

Elizabeth George (b. 1949) US

Although EG has lived all her life in America, mostly in California, where she was a High School teacher for nearly fourteen years (1974–87), she has chosen to set her crime novels in England, where she feels the landscape and sense of history are stronger. All of her novels feature a strong cast of lead characters. Inspector Thomas Lynley of Scotland Yard is, by descent, the Earl of Asherton. His close friend is forensic pathologist Simon Allcourt-St. James, who is now disabled after an accident in a car driven by the drunken Lynley. Simon's wife is Deborah and his laboratory assistant is Lady Helen Clyde, who becomes Lynley's lady friend and later wife. Into this tight group comes Lynley's newly assigned sergeant Barbara Havers who is a complete contrast. She has worked her way up through the ranks and despises the English aristocracy and the old-school network. The series thus provides scope for considerable conflict between the characters, which develops with each book and in turn helps fuel the investigations. EG works on a large canvas – each book is anywhere up to 700 pages – with detailed plots and intense characterization. The first book, *A Great Deliverance*, is set in Yorkshire and, on the face of it, has a straightforward but frightening murder of a father by a daughter, but as Lynley and Havers dig deeper so the family skeletons emerge. The book had an overwhelming reception. It won the Anthony and Agatha awards, was nominated for an Edgar and Macavity, and also won the prestigious French Grand Prix de Littérature Policière – rare for a first novel. The series gained an instant readership, which has grown. Although the crimes may fit into the traditional English mould – there's even a locked-room puzzle in *Payment in Blood* – the telling is far from traditional. The eighth book, *In the Presence of the Enemy*, hit the national bestseller lists for eight weeks and firmly established her as a major writer, a welcome reward for the months of painstaking effort she puts in to developing and plotting each book. EG has written one story about Lynley, 'The Evidence Exposed', included in a collection under that title, plus a non-series neo-gothic suspense novella, *Remember, I'll Always Love You.*

Novels

Thomas Lynley series: *A Great Deliverance* (1988), *Payment in Blood* (1989), *Well-Schooled in Murder* (1990), *A Suitable Vengeance* (1991), *For the Sake of Elena* (1992), *Missing Joseph* (1993), *Playing for the Ashes* (1994), *In the Presence of the Enemy* (1996), *Deception on His Mind* (1997), *In Pursuit of the Proper Sinner* (1999), *A Traitor to Memory* (2001).

Non-series: *Remember, I'll Always Love You* (2001).

Short Stories. *The Evidence Exposed* (1999; rev'd *I, Richard* 2001).

Full name: Susan Elizabeth George.

Where to start: *A Great Deliverance.*

Awards: Agatha and Anthony, best first novel (both 1989), Grand Prix de Littérature Policière (1990).

Website: <www.elizabethgeorgeonline.com>

Similar stuff: Deborah CROMBIE, Faye KELLERMAN.

Final fact: EG was fired from her first teaching job because of union activity, but in her next post she was selected as Orange County Teacher of the Year for her work with remedial students.

Michael Gilbert (b. 1912) UK

MG is the complete and consummate all-rounder in English crime fiction. In addition to over 30 novels and several hundred short stories he has written plays for the theatre, radio and television, compiled books on interesting legal cases, and assembled books on criminology. A reading of all MG's works would leave you well versed in both the breadth and depth of English law as well as providing a copybook course in the art and craft of writing. A solicitor, rising to partner in a major London law firm, MG began writing in 1938 but the War intervened and MG's first book, *Close Quarters*, a locked-room mystery in Cathedral precincts, did not appear until 1947. It introduced Chief Inspector Hazlerigg, a rather stolid, colourless detective who goes into everything in fine detail. These books are a legacy of the Golden Age, a throwback to Freeman Wills Croft, and are a product of their age, with much emphasis on black marketeering. The series produced one certain classic, *Smallbone Deceased*, in which the remains of a law firm's client are found in a deed box. Hazlerigg works with a new member of the firm, Henry Bohun, to solve the case. Bohun, who suffers from para-insomnia and has an excess of energy, reappears in several short stories that were not collected in bookform until twenty years later, as *Stay of Execution*. MG had a delightful habit of reintroducing characters from one series into another so that although most of his novels are stand-alones, there is a feeling of homogeneity, uniting them as a single (and quite outstanding) body of work. His other main continuing character is Scotland Yard officer Patrick Petrella, another methodical detective who, over a long series of short stories and two novels has risen through the ranks to Detective Inspector and dealt with every crime imaginable, ultimately taking on organized crime in London's Docklands. MG specialized in the short story and amongst his most fascinating characters are Mr Calder and Mr Behrends, on the surface two quiet and reserved country gentlemen but in fact two very deadly and ruthless counterintelligent agents. Ellery Queen regarded *Game Without Rules* as one of 'the best volumes of spy stories ever written.'

A selection of just some of MG's non-series books shows the range of his material. His legal expertise emerges in two classic courtroom dramas: *Death Has Deep Roots* (filmed 1956 as *Guilty?* [US *Breakout*]), involving the French resistance and *The Queen against Karl Mullen*, about defending a framed but obnoxious South African secret policeman. During WW2 MG had been a prisoner-of-war and this served as the background for *Death in Captivity* (filmed 1959 as *Danger Within* [US *Blackout*]), which includes an 'impossible crime' about a body in an escape tunnel. He tackles the sordid subject of torture and murder at a public school in *The Night of the Twelfth*. *The Long Journey Home* is a frantic chase novel of a man pursued by various corporate nasties. *The Killing of Katie Steelstock* is one of his most polished and complicated murder mysteries, whilst *The Ninety-Second Tiger* shows that he can parody the whole set up with this spoof about a hack actor who plays a super-hero ends up as a bodyguard to an Arab politician. *Ring of Terror* is set just before the outbreak of WW1 and introduces police constable Luke Pagan who, because he can speak Russian, is involved in investigating an anarchist conspiracy. In the two subsequent novels, set during the War, Pagan is transferred to military intelligence.

MG's work has changed with the times and on every occasion remains the standard against which all other works are measured. One of the founding members of the CWA, MG was honoured by the Association with the Diamond Dagger in 1994. He was also made a Grand Master by the MWA and received the CBE in 1980.

Novels

Inspector Hazlerigg series: *Close Quarters* (1947), *They Never Looked Inside* (1948; as *He Didn't Mind Danger*, US 1949), *The Doors Open* (1949), *Smallbone Deceased* (1950), *Death Has Deep Roots* (1951), *Fear to Tread* (1953).
Patrick Petrella series: *Blood and Judgment* (1959), *Roller-Coaster* (1993).
Knott & Mercer series: *The Body of a Girl* (1972), *Death of a Favourite Girl* (1980; as *The Killing of Katie Steelstock*, US 1980).
Luke Pagan series: *Ring of Terror* (1995), *Into Battle* (1997), *Over and Out* (1998).
Non-series: *Death in Captivity* (1952; as *The Danger Within*, US 1952), *Sky High* (1955; as *The Country-House Burglar*, 1955), *Be Shot for Sixpence* (1956), *After the Fine Weather* (1963), *The Crack in the Teacup* (1966), *The Dust and the Heat* (1967; as *Overdrive*, US 1968), *The Etruscan Net* (1969; as *The Family Tomb*, US 1970), *The Ninety-Second Tiger* (1973), *Flash Point* (1974), *The Night of the Twelfth* (1976), *The Empty House* (1978), *The Final Throw* (1982; as *End-Game*, US 1982), *The Black Seraphim* (1983), *The Long Journey Home* (1985), *Trouble* (1987), *Paint, Gold and Blood* (1989), *The Queen Against Karl Mullen* (1991).

Short Stories
Calder & Behrens series: *Game Without Rules* (1967), *Mr Calder and Mr Behrens* (1982), *The Road to Damascus* (1990).
Patrick Petrella series: *Petrella at Q* (1977), *Young Petrella* (1988).
Jonas Pickett series: *Anything for a Quiet Life* (1990).
Fearne & Bracknell series: *The Mathematics of Murder* (2000).
Non-series: *Stay of Execution* (1971), *Amateur in Violence* (1973), *The Man Who Hated Banks* (1997), *The Curious Conspiracy* (2002).
Plays. *A Clean Kill* (1960), *The Bargain* (1961), *The Shot in Question* (1963), *Windfall* (1963).
Non-fiction. *Dr Crippen* (1953), *The Claimant* (1957), *The Law* (1977), *The Fraudsters* (1987).
Editor. *Crime in Good Company* (1959), *The Oxford Book of Legal Anecdotes* (1986).

Full name: Michael Francis Gilbert.
Where to start: *Smallbone Deceased.*
Awards: Grand Prix de Littérature Policière Best Foreign (1955), Swedish Academy of Detection, Grand Master (1981), MWA Grand Master (1987), Anthony, lifetime achievement (1990), CWA Diamond Dagger (1994).
Similar stuff: Martin EDWARDS, Roy LEWIS and M.R.D. MEEK for investigative solicitors.
Final fact: Amongst MG's clients in his law firm was Raymond Chandler, whose will MG helped prepare.

B.M. Gill (b. 1921) UK

A change of name followed by a change of publisher was what was Welsh author BMG needed to bring her work a wider appreciation. She sold her first novel, *Stranger at the Door*, in 1967. This and its immediate successors were romantic suspense novels under the names Margaret Blake and Barbara Gilmour for the publisher Robert Hale, which specializes in books for libraries. Ten years later, BMG assumed her new name and after an uncharacteristic political thriller, *Target Westminster*, she found a new publisher with Hodder & Stoughton, which in turn brought a deal with the US publisher, Scribner. As a result her next book, *Death Drop*, where a father goes in search of his son's murderer, was nominated for an Edgar award. Each of BMG's books are refreshingly different. They may not always be successful but at least BMG refused to be trapped in a rut. Her three novels featuring Detective Chief Inspector Tom Maybridge are good examples. Maybridge is a quiet, unassuming detective who works his way through his investigations but does not take centre stage. BMG concentrates on the crime and its effects. In *Victims* it's a chilling account of a series of murders in a hospital. *Seminar for Murder* is slightly more light-hearted, involving a murder at a crime writers' convention. *The Fifth Rapunzel* is an emotional study of a teenager whose parents are killed in a car crash. Of her non-series books the most intriguing is *The Twelfth Juror*, which was also nominated for an Edgar and won the CWA Gold

Dagger. It's a courtroom drama with an emphasis on the jury, one of whom has ulterior motives. *Nursery Crimes*, a brutal black comedy about a young girl who is a compulsive murderer, earned BMG another Edgar nomination. With her later novels BMG was moving away from the crime deeper into character studies, much in the vein of Ruth RENDELL's Barbara Vine stories. Her work should be better known for its originality and scope.

Novels

Tom Maybridge series: *Victims* (1980; as *Suspect*, 1981), *Seminar for Murder* (1985), *The Fifth Rapunzel* (1991).

Non-series: *Target Westminster* (1977), *Death Drop* (1979), *The Twelfth Juror* (1984), *Nursery Crimes* (1986), *Dying to Meet You* (1988), *Time and Time Again* (1990).

as Margaret Blake: *Stranger at the Door* (1967), *Bright Sun, Dark Shadow* (1968), *The Rare and the Lovely*, *The Elusive Exile* (1971), *Flight from Fear* (1973), *Courier to Danger* (1973), *Apple of Discord* (1975), *Walk Softly and Beware* (1977).

Real name: Barbara Margaret Trimble
Pen-names: Margaret Blake, B.M. Gill, Barbara Gilmour
Where to start: *Death Drop*.
Awards: CWA Gold Dagger (1984).
Similar stuff: Frances FYFIELD, Ruth RENDELL as Barbara Vine.
Final fact: Before she retired to write BMG had been a schoolteacher and a chiropodist.

Bartholomew Gill (b. 1943) US

BG is an Irish American, who gained his master's degree from Trinity College, Dublin and now lives in New Jersey. He has held a variety of jobs, including a speech-writer, insurance investigator and teacher but has, to all intents, been a full-time writer since 1971. He wrote two non-crime books under his own name before adopting the alias BG to write a crime novel set in Ireland. It features Chief Superintendent Peter McGarr, head of Ireland's Special Crimes Unit, with his headquarters in Dublin and involves an investigation into a yacht club and allegations of gun-running. Any books set in Ireland have to recognize the troubles in Ulster, but BG also knows that life must go on, so these issues are woven into the fabric of life, not placed at the forefront. The first two novels were workmanlike though nothing special but BG steadily developed the character and the series was noticed. As it progressed so the plots became more complex, the characters deeper. In *McGarr and the Method of Descartes* he tackles the IRA issue head on with a plot to assassinate the Rev. Ian Paisley. *McGarr and the Legacy of a Woman Scorned* has the history of Ireland, especially the problem over land ownership, as key to its plot. BG avoids religion in most of the novels, though it rears its head in *McGarr at the Dublin Horse Show* and is the main element in *The Death of an Irish*

Sinner, which involves a fanatical cult. Both *The Death of the Joyce Scholar*, which was shortlisted for an Edgar award, and *Death of an Ardent Bibliophile* are literary puzzles. The one anomaly in the series is McGarr's young wife, who is far too closely involved in the investigations than would seem likely, but otherwise the series is commendable for its portrayal of crime investigation in such a troubled country. BG has written three thrillers under his own name of which *White Rush, Green Fire*, about a calamitous drug deal, best complements BG's other work.

Novels

Peter McGarr series: *McGarr and the Politician's Wife* (1977; as *The Death of an Irish Politician*, 2000), *McGarr and the Sienese Conspiracy* (1977), *McGarr on the Cliffs of Moher* (1978), *McGarr at the Dublin Horse Show* (1980), *McGarr and the P.M. of Belgrave Square* (1983), *McGarr and the Method of Descartes* (1984), *McGarr and the Legacy of a Woman Scorned* (1986), *The Death of the Joyce Scholar* (1989), *The Death of Love* (1992), *Death on a Cold, Wild River* (1993), *Death of an Ardent Bibliophile* (1995), *Death of an Irish Seawolf* (1996), *Death of an Irish Tinker* (1997), *The Death of an Irish Lover* (2000), *The Death of an Irish Sinner* (2001).
as Mark McGarrity: *A Passing Advantage* (1980), *Neon Caesar* (1989), *White Rush, Green Fire* (1991).

Real name: Mark McGarrity.
Pen-name: Bartholomew Gill.
Where to start: *McGarr and the Legacy of a Woman Scorned.*
Similar stuff: John BRADY.
Final fact: McGarrity took his pen-name from his mother's father, Bartholomew Gill, whilst the Peter McGarr pseudonym came from his father's father, Peter McGarrity.

E. X. Giroux (b. 1924) Canada

US-born Canadian author Doris Shannon was in her forties before she turned to writing. Having been a bank clerk until 1949 she then raised two daughters and it was only in the late sixties that she began writing and after eight years' dogged persistence her first book appeared. These early novels, under her married name, are a mixture of historical romance, horror and suspense. *The Whispering Runes* is about a young widow haunted by death. *The Punishment* is pure gothic set in a converted lighthouse with a sinister family. *Little Girls Lost* is a thriller about three women in a small town who vanish. Then she revised one of her earliest unpublished books, *A Death for Adonis*, which appeared under a version of her maiden name. The novel is about retired London barrister Robert Forsythe and his secretary Abigail 'Sandy' Sanderson. Forsythe is asked by a woman to reinvestigate a 25-year old murder for which she believes her father, now dead, was wrongly accused and imprisoned. The case raises questions over the law and justice and causes Forsythe to return to his law practice. The case also raises Forsythe's profile and thereafter he is frequently asked to help on difficult or unsolved cases. Quite often it is

Sandy who does the investigation and Forsythe the deductions. It's an entertaining series with engaging characters and intriguing plots. EXG wrapped it up in *A Death for a Dodo* where Forsythe, recuperating from an accident, finds his fellow patients each have unsolved murders in their past. Thereafter EXG returned to her gothic suspense novels with *The Dying Room*.

Novels

Forsythe & Sanderson series: *A Death for Adonis* (1984), *A Death for a Darling* (1985), *A Death for a Dancer* (1986), *A Death for a Doctor* (1986), *A Death for a Dilletante* (1987), *A Death for a Dietician* (1988), *A Death for a Dreamer* (1989), *A Death for a Double* (1990), *A Death for a Dancing Doll* (1991), *A Death for a Dodo* (1993).

Non-series: *The Dying Room* (1993).

as Doris Shannon: *The Whispering Runes* (1972), *The Punishment* (1980), *Little Girls Lost* (1981), *Family Money* (1984).

Real name: Doris Shannon (*née* Giroux).
Pen-name: E.X. Giroux.
Where to start: *A Death for Adonis*.
Similar stuff: Ann Fallon, M.R.D. MEEK, Sara Woods.
Final fact: EXG's pen-name means just what it says: "ex-Giroux".

Leslie Glass US

LG is the bestselling author of a series featuring first generation Chinese-American Detective Sergeant April Woo who operates in New York's Upper West Side. LG is not Chinese but grew up in the Bronx with a Chinese family and feels a strong attachment to their culture. A frequent contributor to *Cosmopolitan* and *Red Book* magazines, LG also wrote the "Intelligencer" column for the *New York Magazine* and completed two popular mainstream novels, *Getting Away With It* (1976) and *Modern Love* (1983) before she turned to crime fiction. Her first crime novel was *To Do No Harm*, about a coke addict who becomes involved in kidnapping and murder. She followed this with the first of the April Woo books, *Burning Time*. LG fills the books with aspects of the many cultures that live in New York. Woo's former supervisor, with whom she is romantically involved, is a Mexican-American. Woo is herself hampered by her upbringing because of the normal submissiveness and vulnerability of women in Chinese culture, and this aspect is reflected through Woo's mother. LG has included a psychoanalyst, Dr Jason Frank, to cast an alternate perspective upon matters. Although the cases revolve around murder (usually several) the plots are complex, raising many cultural and social issues. For example, *Loving Time* explores malpractice in a mental institution; *Stealing Time* deals with racial issues and abandoned babies. LG is involved in several forensic and psychologic projects, and is founder of the Glass Foundation for research into criminal justice and mental health. She is also the only mystery author to serve as a Trustee of the New York City Police Foundation.

Novels
April Woo series: *Burning Time* (1993), *Hanging Time* (1995), *Loving Time* (1996), *Judging Time* (1998), *Stealing Time* (1999), *Tracking Time* (2000), *The Silent Bride* (2002).
Non-series: *To Do No Harm* (1990).

Where to start: *Burning Time.*
Awards: German Marlowe (2001).
Website: <www.aprilwoo.com>
Similar stuff: S.J. Rozan for another Chinese American detective.
Final fact: The Woo series began because LG wanted to write about psychiatrists who could change their patient's lives but realized she needed a detective to help develop the plot.

John Godey (b. 1912) US

Morton Freedgood has written books under his own name and with his brother as Stanley Morton but all of his crime thrillers are published as John Godey. He is best known for the tense thriller *The Taking of Pelham One Two Three* (filmed 1974), about four terrorists who hijack a New York subway train and hold the passengers to ransom. Although this recognition came towards the end of a long career it saw JG at his most polished and, indeed, his next book, *The Talisman*, though not so well known, is an equally powerful novel about terrorists who steal the remains of the Unknown Soldier. His later books, especially *Fatal Beauty* are all set on the grand thriller scale. JG had been selling stories to *Collier's* and *Good Housekeeping* since the mid-forties and, like his first two novels, these told more personal tales, with individuals as unwitting victims. *The Blue Hour*, for example, finds Henry Calvert's life spiralling out of control in some Woolrichian nightmare, whilst *This Year's Death* is about a woman doctor in love with a fugitive from the law. Over the next twenty years JG's output diminished while he worked as a public relations agent in the film industry. From this middle phase comes *The Fifth House*, where an investigative reporter looks into a hit-and-run accident. Drawing on his movie interests, JG's next two novels featured small-time actor Jack Albany who is mistaken for a Mafia hit-man and is given a new assignment. JG injects much humour into Albany's bungling, a rôle ideally suited to Dick Van Dyke in the film *Never a Dull Moment* (1968). *The Three Worlds of Johnny Handsome* (filmed 1989 as *Johnny Handsome*) is a change of pace and marks the start of JG's final phase of writing. Handsome is a disfigured criminal who has served his time and is given a new face through surgery. Handsome uses this opportunity to seek revenge on the man who framed him. JG may be thought of as a one-hit author but his other works show a resourceful writer.

Novels

Non-series: *The Gun and Mr Smith* (1947), *The Blue Hour* (1948; as *Killer at His Back*, 1955; as *The Next to Die*, UK 1975), *The Man in Question* (1951; as *The Blonde Betrayer*, 1955), *This Year's Death* (1953), *The Clay Assassin* (1959), *The Fifth House* (1960), *The Three Worlds of Johnny Handsome* (1972), *The Taking of Pelham One Two Three* (1973), *The Talisman* (1976), *The Snake* (1978), *Nella* (1981), *Fatal Beauty* (1984).

Jack Albany series: *The Reluctant Assassin* (UK 1966; as *A Thrill a Minute with Jack Albany*, US 1967), *Never Put Off Till Tomorrow What You Can Kill Today* (1970).

Autobiography. *The Crime of the Century and Other Misdemeanors* (1973).

Full name: Morton Freedgood.
Pen-names: John Godey, Stanley Morton.
Where to start: *The Blue Hour* or *The Talisman*.
Similar stuff: Warren ADLER, John LUTZ.

William Goldman (b. 1931) US

WG is one of those mainstream writers that every genre loves to claim, added to which he is also one of the most sought-after film screenwriters. WG's early books, from *The Temple of Gold* (1957) to *Father's Day* (1971) were coming-of-age novels and studies of relationships within families. The one exception was *No Way to Treat a Lady* (filmed 1968), about a serial killer who disguises himself as a woman. In 1963 WG's novel, *Soldier in the Rain* (1960), about a young army recruit trying to win the respect of his commanding officer was adapted for the screen and WG was invited to write a screenplay. WG chose to adapt Victor Canning's spy thriller *Masquerade* (filmed 1965), the first of over 20 films WG would write. His first success was his adaptation of Ross MACDONALD's *The Moving Target* as *Harper* (1966), but his name hit the headlines with his next work, an original screenplay about two desperadoes who escape to Bolivia when the law gets too close, *Butch Cassidy and the Sundance Kid* (1969). His script was originally turned down by most of the studios until 20th Century Fox took the gamble and director George Roy Hill turned it into one of the great blockbusters of the period. WG received an Oscar for his script. He would receive a second Oscar for his adaptation of *All the President's Men* (1976). During a lull in film projects in the early seventies, WG returned to novels and wrote two that would also be major hits when they were adapted for the screen [in fact three if you include his fairy tale fantasy *The Princess Bride* (1973; filmed 1987)]. *Marathon Man* (filmed 1976) is a complex thriller about a research student who becomes entangled with Nazi War criminals in New York, and includes the now famous dentist's torture scene. WG wrote a sequel, which continues the story of Scylla, the superspy, in the surprisingly neglected *Brothers*. *Magic* (filmed 1978) is the chilling story of a ventriloquist whose past comes to haunt him through his dummy. WG's one other novel of note is *Heat* (filmed

1987), about gambling and crime in Las Vegas. *Control* is a less successful and somewhat less believable thriller where reincarnation and time travel play their part in avenging a crime. WG has adapted other crime novels for the screen including *The Hot Rock* (1972), *Misery* (1990) and *Absolute Power* (1997). He has also written about his strong personal views of Hollywood in *Adventures in the Screen Trade* (1983), *Hype and Glory* (1990) and others.

Novels
Non-series: *No Way to Treat a Lady* (1964, originally as by Harry Longbaugh), *Magic* (1976), *Control* (1982), *Heat* (1985; as *Edged Weapons*, UK 1985).
Scylla series: *Marathon Man* (1974), *Brothers* (1986).
Published Screenplays. *Butch Cassidy and the Sundance Kid* (1969), *Four Screenplays with Essays: Marathon Man, Butch Cassidy and the Sundance Kid, The Princess Bride, Misery* (1994), *Five Screenplays with Essays: All the President's Men, Magic, Harper, Maverick, The Great Waldo Pepper* (1997).

Pen-name: Harry Longbaugh.
Where to start: *Magic*.
Awards: Academy Award, best screenplay (1970, 1977), Edgar, Best Motion Picture (1967, 1979), Laurel Award, lifetime achievement in screenwriting (1985).
Similar stuff: Robert L. FISH, Ira LEVIN.
Final fact: The dentist scene in *Marathon Man* was inspired by Goldman's childhood memory of going to a particular dentist who did not believe in using Novocaine.

Joe Gores (b. 1931) US

Others may write about P.I.s, but JG was one, for 12 years (1955–67 – with a break for military service and a year teaching boys English in Kenya). The experience proved valuable in his fiction – indeed it was while he was a P.I. that he sold his first story, "Chain Gang" (*Manhunt*, December 1957) and he has written around a hundred stories since. It was a hard apprenticeship. In one early year he received 300 rejection slips. It paid off, though. He won the Edgar award for "Goodbye Pops" (*EQMM*, 1969), a poignant story of a convict who escapes from prison in order to see his father one last time. With "The Mayfield Case" (*EQMM*, 1967), JG introduced the Dan Kearney Associates (DKA) P.I. agency. This was the first attempt by any writer at an authentic reconstruction of a P.I.'s job, albeit embellished for entertainment value. JG recalls that most of his work had been repossessing cars and that the P.I.s were more often than not called "repos". The DKA stories are collected as *Stakeout on Page Street*. JG did not immediately convert the series into a novel. His first book, the Edgar-winning *A Time of Predators*, presaged Brian GARFIELD's *Death Wish*, as it deals with a college professor who changes his beliefs and resorts to violence when his wife is gang-raped and subsequently kills herself. Then came his first DKA novel, *Dead Skip*, in which two of the agents go looking for a colleague's attacker. There have been four other DKA novels of which *32 Cadillacs*, which was short-listed for the Edgar, was highly praised. It's a wonderful caper and scam novel that is orchestrated like a grand symphony. Of his non-series books, JG's most ambitious was *Hammett* (filmed 1982). Although fictional it is a loving recreation of Hammett as both writer and detective (he had worked for the Pinkerton Agency until 1922) avenging the murder of a friend. In 1975 the producer of the *Kojak* series asked JG if he'd like to write for the show. JG's first *Kojak* script, "No Immunity for Murder" won an Edgar award. For most of the next twelve years JG worked on a number of TV series, including *Columbo* and *Mrs Columbo, The Gangster Chronicles, Magnum P.I.*, *Mickey Spillane's Mike Hammer*, *Remington Steele*, *T.J. Hooker* and *B.L. Stryker*. He also worked on several video screenplays including adapting his own novel *Interface* (video 1982). Since his return to writing novels, one of his best is the strongly autobiographical *Cases*, set in 1953, which follows its protagonist on a wild trip across America in an evocation of a long lost age.

Novels
DKA series: *Dead Skip* (1972), *Final Notice* (1973), *Gone, No Forwarding* (1978), *32 Cadillacs* (1992), *Contract Null and Void* (1996), *Cons, Scams and Grifts* (2001).
Non-series: *A Time for Predators* (1969), *Interface* (1974), *Hammett* (1975), *Come Morning* (1986), *Wolf Time* (1989), *Dead Man* (1993), *Menaced Assassin* (1994), *Cases* (1999).
Short Stories
DKA series: *Stakeout on Page Street* (2000).
Non-series: *Mostly Murder* (1992), *Speak of the Devil* (1999).
Editor. *Tricks and Treats*, with Bill PRONZINI (1976; as *Mystery Writers' Choice*, UK 1977).

Full name: Joseph Nicholas Gores.
Where to start: *Dead Skip*.
Awards: Edgar, best first novel (1970), best short story (1970), best TV segment (1976), Japanese Maltese Falcon (1986).
Similar stuff: Lawrence BLOCK, Donald E. WESTLAKE, Don WINSLOW.
Final fact: When he worked for a P.I. agency, JG had to repossess the car of a Mafia hit-man.

Ed Gorman (b. 1941) US

EG has been an astonishingly prolific writer since he turned full-time in 1989 after 20 years in advertising. Since then he has produced two to three books a year, several pseudonymously, written over a hundred short stories, edited many anthologies and co-founded and edited the news magazine of the mystery field, *Mystery Scene*. He has been dubbed the "Poet of Dark Suspense" and much of his work haunts that ill-defined land between horror and mystery where the emphasis is as much on fear and shock as it is on crime and detection. Even his western fiction trespasses into this darkly psychological territory. EG writes from the soul with deep passion and it is impossible for his work to leave you unaffected. Some of the material is pure horror and supernatural and he has dismissed his Daniel Ransom books as 'trash'. EG has created several series characters, most prominently Jack Dwyer, an ex-cop turned security guard and part-time actor. The books are violent and dark but not as 'noir' as the one Walsh novel to date, *The Night Remembers*, which makes even your brain weep. Other series characters include former FBI psychological profiler Robert Payne; the temperamental and turbulent Tobin, a movie critic whose life is just too complicated; and more recently, Sam McCain, a young attorney in small-town Iowa in the fifties. EG has written more one-off mysteries of late including some superior ones which he signs as E.J. Gorman. These include *The Marilyn Tapes*, which recreates the investigation into Marilyn Monroe's death, and *The First Lady*, a political thriller where the President's wife is accused of murder. One of EG's best psychological noir novels is *Daughter of Darkness*, in which an emotionally and mentally troubled young woman may have murdered a man but she has no memory of it. *Senatorial Privilege* is a vivid recreation of small-town politics and violence.

EG's western fiction should not be overlooked. Like most of his novels they are set in Iowa. The Leo Guild series is about a former lawman turned bounty hunter and are effective historical crime novels. *Grave's Retreat* is an unusual novel about an early baseball hero who becomes entangled in a bank robbery, whilst *Night of Shadows* is an account of the first uniformed policewoman in Cedar Rapids (EG's hometown). Over the 16 years that EG has been writing, his work has become only slightly less intense and dark, but increasingly complex and deep. The light that now shines makes EG's darkness multi-dimensional, illuminating other mysteries and casting further shadows.

Novels

Jack Dwyer series: *Rough Cut* (1985), *New Improved Murder* (1985), *Murder Straight Up* (1986), *Murder in the Wings* (1986), *The Autumn Dead* (1987), *A Cry of Shadows* (1990).

Leo Guild series: *Guild* (1987), *Death Ground* (1988), *Blood Game* (1989), *Dark Trail* (1990).

Tobin series: *Murder on the Aisle* (1987), *Several Deaths Later* (1988).

Jack Walsh series: *The Night Remembers* (1991).

Robert Payne series: *Blood Moon* (1994; as *Blood Red Moon*, UK 1994), *Hawk Moon* (1995), *Harlot's Moon* (1998), *Voodoo Moon* (2000).

Sam McCain series: *The Day the Music Died* (1999), *Will You Still Love Me Tomorrow* (2000), *Wake Up Little Susie* (2001), *Save the Last Dance for Me* (2002).

Non-series: *Grave's Retreat* (1989), *Night Kills* (1990), *Night of Shadows* (1990), *What the Dead Men Say* (1990), *Wolf Moon* (1993), *Shadow Games* (1994), *The Marilyn Tapes* (1995), *Cold Blue Midnight* (1995), *The First Lady* (1995), *Out There in the Darkness* (1995), *Cage of Night* (1996), *Black River Falls* (1996),

Runner in the Dark (1996), *Senatorial Privilege* (1997), *The Silver Scream* (1998), *Trouble Man* (1998), *Daughter of Darkness* (1998), *The Poker Club* (1999).
as Daniel Ransom: *Daddy's Little Girl* (1985), *Toys in the Attic* (1986), *Night Caller* (1987), *The Forsaken* (1988), *Nightmare Child* (1990), *The Serpent's Kiss* (1992), *The Long Midnight* (1993), *The Fugitive Stars* (1995), *Night Screams* (1996), *Zone Soldiers* (1996).
as Christopher Keegan: *Ride Into Yesterday* (1989).
as Chris Shea McCarrick: *Run to Midnight* (1992), *Now You See Her* (1993).
with Richard Chizmar: *Dirty Coppers* (1997)
Short Stories. *Prisoners and Other Stories* (1992), *Dark Whispers* (1993), *Cages* (1995), *Moonchasers* (1996), *Famous Blue Raincoat* (1999), *Such a Good Girl* (2001), *The Dark Fantastic* (2001), *The Long Silence After* (2001).
Non-fiction. *Jim Thompson: The Killers Inside Him*, with Max Allan Collins (1983), *The Fine Art of Murder*, with Martin H. Greenberg, Larry Segriff & Jon L. Breen, *The Dean Koontz Companion*, with Martin H. Greenberg & Bill Munster (1994).
Editor. *The Black Lizard Anthology of Crime Fiction* (1987), *The Second Black Lizard Anthology of Crime Fiction* (1988), *Modern Treasury of Great Detective and Murder Mysteries* (1994), *Women on the Beat* (1995).
with Martin H. Greenberg or other co-editors: *Under the Gun* (1990), *Stalkers* (1990), *Dark Crimes* (1991), *Invitation to Murder* (1991) *Solved* (1991), *Predators* (1993), *Dark Crimes 2* (1993), *Danger in D.C.* (1993), *Night Screams* (1996), *Murder Most Irish* (1996), *Year's 25 Finest Crime and Mystery Stories: 6th Annual Edition* (1997; abr. as *Crime After Crime*, 1999), *The Fatal Frontier* (1997), *Love Kills* (1997), *American Pulp* (1997), *Once Upon a Crime* (1998), *Year's 25 Finest Crime and Mystery Stories: 7th Annual Edition* (1998), *Murder Most Scottish* (1999), *Pure Pulp* (1999), *Felonious Felines* (2000), *The World's Finest Mystery and Crime Stories* (2000), *Sleuths of the Century* (2000), *Pulp Masters* (2001).
Cat Crimes series, with Martin H. Greenberg: *Cat Crimes* (1991), *Cat Crimes II* (1992), *Cat Crimes III* (1992), *Feline and Famous: Cat Crimes Goes Hollywood* (1994) *Cat Crimes Takes a Vacation* (1996), *Cat Crimes for the Holidays* (1997), *Cat Crimes Through Time* (1999)

Full name: Edward Joseph Gorman.
Pen-names: Christopher Keegan, Chris Shea McCarrick, Daniel Ransom.
Where to start: start recent and work back; try *When the Music Died* and *The Marilyn Tapes.*
Awards: Shamus, best short story (1988), Anthony and Macavity, best critical work (1994).
Website: <www.mysteryscene.cjb.net>
Similar stuff: Joe R. LANSDALE, Collin WILCOX's Alan Bernhardt.
Final fact: EG was a petty thief in his youth and was once arrested for stealing a large amount of money, which he had not. Because of his reputation his lawyer told him to plead guilty but EG did not and the police eventually figured out what had happened. It shocked EG so much that he reformed.

Paula Gosling (b. 1939) US (UK resident)

Born in Detroit, Michigan, PG became an advertising copywriter after she graduated from Wayne State University, and was able to continue in that work when she transferred to England in 1964. She had considerable success with her first novel, *A Running Duck*, about a former army sniper who has become a police officer tracking criminal snipers. Not only did this win the John Creasey Memorial Award as the best first novel for that year but it went on to be adapted twice for the cinema, first as the macho action film *Cobra* (1986), starring Sylvester Stallone, and then as *Fair Game* (1995). PG followed with a series of one-off action suspense thrillers such as *The Zero Trap*, where passengers on a plane are kidnapped and taken to a remote house. They have no idea why they are being held and PG cleverly develops the tension through the characters. PG has written two novels about English detective Luke Abbott of the Regional Crime Squad who, in *The Wychford Murders*, is drawn back into the small West country town of his youth. PG is clearly also drawn to small towns of her youth, for although she continues to live in England her imagination has returned to her home state. Six of her last seven novels have been set in small-town Michigan. PG fulfilled the promise of her first award by winning the CWA Gold Dagger with *Monkey Puzzle*, the first of her Jack Stryker series. Stryker is a homicide detective who teams with English professor Kate Trevorne. Although they are also the lead characters in *Backlash*, PG used them as minor characters in the amusing *Hoodwink*. They also appear in *The Body in Blackwater Bay*, which introduced PG's main series featuring Matt Gabriel, sheriff of Blackwater Bay, Michigan, a resort on the shores of the Great Lakes. This series draws on the entire townsfolk as cast, like Deborah ADAMS' Jesus Creek series. In these recent novels PG has moved from mega-action to the micro, and drifts between tension and comedy, but the emphasis remains on character relationships.

Novels

Non-series: *A Running Duck* (1978; rev'd as *Fair Game*, US 1978), *The Zero Trap* (1979), *Loser's Blues* (1980; as *Solo Blues*, 1981), *The Woman in Red* (1983).

Luke Abbott series: *The Wychford Murders* (1986), *Death Penalties* (1991).

Jack Stryker/Blackwater Bay series: *Monkey Puzzle* (1985), *Hoodwink* (1988), *Backlash* (1989), *The Body in Blackwater Bay* (1992), *A Few Dying Words* (1993), *The Dead of Winter* (1995), *Death and Shadows* (1999), *Underneath Every Stone* (2000), *Ricochet* (2002).

as Ainslie Skinner: *Mind's Eye* (1980; as *The Harrowing*, US 1981).

Pen-name: Ainslie Skinner.

Where to start: *A Running Duck* or *The Body in Blackwater Bay*.

Awards: CWA John Creasey Memorial Award (1978), CWA Gold Dagger (1985).

Website: <www.twbooks.co.uk/authors/pgosling.html> and <www.geocities.com/WestHollywood/Heights/9558/paulagosling.htm>

Similar stuff: Deborah ADAMS for small communities, Wendy HORNSBY for academic links.

Laurence Gough (b. 1944) Canada

Hardly known in the UK or US, LG is one of the most popular of crime-fiction writers in his native Canada. He has twice won the Arthur Ellis award and his thriller *Sandstorm* about an apparent plan to assassinate an Arab leader won the Author's Award for Fiction. LG's series features police detectives Jack Willows and Claire Parker in LG's home town of Vancouver. Their cases are rough, no-holds-barred, which tends to throw them together and one of the threads in the series is their growing attachment and Willows' deteriorating marriage. They are methodical police procedurals but with plenty of action. When not writing books, LG writes poetry and plays for CBC radio.

Novels

Willows & Parker series: *The Goldfish Bowl* (1987), *Death on a No.8 Hook* (1988; as *Silent Knives*, US 1988), *Hot Shots* (1989), *Serious Crimes* (1990), *Accidental Deaths* (1991), *Fall Down Easy* (1992), *Killers* (1994), *Heartbreaker* (1995), *Memory Lane* (1996), *Karaoke Rap* (1997), *Shutterbug* (1998), *Funny Money* (2000).

Non-series: *Sandstorm* (1990).

Full name: Laurence Gordon John Gough.
Where to start: *The Goldfish Bowl.*
Awards: Arthur Ellis, best first novel (1988), best novel (1990), Foundation for the Advancement of Canadian Letter, Author's Award for Fiction (1991).
Similar stuff: L.R. WRIGHT for Vancouver setting; Caroline ROE as Medora Sale for Canadian dual sleuths.

Ron Goulart (b. 1933) US

Most of RG's work falls into the categories of fantasy or science fiction, though much of it also has a mystery, crime or espionage theme. RG has a passion for comics and pulp magazines and has written histories of both fields. He began writing at the end of the pulp period, selling his first story in 1952. Many of his early books were pulp-orientated adventures under a host of pen-names. This includes continuing the Avenger series under the Kenneth Robeson name and Flash Gordon adventures as Con Steffanson. Some of his books are genuine detective stories but in an sf setting. The Chameleon Corps series, for instance, starting with *The Sword Swallower* (1968), involves a detective agency of shape changers that can infiltrate alien systems. Max Kearny is a psychic detective whose spooky cases, some of which appear in *Ghost Breaker* (1971), are usually very funny. In fact most of RG's work is humorous or in the field of parody and pastiche, such as the spy spoof *Triple 'O' Seven* (written as Ian R. Jamieson). Just occasionally RG writes genuine, if unconventional, crime fiction. The MWA felt that *After Things Fell Apart*, came close enough to the real world to shortlist it for an Edgar award. It's a parody of the 1960s, set in a Private Inquiry Office in a San Francisco enclave, but could otherwise have been a comic dry run for *All the President's Men*. His most conventional series features Hollywood sleuth, John Easy, who is usually in search of missing women. The books are full of eccentric characters that seem at home in Hollywood. He has written two novels about husband-and-ex-wife team Ben Spanner and H.J. Mavity. In the first they try and solve the mystery of Mavity's ex-boyfriend's death and the riddle of his mysterious final words. Another husband-and-wife team, Bert and Jan Kurrie, turn up in the macabre mystery *A Graveyard of My Own*. Most recently RG has started a series with Groucho Marx as a detective in an entertaining send-up of Hollywood. Amongst his one-off novels is *Ghosting*, where a writer ends up ghosting for the real author who has disappeared and *The Wisemann Originals*, which features two art-world sleuths, Navarro and Briggs, on the trail of an artist who was supposed to have died in a concentration camp. RG has also written close to a hundred mystery stories for magazines and anthologies. A checklist of his mystery stories will be found in his one such collection to date, *Adam and Eve on a Raft*. His work is never predictable and always way off base, which is its charm.

Novels

John Easy series: *If Dying Was All* (1971), *Too Sweet to Die* (1972), *The Same Lie Twice* (1973), *One Grave Too Many* (1974).

Cleopatra Jones series (film novelizations): *Cleopatra Jones* (1973), *Cleopatra Jones and the Casino of Gold* (1975).

Spanner & Mavity series: *Even the Butler Was Poor* (1990), *Now He Thinks He's Dead* (1992).

Groucho Marx series: *Groucho Marx, Master Detective* (1998), *Groucho Marx, Private Eye* (1999), *Elementary, My Dear Groucho* (1999), *Groucho Marx and the Broadway Murders* (2001), *Groucho Marx, Secret Agent* (2002).

Non-series: *After Things Fell Apart* (1970), *Ghosting* (1980), *A Graveyard of My Own* (1985), *The Wisemann Originals* (1989).

Hardy Boys series, as Franklin W. Dixon: *Disaster for Hire* (1989), *The Deadliest Dare* (1989), *Castle Fear* (1990).

as R.T. Edwards, with Otto Penzler based on an outline by Edward D. Hoch: *Prize Meets Murder* (1984).

as Ian R. Jamieson: *Triple 'O' Seven* (1985).

as Josephine Kains: *The Devil Mask Mystery* (1978), *The Curse of the Golden Skull* (1978), *The Green Lama Mystery* (1979), *The Whispering Cat Mystery* (1979), *The Witch's Tower Mystery* (1979), *The Laughing Dragon Mystery* (1980).

Short Stories. *Adam and Eve on a Raft* (2001).

Non-fiction. *The Dime Detectives* (1988), *Lineup Tough Guys* (1966).

Editor. *The Hardboiled Dicks* (1965), *The Great British Detective* (1982).

Full name: Ronald Joseph Goulart.

Pen-names: Josephine Kains, Jillian Kearny, Frank S. Shawn, Joseph Silva, Con Steffanson; house-names, Chad Calhoun, Franklin W. Dixon, R.T. Edwards, Howard Lee, Zeke Masters, Kenneth Robeson; ghost-written under Lee Falk, Ian R. Jamieson.

Where to start: *If Dying Was All.*
Similar stuff: George BAXT, Stuart KAMINSKY.
Final fact: In his teens RG attended a writing course run by Anthony Boucher from his home one evening a week, and it was Boucher who bought his first story.

C.L. Grace *pseudonym, see* Paul C. Doherty

Roderic Graeme *pseudonym, see* Roderic Jeffries

Sue Grafton (b. 1940) US

SG is the author of one of the most popular P.I. series of all time. It features female P.I., Kinsey Millhone, who operates out of Santa Teresa (a thinly disguised Santa Barbara) in California. In the twenty years since the series began SG has been credited with having put women crime writers back on the map. Though this may be a slight exaggeration it is certainly true that her work has helped mould attitudes away from the macho male-dominated image of the hard-boiled P.I. to a more well-rounded, realistic and rational image. Millhone is still a loner, like most P.I.s. Though twice married (and her husbands come back to haunt her in "*E*" and "*O*"), Killhone avoids deep romantic entanglements even though she may become emotionally attached to her clients. Her life – she lost both parents in a car accident when she was five – has made her tough, rebellious, resourceful and capable. At the start of "*A*" she confesses to the first time she had to kill someone. She's the type many people, especially women, can relate to – sharp tongued, angered by charlatanism, but quick witted and determined. She worked briefly for the Police but hated the bureaucracy and the narrow-minded chauvinism. In most books Millhone's investigations, which may begin relatively simply, inevitably unearth a murder or misdemeanour from years past. In "*G*" it's as far back as 50 years whilst in "*B*" it's relatively recent. Whatever the case Millhone applies herself almost regardless of her own safety – she's kidnapped in "*H*". The strength of the books is in the characterization. Not just Millhone but everyone stands out as a well defined character and it's through them that SG weaves her stories.

SG did not start out to be a crime fiction writer, although she is the daughter of renowned lawyer C.W. Grafton (1909–82), who wrote three memorable detective novels during the 1940s. SG had not intended to follow in his footsteps and her first two books, *Keziah Dane* (1967) and *The Lolly-Madonna War* (1969) were mainstream novels. The second was filmed in 1973 and SG was involved with writing the screenplay. This took her to Hollywood where she was a scriptwriter for 12 years during which time she adapted two of Agatha Christie's novels for television. Hollywood taught her to structure a story and write dialogue but she hated the set-up and the interference and the lack of control. It was while she was going through a particularly difficult divorce that Kinsey Millhone gradually took shape and the books have enabled her to regain control of her life and, at the same time, bring pleasure to millions.

Novels

Kinsey Millhone series: *"A" is for Alibi* (1982), *"B" is for Burglar* (1985), *"C" is for Corpse* (1986), *"D" is for Deadbeat* (1987), *"E" is for Evidence* (1988), *"F" is for Fugitive*" (1989), *"G" is for Gumshoe* (1990), *"H" is for Homicide* (1991), *"I" is for Innocent* (1992), *"J" is for Judgment* (1993), *"K" is for Killer* (1994), *"L" is for Lawless* (1995), *"M" is for Malice* (1996), *"N" is for Noose* (1998), *"O" is for Outlaw* (1999), *"P" is for Peril* (2001).

Short Stories. *Kinsey and Me* (1991).

Editor. *Best American Mystery Stories* 1998 (1998).

Awards: Christopher Award, best TV script (1979), Mysterious Stranger Award (1982/3), Anthony, best novel (1986, 1987, 1991), best short story (1987), Shamus, best novel (hardcover) (1986, 1991, 1995), Macavity, best short story (1987), Doubleday Mystery Guild award (1989-94), American Mystery Award (1990, 1992, 1993), Japanese Maltese Falcon (1991).

Books about: *"G" is for Grafton: The World of Kinsey Millhone*, Natalie Hevener Kaufman & Carol McGinnis Kay (1998).

Website: <www.suegrafton.com>

Similar stuff: Ross MACDONALD, Marcia MULLER, Sara PARETSKY.

Final fact: SG has vowed never to have the Millhone books made into films, because the books had been her ticket away from Hollywood, and she has no wish to give them anything back.

Caroline Graham (b. 1931) UK

CG has shown that the day of the traditional English country village setting for mysteries, a la Miss Marple, has not entirely passed, although her Tom Barnaby books, popularized on TV through the *Midsomer Murders* series, are not entirely cosies. CG brings out the eccentric, sinister and macabre in parochial England where secrets lie long buried. Detective Chief Inspector Barnaby is an easy-going detective who prefers traditional methods and is long-suffering of his rather impetuous Detective Sergeant Troy. Prior to starting this series CG had written a mainstream novel, *Fire Dance* (1982), and two children's books. She wrote one other crime novel, *The Envy of the Stranger*, about a psychopath who becomes obsessed by a local radio presenter. This book began as a radio play (1983) and CG, who has been an actress and dancer, has written several radio and TV scripts including adapting *Death of a Hollow Man* for *Midsomer Murders* (1998). CG is also a commentator on royal scandals with *Camilla: The King's Mistress* (1994; updated as *Camilla: Her True Story*, 2000).

Novels

Tom Barnaby series: *The Killings at Badger's Drift* (1987), *Death of a Hollow Man* (1989), *Murder at Madgingley Grange* (1990), *Death in Disguise* (1992), *Written in*

Blood (1994), *Faithful Unto Death* (1996), *Place of Safety* (1999).
Non-series: *The Envy of the Stranger* (1984; rev'd 1994).

Where to start: *The Killings at Badger's Drift.*
Awards: Macavity, best first novel (1989).
Similar stuff: Susannah STACEY, Martha GRIMES, Ann GRANGER.
Final fact: CG also wrote some scripts for the soap opera *Crossroads.*

Ann Granger (b. 1939) UK

With a degree in Modern Languages AG taught English in France for a year before joining the consulate service. Her husband worked in the Foreign Office and as a result AG has travelled widely before settling down to write. Starting with *Summer Heiress* (1981), writing under her married name of Ann Hulme, AG produced a dozen historical romance novels before turning to her first love of crime fiction. Her main series features Meredith Mitchell, a Foreign Service officer temporarily posted to London. In *Say It With Poison*, she is attending her cousin's wedding in the Cotswolds when she meets the placid but determined Chief Inspector Alan Markby. They are soon both involved in an investigation into blackmail and murder. Markby, recently divorced, is attracted to the rather aloof Mitchell who, as the series develops, settles in Bamford, from where Markby operates, but their relationship remains cautious. Mitchell has a natural inquisitiveness that gets her snooping into local crimes and problems in Bamford. These invariably involve murder but sometimes, as in *Shades of Murder*, that may be a hundred years ago or, as in *Flowers for His Funeral*, almost before their very eyes. The series has satisfying plots and strong characterization and, like Caroline GRAHAM's books, shows there is still life in the English village cozy. AG has started a new series about Fran Varaday, an out-of-work, impoverished actress existing in an unsavoury part of London. When her former flat-mate is found dead, Fran begins to investigate her past. Varaday is a resourceful and quick-witted individual. This series is a long way from Mitchell and Markby in setting and social class and is starkly realistic.

Novels

Mitchell & Markby series: *Say it With Poison* (1991), *A Season for Murder* (1991), *Cold in the Earth* (1992), *Murder Among Us* (1992), *Where Old Bones Lie* (1993), *A Fine Place for Death* (1994), *Flowers for his Funeral* (1994), *A Candle for a Corpse* (1995), *A Touch of Mortality* (1996), *A Word After Dying* (1996), *Call the Dead Again* (1998), *Beneath These Stones* (1999), *Shades of Murder* (2000), *A Restless Evil* (2002).
Fran Varaday series: *Asking for Trouble* (1997), *Keeping Bad Company* (1997), *Running Scared* (1998), *Risking it All* (2001).

Real name: Patricia Ann Hulme (*née* Granger).
Pen-names: Ann Granger, Anne Hulme.
Where to start: *Say It With Poison.*

Similar stuff: Ann CLEEVES, Susannah STACEY, June THOMSON.
Final fact: AG's work in the consular service and, after her marriage, with the foreign office took her to embassies in Yugoslavia, Czechoslovakia, Austria, Zambia and Germany

Bill Granger (b. 1941) US

BG, a Chicago journalist, is best known for his series about intelligence agent Devereaux, code name November Man. He works in R Section, a covert unit set up by President Kennedy to "watch the watchers". Because of his rôle Devereaux is a loner though, as this realistic and intelligently plotted espionage series progressed, a romantic involvement develops with female reporter Rita Macklin, who becomes his partner. Several other regular characters emerge, primarily Devereaux's nemesis, Colonel Ready who, in a series within a series, tries to dispose of Deveraux. The first book, *The November Man*, created a stir when three weeks after the book's publication the description of the IRA's plot to assassinate an English peer (Lord Slough, a cousin of the Queen) was almost exactly replicated in the actual murder of Lord Mountbatten. The other books could not rival that but all are fine examples of their kind, especially the mini-sequence *The Infant of Prague*, *Henry McGee is Not Dead* and *The Man Who Heard Too Much*, involving Devereaux's search for missing agent McGee. BG has also written a police procedural series set in Chicago with Special Squad detectives Terry Flynn and Karen Kovac. The first book, *Public Murders*, about a serial killer, won an Edgar award. Mysteriously the next two books appeared under the alias Joe Gash, but the fourth, *The El Murders*, about a series of crimes on Chicago's elevated railway system, reverted to his real name. The Jimmy Drover books are about a forcibly retired newspaper sports columnist who continues to delve into crimes in the sporting world. Of BG's non-series books the best is *Time for Frankie Coolin*, a tough study of a small-time worker who tries to earn an honest buck but whose world goes horribly wrong.

Novels

Devereaux series: *The November Man* (1979), *Schism* (1981), *The Shattered Eye* (1982), *The British Cross* (1983), *The Zurich Numbers* (1984), *Hemingway's Notebook* (1986), *There Are No Spies* (1986), *The Infant of Prague* (1987), *Henry McGee is Not Dead* (1988), *The Man Who Heard Too Much* (1989), *League of Terror* (1990), *The Last Good German* (1991), *Burning the Apostle* (1993).

Flynn & Kovac series (second and third books as Joe Gash): *Public Murders* (1980), *Priestly Murders* (1984), *Newspaper Murders* (1985), *The El Murders* (1987).

Jimmy Drover series: *Drover* (1991), *Drover and the Zebras* (1992), *Drover and the Designated Hitter* (1994).

Non-series: *Sweeps* (1980), *Queen's Crossing* (1982).

as Bill Griffith: *Time for Frankie Coolin* (1982).

Pen-names: Joe Gash, Bill Griffith.
Where to start: *The November Man* or *Public Murders*.

Awards: Edgar, best paperback original (1981).
Similar stuff: John Gardner (for espionage), Jon L. BREEN and Harlan COBEN (for sports detectives).
Final fact: When BG first plotted *The November Man* his IRA target had been Prince Charles but the agent was a little wary of using real people.

John/Jonathan Grant, *see pseudonym* Jonathan Gash

Lesley Grant-Adamson (b. 1942) UK

LG-A was for many years a reporter and newspaper columnist, rising to be a feature writer for *The Guardian*, so it is not too surprising that when she turned to crime and psychological suspense fiction her female investigator would be a gossip columnist, Rain Morgan. LG-A did not want these books to be traditional and while *Patterns in the Dust* and *Wild Justice* are fairly conventional "whodunnits", others are more experimental. In *Curse the Darkness*, for example, she weds the detective story with the suspense novel to create a big contemporary novel about the social inequality of the get-rich-quick eighties. LG-A wrote two books about American con-man Jim Rush wheedling his way into English society, but of her other characters the one that has captured the public interest is female private detective Laura Flynn. She first appeared in *Flynn*, where the search for a missing person (and a missing cat) brings her into confrontation with a shady businessman. LG-A has returned to the character after nearly ten years with several stories, a new book and the chance of a TV series. Several of her one-off novels are studies of past evils. *Dangerous Edge* concerns a child that went missing over 20 years earlier. *Evil Acts*, doubtless inspired by the notorious case of serial killer Fred West in Gloucester (where LG-A worked as a young reporter), concerns a woman who moves into the house of a serial killer. In *Lipstick and Lies*, a woman has to come to terms with her own role in the murder of her mother 40 years earlier. LG-A's books tighten the screw on suspense gradually until there is no turning back.

Novels
Rain Morgan series: *Patterns in the Dust* (1985; as *Death on Widows Walk*, US 1985), *The Face of Death* (1985), *Guilty Knowledge* (1986), *Wild Justice* (1987), *Curse the Darkness* (1990).
Laura Flynn series: *Flynn* (1991; as *Too Many Questions*, US 1991).
Jim Rush series: *A Life of Adventure* (1992), *Dangerous Games* (1994).
Non-series: *Threatening Eye* (1988), *The Dangerous Edge* (1994), *Wish You Were Here* (1995), *Evil Acts* (1996), *The Girl in the Case* (1997), *Lipstick and Lies* (1998), *Undertow* (1999).
Non-fiction. *Writing Crime and Suspense Fiction* (1996).

Full name: Lesley Grant-Adamson (*née* Heycock).
Where to start: *Curse the Darkness* or *The Dangerous Edge*.
Website: <www.crimefiction.co.uk>
Similar stuff: Liza CODY, P.D. JAMES's Cordelia Gray books (for Flynn).

Final fact: When LG-A worked in Gloucester, Mary Bastholm disappeared from a bus stop and a German girl living in a flat above LG-A never came home from a trip to Worcester. Over the years she noticed a pattern of girls vanishing in that area. One day she decided to use Gloucester as the setting to a story about a woman who falls in with a serial killer. LG-A had been writing *Wish You Were Here* for a month before police started digging up the victims of Fred and Rosemary West.

Christine Green (b. 1944) UK

CG is a nurse by training, which provides the background for her series about thirty-something Kate Kinsella. Kinsella opens an investigation agency, but as work is limited she continues to work part-time as a nurse. She rents an office above a funeral parlour whose proprietor, Hubert Humberstone, is a bit quirky but also a good friend. The first three books in the series all involve nurses (either murdered or being stalked) but the fourth, *Deadly Partners*, sends Kinsella off in search of a missing hotelier. CG has also written a police procedural featuring Irish charmer D.I. Connor O'Neill and young detective sergeant Fran Wilson. On the first day of her job the discovery of a dismembered body throws O'Neill and Wilson together in what becomes a taut and well developed series. Another police procedural series, with D.I. Rydell and Sergeant Caldecote, began with *Fire Angels*, about a serial arsonist. As her books have progressed CG has developed from the more traditional type of crime novel to a more tense and atmospheric thriller.

Novels

Kate Kinsella series: *Deadly Errand* (1991), *Deadly Admirer* (1992), *Deadly Practice* (1994), *Deadly Partners* (1996), *Deadly Bond* (2001).

O'Neill & Wilson series: *Death in the Country* (1993), *Die in My Dreams* (1995), *Fatal Cut* (1999).

Inspector Rydell series: *Fire Angels* (2001).

Where to start: *Death in the Country* or *Deadly Partners*.

Website: <www.christine-green.co.uk>

Similar stuff: Mary Kittredge, Anthea FRASER.

Final fact: CG has also written a novel about the original characters of ITV's *Coronation Street* soap series during WW2, *The Way to Victory*.

Stephen Greenleaf (b. 1942) US

SG's San Francisco P.I., John Marshall ("Marsh") Tanner, is perhaps a little too uncomfortably like his creator. Both are lawyers who no longer practise – Tanner because the system drove one of his clients to suicide, SG because the system just overwhelmed him. Tanner is perhaps more of a loner than SG, though the desire may be there. Tanner is also a cynic, so much so that as a character he can become depressing as the series develops especially as he moves into a mid-life crisis. The strength of the series is not Tanner but the cases in which he is involved. SG is remarkable in his ability to seek out the new and the different. The books may often start with Tanner being commissioned to find someone or something, but matters soon develop. In *Fatal Obsession*, which takes Tanner to Iowa, it's about economic struggles in America's heartland. In *Book Case* it's the publishing industry and libel. In *Blood Type* it's about AIDS. In *Southern Cross*, set in South Carolina, it's racism, whilst in *False Conception*, one of his best books, it's about surrogate motherhood. *Beyond Blame* questions the definition of legal insanity, whilst *Flesh Wounds* (which was shortlisted for a Shamus award) explores the impact of computer technology on pornography. SG's one non-series crime book, *Impact*, is a courtroom drama involving the survivor of a plane crash. All of SG's books test the legal system, which is what SG always wanted to do but couldn't as a practising lawyer.

Novels

John Marshall Tanner series: *Grave Error* (1979), *Death Bed* (1980), *State's Evidence* (1982), *Fatal Obsession* (1983), *Beyond Blame* (1986), *Toll Call* (1987), *Book Case* (1991), *Blood Type* (1992), *Southern Cross* (1993), *False Conception* (1994), *Flesh Wounds* (1996), *Past Tense* (1997), *Strawberry Sunday* (1999), *Ellipsis* (2000).

Non-series: *Impact* (1989).

Full name: Stephen Howell Greenleaf.
Awards: Japanese Maltese Falcon (1993).
Similar stuff: Jeremiah HEALY, Ross MACDONALD's Lew Archer.
Final fact: SG had sent the manuscript of his first book to seven or eight publishers without success and was within a week of taking up a legal service job when it was accepted by Dial Press.

D.M. Greenwood UK

DMG is an ecclesiastical officer with the diocese of Rochester in Kent, and her books are ideal for anyone who loves clerical mysteries. They feature the imposing deaconess Theodora Braithwaite who has a highly perceptive no-nonsense outlook on the problems that arise in the cloistered world of the church. *Clerical Errors* finds her involved in a murder that happened in Medewich Cathedral. By the third book, *Idol Bones*, DMG is exposing the undercurrent of church politics and clerical scandal. DMG keeps a balance between the humorous and the macabre and the books are in the traditional English village cozy mystery, but with a slightly dented halo.

Novels

Theodora Braithwaite series: *Clerical Errors* (1991), *Unholy Ghosts* (1992), *Idol Bones* (1993), *Holy Terrors* (1994), *Every Deadly Sin* (1995), *Mortal Spoils* (1996), *Heavenly Vices* (1997), *A Grave Disturbance* (1998), *Foolish Ways* (1999).

Where to start: *Clerical Errors.*
Similar stuff: Kate CHARLES, Jeanne M. Dams, Sister Carol Anne O'MARIE.

John Greenwood *pseudonym, see* John Buxton Hilton

Susanna Gregory (b. 1958) UK

SG is the pen-name of a botanist who spends her winters in the Antarctic studying marine pollution. Prior to earning her PhD at Cambridge, SG worked in the coroner's service. Her American husband, Beau Riffenburgh, is a lecturer on history at Cambridge University and helps her with her research as well as collaborating on the Mappestone books. SG's first series featured Matthew Bartholomew, a physician and teacher at Michaelhouse in the fledgling Cambridge University of the mid-14th century. The books are full of wonderful period detail and atmosphere, with a reliable historical background, and there is never a shortage of murders. Bartholomew brings his knowledge and deductive skills to bear on what amounts to prototype forensic analysis. *Murder in the Holy City*, set in 1100, introduces Sir Geoffrey Mappestone, a Crusader with a desire to learn rather than plunder, who investigates a series of deaths of knights in Jerusalem. In *A Head for Poisoning*, Sir Geoffrey returns home to be with his dying father only to find he has been poisoned. SG's work blends authentic historical detail with a wealth of murder and mystery.

Novels

Matthew Bartholomew series: *A Plague on Both Your Houses* (1996), *An Unholy Alliance* (1996), *A Bone of Contention* (1997), *A Deadly Brew* (1998), *A Wicked Deed* (1999), *A Masterly Murder* (2000), *An Order for Death* (2001), *A Summer of Discontent* (2002).

Sir Geoffrey Mappestone series as Simon Beaufort: *Murder in the Holy City* (1998), *A Head for Poisoning* (1999).

Pen-names: Susanna Gregory, Simon Beaufort.

Where to start: *A Plague on Both Your Houses.*

Similar stuff: Margaret FRAZER, Paul DOHERTY.

Final fact: SG recalls a particularly harrowing incident when she was part of a small team (five people and three tents) camping on Livingston Island, north of the Antarctic Peninsula, when they were hit by a huge storm with winds gusting in excess of 160kph. "The first thing to go was the wind meter, which we never found again. Then all our supplies were ripped from the depot and distributed along the beach. The noise was phenomenal. Then the tent just ripped apart, and we were bombarded by hard snow and large pieces of rock. My husband had to kneel outside and anchor the tent while I did Frankenstein-style stitches to try to hold it all together."

Bill Griffith *pseudonym, see* Bill Granger

Martha Grimes (b. 1931) US

An American, from Pittsburgh, now a Professor of English at Montgomery College, Tacoma Park, Maryland, MG chose England as the setting for her series featuring Inspector Richard Jury of Scotland

Yard. The books emphasis English eccentricities, perhaps almost too much so, as the early ones sail dangerously close to parody. The book titles, and most of the settings, revolve around pubs, which allows MG to explore the strata of English social life, though in the first few books its foibles are exaggerated to the point of grotesqueness. MB has used all the stocks-in-trade of the English cozy mystery but has given them a new polish. Jury is all the things an upper middle-class Scotland Yard detective should be – erudite, tall, handsome, cultured yet concerned, rather like Ngaio Marsh's Roderick Alleyn. In his accomplice, the somewhat unlikely aristocratic professor of French romantic poetry, Melrose Plant, we have a parody of the Bertie Wooster/Peter Wimsey type sleuth with his own obnoxious American Aunt Agatha. The early books are good fun but perhaps a little over-the-top. By the third MG was getting them under control. *The Anodyne Necklace* won the Nero Wolfe award, and the ninth book, *The Five Bells and Bladebone*, hit the *New York Times* best-seller list. MG is mischievous without being cruel, and perceptive without being smug. By *Help the Poor Struggler*, which involves the murder of children, the eccentricity has gone and a pallor of seriousness has shrouded the series, to potent effect. In the recent *The Blue Last* she fuses humour, wit and atmosphere into a powerful story about the consequences, 50 years on, of a WW2 bombing. MG has written several non-series books. These are different in tone to the Jury books, though seem to indicate the direction that the Jury books are taking. They explore dark secrets and violence in small-town America, and have broadened her appeal. *The End of the Pier*, is both a moving story of human relationships and a tense mystery about whether the man convicted of three murders is really guilty or whether the true murderer will strike again. *Hotel Paradise* is about an old hotel now gone to seed but waiting to give up its secrets. MG's versatility is perhaps best demonstrated by *Send Bygraves*, a volume of poetry of which the title poem explores the nature of crime through the conventions of the traditional British mystery. It was writing this poem that caused MG to turn to crime fiction.

Novels

Inspector Jury series: *The Man With a Load of Mischief* (1981), *The Old Fox Deceived* (1982), *The Anodyne Necklace* (1983), *The Dirty Duck* (1984), *Jerusalem Inn* (1984), *The Deer Leap* (1985), *Help the Poor Struggler* (1985), *I Am the Only Running Footman* (1986), *The Five Bells and Bladebone* (1987), *The Old Silent* (1989), *The Old Contemptibles* (1991), *The Horse You Came In On* (1993), *Rainbow's End* (1995), *The Case Has Altered* (1997), *The Stargazey* (1998), *The Lamorna Wink* (1999), *The Blue Last* (2001).

Non-series: *Send Bygraves* (1989), *The End of the Pier* (1992), *Hotel Paradise* (1996), *Biting the Moon* (1999), *The Train Now Departing* (2000).

Where to start: *The Anodyne Necklace*.

Awards: Nero Wolfe award (1983).

Website: <www.marthagrimes.com>
Similar stuff: Deborah CROMBIE, Elizabeth GEORGE, Caroline GRAHAM.
Final fact: MG's *Biting the Moon* is about animal abuse and she donated two-thirds of her royalties to animal abuse organizations in the US.

Terris McMahan Grimes US

TMG popped out of nowhere with her first book *Somebody Else's Child* in 1996 which won her the Chester Himes award, two Anthony awards and an Agatha nomination. It features Theresa Galloway, a black urban mother of two, who tries to hold down a job and cope with her demanding and over-inquisitive mother. In the first book Mother calls Theresa out in the middle of the night because of strange goings-on next door and lands Theresa in a whole pile of trouble. TMG spent 40 years trying to become a writer, to become an overnight success. Born in rural Arkansas and raised in Oakland, she works as a land agent in Sacramento. Mother has continued to involve Theresa in two further adventures, both with the same delightfully fresh approach.

Novels
Theresa Galloway series: *Somebody Else's Child* (1996), *Blood Will Tell* (1997), *Other Duties as Required* (2000).

Awards: Anthony, best first novel & best paperback original (1997), Chester Himes award (1997).
Website: <www.vme.net/dvm/sister-sleuth>
Similar stuff: Natasha COOPER's Willow King, Barbara NEELY's Blanche White.
Final fact: TMG grew up in a cabin in Arkansas with no running water or electricity but they had books. TMG recalls her mother wanted her to become a teacher and the family moved to California to ensure a good education for the children.

John Grisham (b. 1955) US

Known as the "King of the Legal Thriller", JG was one of the best-selling authors of the nineties, with over 60 million books in print. Each of the first six books was filmed. Born in Arkansas, the son of a construction worker, JG graduated from law school in 1981 and served as a practising trial lawyer for 11 years. In 1983 he was elected to the Mississippi House of Representatives. Despite the pressure of his work, JG had the idea for a novel arising from one of his cases involving a 12-year-old rape victim. He wondered what would have happened had the girl's father murdered the rapist and been brought to trial. It took him three years to write *A Time to Kill* (filmed 1996) and another year to find a publisher. He still regards it as his best-written book. His second novel, *The Firm* (filmed 1993), about a bright young lawyer who unwittingly finds he is working for a firm controlled by the Mafia, was sold to Paramount Pictures before it was published and catapulted him into the public eye. It was the best-selling novel of 1991. JG admitted that he had used a formula from a list he saw in *Writer's Digest* – place an innocent and sympathetic hero(ine) in the midst of a life-threatening conspiracy and get them out of it. *The Pelican Brief* (filmed 1993) is his most formula-based novel. A young law student discovers the link between the murder of two Supreme Court judges and suddenly everyone is after her. One reviewer noted that this book was such a brisk page-turner that you could dry your hair with it. JG was more satisfied with *The Chamber* (filmed 1996), about a young lawyer who tries to rescue his racist, psychotic grandfather from Death Row. It is perhaps JG's most accomplished book. He followed his formula of innocents-vs-corruption until his twelfth book, *A Painted House*, set in the Arkansas of JG's childhood at cotton-harvesting time. Although murders are committed this is a social novel of a community in conflict and demonstrates JG's greater breadth as a writer. JG also provided the story-lines for two films: *The Gingerbread Man* (1998), about a psychotic who escapes from an asylum to wreak revenge on the lawyer who put him there, and *Mickey* (2002), about a man on the run from the IRS whose son's talent as a baseball player (JG's favourite sport) threatens to expose him.

Novels. *A Time to Kill* (1989), *The Firm* (1991), *The Pelican Brief* (1992), *The Client* (1993), *The Chamber* (1994), *The Rainmaker* (1995), *The Runaway Jury* (1996), *The Partner* (1997), *The Street Lawyer* (1998), *The Testament* (1999), *The Brethren* (2000), *A Painted House* (2001), *The Summons* (2002).

Where to start: *A Time to Kill.*
Website: <www.randomhouse.com/features/grisham>
Similar stuff: William BERNHARDT, Scott TUROW.
Final fact: JG returned to the courtroom in 1996 to fight the case for the family of a railroad brakeman who was killed when he was pinned between two carriages. JG won the case and his clients were awarded $683,500.

Batya Gur (b. 1947) Israel

A professor of literature and the literary critic on the Israeli paper *Ha'aretz*, BG is the first Israeli writer of detective fiction to be widely recognised in the English-speaking world. Her books feature Chief Inspector Michael Ohayon, a Moroccan-born former history student (who can recite all the names of the Popes and the royal dynasties of Europe), whose misguided marriage forced him out of Cambridge. Thereafter he holds a resentment of academe, especially the pretentious – a feeling that comes to the fore in *Literary Murder*. Patient and compassionate, Ohayon is a contrast to most western police detectives. Though the murders are traditional, the motives and investigations, played out against the culture and social structure of Israel, are not. This is especially true in the third book, *Murder on a Kibbutz*, which was shortlisted for an Anthony award. BG's work helps widen the boundaries of crime fiction. She has had other books published in Israel which have yet to be translated.

Novels
Michael Ohayon series: *The Saturday Morning Murder* (1988; US 1992), *Literary Murder* (1991; US 1993), *Murder on a Kibbutz* (1991; US 1994), *Murder Duet* (US 1999).

Similar stuff: For academic mysteries try Amanda CROSS; for Jewish ethnic elements try Rochelle KRICH or S.T. HAYMON.

Peter Guttridge (b. 1951) UK

A freelance journalist, critic and festival organizer, and a transplanted northerner (born in Burnley, living in Sussex), PG uses all this experience in his series of comic crime novels starring journalist and yoga expert Nick Madrid. He is usually helped or hindered by his friend Bridget Frost, the "Bitch of the Broadsheets". Madrid encounters murder at the world's biggest comic festival (*No Laughing Matter)*; is surrounded by cults and corpses in the New Age romp *A Ghost of a Chance*; tries to survive a rock-music tour when everyone is out to kill the rock star (*Two to Tango*); is up against corporate nasties in *The Once and Future Con*; and enters the sports arena in *Foiled Again*. PG is the crime field's Tom Sharpe.

Novels
Nick Madrid series: *No Laughing Matter* (1997), *A Ghost of a Chance* (1998), *Two to Tango* (1999), *The Once and Future Con* (1999), *Foiled Again* (2001).

Pen-names: none for his fiction but used to use the name Nick Madrid for some journalism.
Website: <www.peterguttridge.com> and <www.twbooks.co.uk/authors/peterguttridge.html>
Similar stuff: Mike RIPLEY, Colin WATSON.
Final fact: PG comments that he "writes obituaries of authors for *The Independent* so is always on the lookout for fellow writers who look a bit poorly."

Jane Haddam *pseudonym, see* Orania Papazoglou

Jean Hager (b. 1932) US

A one-time High School English teacher, JH sold her first book, a children's mystery, *The Whispering House*, in 1970 and turned full-time writer in 1975. She wrote over forty romances and romantic suspense novels under pseudonyms before returning to the mystery field with the first of her books about Mitch Bushyhead, *The Grandfather Medicine*. Bushyhead is half-Cherokee but has been raised in the white tradition and forgotten his roots. Now as chief of police in Buckskin, Oklahoma, he begins to rediscover those roots in the course of his investigations. In a second series, JH introduced Molly Bearpaw, a full-blood Cherokee who is an investigator for the Native American Advocacy League. These books are drawn upon Cherokee tradition and both series are a delightful blend of native culture and modern crime-solving. Books from both series (*Seven

Black Stones and *The Fire Carrier*) have been finalists for the Oklahoma Book Award. JH's work has been alikened to Tony HILLERMAN's in its treatment of native Americans. JH's Iris House series is in more traditional cozy vein. Tess Darcy inherits an old house, which she converts into a bed-and-breakfast establishment. She is clearly not very selective about her guests as murder seems to follow each new intake.

Novels

Mitch Bushyhead series: *The Grandfather Medicine* (1989), *Night Walker* (1990), *Ghostland* (1992), *The Fire Carrier* (1996), *Masked Dancers* (1998).

Molly Bearpaw series: *Ravenmocker* (1992), *The Redbird's Cry* (1994), *Seven Black Stones* (1995), *The Spirit Caller* (1997).

Iris House series: *Blooming Murder* (1994), *Dead and Buried* (1995), *Death on the Drunkard's Path* (1996), *The Last Noel* (1997), *Sew Deadly* (1998), *Weigh Dead* (1999), *Bride and Doom* (2000).

Full name: Wilma Jean Hager
Pen-names: Leah Crane, Marlaine Kyle, Jeanne Stephens; house-names: Amanda McAllister, Sara North.
Where to start: *The Grandfather Medicine.*
Similar stuff: Mary Monica PULVER (for Iris House series), Tony HILLERMAN.
Final fact: JH is herself one-sixteenth Cherokee.

J. P. Hailey *pseudonym, see* Parnell Hall

James W. Hall (b. 1947) US

Kentucky-born JWH is a poet and columnist who teaches creative writing at Florida International University where one of his students was Dennis LEHANE. He has come to be regarded as one of Florida's major writers, his books feeding off the ecology of the state. JWH's main character is Thorn, a complex individual who has a passion for his environment and who grew out of JWH's fascination for Travis McGee. He usually wants to be left alone to fish but gets dragged into major issues, usually involving his side-kick, an Afro-American detective called Sugarman. The first book is rather more conventional. Thorn, who in the past had avenged the death of his parents, now considers how to avenge the murder of his drug-dealing adoptive mother. In later books he becomes something of an eco-warrior, fighting the traffic in apes in *Gone Wild* (a book that had not started out as a Thorn novel) and investigating the slaughter of dolphins in *Red Sky at Night*. *Buzz Cut*, one of the least typical in the series, is set on board a cruise liner where Thorn and Sugarman face a deranged killer. It was shortlisted for the Hammett Prize. Each Thorn book is different as the character evolves with the series. JWH's non-series books could as easily have featured Thorn. *Bones of Coral* uses chemical warfare as its background, *Hard Aground* is a search for lost treasure and *Body Language* is a caper novel involving a major heist. *Rough Draft* involves an ex-cop turned writer who discovers a copy of her first novel full of strange notes and underlinings which she thinks may provide the key to the unsolved murder of her parents.

Novels

Thorn series: *Under Cover of Daylight* (1987), *Tropical Freeze* (1989; as *Squall Line*, UK 1989), *Mean High Tide* (1994), *Gone Wild* (1995), *Buzz Cut* (1996), *Red Sky at Night* (1997), *Blackwater Sound* (2002).
Non-series: *Bones of Coral* (1993), *Hard Aground* (1994), *Body Language* (1998), *Rough Draft* (2000).
Short Stories. *Paper Products* (1990).

Full name: James Wilson Hall.
Where to start: *Under Cover of Daylight*.
Awards: John D. MacDonald award for excellence in Florida fiction (1996), San Francisco Review of Books Critic's Choice Award (1995).
Website: <www.jameswhall.com>
Similar stuff: Carl HIAASEN, Laurence SHAMES.
Final fact: The idea for *Rough Draft* came to JWH when he found one of his own books in a used bookstore filled with strange notes in the margins and passages underlined.

Parnell Hall (b. 1944) US

The character of Stanley Hastings is based firmly on PH's own life. Both are former actors and screenwriters who became private detectives. PH was a detective who assisted lawyers in personal injury cases, such as people tripping over uneven paving. Although he called himself a "detective" it didn't feel like the real thing. *Detective*, which was nominated for both an Edgar and Shamus award, uses that as the starting point when Hastings says he can't help a prospective client, who says drug-runners are trying to kill him, because he isn't a "real" detective. When the man is killed Hastings has to come to terms with his conscience. The rest of the series is Hastings (helped by his wife Alice) trying to be a real detective, usually with humorous results. PH is a great Perry Mason fan and used him as the model for the Steve Winslow series of court-room dramas. He has also started a light-hearted series about Cora Felton, a setter of crosswords who isn't the little old lady everyone thinks she is. In *A Clue for the Puzzle Lady* she becomes involved in a double murder where the victims have crossword clues left on them.

Novels

Stanley Hastings series: *Detective* (1987), *Murder* (1988), *Favor* (1988), *Strangler* (1989), *Client* (1990), *Juror* (1990), *Shot* (1991), *Actor* (1993), *Blackmail* (1994), *Movie* (1995), *Trial* (1996), *Scam* (1997), *Suspense* (1998), *Cozy* (2001).
Steve Winslow series as J.P. Hailey: *The Baxter Trust* (1988), *The Anonymous Client* (1989), *The Underground Man* (1990), *The Naked Typist* (1991), *The Wrong Gun* (1992).

Puzzle Lady series: *A Clue for the Puzzle Lady* (1999), *Last Puzzle and Testament* (2000), *Puzzled to Death* (2001).

Full name: James Parnell Hall.
Pen-names: J.P. Hailey.
Where to start: *Detective.*
Website: <www.parnellhall.com>
Similar stuff: John LUTZ, Howard ENGEL for Stanley Hastings; Thomas CHASTAIN for puzzles and Perry Mason.
Final fact: PH was location manager for and had a bit part in Arnold Schwarzenegger's first film *Hercules in New York* (1969), a rôle he foists upon Stanley Hastings in *Juror*.

Patricia Hall (b. 1940) UK

Yorkshire-born Maureen O'Connor, who writes as PH, is a freelance journalist having previously worked for *The Guardian*, the London *Evening Standard* and the BBC. Her special area of interest is in educational and social concerns and her first mystery, *The Poison Pool*, included a social worker who becomes involved in a murder case when a boy with learning difficulties is accused of the crime. *The Coldness of Killers* was about race relations at a school when an ex-Asian student is found dead. The novel also looked at corruption in local politics, a theme that re-emerged in *Death by Election*, the first of her novels that teams investigative journalist Laura Ackroyd with police inspector Michael Thackeray. All of PH's books are hard-hitting, dealing with social deprivation and corruption and are an accurate if sad reflection of nineties Britain.

Novels

Ackroyd & Thackeray series: *Death by Election* (1993), *Dying Fall* (1994), *In the Bleak Midwinter* (1995; as *Dead of Winter*, US 1997), *Perils of the Night* (1997), *The Italian Girl* (1998), *Dead on Arrival* (1999), *Skeleton at the Feast* (2000), *Deep Freeze* (2001).
Non-series: *The Poison Pool* (1991), *The Coldness of Killers* (1992).

Real name: Maureen O'Connor.
Pen-name: Patricia Hall.
Where to start: *Death by Election.*
Website: <www.twbooks.co.uk/authors/patriciahall.html>
Similar stuff: Lisa CODY, Natasha COOPER's Trish Maguire stories, Abigail PADGETT.
Final fact: PH reflects upon how real life has a nasty way of imitating fiction. A few months after publication of her *Dead on Arrival*, which included twenty illegal immigrants found dead in a lorry, 50 Chinese were found dead in similar circumstances at Dover.

Steve Hamilton (b. 1961) US

SH had one of those dream starts that he still cannot believe. He entered his first novel for the St Martin's Press/PWA best first unpublished P.I. novel contest in 1997 and it won. When it was published, *A Cold Day in Paradise* won both the Edgar and Shamus first novel awards and was nominated for the Anthony and Barry awards. SH had belatedly fulfilled his promise. He had received the Hopwood Award for fiction when studying at the University of Michigan in 1983 and had always intended to continue with his fiction but got sucked into his job as an information developer at IBM. Over 12 years passed before he forced himself to return to writing. The result was his first novel featuring ex-cop and reluctant detective, Alex McKnight, who had been invalided out of the police force years before when he was shot by a psychopath. The bullet remains lodged near his heart. Although the psycho remains in prison, McKnight feels he is again being stalked by him when he reluctantly becomes involved in safeguarding a friend from another. SH has written further novels about McKnight, each one dragging him back into the world to save or protect someone. Set in the bleak cold of northern Michigan, these books are full of atmosphere and pain.

Novels

Alex McKnight series: *A Cold Day in Paradise* (1998), *Winter of the Wolf Moon* (2000), *The Hunting Wind* (2001), *North of Nowhere* (2002).

Awards: St Martin's Press/PWA best first unpublished novel (1997), Edgar and Shamus, best first novel (1999).
Website: <www.authorstevehamilton.com>
Similar stuff: Doug ALLYN, Elmore LEONARD.
Final fact: SH comments that as a "single-digit handicapper", he has yet to find anybody else in the crime fiction field who can play a decent game of golf!

Joseph Hansen (b. 1923) US

JH had been a writer and teacher for several years before he wrote the first of his Dave Brandstetter novels, but it still took three years before Joan Kahn at Harper & Row took the gamble to publish the book. For its day *Fadeout* was a significant novel. Brandstetter, a middle-aged insurance claims investigator, is openly homosexual. JH had made the decision to depict gays as they really are – not to sensationalize or patronize them. There is a natural sympathy for Brandstetter. At the start of the book he has just lost his lover of 20 years to cancer. His relationships are central to the progression of the books, but no more than any heterosexual one would be. Brandstetter is a tenacious investigator who takes nothing for granted. In *Fadeout* he refuses to accept that the body of a drowned singer has disappeared and believes that it is a staged accident. The murder in *Troublemaker* takes Brandstetter into the local gay community whilst in *The Man Everyone Was Afraid Of* a gay activist is arrested for the murder of the chief of police, who was notoriously anti-gay. In all of these stories Brandstetter takes a measured if determined line to find the truth. The later novels suffer by comparison to the early ones if only because by then JH had achieved his aim and Brandstetter's life style was no longer unusual. The best of the later novels is *Early Graves*, where AIDS is central to the plot. JH retired Brandstetter in this book though he came back for three more encores. Writing in the London *Times*, H.R.F. KEATING went so far as to call JH Hammett's "worthy successor". JH's short stories about Hack Bohannon feature a straight P.I. who operates in the remote outback, more often stumbling across crimes than being called in.

Novels
Brandstetter series: *Fadeout* (1970), *Death Claims* (1973), *Troublemaker* (1975), *The Man Everybody Was Afraid Of* (1978), *Skinflick* (1979), *Gravedigger* (1982), *Nightwork* (1984), *The Little Dog Laughed* (1986), *Early Graves* (1987), *Obedience* (1988), *The Boy Who Was Buried This Morning* (1990), *A Country of Old Men* (1991).
Non-series: *Backtrack* (1982), *Steps Going Down* (1985), *Living Upstairs* (1993).
as Rose Brock: *Tarn House* (1971), *Longleaf* (1974).
Short Stories
Brandstetter series: *Brandstetter and Others* (1984) [Note: "Election Day" was also published as a separate booklet (1984).]
Bohannon series: *Bohannon's Book* (1988), *Bohannon's Country* (1993).

Pen-names: Rose Brock, James Colton.
Where to start: *Fadeout.*
Awards: Lambda, best gay mystery (1992), Shamus, lifetime award (1992).
Website: <www.twbooks.co.uk/authors/josephhansen.html>
Similar stuff: Michael NAVA and Mark ZUBRO for other gay investigators.
Final fact: JH wrote two gothic romance novels as Rose Brock. He apparently hated every day of the research and writing for *Longleaf*, yet it became his best selling book.

Paul Harding *pseudonym, see* Paul C. Doherty

William Harrington (1931-2000) US

WH's books fall into three categories, nor far short of "the good, the bad and the ugly! The good are his early courtroom dramas. WH trained as a lawyer and practised from 1958, rising to the office of senior attorney in his home state of Ohio. His first two books were written to bring reality to fictional courtrooms. *Which the Justice, Which the Thief* is written from the viewpoint of a retired judge in a case of armed robbery. *The Power* considers the legal complexity of whether a faith healer who advised a woman to stop taking her medication is guilty of manslaughter. *Trial, Partners, For the Defense* and *Town on Trial* are all first class courtroom dramas though, despite its title, *Trial* is more of a police procedural. Into the "ugly" category fall WH's thrillers and wartime novels, "ugly" because of their occasional concentration on violence and torture. The best of the wartime novels are *The English*

Lady, about a female aviator and English spy and *Oberst*, about the plot to assassinate Hitler, whilst *The Jupiter Crisis* and *Scorpio 5* are high action thrillers. *Virus*, about the search to identify a computer hacker, is the most suspenseful. More recently, however, WH forsook the original direction of his writing to produce a number of spin-off books. The best are his continuation of the series featuring the TV police detective Lieutenant Columbo. WH's eye for detail and understanding of forensics maintains the integrity of this series. WH also served as ghost-writer on the series of books credited to Elliott Roosevelt (1910-90), son of Franklin Delano Roosevelt, who recreated his mother, Eleanor Roosevelt, as an ingenious detective around the White House in the thirties and forties. The series is fun, but the field could have done with more of WH's perceptive courtroom novels.

Novels
Non-series: *Which the Justice, Which the Thief* (1963), *The Power* (1964; as *The Gospel of Death*, UK 1966), *Yoshar the Soldier* (1966), *The Search for Elizabeth Brandt* (1969), *Trial* (1970), *The Jupiter Crisis* (1971), *Mister Target* (1973), *Scorpio 5* (1975), *Partners* (1980), *The English Lady* (1982), *Skin Deep* (1983), *The Cromwell File* (1986), *Oberst* (1987), *For the Defense* (1988), *Endgame in Berlin* (1991), *Virus* (1991), *Town on Trial* (1994).
Columbo series: *The Grassy Knoll* (1993), *The Helter Skelter Murders* (1994), *The Hoffa Connection* (1995), *The Game Show Murder* (1996), *The Glitter Murder* (1997), *The Hoover Files* (1998), *Past Imperfect* with Hilary Grenville (2001).
Eleanor Roosevelt series (ghost-written for Elliott Roosevelt): *Murder and the First Lady* (1984), *The Hyde Park Murder* (1985), *Murder at Hobcaw Barony* (1986), *The White House Pantry Murder* (1987; as *The White House Murder*, UK 1995), *Murder at the Palace* (1988), *Murder in the Rose Garden* (1989), *Murder in the Oval Office* (1989), *Murder in the Blue Room* (1990), *A First Class Murder* (1991), *Murder in the Red Room* (1992), *Murder in the West Wing* (1992), *Murder in the East Room* (1993), *Royal Murder* (1994), *Murder in the Executive Mansion* (1995), *Murder in the Chateau* (1996), *Murder at Midnight* (1997), *Murder in the Map Room* (1998). *Murder in Georgetown* (1999), *Murder in the Lincoln Bedroom* (2000), *Murder at the President's Door* (2001).
Jack Endicott series (ghost-written as Elliott Roosevelt): *The President's Men* (1991), *New Deal for Death* (1993).
Non-fiction. *Manhattan North Homicide* with Thomas McKenna (1996).

Where to start: *Which the Justice, Which the Thief.*
Similar stuff: William BERNHARDT or Jay BRANDON for similar legal thrillers; see p. 547 for other *Columbo* books.

Thomas Harris (b. 1940) US

In Hannibal Lecter TH has created a late 20th-century icon of evil the equivalent of Robert Louis Stevenson's Mr Hyde of a century earlier and one as likely to pass into the language. In three novels of remarkable depth and characterization, TH takes the reader into the psyche of not one but several serial killers to the point where the reader can both understand and even sympathize with the twisted mentality. The first two books, *Red Dragon* (filmed 1986, as *Manhunter*, and 2002) and *The Silence of the Lambs* (filmed 1991), are essentially the same plot. In the first ex-FBI agent Will Graham, who had nearly been killed in arresting Lecter, returns in order to consult Lecter in the hope of understanding and identifying another killer who has been butchering families. Lecter assists Graham but on his own terms, manipulating both the agent and the killer in a bizarre game. Lecter had been a psychiatrist turned murderer who earned the nickname "the Cannibal" because he would eat part of his victim. In *The Silence of the Lambs*, Lecter is again consulted, this time by young female agent Clarice Starling. Both novels are dark and intense but if anything the second novel is more powerful because of the relationship that develops between Lecter and Starling. This continues in *Hannibal* (filmed 2001), set years later after Lecter's escape from prison. Lecter is hunted not only by the police but by Mason Verger, a man convicted of raping children who had once been sent to Dr Lecter, then still a psychiatrist, for treatment. Lecter's treatment had left Verger paralysed and plotting revenge. Some feel that in the climax of *Hannibal*, TH has betrayed the character of Starling but, that aside, the book is another shiveringly perceptive study of the mind of a mass murderer. Even if TH had written nothing else his name has passed into literary legend. The Lecter series has overshadowed TH's first bestseller, *Black Sunday*, itself an intense and powerful journey into the psyche of terrorists who plan to detonate a bomb at the Super Bowl. TH, a former reporter and editor for the Associated Press, has said that he cannot write anything unless he believes it. His research has brought a greater understanding to the motives of a murderer than in any other work of modern crime fiction.

Novels

Hannibal Lecter series: *Red Dragon* (1981; as *Manhunter*, 1986), *The Silence of the Lambs* (1988), *Hannibal* (1999).
Non-series: *Black Sunday* (1975).

Full name: Thomas Harris.
Awards: Anthony, best novel (1989), American Mystery Award, best crime novel (1989), Grand Prix de Littérature Policière Best Foreign (1991).
Website: <www.randomhouse.com/features/thomasharris>
Similar stuff: Robert BLOCH, Jeffrey DEAVER.
Final fact: The character of Hannibal was inspired in part by the case of Ed Gein who was also the inspiration for Robert Bloch's Norman Bates.

Chip Harrison *pseudonym, see* Lawrence Block

Carolyn G. Hart (b. 1936) US

CGH has developed a strong and loyal following with her two distinct series of mysteries. *Death on Demand* introduced Annie Laurance and her future husband Max Darling. Annie owns a mystery bookstore in Broward's Rock, South Carolina (the eponymous Death on Demand) which serves as a focus for gossip and analysis into all the latest local mysteries. Annie is a forceful, inquisitive and engaging individual. Almost every book in the series has been nominated for one or more mystery awards with three of them winning – *Something Wicked*, in which a new production of *Arsenic and Old Lace* leads to murder; *Honeymoon with Murder*, in which Annie and Max marry and where the murder centres on a peeping-tom; and *A Little Class on Murder*, where Annie investigates a suicide at the local college. The other series features Henrietta O'Dwyer Collins (Henrie O to her friends), who was a Pulitzer-prize-winning journalist but has long retired and now brings her years of experience to bear when problems arise amongst her friends. She first appeared in a short story, "Henrie O.'s Holiday", which won a Macavity award. The first book, *Dead Man's Island* (filmed TV 1996), was also an award-winner. Bearing comparison to Agatha Christie's famous *Ten Little Indians*, Henrie O agrees to help a friend who is convinced someone is trying to kill him and joins him on a remote island where he has invited all the likely suspects. CGH took a degree in journalism and worked as a reporter for three years before becoming a full-time writer. Her early books were for the teenage market, starting with *The Secret of the Cellars* (1964). Her first adult mystery was *Flee from the Past*, a suspense novel about a woman who realizes someone else knows her deep secrets. She wrote a number of other suspense novels before turning to her series novels, but has recently written another non-series book, *Letter from Home*, set in a small northeastern Oklahoma town in 1944 and involving a 12-year-old girl whose friend's mother is killed. Its mood is something of a departure for CGH. Although her books are otherwise unashamedly "cozies" on the surface they are rich in texture and characterization and are extremely well plotted. They may appeal to a certain readership, which may be why she has been nominated for and won a cabinet full of Agathas, Anthonies and Macavities but no Edgars, but she has perfected that market and has few equals.

Novels

Death on Demand series: *Death on Demand* (1987), *Design for Murder* (1987), *Something Wicked* (1988), *Honeymoon with Murder* (1989), *A Little Class on Murder* (1989), *Deadly Valentine* (1990), *The Christie Caper* (1991), *Southern Ghost* (1992), *The Mint Julep Murder* (1995), *Yankee Doodle Dead* (1998), *White Elephant Dead* (1999), *Sugarplum Dead* (2000), *April Fool Dead* (2002).

Henrie O series: *Dead Man's Island* (1993), *Scandal in Fair Haven* (1994), *Death in Lovers' Lane* (1997), *Death in Paradise* (1998), *Death on the River Walk* (1999), *Resort to Murder* (2001).

Non-series (selective): *Flee from the Past* (1975), *A Settling of Accounts* (1976), *The Rich Die Young* (1983), *Death by Surprise* (1983), *Castle Rock* (1983), *Skulduggery* (1984).
Short Stories. *Crime On Her Mind* (1999).
Editor. *Crimes of the Heart* (1995), *Love and Death* (2001).

Full name: Carolyn Gimpel Hart (Gimpel is her maiden name).
Where to start: *Death on Demand.*
Awards: Agatha, best novel (1989, 1994), Anthony, best paperback original (1989, 1990), Macavity, best novel (1990), best short story (1993).
Website: <www.carolynhart.com>
Similar stuff: Dorothy CANNELL, Jill CHURCHILL, Joan HESS.
Final fact: A cat sub-plot was added to *Deadly Valentine* when CGH rescued a kitten thrown from a passing car. CGH's own cat, Patch, never accepted the newcomer and this caused CGH to write a book about love and jealousy.

Ellen Hart (b. 1949) US

EH was nearly 40 before she turned to writing. She had worked for 12 years as a chef at the University of Minnesota, so it is not too surprising that food is not far from her books. She writes two series. The first features Jane Lawless, a restaurant owner, and the second features Sophie Greenway, a food critic and magazine editor. Both live in Minneapolis, where EH was born and still lives. Lawless, like EH, is gay, and lives with her partner Cordelia Thorn, the artistic director of a local theatre. In the first few books the two of them become involved in investigating murders in either the restaurant or the theatre worlds, but in later books their horizons broaden and the books become slightly less "cozy". Lawless suffers a serious head injury in *Wicked Games* while assisting a private detective to investigate her new neighbour and this injury leads her into deeper waters in *Hunting the Witch*. Several of the series have been nominated for both the Lambda award for best lesbian mystery and the Minnesota Book award, with four winners. The Sophie Greenway series is also less cozy, as the critic and her husband have to face dark secrets amongst their own friends and relatives and becomes enmeshed in a world of corruption and deceit. The background draws upon EH's own period when she studied and worked at Ambassador College of the Worldwide Church of God in the early seventies only to subsequently discover the corruption amongst the Church's leadership. EH's writings thus reflect deeper truths than one usually expects in traditional mysteries.

Novels

Jane Lawless series: *Hallowed Murder* (1989), *Vital Lies* (1991), *Stage Fright* (1992), *A Killing Cure* (1993), *A Small Sacrifice* (1994), *Faint Praise* (1995), *Robber's Wine* (1996), *Wicked Games* (1998), *Hunting the Witch* (1999), *The Merchant of Venus* (2001).
Sophie Greenway series: *This Little Piggy Went to Murder* (1994), *For Every Evil*

(1995), *The Oldest Sin* (1996), *Murder in the Air* (1997), *Slice and Dice* (2000), *Dial M for Meatloaf* (2001).

Real name: Patricia Boenhardt.
Pen-name: Ellen Hart.
Where to start: *Hallowed Murder* or *This Little Piggy Went to Murder*.
Awards: Lambda Literary Award (1997, 2000), Minnesota Book Award, best crime fiction (1995, 1996).
Website: <www.ellenhart.com>
Similar stuff: Amanda CROSS, Katherine V. FORREST, Sandra SCOPPETTONE.
Final fact: EH originally studied the piano and had anticipated becoming a musician before her degree in theology took her into the Worldwide Church of God.

Jack Harvey *pseudonym, see* Ian Rankin

John Harvey (b. 1938) UK

JH served a busy but comprehensive apprenticeship during the mid-seventies to early eighties. After twelve years as an English teacher he threw himself into full-time writing, producing a number of formulaic series under a dozen pen names. Many of these were westerns or their modern mercenary-orientated equivalent, and he regards them as no more than hack work. Amongst them were a four-book sequence featuring English P.I. Scott Mitchell. He was a complete copy of the American P.I.s, which made him somewhat unrealistic in an English setting, and JH did no more than take him through the usual routine. After this outburst JH returned to University to obtain his degree in American studies, became a part-time lecturer in film and literature at Nottingham University and began scriptwriting for radio and television. This included a series called *Hard Cases* (1987/8) about inner-city problems and the work of a team of probation officers set in Nottingham. The realism presented by the series and the voice of Nottingham itself gave JH the spark to return to novels and create his most complete character, Charlie Resnick. Resnick is a detective with the Nottingham police force. Part-Polish, part-English, he is in his forties and has seen the dark side of life. He is still coming to terms with his wife leaving him. With a shattered confidence and in an increasingly depressing job as the fabric of society in the city crumbles, Resnick struggles to have something to hold on to and throws himself into his job. Resnick's cases are difficult, alienating, dispiriting, frightening, despairing. He encounters child abuse, drugs, prostitution, rape, kidnapping, shocking violence and vicious murders and through it all Resnick brings a light of humanity, determined to resolve matters for his own sanity, let alone those about him. Resnick is one of us trying to get things right. He has been called one of the most fully realized detectives in modern crime fiction and, more than that, he is a true product of his age. JH brought the series to an end after ten novels and they will undoubtedly pass into history as the most authentic reflection of crime in the 1990s. JH adapted two of the Resnick novels, *Lonely Hearts*

(1992) and *Rough Treatment* (1992) for TV, both starring Tom Wilkinson. In addition to adapting *Wasted Years* (1995) and *Cutting Edge* (1996) for radio, JH wrote an original Resnick script, *Slow Burn* (1998) which he later reworked as a short story. Other radio adaptations are planned.

Novels

Scott Mitchell series: *Amphetamines and Pearls* (1976), *The Geranium Kiss* (1976), *Junkyard Angel* (1977), *Neon Madman* (1977).
Charlie Resnick series: *Lonely Hearts* (1989), *Rough Treatment* (1990), *Cutting Edge* (1991), *Off Minor* (1992), *Wasted Years* (1993), *Cold Light* (1994), *Living Proof* (1995), *Easy Meat* (1996), *Still Water* (1997), *Last Rites* (1998).
Non-series: *Frame* (1979), *Blind* (1981), *In a True Light* (2001).
the Deathshop series as Jon Barton: *Kill Hitler!* (1976), *Forest of Death* (1977), *Lightning Strikes* (1977).
the Mercenaries series as Jon Hart: *Black Blood* (1977), *High Slaughter* (1977), *Triangle of Death* (1977), *Guerrilla Attack* (1977), *Death Raid* (1978).
as Terry Lennox: *Dancer Draws a Wild Card* (1985).
as James Mann: *Endgame* (1982).

Short Stories

Charlie Resnick series: *Now's the Time* (1999).

Full name: John Barton Harvey.
Pen-names: Jon Barton, William S. Brady, L.J. Coburn, J.B. Dancer, Jon Hart, William M. James, Terry Lennox, James Mann, John J. McLaglen, Thom Ryder, J.D. Sandon, Michael Syson.
Where to start: *Lonely Hearts*.
Awards: New York Festival Bronze Medal, screenplay for best TV drama series (1992), Sony Radio Drama Silver Award for best radio adaptation (1999), Sherlock, best British Detective (1999), Grand Prix du Roman Noir (2000).
Website: <www.mellotone.co.uk>
Similar stuff: Ian RANKIN.
Final fact: A jazz enthusiast as well as a poet, in 1995 JH recorded several of his poems as *Ghosts of a Chance* with the Second Nature jazz band.

Graham Hastings *pseudonym, see* Roderic Jeffries

S. T. Haymon (1918–95) UK

STH had already written an historical novel and two historical biographies before she turned to writing crime fiction at the age of 60. Over the next 15 years she produced a one-of-a-kind series about Detective Inspector Ben Jurnet of Norfolk CID. Jurnet is a handsome man – his colleagues nickname him "Valentino"', much to his embarrassment. And he is easily embarrassed. Shy, introspective and senstitive, Jurnet hates to intrude upon the victims of the crimes he is investigating, or their relatives, and really just wants the quiet life. He also wants Miriam, a Jewish lady who will only marry him if he converts to Judaism. Jurnet, who believes he may be descended from the brother of Anne Boleyn, also wonders if an ancestor was a Jewish moneylender in Norwich. This background is relevant because the whole series revolves around religious conviction and faith. The first book in the series involves a murder at a shrine to a saint whilst *Ritual Murder* involves the death of a choirboy in a cathedral. Even Druidism arises in *Death of a Warrior Queen*. Jurnet is a fascinating character and the series is a triumph for the traditional English village cozy with a conscious. One only wishes STH had started the series earlier. STH worked for much of her life in broadcasting and her first book was *Television and Radio as a Career* (1963).

Novels
Inspector Jurnet series: *Death and the Pregnant Virgin* (1980), *Ritual Murder* (1982), *Stately Homicide* (1984), *Death of a God* (1987), *A Very Particular Murder* (1989), *Death of a Warrior Queen* (1991), *A Beautiful Death* (1993), *Death of a Hero* (1996).
Autobiography: *Opposite the Cross Keys* (1988) and *The Quivering Tree* (1990), two volumes of memoirs.

Full name: Sylvia Theresa Haymon.
Awards: CWA Silver Dagger (1982).
Similar stuff: Gwendoline BUTLER, B.M. GILL, P.D. JAMES.
Final fact: "Jurnet's House" is one of the oldest buildings in Norwich; it originally belonged to a Jewish merchant and is now used as an Open University centre.

Sparkle Hayter (b. 1958) Canada

SH's Robin Hudson books are amongst the funniest crime novels around. Like SH, Hudson is a TV reporter in a special reports unit. Her life has its ups and downs, mostly downs – in the first book she's been demoted, her husband's run off with another girl and Hudson ends up accused of murder – but through her own resourcefulness she survives. She's glamorous, describing herself as a rumpled Rita Hayworth, witty, and able. The books are fast-paced, strongly character-driven and highly inventive. The plots often ramble, split, twist and turn, but that doesn't matter as it's the journey that counts. Whether it's murder, kidnapping, blackmail or 12 missing chimpanzees, Hudson somehow copes. The first novel was rejected 30 times before publication and went on to win the Arthur Ellis award. Born in Canada, SH came to New York in 1980 and worked in TV for six years. She has since travelled extensively.

Novels
Robin Hudson series: *What's a Girl Gotta Do?* (1994), *Nice Girls Finish Last* (1996), *Revenge of the Cootie Girls* (1997), *The Last Manly Man* (1999), *The Chelsea Girl Murders* (2000).

Full name: Sparkle Vera Lynnette Hayter.
Awards: Arthur Ellis, best first novel (1995), Sherlock, Best Comic Detective (1999).
Similar stuff: Janet EVANOVICH, Joan HESS.

Final fact: SH has written since she was a child but the spark for the Hudson books was ignited through her reading of Simon BRETT's books when she backpacked through India.

Gar Anthony Haywood (b. 1954) US

Readers sat up and paid attention to GAH's first novel, *Fear of the Dark*. It had already won the St Martin's Press/PWA best first unpublished novel award and two years later the Shamus for the best first P.I. novel. It introduced Aaron Gunner, an African-American (like GAH) in Los Angeles. Burned out, down on his luck and planning on getting out of the P.I. work and becoming an electrician (like GAH, who was once a computer maintenance engineer), Gunner is drawn into the violent world of a black revolutionary organization whose leader has been murdered. Racial tension and prejudice is a strong thread throughout this hard-boiled series. GAH's voice is powerful and his depiction of street life in urban America is vivid and unsettling. Gunner is a believable P.I., vulnerable, not necessarily street-wise and far from stereotypical. By contrast GAH's second series is humorous and almost cozy. Retired African-American couple Joe and Dottie Loudermilk (Joe's an ex-cop), decide to sell their house and tour America in a trailer home, leaving behind their five adult offspring. But trouble catches up with them when a dead white man turns up in their toilet. This series is light relief after the Gunner books. Recently GAH has been writing for television including scripts for the series *New York Undercover*.

Novels

Aaron Gunner series: *Fear of the Dark* (1988), *Not Long for This World* (1990), *You Can Die Trying* (1993), *It's Not a Pretty Sight* (1996), *When Last Seen Alive* (1998), *All the Lucky Ones are Dead* (1999).
Joe Loudermilk series: *Going Nowhere Fast* (1994), *Bad News Travels Fast* (1995).

Full name: Gar Anthony Haywood.
Where to start: *Fear of the Dark*.
Awards: St Martin's Press/PWA best first unpublished novel (1987), Shamus, best first novel (1989), Shamus and Anthony, best short story (1996), Chester Himes award (1996).
Similar stuff: Chester HIMES, Walter MOSLEY.
Final fact: Gar is a car nut who almost pursued a career in automotive design straight out of high school. Had all the design jobs not been in Detroit at the time he might never have written a word of fiction.

Victor Headley (b. 1960) Jamaica

VH's direct and unyielding Yardie trilogy, about a young Jamaican drugs courier who rises to become head of a drugs empire, was apparently so realistic that the author received death threats from the Yardies. The first book, *Yardie*, which is set to be filmed, was one of the publishing phenomena of the year, even though it was issued by an independent small press. VH believes that this was the book that got black readers back into the bookshops. Unremitting and almost casual in its attitude to violence the trilogy nevertheless starkly portrayed the gang life of young Jamaicans from the ghetto. VH has continued this theme in his later books though *Off Duty*, the start of a new trilogy, brings a stronger element of humanity to its portrayal of a Jamaican rebel turned cop.

Novels
Yardie trilogy: *Yardie* (1992), *Excess* (1993), *Yush!* (1994).
Non-series: *Fetish* (1995), *Here Comes the Bride* (1997), *The Best Man* (1999), *Off Duty* (2001), *Seven Seals, Seven Days* (2002).

Where to start: *Yardie*.
Similar stuff: Mike PHILLIPS.
Final fact: VH lives in the Republic of the Congo and communicates with the world by e-mail and satellite.

Tim Heald (b. 1944) UK

TH's crime books feature the incredibly inept Simon Bognor, a special investigator for the Board of Trade who is sent to investigate dastardly deeds in all kinds of unlikely places full of eccentric people. Bognor bumbles his way through his investigations, just as likely to be wrong than right, and yet managing to salvage enough at the end. The series is really an opportunity for TH to lampoon various British establishments. It's the church in *Unbecoming Habits,* with monks smuggling out national secrets in jars of honey, the newspaper world in *Deadline* (TH is himself a journalist), and academe in *Masterstroke*. There is a wonderful spoof of the country-house mystery in *Blue Blood Will Out*, whilst the village "cozy" features in both *Red Herrings*, where the VAT inspector is found dead, and *Business Unusual* where Bognor encounters a small-town Mafia. Bognor even becomes a hero amongst the Canadian Mounties in *Murder at Moose Jaw*. It's all good fun with the occasional clever mystery en route. The series was adapted for television as *Bognor* in 1981 with the lugubrious David Horovitch in the title rôle. TH has written real biographies, about Prince Philip, Prince Charles and even Barbara Cartland, and a spoof biography of *Avengers* star John Steed in *Jealous in Honour*.

Novels
Simon Bognor series: *Unbecoming Habits* (1973), *Blue Blood Will Out* (1974), *Deadline* (1975), *Let Sleeping Dogs Die* (1976), *Just Desserts* (1977), *Murder at Moose Jaw* (1981), *Masterstroke* (1982; as *A Small Masterpiece*, US 1982), *Red Herrings* (1985), *Brought to Book* (1988), *Business Unusual* (1989).
Avengers series: *Jealous in Honour: the Authorized Biography of John Steed* (1977).
Editor. *The Newest London Spy* (1987), *The Rigby File* (1989), *A Classic English Crime* (1990), *A Classic Christmas Crime* (1995).

Full name: Timothy Villiers Heald.
Pen-names: David Lancaster.

Where to start: *Unbecoming Habits.*
Similar stuff: James ANDERSON, Simon BRETT, Peter DICKINSON.
Final fact: While at Oxford TH was approached by a man who spoke about possible work in "another branch of the Foreign Office" but TH did not follow it up.

Jeremiah Healy (b. 1948) US

JH is a graduate of Harvard Law School, a former trial lawyer and a former professor at the New England School of Law. He served his military service as a captain in the military police, where he learned about interviewing techniques, and he has made his P.I., John Francis Cuddy, a former US military policeman who had served in Vietnam. The stories are set in Boston, JH's home territory, and also the home of Robert PARKER's P.I., Spenser, so there are inevitable comparisons, but Cuddy is his own man and the series deals with a greater diversity of issues. Having lost his wife to cancer, and lost his job as an insurance claims investigator, Cuddy, dangerously close to becoming an alcoholic, becomes a P.I. He's always willing to help the underdog and through Cuddy JH explores a number of moral concerns. *The Staked Goat* deals with gay-bashing and the aftermath of the Vietnam War. *So Like Sleep* considers whether someone under hypnosis can be a reliable witness. *Swan Dive* involves battered wives. *Right to Die* considers assisted suicide whilst *Rescue* involves surrogate parents and a religious cult. The series is highly charged emotionally and faces crucial issues head on. The Cuddy books have been nominated six times for the Shamus award, and won with *The Staked Goat.* JH took a break from Cuddy with a legal thriller, *The Stalking of Sheilah Quinn*, and is planning a new series.

Novels

John Francis Cuddy series: *Blunt Darts* (1984), *The Staked Goat* (1986; as *The Tethered Goat*, UK 1986), *So Like Sheep* (1987), *Swan Dive* (1988), *Yesterday's News* (1989), *Right to Die* (1991), *Shallow Graves* (1992), *Foursome* (1993), *Act of God* (1994), *Rescue* (1995), *Invasion of Privacy* (1996), *The Only Good Lawyer* (1998), *Spiral* (1999).
Non-series: *The Stalking of Sheilah Quinn* (1998), *Turnabout* (2001).
Short Stories. *The Concise Cuddy* (1998).

Where to start: *Blunt Darts.*
Awards: Shamus, best P.I. novel (1987).
Similar stuff: Stephen GREENLEAF, Robert B. PARKER.
Final fact: JH's first novel, *Blunt Darts*, was rejected 28 times before being published. Then it was selected by the *NYT* as one of the seven best mystery novels of the year.

Mark Hebden (1916–91) UK

Under his real name, John Harris, and the alias Max Hennessy, MH was best known for his war novels and adventure thrillers. He hit the big-time with his third novel, *The Sea Shall Not Have Them* (1953), a tense fight for survival when a plane is shot down over the sea. MH had worked as a merchant seaman before WW2 and in the RAF during the war, so he had witnessed plenty of action. In 1965 he created the Hebden alias for his crime and mystery fiction though the first under that title, *What Changed Charley Farthing* (filmed 1974 as *The Bananas Boat*), is really a humorous caper novel about incompetent gun-running. Next came *Eyewitness* (filmed 1970, aka *Sudden Terror*), a more powerful novel about a young boy who witnesses an assassination attempt on the French President. This set the tone for his next few books, most of which are political thrillers and include his short series about Colonel Mostyn of Intelligence. MH then made a marked change of pace and launched into his long running series about Inspector (later Chief Inspector) Evariste Clovis Desiré Pel of the French police, based in Burgundy. Pel hates his name. In fact he dislikes most things. He chain-smokes, is a hypochondriac and is constantly at odds with his housekeeper – he can't even escape her when he marries later in the series. Pel doesn't realize in what high regard he is held as a detective. His one good trait is his determination. He hates things untidy and must resolve his cases so that they are tied up neatly and he can be left in peace. In this long series Pel encounters just about every type of crime and though he does not get on that well with his colleagues they make a good team, especially Pel's second-in-command, Inspector Darcy. In this respect the novels echo Simenon's Maigret series, but in all other respects they are more like BAANTJER's DeKok. Since MH's death his daughter, Juliet Harris, writing as Juliet Hebden, has continued the series, starting with *Pel Picks Up the Pieces* (1993).

Novels

Colonel Mostyn series: *Mask of Violence* (1970), *A Pride of Dolphins* (1974), *The League of 89* (1977).

Inspector Pel series: *Death Set to Music* (1979; as *Pel and the Parked Car*, 1995), *Pel and the Faceless Corpse* (1979), *Pel Under Pressure* (1980), *Pel is Puzzled* (1981), *Pel and the Staghound* (1981), *Pel and the Bombers* (1982), *Pel and the Predators* (1984), *Pel and the Pirates* (1984), *Pel and the Prowler* (1985), *Pel and the Paris Mob* (1986), *Pel among the Pueblos* (1987), *Pel and the Touch of Pitch* (1987), *Pel and the Picture of Innocence* (1988), *Pel and the Party Spirit* (1989), *Pel and the Missing Persons* (1990), *Pel and the Promised Land* (1991), *Pel and the Sepulchre Job* (1992).

Non-series: *What Changed Charley Farthing* (1965), *Eyewitness* (1966), *The Errant Knights* (1968), *Portrait in a Dusty Frame* (1969; as *Grave Journey*, US 1970); *A Killer for the Chairman* (1972), *The Dark Side of the Island* (1973).

Real name: John Harris.
Pen-names: Mark Hebden, Max Hennessy.
Where to start: *Death Set to Music*.
Similar stuff: A.C. BAANTJER, Nicolas FREELING's Henri Castang.

William Heffernan (b. 1937) US

Although he won an Edgar for his Paul Devlin novel *Tarnished Blue*, and was a three-time Pulitzer Prize winner during his days as an investigative reporter in New York and Buffalo, WH does not seem as well known in the mystery community as perhaps he should be. He will probably become best remembered for the non-criminous *The Dinosaur Club* about a group of men forced into retirement who plot revenge against their former employee. But he has also written several international thrillers, including the tense *Corsican Honor* about the clash between a renegade CIA agent and a Mafia assassin. The Devlin series is about a NYPD detective who hopes for the quiet life and becomes Chief of Police in Vermont looking for early retirement only to be called out of retirement, in *Scarred*, to catch a serial killer. The plots in each book revolve around betrayal and obsession, from the psychotic murderer in *Ritual* to the NYPD police captain who is betrayed and murdered in *Tarnished Blue*. These books are strong on action and atmosphere with a relentless drive. WH has also written an historical crime novel, *Beulah Hill*, set in Vermont in 1933 with a powerful portrayal of bigotry and injustice.

Novels

Paul Devlin series: *Ritual* (1989), *Blood Rose* (1991), *Scarred* (1993), *Tarnished Blue* (1995), *Winter's Gold* (1997), *Red Angel* (2000), *Unholy Order* (2002).
Non-series: *Broderick* (1980), *Caging the Raven* (1981), *The Corsican* (1983), *Acts of Contrition* (1986), *Toltec* (1989), *Corsican Honor* (1992), *The Dinosaur Club* (1997), *Cityside* (1999), *Beulah Hill* (2001).

Where to start: *Ritual.*
Awards: Edgar, best paperback original (1996).
Website: <homepages.together.net/~dsychn/>
Similar stuff: John Bingham and Ted Wood for other detectives called back from the quiet life.

Lauren Henderson (b. 1966) UK

LH's books, which have been dubbed "Tart Noir", feature metal-sculptress Samantha Jones and are flagrant designer-nineties gems. Independent, witty, impulsive and with a strong fighting spirit, Sam takes on any challenge regardless. In *Dead White Female* she is annoyed when the police dismiss the death of her former art tutor as an accident and when the rest of her circle clam up, Sam goes for broke. *Too Many Blondes* follows a similar pattern but *Black Rubber Dress* gets us into the world of merchant bankers, *Freeze My Margarita* into fetishism and the theatre, *The Strawberry Tattoo* into the New York artworld, and *Chained!* into animals' rights. LH read English at Cambridge University and for a while was a journalist at *Marxism Today* before graduating to the *New Statesman* and *The Observer*.

Novels

Sam Jones series: *Dead White Female* (1995), *Too Many Blondes* (1996), *Black Rubber Dress* (1997), *Freeze My Margarita* (1998), *The Strawberry Tattoo* (1999), *Chained!* (2000), *Pretty Boy* (2001).

Website: <www.twbooks.co.uk/authors/lhenderson.html> and features on <www.tartcity.com>
Similar stuff: Stella DUFFY, Sparkle HAYTER.
Final fact: LH has also written an anti-Bridget Jones novel *My Lurid Past*.

Sue Henry (b. 1940) US

For those still missing *Northern Exposure*, SH's series featuring Alaskan state trooper Alex Jensen and dog-sled racer Jessie Arnold, should partly fill the gap. The characters were introduced in *Murder on the Iditarod Trail*, where a series of apparently "accidental' deaths occur on the world's biggest dog-sled race. The book not only won both the Anthony and Macavity awards but it was rapidly made into a TV movie, *The Cold Heart of a Killer* (1996). SH was an administrator at the Anchorage Adult Learning Center, University of Alaska from which she has now retired to devote herself to writing and teaching mystery writing. Since 1995 she has produced a regular annual volume using the remarkable beauty, danger, weather and wilderness of Alaska as both hero and villain in a series of highly original novels.

Novels

Arnold & Jensen series: *Murder on the Iditarod Trail* (1991), *Termination Dust* (1995), *Sleeping Lady* (1996), *Death Takes Passage* (1997), *Deadfall* (1998), *Murder on the Yukon Quest* (1999), *Beneath the Ashes* (2000), *Dead North* (2001), *Cold Company* (2002).

Awards: Anthony and Macavity, best first novel (1992).
Similar stuff: For other mysteries set in Alaska try Aaron ELKINS (*Icy Clutches*), Elizabeth Quinn, Dana STABENOW.
Final fact: SH is still overwhelmed by the beauty of Alaska. In 1999, during a writer's retreat, she was taken aback by a vivid star-shaped Aurora Borealis, so bright that it cast shadows.

Joe L. Hensley (b. 1926) US

JLH was progressively an attorney, state legislator and circuit judge in his native Indiana until his retirement in 1988. He had started writing in the early fifties, selling stories to the science-fiction and crime-fiction magazines, but apart from *The Color of Hate* he did not begin to produce novels until the seventies. Almost all of JLH's books feature small-town attorneys who take on major issues. *The Color of Hate* remains a good example. A black ex-convict is charged with raping and murdering a white woman. The town has already decided his guilt and the defence lawyer has a mountain of prejudice to overcome. (This book was revised in the eighties to make the lawyer a Vietnam veteran and move the setting to Georgia.) Many books feature attorney Donald Robak, who operates out of Bington in Indiana, a fictionalized version of JLH's Bloomington, where he was born, and Madison, where he lives. Robak frequently finds himself with clients that the rest of the town would like to lynch, such as a disgraced ex-cop in *Outcasts* or a young girl charged with stabbing her carers to death in *Minor Murders*. Perhaps the best of the series is *Robak's Cross*, where Robak defends an alcoholic charged with murdering his wife. An unusual non-series book is *Rivertown Risk*, related by a judge who receives death threats during a murder trial in a corrupt town.

Novels
Robak series: *Deliver Us to Evil* (1971), *Legislative Body* (1972), *Song of Corpus Juris* (1974), *A Killing in Gold* (1978), *Minor Murders* (1979), *Outcasts* (1981), *Robak's Cross* (1985), *Robak's Fire* (1986), *Robak's Run* (1990), *Robak's Witch* (1997), *Robak in Black* (2001).
Non-series: *The Color of Hate* (1960; rev'd as *Color Him Guilty*, 1987), *The Poison Summer* (1974), *Rivertown Risk* (1977), *Fort's Law* (1987), *Grim City* (1994), *Loose Coins* with Guy M. Townsend (1998).
Short Stories. *Final Doors* (1981), *Robak's Firm* (1987), *Deadly Hunger* (2001).

Full name: Joseph Louis Hensley.
Where to start: *Deliver Us to Evil.*
Similar stuff: William BERNHARDT, Jay BRANDON, William HARRINGTON.
Final fact: Harlan Ellison tells how the nerves in one of JLH's hands are dead as a result of a fire which allows JLH to pound his fist against a brick wall with no apparent pain.

Evelyn Hervey *pseudonym, see* H.R.F. Keating

Joan Hess (b. 1949) US

At first glance both of JH's two long-runing series may seem traditional cozy mysteries, but they are only to a degree. Both have small town settings, and both are generally light-hearted, but both also have deeper levels and can shift from humour to pathos very quickly. One reviewer remarked that it was difficult to say whether JH's mysteries were "pure fun or clever social commentary" and, of course, they're both. The Claire Malloy series is set in Farberville, a lightly fictionalized version of JH's hometown of Fayetteville, Arkansas. Malloy, who narrates the stories, is a young widow who runs a bookstore and looks after a rapidly maturing teenage daughter, Caron. Emotions run high throughout the series, and though there are frequent comic scenes there is also much soul-searching and grief. The first book, *Strangled Prose*, is not typical of the series. Malloy holds a signing party for an author whose book casts thinly disguised aspersions on the local townsfolk, including Malloy's dead husband, so it's little surprise when the author is killed. In later books

Malloy ventures out of her store to prime murder locales such as a "murder weekend" in the confusingly titled *The Murder at the Murder at the Mimosa Inn*, or a private school in *Dear Miss Demeanor*. The books have become more light-hearted as the series has progressed, although *Roll Over and Play Dead*, about stolen pets, is more downbeat. A familiarity with the cast of characters can lead to a certain sameness, but such is not the case with the ever-inventive series set in backwoods Arkansas in Maggody (population 755) where chief of police Arly Hanks has her work cut out. Here JH introduces a larger cast of characters and a never-ending stream of visitors from a Hollywood film crew in *Mortal Remains in Maggody* to an evangelical sect in *Miracles in Maggody*. The town comes alive in this series and every mystery is an adventure. JH began a third series of botanical mysteries under the alias Joan Hadley. Theo Bloomer is a retired florist who has to keep rescuing his niece Dorrie from trouble. The series did not sell so well and was dropped after two books. JH has won both the Agatha and Macavity awards for her short fiction, and has been nominated six times for her novels. *A Diet to Die For*, a Claire Malloy novel about fad diets, won the American Mystery Award for best traditional novel.

Novels

Claire Malloy series: *Strangled Prose* (1986), *The Murder at the Murder at the Mimosa Inn* (1986), *Dear Miss Demeanor* (1987), *A Really Cute Corpse* (1988), *A Diet to Die For* (1989), *Roll Over and Play Dead* (1991), *Death by the Light of the Moon* (1992), *Poisoned Pins* (1993), *Tickled to Death* (1994), *Busy Bodies* (1995), *Closely Akin to Murder* (1996), *A Holly, Jolly Murder* (1997), *A Conventional Corpse* (2000).

Maggody series: *Malice in Maggody* (1987), *Mischief in Maggody* (1988), *Much Ado in Maggody* (1989), *Madness in Maggody* (1990), *Mortal Remains in Maggody* (1991), *Maggody in Manhattan* (1992), *O Little Town of Maggody* (1993), *Martians in Maggody* (1994), *Miracles in Maggody* (1995), *The Maggody Militia* (1997), *Misery Loves Maggody* (1998), *Murder@Maggody.com* (2000), *Maggody and the Moonbeams* (2001).

Theo Bloomer series as Joan Hadley: *The Night-Blooming Cereus* (1986), *The Deadly Ackee* (1988).

Short Stories: *Death of a Romance Writer* (2002).

Editor. *Funny Bones* (1997), *Year's 25 Finest Crime and Mystery Stories: Sixth Annual Edition* with Ed Gorman & Martin H. Greenberg (1997; abr. as *Crime After Crime*, 1999), *Malice Domestic 9* (2000).

Pen-name: Joan Hadley.

Where to start: *Malice in Maggody*.

Awards: American Mystery Award, best traditional novel (1990), Agatha and Macavity, best short story (1991).

Website: <www.joanhess.com> and <www.maggody.com>

Similar stuff: Deborah ADAMS, Carolyn G. HART.

Final fact: The name Maggody came from a tiny village in Jamaica called Maggotty.

Carl Hiaasen (b. 1953) US

CH is the closest Florida has to a conscience. His books hold a mirror up to the sleaze, crime and corruption in the sunshine state. By tweaking the bizarre and fine-tuning the eccentric, CH allows us to laugh at ourselves and point the finger of guilt at others. CH's first three novels were collaborations with journalist colleague William Montalbano and are not typical. They are more serious fight-or-flight revenge novels, though *Trap Line*, about corruption in the Conch-fishing world, has some nascent CH touches. He found his own voice with *Tourist Season*, a wonderfully zany caper novel where a series of increasingly bizarre deaths leads reporter-turned-P.I., Brian Keyes, further into a Marx-Brothers world. From there on CH was on a roller-coaster ride. Each novel, though serious and suspenseful in its own right, uses the quirky and unusual to potent effect. There's the plastic surgeon with the shakes and the hit-man with gross skin problems in *Skin Tight*, where retired State investigator Mick Stranahan has to defend himself with a stuffed marlin head. There's the man with the tranquilizer gun and a roomful of skulls who is Bonnie Lamb's only hope to find her missing husband in *Stormy Weather*. There's the intellectually challenged white supremist Bodean Gazzer who takes objection to sharing his lottery win with a black woman in *Lucky You*. Every CH novel starts with the slightly odd and heads off down bizarre alleys. So far only one of CH's books has been filmed, *Striptease* (1996). CH has resisted the demands by Hollywood to create a regular series character. Apart from homicide detective Al Garcia, who appears now and then, the only "by popular demand" character is former state governer Skink, who had a breakdown and hid in the Everglades and pops up occasionally to challenge right and wrong. Skink has become something of an eco-champion and environmental issues are at the core of several of CH's novels, especially *Native Tongue* and *Sick Puppy*. CH has been a reporter since he obtained his degree in journalism at the University of Florida in 1974. He has written regularly for the Miami *Herald* since 1976, where he worked for a while with Edna BUCHANAN. Some of his hard-hitting, challenging columns, reprinted as *Kick Ass* and *Paradise Screwed*, serve to demonstrate that life continues to be weirder than fiction.

Novels. *Tourist Season* (1986), *Double Whammy* (1987), *Skin Tight* (1989), *Native Tongue* (1991), *Striptease* (1993), *Stormy Weather* (1995), *Lucky You* (1997), *Sick Puppy* (1999), *Basket Case* (2002).
with William D. Montalbano: *Powder Burn* (1981), *Trap Line* (1982), *A Death in China* (1984).
Non-fiction. *Team Rodent* (1998), *Kick Ass* (1999), *Paradise Screwed* (2001).
Where to start: *Tourist Season.*
Awards: Anthony Bookseller's Award (1992), CWA Last Laugh (1992), Dilys (1992).

Website: www.carlhiaasen.com
Similar stuff: James W. HALL, Laurence SHAMES.
Final fact: CH keeps snakes as pets and has written two songs with Warren Zevon on his album *Mutineer*.

George V. Higgins (1939–99) US

The problem with starting your writing career with a mini-masterpiece is that you are always having to live up to it. GVH didn't always, though his hit rate was impressive. GVH began life as a reporter on the Providence, Rhode Island *Journal* in 1962, but having achieved his law degree in 1967 he was admitted to the Massachusetts Bar. He was a prosecuting attorney for the Commonwealth of Massachusetts and later District of Massachusetts from 1969–73, during which time GVH was involved in several cases concerning the Mafia. He established his own private practice in 1974 and also served as instructor in trial practice at Boston College Law School. All of this was formidable background when GVH turned to writing novels and he scored first time out with *The Friends of Eddie Coyle* (filmed 1973), a powerful, realistic story of a no-good hoodlum and police informer who tries unsuccessfully to stay out of trouble. The realism in the novel comes from GVH's dialogue. He maintained he always kept his "ears open" and through his years in the courts GVH had mastered the criminal patter. His stories are told through dialogue with a skill mastered by few others. Only Elmore LEONARD is spoken of in the same breath as GVH. GVH did not like to be regarded as a crime writer, maintaining that he wrote "novels", as if there were a literary distinction. Although some of his books are closer to the mainstream, most of them deal with crime in some form. There's City Hall politics and corruption in *A Choice of Enemies*, *Impostors* or *A Change of Gravity*, or small-time crooks with whom GVH showed some sympathy, in *The Judgement of Deke Hunter* or *Trust*. Despite his work as an attorney GVH did not write as many legal thrillers or courtroom dramas as one might expect. There are five books featuring 40-something lawyer Jerry Kennedy, who spends his life defending people he knows are guilty and trying to patch deals. There's little plot in the first three Kennedy books, though a lot still happens, usually to Kennedy's detriment. One of the best of GVH's courtroom novels is *Outlaws* about a gang of urban terrorists brought to trial. Critics felt that by his later books GVH had become complacent but that is certainly not true of *The Mandeville Talent*, where an attorney tries to solve the death of his wife's grandfather, *Bomber's Law*, about the hunt for a Mob hit-man, or *At End of Day*, his last novel, based on a true story about two gangsters and their relationship with the FBI.

Novels

Non-series: *The Friends of Eddie Coyle* (1972), *The Digger's Game* (1973), *Cogan's Trade* (1974), *The Judgment of Deke Hunter* (1976), *Dreamland* (1977), *A Year or*

So With Edgar (1979), *The Patriot Game* (1982), *A Choice of Enemies* (1984), *Impostors* (1986), *Outlaws* (1987), *Wonderful Years, Wonderful Years* (1988), *Trust* (1989), *Victories* (1990), *The Mandeville Talent* (1991), *Bomber's Law* (1993), *Swan Boats at Four* (1995), *A Change of Gravity* (1997), *The Agent* (1999), *At End of Day* (2000).

Jerry Kennedy series: *Kennedy for the Defense* (1980), *The Rat on Fire* (1981), *Penance for Jerry Kennedy* (1985), *Defending Billy Ryan* (1992), *Sandra Nichols Found Dead* (1996).

Short Stories. *The Sins of the Fathers* (1988).

Non-fiction. *The Friends of Richard Nixon* (1975), *Style Versus Substance* (1984), *On Writing* (1990).

Full name: George Vincent Higgins.

Where to start: *The Friends of Eddie Coyle.*

Similar stuff: Elmore LEONARD, Ted LEWIS.

Final fact: As a defence attorney, GVH's clients included Watergate conspirator G. Gordon Liddy and Black Panther activist Eldridge Cleaver.

Patricia Highsmith (1921–95) US

PH's novels and stories are, at their extreme, macabre expeditions into fear, more horror than crime, like Roald Dahl's *Tales of the Unexpected.* Even her less extreme works are bleak and unremitting, pushing the acceptable boundaries of suspense. Graham Greene remarked that the world of a PH novel is "claustrophobic and irrational which we enter each time with a sense of personal danger.' At the heart of her crime novels is the simple idea that anyone can be a murderer, over which she laid the complexity that anyone could be mistaken for a murderer. In *Strangers on a Train* (filmed 1951 and 1969, last as *Once You Kiss a Stranger*) two men meet on a train and in discussion realize that they could each rid the other of their burdens – one of a wife, the other of a domineering mother. PH took this idea one step further in *The Blunderer* (filmed 1963 as *The Murderer*), where a man's wife dies accidentally but people become suspicious when he regularly visits another who had murdered his wife by a similar method. The ease with which someone could accept murder was the basis for her character Tom Ripley who first appears in *The Talented Mr Ripley* (filmed 1960 [as *Plein Soleil*] and 1999). Ripley is on the surface a friendly if nervous individual but he has no qualms in disposing of people to further his own aims. He is utterly ruthless and it is unsettling how easily PH makes him appealing to the reader. Like Thomas HARRIS would later with Hannibal Lecter, PH takes us into the mind of Tom Ripley allowing us to associate with his actions. Ripley becomes even more ruthless in the later novels and yet PH still sustains the reader's sympathy. Several of PH's novels and stories have been filmed by European directors including *Ripley's Game* (filmed 1977 as *The American Friend*). PH's other novels move away from crime towards suspense and fantasy, such as *Edith's Diary*, where an old lady creates an escapist world.

There is a strong feeling in PH's work that she, too, is trying to escape, deep-rooted memories from her childhood. Her parents, both artists, separated before she was born and PH did not meet her real father until she was 12. She lived with her grandmother and remained a loner, eventually settling in Europe in 1963 (mostly in France or East Anglia in England). She also showed talent as an artist and sculptress but writing remained her true passion.

Novels
Ripley series: *The Talented Mr Ripley* (1955), *Ripley Under Ground* (1970), *Ripley's Game* (1974), *The Boy Who Followed Ripley* (1980), *Ripley Under Water* (1992).
Non-series: *Strangers on a Train* (1950), *The Blunderer* (1954; as *Lament for a Lover*, 1956), *Deep Water* (1957), *A Game for the Living* (1958), *This Sweet Sickness* (1960), *The Cry of the Owl* (1962), *The Two Faces of January* (1964), *The Glass Cell* (1964), *The Story-Teller* (1965; as *A Suspension of Mercy*, UK 1965), *Those Who Walk Away* (1967), *The Tremor of Forgery* (1969), *A Dog's Ransom* (1972), *Edith's Diary* (1977), *The People Who Knock on the Door* (1983), *Found in the Street* (1986).
Short Stories. *The Snail-Watcher* (1970; as *Eleven*, UK 1970), *Little Tales of Misogyny* (Germany, 1974; UK 1977), *The Animal Lover's Book of Beastly Murder* (1986), *Slowly, Slowly in the Wind* (1979), *The Black House* (1981; exp. US 1988), *Mermaids on the Golfcourse* (1988), *Tales of Natural and Unnatural Catastrophes* (1988), *Chillers* (1990), *Selected Stories* (2001).
Non-fiction. *Plotting and Writing Suspense Fiction* (1966; rev'd 1990).

Full name: Mary Patricia Plaugman (assumed stepfather's name, Highsmith).
Pen-name: Claire Morgan.
Where to start: *Strangers on a Train.*
Awards: French Grand Prix de Littérature Policière, best foreign (1958), CWA, best foreign (1964), Swedish Academy of Detection, Grand Master (1979).
Similar stuff: Roald Dahl, Shizuko NATSUKI, Ingrid NOLL.
Final fact: After PH left college she spent some time providing story-lines for the comics and it is believed she worked on scripts for *Black Terror* and possibly *Captain America.*

John Spencer Hill (1943–98) Canada

JSH was a Professor of English at the University of Ottawa with a wide range of interests, having published books on John Milton, Samuel Taylor Coleridge, John Keats and Euripedes. He was also the editor of *The Romantic Imagination* (1977). He had a special interest in the Renaissance period and this inspired his first mystery novel, *The Last Castrato.* An American student visits Florence to study a secret Renaissance musical brotherhood and her life becomes enmeshed with Inspector Carlo Arbati who is investigating the murder of a local cardinal. JSH carries the story along at a strong pace while still delivering fascinating insights into the Renaissance period and especially the cult of the *castrati.* Arbati, who is also something of a poet, reappears in *Ghirlandaio's Daughter* where he becomes involved in investigating an art fraud. This could have become a fine series but JSH died of a massive heart attack aged only 54.

Novels
Carlo Arbati series: *The Last Castrato* (1995), *Ghirlandaio's Daughter* (1996).

Full name: John Spencer Hill.
Awards: Arthur Ellis award (1996), San Francisco Review of Books, Critics' Choice award (1996), Harlequin/Worldwide Library Prize (1996) all for best first mystery novel.
Similar stuff: Michael DIBDIN (for Italian police), Elizabeth EYRE, Derek WILSON.
Final fact: A John Spencer Hill Award for Fiction was established after JSH's death.

Reginald Hill (b. 1936) UK

RH is the author of the popular police detective series featuring Dalziel and Pascoe and has been dubbed Britain's "finest living crime writer' by the *Daily Telegraph*. Having earned his degree in English at Oxford in 1960, RH taught at secondary school and college before becoming a full-time writer in 1981. By then he was an established writer with 20 books to his credit. *A Clubbable Woman* introduced Superintendent Andrew Dalziel and Sergent Peter Pascoe of the Mid-Yorkshire C.I.D. Dalziel, known as Fat Andy, is coarse and blunt, with few social graces, but has an intuitive understanding of human nature. Pascoe is college-educated and ambitious – he rises through the ranks as the series progresses. Sensitive, with a more liberal attitude to people, Pascoe finds Dalziel obnoxious but respects his instincts and insights. The development over the years from their initial antipathy towards a complementary team is one of the strengths of the series. RH is able to balance sharp wit and intelligent observation against the emotions arising from murder, fear and loss, which bring a stark realism to his books. He also uses the Yorkshire background to good effect. *Under World*, for instance, takes place during a national miners' strike. *Pictures of Perfection* is a study of how social change is destroying the traditional country way of life. Occasionally the characters venture further afield. *An April Shroud* has Pascoe on honeymoon and Dalziel stumbling over a mystery while trapped with a funeral procession when on holiday in Lincolnshire. *Recalled to Life* sends Dalziel to New York to resolve an old miscarriage of justice. RH likes to experiment. Not only has he gone back to the very beginning and recounted when Dalziel and Pascoe first met in "The Last National Serviceman" (in *Asking for the Moon*) but looked ahead and in *One Small Step* tells of the first murder on the Moon in 2010. Both *Child's Play* and *Under World* were shortlisted for the CWA Gold Dagger Award, which RH finally won with *Bones and Silence*. More recently the stark and poignant *On Beulah Height* won the Barry Award. The series has adapted well to TV and the adaptation of *On Beulah Height* (1999) won the Edgar.

RH has not taken it easy between Dalziel and Pascoe novels but has written almost an equal amount of non-series books. These include espionage novels (*The Spy's Wife* and *Traitor's Blood*), a tale of military revenge (*A Very Good Hater*), suspense (*Fell of Dark*), a secret life (*Death of a Dormouse*), psychological drama (*Another Death in Venice*) and even attempts by the freemasons to undermine the British government (*Who Guards the Prince?*). In the story "Bring Back the Cat!" (in *There Are No Ghosts in the Soviet Union*) RH introduced the balding West Indian P.I. Joe Sixsmith who operates out of Luton. RH found the character's honesty and basic humanity so appealing that he developed him into a new series. The first book, *Blood Sympathy*, was shortlisted for the CWA's Last Laugh award. RH's fiction can be bleak – he has even written a pseudonymous novel [*Albion! Albion!* as Dick Morland (1974) where football hooligans take over running the country] – but at their heart they show the unquenchable human spirit and determination for justice.

Novels

Dalziel & Pascoe series: *A Clubbable Woman* (1970), *An Advancement of Learning* (1971), *Ruling Passion* (1973), *An April Shroud* (1975), *A Pinch of Snuff* (1978), *A Killing Kindness* (1980), *Deadheads* (1983), *Exit Lines* (1984), *Child's Play* (1987), *Under World* (1988), *Bones and Silence* (1990), *One Small Step* (1990), *Recalled to Life* (1992), *Pictures of Perfection* (1994), *The Wood Beyond* (1996), *On Beulah Height* (1998), *Arms and the Woman* (2000), *Dialogues of the Dead* (2001), *Death's Jest Book* (2002).

Joe Sixsmith: *Blood Sympathy* (1993), *Born Guilty* (1995), *Killing the Lawyers* (1997), *Singing the Sadness* (1999).

Non-series: *Fell of Dark* (1971), *A Fairly Dangerous Thing* (1972), *A Very Good Hater* (1974), *Another Death in Venice* (1976), *The Spy's Wife* (1980), *Who Guards a Prince?* (1982; as *Guardians of the Prince*, 1983), *Traitor's Blood* (1983), *No Man's Land* (1985), *The Collaborators* (1987), *The Four Clubs* (1997).

as Patrick Ruell: *The Castle of the Demon* (1971), *Red Christmas* (1972), *Death Takes the Low Road* (1974), *Urn Burial* (1975), *The Long Kill* (1986; as by RH 1998), *Death of a Dormouse* (1987), *Dreams of Darkness* (1989; as by RH 1997), *The Only Game* (1991).

Short Stories. *Pascoe's Ghost* (1979), *There Are No Ghosts in the Soviet Union* (1987), *Brother's Keeper* (1992), *Asking for the Moon* (1994).

Full name: Reginald Charles Hill.
Pen-names: Dick Morland, Patrick Ruell, Charles Underhill.
Where to start: *A Clubbable Woman.*
Awards: CWA Gold Dagger (1990), Diamond Dagger (1995), Short Story Dagger (1997), Barry award (1999), Macavity, best short story (2001).
Website: <www.randomhouse.com/features/reghill/>
Similar stuff: Pauline BELL, Peter ROBINSON, Peter TURNBULL.
Final fact: Under the pen-name of Charles Underhill RH wrote two rollicking historical adventure novels about Captain Fantom, a "soldier of misfortune, hard man and ravisher."

Tony Hillerman (b. 1925) US

Crime fiction doesn't come much better than in the books of TH or, for that matter, much different. Born in Sacred Heart, Oklahoma, TH was raised and educated amongst the Pottawatomie and Seminole Indians and has had a lifelong interest in and respect for the cultures, beliefs and values of the native Americans. After a distinguished service in the army during WW2 and a career as a journalist, newspaper editor and finally lecturer in journalism, TH put his knowledge into the novel *The Blessing Way*. This introduced Navajo police lieutenant Joe Leaphorn who investigates what appears to be a ritual murder and finds himself on the trail of the Wolf-Witch. Thankfully TH ignored the advice of his then literary agent to "drop all that Indian stuff." The novel was short-listed for the Edgar first novel award and the follow-up, *Dance Hall of the Dead*, where Leaphorn has to track a murderer across the deserts of New Mexico and Arizona, went on to win the Edgar for best novel. The third novel, *Listening Woman*, where a blind Navajo woman is "witness" to a crime, was also shortlisted for the Edgar. TH then introduced a new detective, Sergeant Jim Chee. Whereas Leaphorn is unsure about his native American beliefs, because he has become Americanized, Chee is a devout young believer. He thus has a different perspective on the crimes he investigates, less sceptical and more insightful. The first three Chee novels strongly contrast Navajo and American values. The Chee novels include *The Dark Wind* (filmed 1991), where a plane crashes into the desert and a shipment of cocaine vanishes. In *Skinwalkers* TH brought Chee and Leaphorn together. It was not a meeting of minds. Leaphorn tells Chee that though he respects him he does not like him. The two conduct their investigations in their own way and this allows TH to explore in more depth the conflict between cultures. *A Thief of Time*, finds Leaphorn further questioning his beliefs when the tragic death of his wife leads Leaphorn to reconsider the Navajo beliefs about the dead. This novel, which was nominated for an Edgar and won the Macavity award, is not only a search for the murderer of an archeologist but also a quest into the past and the mysteries of the lost Anasazi tribe, and is regarded by many as the best of the series. TH's descriptions of ceremonial rituals in his novels are so accurate that he was cross-examined by Zuñi elders to see whether any of their people had revealed secrets. TH has written two non-series crime novels. *Fly on the Wall* has a journalist investigating political corruption and *Finding Moon* sends a newspaper editor back to Vietnam to look for his dead brother's lost daughter. The fascination with the Chee and Leaphorn series has resulted in various spin-off books. TH has produced several descriptive guides to the American southwest, including *Rio Grande* (1975) and *Indian Country* (1987). He has also compiled a book of native American stories, *The Great Taos Bank Robbery* and the Zuñi myth, *The Boy Who Made Dragonfly* (1972). Further anecdotes are told in his autobiography *Seldom Disappointed.*

Novels
Joe Leaphorn series (with Jim Chee after book 3): *The Blessing Way* (1970), *Dance Hall of the Dead* (1973), *Listening Woman* (1978), *Skinwalkers* (1987), *A Thief of Time* (1988), *Talking God* (1989), *Coyote Waits* (1990), *Sacred Clowns* (1993), *Fallen Man* (1996), *The First Eagle* (1998), *Hunting Badger* (1999), *The Wailing Wind* (2002).
Jim Chee alone: *People of Darkness* (1980), *The Dark Wind* (1982), *The Ghostway* (1984), thereafter with Leaphorn. These three novels collected as *The Jim Chee Mysteries* (1990).
Non-series: *The Fly on the Wall* (1971), *Finding Moon* (1995)
Non-fiction (selective). *The Great Taos Bank Robbery and Other Indian Country Affairs* (1973)
Editor. *The Mysterious West* (1994), *Oxford Book of American Detective Stories*, with Rosemary Herbert (1996), *The Best American Mystery Stories of the Century*, with Otto Penzler (2000).
Autobiography. *Seldom Disappointed* (2001).
Books about: *Words, Weather and Wolfmen: Conversations with Tony Hillerman* by TH & Ernie Bulow (1989; rev'd as *Talking Mysteries*, 1991); *The Tony Hillerman Companion* ed. Martin H. Greenberg (1995), *Tony Hillerman: A Critical Companion* by John M. Reilly (1996), *Tony Hillerman's Navaholand* by Laurance D. Linford (2001).

Full name: Anthony Grove Hillerman.
Where to start: *The Blessing Way* or *Skinwalkers*.
Awards: Shaffer award for reporting (1952), Edgar, best novel (1974), Grand Prix de Littérature Policière Best Foreign (1987), Western Writers Silver Spur, best novel (1987), Anthony, best novel (1988), Macavity, best novel (1989), Nero Wolfe award (1991), MWA Grand Master (1991), Macavity, best biographical/critical work (1992), Swedish Academy of Detection, Grand Master (1993), Anthony, lifetime achievement (1994), best anthology (1995). Most meaningful to TH, though, is the "Special Friends to the Dineh" award granted by the Navajo nation in 1987 for "authentically portraying the strength and dignity of traditional Navajo culture."
Website: unofficial homepage at <www.umsl.edu/~smueller/>
Similar stuff: Brian GARFIELD's Sam Watchman, Thomas PERRY's Jane Whitefield, Alanna KNIGHT's *Angel Eyes* and the works of Jean HAGER and J.A.JANCE.
Final fact: When in Paris in 1987 TH had to fetch some medicine from the doctor because his wife was ill. On the way he bumped into a man and they got talking. Clearly the man was overcome by sympathy at TH's plight because after their conversation he returned to him the wallet and travellers' cheques he had lifted from TH's pocket!

John Buxton Hilton (1921–86) UK

JBH did not turn to writing until he was almost 50 and in fact the majority of his writing followed his retirement as an Inspector of Schools and, previously, a grammar school headmaster and teacher of languages. JBH was in the Intelligence Corps during WW2. Combine these qualities and you have much of the character of JBH's chief character, Inspector (later Superintendent) Kenworthy of Scotland Yard – smart, wily, exacting and determined. Kenworthy's cases take him all over England, and most of them have causes rooted deep in the past. During this long series Kenworthy rises through the ranks but is eventually forced into early retirement and the final few cases find him investigating cases privately. Fine though this series is – solid and reliable police procedurals – JBH's best work lay in his other two series. The books featuring Thomas Brunt are set in the Peak District (where JBH was born and raised) in the late Victorian and Edwardian periods. Brunt is a village constable in *The Quiet Stranger* but has reached Inspector by the time of *Mr Fred* set just before WW1. These books are an excellent evocation of the difficult and strenuous country life at this time and the isolation of many of the people. They are amongst the best historical detective stories of their day. JBH's other series, written as John Greenwood, is more light-hearted. Set in the present on the Yorkshire/Lancashire borders where JBH was for many years a head-master, they feature Inspector Mosley, a friendly, kind-hearted seemingly innocuous fellow whose skills are not appreciated by his superiors but who nevertheless solves murders simply and quietly. The delight of this series is how Mosley uses his knowledge, experience and network of friends to resolve matters that the more bureaucratic and so-called "modern' detective cannot. It is a shame that JBH started writing so late in life and that he did not have time to write more about Brunt and Mosley.

Novels

Superintendent Kenworthy series: *Death of an Alderman* (1968; as *Dead Man's Path*, US 1992), *Death in Midwinter* (1969), *Hangman's Tide* (1975), *No Birds Sang* (1975; as *Target of Suspicion*, US 1994), *Some Run Crooked* (1978), *The Anathema Stone* (1980; as *Fatal Curtain*, US 1990), *Playground of Death* (1981), *Surrender Value* (1981; as *Twice Dead*, US 1992), *The Green Frontier* (1982; as *Focus on Crime*, US 1993), *The Sunset Law* (1982), *The Asking Price* (1983; as *Ransom Game*, US 1992), *Corridors of Guilt* (1984), *The Hobbema Prospect* (1984; as *Cradle of Crime*, US 1991), *Passion in the Park* (1986; as *Holiday for Murder*, US 1991), *Moondrop to Murder* (1986), *The Innocents at Home* (1986; as *Lesson in Murder*, US 1991), *Displaced Persons* (1987).

Inspector Brunt series: *Rescue from the Rose* (1976), *Gamekeeper's Gallows* (1976), *Dead-Nettle* (1977), *Mr. Fred* (1983), *The Quiet Stranger* (1985), *Slickensides* (1987).

Inspector Mosley series as John Greenwood: *Murder, Mr. Mosley* (1983), *Mosley by Moonlight* (1984), *Mosley Went to Mow* (1985; as *The Missing Mr. Mosley*, US 1985), *Mists Over Mosley* (1986), *The Mind of Mr. Mosley* (1987), *What Me, Mr. Mosley?* (1987).

Pen-name: John Greenwood.
Where to start: *Rescue from the Rose* or *Murder, Mr. Mosley*.
Similar stuff: Eric WRIGHT's Charlie Salter, Reginald HILL.
Final fact: Kenworthy and Mosley were the names of JBH's cats.

Chester Himes (1909–84) US

CH was one of the first major voices amongst black writers in crime fiction. Born into a well-educated family in Missouri, where his father taught at the local black college, CH was himself expelled from Ohio State University, after the family had moved to Cleveland, for taking students to a gambling den. CH entered into a life of crime and was imprisoned for armed robbery in 1928. While in prison he read Hammett's stories in *Black Mask* and believed he could do as well. He never sold to *Black Mask*, but after placing stories in several African-American magazines, starting with "His Last Day" (*Abbott's Monthly*, 1932), he began to sell to *Esquire* and other prestigious markets. This facilitated his early release in 1936, and though he continued to write for newspapers and magazines no publishers would consider his books and CH ended up working in the shipyards in California during WW2. It was not until 1945 that Doubleday published *If He Hollers Let Him Go*, an autobiographical account of racism in the defence industry. Struggling to sell his books CH moved to Europe in 1953, settling in Paris. The French had a strong interest in hard-boiled crime fiction and CH was encouraged to write. With the help of editor Marcel Duhamel, CH began to find a market in France and through them markets in the US. He began a series of books about two black New York police detectives, Coffin Ed Johnson and Grave Digger Jones. They have the worst of both worlds. Despised by the whites and distrusted by the blacks, the two are seldom assigned major cases but instead patrol the streets in Harlem and follow what comes along. Coffin Ed is driven to fits of rage which are worse after his face is disfigured when acid is thrown at him in the first novel, *For Love of Imabelle*. Jones frequently has to stop him fighting and even killing people. The French appreciated CH's work far more than in his home country where it was too unpalatable. The first novel won the French Grand Prix, but CH never won a literary award in the US. As the novels progress the two detectives are drawn deeper into the underworld of crime. In *The Real Cool Killers* it's the trade in young black girls. In *All Shot Up* (which features one of the most exciting car chases in all crime fiction) it's a big heist and a corrupt homosexual politician; while in *Cotton Comes to Harlem* (filmed 1970) it's a corrupt preacher with a major con scheme. In *The Heat's On* (filmed 1972 as *Come Back, Charleston Blue*) it's drugs and a series of savage murders. During the sixties the racial tension in America boiled over and CH's last completed crime novel, *Blind Man with a Pistol* ends with Digger and Ed overwhelmed by a race riot and shooting at rats. He found it impossible to complete *Plan B*, because the scale of violence choked even him. CH's books were extremely violent for their day but he was only holding a mirror up to reality. CH's *A Case of Rape* was too strong for American publishers and though published in France in 1968 did not see a US edition until 1980. Amongst his other novels is *Cast the First Stone*, which told of his life in prison. CH was the first black writer to depict honestly and openly the scale of crime, social upheaval and racism in New York, and he paved the way for the next generation of black writers. CH died in Spain, still unappreciated in his homeland. Eventually in 1996 a Chester Himes award was initiated for the best black fiction.

Novels

Coffin Ed & Grave Digger Jones series: *For Love of Imabelle* (1957; as *A Rage in Harlem*, 1965), *The Crazy Kill* (1959), *The Real Cool Killers* (1959), *All Shot Up* (1960), *The Big Gold Dream* (1960), *Cotton Comes to Harlem* (1965), *The Heat's On* (1966; as *Come Back, Charleston Blue*, 1970), *Blind Man With a Pistol* (1969; as *Hot Day, Hot Night*, 1970), *Plan B* (France 1983; US 1993). These have been reissued in three volumes under the generic title *The Harlem Cycle*.

Non-series: *Cast the First Stone* (1952), *Run Man Run* (1966), *Une Affaire de Viol* (France 1968; as *A Case of Rape*, US 1980)

Short Stories. *The Collected Stories of Chester Himes* (1990).

Autobiography: *The Quality of Hurt* (1972), *My Life of Absurdity* (1976).

Books about: *Chester Himes* by James Lundquist (1976), *Two Guns from Harlem* by Robert E. Skinner (1989), *Conversations with Chester Himes* by Robert E. Skinner and Michel Fabre (1995), *The Several Lives of Chester Himes* by Edward Margolies and Michel Fabre (1997), *Chester Himes: A Life* by James Sallis (2000).

Full name: Chester Bomar Himes.

Where to start: *The Crazy Kill.*

Awards: Grand Prix de Littérature Policière Best Foreign (1959).

Website: <www.math.buffalo.edu/~sww/Himes/>

Similar stuff: Clarence COOPER Jr., Walter MOSLEY, Ernest TIDYMAN.

Tami Hoag (b. 1959) US

In 1999 TH achieved the unprecedented record of having five books hit the *New York Times* bestseller list in the space of 20 months. Born in Minnesota but now living in Virginia, TH has held a variety of jobs, from selling designer toilet seats to training show horses (and horses remain one of her passions), before she sold her first book, *The Trouble With JJ*, in 1988. This and the next 14 were all romance titles, but steadily TH injected more mystery and suspense until, by *Still Waters*, she had crossed the divide. That book, though still at its core a romance novel, is about the relationship between a young fiery newspaperwoman, who moves to small-town Minnesota, and the local sheriff, who was once a professional athlete. The woman encounters a dead body and becomes the prime suspect. TH regards *Night Sins* (filmed 1997 TV) as her first real mystery-suspense novel. Also set in small-town Minnesota it concerns the disappearance of a young boy and a connection with a murder 26 years before. *Guilty as Sin* follows on immediately after these events in a relentless sequel. These two are available as the *Tami Hoag Omnibus*. *A Thin Dark Line* shares a common background and characters with her romantic suspense novel *Cry Wolf*, the Louisiana Bayou country, though it is not a sequel. It concerns a cop, ostracized by her colleagues, who becomes the obsession of a serial killer. There's another serial killer, this one called "The Cremator" in *Ashes to Ashes*. TH became fascinated with the local Minneapolis police detective Sam Kovac who appears in that novel and reintroduced him in a taut police procedural *Dust to Dust* where he investigates the death of a fellow gay police officer. TH's transition from romance writer to crime writer has been more successful than most because of her strong characterization and attention to detail.

Novels

Non-series: *Still Waters* (1992), *Cry Wolf* (1993), *Dark Paradise* (1994), *A Thin Dark Line* (1997).

Deer Lake sequence: *Night Sins* (1996), *Guilty as Sin* (1997).

Kovac & Liska series: *Ashes to Ashes* (1999), *Dust to Dust* (2000).

Similar stuff: Clare FRANCIS, Nicci FRENCH, Ruth RENDELL as Barbara Vine.
Final fact: TH has been a successful competitor in dressage competitions, placing second in the Florida Grand Prix in February 2001.

Edward D. Hoch (b. 1930) US

EDH is a literary phenomenon. He is the sole surviving writer of mysteries to earn his living by writing short fiction alone. In the heyday of the pulp magazines that was easy, but the pulps folded about the time EDH started writing, and with today's limited markets it is staggering that EDH has notched up over 860 stories. He is still producing at the rate of about 20 per year, so he should reach the magic 1,000 before his 80th birthday, a record that no other writer is likely to attain. EDH's achievement has been recognized by his elevation to a MWA Grand Master plus lifetime achievements awards from both the PWA and the Bouchercon committee. EDH has written very few novels and three of those, the series featuring Computer Cops Carl Crader and Earl Jazine, are set in the future. Only *The Shattered Raven*, about a murder before a full audience at the MWA Edgar Awards banquet, is a bona fide contemporary mystery, though he has ghosted an Ellery Queen novel. Only a small proportion of EDH's stories have been collected in book form, though these are at last gathering pace. A fair proportion of his work falls into one of nearly 30 character series, though not all have run extensively. His earliest was Simon Ark who appeared in EDH's first story, "Village of the Dead" (*Famous Detective Stories*, 1955). Ark is a mysterious character who purports to be a 2,000 year-old Coptic priest. Although the stories have some arcane or bizarre element they are always rationalized. Others who have stayed the course over the years include Ben Snow, a gunslinger in the Old West; Captain Leopold, chief of police in an upstate New York city; Jeffrey Rand, a spy, later retired, who is an expert in codes and cryptograms; Nick Velvet, a thief who steals only valueless objects; Dr Sam Hawthorne, a retired doctor who recounts his cases from between the Wars; and the Interpol series with two protagonists Sebastian Blue and Laura Charme not unlike the original "Avengers". EDH's stories all follow a traditional form but he loves to play tricks and he is the modern champion of the impossible crime. All of the Sam Hawthorne stories are "impossibles". Two of the Captain Leopold "impossibles" were adapted for the TV series *McMillan and Wife*. Other stories have been adapted for the TV series *The Alfred Hitchcock Hour*, *Night Gallery* and *Tales of the Unexpected* but only one has been made into a full-length feature film, *It Takes All Kinds* (1969), based on "A Girl Like Cathy" (1966). In addition to the books listed below are seven collections published only in Japan and two mystery stories for teenagers collected as *The Monkey's Clue and The Stolen Sapphire* (1978).

Novels
Crader and Jazine series: *The Transvection Machine* (1971), *The Fellowship of the Hand* (1973), *The Frankenstein Factory* (1975).
Non-series: *The Shattered Raven* (1969).
Ghosted for Ellery Queen: *The Blue Movie Murders* (1972).
Short Stories
Simon Ark series: *The Judges of Hades* (1971), *City of Brass* (1971), *The Quests of Simon Ark* (1984).
Nick Velvet stories: *The Spy and the Thief* (1971) also includes Rand stories, *The Thefts of Nick Velvet* (1978), *The Velvet Touch* (2000).
Captain Leopold series: *Leopold's Way* (1985).
Jeffrey Rand series: *The Spy and the Thief* (1971) also includes Nick Velvet stories, *The Spy Who Read Latin* (1991), *The Old Spies Club* (2001).
Sam Hawthorne series: *Diagnosis: Impossible* (1996).
Ben Snow series: *The Ripper of Storyville* (1997).
Non-series: *The Night My Friend* (1991), *The Night People* (2001).
Editor. *Dear Dead Days* (1972), *All But Impossible* (1981), *Twelve American Detective Stories* (1997).
Annuals: *Best Detective Stories of the Year*, 6 volumes (1976–81), *The Year's Best Mystery and Suspense Stories*, 14 volumes (1982–95).
with Martin H. Greenberg: *Great British Detectives* (1987), *Women Write Murder* (1987), *Murder Most Sacred* (1989).

Full name: Edward Dentinger Hoch.
Pen-names: Irwin Booth, Anthony Circus, Stephen Dentinger, Pat McMahon, R.E. Porter (reviews only), R.L. Stevens, Mr. X. Has also ghost-written as Ellery Queen.
Where to start: Almost anywhere but perhaps *Leopold's Way* or *The Thefts of Nick Velvet*.
Awards: Edgar, best short story (1968), Anthony, best short story (1998, 2001), Golden Derringer, lifetime achievement (1998), Shamus, lifetime achievement (2000), Anthony, lifetime achievement (2001), MWA Grand Master (2001).
Similar stuff: Thomas CHASTAIN, John Dickson Carr, Ellery Queen, Francis M. NEVINS, Bill PRONZINI, Henry SLESAR.

Final fact: EDH has had a story (sometimes more) in *every* issue of *EQMM* since May 1973.

William Hoffman (b. 1925) US

In a career that has stretched over nearly 50 years WH has produced 11 novels and 4 short-story collections, all highly acclaimed, bringing him a cabinet full of awards. His work concentrates on the lives and conflicts of the American south and inevitably some of those lives encounter crime and danger, even though WH would not regard himself as a crime writer. *Tidewater Blood* won the Hammett Prize for excellence in crime writing. It is about Charles LeBlanc, a dishonourably discharged Vietnam vet who now lives deep in the Virginia swamp territory. He is arrested on suspicion of the deaths of other members of his family from whom he has become estranged and when he's released without enough evidence he goes on the trail of the real killer. It's a rich novel, full of a sense of place and time. It served to remind crime fiction fans of WH's work, as two of his earlier novels are of interest. *A Walk to the River* is about the effects on a small community when the local minister is accused of rape. *Godfires* is a full blown southern gothic about murder and obsession. With the success of *Tidewater Blood* WH has written a further dark novel, *Blood and Guile*, when the truth of a man's death on a hunting trip is kept secret.

Novels (selective). *A Walk to the River* (1970), *Godfires* (1985), *Tidewater Blood* (1998), *Blood and Guile* (2000).

Where to start: *Tidewater Blood.*
Awards: Hammett prize (1999).
Books about: *The Fictional World of William Hoffman* by William L. Frank (2000).
Similar stuff: Thomas H. COOK
Final fact: WH should not be confused with another William Hoffman who co-authors and sometimes ghost-writes true-crime accounts with John Dillman, Lake Headley, Eddie Maloney and others.

Samuel Holt *pseudonym, see* Donald E. Westlake

Wendy Hornsby (b. 1947) US

Born and raised in Los Angeles, the setting for all her books, WH is a Professor of History. Her first main character, Kate Teague was also a history professor who, in *No Harm*, becomes involved with Latino police detective Roger Tejeda, who is investigating her uncle's death. This book and its sequel are both violent hard-edged police procedurals. But they were just a training ground for WH whose work really blossomed with her next series. Maggie MacGowen is a documentary film-maker who comes to Los Angeles in *Telling Lies* to find her sister has been gunned down. She becomes involved with police detective Mike Flint. The strength of this book and its sequels is the sense of place and the realistic characters. One reviewer went so far as to say that no one since Chandler had "captured downtown Los Angeles the way Hornsby does." *77th Street Requiem*, which is based on an actual LAPD case, was named as one of the six best mysteries of the year by *Publisher's Weekly*.

Novels

Kate Teague series: *No Harm* (1987), *Half a Mind* (1990).

Maggie MacGowen series: *Telling Lies* (1992), *Midnight Baby* (1993), *Bad Intent* (1994), *77th Street Requiem* (1995), *A Hard Light* (1997).

Short Stories. *High Heels Through the Headliner* (1994), *Nine Sons* (2002).

Full name: Wendy Nelson Hornsby.
Where to start: *Telling Lies*.
Awards: Orange Coast fiction award (1987), Edgar, best short story (1992), American Mystery Award, best short story (1992), American Reader award (1992), Reviewers' Choice award (1993).
Similar stuff: Faye KELLERMAN, Rochelle Majer KRICH.
Final fact: For her research on *Telling Lies*, WH summoned up the courage to visit a morgue. She was glad she did it but it was an experience she would never forget. It assails all five senses. It's not just the sight of all those dead bodies, and the fear of touching them, but the smell and the taste in the air and the sound of the autopsy. "When the top of the skull is removed," she commented, "it pops like a champagne cork."

Matilda Hughes *pseudonym, see* Charlotte MacLeod

David Hunt *pseudonym, see* William Bayer

E. Howard Hunt (b. 1918) US

EHH might just have been remembered as a capable if moderate author of espionage and detective fiction if, as consultant to President Nixon, he had not become convicted on six counts of conspiracy in the Watergate scandal in 1972. He served two terms of imprisonment from 1973–4 and 1975–7. When it was learned that he had been writing spy fiction under various pen-names his books were rushed back into print. EHH had been a war correspondent for *Life* and after WW2 entered the US State Department serving as an attaché to several embassies throughout the world. These assignments were usually covers for his CIA spying activities and his rôle as a spy is rather accurately recreated in his books featuring agent Peter Ward. Of equal interest, and amongst his better work, are his novels featuring Washington accountant Steve Bentley who works undercover as a P.I. At the time of Watergate the press took great delight in highlighting that *Angel Eyes* is about a tape recording that could destroy a political career. "Don't think I can't smell a cover-up," Bentley says rather ironically. Since Watergate EHH has continued to write political thrillers including a series featuring ex-DEA agent Jack Novak who continues as a special investigator acting just like any fifties sexist hoodlum. The seventh book in the series, *Sonora*, takes us back to the start of Novak's career.

Novels

Jack Novak series: *Cozumel* (1985), *Guadalajara* (1986), *Mazatlan* (1987), *Ixtapa* (1994), *Islamorada* (1995), *Izmir* (1996), *Sonora* (2000).

Non-series: *Maelstrom* (1948; as *Cruel is the Night*, 1955), *Bimini Run* (1949), *The Violent Ones* (1950), *Dark Encounter* (1950), *The Judas Hour* (1951), *Whisper Her Name* (1952), *Lovers are Losers* (1953), *The Berlin Ending* (1973), *The Hargrave Deception* (1980), *The Gaza Intercept* (1981), *The Kremlin Conspiracy* (1985), *Murder in State* (1990), *Body Count* (1991), *Chinese Red* (1992), *The Paris Edge* (1995), *Dragon Teeth* (1997), *Guilty Knowledge* (1999).

as Gordon Davis: *I Came to Kill* (1953), *House Dick* (1961; as *Washington Payoff* by EHH, 1975), *Counterfeit Kill* (1963; as by EHH, 1975), *Ring Around Rosy* (1964; as *From Cuba With Love* by EHH, 1974), *Where Murder Waits* (1965; as by EHH, 1973).

as Robert Dietrich: *One for the Road* (1954), *The Cheat* (1954), *Be My Victim* (1956).

Steve Bentley series as Robert Dietrich: *Murder on the Rocks* (1957), *The House on Q Street* (1959), *End of a Stripper* (1959), *Mistress to Murder* (1960), *Murder on her Mind* (1960), *Angel Eyes* (1961), *Steve Bentley's Calypso Caper* (1961), *Curtains for a Lover* (1961), *My Body* (1962).

as P.S. Donoghue: *The Dublin Affair* (1988), *The Sankov Confession* (1989).

Peter Ward series as David St. John: *On Hazardous Duty* (1965; as *Hazardous Duty*, UK 1966; as by EHH, 1972), *Return from Vorkuta* (1965; as EHH, 1972), *The Towers of Silence* (1966; as EHH, 1974), *Festival for Spies* (1966; as EHH, 1973), *The Venus Probe* (1966; as EHH, 1974), *One of Our Agents is Missing* (1967; as EHH, 1973), *The Mongol Mask* (1968), *The Sorcerers* (1969), *Diabolus* (1971), *The Coven* (1972).

Autobiography. *Undercover: Memoirs of an American Secret Agent* (1974).

Full name: Everette Howard Hunt, Jr.
Pen-names: John Baxter, Gordon Davis, Robert Dietrich, P.S. Donoghue, David St John.
Where to start: for spy fans, any of the Peter Ward books, otherwise *Angel Eyes*.
Similar stuff: Ross THOMAS.
Final fact: EHH's life is full of incidents for conspiracy theorists. He was accused of being involved in the Kennedy assassination but won a libel suit against the accuser. He was involved in the Bay of Pigs incident and recruited Cubans to assist in the Watergate break-in. His wife, who was collecting money for his defence in Watergate died in a mysterious plane crash in December 1972. EHH uttered the immortal words: "No one is entitled to the truth."

Evan Hunter, *see pseudonym* Ed McBain

Martin Inigo *pseudonym, see* Edward Marston

Elizabeth Ironside UK

EI's first novel won the John Creasey Memorial Award and was shortlisted for the Betty Trask Award. It features George Sinclair, a security officer at the Foreign Office who is sent to the British High Commission to investigate the death of a senior diplomat. EI is married to a diplomat and has lived in France, India and Russia, so she creates an authentic atmosphere. EI's other books all start in that comfortable world of the privileged but things soon fall apart. In *Death in the Garden*, which was shortlisted for the Golden Dagger award, the mystery surrounding the death of an MP in 1925 is only resolved 70 years later. In *The Accomplice* the body of a child is found in a rose garden and events stir up memories for an elderly Russian exile. *The Art of Deception*, which shifts between London and Moscow, is an intriguing exploration of truth and lies when a man rescues a woman from a mugging only to be drawn into a world of deception. *A Good Death* is a change of pace and setting. It takes place in France in the final days of WW2 where the Resistance is meting out retribution to Nazi collaborators. All of EI's books show how thin the veneer of security and respectability is in an otherwise harsh and uncertain world.

Novels. *A Very Private Enterprise* (1984), *Death in the Garden* (1995), *The Accomplice* (1996), *The Art of Deception* (1998), *A Good Death* (2000).

Where to start: *A Very Private Enterprise.*
Awards: John Creasey Memorial Award (1984).
Similar stuff: Veronica STALLWOOD.
Final fact: *A Good Death* arose out of local knowledge around EI's home in south-west France where the Resistance was strong in WW2.

Robert R. Irvine (b. 1936) US

RRI was born and raised in Mormon territory in Utah, though he has long since lived in California with his wife Angela. He obtained his degree in anthropology and art history but after his military service in counter-intelligence (1959–61) he took up a career in journalism, becoming a TV newswriter in 1964 and remaining a writer and director for TV and radio for the next 20 years. Not surprisingly his first few books all have a TV background. Four feature overweight Vietnam veteran Bob Christopher who debuted in the Edgar-nominated *Jump Cut*. Christopher is a TV field reporter who becomes deeply involved in his stories. After a short break in the early eighties, when RRI produced two horror novels, he then returned with a more substantial series featuring ex-pro football player, Moroni Traveler, who works with his father, Martin, as a P.I. Moroni is named after the Mormon's founding angel but has himself renounced the church. The novels, set in and around Salt Lake City, draw upon Mormonism for their background. In the first, *Baptism for the Dead*, Moroni is asked by a client to find whether her mother is still alive in order that she may be baptized retrospectively. The control that the church has over Salt Lake City permeates the books and Moroni's investigations, and RRI draws upon interesting historical details. *The Great Reminder*, for instance, explores the repercussions of prisoners of war being quartered in Utah during WW2. The consequences of nuclear bomb testing in Utah is the background to *Pillar of Fire* where the Church of Latter Day Saints hires Traveler to investigate a purported faith healer. The books contain a fascinating cast of characters which RRI's wife, Angie, has utilized in several short stories in *EQMM*. Angie Irvine is a computer technologist and she and her husband have collaborated under the name Val Davis on an unusual new series that will delight aircraft buffs. It features archaeologist Nicolette "Nicky" Scott who enjoys finding old aircraft. In *Track of the Scorpion* it's a B-17 bomber, buried for 50 years in the New Mexico desert, and Scott's investigations unearth a military conspiracy. There's another such conspiracy in *Flight of the Serpent* whilst *Wake of the Hornet* takes Nicky to a remote Pacific island where the natives worship planes. By *The Return of the Spanish Lady* her expertise has been recognized by the Smithsonian Institute who commission Scott to locate a Japanese plane shot down over Alaska. Between them RRI and his wife have produced some highly original fiction.

Novels

Bob Christopher series: *Jump Cut* (1974), *Freeze Frame* (1976), *Horizontal Hold* (1978), *Ratings are Murder* (1985).

Moroni Traveler series: *Baptism for the Dead* (1988), *The Angel's Share* (1989), *Gone to Glory* (1990), *Called Home* (1991), *The Spoken Word* (1992), *The Great Reminder* (1993), *The Hosanna Shout* (1994), *Pillar of Fire* (1995).

Nicolette Scott series as Val Davis: *Track of the Scorpion* (1996), *Flight of the Serpent* (1998), *Wake of the Hornet* (2000), *Return of the Spanish Lady* (2001).

Non-series: *The Face Out Front* (1977), *Barking Dogs* (1994).

Full name: Robert Ralstone Irvine.
Pen-name: Val Davis (with Angie Irvine).
Where to start: *Baptism for the Dead*.
Similar stuff: William DEANDREA's Matt Cobb series.
Final fact: RRI's great-grandmother pulled a handcart across the Great Plains to join her husband, who was a surveyor on the railroad at Salt Lake City. Four generations later RRI's wife Angie taught the Apollo astronauts how to use their on-board computers for the Moon trips.

Eugene Izzi (1953–96) US

During his relatively short career EI was regarded as one of the hottest crime writers around and his tragic death by hanging (verdict suicide but doubts remain) catapulted him to cult status. It was a long time coming. EI was a high-school drop-out whose father had been a petty criminal and EI also ended up on the streets. A period in the army encouraged him to write, imitating Mickey SPILLANE, but he was unable to find a publisher for six years, during which time he worked in a steel mill until laid off. His first published book was *The Take* about a former cop who had served time for being on "the take" and was now a burglar planning that one last job. Several of EI's books follow that formula: a good guy gone bad through circumstance hoping to make good again after one last great heist. *Invasions* is one such example, where a burglar plans the perfect heist. EI knew the street life and crooked world of Chicago and it is all reflected in his books. EI had hoped that *Tribal Secrets* would be his breakthrough novel. It's about the son of a Mafia hit-man who tries to break with his family and become a TV star. The book sold poorly and EI's dispute with his publisher meant he had to use an alias on his next three books. He chose Nick Gaitano and wrote a series about Detective Jake Phillips of the Special Victims unit. These are three very powerful novels, and are best read as one unit, as we follow Phillips' difficult job that eventually takes its toll on his health and his family. EI was a prolific writer and two further books appeared after his sudden death. *A Matter of Honor*, about racial conflagration in Chicago, was the book he was working on when he died and includes a scene identical to EI's own death by hanging outside his 14th-floor office window. *The Criminalist* is also amongst his best works and features a detective who had shunned promotion who looks into the murder of a prostitute that echoes a crime he recalls from 20 years ago. EI's work was rough-edged because of the speed with which he wrote, but they all have a power and vivacity that makes them amongst the most potent crime fiction of the last 20 years.

Novels. *The Take* (1987), *Bad Guys* (1988), *The Eighth Victim* (1988), *The Booster* (1989), *King of the Hustlers* (1989), *Invasions* (1990), *The Prime Roll* (1990), *Prowlers* (1991), *Tribal Secrets* (1992), *Tony's Justice* (1993), *Bulletin from the Street* (1995), *Safe Harbour* (1995), *A Matter of Honor* (1997), *The Criminalist* (1998).
Jake Phillips series as Nick Gaitano: *Special Victims* (1994), *Mr. X* (1995), *Spent Force* (1996; as *Jaded*, US 1996).

Full name: Eugene "Guy" Izzi.
Pen-name: Nick Gaitano.
Where to start: *The Take.*
Similar stuff: Barbara D'AMATO, Sam REAVES for similar stories set in Chicago.
Final fact: The official verdict on EI's death was suicide, though it was conjectured that it may have been murder or an accident, with EI testing out a scene from his own book. If it was murder it was a locked-room crime as officials had to break in to his office to rescue his body. EI was wearing a bullet-proof vest and there was a gun on the floor. He left no suicide note, though a psychologist said that his novel, *A Matter of Honor*, was one long suicide note. EI had told friends that he had received threats from a militant group he had been researching for the book.

Nancy Baker Jacobs (b. 1944) US

Though currently a college professor and lecturer in journalism NBJ has, over the years, been a reporter, scriptwriter and private investigator. She thus writes from experience, and her books are strong on social issues, particularly dealing with children and vicitimization in the family. Under her maiden name of Nancy Baker she had written several self-help guides for women including *New Lives for Former Wives, Displaced Homemakers* (1980) plus a book exposing the black-market in adoption, *Baby Selling* (1978) and these themes recur in her books. Her first novel is the relatively minor *Deadly Companion*, about a psychotic nurse who murders elderly patients, but when she returned to fiction five years later she had matured significantly dealing with more complex issues. *The Turquoise Tattoo* introduces Minneapolis P.I. Devon MacDonald who tries to find the half-brother of a boy dying of leukemia who needs a bone-marrow transplant. The boy's natural father was a Jewish doctor, but his adoptive father is an Aryan supremacist. *A Slash of Scarlet* has MacDonald set a trap to catch a con-artist that goes horribly wrong. In *The Silver Scalpel* MacDonald confronts an anti-abortion group when several pregnant teenagers disappear. Her non-series books follow similar themes. *See Mommy Run* has a mother take her young child away from the sexually abusing father. In *Daddy's Gone A-Hunting* a talkshow host finds that a fan has become obsessed with the host's young daughter.

Novels

Non-series: *Deadly Companion* (1986), *See Mommy Run* (1992), *Cradle and All* (1995), *Daddy's Gone A-Hunting* (1995), *Rocking the Cradle* (1996), *Double or Nothing* (2001).

Devon MacDonald series: *The Turquoise Tattoo* (1991), *A Slash of Scarlet* (1992), *The Silver Scalpel* (1993).

Pen-name: Nancy C. Baker.
Where to start: *The Turquise Tattoo* or *See Mommy Run*.
Similar stuff: Liza CODY, Natasha COOPER, Karen KIJEWSKI.

Michael Jahn (b. 1943) US

Like many writers MJ, a former rock music critic for the *New York Times*, worked his way into writing through TV and film tie-ins and producing series novels under a publisher's "house" name. His first dozen or more books include spin-offs from the *Six Million Dollar Man* and *Rockford Files* series, initiating the Omega Sub sf series (about the crew of a submarine that survives the Final War) as J.D. Cameron and producing the book-of-the-film *The Invisible Man* (1975). He continued to produce sf, spy and historical novels until the early eighties and in the midst of this farrago were two original NYPD police thrillers *The Quark Maneuver* and *Killer on the Heights*. Both heavily influenced by Kurt Vonnegut with short staccato sections and an almost recursive style, the first won the

Edgar award for best paperback original. After over 30 books MJ, who had been writing as Mike Jahn, spruced himself up as Michael Jahn and turned in what became his first hardcover novel and the first in the Bill Donovan series. At the outset Donovan is a rather mixed-up NYPD cop with a murky past and weighed down by self-recrimination over his father's death. In *Night Rituals* Donovan tracks down the perpetrator of a series of grisly ritual murders in Riverside Park. During the series, as Donovan straightens himself out, we are taken on a tour of key locations in New York that has become one of the strong features of the series – including the Cathedral of St John the Divine (in *City of God*), the American Museum of Natural History, Times Square (in *Murder on Theatre Row*), Central Park. Both the City and its inhabitants come alive in this vivid and exciting series.

Novels

Bill Donovan series: *Night Rituals* (1982), *Death Games* (1987), *City of God* (1992), *Murder in the Museum of Natural History* (1994), *Murder on Theatre Row* (1997), *Murder on Fifth Avenue* (1998), *Murder in Central Park* (2000), *Murder on the Waterfront* (2001).
Rockford Files TV tie-ins: *The Unfortunate Replacement* (1975), *The Deadliest Game* (1976).
Switch TV tie-ins: *Switch* (1976), *Switch #2* (1976).
Nick Carter series as Nick Carter: *Cauldron of Hell* (1981).
Non-series: *The Quark Maneuver* (1977), *Killer on the Heights* (1977). *Shearwater* (1980).

Full name: Joseph Michael Jahn.
Pen-names: work under house names J.D. Cameron, Nick Carter, John Darby, Jan Michaels, Lee Davis Willoughby.
Where to start: *Night Rituals*.
Awards: Edgar, best paperback original (1978).
Website: <home.att.net/~medj/>
Similar stuff: New York features strongly in the works of Thomas ADCOCK, Leslie GLASS, Robert J. RANDISI, Lawrence SANDERS, Dorothy UHNAK.
Final fact: MJ recalls the one time he was nearly burgled, he was in bed and heard the bedroom window being lifted. In as good a Clint Eastwood impression as he could muster he said, "You don't really want to do that, do you?" To which came a quick, "No", and the burglar ran away.

Maxim Jakubowski (b. 1944) UK

When sex meets violence there's crime. That's the impact in MJ's fiction. Dubbed "the King of the Erotic Thriller", MJ's books are really erotica trapped within a turbulence of high-action crime. They're also the book equivalent of "road" movies. MJ's characters can't stay in one place. In *It's You That I Want to Kiss* a couple are pursued across the US by a psychopath. Although the premise of *Because She Thought She Loved Me* is internet pornography, it soon becomes another chase from London to

Paris to New York. *On Tenderness Express* is MJ's first P.I. novel. Martin Jackson calls himself a liar and "unconvincing', the narrative challenging the truth as once again we are on a quest with Jackson hunting a man's wife and a woman's sister from London to Amsterdam and then across America. MJ's work provides bleak and disturbing reflections of the downside of life. MJ has also written a heroic-fantasy novel and several rock-music books under two pseudonyms, though these are one of the few things MJ chooses not to expose. MJ was originally better known in the field of science fiction where his first story in English appeared in 1969 (he had sold earlier fiction in France since 1962). He has also compiled several anthologies and reference works in France and the UK. Since the mid-eighties he has made a significant contribution to the re-emergence of crime fiction in Britain through his period as a publisher – when he revived lost noir and hard-boiled classics in the Black Box and Blue Murder series – and as an anthologist. Four stories from MJ's anthologies have won major crime-fiction awards and he has done much to encourage new writers and provide markets for experimental new crime. Especially significant are *London Noir*, *No Alibi* and the *Fresh Blood* series he compiled with Mike RIPLEY. He also won an Anthony award for his handy compilation *100 Great Detectives*.

Novels. *It's You That I Want to Kiss* (1996), *Because She Thought She Loved Me* (1997), *On Tenderness Express* (2000), *Kiss Me Sadly* (2002).
Short Stories. *Life in the World of Women* (1996).
Non-fiction. *100 Great Detectives* (as editor) (1991), *The Mammoth Book of Jack the Ripper* with Nathan Braund (1999).
Editor. *New Crimes* (1989), *New Crimes 2* (1990), *New Crimes 3* (1991), *Murders for the Fireside* (1992), *Constable New Crimes 1* (1992), *Constable New Crimes 2* (1993), *Crime Yellow* (1994), *More Murders for the Fireside* (1994), *Royal Crimes*, with Martin H. Greenberg (1994), *London Noir* (1994), *No Alibi* (1995), *The Mammoth Book of Pulp Fiction* (1996), *Fresh Blood 1*, with Mike Ripley (1996), *Fresh Blood 2*, with Mike Ripley (1997), *Fresh Blood 3*, with Mike Ripley (1999), *Past Poisons* (1998), *Chronicles of Crime* (1999), *Murder Through the Ages* (2000), *The Mammoth Book of Pulp Action* (2001), *The Mammoth Book of Comic Crime* (2002), *Future Noir* (2002).

Awards: International SF Association Karel Award for best sf translation (1984), Anthony, best critical/biographical (1992).
Similar stuff: Stella DUFFY, Rob KANTNER, Charles WILLEFORD.
Final fact: MJ owns the UK's biggest crime-fiction bookshop, Murder One.

Bill James (b. 1929) UK

Although best known today as Bill James, with his novels featuring Chief Superintendent Harpur, Welsh author and journalist James Tucker began writing under his own name and has written more books under the alias David Craig. Tucker's first three books, starting with *Equal Partners* in 1960, were non-criminous, but in 1968 he adopted the alias David Craig for a trilogy of novels featuring Home Office agent Roy Rickman set in a future Britain on the brink of becoming a Russian satellite state. The Craig name appeared on several more espionage novels and action thrillers including *Whose Little Girl Are You?*, about alcoholic ex-policeman Jim Naboth, who is involved in the search for a kidnapped girl. It was filmed as *The Squeeze* (1977) starring Stacey Keach. Also under the David Craig alias is *Faith, Hope and Death*, which promised a new series featuring detective Peter Gale who investigates a murder in a hospital. After a couple of crime novels set in the 1930s, published under his own name, the BJ alias appeared with *You'd Better Believe It*. This introduced two high-ranking police officials, Assistant Chief Constable Iles and Chief Superintendent Harpur. They are friends and both are fervent in their desire to capture criminals at whatever cost and no matter what rules they break. It is a bleak and pessimistic series where BJ explores his belief that it is impossible to control crime solely by legitimate means. Like George V. HIGGINS, whom BJ cites as a major influence, BJ's dialogue is sharp and delineating, his plots violent yet realistic. Yet there is also a strong vein of black humour. Peter GUTTRIDGE has described the series as "achingly funny". As the series progresses the amoral Iles stoops even to possible murder to protect his world and in *In Good Hands* Harpur is charged to investigate Iles. In later novels Iles and Harpur uncover corruption elsewhere in the force. The novels raise the challenging question of how far can you use evil to fight evil. In 1995 BJ resurrected his David Craig persona for a new series set around his native Cardiff featuring police detectives David Brade and Glyndwr Jenkins. Though less bleak than the Harpur and Iles series they are equally tough and unforgiving and paint a dire portrait of nineties Wales attempting to revive its fortunes.

Tucker has also written two novels about female detective Kerry Lake, both published under the alias Judith Jones, though the third novel, *Double Jeopardy*, has appeared under the BJ alias. In 2001 BJ returned to espionage with *Split*, featuring the British spy Simon Abelard, of mixed race, from Cardiff's dockland. Tucker's output is diverse, potent and rewarding.

Novels

Harpur & Iles series: *You'd Better Believe It* (1985), *The Lolita Man* (1986), *Halo Parade* (1987), *Protection* (1988), *Come Clean* (1989), *Take* (1990), *Club* (1991), *Astride a Grave* (1991), *Gospel* (1992), *Roses, Roses* (1993), *In Good Hands* (1994), *The Detective is Dead* (1995), *Top Banana* (1996), *Panicking Ralph* (1997), *Lovely Mover* (1998), *Eton Crop* (1999), *Kill Me* (2000), *Pay Days* (2001).

Simon Abelard series: *Split* (2001).

Roy Rickman series as David Craig: *The Alias Man* (1968), *Message Ends* (1969), *Contact Lost* (1970).

Bellecroix & Roath series as David Craig: *Young Men May Die* (1970), *A Walk at Night* (1971).

David Brade series as David Craig: *Forget It* (1995), *The Tattooed Detective* (1998), *Torch* (1999), *Bay City* (2000).
Non-series as David Craig: *Up from the Grave* (1971), *Double Take* (1972), *Bolthole* (1973; as *Knifeman*, US 1973), *Whose Little Girl Are You?* (1974; as *The Squeeze,* US 1974), *A Dead Liberty* (1974), *The Albion Case* (1975), *Faith, Hope and Death* (1976).
as James Tucker: *Blaze of Riot* (1979), *The King's Friends* (1982; as by BJ, 1996).
Kerry Lake series (first two as Judith Jones): *Baby Talk* (1998), *After Melissa* (1999), *Double Jeopardy* (2002).

Real name: Allan James Tucker.
Pen-names: David Craig, Bill James, James Tucker, Judith Jones.
Where to start: *You'd Better Believe It.*
Website: <www.twbooks.co.uk/authors/billjames.html>
Similar stuff: John HARVEY, William MCILVANNEY, Ian RANKIN, plus Roy LEWIS for a Welsh police series.
Final fact: When BJ was fourteen he contracted whooping cough and couldn't go to school. Instead he visited a small subscription library and withdrew a crime novel a day, rather than study for the school certificate. He failed the certificate but established the roots for a career.

P. D. James (b. 1920) UK

Like her namesake, M.R. James, in the world of supernatural fiction, it is certainly quality not quantity that counts in the work of PDJ. A total of just 15 novels in 30 years shows that here you have very fine wine indeed, one that has matured through the application of considerable thoughtful planning. She has been christened the "Queen of Crime", not a title that she would claim herself but one that places her on a pedestal as a natural successor to Agatha Christie, Margery Allingham and Ngaio Marsh. In fact her works bear little comparison with those masters other than that she works firmly in the field of the traditional mystery. Most of her books feature Adam Dalgliesh of Scotland Yard. He is an Inspector in the first novel, a Superintendent in most of the others but is now a Commander. Dalgliesh is a private, introverted person, sensitive – he is a published poet – and a loner, still suffering inwardly from the death of his wife in childbirth. He could be perceived as a modernized descendent of Marsh's Roderick Alleyn, and PDJ has thought of him as the idealized person she might have been had she been a man. Dalgliesh has no regular Watson-like assistant to hand, but investigates his cases alone, ever thoughtful, ever insightful. The novels are amongst the best examples of the English "country house" mystery, though you may substitute clinics, hospitals, research laboratories or any enclosed environment for the "house". This limits the cast of suspects and allows PDJ to develop each character. Even the minor characters in her books have a richness. At the time of her fifth book, *The Black Tower*, Robin Winks of *The New Republic*, said that "P.D. James shows far more awareness of the complex nature of human beings than Dorothy Sayers did, writes with a more civilized style than Margery Allingham did, and provides more realistic and puzzling plots than Dame Ngaio has done in recent years." PDJ's starting point is her setting and this inspires her to create her characters and then the crime. In *Cover Her Face* it is a home for unwed mothers (this book was written in 1960 when such matters were still a village scandal). In *A Mind to Murder* it is a psychiatric clinic. This was close to PDJ's heart. Her husband, Dr Connor White, had served in the Royal Army Medical Corps in WW2 but had returned home a schizophrenic and, until his death in 1964, was frequently in mental hospitals. *Shroud for a Nightingale*, the first of her novels to receive an award (the CWA Silver Dagger), is also set in a hospital environment, this time a nursing school, whilst *The Black Tower*, her next award-winner, is set in an isolated home for the disabled. It was ten years between that novel and her next Dalgliesh case but *A Taste for Death*, which received a CWA Silver Dagger, a Macavity and the French Grand Prix de Littérature Policière Best Foreign, is regarded by many as her best novel. Not only is it a complex psychological murder mystery, but it is one that gets to the very roots of Christian faith and understanding. H.R.F. KEATING included it in his hundred best crime and mystery books, stating that PDJ had "succeeded in widening the scope of the crime novel in a way that has hardly been done before." The Dalgliesh series has been admirably adapted for TV with Roy Marsden as the Superintendent, adding to her success. There have been similar adaptations of her books featuring the first modern female P.I., Cordelia Gray who, in *An Unsuitable Job for a Woman* (filmed 1981; TV series 1998), in which Dalgliesh has a minor rôle, inherits a detective agency from her colleague who has killed himself. PDJ has written two non-series books. *Innocent Blood* is a finely crafted, highly compassionate novel of a woman who had been adopted as a child and learns the worst when she tries to find her natural parents. *The Children of Men* is an untypical, almost old-fashioned novel of an Orwellian infertile future where no children have been born for a quarter of a century and the human race faces extinction. Fans of PDJ will want to read her own book of reminiscences, *Time to be in Earnest*, which reveals much about her lonely childhood, her pre-war work in the theatre and her days as a Home Office "bureaucrat". She was awarded the OBE in 1983 and was created Baroness James of Holland Park in 1991.

Novels

Commander Dalgliesh series: *Cover Her Face* (1962), *A Mind to Murder* (1963), *Unnatural Causes* (1967), *Shroud for a Nightingale* (1971), *The Black Tower* (1975), *Death of an Expert Witness* (1977), *A Taste for Death* (1986), *Devices and Desires* (1989), *Original Sin* (1994), *A Certain Justice* (1998), *Death in Holy Orders* (2001). Cordelia Gray series: *An Unsuitable Job for a Woman* (1972), *The Skull Beneath the Skin* (1982).

Non-series: *Innocent Blood* (1980), *The Children of Men* (1992).
Non-fiction. *The Maul and the Pear Tree*, with Thomas A. Critchley (1971).
Editor. *Sightlines,* with Harriet Harvey Wood (2001).
Autobiography. *Time to be in Earnest* (1999).

Full name: Phyllis Dorothy White (*née* James).
Where to start: *Cover Her Face.*
Awards: CWA Silver Dagger (1971, 1975, 1986), Macavity, best novel (1987), Grand Prix de Littérature Policière Best Foreign (1988), CWA Diamond Dagger (1987), Swedish Academy of Detection, Grand Master (1996), MWA Grand Master (1999), Fellow of the Royal Society of Arts (1985), Fellow of the Royal Society of Literature (1987).
Books about: *P.D. James* by Norma Siebenheller (1981), *P.D. James* by Richard B. Gidez (1986).
Similar stuff: Elizabeth GEORGE, Ruth RENDELL, Minette WALTERS.
Final fact: One of PDJ's roles when she worked for the Home Office involved the appointment of scientists and pathologists to the forensic research laboratories and as an adviser to ministers on the legal problems related to juvenile crime.

Russell James (b. 1942) UK

RJ was for a while something of a lone voice in British crime fiction. In his own words, most people write "anti-crime novels", in other words detective or puzzle stories. RJ writes crime novels about villains and their victims and, as such, he has been compared more to the American hard-boiled school, while Ian RANKIN dubbed him the "Godfather of British noir". His books explore the dog-eat-dog world of the petty criminal ruled by the more dominating gangsters. He has no regular series but there is a consistency to his world as occasional characters do recur, most notably his arch villain and art fence, Gottfleisch. RJ's debut novel, *Underground*, was a powerful tour-de-force, a first person narrative by a nameless villain who has been lying low for several years but is now on the run. *Daylight* finds Gottfleisch's debt collector entering the dangerous world of the Russian gangs. *Payback* is reminiscent of Ted LEWIS's *Jack's Return Home*, as Floyd Carter investigates the death of his brother. Amongst RJ's other powerful novels is the landmark *Painting in the Dark*, which spans over 70 years and explores both the world of the Nazis and Fascist Britain of the thirties and the world of the present as Gottfleisch tries to get his hands on some long forgotten paintings of Hitler and his cohorts. RJ shines his torch into the crevices of the British underworld and turns what crawls out into some of the best crime fiction being written today.

Novels. *Underground* (1989), *Daylight* (1990), *Payback* (1991), *Slaughter Music* (1994), *Count Me Out* (1996), *Oh No, Not My Baby* (1999), *Painting in the Dark* (2000), *The Annex* (US 2002), *Pick Any Title* (2002).

Where to start: *Count Me Out.*
Website: <www.russelljames.co.uk>
Similar stuff: Elmore LEONARD, Mark TIMLIN.

Final fact: As befits a low-life thriller writer, RJ is an active member of the Voluntary Euthanasia Society.

J. A. Jance (b. 1944) US

JAJ was already popular for her series featuring Seattle homicide police detective Jonas P. Beaumont ("Beau"), which she had been writing since 1985, yet when *Kiss of the Bees* hit the *New York Times* bestseller lists this non-Beaumont novel instantly established her name. *Kiss of the Bees* picks up the action twenty years after an earlier book *Home of the Hunter*, which was a total rewrite of JAJ's abortive unpublished first novel. That concerned a psychopath, released from prison after serving only six years for the murder of a Papago Indian child, who stalks the woman who testified against him. *Kiss of the Bees* follows the life of that woman and her son after the psychopath's death. JAJ had wanted to write since her childhood but her overbearing and alcoholic husband stifled her talent. Working full time as a teacher of English to native Americans and later as a school librarian, JAJ wrote poetry in secret (later published as *After the Fire*, 1984) and also three children's books. Following her divorce in 1982, when she left Arizona for Seattle, she began her series about J.P. Beaumont, himself an alcoholic, and an ill-tempered man full of resentment and inner anger. JAJ drew her inspiration in part from John MacDonald's Travis McGee. The series is told in the first person so we live J.P.'s anguish and follow him through his alcoholism into rehabilitation in *Minor in Possession*. Thereafter he steadily rebuilds his life. This is against a background of violent and often soul-searching crimes. The first novel, *Until Proven Guilty*, is about a murdered child and child beating. JAJ also writes a series featuring Joanna Brady. In *Desert Heat* her husband, a candidate for sheriff of Cochise County, Arizona, is killed and Joanna takes his place. This series allows JAJ to explore native American culture in more detail. In both series the characters age along with the books, allowing a greater connection but also demanding that the books be read in sequence.

Novels

J.P. Beaumont: *Until Proven Guilty* (1985), *Injustice for All* (1986), *Trial by Fury* (1986), *Taking the Fifth* (1987), *Improbably Cause* (1988), *A More Perfect Union* (1988), *Dismissed with Prejudice* (1989), *Minor in Possession* (1990), *Payment in Kind* (1991), *Without Due Process* (1992), *Failure to Appear* (1993), *Lying in Wait* (1994), *Name Withheld* (1995), *Breach of Duty* (1999), *Birds of Prey* (2001).

Joanna Brady: *Desert Heat* (1993), *Tombstone Courage* (1994), *Shoot, Don't Shoot* (1995), *Dead to Rights* (1996), *Skeleton Canyon* (1997), *Rattlesnake Crossing* (1998), *Outlaw Mountain* (1999), *Devil's Claw* (2000), *Paradise Lost* (2001).

Diana Walker sequence: *Hour of the Hunter* (1991), *Kiss of the Bees* (2000).

Full name: Judith Ann Jance.
Where to start: *Hour of the Hunter*.

Awards: American Mystery Award, best crime novel (1993).
Website: <www.jajance.com>
Similar stuff: Elizabeth LININGTON, plus Tony HILLERMAN for native culture.
Final fact: JAJ's first unpublished novel ran to over 1,200 pages as no one had told her there were things you could leave unsaid.

Sébastien Japrisot (b. 1931) France

Over a period of forty years the French novelist and screenwriter has produced some of the most surreal and bizarre crime fiction available in English. SJ loves to experiment with perspective, time, identity, and to twist the fabric of reality to confuse and challenge the reader into questioning the truth. Even in his earliest such novel, *The Sleeping Car Murders* (filmed 1965), which tells the story of the death of a girl from the different viewpoints of those on the train, you get a bewildering array of alternatives even though the killer soon becomes obvious. *Trap for Cinderella* (filmed 1965), which won the French Grand Prix de Littérature Policière, turns the screw tighter. The heroine has lost her memory and does not know whether she is a murderer or a replacement for the victim. Something similar happens in *The Lady in the Car With Glasses and a Gun* (filmed 1970), which won the CWA award for best foreign novel. A woman meets with an absurd accident and thereafter events become bewildering as she apparently relives the day, becoming victim, murderer, witness and detective all at once. *Rider on the Rain* (filmed 1969) sets up another vortex of crime and punishment after a brutal rape. Perhaps the most intriguing of his novels is *A Very Long Engagement* in which five French soldiers are abandoned to the Germans on the front line because of their cowardice. The men are subsequently reported dead but later events suggest that maybe the outcome was different. All of SJ's crime novels are Escher-like puzzles providing a delightful diversion from more traditional fiction.

Novels. *The 10:30 from Marseilles* (1962; US 1963; as *The Sleeping Car Murders*, UK 1978), *Trap for Cinderella* (1962; US 1965), *The Lady in the Car with Glasses and a Gun* (1966; US, 1967), *Goodbye, Friend* (1968; US 1969), *One Deadly Summer* (1978; US 1980), *The Passion of Women* (1986; US 1990; as *Women in Evidence*, UK 1990), *A Very Long Engagement* (1991; US 1993), *Rider on the Rain* (1969; US, 1999).

Real name: Jean Baptiste Rossi.
Pen-name: Sébastien Japrisot.
Where to start: *The Sleeping Car Murders* though almost anywhere will do.
Awards: Grand Prix de Littérature Policière best novel (1963), Prix d'Honneur (1966), CWA best foreign novel (1968), Swedish Academy of Detection, Best Foreign (1981).
Similar stuff: Jorge Luis Borges, Mark MCSHANE, Daniel ODIER, James SALLIS.

Quintin Jardine (b. 1945) UK

QJ is a former journalist who, since 1986, has been an independent public relations consultant, but previously advised government ministers on public relations and was involved with media coverage of royal visits. In 1993 he began his series featuring Robert Skinner, Edinburgh's Assistant (later Deputy) Chief Constable. Despite his high rank, Skinner becomes involved in a wide variety of violent and sadistic crimes. Murder, arson, terrorism and drugs are order of the day, and the graphic scenes make this series strong on realism and a formidable counter to traditional crime fiction. Like John HARVEY and Ian RANKIN, QJ pulls no punches in his treatment of modern-day inner-city crime. The recent *Gallery Whispers*, which starts with what looks like a case of euthanasia, is almost tame by comparison until the full impact of the crime is understood. QJ also writes a series about private-enquiry agent Oz Blackstone. This is comparatively light and is played out against a broader European canvas. Blackstone and his partner Primavera Phillips are initially successful and with increased finances hope to say goodbye to the private-enquiry business, but life's never that simple. In each of the books Oz's mettle is well and truly tested. The first book was originally issued under the alias Matthew Reid at the publisher's suggestion though they subsequently realized it did not help sales. The name was removed for the paperback edition and QJ is adamant that he has "gone for good."

Novels

Bob Skinner series: *Skinner's Rules* (1993), *Skinner's Trail* (1994), *Skinner's Festival* (1994), *Skinner's Round* (1995), *Skinner's Ordeal* (1996), *Skinner's Mission* (1997), *Skinner's Ghosts* (1998), *Murmuring the Judges* (1998), *Gallery Whispers* (1999), *Thursday Legends* (2000), *Autographs in the Rain* (2001), *Head Shot* (2002). Oz Blackstone series: *Blackstone's Pursuits* (1996), *Coffin for Two* (1997), *Wearing Purple* (1998), *Screen Savers* (2000).

Where to start: *Skinner's Rules.*
Website: <www.jthin.co.uk/jardine.htm>
Similar stuff: John HARVEY, Peter TURNBULL.
Final fact: A couple of months before *Skinner's Rules* was published QJ was invited to meet the Assistant Chief Constable of Lothian and Borders police. QJ was astonished to find that the officer fitted Skinner's description to a "T" – a little over six feet tall, strongly built with steel-grey hair. QJ commented that "the saving grace was that he's a Yorkshireman!"

Michael Jecks (b. 1960) UK

After studying to be an actuary and then successfully selling computers and computer software for 13 years MJ finally turned his talents to writing and produced the first of his best-selling series of historical mysteries. Set in Devon in the early 14th century, during the reign of Edward II, they feature Simon Puttock, bailiff of Lydford Castle, who is responsible for law and order across the Stannaries (or tin mines) of Dartmoor, and Sir Baldwin Furnshill, a dispossessed and disgruntled former Templar Knight and now Keeper of the King's Peace in Crediton. The books bring alive a fascinating and turbulent period of history and MJ is continually studying the laws of the time, the quality of life and especially the unique regulations that applied to the stannaries and the world of Dartmoor. These books are strong on atmosphere and period detail.

Novels

Puttock & Furnshill series: *The Last Templar* (1995), *The Merchant's Partner* (1995), *A Moorland Hanging* (1996), *The Crediton Killings* (1997), *The Abbot's Gibbet* (1998), *The Leper's Return* (1998), *Squire Throwleigh's Heir* (1999), *Belladonna at Belstone* (1999), *The Traitor of St. Giles* (2000), *The Boy Bishop's Glovemaker* (2000), *The Tournament of Blood* (2001), *The Sticklepath Strangler* (2001), *The Devil's Acolyte* (2002).

Website: <www.michaeljecks.co.uk> and <www.twbooks.co.uk/authors/mjecks.html>

Similar stuff: Edward MARSTON, Susanna GREGORY, Bernard Knight, P.C. DOHERTY's Brother Athelstan series.

Final fact: When MJ turned to writing he picked on the character of Sir Baldwin because MJ had found a beautiful place called Fursdon which had first been inhabited by a knight in the 14th century. After MJ moved to Devon he discovered that his house was built over a mine still owned by the Fursdon family. In other words the area he had moved to was owned by the family of the main character in his books!

William Jefferies *pseudonym, see* Jeffery Deaver

Roderic Jeffries (b. 1926) UK

Although the author of over 140 crime novels and thrillers, including over 20 for children, under half a dozen pseudonyms, RJ's works are mostly ingenious variations on just one or two themes. There are the police procedurals, exemplified by his Inspector Alvarez and Constable Kerr books, and there are the psychological suspense novels of the innocent who becomes embroiled in a crime and has to prove his innocence, either through crafty courtroom strategies or by hunting the criminal. RJ is the son of Graham Montague Jeffries (1900–82) another prolific writer of mystery novels, and both have careers spanning over 50 years. After serving in the Merchant Navy during and after the War, RJ studied law and became a barrister in 1952 but he soon found writing was his true vocation. He began by continuing the adventures of Richard Verrell, which had been started by his father (under the alias Bruce Graeme) in the million-selling *Blackshirt* (1925). In fact Bruce Graeme created an entire Blackshirt dynasty but RJ, writing as Roderic Graeme, concentrated on Verrell, a successful mystery writer by day who becomes a gentleman thief by night. By the mid-sixties RJ was writing up to four books a year under various pseudonyms. As Peter Alding he wrote a complex series of police procedurals featuring the hard-working and cynical Inspector Fusil and the younger more optimistic Constable Kerr. The intrigue of this series, as in many of RJ's books, is in separating truth from fiction and contrasting the ingenuity of the criminal against the unreliability of the public. In recent years RJ's output has settled down to a regular twice-yearly output under his own name and that of Jeffrey Ashford, both names producing sufficient in quantity and quality for any one career and reputation. The Ashford books feature no regular series apart from two early titles, *Investigations are Proceeding* and *Enquiries are Continuing* which explore how the police have to defend themselves against the potential for corruption. Temptation, ambition and folly are the basis for *Bent Copper* whilst *The Anger of Fear* is an excellent study of the human chemistry within the police force. The Ashford books are at their best when demonstrating how easy it is to frame the innocent (because the public is so gullible) and how hard it is to prove the criminal guilty (because the best criminals are clever). Good variations on this are *The Burden of Proof*, *Consider the Evidence*, *The Hands of Innocence*, *An Ideal Crime* and the clever *Counsel for the Defence*. Pressure is brought on a witness in *Forget What You Saw*, whilst an innocent man finds how easy it is to get drawn into crime in *Slow Down the World* and *Presumption of Guilt*. Some of the early books under his own name also plough this terrain – *Evidence of the Accused*, *Dead Against the Lawyers* and *An Embarrassing Death*. Since moving to Majorca in 1972, RJ has reserved his own name for his long-running series featuring Spanish police detective Inspector Alvarez. These have been dubbed "ex-pat cozies" and certainly RJ, who has written his fair share of country house murders (*Death in the Coverts* and *Guilt With Honour* being amongst the best), has reworked the formula with the determined but practical Inspector working his way through suspects within the closed community of small towns in Majorca. RJ is a master of his art. His novels are full of red herrings, multiple twists and turns and frequent surprise endings – *Unseemly Ending* being a prime example. Alvarez, like other of RJ's police officers, are prepared to take the law into their own hands in order to exact justice. As in most of RJ's novels, there is the constant puzzle of what constitutes truth and justice. RJ's books demonstrate the transition from the end of the classic period to the modern by blending the best of the old with the best of the new.

Novels

Enrique Alvarez series: *Mistakenly in Mallorca* (1974), *Two-Faced Death* (1976), *Troubled Deaths* (1977), *Murder Begets Murder* (1979), *Just Desserts* (1980), *Unseemly End* (1981), *Deadly Petard* (1983), *Three and One Make Five* (1984), *Layers of Deceit* (1985), *Almost Murder* (1986), *Relatively Dangerous* (1987), *Death Trick* (1988), *Dead Clever* (1989), *Too Clever by Half* (1990), *A Fatal Fleece* (1991), *Murder's Long Memory* (1992), *Murder Confounded* (1993), *Death Takes Time*

(1994), *An Arcadian Death* (1995), *An Artistic Way to Go* (1996), *A Maze of Murders* (1997), *An Enigmatic Disappearance* (2000), *An Artful Death* (2000), *The Ambiguity of Murder* (2001), *Definitely Deceased* (2001), *Seeing is Deceiving* (2002).
Non-series: *Evidence of the Accused* (1961), *Exhibit No. Thirteen* (1962), *Police and Detection* (1962; as *Against Time!*, US 1964), *The Benefits of Death* (1963), *An Embarrassing Death* (1964), *Police Dog* (1965), *Police Car* (1965; as *Patrol Car*, US 1967), *Dead Against the Lawyers* (1966), *Death in the Coverts* (1966), *A Deadly Marriage* (1967), *A Traitor's Crime* (1968), *River Patrol* (1969; as *Police Patrol Boat*, US 1971), *Dead Man's Bluff* (1970), *Trapped* (1972).
Blackshirt series as Roderic Graeme: *Concerning Blackshirt* (1952), *Blackshirt Wins the Trick* (1953), *Blackshirt Passes By* (1953), *Salute to Blackshirt* (1954), *The Amazing Mr. Blackshirt* (1955), *Blackshirt Meets the Lady* (1956), *Paging Blackshirt* (1957), *Blackshirt Helps Himself* (1958), *Double for Blackshirt* (1958), *Blackshirt Sets the Pace* (1959), *Blackshirt Sees it Through* (1960), *Blackshirt Finds Trouble* (1961), *Blackshirt Takes the Trail* (1962), *Blackshirt on the Spot* (1963), *Call for Blackshirt* (1963), *Blackshirt Saves the Day* (1964), *Danger for Blackshirt* (1965), *Blackshirt at Large* (1966), *Blackshirt in Peril* (1967), *Blackshirt Stirs Things Up* (1969).
as Hastings Draper: *Wiggery Pokery* (1956), *Wigged and Gowned* (1958), *Brief Help* (1961).
as Graham Hastings: *Twice Checked* (1959), *Deadly Game* (1961).
as Jeffrey Ashford: *Counsel for the Defence* (1960), *The Burden of Proof* (1962), *Will Anyone Who Saw the Accident…* (1963; as *Hit and Run*, 1966), *The Hands of Innocence* (1965), *Consider the Evidence* (1966), *Forget What You Saw* (1967), *Prisoner at the Bar* (1969), *To Protect the Guilty* (1970), *Bent Copper* (1971), *A Man Will be Kidnapped Tomorrow* (1972), *The Double Run* (1973), *The Colour of Violence* (1974), *Three Layers of Guilt* (1975), *Slow Down the World* (1976), *Hostage to Death* (1977), *The Anger of Fear* (1978), *A Recipe for Murder* (1980), *The Loss of the Culion* (1981), *Guilt With Honour* (1982), *A Sense of Loyalty* (1983), *Presumption of Guilt* (1984), *An Ideal Crime* (1985), *A Question of Principle* (1986), *A Crime Remembered* (1987), *The Honourable Detective* (1988), *A Conflict of Interests* (1989), *An Illegal Solution* (1990), *Deadly Reunion* (1991), *Twisted Justice* (1992), *Judgment Deferred* (1993), *The Bitter Bite* (1994), *The Price of Failure* (1995), *Loyal Disloyalty* (1996), *A Web of Circumstances* (1997), *The Cost of Innocence* (1998), *An Honest Betrayal* (1999), *Murder Will Out* (2000), *Looking-glass Justice* (2001), *A Truthful Injustice* (2002).
Inspector Kerry series as Jeffrey Ashford: *Investigations are Proceeding* (1961; as *The D.I.*, US 1962), *Enquiries Are Continuing* (1964; as *The Superintendent's Room*, US 1965).
as Julian Roberts: *A Case of Give a Dog* (1966).
Constable Kerr series as Peter Alding: *The C.I.D. Room* (1967; as *All Leads Negative*, US 1967), *Circle of Danger* (1968), *Murder Among Thieves* (1969), *Guilt Without Proof* (1970), *Despite the Evidence* (1971), *Call Back to Crime* (1972), *Field of Fire* (1973), *The Murder Line* (1974), *Six Days to Death* (1975), *Murder is Suspected* (1977), *Ransom Town* (1979), *A Man Condemned* (1981), *Betrayed by Death* (1982), *One Man's Justice* (1983).

Full name: Roderic Graeme Jeffries.
Pen-names: Peter Alding, Jeffrey Ashford, Hastings Draper, Roderic Graeme, Graham Hastings, Julian Roberts.

Where to start: *Counsel for the Defence* or *Mistakenly in Mallorca.*
Similar stuff: Manuel Vázquez MONTALBÁN and David SERAFIN for other police series set in Spain.

E. Richard Johnson (1938–97) US

There have been several writers who began their writing careers in prison, but ERJ is the only crime novelist whose entire writing career was in gaol. He was in Stillwater State Prison from 1964 to 1990 (apart from when he escaped in 1975 and 1978) for armed robbery. He had dropped out of High School and served in the Army field intelligence unit from 1956–60. After his discharge he held no regular job but was a logger, ranch hand and forester while entering on his life of crime. In prison he began to write out of borèdom, teaching himself from a *Writer's Digest* short-story course. His first book, *Silver Street*, sold first time out to indefatigable editor Joan Kahn. It introduced his hard-bitten, believable, though at times naïve, detective Tony Lonto who is on the trail of a pimp killer. ERJ was astonished when the book won an Edgar award. Lonto returns in *The Inside Man*, where he has to identify a bent cop. ERJ writes life as he knows it – vicious, uncompromising, unforgiving. The books are described as "urban nightmares". They constantly relive ERJ's own outlook on life, especially *Cage Five is Going to Break* about prison life. It is ERJ's least satisfying book, perhaps because it was too close to home. ERJ's best non-series book is *Mongo's Back in Town* (filmed TV 1971) about a contract killer brought in by his brother to dispose of a gang rival but who turns up at the same time as a series of other murders. ERJ also wrote two books about hired assassin Jericho Jones the second of which, *The Cardinalli Contract*, is a rerun of *The Godfather*. By 1971 ERJ was getting into drugs. He wrote about it in *The God Keepers*, and soon after he was a hopeless heroin addict. It was not until 1979 that he was rehabilitated and returned to writing. He was unable to sell another novel, though, until 1986 when he returned to Tony Lonto. *Blind Man's Bluff* is about an especially nasty murder by torture whilst *The Hands of Eddy Loyd* is a murder without a body. ERJ was released from prison in 1990 full of ideas for farming and writing but his life collapsed around him and an increasing dependency on alcohol led to an early death.

Novels

Tony Lonto series: *Silver Street* (1968; as *The Silver Street Killer*, UK 1969), *The Inside Man* (1969), *Blind Man's Buff* (1987), *The Hands of Eddy Loyd* (1988), *Dead Flowers* (1990).

Jericho Jones series: *The Judas* (1971), *The Cardinalli Contract* (1975).

Non-series: *Mongo's Back in Town* (1969), *Cage Five is Going to Break* (1970), *The God Keepers* (1970), *Case Load – Maximum* (1971).

Full name: Emil Richard Johnson.
Where to start: *Silver Street* or *Mongo's Back in Town.*

Awards: Edgar, best first novel (1969).
Similar stuff: Edward BUNKER for other prison-based novels.
Final fact: ERJ was an expert on survival and wrote a handbook on it, *Fur, Food and Survival* (1988), which is still recommended today.

Stuart M. Kaminsky (b. 1934) US

Born and raised in Chicago, SMK studied as a journalist and worked for the Office of Public Information at the universities of Illinois, Michigan and Chicago before teaching at Northwestern University in 1972. He became the Director of the Florida State University Conservatory of Motion Picture, Television and Recording Arts in 1989. He has written several screenplays as well as film biographies of Don Siegel, Clint Eastwood, John Huston and others. He has been a full-time writer since 1994 sometimes producing up to four books a year. He began selling short fiction in 1966 but his first novel, *Bullet for a Star*, did not appear until 1977. This introduced his 1940s impoverished Hollywood detective Toby Peters, who always seems down on his luck, despite rubbing shoulders with the stars, and has to share his office with an eccentric dentist. The books are set in the rather unreal world of the movie industry and each adventure centres around a noted film star. In the first it's Errol Flynn. In the second, *Murder on the Yellow Brick Road*, which is one of the best of the series, it's Judy Garland who calls in Peters when a munchkin is murdered on the set of *The Wizard of Oz*. Later books have included the Marx Brothers (*You Bet Your Life*), Bela Lugosi (*Never Cross a Vampire*), Mae West (*He Done Her Wrong*) and, more recently, W.C. Fields and Charlie Chaplin. The Peters books are clearly written for fun. In a more serious vein is Inspector Porfiry Rostnikov of the Moscow Police. Rostnikov is an honourable man, and a father-like figure to his team, who suffers from a war wound but tries to keep fit. He is distrusted by the KGB and his superiors, partly because he does not do things by the book, but also because he is married to a Jew. Every problem is put in his way and he is often transferred to especially difficult cases. This includes some of SMK's best work, including the Edgar-winning *A Cold Red Sunrise*, where Rostnikov becomes involved in a government conspiracy while investigating the death of a child. The fall of Soviet Russia does not make things any easier for Rostnikov, if anything the increase in lawlessness makes it harder. Posted to the Office of Special Investigations, in *Fall of a Cosmonaut* we find him and his team working on three disparate cases which are ingeniously woven together. SMK also writes a series featuring 60-something Chicago police detective Abe Lieberman. This series is rich in Jewish culture wonderfully contrasted with the Catholic faith through Lieberman's partner Bill Hanrahan – the two are nicknamed "the Rabbi and the Priest". The series is also downbeat and fatalistic. Like Rostnikov, Lieberman acts like an outsider, coping with a world that owes him no favours. SMK's latest series (aside from his TV spin-off Jim Rockford books) grew out of a series of short stories. It features enquiry agent Lew Fonesca, who operates out of Sarasota, Florida, where SMK now lives. Fonesca is still struggling to come to terms with the death of his wife in a car accident three years ago and strives to recover by helping others, though this inevitably leads him into trouble. SMK has written two non-series novels, both powerful suspense thrillers. In *When the Dark Man Calls* (filmed 1988 as *Fréquence meurtre* and 1995) a woman is menaced by the murderer of her parents 20 years before, whilst in *Exercise in Terror* (filmed 1993 as *Hidden Fears*) it's a widow stalked by the murderer of her husband. SMK is the editor-in-chief of Mystery Vault Books, launched in 2001.

Novels
Toby Peters series: *Bullet for a Star* (1977), *Murder on the Yellow Brick Road* (1978), *You Bet Your Life* (1979), *The Howard Hughes Affair* (1979), *Never Cross a Vampire* (1980), *High Midnight* (1981), *Catch a Falling Clown* (1982), *He Done Her Wrong* (1983), *The Fala Factor* (1984), *Down for the Count* (1985), *The Man Who Shot Lewis Vance* (1986), *Smart Moves* (1987), *Think Fast, Mr Peters* (1988), *Buried Caesars* (1989), *Poor Butterfly* (1990), *The Melting Clock* (1991), *The Devil Met a Lady* (1993), *Tomorrow is Another Day* (1995), *Dancing in the Dark* (1996), *A Fatal Glass of Beer* (1997), *A Few Minutes Past Midnight* (2001), *To Catch a Spy* (2002).
Inspector Rostnikov series: *Death of a Dissident* (1981; as *Rostnikov's Corpse*, UK 1981), *Black Knight in Red Square* (1984), *Red Chameleon* (1985), *A Fine Red Rain* (1987), *A Cold Red Sunrise* (1988), *The Man Who Walked Like a Bear* (1990), *Rostnikov's Vacation* (1991), *Death of a Russian Priest* (1993), *Hard Currency* (1995), *Blood and Rubles* (1996), *Tarnished Icons* (1997), *The Dog Who Bit a Policeman* (1998), *Fall of a Cosmonaut* (2000), *Murder on the Trans-Siberian Express* (2001).
Abe Lieberman series: *Lieberman's Folly* (1990), *Lieberman's Choice* (1993), *Lieberman's Day* (1995), *Lieberman's Thief* (1995), *Lieberman's Law* (1996), *The Big Silence* (2000), *Not Quite Kosher* (2001).
Rockford Files series: *The Green Bottle* (1996), *Devil on My Doorstep* (1998).
Lew Fonesca series: *Vengeance* (1999), *Retribution* (2001).
Non-series: *When the Dark Man Calls* (1983), *Exercise in Terror* (1985).
Short Stories. *Opening Shots* (1991).
Editor. *Mystery in the Sunshine State* (1999).

Full name: Stuart Melvin Kaminsky.
Where to start: *Murder on the Yellow Brick Road* or *Death of a Dissident*.
Awards: Edgar, best novel (1989), Prix du Roman d'Aventure (1991).
Website: <www.stuartkaminsky.com>
Similar stuff: for Hollywood stars, George BAXT; for Moscow Martin Cruz SMITH; for Jewish PI, Howard ENGEL's Benny Cooperman.
Final fact: SMK wrote the dialogue for Sergio Leone's *Once Upon a Time in America* (1984).

Jonathan Kane *pseudonym, see* Derek Wilson

Rob Kantner (b. 1952) US

Despite having won four Shamus awards and two further nominations, RK's Ben Perkins series is surprisingly unknown, probably because it was only published in paperback, and only in the US. Perkins is a retired union enforcer who is now a maintenance and security guy at an up-market apartment complex in a suburb of Detroit. Always nosey and tinkering with things – a regular "fixer" – Perkins does a lot of "private eyeing" on the side. His cases are tough and uncompromising – in *Dirty Work* it's a series of rape stranglings, in *The Red, White and Blues* it's the kidnapping of a newborn baby and other patients from various hospitals, in *Concrete Hero* it's internet porn and auto-eroticism. Perkins can look after himself, but he also has an army of friends and relatives who he can call upon. The series stopped when RK started his own consultancy business in quality management, though a few short stories continue to appear. There are sufficient stories about Perkins since the first in 1982 for at least two collections.

Novels

Ben Perkins series: *The Back-Door Man* (1986), *The Harder They Hit* (1987), *Dirty Work* (1988), *Hell's Only Half Full* (1989), *Made in Detroit* (1990), *The Thousand-Yard Stare* (1991), *The Quick and the Dead* (1992), *The Red, White and Blues* (1993), *Concrete Hero* (1994).

Full name: T. Robin Kantner (the T. stands for nothing).
Awards: Shamus, best short story (1987), Shamus, best paperback original (1987, 1989, 1990).
Website: none for his fiction, but <www.9sg.com> for his business.
Similar stuff: Loren ESTLEMAN's Amos Walker.
Final fact: RK reflects that "after 30 years in metro Detroit I now live in a remote area of central Michigan, on a 40 acre horse farm. Closest town is 2 miles away and has 200 people."

Dan Kavanagh (b. 1946) UK

DK is the persona adopted by Julian Barnes for his series of crime novels about the former London bi-sexual policeman turned P.I. Nick Duffy. The series reflects the highs and lows of seedy and corrupt eighties London, where new money helps finance old sins. In *Duffy* he's on the streets of Soho, in *Fiddle City* it's corruption at Heathrow airport, in *Putting the Boot In* it's football hooliganism and shady dealings and in *Going to the Dogs* it's the closest DK gets to a country house murder – though it's far from "cozy". The DK books were written while Barnes was establishing himself as a novelist and literary critic. After graduating from Oxford in modern languages he worked as a lexicographer for the *Oxford English Dictionary* for a few years before becoming a literary and television critic. His first book, *Metroland* (1980), is a highly personal view of growing up in London. He established his reputation with *Flaubert's Parrot* (1984), which was shortlisted for the Booker Prize. The only book under his own name to venture close to crime fiction is *The Porcupine* (1992), a fascinating study of a deposed Communist Party leader after the fall of communism in Eastern Europe on trial for crimes against his country.

Novels

Duffy series: *Duffy* (1980), *Fiddle City* (1981), *Putting the Boot In* (1985), *Going to the Dogs* (1987).

Real name: Julian Barnes.
Pen-name: Dan Kavanagh.
Where to start: *Duffy*.
Awards: None for his crime fiction. The Somerset Maugham Award for *Metroland* (1981), Geoffrey Faber Memorial Prize for *Flaubert's Parrot* (1985), Prix Medicis for *Flaubert's Parrot* (1986), E.M. Forster Award (1986), Gutenberg Prize (1987), Grinzane Cavour Prize (1988) and Prix Femina for *Talking It Over* (1992).
Website: <www.julianbarnes.com>
Similar stuff: Derek RAYMOND, Mark TIMLIN.
Final fact: Barnes was one of several authors who sued Professor Mark Hogarth in 2000 for the right to use his own name in his website. Hogarth had originally registered the domain name and then sought to sell the site to Barnes for a percentage of his royalties.

Paul Kavanagh *pseudonym, see* Lawrence Block

H. R. F. Keating (b. 1926) UK

HRFK is one of the doyens of British crime fiction with a career spanning over forty years, his contribution recognized by the CWA's award of the prestigious Diamond Dagger. He is also one of the field's most astute critics and commentators, serving as the crime-fiction reviewer for *The Times* from 1967–83 and having compiled ten compendia on the history and major books of the field. He is best known for his novels featuring Inspector Ganesh Ghote (pronounced Go-tay) of the Bombay C.I.D. Ghote first appeared in the award-winning *The Perfect Murder* (filmed 1990) – a clever title, where "perfect" is a person's name not an adjective. In fact it's a completely bungled attempted murder but that makes it a more complex crime and with so many red herrings and distractions it is only Ghote's determination and application that sees him through. Several of the crimes in the Ghote series go wrong and HRFK's ability to develop the fallible human side of villain, victim and detective is what gives this series its appeal. It also enables HRFK to consider the moral issues of crime especially when played out against changing values and the clash of cultures. Ghote is frequently harrassed and undervalued by his superiors, but he goes about his business quietly and unassumingly. It is only in moments of utter frustration, as in *Inspector Ghote Trusts the*

Heart, that he will take matters into his own hands. He is never as in control as he would like to be but copes, mostly because he is at one with the world about him. This is contrasted in *Inspector Ghote Hunts the Peacock* and *Go West Inspector Ghote*, where he appears out of his depth when outside of India. The Ghote novels draw heavily on the multicultural world of India, which is all the more surprising because HRFK did not visit there until he was ten years into the series. *Breaking and Entering*, a wonderfully ingenious "locked room" murder brings the series full circle and HRFK has suggested that it may be the last Ghote novel.

The Ghote series accounts for only a half of HRFK's output, though the award-winning *The Murder of the Maharajah*, which is a clever pastiche of the English country house cozy transplanted to a maharajah's palace, features Ghote's father as one of the minor characters. HRFK has created other series characters. There is the endearing and resourceful cleaning lady, Mrs Craggs who appears in several short stories and the amusing *Death of a Fat God*, about antics in an opera company. Under the alias Evelyn Hervey he wrote three novels about Victorian governess Harriet Unwin, somewhat in the style of Anne PERRY. In *The Governess* Unwin is accused of the murder of the master of the house and has to prove her innocence. In *The Man of Gold* she sets about trying to prove the innocence of the new Master in another murder. HRFK is very much at home in the Victorian period where, as in the Ghote novels, there is a considerable pace of change and the clash between the class systems. Both *The Underside* and *A Remarkable Case of Burglary* have Victorian settings and HRFK has also written several Sherlock Holmes pastiches.

HRFK is never one to be complacent. The recent *Jack the Lady Killer* is an historical mystery set in the Punjab in 1935 but is a novel written entirely in verse. It is a reminder that in his early work HRFK was always one to experiment and break moulds. *Death and the Visiting Firemen*, *Zen There Was Murder*, *A Rush on the Ultimate* and *The Dog It Was that Died* may not have been critical successes but they were cleverly contrived mysteries that worked on several levels from the deeply philosophical to simple farce. Recently HRFK has experimented again with a sequence of novels, beginning with *The Rich Detective*, which looks at the different motives, lifestyles and driving forces of the detectives themselves. Detective Chief Inspector Harriet Martins in *The Hard Detective* proved such an appealing character that she has returned in *A Detective in Love* and may yet be the start of another series.

Novels

Inspector Ghote series: *The Perfect Murder* (1964), *Inspector Ghote's Good Crusade* (1966), *Inspector Ghote Caught in Meshes* (1967), *Inspector Ghote Hunts the Peacock* (1968), *Inspector Ghote Plays a Joker* (1969), *Inspector Ghote Breaks an Egg* (1970), *Inspector Ghote Goes by Train* (1971), *Inspector Ghote Trusts the Heart* (1972), *Bats Fly Up for Inspector Ghote* (1974), *Filmi, Filmi, Inspector Ghote* (1976), *Inspector*

Ghote Draws a Line (1979), *Go West, Inspector Ghote* (1981), *The Sheriff of Bombay* (1984), *Under a Monsoon Cloud* (1986), *The Body in the Billiard Room* (1987), *Dead on Time* (1988), *The Iciest Sin* (1990), *Cheating Death* (1991), *Doing Wrong* (1993), *Asking Questions* (1996), *Bribery, Corruption Also* (1999), *Breaking and Entering* (2000).
Non-series: *Death and the Visiting Firemen* (1959), *Zen There Was Murder* (1960), *A Rush on the Ultimate* (1961), *The Dog It Was that Died* (1962), *Death of a Fate God* (1963), *Is Skin Deep, Is Fatal* (1965), *A Remarkable Case of Burglary* (1975), *Murder by Death* as Henry Keating (1976) *The Murder of the Maharajah* (1980), *The Rich Detective* (1993), *The Good Detective* (1995), *The Bad Detective* (1996), *The Soft Detective* (1997), *Jack the Lady Killer* (1999).
Harriet Martins series: *The Hard Detective* (2000), *A Detective in Love* (2001).
Harriet Unwin series as Evelyn Hervey: *The Governess* (1984), *The Man of Gold* (1985), *Into the Valley of Death* (1986).
Short Stories. *Mrs Craggs: Crimes Cleaned Up* (1985), *Inspector Ghote: His Life and Crimes* (1989), *Inspector Ghote and Some Others* (1991), *In Kensington Gardens Once* (1997).
Non-fiction. *Murder Must Appetize* (1975), *Agatha Christie: First Lady of Crime* (1977), *Crime Writers: Reflections on Crime Fiction* (1978), *Sherlock Holmes: The Man and His World* (1979), *Great Crimes* (1982), *Whodunit?* (1982), *Crime and Mystery: The 100 Best Books* (1987), *Writing Crime Fiction* (1986), *The Bedside Companion to Crime* (1989), *Crime Waves* (1991).
Editor. *The Man Who …* (1992).

Full name: Henry Reymond Fitzwalter Keating.
Pen-name: Evelyn Hervey.
Where to start: *The Perfect Murder*.
Awards: CWA Gold Dagger (1964, 1980), American Mystery Award, best scholarly work (1988), Macavity, best critical (1990), The George N. Dove Award (1995), CWA Diamond Dagger (1996).
Website: <www.twbooks.co.uk/authors/hrfkeating.html>
Similar stuff: Paul Mann's George Sansi series is also set in Bombay.
Final fact: When HRFK worked as a sub-editor at *The Times* he sat in the exact same chair as Graham Greene had years before.

Faye Kellerman (b. 1952) US

Though she has a doctorate in dental surgery, FK, who married author Jonathan KELLERMAN in 1972, pursued a career in real estate until she became a full-time writer. All but two of her books feature Detective Sergeant (rising to Lieutenant) Peter Decker of the LAPD. In *The Ritual Bath*, which involves the rape of an orthodox Jew, he meets a young widow, Rina Lazarus. The novels have followed their relationship: they have married by the time of *Day of Atonement* and their first child is born in *Grievous Sin* (which allows for the investigation of a kidnapped baby from the hospital). Decker had been born a Jew but had been raised by Baptist parents so he needs to readopt his faith, which causes a struggle in *Milk and Honey*. FK uses this framework to explore religious and family tensions as backgrounds to crimes and guilt, which gives the books a robust framework. Decker had a daughter, Cindy, by his first marriage and she matures through the novels becoming a police officer in *Stalker*, which is written almost entirely from her perspective. FK likes to experiment with various viewpoints. *Justice* is told almost entirely from the viewpoint of a student whose classmate, a Prom Queen, is murdered. The series is strong on both characterization and motivation with realistic plot lines. FK has written two non-series books. *The Quality of Mercy* is an historical novel set at the time of Shakespeare and considers his relationship with the daughter of Queen Elizabeth's physician. It has a minor crime theme about smuggling Jews out of Spain at the time of the Inquisition. *Moon Music* is set in Las Vegas and involves Native American mysticism in a series of brutal murders.

Novels

Decker and Lazarus series: *The Ritual Bath* (1985), *Sacred and Profane* (1987), *Milk and Honey* (1990), *Day of Atonement* (1991), *False Prophet* (1992), *Grievous Sin* (1993), *Sanctuary* (1994), *Justice* (1995), *Prayers for the Dead* (1996), *Serpent's Tooth* (1997), *Jupiter's Bones* (1999), *Stalker* (2000), *The Forgotten* (2001), *Stone Kiss* (2002).

Non-series: *The Quality of Mercy* (1988), *Moon Music* (1998).

Full name: Faye Kellerman (*née* Marder).
Where to start: *The Ritual Bath*.
Awards: Macavity, best first novel (1987).
Similar stuff: S.T. HAYMON, Wendy HORNSBY, Rochelle Majer KRICH.
Final fact: In March 1999 FK filed a lawsuit against the scriptwriters and film company that made *Shakespeare in Love* claiming that the story was taken from her book *The Quality of Mercy*. The case has yet to be settled.

Jonathan Kellerman (b. 1949) US

JK is a clinical psychologist with a special interest in child psychology. Born in New York he grew up in Los Angeles where he lives with his wife, the author Faye KELLERMAN. He has brought his expertise to a series of bestselling novels featuring child psychologist Dr Alex Delaware. The first, the award-winning *When the Bough Breaks* (filmed TV 1986), which took two years to sell because it was regarded as too controversial, deals with a ring of child molesters. Delaware, who had retired through stress, has to coax memories from a child witness to a double murder. In *Blood Test*, a child goes missing from a motel room spattered with blood. Each book is a complex study of the psychological causes and consequences of crime delving into family backgrounds, upbringing and relationships. Delaware works with LA homicide detective Milo Sturgis, who is homosexual and rather a loner in his work. Though they both have common goals in resolving the crimes they have different methods of dealing with it. Although children remain key to the books, Delaware serves increasingly as a profiler and psychological analyst. *The Clinic*, for instance, requires Delaware to dig into the childhood of a murdered psychologist to find a motive for her death. *Monster* concerns a psychotic, imprisoned in a secure unit, who somehow predicts violent murders elsewhere. *Dr Death* deals with assisted suicide. The gradual unravelling of these cases through exploring the human psyche is as fascinating as it is compelling. In addition to two books on psychology and two children's books, JK has written two non-series thrillers. *The Butcher's Theatre* is about the search for a psychopath in Jerusalem. *Billy Straight*, like *When the Bough Breaks*, is about the search for a young boy who witnessed a murder. JK's popularity is evident with over 20 million copies in print.

Novels

Alex Delaware series: *When the Bough Breaks* (1985; as *Shrunken Heads*, UK 1985), *Blood Test* (1986), *Over the Edge* (1987), *Silent Partner* (1989), *Time Bomb* (1990), *Private Eyes* (1991), *Devil's Waltz* (1992), *Bad Love* (1994), *Self-Defence* (1994), *The Web* (1995), *The Clinic* (1996), *Survival of the Fittest* (1997), *Monster* (2000), *Dr Death* (2000), *Flesh and Blood* (2001).

Non-series: *The Butcher's Theatre* (1988), *Billy Straight* (1998).

Awards: Edgar, Anthony and Macavity, best first novel (1986), Samuel Goldwyn Creative Writing Award (1971),

Website: <www.mysterynet.com/jkellerman/>

Similar stuff: P.M. CARLSON, Val MCDERMID, Maxine O'CALLAGHAN, Benjamin SCHUTZ.

Final fact: JK still managed to produce two novels during 1988/89 when he was diagnosed with cancer of the thyroid and was undergoing treatment. He felt that his own need to write and be productive helped pull him through.

Judith Kelman (b. 1945) US

JK's books are in the mould of Mary Higgins CLARK's, though most are rather more formulaic and have less variety. They are all psychological suspense novels of women or children at the mercy of a vicious murderer. Her first, *Prime Evil*, is not her best but sets the tone. A pregnant and unmarried woman comes to an old rambling farmhouse to sort out the papers of a reclusive author and her eccentric husband. Before long she finds herself menaced by a dark family secret. *While Angels Sleep* is in a similar vein. Her second novel, *Where Shadows Fall*, was better. A mother determines to find the truth about her son's apparent suicide – the 12th in a series of such unusual deaths. This book was sufficiently successful to demand a sequel, *Hush Little Darlings*, in which the mother, Sarah Spooner, delves into the life of a mysterious criminal who abducts prepubescent girls who later have no memory of their ordeal. JK loves to explore the mind of the criminal and his effect on the world about him. *Someone's Watching* (filmed TV 1993), perhaps JK's best known book, is a violent study of a psychopath who enjoys running children down in his car. Other psychopaths with a delight in murdering or molesting children appear in *The House on the Hill* and *More Than You Know*. Other novels, such as *If I Should Die*, *One Last Kiss* and *Fly Away Home* concentrate on the psychology of the parent or of an adult who believes they may be going crazy and have no recollection of crimes. JK's most recent books have started to vary the formula. *After the Fall* is an ingenious legal thriller about a teenager charged with rape. *Summer of Storms* is about a murder that happened 30 years ago but which comes to life again to haunt the victim's younger sister. JK's books are strong on suspense and atmosphere.

Novels

Non-series: *Prime Evil* (1986), *While Angels Sleep* (1988), *Someone's Watching* (1991), *The House on the Hill* (1992), *If I Should Die* (1993), *One Last Kiss* (1994), *More Than You Know* (1996), *Fly Away Home* (1997), *After the Fall* (1999), *Summer of Storms* (2001).
Sara Spooner sequence: *Where Shadows Fall* (1987), *Hush Little Darlings* (1989).

Full name: Judith Ann Kelman.
Where to start: *Hush Little Darlings* or *One Last Kiss*.
Website: <www.jkelman.com>
Similar stuff: Mary Higgins CLARK, Marilyn WALLACE.
Final fact: JK gave up a career as a speech therapist and educational consultant and gave herself a year in which to become an author. Before the year was out she had sold her first novel and two articles for major magazines.

Harry Kemelman (1908–96) US

HK was a teacher before WW2 but then held several government posts and was a wage analysis consultant at the time he sold his first story, "The Nine-Mile Walk" to *EQMM* in 1947, where it was subsequently voted by readers as the year's best first story. It introduced HK's character Nicky Welt, an English professor who is something of an armchair detective. He solves a crime described to him by his friend, the district attorney, while they are playing chess. This delightful series ran in the pages of *EQMM* over the next 20 years and was collected as *The Nine-Mile Walk*. By then HK had introduced a new detective, Rabbi David Small. These books are also small-town cozies, set in Barnard's Crossing, Massachusetts, and Small is rather like a male Jewish Miss Marple. He knows all the people in his community, he knows how the small things in life can be so important, and he has an astute logic, sharpened by his religious training, which allows him to make deductions overlooked by others. In the first book, *Friday the Rabbi Slept Late* (filmed TV 1976 as *Lanigan's Rabbi*), Small becomes a suspect in a murder case and has to prove his innocence. This bonds his friendship with Police Chief Hugh Lanigan, who is a regular through the series. HK took on contemporary issues as the series progressed including drug smuggling, international terrorism and fanatical religious cults. The last book in the series, *The Day the Rabbi Left Town*, is more a series of lectures on the history and customs of Judaism than a mystery. Similarly, *Conversations with Rabbi Small* (1981) is not a mystery novel but a series of reflections on the Jewish faith. Rabbi Small is a fine example of a true ethnic detective.

Novels

Rabbi Small series: *Friday the Rabbi Slept Late* (1964), *Saturday the Rabbi Went Hungry* (1966), *Sunday the Rabbi Stayed Home* (1969), *Monday the Rabbi Took Off* (1972), *Tuesday the Rabbi Saw Red* (1973), *Wednesday the Rabbi Got Wet* (1976), *Thursday the Rabbi Walked Out* (1978), *Someday the Rabbi Will Leave* (1985), *One Fine Day the Rabbi Bought a Cross* (1987), *The Day the Rabbi Resigned* (1992), *The Day the Rabbi Left Town* (1996).

Short Stories

Nicky Welt series: *The Nine-Mile Walk* (1967).

Awards: Edgar, best first novel (1965).
Similar stuff: Howard ENGEL, Stuart KAMINSKY.
Final fact: The first Rabbi Small book was not originally written as a mystery but was about the building of a local synagogue for which HK hoped to raise some money. His editor suggested turning it into a crime novel.

Jerry Kenneally (b. 1938) US

JK's Nick Polo is a former San Francisco cop turned P.I., just like his creator. JK has been a licensed P.I. since 1971 and does things by the book, which is why he likes writing the Nick Polo series so that he can bend the rules. *Polo Solo* starts off with Polo in prison after trusting a dodgy lawyer but he wins his freedom, and a P.I. licence, by helping solve a case of blackmailing against the city's female mayor. Polo doesn't have all the angst of so many P.I.s, though his parents were killed in a plane crash, but he is a compulsive gambler and is prepared to take risks. Several of his cases arise out of his gambling. In *Polo, Anyone?* he sets up a sting to catch a poker cheat, while in *Polo's Ponies* its horse racing where, intriguingly, a horse is the murder weapon. Polo's later cases operate on a bigger scale, especially *All That Glitters*, where Polo becomes involved in the quest for a lost amulet once owned by Genghis Khan. Since then JK has written standalone thrillers. Both *The Suspect* and *The Other Eye*, like *All That Glitters*, involve major art thefts. *The Conductor* is about a terrorist turned assassin. *The Hunted* concerns the search for a young witness to a murder. JK's books have plenty of action and suspense and occasional wit.

Novels

Nick Polo series: *Polo Solo* (1987), *Polo, Anyone?* (1988), *Polo's Ponies* (1988), *Polo in the Rough* (1989), *Polo's Wild Card* (1990), *Green With Envy* (1991), *Special Delivery* (1992), *Vintage Polo* (1993), *Beggar's Choice* (1994), *All That Glitters* (1997).
Non-series: *Nobody Wins*, as G.P. Kennealy (1978), *The Conductor* (1996), *The Suspect* (1998), *The Hunted* (1999), *The Other Eye* (2000).

Where to start: *Polo's Ponies* or *The Suspect.*
Similar stuff: Joe GORES.
Final fact: JK recalls that when he was a young, naïve San Francisco policeman, walking a beat in North Beach, he saw a plainclothes inspector leaving a delicatessen with a large Prosciutto ham under his arm as a courtesy package from a merchant who liked to see cops hang around his establishment. He dropped the ham into the trunk of an unmarked car and said, "You know kid, it's not all red lights and sirens."

Michael Kenyon (b. 1931) UK (but US resident)

Despite their titles and the inherent seriousness throughout, all of MK's books are humorous mysteries, sometimes verging on the farcical, but always tremendous fun. *May You Die in Ireland* doesn't suggest it's a barrel of laughs, but in fact MK provides a spoof on the traditional mystery with an American professor who inherits a castle in Ireland without realising that his background makes him something of a human time-bomb. MK later admitted that he was rather contemptuous of the crime and thriller field when he began, hence his rather flagrant send-ups, but he soon came to respect the field and his later books take on a more reverential parody. His best works fall into two series. There is Superintendent O'Malley, the rather lugubrious detective of the Irish garda around whom things seem to happen. And there is the Bard of the Yard, the cockney Chief Inspector Enry Peckover who, much to the annoyance of his fellow officers, insists on quoting spontaneously composed verse at a moment's notice. How Peckover ever became a Chief Inspector is a miracle since he was demoted at least twice. Peckover and O'Malley meet in the first of the series, *Zigzag*. In all of MK's books the crimes are always serious, especially the rape and murder in *The Rapist*, but it's the fallout from the crime and its investigation that provides the opportunities for MK's caustic and at times goonish wit. Peter LOVESEY selected Peckover as one of his favourite detectives in *100 Great Detectives*, noting that "Line for line, Michael Kenyon's is the wittiest and freshest of all crime fiction." MK was born in Yorkshire and spent most of his working life in England as a reporter (including a stint on the *Guardian*, from 1960-64) but has since made the United States his home where he demonstrates his knowledge of food and cooking by regular columns for the *Gourmet* magazine.

Novels

Superintendent O'Malley series: *The 100,000 Welcomes* (1970), *The Shooting of Dan McGrew* (1972), *A Sorry State* (1974), also in Peckover novel *Zigzag*.
Inspector Peckover series: *Zigzag* (1981; as *The Elgar Variation*, US 1981), *The God Squad Bod* (1982; as *The Man at the Wheel*, US 1982), *A Free-Range Wife* (1983), *A Healthy Way to Die* (1986), *Peckover Holds the Baby* (1988), *Kill the Butler!* (1991), *Peckover Joins the Choir* (1992), *Peckover and the Bog Man* (1994).

Non-series: *May You Die in Ireland* (1965), *The Whole Hog* (1967; as *The Trouble With Series Three*, US 1967), *Out of Season* (1968), *Green Grass* (1969), *Mr. Big* (1975; as by Daniel Forbes in US), *The Rapist* (1977; as by Daniel Forbes in US), *Deep Pocket* (1978; as *The Molehill File*, US 1978).

Where to start: *Zigzag*.
Similar stuff: Peter DICKINSON for the irreverent humour.
Final fact: In *A French Affair* (1992) MK wrote an account of the years his family lived in France.

Sean A. Key *pseudonym, see* William J. Coughlin

William X. Kienzle (1928–2001) US

WXK, like his character Father Robert Koesler, was a diocesan Catholic priest in Detroit and editor of the weekly Catholic paper. Koesler is a fan of mystery stories and brings this and his strong religious conviction to bear when he becomes involved in a series of murders of priests and nuns in *The Rosary Murders* (filmed 1987). Thereafter Koesler finds himself frequently consulted by Inspector Koznicki of the Detroit police when Catholic-related problems arise. Despite the violence of some of the murders the series is in the traditional mode, with plenty of red herrings and lengthy explanations. The series benefits from WXK's rich discussion of key issues, frequently associated with his faith. The books are for those who like their novels leisurely.

Novels

Father Koesler series: *The Rosary Murders* (1979), *Death Wears a Red Hat* (1980), *Mind Over Murder* (1981), *Assault With Intent* (1982), *Shadow of Death* (1983), *Kill and Tell* (1984), *Sudden Death* (1985), *Deathbed* (1986), *Deadline for a Critic* (1987), *Marked for Murder* (1988), *Eminence* (1989), *Masquerade* (1990), *Chameleon* (1991), *Body Count* (1992), *Dead Wrong* (1993), *Bishop as Pawn* (1994), *Call No Man Father* (1995), *Requiem for Moses* (1996), *The Man Who Loved God* (1997), *The Greatest Evil* (1998), *No Greater Love* (1999), *Till Death* (2000), *The Sacrifice* (2001), *The Gathering* (2002).

Full name: William Xavier Kienzle (pronounced Kin-zell).
Pen name: Mark Boyle (for non-fiction).
Similar stuff: Ralph MCINERNY's Father Dowling series, Andrew Greeley's "Blackie" Ryan books.
Final fact: WXK originally proposed calling his second novel *I Had Intercourse With a Bear*!

Karen Kijewski (b. 1943) US

KK was a high school English teacher in Massachusetts before she returned to her native California, as a full-time writer. She entered *Katwalk* for the St Martin's Press/PWA first unpublished novel competition in 1988 and it not only won but went on to win the Anthony and Shamus awards. It launched her series about Kat Colorado, a 40-something Sacramento P.I., former reporter and occasional bartender, as KK was for ten years. Though the series follows some of the hard-boiled conventions – certainly Kat has a sad and violent upbringing, and she faces various dangers in her investigations – its overall tone remains fairly light, with Kat's wry observations on events plus an engaging cast of characters. These include advice columnist Charity Collins who, in the first book, sends Kat after her husband who has absconded with $200,000, which leads Kat to the sleazy side of Las Vegas. In *Katapult* Kat goes after the murderer of her own cousin. KK is at her best when observing individuals' lives, motives and dirty dealings. This comes to the fore strongly in *Kat's Cradle* where a young girl is about to come into an inheritance but needs documentary proof of her mother's death. Kat's investigations unearth a trail of deceit. Although these novels do not have the impact of those by Sue GRAFTON or Sara PARETSKY, the plots are well crafted with strong characters.

Novels
Kat Colorado series: *Katwalk* (1989), *Katapult* (1990), *Kat's Cradle* (1992), *Copy Kat* (1992), *Wild Kat* (1993), *Alley Kat Blues* (1995), *Honky Tonk Kat* (1996), *Kat Scratch Fever* (1997), *Stray Kat Waltz* (1998).

Full name: Karen Kijewski (pronounced Kee-eff-ski).
Awards: St Martin's Press/PWA best first unpublished novel (1988), Anthony and Shamus, best first novel (1990).
Website: <embers.tripod.com/~kat_colorado/> [unofficial]
Similar stuff: Linda BARNES, Sara PARETSKY.

Frank King, *see under pseudonym* Lydia Adamson

Laurie R. King (b. 1952) US

LRK, born and raised in California, turned to writing while she was raising her family and after she had graduated from theological college. Her first published book, *A Grave Talent*, was her fourth written and introduced the recently promoted San Francisco police detective Kate Martinelli and her new partner Inspector Alonzo Hawkin. In the first case the duo are investigating the murder of three girls in a community of artists. The strength of the book, apart from the intricate plotting and excellent characterization, is in Martinelli's own dilemma over her sexuality and her eventual coming out at the end of the book. It is also a fascinating study of the relationship of art to women. The book not only won the Edgar for best first novel but was nominated for the CWA John Creasey award and the Anthony. A second Martinelli novel, *To Play the Fool*, reworks the themes of the first book to some extent with another enigmatic individual, a latter-day Shakespearean fool. The series has considerable depth peopled with enigmatic characters and dark emotions. These are not so much detective novels as explorations of how people find solutions to coping with whatever life throws at them –

whether as villain or victim. Despite the popularity of this series LRK is better known for her other series featuring the young American Mary Russell who, in *The Beekeeper's Apprentice*, meets a semi-retired Sherlock Holmes on the Sussex Downs. This first book (which was LRK's second completed novel) is almost a comedy of manners, as its purpose is to match Holmes, the epitomé of the logical, enquiring late Victorian against a modern, liberated young woman. LRK did not see it as a Holmesian pastiche, but later books in the series have slipped quite comfortably into that mode, although the marriage of Holmes and Russell was something of a shock to pure Sherlockians in *A Letter of Mary*. The first book was nominated for an Agatha whilst the second won the Nero Wolfe award. The fourth, *The Moor*, takes Holmes back to the scene of *The Hound of the Baskervilles.* LRK has written two non-series books. The first of these, *The Birth of a New Moon*, could yet herald a new series. It features Anne Waverly, an occasional FBI consultant, whose husband and daughter died in a mass suicide pact within a strange cult. Anne is called upon by the FBI to investigate a sinister religious community, which brings back echoes of her past. *Folly* starts with a similar premise, a woman struggling to come to terms with the loss of her husband and daughter, but follows a very different thread as, while seeking solitude, she stumbles across a dark secret in her family history. Although LRK's books may be categorized as police procedurals, Holmesian pastiches and psychological suspense they are all character-driven explorations of life.

Novels

Kate Martinelli series: *A Grave Talent* (1993), *To Play the Fool* (1995), *With Child* (1996), *Night Work* (1999).

Mary Russell series: *The Beekeeper's Apprentice* (1994), *A Monstrous Regiment of Women* (1995), *A Letter of Mary* (1996), *The Moor* (1998), *O Jerusalem* (1999), *Justice Hall* (2002).

Non-series: *The Birth of a New Moon* (1999; as *A Darker Place*, US 1999), *Folly* (2001).

Where to start: *A Grave Talent* unless you are a Holmes fan, in which case *The Beekeeper's Apprentice.*

Awards: Edgar, best first novel (1994), Nero Wolfe award (1996).

Similar stuff: Frances FYFIELD, Gillian LINSCOTT.

Final fact: LRK's first completed book is the as yet unpublished *Daughters of Men*, a futuristic novel where almost all men are wiped out and a small colony of women survive.

Michael Kirk *pseudonym, see* Bill Knox

Alanna Knight (b. 1923) UK

AK began her writing career with a long series of romantic suspense novels, the first of which, *Legend of the Loch* (1969) won her the Romantic

Novelists' Association best first novel award. All of her books draw upon the spirit of the Scottish heritage. One, *The Passionate Kindness* (1974), was about the romance between Robert Louis Stevenson and Fanny Osbourne. AK became fascinated with Stevenson, leading her to compile *The Robert Louis Stevenson Treasury* (1982) plus two further tributes to the author and a play, *The Private Life of Robert Louis Stevenson* (1984). This research brought her into close contact with the Edinburgh of the late 19th century, an ideal setting for a murder mystery and thus was born her series featuring Inspector Jeremy Faro. There's something of Stevenson in Faro – both have a rather fatalistic outlook and a tragic past, and both have stepsons. In Faro's case it's Dr Vincent Laurie who frequently becomes involved in Faro's cases. In the first, *Enter Second Murderer*, Faro reopens an old case where the perpetrator had been caught and hanged as events now suggest there was another murderer. *Blood Line* is a fascinating novel, not unlike the work of Josephine Tey, where Faro's investigations cause him to consider a royal crime three centuries ago. The Faro books are rich in atmosphere and suspense. Recently AK has started a companion series featuring Faro's daughter, Rose McQuinn who, after tragedy in America, returns to Scotland to restart her life and in soon entangled in an unsolved murder. Of her non-series books, *Angel Eyes* is the most unusual. Set in Arizona, where AK spends some of her winters, it involves a Navajo P.I. and brings together Celtic legends and those of the Anasazi. *The Dagger in the Crown* is a historical mystery set at the time of Mary Queen of Scots. AK has also written three mystery novels for children and adolescents, *The Royal Park Murder* (1998), *The Monster in the Loch* (1998) and *Dead Beckoning* (1999).

Novels

Inspector Faro series: *Enter Second Murderer* (1988), *Bloodline* (1989), *Deadly Beloved* (1990), *Killing Cousins* (1990), *A Quiet Death* (1991), *The Evil That Men Do* (1992), *To Kill a Queen* (1992), *The Missing Duchess* (1994), *The Bull Slayers* (1995), *Murder by Appointment* (1996), *The Coffin Lane Murders* (1998), *The Shooting Party Murders* (2001).

Rose McQuinn series: *The Inspector's Daughter* (2000), *Dangerous Pursuits* (2002).

Non-series: *The Sweet Cheat Gone* (1992), *The Outward Angel* (1993), *Angel Eyes* (1997), *The Dagger in the Crown* (2001).

Full name: Alanna Knight (*née* Cleet).
Pen-name: Margaret Hope (for romances).
Where to start: *Enter Second Murderer*.
Similar stuff: Anne PERRY, Amy MYERS.
Final fact: While researching the life of Robert Louis Stevenson, AK discovered, buried in an archive and forgotten for a hundred years, his magic lantern slides of his years in Samoa.

Bill Knox (1928–99) UK

BK was in newspapers and journalism all his life, from a copy boy at 16 to presenting the Scottish TV series *Crime Desk* at 60. For many years he was a crime reporter and his knowledge of police procedures in his native Glasgow was profound. This enabled him to write thoroughly realistic books at a remarkable rate – often four a year over many years. His series featuring Detective Chief Inspector Colin Thane and his partner Inspector Phil Moss is one of the longest-running of all police procedurals, yet it never flagged in its inventiveness or relevance. Thane is an intuitive detective who doesn't always let facts get in the way and relies upon Moss for the dogged research and deduction. The novels are always ingeniously constructed and the investigation of often quite complex crimes is meticulous and determined. Over the years their thoroughness has not diminished and the crimes have kept pace with time – from a major swindle and murder within a department store in *Death Department* to high-tech crime in the computer world in *Death Bytes*. The 19th book in the series, *The Crossfire Killings*, won BK the *Police Review* award as the most authentic police procedural of the year. Under his own name BK also wrote a series about Webb Carrick who patrols the seas and islands off the Scottish coast for the Scottish Fishery Protection Service. His work brings him up against smuggling, gunrunning, espionage and even murder, and he frequently has to fight against the superstitions of the islanders. This unusual series vividly recreates the Scottish islands and culture with a fascinating array of incidents from sea-serpent sightings in *The Klondyker* to a WW2 wreck in *Bombship* and a Soviet spy ship in *Bloodtide*.

BK has also written three further series under the name Robert MacLeod, all of which allow him to display his knowledge of the world beyond Scotland. The Talos Cord series, about a UN troubleshooter, is the closest BK comes to a straight spy series. There are six books about Andrew Laird, an international marine insurance claim investigator. Jonathan Gaunt is an external auditor for the Scottish Remembrancer's Office in Edinburgh, and is really a land-based version of Laird. All three series are action thrillers and lack the local colour, intensity and realism of BK's Scottish novels. BK has adapted several of his novels for radio and TV, and conversely adapted several episodes from Eddie Boyd's series *The View from Daniel Pike* (TV 1971–3), about an unglamorous Glasgow P.I. and debt collector, for a story collection. He also compiled a volume of famous trials in Glasgow, as *Court of Murder*.

Novels

Thane and Moss series: *Deadline for a Dream* (1957; as *In at the Kill*, US 1961), *Death Department* (1959), *Leave it to the Hangman* (1960), *Little Drops of Blood* (1962), *Sanctuary Isle* (1962; as *The Grey Sentinels*, US 1963), *The Man in the Bottle* (1963; as *The Killing Game*, US 1963), *The Taste of Proof* (1965), *The Deep Fall* (1966; as *The Ghost Car*, US 1966), *Justice on the Rocks* (1967), *The Tallyman* (1969), *Children of the Mist* (1970; as *Who Shot the Bull?*, US 1970), *To Kill a Witch* (1971), *Draw Batons!* (1973), *Rally to Kill* (1975), *Pilot Error* (1977), *Live Bait*

(1978), *A Killing in Antiques* (1981), *The Hanging Tree* (1983), *The Crossfire Killings* (1986), *The Interface Man* (1989), *The Counterfeit Killers* (1996), *Blood Proof* (1997), *Death Bytes* (1998), *The Lazarus Widow*, completed by Martin EDWARDS (1999)
Webb Carrick series: *The Scavengers* (1964), *Devilweed* (1966), *Blacklight* (1967), *The Klondyker* (1968; as *Figurehead*, US 1968), *Blueback* (1969), *Seafire* (1970), *Stormtide* (1972), *Whitewater* (1974), *Hellspout* (1976), *Witchrock* (1977), *Bombship* (1980), *Bloodtide* (1982), *Wavecrest* (1985), *Dead Man's Mooring* (1987), *The Drowning Nets* (1991).
Talos Cord series as Robert MacLeod: *Cave of Bats* (1964), *Lake of Fury* (1966; as *The Iron Sanctuary*, US 1968), *Isle of Dragons* (1967), *Place of Mists* (1969), *Path of Ghosts* (1971), *Nest of Vultures* (1973),
Jonathan Gaunt series as Robert MacLeod (in UK) and as Noah Webster (in US): *A Property in Cyprus* (1970; as *Flickering Death*, US 1971), *A Killing in Malta* (1972), *A Burial in Portugal* (1973), *A Witchdance in Bavaria* (1975), *A Pay-Off in Switzerland* (1977), *An Incident in Iceland* (1979), *A Problem in Prague* (1981), *A Legacy from Tenerife* (1984), *A Cut in Diamonds* (1985), *The Money Mountain* (1987; as *A Flight from Paris*, US 1987), *The Spanish Maze Game* (1990).
Andrew Laird series as Robert MacLeod (in UK) and as Michael Kirk (in US): *All Other Perils* (1974), *Dragonship* (1976), *Salvage Job* (1978), *Cargo Risk* (1980), *Mayday from Malaga* (1983), *Witchline* (1988).
Non-series: *The Cockatoo Crime* (1958), *Death Calls the Shots* (1961), *Die for Big Betsy* (1961), *The Drum of Ungara* (1963; as *Drum of Power* by Robert MacLeod, UK 1964).
Short Stories. *The View From Daniel Pike*, with Edward Boyd (1974), *Scottish Tales of Crime* (1989).
Non-fiction. *Court of Murder* (1968).

Full name: William Knox.
Pen-names: Robert MacLeod, Michael Kirk, Noah Webster.
Where to start: Anywhere in the Thane and Moss series, such as *Rally to Kill* or *The Crossfire Killings*.
Awards: *Police Review* award (1986).
Similar stuff: Gavin Black, Peter TURNBULL.
Final fact: BK used to have the final proofs of his novels checked by a professional, such as a police detective, to ensure accuracy.

Rochelle Majer Krich (b. 1947) US

RMK was born in Germany, the child of Polish Jews who were Holocaust survivors, but was raised and educated in the US. She was an English teacher at a private high school for 18 years and received two awards for her professionalism. Her first book, *Where's Mommy Now?* (filmed 1995 as *Perfect Alibi*), a surprisingly conventional gothic suspense novel about a mother who, unbeknown to her, has become the victim of her children's nanny, won the Anthony award. Most of RMK's later books draw upon her Orthodox Jewish upbringing, especially in her series about LAPD homicide detective Jessie Drake. The first book, *Fair Game*, which received an Agatha nomination, concerns a serial killer who likes to play games with the police. It is with *Angel of Death*, another Agatha nominee, that RMK develops the Jewish thread. A lawyer, Barry Lewis, is the son of Holocaust survivors but finds he has to defend a group of neo-Nazis and holocaust deniers. The inevitable murder causes Jessie to discover matters about her own origins. This flows over into *Blood Money*, where an elderly survivor of the concentration camps is found murdered and leads Jessie to the discovery of other connected deaths. There are strong Jewish themes in *Till Death Do Us Part* and *Speak No Evil*. RMK is also working on a new series about crime writer Molly Blume, an Orthodox Jew who turns investigator.

Novels

Jessie Drake series: *Fair Game* (1993), *Angel of Death* (1994), *Blood Money* (1999), *Dead Air* (2000), *Shadows of Sin* (2001).

Non-series: *Where's Mommy Now?* (1990), *Till Death Do Us Part* (1992), *Nowhere to Run* (1994), *Speak No Evil* (1998), *Fertile Ground* (1998).

Where to start: *Till Death Do Us Part* or *Fair Game*.
Awards: Anthony, best paperback original (1991).
Website: <www.rochellekrich.com>
Similar stuff: Faye KELLERMAN, Harry KEMELMAN.
Final fact: Jessie Drake was originally a male detective (who had appeared in *Where's Mommy Now?*) but the novel was rejected 16 times. RMK reworked it with a female detective and it sold first time out.

Mary Kuhfeld, *see under* Mary Monica Pulver

Michael Kurland (b. 1938) US

MK is probably better known as a science fiction writer, though little of his sf is conventional, and some of it contains strong mystery elements. MK has held a number of jobs, including editing the rock music magazine *Crawdaddy* for a while and teaching English. His first book, *Ten Years to Doomsday* (1964), written with Chester Anderson, was science fiction. His early spy novels, comparable to the *Man from U.N.C.L.E.* series and influenced by the espionage novels of Manning Coles, are also high on technology. His first proper mystery, *The Secret of Benjamin Square*, was written under the alias Jennifer Plum and is a gothic suspense novel set in an old house in Victorian London. MK returned to the Victorian period for his sequels to the Sherlock Holmes series where he resurrects the "Napoleon of Crime", Professor Moriarty, starting with *The Infernal Device*, which was nominated for both an Edgar award and an American Book Award. MK was a long-time friend of sf writer Randall Garrett and in *Ten Little Wizards* and *A Study in Sorcery* he continued Garrett's series about Lord Darcy. Although ostensibly science fiction – they are set in an alternate timeline where magic still operates, though by strict scientific rules – the stories are bona fide mysteries. MK's own series features 1930s newspaper columnist Alexander Brass, who reports on the rich and the famous. In *Too Soon Dead*, while investigating the owner of some compromising photos, Brass finds himself involved with an anti-Nazi group. Both books wonderfully recreate the Depression era and it is to be hoped there will be more in the series. MK has also compiled a series of useful guides, which no crime-fiction writer should be without. *How to Solve a Murder* looks at forensic detection while *How to Try a Murder* runs through the trial process.

Novels
Moriarty series: *The Infernal Device* (1979), *Death by Gaslight* (1982), *The Great Game* (2001). First two reissued with a short story as *The Infernal Device and Others* (2001).
Lord Darcy series: *Ten Little Wizards* (1988), *A Study in Sorcery* (1989).
Alexander Brass series: *Too Soon Dead* (1997), *The Girls in the High-Heeled Shoes* (1998).
Man from W.A.R. series: *Mission: Third Force* (1967), *Mission: Tank War* (1968), *A Plague of Spies* (1969).
as Jennifer Plum: *The Secret of Benjamin Square* (1972).
Non-fiction. *Gallery of Rogues* (1994), *How to Solve a Murder* (1995), *How to Try a Murder* (1997), *The Complete Idiot's Guide to Unsolved Mysteries* (2000).
Editor. *My Sherlock Holmes* (2002).

Full name: Michael Joseph Kurland.
Pen-name: Jennifer Plum.
Where to start: *Too Soon Dead.*
Website: <www.michaelkurland.com>
Similar stuff: Other 1930s books, see Nate Heller series by Max Allan COLLINS and Loren ESTLEMAN's Detroit series.
Final fact: When living in New York, MK received a call from a friend in Los Angeles asking him who he thought was signing books in a local sf book store. When MK expressed a blank the friend said, 'You are.' It turned out an impostor was signing MK's books!

Lynda La Plante (b. 1946) UK

Dubbed by the press "the novelist with the million-dollar quill" and "the Queen of the Best Sellers", LLP revolutionized crime fiction on British TV with her hard-hitting series *Prime Suspect* and *Trial and Retribution*. Born in Liverpool, LLP trained for the stage and worked with the National Theatre and Royal Shakespeare Company before she began to appear on TV in 1978 with parts in *The Sweeney* and *The Professionals.* Frustrated that there were not good acting parts for women LLP began to write her own scripts, hitting the jackpot with *The Widows* (TV, 1982; remade for US TV 2000). When four robbers are killed during a raid on a security van their widows, under the leadership of Dolly Rawlins, decide to pull off the raid themselves. A brilliantly plotted, scripted and acted TV serial, it pressed all the right buttons and led to two sequels. LLP novelized the TV serial and then wrote three one-off novels before her next TV series. The first novel, *The Legacy* (1987), with its sequel *The Talisman* (1988) is a family saga of greed and ambition. *Bella Mafia* (filmed TV 1997), is similar, but tells of a Mafia Don who turns informer and his family suffers the consequences. LLP's next TV project was *Prime Suspect*, the first of the powerful TV series featuring D.C.I. Jane Tennison, who, despite her rank, struggles against strong anti-feminist views in the police force and against her own vulnerability. The series was showered in awards. LLP established her own La Plante Productions in 1995 and her productions include *The Governor* (remade for US TV as *The Warden*, 2000), about the woman governor of a high security all-male prison, and *Trial and Retribution*, the groundbreaking split-screen series about Superintendent Mike Walker. All of LLP's crime series tackle violent contemporary issues with few holds barred. LLP has continued to write separate novels, although all of these have also been optioned for TV or the cinema. In *Entwined* a murder brings together twin sisters who have not seen each other since they were separated in a Nazi concentration camp. *Cold Shoulder* (TV 2000) introduces LLP's P.I. Lorraine Page, a former LAPD homicide lieutenant who lost her job when she killed an innocent boy on duty. In *Cold Blood*, Page, struggling with her alcoholism, goes in search of the daughter of a fading actress, and becomes enmeshed in the world of voodoo. Other relevant TV series written by LLP include *Seekers* (1993), about the wives of a bigamist who take over his detective agency when he goes missing; *Framed* (1992), where a policeman on holiday in Spain goes on the trail of a supergrass, *Killer Net* (1998), which explores the violent consequences of dating via the internet; and *Mind Games* (2000), about a female psychological profiler. LLP has already earned her place in the TV Hall of Fame but there is doubtless plenty more yet to come.

Novels

Dolly Rawlins series: *The Widows* (1983), *The Widows II* (1985), *She's Out* (1995).
Jane Tennison series: *Prime Suspect* (1991), *Framed: Prime Suspect 2* (1992), *Prime Suspect #3* (1993).
Lorraine Page series: *Cold Shoulder* (1994), *Cold Blood* (1996), *Cold Heart* (1998).
Helen Hewitt series: *The Governor* (1995), *The Governor II* (1996).
Mike Walker series: *Trial and Retribution* (1997), *Trial and Retribution II* (1998), *Trial and Retribution III* (1999), *Trial and Retribution IV* (2000).
Non-series: *Bella Mafia* (1990).

Short Stories. *Seekers* (1993).

Where to start: *Prime Suspect.*

Awards: BAFTA Award (1992, 1994), British Broadcasting Award (1992), Royal TV Society Writers Award (1992), Edgar, best TV presentation (1993), Prix du Roman d'Aventure (1992), Emmy Award (1994), Anthony, best TV series (1995), *Liverpool Echo* Arts Award, best TV writer (1997), Dennis Potter writer's award (2001).

Website: <www.laplanteproductions.com>
Similar stuff: Edna BUCHANAN, Wendy HORNSBY.
Final fact: LLP used to act under the name Lynda Marchal and appeared in *Rentaghost* in 1980 as a ghost with an allergy to flowers. LLP also claims that because of her red hair and feisty attitude she played more prostitutes on TV than anyone else.

Ed Lacy (1911–68) US

Because most of EL's novels appeared as paperback originals with provocative titles, it's easy to dismiss him as a hack. That would be a serious mistake. EL took his work seriously, sold to many of the major slick markets and appeared mostly in paperback because his ideas were frequently too risque at the time for most hardcover publishers to accept. One exception was Harper's which published the cream of EL's work including his award-winning *Room to Swing*. This introduced the first significant treatment of a black American P.I., Toussaint Moore, preceding John BALL's Virgil Tibbs. Though he lives in Harlem, Moore is fairly affluent, but a case that backfires ends up with him being pursued by the cops for murder and he heads to Ohio in pursuit of the real killer. In Ohio he has to face southern bigotry and EL draws a vivid and powerful picture. EL was married to a black lady and counted many African Americans amongst his friends so his portrayal is as authentic as any white man achieved in the fifties. EL created a black cop with Lee Hayes who, in *Harlem Underground*, is assigned to track down a gang leader. EL was not really a series writer, though he returned to Toussaint Moore and Lee Hayes for one further novel apiece, and wrote two novels featuring brash new NYPD cop Dave Wintino. EL wrote several other P.I. novels, including *Sin in Their Blood*, *Strip for Violence* and *Bugged for Murder*, though the majority of his work explores the lives of individuals trapped in a world of crime. *The Men From the Boys* is a most unusual novel of a violent man and ex-cop, Marty Bond, who believes he has cancer. Unable to kill himself he sets off to investigate a crime in the hope that he is killed. EL achieves the remarkable feat of drawing reader sympathy for a nasty individual. *Go For the Body*, which unusually for EL is set in Paris, is about a black American boxer who becomes caught up in a crime syndicate. EL had a passion for boxing and it features in many of his books. His first ever published book, a non-crime novel, *Walk Hard – Talk Loud* (1940 as Len Zinberg) is about boxing and became a play on Broadway. Unfortunately, none of EL's books are currently in print, a sad reflection on an otherwise memorable author.

Novels

Dave Wintino series: *Lead With Your Left* (1957), *Double Trouble* (1965).
Toussaint Moore series: *Room to Swing* (1957), *Moment of Untruth* (1964), *Pity the Honest* (1964).

Lee Hayes series: *Harlem Underground* (1965), *In Black and Whitey* (1967). Non-series: *The Woman Aroused* (1951), *Sin in Their Blood* (1952; as *Death in Passing*, UK 1959), *Strip for Violence* (1953), *Enter Without Desire* (1954), *Go for the Body* (1954), *The Best That Ever Did It* (1955; as *Visa to Death*, 1956), *The Men from the Boys* (1956), *Breathe No More My Lady* (1958), *Devil for the Witch* (1958), *Be Careful How You Live* (1958; as *Dead End*, 1960), *Shakedown for Murder* (1958), *Blonde Bait* (1959), *The Big Fix* (1960), *A Deadly Affair* (1960), *Bugged for Murder* (1961), *The Freeloaders* (1961), *South Pacific Affair* (1961), *The Sex Castle* (1963; as *Shoot it Again*, 1969), *The Napalm Bugle* (1968), *The Big Bust* (1969).
Short Stories. *Two Hot to Handle* (1963).

Full name: Leonard S. Zinberg.
Pen-names: Steve April, Ed Lacy.
Where to start: *The Men from the Boys* or *Room to Swing*.
Awards: Edgar, best novel (1958).
Similar stuff: Evan Hunter [Ed McBain], Dan J. Marlowe, Charles Willeford.

Deryn Lake (b. 1937) UK

DL is the pen-name of bestselling historical novelist Dinah Lampitt. Her historical novels, which began with *Sutton Place* (1983) are strong on period and atmosphere. Although not mysteries, the Sutton Place trilogy, which continued with *The Silver Swan* (1984) and *Fortune's Soldier* (1985), follows the apparent consequences of a curse down through the centuries. With the dwindling interest in costume-drama historicals, DL switched to historical mysteries using as her investigator John Rawlings, a real character who lived in the mid-18th century. An apothecary, Rawlings was closely associated with John Fielding, the founder of the Bow Street Runners, and the team of Rawlings and Fielding make a formidable pair. The books are thoroughly researched with rich characterization. The novels are generally set in London but *Death on the Romney Marsh* takes Rawlings to this remote part of Kent, where he becomes involved in conspiracy and espionage. In *Death in the West Wind* we find Rawlings married and on honeymoon in the West Country but rapidly involved in murder and the strange Society of Angels.

Novels
John Rawlings series: *Death in the Dark Walk* (1994), *Death at the Beggar's Opera* (1995), *Death at the Devil's Tavern* (1996), *Death on the Romney Marsh* (1998), *Death in the Peerless Pool* (1999), *Death at Apothecaries' Hall* (2000), *Death in the West Wind* (2001).

Real name: Dinah Lampitt.
Pen-name: Deryn Lake.
Website: <www.twbooks.co.uk/authors/derynlake.html>
Similar stuff: Bruce Cook.
Final fact: DL encountered John Rawlings when hired by Canada Dry to check the history of their new acquisition, the makers of soda and tonic waters, H.D.

Rawlings. DL discovered that John Rawlings had invented carbonated water in England in 1754.

M. D. Lake (b. 1934) US

MDL is the pen-name of Allen Simpson, a former Professor of Scandinavian Studies at the University of Minnesota who took early retirement to write full-time. His books feature Peggy O'Neill, security cop on a university campus with an inordinate amount of murders. O'Neill is persistent and strong-willed with a heavy dose of curiosity. The books are traditional mysteries and MDL develops clever puzzles that require judicious unravelling. In the award-winning *Poisoned Ivy* a poisoned apple meant for the university's unpopular dean is eaten by an innocent victim. In *Once Upon a Crime* a visiting Danish scholar who is to open a symposium on Hans Christian Andersen is bludgeoned to death with a statuette of the Little Mermaid. These are relatively light-hearted academic mysteries clearly written by someone wreaking vengeance on his past colleagues.

Novels

Peggy O'Neill series: *Amends for Murder* (1989), *Cold Comfort* (1990), *Poisoned Ivy* (1991), *A Gift for Murder* (1991), *Murder by Mail* (1993), *Once Upon a Crime* (1994), *Grave Choices* (1995), *Flirting With Death* (1996), *Midsummer Malice* (1997), *Death Calls the Tune* (1999).

Real name: James Allen Simpson.
Pen-name: M.D. Lake.
Awards: American Mystery Award, best paperback original (1993), Agatha, best short story (1994, 1998).
Similar stuff: Bill CRIDER's Carl Burns, Charlotte MACLEOD's Helen Shandy.
Final fact: Simpson was told to use a pseudonym, preferably sexless, so that readers would not know it was a man writing a woman's viewpoint. He chose M.D. Lake because his wife's family live at Medicine Lake, and he equated "medicine" to a doctor, or "M.D.".

Jane Langton (b. 1922) US

The artist, broadcaster and teacher JL is as well known for her children's books as for her mystery novels, and at times both exhibit the same unfettered flights of fancy. Not many authors can blend the inspiration of Edith Nesbit, Dorothy L. Sayers and John D. MacDonald into their work but JL does it with mischievous aplomb. Her detective is Homer Kelly, a lawyer and former police lieutenant who has become a Professor of American literature at Harvard. He is tall, ungainly and eccentric, given to quoting verse, especially Thoreau or Emily Dickinson, and delving into his mysteries as he would any thesis. Kelly meets his future wife Mary in the first book *The Transcendental Murder*, where the local police in Concord ask for his help when a body turns up during the annual Paul Revere pageant. Most of the settings are in and around

Boston, though the wonderful *Dark Nantucket Noon* concerns a murder in a lighthouse during a solar eclipse. A murder at an Emily Dickinson symposium at Amherst is the basis for the award-winning *Emily Dickinson is Dead*. Little things mean a lot in Kelly mysteries, whether it's tadpoles in the water fountain in *Murder at the Gardner* or how a spider spins its web in *Natural Enemy*, one of the best in the series. These are academic mysteries de-luxe, thick with atmosphere, delightfully quirky and remarkably astute. That the Bouchercon committee is able to award JL a lifetime achievement award on the strength of one series is testament to its individuality.

Novels

Homer Kelly series: *The Transcendental Murder* (1964; as *The Minute Man Murder*, 1976), *Dark Nantucket Noon* (1975), *The Memorial Hall Murder* (1978), *Natural Enemy* (1982), *Emily Dickinson is Dead* (1984), *Good and Dead* (1986), *Murder at the Gardner* (1988), *The Dante Game* (1991), *God in Concord* (1992), *Divine Inspiration* (1993), *The Shortest Day* (1995), *Dead as a Dodo* (1996), *The Face on the Wall* (1998), *The Thief of Venice* (1999), *Murder at Monticello* (2001), *The Escher Twist* (2002).

Full name: Jane Langton (*née* Gillson)
Awards: Nero Wolfe award (1984), Anthony, lifetime achievement (2000).
Similar stuff: J.S. BORTHWICK, Amanda CROSS, Paula GOSLING.
Final fact: JL illustrates most of her own books, which may well add to their collectibility in future years.

Joe R. Lansdale (b. 1951) US

Like the best of the modern-day neo-pulp writers JRL brings his dark visions to a variety of fields – horror, science fiction, westerns as well as mystery – and also like all true writers he has had his quota of casual jobs – from ditch digger to plumber's mate – before he turned to writing full time in 1981. Since then this Texan martial arts expert (he runs a martial arts studio) has won an armful of awards and a considerable following for his roller-coaster paeans to pain and banal violence. His darker material has been called "country noir". JRL's roots have drawn succour as much from the comic-book tradition (to which he also contributes) as the hard-boiled school – it's a merger of *Vault of Horror* with *Dime Detective*, a true child of Ray Bradbury and Robert BLOCH. His early work was predominantly horror fiction, though it was only a short step from that to what JRL calls "dark suspense". Not surprisingly JRL is adept at depicting villains. In *Act of Love* it is a crazed serial killer, in *Cold in July* it's the vengeful father whose son was killed in the act of breaking and entering, in *The Nightrunners* it's a whole pack of vicious teenagers, one of whom is possessed. JRL calls himself a storyteller more than a writer because his stories are full of fascinating characters entangled with events that career along at a relentless pace almost regardless of plot. His series featuring the odd couple Hap Collins (a straight white man) and Leonard Pine (a black gay man) has more by way of structure. In *Savage Season*, a treasure hunt turns nasty when they encounter a murdering drug-dealer called "Soldier'. In *Mucho Mojo*, they discover several skeletons of children under the floorboards of Pine's deceased uncle's house leading them on a trail to prove the uncle's innocence. In the more recent *Captains Outrageous* they end up on a trail of murder and intrigue in Mexico. JRL's award-winning *The Bottoms* is his most conventional novel. Its portrayal of racial tension in East Texas during the Depression years of the early thirties and its consequences in a murder investigation is both harrowing and moving. It's a sign of a less wild, more profound story-teller.

Novels
Collins & Pine series: *Savage Season* (1990), *Mucho Mojo* (1994), *Two-Bear Mambo* (1995), *Bad Chili* (1997), *Rumble Tumble* (1998), *Captains Outrageous* (2001).
Non-series: *Act of Love* (1980), *The Nightrunners* (1983), *Cold in July* (1989), *Freezer Burn* (1999), *Waltz of Shadows* (1999), *The Bottoms* (2000).
as Ray Slater: *Texas Night Riders* (1983).
Short Stories. (selective, includes some horror and non-fiction). *By Bizarre Hands* (1989), *Stories by Mama Lansdale's Youngest Boy* (1991; exp. as *Bestsellers Guaranteed*, 1993), *Writer of the Purple Rage* (1994), *Electric Gumbo* (1994), *Fist Full of Stories (and Articles)* (1996), *The Good, the Bad & the Indifferent* (1997), *Private Eye Action As You Like it*, with Lewis Shiner (1998), *High Cotton* (2000).
Editor. *Dark at Heart*, with Karen Lansdale (1992)

Full name: Joe Richard Harold Lansdale.
Pen-names: Ray Slater; plus house name Jack Buchanan (Vietnam war series).
Where to start: *Cold in July* or *Mucho Mojo*.
Awards: Bram Stoker award, best horror short story (1989, 1990), best horror novella/long fiction (1993, 1998, 2000), other media (1994); American mystery award, best novel (1989), British Fantasy Society award, best short story (1990), the Horror Critics Award (1993), Booklist Editor's Award (1993), Critic's Choice Award (1994), *New York Times* Notable Book award (1996), the International Crime Writer's "Shot in the Dark" award (1996), Edgar, best novel (2001), Herodotus (2001), Inkpot Award (2001).
Website: <www.joerlansdale.com>
Similar stuff: Ed GORMAN, Loren ESTLEMAN, Bill CRIDER.
Final fact: JRL is one of the few writers authorized by the Edgar Rice Burroughs estate to write a Tarzan novel. He completed an adventure started by Burroughs and published as *Tarzan: The Lost Adventure* (1997).

Emma Lathen US

EL is the better-known pen-name used by Mary Jane Latsis (1927–97) and Martha Henissart (b. 1929), who also write as R.B. Dominic. Henissart worked in the financial world, though by training she was a lawyer. Latsis was an economist and worked for the United Nations. As Lathen they created the elegant, silver-haired Wall Street banker John

Putnam Thatcher. The idea of a banker as a detective may not seem immediately exciting, but Latsis and Henissart became adept at allowing the characters to explain the financial issues without getting in the way of the mystery. These are sophisticated novels with a cast rich in characters you want to meet and plots that are compelling. Thatcher is the executive vice-president of the Sloan Guaranty Trust, and a quiet, reserved widower who has remained 60-something throughout the 30 years of the series. He is extremely observant, indeed his comments on people and life are part of the books' appeal. The bank is pleased that Thatcher is always on hand to sort out any messy business that gets in the way of profits. Assisted by his overly efficient secretary Miss Corsa and his fussy colleague Everett Gabler, Thatcher's cases take him all over the world and involve him in matters varying from dog shows to civil rights, and the Olympics to the oil crisis. *Murder Against the Grain*, about chicanery during a Russian wheat deal, won the authors the CWA Gold Dagger award. The authors' other series moves in even higher circles. This features Ohio Congressman Ben Safford who is always anxious about being re-elected and thus feels obliged to please his electorate, but is drawn into issues that might otherwise hinder his chances. Of necessity these tend to be related to political corruption or major crises. Both series are intelligently written with wry observations on the political and financial worlds. The final Thatcher novel was nearly finished at the time of Latsis's death but has yet to be completed.

Novels

John Putnam Thatcher series: *Banking on Death* (1961), *A Place for Murder* (1963), *Accounting for Murder* (1964), *Murder Makes the Wheels Go 'Round* (1966), *Death Shall Overcome* (1966), *Murder Against the Grain* (1967), *A Stitch in Time* (1968), *Come to Dust* (1968), *When in Greece* (1969), *Murder to Go* (1969), *Pick up Sticks* (1970), *Ashes to Ashes* (1971), *The Longer the Thread* (1971), *Murder Without Icing* (1972), *Sweet and Low* (1974), *By Hook or By Crook* (1975), *Double, Double, Oil and Trouble* (1978), *Going for the Gold* (1981), *Green Grow the Dollars* (1982), *Something in the Air* (1988), *East is East* (1991), *Right on the Money* (1993), *Brewing Up a Storm* (1996), *A Shark Out of Water* (1997).

Ben Safford series as R.B. Dominic: *Murder Sunny Side Up* (1968), *Murder in High Places* (1969), *There is No Justice* (1971; as *Murder Out of Court*, UK 1971), *Epitaph for a Lobbyist* (1974), *Murder Out of Commission* (1976), *The Attending Physician* (1980), *A Flaw in the System* (1983; as *Unexpected Developments*, US 1984).

Real names: Mary Jane Latsis and Martha Henissart.
Pen-name: R.B. Dominic, Emma Lathen.
Where to start: *Come to Dust* and *Pick up Sticks* are the least financially challenging.
Awards: CWA Gold Dagger (1967), Ellery Queen Award (1983), Agatha, lifetime achievement (1997).
Similar stuff: Arthur Maling, Janet NEEL, David WILLIAMS.

Final fact: Each author wrote alternate chapters, Latsis starting the book and Henissart always finishing it. Latsis once annoyed Henissart by killing off one of her partner's favourite characters.

Janet Laurence (b. 1937) UK

A former public relations executive, JL was also a teacher of cookery courses and has written several cookbooks, such as *A Little French Cookbook* (1989), *A Little Scandinavian Cookbook* (1990) and *Simply Delicious* (2001). She has created a series featuring Cordon-bleu chef, caterer and writer Darina Lisle where the food is every bit as tempting as the recipes for murder. In *A Deepe Coffyn*, Darina's offensive cousin Digby Cary is killed at the symposium for the Society of Historical Gastronomes, and Darina finds herself having to prove her innocence. In this first novel she meets police sergeant William Pigram with whom she soon becomes romantically entangled. Though traditional cozies, these books are ingeniously plotted and constantly enjoyable. In a remarkable change of setting, JL has started a new series of historical mysteries set in the 1740s featuring the famous Venetian painter Canaletto. No sooner has he arrived in Britain in the first novel than he is set upon and nearly killed. A stickler for detail, JL brings London alive and blends fact and fiction seamlessly.

Novels

Darina Lisle series: *A Deepe Coffyn* (1989), *A Tasty Way to Die* (1990), *Hotel Morgue* (1991), *Recipe for Death* (1992), *Death and the Epicure* (1993), *Death at the Table* (1994), *Death a la Provencale* (1995), *Diet for Death* (1996), *Appetite for Death* (1998), *The Mermaid's Feast* (2000).

Canaletto series: *Canaletto and the Case of the Westminster Bridge* (1998), *Canaletto and the Case of the Privvy Garden* (1999), *Canaletto and the Case of Bonnie Prince Charlie* (2002).

Non-series: *To Kill the Past* (1995).

Full name: Janet Laurence.
Pen-names: Julia Lisle (for general fiction).
Similar stuff: Diane Mott DAVIDSON and Amy MYERS for other culinary sleuths, Derek WILSON for artworld and historical mysteries.
Final fact: JL reveals that research can produce unexpected results. While being given a tour of New Covent Garden for *A Tasty Way to Die*, she wanted to check with her guide whether it was realistic for one of her characters to have started as a barrow boy and ended up as a highly successful wholesaler owning a Queen Anne house in Highgate and a Rolls Royce. Her guide responded: "But I started as a barrow boy. I have a Queen Anne house in Highgate and that's my Rolls Royce out there." JL found it hard to persuade him that she had known nothing about his background.

Peter Lear *pseudonym, see* Peter Lovesey

Dennis Lehane (b. 1965) US

DL's first non-series novel, *Mystic River*, shot to the top of the bestseller lists and was optioned for filming by Clint Eastwood. The novel explores the relationship between three men who have known each other since childhood but whose lives have gone very different ways – one a cop, one an ex-con and the other a victim of child abduction. DL's work is raw, tough and violent. He takes the reader and his characters to hell and doesn't always bring them back. His early books all featured the private detective team of Patrick Kenzie and Angie Gennaro, who operate out of the "mean streets" of Boston. They have also known each other since childhood and their relationship is part of the spark of the series. Their investigations find them involved with rapists, child abusers, serial killers and other psychopaths and it's a wonder either of them survive. Even as he writes DL expects to find himself killing off one or other of them. DL is firmly of the belief that the world owes no one any favours and things do not end happily ever after. His work is the stuff of nightmares. Plot summaries do not suffice in what is a very complex series with intense characterization. DL's work may yet prove to be the yardstick by which nineties hard-boiled crime fiction will be measured.

Novels

Kenzie and Gennaro series: *A Drink Before the War* (1994), *Darkness, Take My Hand* (1996), *Sacred* (1997), *Gone Baby Gone* (1998), *Prayers for Rain* (1999). Non-series: *Mystic River* (2001).

Awards: Shamus, best first novel (1995), Nero Wolfe award (1998), Barry award, best novel (1999), Dilys Award (1999, 2002).
Website: <www.dennislehanebooks.com>
Similar stuff: James ELLROY, George PELECANOS, Robert PARKER.
Final fact: *Mystic River* drew its roots from an incident in DL's own childhood when he was fighting with a friend and was picked up by the cops and taken home. DL's mother was furious – not because of the fighting, but what if they had not been real cops?

Donna Leon (b. 1942) US

DL's books feature Guido Brunetti, Commissario of the Questura in Venice. DL has lived in Venice for over 20 years, where she teaches English literature at a nearby university on the US Air Force base. She is a New Yorker of Irish/Spanish descent and has lived in China and the Middle East so has a strong cosmopolitan view of the world. Brunetti is a man of principle and has to work carefully both within his professional world – where his senior wants quick solutions that fuel his own advancement – and his private life. His wife, Paola, is from a wealthy and influential family. In the first book, which was awarded the prestigious Suntory Prize in Japan, Brunetti investigates the death of a famous conductor at the opera house. Paola finds herself in trouble in *Fatal Remedies* where her actions place Brunetti at risk. *Friends in High Places*, a multi-layered story of government corruption, received the CWA Silver Dagger. These are pleasingly different police procedurals, not only for their setting – DL reveals the Venice behind the tourist veneer – but also their complications as Brunetti works through a maze of bureaucracy and corruption. The series bears some similarity to Michael DIBDIN's Zen books, except that Brunetti is less of a renegade, and more circumspect in his investigations. The series is best read in sequence as later books refer to earlier events and characters.

Novels
Commissario Brunetti series: *Death at La Fenice* (1992), *Death in a Strange Country* (1993), *The Anonymous Venetian* (1994; as *Dressed for Death*, UK 1994), *A Venetian Reckoning* (1995; as *Death and Judgment*, US 1995), *Acqua Alta* (1996; as *Death in High Water*, US 1996), *The Death of Faith* (1997; as *Quietly in Their Sleep*, US 1997), *A Noble Radiance* (1998), *Fatal Remedies* (1999), *Friends in High Places* (2000), *A Sea of Troubles* (2001).

Awards: Japan's Suntory Prize, best suspense novel (1992), CWA Silver Dagger (2000).
Website: <www.phys.uni-paderborn.de/~stern/leon/books/> and <www.twbooks.co.uk/authors/donnaleon.html>
Similar stuff: Michael DIBDIN, Magdalen NABB, Julian RATHBONE.
Final fact: DL was first inspired to write a crime novel when attending an opera at La Fenice and found the conductor so obnoxious that she and a friend plotted how best to kill him.

Elmore Leonard (b. 1925) US

Today EL is lauded as "our greatest crime novelist" (*Washington Post*), "the greatest crime writer of our time" (*New York Times*) and even "a literary genius" (*Sunday Times*), making him one of the few writers whose critical success accords with his general popularity. Yet EL comes from no literary background and the plaudits serve only to highlight a writer who has succeeded better than most in making his stories reflect the harsh realism of life whilst sustaining a fast and often amusing pace. This comes from EL's pulp-writing apprenticeship. He grew up writing western stories for the pulp magazines in the 1950s while he worked by day as an advertising copywriter in Detroit, where he settled after his military service. EL had tremendous success with his westerns graduating to novels – *The Bounty Hunters* (1953) – and to films – *Three-Ten to Yuma* (1957). As the popularity for westerns faded during the sixties, EL turned to crime fiction, starting with *The Big Bounce* (filmed 1969), about a petty thief who falls too heavily under the thumb of an ambitious woman. Most of EL's books concentrate on the world of the criminal rather than the police and there is seldom much detection in his novels. With *Fifty-Two Pickup* (filmed 1986), a cleverly wrought story of a blackmail victim who fights back, EL showed parallels with George V. Higgins by telling the story through dialogue, often profane, usually violent, but also witty. EL has a tremendous gift for creating character and place, and out of that comes such plot as EL needs. An assignment for the *Detroit News* to write about the local police resulted in *City Primeval*, one of EL's few novels told from the police perspective. He prefers to explore the survival of the fittest, depicting likeable enough low-life who have strayed into shark-infested waters and do their best to survive. Amongst the best of these novels are *Swag* and *Stick* (filmed 1985), featuring car thief Ernest "Stick" Stickley. In the first, Stick teams up with car salesman Frank Ryan in a series of armed robberies – this book was later retitled *Ryan's Rules* because it was noted for Ryan's ten rules for success in armed robbery. Stick serves time and on his release is back into car theft in *Stick* when he becomes involved with a drug dealer and is soon fighting for his life. There was to be a third Stick novel but the character mutated into Joe LaBrava, a former secret-service agent turned photographer. In the award-winning *LaBrava*, which has one of the richest casts of any of EL's novel, La Brava ends up in Miami trying to save a former film star from a major extortion scam. The spirit of Stick endures in other characters, such as Chili Palmer in *Get Shorty* (filmed 1995) and *Be Cool*, and Harry Arno in *Pronto* (filmed TV 1997). Palmer is a relatively mild-mannered and likeable Mobster who, in the first book, goes to Hollywood to collect a debt from someone who faked their death and ends up becoming a movie producer, giving EL an opportunity to fuse what little distinction there is in Hollywood between fact and fiction. Harry Arno is a small-time operator in Miami who has pressure brought upon him by the Feds to grass on his Mafia boss and as the pressure grows Harry flees to Italy, allowing EL to play one side of the Mafia off against the other. In all of EL's books it is through characters like Stick, LaBrava or Chili that you live the story as they cast their perspective on bigger and often crazier fish. All of EL's characters are memorable, such as the crackpot rule-bending judge Bob Gibbs in *Maximum Bob* (TV series 1998) or the psychopathic Teddy Magyk who plots revenge on the Miami cop who arrested him years before in *Glitz* (filmed TV 1988). Just occasionally EL changes the scene entirely. *Cuba Libre* is an historical novel set during the Spanish-American War of 1898 but allowing EL plenty of scope to introduce the low-life who use any opportunity to make a profit. In a career now into its sixth decade EL has made legends out of his pulp fiction roots and given hard-boiled crime fiction a literary acceptability.

Novels

"Stick" Stickley series: *Swag* (1976; as *Ryan's Rules*, 1978), *Stick* (1983).
Chili Palmer series: *Get Shorty* (1990), *Be Cool* (1999).
Raylan Givens series: *Pronto* (1993), *Riding the Rap* (1995).
Non-series: *The Big Bounce* (1969), *The Moonshine War* (1969), *Valdez is Coming*

(1970), *Fifty-Two Pickup* (1974), *Mr Majestyk* (1974), *Unknown Man No. 89* (1977), *The Hunted* (1977), *The Switch* (1978), *Gold Coast* (1980), *City Primeval* (1980), *Split Images* (1982), *Cat Chaser* (1982), *La Brava* (1983), *Escape from Five Shadows* (1985), *Glitz* (1985), *Bandits* (1986), *Touch* (1987), *Freaky Deaky* (1988), *Killshot* (1989), *Maximum Bob* (1991), *Rum Punch* (1992), *Out of Sight* (1996), *Cuba Libre* (1998), *Pagan Babies* (2000), *The Hunted* (2000), *Tishomingo Blues* (2002).
Short Stories. *The Tonto Woman and Other Western Stories* (1998).

Full name: Elmore John Leonard, Jr.
Pen-names: Dutch Leonard, Emmet Long.
Where to start: *Fifty-Two Pickup* or *Swag*.
Awards: Edgar, best novel (1984), Swedish Academy of Detection, Best Foreign (1985), Grand Prix de Littérature Policière Best Foreign (1986), American Mystery Award, best crime novel (1988, 1989), Hammet Prize (1992), MWA Grand Master (1992).
Books about: *Elmore Leonard* by David Geherin (1989), *Get Dutch!* (biography) by Paul Challen (2001).
Website: <www.elmoreleonard.com>
Similar stuff: Lawrence BLOCK, George V. HIGGINS, Donald E. WESTLAKE.
Final fact: After *City Primeval* EL wrote another novel featuring detective Raymond Cruz only to find he could not use the name because the film rights to the book and character had been sold. EL thus changed the name throughout to Walter Kouza but missed one spot, which is why Raymond appears out of nowhere in the middle of *Split Images*.

Jonathan Lethem (b. 1964) US

There are those who will say that JL belongs more properly in a science-fiction encyclopedia. Certainly most of his stories are science fiction, published in genre magazines and anthologies. His first novel, *Gun With Occasional Music*, is set in a depressing 21st century, drawing paranoid visions from Philip K. Dick and Kurt Vonnegut. But it is primarily a detective novel where a P.I. (Private Inquisitor) struggles to find the murderer of his employer and to free the accused innocent. JL admits he was trying to wed the hard-boiled tradition with the dystopian. Since then, JL has succeeded in being recognized by the literary establishment, even though *Amnesia Moon* (1995), *As She Climbed Across the Table* (1997) and *Girl in Landscape* (1998) are also science fiction, each with its own individual surreal quirkiness. Where JL made the giant leap was with *Motherless Brooklyn*, another quirky novel but firmly in the field of crime fiction. It features Lionel Essrog, one of four street orphans taken in by local tough guy Frank Minna as part of his detective agency. When Minna is murdered Essrog goes on an odyssey of detection to find the murderer. What makes this different is that Essrog, who narrates the story, has Tourette's syndrome, which means the book is complete with his frequent outbursts and impromptu observations. This gives the book a manic and feverish drive that is refreshingly different. The world is waiting to see what Lethem will do next.

Novels (selective) *Gun With Occasional Music* (1994), *Motherless Brooklyn* (1999).

Full name: Jonathan Allen Lethem.
Where to start: *Motherless Brooklyn.*
Awards: Locus Award, best first novel (1995), IAFA Crawford Award (1995), National Book Critics Circle Award for Fiction (1999), CWA Gold Dagger (2000).
Similar stuff: Paul AUSTER, Jerome CHARYN.
Final fact: JL also works with the jazz group 1001 Noirs, reading his stories to their music.

Ira Levin (b. 1929) US

IL is best known for his bestselling occult thriller *Rosemary's Baby* (1967) which kick-started the revival of interest in horror fiction in the late sixties. He is by profession a playwright, but his first book was also a crime novel and an ingenious one. *A Kiss Before Dying* is presented in three parts, each from a different perspective. The first part shows the events up to a murder made to look like a suicide. The second part is from the viewpoint of the victim's sister who remains supicious of her death, which leads to her own murder. The final part brings in another sister and her investigations. The book won an Edgar Award for the best first novel and has twice been filmed (1956 and 1991). IL has not written another traditional crime novel, though *The Boys from Brazil* (filmed 1978), a thriller about a neo-Nazi plot to clone Hitler, and *Sliver* (filmed 1993), a neo-gothic suspense novel about a woman spied upon in a high-rise apartment, fit into the broader crime spectrum, while *The Stepford Wives* (filmed 1975) is more in the science-fiction field. Amongst his stage plays IL has produced at least one enduring masterpiece, *Deathtrap* (filmed 1982), Broadway's longest running thriller. It's about a student who writes the perfect play and about his mentor who decides to kill the student and pass the play off as his own. The intricate plot and the twists between real events and the play-within-a-play, give this a rare satisfying quality. IL's other plays include *Dr Cook's Garden* (filmed TV 1970), about a kindly yet murderous small-town doctor, and two psychological suspense chillers, *Interlock* and *Veronica's Room*. IL has even written a musical about a cat burglar, *Drat! That Cat!* (1965).

Novels (selective) *A Kiss Before Dying* (1953), *The Boys from Brazil* (1976), *Sliver* (1991).
Plays (selective). *Interlock* (1958), *Dr Cook's Garden* (1968), *Veronica's Room* (1974), *Deathtrap* (1978).

Where to start: *A Kiss Before Dying*.
Awards: Edgar, best first novel (1954), best play (1980).
Similar stuff: Anthony SHAFFER.

Paul Levine (b. 1948) US

PL is a former Miami civil trial lawyer who began his working life as a journalist on the *Miami Herald* after spending his childhood and youth in small-town Pennsylvania. He turned to writing when he began to dislike his cases and his clients. It was a therapeutic outlet for his cynicism. His books are legal thrillers. Most feature ex-football linebacker turned lawyer Jake Lassiter. In the first novel, *To Speak for the Dead*, which became a bestseller and was adapted for TV as *Justice on the Bayou* (1995), Lassiter is caught in a dilemma between defending a surgeon of malpractice over the death of a patient, and a plea by the victim's daughter for Lassiter to prove the surgeon guilty of murder. Lassiter reflects PL's own increasingly bleak views on the legal process but also his hopes to get it right in the end. The cases are unusual – the kind that PL wanted and never got. *Night Vision* is an early novel about murder arising from internet dating. *False Dawn* involves an international crime ring. *Mortal Sin* finds Lassiter defending a Mobster in a wrongful death suit. *Flesh and Bones* is perhaps his most testing case as he has to defend a supermodel on the charge of murdering her father, which was done in broad daylight with a dozen witnesses. His non-Lassiter novel, *9 Scorpions*, arose from a challenge PL set himself to work out how the Supreme Court could be corrupted. PL has written several TV scripts including the series *You and the Law* (1977-82) and *JAG* (1995).

Novels

Jake Lassiter series: *To Speak for the Dead* (1990), *Night Vision* (1991), *False Dawn* (1993), *Mortal Sin* (1994), *Slashback* (1995), *Fool Me Twice* (1996), *Flesh and Bones* (1997).
Non-series: *9 Scorpions* (1998).

Awards: John D. Macdonald Award for fiction (1994).
Similar stuff: William J. COUGLIN, John GRISHAM, Scott TUROW.

Michael Z. Lewin (b. 1942) US

Entering the world of MZL is like entering a community. Most of his books are set in Indianapolis and are peopled by many of the same characters, though different ones take the lead. Paramount is Albert Samson, a low-key fairly soft-boiled P.I., who takes on simple cases that develop into complicated ones. In *The Enemies Within*, for instance, an innocent request to find a lost manuscript ends up as a murder investigation, whilst in *Out of Season*, a request to trace someone's parents ends up unearthing a major cover-up. Samson is not some angst-ridden detective, though life has generally dealt him a low set of cards. But he gets pleasure in helping sort out people's lives and catching a crook or two is an added bonus. Samson's girlfriend (the relationship hasn't developed much over 20 years) is a social worker, Adele Buffington, who features in most books and has a case of her own in *And Baby Will Fall*. Now and again Samson leaves the work to the local police force under detective Leroy Powder, whilst in *Underdog*, a new character, a dwarf down-and-out called Jan Moro, carries the day. You get a strong, satisfying feel of a community trying to help itself. Somewhat oddly, no sooner had MZL, who had been a science teacher since he left college, finished the first book in 1971, than he moved to England, settling in Somerset. It took him over 20 years to begin a new series set in Somerset (in Bath) involving a family of Anglo-Italians who have established the Lunghi Detective Agency. All of MZL's books are written with a sly wit, a keen observation of character, an honourability (Samson even goes to prison at one point rather than expose a gang of would-be Robin Hood do-gooders) and a quiet acceptance of fate. His books are seldom predictable – who else would write a book for adolescents about the fate of two girls in the 19th century who dress as men (*Cutting Loose*) or a series of stories about Rover, a four-legged good Samaritan (*Rover's Tails*). MZL's work is to be savoured.

Novels

Albert Samson series: *Ask the Right Question* (1971), *The Way We Die Now* (1973), *The Enemies Within* (1974), *The Silent Salesman* (1978), *Missing Woman* (1981), *Out of Season* (1984; as *Out of Time*, UK 1984), *And Baby Will Fall* (1988; as *Child Proof*, UK 1988), *Called by a Panther* (1991).

Leroy Powder series: *Night Cover* (1976), *Hard Line* (1982), *Late Payments* (1986).

Lunghi Agency series: *Family Business* (1995), *Family Planning* (1999).

Non-series: *The Next Man* (1976), *Outside In* (1980), *Underdog* (1993), *Cutting Loose* (1999).

Short Stories. *Telling Tails* (1994), *The Reluctant Detective* (2001).

Editor (with others). *1st Culprit* (1992), *2nd Culprit* (1993), *3rd Culprit* (1994).

Full name: Michael Zinn Lewin.

Where to start: *Night Cover*.

Awards: Japanese Maltese Falcon (1988), German Marlowe (1992), Mystery Masters Award (1994).

Similar stuff: Sandra SCOPPETTONE produces a similar "friends & family" feel without the family.

Roy Lewis (b. 1933) UK

Welsh by birth and upbringing, RL lives within sight of the English Lake District and the Yorkshire Dales. He was a teacher and lecturer at various schools and colleges before becoming a school inspector and later college principal. He is a qualified lawyer and barrister and, since 1964, has produced over 20 books on various aspects of the law, mostly technical but including such interesting items as *The Victorian Bar* (1982). He turned to writing fiction in order to broaden the use of his technical knowledge. He first wrote a fairly traditional police procedural series about Inspector John Crow, but RL became increasingly interested in the background and settings of crime and developed two new series. The most fascinating features Arnold Landon, an archaeologist and antiquarian who works at the Department of Museum and Antiquities and frequently encounters dark deeds during his research. His sparring partner is DCI Culpepper. This series allows RL to explore subjects as diverse as the Knights Templar, Celtic bog-people, and even drug dealing and corporate corruption. RL's other series features Eric Ward, a police officer who was forced to retire from the service because he suffered from glaucoma and becomes a solicitor. Later in the series an operation helps cure his disability but the early novels, in which he has bouts of intense suffering, are highly original. Ward, however, seems to be one of life's victims. In *A Form of Death*, Ward discovers his wife is having an affair and Ward turns to the arms of another only to find she is killed and he is the prime suspect. Most of RL's books are set in the north of England but some of his non-series titles, such as *Witness My Death* and *A Distant Banner,* are fine evocations of the Welsh hills and dark valleys.

Note: RL should not be confused with Roy Harley Lewis, an antiquarian book dealer and expert on bookbinding, who wrote five bibliomysteries featuring book dealer Matthew Coll, starting with *A Cracking of Spines* (1980).

Novels

Inspector Crow series: *A Lover Too Many* (1969), *Error of Judgement* (1971), *A Secret Singing* (1972), *Blood Money* (1973), *A Question of Degree* (1974), *A Part of Virtue* (1975), *Nothing But Foxes* (1977), *A Relative Distance* (1981).

Eric Ward series: *A Certain Blindness* (1980), *Dwell in Danger* (1982), *A Limited Vision* (1983), *Once Dying, Twice Dead* (1984), *A Blurred Reality* (1985), *A Premium on Death* (1986), *The Salamander Chill* (1988), *A Necessary Dealing* (1989), *A Kind of Transaction* (1991), *A Form of Death* (2000), *The Nightwalker* (2001).

Arnold Landon series: *A Gathering of Ghosts* (1982), *Most Cunning Workmen* (1984), *A Trout in the Milk* (1986), *Men of Subtle Craft* (1987), *The Devil is Dead* (1989), *A Wisp of Smoke* (1991), *A Secret Dying* (1992), *Bloodeagle* (1993), *The Cross Bearer* (1994), *A Short-Lived Ghost* (1995), *Angel of Death* (1995), *Suddenly as a Shadow* (1997), *The Shape-Shifter* (1998), *The Ghost Dancers* (1999), *An Assumption of Death* (2000), *Dead Secret* (2001).

Non-series: *A Wolf by the Ears* (1970), *The Fenokee Project* (1971), *A Fool for a Client* (1972), *Of Singular Purpose* (1973), *Double Take* (1975), *Witness My Death* (1976), *A Distant Banner* (1976), *An Uncertain Sound* (1978), *An Inevitable Fatality* (1978), *A Violent Death* (1979), *Seek for Justice* (1981).

Full name: John Royston Lewis.

Pen-name: David Springfield.

Where to start: *A Gathering of Ghosts* or *Witness my Death.*

Similar stuff: Martin EDWARDS's Harry Devlin, Aaron ELKINS's Chris Norgren; David WILLIAMS for other Welsh books.

Ted Lewis (1940–82) UK

TL began his career as an artist but income was patchy and he drifted into various jobs only to be amazed when his first attempt at writing – a semi-autobiographical novel of an art-school romance, *All the Way Home and*

All the Night Through (1965) – sold first time out. TL turned his hand to writing women's romances for magazines, but his next book was his one claim to fame. *Jack's Return Home* is better known under its film title *Get Carter*. In fact this novel of a Mobster hit-man who thrashes his way through the underworld to find his brother's killer has been filmed three times – 1971 (with Michael Caine), 1972 as *Hit Man*, and 2000 (with Sylvester Stallone). TL was never able to regain the success of that book. At his publisher's urging he wrote two further Jack Carter novels, set earlier in his violent career, plus a half-dozen other novels, not all crime fiction. Of the others the best is *Billy Rags*, based on the life of a notorious bank robber who escapes from a maximum security prison. Unfortunately TL's life was ruined by alcoholism and financial problems resulting in a broken marriage. He completed one last book, *G.B.H.*, which was an attempt to recover the power of *Get Carter*, but was unable to write more and died of a heart attack aged only 42. *Get Carter*, however, remains as one of the first realistic English Mobster books of the sixties, opening a new vein in crime fiction.

Novels

Jack Carter series: *Jack's Return Home* (1970; as *Get Carter*, 1971), *Jack Carter's Law* (1974; as *Jack Carter and the Law*, US 1975), *Jack Carter and the Mafia Pigeon* (1977).

Non-series: *Plender* (1971), *Billy Rags* (1973), *Boldt* (1976), *G.B.H.* (1980; as *Grievous Bodily Harm*, US 1980).

Full name: Edward Lewis
Where to start: *Get Carter*.
Similar stuff: George V. HIGGINS.
Final fact: TL was one of the artists who worked on the Beatles' cartoon *Yellow Submarine*.

Douglas Lindsay (b. 1964) UK

A spoof on the serial killer plot has long been overdue, and Scottish writer and former Ministry of Defence worker DL has made it unmistakably his own. Barney Thomson is an unhappy barber who ends up killing his employer by accident (though he'd long considered it). Unfortunately it's at the same time as the Glasgow police are hunting a serial killer and Barney ends up as number one suspect. As the series progresses Barney becomes a serial killer, all by accident, and at one point finds himself surrounded by an entire monastery full of them. The series succeeds in thumbing its nose at the serial killer genre whilst still retaining an obvious affection for the field.

Novels

Barney Thomson series: *The Long Midnight of Barney Thomson* (1999), *The Cutting Edge of Barney Thomson* (2000), *A Prayer for Barney Thomson* (2001), *Barney Thomson and the Face of Death* (2002).

Website: <www.barney-thomson.com>
Similar stuff: Peter GUTTRIDGE.
Final fact: The first book was conceived and written in Senegal.

Elizabeth Linington (1921–88) US

EL's first book, *The Proud Man* (1955), is set in turbulent 16th-century Ireland. She thought of herself primarily as a historical writer, but she wrote only half a dozen such novels before she shifted into crime fiction in order to sustain an income. In the end crime fiction took over and she produced three books a year under various by-lines becoming known as the "Queen of the Police Procedurals". She created four long-running series. As Dell Shannon (not to be confused with the singer Del Shannon who was in the charts at this same time) she wrote about Lieutenant Luis Mendoza of the LAPD. Of Mexican descent, Mendoza was learned, but also liked fast cars and rich living in which he could indulge due to an inheritance. As Lesley Egan she created two series both emerging out of the first book *A Case for Appeal*. This featured Detective Vic Varallo of Glendale, in suburban Los Angeles and the lawyer Jesse Falkenstein, and both characters thereafter went their own way. Finally, under her own name, EL created Sergeant Ivor Maddox based in Hollywood. The first book in that series, *Greenmask!*, sees EL in mischievous mood as her police officers find leads in 1920s mystery novels to solve a current murder. The Maddox books were all published in the UK under the pen-name Anne Blaisdell, which EL had originally concocted for a gothic suspense melodrama *Nightmare* (filmed 1965 as *Die! Die! My Darling*, aka *Fanatic*). All of EL's series are similar in mood. They are generally upbeat, the police are always good guys and never corrupt (though in *Some Avenger, Rise!* Falkenstein has to defend an LAPD sergeant on a charge of bribery), and there is a strong emphasis on family life, which may seem a little strange as EL never married. Collecting EL today is difficult as her work is all out of print, but she was highly regarded in her day, especially for the realism of her cases and for the authenticity of her procedural work which, though now dated, is highly redolent of the period.

Novels

Sergeant Maddox series (as EL in US but issued in UK as by Anne Blaisdell): *Greenmask!* (1964), *No Evil Angel* (1964), *Date With Death* (1966), *Something Wrong* (1967), *Policeman's Lot* (1968), *Practice to Deceive* (1971), *Crime by Chance* (1973), *Perchance of Death* (1977), *No Villain Need Be* (1979), *Consequence of Crime* (1980), *Skeletons in the Closet* (1982), *Felony Report* (1984), *Strange Felony* (1986). Detective Mendoza series as Dell Shannon: *Case Pending* (1960), *The Ace of Spades* (1961), *Extra Kill* (1962), *Knave of Hearts* (1962), *Death of a Busybody* (1963), *Double Bluff* (1964), *Mark of Murder* (1964), *Root of all Evil* (1964), *The Death-Bringers* (1965), *Death by Inches* (1965), *Coffin Corner* (1966), *With a Vengeance* (1966), *Chance to Kill* (1967), *Rain with Violence* (1967), *Kill with*

Kindness (1968), *Schooled to Kill* (1969), *Crime on Their Hands* (1969), *Unexpected Death* (1970), *Whim to Kill* (1971), *The Ringer* (1971), *Murder with Love* (1972), *With Intent to Kill* (1972), *No Holiday for Crime* (1973), *Spring of Violence* (1973), *Crime File* (1974), *Deuces Wild* (1975), *Streets of Death* (1976), *Appearances of Death* (1977), *Cold Trail* (1978), *Felony at Random* (1979), *Felony File* (1980), *Murder Most Strange* (1981), *The Motive on Record* (1982), *Exploit of Death* (1983), *Destiny of Death* (1984), *Chaos of Crime* (1985), *Blood Count* (1986), *The Dispossessed* (1988).

Jesse Falkenstein series as Lesley Egan: *A Case for Appeal* (1961), *Against the Evidence* (1962), *My Name is Death* (1964), *Some Avenger, Rise!* (1966), *A Serious Investigation* (1968), *In the Death of a Man* (1970), *Paper Chase* (1972), *The Blind Search* (1977), *Look Back on Death* (1979), *Motive in Shadow* (1980), *The Miser* (1981), *Little Boy Lost* (1983).

Vic Varallo series as Lesley Egan: *The Borrowed Alibi* (1962), *Run to Evil* (1963), *Detective's Due* (1965), *The Nameless Ones* (1967), *The Wine of Violence* (1969), *Malicious Mischief* (1971), *Scenes of Crime* (1976), *A Dream Apart* (1978), *The Hunter and the Hunted* (1979), *A Choice of Crimes* (1980), *Random Death* (1982), *Crime for Christmas* (1983).

Non-series (as EL): *Alter Ego* (1988).

Non-series as Anne Blaisdell: *Nightmare* (1961).

Non-series as Lesley Egan: *Chain of Violence* (1985), *The Wine of Life* (1985).

Non-series as Dell Shannon: *The Manson Curse* (1990), *Sorrow to the Grave* (1992).

Short Stories

As Dell Shannon: *Murder by the Tale* (1987)

Full name: Barbara Elizabeth Linington.
Pen-names: Anne Blaisdell, Lesley Egan, Egan O'Neill, Dell Shannon.
Where to start: *A Case for Appeal* or *Greenmask!*
Similar stuff: Anthea FRASER, J.A. JANCE.
Final fact: Much of EL's research was drawn from the "confessions" magazines.

Gillian Linscott (b. 1944) UK

A former journalist and BBC Parliamentary reporter, GL became a full-time writer in 1990. Her first series of books feature Birdie Linnet, a former policeman, forced to resign, who finds himself in France on the trail of his wife who has run away with another man. When that man's body turns up in the dunes, Linnet is the prime suspect. This series is light-hearted with a wry observation on 1980s yuppie culture. Linnet later becomes a fitness trainer but trouble follows him over the globe. GL's next series features Nell Bray, a well-educated, upper-middle-class girl who becomes a suffragette in the Edwardian era. In the first book, *Sister Beneath the Sheet*, Bray has only just been released from prison for throwing a brick through the Prime Minister's window when Emmeline Pankhurst sends her to Biarritz to collect a fortune bequeathed to the suffragette movement by a high-class prostitute who has been found dead. This series, which is written with considerable passion, intensity and conviction, and not a little satire on the political situation of the period, follows the suffragette movement through to the post-war years. *Absent Friends*, which won both the CWA Ellis Peters award and the Herodotus, takes place at the time of the first election when women had the vote and Nell Bray stands as a candidate amidst suspicion that the former candidate had been murdered. GL has written two non-series mysteries of which *Unknown Hand* is an intriguing if fantastical bibliomystery and *Murder I Presume*, involving a clash between explorers soon after the death of David Livingstone, is another historical.

Novels

Birdie Linnet series: *A Healthy Body* (1984), *Murder Makes Tracks* (1985), *Knightfall* (1986), *A Whiff of Sulphur* (1987).

Nell Bray Series: *Sister Beneath the Sheet* (1991), *Hanging on the Wire* (1992), *Stage Fright* (1993), *Widow's Peak* (1994; as *An Easy Day for a Lady*, US 1995), *Crown Witness* (1995), *Dead Man's Music* (1996; as *Dead Man's Sweetheart*, US 1997), *Dance on Blood* (1998), *Absent Friends* (1999), *The Perfect Daughter* (2000), *Dead Man Riding* (2002).

Non-series: *Unknown Hand* (1988), *Murder, I Presume* (1990).

Where to start: *Sister Beneath the Sheet.*

Awards: CWA Ellis Peters Historical Dagger (2000), Herodotus, best international historical mystery (2000).

Website: <www.twbooks.co.uk/authors/glinscott.html> and <www.gillianlinscott.co.uk>

Similar stuff: Laurie R. KING for other feminist views of the early 20th century; Lesley GRANT-ADAMSON for contemporary setting.

Final fact: GL keeps a trampoline in the garden and when stuck on a plot goes out and bounces for a bit to shake ideas up.

Laura Lippman (b. 1959) US

LL has the enviable record that each of her first four books was nominated for one of the major mystery fiction awards, winning a total of six awards out of thirteen nominations. The series features Tess Monaghan, a former reporter in Baltimore, who turns informal P.I. when her paper ceases publication. Though tough and determined, she rather bungles her way through her first case, in *Baltimore Blues*, where she tries to help a friend who's implicated in the murder of a lawyer. In *Charm City* she is still learning the ropes in what is a curiously complicated case of a murdered business tycoon and financial corruption. The series really took off with *Butchers Hill*, inspired by a real case of the death of a teenager. Tess is hired to find the young witnesses of a crime which happened years before only for them to die as she finds them. The series is all the more fascinating because of Tess's vulnerability. LL hails from Georgia but has lived in Baltimore since 1965. Like her father before her she is a journalist, and was named the best writer for the *Baltimore Sun* in 1996.

Novels

Tess Monaghan series: *Baltimore Blues* (1997), *Charm City* (1997), *Butcher's Hill* (1998), *In Big Trouble* (1999), *The Sugar House* (2000), *In a Strange City* (2001), *The Last Place* (2002).

Awards: Edgar, best paperback original (1998), Shamus, best paperback original (1998, 2000), Agatha, best novel (1999), Anthony, best paperback original (1999, 2000), Nero Wolfe (2001).
Website: <www.lauralippman.com>
Similar stuff: Edna BUCHANAN, Mary Willis WALKER.
Final fact: LL studied journalism at Northwestern University where one of her professors was Stuart KAMINSKY.

Nancy Livingston (1935–94) UK

NL had a varied life from actress to airline stewardess to TV production assistant and radio and TV scriptwriter before she turned to writing full-time in 1989. She originally wanted to write family sagas and achieved that aim with *The Far Side of the Hill* (1987), but before then was advised to write crime fiction. Her choice of hero was a little unusual, but that's what marks him out. G.D.H. Pringle is a widower and a retired tax inspector who is used to detecting fraud. He is occasionally called upon to investigate other crimes. His first case happens by chance, when he becomes involved in a murder at a health farm in France. As you'd expect from a tax inspector, Pringle is suspicious, persistent, astute yet surprisingly modest, and looks like someone from the 1950s. He solves the case much to the annoyance of the incumbent police inspector and to the admiration of the new one. Pringle is usually accompanied by his lady-friend, Mavis Bignell, a widow whom he met when she served as a nude model at an art class. Once NL got into her stride she introduced all manner of eccentric characters into the series with increasingly convoluted plots. Most of the series lampoon the traditional English mystery, though NL deftly balances the humour with pathos. Some are set in England, but Pringle frequently travels abroad. The least traditional is *Death in a Distant Land*, set in Australia, involving drug-smuggling and a missing child. Despite its rather more sombre tone, it won the *Punch* award for that year's most comic novel. It is sad that NL had such a short writing career, dying at the age of 58.

Novels

Mr Pringle series: *The Trouble at Aquitaine* (1985), *Fatality at Bath and Wells* (1986), *Incident at Parga* (1987), *Death in a Distant Land* (1988), *Death in Close-Up* (1989), *Mayhem in Parva* (1990), *Unwillingly to Vegas* (1991), *Quiet Murder* (1992).

Awards: CWA *Punch* Award for best comic mystery (1988).
Similar stuff: Ruth Dudley EDWARDS, Kay MITCHELL.

MacDonald Lloyd *pseudonym, see* Don Winslow

Dick Lochte (b. 1944) US

Critic and reviewer DL is not a prolific novelist – nine books spread over thirty-three years (six of them mysteries) – but it's the quality that counts. His books are always original and experimental, especially with using multi-perspective narratives. His first two mysteries, both set in LA where DL now lives, feature an odd couple: the Bogart-obsessed middle-aged P.I. Leo Bloodworth, and young teenager Serendipity Dahlquist who aspires to be a private detective. DL tells the story through each character's differing viewpoint – Dahlquist's modern young view versus Bloodworth's traditional. In addition Bloodworth is dogged and persistent, Dahlquist sharp and intuitive. It makes for a fascinating pairing and the first book, *Sleeping Dog*, was nominated for all the major mystery awards winning the Nero. DL then switched locale to his native New Orleans for two books featuring P.I. Terry Manion. Here the crimes and narrative are more complex. In *Blue Bayou*, Manion investigates the murder of his mentor, J.J. Legendre, which unravels associations with Manion's own father whose apparent suicide had also remained a mystery. In *The Neon Smile*, DL achieves a remarkable alternate perspective by recounting a 1965 investigation of an unsolved crime by Legendre alongside Manion's investigation 30 years later. Most recently DL has teamed with Los Angeles DA prosecutor Christopher Darden, who was involved in the O.J. Simpson trial, to write a fast-paced legal thriller series about ambitious young black prosecutor Nikki Hill. It is hoped that DL will continue to experiment.

Novels
Dahlquist & Bloodworth series: *Sleeping Dog* (1985), *Laughing Dog* (1988).
Terry Manion series: *Blue Bayou* (1992), *The Neon Smile* (1995).
Nikki Hill series with Christopher Darden: *The Trials of Nikki Hill* (1999), *L.A. Justice* (2001).
Short Stories: *Lucky Dog and Other Tales of Murder* (2000).

Full name: Richard Samuel Lochte.
Where to start: *Sleeping Dog*.
Awards: Nero Wolfe award (1985).
Similar stuff: Carol O'CONNELL, Don WINSLOW.
Final fact: DL also helped veteran jockey Bill Shoemaker on his three racetrack mysteries featuring jockey Coley Killebrew starting with *Stalking Horse* (1994).

Roger Longrigg (1929–2000) UK

RL was an accomplished writer for over 40 years, adopting a new persona each time he explored a new territory. Under his own name he was best known for his humorous, often satirical novels of city and country life. Only one of these books, *The Desperate Criminals*, a zany romp set in the south of France, really falls within the crime-fiction field. As Ivor Drummond he wrote a series featuring three rich jetsetting adventurers,

Lady Jennifer Norrington, Count Alessandro di Ganzarello and Coleridge Tucker III – Jenny, Sandro and Colly for short. Their adventures, rather like the agents from U.N.C.L.E., took them all over the world fighting larger-than-life criminals from Thuggees in India (*The Necklace of Skulls*) to poachers in Africa (*The Frog in the Moonflower*). It is his Frank Parrish persona that is closest to crime fiction, though far from traditional. Under this name he created village poacher and petty thief Dan Mallett who becomes an unlikely crimefighter and amateur sleuth. In several books Mallett's reputation makes him a likely suspect when something goes wrong, even murder as in *Sting of the Honeybee* and *Bait on the Hook*, but elsewhere Mallett becomes something of a local hero. In *Fire in the Barley*, which was shortlisted for an Edgar award, he has to overcome a protection racket, while in *Sting of the Honeybee* he takes on an organized crime boss. These books show not only RL's humour but his knowledge of the countryside. Under his own name he has written books on foxhunting, horse racing and the English squire. As Laura Black RL wrote several historical gothic romances set mostly in Scotland, starting with *Glendraco* (1977). His last major incarnation was as Domini Taylor under which name he wrote several psychological horror stories. A few verged on the supernatural, such as *Gemini*, about a pair of unusual twins, but most dealt with vengeful females such as the embittered Helena in *Mother Love* (TV series 1989) or the spiteful Rosalind in *Suffer Little Children*, or the femme fatale in *Praying Mantis.* Arguably the best of his Taylor books is *Not Fair*, in which a woman is injured in a hit-and-run meant to kill her. Surviving as an invalid she realizes the murderer is still after her. Under the name Grania Beckford RL wrote a sequel to Jane Austen's *Persuasion* called *Virtue and Vices* (1980). Under one name or another RL had something for everyone.

Novels

Non-series: *The Desperate Criminals* (1971).

Jenny, Sandro & Colly series as Ivor Drummond: *The Man With the Tiny Head* (1969), *The Priests of the Abomination* (1970), *The Frog in the Moonflower* (1972), *The Jaws of the Watchdog* (1973), *The Power of the Bug* (1974), *The Tank of Sacred Eels* (1976), *The Necklace of Skulls* (1977), *A Stench of Poppies* (1978), *The Diamonds of Loreta* (1980).

Dan Mallett series as Frank Parrish: *Fire in the Barley* (1977), *Sting of the Honeybee* (1978), *Snare in the Dark* (1982), *Bait on the Hook* (1983), *Face at the Window* (1984; as *Death in the Rain*, US 1984), *Fly in the Cobweb* (1986), *Caught in the Birdlime* (1987; as *Bird in the Net*, US 1988), *Voices from the Dark* (1993).

as Domini Taylor: *Mother Love* (1983), *Gemini* (1984), *Suffer Little Children* (1987; as *Teacher's Pet*, US 1987), *Praying Mantis* (1988), *Siege* (1989), *Not Fair* (1992), *The Eye Behind the Curtain* (1993), *The Tiffany Lamp* (1994), *Pig in the Middle* (1996).

Full name: Roger Erskine Longrigg.

Pen-names: Megan Barker, Laura Black, Grania Beckford, Ivor Drummond,

Rosalind Erskine, Frank Parrish, Domini Taylor.
Where to start: *Fire in the Barley*.
Similar stuff: Jonathan GASH for the Frank Parrish novels.
Final fact: RL's most notorious book was *The Passion-Flower Hotel* (1962; filmed 1978), purportedly written by a fifteen-year-old school-girl, Rosalind Erskine, and being her story of sex-for-sale at a boarding school. The film provided an early rôle for Nastassja Kinski who was apparently so appalled with the film that she wished she could destroy every copy.

Marc Lovell *pseudonym, see* Mark McShane

Peter Lovesey (b. 1936) UK

PL was a college lecturer and department head when he decided to enter a publisher's contest for a crime novel with £1000 as first prize, a significant sum in 1970. PL won with his highly original *Wobble to Death*. The public interest in historical mysteries had yet to emerge, though there was always an interest in the Victorians. PL's creation of Sergeant Cribb and Constable Thackeray, set in the 1880s, tapped into that vein and brought alive the quirkiness of the Victorian world. Unlike other authors, who make their detectives larger-than-life and full of idiosyncracies, Cribb was as solid as a rock and was the one point of assurety around which this strange world revolved. In *Wobble* it was murder at a marathon walking contest. In *The Detective Wore Silk Drawers* it's the illegal world of bare-knuckle boxing. *Abracadaver* is set amidst unusual entertainers in the music hall; *Mad Hatter's Holiday* follows the growing fascination for the seaside whilst *A Case of Spirits* involves spiritualism. PL wound the Cribb series up after eight books but continued with other historical mysteries. *Keystone* is set in the dangerous world of the stuntman in the early movie industry of 1915. *The False Inspector Dew* is a case of mistaken identity on an Atlantic liner in 1921 and won PL the CWA Gold Dagger. With *Bertie and the Tinman* PL returned to the Victorian period. Bertie is the Prince of Wales and the future Edward VII, whose colourful life in reality brought him into disrepute more than once. In three novels and two short stories the Prince displays his skills as a detective. In the delightful *Bertie and the Crime of Passion* he co-opts the Divine Sarah Bernhardt as his sleuthing partner investigating a murder at the Moulin Rouge in Paris. Apart from the novels written as Peter Lear, which include the bestselling *Goldengirl*, about developing a special athlete for the Olympics, PL did not write a contemporary mystery until *The Last Detective*, which introduced his forceful and single-minded police detective Peter Diamond. Diamond is perhaps the most appealing of all of PL's intriguing characters. In *The Last Detective*, which won the Anthony award, Diamond is forced to resign because of his frustration with modern methods of operating and in *Diamond Solitaire* we find he still can't hold down a job and so takes up private sleuthing. *The Summons* marks his way back to the Force when a man Diamond had arrested for murder years before escapes and takes a hostage. Diamond discovers he is innocent so must find the real killer before the hostage is harmed. With *Bloodhounds* Diamond is back with CID and this delicious locked-room mystery is regarded by many as one of the best of the series. It was awarded both the CWA Silver Dagger and the Macavity. PL is one of the more original writers working in the traditional mode and is never afraid to experiment, especially in the short story form. "Youdunnit" (1989) ingeniously makes the reader the murderer. In all of his books PL creates solid characters in bizarre circumstances who are able to bring order back from chaos. In 2000 the CWA awarded PL the Diamond Dagger for his achievements.

Novels

Sergeant Cribb series: *Wobble to Death* (1970), *The Detective Wore Silk Drawers* (1971), *Abracadaver* (1972), *Mad Hatter's Holiday* (1973), *Invitation to a Dynamite Party* (1974; as *The Tick of Death*, US 1974), *A Case of Spirits* (1975), *Swing, Swing Together* (1976), *Waxwork* (1978).

Bertie series: *Bertie and the Tinman* (1987), *Bertie and the Seven Bodies* (1990), *Bertie and the Crime of Passion* (1993).

Peter Diamond series: *The Last Detective* (1991), *Diamond Solitaire* (1992), *The Summons* (1995), *Bloodhounds* (1996), *Upon a Dark Night* (1997), *The Vault* (2000), *Diamond Dust* (2002).

Non-series: *The False Inspector Dew* (1982), *Keystone* (1915), *Rough Cider* (1986), *On the Edge* (1989), *The Reaper* (2000).

Non-series as Peter Lear: *Goldengirl* (1977), *Spider Girl* (1980), *The Secret of Spandau* (1986).

Short Stories. *Butchers and Other Stories of Crime* (1985), *The Staring Man* (1988), *The Crime of Miss Oyster Brown* (1994), *Do Not Exceed the Stated Dose* (1998), *The Sedgemoor Strangler* (2001).

Editor. *The Black Cabinet: Stories Based on True Crime* (1989).

Full name: Peter Harmer Lovesey.

Pen-name: Peter Lear.

Where to start: Almost anywhere but for historicals try *Abracadaver* or *Bertie and the Crime of Passion*; otherwise *The Last Detective*.

Awards: CWA Silver Dagger (1978, 1995, 1996), CWA Gold Dagger (1982), Grand Prix de Littérature Policière Best Foreign (1985), Prix du Roman d'Aventures (1987), Anthony, best novel (1992), Barry, best novel (1997), Macavity, best novel (1997), CWA Diamond Dagger (2000).

Website: <www.twbooks.co.uk/authors/peterlovesey.html>

Similar stuff: Donald THOMAS.

Final fact: PL has long been fascinated by track and field athletics and is one of the NUTS (National Union of Track Statisticians). He has written a study of five great runners, *The Kings of Distance* (1968), as well as *The Official Centenary History of the Amateur Athletics Association* (1979) and most recently *An Athletics Compendium* (2001).

Phil Lovesey (b. 1963) UK

The son of author Peter LOVESEY, PL trained as an artist and earned a degree in film and TV studies before becoming what he terms as "London's laziest copywriter" in various advertising agencies. In 1994 he began writing short stories and was a finalist in the MWA's 50th anniversary short story competition in 1995 with "Double Event", a clever twist on the serial-killer-plays-games-with-the-police plot. It was a small hint of the direction his early novels would take, all of which are sinister studies of dark motives and displaced psychologies. *Death Duties* traces connections between a bizarre 1969 patricide and a present-day murder. *Ploughing Potter's Field* delves deep into the mind of a sociopath in a study of pure evil. *When the Ashes Burn* explores a serious development in juvenile crime. PL's novels explore the roots of crime deep into the tainted soil.

Novels. *Death Duties* (1998), *Ploughing Potter's Field* (1999), *When the Ashes Burn* (2000), *The Screaming Tree* (2002).

Full name: Philip Lovesey.
Website: <www.twbooks.co.uk/authors/phillovesey.html>
Similar stuff: Val MCDERMID.
Final fact: PL plays drums and has a proper Tin Pan Alley in his country garden which he likes to thrash around while thinking up horrible crimes.

John Lutz (b. 1939) US

By the time JL turned to full-time writing in 1975, after years in various jobs ranging from theatre usher and truck driver to a switchboard operator for the St Louis Metropolitan, he was already a well established short-story writer with scores of sales to the mystery magazines since his first in 1963. He had a talent for an unusual plot and an intriguing gimmick, producing neat tales of revenge, suspense or encroaching madness, the best of which will be found in *Better Mousetraps* and *Until You Are Dead*. JL brought the same tenseness and diversity to his novels. Most of the non-series books are suspense thrillers ranging from the self-destructive flight of a psychotic in his first book, *The Truth of the Matter* to the roommate from hell in *SWF Seeks Same*, better known under its film title as *Single White Female* (filmed 1992). Lutz reworked the theme of *SWF* in *The Ex* (filmed 1997), this time with the neighbour from hell, who also happens to be her victim's ex-wife. JL's other books include a thriller about a community going berserk for fear of an apparent lake monster in *Bonegrinder*, a genuinely frightening assassin in *The Shadow Man*, whose protagonist appears to be able to kill from beyond his prison cell and, in the light of 11 September carnage in New York, the rather chilling *Jericho Man* about a maniac who builds time bombs into the very fabric of skyscrapers under construction. JL has developed two strong series detectives. Alo Nudger is a St Louis P.I. who resigned from the police force because of a stomach disorder and he is always taking antacid tablets. Nudger is something of a loser, highly strung, fearful of guns with a tragic history in past wives. But he's a compassionate fellow who cares for his clients and tries to do his best for them, even though he takes ages over it and events often overtake him. In his debut, *Buyer Beware*, he's hired by two different people to solve the same case – to trace a missing woman and her child – and the case leads him into a nightmare world of corporate madness. Fred Carver, who operates out of Orlando, Florida, is another ex-cop, invalided out when he was knee-capped by a young thug. His life is as tragic as Nudger's – in the second novel, *Scorcher*, his own son is murdered by a maniac with a home-made flamethrower. Unlike Nudger, though, Carver becomes mean and vengeful. Both series reflect the skill for original plotting and clever twists displayed in JL's many short stories.

Novels
Alo Nudger series: *Buyer Beware* (1976), *Nightlines* (1985), *The Right to Sing the Blues* (1986), *Ride the Lightning* (1987), *Dancer's Debt* (1988), *Time Exposure* (1989), *Diamond Eyes* (1990), *Thicker Than Blood* (1993), *Death by Jury* (1995), *Oops!* (1998).
Fred Carver series: *Tropical Heat* (1986), *Scorcher* (1987), *Kiss* (1988), *Flame* (1990), *Bloodfire* (1991), *Hot* (1992), *Spark* (1993), *Torch* (1994), *Burn* (1995), *Lightning* (1996).
Oxman & Tobin series: *The Eye* with Bill Pronzini (1984), *Shadowtown* (1988),
Non-series: *The Truth of the Matter* (1971), *Bonegrinder* (1977), *Lazarus Man* (1979), *Jericho Man* (1980), *The Shadow Man* (1981), *SWF Seeks Same* (1990; as *Single White Female*, 1992), *Dancing With the Dead* (1992), *The Ex* (1996), *Final Seconds* with David August (1998), *The Night Caller* (2001).
Short Stories. *Better Mousetraps* (1988), *Shadows Everywhere* (1994), *Until You Are Dead* (1998), *The Nudger Dilemmas* (2001).

Full name: John Thomas Lutz.
Pen-name: John Bennett, Tom Collins, Van McCloud, Paul Shepparton, Elwin Strange, John Barry Williams.
Where to start: *Nightlines* or *Tropical Heat* or *The Shadow Man*.
Awards: Shamus, best short story (1983), best hardcover novel (1989), lifetime achievement (1995), Edgar, best short story (1986), PWA Lifetime Achievement (1995), Derringer, lifetime (2001).
Similar stuff: Michael CONNELLY, Robert CRAIS, Bill PRONZINI.
Final fact: JL called his character Nudger because he "nudges" his cases along, unlike Spillane's Mike Hammer who "hammers" them home.

Dennis Lynds, *see* Michael Collins

Gayle Lynds, *see under* Michael Collins

Arthur Lyons (b. 1946) US

AL is the creator of Jacob Asch, a divorced, half-Jewish former investigative journalist who, after six months in prison for contempt of court, decides to become a P.I. Cynical, tough, persistent and given to bursts of uncontrolled temper, Asch finds himself investigating bleak and often disturbing crimes. AL's own investigations into satanism provided the background for the debut novel *The Dead Are Discreet*. AL explores the vulnerability and manipulation of individuals, from religious cults in *All God's Children*, prostitution in *Dead Ringer* and doctors and the sex trade in *At the Hands of Another*. In *Castles Burning* (filmed TV 1986 as *Slow Burn*) it about the rebelliousness of youth leading to a missing child. Asch has been compared favourably to Philip Marlowe and Sam Spade and AL certainly works in the hard-boiled tradition though Asch is no stereotype. He's his own man with a strong if flexible moral code. AL has written two medical thrillers with Los Angeles' chief medical examiner, Thomas Noguchi. AL was a restaurateur in Palm Springs, California where he also served as mayor and recently launched the Palm Springs Film Noir Festival.

Novels

Jacob Asch series: *The Dead Are Discreet* (1974), *All God's Children* (1975), *The Killing Floor* (1976), *Dead Ringer* (1977), *Castles Burning* (1980), *Hard Trade* (1982), *At the Hands of Another* (1983), *Three With a Bullet* (1985), *Fast Fade* (1987), *Other People's Money* (1989), *False Pretenses* (1994).

Dr Parker series, with Thomas T. Noguchi: *Unnatural Causes* (1988), *Physical Evidence* (1990).

Non-fiction (selective) *The Second Coming: Satanism in America* (1970; as *Satan Wants You: The Cult of Devil Worship*, UK 1971); *The Blue Sense: Psychic Detectives and Crime*, with Marcello Truzzi (1991); *Death on the Cheap: The Lost B Movies of Film Noir* (2000).

Similar stuff: Howard ENGEL, Roger L. SIMON, Collin WILCOX.

Final fact: AL's collaborator, Thomas Noguchi (b. 1927), was the doctor who performed the autopsies on Marilyn Monroe and Robert Kennedy.

Peter MacAlan see under pseudonym Peter Tremayne

Ed McBain (b. 1926) US

Under various pen-names, EM has written around one hundred books, over half of which feature the officers of the 87th Precinct in the fictional city of Isola (based on New York). Although EM did not invent the police procedural he did more than most in establishing it as a genre. Although the series is an ensemble piece, with Lieutenant Byrnes in charge overall, the main character is Detective Steve Carella, who in the first book, *Cop Hater* (filmed 1958), tracks down a maniac who is killing cops. The characters have experienced enough for several lifetimes, but few of them seem to have aged and remain perpetually 30-something, though Carella has married and raised children during the series. A few have come and gone. The bullying Roger Haviland was killed-off in *Killer's Choice* but an equally violent, loutish cop Andy Parker took over in *Tricks*. There is also the racist Fat Ollie Weeks who is tolerated because he's so good at his job. The Precinct has covered just about every crime during the course of the series – in *Hail, Hail the Gang's All Here!* he manages to keep 14 separate story-lines going. He occasionally ventures into less common territory including the supernatural in *Ghosts*, politics in *Hail to the Chief* and a planned terrorist attack in the uncannily timely *Money, Money, Money*. A feature of several of the novels since *The Heckler* is the master criminal nemesis of the Precinct known only as "the Deaf Man' whose arch-plans the Precinct manages to scupper at the last minute only for him to rise again. In *He Who Hesitates* the police remain in the background and the story is told entirely from the viewpoint of a murderer who commits a perfect crime. Despite its length, or maybe because of it, the series continues to be original and topical, perhaps no longer setting standards but certainly remaining a yardstick for other aspiring writers.

The name Ed McBain was concocted to cover the author's less "sophisticated" material, keeping his more significant pen-name, Evan Hunter, for serious mainstream novels. EM was born Salvatore Lombino under which name his first stories appeared in the science-fiction magazines from 1951 on. After serving in the Navy during and just after the War, he obtained a degree in English and taught briefly in vocational high schools before taking a job at Scott Meredith's Literary Agency, through whose auspices he began to sell regularly. It was Meredith who advised Lombino to change his name because of racial attitudes to Italian Americans at the time and he took the name Evan Hunter, later adopting it legally. It was as Hunter that he had his first major success with the semi-autobiographical *The Blackboard Jungle* (filmed 1955), which dealt with the rising problem of juvenile deliquency in vocational schools. This theme also features in the stories collected as *The Jungle Kids* and in his science-fiction novel *Tomorrow's World* (1956 as by Hunt Collins) which portrays a future dominated by drug addicts and pushers. During the fifties Hunter was a prolific writer, producing books and magazine stories under many pen-names. Originally under the Hunter name he produced a series of stories for the hard-boiled magazine *Manhunt* featuring Matt Cordell, a desperate alcoholic ex-P.I. who has lost his wife and his licence. In the first story, "Die Hard" (1953), he has a dead body on his hands. When these were collected as *I Like 'em Tough* the P.I.'s name was changed to Curt Cannon and that became the by-line on the book. The Cannon adventures are regarded as amongst the toughest and most shocking of all P.I. stories, perhaps second only to Mike Hammer. The books bearing the Hunter name continued to deal with strong social issues such as drugs, marital infidelity and youth violence. *A*

Matter of Conviction (filmed 1961 as *The Young Savages*), for example, is a convincing legal drama of an attorney prosecuting three juvenile delinquents charged with murder. However the scope for the name later broadened to cover war novels and family sagas and more light-hearted crime novels such as *A Horse's Head* (filmed France 1970) and *Every Little Crook and Nanny* (filmed 1972). *Buddwing* (filmed 1966) is a Woolrichian style nightmare of a man who wakes on a park bench with no memory of who he is. *Paper Dragons* explores the crime of plagiarism. *Nobody Knew They Were There* deals with terrorism. *Lizzie* is a recreation of the Lizzie Borden case. *Privileged Conversation* is the story of a psychiatrist who has an affair with a woman who is being stalked. Hunter has written several plays and adapted several of his books as films or for TV series. He also wrote the screenplay for the Hitchcock thriller *The Birds* (1963).

While Hunter was working the mainstream, McBain was growing in popularity and, by the mid-eighties overtook Hunter in sales and hit the best seller lists. In addition to the 87th Precinct novels he started a new series about Florida-based lawyer Matthew Hope. Hope spends more time investigating than in the courtroom. His civil cases tend to lead to murder so he turns unofficial P.I. Each book is modelled on a classic fairy tale. The first, *Goldilocks*, is about a man whose wife and children are murdered whilst he is having an affair. *Cinderella* concerns a young woman who steals Mob money in order to improve her lot. Hope lives in the same universe as the 87th Precinct as Steve Carella becomes involved in a case in *The Last Best Hope*.

Most recently the Hunter and McBain personas have come together in *Candyland*, an interesting experiment that begins as a Hunter novel – about a middle-aged man who suddenly ruins his life in an evening of debauchery – and then switches to a McBain police procedural. In a career spanning over 50 years and with a reputed 100 million books in print, EM may no longer be in the engine-room of crime fiction, but he continues to entertain and occasionally surprise. In recognition of his career EM has the rare distinction of being awarded a Grand Master by the MWA and a Diamond Dagger by the CWA.

Novels

87th Precinct series: *Cop Hater* (1956), *The Mugger* (1956), *The Pusher* (1956), *The Con Man* (1957), *Killer's Choice* (1957), *Killer's Payoff* (1958), *Lady Killer* (1958), *Killer's Wedge* (1958), *"Til Death* (1959), *King's Ransom* (1959), *Give the Boys a Great Hand* (1960), *The Heckler* (1960), *See Them Die* (1960), *Lady, Lady, I Did It!* (1961), *Like Love* (1962), *Ten Plus One* (1963), *Ax* (1964), *He Who Hesitates* (1965), *Doll* (1965), *Eighty Million Eyes* (1966), *Fuzz* (1968), *Shotgun* (1969), *Jigsaw* (1970), *Hail, Hail, the Gang's All Here!* (1971), *Sadie When She Died* (1972), *Let's Hear it for the Deaf Man* (1973), *Hail to the Chief* (1973), *Bread* (1974), *Blood Relatives* (1975), *So Long As You Both Shall Live* (1976), *Long Time No See* (1977), *Calypso* (1979), *Ghosts* (1980), *Heat* (1981), *Ice* (1983), *Lightning*

(1984), *Eight Black Horses* (1985), *Poison* (1987), *Tricks* (1987), *Lullaby* (1989), *Vespers* (1990), *Widows* (1991), *Kiss* (1992), *Mischief* (1993), *Romance* (1995), *Nocturne* (1997), *The Big Bad City* (1999), *The Last Dance* (2000), *Money, Money, Money* (2002).
Matthew Hope series: *Goldilocks* (1977), *Rumpelstiltskin* (1981), *Beauty and the Beast* (1982), *Jack and the Beanstalk* (1984), *Snow White and Rose Red* (1985), *Cinderella* (1986), *Puss in Boots* (1987), *The House That Jack Built* (1988), *Three Blind Mice* (1990), *Mary, Mary* (1992), *There Was a Little Girl* (1994), *Gladly the Cross-Eyed Bear* (1996), *The Last Best Hope* (1998).
Non-series: *The Sentries* (1965), *Where There's Smoke* (1975), *Guns* (1976), *Another Part of the City* (1985), *Downtown* (1989).
as John Abbott: *Scimitar* (1992).
as Curt Cannon: *I'm Cannon for Hire* (1958).
as Hunt Collins: *Cut Me In* (1954; as *The Proposition*, 1955).
as Ezra Hannon: *Doors* (1975; as by Ed McBain, 1976).
as Evan Hunter (selective): *The Big Fix* (1952), *The Evil Sleep!* (1952; as *So Nude, So Dead* by Richard Marsten, 1956), *Don't Crowd Me* (1953; as *The Paradise Party*, UK 1968), *The Blackboard Jungle* (1954), *Second Ending* (1956; as *Quartet in H*, 1957), *A Matter of Conviction* (1959; as *The Young Savages*, 1966), *Buddwing* (1964), *The Paper Dragon* (1966), *A Horse's Head* (1967), *Nobody Knew They Were There* (1971), *Every Little Crook and Nanny* (1972), *Lizzie* (1984), *Criminal Conversation* (1994), *Privileged Conversation* (1996), *Candyland* (2001), *Moment She was Gone* (2002).
as Richard Marsten: *Runaway Black* (1954; as *Runaway* by Ed McBain, 1992), *Murder in the Navy* (1955; as *Death of a Nurse* by Ed McBain, 1968), *The Spiked Heel* (1956), *Vanishing Ladies* (1957), *Even the Wicked* (1958; as by Ed McBain, UK 1979), *Big Man* (1959; as by Ed McBain, UK 1978).
completed for Craig Rice: *The April Robin Murders* (1958).

Short Stories

87th Precinct series: *The Empty Hours* (1962), *And All Through the House*, single story (1986), *McBain's Ladies* (1988), *McBain's Ladies Too* (1989)
Non-series: *The McBain Brief* (1982; abr. as *The Interview*, Finland 1986), *Driving Lessons* (2000), *Running from Legs* (2000).
as Curt Cannon: *I Like 'em Tough* (1958).
as Evan Hunter: *The Jungle Kids* (1956), *The Last Spin* (UK 1960), *Happy New Year, Herbie* (1963), *The Beheading* (UK 1971), *Seven* (UK 1972; abr. as *The Easter Man*, US 1972), *Barking at Butterflies* (2000).

Non-fiction. *Me and Hitch* (1997).

Editor. *Crime Squad* (UK 1968), *Homicide Department* (UK 1968), *Downpour* (UK 1969), *Ticket to Death* (UK 1969), *The Best American Mystery Stories 1999* with Otto Penzler (1999).

Real name: Evan Hunter, changed legally from Salvatore Alberto Lombino.
Pen-names: Curt Cannon, Hunt Collins, Ezra Hannon, Ed McBain, Richard Marsten
Where to start: For McBain almost anywhere but *Hail, Hail, the Gang's All Here!* is an excellent example. For Hunter try either *Buddwing* or *A Matter of Conviction*.
Awards: Swedish Academy of Detection, Grand Master (1976), MWA Grand

Master (1986), CWA Diamond Dagger (1998), American Mystery Award, best police procedural (1988, 1991, 1992, 1993).
Similar stuff: Thomas ADCOCK, William BAYER.
Website: <www.edmcbain.com>
Final fact: In the tradition of Agatha Christie and Poirot, EM has apparently plotted the last 87th Precinct novel, *Exit*, to be published after his death.

Barbara Taylor McCafferty (b. 1946) US

Kentucky-resident BTM was an art director and advertising copywriter before she dropped her first name and began writing mysteries as Taylor McCafferty. Her first series features P.I. Haskell Blevins, a former police detective who has left his job and his wife and retired to the small Kentucky town of his birth. Not much work comes along but when it does it soon develops in strange ways, as in *Pet Peeves* where he finds himself investigating the murder of an old lady's pets – as well as the death of the old lady. Animals feature strongly in this series, not least Blevins's daft dog Rip. The series is light-heartedly eccentric. Under the alias Tierney McClellan BTM has written about 40-something real-estate agent Schuyler Ridgway of Louisville, Kentucky. In another light-hearted though less comic series, Ridgway finds herself involved in a variety of murders and a prime suspect in the first, *Heir Condition*. More recently, BTM has teamed up with her twin sister, Beverly Taylor Herald, to write a series about twin sisters Bert and Nan Tatum. Inspired by the Bobbsey Twins, this series has a certain fascination. Chapters alternate between each twin's viewpoint and place an emphasis on the bond and rapport between twins even though they are complete opposites. Nan, who is a country music DJ, is apparently modelled on Beverly whilst Bert, who is the more strait-laced of the two, reflects Barbara's views. It's also set in Louisville, Kentucky, and is perhaps the more intriguing of the three series.

Novels

Haskell Blevins series: *Pet Peeves* (1990), *Ruffled Feathers* (1992), *Bed Bugs* (1992), *Thin Skins* (1994), *Hanky Panky* (1995), *Funny Money* (2000).
Schuyler Ridgway series as Tierney McClellan: *Heir Condition* (1995), *Closing Statement* (1995), *A Killing in Real Estate* (1996), *Two-Story Frame* (1997).
Bert & Nan Tatum series with Beverly Taylor Herald: *Double Murder* (1997), *Double Exposure* (1997), *Double Cross* (1998), *Double Dealer* (2000), *Double Date* (2001).

Pen-names: Taylor McCafferty, Tierney McClellan.
Where to start: *Double Murder* or *Pet Peeves.*
Website: <www.mysterytwins.com>
Similar stuff: Deborah ADAMS, Dorothy CANNELL, Ann GEORGE.
Final fact: When collaborating, Beverly writes the first draft and Barbara does the final polish.

Wendell McCall *pseudonym, see* Ridley Pearson

Tierney McClellan *pseudonym, see* Barbara Taylor McCafferty

James McClure (b. 1939) South Africa

JM is a South-African born Brit whose novels helped expose the horrors of the apartheid regime. He had worked as a photographer, teacher and finally journalist in Natal before coming to Britain in 1965. *The Steam Pig* was the first of eight novels he wrote featuring Afrikaan police lieutenant Tromp Kramer and his Zulu assistant, Sergeant Mickey Zondi. Kramer is gruff and not especially bright, but he is persistent and he is not blinkered by the apartheid way of life, though he abides by it even to the extent of masking his admiration for Zondi who has sound detective skills. Zondi also speaks three native languages, which enables Kramer to take investigations into tribal areas otherwise out of reach. The relationship between the two officers is one of the strengths of the series. *The Steam Pig* underlines the iniquity of apartheid by tracing its effects upon an individual who turns to crime after he and his family are reclassified from white to "coloured' and consequently lose many privileges. The book won the CWA Gold Dagger. Perhaps surprisingly only one of the books was banned in South Africa – *The Sunday Hangman*, because it revealed too much about the prison regime – but otherwise the books were seen as an accurate reflection of life by the South African authorities. That alone is a condemnation of the authorities and a mark of success for JM. He wrote one non-series novel set in South Africa, *Rogue Eagle*, about the secret Afrikaaner organization the Broederbond, the real power behind the government. This won the CWA Silver Dagger. Anyone wishing to read the Kramer and Zondi series in sequence should begin with *The Song Dog*, which is set in 1962 and tells the story of how they came together.

Novels

Kramer & Zondi series: *The Steam Pig* (1971), *The Caterpillar Cop* (1972), *The Gooseberry Fool* (1974), *Snake* (1975), *The Sunday Hangman* (1977), *The Blood of an Englishman* (1980), *The Artful Egg* (1984), *The Song Dog* (1991).
Non-series: *Four and Twenty Virgins* (1973), *Rogue Eagle* (1976), *Imago* (1988).
Non-fiction. *Killers* (1976), *Spike Island: Portrait of a Police Division* (1980), *Copworld: Policing on the Streets of San Diego* (1985).

Full name: James Howe McClure.
Where to start: *The Song Dog*.
Awards: CWA Gold Dagger (1971), Silver Dagger (1976).
Similar stuff: Gillian Slovo.
Final fact: An internet web search engine has been named after Sergeant Zondi.

Val McDermid (b. 1955) UK

A journalist for 15 years, having been nominated the National Trainee Journalist of the Year in 1977, VM turned to full-time writing in 1991. By then her first three books had been published, all to critical acclaim, and with Sara PARETSKY citing her as one of her favourite authors. These books feature the Scottish journalist Lindsay Gordon. The first book, *Report for Murder*, is in many ways a classic English mystery – set in a girls' public school with a body in a locked room. It is against such a setting that VM can contrast Gordon, who is described as a hard-drinking, socialist, lesbian feminist. It was the next two books that helped establish Gordon. She becomes involved in an intelligence cover-up at a women's protest camp and the consequences of this spill over into *Final Edition* where she finds herself pitched against authority. In subsequent books Gordon pursues major political and social concerns leading to embezzlement, corruption and murder. VM next created Kate Brannigan, a red-headed P.I. who operates out of Manchester. She has been compared favourably to Paretsky's Warshawski, and is certainly as feisty, dominant and in control. This series is less political and more violent, though both series have wonderfully convoluted plots. Brannigan's investigations tend to start from something straightforward, if admittedly bizarre, such as missing conservatories in *Kick Back*, car sales fraud in *Crackdown*, or art theft in *Clean Break*, but rapidly descend into a world that is dark and nasty. In *Crackdown*, which was shortlisted for the CWA Gold Dagger and the Anthony award, it sucks Kate down into child pornography, drug trafficking and gangland enforcers. As part of her research for her books VM interviewed many female P.I.s and compiled her findings into *A Suitable Job for a Woman*. VM's third series featured clinical psychologist and profiler Tony Hill who, in the award-winning *The Mermaids Singing*, pits his wits and his life against a gay serial killer. In the sequel, *The Wire in the Blood*, Hill is now the head of a National Profiling Task Force, which becomes a target for a new serial killer. This series has been adapted for TV. VM's novels have become progressively darker, more intense but more fully realized. She has written two non-series books, which are the most haunting to date. The multi-award-winning *A Place of Execution* looks back nearly 40 years to the time of the Brady and Hindley Moors murders and to another unsolved case of a missing child. This book grabbed the media attention and pushed VM further up the ladder of recognition. *Killing the Shadows* has an element of self-satire, as it concerns a serial killer who is murdering specific crime novelists, but the investigation has even more sinister consequences. VM has created a strong body of work featuring dominant and forceful women investigators.

Novels

Lindsay Gordon series: *Report for Murder* (1987), *Common Murder* (1989), *Final Edition* (1991; as *Open and Shut*, US 1991; as *Deadline for Murder*, US 1997),),

Union Jack (1993; as *Conferences are Murder*, US 1999), *Booked for Murder* (1996).
Kate Brannigan series: *Dead Beat* (1992), *Kick Back* (1993), *Crackdown* (1994), *Clean Break* (1995), *Blue Genes* (1996), *Star Struck* (1998).
Dr Hill series: *The Mermaids Singing* (1995), *The Wire in the Blood* (1998), *The Last Temptation* (2002).
Non-series: *A Place of Execution* (1999), *Killing the Shadows* (2000).
Short stories. *The Writing on the Wall* (1997).
Non-fiction. *A Suitable Job for a Woman* (1995).

Where to start: *Crackdown* or *The Mermaids Singing*.
Awards: CWA Gold Dagger (1995), Le Masque de l'annee (1997), Le Grand Prix des Romans d'Aventures (1998), Barry, best British crime novel (2000), Dilys Award (2001), Anthony, best novel (2001), Macavity, best novel (2001).
Website: <www.twbooks.co.uk/authors/valmcdermid.html>
Similar stuff: Ruth RENDELL, Lesley GRANT-ADAMSON.
Final fact: VM was the first ever undergraduate from a Scottish state school to attend St Hilda's College, Oxford.

Gregory McDonald (b. 1937) US

GM had not planned to become a writer let alone a mystery writer, and certainly not one known for his humorous works, but *Fletch* (filmed 1985) changed all that. With a degree from Harvard and a few years as a marine insurance engineer and a teacher, GM became a reporter and critic for the *Boston Globe* in 1966. His first novel, *Running Scared* (filmed 1972), had been a provocative account of two students and how one allows the other to ultimately commit suicide. The book was highly controversial and GM did not write another novel for ten years. When he did it was a complete *volte face* and introduced "Fletch" – Irwin M. Fletcher – to the world. At the outset Fletch is an undercover reporter looking for a story amongst the junkies and drug pushers of the beaches of southern California. He is approached by a man who is terminally ill but cannot face the outcome so offers Fletch $3 million to kill him. The novel reveals how Fletch gets his news story and keeps the $3 million without having to become a murderer. The book had been a one-off, but by public demand Fletch returned in *Confess, Fletch*. Because of his wealth Fletch can infiltrate areas of interest and act like an unofficial P.I. Both books won the Edgar award. One of the delightful characters in the second book was Francis Xavier Flynn, a droll, sarcastic Boston police inspector who trails Fletch about trying to get him to confess to murder. Flynn proved sufficiently popular to demand his own series but GM took the character in a different direction. In *Flynn* he emerges as something of a senior espionage agent, undercover as a cop, who becomes involved in a terrorist campaign in Boston. Less light-hearted, the Flynn books have not been so successful. Thereafter GM took Fletch through a series of books, writing two that happen before *Fletch*. In fact the chronological sequence of the books is at considerable variance to their publication date. Anyone wishing to follow Fletch's life through from his young days should read *Fletch Won*, *Fletch Too*, *Fletch and the Widow Bradley*, *Fletch*, *Carioca Fletch*, *Confess, Fletch*, *Fletch's Fortune*, *Fletch's Moxie* and *Fletch and the Man Who*, where we find Fletch on a Presidential campaign. The second film, *Fletch Lives* (1989), is not based on any of the books. GM later began a new series – "Fletch – The Next Generation" – where an older Fletch meets an escaped convict who claims to be his son. The series involves much the same high jinks but is really only related to the original sequence by name. GM has also written two novels about Skylar Whitfield, a young musical prodigy from small-town Tennessee who also proves to be a smart sleuth. As GM feared, his non-mysteries have been overshadowed by Fletch. Several of them still fall into the crime category, although *Safekeeping*, about the adventures of a ten-year-old who ends up on the run from a Mob hit-man, is also light-hearted. *The Brave* (filmed 1997) is entirely different. It is a tense, moving novel about an unemployed, alcoholic ex-con native American who agrees to be the victim in a "snuff" film in the hope that the money will help his family. All of GM's books cast an oblique eye on American society usually to humorous but sometimes to chilling effect.

Novels

Fletch series: *Fletch* (1974), *Confess Fletch* (1976), *Fletch's Fortune* (1978), *Fletch and the Widow Bradley* (1981), *Fletch's Moxie* (1982), *Fletch and the Man Who* (1983), *Carioca Fletch* (1984), *Fletch Won* (1985), *Fletch Too* (1986).
Son of Fletch series: *Son of Fletch* (1993), *Fletch Reflected* (1994).
Flynn series: *Flynn* (1977), *The Buck Passes Flynn* (1981), *Flynn's In* (1984), *Flynn's World* (1999); also in *Confess Fletch*.
Skylar series: *Skylar* (1995), *Skylar in Yankeeland* (1997).
Non-series: *Running Scared* (1964), *Who Took Toby Rinaldi?* (1980; as *Snatched*, UK 1980), *Safekeeping* (1985), *The Brave* (1991).
Editor. *Last Laughs* (1986).

Full name: Gregory Christopher McDonald.
Where to start: *Fletch*.
Awards: Edgar, best first mystery (1975), best paperback original (1977), Alex Haley award (1992), French Trophée 813 (1997).
Website: <www.gregorymcdonald.com>
Similar stuff: Laurence SHAMES.
Final fact: GM has worked as a Peace Corps volunteer and the civil rights movement and was named Humanitarian of the Year in 1989 and Citizen of the Year in 1990.

John D. MacDonald (1916–86) US

Think of JDM and you probably think of Travis McGee. In fact JDM came to McGee late in life. He had already written over 40 books and several hundred short stories and was loath to accede to publisher pressure to create a regular series character because he felt it would be constraining. He also disliked the limitations of the first-person narrative.

Yet JDM was such a skilled writer and a born storyteller that such restrictions are not evident and JDM's books are every bit as readable now as they were thirty or more years ago. JDM was born in Pennsylvania, but studied at Syracuse University and Harvard. After WW2, in which he served as a lieutenant-colonel in the Office of Strategic Services (the forerunner of the CIA), he settled in Florida and began to write stories for the magazines. Most of his output was crime and detective fiction but he also wrote science fiction, sports stories and westerns. He was extremely prolific and only a handful of these stories have been collected – see *The Good Old Stuff* and *More Good Old Stuff*. As the pulps died, JDM shifted to the paperbacks – in fact about two-thirds of his output was published in the US as paperback originals in editions that are now highly collectible. JDM wrote with all the flair and gusto of the pulp writers, telling a fast-paced action story with recognizable characters in an almost cinematic style. His early paperbacks are all in this mode. The first, *The Brass Cupcake*, is about an ex-cop who left the police force because he would not go along with their corrupt "arrangements" and falls in love with a girl suspected of murdering her aunt. Corruption is a key theme in JDM's books, along with the outsider who will not conform. There are some powerful books from this early period, especially *Dead Low Tide* (the first of his maniac killer novels) and *Murder in the Wind* (where refuge from a hurrican brings a motley crew of characters together). His best known book from the fifties is *The Executioners*, twice filmed as *Cape Fear* (1962 and 1991), one of the all-time great convict-seeks-revenge novels. JDM continued to write one-off novels of powerful suspense throughout the sixties, particularly *The Drowner* and *The Last One Left*, arguably his two best novels. However in 1963 Richard PRATHER, whose books were Fawcett's best sellers, left for another publisher and editor-in-chief Knox Burger persuaded JDM to create a series character. Travis McGee is not an official P.I. He has no licence and he does not look for business. He's an ex-pro-footballer who lives in retirement on his boat, the *Busted Flush*, off the coast of Florida at Fort Lauderdale. He occasionally emerges to help out his friends or a damsel in distress against the forces of corruption. McGee does not take on a job unless he believes in it, and his conviction is what makes his character. There are the inevitable stereotypical P.I. traits – he drinks and complains a lot, he's a bit of a bum, and he charms and beds women (with miraculous therapeutic effect), but McGee is not otherwise like previous detectives. He admits to and recognizes his own weaknesses and vulnerabilities. He knows he could better himself and deals with it by combatting corruption and seeking revenge for those who have been wronged – a true knight errant. The first novel, *The Deep Blue Goodbye*, where he goes on the trail of a thug who had ruined a woman's life, establishes the formula. *Nightmare in Pink* is of historical significance as one of the first major crime novels to include the use of LSD. A few later novels varied the formula and these include some of his best books – *Bright Orange for the Shroud*, *Darker Than Amber* (filmed 1970) and *A Tan and Sandy Silence*. All of the McGee titles are colour-coded. *The Green Ripper*, where McGee seeks revenge for the death of his lover, is the least typical of the series – some love it, some hate it. *The Empty Copper Sea* was adapted for TV (1983) as a pilot for a projected series that never eventuated. With JDM you are always guaranteed a good story, strong action and some homespun philosophy. Even though many are formulaic, JDM knew what made that formula work.

Novels

Travis McGee series: *The Deep Blue Goodbye* (1964), *Nightmare in Pink* (1964), *A Purple Place for Dying* (1964), *The Quick Red Fox* (1964), *A Deadly Shade of Gold* (1965), *Bright Orange for the Shroud* (1965), *Darker Than Amber* (1966), *One Fearful Yellow Eye* (1966), *Pale Gray for Guilt* (1968), *The Girl in the Plain Brown Wrapper* (1968), *Dress Her in Indigo* (1969), *The Long Lavender Look* (1970), *A Tan and Sandy Silence* (1972), *The Scarlet Ruse* (1973), *The Turquoise Lament* (1973), *The Dreadful Lemon Sky* (1974), *The Empty Copper Sea* (1978), *The Green Ripper* (1979), *Free Fall in Crimson* (1981), *Cinnamon Skin* (1982), *The Lonely Silver Rain* (1985).

Non-series: *The Brass Cupcake* (1950), *Judge Me Not* (1951), *Murder for the Bride* (1951), *Weep for Me* (1951), *The Damned* (1952), *Dead Low Tide* (1953), *The Neon Jungle* (1953), *All These Condemned* (1954), *Area of Suspicion* (1954; rev'd 1961), *A Bullet for Cinderella* (1955; as *On the Make*, 1960), *Cry Hard, Cry Fast* (1955), *April Evil* (1956), *Murder in the Wind* (1956; as *Hurricane*, UK 1957), *You Live Once* (1956; as *You Kill Me*, 1961), *Death Trap* (1957), *The Empty Trap* (1957), *The Price of Murder* (1957), *A Man of Affairs* (1957), *Clemmie* (1958), *The Executioners* (1958; as *Cape Fear*, 1962), *Soft Touch* (1958; as *Man-Trap*, UK 1961), *The Deceivers* (1958), *The Beach Girls* (1959), *The Crossroads* (1959), *Deadly Welcome* (1959), *The End of the Night* (1960), *The Only Girl in the Game* (1960), *Slam the Big Door* (1960), *One Monday we Killed them All* (1961), *Where is Janice Gantry?* (1961), *A Flash of Green* (1962), *A Key to the Suite* (1962), *The Drowner* (1963), *On the Run* (1963), *The Last One Left* (1967), *One More Sunday* (1984), *Barrier Island* (1986).

Short Stories. *Border Town Girl* (1956; as *Five Star Fugitive*, UK 1970), *End of the Tiger* (1966), *Seven* (1971), *The Good Old Stuff* (1982), *Two* (1983), *More Good Old Stuff* (1984).

Non-fiction. *No Deadly Drug* (1968).

Editor. *The Lethal Sex* (1959).

Full name: John Dann MacDonald.

Pen-names: John [Wade] Farrell, Robert Henry, John Lane, Scott O'Hara, Peter Reed, Harry Reiser (all on short stories for magazines).

Where to start: Of the non-McGee books, *The Brass Cupcake* and *The Drowner*.

Awards: Benjamin Franklin award, short story (1955), Grand Prix de Littérature Policière Best Foreign (1964), MWA Grand Master (1972), American Book Award (1980).

Books about: *John D. MacDonald and the Colourful World of Travis McGee* by Frank D. Campbell (1977), *John D. MacDonald* by David Geherin (1982), *A Friendship: The Letters of Dan Rowan and John D. MacDonald 1967–74* (1986), *A*

MacDonald Potpourri by Walter & Jean Shine (1988), *The Red Hot Typewriter* by Hugh Merril (2000).

Website: Plenty of fan ones. Try <members.bellatlantic.net/~mwarble/slipf18.htm> for starters.

Similar stuff: JDM establish a template which has inspired many, including Marvin H. Albert, James W. HALL and J.A. JANCE.

Final fact: JDM was going to call his hero Dallas McGee, but the assassination of President Kennedy in Dallas soured that idea so JDM picked the name from a US Air Force base.

Ross Macdonald (1915–83) US/Canada

Even 25 years after his death RM is still regarded amongst the first rank of American crime novelists. William GOLDMAN called his Lew Archer books "the finest series of detective novels ever written by an American." Many regard RM as the banner-man who led crime fiction out of the hard-boiled ghetto into the literary establishment. Whatever the hyperbole, RM's work is distinctive. RM's real name was Kenneth Millar. He was the son of a newspaper editor and though born in California was raised and educated in his parents' native Canada. He married Margaret Sturm in 1938 (see Margaret MILLAR) and became a teacher of English and History before serving in the US Naval Reserve in WW2. After the War he and his family settled in California. His first book, *The Dark Tunnel*, is a Buchanesque pursuit novel of a man trying to outwit a Nazi spy, and is not typical of his later work. More in vogue is *Blue City* (filmed 1986), about a man's return to his home town where he faces a few home truths and turns the stones over on the town's corruptive practices. Like the later Lew Archer novels, here Millar wanted to get at the root causes of crime. These first four books were published under his own name, which he planned to retain for more serious works and adopted a new persona for crime fiction. Although he also wanted to avoid confusion with his wife who was establishing her own reputation, Millar only confused matters more by adopting the name John Macdonald, seemingly unaware of the growing reputation of John D. MacDonald. On later books he expanded this as John Ross Macdonald, but it was not until 1956 that he dropped this on his books in the US (it was retained by UK publishers until 1960). *The Moving Target* (filmed *Harper*, 1966) introduced Lew Archer, many readers' favourite P.I. Archer does not like to reveal much about himself though over time we learn that he was mid-30s in the first novel (and aged steadily). He had worked for the Long Beach police force but had resigned (or been fired) over a matter relating to corruption. He served in Intelligence during the War and then set up as a P.I. in Hollywood. He married Sue, but she soon divorced him. Archer is not embittered, and does not shoulder centuries of angst like other P.I.s. Neither is he an alcoholic. The first few Archer novels are, nevertheless, firmly in the hard-boiled tradition. In *The Moving Target*, Archer is hired to find a missing millionaire and RM uses this theme to explore the millionaire's business practices and how these impact on the world about him. In later novels, however, RM concentrated on family relationships, the interraction between individuals and how and why such relationships fail. Although the end result is inevitably crime, RM preferred to say that he wrote about "human error". This emphasizes the psychological aspect of Archer's detective work, a theme which took a giant leap in the groundbreaking *The Galton Case*, where a mother hires Archer to find her son whom she hasn't seen for over 20 years. This book was written after RM had himself undergone a period of psychotherapy, and it brought a new dimension to his work. Thereafter Archer became as much a psychologist as a P.I., keen to know why the crimes had occurred. From here on RM hit the peak of his career. His books hit the bestseller lists and he rose from cult to classic status. In addition to *Harper* there have been two other Lew Archer films, *The Drowning Pool* (1975) and *The Underground Man* (TV 1974). The latter led to a short TV series (1975).

RM long maintained that he wanted "to deal with life-and-death problems in contemporary society." Those problems are labelled crime fiction by publishers but are really problems of everyday life. By taking this inside-out approach RM legitimized crime fiction. He fused the gritty realism of Hammett with the knight errantry of Chandler but then wove this back into the fabric of society and patterned it with the disintegration of human lives and relationships. He thereby transcended the crime-fiction genre and gave it a respectability it had hitherto lacked in the US.

Novels

Lew Archer series (as John or John Ross Macdonald on first 5 books): *The Moving Target* (1949; as *Harper* by RM, 1966), *The Drowning Pool* (1950), *The Way Some People Die* (1951), *The Ivory Grin* (1952; as *Marked for Murder*, 1953), *Find a Victim* (1954), *The Barbarous Coast* (1956), *The Doomsters* (1958), *The Galton Case* (1959), *The Wycherly Woman* (1961), *The Zebra-Striped Hearse* (1962), *The Chill* (1964), *The Far Side of the Dollar* (1965), *Black Money* (1966), *The Instant Enemy* (1968), *The Goodbye Look* (1969), *The Underground Man* (1971), *Sleeping Beauty* (1973), *The Blue Hammer* (1976).

Chet Gordon series as Kenneth Millar: *The Dark Tunnel* (1944; as *I Die Slowly*, 1955), *Trouble Follows Me* (1946; as *Night Train*, 1955).

Non-series: *The Ferguson Affair* (1960).

Non-series as Kenneth Millar: *Blue City* (1947), *The Three Roads* (1948).

Non-series as John Ross Macdonald: *Meet Me at the Morgue* (1953; as *Experience With Evil*, UK 1954),

Short Stories. *The Name is Archer* (1955; abr. UK 1976), *Lew Archer, Private Investigator* (1977), *Strangers in Town: Three Newly Discovered Mysteries* (2001).

Non-fiction. *On Crime Writing* (1973).

Editor. *Great Stories of Suspense* (1974).

Real name: Kenneth Millar.

Pen-names: John Macdonald, John Ross Macdonald, Ross Macdonald.

Where to start: *The Moving Target* or *The Galton Case.*
Awards: CWA Gold Dagger (1965), Popular Culture Association Award of Excellence (1973), MWA Grand Master (1974), Swedish Academy of Detection, Grand Master (1976), PWA Lifetime achievement (1982).
Books about: *Ross Macdonald* by Jerry Speir (1978), *Self-Portrait: Ceaselessly Into the Past* edited by Ralph Sipper (1981), *Ross Macdonald* by Tom Nolan (1999).
Website: "The Ross Macdonald Files" is at <http://hem1.passagen.se/caltex/index.html>
Similar stuff: Many, but see in particular Jerome CHARYN, Michael COLLINS, Stephen GREENLEAF, Sara PARETSKY.
Final fact: RM's publisher, A.A. Knopf, did not want to publish the first Lew Archer novel urging Millar to concentrate on his more serious work. Millar persisted, though, encouraged by W.H. Auden who advised Millar that he should treat crime fiction the same as any other serious literature.

Mark McGarrity, *see pseudonym* Bartholomew Gill

Jill McGown (b. 1947) UK

Born in Argyll, JM has lived in Northamptonshire since she was ten. She turned to writing full time after she was made redundant from the British Steel Corporation in 1980. Her first novel, *A Perfect Match*, introduced her police detectives Chief Inspector Lloyd (who, like Morse, prefers not to reveal his first name) and his partner (and later lover) Sergeant (later Inspector) Judy Hill. JM did not immediately develop a series, although she has concentrated on these characters since 1992, creating a thoroughly pleasing body of work. Hill is the intuitive one of the partnership, though her insights arise from a logical assessment. Lloyd can be overly dramatic and infuriatingly smug, but his determination and insusceptibility allows him to see beyond the simple solution. The plots of the series are in the traditional English mystery mode but JM accords them a modern treatment and perspective without overt sensationalism. *A Shred of Evidence* was dramatized for TV as *Lloyd and Hill* (2001) with Philip Glenister and Michelle Collins. At the outset JM concentrated more on one-off novels where the perspective was primarily from the victim's viewpoint. *The Stalking Horse* is especially effective, following the actions of a prisoner released after serving 16 years for a crime he did not commit and determined to find out who did. These novels place greater emphasis on suspense and JM has moved back once into that field with the pseudonymous *Hostage to Fortune*, about a disintegrating marriage sparked by a pools win. JM's work deserves to be better known.

Novels

Lloyd & Hill series: *A Perfect Match* (1983), *Redemption* (1988; as *Murder at the Old Vicarage*, US 1989), *Death of a Dancer* (1989; as *Gone to Her Death*, US 1990), *The Murders of Mrs Austin and Mrs Beale* (1991), *The Other Woman* (1992), *Murder*

... *Now and Then* (1993), *A Shred of Evidence* (1995), *Verdict Unsafe* (1996), *Picture of Innocence* (1998), *Plots and Errors* (1999), *Scene of Crime* (2001), *Births Deaths and Marriages* (2002).
Non-series: *Record of Sin* (1985), *An Evil Hour* (1986), *The Stalking Horse* (1987), *Murder Movie* (1990).
as Elizabeth Chaplin: *Hostage to Fortune* (1992).

Pen-name: Elizabeth Chaplin.
Where to start: *A Perfect Match.*
Website: <www.jillmcgown.com> and
<www.twbooks.co.uk/authors/jillmcgown.html>
Similar stuff: Jane ADAMS, Paula GOSLING, Jenny MELVILLE.
Final fact: JM was taught Latin by Colin DEXTER when he was senior classics master at Corby Grammar School.

Patrick O. McGuire *pseudonym, see* James Mitchell

William McIlvanney (b. 1936) UK

The works of poet and novelist WM are perfect examples of where crime fiction and the literary mainstream are but two sides of the same coin. Scottish by birth but of Irish descent, WM grew up in the working-class area of Kilmarnock. His academic achievements were excellent and he became an English teacher, rising to assistant rector of Greenwood Academy before retiring to write full time in 1975. His "straight" work, including *Remedy is None* (1966), *Docherty* (1975) and *The Kiln* (1996), looks at the lives of individuals with the same background as WM, struggling for survival in Scotland's declining industrial years. The same background provides the setting for his detective fiction featuring the highly philosophical Inspector Jack Laidlaw of Glasgow C.I.D. The novels are essentially quests by Laidlaw into the meaning of life and the fabric of society, with the crime being the starting point. In *Laidlaw* it is the search for a rapist whose identity is known from the start. In *The Papers of Tony Veitch* it's to find the murderer of a vagrant. In *Strange Loyalties* it's to understand why Laidlaw's brother was killed. En route WM provides a harsh but reassuring outlook on what makes people keep going. One non-series book, *The Big Man* (filmed 1991), about rivalry between factions of the underworld which becomes focused in a bare-knuckle boxing match, defiantly forges the link between WM's crime fiction and straight fiction.

Novels
Laidlaw series: *Laidlaw* (1977), *The Papers of Tony Veitch* (1983), *Strange Loyalties* (1991).

Awards: Faber Memorial Prize (1967), Whitbread award (1975), CWA Silver Dagger (1977, 1983), Saltire Scottish Book of the Year award (1997).
Similar stuff: Quintin JARDINE, Denise MINA, Ian RANKIN.
Final fact: WM is one of Sean Connery's favourite authors.

Ralph McInerny (b. 1929) US

Born in Minneapolis, but long resident in Notre Dame, Indiana, RM has been a lecturer in philosophy for over 40 years and is an acknowledged expert on St Thomas Aquinas. He has written over 20 volumes on philosophy, ethics and religion and yet that output is more than equalled by his 50-plus mystery novels and collections. He is best known for the series featuring secular priest Father Roger Dowling in the township of Fox River, Illinois. Dowling is a recovering alcoholic and expert in canonical law. His interest in crime is not for retribution but to resolve the spiritual issue. As RM has observed, Dowling may be "soft on crime but he is hard on sin." The regular police presence in each book is Captain Phil Keegan, a former seminarian who thus has sympathies with Dowling but he provides the official cut and thrust to Dowling's theosophical parries. The books are traditional classic cozies but with strong doctrinal themes, and are more insightful than the loosely adapted TV series (1987–91) starring Tom Bosley, which developed a life of its own. RM developed a companion series featuring the cantakerous elderly Sister Mary Teresa, nicknamed "Attila the Nun" because of her forceful character. The puns in the book titles, such as *Nun Plussed*, serve to emphasize the light-hearted nature of this series. Recently RM has found time to create further series. *Cause and Effect* introduced Andrew Broom, one of two rival attorneys in the small town of Wyler, Indiana, which scarcely has enough crime for one law firm. Their animosity is such that when major crimes do erupt it becomes no-holds-barred. *On This Rockne* introduced the Knight Brothers in a series of academic mysteries. One brother is a P.I. while the other is philosophy professor at the University of Notre Dame, Indiana (where RM taught philosophy). RM has written several one-off novels of which *The Red Hat*, about political and theological struggles within the Vatican, shows the serious and deeply committed side of RM's nature. *Still Life* opens yet another series featuring Captain Manfredi of the Fort Elbow, Ohio police force, who is facing retirement when the opportunity arises to look into a 30-year-old crime. *Booklist* summed up RM's work when its reviewer wrote, "No drugs, no guns, no orgies – just good storytelling."

Novels

Father Dowling series: *Her Death of Cold* (1977), *The Seventh Station* (1977), *Bishop as Pawn* (1978), *Lying Three* (1979), *Second Vespers* (1980), *Thicker Than Water* (1981), *A Loss of Patients* (1982), *The Grass Widow* (1983), *Getting a Way with Murder* (1984), *Rest in Pieces* (1985), *The Basket Case* (1987), *Abracadaver* (1989; as *Sleight of Hand*, UK 1989), *Judas Priest* (1991), *Desert Sinner* (1992), *Seed of Doubt* (1993), *A Cardinal Offence* (1994), *The Tears of Things* (1996), *Grave Undertakings* (2000), *Triple Pursuit* (2001).

Father Dowling spin-off series for younger readers: *The Case of the Dead Winner* (1995), *The Case of the Constant Caller* (1995).

Andrew Broom series: *Cause and Effect* (1987), *Body and Soil* (1989), *Frigor Mortis* (1989), *Savings and Loam* (1990), *Mom and Dead* (1994), *Law and Ardor* (1995), *Heirs and Parents* (2000).
Brothers Knight series: *On This Rockne* (1997), *Lack of the Irish* (1998), *Irish Tenure* (1999), *The Book of Kills* (2000), *Emerald Aisle* (2001).
Captain Manfredi series: *Still Life* (2000).
Sister Mary Teresa series as Monica Quill: *Not a Blessed Thing!* (1981), *Let Us Prey* (1982), *And Then There Was Nun* (1984), *Nun of the Above* (1985), *Sine Qua Nun* (1986), *The Veil of Ignorance* (1988), *Sister Hood* (1991), *Nun Plussed* (1993), *Half Past Nun* (1997).
Non-series: *Romanesque* (1978), *The Noonday Devil* (1985), *The Search Committee* (1990), *Easeful Death* (1991), *Infra Dig* (1992), *The Red Hat* (1998).
Non-series as Edward Mackin: *The Nominative Case* (1990).

Short Stories
Father Dowling series: *Four on the Floor* (1989).
Sister Mary Teresa series: *Death Takes the Veil* (2001).

Full name: Ralph Matthew McInerny.
Pen-names: Edward Mackin, Monica Quill.
Where to start: Try the non-series books like *Romanesque* and *The Red Hat* first before easing into the series.
Awards: Bouchercon Committee Lifetime Achievement award (1993).
Website: None specifically for McInerny but there are several devoted to the Father Dowling TV series, including <members.aol.com/sherryberry88/dowling.html>
Similar stuff: Andrew M. Greeley, William X. KIENZLE, Sister Carol Anne O'MARIE.
Final fact: RM was encouraged to write the Father Dowling series by his agent who was reading Harry KEMELMAN's Rabbi Small mysteries.

Donald MacKenzie (1918–93) Canada

DM styled himself as a playboy and a professional thief who, after his final term in prison in 1948, turned to writing. He produced two volumes of autobiography that rather glamorized his life but were critical of the judicial and prison systems, an element that came through strongly in his novel *The Juryman*. His early novels are less idealized and draw from direct experience. They depict petty criminals who are victims of circumstance and fall prey to bigger fish – there is no honour amongst thieves in DM's books. In *Nowhere to Go* (filmed 1958) a thief is sprung from jail by his over-greedy accomplice in order to find where he stashed the money. *Scent of Danger* (filmed 1960 as *Moment of Danger* and (US) *Malaga*) has a jewel thief pursuing his double-crossing partner to Spain. *Zaleski's Percentage* introduced the character of Detective Inspector John Raven of Scotland Yard. Raven is honest but is happy to bend the rules in the interest of justice. He became the central character in a long-running series. Forced to leave the police, Raven becomes a freelance investigator. The best books are *Raven and the Ratcatcher*, *Raven Settles a Score* and

Raven's Revenge which form a trilogy about Raven's battle against a corrupt senior police officer. DM's writing career stretched over nearly forty years – he even turned a hand to a few spy novels, such as *Salute from a Dead Man* – and though his later novels have a more humanizing tone he was still adept at depicting the underworld and the relationship between criminals. Despite a degree of repetition he brought to the field a slightly jaundiced but nevertheless perceptive eye.

Novels

Henry Chalice series: *Salute from a Dead Man* (1966), *Death is a Friend* (1967), *Sleep is for the Rich* (1971).

John Raven series: *Zaleski's Percentage* (1974), *Raven in Flight* (1976), *Raven and the Ratcatcher* (1977), *Raven and the Kamikaze* (1977), *Raven Settles a Score* (1979), *Raven Feathers His Nest* (1978; as *Raven After Dark*, US 1979), *Raven and the Paperhangers* (1980), *Raven's Revenge* (1982), *Raven's Longest Night* (1983), *Raven's Shadow* (1984), *Nobody Here by that Name* (1986), *A Savage State of Grace* (1988), *By Any Illegal Means* (1989), *Loose Cannon* (1991), *The Eyes of the Goat* (1992), *The Sixth Deadly Sin* (1993).

Non-series: *Nowhere to Go* (1956; as *Manhunt*, US 1957), *The Juryman* (1957), *Scent of Danger* (1958; as *Moment of Danger*, 1959), *Dangerous Silence* (1960), *Knife Edge* (1961), *The Genial Stranger* (1962), *Double Exposure* (1963; as *I Spy*, US 1962), *Cool Sleeps Balaban* (1964), *The Lonely Side of the River* (1965), *Salute from a Dead Man* (1966), *Death is a Friend* (1967), *Three Minus Two* (1968; as *The Quiet Killer*, US 1968), *Dead Straight* (1969), *Night Boat from Puerto Vedra* (1970), *The Kyle Contract* (1970), *Sleep is for the Rich* (1971; as *The Chalice Caper*, 1974), *Postscript to a Dead Letter* (1973), *The Spreewald Collection* (1975). *Deep, Dark and Dead* (1978), *The Last of the Boatriders* (1981),

Autobiography. *Occupation: Thief* (1955; as *Fugitives*, UK 1955), *Gentleman at Crime* (1956).

Where to start: *Raven in Flight* or *Raven and the Ratcatcher*.
Similar stuff: E. Richard JOHNSON for other books by a prison inmate; G.F. NEWMAN or Julian RATHBONE for books about corruption.

Jack MacLane *pseudonym, see* Bill Crider

Charlotte Macleod (b. 1922) Canada/naturalized US

CM was dubbed the "Queen of the Whimsical Whodunnits" and the success of her books demonstrated, in the late 1970s, that there was a significant readership for the traditional cozy mystery, and CM's books are pure tinseltown tongue-in-cheek cozies. A Canadian by birth (from New Brunswick), CM lived most of her adult life in Boston where she worked in an advertising agency. Her first books were for children and teenagers, including the mystery adventures *Mystery of the White Knight* (1964) and *Next Door to Danger* (1965). She moved on to books for adults with two series. The first features Peter Shandy, a professor at the Balaclava Agricultural College, renowned for his newly developed rutabaga. In the first book, *Rest You Merry*, Peter becomes entangled in the death of a faculty member's wife, during the course of which he has a romance with the librarian Helen Marsh, who becomes his wife. She's kidnapped in *The Luck Runs Out* though there's more concern for the college's prize-winning pig, which has also gone missing. CM has written herself into the series as Catriona McBogle, who lives on the Maine coast and which allows for adventures away from the college of which *Vane Pursuit* is the best. *The Corpse in Oozak's Pond*, in which the long-dead body of the founder of the College turns up in a local pond, won the Nero Wolfe award and was nominated for an Edgar.

CM's second series features Sarah Kelling, a widow who also ends up married during the first book to art connoisseur Max Bittersohn. These books are ensemble pieces as half the population of Beacon Hill, Boston seems to consist of Sarah's relatives. Sarah and Max usually investigate their mysteries together but Max undertakes his own delving into a stolen *object d'art* in *The Convivial Codfish*. Under her Alisa Craig alias CM has created two even more eccentric series. Madoc Rhys is a Royal Canadian Mounted Policeman in New Brunswick whose wife Janet becomes involved in his quirky if highly atmospheric investigations. Most bizarre of all are the adventures of Osbert Monk, a writer of westerns and his wife Dittany, a member of the Grub-and-Stake Gardening and Roving Club in Lobelia Falls, Ontario. One reviewer summarized CM's books as having "generous dollops of warmth, wit and whimsy". If you like light mystery and romance with larger-than-life characters and totally unrealistic escapism, CM has it by the cartload.

Novels

Peter Shandy series: *Rest You Merry* (1978), *The Luck Runs Out* (1979), *Wrack and Rune* (1982), *Something the Cat Dragged In* (1983), *The Curse of the Giant Hogweed* (1985), *The Corpse in Oozak's Pond* (1986), *Vane Pursuit* (1989), *An Owl Too Many* (1991), *Something in the Water* (1994), *Exit the Milkman* (1996).

Kelling & Bittersohn series: *The Family Vault* (1979), *The Withdrawing Room* (1980), *The Palace Guard* (1981), *The Bilbao Looking Glass* (1983), *The Convivial Codfish* (1984), *The Plain Old Man* (1985), *The Recycled Citizen* (1988), *The Silver Ghost* (1987), *The Gladstone Bag* (1989), *The Resurrection Man* (1992), *The Odd Job* (1995), *The Balloon Man* (1998).

Inspector Rhys series as Alisa Craig: *A Pint of Murder* (1980), *Murder Goes Mumming* (1981), *The Dismal Thing to Do* (1986), *Trouble in the Brasses* (1989), *The Wrong Rite* (1992).

Dittany & Osbert Monk series as Alisa Craig: *The Grub-and-Stakers Move a Mountain* (1981), *The Grub-and-Stakers Quilt a Bee* (1985), *The Grub-and-Stakers Pinch a Poke* (1988), *The Grub-and-Stakers Spin a Yarn* (1990), *The Grub-and-Stakers House a Haunt* (1993).

Non-series as Alisa Craig: *The Terrible Tide* (1983).

Short Stories. *Grab Bag* (1987).

Non-fiction. *Had She But Known: a Biography of Mary Roberts Rinehart* (1994).

Editor. *Mistletoe Mysteries* (1989), *Christmas Stockings* (1991).

Full name: Charlotte Matilda Hughes MacLeod.
Pen-names: Alisa Craig, Matilda Hughes.
Where to start: *The Family Vault* or *The Corpse in Oozak's Pond.*
Awards: Nero Wolfe award (1987), Bouchercon Committee Lifetime achievement (1992), Malice Domestic lifetime achievement (1998), American Mystery Award, best traditional novel (1988, 1989,1991), best paperback original (1989, 1990).
Similar stuff: Carolyn G. HART, Jane LANGTON, Nancy PICKARD.

Robert MacLeod *pseudonym, see* Bill Knox

Mark McShane (b. 1929) Australia/UK

Australian-born, raised in Lancashire, now resident in Spain and with some books published only in France or Germany, MM seems to defy national boundaries just as much as he does genre definitions. His work is wonderfully eccentric and bizarre and ideal for those who want something out of the ordinary. His first book, *The Straight and the Crooked*, about four men who plan a bank robbery, was relatively straightforward but thereafter he explored the unusual. *Séance on a Wet Afternoon* (filmed 1964), his best known book, is about a woman and her husband who plan a kidnapping and predict it in a séance in order to prove her mediumistic powers. *The Passing of Evil* is about a femme fatale. *The Girl Nobody Knows* features former Detective Sergeant Norman Pink who at last stumbles across a clue that may help identify a child killed in a train crash 12 years before. In *The Crimson Madness of Little Doom* an entire village is subjected to anonymous letters. *Ill Met by a Fish Shop on George Street*, despite the title, is a simple but suspenseful story of a murderer who had fled to Australia 30 years before and is suddenly recognized by the one person who can link him to the murder. *The Singular Case of the Multiple Dead*, about an inept gang of crooks, has been compared to *The Lavender Hill Mob*. There's another bunch of losers in *The Imitation Thieves* under his Marc Lovell alias, this time operating in Canada and pursued by another gang of criminals. As Lovell MM explored the pseudo-psychic. *A Presence in the House* features Canadian psychologist Andrew Bailey discovering the true evil of an old house. Bailey returns in *Hand Over Mind* to investigate the case of a girl who is apparently producing cryptic letters through automatic writing. *The Blind Hypnotist* and its sequel *The Second Vanetti Affair* are both novels about the use of hypnotism in manipulating and abducting victims. In *Shadows and Dark Places* a girl believed killed in an explosion starts making phone calls. MM's longest sustained series features the unlikely but highly effective spy "Apple" Porter who is 6 ft 7 in tall and blushes all too easily, yet he still gets the girl. Not all of MM's books are amusing. When the unusual and violent come together they are deeply profound and disturbing. In

Untimely Ripped, a detective discovers the dark side of himself. In *Just a Face in the Dark* a charismatic stranger causes 15 deaths, none by his own hand. His last book, *Mourning Becomes the Hangman,* concerns a man who is wrongfully jailed, escapes to seek revenge but is murdered. MM is the Punch-and-Judy man of surreal crime.

Novels

Myra Savage series: *Séance on a Wet Afternoon* (1961; as *Séance*, US 1962), *Séance for Two* (1972),

Norman Pink series: *The Girl Nobody Knows* (1966), *Night's Evil* (1966), *The Way to Nowhere* (1967).

Jason Galt series as Marc Lovell: *The Blind Hypnotist* (1976), *The Second Vanetti Affair* (1977).

Andrew Bailey series as Marc Lovell: *A Presence in the House* (1972), *Hand Over Mind* (1979).

Appleton Porter series as Marc Lovell: *The Spy Game* (1980), *The Spy With His Head in the Clouds* (1982), *Spy on the Run* (1982), *Apple Spy in the Sky* (1983), *Apple to the Core* (1983), *How Green Was my Apple* (1984), *The Only Good Apple in a Barrel of Spies* (1984), *The Spy Who Got His Feet Wet* (1985), *The Spy Who Barked in the Night* (1986), *Good Spies Don't Grow on Trees* (1986), *That Great Big Trench Coat in the Sky* (1988), *The Spy Who Fell Off the Back of a Bus* (1988), *Ethel and the Naked Spy* (1989), *Comfort Me With Spies* (1990).

Non-series: *The Straight and the Crooked* (1960), *The Passing of Evil* (1961), *Untimely Ripped* (1962), *The Crimson Madness of Little Doom* (1967), *Ill Met by a Fish Shop on George Street* (1968), *The Singular Case of the Multiple Dead* (1969), *The Man Who Left Well Enough* (1971), *The Othello Complex* (France 1974), *The Headless Snowman* (France 1974), *Lashed but not Leashed* (1976), *Lifetime* (1977), *The Hostage Game* (1979), *The Halcyon Way* (1979), *Just a Face in the Dark* (1987), *Once Upon a Fairy Tale* (1990), *Mourning Becomes the Hangman* (1991).

Non-series as Marc Lovell: *The Ghost of Megan* (1968; as *Memory of Megan*, 1970), *The Imitation Thieves* (1971), *An Enquiry Into the Existence of Vampires* (US 1974; as *Vampires in the Shadows*, UK 1976), *Dreamers in a Haunted House* (1975), *The Guardian Spectre* (1977), *Fog Sinister* (1977), *A Voice from the Living* (1978), *And They Say You Can't Buy Happiness* (1979), *Shadows and Dark Places* (1980), *The Last Séance* (1982), *Looking for Kingford* (Germany, 1983)

Pen-name: Marc Lovell.

Where to start: *The Girl Nobody Knows* and *The Singular Case of the Multiple Dead* for sheer contrast.

Similar stuff: Difficult, but try Jerome CHARYN and Peter DICKINSON.

Final fact: MM holds the record for the longest word ever used in a crime fiction novel. Praetertranssubstantiationalistically appears in *Untimely Ripped* and is 37 letters long. It means "surpassing the Roman Catholic ritual of turning the holy communion bread and wine into the body and blood of Christ."

Barry Maitland (b. 1941) UK/Australia

It's tempting to say that an architect should have well structured novels, but in the case of BM that's true. Born in Scotland, raised in London, educated at Cambridge and now professor of architecture at the

University of Newcastle in Australia, BM has written five highly acclaimed crime novels. *The Marx Sisters* introduced the team of Detective Chief Inspector David Brock of Scotland Yard and his young protege Sergeant Kathy Kolla. The novel starts deceptively as a traditional English mystery with Kolla investigating the death of an elderly lady who lived with her two sisters, but as the story develops so the atmosphere darkens. This compelling novel was shortlisted for the John Creasey award. The same darkening mystery enshrouds *The Malcontenta*, which won the Australian Ned Kelly award. These books are as much whydunits as whodunits and BM's eye for architecture and landscape creates strong imagery, which adds to the plot's suspense. The later novels have continued to deliver, making this a striking new series.

Novels

Brock & Kolla series: *The Marx Sisters* (1994), *The Malcontenta* (1995), *All My Enemies* (1996), *The Chalon Heads* (1999), *Silvermeadow* (2002).

Awards: Ned Kelly award (1996).

Similar stuff: Dorothy SIMPSON, Ruth RENDELL.

Final fact: Amongst BM's other books is a volume on shopping malls.

John Malcolm (b. 1936) UK

JM is an expert on antiques and founder of the British Antique Collectors Club. Under his own name of John Andrews he has written volumes about antique furniture and this expertise is abundant in his series featuring art investment specialist Tim Simpson. Tim's job is to advise his bank on works of art for investment and as a consequence he becomes involved in investigating forgeries, art theft and even murder. Unlike Jonathan GASH's Lovejoy, who may be an antiques expert but is out for what he can get, Simpson is trying to foil the art thiefs and the intriguing plots and wealth of knowledge makes this what the *Library Journal* called "one of the finest series being written today."

Novels

Tim Simpson series: *A Back Room in Somers Town* (1984), *The Godwin Sideboard* (1984), *The Gwen John Sculpture* (1985), *Whistler in the Dark* (1986), *Gothic Pursuit* (1987), *Mortal Ruin* (1988), *The Wrong Impression* (1990), *Sheep, Goats and Soap* (1991), *A Deceptive Appearance* (1992), *The Burning Ground* (1993), *Hung Over* (1994), *Into the Vortex* (1996), *Simpson's Homer* (2001).

Full name: John Malcolm Andrews.

Similar stuff: Iain PEARS, Derek WILSON.

Final fact: JM is almost certainly the only British writer of crime fiction to have received part of his education in Uruguay.

Michael Malone (b. 1942) US

Crime fiction magus Otto Penzler called *Uncivil Seasons* "one of the few nearly perfect novels in the history of detective fiction". It introduced two police detectives in Hillston, North Carolina (MM's home state): the wayward Lieutenant Justin Savile, a womanizer who loves the bottle, and the arrogant and impatient redneck Police Chief Cuddy Mangum. Despite their faults the two are die-hard cops, determined to root out the truth, no matter what the consequences. Both *Uncivil Seasons* and its sequel *Time's Witness* depict a North Carolina struggling to shake off the shackles of the past whilst uncertain how to face the future and Mangum and Savile have an uphill struggle with local prejudices and dirty tricks. MM had started writing while at University (Harvard) studying for his PhD in English. His first book *Painting the Roses Red* (1975), was a typical coming-of-age novel set in a graduate school, but he subsequently wrote several humorous small-town novels including *Dingley Falls* (1980), *Handling Sin* (1986) and *Foolscap* (1991). Whilst serving as writer-in-residence at the University of Pennsylvania he was invited to become the head writer on the daytime soap drama *One Life to Live*. He remained with the show for six years, 1991–6, radically improving its ratings and winning an Emmy Award (1994). That period temporarily robbed crime fiction of a vibrant talent, but he has now returned to the field. He has written a cluster of short stories, including the award-winning "Red Clay" (1996), which steadily unfolds the truth about a notorious 1959 murder involving a fading movie star. He has also written the third in the Savile and Mangum series, *First Lady*, where they pit their wits against a serial killer. Hopefully there will be more to come.

Novels

Mangum & Savile series: *Uncivil Seasons* (1983), *Time's Witness* (1989), *First Lady* (2001).

Full name: Michael Christopher Malone.
Awards: Edgar, best short story (1997).
Website: (unofficial)
<http://members.tripod.com/magnifmalonian/index_m.htm>
Similar stuff: K.C. CONSTANTINE, Stephen GREENLEAF.
Final fact: MM's PhD was on archetypes of innocence and eroticism in American film and was published as *Heroes of Eros* in 1979.

Shane Maloney (b. 1953) Australia

SM's work is only now being discovered in the US and Europe but he has already established a strong following in Australia for his humorous and perceptive novels of political chicanery featuring Murray Whelan and set in Melbourne during the 1980s. Whelan is a political minder and is sent by his boss, Angelo Agnelli, on various missions to investigate likely trouble spots and ward off bad news. In Whelan's world, though, that bad news comes in big packages. In *Stiff* it's the frozen body of the Turkish manager of a meat-packing plant. In *The Brush-Off* it's an artist found dead in the moat of a public arts building. In *Nice Try* it's murder amongst the athletes during the bid for the Olympics. In *The Big Ask* it's a corrupt trade union. Maloney maintains a hard-boiled interior to the books whilst sugar-coating them in his brand of wit and satire. He has himself led a varied life from Director of the Melbourne Comedy Festival to the Cultural Director of Melbourne's Olympic bid to a rock concert promoter and a senior arts officer, so he writes from experience.

Novels

Murray Whelan series: *Stiff* (1994), *The Brush-Off* (1996), *Nice Try* (1998), *The Big Ask* (2001).

Awards: Ned Kelly, best novel (1997).
Similar stuff: Try Jon CLEARY.
Final fact: SM was once a contestant on the Australian TV version of "Sale of the Century".

Jessica Mann (b. 1937) UK

Although JM's main continuing series features archaeologists, allowing JM to demonstrate her expertise in the subject (she has degrees in archaeology and Anglo-Saxon), they are not archaeological mysteries like, say, the work of Aaron ELKINS. They should be seen in the context of JM's non-series works, most of which explore attitudes and conventions in society, often within the enclosed worlds of institutions big or small. For instance her first book, *A Charitable End*, is about decidedly uncharitable exploits amongst a Scottish charity. The two Thea Crawford novels depict the antagonisms and conflicts that arise at a university following her appointment as professor of archaeology. *Captive Audience*, when a body is discovered during student riots, is especially effective. *No Man's Island*, which sets Crawford's student Tamara Hoyland off on her own adventures as something of an undercover agent, takes place on a remote British island where the locals find ways to stop the government usurping the island for oil. *The Sting of Death* has a town split into factions over the development of a campsite. In all of these books JM establishes complex relationships and strong motives for corruption and crime. Other books focus these motives on the individual. *Mrs Knox's Profession*, for example, follows the disintegration of a woman in a mid-life crisis when a child she is looking after is kidnapped. *Funeral Sites* pits a woman against her brother-in-law, an ambitious politician, whom she is convinced murdered his wife. Several of JM's books are set in Cornwall, where she now lives, though she was born and raised in London. She is a journalist, reviewer and broadcaster and has written a study of five classic British female crime fiction writers *Deadlier Than the Male*.

Novels

Thea Crawford series: *The Only Security* (1973; as *Troublecross*, US 1973), *Captive Audience* (1975).

Tamara Hoyland series: *Funeral Sites* (1981), *No Man's Island* (1983), *Grave Goods* (1984), *A Kind of Healthy Grave* (1986), *Death Beyond the Nile* (1988),

Faith, Hope and Homicide (1991).
Non-series: *A Charitable End* (1971), *Mrs Knox's Profession* (1972), *The Sticking Place* (1974), *The Eighth Deadly Sin* (1976), *The Sting of Death* (1978), *Telling Only Lies* (1992), *A Private Inquiry* (1996), *The Survivor's Revenge* (1998), *Under a Dark Sun* (2000), *Hanging Fire* (2000), *The Voice from the Grave* (2002).
Non-fiction. *Deadlier Than the Male* (1981).

Where to start: *Funeral Sites.*
Similar stuff: Amanda CROSS, Paula GOSLING, Susan MOODY.
Final fact: JM has taken part in the radio programme *Round Britain Quiz.*

Dan J. Marlowe (1914–86) US

DJM's books all appeared first as paperback originals and are less easy to come by today though they are revered by collectors. Although he wrote his books entirely to formula – they are all hard-hitting violent gangster/P.I. escapades – he packed them with so much energy that they nearly self-destruct. His most memorable book was *The Name of the Game is Death* which Bill PRONZINI called "about as good as original paperback writing can get." It was the first of his Earl Drake novels. Drake (originally called Chet Arnold) was a vicious killer and bank robber. He's injured in a robbery and his partner escapes, mailing money back to Drake. Then the money stops coming. Once recovered, Drake goes in search of his partner, leading to a cataclysmic climax. DJM was nothing like his characters. He was an accountant and city councillor, serving as mayor of Harbor Beach, Michigan. He turned to writing when his wife died in 1957. His first series of books featured the super-tough hotel detective Johnny Killain, as likely to punch his way through a door as open it. There was no sophistication in these books but they were very popular, not least amongst prison inmates. DJM was contacted by bank robber Al Nussbaum (1935–96) who, in a succession of letters, gave him the inside dope on safe-cracking, ballistics, alarm systems – the works. Thereafter DJM's books became so authentic that he had to dumb them down rather than be charged with writing a do-it-yourself bank-robbing guide. His newly acquired knowledge is very evident in the bank-heist novels *Four for the Money* and *One Endless Hour*. The latter reintroduced Earl Drake. Having undergone plastic surgery he is now known as "the man with nobody's face". He becomes an honourable villain, if there is such a thing, pitting himself against the Mafia. The government decided he was safer on their side and in *Flashpoint*, which won an Edgar, he became an undercover agent infiltrating a gang of Middle-Eastern terrorists. Although the series weakened over time there is still plenty of action. Of the non-series books the best is probably *The Vengeance Man*, where a man ends up on the run after killing his wife and her lover.

Novels

Johnny Killain series: *Doorway to Death* (1959), *Killer With a Key* (1959), *Doom Service* (1960), *The Fatal Frails* (1960), *Shake a Crooked Town* (1961).

Earl Drake series: *The Name of the Game is Death* (1962; as *Operation Overkill*, UK 1973), *One Endless Hour* (1969; as *Operation Endless Hour*, UK 1975), *Operation Fireball* (1969), *Flashpoint* (1970; as *Operation Flashpoint*, UK 1972), *Operation Breakthrough* (1971), *Operation Drumfire* (1972), *Operation Checkmate* (1972), *Operation Stranglehold* (1973), *Operation Whiplash* (1973), *Operation Hammerlock* (1974), *Operation Deathmaker* (1975), *Operation Counterpunch* (1976).
Non-series: *Backfire* (1961), *Strong Arm* (1963), *Never Live Twice* (1964), *Death Deep Down* (1965), *Four for the Money* (1966), *The Vengeance Man* (1966), *The Raven is a Blood Red Bird* with William Odell (1967), *Route of the Red Gold* (1967).
as Gar Wilson: *Guerilla Games* (1982).

Full name: Dan James Marlowe.
Pen-names: Albert Avellano (in magazines), Gar Wilson (house name).
Where to start: *The Name of the Game is Death*.
Awards: Edgar, best paperback original (1971).
Similar stuff: Ed LACY, Evan Hunter [Ed MCBAIN].
Final fact: In gratitude to Al Nussbaum, DJM aided him at his parole hearing and helped him get started as a short-story writer. In turn Nussbaum cared for DJM in his final years after a stroke.

Margaret Maron US

Born and raised in North Carolina, MM met her husband (a former Naval officer) in the Pentagon. After a tour of duty in Naples, they settled in New York where he taught art at Brooklyn College, while she gave herself a writing course. Though MM had aspired to be a poet, she began to sell stories, mostly mysteries, to the magazines, starting with "The Death of Me" (*AHMM*, 1968). After twelve years she graduated to novels. *One Coffee With* introduced NYPD Lieutenant Sigrid Harald, an emotionally insecure individual whose cool-as-ice demeanour belies the turmoil within. MM regards the series as one long serial – in fact the first eight books span only one year and have reached a natural conclusion. The books benefit from being read in sequence, as clues for a crime in a later book are planted in earlier volumes and the characters do evolve and change. In the first volume, involving a murder at a College's Art Department, Harald meets the College's Head, Oscar Nauman, and they later become lovers. During the year covered by the books Harald's character grows but a tragedy in the eighth volume puts her spiritual and physical strength to the test. In the early eighties MM moved back to North Carolina and wrote a novel, *Bloody Kin*, set on a version of her old family farm. Originally a one-off book – it concerns Kate Honeycutt, who returns to North Carolina after her husband's death but discovers he was murdered – MM subsequently used the same setting and some of the same characters in her first Deborah Knott novel, *Bootlegger's Daughter*. This book made a clean sweep of the premier American mystery awards, something not previously achieved. The character had earlier appeared in a short story, "Deborah's Judgement" (1991), which won both the Agatha and Macavity awards, thus giving the series an auspicious start. Knott is a North Carolina attorney (who rises to Judge). She is the opposite of Harald – confident, assured, experienced and the first-person narrative of the stories provides more certainty to her actions. Through this multi-award winning series, MM has evoked a strong Southern setting and an absorbing world.

Novels

Sigrid Harald series: *One Coffee With* (1981), *Death of a Butterfly* (1984), *Death in Blue Folders* (1985), *The Right Jack* (1987), *Baby Doll Games* (1988), *Corpus Christmas* (1989), *Past Imperfect* (1991), *Fugitive Colors* (1995).
Deborah Knott series: *Bootlegger's Daughter* (1992), *Southern Discomfort* (1993), *Shooting at Loons* (1994), *Up Jumps the Devil* (1996), *Killer Market* (1997), *Home Fires* (1998), *Storm Track* (2000), *Uncommon Clay* (2001), *Slow Dollar* (2002).
Non-series: *Bloody Kin* (1985).

Short Stories. *Lieutenant Harald and the Treasure Island Treasure* (booklet 1991), *Shoveling Smoke* (1997).
Where to start: *Bootlegger's Daughter*.
Awards: Agatha and Macavity, best short story (1992), Agatha, best novel (1993, 1997, 2001), Anthony, best novel (1993), Edgar, best novel (1993), Macavity, best novel (1993).
Website: <www.margaretmaron.com>
Similar stuff: Charlaine Harris, Joan HESS.
Final fact: Living in the country MM has become fascinated with orb-weaving spiders and has documented on film the entire life cycle of a Black-and-Yellow Argiope from the moment it emerges from the egg sac through courtship and mating to senility and death.

William Marshall (b. 1944) Australia

WM writes amongst the most anarchic police procedurals available. In fact police procedural is not really apt, but then most of WM's books defy simplistic categorization. After a few years as a playwright and journalist, WM moved to Hong Kong and there completed his first novel, *The Fire Circle*, a murder mystery set in the Australian outback. Suitably inspired, after a couple of war novels, WM launched into his series set at Yellowthread Street, a police station in Hong Kong. The first novel has no real plot but takes the reader at pell-mell pace through a whirlwind night at the precinct where anything can happen. WM's characters – DCI Harry Feiffer, and DIs O'Yee, Spencer and Auden – are wildly eccentric and take the bizarre cases in their stride. In *Gelignite* they encounter a serial bomber. In *The Hatchet Man* a psychotic starts chopping people up at the cinema. In *Thin Air* a maniac kills all the passengers on an airline flight. In *Skullduggery* a raft is washed ashore bearing a man's skeleton and an assortment of oddities. *Perfect End* has a series of police murders take place during a typhoon. That book is not the end, though, as WM has continued the series through "to the end" and the handover of Hong

Kong to China. He also wrote two similar novels set at a police station in the Philippines, but genius is a rare commodity and doesn't spread too thin. Having moved to New York at the end of the eighties, WM began a new series set in the City in the 1880s and featuring "modern" detective, Virgil Tillman, and his intellectually challenged partner Ned Muldoon. The first book, *The New York Detective*, is extremely evocative of the period. It remains to be seen whether WM will write more.

Novels

Yellowthread series: *Yellowthread Street* (1975), *Gelignite* (1976), *The Hatchet Man* (1976), *Thin Air* (1977), *Skulduggery* (1979), *Sci Fi* (1981), *Perfect End* (1981), *War Machine* (1982), *The Far Away Man* (1984), *Roadshow* (1985), *Head First* (1986), *Frogmouth* (1987), *Out of Nowhere* (1988), *Inches* (1994), *Nightmare Syndrome* (1997), *To the End* (1998).

Manila Bay series: *Manila Bay* (1986), *Whisper* (1988).

Virgil Tillman series: *The New York Detective* (1989), *Faces in the Crowd* (1991).

Non-series: *The Fire Circle* (1969).

Full name: William Leonard Marshall.

Where to start: *Yellowthread Street.*

Similar stuff: Peter DICKINSON for eccentricity, Gavin Black for Far East, Caleb CARR and Maan MEYERS for old New York.

Final fact: WM believes he is the only person who was born in Australia, raised in Europe and lived in Asia to have set a book in New York in 1883.

Richard Marsten, *see pseudonym* Ed McBain

Edward [or A. E.] Marston (b. 1940) UK

EM is the best-known pen-name of Welsh author and playwright Keith Miles. He has had a diverse, varied and prolific writing career. After studying at University College, Oxford and teaching modern history at Wulfrun College, Wolverhampton for three years, EM turned to writing full-time. He had already produced, written and appeared in several plays while at university and had also taught drama to inmates at Winson Green prison. He was approached by the BBC, which marked the start of his extensive career as a writer of plays for radio and television – over 40 original plays plus some 600 individual episodes for drama series, in addition to plays he has written or adapted for the theatre. These plays included *Spiggott*, an occasional series for radio (between 1972 and 1981) about Bow Street Runner Ben Spiggott in the 1820s, and *Crime Buster* (1968) a 13-part series for TV, about journalist Ray Saxon who involves himself in uncovering shady practices in various sports. Miles is as fascinated with sports almost as much as the theatre and has written books about snooker, athletics and rugby, and when he came to write fiction his first series featured Alan Saxon, a professional golfer. *Bullet Hole* involves greed, ambition, sex and murder at the British Open at St Andrews. The series took Saxon to other tournaments across the globe but it stopped after four books, though Miles completed a fifth title, *Bermuda Grass*. An earlier projected fifth title, *Stone Dead* was issued under the name Martin Inigo and reworked to feature Don Hawker, a former Olympic athlete turned sports reporter. Its sequel *Touch Play* was set in the world of professional tennis. During this time Miles also wrote over twenty books for children many of which had mystery elements tied in with the sporting and other adventures.

By now Miles had turned to the historical mystery and the Marston persona was created. His first series, starting with *The Queen's Head*, is set in the world of the Elizabethan theatre and involves Lord Westfield's Men, a group of actors who perform in the courtyards of inns and are managed by Nicholas Bracewell. There is often antagonism between the actors and dramatists and the theatre allowed EM to explore a wide cross-section of the Elizabethan world from the Queen down to the lowliest subject. EM brings the Elizabethan world alive with all its intrigue, eccentricities, wit and lustiness. The seventh book in the series, *The Roaring Boy*, was shortlisted for the Edgar award. *The Wolves of Savernake* is set in the years after the Norman conquest of England and introduced a new series featuring Norman soldier Ralph Delchard and Breton-Saxon lawyer Gervase Bret. They are part of the commission surveying England and compiling what became the Domesday Book, an excellent framework for encountering and resolving crimes. EM has recently started three more series. Under his own name he has written about Merlin Richards, a Welsh architect who emigrates to the United States in the late 1920s to become a student of Frank Lloyd Wright. His commissions, in the years leading to the Depression, invariably bring him into contact with crime and corruption. As EM he has started a series with another architect, Christopher Redmayne, who has the opportunity to help rebuild London after the Great Fire in 1666. Another colourful period, EM captures the excitement, gaiety and freedom following Charles II's restoration. Through Redmayne, and his friend Constable Jonathan Bale, EM peels back the layers of society and reveals the turbulence beneath. Finally, as Conrad Allen, he has started a nautical series set on the great ocean liners in the Edward period and involving American P.I. George Porter Dillman. EM has an eye for period detail and creates mysteries arising out of the fabric of their time.

Novels

Nicholas Bracewell series: *The Queen's Head* (1988), *The Merry Devils* (1989), *The Trip to Jerusalem* (1990), *The Nine Giants* (1991), *The Mad Courtesan* (1992), *The Silent Woman* (1992), *The Roaring Boy* (1995), *The Laughing Hangman* (1996), *The Fair Maid of Bohemia* (1997), *The Wanton Angel* (1999), *The Devil's Apprentice* (2001), *The Bawdy Basket* (2002).

Domesday series: *The Wolves of Savernake* (1993), *The Ravens of Blackwater* (1995), *The Dragons of Archenfield* (1995), *The Lions of the North* (1996), *The*

Serpents of Harbledown (1996), *The Stallions of Woodstock* (1997), *The Hawks of Delamere* (1998), *The Wildcats of Exeter* (1999), *The Foxes of Warwick* (1999), *The Owls of Gloucester* (2000), *The Elephants of Norwich* (2000).
Restoration series: *The King's Evil* (1999), *Amorous Nightingale* (2000), *The Repentant Rake* (2001).
Alan Saxon series as Keith Miles: *Bullet Hole* (1986), *Double Eagle* (1987), *Green Murder* (1990), *Flagstick* (1991), *Bermuda Grass* (2002).
Merlin Richard series as Keith Miles: *Murder in Perspective* (1997), *Saint's Rest* (1999).
Don Hawker series as Martin Inigo: *Stone Dead* (1991), *Touch Play* (1991).
George Dillman series as Conrad Allen: *Murder on the Lusitania* (2000), *Murder on the Mauretania* (2001), *Murder on the Minnesota* (2002).
Real name: Keith Miles.
Pen-names: Conrad Allen, Martin Inigo, A.E. Marston, Edward Marston, Christopher T. Mountjoy.
Where to start: *The Queen's Head*.
Website: <www.twbooks.co.uk/authors/aemarston.html> for Marston titles only.
Similar stuff: Paul DOHERTY, Patricia FINNEY, Susanna GREGORY, Philip Gooden.
Final fact: Keith Miles was teaching his drama group at Winson Green Prison on the very evening before the last man was executed there in November 1962. To keep their minds off the occasion they read *Cat on a Hot Tin Roof*.

Dominic Martell *pseudonym, see* Sam Reaves

Sarah J. Mason (b. 1949) UK

The pleasure of SJM's fiction is that she likes to take the traditional and convert it into the eccentric. This has grown over time. Her first book, *Let's Talk of Wills*, was fairly conventional set in an old English country house cut off by flood waters. Shortly after, through the recommendation of her editor, SJM took over from Hampton Charles (see James MELVILLE) on the continuation of Heron CARVIC's Miss Seeton series. She wrote these under the alias Hamilton Crane, writing more novels than the previous two authors in total and developing Miss Seeton's eccentric ways and her relationship with Chief Superintendent Delphick of Scotland Yard. SJM has now brought this series to a close with a final flourish in which she takes Miss Seeton back to her prime of life when she becomes involved with the Ministry of Information during WW2. Under her own name SJM began her own series in 1993 featuring two oddly matched police detectives, Superintendent Trewley and his new female assistant Sergeant Stone. Like the Miss Seeton books, these stories set up unusual deaths and bizarre circumstances. In the first a body is found in a maze during a summer festival. In the next a body turns up on the frozen fish counter at a grocer's. A baker choked to death by her own rising dough, a research chemist killed by a gas leak, an optician kidnapped after a bank robbery – all these are part of the crazy world of Trewley and Stone. The *pièce de resistance*, though, has to be in *Sew Easy to Kill*, where SJM devises a sewing machine as a murder weapon. As a result of the CWA's conference in Kent in 1997, SJM was able to visit the vessel her father commanded at Dunkirk. This led to *Miss Seeton's Finest Hour* having a meticulously researched WW2 setting and SJM's subsequent interests have continued in that direction.

Novels

Trewley & Stone series: *Murder in the Maze* (1993), *Frozen Stiff* (1993; as *Deep-frozen Death*, 1999), *Corpse in the Kitchen* (1993; as *Corpse in the Case*, 1999), *Dying Breath* (1994; as *Murder from Memory*, 1999), *Sew Easy to Kill* (1996), *Seeing is Deceiving* (1997).

Miss Seeton series as Hamilton Crane: *Miss Seeton Cracks the Case* (1991), *Miss Seeton Paints the Town* (1991), *Hands Up, Miss Seeton* (1992), *Miss Seeton by Moonlight* (1992), *Miss Seeton Rocks the Cradle* (1992), *Miss Seeton Goes to Bat* (1993), *Miss Seeton Plants Suspicion* (1993), *Starring Miss Seeton* (1994), *Miss Seeton Undercover* (1994), *Miss Seeton Rules* (1994), *Sold to Miss Seeton* (1995), *Sweet Miss Seeton* (1996), *Bonjour, Miss Seeton* (1997), *Miss Seeton's Finest Hour* (1999).

Non-series: *Let's Talk of Wills* (1985).

Full name: Sarah Jill Mason.
Pen-name: Hamilton Crane.
Where to start: *Murder in the Maze*.
Similar stuff: Catherine AIRD, K.K. BECK, Charlotte MACLEOD.
Final fact: SJM recalls that her first "criminal" experience was when she was taken from her pram outside a sweetshop by a bewhiskered tramp who said he only wanted to cuddle her, but he was forcibly driven away by SJM's mother.

Sujata Massey (b. 1964) UK/India

Although SM was born in Britain and holds British citizenship, her father is Indian, her mother German and she was educated, from the age of five, in America. To cap all that her series is about Rei Shimura, a young antiques dealer of mixed Japanese-American parentage, who leaves California to settle in Japan both as an antiques dealer and a teacher. SM had taught English in Japan for two years and became steeped in the culture. In the first book, *The Salary Man's Wife*, a beautiful woman is murdered in a holiday inn and Rei is drawn into the investigation. Although the series is modelled on the conventional English mystery format, its Japanese setting allows SM to blend the modern with the traditional. The writing is like silk drawn over razor blades, serene yet deadly. Each of the first four books was nominated for one or more awards and the series has so far won both the Agatha and Macavity. SM lives in Baltimore and was for five years a reporter for the *Baltimore Evening Sun*. She had written her first novel while living in Japan and upon her return to the US entered it for the Malice Domestic Unpublished Writers Contest in 1996, which she won, selling the book to a publisher six weeks later.

Novels

Rei Shimura series: *The Salaryman's Wife* (1997), *Zen Attitude* (1998), *The Flower Master* (1999), *The Floating Girl* (2000), *The Bride's Kimono* (2001).

Awards: Agatha, best first novel (1998), Macavity, best novel (2000).
Website: <www.interbridge.com/sujata/>
Similar stuff: James MELVILLE and Janwillem VAN DE WETERING for books by western writers set in modern-day Japan, plus works by Japanese writers Seichō MATSUMOTO, Shizuko NATSUKI and Masako TOGAWA.
Final fact: SM travelled extensively with her parents as a child and this left her with a lasting desire to want to tell stories set in other places.

Lia Matera (b. 1952) Canada

Born in Vancouver, LM came to the US in 1958. She received her law degree from Hastings College, San Francisco and became a practising attorney and a teaching fellow at Stanford Law School. Both of her series of books are about San Francisco-based attorneys, though the characters are very different. Willa Jannson first appears in *Where Lawyers Fear to Tread*, nominated for both an Anthony and Macavity award. In this book she is still a law student struggling to find her own voice beside her radically left-wing parents and to live up to her, and their, ideals. She becomes a suspect in the death of a law review editor. Willa's life never runs smooth. She keeps getting into trouble because of her views, and the generation conflict continues to cause problems in later volumes. Laura Di Palma, LM's other attorney, is the opposite. A corporate lawyer, she is assured, confident, high profile and prepared to go those extra steps. The cases she takes on are darker, more controversial and, though her life doesn't run smoothly either, that's her choice. Four of LM's books have been nominated for major mystery awards, and she won the Shamus for her short story "Dead Drunk", which can be found in her collection *Counsel for the Defense*. That volume also includes "Dream Lawyer", which brings her two main characters together.

Novels

Willa Jansson series: *Where Lawyers Fear to Tread* (1987), *A Radical Departure* (1988), *Hidden Agenda* (1988), *Prior Convictions* (1991), *Last Chants* (1996), *Star Witness* (1997), *Havana Twist* (1998).
Laura Di Palma series: *The Smart Money* (1988), *The Good Fight* (1990), *A Hard Bargain* (1992), *Face Value* (1994), *Designer Crimes* (1995).
Short Stories. *Counsel for the Defense* (2000).
Editor. *Irreconcilable Differences* (1999).

Where to start: *Where Lawyers Fear to Tread.*
Awards: Shamus, best short story (1997).
Website: <www.scruz.net/~lmatera/liamatera.html>
Similar stuff: Lisa SCOTTOLINE.

Seichō Matsumoto (1909–92) Japan

SM was the first writer of modern crime fiction in Japan, rebelling against the popular supernatural theme of pre-WW2 mysteries. From a working-class background in Kokura, SM held a variety of jobs until he began writing in 1950, winning the prestigious Akutagawa prize for *Aru Kokura nikki den* ("A Story of the Kokura Diary", 1952), about a man researching another's life. He wrote in a variety of fields, mostly historical, but began writing mysteries in 1955. His collection of "social detective" stories, *Kao* ("The Face', 1956), which emphasized the causes and motives for crime, won the Mystery Writers of Japan prize in 1957. He had considerable success with the best-selling *Ten to sen* (*Points and Lines*) where the persistent Inspector Toragay is convinced that what appears to be a double suicide is in fact a double murder. A sequel, *Jikan no Shuzoku* ("The Spirit of the Times", 1962) remains untranslated. In fact few of SM's forty-plus mysteries have been translated into English, though a dozen or so have been made into films, of which *Harikomi* (1957, aka *Stakeout*) and *Kuroi gashû: Aru sonan* (1961 aka *Death on the Mountain*) are still commercially available. The book many consider his best, *Suna no utsawa*, is available as *Inspector Imanishi Investigates.* Through solid basic detective work and intriguing clues, including a particular Japanese dialect, Imanishi works his way through the strata of Japanese society in pursuit of his murderer. A collection of six stories, including "The Face", is available as *The Voice.*

Novels *(in translation only). Points and Lines* (Japan 1957; US 1970), *Inspector Imanishi Investigates* (Japan 1961; US 1989).
Short Stories. *The Voice* (US 1989).

Real name: Matsumoto Kiyoharu.
Pen-name: Seichō Matsumoto.
Awards: Akutagawa Literary Prize (1952), Mystery Writers of Japan Prize (1957).
Similar stuff: Shizuko NATSUKI, Masako TOGAWA, Akimitsu Takagi, plus works by Sujata MASSEY and James MELVILLE.
Final fact: SM owned his own film company, Kiri Productions, and supervised the production of films based on his work.

M.R.D. Meek (b. 1918) UK

MRDM turned to writing crime fiction late in life, after her retirement as a solicitor. She was born in Scotland and worked as a secretary and clerk before WW2, but after the War studied law and earned a law degree with honours in 1966. Her books feature solicitor Lennox Kemp who in the hard-to-find first book, *With Flowers That Fell*, is disbarred by the Law Society and turns to working for a detective agency. Most of his work involves divorce or other marital problems and even as he works his way back as a solitor, being reinstated in *The Split Second*, his cases still frequently revolve around family discord out of which Kemp tries to salvage what he can. MRDM builds concisely plotted stories with sharp observation and finely drawn characters. We don't learn much about Kemp himself – he's "short, fat and forty" with an interest in women – though he remains single until *Postscript to Murder* – but through him we learn a lot about others. The series has been likened to the work of P.D. JAMES with a dash of Ross MACDONALD. MRDM has also written two mysteries as Alison Cairns.

Novels

Lennox Kemp series: *With Flowers That Fell* (1983), *The Sitting Ducks* (19840, *Hang the Consequences* (1984), *The Split Second* (1985), *In Remembrance of Rose* (1987), *A Worm of Doubt* (1987), *A Mouthful of Sand* (1988), *A Loose Connection* (1989), *This Blessed Plot* (1990), *Touch and Go* (1992), *Postscript to Murder* (1996), *A House to Die For* (1999), *If You Go Down to the Woods* (2001).

Toby Wilde series as Alison Cairns: *Strained Relations* (1983), *New Year Resolution* (1984).

Full name: Margaret Reid Duncan Meek.
Pen-name: Alison Cairns.
Where to start: *With Flowers That Fell* if you can find it, otherwise *Hang the Consequences.*
Similar stuff: Martin EDWARDS, Roy LEWIS.

James Melville (b. 1931) UK

Originally a local government officer and then a schoolteacher in the early fifties, JM became a British Council Officer in 1960 and thereafter spent his career in cultural diplomacy and educational development in Indonesia, Japan and Hungary. He returned to Japan as Head of the British Council in 1979. Most of his books are set in Japan and feature Superintendent Tetsuo Otani, chief of police in the city of Kobe. They are set in a contemporary Japan facing many cultural and social changes and many of the crimes arise out of conflict between the old and the new or the traditional with the foreign. JM provides a telling insight into the Japanese view of the foreigner. In *The Chrysanthemum Chain*, for instance, a member of the British consulate is dragged into the sordid world of organized crime. Otani is sensitive to these issues and conducts his investigations genially and assuredly, whilst keeping his two principal assistants under control. The series brings Japanese culture and tradition alive, admittedly through the eyes of a westerner, but one with a strong affinity for the country. It came to a close with the highly personal *The Body Wore Brocade*, narrated by Otani after his retirement. JM was the first author to revive the humorous Miss Seeton series originated by Heron CARVIC and continued by Sarah J. MASON. JM has written two other mysteries based on his experiences in the British Council in Hungary and Indonesia and featuring a quasi alter-ego and suspected spy,

Ben Lazenby. He has also written two historical novels, *The Imperial Way* (1986) and *A Tarnished Phoenix* (1990), which explore the tensions in Japan before and after WW2, and (under his own name) *The Chrysanthemum Throne* (1997), a study of the Japanese imperial dynasty through the ages.

Novels

Tetsuo Otani series: *The Wages of Zen* (1979), *The Chrysanthemum Chain* (1980), *A Sort of Samurai* (1981), *The Ninth Netsuke* (1982), *Sayonara, Sweet Amaryllis* (1983), *Death of a Daimyo* (1984), *The Death Ceremony* (1985), *Go Gently, Gaijin* (1986), *Kimono for a Corpse* (1987), *The Reluctant Ronin* (1988), *A Haiku for Hanae* (1989), *The Bogus Buddha* (1990), *The Body Wore Brocade* (1992).
Ben Lazenby series: *Diplomatic Baggage* (1995), *The Reluctant Spy* (1995).
Miss Seeton series as Hampton Charles: *Miss Seeton, by Appointment* (1990), *Advantage Miss Seeton* (1990), *Miss Seeton at the Helm* (1990).

Real name: Roy Peter Martin.
Pen-name: Hampton Charles, James Melville.
Where to start: *The Wages of Zen.*
Similar stuff: Janwillem VAN DE WETERING for books by a western writer set in modern-day Japan, plus works by Japanese writers Seichō MATSUMOTO, Shizuko NATSUKI and Masako TOGAWA.
Final fact: When JM was Cultural Counsellor at the British Embassy in Tokyo he met the then Crown Prince (now Emperor) of Japan on many occasions and was able to advise him on his personal correspondence in English.

Jennie Melville *pseudonym, see* Gwendoline Butler

Annette and Martin Meyers (both b. 1934) US

New Yorker AM spent 16 years as assistant to Broadway producer Hal Prince before spending another 16 years as a headhunter and consultant on Wall Street. She married actor MM in 1963. Both had aspirations to be writers and MM, with plenty of time between engagements, scored first. He wrote a series about Irish-American P.I. Patrick Hardy who was a foodaholic (rather than alcoholic) and lazy and tended to land in trouble rather than go looking for it. The series lasted for five hastily written books before it was back to the boards. AM eventually scored with *The Big Killing*, the first of her books about corporate headhunters Xenia Smith and Leslie Wetzon whose research causes them to stumble over almost as many dead bodies as live ones. The series allowed AM to draw upon her experiences on Wall Street and in the theatre. Wetzon, a former chorus girl, is the real sleuth, whilst Smith is over-ambitious and manipulative. The success of the series opened other doors and in 1992 AM and MM collaborated on a series of historical mysteries which has steadily been recreating the history of New York, and what was New Amsterdam, from the 1660s to the 1890s. The books do not run in chronological sequence but have a common thread in the family of Pieter Tonneman, the first

Sheriff of New York and the eponymous Dutchman of the first book. The authors combined the first two letters of their Christian names to create a suitably Dutch-sounding pseudonym, Maan Meyers. This thoroughly researched series is their most original work to date. It includes a Civil War thriller, *The Lucifer Contract*. With *Free Love*, AM has started a new series featuring poet/detective Olivia Brown set in Greenwich Village in the 1920s and recreating the artistic bohemian life.

Novels

Patrick Hardy series by Martin Meyers: *Kiss and Kill* (1975), *Spy and Die* (1976), *Red is for Murder* (1976), *Hung Up to Die* (1976), *Reunion for Death* (1976).
Smith & Wetzon series by Annette Meyers: *The Big Killing* (1989), *Tender Death* (1990), *The Deadliest Option* (1991), *Blood on the Street* (1992), *Murder: The Musical* (1993), *These Bones Were Made for Dancin'* (1995), *The Groaning Board* (1997).
Olivia Brown series by Annette Meyers: *Free Love* (1999), *Murder Me Now* (2001).
Tonneman family series as Maan Meyers: *The Dutchman* (1992), *The Kingsbridge Plot* (1993), *The High Constable* (1994), *The Dutchman's Dilemma* (1995), *The House on Mulberry Hill* (1996), *The Lucifer Contract* (1998).
Non-series by Martin Meyers: *Suspect* (1987).

Full names: Annette Meyers (*née* Brafman) and Martin Meyers.
Pen-name: Maan Meyers.
Where to start: *The Big Killing* or *The Dutchman*.
Website: <www.meyersmysteries.com>
Similar stuff: Caleb CARR for Old New York; Emma LATHEN for Wall Street; Jane DENTINGER for Broadway.
Final fact: Annette worked with Hal Prince on the Broadway productions of *Fiddler on the Roof*, *Cabaret* and *A Little Night Music* amongst others.

Maan Meyers *pseudonym, see* Annette and Martin Meyers

Barbara Michaels *pseudonym, see* Elizabeth Peters

Keith Miles, *see pseudonym* Edward Marston

Margaret Millar (1915–94) Canada

MM's roots were firmly in the classic age of crime fiction. Her first book, *The Invisible Worm*, which introduced the psychiatrist detective Dr Paul Prye, appeared back as far as 1941 and betrayed some of the light-hearted whimsy prevalent in suspense fiction of the time. But her career stretched over 46 years and she outlived her husband, Kenneth Millar (better known as Ross MACDONALD) and, rather more tragically, their one daughter, Linda, who died in 1970. Her best books did not start to appear until the mid-fifties and she established some features in suspense fiction which have since been overused but never bettered. The third Prye book, *The Devil Loves Me*, introduced Inspector Sands of the Toronto Police Department who continued in two further novels. The last of these, *The Iron Gates*, is the best and pointed the way MM's later books would go – a puzzling, convoluted plot, a strong psychological element and a surprise ending. The twist at the end became MM's *forté*, and is seen at its best in the award-winning study in madness, *Beast in View*, about a woman menaced by a crank phone caller, and *Listening Walls*, where a woman's death is just the start of a labyrinthine puzzler. Private detectives do not feature strongly in MM's fiction, probably because her husband was writing enough for both of them, but she does use P.I.s in *A Stranger in My Grave*, an eerie novella about a woman who dreams of her own grave, and *How Like an Angel*, in which compulsive gambler Joe Quinn finds himself investigating a religious cult. In all of these books MM creates a wonderful atmosphere of suspense and suspicion, and it is the latter that she develops even more strongly in *The Fiend*, where a man who is friendly with children becomes the prime suspect when a little girl disappears. Hypocrisy, guilt and deep secrets are also key to her two major courtroom dramas, *Beyond This Point are Monsters* and *Spider Webs*, in which she cleverly peels away layers of truth and deception. Amongst her last books three feature Hispanic lawyer Tom Aragon of which the best is *Mermaid*, involving a search for a mentally retarded woman. The most emotional of her last books, however, is *Banshee*, where a young girl disappears and is later found dead. The book explores the effects of her loss, discovery and the investigation upon her family. MM lived for too long in the shadow of her husband though she deservedly received both the Grand Master award from the MWA and the Derrick Murdoch Award from the Crime Writers of Canada. MM was also a keen conservationist and her activities led to her being named Woman of the Year by the *Los Angeles Times* in 1965. Her study of the local Californian wildlife was published as *The Birds and the Beasts Were There* (1968).

Novels

Dr Prye series: *The Invisible Worm* (1941), *The Weak-Eyed Bat* (1942), *The Devil Loves Me* (1942).

Inspector Sands series: *Wall of Eyes* (1943), *The Iron Gates* (1945; as *Taste of Fears*, UK 1950); also in the Prye novel *The Devil Loves Me*.

Tom Aragon series: *Ask For Me Tomorrow* (1976), *The Murder of Miranda* (1979), *Mermaid* (1982).

Non-series: *Fire Will Freeze* (1944), *Do Evil in Return* (1950), *Rose's Last Summer* (1952; as *The Lively Corpse*, 1956), *Vanish in an Instant* (1952), *Beast in View* (1955), *An Air That Kills* (1957; as *The Soft Talkers*, UK 1957), *The Listening Walls* (1959), *A Stranger in my Grave* (1960), *How Like an Angel* (1962), *The Fiend* (1964), *Beyond This Point Are Monsters* (1970), *Banshee* (1983), *Spider Webs* (1986).

Full name: Margaret Ellis Millar (*née* Sturm)

Where to start: *Beast in View*.
Awards: Edgar, best novel (1956), MWA Grand Master (1983), Derrick Murdoch Award (1986).
Similar stuff: Ruth RENDELL, Minette WALTERS.
Final fact: MM is noted for the quotation, "Life is something that happens to you while you're making other plans."

Denise Mina (b. 1966) UK

DM's trilogy featuring ex-psychiatric patient and survivor of child sexual abuse, Maureen O'Donnell, is a powerful sequence of work. DM studied law and psychiatry at Glasgow for her PhD though did not complete the course, opting for full-time writing. Her work also draws upon her direct experiences as an auxiliary nurse and health-care worker and paints a bleak picture of inner city Glasgow. O'Donnell is from a dysfunctional family with an alcoholic mother, an abusive father and a drug-dealing brother. In the award-winning *Garnethill*, after a night of drinking with a friend, she wakes to find him dead and she becomes the prime suspect. *Exile* finds her travelling to London to discover what happened to a client at a shelter for abused women in Glasgow who turns up dead in the Thames. *Resolution* piles on the agonies of life while Maureen tries to solve a third murder. O'Donnell may seem an unlikely sleuth but she is entirely believable as is the grim and relentless world about her. If further proof were needed that DM is a talent to watch, her first short story "Helena and the Babies" (*Fresh Blood 3*, 1999), set in a nursing home, won the CWA Short Story Dagger.

Novels

Maureen O'Donnell series: *Garnethill* (1999), *Exile* (2000), *Resolution* (2001).

Awards: CWA John Creasey Award (1998), CWA Short Story Dagger (2000).
Similar stuff: William MCILVANNEY for other Glasgow inner-city problems; Abigail PADGETT.
Final fact: DM claims she can do a passable Elvis impersonation.

James Mitchell (b. 1926) UK

A native of South Shields, County Durham, JM held several jobs while obtaining his diploma in education, including working in a shipyard and briefly as an actor. He then spent ten years as a college lecturer during which time he wrote a few action thrillers and war novels as well as the gangster novel *Here's a Villain!* He also wrote a stage play for the Newcastle Arts Theatre and this gave him an opening to television which broadcast his first teleplay, *Soldier in the Snow*, set at the time of the Peninsula War, in 1960. Thereafter his joint careers as a novelist and scriptwriter went hand-in-hand. He had some success with a series of novels featuring government agent John Craig a violent but essentially moral man who finds himself trapped in his work for British Intelligence.

The last of these, *Innocent Bystanders*, was filmed in 1972 from JM's script. JM reworked the idea to create a new character, David Callan. He is a government assassin who wants to retire but is manipulated by his boss, Hunter, into always undertaking "one last job". Callan first appeared in the one-off TV play *A Magnum for Schneider* (1967) which became the pilot for a new TV series, *Callan* (1967–72), starring Edward Woodward. The series, and the books arising, followed the tension and agony of Callan, trapped in his world, but increasingly in sympathy with his chosen victims. It was one of the more intelligent series of its time. JM has written another espionage novel, *KGB Kill*, plus an interesting series about London P.I. Ron Hoggett. Hoggett specializes in finding missing things, from coins to horses, and he's so good at his work that in the first book, *Sometimes You Could Die*, a millionaire hires him to find his wife's murderer. More light-hearted than either the Craig or Callan series, it shows another facet of JM's versatility.

Novels

Callan series: *A Magnum for Schneider* (1969; as *A Red File for Callan*, US 1971; as *Callan*, 1974), *Russian Roulette* (1973), *Death and Bright Water* (1974), *Smear Job* (1975).

Ron Hoggett series: *Sometimes You Could Die* (1985), *Dead Ernest* (1986), *Dying Day* (1988).

John Craig series as James Munro: *The Man Who Sold Death* (1964), *Die Rich, Die Happy* (1965), *The Money That Money Can't Buy* (1967), *The Innocent Bystanders* (1969).

Non-series: *Here's a Villain!* (1957; as *The Lady is Waiting*, US 1958), *A Way Back* (1959), *Among Arabian Sands* (1962), *Ilion Like a Mist* (1969; as *Venus in Plastic*, 1970), *The Winners* (1970), *The Evil Ones* (1982), *KGB Kill* (1987).

as Patrick O. McGuire: *A Time for Murder* (1955), *Fiesta for Murder* (1962).

Full name: James William Mitchell.
Pen-names: Patrick O. McGuire, James Munro.
Where to start: *The Man Who Sold Death* or *A Magnum for Schneider*.
Similar stuff: Brian GARFIELD.
Final fact: Mitchell also co-created the TV legal drama series *Justice* with Margaret Lockwood and Anthony Valentine.

Kay Mitchell UK

Yorkshire born and raised KM, a former nurse, midwife and health visitor, has written two series that reflects two sides of her character, the methodical and the mischievous. The first series features Chief Inspector John Morrissey, a family man who lives in Malminster. He encounters violent crimes in an otherwise conventional village setting, complete with its usual scandal, gossip and skeletons in the cupboard. These novels are cozies with the light off, especially for the young or the unconventional who seem prime victims in the series. Students, young girls, vagrants and the homeless all find themselves dead or missing in this series where

Morrissey brings a methodical and humane eye to his investigations. On the flip side we have the Leah Hunter series under the alias Sarah Lacey. Hunter is a twenty-five year old tax inspector who is extremely nosey and inquisitive and needs little excuse to follow up mysteries especially when, in the first book, a handsome man, with a dodgy tax record, drops dead in her arms. This is the more light-hearted and mischievous side of KM's writing but no less enjoyable.

Novels

Chief Inspector Morrissey series: *A Lively Form of Death* (1990), *In Stony Places* (1991), *A Strange Desire* (1993; as *Roots of Evil*, US 1993), *A Portion for Foxes* (1995), *A Rage of Innocents* (1997).

Leah Hunter series as Sarah Lacey: *File Under: Deceased* (1992), *File Under: Missing* (1993), *File Under: Arson* (1994), *File Under: Jeopardy* (1995), *File Under: Justice* (1998).

Pen-names: Sarah Lacey.
Where to start: *A Lively Form of Death.*
Website: <www.twbooks.co.uk/authors/kaymitchell.html>
Similar stuff: Caroline GRAHAM, Ann GEORGE, Nancy LIVINGSTON.

Gwen Moffat (b. 1924) UK

Though born in Sussex GM now lives in Cumbria, close to the Lakeland Fells and has spent most of her life venturing into remote and inaccessible areas. She is a mountaineer and guide and has written about her experiences and interests in scores of books including her autobiography *Space Below My Feet* (1961; rev'd 2001). GM realized that for everyday people to be involved in investigating crime it helps to have a specialism that allows them access to places authorities cannot go, and what better than remote mountains or difficult terrain? Moreover the dynamics in remote communities allow for interesting situations. The heroes of GM's books have a love for nature and isolation and are tied to the landscape either as explorers, rescuers or walkers. Her main character is Melinda Pink, a magistrate who is also a mountaineer, explorer and writer. She stumbles over crimes and dark secrets in Wales and Scotland and, since GM explored the California trail, Arizona, Montana, Oregon, Utah, New Mexico and Washington State. In all of these places GM brings alive small, local communities which cling to the landscape for their livelihood. Another occasional character is Jack Pharaoh, invalided out of the RAF Mountain Rescue but who can't keep away from search-and-rescue emergencies. GM's pleasure in nature and the environment leads to passionate novels full of atmosphere and feeling as well as tension and mystery. Her books are not simply mountaineering mysteries but display a care for the whole environment. In *Persons Unknown* it's nuclear energy, in *Rage* it's endangered species, in *Quicksand* it's the media invasion of remote communities. She also deals with adultery in *Deviant Death*, incest in *The Lost Girls* and a totally dysfunctional family in *Private Sins*. GM's works are rare and distinctive.

Novels
Melinda Pink series: *Lady With a Cool Eye* (1973), *Miss Pink at the Edge of the World* (1975), *Over the Sea to Death* (1976), *A Short Time to Live* (1976), *Persons Unknown* (1978), *Die Like a Dog* (1978), *Last Chance Country* (1983), *Grizzly Trail* (1984), *Snare* (1987), *The Stone Hawk* (1989), *Rage* (1990), *The Raptor Zone* (1990), *Veronica's Sisters* (1992), *The Lost Girls* (1998), *Private Sins* (1999), *Retribution* (2002).
Jack Pharaoh series: *Pit Bull* (1991), *The Outside Edge* (1993).
Non-series: *Deviant Death* (1973), *The Corpse Road* (1974), *Cue the Battered Wife* (1994), *A Wreath of Dead Moths* (1998), *Running Dogs* (1999), *Quicksand* (2001).

Where to start: *Lady With a Cool Eye.*
Website: <www.twbooks.co.uk/authors/gmoffat.html>
Similar stuff: Nevada BARR, Ann CLEEVES.
Final fact: GM was the first woman in Britain to become a professional rock-climbing guide and has been a member of mountain rescue teams in Britain and the Swiss Alps.

Miriam Grace Monfredo (b. 1940) US

MGM has established a strong following with her series set in Seneca Falls, New York in the mid-19th century. The main character is Glynis Tryon, a librarian of independent character who falls out with her family because of her refusal to marry. Her emerging feminist views bring her into contact with the women's rights movement that met in Seneca Falls in 1848. The series continues through other key historical events and most recently has reached the Civil War. The series may at heart be a traditional historical cozy, but it is steeped with the social and ethnic tensions and reforms of the age, which bring the period and the characters alive. *Seneca Falls Inheritance* was short-listed for both the Agatha and Macavity awards for best first novel. MGM was herself a librarian and newspaper feature writer and is now director of a legal and historical research firm.

Novels
Seneca Falls series: *Seneca Falls Inheritance* (1992), *North Star Conspiracy* (1993), *Blackwater Spirits* (1995), *Through a Gold Eagle* (1996), *The Stalking Horse* (1998), *Must the Maiden Die* (1999), *Sisters of Cain* (2000), *Brothers of Cain* (2001).
Editor with Sharan NEWMAN. *Crime Through Time* (1997), *Crime Through Time II* (1998).

Website: <www.miriamgracemonfredo.com>
Similar stuff: Gillian LINSCOTT, Annette & Martin MEYERS.

Manuel Vázquez Montalbán (b. 1939) Spain

Only a small proportion of MVM's books are available in English even though he is highly regarded in his native Spain, where he was won the Planeta, the equivalent of the Booker Prize. He is one of the leading postmodern Spanish crime-fiction writers with his long-running series featuring the unconventional P.I. Pepe Carvalho. Carvalho is an ex-CIA agent and former Communist who has trouble coming to terms with the changes in post-Franco Spain and in his beloved Barcelona. He believes it is his mission to expose hypocrisy and corruption. He is also overweight and loves food. He has his own personal cook. The first book in the series, *Yo maté a Kennedy* ("I Have Killed Kennedy", 1972; not available in English), looked back to his early career when the CIA called him in to assassinate Kennedy. His P.I. days started in *Tatuaje* (1974), also untranslated, where he has to identify a body fished out of the sea with its face eaten off. The translations begin with book three, *The Angst-Ridden Executive*, where an old friend dies trying to contact Carvalho and his widow asks for Carvalho's help. Football devotees will like *Off-Side*, where the new manager of Barcelona F.C. starts receiving death threats. All of the novels are explosive and passionate, with frequent insights into political chicanery and CIA manipulation. None of this is like MVM himself, a mild-mannered man though with strong views. He often appears on Spanish television and is renowned for his poetry. He has written many books of essays and other fiction, some of it drawing upon major crime cases. The award-winning *Galíndez* recreates an attempt in the late 1980s to unravel the disappearance of an outspoken critic in the Dominican Republic in 1956. *El Estrangulador* (1994; not translated) is about the Boston strangler.

Novels

Pepe Carvalho series: *The Angst-ridden Executive* (1977; UK 1989), *Southern Seas* (1979; UK 1986), *Murder in the Central Committee* (1981; UK 1984), *Off Side* (1988; UK 1996), *Olympic Death* (1988; UK 1992).
Non-series: *Galíndez* (1990; US 1992).

Awards: Planeta Prize (1979), Grand Prix de Littérature Policière Best Foreign (1981), National Fiction Prize, Spain (1991), Swedish Academy of Detection, Best Foreign (1992).
Website: <www.vespito.net/mvm.html>
Similar stuff: Roderic JEFFRIES, Julian RATHBONE, David SERAFIN.
Final fact: MVM is himself something of a gourmet and has compiled a Pepe Carvalho cookbook.

Susan Moody (b. 1940) UK

SM was a creative writing tutor at Bedford Prison from 1983–5 before she turned to full-time writing. She has created two series characters. Penny Wanawake is a black freelance photographer, the daughter of Lady Hurley and an African ambassador to the UN. SM had lived in Tennessee during the sixties and seen racial issues first hand, so wanted to explore them from an English viewpoint. Penny is rich with a jet-set lifestyle, but is also aware of her background and is keen to channel money into impoverished third-world countries. In *Penny Black* she sets up a scam with her lover, an antique dealer and jewel thief, to steal jewelry from the rich and send the proceeds to famine victims. This lifestyle inevitably brings Penny into conflict with a wide range of characters and she is frequently involved in either investigating or avenging the death or kidnapping of friends. SM's other series is totally different. Much more light-hearted, it features the overweight and meek Cassie Swann, a bridge expert who earns money through both playing and teaching the game. In her first case, *Takeout Double*, it is her knowledge of bridge that proves that the sudden death of three people was not a bizarre accident but foul play. Swann is a more introspective and vulnerable individual than the flamboyant Wanawake. Her soul is bared in *Grand Slam* and *King of Hearts* where she investigates the death of her own father 20 years ago. By the time of *Sacrifice Bid*, Swann is finding making a living difficult and in *Dummy Hand* she is the victim of a hit-and-run driver. This all makes Swann a more sympathetic and intriguing heroine. SM regards these detective series as basic work and enjoys writing more literary suspense novels when opportunity allows. These include some of her most atmospheric writing. *Hush-a-Bye* concerns the kidnapping of a baby. In *Falling Angel* a woman investigates the murder of her sister. *House of Moons* explores present-day consequences of disasters during the Spanish Civil War, whilst in *The Italian Garden* a mother has to cope with realizing that her daughter's death may not have been suicide. In all of SM's books there is a strong emphasis on family ties and the repercussion of past events. SM has also written a sequel to Frances Hodgson Burnett's *The Secret Garden* called *Misselthwaite* (1995) which reveals what happens to the children in adulthood.

Novels
Penny Wanawake series: *Penny Black* (1984), *Penny Dreadful* (1984), *Penny Post* (1985), *Penny Royal* (1986), *Penny Wise* (1988), *Penny Pinching* (1989), *Penny Saving* (1990).
Cassie Swann series: *Takeout Double* (1993; as *Death Takes a Hand*, US 1994), *Grand Slam* (1994), *King of Hearts* (1995), *Doubled in Spades* (1996), *Sacrifice Bid* (1997), *Dummy Hand* (1998).
Non-series: *Playing With Fire* (1990; as *Mosaic*, US 1991), *Hush-a-Bye* (1991), *House of Moons* (1993), *The Italian Garden* (1994), *Falling Angel* (1998).

Full name: Susan Elizabeth Moody (*née* Horwood).
Pen-name: Susannah James.
Where to start: *Hush-a-Bye*.
Similar stuff: Liza Cody, Gar Anthony Haywood.
Final fact: SM wrote *Love Over Gold* (1993) as Susannah James, the novel which told the story of the romance of the Gold Blend coffee couple in the long-running TV advert.

Ian Morson (b. 1947) UK

Born in Derby but working most of his life as a librarian in London, IM now lives in Cornwall where he is able to indulge his interests in nature conservation and amateur dramatics. He also writes historical mysteries. His first series features Regent Master William Falconer of the fledgling Oxford University in the mid-13th century. Falconer is a daringly progressive teacher in what are turbulent times of civil war. He is keenly observant and has, as his mentor, the legendary Roger Bacon. The key to all historical mysteries is to blend an authentic detective tale with the cultural and historical resonances of the period and IM achieves that superbly. You can taste and feel Oxford as he brings alive some of the more unusual moments of England's history. Falconer is an excellent sleuth who uses logic based on his studies of Aristotelean philosophy. The fifth book, *Falconer and the Great Beast*, set in 1268 when Oxford played host to the Tartars, was shortlisted for the CWA Ellis Peters Historical Dagger award. IM is currently working on a new series set in the Mongol Empire.

Novels

Falconer series: *Falconer's Crusade* (1994), *Falconer's Judgement* (1995), *Falconer and the Face of God* (1996), *A Psalm for Falconer* (1997), *Falconer and the Great Beast* (1999).

Website: <website.lineone.net/~ian.morson/>
Similar stuff: Susannah GREGORY, Paul DOHERTY, Ellis PETERS.
Final fact: IM is dogged by a non-existent middle name born somewhere in the depths of the Net. This name, "Nairne", is obviously so lonely, yet so enamoured of "Ian" and "Morson" that it constantly seeks to insinuate itself between the two names.

John Mortimer (b. 1923) UK

JM is best known as the creator of that lovable if eccentric barrister Horace Rumpole. Despite the hopes of Mrs Rumpole ("She-Who-Must-Be-Obeyed") that Horace will follow in the footsteps of "Daddy", take silk and become a Head of Chambers, Rumpole has little such ambition. He's an Old Bailey "hack" who comes alive in court when given the chance to fight the case for the underdog. Rumpole always acts for the defence, even for the guilty when he knows there are mitigating circumstances. Rumpole is at the same time an amusing and a sad individual. His wry observations cast a cynical viewpoint on life at Chambers and the procedures in Court, and he has a distant relationship with his wife and their son, but his occasional moments of triumph for justice make him something of a shambling knight errant. Rumpole first appeared in a TV play, *Rumpole at the Bailey* (1975) and then a successful series (1978–92) with Leo McKern in the title rôle. JM adapted the episodes as short stories which have appeared in various volumes and compendia and which he continues to write, though the TV series has finished. JM was called to the Bar in 1948 and, unlike Rumpole, was made a Q.C. in 1966. He nevertheless regards himself as primarily a writer. Apart from the Rumpole series few of his books and plays are crime fiction. During WW2 JM served in a unit making documentary films and this formed the basis of his first book, *Charade*, in which a naïve young scriptwriter becomes suspicious over an apparent accidental death during the filming of a training exercise. JM's first play, *The Dock Brief* (radio 1957; in *Three Plays*; filmed 1962) concerns an unsuccessful barrister who is chosen to defend a murderer. *Like Men Betrayed* is a strongly autobiographical novel about estrangement between father and son and the belief by the father that his son is up to something illegal. Like others of JM's books, such as *Dunster* and *Felix in the Underworld*, it explores moments lost and a gradual spiralling out of control of once-strong relationships. JM's own father, the model for Rumpole, was a distinguished if eccentric barrister who specialized in divorce cases. *Summer's Lease* is unusual for JM in that it is primarily a suspense novel, concerning a mother on holiday with her family in Italy becoming embroiled in a series of mysterious events. JM also scripted the TV series *Under the Hammer* (1993) set in an auction house where two of the staff, Maggie Perowne and Ben Glazier, become over zealous in their research in verifying the items for auction. JM was awarded the CBE in 1986 and received a knighthood in 1998.

Novels. *Charade* (1947), *Like Men Betrayed* (1953), *Summer's Lease* (1988), *Dunster* (1992), *Felix in the Underworld* (1997).
Short Stories
Rumpole series: *Rumpole of the Bailey* (1978), *The Trials of Rumpole* (1979), *Rumpole's Return* (1980), *Regina v Rumpole* (1981; abr. as *Rumpole for the Defence*, 1982), *Rumpole and the Golden Thread* (1983), *Rumpole's Last Case* (1987), *Rumpole and the Age of Miracles* (1988), *Rumpole à la Carte* (1990), *Rumpole on Trial* (1992), *Rumpole and the Angel of Death* (1995), *Rumpole Rests His Case* (2001).
Maggie Perowne series: *Under the Hammer* (1994).
Published Plays. *Three Plays* (1958), *The Judge* (1967)
Editor. *Great Law and Order Stories* (1990); Non-fiction: *Famous Trials* (1984), *The Oxford Book of Villains* (1992).
Autobiography. *Clinging to the Wreckage* (1982), *Murderers and Other Friends* (1994), *The Summer of a Dormouse* (2000).

Full name: John Clifford Mortimer.
Pen-name: Geoffrey Lincoln.
Where to start: *Rumpole of the Bailey*.
Awards: Italia Prize, radio play (1958), Screenwriters Guild Award, television play (1970), British Academy Award, TV series (1980).
Similar stuff: Michael GILBERT.
Final fact: JM led the successful defence in the groundbreaking court case in 1960 over whether D.H. Lawrence's *Lady Chatterley's Lover*, published for the first time in Britain by Penguin Books, contravened the Obscene Publications Act.

Walter Mosley (b. 1952) US

Many critics have seen WM as the natural successor to Chester HIMES, except that although WM's books explore the increasingly violent and despairing interracial relationships in the US (specifically Los Angeles) from the 1940s to 1960s, his work is less bleak and retains a glimmer of hope that matters will change. WM is the son of a Russian-Jewish schoolteacher and a black father who was a school janitor. His character of Ezekiel "Easy" Rawlins is based to some extent on his father. WM first wrote about him in *Gone Fishin'* in the late 1980s, though that book was not published until 1997. It is set in Houston, Texas in 1939 and charts the early relationship between Rawlins and his psychopathic friend Mouse Alexander. It is an introductory novel and lacks the impact of *Devil in a Blue Dress* (filmed 1995). It is now 1948 and Rawlins lives in the Watts area of Los Angeles. Jobless and penniless Rawlins accepts money from a rich white man to find a girl who used to frequent black nightclubs but has gone missing. Rawlins realizes too late what he has let himself in for. This formula is repeated with believable effect through the rest of the series as Rawlins is manipulated by the rich and powerful (and white) to infiltrate areas he knows but which are beyond their bounds. A reluctant sleuth, Rawlins has his own code, like the hard-boiled P.I.s, which this series emulates, and struggles to do the right thing despite knowing his own limitations and the cultural boundaries placed about him. WM developed a new twist on the theme with Socrates Fortlow, another African American, imprisoned for 27 years for murder and now trying to redeem his misspent youth. He can see the error of his ways and the traps into which so many of today's youth are falling, but his attempts to help only lead him back into trouble. Fortlow has appeared in a run of short stories collected as *Always Outnumbered, Always Outgunned* (filmed 1998) and an episodic novel. Since then WM has experimented with science fiction in *Blue Light* (1998) and his Futureland stories, but he has returned to his roots with *Fearless Jones*, introducing two new black characters not unlike Easy and Mouse, who try to survive by their wits in 1950s Los Angeles.

Novels

Easy Rawlins series: *Devil in a Blue Dress* (1990), *A Red Death* (1991), *White Butterfly* (1992), *Black Betty* (1994), *A Little Yellow Dog* (1996), *Gone Fishin'* (1997), *Bad Boy Brawly Brown* (2002).
Socrates Fortlow series: *Walkin' the Dog* (1999).
Non-series: *Fearless Jones* (2001).

Short Stories

Socrates Fortlow series: *Always Outnumbered, Always Outgunned* (1997).

Where to start: *Devil in a Blue Dress* or *Gone Fishin'* if you want strict chronological order.

Awards: CWA John Creasey Memorial Award (1991), Shamus, best first novel (1991), O. Henry Award (1996), Chester Himes award (1999).

Website: <www.twbookmark.com/features/waltermosley/index.html> though there's also a good site at <www.math.buffalo.edu/~sww/mosley/mosley_walter_primer.html>
Similar stuff: Chester HIMES.
Final fact: Former US President Bill Clinton cited WM as one of his favourite writers in 1992.

Christopher T. Mountjoy, *see under pseudonym* Edward Marston

Patricia Moyes (1923–2000) Anglo-Irish

PM's work is firmly in the traditional mould, though infused with contemporary wit and wry observation and a recognition of changing values. Born in Ireland, the daughter of a judge in the Indian Civil Service, PM was raised and educated in England and in later years lived in various countries including Switzerland, the Netherlands and the British Virgin Islands, where she died. Her mystery novels, all of which feature Chief Superintendent Henry Tibbett of Scotland Yard and his wife Emmy, reflect PM's travels. The first book, *Dead Men Don't Ski*, starts with one of those intriguing puzzles, the discovery of a dead man in a ski-lift, and the resultant book was warmly received in both UK and US, launching PM on a career spanning 40 years and 41 books. Tibbetts is a methodical detective with a nose for the unusual and an intuitive streak. His wife is a key character in the books and in some ways reflects PM herself. In *Johnny Under Ground*, her wartime background provides a key to solving a murder. *Who Saw Her Die?*, about the seemingly natural death of an old lady at her birthday party, was nominated for an Edgar award, though most critics agree that PM's best book was *Falling Star*, where an actor dies on a film set. This draws on PM's own experiences as a secretary at Peter Ustinov Productions, where she worked from 1945–53 before becoming an assistant editor on *Vogue* magazine. PM's books are full of strong characters, fascinating plots and authentic detective work. Her other books include a children's mystery, *Helter-Skelter* (1968) and several books about cats.

Novels

Henry Tibbett series: *Dead Men Don't Ski* (1959), *The Sunken Sailor* (1961; as *Down Among the Dead Men*, US 1961), *Death on the Agenda* (1962), *Murder à la Mode* (1963), *Falling Star* (1964), *Johnny Under Ground* (1965), *Murder Fantastical* (1967), *Death and the Dutch Uncle* (1968), *Who Saw Her Die?* (1970); as *Many Deadly Returns*, US 1970), *Season of Snows and Sins* (1971), *The Curious Affair of the Third Dog* (1973), *Black Widower* (1975), *To Kill a Coconut* (1977; *The Coconut Killings*, 1977), *Who is Simon Warwick?* (1978), *Angel Death* (1980), *A Six-Letter Word for Death* (1983), *Night Ferry to Death* (1985), *Black Girl, White Girl* (1989), *Twice in a Blue Moon* (1993).

Short Stories. *Who Killed Father Christmas?* (1996).

Awards: Malice Domestic lifetime achievement (1999).
Similar stuff: Marian BABSON, Roger ORMEROD, Dorothy SIMPSON.
Final fact: PM started writing when she suffered a skiing accident in Switzerland and needed something to do.

Marcia Muller (b. 1944) US

MM created the first American female contemporary P.I. in the shape of Sharon McCone. McCone is in her 30s in the first book, *Edwin of the Iron Shoes*, and operates from the All Souls Legal Co-operative in San Francisco, though in later books she sets out on her own. She's less sure of herself at the outset, and bolsters her confidence with a .357 Magnum, but in later books as her confidence grows, she resorts to it less, even though her investigations become tougher and darker. The first few books have varied plots, broadening the usual grist of the P.I. mill, especially *Games to Keep the Dark Away*, involving deaths in a hospice and a missing social worker. The series moved up a notch with the award-winning *The Shape of Dread*, where McCone finds herself delving into the world of a murder victim, and *Wolf in the Shadows*, another award winner, involving a disappearance, a kidnapping and a murder. In these books McCone's character visibly grows as the demands of her work expose her vulnerability and cause her to become tougher. *Listen to the Silence* delves further into McCone's past with the death of her father and her research into her native American background. Throughout the series McCone has gathered around her an intriguing array of characters and several have adventures of their own in separate stories, providing additional perspectives on McCone. This not only brings a satisfying roundness to McCone's world but, brings more depth and shade to her character. MM has written two further series, both of which she has now laid to rest. Elena Oliverez is a Mexican-American art museum curator in Santa Barbara and Joanna Stark is an art-security consultant. Although these series are more lightweight than the McCone books, they are well plotted, with a wealth of information about the art world. It is a subject of special interest to MM, as several of the early McCone books also involved missing art or religious treasures. MM was born in Detroit but settled in San Francisco in 1967 when she joined the staff of *Sunset* magazine. She held a variety of other jobs including running a writers' editorial service, Invisible Ink (from 1979–83) with future novelist Julie SMITH. She married (in 1992), as her second husband, author Bill PRONZINI, with whom she had already collaborated on a number of writing and editing projects including *Double*, which brought McCone together with Pronzini's Nameless detective. She has written one solo stand-alone novel, *Point Deception*, featuring Rhoda Swift, deputy sheriff of Soledad County, California, who is worried that the 13th anniversary of a series of unsolved murders may have unleashed another bout of murders.

Novels
Sharon McCone series: *Edwin of the Iron Shoes* (1977), *Ask the Cards a Question* (1982), *The Cheshire Cat's Eye* (1983), *Games to Keep the Dark Away* (1984), *Leave a Message for Willie* (1984), *Double* with Bill Pronzini (1984), *There's Nothing to be Afraid Of* (1985), *Eye of the Storm* (1988), *There's Something in a Sunday* (1989), *The Shape of Dread* (1989), *Trophies and Dead Things* (1990), *Where Echoes Live* (1991), *Pennies on a Dead Woman's Eyes* (1992), *Wolf in the Shadows* (1993), *Till the Butchers Cut Him Down* (1994), *A Wild and Lonely Place* (1995), *The Broken Promise Land* (1996), *Both Ends of the Night* (1997), *While Other People Sleep* (1998), *A Walk Through the Fire* (1999), *Listen to the Silence* (2000), *Dead Midnight* (2002).
Elena Oliverez series: *The Tree of Death* (1983), *The Legend of the Slain Soldiers* (1985), *Beyond the Grave* with Bill Pronzini (1986).
Joanna Stark series: *The Cavalier in White* (1986), *There Hangs the Knife* (1988), *Dark Star* (1989).
Non-series: *The Lighthouse* with Bill Pronzini (1987), *Point Deception* (2001).
Short Stories. *Deceptions* (1991), *The McCone Files* (1995), *McCone and Friends* (1999).
Non-fiction *see under Bill Pronzini.*
Editor with Bill Pronzini. *The Web She Weaves* (1983), *Child's Ploy* (1984), *Witches' Brew* (1984), *Dark Lessons* (1985), *She Won the West* (1985), *Chapter and Hearse* (1985), *Kill or Cure* (1985), *The Wickedest Show on Earth* (1985), *The Deadly Arts* (1985), *Lady on the Case* (1988), *A Century of Mystery, 1980–89* (1996), *Detective Duos* (1997).

Where to start: The McCone books are best read in sequence but if you want to dip in then start with either *Leave a Message for Willie*, *There's Nothing to be Afraid Of* or *The Shape of Dread*.
Awards: Macavity, best critical (1987), American Mystery Award, best novel (1989), Shamus, best short story (1991), Anthony, best novel (1994), best short story collection (1996), PWA lifetime achievement (1993).
Website: (unofficial) <www.interbridge.com/marciamuller/>
Similar stuff: Sue GRAFTON, Sara PARETSKY for strong female P.I.; Aaron J. ELKINS for art/museum crimes.
Final fact: MM is thorough in her research for her books though sometimes this goes a bit too far and she admits to nearly shooting herself in the foot with a .357 Magnum and almost being arrested for straying too close to the US-Mexico border. She also learned to fly even though she's afraid of heights.

James Munro *pseudonym, see* James Mitchell

Warren Murphy (b. 1933) US

WM is the co-creator of the long-running and highly successful series featuring Remo Williams, "The Destroyer". The roots for the series go back to 1963. WM was then a Jersey City political consultant, having previously been a reporter and editor in the years since his military service in the Korean War. WM was friends with political reporter Richard Ben Sapir (1936–87) and the two put together a proposal for a book about a former cop and Vietnam vet, Remo Williams, who had been framed for murder and executed. However he had been saved to work as a government law enforcer by a secret organization called CURE. Williams was trained in martial arts by a Korean called Chiun. No publisher was interested until after the success of Don PENDLETON's Executioner series and the first novel, *Created: The Destroyer* (filmed 1985 as *Remo Williams: The Adventure Begins*), appeared in 1971. By then it had mutated into a spoof on the super-spy series of the sixties and as the series grew and developed it took on more fantastical plots and porportions and shifted into the realms of science fantasy. WM and Sapir wrote the first 35 books before Sapir moved on to write bigger and greater books. WM wrote another six on his own but then brought in other collaborators including Robert RANDISI and his future wife Molly Cochran. Sapir also collaborated on a few more. By 1984, most of the writing was being done by others, even though Sapir and WM's names continued to appear on the books, even after Sapir's untimely death. Most of the writing since book #70 (*The Eleventh Hour*, 1987) has been by Will Murray who handed the baton on to Jim Mullaney in 1998.

WM has continued to be prolific with other series and one-off novels. His first solo-series featured two New York cops, Ed Razoni, who is white and given to occasional crazy outbursts and his partner and calming influence, the black detective and family man William "Tough" Jackson. The characters bear a close resemblance to the cops Riggs and Murtaugh in *Lethal Weapon* (1987) and though the influence was never acknowledged it is perhaps pertinent that WM was brought in as co-scriptwriter on *Lethal Weapon 2* (1989). WM's next series featured freelance insurance investigator Julian "Digger" Burroughs, based in Las Vegas. He drinks, smokes and gambles too much and is generally pretty hopeless at his job, which he only keeps because the boss likes him. The cases are usually solved by his lover Koko. After four books WM changed publisher and, for contractual reasons, converted Digger to Devlin "Trace" Tracy and Koko to Chico, but the plots carried on as before. This series seemed to capture the fans' fancy though, because of the OTT characterization of Trace, with his sharp and incisive dialogue but hopeless detective skills. Four of the books were nominated for Shamus awards and *Pigs Get Fat* won an Edgar. The series later mutated into the short-lived TV series *Murphy's Law* (1988–9) with the character now named Daedalus Murphy and a reformed drinker/smoker/gambler! WM's Grandmaster trilogy (of which only two books have appeared), co-authored with his wife, are an unusual blend of espionage thriller and psychological suspense built around the world of the chess champion. The first book won an Edgar award.

Of his one-off novels most, with the exception of *Leonardo's Law*, which is one for the locked-room fans, are political thrillers. *The Ceiling of*

Hell, which has a former secret service agent turned PI stumble across a nest of neo-Nazis in the US, won a Shamus award. *Scorpion's Dance*, may seem frighteningly predictive, as it has Soviet and American forces combine to stop an Arab terrorist.

Novels

Destroyer series: with Richard Sapir, #1, *Created: The Destroyer* (1971) to #34, *Chained Reaction* (1980); solo or in collaboration with various authors #35, *Last Call* (1978) to #44, *Balance of Power* (1981) plus #48, *Profit Motive* (1982), #52, *Fool's Gold* (1983), #55, *Master's Challenge* (1984) to #62, *The Seventh Stone* (1985), #69, *Blood Ties* (1987) to #73, *Line of Succession* (1988), and #94, *Feeding Frenzy* (1993). Also film novelization *Remo: The First Adventure* (1985).

Razoni & Jackson series: *One Night Stand* (1973), *Dead End Street* (1973), *City in Heat* (1973), *Down and Dirty* (1974), *Lynch Town* (1974), *On the Dead Run* (1975); also in Tracy novel *Too Old a Cat*.

Digger Burroughs series: *Smoked Out* (1982; as *Digger Smoked Out*, 1994), *Fool's Flight* (1982), *Dead Letter* (1982), *Lucifer's Weekend* with Robert J. Randisi (1982).

Trace Tracy series: *Trace* (1983), *Two Steps from Three East* (1983), *And 47 Miles of Rope* (1984), *When Elephants Forget* (1984), *Pigs Get Fat* (1985), *Once a Mutt* (1985), *Too Old a Cat* (1986), *Getting Up with Fleas* (1987).

Grandmaster series with Molly Cochran: *Grandmaster* (1984), *High Priest* (1987).

Non-series: *Leonardo's Law* (1978), *Atlantic City* with Frank Stevens (1979), *The Red Moon* (1982), *The Ceiling of Hell* (1984), *The Hand of Lazarus* with Molly Cochran (1988), *The Sure Thing* (1988), *The Temple Dogs* with Molly Cochran (1989), *Jericho Day* (1989), *Scorpion's Dance* (1990), *Destiny's Carnival* (1992), *Honor Among Thieves* (1992).

with Molly Cochran as Dev Stryker: *Deathright* (1993), *End Game* (1994).

Full name: Warren Burton Murphy.
Pen-name: Dev Stryker.
Where to start: Unless you want to read The Destroyer series start with *One Night Stand* or *Trace*.
Awards: Edgar, best paperback original (1985, 1986), Shamus, best paperback original (1985), best short story (1999).
Website: <http://warrenmurphy.tripod.com> and <www.sinanju.com>
Similar stuff: Don PENDLETON, Max Allan COLLINS.
Final fact: When *The Eiger Sanction* (1972) was adapted for the movie (1975), WM was brought in to script most of the snappy dialogue.

Amy Myers (b. 1938) UK

For twenty years AM was a director of the London-based publisher William Kimber, and while there edited a series of ghost story anthologies starting with *After Midnight Stories* (1985). With the inevitable changes and mergers that followed the publisher's retirement in 1988, AM decided to further her own writing. In addition to romantic sagas under the alias Harriet Hudson and other historical novels under other names, AM produced a series of light-hearted detective novels featuring Victorian Anglo-French master chef Auguste Didier. AM came up with the idea while she and her husband lived for a while in Paris. We first meet the egotistical Didier in *Murder in Pug's Parlour*, set in AM's native Kent where she still lives. He is chef at Stockbery Towers and comes under investigation when the Duke's steward dies of poison. Didier has to solve the murder to clear himself. The book introduces Inspector Egbert Rose of Scotland Yard and he and Didier cross swords and ideas throughout the series. Didier later establishes his own restaurant in London. The series is great fun with an authentic period feel and memorable characters. Each book takes us forward roughly a year at a time and has reached the early Edwardian period. AM has recently developed a new crime series featuring the exploits of chimney sweep Tom Wasp and his apprentice Ned in London's east end in the 1860s. The first novel has so far only appeared in Germany as *Tom Dickens und die Geliebte des Malers* (2001), but he has made his debut in English in several short stories in *EQMM*. AM has written other mystery stories ranging from Didier to Aphrodite, the Goddess of Love, and a collection is in the offing.

Novels

Auguste Didier series: *Murder in Pug's Parlour* (1986), *Murder in the Limelight* (1987), *Murder at Plum's* (1989), *Murder at the Masque* (1991), *Murder Makes an Entrée* (1992), *Murder Under the Kissing Bough* (1992), *Murder in the Smokehouse* (1994), *Murder at the Music Hall* (1995), *Murder in the Motor Stable* (1996), *Murder With Majesty* (1999), *Murder in the Queen's Boudoir* (2000).

Pen-names: Alice Carr, Laura Daniels, Harriet Hudson.
Website: <www.twbooks.co.uk/authors/amymyers.html>
Similar stuff: Alanna KNIGHT, Elizabeth PETERS or, for culinary detectives, Diane Mott DAVIDSON and Janet LAURENCE.
Final fact: AM recalls that long ago, when Auguste Didier was not even a twinkle in her eye, she worked as a waitress at a restaurant priding itself on its food. "I was not a very good waitress," she relates, "and two women at one table reduced me to tears. The staff crowded round me in the kitchen. 'Don't let those two Lesbians upset you,' one said, to which I innocently replied: 'Lesbians? I thought they were Belgians.'"

Magdalen Nabb (b. 1947) UK

MN was born in Lancashire and trained as a potter but in 1975 she moved lock, stock and barrel to Italy, despite knowing no Italian, and has remained there, in Florence, earning her career as a writer. Apart from a collaborative novel, all of her crime fiction books feature Marshal Salvatore Guarnaccia of the Carabinieri in Florence. He has been described as the "most Maigret-like of contemporary policemen" and the first book, *Death of an Englishman*, was indeed praised by no less than Simenon himself. MN has observed just how secretive a city Florence is and how much Guarnaccia has to cope with this wall of silence. The first book looked at an expat English community in Tuscany, but later novels have shifted their focus to Florentine life, starting with *The Marshal and the Madwoman*. Guarnaccia is methodical and dogged but likeable, just like Maigret or Donna LEON's Brunetti. MN paints a beautiful picture of the Tuscan countryside and of Florence. The Guarnaccia novels have to contend for MN's time with her successful series of children's books about Josie Smith, set in Lancashire, which is the basis of the TV series, which MN also scripts.

Novels
Marshal Guarnacci series: *Death of an Englishman* (1981), *Death of a Dutchman* (1982), *Death in Springtime* (1983), *Death in Autumn* (1985), *The Marshal and the Murderer* (1987), *The Marshal and the Madwoman* (1988), *The Marshal's Own Case* (1990), *The Marshal Makes His Report* (1991), *The Marshal at the Villa Torrini* (1993), *The Marshal and the Forgery* (1995), *The Monster of Florence* (1996), *Property of Blood* (2001).
Non-series: *The Prosecutor* with Paolo Vagheggi (1986).

Website: <www.twbooks.co.uk/authors/mnabb.html>
Awards: Guardian Children's Fiction award (1989), Smarties Book Prize (1991).
Similar stuff: Nicolas FREELING, Donna LEON, Per WAHLÖÖ.

Reggie Nadelson US

RN is an American journalist and documentary filmmaker who has had considerable success with her series of books about Russian-born New York cop (and later P.I.) Artie Cohen. Despite his background Cohen wants to be American but his heritage continues to haunt him. In the first book a friend of his father's, a former KGB agent, is murdered on a live TV show and Artie finds himself dealing with the Russian Mafia. In *Hot Poppies* he investigates the trade in illegal immigrant girls. With *Bloody London* RN moved up a gear exploring the cancerous infiltration of London and New York by the fallout from the end of Soviet Russia. This sets Artie on a roller-coaster ride which continues in *Sex Dolls* when his long-time girl friend, Lily, is beaten and raped, and Artie goes on the trail of her attackers. RN plans at least two more Artie Cohen books and as each one fires off the back of the previous they are building into a powerful body of work.

Novels. Artie Cohen series: *Red Mercury Blues* (UK 1995; as *Red Hot Blues*, US 1998), *Hot Poppies* (1997), *Bloody London* (1999), *Sex Dolls* (2002).

Full name: Regina Nadelson.
Similar stuff: Clare CURZON as Rhona Petrie; Martin Cruz SMITH.
Final fact: RN had not planned to write a series from a man's viewpoint. Lily was originally the central character but Artie appeared and wouldn't let go.

Shizuko Natsuki (b. 1938) Japan

SN is regarded as one of Japan's premier mystery writers with over 40 books to her credit since her first, *Tenshi ga kiete yuku* ("The Angel Has Gone"), in 1969, yet only a handful have been translated into English and are presently only available in the US. SN places great emphasis on the family and social background of characters and their reactions when their world collapses, sometimes in the form of a dumbfounding puzzle as in her first bestseller, *Johatsu* ("Disappearance", 1973) where a woman disappears from a plane in flight. One of her most popular books is *Murder at Mr Fuji* (filmed 1984 as *The Tragedy of W*, a rather liberal adaptation), where a grandchild claims responsibility for the death of her grandfather, even though that looked like an accident. The family weaves a complex web of alibis and lies, which the police have to unravel. There is a similar feel about *Portal of the Wind*, which starts with several apparently unrelated deaths or accidents but behind which is a staggering secret. *The Third Lady* has been alikened to HIGHSMITH's *Strangers on a Train*, since both revolve around an exchange of murders, but SN's novel is far more complex. Some forty of SN's stories have been adapted for the Japanese TV series *Shizuko Natsuki Suspense*, but her work still needs better exposure in the West.

Novels. *The Third Lady* (1978; US 1987), *Portal of the Wind* (1980; US 1990), *Murder at Mt Fuji* (1982; US 1984), *The Obituary Arrives at 2 o'Clock* (1983; US 1988), *Innocent Journey* (US 1989), *Death From the Clouds* (1988; US 1991).

Where to start: *Murder at Mt Fuji*.
Similar stuff: Seichō MATSUMOTO, Akimitsu Takagi.
Final fact: SN is a passionate player of the Japanese board game of Go and had a special set of pieces made in green so as to avoid the acute eyestrain from which she is suffering.

Michael Nava (b. 1954) US

MN is a California attorney who obtained his degree from Stanford University in 1981 and worked as a research attorney at the California Court of Appeals from 1986–95 before establishing his own private law practice in San Francisco. He is the author of the highly popular series about gay Latino criminal defence attorney Henry Rios. MN, who is gay himself, has chronicled the turbulent life of Rios through his alcoholism and the loss of one lover to AIDS, and another murdered. The series inevitably explores gay issues, but though these are frequently the driving forces for the plot the strength of the books is in the development of the characters and the relationship between individuals and families. Rios is at times only an average lawyer but he is one of those who struggles between what is morally right and what is legally just, which makes for challenging discoveries.

Novels
Henry Rios series: *The Little Death* (1986), *Goldenboy* (1988), *How Town* (1990), *The Hidden Law* (1992), *The Death of Friends* (1996), *The Burning Plain* (1997), *Rag and Bone* (2001).
Editor. *Finale* (1989).

Awards: Lambda, best gay mystery novel (1989, 1991, 1993, 1997).
Similar stuff: Mark ZUBRO.
Final fact: At the end of the last book, *Rag and Bone*, MN also announced this was to be his last mystery.

Janet Neel (b. 1940) UK

Qualified as a solicitor, JN (who was born at Oxford but educated at Cambridge) has seen a career as a civil servant and merchant banker as well as founding two successful London restaurants. In 1988 she turned to writing, starting her series featuring DCI John McLeish of the London Metropolitan Police and strong-willed businesswoman Francesca Wilson whom he marries in book four. JN draws upon her own background in developing Wilson, whose job in the Department of Trade and Industry is to try and save large businesses that are going bankrupt. In *Death's Bright Angel*, which won the CWA John Creasey Memorial Award, a director of one such business is murdered while in London and this brings Wilson in touch with McLeish. The series follows their relationship against a background of crime and corruption in commerce and academe. It is intelligently written with strong characters facing contemporary problems. *Death Among the Dons*, where the newly married Francesca finds herself working at a women's college, was shortlisted for the CWA Gold Dagger. JN has written other novels under her married name of Janet Cohen, including a financial thriller, *The Highest Bidder* (1992).

Novels
McLeish & Wilson series: *Death's Bright Angel* (1988), *Death on Site* (1989), *Death of a Partner* (1991), *Death Among the Dons* (1993), *A Timely Death* (1996), *To Die For* (1998).

Awards: CWA John Creasey Memorial Award (1988).
Similar stuff: Frances FYFIELD, Emma LATHEN.
Final fact: JN also designs war games for the US market.

Barbara Neely (b. 1941) US

BN made a considerable impact with her first book about black, 40-something, well-built domestic worker Blanche White (a name selected with considerable irony), which won three best first novel awards. Blanche is a formidable character. Strong-willed, determined, intelligent but not averse to getting her own back once in a while. At the start of the first book she escapes custody after being charged with issuing dud cheques and keeps her head down for a while taking the job of a housekeeper with an old-style white southern family. This allows BN, through White, to comment upon relationships between black and white people and between blacks and other blacks. When a wealthy old woman is killed Blanche feels she must solve the crime before she becomes the prime suspect. BN had not planned a series but the character took over. BN is a reluctant sleuth but good at it and her down-to-earth, intuitive but uncomplicated attitude is refreshing as she unravels communities and lives and pieces the clues back together. By the fourth book Blanche has tired of being a domestic worker and become a caterer. Although BN always loved writing, and had produced poetry and short stories, she had not planned to be a novelist. Her degree was in Urban Planning and her first job was to develop a women's correctional facility in Pennsylvania. She has also been a producer for the African News Service.

Novels

Blanche White series: *Blanche on the Lam* (1992), *Blanche Among the Talented Tenth* (1994), *Blanche Cleans Up* (1998), *Blanche Passes Go* (2000).

Awards: Agatha, Anthony and Macavity, best first novel (1993).
Website: <www.blanchewhite.com>
Similar stuff: Eleanor Taylor BLAND, Terris McMahan GRIMES.
Final fact: When interviewed for her first job BN had heard the appointment had already been fixed. So she told the interviewers what she thought of them and their plans for a women's correctional unit and she got the job!

Francis M. Nevins (b. 1943) US

An attorney by profession FMN is a Professor at the Saint Louis University School of Law where he has taught estate and copyright law since 1971. But he is far better known in the world of crime fiction (and western fiction) for his encyclopedic knowledge of the field with which he has compiled many single-author story collections and reference works. These include a study of Ellery Queen's life and works and the prizewinning biography of Cornell Woolrich, *First You Dream, Then You Die*. These works aside, FMN has also been a steady writer of short stories since 1972 and an occasional writer of novels. His main character is Loren Mensing, a law-school professor, who, in *Publish and Perish*, becomes involved in the suspicious death of an author whose will he had drawn up. Mensing becomes an occasional consultant for the police and has an astute, almost photographic mind. The stories are in the traditional Ellery Queen mode. His other character is Milo Turner, a con-man who creates a new persona for himself in *The 120-Hour Clock* in order to investigate the death of his lover. Mensing has a walk-on part in this book, which is FMN's best to date. Amongst his short fiction are three stories featuring Gene Holt, whom FMN thinks of as a female Inspector Morse. FMN's characters have strong views and will not be deterred. His books are for those who love devious plots, cunning puzzles and smart detection.

Novels
Loren Mensing series: *Publish and Perish* (1975), *Corrupt and Ensnare* (1978), *Into the Same River Twice* (1996), *Beneficiaries' Requiem* (2000).
Milo Turner series: *The 120-Hour Clock* (1986), *The Ninety Million Dollar Mouse* (1987).
Short Stories. *Night of Silken Snow* (2001).
Non-fiction. *The Mystery Writers Art* (editor) (1970), *Royal Bloodline: Ellery Queen, Author and Detective* (1974), *The Sound of Detection: Ellery Queen's Adventures in Radio* (1983), *Cornell Woolrich: First You Dream, Then You Die* (1988).
Editor with Martin H. Greenberg (anthologies only). *Hitchcock in Prime Time* (1985), *Mr President – Private Eye* (1989).

Full name: Francis Michael Nevins.
Where to start: *The 120-Hour Clock*.
Awards: Special Edgar (1975), Edgar, best biographical work (1989).
Similar stuff: Ellery Queen, Lesley GRANT-ADAMSON and Daniel ODIER for other con-artists.
Final fact: FMN is an advocate for literature's most maligned animal, the toad, and one of the reasons he wrote the story "Toad Cop" (in *Night of Silken Snow*) was to win friends for the sweet-voiced little amphibian. FMN tries to smuggle the word "toad" into almost everything he writes – including scholarly articles for law journals.

G. F. Newman (b. 1946) UK

Throughout his life GFN has been something of a maverick. His books, starting with his series about the bent cop Inspector Terry Sneed, consider corruption in all levels of society and constantly test the question "does the end justify the means?". In the "Bastard" trilogy, starting with *Sir, You Bastard* (filmed 1974 as *The Take*), Sneed is unscrupulous and does what he needs to feather his own nest and further his own advancement, whether that's blackmailing his superiors, working with criminals or falsifying convictions. Yet he is a good detective and his methods achieve results. Even so, as he advances he discovers that the higher echelons of business and politics are equally as corrupt. In *The Guvnor*, another cop, DCI John Fordham, is corrupt only so far as it helps him achieve justice, and not for his own benefits. Even so his actions, usually trading one criminal off against another, backfire. GFN's main impact was through TV and in particular his series of four connected plays under the generic title *Law and Order* (1978) which looked at crime and punishment through the eyes of a detective, criminal, lawyer and prison officer. Corruption was prevalent and caused an outcry from viewers. GFN has never shirked from confrontation or challenging blinkered beliefs – he believes it is part of his karma to make people aware of the corruption in society. He explored police corruption in a further TV series *Black and Blue* (1992) and looked at corruption within the courts in *Judge John Deed* (2001). In some of his books GFN's uncovering of corruption is writ large, as in *The List*, where it's corruption in the FBI, or *The Men With Guns*, where it's in the CIA. Elsewhere it's at a personal level, such as pedophilia in *The Obsession* or child abuse in *Charlie and Joanna*. Whatever his target, GFN's work is a constant thorn in the side of our collective conscience.

Novels

Inspector Sneed series: *Sir, You Bastard* (1970; as *Rogue Cop*, US 1973), *You Nice Bastard* (1972), *The Price* (1974; as *You Flash Bastard*, 1978).
Law and Order series: *A Detective's Tale* (1977), *A Prisoner's Tale* (1977), *A Villain's Tale* (1977). Revised and issued in omnibus as *Law and Order* (1983).
Non-series: *The Abduction* (1972), *The Split* (1972), *The Guvnor* (1977; as *Trade-Off*, US 1979), *The List* (1979), *The Obsession* (1980), *Charlie and Joanna* (1981), *The Men With the Guns* (1982), *Set a Thief* (1986), *The Testing Ground* (1987), *Trading the Future* (1992), *Circle of Poison* (1995).
Published Plays. *Operation Bad Apple* (1982), *The Testing Ground* (1989).

Full name: Gordon Frank Newman.
Awards: BAFTA Writer's award (1992), BAFTA, best play (1996).
Where to start: *Law and Order*.
Similar stuff: Peter DOYLE and Derek RAYMOND.
Final fact: Even in his childhood GFN was something of an anarchist. He lost two and a half fingers on his left hand when he was 11 in an accident while he was making a bomb.

Sharan Newman (b. 1949) US

SN has a degree in medieval literature and is a keen student of medieval history. Although her early novels were fantasy, including a trilogy about Queen Guinevere, with *Death Comes as Epiphany* she started a mystery series set in the 12th century. It features Catherine LeVendeur, a young lady who has come to study at the famous Convent of the Paraclete, run by the abbess Heloïse, renowned for her love affair with Peter Abelard. It is their relationship, and a lost manuscript, that is the start of Catherine's first investigation. The book won the Macavity award and was shortlisted for the Agatha and Anthony. The series is steeped in historical atmosphere, painting a rich tapestry of medieval Europe, with episodes set in Paris, Spain, Germany and England.

Novels

Catherine LeVendeur series: *Death Comes as Epiphany* (1993), *The Devil's Door* (1994), *The Wandering Arm* (1995), *Strong as Death* (1996), *Cursed in the Blood* (1998), *The Difficult Saint* (1999), *To Wear a White Cloak* (2000).
Editor. *Crime Through Time* 3 volumes (1997, 1998, 2000), first two with Miriam Grace MONFREDO.

Full name: Sharan Elizabeth Newman (*née* Hill).
Awards: Macavity, best first novel (1994), Herodotus, best US historical mystery (1999).

Website: <www.hevanet.com>
Similar stuff: Margaret FRAZER, Ellis PETERS, Kate SEDLEY.
Final fact: SN confesses that she feels more at home in the Middle Ages than the present day.

Ingrid Noll (b. 1935) Germany

The daughter of a physician, IN was born in Shanghai and raised and educated in China. Although she always wanted to be a writer, and had dabbled with stories when still a child, it was not until she was 55, when her family had grown, that she tried again, with considerable success. IN is now the bestselling German writer of crime fiction. Only three of her seven books to date have been translated into English. They are all dark psychological thrillers exploring obsession, power and control. *Hell Hath No Fury* (filmed TV 2000) is about a woman in her fifties who believes she has at last found the love of her life and will stop at nothing to keep him. In *Head Count* (filmed 1999) two childhood friends, who used to invent fantasy lives, meet again and this time find fantasy and reality merging. In *The Pharmacist* (filmed 1997) a woman, who looks after wayward individuals, finds she has taken on more than she bargained for.

Novels. *Hell Hath No Fury* (1991; UK 1996), *Head Count* (1993; UK 1997), *The Pharmacist* (1994; UK 1998).

Awards: Glauser, best novel (1994).
Similar stuff: Patricia HIGHSMITH, Ruth RENDELL as Barbara Vine.

Joyce Carol Oates (b. 1938) US

Almost all of JCO's fiction looks at the potential for violence through the repressive nature of society, especially the cultural or generation divide. However, when she wrote *Lives of the Twins* (filmed TV 1991), she regarded this as different from her previous work and sold it under a pseudonym. The book is a psychological thriller about a girl who marries a psychiatrist only to discover he is one of twins and the brother is identical in every way. The idea of twins, doubles and the polarization of good and evil fascinated the "Smith" side of JCO and she explored it in several books. In *Soul/Mate* a psychopath kills because he believes he is one of the elite in which his devil-half has awakened. In *Snake Eyes* a convicted killer is paroled and seeks out the lawyer who saved him from the electric chair and whose family, which includes twins, he now infiltrates. *You Can't Catch Me* concerns a man who finds his life dogged by a double whose life is the exact opposite. The theme reaches a pinnacle in *Starr Bright Will Be With You Soon*, about a female serial killer who seeks refuge with her estranged twin sister. Throughout the Smith titles, JCO explores the Jekyll and Hyde factor in us all.

While these books were a departure for JCO they were not a million miles from the progression her work had been taking, exploring opposing tensions within families, particularly across generations or between siblings. As far back as *Expensive People*, JCO considered a son who, seeking to escape the suffocation of his affluent parents, turns to murder. In *Angel of Light* it is the children who believe that their father's apparent suicide may have been arranged by their mother. In *American Appetites* the violence erupts between husband and wife while in the award-winning *Because It is Bitter and Because it is my Heart*, it is racial tension and a witness to murder that leads to a bizarre bond. JCO's exploration of opposites reacting is at its most potent in *Foxfire* (filmed 1996) about a girl gang that unites against men in an orgy of vengeance.

Another strand of JCO's work is her Gothic sequence that began with *Bellefleur* (1980). The first two books are eccentric fabulations rather than mysteries but the third book, *The Mysteries of Winterthurn*, a linked sequence of three short novels, is a gothic detective story. Over a period of years at the end of the 19th century, detective Xavier Kilgarven is brought back three times to Winterthurn, the place of his birth, to unravel three baffling outbreaks of murder. This is JCO's only detective fiction, though it is far from traditional. The *outré* atmosphere of this series has continued in many of her short stories, some of which are supernatural but others of which are mysteries and will be found in *Haunted* and *Faithless*. The mood also infects *Zombie*, one of her most disturbing books, which sees life through the mind of a soulless, dispassionate murderer. JCO is one of America's major literary talents – twice nominated for the Nobel Prize – and a keen observer of the passions and tensions that smoulder under the surface of society.

Novels. *Expensive People* (1968), *Angel of Light* (1981), *The Mysteries of Winterthurn* (1984), *American Appetites* (1989), *Because it is Bitter and Because it is my Heart* (1990), *Foxfire* (1993), *Zombie* (1995), *Man Crazy* (1997), *My Heart Laid Bare* (1998), *Beasts* (2002).
as Rosamund Smith: *Lives of the Twins* (1987; as *Kindred Passions*, UK 1988), *Soul/Mate* (1989), *Nemesis* (1990), *Snake Eyes* (1992), *You Can't Catch Me* (1995), *Double Delight* (1997), *Starr Bright Will be With You Soon* (1999), *The Barrens* (2001).
Short Stories. *Haunted: Tales of the Grotesque* (1994), *Faithless: Tales of Transgression* (2001).

Pen-name: Rosamund Smith.
Where to start: *The Mysteries of Winterthurn* or *Lives of the Twins*.
Awards: Rosenthal Award (1968), National Book Award (1970), Bram Stoker Award (1996).
Books about: *Invisible Writer* by Greg Johnson (1998).
Website: <www.usfca.edu/~southerr/>
Similar stuff: Andrew VACHSS, Minette WALTERS.
Final fact: JCO adopted a pen-name to see if an agent and publisher would buy her fiction, not knowing it was by her. They did but, when the truth leaked out, JCO found she had upset both her regular agent and her publisher.

Maxine O'Callaghan (b. 1937) US

Some people may have been surprised when MO'C received the PWA Lifetime Achievement Award in 1999. She had written only a dozen novels, some of which were not crime fiction, and none of them individually had received awards. But it was belated recognition for the author who created the first modern American independent female P.I., Delilah West, who appeared in the story "A Change of Clients" (*AHMM*, November 1974). In that story her husband had died and she inherited the West & West detective agency. MO'C later reworked this for the first novel, *Death is Forever*, in which Delilah is the prime suspect for the murder of the man who killed her husband and she has to unravel the complex web of intrigue to prove her innocence. Through the first few novels Delilah struggles to cope with the loss of her husband and to make ends meet and her vulnerability leaves her open not only to approaches from other men but also as a prime victim. Not especially recognized for her achievement at the time, as she was rapidly overshadowed by Marcia MULLER, Susan GRAFTON and Sara PARETSKY, MO'C has at last entered the Hall of Fame. Amongst her other books is a short series featuring the emotionally empathic child psychologist Anne Menlo.

Novels
Delilah West series: *Death is Forever* (1980), *Run From Nightmare* (1981), *Hit and Run* (1989), *Set-Up* (1991), *Trade-Off* (1994), *Down for the Count* (1997).
Anne Menlo series: *Shadow of a Child* (1996), *Only in the Ashes* (1997).
Non-series: *Dark Visions* (1988), *Something's Calling Me Home* (1991), *Dark Time* (1992).
Short Stories. *Deal with the Devil* (2001).

Full name: Helen Maxine O'Callaghan.
Pen-name: Marissa Owens (on romance novel).
Where to start: *Death is Forever*.
Awards: PWA Lifetime Achievement (1999).
Similar stuff: P.D. JAMES's Cordelia Gray; Jonathan KELLERMAN for child psychology.

Carol O'Connell (b. 1947) US

American painter CO'C caused quite a stir when rights to her first book, *Mallory's Oracle*, which she sold first to a UK publisher, were subsequently sold back to a US publisher for $800,000. The book was nominated for an Edgar but none of the series has yet won an award even though they have proved popular. Their power lies in the character of Kathleen Mallory herself. Now a sergeant in the NYPD, she had been a streetwise urchin adopted by homicide cop Lou Markowitz, and she remains distant and unpredictable. No one's quite sure how damaged her psyche is or just what happened about her real parents. Mallory is a computer expert and can hack into any system. At the start of the first book Markowitz is found dead alongside the third of three elderly women victims who have been murdered. Although on compassionate leave, Mallory teams up with her P.I. friend Charles Butler and follows a trail through the murky world of stage magic and cod spiritualism to find the murderer. Over the next three books, each with their intense and often grotesque murders, a little bit more of Mallory's early life is revealed, coming to a climax in *Flight of the Stone Angel*. This four-book sequence has to be read complete for its full power to be appreciated and stands as one of the more striking crime series of the 1990s. CO'C has returned to Mallory in a fifth book and it remains to be seen where else she will be taken. *Judas Child* was a one-off book with the potential for a series and concerns State Police Investigator Rouge Kendall's search for a serial killer who murders a young girl every Christmas. The first, fifteen years ago, had been Kendall's twin sister. CO'C's books are uncompromising, explosively emotional and vivid.

Novels
Mallory series: *Mallory's Oracle* (1994), *The Man Who Cast Two Shadows* (1995; as *The Man Who Lied to Women*, UK 1995), *Killing Critics* (1996), *Flight of the Stone Angel* (1997), *Shell Game* (1999).
Non-series: *Judas Child* (1999).

Where to start: *Mallory's Oracle*.
Website: <www.twbooks.co.uk/authors/coconn1.html>
Similar stuff: Abigail PADGETT, Don WINSLOW.
Final fact: CO'C's first completed novel was really a prequel to *Mallory's Oracle*, but she felt it didn't work and took it as an omen when it was lost in the post. Nevertheless it had served a purpose as it got the needless background out of the way and allowed CO'C to get right on with the action.

Daniel Odier (b. 1945) Switzerland

DO is a Swiss artist and music critic who, following a tour of the Far East in 1968 studied taosim and tantrism and now runs a Tantra/Chan study centre in Paris. He has written several books under his own name, plus novels under the alias Delacorta. Most of these feature classical pianist turned con-man and criminal mastermind Serge Gorodish and his kinky nymphette companion Alba. Gorodish is a modern-day punk Raffles. He enjoys committing crimes for their own sake, like works of art. In the first, and best-known, *Diva* (filmed 1981), Gorodish learns of a bootleg tape of an opera singer who has refused to have her voice recorded but it becomes switched with a surveillance tape and Gorodish isn't the only one looking for it. The books are a light-hearted mixture of underground punk and homage to hard-boiled American fiction. The later volume, *Alba*, finds Gorodish in America on the trail of his partner who has been sucked into a weird cult. DO has also written *The Rap Factor*, about a super-funky P.I. with a philosophy degree, who tries to solve the murder of a young rap artist. The books are apparently best read in the original French.

Novels
Serge Gorodish series as Delacorta: *Diva* (1978; US 1983), *Nana* (1979; US 1984), *Luna* (1979; US 1985), *Rock* (1981; as *Lola*, US 1986), *Vida* (1985; UK 1986), *Alba* (1988; UK 1989).
Non-series as Delacorta: *The Rap Factor* (1992; US 1993).

Pen-name: Delacorta
Where to start: *Diva.*
Similar stuff: Lesley GRANT-ADAMSON and Francis M. NEVINS for other con-artists.

Lillian O'Donnell (b. 1926) US

LO'D was born in Italy of Hungarian extraction, but is an American citizen. She was a stage and TV actress from the age of 14 until her marriage in 1954, and she turned to writing a few years later. For the first ten years she produced one-off suspense novels. *Death of a Player* used her theatrical background but though *Babes in the Wood* may sound similar it is actually about a newly wed wife who becomes the prime suspect when the children who should inherit from her husband all start to die. LO'D found her forté when she created young NYPD cop Nora Mulcahaney in what has become the longest-running police procedural series featuring a lead policewoman. Mulcahaney is fresh from police academy in the first book, which deals with women receiving a series of threatening phone calls, and she ages steadily as the series progresses, being in her 40s in *Blue Death*. The series focuses on her and her family (rather like Mary-Beth in *Cagney and Lacey*) and are not rigid procedurals. Nevertheless LO'D creates a convincing New York environment and crime scene and the series has kept track of the increasing and varied forms of violence arising on the streets. Mulcahaney usually has the luxury of dealing with just one crime at a time, and anything else arising is related. *No Business Being a Cop* was filmed for TV as *Prime Target* (1989). LO'D's other series lack the sparkle of the Mulcahaney books. Mici (pronounced Mitzy) Anholt is an Hungarian-American and former ballet dancer who becomes a criminal justice investigator for the Crime Victims Compensation Board. She is an appealing and sympathetic character but somewhat impulsive and lightweight. Much the same applies to Gwenn Ramadge, a former model who inherits a detective agency from her boss.

Novels
Norah Mulcahaney series: *The Phone Calls* (1972), *Don't Wear Your Wedding Ring* (1973), *Dial 577 R-A-P-E* (1974), *The Baby Merchants* (1975), *Leisure Dying* (1976), *No Business Being a Cop* (1979), *The Children's Zoo* (1981), *Cop Without a Shield* (1983), *Ladykiller* (1984), *Casual Affairs* (1985), *The Other Side of the Door* (1987), *A Good Night to Kill* (1989), *A Private Crime* (1991), *Pushover* (1992), *Lockout* (1994), *Blue Death* (1998).
Mici Anhalt series: *Aftershock* (1977), *Falling Star* (1979), *Wicked Designs* (1980).

Gwenn Ramadge series: *A Wreath for the Bride* (1990), *Used to Kill* (1993), *The Raggedy Man* (1995), *The Goddess Affair* (1997).
Non-series: *Death on the Grass* (1960), *Death Blanks the Screen* (1961), *Death Schuss* (1963), *Murder Under the Sun* (1964), *Death of a Player* (1964), *Babes in the Wood* (1965), *The Sleeping Beauty Murders* (1967), *The Face of the Crime* (1968), *The Tachi Tree* (1968), *Dive Into Darkness* (1971).

Full name: Lillian O'Donnell (*née* Udvardy).
Where to start: *The Phone Calls.*
Awards: American Mystery Award, best police procedural (1990).
Similar stuff: Susan DUNLAP, Dorothy UHNAK.
Final fact: LO'D was the first woman stage manager in New York.

Sister Carol Anne O'Marie (b. 1933) US

The idea of a nun writing mysteries conjures up the image of perhaps the ultimate cozy, but it isn't quite like that. Although in her 70s, Sister Mary Helen, who is modelled on a former principal of CAO'M's convent, is a very modern-thinking nun even if traditional in her everyday life. Retired after nearly 50 years of teaching (similar to her slightly younger creator), Sister Mary Helen has gone to undertake research at the Mount St Francis College for Women in San Francisco. A professor is murdered and soon the Sister is involved in a scheme to exploit illegal Portuguese immigrants. Thereafter the Sister remains at the College. The police representatives in the series are detectives Dennis Gallagher and Kate Murphy. Murphy was an alumna of the college and thus finds herself frequently consulted by (and consulting) the Sister. CAO'M believes that crime novels are today's equivalent of the medieval morality play, depicting good vs evil. Sister Mary Helen believes that God is directing her to do good in the solving of crimes, though there is no supernatural intervention. She does it all through keen observation and what she sees betrayed in people's eyes. Since 1990 CAO'M has been running a shelter for homeless women in Oakland.

Novels

Sister Mary Helen series: *A Novena for Murder* (1984), *Advent of Dying* (1986), *The Missing Madonna* (1988), *Murder in Ordinary Time* (1991), *Murder Makes a Pilgrimage* (1993), *Death Goes on Retreat* (1995), *Death of an Angel* (1997), *Death Takes Up a Collection* (1998), *Requiem at the Refuge* (2000), *Advent of Dying* (2001), *The Corporal Works of Murder* (2002).

Similar stuff: D.M. GREENWOOD, Ralph MCINERNY writing as Monica Quill.
Final fact: CAO'M came second in a Bell Ringing contest in 1979.

Roger Ormerod (b. 1920) UK

The *Sunday Times* described RO as "eclectic" and "underrated", adding that he "can be relied upon to come up with the startling goods." RO is at the top level of that legion of second-tier British crime-fiction writers who produce reliable, original and highly entertaining work, yet do not receive the recognition they deserve. Much of his work is now out of print and difficult to find. Most of his books fall into two main series. The first features two private detectives, David Mallin and George Coe, sometimes together, sometimes individually. The books are modelled on the standard hard-boiled American format but toned down and refurbished for English readers. RO delights in creating puzzles. *The Weight of Evidence* is one of the most complicated "locked-room" murder mysteries of recent years, while *Cart Before the Hearse* has the detectives knowing the murderer but not knowing the victim. After 16 books in this sequence RO opted for a new series. In *Face Value*, Detective Inspector Richard Patton is only three days from retirement when he becomes involved in a missing persons case and, just to complicate matters, becomes romantically entangled with the missing (later dead) person's wife. In later books Patton achieves his retirement but is constantly being called out by friends and family to help solve problems, including previously unsolved cases, such as in *An Alibi Too Soon* and *The Night She Died*. This series is refreshingly inventive and shows a keen knowledge of police procedures. RO was for many years a county court officer, so knew the day-to-day processes related to summonses and petty crime. He also worked in the Department of Social Security before, at the age of 52, opting to become a postman, which gave him plenty of time to think up plots. One of the best of his non-series books is *Seeing Red*, in which a detective sergeant, currently suspended from duty, becomes interested in the truth behind a purported accidental death. It is amongst his one-off books that you will find RO at his most eclectic, such as in the wildly off-the-wall *The Seven Razors of Ockam* in which a whole town runs amok. RO's books are worth seeking out for their rock-solid dependability.

Novels

Mallin & Coe series: *Time to Kill* (1974), *The Silence of the Night* (1974), *Full Fury* (1975), *A Spoonful of Luger* (1975), *Sealed With a Loving Kill* (1976), *The Colour of Fear* (1976), *A Glimpse of Death* (1976), *Too Late for the Funeral* (1977), *This Murder Comes to Mind* (1977), *A Dip Into Murder* (1978), *The Weight of Evidence* (1978), *The Bright Face of Danger* (1979), *The Amnesia Trap* (1979), *Cart Before the Hearse* (1979), *More Dead Than Alive* (1980), *One Deathless Hour* (1981).

Inspector Patton series: *Face Value* (1983; as *The Hanging Doll Murder*, US 1984), *Still Life With Pistol* (1986), *An Alibi Too Soon* (1987), *An Open Window* (1988), *Guilt on the Lily* (1989), *Death of an Innocent* (1989), *No Sign of Life* (1990), *When the Old Man Died* (1991), *Shame the Devil* (1993), *Mask of Innocence* (1994), *Stone Cold Dead* (1995), *The Night She Died* (1997).

Philippa Lowe series: *Hung in the Balance* (1990), *Bury Him Darkly* (1991), *A Shot at Nothing* (1993).

Non-series: *Double Take* (1980), *Seeing Red* (1984), *Dead Ringer* (1985), *A Death to Remember* (1986), *The Second Jeopardy* (1987), *By Death Possessed* (1988), *Farewell Gesture* (1991), *Third Time Fatal* (1992), *The Key to the Case* (1992), *And*

Hope to Die (1995), *Landscape with Corpse* (1996), *Curtain of Beads* (1996), *The Vital Minute* (1996), *The Seven Razors of Ockham* (1997), *Parting Shot* (1998), *Final Toll* (1999).

Where to start: *The Weight of Evidence*, *Face Value* and *Seeing Red*.
Similar stuff: Jonathan ROSS, Miles TRIPP.

Abigail Padgett (b. 1942) US

AP has had a long and varied career, primarily in sociology and rehabilitation and, more recently, as a court investigator for the Child Protection Services. Though she turned full-time writer in 1988 she is still an advocate for the mentally ill. All of this background, together with AP's interests in native American art and culture, feed into her intense books. The first, *Child of Silence*, which introduced Barbara Joan "Bo" Bradley, a child abuse investigator, concerns the discovery of an abandoned four-year-old deaf child on an Indian reservation. An attempt is made to murder the child and Bo, despite her code of practice not to get personally involved, determines to find out the truth. Bradley is a manic depressive, although these mood swings can heighten her awareness, giving at times an almost mystical feel to her perceptions. The book was shortlisted for the Agatha, Anthony and Macavity awards. *Strawgirl*, which was listed by the *Los Angeles Times* amongst the ten best mysteries of the year, is even more potent. An infant girl has been raped and murdered and Bo tries to rescue her sister from a controversial New Age cult. The series is an emotional whirlpool that leaves no one unscathed. Her second series features Blue McCarron, a social psychologist who is asked by a man to help his sister who has confessed to murdering someone and storing his body in a freezer. Blue applies her knowledge of primate behaviour (she has made a study of apes) to the case. It's an unusual but effective scenario. AP has cast a new light on crime fiction and woven suspense into the shadows.

Novels
Bo Bradley series: *Child of Silence* (1993), *Strawgirl* (1994), *Turtle Baby* (1995), *Moonbird Boy* (1996), *The Dollmaker's Daughters* (1997).
Blue McCarron series: *Blue* (1998), *The Last Blue Plate Special* (2000).
Non-Fiction. Weep for the Living (2000).

Full name: Mary Abigail Padgett.
Where to start: *Child of Silence*.
Website: <www.twbookmark.com/authors/66/264/>
Similar stuff: Carol O'CONNELL, Nancy PICKARD.

Emma Page (b. 1921) UK

EP works firmly in the traditional English village mystery field somewhere in the heart of England not a million miles from EP's own home territory in Worcestershire. EP's father had been a policeman and her

Inspector Kelsey (we never know his first name) doubtless bears many of his traits. He is a methodical detective who perseveres to find the truth even when matters at first seem cut-and-dried, as in *Every Second Thursday*, when he becomes suspicious of the purported suicide of an elderly lady. Most of EP's books feature elderly women, including the early non-series *Family and Friends* where a once beautiful woman has turned awkward with age and there are plenty of candidates wanting her dead. EP depicts the intricate networks that people develop and how these must be unravelled to discover the truth.

Novels

Kelsey & Lambert series: *Missing Woman* (1980), *Every Second Thursday* (1981), *Last Walk Home* (1982), *Cold Light of Day* (1983), *Scent of Death* (1985), *Final Moments* (1987), *A Violent End* (1988), *Deadlock* (1991), *Mortal Remains* (1992), *In the Event of My Death* (1994), *Murder Comes Calling* (1995), *Hard Evidence* (1996), *Intent to Kill* (1998), *Say It With Murder* (2000).

Non-series: *In Loving Memory* (1970), *Family and Friends* (1972), *A Fortnight by the Sea* (1973; as *Add a Pinch of Cyanide*, US 1973), *Element of Chance* (1975).

Full name: Honoria Tirbutt (*née* O'Mahoney).
Pen-name: Emma Page.
Where to start: *Missing Woman.*
Similar stuff: Catherine AIRD.

Orania Papazoglou (b. 1951) US

Although OP's first series of books came out under her own name, she is probably better known now as Jane Haddam, under which she writes the Gregor Demarkian books. OP was born in America of Greek descent, and her first job was an editorial assistant on *Greek Accent*. She still continues to write magazine journalism, but she turned full-time writer in 1983 partly prompted by meeting, and subsequently marrying, the writer William DEANDREA. Her early books were humorous mysteries. Patience Campbell McKenna, "Pay" to her friends, is a thin, diet freak, chain-smoking journalist who also writes romance novels for extra cash. In *Sweet, Savage Death*, her close friend, America's leading romance writer, is found dead in the river and Pay's agent turns up dead in her room, door bolted on the inside. Pay is attending a romance-writers conference and turns sleuth, convinced the murderer is there. In the later novels OP continues to combine the world of romance fiction with crime and murder in an entertaining mix. OP has also written several standalone suspense novels under her own name and pseudonyms of which *Graven Image*, as Ann Paris, allows her to exploit her Greek background. *Watcher in the Garden* is about a stalker, while both *Sanctity* and *Charisma* involve murders amongst nuns or (in *Charisma*) ex-nuns. However, since 1990 OP has concentrated primarily on her Demarkian series. Demarkian was the founder of the FBI Department of Behavioral Sciences but retired with his wife's imminent death and subsequently moved back to the Armenian community of his youth in Philadelphia. OP has transferred her Greek Orthodox upbringing to the Armenian community and each novel starts with a wealth of fascinating ethnic background. Demarkian remains a consultant to the police who need his skills in understanding criminal behaviour as well as his specialist knowledge in poisons. He also helps when crimes cross police jurisdiction boundaries. He is helped in his investigations by Father Tibor Kasparian of the Armenian church and by his girlfriend, Bennis Hannaford, a writer, and a romanticized image of OP herself. Each adventure revolves around a particular holiday, though that is usually just the trigger to the crime. At the heart of them all is character and community, not just religious or ethnic communities, but any group or gathering, such as a New Age movement in *Bleeding Hearts*, or a keep-fit organization in *Fountain of Death*. These books are more downbeat than the Pay McKenna series and paint a bleak picture of the innocent gullibility of many individuals that leave them open to crime. OP is painstaking in her research to ensure she gets the small details correct and is thorough in her plotting, as the story-lines are frequently complex.

Novels

Patience McKenna series: *Sweet, Savage Death* (1984), *Wicked, Loving Murder* (1985), *Death's Savage Passion* (1986), *Rich Radiant Slaughter* (1988), *Once and Always Murder* (1989).
Non-series: *Sanctity* (1986), *Charisma* (1992).
Gregor Demarkian series as Jane Haddam: *Not a Creature was Stirring* (1990), *Precious Blood* (1991), *Act of Darkness* (1991), *Quoth the Raven* (1991), *A Great Day for the Deadly* (1992), *Feast of Murder* (1992), *A Stillness in Bethlehem* (1992), *Murder Superior* (1993), *Bleeding Hearts* (1994), *Dear Old Dead* (1994), *Festival of Deaths* (1994), *Fountain of Death* (1995), *And One to Die On* (1996), *Baptism in Blood* (1996), *Deadly Beloved* (1997), *Skeleton Key* (2000), *True Believers* (2001), *Somebody Else's Music* (2002).
as Angelica Parr: *Watcher in the Garden* (1989).
as Ann Paris: *Graven Image* (1987), *Arrowheart* (1988).

Pen-names: Jane Haddam, Angelica Paar, Ann Paris.
Where to start: *Not a Creature was Stirring*.
Similar stuff: Carolyn G. HART, Les ROBERTS.
Final fact: OP met William DeAndrea when she went to collect a couple of his books that she had ordered from the Murder Ink bookstore and there he was on the other side of the counter.

Sara Paretsky (b. 1947) US

SP rapidly earned a formidable reputation for her books featuring Chicago P.I. V.I. Warshawski. The V.I. stands for Victoria Iphegenia, and you can call her Vic but never Vicki. She is tough, resilient and determined. We first meet her, in *Indemnity Only*, in the dark (the fuses have blown), and this is a fitting metaphor for the start of the series. Not only does it cast a veil of secrecy over V.I. – she remains her own person and though we learn much about her, she only tells you as much as you need to know and she remains fearlessly in control. It also conjures up in seconds the sombre and dark world of the P.I., capturing the image of the black-and-white P.I. movies of the forties and establishing a comfortable traditional mood despite the vibrant contemporary nature of the books. Warshawki is the daughter of a Polish cop and an Italian-Jewish opera singer. She was a former civil rights protester and public defender and, like Ross MACDONALD's Lew Archer, has a special interest in corporate crime. She goes for the corrupt leaders of big business or social institutions. SP worked in insurance for ten years before becoming a full-time author, and before that had worked as a writer, publicist and organizer with many Chicago businesses. In addition to the insurance business, which features in several of her books, her targets include the Catholic Church (*Killing Orders*), the Health service (*Bitter Medicine*), local politics (*Blood Shot* – which received the CWA Silver Dagger), the police (*Burn Marks*), the entertainment industry and private security (both in *Hard Time*). Although her first case is on behalf of a union leader, most of her cases arise out of family or friends. This establishes a more personal link between detective and client and heightens often very private issues. In the recent *Total Recall*, a case brings back horrendous memories of the Nazi concentration camps with tendrils that are still alive today. The Warshawski novels were not only in the vanguard of the female P.I. but amongst the toughest and most uncompromising. One film has been made, *V.I. Warshawski* (1991), starring Kathleen Turner, not based on any specific novel and not adequately reflecting SP's creation. Although SP has written several non-series short stories (some of which will be found in *A Taste for Life*), she has so far written only one stand-alone novel, *Ghost Country*. It is about a group of homeless women and the frightening consequences when they begin to worship at a shrine that they have created and believe has been visited by the Holy Spirit. SP was born in Ames, Iowa, but has lived in Chicago for over thirty years. She was the driving force behind founding the Sisters in Crime organization in 1986.

Novels

V.I. Warshawski series: *Indemnity Only* (1982), *Deadlock* (1984), *Killing Orders* (1985), *Bitter Medicine* (1987), *Blood Shot* (1988; as *Toxic Shock*, UK 1988), *Burn Marks* (1990), *Guardian Angel* (1992), *Tunnel Vision* (1994), *Hard Time* (1999), *Total Recall* (2001).

Non-series: *Ghost Country* (1998).

Short Stories. *A Taste of Life* (1995), *Windy City Blues* (1995; as *V.I. for Short*, UK 1995).

Editor. *A Woman's Eye* (1991), *Women on the Case* (1996).

Where to start: The first three novels are available in a single-volume omnibus, *V.I. Warshawski* (1993).

Awards: CWA Silver Dagger (1988), Anthony, best anthology (1992), German Marlowe Award (1993), Mark Twain award, distinguished contribution to Midwest Literature (1996), CWA Diamond Dagger (2002).
Website: <www.saraparetsky.com>
Similar stuff: Linda BARNES, Sue GRAFTON, Marcia MULLER.
Final fact: SP was named "Woman of the Year" by *Ms.* magazine in 1987.

Edith Pargeter *see pseudonym* Ellis Peters

Ann Paris *pseudonym, see* Orania Papazoglou

Robert B. Parker (b. 1932) US

Parker's Boston based hard-boiled P.I. Spenser (no first name) has been called the direct lineal descendant of Chandler's Philip Marlowe, and to some degree he is, more so than, say, Ross MACDONALD's Lew Archer. But this similarity is primarily in the first novel only, *The Godwulf Manuscript*, where a search for a lost manuscript uncovers a traffic in drugs. Even then differences are apparent. Spenser is not averse to killing with his own bare hands (he's an ex-boxer and keeps in training), he is far less a loner, he's a good cook and he spouts poetry. From the second book Spenser begins a relationship with Susan Silverman, a guidance counsellor for a missing boy he's trying to trace. Susan remains his companion for most of the series, though their relationship cools with *Valediction*, and *A Catskill Eagle* deals with her rescue. Spenser is a Marlowe for the liberated, feminist world of the seventies and beyond. He has a code of ethics – in fact he constantly broods over this – but has no qualms in consorting with gangsters if it achieves his aims. The award winning *Promised Land*, where Spenser is on the trail of a missing wife, introduces Hawk, a black, immensely strong "minder", who becomes a close ally. *Promised Land* is one of the best all-round Spenser novels where characters and relationships take on a more substantial form, and was the first to be adapted as a TV film (1985). With the next novel, *The Judas Goat*, the action moves up a gear as Spenser and Hawk go in search of a group of terrorists. The novels of the late eighties and early nineties are only slightly less violent than the earlier books, and his main opposition remains organized crime, but they are more socially aware and less action-orientated. Spenser becomes involved in corruption in college basketball (*Playmates*), a housing ghetto (*Double Deuce*), even an academic mystery (*Hush Money*). The series has kept pace with the times, though neither Spenser nor Susan age much. The length of the series has inevitably resulted in a loss of freshness – most diehard Spenser fans believe the first four books are the ultimate in P.I. fiction – but the large cast of characters and the increasing complexity of Spenser's life continues to keep the books in the bestseller lists. The series was adapted for television as

Spenser for Hire (1985–8) with Robert Urich in the title rôle. There have also been eight further TV films made starting with *Ceremony* (1993), all adapted from the novels, with Urich again in the main rôle until *Small Vices* (1999) when Joe Mantegna took over. RBP's preferred actor would have been Robert Mitchum in his heyday. The popularity of the Spenser series has added to the tourist attraction of Boston. RBP has written a guide, *Spenser's Boston*, and a beautiful coffee-table book *Boston: History in the Making*.

The Spenser series alone would have been sufficient homage to Chandler but RBP was commissioned to complete Chandler's Marlowe novel, *Poodle Springs*, and he wrote a new Marlowe adventure, *Perchance to Dream*, a sequel to *The Big Sleep*. RBP's own doctoral dissertation "The Private Eye in Hammett and Chandler', written in 1971, was edited and issued as a limited edition volume in 1984.

RBP has written a few one-off novels. *Wilderness* concerns a man who witnesses a murder and he and his wife are subsequently threatened if they involve the police, so he goes after the murderer himself. *All Our Yesterdays* is a family saga of love and crime, whilst *Love and Glory* is a romance with no crime element. Recently RBP started two new series. *Night Passage* features Jesse Stone, who had been fired from his job as a homicide detective with the LAPD because he is an alcoholic but he gets hired as Chief of Police in Paradise, Massachusetts. *Family Honor* is the first of the Sunny Randall books. Sunny is an ex-cop and the daughter of a policeman, who resigns from the force when only 32 and becomes a P.I. These two series are promising but less cohesive than the Spenser books. RBP has also written a western novel, *Gunman's Rhapsody*, featuring Wyatt Earp.

RBP was 40 before he turned to writing. He had previously worked in insurance and advertising before entering academe as a lecturer and achieving a professorship in 1977. He married in 1956 and has written two non-fiction books with his wife of which *Three Weeks in Spring* (1978) is a touching account of her battle with breast cancer.

Novels

Spenser series: *The Godwulf Manuscript* (1973), *God Save the Child* (1974), *Mortal Stakes* (1975), *Promised Land* (1976), *The Judas Goat* (1978), *Looking for Rachel Wallace* (1980), *A Savage Place* (1981), *Early Autumn* (1981), *Ceremony* (1982), *The Widening Gyre* (1983), *Valediction* (1984), *A Catskill Eagle* (1985), *Taming a Sea-Horse* (1986), *Pale Kings and Princes* (1987), *Crimson Joy* (1988), *Playmates* (1989), *Stardust* (1990), *Pastime* (1991), *Double Deuce* (1992), *Paper Doll* (1993), *Walking Shadow* (1994), *Thin Air* (1995), *Chance* (1996), *Small Vices* (1997), *Sudden Mischief* (1998), *Hush Money* (1999), *Hugger Mugger* (2000), *Potshot* (2001), *Widow's Walk* (2002).

Philip Marlowe series: *Poodle Springs* completed for Raymond Chandler (1989), *Perchance to Dream* (1991).

Jesse Stone series: *Night Passage* (1997), *Trouble in Paradise* (1998), *Death in Paradise* (2001).

Sunny Randall series: *Family Honor* (1999), *Perish Twice* (2000).
Non-series: *Wilderness* (1979), *All Our Yesterdays* (1994), *Gunman's Rhapsody* (2001).
Short Stories. *Surrogate* single Spenser story (1982).
Non-fiction. *The Private Eye in Hammett and Chandler* (1984), *Parker on Writing* (1985), *Spenser's Boston* (1994).

Full name: Robert Brown Parker.
Where to start: Unless you want to read the series in order try *Promised Land* as a sampler.
Awards: Edgar, best novel (1977), Japanese Maltese Falcon (1983), PWA, life achievement (1995), Sherlock, Best Detective Created by an American (1999).
Website: The Unofficial website, "The Spensarium" is at <www.linkingpage.com/spenser/>. The amazingly detailed Spenser site is at <www.mindspring.com/~boba4/> and you may also like to check out another detailed site at <www.geocities.com/Athens/Academy/5473/>
Similar stuff: Jeremiah HEALY's Cuddy books to a degree.
Final fact: RBP created the character of Sunny Randall especially for his friend, the actress Helen Hunt.

Angelica Parr *pseudonym, see* Orania Papazoglou

Frank Parrish *pseudonym, see* Roger Longrigg

James Patterson (b. 1947) US

JP was a leading advertising executive before he turned to fiction. He created award-winning campaigns for Kodak, Burger King and Toys R' Us and later wrote about American cultural images with colleague Peter Kim in *The Day America Told the Truth* (1991). By then he was already an established bestselling author. His first book, *The Thomas Berryman Number*, about a manhunt for a ruthless assassin, won an Edgar award. During his next few books he was striving to find a niche in the thriller market. The books are enjoyable if near misses. JP remained dissatisifed with *Virgin* (filmed 1991 as *Child of Darkness, Child of Light*), about two girls, one of whom is apparently giving birth to the Messiah and the other to Satan, and recently completely rewrote it in a detective form as *Cradle and All*. Another, *Black Market*, where a terrorist group working for a shadowy international figure try to destroy the financial centre of New York, feels chillingly prophetic. JP hit his stride with *The Midnight Club* about a tough, streetwise but invalided New York cop on the trail of the leader of an international crime ring. This was followed with his first major bestseller and the first in his series featuring Alex Cross, *Along Came a Spider* (filmed 2001). Cross is a tall, black, athletic Washington D.C. homicide detective who holds a PhD in psychology and ran a private practice before joining the police. His qualifications mean that if there's a serial killer or psychopath about, Cross is on the case. In *Kiss the Girls* (filmed 1997) he's up against two serial killers in a case of "twinning". The cunning psychopath of the first novel, Gary Soneji, returns in *Cat and Mouse* as Cross's nemesis. JP repeats this approach in *Roses are Red* and *Violets are Blue* when he is up against a vicious killer known as "The Mastermind". JP had five number one bestsellers in a row – four of them being Alex Cross books and the fifth being his fantasy about genetically-engineered flight, *When the Wind Blows*. JP's new series concerns four professional women in San Francisco – a homicide detective, a medical examiner, an assistant district attorney and a newspaper reporter – join forces in *1st to Die* (filmed TV series 2001) to catch yet another serial killer. JP's style is clipped, fast paced and skims along like a stone over water. He has also written two non-crime novels with Peter de Jonge and a tear-jerking romance *Suzanne's Diary for Nicholas* (2001).

Novels
Alex Cross series: *Along Came a Spider* (1993), *Kiss the Girls* (1995), *Jack and Jill* (1996), *Cat and Mouse* (1997), *Pop Goes the Weasel* (1999), *Roses Are Read* (2000), *Violets are Blue* (2001).
Women's Murder Club series: *1st to Die* (2001), *2nd Chance* (2002).
Non-series: *The Thomas Berryman Number* (1976), *The Season of the Machete* (1977), *The Jericho Commandment* (1979), *Virgin* (1980; rev'd as *Cradle and All*, 2000), *Black Market* (1986), *The Midnight Club* (1989), *Hide and Seek* (1996), *See How They Run* (1997), *When the Wind Blows* (1998).

Full name: James Brendan Patterson.
Where to start: *Along Came a Spider*.
Awards: Edgar, best first novel (1977).
Website: <www.twbookmark.com/features/jamespatterson/index.html>
Similar stuff: Jonathan KELLERMAN.
Final fact: JP's first book was rejected 31 times before being accepted.

Richard North Patterson (b. 1947) US

RNP was a practising attorney specializing in commercial law until he was at last able to turn to writing full-time in 1993, following the success of *Degree of Guilt* (filmed TV mini-series 1995). This was his second novel about trial lawyer and special investigator Christopher Paget and, like many of RNP's books, is part-legal/part-political thriller. Paget had first appeared in *The Lasko Tangent*, in which the Economic Crimes Commission employs Paget to find sufficient evidence to convict a corrupt but influential millionaire who is friends with the President. RNP's next two books were less successful. *The Outside Man* involves another lawyer up against the rich and influential as he tries to find the murderer of a friend's wife. *Escape the Night* turns the mirror around and looks at terror within the world of the rich, as a man finds himself menaced by the terror that claimed his parents years before. With *Private Screening*, however, RNP began to establish his own fictional network. From here on most of his books feature one or two common characters within a consistent fictional world – he calls them his "repertory company". In *Private Screening* a presidential candidate is murdered and a terrorist, known as the Phoenix, mounts a televised trial of the accused, with the viewers as the jury. The defending attorney, Tony Lord, reappears in *Silent Witness*, where we learn that in his youth he had been accused of murder, and when he returns to his hometown years later, events start to repeat themselves. The prosecuting attorney in that novel, Stella Marz, reappears in *Dark Lady*, where her future is threatened by two separate but possibly connected murders. Meanwhile, in *No Safe Place*, Kerry Kilcannon, the brother of the candidate assassinated in *Private Screening*, finds he is under threat by an anti-abortionist who does not want to see Kilcannon as the next President. Kilcannon's influence continues in *Protect and Defend* where Caroline Masters, who had appeared in the Paget novel *Degree of Guilt*, is nominated to take the post as first woman Head of the Supreme Court. RNP's work, more than that of John GRISHAM's or Scott TUROW's, with which it has been compared, shows the interaction and influence of politics and wealth upon the legal system.

Novels

Christopher Paget/Caroline Masters series: *The Lasko Tangent* (1979), *Degree of Guilt* (1992), *Eyes of a Child* (1994), *The Final Judgment* (1995; as *The Summer of Caroline*, UK 1996; as *Caroline Masters*, 2000), *Protect and Defend* (2000).

Tony Lord/Stella Marz series: *Private Screening* (1985), *Silent Witness* (1997), *Dark Lady* (1999).

Non-series: *The Outside Man* (1981), *Escape the Night* (1983), *No Safe Place* (1998).

Where to start: *Private Screening.*

Awards: Edgar, best first novel (1980), Grand Prix de Littérature Policière Best Foreign (1995).

Similar stuff: William BERNHARDT, Jay BRANDON, Robert K. TANENBAUM.

Final fact: RNP vowed to complete his first novel by the time he was 30. He did with days to spare and on his birthday he found in his mailbox – a rejection slip!

Barbara Paul (b. 1931) US

BP's work has a voice of its own. Although it falls within traditional boundaries her treatment is sufficiently distinctive to make the books harder to define. This may come from BP's theatrical background. She earned her degree in Theatre and has been a drama teacher and director. Her novels have a theatricality about them, with people moving in and out of the spotlight. Her writing career began with several science-fiction novels, including the *Star Trek* related *The Three-Minute Universe* (1988), but she soon shifted to crime fiction which has been the bulk of her output. Her first mystery, *The Fourth Wall*, is a powerful story of revenge. It is an example of her novels of manipulation in which her characters serve almost like scene-shifters, shaping the world about them. The theatrically entitled *First Gravedigger* has an antiques dealer arranging a murder in order to purloin an antique chair. In *Kill Fee* (filmed TV 1990 as *Murder C.O.D.*) a murderer kills people and then blackmails those who would most profit from the death. BP wrote a series of historical opera whodunits featuring Enrico Caruso and Geraldine Ferrar, but generally she avoided developing a series character. Her main heroine, Marian Larch, developed more by chance. She is a NYPD homicide detective who in *The Renewable Virgin* is just one of the characters whose viewpoint BP explores. She appears only at the end of *He Huffed and He Puffed*, another manipulative blackmail novel. It was not until *You Have the Right to Remain Silent* and its direct sequel *The Apostrophe Thief*, the latter a bizarre play within a play, that Larch strode centre stage and she has since dominated BP's writing. All of BP's books are worth exploring. Through ingenious use of perspective and stage direction she casts a different light on traditional themes.

Novels
Marian Larch series: *The Renewable Virgin* (1985), *He Huffed and He Puffed* (1989), *Good King Sauerkraut* (1989; as *King of Misrule*, UK 1990), *You Have the Right to Remain Silent* (1992), *The Apostrophe Thief* (1993), *Fare Play* (1995), *Full Frontal Murder* (1997).
Enrico Caruso series: *A Cadenza for Caruso* (1984), *Prima Donna at Large* (1985), *A Chorus of Detectives* (1987).
Non-series: *The Fourth Wall* (1979), *Liars and Tyrants and People Who Turn Blue* (1980), *First Gravedigger* (1980), *Your Eyelids are Growing Heavy* (1981), *Kill Fee* (1985), *But He Was Already Dead When I Got There* (1986), *In-laws and Outlaws* (1990; as *Death Elsewhere*, UK 1991).
Short Stories. *Jack be Quick* (1999).

Full name: Barbara Jeanne Paul.
Where to start: *The Fourth Wall.*
Website: <www.barbarapaul.com>
Similar stuff: Marian BABSON, Jane DENTINGER, Annette MEYERS.
Final fact: BP was astonished to see the film *Murder C.O.D.* which had been based on her book *Kill Fee*, but about which she knew nothing. The book had been optioned several years before but that option had lapsed. It seems no one had checked or thought to tell the author!

Michael Pearce (b. 1933) UK

MP was raised in what was then called the Anglo-Egyptian Sudan and has retained an active interest in the region. His knowledge of Egyptian and surrounding cultures is crucial to the events related in his delightful series featuring Captain Gareth Owen, the Mamur Zapt, or head of the secret police in Cairo in the years leading up to the First World War. At that time the British retained a strong hold over Egyptian affairs, though there were continuing tensions with the Turks and other nations, such as the French, who believe they have controlling rights in the region. The Mamur Zapt keeps a watchful eye over all of this, intervening where necessary and sometimes getting involved more than he wishes. MP writes with a sharp, incisive style, with never a word wasted, telling more in a sentence than other writers tell in a whole page. He is witty, observant and ingenious, his narrative skidding over turbulent situations with typical British aplomb. Though light-hearted at the core the stories are serious, and MP's commentary upon the British and the Egyptian cultures says much about how Anglo-Egyptian relationships worked. *The Mamur Zapt and the Spoils of Egypt* won the CWA Last Laugh award, whilst both *Death of an Effendi* and *A Cold Touch of Ice* were shortlisted for the CWA Ellis Peters Historical Dagger. MP also worked as a Russian interpreter and his understanding of Russian politics at the turn of the last century is the basis for a new series featuring Dmitri Kameron, a lawyer of Scottish-Russian descent who is working in Russia in the 1890s. In the first book, *Dmitri and the Milk Drinkers*, Dmitri believes the potential for reform is opening in Czarist Russia but when he is sent to trace a missing woman the opposition he encounters suggests to him that there are plenty who are against such changes. MP's shrewd observations on British and Russian imperialism add the spice to both these entertaining series. MP has also written a non-crime novel, more a comedy of manners, *The Dragoman's Story* (2000), which explores the Victorian attitude to other cultures.

Novels

Mamur Zapt series: *The Mamur Zapt and the Return of the Carpet* (1988), *The Mamur Zapt and the Night of the Dog* (1989), *The Mamur Zapt and the Donkey-Vous* (1990), *The Mamur Zapt and the Men Behind* (1991), *The Mamur Zapt and the Girl in the Nile* (1992), *The Mamur Zapt and the Spoils of Egypt* (1993), *The Mamur Zapt and the Camel of Destruction* (1993), *The Snake-Catcher's Daughter* (1994), *The Mingrelian Conspiracy* (1995), *The Fig Tree Murder* (1996), *The Last Cut* (1998), *Death of an Effendi* (1999), *A Cold Touch of Ice* (2000), *The Face in the Cemetery* (2001).

Dmitri Kameron series: *Dmitri and the Milk Drinkers* (1997), *Dmitri and the One-Legged Lady* (1999).

Where to start: *The Mamur Zapt and the Return of the Carpet.*
Awards: CWA Last Laugh (1993).
Website: <www.twbooks.co.uk/authors/mpearce.html>
Similar stuff: Elizabeth PETERS for Egypt; Peter DICKINSON for style.
Final fact: MP reports that he started writing in a garden on the bank of the Nile. The night before he couldn't sleep because of the drumming across the river. In the morning he found the cause for the noise – people were still diving for a body and trying to avoid the crocodiles.

Iain Pears (b. 1955) UK

IP is an art historian, journalist and television consultant. He was a correspondent for Reuters from 1982 to 1990 and since 1987 has been a Getty Fellow in the Arts and Humanities at Yale University. His detailed knowledge of art, which he has demonstrated in several non-fiction books, is also at the centre of his series featuring British art dealer Jonathan Argyll. Argyll has settled in Rome where he is affiliated with General Bottando of the Italian National Art Theft Squad, though the international nature of art crime means that Argyll frequently travels abroad, usually to England or as far as Los Angeles in *The Bernini Bust*. In the first book, *The Raphael Affair*, Argyll is himself arrested for breaking into a church looking for a long-lost Raphael, only to find the painting is missing. Argyll's investigations are never simple, as the masterminds behind art crime are always shadowy and distant. Pears's knowledge adds considerable colour to this rewarding series. In a surprise change of pace IP wrote a complex historical mystery, the bestselling *An Instance of the Fingerpost*, set in post-Restoration England where he reveals four separate witnesses' stories of a murder. IP's thorough research makes this novel both an historical and a mysterious experience.

Novels

Jonathan Argyll series: *The Raphael Affair* (1990), *The Titian Committee* (1991), *The Bernini Bust* (1992), *The Last Judgement* (1993), *Giotto's Hand* (1995), *Death and Restoration* (1996), *The Immaculate Deception* (2000).
Non-series: *An Instance of the Fingerpost* (1997).

Awards: Swedish Academy of Detection, Martin Beck (1999).
Similar stuff: John MALCOLM, Derek WILSON.

Ridley Pearson (b. 1953) US

After two early spy novels and a hostage thriller RP established himself as a writer to watch with *Undercurrents* the first of his novels featuring Sergeant Lou Boldt of Seattle's special forensic task force in the homicide bureau. Boldt teams with police psychologist Daphne Matthews to recreate the mind of a serial killer. All of the Boldt and Matthews series place emphasis on detailed research and microscopic analysis of clues. RP was one of the first authors to use forensic science as the main pillar of his plot; he regards these books as firmly in the tradition of Sherlock Holmes. His non-series crime thrillers, starting with *Probable Cause*, are also strong on forensics. In RP's books the more complicated the plot and the more demanding the analysis, the better. *Hard Fell* is an especially ingenious puzzle concerning a murder in a flight simulator. RP's high-tech research takes him to the cutting edge of forensics. Perhaps his most controversial book has been *Chain of Evidence*, which suggests a crime gene, and this was discussed at a genetics conference with considerable news coverage. A method of arson that he devised in *Beyond Recognition* repeated itself in fact some while later. *Undercurrents* helped a prosecuting attorney solve a real-life murder by applying research used in the book. RP became the first American to be awarded the Raymond Chandler Fulbright fellowship at Oxford University.

Novels

Boldt & Matthews series: *Undercurrents* (1988), *The Angel Maker* (1993), *No Witnesses* (1994), *Beyond Recognition* (1997), *The Pied Piper* (1998), *The First Victim* (1999), *Middle of Nowhere* (2000), *The Art of Deception* (2002).
Chris Klick series as Wendell McCall: *Dead Aim* (1988), *Aim for the Heart* (1990), *Concerto in Dead Flat* (1999).
Non-series: *Never Look Back* (1985), *Blood of the Albatross* (1986), *The Seizing of Yankee Green Mall* (1987; as *Hidden Charges*, 1983), *Probable Cause* (1990), *Hard Fall* (1992), *Chain of Evidence* (1995), *Parallel Lies* (2001).

Pen-name: Wendell McCall.
Where to start: *Undercurrents* or *Probable Cause*.
Website: <www.ridleypearson.com>
Similar stuff: Patricia CORNWELL, Clare CURZON, Kathy REICHS.
Final fact: RP composes music and plays bass guitar in the band Rock Bottom Remainders alongside Stephen King, Amy Tan and Dave Barry. His album *Big Lost Rainbow* is still available.

George Pelecanos (b. 1957) US

GP is a Greek-American, living just outside Washington D.C., who turned to writing after several years of running a chain of electronic stores. He had previously held several jobs, including shoe salesman, since he had left college where he obtained his degree in film studies and also took a course in the hard-boiled novel. Those two interests have since taken over his life. Until recently he managed an independent film production company, Circle Films, which was responsible for the Coen Brothers' films *Raising Arizona*, *Miller's Crossing* and *Barton Fink*. His first book, *A Firing Offense*, introduced Nick Stefanos, who works in a chain of music stores, who is asked to search for a missing boy. Finding he has a gift for the work Stefanos applies for his P.I.'s licence. *Nick's Trip* charts his first big job as a P.I. but the dirt really starts flying in *Down by the River Where the Dead Men Go*, which is one of GP's bleakest novels. The books are fast, violent, laced with black humour and punctuated with many musical references. GP uses music to help create his characters and set a mood. This becomes even more important when, with *The Big Blow Down*, GP turned the clock back to trace the history of the Greek and Italian immigrant communities around Washington D.C. from the late thirties to the present day. These books are peopled with the earlier generation of the Stefanos books, in particular Dimitri Karras and Marcus Clay. The most powerful of these books is *King Suckerman*, set in the fifties, where Karras and Clay find themselves up against two violent killers in the 1970s. That book won awards in Germany and Japan and was shortlisted for the CWA Golden Dagger award. With *Right as Rain* GP started a new series featuring black ex-cop turned P.I., Derek Strange, who is asked to help clear the reputation of a black policeman who had been killed "in the line of duty" by a white cop. The white cop, Terry

Quinn, though cleared of the offence, has done much soul-searching since, and has himself left the force. In an odd twist he teams up with Strange to reinvestigate the case. The scenario allows GP to explore racial issues in a city that tries to ignore the matter. Because of his subject matter and the manner in which he evokes time and place GP's books will become a chronicle of their period and a keystone of modern crime fiction.

Novels

Nick Stefanos (& others) series: *A Firing Offense* (1992), *Nick's Trip* (1993), *Down By the River Where the Dead Men Go* (1995); *The Big Blowdown* (1996), *King Suckerman* (1997), *The Sweet Forever* (1998), *Shame the Devil* (2000).
Strange & Quinn series: *Right as Rain* (2001), *Hell to Pay* (2002).
Non-series: *Shoedog* (1994).

Where to start: *A Firing Offense* or *The Big Blowdown*.
Awards: Japanese Maltese Falcon (1999), German Marlowe (1999).
Similar stuff: James ELLROY, Elmore LEONARD.
Final fact: When still a kid GP accidentally shot a best friend in the face with a .38 special. Fortunately the friend survived but the incident made GP "rabidly antigun".

Don Pendleton (1927–95) US

Long before there was Rambo there was Mack Bolan, dubbed the "Executioner". Bolan was a guerilla warfare specialist and sniper in Vietnam who, in *War Against the Mafia* (1969), returns home to the funeral of his parents and sister, who had been killed by the Mafia. Thereafter Bolan blasted his way through city after city in an orgy of revenge and an increasing arsenal of firepower, slaughtering as many Mafiosi as he can. There is no subtlety to these books and very little plot, but it did spawn a whole new sub-genre of macho heroic action adventure novels and thus ushered in not just David Morrell's Rambo but Warren Murphy's "Destroyer", Barry Malzberg's "Lone Wolf" and a host of other gun-crazy vigilantes. The success of the series took DP (and his publisher, Pinnacle Books) by surprise and eventually led to legal wrangles with Pinnacle trying to own the character. Pendleton won and took the character away from Pinnacle. In his final series of books for them he has Bolan granted a pardon in order to become head of a government anti-terrorist unit. In a final sequence of novels Bolan has a week's grace in which to wipe out as many Mafia strongholds as he can. *Satan's Sabbath* was the last Executioner novel DP would write. Thereafter all of the books – now around 400 in total – have been ghost-written by a variety of authors, though DP and his wife Linda supervised the adaptation of the series for comic-book format in 1992. DP wrote two new series, neither of which proved successful. *Ashes to Ashes* introduced Ashton Ford, a former spy with psychic powers. *Copp for Hire* introduced Joe Copp, a Hollywood P.I. who shoots first and asks questions later. After the first

Executioner novel, little of DP's work is of particular interest apart from noting its impact and popularity. It represents the nadir of formula pulp-style fiction. DP, who was born in Little Rock, Arkansas had served in the Navy during WW2 and the Korean War and later worked as a railroad telegrapher, air-traffic control officer and aerospace engineer before he turned to full-time writing in 1967. He wrote a few science-fiction novels and soft-porn books before he began the phenomenally successful Executioner series. Towards the end of his life DP collaborated with his wife on producing books on self-awareness.

Novels

Executioner series (by DP only): *War Against the Mafia* (1969), *Death Squad* (1969), *Battle Mask* (1970), *Miami Massacre* (1970), *Continental Contract* (1971), *Assault on Soho* (1971), *Nightmare in New York* (1971), *Chicago Wipe-Out* (1971), *Vegas Vendetta* (1971), *Caribbean Kill* (1972), *California Hit* (1972), *Boston Blitz* (1972), *Washington IOU* (1972), *San Diego Siege* (1972), *Panic in Philly* (1973), *Jersey Guns* (1974), *Texas Storm* (1974), *Detroit Deathwatch* (1974), *New Orleans Knockout* (1974), *Firebase Seattle* (1975), *Hawaiian Hellground* (1975), *Canadian Crisis* (1975), *St Louis Showdown* (1975), *Colorado Kill-Zone* (1976), *Acapulco Rampage* (1976), *Dixie Convoy* (1976), *Savage Fire* (1977), *Command Strike* with Mike Newton and Stephen Mertz (1977), *Cleveland Pipeline* with Mike Newton and Stephen Mertz (1977), *Arizona Ambush* with Mike Newton (1977), *Tennessee Smash* with Mike Newton (1978), *Monday's Mob* (1978), *Terrible Tuesday* (1979), *Wednesday's Wrath* (1979), *Thermal Thursday* (1979), *Friday's Feast* (1979), *Satan's Sabbath* (1980).
Ashton Ford series: *Ashes to Ashes* (1986), *Eye to Eye* (1986), *Heart to Heart* (1987), *Life to Life* (1987), *Mind to Mind* (1987), *Time to Time* (1988).
Joe Copp series: *Copp for Hire* (1987), *Copp on Fire* (1988), *Copp in Deep* (1989), *Copp in the Dark* (1990), *Copp on Ice* (1991), *Copp in Shock* (1992).

Full name: Donald Eugene Pendleton.
Pen-names: Dan Britain (on sf), Stephan Gregory (on soft porn).
Website: <www.donpendleton.com>
Similar stuff: Warren MURPHY.
Final fact: DP was an engineering administrator during NASA's Apollo Moonshot programme.

Daniel Pennac (b. 1944) France

Born in Casablanca and raised in Africa, Asia and Europe, DP now lives, teaches and writes in France. Amongst his dozen or so books are a series that are being hailed as amongst the most literary of all French crime fiction. Known oddly as the Belleville Quartet, even though there are five books (and a play), they are semi-surreal fabulisms only just keeping one foot on the ground. They concern the odd life of Benjamin Malaussène, who lives in the Belleville quarter of Paris, along with a bizarre family and a smelly dog. He is a professional scapegoat, which means that he is hired to take all the blame if anything goes wrong. Unfortunately people start dying in the store where he works and Malaussène decides he ought to work out what's happening. In the award-winning *The Fairy Gunmother* he now works for a publisher, taking the brunt of complaints. Various old people are being killed by the equivalent of a Monty Python "Hell's Granny". In *Write to Kill* Malaussène agrees to double for his publisher's bestselling writer, who wants to remain incognito. Unfortunately on his first outing Malaussène is shot and the rest of the novel is a rather surreal and cerebral manhunt. In *Passion Fruit* there is death at Malaussène's sister's wedding and Malaussène, convinced he will get the blame, tries to solve the murder. A fifth novel, *Monsieur Malaussène*, has yet to be translated. It is something of a magnum opus, where Malaussène takes the rap for 21 murders. DP's fiction is about as far from conventional crime fiction as you can go and still feel in the same genre.

Novels

Malaussène series: *The Scapegoat* (1985; UK 1998), *The Fairy Gunmother* (1987; UK 1997), *Write to Kill* (1989; UK 1999), *Monsieur Malaussène* (1995; no trans.), *Passion Fruit* (1999; UK 2001).

Awards: French Trophée 813 (1987).
Similar stuff: Nearest English equivalent is a blend of Peter DICKINSON and James SALLIS.

Anne Perry (b. 1938) UK

It took AP over 20 years to sell her first book. After considerable childhood problems (*see below*) she supported herself through a variety of jobs, including air stewardess and property underwriter. Her early attempts were all historical fiction and it was not until she added the element of mystery that they sold. Most of her books are set in the late Victorian period. Her first series features Inspector (later Superintendent) Pitt of the Bow Street Police in London. Pitt has married into an upper-class family, which leads to much cultural conflict. Pitt's wife, Charlotte, has strong views and a mind of her own, and is very supportive of her husband. She plays a large part in the investigation of the crimes, sometimes with other members of her family, through their knowledge of the higher echelons of society. However, she is also given to considerable moralizing. AP converted to Mormonism in 1967, and her views inevitably permeate the books. In a few novels, such as *Ashworth Hall*, Pitt takes something of a back seat. He is tolerant and flexible and sometimes not as bright as you'd expect him to be. The Pitt series is full of contrasts, in the characters, the social classes, the attitudes of the day, the London environment and amongst Pitt's own police colleagues, allowing for tension and conflict. The first book in the series, *The Cater Street Hangman*, in which Pitt and Charlotte meet, was made into a TV film in 1998 as a pilot for a series. AP's second series is darker. It features William Monk, a private detective again in the 1890s who, following an accident, has lost his memory. The books are therefore not only quests to solve crimes but a search by Monk to find his past life. He is helped by a friend, Hester Latterly, another strong-willed woman who trained as a nurse, and a barrister Oliver Rathbone. This series allows for a greater diversity than the Pitt novels and involve both investigations and courtroom scenes. Both series are excellent in their exploration of the mood, hypocrisy, social injustice and mixed values of Victorian England. AP has ventured into other territory more recently. Amongst her novels *The One Thing More* is an effective murder mystery set in the midst of the French Revolution. She has also started a spiritual fantasy series with *Tathea* (1999), which allowed her to rework one of her early, unsold historical novels and use it as a vehicle for her religious views. AP's short stories allow for more variety. She has written enough for a collection, which would be a welcome addition to her books. Some of the incidental characters from her novels have spilled out into stories of their own. Charlotte Pitt's great aunt Vespasia turns up in "An Affair of Inconvenience" (1998), whilst Oliver Rathbone's father, Henry, who is based on AP's own father, does some armchair detection in "The Blackmailer" (1996). AP's award-winning "Heroes" introduces an army chaplain serving in the trenches during WW1 who uncovers a mystery that raises questions of ethics and morality. Her stories and recent novels suggest we have only just started to see AP's true versatility.

Novels

Thomas Pitt series: *The Cater Street Hangman* (1979), *Callander Square* (1980), *Paragon Walk* (1981), *Resurrection Row* (1981), *Rutland Place* (1983), *Bluegate Fields* (1984), *Death in the Devil's Acre* (1985), *Cardington Crescent* (1987), *Silence in Hanover Close* (1988), *Bethlehem Road* (1990), *Highgate Rise* (1991), *Belgrave Square* (1992), *Farrier's Lane* (1993), *The Hyde Park Headsman* (1994), *Traitor's Gate* (1995), *Pentecost Alley* (1996), *Ashworth Hall* (1997), *Brunswick Gardens* (1998), *Bedford Square* (1999), *Half Moon Street* (2000), *The Whitechapel Conspiracy* (2001), *Southampton Row* (2002).

William Monk series: *The Face of a Stranger* (1990), *A Dangerous Mourning* (1991), *Defend and Betray* (1992), *A Sudden, Fearful Death* (1993), *The Sins of the Wolf* (1994), *Cain His Brother* (1995), *Weighed in the Balance* (1996), *The Silent Cry* (1997), *Whited Sepulchres* (1997; as *A Breach of Promise*, US, 1998), *The Twisted Root* (1999), *Slaves and Obsessions* (2000), *A Funeral in Blue* (2001).

Non-series: *The One Thing More* (2000).

Editor. *Malice Domestic 6* (1997), *Death by Horoscope*, with Martin H. Greenberg (2001).

Real name: Juliet Marion Hulme.
Pen-name: Anne Perry.
Where to start: *The Cater Street Hangman* and *The Face of a Stranger*.
Awards: American Mystery Award, best traditional mystery (1993), Herodotus, lifetime achievement (1999), Edgar, best short story (2000).

Website: < www.anneperry.net>
Similar stuff: Alanna KNIGHT, Peter LOVESEY.
Final fact: As a result of the film *Heavenly Creatures* (1994) it was revealed that in 1954 AP, then Juliet Hulme and living in New Zealand, had helped a teenage friend murder that friend's mother. She was convicted and served a prison sentence of just over five years. After her release Juliet returned to England and took on a new identity. She later claimed that at the time she was taking a potent medication that was later taken off the market. AP had suffered a traumatic childhood. When only two years old she was caught in a bombing raid during the London blitz, which left her with recurrent nightmares. She was frequently ill, nearly dying from pneumonia when she was five. She was in and out of schools and sanatoria at the time and was described as being "traumatized by the accumulation of repeated separations from her family." AP was an intelligent child with an IQ of 170.

Thomas Perry (b. 1947) US

TP's writing skills are diverse so that at one moment he can hold you in tight suspense and the next have you chuckling over the daring delights of his plots. His first book, *The Butcher's Boy*, which won an Edgar, is one of those rare titles which make you root for the contract killer. The anonymous hit-man (who later calls himself Michael Schaeffer, but you never know his real name) has been double-crossed by the Mafia so starts to kill off Mob members. He is pursued by a female FBI agent and another Mob hit-man. The chase continues in *Sleeping Dogs*, set ten years later when Schaeffer has settled in England but is spotted. TP's second book, *Metzger's Dog*, nominated by the *New York Times* as a notable book of the year, couldn't be more different. It's about a gang who, during a heist, also pick up a dog and a manuscript. Trying to trade in the manuscript they are double-crossed and so plot their revenge. Metzger, by the way, is a cat! TP then brought the two styles together in *Island*, one of the great serio-comic caper adventures. TP has also established a following for his series featuring Jane Whitefield, a half-Irish, half Seneca Indian "guardian", who helps people in trouble take on new identities and "disappear". She first appears in *Vanishing Act*, where she helps a woman who is trying to escape from her sadistic husband but is being pursued by a P.I. Whitefield takes many personal risks in the process which is why, when she becomes married at the end of *Shadow Woman*, her husband asks her to retire. She returns, however, in two further books, the last of which takes on the Mafia. There are lots of chases and confrontations in TP's books, which are always ingenious, exciting and different.

Novels

Michael Schaeffer series: *The Butcher's Boy* (1982), *Sleeping Dogs* (1992).
Jane Whitefield series: *Vanishing Act* (1995), *Dance for the Dead* (1996), *Shadow Woman* (1997), *The Face Changers* (1998), *Blood Money* (2000).
Non-series: *Metzger's Dog* (1983), *Big Fish* (1985), *Island* (1987), *Death Benefits* (2001), *Pursuit* (2002).

Where to start: For sheer contrast try both *The Butcher's Boy* and *Metzger's Dog*.
Awards: Edgar, best first novel (1983).
Similar stuff: Donald E. WESTLAKE.
Final fact: TP became a writer of crime fiction more or less by accident. He did not really know the field and before he wrote *The Butcher's Boy* had written, but not tried to sell, a science-fiction novel and a lost-race book *a la* H. Rider Haggard.

Elizabeth Peters (b. 1927) US

EP is in real life Dr Barbara Mertz, a qualified Egyptologist and archaeologist who has written several detailed books on the subject including *Temples, Tombs and Hieroglyphs* (1964) and *Red Land, Black Land: The World of the Ancient Egyptians* (1966). It is no surprise, therefore, that currently her most popular books are those set amongst the tombs and temples of Egypt, featuring Victorian archaeologists Amelia Peabody and her husband Radcliffe Emerson. The couple meet in *Crocodile on the Sandbank* when Amelia sets off on a Grand Tour having just come into her inheritance. Both she and her future husband are strong-willed and opinionated so the series is full of light-hearted sparkle and banter. The books are loving pastiches of the traditional mystery, emulating Christie and Conan Doyle – even H. Rider Haggard in *The Last Camel Dies at Noon*. The series has galloped through the years. We watch the Emersons' son, Ramses, grow up into a precocious teenager. *Lord of the Silent* brings the series up to WW1. The Peabody books had to some extent been presaged by the first book under the EP alias, *The Jackals's Head*, a contemporary archaeological mystery set in Egypt. In *The Dead Sea Cipher*, an antiquarian thriller set in the Holy Land, we see a glimmer of the Vicky Bliss series. Bliss first appears in *Borrower of the Night*. She is an antiquarian and historian in search of a lost shrine who encounters a murderer in an ancient German castle. Throughout the series various villains try and stop Vicky finding her art treasures. EP's other early series is firmly in the cozy tradition. Jacqueline Kirby is a romance novelist who, in *The Seventh Sinner* turns sleuth to solve the murder of one of a group of art students in Rome. The keynote of this series is *The Murders of Richard III*, where Jacqueline applies her mind to solving the real fate of the princes in the Tower only to find that somene is trying to bump off the present-day Richard III re-enactors. The EP alias was created when her publisher felt she was becoming too prolific under her alter ego Barbara Michaels. Most of the Michaels' books are gothic suspense with very little crime content and a strong element of the supernatural, and thus beyond the coverage of this encyclopedia. Nevertheless, mystery fans will enjoy *Shattered Silk*, about a stalker, which is the second in a loosely connected series set in an old house, that starts with *Ammie, Come Home*, where a séance unleashes secrets from the past. Also of interest is the gothic bibliomystery *Houses of Stone* (1993) where the desire to own a rare 19th-century manuscript leads to frightening consequences. Like Charlotte

MacLeod, EP's works were amongst those that rekindled the traditional mystery form for a new readership.

Novels

Jacqueline Kirby series: *The Seventh Sinner* (1972), *The Murders of Richard III* (1974), *Die for Love* (1984), *Naked Once More* (1989).
Vicky Bliss series: *Borrower of the Night* (1973), *Street of the Five Moons* (1978), *Silhouette in Scarlet* (1983), *Trojan Gold* (1987), *Night Train to Memphis* (1994).
Amelia Peabody series: *Crocodile on the Sandbank* (1975), *The Curse of the Pharaohs* (1981), *The Mummy Case* (1985), *Lion in the Valley* (1986), *The Deeds of the Disturber* (1988), *The Last Camel Died at Noon* (1991), *The Snake, the Crocodile and the Dog* (1992), *The Hippopotamus Pool* (1996), *Seeing a Large Cat* (1997), *The Ape Who Guards the Balance* (1998), *The Falcon at the Portal* (1999), *He Shall Thunder in the Sky* (2000), *Lord of the Silent* (2001), *The Golden One* (2002).
Non-series: *The Jackal's Head* (1968), *The Camelot Caper* (1969; as *Her Cousin John*, 1970), *The Dead Sea Cipher* (1970), *The Night of Four Hundred Rabbits* (1971; as *Shadows in the Moonlight*, UK 1975), *Legend in Green Velvet* (1976; as *Ghost in Green Velvet*, UK 1977), *Devil-May-Care* (1977), *Summer of the Dragon* (1979), *The Love Talker* (1980), *The Copenhagen Connection* (1982).
Cheryl Cardoza series as Barbara Michaels: *Ammie, Come Home* (1968), *Shattered Silk* (1986), *Stitches in Time* (1995).
Editor. *Malice Domestic 1*, with Martin H. Greenberg (1992).

Real name: Barbara Louise Mertz (*née* Gross).
Pen-names: Barbara Michaels, Elizabeth Peters.
Where to start: *The Jackal's Head*.
Awards: Agatha, best novel (1990), Bouchercon committee, Grand Master (1986), MWA, Grand Master (1998), American Mystery Award, best romantic suspense (1988, 1989, 1990), best traditional mystery (1992).
Website: <www.mpmbooks.com/>
Similar stuff: Margot Arnold and Jessica Mann for archaeology; Marcia Muller for art investigations; Michael Pearce for period Egypt; Lauren Haney, Lynda Robinson for ancient Egypt.
Final fact: On one trip to Egypt EP acted as a tour guide for fellow writers Charlotte and Aaron Elkins.

Ellis Peters (1913–95) UK

Edith Pargeter, the real persona behind Ellis Peters, had a writing career that spanned nearly 50 years and some 90 books, but it was only in her last 10 or so years that she became internationally recognized through her books featuring Brother Cadfael. The popularity of those books created a whole new publishing niche – the historical detective story. It had been around before EP, but with Cadfael's success publishers suddenly recognized a new genre to promote and an industry began. EP was a prolific writer – she was known at school as "the girl who never stopped writing". Her early novels cover a wide range of subject matter, from ancient Rome (her first book, *Hortensius, Friend of Nero*, 1936) to romance (*Iron-Bound*, 1936), to a femme fatale (*Day Star* as Peter Benedict, 1937), even a supernatural fable, *The City Lies Foursquare* (1939). Her first crime novel appeared as by Jolyon Carr, *Murder in the Dispensary*, drawn directly from EP's experience as a chemist's assistant from 1933 to 1940. During WW2 she served in the Women's Royal Navy Service (for which she received a British Empire Medal). EP shuddered at the memory of those early novels in later years, but they are, of course, highly collected now and *Murder in the Dispensary* was reissued in a special limited edition in 1999. EP established herself with her wartime trilogy starting with *The Eighth Champion of Christendom* (1945) and despite her interest in crime fiction she saw herself as a mainstream writer. In later years she argued that there should not be a distinction and that crime-fiction writers produced as much fine literature as the *literati*. Most of her books of the fifties are mainstream, influenced by her travels and her love of Czechslovakia. She became a translator of books from the Czech and was awarded the Czechoslovak Society for International Relations Gold Medal in 1968. It was not until the sixties that her output bifurcated and the Ellis Peters persona emerged to cover crime fiction, while the Pargeter name remained on her general fiction and an increasing number of historical novels.

Apart from a few non-series books, EP's crime fiction falls into two main series. The first features Inspector Felse and his family. He had appeared in an early Pargeter book, *Fallen Into the Pit*, when he was still Sergeant Felse and he has to deal with the murder of a former German prisoner-of-war who had remained in the locality. The book is set in EP's native Shropshire which she has renamed Midshire. Typical of so much of EP's output, the book was not so much a crime novel as a novel about society, the tensions that lead to crime and its after-effects. EP resurrected Felse in *Death and the Joyful Woman*, which went on to win the Edgar award as that year's best novel. The novel focuses on Inspector Felse's son, Dominic, and the problems that arise when he is privy to information in a case in which he has a personal interest. Felse's family features in many of the novels, especially those set outside Midshire. In *A Nice Derangement of Epitaphs* they are on holiday in Cornwall when they stumble across a drowned body. *The Piper on the Mountain* has Dominic, now a student, involved in a mysterious death in Czechoslovakia, while *Mourning Raga* and *Death to the Landlords!* takes Dominic to India. In the second title he becomes involved with terrorists. By contrast *The Grass-Widow's Tale* has Felse's wife, Bunty, alone at home and the victim of a violent gang. Although at their core the Felse series may be mistaken for a traditional English village mystery series, nothing could be further from the truth. These are novels about a family coping with the consequences of the father being a policeman.

While writing the Felse books EP was also producing a series of excellent historical novels set in the Middle Ages, mostly in Shrewsbury or the Marches. The first Cadfael book, *A Morbid Taste for Bones* had been intended as a one-off and had arisen out of an interest EP had in the translation of the bones of St Winifred from Wales to Shrewsbury Abbey. Just as her Felse novels are contemporary literature into which crime intrudes, so the Cadfael books were historical fiction where crime happens. The idea that the reliquary for the bones was an ideal place to hide a body led to her first historical whodunnit. Soon, another idea that an extra body turns up amongst the dead during the siege of Shrewsbury in 1138, brought Cadfael back in *One Corpse Too Many*. Even in these first two books Cadfael and the brothers at the monastery are well-rounded figures. Cadfael is a Welshman in his 60s who has seen life, including serving in the Crusades, and who has retired to the monastery in his later years. There he tends the herb garden, but his knowledge of the world, his eye for detail, and his expertise in herbs, medicines and poisons means he frequently helps the local sheriff in solving crimes. These are set during the turbulent times of the Civil War between King Stephen and the Empress Matilda, a period that EP recreates in sharp detail, bringing the life and characters alive. With the third novel, *Monk's-Hood*, for which EP received the CWA Silver Dagger, we learn more of Cadfael's early life and his skill at detecting poisons. By then the character of Cadfael had established itself and the series took off. All of the novels are firmly related to actual historical events, which makes them historical novels first and mysteries second. In some of the later novels, especially *The Summer of the Danes*, the crime does not happen till the end of the book and is easily solved. EP's work clearly demonstrates how you can produce quality literature that works as mainstream, as historical and as mystery fiction. For her remarkable abilities she received the CWA Diamond Dagger in 1993, and the OBE in 1994. The success of the Cadfael books not only established a new publishing genre, it created a tourist boom in Shrewsbury, several spin-off books about Cadfael country, and a TV series *Cadfael* (1994–8) with Derek Jacobi in the title rôle. The CWA established an Ellis Peters award for the year's best historical detective novel in 1999. EP's legacy will be appreciated for many years to come.

Novels

Felse series (as Edith Pargeter on first book): *Fallen Into the Pit* (1951; as by EP, 1994), *Death and the Joyful Woman* (1961), *Flight of a Witch* (1964), *A Nice Derangement of Epitaphs* (1965; as *Who Lies Here?* US 1976), *The Piper on the Mountain* (1966), *Black is the Colour of my True Love's Heart* (1967), *The Grass-Widow's Tale* (1968), *The House of Green Turf* (1969), *Mourning Raga* (1969), *A Knocker on Death's Door* (1970), *Death to the Landlords!* (1972), *City of Gold and Shadows* (1973), *Rainbow's End* (1978).

Brother Cadfael series: *A Morbid Taste for Bones* (1977), *One Corpse Too Many* (1979), *Monk's-Hood* (1980), *Saint Peter's Fair* (1981), *The Leper of Saint Giles* (1981), *The Virgin in the Ice* (1982), *The Sanctuary Sparrow* (1983), *The Devil's Novice* (1983), *Dead Man's Ransom* (1984), *The Pilgrim of Hate* (1984), *An Excellent Mystery* (1985), *The Raven in the Foregate* (1986), *The Rose Rent* (1986),

The Hermit of Eyton Forest (1987), *The Confession of Brother Haluin* (1988), *The Heretic's Apprentice* (1989), *The Potter's Field* (1989), *The Summer of the Danes* (1991), *The Holy Thief* (1992), *Brother Cadfael's Penance* (1994).
Non-series: *Death Mask* (1959), *The Will and the Deed* (1960); as *Where There's a Will*, US 1960), *Funeral of Figaro* (1962), *The Horn of Roland* (1974), *Never Pick Up Hitch-Hikers!* (1976).
Non-series as Edith Pargeter: *Holiday with Violence* (1952), *Most Loving Mere Folly* (1953).
as Jolyon Carr: *Murder in the Dispensary* (1938), *Freedom for Two* (1939), *Masters of the Parachute Mail* (1940), *Death Comes by Post* (1940).
as John Redfern: *The Victim Needs a Nurse* (1940).
Short Stories
as Edith Pargeter: *The Assize of the Dying* (1958), *The Lily Hand* (1965).
as Ellis Peters: *A Rare Benedictine* (1988).

Real name: Edith Mary Pargeter.
Pen-names: Peter Benedict, Jolyon Carr, Ellis Peters, John Redfern.
Where to start: *Death and the Joyful Woman* and *One Corpse Too Many*.
Awards: Edgar, best novel (1963), CWA Silver Dagger (1980), CWA Diamond Dagger (1993).
Books about: *Edith Pargeter: Ellis Peters* by Margaret Lewis (1994), *The Cadfael Companion* by Robin Whiteman (1991; rev'd US 1995).
Website: None specific but of interest are two Cadfael sites <www.iw.net/~csonne/> and <home.earthlink.net/~chinmom/cadfael.html>
Similar stuff: Margaret FRAZER, Susanna GREGORY, Candace ROBB.
Final fact: There is a Brother Cadfael rose bush, an old-fashioned, fragrant rose with pink flowers, which was introduced at the Chelsea Flower Show in 1990.

Rhona Petrie *pseudonym, see* Clare Curzon

Dennis Phillips, *see under pseudonym* Philip Daniels

Mike Phillips (b. 1946) UK

MP is a journalist and lecturer who came to Britain from Guyana in 1956. His first series of books feature Jamaican investigative journalist Samson Dean who lives in London. The series is full of Jamaican patois and the life of the streets and portrays a young immigrant struggling to better himself in Britain whilst conscious of his countrymen falling into a life of crime. One of the key elements of MP's books is in showing how crime can easily become a way of life. His books aren't traditional whodunits or detection, but are about crime. In *Blood Rights*, Dean is asked to find the missing daughter of an MP and the trail leads him into the world of drugs. In *The Late Candidate*, which received the CWA Silver Dagger, Dean is shocked to discover the life led by a childhood friend and politician who has died in suspicious circumstances. *Point of Darkness* takes Dean to New York looking for an old friend's daughter only to, once again, encounter a world of violence and corruption. In *An Image to Die For* Dean is helping a TV producer on a crime programme only to find his life in danger through deceit and double dealing. MP also wrote the novel of the film *Boyz 'n the Hood*, which uses ideas similar to MP's own, showing how the lives of two childhood friends are affected by their environment as they grow older. MP's work likes to explore racial and cultural ideologies and their effects upon individuals and society. In recent books MP has broadened his canvas with more ambitious thrillers. The eponymous Beninoise mask of *The Dancing Face* is a talisman everyone is after and some will stop at nothing to acquire. *A Shadow of Myself* considers the fallout from the former Soviet Union and its effects in Central Europe.

Novels
Samson Dean series: *Blood Rights* (1989), *The Late Candidate* (1990), *Point of Darkness* (1994), *An Image to Die For* (1995).
Non-series: *Boyz 'n the Hood* (1991), *The Dancing Face* (1997), *A Shadow of Myself* (2000).

Full name: Michael Ray Phillips.
Where to start: *Blood Rights.*
Awards: CWA Silver Dagger (1990).
Website: <www.twbooks.co.uk/authors/mikephillips.html>
Similar stuff: Victor HEADLEY.
Final fact: MP once set up and ran a hostel for homeless black youths in Notting Hill and moved on to become a community activist in Manchester and Birmingham.

Nancy Pickard (b. 1945) US

A former journalist, from Kansas, NP has earned a solid reputation and a cupboard full of awards and nominations for her series of mysteries featuring Jenny Cain, the director of a charitable foundation in the fictional town of Port Frederick, Massachusetts. Her investigations arise when assessing or disbursing the foundation's grants. The series works a fine balance between the light-hearted traditional small-town cozy, with its small cast of local characters and eccentrics, and the more poignant and at times depressing world of Cain's dysfunctional family. Her mother is institutionalized, her father's business bankrupt (which affected half the town) and she and her sister are always at odds. It is this mixture of humour and pathos that makes the series so readable. Since that first book the series and characters have grown. The multi-award winning *I.O.U.*, in which Cain delves into her mother's past, is an emotionally charged story in which many readers have found comfort in coping with the loss of a parent. On the lighter side we have the delightful opener, in *No Body*, of a graveyard bereft of corpses. NP does not shirk from significant social issues such as domestic violence in *Marriage is Murder* or the homeless in *Dead Crazy*. The books are straightforward but thought-provoking. Her new series, featuring investigative crime writer Marie Lightfoot, is more complex. The twist of this series is in investigating crimes after the arrest and conviction. The Edgar nominated *The Whole Truth* deals with a child-killer who escapes from the court during his trial and Lightfoot's research places her in grave danger. In *Ring of Truth* Lightfoot looks into the verdict of a rape and murder trial where one man is convicted but the other released. This series allows NP to test preconceptions and misconceptions. NP has also taken over the Eugenia Potter series of culinary mysteries from the late Virginia Rich. NP is a prolific writer of short stories, which have also won awards, and a selection is available as *Storm Warnings.*

Novels

Jenny Cain series: *Generous Death* (1984), *Say No To Murder* (1985), *No Body* (1986), *Marriage is Murder* (1987), *Dead Crazy* (1988), *Bum Steer* (1990; as *Cross Bones*, UK 1990), *I.O.U.* (1991), *But I Wouldn't Want to Die There* (1993), *Confession* (1994), *Twilight* (1995).

Eugenia Potter series: *The 27-Ingredient Chili Con Carne Murders* completed for Virginia Rich (1993), *The Blue Corn Murders* (1998), *The Secret Ingredient Murders* (2002).

Marie Lightfoot series: *The Whole Truth* (2000), *Ring of Truth* (2001)

Short Stories. *Afraid All the Time* (booklet 1992), *Storm Warnings* (1999).

Editor. *Malice Domestic 3*, with Martin H. Greenberg (1994), *The First Lady Murders* (1999), *Mom, Apple Pie and Murder* (1999).

Where to start: *Generous Death.*

Awards: Anthony, best paperback original (1986), best short story (1990), Macavity, best novel (1988, 1992), best short story (1990), American Mystery Award, best short story (1990), Agatha, best novel (1991, 1992), best short story (2000), Shamus, best short story (1992).

Similar stuff: Carolyn G. HART, Jane LANGTON.

Final fact: NP's first book was published at the same time her son was born. Her parents were reading the book while awaiting the birth of their grandchild. NP said that it "felt as if I had given birth to twins."

Robert L. Pike *pseudonym, see* Robert L. Fish

Jeremy Potter (1922–97) UK

JP was manager, later deputy chairman of the *New Statesman* from 1951–69 and head of Independent Television's publishing arm from 1970–9 – he wrote two volumes of the official history of commercial television. His crime novels, though, are not as well known as they should be. He was a champion of the Plantagenet king Richard III and wrote in his defence in *Good King Richard?* (1983). He was Chairman of the Richard III Society from 1971–89 and became its President just before his death. Like Lillian de la Torre, JP delighted in reconstructing historical mysteries in the form of novels. His best is *A Trail of Blood*, set at the time of the dissolution of the monasteries in the reign of Henry VIII. A monk is sent on a secret mission to find any surviving Yorkist heirs, which means investigating the fate of the princes in the Tower. JP repeated his formula in further novels, recreating the death of William II in *Death in the Forest*, considering an unsolved 17th-century murder of a London magistrate in *The Primrose Hill Murder* and exploring the disappearance of the steward of a manor house in the early 19th century in *The Mystery of Campden Wonder*. Although JP wrote a couple of conventional police procedurals featuring Sergeant (later Inspector) Hiscock, plus a couple of sporting mysteries (*Hazard Chase* and *Foul Play*) it is his historical mysteries that were his forté and for which he should be remembered.

Novels
Inspector Hiscock series: *Death in Office* (1965), *The Dance of Death* (1968).
Non-series: *Hazard Chase* (1964), *Foul Play* (1967), *A Trail of Blood* (1970), *Going West* (1972), *Disgrace and Favour* (1975), *Death in the Forest* (1977), *The Primrose Hill Murder* (1992), *The Mystery of the Campden Wonder* (1995).

Full name: Ronald Jeremy Potter.
Where to start: *A Trail of Blood*.
Similar stuff: Lillian de la Torre, Paul DOHERTY, Josephine Tey.
Final fact: JP helped stage a modern-day TV trial of Richard III in 1984 with the former Lord Chancellor presiding as judge.

Richard S. Prather (b. 1921) US

RSP's Shell Scott books were second only to Mickey Spillane's Mike Hammer as the biggest-selling P.I. novels of the fifties, with over 40 million in print. Los Angeles based Scott, though, was unlike any other P.I. of his time, particularly in the later books. Here was no emotionally distraught crusader against crime. Ex-marine Scott, with his blonde, near white crewcut hair and his egg-blue cadillac convertible, did everything because he enjoyed it and set out to have fun, despite the violence. Although RSP can stage good fight scenes the violence is pretty kid-glove stuff. The title of one of the short stories, "Babes, Bodies and Bullets", just about sums up a Scott adventure, in that order. "Babes" dominate his books, frequently unclothed, though Scott does not always take advantage of them. Scott's quite happy to be unclothed as well – *Strip for Murder*, the book that really established the fun-loving image, has him investigating a nudist colony. A helpless damsel is usually Scott's client, and he can't refuse a pretty face. The fantasy world of P.I.s that RSP created certainly influenced at least one person who told RSP he became a P.I. through reading the books. The books were an influence on the more happy-go-lucky P.I.'s who began to appear on TV in the fifties, and some of the sexy secret agent books of the sixties. However none of the Scott books has been adapted for TV or film and, with changing trends in the mid-sixties and a legal wrangle with his publisher, they fell out of print. A

Shell Scott Mystery Magazine issued in 1966 ran for only nine issues. RSP continued to write books, however, and the series is now being reissued as e-books, with the promise of new titles. Two of the Scott books were originally issued under pen-names with Scott rewritten as another character, but were subsequently reissued with Scott reinstated. One of the more popular Scott books was written in collaboration with Stephen Marlowe, *Double in Trouble*, and also features Marlowe's detective Chester Drum – each author wrote alternate chapters. RSP also wrote a *Dragnet* novel, tied in to the popular TV series, which showed he was capable of more serious material if he chose.

Novels
Shell Scott series: *Case of the Vanishing Beauty* (1950), *Bodies in Bedlam* (1951), *Everybody Had a Gun* (1951), *Find This Woman* (1951), *Way of a Wanton* (1952), *Lie Down, Killer* (1952), *Dagger of Flesh* (1952), *Darling, It's Death* (1952), *Ride a High Horse* (1953; as *Too Many Crooks*, 1956), *Always Leave 'em Dying* (1954), *Strip for Murder* (1955), *The Wailing Frail* (1956), *Slab Happy* (1958), *Take a Murder, Darling* (1958), *Over Her Dead Body* (1959), *Double in Trouble* with Stephen Marlowe (1959), *Dance With the Dead* (1960), *Dig That Crazy Grave* (1961), *Kill the Clown* (1962), *Dead Heat* (1963), *Joker in the Deck* (1964), *The Cockeyed Corpse* (1964), *The Trojan Hearse* (1964), *Kill Him Twice* (1965), *Dead Man's Walk* (1965), *The Meandering Corpse* (1965), *The Kubla Khan Caper* (1966), *Gat Heat* (1967), *The Cheim Manuscript* (1969), *Kill Me Tomorrow* (1969), *Dead Bang* (1971), *The Sweet Ride* (1972), *The Sure Thing* (1975), *The Amber Effect* (1986), *Shellshock* (1987).
Non-series: *Pattern for Panic* (1954; rev'd as Shell Scott novel, 1961).
as David Knight: *Pattern for Murder* (1952 as Knight; rev'd as Shell Scott novel *The Scrambled Yeggs*, 1958), *Dragnet: Case No. 561* (1956).
as Douglas Ring: *The Peddler* (1952; as by RSP, 1963).
Short Stories
Shell Scott series: *Three's a Shroud* (1957), *Have Gat – Will Travel* (1957), *Shell Scott's Seven Slaughters* (1961), *The Shell Scott Sampler* (1969), *Hot Rock Rumble and The Double Take* (1995).
Editor. *The Comfortable Coffin* (1960).

Full name: Richard Scott Prather.
Pen-names: David Knight, Douglas Ring.
Where to start: *The Amber Effect* – Scott never ages.
Awards: PWA, lifetime achievement (1986).
Website: Shell Scott site at <user.dtcc.edu/~ddavis/>
Similar stuff: Michael Avallone.
Final fact: From 1974–80 RSP ran what was probably the only organic avocado farm in the US.

Bill Pronzini (b. 1943) US

BP has been a prolific writer and editor for over 35 years, since his first short story sale in 1966. He has published over a hundred short stories mostly crime and mystery but including science fiction, horror, westerns and adventure. The best of his non-series work has appeared in half a dozen collections but there are plenty more of these crisp, sharp stories to be preserved in book form. His story "Liar's Dice" (*EQMM*, 1992) was the basis for the TV film *Tails You Live, Heads You're Dead* (1995). One of his earliest stories, "Sometimes There is Justice" (*AHMM*, 1968), introduced his best-known character, the Nameless Detective, a former cop with many contacts still in the force. BP could not think of a suitable name and when he wrote the first novel, *The Snatch*, his editor, Lee Wright, suggested keeping him as "Nameless" as a marketing ploy. It worked. It meant Nameless could represent Everyman, though BP has admitted that when he writes about Nameless it's an older version of himself that he sees. This long-running series allows us to see Nameless age and mature. In the early books he is rather introspective, worried about his health and abhors the violence he encounters – he won't carry a gun. We follow him through various crises. There is his cancer scare in *Blowback*, which changes his outlook on the world, making him more determined to enjoy life and even prepared to enter into a relationship (though it's not until *Hardcase* that he marries his partner, Kerry). There is his ordeal in *Shackles*, where he is captured by an unidentified villain, chained in a remote mountain-cabin and left to die from starvation. There is no "with one bound he was free" in this novel and thereafter Nameless is a more serious, cautious but determined individual. The early books are more in the classic tradition. Like BP, Nameless is a collector of pulp magazines and the award-winning *Hoodwink* is a double locked-room puzzle set at a pulp collectors' convention. However the later ones, written during BP's growing relationship with and later marriage to Marcia MULLER (in 1992), are more character-driven with greater consideration of social and cultural issues. *Epitaphs* for instance considers the changes and tensions in the Italian-American quarter. BP had intended that *Bleeders* be the last Nameless novel, but he has since revised the format to allow Nameless some form of retirement whilst keeping the business going.

BP has developed a few other series characters of which the most different is John Quincannon. Set in San Francisco in the 1890s, Quincannon is a former secret service agent who has set up a detective agency with his partner Sabina Carpenter, a former Pinkerton agent. The transformation of roles happens in *Quincannon* but the more investigative cases appear in a series of short stories collected as *Carpenter & Quincannon*. His other characters include Carmody, a hard-nosed American bodyguard and wheeler-dealer who operates out of the Spanish island of Majorca. He has appeared in several stories and a novel, all of which are collected in *Carmody's Run*. Dan Connell is a Far East pilot, a relic from the old pulp adventure days, who has to get himself out of difficult situations.

BP's non-series books are all worth exploring. His first, *The Stalker*, which was short listed for the Edgar award for best first novel, is about a gang of hijackers who, years later, are being killed off one by one. *Snowbound*, which won the prestigious French Grand Prix, deals with an attempt to loot an entire snowbound village. *Blue Lonesome* concerns a man who becomes obsessed by the suicide of a woman he scarcely knew. *Nothing but the Night* is a powerful study of two individuals, both with traumatic memories, one of whom wants the other one dead.

BP is a passionate devotee of crime-fiction and has written extensive studies of the field and compiled numerous anthologies. Devotees will delight in BP's affectionate study of the worst in crime fiction, *Gun in Cheek* and *Son of Gun in Cheek*, along with his similar treatment of western fiction *Six Gun in Cheek*. He and his wife consider the range of crime fiction in *1001 Midnights*.

Novels

Nameless series: *The Snatch* (1971), *The Vanished* (1973), *Undercurrent* (1973), *Blowback* (1977), *Twospot* with Collin Wilcox (1978), *Labyrinth* (1980), *Hoodwink* (1981), *Scattershot* (1982), *Dragonfire* (1982), *Bindlestiff* (1983), *Quicksilver* (1984), *Nightshades* (1984), *Doubles* with Marcia Muller (1984), *Bones* (1985), *Deadfall* (1986), *Shackles* (1988), *Jackpot* (1990), *Breakdown* (1991), *Quarry* (1992), *Epitaphs* (1992), *Demons* (1993), *Hardcase* (1995), *Sentinels* (1996), *Illusions* (1997), *Boobytrap* (1998), *Crazybone* (2000), *Bleeders* (2001).

Carmody series as Alex Saxon: *A Run in Diamonds* (1973).

Dan Connell series as Jack Foxx: *The Jade Figurine* (1972), *Dead Run* (1975).

Quincannon series: *Quincannon* (1985), *Beyond the Grave* with Marcia Muller (1986).

Oxman & Tobin series with John LUTZ: *The Eye* (1984).

Non-series: *The Stalker* (1971), *Panic!* (1972), *Snowbound* (1974), *Games* (1976), *Masques* (1981), *The Lighthouse* with Marcia Muller (1987), *With an Extreme Burning* (1994; as *The Tormentor*, 2000), *Blue Lonesome* (1995), *Nothing But the Night* (1999), *In an Evil Time* (2001), *Step to the Graveyard Easy* (2002).

with Barry N. Malzberg: *The Running of Beasts* (1976), *Acts of Mercy* (1977), *Night Screams* (1979).

Non-series as Jack Foxx: *Freebooty* (1976; as by BP, 1992), *Wildfire* (1978; rev'd as *Firewind*, 1989).

Non-series as William Jeffrey (with Jeffrey Wallmann): *Day of the Moon* (1983).

See also collaborations listed under Marcia Muller.

Short Stories

Nameless series: *Casefile* (1983), *Spadework* (1996).

Carmody series: *Carmody's Run* (1993).

Quincannon series: *Carpenter and Quincannon* (1998).

Non-series: *Graveyard Plots* (1985), *Small Felonies* (1988), *Cat's Paw* (1991), *Stacked Deck* (1991), *Sleuths* (1999), *Night Freight* (2000), *Oddments* (2000), *More Oddments* (2001), *Problems Solved*, with Barry N. Malzberg (2002).

Non-fiction. *Gun in Cheek* (1982), *1001 Midnights* with Marcia Muller (1986), *Son of Gun in Cheek* (1987), *Sixgun in Cheek* (1990).

Editor. *Tricks and Treats* with Joe GORES (1976; as *Mystery Writers Choice*, UK 1977), *Midnight Specials* (1977), *Dark Sins, Dark Dreams* with Barry N. Malzberg (1977), *The Edgar Winners* (1980), *The Arbor House Treasury of Detective and Mystery Stories from the Great Pulps* (1983).
with Martin H. Greenberg (and others): *The Mystery Hall of Fame* (1984), *Murder in the First Reel* (1985), *13 Short Mystery Novels* (1985), *13 Short Espionage Novels* (1985), *Women Sleuths* (1985), *Police Procedurals* (1985), *Great Modern Police Stories* (1986), *101 Mystery Stories* (1986), *Locked Room Puzzles* (1986), *Mystery in the Mainstream* (1986; as *Crime and Crime Again*, 1990), *Prime Suspects* (1987), *Uncollected Crimes* (1987), *Suspicious Characters* (1987), *Manhattan Mysteries* (1987), *Criminal Elements* (1987), *13 Short Detective Novels* (1988), *Cloak and Dagger* (1988), *The Mammoth Book of Private Eye Stories* (1988), *Homicidal Acts* (1989), *Felonious Assaults* (1989), *Hard-Boiled* with Jack Adrian (1995), *American Pulp* (1997), *Pure Pulp* (1999).
See also collaborations listed under Marcia Muller.

Full name: William John Pronzini.
Pen-names: J.V. Drexel, Jack Foxx, Alex Saxon, William Jeffrey (with Jeffrey Wallman), John Barry Williams; house names Robert Hart-Davis, Brett Halliday.
Where to start: The Nameless series is best read in sequence but if you want a sample go for *Shackles*. Of his non-series book, *Blue Lonesome* is a good starting point.
Awards: Shamus, best hardcover novel (1982, 1999), best short story (1984), PWA Lifetime Achievement (1987), Macavity, best critical (1987, 1988), Grand Prix de Littérature Policière Best Foreign (1989), American Mystery Award, best P.I. novel (1991).
Similar stuff: Michael COLLINS, Joe GORES.
Final fact: BP's most unusual writing job was in the mid-70s when he was commissioned by the female head of a San Francisco call-girl ring to compile an "etiquette manual" for her girls! Do's and don'ts in dealing with customers, how to dress, how to handle trouble situations, and so on. BP worked from some hastily scribbled notes. The "manual" was privately printed in pamphlet form but BP never received a copy. It must be one of his most collectable items.

Mary Monica Pulver (b. 1943) US

MMP's work is difficult to tie down as each series is as different as the pen-names they appear under. Her first novel, *Murder at the War*, which was nominated for an Anthony award, introduced Illinois police detective Peter Brichter and his wife Kori Price, who breeds horses. Their first adventure is light-hearted. Brichter and his wife are members of the Society for Creative Anachronism (as is MMP) and a murder occurs in the midst of a recreation of a medieval battle. The second book, *The Unforgiving Minutes*, is darker and more gritty and takes place before the first book, showing how Brichter and Price came together when Brichter reopened a 14-year-old murder case. The rest of the series alternates between lighter and darker touches, with *Original Sin* being an atmospheric snowbound country house murder case. Horse lovers will want to read *Show Stopper* as it takes place at a horse show. MMP next worked on an historical series featuring Dame Frevisse with her friend Gail Fraser under the alias Margaret FRAZER. Her third series, as Monica Ferris, are needlework mysteries with a pattern included with each novel. The title of the first book, *Crewel World*, refers to a needlework and wool store run by wealthy widow, Margot Berglund, whose older and less benign sister, Betsy, has come to stay with her. There are plenty of candidates who want Margot out of the shop so when she is murdered and the shop trashed, Betsy takes it upon herself to investigate. Although the series is essentially a small-town cozy, with a fascinating cast of characters, MMP has a flair for originality and the plots are always diverse and fascinating. MMP has also written occasional stories about medieval monk and sleuth Father Hugh and, with her husband (as Al and Mary Kuhfeld) a series about Minnesota detectives Hafner and Nygaard. This has appeared entirely in *AHMM* and has yet to be collected.

Novels

Peter Brichter series: *Murder at the War* (1987; as *Knight Fall*, 1992), *The Unforgiving Minutes* (1988), *Ashes to Ashes* (1988), *Original Sin* (1991), *Show Stopper* (1992).

Dame Frevisse series with Gail Fraser as Margaret Frazer: *The Novice's Tale* (1992), *The Servant's Tale* (1993), *The Outlaw's Tale* (1994), *The Bishop's Tale* (1994), *The Boy's Tale* (1995), *The Murderer's Tale* (1996).

Betsy Devonshire series as Monica Ferris: *Crewel World* (1999), *Framed in Lace* (1999), *A Stitch in Time* (2000), *Unraveled Sleeve* (2001), *A Murderous Yarn* (2002).

Full name: Mary Monica Pulver Kuhfeld.
Pen-names: Margaret of Shaftesbury, Monica Ferris, Margaret Frazer.
Where to start: *The Unforgiving Minutes* or *Crewel World*.
Website: <members.aol.com/MaryPulver/>
Similar stuff: Deborah ADAMS, Jo BANNISTER, both for horse-related mysteries; Dorothy CANNELL and Ann GEORGE.
Final fact: When MMP was researching the Peter Brichter series, she acquired an improved seat on a horse, researching the Dame Frevisse series left her with a smattering of medieval church Latin, and researching her needlework series gave her scarves, a sweater, wall hangings, Christmas tree ornaments, and a pair of socks.

Mario Puzo (1920–99) US

The Godfather is one of the ten best-selling novels of all time with over 20 million copies sold. It has been called "the definitive gangster novel" and led to one of the most successful films of all time. The book is the story of Don Vito Corleone, head of a New York Mafia family, and how he controls the Mafia underworld and the tensions within his own family at the time of his death. Although MP did not regard it as his best book, his portrayal of the seemingly just, reasonable, even benevolent Godfather whose demeanour masks a man of infinite evil power, is masterful. MP had not really wanted to write *The Godfather*, and only finished it because he needed the final portion of the advance. After the success of the book he returned to the world of the Mafia three times. *The Sicilian* (filmed 1987) is about Michael Corleone, exiled to Sicily, who has been commanded to return with a young Sicilian bandit, Salvatore Guiliano, who is regarded as a local hero. *The Last Don* (filmed TV 1997) portrays the rivalry between two other New York families, the Clericuzios and the Santadios, and their links to Las Vegas and Hollywood. *Omerta* brings to life another family, the Apriles, and the quest for revenge by Astorre when his uncle, Don Raymonde, is killed. Two other books can be loosely linked to these. *The Fortunate Pilgrim* (filmed TV series 1988), an early book, is almost a prequel to *The Godfather*. It is set in the Hell's Kitchen area of New York (where MP was born) in the early years of the 20th century and follows the growth of an immigrant Italian family held together by their strong mother. *Fools Die* is about the corruption in the world of gambling and the movies. MP also collaborated with Francis Ford Coppola on the scripts for the three films, *The Godfather* (1972), *The Godfather, Part II* (1974) and *The Godfather, Part III* (1990) and won an Academy Award for the first two. The third is not based on any book, but considers the future of Michael Corleone as he tries to become a legitimate businessman.

Two other books are of interest. In *The Fourth K*, a new member of the Kennedy family is elected President, but when his daughter is kidnapped by terrorists it sets him on a course of political destruction. *The Family* was MP's last book, completed after his death by his partner, Carol Gino, where he recreates the life and crimes of the notorious Borgias in 15th-century Rome. Under his pen-name, Mario Cleri, MP wrote *Six Graves to Munich* (filmed 1983 as *A Time to Die*). It's a post-war revenge novel set in 1948 where a WW2 veteran seeks revenge on four Nazis responsible for the death of his wife. MP had served in the USAF during WW2 and stayed on in Germany for a short while after the War as a civilian public relations officer for the Air Force. He returned to New York where he worked for the Defence Department for twenty years. He sold his first novel, *Dark Arena*, another WW2 revenge story, in 1955. MP also worked on the scripts for the films *Earthquake* (1974), *Superman* (1978), *Superman II* (1980) and *Christopher Columbus: The Discovery* (1992).

Novels

Godfather series: *The Godfather* (1969), *The Sicilian* (1984), *The Last Don* (1996), *Omerta* (2000).
Non-series: *The Fortunate Pilgrim* (1965), *Fools Die* (1978), *The Fourth K* (1990), *The Family* with Carol Gino (2001).
as Mario Cleri: *Six Graves to Munich* (1967).

Awards: Oscar, best script (1972, 1974).
Books about: *The Godfather Papers & Other Confessions* by Mario Puzo (1972).

Website: The Official Mario Puzo Library is at <www.jgeoff.com/puzo/>
Similar stuff: Leonard SCIASCIA.
Final fact: After MP's death the FBI disclosed that they had been investigating MP in the mid-sixties on charges that he was accepting bribes to help young men avoid the army draft.

Monica Quill *pseudonym, see* Ralph McInerney

Simon Quinn *pseudonym, see* Martin Cruz Smith

Sheila Radley (b. 1928) UK

SR has written some of the best English village mysteries of recent years. These are not traditional cozies. SR's interest was in motive. She believed that most people are not criminally minded but are driven to crime by overwhelming pressures. Sometimes those crimes turn nasty, such as the drowned girl in *Death and the Maiden* or the decapitated cat and the threat "Your Turn Next" in *Blood on the Happy Highway*. SR's detective, based in Suffolk, is Inspector (later Chief Inspector) Douglas Quantrill, a rather old-style family man policeman who understands people. He is assisted by high-flyer Sergeant Martin Tate in the first three books and thereafter by a female sergeant, reflecting the changing times. SR was ideally placed to observe village life. For 14 years, until she turned full-time writer in 1978, she had run the village store and post office in Banham, Norfolk, a rôle that is especially pertinent in *Cross My Heart and Hope to Die*, when an elderly couple disappear just after drawing their pension. SR wrote three romantic suspense novels under the alias Hester Rowan before starting the Quantrill books. Her specialism had been in history, however, in which she achieved her B.A. with honours in 1951, before entering the WRAF. She achieved a long-held ambition in 1998 with the publication of her historical mystery novel *New Blood from Old Bones*.

Novels

DCI Quantrill series: *Death and the Maiden* (1978; as *Death in the Morning*, US 1979), *The Chief Inspector's Daughter* (1981), *A Talent for Destruction* (1982), *Blood on the Happy Highway* (1983; as *The Quiet Road to Death*, US 1984), *Fate Worse Than Death* (1985), *Who Saw Him Die?* (1987), *This Way Out* (1989), *Cross My Heart and Hope to Die* (1992), *Fair Game* (1994).
Non-series: *New Blood from Old Bones* (1998).
as Hester Rowan: *Overture in Venice* (1976), *The Linden Tree* (1977), *Snowfall* (1978; as *Alpine Encounter*, US 1979).

Real name: Sheila Robinson.
Pen-names: Sheila Radley, Hester Rowan.
Where to start: *Death and the Maiden.*
Similar stuff: Ruth RENDELL's Wexford novels; Jill MCGOWN, Minette WALTERS.

Robert J. Randisi (b. 1951) US

RJR is a prolific writer with some 350 novels to his credit, around 90% of which are westerns. These include the Gunsmith series (over 250 titles), written as J.R. Roberts, a number of which are also mysteries, as are the Bounty Hunter series written as Joshua Randall and the Angel Eyes series as W.B. Longley. But RJR has also written the genuine article, mostly featuring P.I.s. RJR has a passion for P.I.s. He founded the Private Eye Writers of America in 1981 and inaugurated the Shamus Awards. He has compiled a number of private-eye anthologies and co-founded (with Ed Gorman) the magazine *Mystery Scene* in 1985. He's even brought other authors' P.I.s into his own books. His first P.I. was Miles "Kid" Jacoby, an ex-boxer who, in *Eye in the Ring*, gains his P.I. licence. In the second novel, *The Steinway Collection* (developed from a 1977 short story which first introduced the character), which revolves around a collection of old pulp magazines, Jacoby consults both Bill PRONZINI's Nameless and the author Stuart KAMINSKY over the magazines, as well as running into Michael COLLINS's Dan Fortune. In this series Jacoby learns as he goes along and the reader learns with him. RJR's first book, *The Disappearance of Penny*, introduced womanizer Henry Po, an investigator for the New York Racing Commission, who has also appeared in five stories collected as *Black and White Memories* (along with other P.I. stories). Nick Delvecchio, a thoroughbred hard-boiled P.I. from Brooklyn, has appeared in two novels and a story collection. RJR's most fully realized series, however, does not feature a P.I., but NYPD detective Joe Keough. RJR worked as an admin. assistant for the NYPD until he became a full-time writer in 1982, and this provided him with considerable background material. Keough is a renegade cop who, in *Alone With the Dead*, is banished to Brooklyn. There he becomes the only one who believes that some of the murders by a serial killer known as The Lover are copy-cat killings. Cold-shouldered by his colleagues, Keough sets out to find both murderers. In *In the Shadow of the Arch*, Keough has relocated to St Louis where he becomes involved in several cases of kidnapping and murder. RJR further develops Keough's character in the third novel, *Blood on the Arch*, and looks set to have a fine series. Of RJR's non-series books *The Sixth Phase* is a powerful thriller where detectives discover that a series of apparently unconnected murders are all by one killer, but have no other clues. Also worth checking is *The Ham Reporter*, set in 1911 when Bat Masterson teams up with Damon Runyon to solve a mystery. RJR has collaborated with his partner, Christine Matthews, on a series featuring amateur sleuths Gil Hunt, a St Louis bookstore owner, and his wife, Claire, a local celebrity.

Novels

Miles Jacoby series: *Eye in the Ring* (1982), *The Steinway Collection* (1983), *Full Contact* (1984), *Separate Cases* (1990), *Hard Look* (1993), *Stand-Up* (1994).

Nick Delvecchio series: *No Exit from Brooklyn* (1987), *The Dead of Brooklyn* (1991).
Joe Keough series: *Alone With the Dead* (1995), *In the Shadow of the Arch* (1997), *Blood on the Arch* (2000), *East of the Arch* (2002).
Nick Carter series (as Nick Carter): *Pleasure Island* (1981), *Chessmaster* (1982), *The Mendoza Manuscript* (1982), *The Greek Summit* (1983), *The Decoy Hit* (1983), *The Caribbean Coup* (1984).
Destroyer series, with or ghost-written as Warren MURPHY: *Dangerous Games* (1980), *Midnight Man* (1981), *Lucifer's Weekend* (1982), *Total Recall* (1984).
Gil & Claire Hunt series with Christine Matthews: *Murder is the Deal of the Day* (1999), *The Masks of Auntie Laveau* (2002).
Non-series: *The Disappearance of Penny* (1980), *The Ham Reporter* (1986), *The Turner Journals* as Robert Leigh (1996, as *The Sixth Phase,* 2000).
Short stories. *Delvecchio's Brooklyn* (2001), *Black and White Memories* (2002).
Non-fiction. *Writing the Private Eye Novel* (1997).
Editor. *The Eyes Have It* (1984), *Mean Streets* (1986), *An Eye for Justice* (1988), *Under the Gun* with Ed GORMAN & Martin H. Greenberg (1990), *Justice for Hire* (1990), *Deadly Allies* with Marilyn Wallace (1992), *Deadly Allies II* with Susan DUNLAP (1994), *The Eyes Still Have It* (1995), *First Cases* (1996), *Lethal Ladies* with Barbara Collins (1996), *First Cases 2* (1997), *Lethal Ladies 2* with Christine Matthews (1997), *First Cases 3* (1999), *The Shamus Game* (2000), *Mystery Street* (2001). Also audio-anthologies *For Crime Out Loud* (2 vols. 1995/6).
Full name: Robert Joseph Randisi.
Pen-names: Lew Baines, Tom Cutter, Robert Lake, Paul Ledd, W.B. Longley, Joseph Meek, Joshua Randall, J.R. Roberts, Jon Sharpe, Cole Weston (all on westerns), Spenser Fortune, Robert Leigh; house names, Nick Carter, Jack Hild.
Where to start: *Alone With the Dead.*
Awards: Southwest Mystery/Suspense Convention, Lifetime Achievement (1993).
Website: Nothing on his mystery fiction but <www.readthewest.com/randisi.htm> covers some of his western output.
Similar stuff: Michael COLLINS, Loren ESTLEMAN, Bill PRONZINI.
Final fact: RJR once wrote one of his Angel Eyes western novels in three-and-a-half days. He also had a flying streak with *The Dead of Brooklyn* where he allowed himself three months and wrote it in eleven days.

Ian Rankin (b. 1960) UK

After a slow but steady start IR has emerged in the nineties as one of Britain's major writing talents, primarly for his series featuring Detective Inspector John Rebus of the Lothian and Borders police. A Scot, born in Cardenden in Fife, IR was not acquainted with crime fiction when he began writing. Originally inspired by music, he had written lyrics for pop songs (he even performed briefly in a punk band), which turned into writing poetry and from there to short stories. His first book, *The Flood* (1986), written when he should have been studying for a PhD at Edinburgh, was a coming-of-age book. He then sought to rework the Jekyll and Hyde theme in Edinburgh, choosing a police detective and a villain as the two conflicting sides. This became *Knots and Crosses*, the first of the Rebus novels, though it was only when it was completed that IR realized he had written crime fiction and that it proved a good vehicle for his exploration of social issues. The Rebus novels have been dubbed "Tartan noir" by James ELLROY, an epithet also bequeathed upon Christopher BROOKMYRE. IR has taken a cynical and antisocial individual and placed him in a secretive, repressive and conspiratorial city. Rebus is ex-SAS, middle-aged (and grows older with the series), rebellious, angry and goes his own way. He frequently frustrates his own life, which adds to his anger and determination. He's as likely to get something wrong as right. He gets results, often at great personal cost, partly through his pig-headedness but mostly because of his knowledge of Edinburgh, its people and its life. IR deals with major and usually violent social issues, sometimes several in one book. Child abduction, satanism, serial killers, gun-running, war criminals, a trade in refugees, paedophilia, political corruption, all these take Rebus to the edge. Perhaps the darkest of the novels is *Black and Blue*, which won IR the CWA Gold Dagger and earned him an Edgar nomination. It was also the first of the series he was completely satisfied with. IR had selected an unsolved series of crimes committed in Glasgow by Bible John in the sixties that are now being recreated by a copy-cat killer. The Rebus series is being adapted for TV and IR sees a finite lifetime to the run of Rebus books, but until then he is creating a formidable body of work.

Besides the Rebus books IR has written several thrillers. His favourite remains a complicated Le Carré style spy novel, *The Watchman*. *Westwind* is more of a light-hearted caper, and not in IR's usual idiom. He wrote three books as Jack Harvey. *Witch Hunt* has a female assassin after a politician; *Bleeding Hearts* has an unscrupulous P.I. tracking another assassin; while *Blood Hunt* used the BSE scare to explore a government cover-up. IR is at his best, though, when exploring the dark and sinister side of Edinburgh. He has written two radio plays ("The Serpent's Back", 1995 and "The Third Gentleman", 1997), the first adapted as a story, set in 18th-century Edinburgh and featuring the roguish Cullender, a "caddy", a personal escort who looks after the safety of visitors, and knows how to sort out any problems. There is a promise of more to come.

Novels

Rebus series: *Knots and Crosses* (1987), *Hide and Seek* (1991), *Wolfman* (1992; as *Tooth and Nail*, US 1996), *Strip Jack* (1992), *The Black Book* (1993), *Mortal Causes* (1994), *Let It Bleed* (1995), *Black and Blue* (1997), *The Hanging Garden* (1998), *Dead Souls* (1999), *Death is Not the End* (2000), *Set in Darkness* (2000), *The Falls* (2001), *Resurrection Men* (2002).

Non-series: *Watchman* (1988), *Westwind* (1990).

as Jack Harvey: *Witch Hunt* (1993), *Bleeding Hearts* (1994), *Blood Hunt* (1995).

Short Stories
Rebus series: *A Good Hanging and Other Stories* (1992).
Non-series: *Herbert in Motion* (1997).

Full name: Ian James Rankin.
Pen-name: Jack Harvey.
Where to start: *Knots and Crosses*.
Awards: Raymond Chandler-Fulbright Fellowship (1991/2); CWA short story dagger (1996), Gold Dagger (1997), Sherlock, Best British Detective (2001).
Website: <www.ianrankin.com>
Similar stuff: Christopher BROOKMYRE, John HARVEY, Quintin JARDINE.
Final fact: The first time IR visited a police station to undertake research he became the subject of their enquiries. It seems that the plot he was researching was similar to a case they were investigating and IR almost became a suspect.

Daniel Ransom *pseudonym, see* Ed Gorman

Julian Rathbone (b. 1935) UK

The majority of JR's books fall into the category of international political thriller though, with the exception of a few, such as *A Spy of the Old School*, they are not fully fledged spy or espionage adventures. Most of his early books are set in Turkey or the Middle East. Three feature Turkish policeman Colonel Nur Bey who has to help British ex-pats out of trouble, such as an assassination plot in *Diamonds Bid* or drug-smuggling in *Trip Trap*. Five further novels, with no continuing characters, are set in Spain. *Carnival!* is the most straightforward – a television crew film a murder. *Bloody Marvellous* is a drug-smuggling double cross while *A Raving Monarchist* has a political assassination plot. *Lying in State* concerns the discovery of a revealing tape by the now-dead dictator Peron of Argentina. Set during the preparations for the Barcelona Olympics *Dangerous Games* has a rather unwelcome killer on the loose. For his series about Police Commissioner Jan Argand, JR invented a fictitious European country, Brabt, where Argand faces pressures arising through big business, the US military or antinuclear demonstrations. More recently JR has developed several books dealing with ecological issues. *Zdt* deals with a strain of maize that is discovered in Costa Rica and which a rival agricultural business tries to sabotage. *The Pandora Option* deals with attempts to contaminate Iranian grain siloes, a plot not too dissimilar to the earlier *Kill Cure*, where antibiotics meant for Bangladesh are mixed with virulent poisons. *Accidents Will Happen* introduces the Eco-Cops, led by the German Renata Fechter, who investigates major ecological scandals or disasters. Other political thrillers include *The Crystal Contract*, about drug smuggling, and *Sand Blind*, about Iraq's designs on Kuwait. Over the years JR has also shown an interest in the historical novel including his Booker-award nominated *Joseph* and the bestselling *The Last English King*. His recent *Homage*, was therefore a surprise. It's a post-modern P.I. story of a 50-something down-at-heel

British private detective summoned to California looking for a colleague. Needless to say the book soon takes on international overtones, but it remains at heart a tribute to the world of Chandler with a zest of Crais and Crumley. JR continues to demonstrate his ability to juggle the human element amidst a world of corruption, violence and despair.

Novels

Nur Bey series: *Diamonds Bid* (1967), *Hand Out* (1968), *Trip Trap* (1972).

Jan Argand series: *The Euro-Killers* (1979), *Base Case* (1981), *Watching the Detectives* (1983).

Eco-cops series: *Accidents Will Happen* (1995), *Brandenburg Concerto* (1998).

Non-series: *With My Knives I Know I'm Good* (1969), *Kill Cure* (1975), *Bloody Marvellous* (1975), *Carnival!* (1976), *A Raving Monarchist* (1978), *A Spy of the Old School* (1982), *Lying in State* (1985), *Zdt* (1986; rev'd as *Greenfinger*, US 1987), *The Crystal Contract* (1988), *The Pandora Option* (1990), *Dangerous Games* (1991), *Sand Blind* (1993), *Homage* (2001).

Where to start: *Lying in State* or *Accidents Will Happen*.
Awards: CWA short story dagger (1993).
Similar stuff: Eric Ambler, John Le Carré, Ross THOMAS.
Website: <www.julianrathbone.com>
Final fact: The actor Basil Rathbone was JR's father's cousin.

Derek Raymond (1931–94) UK

The *Sunday Times* described DR as a man "who was on the down escalator all his life." Like other renegade talents DR never found his true niche and drifted wastrel-like through the world, living in Spain, Paris, New York, Tangiers, London doing whatever jobs came along, mostly as a waiter and taxi-driver. He had a burst of fortune in the sixties with several gritty novels of London lowlife, starting with *The Crust on Its Uppers* (1962). By their very nature these books plumbed human depths and touched on criminal activities without really being crime novels. They appeared under DR's real name, or close to it, of Robin Cook, but when he re-emerged as a writer in the eighties that name was better known as the US author of medical thrillers, so DR adopted a new persona. This brought him fame late in life. He wrote a series of books about "the Factory", the nickname given to a police unit in Soho which worked for A14 – the Department of Unexplained Deaths. This unit mopped up all the deaths of people no one cared about – people whom DR knew well: tramps, vagrants, the homeless, prostitutes. Seen as a dead-end job (literally) the detectives in the unit are themselves outcasts. The unnamed protagonist is uncouth, bent and violent, almost a necessity for the company they need to keep. The French were more appreciative of DR's works than the British. The first two books received French awards and were filmed in France: *He Died With His Eyes Open* (filmed 1985) and *The Devil's Home on Leave* (filmed 1987). Although these books are bleak and noisome – *I Was Dora Suarez* has been called "one of the most gruesome books ever published" – they are also honest and portray a life too many traditional crime novels try to avoid. DR painted the underbelly of London in all its shades of black.

Novels

Factory series: *He Died With His Eyes Open* (1984), *The Devil's Home on Leave* (1985), *How the Dead Live* (1986), *I Was Dora Suarez* (1990), *Dead Man Upright* (1993).
Non-series: *Not Till the Red Fog Rises* (1994)

Real name: Robert William Arthur Cook.
Pen-names: Robin Cook, Derek Raymond.
Awards: Prix Mystère Etranger de la Critique de la Presse Français (1984), Meilleur Roman Policier (1986), Trophy 813 Award, (1995.)
Book about: *The Hidden Files*, quasi-autobiography (1992).
Similar stuff: Mark TIMLIN.
Final fact: DR's literary executor, John Williams, hopes to get further unpublished work into print, including *Nightmare in the Street*, a French *policier*, of which the opening chapter has been printed in the anthology *Fresh Blood* (1996).

Sam Reaves (b. 1954) US

SR's work has been highly acclaimed under both his pseudonyms. His first series features Vietnam veteran Cooper MacLeish who finds it difficult to settle back home and has become a taxi-driver in Chicago. The stories are dead-centre traditional hard-boiled P.I. adventures. In *A Long Cold Fall* MacLeish goes looking for the son of an old friend who has apparently committed suicide, and learns the boy may be his own. In later novels MacLeish manages to get himself entangled in things far more sinister than they at first seem. By *A Long Cold Fall* he's trying to have a quieter life and has become a chauffeur, which is fine until his boss's son is killed and MacLeish finds himself having to protect his boss in the midst of a drug war. SR then switched personalities and as Dominic Martell wrote a trilogy of thrillers set in Europe. SR, who has worked as a teacher and translator, has lived in Spain and France as well as the Middle East and uses this background for this fast-paced series. They feature Pascual Rose, a repentant ex-terrorist who is trying to keep a low profile in Barcelona but in each novel is drawn out into the open. In *Lying Crying Dying* he meets former girlfriend Katixa who is on the run with a suitcase full of cash stolen from an ETA kidnapping and seeks Pascual's help. In *The Republic of Night* the French police want his help in tracing a Syrian terrorist. In *Gitana* Spanish authorities want to know why Pascual's name is linked to a murder victim. SR's work has the authentic touch.

Novels

Cooper MacLeish series: *A Long Cold Fall* (1991), *Fear Will Do It* (1992), *Bury It Deep* (1993), *Get What's Coming* (1995).

Pascual Rose series as Dominic Martell: *Lying Crying Dying* (1998), *The Republic of Night* (1999), *Gitana* (2001).
Real name: Samuel Allen Salter.
Pen-names: Dominic Martell, Sam Reaves.
Website: <www.martell-reaves.com>
Similar stuff: Linda BARNES for taxi-driving P.I., Manuel Vázquez MONTALBÁN and David SERAFIN for Spanish crime.

Kathy Reichs (b. 1950) Canada

KR's first book, *Déjà Dead*, was accompanied by the kind of publicity hype that new authors only dream of. As a result the book topped best-seller lists in Canada and Britain and earned the Arthur Ellis award for best first novel. It introduced Dr Temperance Brennan, a forensic anthropologist for the state of North Carolina and the province of Quebec. Brennan believes that bones discovered on the site of an old monastery are of the latest victim of a serial killer, a view not held by the mysoginistic detective assigned to the case. Headstrong and determined, Brennan decides to prove her point. Brennan is based in Montreal, allowing KR to explore the cultural issues in this bi-lingual city. KR is herself one of only 50 certified forensic anthropologists operating in North America. She works for the province of Quebec and the Office of the Chief Medical Examiner for the State of North Carolina, where she also teaches. She has written such detailed studies as *Hominid Origins* (1983) and *Forensic Osteology* (1997). Although KR is not as headstrong as Brennan, the books adequately reflect her expertise and knowledge and are certainly the most detailed books of this nature. The deductions drawn from her analysis of remains would have impressed even Sherlock Holmes.

Novels

Temperance Brennan series: *Déjà Dead* (1997), *Death du Jour* (1999), *Deadly Decisions* (2000), *Fatal Voyage* (2001), *Grave Secrets* (2002).

Full name: Kathleen Joan Reichs.
Awards: Arthur Ellis, best first novel (1998).
Website: <http://literati.net/Reichs/>
Similar stuff: Beverly CONNOR, Patricia D. CORNWELL
Final fact: KR investigates around 80 cases a year, some of which may prove to be animal remains or historical bones, but most are recent deaths.

Ruth Rendell (b. 1930) UK

Whether judged by literary quality, by the depth, breadth, scale or originality of her output, or simply by the number of major awards she has received, RR is the pre-eminent British woman writer of crime and mystery fiction. Her 60-plus books cover the full range from police procedural to psychological suspense, the latter most evident in the books written as Barbara Vine. RR's strength is in charting the collapse of the status quo, where pressures from society or within push an individual over the edge. This was evident from her first book, *From Doon with Death*, which introduced her only continuing character, Chief Inspector Reginald Wexford. A husband finds his wife is missing, something completely out of character, yet it seems her fate is wrapped up with something unresolved in her distant past. Wexford, along with his main sidekick, Inspector Mike Burden, operates from Kingsmarkham, a fictional town in Sussex. Wexford is not an attractive man, but he is sharp, witty and pragmatic, with a keen understanding of what makes people tick. Burden is more rigid, and keeps himself to himself. Wexford helps him get through the loss of his wife early in the series. The inevitable limitations of crime in the average English town means that occasionally RR changes the scenery. *Murder Being Once Done* takes place in London, whilst part of *Speaker of Mandarin* is set in China. The strength of the series lies in the character of Wexford himself and his relationship not only with Burden but with the victims and suspects in the crime – how he treats them and how they perceive him. RR is adept at employing red herrings and many twists and turns in taking the reader by surprise, but you never feel Wexford is out of his depth.

By contrast her non-series books are deliberately constructed to make everyone feel out of control. These are mostly novels of either psychological suspense or psychological manipulation. As RR developed this style she created a new persona, Barbara Vine, for the more extreme, but that pattern was already there in the earlier RR novels. *A Demon in My View* was her first award-winning novel, which explores the reactions of an obsessional killer when his routine, secure world is changed forever by an odd coincidence. *Master of the Moor* turns the premise on its head. A man, who feels a failure to his wife and family, finds solace on the moor, but his one hideaway is forfeit when he discovers a dead body. Opportunity presents itself to another failure in *Make Death Love Me*. In these, and other books, RR delves deep into the psyche of individuals who have built barriers around themselves that are suddenly breached. It is used to most stunning effect in what many critics regard as RR's best novel, *A Judgement in Stone*, the story of how and why an illiterate servant ends up slaughtering her employers. This same approach is adopted for the Barbara Vine books, only this time showing how secrets buried deep in the past will out. In *A Dark-Adapted Eye* it's a 30-year-old murder case that was solved and closed but is suddenly reopened. In *A Fatal Inversion* it's a 10-year-old murder that suddenly comes to light. Both these, the first two Vine books, won major awards. Despite certain similarities between books, RR's work is notable for its originality, especially in its plotting and treatment. *The Lake of Darkness*, where a man unwittingly pays a professional assassin who thereupon assumes a service, is arguably her most ingeniously developed and crafted novel.

RR is also the author of many short stories, mostly of the suspense type, though including several Wexford cases and a few supernatural tales. All are worth reading for their deftness and precision. RR is one of the most skilled and accomplished of writers. Many of RR's books and stories, including the Wexford series, have been filmed for TV, usually under the generic title of *The Ruth Rendell Mysteries*, since 1986. In recognition of her achievement she is one of the few writers to have been awarded a Diamond Dagger by the CWA and made a Grand Master by the MWA. She is a Fellow of the Royal Society of Literature and was made a CBE in 1996. In 1997 she was created a life peer and became Baroness Rendell of Babergh. Her motto is *Vixi scripsi* ("I have lived, I have written").

Novels
Inspector Wexford series: *From Doon With Death* (1964), *A New Lease of Death* (1967; as *Sins of the Fathers*, US 1970), *Wolf to the Slaughter* (1967), *The Best Man to Die* (1969), *A Guilty Thing Surprised* (1970), *No More Dying Then* (1971), *Murder Being Once Done* (1972), *Some Lie and Some Die* (1973), *Shake Hands for Ever* (1975), *A Sleeping Life* (1978), *Put on by Cunning* (1981; as *Death Notes*, US 1981), *The Speaker of Mandarin* (1983), *An Unkindness of Ravens* (1985), *The Veiled One* (1988), *Kissing the Gunner's Daughter* (1992), *Simisola* (1994), *Road Rage* (1997), *Harm Done* (1999).
Non-series: *To Fear a Painted Devil* (1965), *Vanity Dies Hard* (1965; as *In Sickness and in Health*, US 1966), *The Secret House of Death* (1968), *One Across, Two Down* (1971), *The Face of Trespass* (1974), *A Demon in my View* (1976), *A Judgement in Stone* (1977), *Make Death Love Me* (1979), *The Lake of Darkness* (1980), *Master of the Moor* (1982), *The Killing Doll* (1984), *The Tree of Hands* (1984), *Live Flesh* (1986), *Heartstones* novella (1987), *Talking to Strange Men* (1987), *The Bridesmaid* (1989), *Going Wrong* (1990), *The Crocodile Bird* (1993), *The Keys to the Street* (1996), *A Sight for Sore Eyes* (1998), *Adam and Eve and Pinch Me* (2001).
as Barbara Vine: *A Dark-Adapted Eye* (1986), *A Fatal Inversion* (1987), *The House of Stairs* (1988), *Gallowglass* (1990), *King Solomon's Carpet* (1991), *Asta's Book* (1993), *Anna's Book* (1993), *No Night is Too Long* (1994), *The Brimstone Wedding* (1996), *The Chimney Sweeper's Boy* (1998), *The Grasshopper* (2000), *The Blood Doctor* (2002).
Short Stories
Wexford series: *Means of Evil* (1979).
Other: *The Fallen Curtain* (1976), *The Fever Tree* (1982), *The New Girl Friend* (1985), *The Copper Peacock* (1991), *Blood Lines* (1995), *"Piranha to Scurfy"* (2001).
Editor. *The Reason Why* (1996).

Full name: Ruth Barbara Rendell (*née* Grasemann).
Pen-names: Barbara Vine.
Where to start: The Wexford books are best read in sequence starting with the first *Wexford Omnibus*. With the non-series books you are spoiled for choice but try *A Demon in My View* or *A Dark-Adapted Eye* before *A Judgement in Stone* and *The Lake of Darkness*.
Awards: CWA Gold Dagger (1976, 1986, 1987, 1991), CWA Silver Dagger (1984), CWA Diamond Dagger (1991); Edgar, best short story (1975, 1984), best

novel (1987); Swedish Academy of Detection, Best Foreign (1980), Swedish Academy of Detection, Grand Master (1996), MWA Grand Master (1997).
Website: <www.twbooks.co.uk/authors/rendell.html>
Similar stuff: P.D. JAMES, Minette WALTERS, Robert BARNARD.
Final fact: RR's first job was as a journalist. She purportedly resigned because she filed a story about an after-dinner speech based on advance notes and did not attend the meeting. Unfortunately the speaker collapsed and died during his speech.

Nicholas Rhea (b. 1936) UK

NR brought to the rural Yorkshire police what James Herriott had to the rural Yorkshire vet with his series about young police constable Nick Rhea who patrolled part of the Yorkshire Moors during the 1960s. This series of semi-autobiographical reminiscences was adapted into the popular TV series *Heartbeat*. Rather than concentrate on crime, NR recreated the day-to-day life of a young "bobby" complete with all the local characters and countryside. They reflect much of NR's own career in the police force. He joined as a young cadet in 1952, became a constable in 1956, rose to the rank of Inspector and retired to write full time in 1982, having spent his last few years as the press and public relations officer. Under his own name of Peter N. Walker, NR had been writing crime novels for 15 years before his retirement. His first series featured Detective-Sergeant James Aloysius Carnaby-King, a rather flamboyant character who had a private income in addition to his police salary, which enabled him to pursue undercover work. As Walker he also wrote a short series about patrol officer Jock Patterson plus a variety of non-series books all of which reflect aspects of Walker's life on the force. One novel, *Murder After the Holiday*, under the Andrew Arncliffe alias, won Walker the *Police Review* award from the CWA for its authentic police procedure detail. Since his retirement, in addition to writing the Constable Nick series, plus novelizations of the *Emmerdale Farm* soap series and books about Yorkshire, NR has created two new characters. Detective Superintendent Pemberton is a high-flier in the North Yorkshire CID whose dedication to his work means he invariably receives the more complicated cases. These include a mock murder investigation that turns real in *False Alibi* to the discovery that a death in 1916 had been a murder that was never solved in *Family Ties*. The other series features the eccentric and superstitious D.I. Montague Pluke, a small-town detective who nevertheless operates on a big scale, especially when, in *Omens of Death*, the first ever murder happens in his small town allowing Pluke to prove himself at last. Although NR's books are all based on years of experience he never takes himself too seriously and that is what makes his books such a pleasant read.

Novels

Nick Rowan/*Heartbeat* novelizations: *Constable on Call* (1993), *Constable in Control* (1994) .

Superintendent Pemberton series (first two titles as by Peter N. Walker): *False Alibi* (1991), *Grave Secrets* (1992), *Family Ties* (1994), *Suspect* (1995), *Confession* (1997), *Death of a Princess* (1999), *The Sniper* (2001).
Montague Pluke series: *Omens of Death* (1997), *Superstitious Death* (1998), *A Well-Pressed Shroud* (2000), *Garland for a Dead Maiden* (2002).
Carnaby series as Peter N. Walker: *Carnaby and the Hijackers* (1967), *Carnaby and the Gaolbreakers* (1968), *Carnaby and the Assassins* (1968), *Carnaby and the Conspirators* (1969), *Carnaby and the Saboteurs* (1970), *Carnaby and the Eliminators* (1971), *Carnaby and the Demonstrators* (1972), *Carnaby and the Infiltrators* (1974), *Carnaby and the Kidnappers* (1976), *Carnaby and the Counterfeiters* (1980), *Carnaby and the Campaigners* (1984).
Jock Patterson series as Peter N. Walker: *Panda One on Duty* (1971), *Panda One Investigates* (1973), *Witchcraft for Panda One* (1978), *Siege for Panda One* (1981).
Ross MacAllister series as Christopher Coram: *Death in Ptarmigan Forest* (1970), *Death on the Motorway* (1973), *Murder by the Lake* (1975), *Murder Beneath the Trees* (1979), *Prisoner on the Dam* (1982), *Prisoner on the Run* (1985).
Non-series as Andrew Arncliffe: *Murder After the Holiday* (1985).
Non-series as Christoper Coram: *A Call to Danger* (1968), *A Call to Die* (1969).
Non-series as Tom Ferris: *Espionage for a Lady* (1969).
Non-series as Peter N. Walker: *Fatal Accident* (1970), *Special Duty* (1971), *Identification Parade* (1972), *Major Incident* (1974), *The Dovingsby Death* (1975), *Missing from Home* (1977), *The MacIntyre Plot* (1977), *Target Criminal* (1978), *The Carlton Plot* (1980), *Teenage Cop* (1982), *Robber in a Mole Trap* (1984).

Short Stories

Constable Series: *Constable on the Hill* (1979), *Constable on the Prowl* (1980), *Constable Around the Village* (1981), *Constable Across the Moors* (1982), *Constable in the Dale* (1983), *Constable by the Sea* (1985), *Constable Along the Lane* (1986), *Constable Through the Meadow* (1988), *Constable at the Double* (1988), *Constable in Disguise* (1989), *Constable Among the Heather* (1990), *Constable by the Stream* (1991), *Constable Around the Green* (1993), *Constable Beneath the Trees* (1994), *Constable in the Shrubbery* (1995), *Constable versus Greengrass* (1995), *Constable About the Parish* (1996), *Constable at the Gate* (1997), *Constable at the Dam* (1997), *Constable Over the Stile* (1998), *Constable Under the Gooseberry Bush* (1998), *Constable in the Farmyard* (1999), *Constable Around the Houses* (2000), *Constable Along the Highway* (2001), *Constable Over the Bridge* (2001), *Constable Goes to Market* (2002), *Constable along the Riverbank* (2002). [Note: some paperback reprintings are omnibus volumes of two or three novels.]

Non-fiction (selective).

as Peter N. Walker: *The Courts of Law* (1971), *Punishment: an Illustrated History* (1972), *Murders and Mysteries from the North York Moors* (1988), *Murders and Mysteries from the Yorkshire Dales* (1991), *Heartbeat of Yorkshire* (1993).

Real name: Peter Norman Walker.
Other pen-names: Andrew Arncliffe, Christopher Coram, James Ferguson, Tom Ferris.
Where to start: The Constable series aside, try the first Pemberton novel, *False Alibi*.
Awards: CWA *Police Review* Award (1986).

Website: <www.heartbeat.demon.co.uk> and <www.twbooks.co.uk/authors/nrhea.htm>
Similar stuff: Pauline BELL, Peter ROBINSON.
Final fact: In 1982 Walker was the first police PR man to deal directly with the media from the scene of a murder investigation. It was during the manhunt for Barry Prudom who had murdered two policemen and a pensioner. Police handling of the situation probably saved the lives of two other pensioners and, for his role, Walker received the Chief Constable's commendation. The experience now serves as a police training model.

Robert Richardson (b. 1940) UK

A journalist and former newspaper editor, Manchester-born RR met with success with his first novel, *The Latimer Mercy*, which won the John Creasey Memorial award. It was the first to feature amateur sleuth Augustus Maltravers, also a former journalist turned novelist and playwright. Although Maltravers is an amateur detective in the classic sense, RR is not always traditional in his approach to either the detection or solution to the crime. In *Bellringer Street*, for instance, the police solve the primary crime because Maltravers has become interested in a secondary crime. In *The Dying of the Light* Maltravers solves a murder but keeps his solution from the police. The premise of the series allows for some interesting bibliomysteries. *The Latimer Mercy* is about the theft of a 16th-century Bible. *The Book of the Dead* is especially clever as RR weaves into the mystery a hitherto "lost" Sherlock Holmes story. After six novels RR tired of Maltravers and changed direction completely to produce several psychological suspense novels, which he has found more artistically satisfying. *The Hand of Strange Children*, which was nominated for a CWA Gold Dagger, is about three siblings and their guilt about the death of their father. *Significant Others* is about a newspaper columnist who goes into hiding but is attacked, only no one knows where she is. *Victims* returns to a small village several years after a mass murder and considers the long-term effects. RR is not a prolific writer but his books are well crafted and highly satisfying.

Novels

Augustus Maltravers series: *The Latimer Mercy* (1985), *Bellringer Street* (1988), *The Book of the Dead* (1989), *The Dying of the Light* (1990), *Sleeping in the Blood* (1991; as *Murder in Waiting*, 1991), *The Lazarus Tree* (1992).
Non-series: *The Hand of Strange Children* (1993), *Significant Others* (1995), *Victims* (1997).

Full name: Robert Oliver Richardson.
Where to start: *The Latimer Mercy* for traditional fare or *The Hand of Strange Children*.
Awards: CWA John Creasey Memorial (1985).
Website: <www.twbooks.co.uk/authors/rrichardson.html>
Similar stuff: Veronica STALLWOOD for another author-sleuth; Ruth RENDELL.

Rick Riordan (b. 1964) US

RR fulfilled expectations when, after his first book won the Shamus award for best first P.I. novel his second in the series went on to win an Edgar. These launched his character Tres Navarre, an unlicensed P.I. and a tai-chi expert with a PhD in medieval English and a fondness for Chaucer, who lives in RR's native city of San Antonio, Texas. He is the son of a former sheriff who had been murdered years before and in the first book Tres returns to San Antonio, an outcast from academe, to delve further into his father's death. These books have a strong sense of place. RR began them out of a nostalgia for Texas while he was teaching middle-school students in San Francisco. The books have made a powerful impact. After the first four RR has developed a strong community feel in the novels, particularly in *The Devil Went Down to Texas*, where a crime unravels beneath the waters of a dammed lake. RR is certainly a name to follow.

Novels

Tres Navarre series: *Big Red Tequila* (1997), *The Widower's Two-Step* (1998), *The Last King of Texas* (2000), *The Devil Went Down to Austin* (2001).

Awards: Anthony, best paperback original (1998), Shamus, best first novel (1998), Edgar, best paperback original (1999).
Website: <www.rickriordan.com>
Similar stuff: Bill CRIDER.
Final fact: RR used to sing in a folk group called Shenandoah.

Jack Ripley *pseudonym, see* John Wainwright

Mike Ripley (b. 1952) UK

MR's series about trumpet-playing taxi-driving Londoner Roy (Fitzroy) Maclean Angel are amongst the funniest crime novels currently being written and have twice won the CWA's Last Laugh award. Angel doesn't exactly go looking for trouble but mixes with all the wrong people and gets entangled in the dodgiest of enterprises and trouble soon finds him. In *Angel Confidential* he teams up with rather inept P.I. Veronica Blugden who becomes a regular in the series. His antics take him into animal rights, drug smuggling, counterfeiting, bootlegged booze, the fashion business, even the movie industry in *Lights, Camera, Angel*, but as nothing much ever goes right for Angel, you know wherever he is, murder, mayhem and amusement are never far away. MR was the crime reviewer for the *Daily Telegraph* and now for the *Birmingham Post* and *The Good Book Guide* and has also written occasional TV and radio scripts, including ones for the *Lovejoy* series. He co-edits the *Fresh Blood* anthologies with Maxim JAKUBOWSKI and was the creator of the annual Sherlock Awards for fictional detectives. After 20 years in journalism and public relations MR became an archaeologist specializing in Roman Britain.

Novels

Angel series: *Just Another Angel* (1988), *Angel Touch* (1989), *Angel Hunt* (1990), *Angel in Arms* (1991), *Angel City* (1994), *Angel Confidential* (1995), *Family of Angels* (1996), *That Angel Look* (1997), *Bootlegged Angel* (1999), *Lights, Camera, Angel* (2001), *Angel Underground* (2002).
Non-series: *Double Take* (2002).
Editor, with Maxim Jakubowski. *Fresh Blood* (1996), *Fresh Blood 2* (1997), *Fresh Blood 3* (1999).

Full name: Michael David Ripley.
Awards: CWA Last Laugh (1989, 1991).
Website: <www.twbooks.co.uk/authors/mikeripley1.html>
Similar stuff: Peter GUTTRIDGE.
Final fact: MR's first editor at the legendary Collins Crime Club was Agatha Christie's last editor. She accepted the first Angel novel within eight days and her first words to MR were: "How many more can you do?"

Candace Robb (b. 1950) US

CR's series featuring Owen Archer began as an historical short story, without Archer, but soon grew into a mystery novel. The books are set in York, England, in the 1360s. Archer is a former captain of archers but the loss of sight in his left eye means he can no longer serve. He has become a spy for John Thoresby, Lord Chancellor of England and Archbishop of York. In *The Apothecary Rose* Archer is sent to York to look into a couple of suspicious deaths and takes cover as an apprentice to the apothecary whose medicine seems to have proved fatal. The apothecary is also ill and Archer finds himself working alongside Lucie Wilton, the apothecary's wife, and soon to be widow. By the second novel Archer and Lucie have married. The novels benefit from detailed historical research and recreate 14th-century England in all its glory and misery, especially during the plague. Other key characters of the time appear, including fellow spy Geoffrey Chaucer. CR has recently started a new series set in Scotland in the turbulent years at the end of the 13th century and the war with England. Her heroine is Margaret Kerr, struggling to find the truth about her missing husband. CR has an MA in medieval literature. Born in North Carolina, she lives in Seattle where she teaches a creative writing course.

Novels

Owen Archer series: *The Apothecary Rose* (1993), *The Lady Chapel* (1994), *The Nun's Tale* (1995), *The King's Bishop* (1996), *The Riddle of St Leonard's* (1997), *A Gift of Sanctuary* (1998), *A Spy for the Redeemer* (1999), *The Cross-legged Knight* (2002).
Margaret Kerr series: *A Trust Betrayed* (2000).

Website: <www.candacerobb.com>
Similar stuff: Margaret FRAZER, Paul DOHERTY, Susanna GREGORY.
Final fact: CR shares her birthday with Agatha Christie.

Gillian Roberts (b. 1939) US

Philadelphia born and bred, Judith Greber originally planned to write a mystery story for her first book but the US market was not quite ready for a humorous mystery series with a woman detective, so the former high-school teacher shelved the idea and turned to writing mainstream novels. Five years later the market had changed. Greber resurrected her first novel but, because she was now identified with mainstream novels, a new persona was born and *Caught Dead in Philadelphia*, which sold within a week, appeared as by GR. It introduced Amanda Pepper, also a high school English teacher in Philadelphia. Amanda (or Mandy) is a 30-something spinster, always helpful and obliging. In the first book Mandy allows a distraught fellow teacher to take refuge in her apartment only to find the woman dead when she returns home. Amanda becomes a prime suspect. During this investigation Mandy meets detective C.K. Mackenzie who provides an element of cautious romance. There's a strong literary thread in all of the books, most intriguingly in *I'd Rather be in Philadelphia*, where GR succeeds in weaving together *The Taming of the Shrew* with a book about battered wives that contains notes in the margin which send Mandy off trying to stop a murder. Though the books are generally light-hearted, the plots are serious and intelligently developed. With her move to California, GR has started a new series set in San Raphael about 50-something P.I. Emma Howe and her new and much younger trainee partner, single mother Billie August. This is a complete change from the Pepper books – stark characterization, fast pace and deadly serious. The relationship between Emma and Billie sizzles in the first book *Time and Trouble* where there is a desperate race to find a missing girl believed to be abducted by a bizarre cult. GR has put her experience into a how-to book, *You Can Write a Mystery*.

Novels

Amanda Pepper series: *Caught Dead in Philadelphia* (1987), *Philly Stakes* (1989), *I'd Rather be in Philadelphia* (1992), *With Friends Like These . . .* (1993), *How I Spent My Summer Vacation* (1994), *In the Dead of Summer* (1995), *The Mummer's Curse* (1996), *The Bluest Blood* (1998), *Adam and Evil* (1999), *Helen Hath No Fury* (2000).
Emma Howe series: *Time and Trouble* (1998), *Whatever Doesn't Kill You* (2001).
Short Stories. *Where's the Harm in That* (1999).
Non-fiction. *You Can Write a Mystery* (1999).

Real name: Judith Greber.
Awards: Anthony, best first mystery (1988).
Website: <www.gillianroberts.com>
Similar stuff: Orania PAPAZOGLOU, Nancy PICKARD, Lisa SCOTTOLINE.

Julian Roberts *pseudonym, see* Roderic Jeffries

Les Roberts (b. 1937) US

Having been a singer, actor and jazz pianist, LR spent 24 years in Hollywood writing or producing over 2,500 half-hours of network and syndicated TV, including working on *The Lucy Show*, *The Man from U.N.C.L.E.* and *Hollywood Squares*. In 1986 he converted an unsold script into his first novel, *An Infinite Number of Monkeys*, which won the first St Martin's Press/PWA award for the best first unpublished P.I. novel and was later shortlisted for both the Shamus and Anthony awards. It introduced his actor-turned-P.I., Saxon (we never learn his first name), who operates out of Los Angeles. Like LR, Saxon is a transplanted Chicagoan with an ambivalence about Hollywood and therefore, unlike other Hollywood-based P.I.s, LR brings a caustic realism to the setting. The Saxon series is spread over several years and we watch him age and grow in cynicism along with his self-adopted son, Marvel, a black street kid that Saxon took in and raised as his own. LR has put the Saxon series on hold though the character has appeared both on and off-stage in LR's second series. This is set in Cleveland, where LR now lives, and features Slovenian P.I. Milan Jacovich. Jacovich is more strongly realized than Saxon. An ex-cop turned security consultant, he is well educated (with a master's degree) and proud of his ethnic heritage and working class roots. His work allows LR to explore matters on both the big scale of corporate business, and at an individual level. Divorced and lonely, finding it difficult to establish a new relationship, Jacovich is nevertheless a very likeable individual with strong moral values that guide his actions. Most critics agree that the series has improved with each successive book although the series opener, *Pepper Pike*, was nominated for an Anthony, and the fifth title, *The Lake Effect*, where Jacovich has to repay a debt to the head of the local Mafia, was shortlisted for a Shamus award. It is certainly true that recent books have taken on more challenging subject matter and Jacovich has grown in character as a result. Perhaps the best example to date has been *The Indian Sign* where he becomes involved not only in a case of corporate corruption but also in the kidnapping of a Native American child. LR has spread his wings further with a one-off novel *The Chinese Fire Drill*, labelled an "international thriller". Set in Hong Kong it involves murder, smuggling, kidnapping and piracy. In a poll conducted online by <cleveland.com>, LR was voted "Cleveland's Favorite Author".

Novels

Saxon series: *An Infinite Number of Monkeys* (1987), *Not Enough Horses* (1988), *A Carrot for the Donkey* (1989), *Snake Oil* (1990), *Seeing the Elephant* (1992), *The Lemon Chicken Jones* (1994); also in Jacovich novel *A Shoot in Cleveland*.

Milan Jacovich series: *Pepper Pike* (1988), *Full Cleveland* (1989), *Deep Shaker* (1991), *The Cleveland Connection* (1993), *The Lake Effect* (1994), *The Duke of Cleveland* (1995), *Collision Bend* (1996), *The Cleveland Local* (1997), *A Shoot in*

Cleveland (1998), *The Best Kept Secret* (1999), *Indian Sign* (2000), *The Dutch* (2001), *The Irish Sports Pages* (2002).
Non-series: *The Chinese Fire Drill* (2001).
Short stories. *The Scent of Spiced Oranges* (2002).

Where to start: *Pepper Pike*.
Awards: St Martins' Press/PWA Best First P.I. Novel (1986), Cleveland Arts Prize for Literature (1992).
Website: <www.lesroberts.com>
Similar stuff: Orania PAPAZOGLOU, Roger L. SIMON, Ron GOULART's John Easy.
Final fact: LR met John Wayne when he was appearing on *Rowan and Martin's Laugh-In* and after the show Wayne invited him and others out for a drink. Needless to say the Duke drank them all under the table.

Peter Robinson (b. 1950) UK/Canada

A Yorkshireman, PR has lived in Canada for over 20 years where he has been an English instructor at a number of colleges. His first book was written while he was studying for his PhD at the University of York. It features his main character, Detective Chief Inspector Alan Banks who has recently moved to the Yorkshire Dales from London. The books are set in Swainsdale, a fictional composite of the Dales. Though this is Herriott country, there is nothing cozy or nostalgic about PR's hard-biting series. The crimes are frequently vicious, the motives complicated and the investigations under pressure. A key feature of many of the series is the large cast of possible suspects through which Banks and his colleagues have to investigate. Moreover Banks' increasingly complicated home life and growing tension at work helps raise these books above the norm. Most of the series have been nominated for awards and five have won. These include *In a Dry Season*, which won three awards including the prestigious French Grand Prix de Littérature Policière. It's an investigation that opens up old wounds and takes Banks back to the War years. PR has written only two non-series books so far. *Caedmon's Song* concerns a student who survives a serial killer but is psychologically as well as physically damaged. *No Cure for Love* is, unusually for PR, set in Los Angeles and concerns a British actress in a popular TV detective series who begins to receive threatening letters. PR has also won awards for his short fiction some of which has been collected as *Not Safe After Dark*.

Novels
Alan Banks series: *Gallows View* (1987), *A Dedicated Man* (1988), *A Necessary End* (1989), *The Hanging Valley* (1989), *Past Reason Hated* (1991), *Wednesday's Child* (1992), *Final Account* (1994; as *Dry Bones That Dream*, UK 1995), *Innocent Graves* (1996), *Dead Right* (1997; as *Blood at the Root*, US 1997), *In a Dry Season* (1999), *Cold is the Grave* (2000), *Aftermath* (2001).
Non-series: *Caedmon's Song* (1990), *No Cure for Love* (1995).
Short Stories. *Not Safe After Dark* (1998).

Awards: Arthur Ellis, best short story (1991, 2001), best novel (1992, 1997, 2001), Macavity, best short story (1998), Anthony, best novel (2000), Barry, best novel (2000), Grand Prix de Littérature Policière (2001), Swedish Martin Beck (2001), Edgar, best short story (2001).
Website: <www.inspectorbanks.com>
Similar stuff: Pauline BELL, Reginald HILL and Peter TURNBULL for other tough Yorkshire police series.
Final fact: PR submitted his first novel on spec to Viking Penguin. That meant it ended up in their "slush pile" of unsolicited manuscripts and it was the only one from that pile to be selected for publication that year.

Caroline Roe (b. 1943) Canada

Writing originally under her maiden name, Medora Sale, CR, a former English teacher with a Ph.D. in medieval studies, produced a popular series featuring Toronto police detective John Sanders. The first volume, *Murder on the Run*, about an investigation into a serial killer that becomes complicated by copycat killings, won CR the Arthur Ellis award for best first novel. In the second novel, *Murder in Focus*, set in Ottawa, Sanders meets architectural photographer Harriet Jeffries (CR's husband is a photographer) and romance blossoms. The rest of the series becomes a mixture of light romance and complicated crime investigation, but they certainly aren't cozies, being more like sugar mixed with powdered glass. The series ceased when the market for feminist crime fiction dried up in Canada. After a brief pause CR re-emerged under her married name with a series of historical mysteries featuring Isaac, a blind Jewish physician living in Girona, Spain in the 1350s. The Bishop of Girona is Isaac's main patient and patron and Isaac undertakes investigations on his behalf, his blindness being no handicap but sharpening his other faculties. Doctors have always worked well as investigators and Isaac is no exception. This series is rich in atmosphere and period detail. The third novel, *An Antidote for Avarice*, won CR the Barry Award.

Novels

Chronicles of Isaac series: *Remedy for Treason* (1998), *Cure for a Charlatan* (1999), *Antidote for Avarice* (1999), *Solace for a Sinner* (2000), *A Potion for a Widow* (2001).
Inspector Sanders series as Medora Sale: *Murder on the Run* (1986), *Murder in Focus* (1989), *Murder in a Good Cause* (1990), *Sleep of the Innocent* (1991), *Pursued by Shadows* (1992), *Short Cut to Santa Fe* (1994).

Full name: Caroline Medora Roe (*née* Sale)
Awards: Arthur Ellis, best first novel (1987), Barry, best paperback original (2000).
Similar stuff: Umberto ECO, Susanna GREGORY, Kate SEDLEY.
Final fact: CR has an ear for languages and is fluent in not only modern French, Catalan and Spanish but the medieval versions as well.

Nancy Taylor Rosenberg (b. 1946) US

NTR draws for her work upon her years of experience as a police officer with the Dallas Police Department and subsequently a superior court investigator with the Ventura County Probation Department. Her first book, *Mitigating Circumstances*, challenged the professional status quo. It featured District Attorney Lily Forrester, new head of the Sex Crimes Division, who had been a victim of incest in her childhood and is now subject to more violence when she and her teenage daughter are raped. Forrester finds the traditionally strong male preserve of the legal system is a barrier rather than an aid as events drive her towards a violent solution. The book was a major success, not only hitting the bestselling lists but becoming a Literary Guild Selection and being optioned for the cinema. NTR originally treated that book as a one-off but eventually returned to Forrester in a direct sequel *Buried Evidence*, where Forrester's past actions threaten to be revealed. NTR's other books have generally been called legal thrillers, but they do not all fall into that category, least of all *California Angel* (1995), which is a fantasy, not a mystery, about a teacher who discovers she has angelic powers. Her books are more about strong-willed women who fight the system. In *Interest of Justice* it's a female judge trying to find the murderer of her sister; in *First Offence* it's a probation officer who is shot and wounded; in *Trial by Fire* it's a prosecuting attorney who has to cope with her past and in *Abuse of Power* it's a female cop who has to speak out against a fellow officer and take the consequences. All of her books have been bestsellers.

Novels

Lily Forrester series: *Mitigating Circumstances* (1993), *Buried Evidence* (2000).
Non-series: *Interest of Justice* (1993), *First Offence* (1994), *Trial by Fire* (1996), *Abuse of Power* (1997), *Conflict of Interest* (2002).

Where to start: *Mitigating Circumstances.*
Website: <www.nancytrosenberg.com>
Similar stuff: Amelia PADGETT, Lisa SCOTTOLINE.
Final fact: NTR worked as a photographic model in the mid-sixties before studying criminology.

Jonathan Ross (b. 1916) UK

Not to be confused with the radio and television personality of the same name, JR was the pen-name of police detective John Rossiter. Apart from three years in the RAF during WW2, JR was with the Wiltshire Constabulary for 30 years, rising to the rank of Detective Chief Superintendent. He translated that experience into a series featuring Inspector, later Superintendent, George Rogers. JR has stated that his novels depict police work "as it is", and although allowing for authorial licence to remove the daily routine, this is as close as you get to authentic British police procedurals. Rogers has no special talents, but years of experience have honed his detective skills and brought him a rapport with and sensitivity to the criminal mind and its motives. JR likes to develop complex puzzles which are unravelled doggedly with no Holmesian leaps in deduction – in fact Rogers and his partner, Lingard, frequently follow wrong lines of enquiry. We are presented with such tantalizing problems as a murder weapon and a body that aren't connected (*Diminished by Death)* to a mummified body found in a long-empty house (*A Rattling of Old Bones*) to a body in the woods that seems to have fallen from the clouds (*Dropped Dead*). Unlike other novels of the period JR places much emphasis on autopsies and the fundamentals of police work. He also, more plausibly than many authors, presents the frustrations that affect police in their investigations and the need to cut corners. *Dark Blue and Dangerous* is a revealing investigation of a police sergeant who is found drowned. In a non-series but thematically linked sequence, written under his own name, JR looked at how the police may feel let down by the courts and take matters into their own hands to seek justice (in *The Villains*) and likewise the effect upon the victims (in *The Victims*). In the early seventies JR also had some moderate success with a series featuring secret service agent Roger Tallis. JR's books are too rapidly being forgotten but they are amongst the most authentic of their kind.

Novels

Inspector/Superintendent Rogers series: *The Blood Running Cold* (1968), *Diminished by Death* (1968), *Dead at First Hand* (1969), *The Deadest Thing You Ever Saw* (1969), *Here Lies Nancy Frail* (1972), *The Burning of Billy Toober* (1974), *"I Know What It's Like to Die"* (1976), *A Rattling of Old Bones* (1979), *Dark Blue and Dangerous* (1981), *Death's Head* (1982), *Dead Eye* (1983), *Dropped Dead* (1984), *Burial Deferred* (1985), *Fate Accomplished* (1987), *Sudden Departures* (1988), *A Time for Dying* (1989), *Daphne Dead and Done For* (1990), *Murder be Hanged* (1992), *The Body of a Woman* (1994; as *None the Worse for a Hanging*, US 1995), *Murder, Murder Burning Bright* (1996).

Tallis series as John Rossiter: *The Murder Makers* (1970), *The Deadly Green* (1970), *A Rope for General Dietz* (1972), *The Golden Virgin* (1975; as *The Deadly Gold*, US 1975).

Non-series as John Rossiter: *The Victims* (1971), *The Manipulators* (1973), *The Villains* (1974).

Real name: John Rossiter.
Pen-name: Jonathan Ross.
Where to start: Best read in sequence but the early novels have dated slightly. *A Rattling of Old Bones* is a good starting point.
Similar stuff: Roger ORMEROD, Peter Walker/Nicholas RHEA.

Kate Ross (1956–98) US

The tragic death of KR from cancer at the age of only 41 robbed the mystery field of a delightful talent. A Boston trial lawyer and student of legal history, KR became fascinated with the British Regency period of the 1820s and used this as the setting for her books about Julian Kestrel, a dandy but dabbler in puzzlers. In *Cut to the Quick* Kestrel finds himself having to identify a dead woman found in his bed and solve her murder before his valet, the reformed pickpocket Dipper, is held to account. KR admirably captured the period and, over the next few books revealed more about Kestrel's own dubious background which comes to the fore in the wonderfully gothic *The Devil in Music*, set in Italy, which won the Agatha award.

Novels
Julian Kestrel series: *Cut to the Quick* (1993), *A Broken Vessel* (1994), *Whom the Gods Love* (1995), *The Devil in Music* (1997).

Full name: Katherine Ross.
Awards: Gargoyle, best novel (1994), Agatha, best novel (1998).
Similar stuff: Bruce COOK (as Bruce Alexander), Deryn LAKE.
Final fact: KR also had a degree in ancient Greek and loved to read Euripides in his original tongue.

John Rossiter *see pseudonym* Jonathan Ross

Jennifer Rowe (b. 1948) Australia

To Australian children JR is better known under her alias Emily Rodda, under which she has written around 50 children's books since her first, *Something Special* in 1984. She has since won the Australian Children's Book of the Year award five times. Formerly head of the publishing company Angus & Robertson and then editor of the prestigious *Australian Women's Weekly*, JR turned to writing full-time in 1994. Her first series of adult books featured TV researcher Verity "Birdie" Birdwood who debuted in *Grim Pickings* (TV mini-series 1989). The series is in the traditional mould, light-hearted with clever puzzle plots. The first, a murder amongst seasonal fruit pickers in JR's native Blue Mountains near Sydney, is perhaps the most original. JR draws upon her publishing experience for the background of *Murder by the Book*, where someone is killing Australia's leading authors. The last in the series, *Lamb to the Slaughter*, where a man convicted of the murder of his wife is released with a pardon only to be found dead the next day, showed that JR was moving towards a greater emphasis on policing methods. She had already contributed to the police TV series *Blue Heelers*, and in 1996, was asked by TV producer Hal McElroy to develop a new police procedural series. The result was *Murder Call* (1997–9) which ran for 56 episodes. JR wrote all of the first series and contributed several scripts to the second. It features senior homicide detectives Tessa Vance and Steve Hayden, who start at odds with each other, and the series emphasizes the pressure of the work and the constant race against time. JR wrote two novels based on episodes from the series, *Deadline*, where Vance and Hayden try and track down a cunning serial killer and

Something Wicked, with a bizarre death at the isolated home of a former rock star. JR brings considerable panache and originality to traditional themes.

Novels

Verity Birdwood series: *Grim Pickings* (1987), *Murder by the Book* (1989), *The Makeover Murders* (1992), *Stranglehold* (1993), *Lamb to the Slaughter* (1995).
Tessa Vance series: *Deadline* (1997; as *Suspect*, US 1998), *Something Wicked* (1998).

Short Stories

Verity Birdwood series: *Death in Store* (1991).
Editor. *Love Lies Bleeding* (1994).

Real name: Jennifer June Rowe.
Pen-name: Emily Rodda.
Website: for her children's books <www.emilyrodda.com>
Similar stuff: Paula GOSLING, Carolyn G. HART, Jill MCGOWN.

Laura Joh Rowland (b. 1954) US

New Orleans resident LJR is a granddaughter of Chinese and Korean American immigrants. Although her original passion was for painting, she has worked as a chemist, microbiologist, sanitary inspector and quality engineer before she became a full-time writer. She carved her own niche with her first book, *Shinju*, set in 17th-century Japan, which introduced her detective, Sano Ichiro, a samurai and soon-to-be appointed Most Honorable Investigator to the Shogun in Edo (the old name for Tokyo). In the first book, which received nominations for both the Hammett and Anthony awards, Sano investigates a "shinju', or ritual double suicide, whilst *Bundori* finds him on the trail of a serial killer. The series is vibrant with Japanese period culture. It gathers pace with *The Concubine's Tattoo* where Sano finds that his new wife, the Lady Reiko, is every bit as good a detective as he. The series scores highly on originality, characterization and atmosphere.

Novels

Sano Ichiro series: *Shinju* (1994), *Bundori* (1996), *The Way of the Traitor* (1997; as *Irizumi*, UK 1998), *The Concubine's Tattoo* (1998), *The Samurai's Wife* (2000), *Black Lotus* (2001), *The Pillow Book of Lady Wisteria* (2002).

Website:
<http://ourworld.compuserve.com/homepages/laurajohrowland/ljr.html>
Similar stuff: Dale FURUTANI.
Final fact: Amongst LJR's jobs when she was a quality engineer at Lockheed Martin was to help build the external fuel tank for the Space Shuttle.

S. J. Rozan (b. 1950) US

A practising architect, SJR now spends about half her time as a writer. Though of Jewish descent, SJR has chosen as her P.I.s a Chinese-American in her 20s and a former sailor in his 40s. In fact SJR went out of her way to make the two individuals as opposite as possible and then was inspired to alternate the viewpoint with each book. Lydia Chin is the narrator of *China Trade*, the first book published but the second completed. She is on the trail of stolen porcelain which leads her into New York's Chinatown and conflict with the gangs. Bill narrates the next book, *Concourse*, about deaths at the Bronx Home for the Aged, and this won SJR the Shamus Award. Interestingly her next award, the Anthony, came with the next Bill-narrated story, *No Colder Place*, where he is investigating deaths in the construction industry. SJR's research is thorough, including travelling to Hong Kong for *Reflecting the Sky* and indulging in one of her favourite sports, American football, for *Winter and Night*. The dual perspectives allow SJR to explore deeper into aspects of New York culture and society, and especially the matters of alienization and victimization. It also adds variety to what is almost two series in one.

Novels

Lydia Chin & Bill Smith series: *China Trade* (1994), *Concourse* (1995), *Mandarin Plaid* (1996), *No Colder Place* (1997), *A Bitter Feast* (1998), *Stone Quarry* (1999), *Reflecting the Sky* (2001), *Winter and Night* (2002).

Full name: Shira Judith Rozan.
Awards: Shamus, best novel (1996), Anthony, best novel (1998).
Website: <www.sjrozan.com>
Similar stuff: Leslie GLASS for another Chinese American detective.
Final fact: To research her story "Hoops", SJR took up basketball in middle age. The story was published, even nominated for an Edgar, but SJR couldn't drop the basketball habit and now plays at least twice a week. She just hopes she doesn't do a story involving sky diving!

Patrick Ruell *pseudonym, see* Reginald Hill

Mark Sadler *pseudonym, see* Michael Collins

David St. John *pseudonym, see* E. Howard Hunt

Medora Sale *pseudonym, see* Caroline Roe

James Sallis (b. 1944) US

It's all too tempting to try and shoe-horn the work of JS into several categories – science fiction, mystery, noir – but he really defies categorization being a genuine *sui generis* man of letters. Born and raised in Arkansas, JS is widely travelled and spent much time in England in the late sixties where he was associated with Michael Moorcock and *New Worlds*. JS delighted in the *avant garde* and surreal and his early fictions and narratives were typical of the approach Moorcock was encouraging in speculative writings. JS was also fascinated by those writers who were outcasts from society but whose work challenged convention, such as Dave Goodis and Chester HIMES. Himes influenced him strongly and he has recently written a biography of the author. JS's own P.I. novels have been compared to the work of Himes and Walter MOSLEY. They feature Lew Griffin, a black, cynical New Orleans-based professor, poet and novelist who is also a reformed alcoholic and blues afficionado. His explorations, frequently in search of missing women and children, became a haunting study of life itself. JS's approach is postmodern and non-linear, making his novels nonconformist and challenging, as you'd expect, and the result is a unique perspective on the dark side of life. One of the most unusual is *Bluebottle*, in which Griffin is shot at the outset and does not regain consciousness for a year by which time the trail he has to follow has gone long cold. In addition to his volumes of poetry and his studies of the jazz guitar JS has written a surreal novel, *Renderings* (1995), and an unconventional spy novel, *Death Will Have Your Eyes.* He has also written the screenplay for a thriller *Big Green.*

Novels
Lew Griffin series: *The Long-Legged Fly* (1992), *Moth* (1993), *Black Hornet* (1994), *Eye of the Cricket* (1997), *Bluebottle* (1999), *Ghost of a Flea* (2001).
Non-series: *Death Will Have Your Eyes* (1997).
Short Stories. *Time's Hammers* (2000).
Non-fiction. *Difficult Lives: Jim Thompson–David Goodis–Chester Himes* (1993), *Gently Into the Land of Meateaters* essays (2000), *Chester Himes: A Life* (2000).

Website: <www.btinternet.com/~richnabi/>
Similar stuff: Chester HIMES, Walter MOSLEY for background; Sébastien JAPRISOT for perspective and style.

Lawrence Sanders (1920–98) US

A former journalist and editor of technical magazines, LS became one of the most popular writers of hefty "blockbuster" crime novels in his day, over 20 of them hitting the bestseller lists. His early books are his best – inventive, influential, ingenious – and the smartest of them all is *The Anderson Tapes* (filmed 1970), which won an Edgar award. It's a highly sophisticated and complicated caper novel about an ex-con's plans to rob an entire apartment block but what is remarkable is that LS tells the whole story through reports, official documents and other surveillance paraphernalia. A minor character at the end of the novel who pulls all the threads together is Captain Edward X. "Iron Balls" Delaney, commander of New York's 251st Precinct. LS next built a major novel around him, *The First Deadly Sin* (filmed 1980), in which Delaney pits himself against the cunning of a random killer who slaughters his victims with an ice axe. The two individuals are driven by pride, the sin of the title, and LS continued the series, bringing Delaney out of retirement as a consultant, with plots worked around the sins of greed, lust and anger. *The Third*

Deadly Sin is especially innovative as LS develops a woman serial killer whose rage is fuelled by PMT. LS did not complete the sequence, growing tired of any one single character. He began another sequence based around the Ten Commandments, but used a different detective in each book. These are usually investigators working on behalf of big corporations. In *The Sixth Commandment* it's Samuel Todd, who works for a large New York Foundation and investigates likely beneficiaries of the organization's funds. In *The Tenth Commandment* it's Joshua Bigg, an investigator for a law firm, while in *The Seventh Commandment* it's Dora Conti, an insurance investigator. Before the success of *The Anderson Tapes*, LS had created another insurance investigator, "Wolf" Lannihan, in a series of stories he wrote for *Swank Magazine* in 1968–9 later collected as *Tales of the Wolf.* These stories were laced with plenty of graphic sex, an element increasingly common in LS's books, especially his non-series books. It's also true of the stories that make up the two books of adventures of Timothy Cone, an ex-Marine, strong, tall and unpredictable, who works for a firm dealing in corporate intelligence and industrial espionage. Towards the end of his career LS toned down his work and lightened it for a series featuring Archy McNally, a Fletch-like Florida playboy who serves as a P.I. on behalf of his father's law practice in Palm Beach. The series makes the most of the eccentricities of Florida's rich and famous, but it is uncharacteristic fare for LS and dangerously close to a Florida cozy. The series has been continued after LS's death by Vincent Lardo, who rapidly mastered the style, suggesting to some that Lardo may have had a hand in the earlier books. Although LS's books always remained popular he found it all too easy to rest on his laurels in later years and not develop the talent he clearly possessed.

Novels

Edward X. Delaney series: *The Anderson Tapes* (1970), *The First Deadly Sin* (1973), *The Second Deadly Sin* (1977), *The Third Deadly Sin* (1981), *The Fourth Deadly Sin* (1985).

Peter Tangent series: *The Tangent Objective* (1976), *The Tangent Factor* (1978).

Archy McNally series: *McNally's Secret* (1991), *McNally's Luck* (1992), *McNally's Risk* (1993), *McNally's Caper* (1994), *McNally's Trial* (1995), *McNally's Puzzle* (1996), *McNally's Gamble* (1997). Series continued by Vincent Lardo, *McNally's Dilemma* (1999), *McNally's Folly* (2000), *McNally's Chance* (2001).

Commandment series: *The Sixth Commandment* (1979), *The Tenth Commandment* (1980), *The Eighth Commandment* (1986), *The Seventh Commandment* (1991).

Non-series: *The Tomorrow File* (1975), *The Case of Lucy Bending* (1982), *The Seduction of Peter S.* (1983), *The Passion of Molly T.* (1984), *The Loves of Harry Dancer* (1986; as *The Loves of Harry D.*, UK 1986), *Capital Crimes* (1989), *Stolen Blessings* (1989), *Sullivan's Sting* (1990), *Private Pleasures* (1994), *Guilty Pleasures* (1998).

as Lesley Andress: *Caper* (1980).

as Mark Upton: *The Dream Lover* (1978; as by LS, 1987), *Dark Summer* (1979; as by LS, 1988).

Short Stories

Wolf Lannihan series: *Tales of the Wolf* (1986).

Timothy Cone series: *The Timothy Files* (1987), *Timothy's Game* (1988).

Pen-names: Lesley Andress, Mark Upton.

Where to start: *The Anderson Tapes* or *The First Deadly Sin*.

Awards: Edgar, best first novel (1971).

Similar stuff: Larry BEINHART, Michael JAHN.

Walter Satterthwait (b. 1946) US

Something of a nomad, WS has lived in many countries in Europe as well as maintaining a home in Santa Fe, New Mexico. He held a variety of jobs from bartender to encyclopedia salesman before settling down to write full-time. Apart from two early action novels about drug smuggling, WS's main body of work began with *Wall of Glass*. This introduced his Santa Fe P.I. Joshua Croft and his partner, the brains of the operation, Rita Mondragon. Although the first novel, where Croft goes in search of a missing necklace and discovers the world of the wealthy, is fairly traditional, the series soon carved a special niche. This is partly because of its slant on New Age and American Indian culture, which began in *At Ease With the Dead*, but mostly because of the continuing danger to Rita that comes to a head in *Accustomed to the Dark*. She is shot and in a coma and Croft goes on a quest to find her assailant. Alternating with the Croft series is a series of historical mysteries built around real people. The first, *Miss Lizzie*, depicts Lizzie Borden as a detective years after the notorious murder case, but it was with *Wilde West*, which brought Oscar Wilde to the old frontier that the series took off. In *Escapade* WS introduced two Pinkerton detectives in an adventure which also paired Harry Houdini and Arthur Conan Doyle. The detectives, Philip Beaumont and his partner, the British Jane Turner, returned in *Masquerade*, set amongst the literary ex-pats in Paris in 1923, including Hemingway, Gertrude Stein and James Joyce. WS has written several stories set in East Africa detailing the investigations of Sergeant M'butu and Constable Kobari of the Kenyan police, which have been collected as *The Gold of Mayani*. WS's books bring you both variety and excitement.

Novels

Joshua Croft series: *Wall of Glass* (1988), *At Ease With the Dead* (1990), *A Flower in the Desert* (1992), *The Hanged Man* (1993; as *The Death Card*, UK 1994), *Accustomed to the Dark* (1996).

Turner & Beaumont series: *Escapade* (1995), *Masquerade* (1998).

Non-series: *Cocaine Blues* (1980), *The Aegean Affair* (1982), *Miss Lizzie* (1989), *Wilde West* (1991).

Short Stories. *The Gold of Mayani* (1995).

Where to start: *Wall of Glass* or *Miss Lizzie*.
Awards: Prix du Roman d'Aventures (1996).
Books about: *Sleight of Hand: Conversations with Walter Satterthwait* by Ernie Bulow (1993).
Website: <http://freenet.vcu.edu/education/literature/Walter_Satterthwait.html>
Similar stuff: For historical mysteries with real people, Max Allan COLLINS, Howard ENGEL. Ed MCBAIN has also written a Lizzie Borden novel.
Final fact: To help promote his book *Masquerade*, WS bought a Winnebago motorhome and had the book cover and title painted on the side.

Andrew Saville *pseudonym, see* Andrew Taylor

Steven Saylor (b. 1956) US

SS is best known for his Roma Sub Rosa series, which features the investigator Gordianus the Finder. The books are set in the final years of the Roman Republic in the mid-1st Century BC at the time of Cicero, Crassus, Pompey and the rise to power of Julius Caesar. SS is a known authority on ancient Rome and each book is set against a specific historical incident and is packed with authentic detail. The first book, *Roman Blood*, involves Cicero's first major murder trial as a young advocate and he is helped by Gordianus, which is the start of their difficult relationship, so important in later books. The series spans several decades and we see Gordianus age and the world about him change. The rebellion of Spartacus is the background to *Arms of Nemesis*, the conspiracy of Catilina features in *Catilina's Riddle* and the civil war between Caesar and Pompey begins in *Rubicon*. Gordianus is an engaging individual, not averse to bending the rules, as is most evident in *Rubicon*, but with strong emotional attachments especially to his mute son Eco, his adopted son Meto and his slave partner, later his wife, Bethesda. He is driven by a kind heart and a desire to see matters righted, even when he has little control over events. Though now a full-time writer SS was previously a magazine and newspaper editor. He moved to San Francisco from his native Texas in 1980 but still has a strong attachment to Texas. His novel *A Twist at the End* recreates in remarkable detail a series of murders in Austin, Texas in 1885 and features as the investigator a young William S. Porter, later to be world famous as the writer O. Henry. SS writes with a dedication for accuracy but with a lightness of touch that allows you to taste, smell and live his worlds without being overwhelmed by them.

Novels

Gordianus series: *Roman Blood* (1991), *Arms of Nemesis* (1992), *Catilina's Riddle* (1993), *The Venus Throw* (1995), *A Murder on the Appian Way* (1996), *Rubicon* (1999), *Last Seen in Massilia* (2000), *A Mist of Prophecies* (2002).
Non-series: *A Twist at the End* (2000; as *Honour the Dead*, UK 2001), *Have You Seen Dawn?* (2003).

Short Stories

Gordianus series: *The House of the Vestals* (1997).

Full name: Steven Warren Saylor.
Awards: Robert L. Fish, best first story (1993), Lambda Award (1994), Critics' Choice Award (1995), Herodotus Award (2000), Writers League of Texas, Violet Crown award (2001).
Website: <www.stevensaylor.com>
Similar stuff: Lindsey DAVIS.
Final fact: SS's childhood interest in the ancient world was inflamed by the movies of the day, spectacles such as *Spartacus, Ben Hur* and *Hercules*, but most especially the 1963 version of *Cleopatra*. As a boy he saw it at a drive-in theatre in Texas where the projectionist saw fit to censor Elizabeth Taylor's nude scene. SS continues: "My outrage was so intense that I've been on a quest to find the naked truth about Cleopatra ever since. Finally, after nine volumes, the Roma Sub Rosa series is drawing very close to Gordianus's encounter with the Queen of the Nile."

Benjamin Schutz (b. 1949) US

Despite a certain terseness of style and a florid prose that is not to everyone's taste, the devotees of BS's series featuring Washington D.C.'s P.I. Leo Haggerty regard it as one of the best. The novels have thrice been nominated for the Shamus award winning once, whilst the short story, "Mary, Mary, Shut the Door" won both the Shamus and Edgar. BS lives in Northern Virginia where he is a clinical and forensic psychologist specializing in child abuse. The first two novels both deal with missing young girls and the sordid world of drugs and pornography. With *A Tax in Blood*, BS broadened his scope to terrorism whilst *A Fistful of Empty* looks at espionage in the pharmaceutical industry. Haggerty is a strongly moralistic man but is prepared to work with a less scrupulous sidekick (who meets his fate in *A Fistful of Empty*) and an intelligent girlfriend who also acts as his sounding board. BS has not written a new Haggerty novel for some years but he continues to write the occasional non-series short story. BS has also written a study of the law for the psychotherapist in *Legal Liability in Psychotherapy* (1982).

Novels

Leo Haggerty series: *Embrace the Wolf* (1985), *All the Old Bargains* (1985), *A Tax in Blood* (1987), *The Things We Do for Love* (1989), *A Fistful of Empty* (1991), *Mexico is Forever* (1994).

Full name: Benjamin Merrill Schutz.
Awards: Edgar, best short story (1993), Shamus, best hardcover novel (1988), best short story (1993).
Similar stuff: Jonathan KELLERMAN, Maxine O'CALLAGHAN.

Leonardo Sciascia (1921–89) Italy

LS is still regarded, more than a decade after his death, as Italy's foremost writer of crime fiction. Born in Sicily, he grew up in a world where the Mafia was an unspoken reality and it was LS who broke the code of silence in the late 1950s with several books about the Mob. His early books, written while he was still a teacher and school administrator, were political thrillers and satires, starting with *Favole della dittatura* ("Fables of Dictatorship") in 1950. LS was himself a communist. Despite its title, *Sicilian Uncles* is not a book about the Mafia, but a sequence of four novellas which looks at the major 20th-century crises in Sicily which created the climate in which the Mafia could thrive, a development he would explore further in *Equal Danger* and *Candido*. His major breakthrough was in 1961 with *The Day of the Owl*, about the investigation of a local police captain into the Mafia murder of a small-town building contractor. The power of this novel is that Captain Bellodi knows that everybody else knows what happened but the code of silence forbids anyone to tell. In *The Council of Egypt* an abbot exploits that silence by forging an ancient document which apparently establishes claims by Neapolitan families over Sicily. In *To Each His Own* a schoolteacher looks into the death of a local pharmacist who was shot after he ignored a threatening letter. Mysterious notes or phone calls leading to death also arise in "The Knight and Death" and "A Straightforward Tale", novellas collected in *The Knight and Death*. LS's tales are highly atmospheric and place the reader in the position of an observer who watches terrible events unfold as in *One Way or Another*, in which a painter is such a witness. In the stories in *Death of an Inquisitor*, LS uses his analytical skills to re-explore unsolved mysteries since the time of the Inquisition, whilst *The Mystery of Majorana* looks into the disappearance of a physicist in 1938. Most of LS's later books deal with the analysis or retelling of true crime stories such as the murder of the politician Aldo Moro in 1978 in *The Moro Affair*. Most of his true crime books have yet to be translated and include *Nero su Nero* (1979), a history of crime in Italy.

Novels. *Mafia Vendetta* (1961; UK 1963; as *The Day of the Owl*, UK 1984), *The Council of Egypt* (1963; UK 1966), *A Man's Blessing* (1966; US 1968; as *To Each His Own*, UK 1989), *Equal Danger* (1971; US 1973), *One Way or Another* (1974; US 1977), *Candido; or, a Dream Dreamed in Sicily* (1982; UK 1984).
Short Stories. *Sicilian Uncles* (1958; UK 1986), *Death of an Inquisitor* (1964; UK 1990), *The Knight and Death* (1988; UK 1991; exp. as *Open Doors and Three Novellas*, 1987; US 1992), *The Wine-Dark Sea* (1973; UK 1985).
Non-fiction. *The Mystery of Majorana* (1975; UK 1987 with *The Moro Affair*, 1978), *1912+1* (1986; UK 1989).

Full name: Leonardo Sciascia (pronounced "Sha-sha").
Where to start: *The Day of the Owl*.
Book about: *Il Maestro di Regalpetra* by Matteo Collura (Italy, 1996), not translated.
Similar stuff: Michael DIBDIN, Mario PUZO.

Final fact: LS fell out of favour in Italy in his last years because of an article he wrote that undermined the investigative work into the Mafia and which was believed to have contributed to the murders of two major investigators.

Sandra Scoppettone (b. 1936) US

SS is best known today as the author of the series about Greenwich Village lesbian female P.I. Lauren Laurano. The delight of Laurano is that she has no hang-ups about life or her sexuality. In fact, apart from her fear of insects, she lives a well-adjusted life with her lover, family and friends, and that bond of friendship is important to her throughout her adventures. She also has a passion for chocolate, a good sense of humour and an ability with (though fear of) computers, all of which she needs for the cases she takes on. In *Everything You Have is Mine* Laurano is the only person a rape victim will talk to and when that victim is murdered Laurano is left to decipher the clues. In later books it is usually friends who come to her for help, or end up beyond help. SS wonderfully contrasts a happy, well-rounded life with the violence and tragedy of victims. SS started writing in the late 1960s, beginning with books for children and young adults. One of these, *Playing Murder* (1985), was nominated for an Edgar award. Her first adult crime novel was *Some Unknown Person* about a young girl, the victim of child abuse drugs and drink who is found dead, possibly murdered. With *A Creative Kind of Killer*, SS wanted to tell the story from the viewpoint of its male detective, Fortune Fanelli, an ex-cop turned P.I. on the trail of a killer. She adopted a male persona, Jack Early. The book went on to win a Shamus award and Early was being compared to Elmore Leonard. SS was annoyed that the success came because most people believed the author was a man and that now she had to stay as Jack Early in order to make more money. She wrote two more Early novels before putting the name to rest. The last of these, *Donato & Daughter* (filmed 1993), had a female for the lead character, a police lieutenant who teams up with her estranged father, a police sergeant, to find a serial killer who is murdering nuns. SS was amongst the vanguard of female P.I. writers though no one knew it.

Novels

Lauren Laurano series: *Everything You Have is Mine* (1991), *I'll Be Leaving You Always* (1993), *My Sweet Untraceable You* (1994), *Let's Face the Music and Die* (1996), *Gonna Take a Homicidal Journey* (1998).
Non-series: *Some Unknown Person* (1977), *Such Nice People* (1980), *Innocent Bystanders* (1983).
as Jack Early (all reissued as by SS in 1995): *A Creative Kind of Killer* (1984), *Razzamatazz* (1985), *Donato & Daughter* (1988).

Pen-names: Jack Early.
Where to start: *Some Unknown Person* or *A Creative Kind of Killer*.
Awards: Shamus, best novel (1985).

Website: <www.imt.net/~gedison/scoppett.html>
Similar stuff: Sue GRAFTON, Marcia MULLER, Lillian O'DONNELL, Dorothy UHNAK.
Final fact: Cybill Shepherd appears as a character in *My Sweet Untraceable You* and was more than happy for SS to "say anything you want about me!"

Lisa Scottoline (b. 1955) US

LS was a trial lawyer with a major firm in Philadelphia and uses her experience in a series of bestselling legal thrillers. All are set in Philadelphia loosely built around attorneys in the firm Rosato & Associates, though each book has a different lead character. In *Everywhere That Mary Went* it's Mary DiNunzio, a widow who has struggled for eight years to become a partner in her law firm and who now becomes threatened by a stalker. The book was nominated for an Edgar. Her second, *Final Appeal*, won the award. This is about divorced mother and lawyer Grace Rossi who is assigned a death penalty appeal and, with the death of the Judge, also finds herself on a trail of judicial corruption. Her sixth book, *Mistaken Identity*, where the head of the law firm, Bennie Rosato, finds that her new client, who is accused of murdering her lover, a police detective, claims to be Rosato's lost twin sister, entered the *New York Times* bestseller lists, as have her subsequent books. Other books explore police brutality (*Legal Tender*), sexual harassment (*Running from the Law*) and the central question of what justice really is (*Rough Justice*).

Novels. *Everywhere That Mary Went* (1993), *Final Appeal* (1994), *Running from the Law* (1995), *Legal Tender* (1996), *Rough Justice* (1997), *Mistaken Identity* (1999), *Moment of Truth* (2000), *The Vendetta Defense* (2001), *Courting Trouble* (2002).

Where to start: Best read in order but as a good starter try *Final Appeal* or *Mistaken Identity*.
Awards: Edgar, best paperback original (1995).
Website: <www.scottoline.com>
Similar stuff: William BERNHARDT, Jeremiah HEALY, Lia MATERA.
Final fact: LS's books are used by the various Bar associations to highlight legal ethics.

Kate Sedley (b. 1926) UK

A former civil servant, KS turned to writing in 1968 producing a series of historical novels published under her maiden name of Brenda Honeyman. Starting with *Richard by the Grace of God* (1968) most of these were set in the turbulent 15th century with the events leading up to and during the Wars of the Roses, the clash for the throne between the Houses of Lancaster and York. After a period of writing rather more contemporary historical romances under her married name of Brenda Clarke, KS returned to the Wars of the Roses as the setting for her series of historical mysteries featuring Roger the Chapman. Roger is a lapsed Benedictine monk who has turned "chapman" or pedlar and thus travels throughout England. He becomes acquainted with the Duke of Gloucester, the future Richard III, and as the series develops Roger finds himself acting as both sleuth and spy for the Duke. The series is as fascinating for KS's portrayal of the troubled Duke as it is for the historical atmosphere and the investigations Roger undertakes, which are tailor-made for the period. Roger is an excellent investigator applying both intelligence and a keen eye for human nature.

Novels

Roger the Chapman series: *Death and the Chapman* (1991), *The Plymouth Cloak* (1992), *The Hanged Man* (1993; as *The Weaver's Tale*, US 1994), *The Holy Innocents* (1994), *The Eve of St Hyacinth* (1995), *The Wicked Winter* (1996), *The Brothers of Glastonbury* (1997), *The Weaver's Inheritance* (1998), *The Goldsmith's Daughter* (2001), *The Lammas Feast* (2002).

Real name: Brenda Margaret Lilian Clarke (*née* Honeyman).
Pen-names: Brenda Honeyman, Kate Sedley.
Similar stuff: Susanna GREGORY, Paul DOHERTY, Candace ROBB.
Final fact: The young Brenda Clarke was a section leader in the British Red Cross during WW2.

Tom Sehler *pseudonym, see* Rex Burns

Francis Selwyn *pseudonym, see* Donald Thomas

David Serafin (b. 1936) UK

DS is the pseudonym used by Oxford professor and medievalist Ian Michael on his series of police procedurals set in Spain. They feature Superintendent Luis Bernal, a portly, almost Poirot-like character, who is methodical and unruffled, relying heavily on his team to help solve his crimes. The first two books are more traditional police cases, especially the suspenseful *Madrid Underground*, where Bernal is pitted against a psychopath working in the Madrid underground rail network. Thereafter Bernal becomes more of a political troubleshooter, dealing with terrorists and political coups. Most of the stories are set in Madrid but *Port of Light* takes Bernal to the Canary Islands. The series is historically interesting because it depicts the turbulent years as Spain emerges from the shadow of Franco and re-establishes itself as a kingdom.

Novels

Superintendent Bernal series: *Saturday of Glory* (1979), *Madrid Underground* (1982), *Christmas Rising* (1982), *The Body in Cadiz Bay* (1985), *Port of Light* (1987), *The Angel of Torremolinos* (1988).

Real name: Ian David Lewis Michael.
Pen-name: David Serafin.
Awards: CWA John Creasey Memorial Award (1979).

Similar stuff: Delano Ames's Juan Llorca series, Manuel Vázquez MONTALBÁN, Roderic JEFFRIES Alvarez series.

Anthony Shaffer (1926–2001) UK

AS was best known as a playwright, in particular for his multi-award winning *Sleuth* (produced 1970; filmed 1973) about a deadly confrontation between an ageing mystery writer and his wife's lover. AS was born in Liverpool, the eldest of identical twins. Both he and his brother Peter achieved considerable success for their plays. Early in their careers they collaborated under the name Peter Antony. This included several short stories (none of which has been collected) and three odd novels which feature the enigmatic Mr Verity (renamed Mr Fathom in the last book) who, rather like Agatha Christie's Harley Quin, mysteriously appears at the time a crime is about to be committed. Both AS and his brother were great devotees of the golden age mystery which they liked to parody. AS studied law and practised as a barrister in the early fifties but in 1955 established his own company for producing TV commercials which took up most of his time for the next 14 years. He did find time to write his first play, *The Savage Parade* (1963; later revised as *This Savage Parade*, 1987), which deals with the Eichmann trial and three Jews seeking justice for their treatment during the War. With the success of *Sleuth*, which ran for 2,359 performances in London and a further 1,222 on Broadway, AS returned to plays, initially concentrating on screenplays. This included the script for the Hitchcock film *Frenzy* (1972) and the cult classic *The Wicker Man* (filmed 1973), which AS later adapted as a novel with the film's director Robin Hardy. The story is really about the confrontation between Christianity and paganism but is told in the form of a detective novel with a search by a pious Scottish police officer for a missing girl on a remote island. AS's other stage plays include *Murderer* (produced 1975; rev'd 1987), about a struggling artist who seeks fame by committing the perfect murder and then confessing to it, and *The Case of the Oily Levantine* (produced 1979; rev'd as *Whodunnit*, US 1982), a parody of the country house murder. He also wrote the screenplay *Absolution* (filmed 1981; retitled *Murder by Confession* for TV), based on his novel, a dark psychological thriller about revenge at a militaristic Catholic school. In addition to his own books, AS adapted several of Agatha Christie's novels for the screen including *Death on the Nile* (1978), *Evil Under the Sun* (1982) and *Appointment with Death* (1988). AS's creative and mercurial mind allowed him to rework old themes with remarkable freshness and ingenuity.

Novels

Non-series: *The Wicker Man* with Robin Hardy (1978), *Absolution* (1979).
Mr Verity series with Peter Shaffer (first two as Peter Antony): *The Woman in the Wardrobe* (1951), *How Doth the Little Crocodile?* (1952), *Withered Murder* (1955).

Published Plays. *Sleuth* (1971), *Murderer* (1979), *Whodunnit* (1983), *This Savage Parade* (1988).
Autobiography. *So What Did You Expect?* (2001).

Full name: Anthony Joshua Shaffer.
Pen-names: Peter Antony (with Peter Shaffer).
Awards: Tony, best play (1971), Antoinette Perry award, best play (1971), Edgar, best stage play (1971), best screenplay (1973).
Similar stuff: Ira LEVIN.
Final fact: The first stage performance of *The Savage Parade* lasted one night.

Laurence Shames (b. 1951) US

LS was a journalist but left the confines of New York and New Jersey for the open skies of Florida. Before turning to his comic novels LS had written several non-fiction books including ghost-writing *Boss of Bosses* (1991), a study of the FBI against the Mafia, for Joseph O'Brien and Andris Kurins. That provided him with a detailed background for his series of novels all set in Key West, Florida and all revolving around escapades of the Mob. Although most of the books aren't connected by continuing characters there is a homogeneity that makes them feel like one long series. *Florida Straits* introduces Joey Goldman who despairs of ever running the Mob in New York so goes to Key West thinking he can rule the roost down there with a few scams and minor operations. That's fine till his bumbling half-brother turns up. In the sequel, *Sunburn*, which won the CWA Last Laugh award, things get even more frenetic when Goldman's father decides to retire to Key West and write his memoirs. The humour of the books derives from the characters rather than the events. They have been described as if Woody Allen wrote Chandler, and there's a lot of truth in that, though you need to mix in some of James W. HALL and Carl HIAASEN. *Scavenger Reef* is an excellent caper novel of an artist who is presumed dead and the value of his paintings rocket, which makes it a bit awkward when he turns up alive. Some of LS's more recent work, such as *Mangrove Squeeze*, involving the Russian Mafia muscling in on the Americans, gets a bit too close to reality to be amusing, and LS hates violence. But *Welcome to Paradise*, a wonderful farce on mistaken identity, and *The Naked Detective*, about a detective who makes every effort to be a failure and is hired by a man in drag to find a missing man (who is really the man in drag) mark a spectacular return to form.

Novels
Joey Goldman series: *Florida Straits* (1992), *Sunburn* (1995).
Non-series: *Scavenger Reef* (1994), *Tropical Depression* (1996), *Virgin Heat* (1997), *Mangrove Squeeze* (1998), *Welcome to Paradise* (1999), *The Naked Detective* (2000).

Where to start: *Scavenger Reef* or *Sunburn*.
Awards: CWA Last Laugh (1995).
Website: <www.twbooks.co.uk/authors/lshames.html>

Similar stuff: Carl HIAASEN, Greg McDONALD.
Final fact: Before he was a journalist LS worked as a cab driver, shoe salesman, furniture mover, gym teacher, lifeguard and pollster but, unlike one of his characters, he was never a bra salesman.

Dell Shannon *pseudonym, see* Elizabeth Linington

Simon Shaw (b. 1956) UK

Simon Shaw is an actor who has used his theatrical background for a series of surreal black humour crime novels. They feature Philip Fletcher, a lecherous and egotistical actor who stops at nothing, including murder, to achieve his aims. After we learn his murderous ways in *Murder Out of Tune*, Fletcher has to turn detective in *Bloody Instructions* to avoid being accused of a murder he did not commit. SS brings the world of the theatre alive in all its eccentricities and rivalries. *The Villain of the Earth*, where Fletcher once again has to watch his back when the director of his new show ends up dead, won SS his second Last Laugh award from the CWA. He had previously won it for his first non-Fletcher book, *Killer Cinderella*. Although it lacks the theatrical background this could as easily have been a Fletcher novel. A husband murders his wife and then impersonates her with increasingly complicated and amusing consequences. Recognizing that there are only so many variations to a theme SS has recently rested Fletcher and written two darker and more sinister novels featuring a female P.I.

Novels

Philip Fletcher series: *Murder Out of Tune* (1988), *Bloody Instructions* (1991), *Dead for a Ducat* (1992), *The Villain of the Earth* (1994), *The Company of Knaves* (1996), *Act of Darkness* (1997).
Grace Cornish series: *Killing Grace* (2000), *Selling Grace* (2003).
Non-series: *Killer Cinderella* (1990).

Where to start: *Killer Cinderella*.
Awards: CWA, Last Laugh (1990, 1994).
Similar stuff: Simon BRETT.
Final fact: SS has always wanted to write and even when a young boy he used to regale the family au pair with bloodthirsty stories.

Roger L. Simon (b. 1943) US

RLS's Moses Wine books are more than a series of amusing and deeply thought-provoking P.I. novels, they are a chronicle of American society over the last 30 years. Even RLS thinks of them as almost a personal diary. They follow RLS from his days as a pot-smoking, laid-back hippy in the early seventies to a divorced single parent of two sons, having become enmeshed in the establishment he had once rebelled against. The series charts Wine being buffeted by the dramas of the day. *The Big Fix*, which

Ross MACDONALD called "a landmark in its field", saw him involved in a case of election fixing and the search for a missing politician. The book earned RLS the CWA John Creasey Memorial Award and he later received an Oscar nomination for his screenplay for the book, filmed in 1978 starring Richard Dreyfuss. Thereafter he's involved in murder and the sexual revolution (*Wild Turkey*), China and the communist revolution (*Peking Duck*), the advance of the yuppies (*California Roll*) and terrorism in Jerusalem (*Raising the Dead*). Throughout this RLS struggles to bring up his two young sons, one of the more touching elements of the series, which makes *The Lost Coast*, which brings together many of the threads of the series, all the more poignant. His son Simon, now at university and becoming like the younger Moses, is accused of murder and Moses enters a world of guilt and uncertainty. RLS has only written a Moses Wine novel when he felt he had something to say. The rest of his time is heavily filled in writing screenplays and occasionally directing films. It is to be hoped he still has some things to say about Wine, who has become symbolic of everyday America.

Novels

Moses Wine series: *The Big Fix* (1973), *Wild Turkey* (1975), *Peking Duck* (1979), *California Roll* (1985), *The Straight Man* (1986), *Raising the Dead* (1988), *The Lost Coast* (1997).

Full name: Roger Lichtenberg Simon.
Awards: CWA, John Creasey Memorial Award (1974)
Similar stuff: Arthur LYONS, Les ROBERTS.
Final fact: RLS turned up as Dr Greenberg in an episode of the *Father Dowling Mysteries,* "Passionate Painter", in 1990.

Dorothy Simpson (b. 1933) UK

Born and raised in Wales but resident in Kent since 1955, where she was first a teacher and then a marriage guidance counsellor, DS is the author of the long-running series featuring family man Detective Inspector Luke Thanet. The books are set in the fictional town of Sturrenden, in Kent, and are traditional police procedurals. No sensationalism, but plenty of red herrings, suspects and puzzles woven together by fascinating investigation. DS likes to explore the motives for the crimes, and their effects, making these books as much whydunnits as whodunnits. The series may have a cozy feel, but the crimes and their causes are seldom comfortable, as DS likes to probe under the surface of everday life finding the foibles and secrets beneath. The murdered wife with a secret in *The Night She Died*; the drab, middle-aged spinster who had another life in *Six Feet Under*; the missing girl from the strongly religious family in *Close Her Eyes*; the woman who returned but was not wanted in *Last Seen Alive* (which received the CWA Silver Dagger) right through to the flirtatious barrister's wife who ends up at the bottom of a well in *Dead and Gone*.

DS's only non-series book was her first, *Harbingers of Fear*, also set in Kent, about a mother-to-be who starts to receive threatening messages. Like all her books it is a compulsive puzzle.

Novels

Inspector Thanet series: *The Night She Died* (1981), *Six Feet Under* (1982), *Puppet for a Corpse* (1983), *Close Her Eyes* (1984), *Last Seen Alive* (1985), *Dead on Arrival* (1986), *Element of Doubt* (1987), *Suspicious Death* (1988), *Dead by Morning* (1989), *Doomed to Die* (1991), *Wake the Dead* (1991), *No Laughing Matter* (1993), *A Day for Dying* (1995), *Once Too Often* (1998), *Dead and Gone* (2000).
Non-series: *Harbingers of Fear* (1977).

Full name: Dorothy Simpson (*née* Preece).
Where to start: The Thanet books are now available in five *Omnibus* volumes and it's worth starting with the first.
Awards: CWA Silver Dagger (1985).
Similar stuff: W.J. BURLEY, Jill MCGOWN, Roger ORMEROD.
Final fact: As a result of *Last Seen Alive* a reader contacted DS for help over a claim by a man that he was an illegitimate half-brother. DS was able to help advise on DNA testing, then in its infancy, which proved the man's claims to be false.

Josef Škvorecký (b. 1924) Czechoslovakia

JS is a leading Czech writer who was forced to flee the country in 1969, after the Russian invasion, because of his political views. He had already been fired from his job in 1958, following publication of his first book, *The Cowards*, because of its portrayal of post-war Czechoslovakia. JS and his wife settled in Canada and established a small Czech publishing house. Most of his books are satires exploring relationships against the social and political upheaval of Czechoslovakia. Occasionally he would use detective fiction to explore his points. His series featuring Lieutenant Boruvka shows a police officer coping with bureaucracy in a world further complicated by the Russian invasion. Like JS in the final book, *The End of Lieutenant Boruvka*, he escapes to Canada. JS avoided the Czech censors by portraying Boruvka as a seemingly ordinary individual going about his daily toil. JS wrote two other political satires with mystery elements. *Miss Silver's Past* (filmed 1969) is about an editor in a publishing house struggling to find books of any value, whilst *The Miracle Game* is about the consequences of and investigation into an apparent miracle when a statue bows to a church congregation. However, his best work of this period is *Sins for Father Knox*, which concerns Eve Adam, a nightclub singer who encounters crimes in her travels. In each story JS deliberately breaks one of the ten rules of fair play in detective fiction established by Monsignor Ronald Knox in 1929. It is unfortunate that not all of JS's crime fiction has been translated. Before he fled Czechoslovakia, he had plotted a series of crime novels with his friend, the poet, Jan Zábrana. JS was then still under a publishing ban, so these books appeared under Zábrana's name, though they were wholly written by JS. They featured an investigator, Dr. Pivoňky at different periods during the 20th century. Although five were planned only three were published. They are *Vražda pro stestí* ("Murder for Luck", 1960) set in the early thirties, *Vražda se zárukou* ("Guaranteed Murder", 1964) set just before WW2 and *Vražda v zastoupení* ("Murder by Proxy", 1967) set during the War. More recently JS has written two detective novels with his wife, Zdena Salivarová- Škvorecká, *Krátké setká í, s vrazdou* ("A Short Encounter, with Murder", 1999) and *Setkání po letech, s vrazdou* ("A Reunion, with Murder", 2001). Though set in Canada they too are only available in Czech. JS has written just one book directly in English, *Two Murders in My Double Life*, featuring his alter ego Danny Smiricki. It weaves together two stories. One is about a murder at a college where Smiricki teaches and which draws him into the investigation; the other is about Smiricki's wife who is haunted by a past transgression in Czechoslovakia, which now threatens her life. JS was nominated for a Nobel Prize in 1982.

Novels

Lieutenant Boruvka series: *The Return of Lieutenant Boruvka* (Can 1990).
Danny Smiricki series: *Miss Silver's Past* (Czech 1969; Can 1975), *The Miracle Game* (Can 1990), *Two Murders in My Double Life* (Can 1999).

Short Stories

Lieutenant Boruvka series: *The Mournful Demeanour of Lieutenant Boruvka* (Czech 1966; UK 1973), *The End of Lieutenant Boruvka* (Can 1989).
Eve Adam series: *Sins for Father Knox* (Czech 1988; Can 1988).

Full name: Josef Volcav Škvorecký.
Pen-name: Jan Zábrana.
Where to start: *Sins for Father Knox*.
Awards: Neustadt International Prize for Literature (1980), Governor General's Award (1984), Echoing Green Foundation Literary Prize (1990), Czech Order of the White Lion (1990), Arthur Ellis, best short story (1990), Toronto Arts Award for Literature (1999), Czech State Prize for Literature (1999).
Autobiography: *Headed for the Blues* (1997).
Similar stuff: Manuel Vázquez MONTALBÁN and Gillian SLOVO for equivalent portrayals of life in Spain and South Africa respectively.
Final fact: JS discovered crime fiction when he was in hospital with hepatitis in 1960 when doctors believed that the disease could be transmitted by books. So any books brought into the hospital stayed there.

Henry Slesar (1927–2002) US

HS was an exceedingly prolific and inventive writer but his work was too little known, even in his native America. That's because he was predominantly a writer of short stories (over 500 in various magazines) and a prolific TV scriptwriter. He was head writer for the daytime US mystery soap serial *Edge of Night* from 1968 to 1983 and this served as the thinly veiled background to his novel *Murder at Heartbreak Hospital* (filmed

2001 as *Heartbreak Hotel*). One of the story-lines from the series was novelized as *The Seventh Mask*. He also contributed many scripts to other TV suspense series, in particular *Alfred Hitchcock Presents*. Some of his original stories from that series are collected as *Death on Television*. He also adapted three stories from the *Inner Sanctum* radio series for TV as *Seduction* (1992) and contributed over 40 scripts to *Radio Mystery Theatre* during the 1980s. He wrote six stage plays (with 26 productions) of which only *The Veil* has been published. HS's career was in the advertising industry, eventually becoming head of his own company, and it is the advertising world and corporate business that's the background to HS's award-winning first crime novel, *The Gray Flannel Shroud*, featuring adman-turned-sleuth Dave Robbins. *Enter Murderers* is about a group of actors who stage a bogus murder-and-arrest scam in order to extort money from a rich man. HS's best novel is *The Thing at the Door*, a highly suspenseful psychological drama about a girl coming-of-age and facing terrors from her past. HS was also the master of the interactive short puzzle story and a collection of these, featuring Inspector Cross, was published as *Acrostic Mysteries*.

Novels. *The Gray Flannel Shroud* (1959), *Enter Murderers* (1960), *The Bridge of Lions* (1963), *The Seventh Mask* (1969), *The Thing at the Door* (1974), *Murder at Heartbreak Hospital* (1993).
Short Stories. *A Bouquet of Clean Crimes and Neat Murders* (1960), *A Crime for Mothers and Others* (1962), *Acrostic Mysteries* (1985), *Murders Most Macabre* (1986), *Death on Television* (1989).
Published play: *The Veil* (1997).

Full name: Henry Slesar.
Pen-names: O.H. Leslie, Lee Saber, Jay Street plus several house names in magazines.
Where to start: *The Thing at the Door*.
Awards: Edgar, best first novel (1960), Emmy award (1974), Derringer, lifetime (2000), best puzzle story (2001).
Similar stuff: Thomas CHASTAIN, Ed HOCH, Parnell HALL.
Final fact: HS comments on how life imitates art. "The Hitchcock producers were visited by the FBI, when a woman duplicated a murder depicted on screen in one of my teleplays. And in England, a man attempted to duplicate an embezzlement scheme identical to the one in my teleplay. Fortunately, one of the bobbies had seen the show and he was nabbed." (The papers called it "The Alfred Hitchcock Caper.")

Iceberg Slim (1918–92) US

Robert Beck, who was known on the streets of Chicago as Iceberg Slim, operated for over 20 years as a pimp until his third term of imprisonment in 1960, when 10 months of solitary confinement eventually forced him to change. He turned to writing and became a bestseller. He first wrote the story of his life, *Pimp*, with the hope of turning people away from crime, though its depiction of the harsh ghetto life is in itself a compelling read. With his first novel, *Trick Baby* (filmed 1973), IS told the story of White Folks, a white Negro who, through his looks, is able to deceive white people and thus become a clever con-man. His adventures continue in *Long White Con*. *Mama Black Widow* is the story of an ageing schizophrenic and transvestite, Otis Tilson, and his overbearing mother who infects with her bigotry all those near her. With *Death Wish*, IS took on the Chicago Mafia in a bloodthirsty novel of rivalry and hatred. His final novel, *Doom Fox*, was not published until six years after his death. Written in his usual harsh and uncompromising style, this saga of three generations of ghetto life is perhaps his bleakest work. IS's work is reckoned the best in its portrayal of the ghetto street life, though it was not always appreciated by the Black power movements who believed it contributed towards the "blaxploitation" films of the early 70s.

Novels
White Folks series: *Trick Baby* (1967), *Long White Con* (1977).
Non-series: *Mama Black Widow* (1970), *Death Wish* (1976), *Doom Fox* (1998).
Short stories. *Airtight Willie and Me* (1979).
Autobiography. *Pimp* (1967), *The Naked Soul of Iceberg Slim* (1971).

Full name: Robert Maupin Beck III.
Pen-name: Iceberg Slim.
Where to start: *Trick Baby*.
Similar stuff: Clarence COOPER, Jr., Chester HIMES.
Final fact: IS also released an album of his poetry, *Reflections*, which shows his hypnotic voice.

Gillian Slovo (b. 1952) South Africa

GS was born in South Africa, the daughter of two active anti-apartheid campaigners, and her book *Every Secret Thing* is a vivid and frequently painful memoir of her childhood, the murder of her mother and the political climate in South Africa. GS came to England in 1964 where she has worked as a writer, journalist and film/TV producer. Her novel, *Ties of Blood*, is also strongly autobiographical, and tells of two families, one white, one black, and their struggle through four generations in South Africa. When GS turned to writing she first chose the detective genre because, she says, it is "about the gradual uncovering of secrets." She created the character of Kate Baeier, a London-based P.I. of Portuguese descent. Baeier is a strong-minded socialist and feminist and politically active. All of the books have major political implications. In *Morbid Symptoms* it is apartheid and its ramifications in England. In *Death by Analysis* it's the IRA whilst *Death Comes Staccato*, which focuses on child abuse and incest, also explores police corruption and corporate exploitation. GS stopped writing about Baeier for a few years and we learn Baeier has become a war correspondent and journalist when she returns in two further powerful novels, finding her own life threatened. In the meantime GS has written two other political thrillers: *The Betrayal*, about division and a failure of trust amongst ANC activists in South Africa, and *Red Dust*, set in present-day South Africa and a confrontation between characters from the past. *Façade* is a change of pace, though is still about the discovery of secrets. This time it's an actress who, through the intervention of a stranger, begins to question the accepted truths about her parents. All of GS's books are profound and thought-provoking and challenge the status quo.

Novels
Kate Baeier series: *Morbid Symptoms* (1984), *Death by Analysis* (1986), *Death Comes Staccato* (1987), *Catnap* (1994), *Close Call* (1995).
Non-series: *Ties of Blood* (1989), *The Betrayal* (1991), *Façade* (1993), *Red Dust* (2000).
Autobiography. *Every Secret Thing* (1997).

Where to start: *Morbid Symptoms* or *The Betrayal*.
Website: <www.twbooks.co.uk/authors/gillianslovo.html>
Similar stuff: James McClure.

Joan Smith (b. 1953) UK

JS was drawn to writing crime fiction when she covered the Yorkshire Ripper murders as a journalist for both radio and the *Sunday Times*. She became fascinated with the effects of male hatred upon women, which led to her book of essays *Misogynies* (1989) and also the first of her Loretta Lawson books, *A Masculine Ending* (filmed TV 1992). Lawson is a university lecturer and a feminist in the cloistered world of strong chauvanist attitudes. It is these attitudes which affect the outcome of Lawson's investigations into deaths in the first two books, causing JS to challenge conventionality. In the third book, *Don't Leave Me This Way* (filmed TV 1993), Lawson, shattered by the lack of support from the police in London, moves to Oxford, the setting for *What Men Say*, one of the best of the series where JS demonstrates how preconceived attitudes affect a crime investigation. JS has concentrated on her other non-fiction writings but it is hoped she will soon return to Loretta Lawson.

JS should not be confused with the Canadian writer Joan Smith (b. 1932), who writes mostly Regency novels but has also written several murder mysteries including the Berkeley Brigade series about four aristocratic investigators that began with *Murder Will Speak* (1996).

Novels
Loretta Lawson series: *A Masculine Ending* (1987), *Why Aren't They Screaming?* (1988), *Don't Leave Me This Way* (1990), *What Men Say* (1993), *Full Stop* (1996).

Similar stuff: Amanda Cross, Veronica Stallwood.

Final fact: JS's book *Different for Girls* is a series of essays on female icons and how attitudes are influenced by preconceived feelings on gender. It includes a chapter on Princess Diana and was published in the very week of her death.

Julie Smith (b. 1944) US

Born in Maryland but raised in Georgia, JS was educated in Mississippi and then took a journalist job in New Orleans. She later moved to San Francisco but recently returned to New Orleans, the setting for her Skip Langdon novels. Her first series character was Rebecca Schwartz, a San Francisco Jewish feminist attorney. In *Death Turns a Trick*, Rebecca returns home after being caught in a police raid on a bordello, where she was playing piano, only to find a prostitute dead in her apartment. The series has a light touch and is fun whilst being clever and tightly plotted. JS briefly created another character, Paul McDonald, a writer turned part-time P.I. who in *True-Life Adventure* investigates the death of his boss. The two books are mock hard-boiled, and JS is just having fun. The second book, *Huckleberry Fiend* is an excellent literary mystery about a hunt for a lost Mark Twain manuscript. After these apprentice novels JS dived in at the deep end with her character Skip Langdon. She is a tall, self-aware but not always confident New Orleans police detective who pushes herself into ever more dangerous situations. This series is far more serious than the others, with strong characterization and complex plots dealing with major issues. The first novel, *New Orleans Mourning*, starts with a murder during Mardi Gras, and Skip's investigation leads her into New Orleans's high society with its complex web of secrets. The book earned JS an Edgar award for that year's best novel. She was the first American woman writer to win an Edgar in that category since Charlotte Armstrong in 1957. The series has maintained its high quality. The eighth novel, *82 Desire*, introduced the character of Talba Wallis, a young black computer whiz who performs her own poetry under the name Baroness de Pontalba and is also a P.I. Her boss, who was investigating a missing businessman, is killed and Talba contacts Skip to see what connection there may be. Talba was too much of a character to be contained in one book so JS gave her her own novel in *Louisiana Hotshot*, with promise of more to come. In researching Talba's background JS even went through the process to gain her own P.I. licence so that she is now an official private eye. She also ran a writers' editorial service, Invisible Ink (from 1979–83) with novelist Marcia MULLER.

Novels

Rebecca Schwartz series: *Death Turns a Trick* (1982), *The Sourdough Wars* (1984), *Tourist Trap* (1986), *Dead in the Water* (1991), *Other People's Skeletons* (1993).
Paul MacDonald series: *True-Life Adventure* (1985), *Huckleberry Fiend* (1987).

Skip Langdon series: *New Orleans Mourning* (1990), *The Axeman's Jazz* (1991), *Jazz Funeral* (1993), *New Orleans Beat* (1994), *House of Blues* (1995), *The Kindness of Strangers* (1996), *Crescent City Kill* (1997), *82 Desire* (1998).
Talba Wallis series: in Skip Langdon *82 Desire*; *Louisiana Hotshot* (2001).
Short Stories. *Mean Rooms* (2000).

Real name: Julienne Drew Smith.
Where to start: *New Orleans Mourning*.
Awards: Edgar, best novel (1991).
Website: <www.juliesmithauthor.com>
Similar stuff: Margaret MARON, Dick LOCHTE's Terry Manion books, Gillian ROBERTS.
Final fact: During JS's days with the *San Francisco Chronicle* she interviewed cult leader Jim Jones and after she filed her profile there were rumours she was on a hit list. She had to take cover in a safe house for a week.

Martin Cruz Smith (b. 1942) US

Former reporter MCS, then writing simply as Martin Smith, was short-listed for the Edgar best first mystery novel award for *Gypsy in Amber*, which introduced Roman Grey, a gypsy art dealer and investigator with a psychic gift. MCS has disowned most of these early books, including the series about Francis Xavier Killy, a lay brother investigator for the Vatican known as "The Inquisitor", which MCS wrote as Simon Quinn. Restyling himself as Martin Cruz Smith, he hit the big time with *Nightwing* (filmed 1979), where investigations into the deaths of several native Americans leads to the discovery of a new plague spread by bats. MCS's main reputation, though, lies with his series featuring Arkady Renko, the Chief Homicide Investigator for the Prosecutor's Office in Moscow. He first appeared in the mega-selling *Gorky Park* (filmed 1983) where his investigations into a triple murder lead him into a world of subterfuge, deception and double-dealing. The novel, which won the CWA Gold Dagger, was praised for its detail and MCS has become renowned for the depth of his research. He has written three further Renko novels. In the stark *Polar Star*, Renko is in exile in Siberia and investigates a murder on a factory ship in the Bering Sea. *Red Square* brings him back to Moscow at the time of the fall of the Soviet Union, the collapse providing the background to his investigation into the death of an informer. *Havana Bay*, which won the Hammett Prize, brings Renko to Cuba in search of a missing friend but he soon becomes involved in a series of murders. The Renko series are top quality police procedurals blended with the political thriller. Of his non-series books *Rose* is slightly unusual. Set in Lancashire, England, in 1872, it is the story of an engineer and explorer who is sent to find a missing curate but whose investigation creates animosity amongst the mining community. Even including his early journeyman work, MCS can never be accused of resting on his laurels. His novels are always inventive, credible and different.

Novels
Roman Grey series: *Gypsy in Amber* (1971), *Canto for a Gypsy* (1972).
Arkady Renko series: *Gorky Park* (1981), *Polar Star* (1989), *Red Square* (1992), *Havana Bay* (1999).
Inquisitor series as Simon Quinn: *His Eminence, Death* (1974), *Nuplex Red* (1974), *The Devil in Kansas* (1974), *The Last Time I Saw Hell* (1974), *The Midas Coffin* (1975), *Last Rites for the Vulture* (1975)
Non-series (film novelization) as Simon Quinn: *The Human Factor* (1975).
as Nick Carter: *The Inca Death Squad* (1972), *Code Name: Werewolf* (1973), *The Devil's Dozen* (1973).
Non-series: *The Analog Bullet* (1972), *Nightwing* (1977), *Stallion Gate* (1986), *Rose* (1996).
Editor. Death by Espionage (1999).

Full name: Martin William Cruz Smith.
Pen-names: Jake Logan, Martin Quinn, Simon Quinn; house name Nick Carter.
Where to start: *Gorky Park*.
Awards: CWA Gold Dagger (1981), Hammett Prize (1997, 2000).
Website: <http://literati.net/MCSmith/SmithBooks.htm>
Similar stuff: Stuart KAMINSKY, Reggie NADELSON.
Final fact: MCS's first book, *The Indians Won* (1970), considered an alternative America where the native Indians regained control.

Rosamund Smith *pseudonym, see* Joyce Carol Oates

Walter Sorrells (b. 1962) US

WS is something of a split personality. Under his own name he has written three powerful legal thrillers. The first, *Power of Attorney*, is about an Atlanta attorney who is framed for the murder of a con-man. The third, *Cry for Justice*, features another Atlanta attorney on the verge of being disbarred for allegedly bribing a witness who discovers he is the next target of a lawyer-hating serial killer. Good though these were there was something different about *Will to Murder* which introduced stubborn Atlanta tax lawyer Mae-mae Cosgrove, whose client is murdered. She is a delightfully quirky character and, following his publisher's suggestion, WS reworked her as a sassy Atlanta P.I. Sunny Childs, beginning a new series under the persona Ruth Birmingham. The first novel, *Atlanta Graves*, which involves Sunny in art theft, forgery and murder, was nominated for an Edgar award. The second, *Fulton County Blues*, a superbly crafted novel of Sunny's investigation into the death of a former Vietnam vet and the mystery surrounding her father's own death, took the Edgar the following year. WS has written three more Sunny Childs novels as well as ghost-writing a legal thriller, *Proof of Intent*, for the late William J. COUGHLIN. He has also written a hypertext novel, *The Heist*, and has several stories on the Web under the name Orvis Slayton.

Novels

Non-series: *Power of Attorney* (1994), *Will to Murder* (1996), *Cry for Justice* (1996). Sunny Childs series as Ruth Birmingham: *Atlanta Graves* (1998), *Fulton County Blues* (1999), *Sweet Georgia* (2000), *Blue Plate Special* (2001), *Cold Trail* (2002).

Pen-names: Ruth Birmingham, Orvis Slayton.
Where to start: *Will to Murder* or *Atlanta Graves*.
Awards: Edgar, best paperback original novel (2000).
Website: <www.mindspring.com>
Similar stuff: Rosemary AUBERT, Joe L. HENSLEY, Stuart WOODS.
Final fact: A martial artist, WS holds a black belt in Japanese shito-ryu karate.

Mickey Spillane (b. 1918) US

MS still holds the record as the biggest-selling American writer of crime fiction, with around 200 million copies sold over 50 years. He may well hold the record for the fastest-selling crime novel – the paperback edition of *The Long Wait* sold 3 million copies in a single week in 1952. MS had been writing for the comic books before WW2, during which he served as a flying instructor. He returned to the comics after the War but was unable to sell a character he had developed called Mike Danger, a private detective, so he rewrote him in book form as that most vengeful of P.I.s, Mike Hammer. Hammer was a natural descendant of Carroll John Daly's Race Williams, with none of the glamour or style of Chandler or Hammett. Through the Hammer books, MS influenced a generation of writers and his legacy can be traced through the sixties and seventies with the likes of Brian GARFIELD's *Death Wish*, Don PENDLETON's Executioner series, and David Morrell's Rambo. Hammer is a one-man crusader against evil who steps outside the law to become judge, jury and executioner, hence the title of the first book, *I, the Jury* (filmed 1953, 1982). Hammer's wartime friend has been killed and Hammer vows to track down and execute the murderer, which he does, culminating in a memorable ending. In later novels Hammer acquires a conscience about that murder and though he vows never to kill another woman it does not stop him killing others in his crusade against anything he sees as corrupt, from thugs to perverts to communists to corporate corruption. His approach brought the establishment against him, believing that his work was in itself corrupting the youth of the nation. What those critics failed to see was that Mike Hammer was a natural extension of the War years where the nation's youth had been turned into killing machines by the Army and that crusade was continued within America during the McCarthy era against the new enemy, communism. In *One Lonely Night*, arguably *the* classic Hammer novel, Hammer goes on a crusade against communists, who have kidnapped his secretary and assistant, the ever-beautiful Velda. His approach is challenged by a Judge who argues that Hammer enjoys killing, which makes him every bit as bad as those he kills.

This causes Hammer more mental anguish and forces him to understand himself and his purpose. The end result is that he sees himself almost as the "Hammer of God", fighting the fight of good against evil. This incensed the critics even more, but to the public Hammer was their answer to decay and corruption, not its cause, and they loved him.

Nevertheless after seven major bestsellers MS stopped writing novels, though he continued to produce short stories and work for comic strips. Some claim that he hit a writer's block or that he tired of the critical backlash, but it was more likely due to his religious conversion. MS had become a Jehovah's Witness in 1952 and his work for what they call the "Truth" would have eaten into his writing time and curbed his desire. When he returned to writing in the sixties Hammer had mellowed slightly and the writing become more measured. MS created a new character, Tiger Mann, an agent working for an espionage organization funded by a radical right-wing billionaire. The first book, *Day of the Guns*, has strong echoes of *I, the Jury*. Mann believes he recognizes a former female Nazi spy whom he had vowed to kill. This series lacks both the conviction and the power of the Hammer books and faded away after five titles. MS wrote a few one-off books, though they are all really Hammer clones. *The Erection Set* and *The Last Cop Out*, the only two books MS wrote in the third person, replace the Mafia as the latest villains.

MS proved he was not just a single formula writer when he produced two children's books, the first of which, *The Day the Sea Rolled Back* (1979), earned him a Junior Literary Guild Award. He also demonstrated he was a capable actor, taking the rôle of Hammer in *The Girl Hunters* (filmed 1963), and he became well known for his Miller beer adverts during the 1970s. The first Hammer film was *I, the Jury* with Biff Elliot as Hammer followed by *Kiss Me Deadly* (filmed 1955) with Ralph Meeker and *My Gun is Quick* (filmed 1957) with Robert Bray. MS did not like any of the films, other than his own. TV adaptations began as early as 1958 with Darrin McGavin in the rôle, though Stacy Keach would become most closely associated with the character in *Mickey Spillane's Mike Hammer* (1984–5). MS was married three times. His second wife, the actress Sherri Malinou, served as the model for several of the later Hammer book covers.

Novels

Mike Hammer series: *I, the Jury* (1947), *My Gun is Quick* (1950), *Vengeance is Mine!* (1950), *The Big Kill* (1951), *One Lonely Night* (1951), *Kiss Me, Deadly* (1952), *The Girl Hunters* (1962), *The Snake* (1964), *The Twisted Thing* (1966), *The Body Lovers* (1967), *Survival... Zero!* (1970), *The Killing Man* (1989), *Black Alley* (1996).

Tiger Mann series: *Day of the Guns* (1964), *Bloody Sunrise* (1965), *The Death Dealers* (1965), *The By-Pass Control* (1966).

Non-series: *The Long Wait* (1951), *The Deep* (1961), *The Delta Factor* (1967), *The Erection Set* (1972), *The Last Cop Out* (1973).

Short Stories. *Me, Hood!* (UK 1963), *The Flier* (UK 1964), *Return of the Hood* (UK 1964; rev'd as *Me, Hood!*, US 1969), *Killer Mine* (UK 1965), *The Tough Guys* (1969), *Tomorrow I Die* (1984).
Comic-strip collections
Mike Hammer series: *The Sudden Trap* (1982), *Comes Murder* (1985).
Editor with Max Allan COLLINS: *Murder is My Business* (1994), *Vengeance is Hers* (1997), *Private Eyes* (1998), *A Century of Noir* (2002).

Full name: Frank Morrison Spillane.
Pen-name: Frank Morrison, Mickey Spillane.
Where to start: *I, the Jury*.
Awards: Junior Literary Guild Award (1979), PWA, lifetime achievement (1983), Shamus, best PI story (1990), MWA Grand Master (1995).
Books about: *One Lonely Knight: Mickey Spillane's Mike Hammer* by Max Allan Collins & James L. Traylor (1984).
Website: unofficial Mike Hammer site
<www.interlog.com/~roco/hammer.html>
Similar stuff: Michael AVALLONE, Ed McBAIN as Curt Cannon, Mark TIMLIN.
Final fact: In the early fifties MS became involved with a circus and did some trampoline work as well as being shot out of a cannon.

Elizabeth Daniels Squire (1926–2001) US

EDS came from a newspaper family in North Carolina and was a reporter herself all her life, serving at one time and another as a police reporter in Connecticut and a correspondent from Beirut. She also wrote a nationally syndicated column "How to Read Your Own Hand", converting that information into a book, *Palmistry Made Practical* (1960). EDS used an episode from family history, where her grandfather received death threats and was shot at, as the inspiration for her first novel, *Kill the Messenger*, where a newspaper proprietor is killed and just about everyone is suspect. But EDS, who was notoriously absent-minded, will be remembered mostly for her delightful series about Peaches Dann, a widow in her 50s who has a terrible memory. So does her 83-year-old father, though he's convinced someone's on his roof and when his sister is killed Peaches helps solve the murder. She finds her memory-prompting techniques (which she's compiling into a book *How to Survive Without a Memory*) are useful in her investigations. These continue in *Remember the Alibi*, where her father is again vulnerable, this time to a con-artist who befriends the elderly, acquires their money and then makes their death look like suicide. Thereafter locals consult her to help solve mysteries and in the final book she becomes a reporter embroiled in a murder investigation. The Peaches Dann short story, "The Dog Who Remembered Too Much", won EDS an Agatha award and was shortlisted for an Anthony. This is a traditional cozy series but with a charming new twist.

Novels

Peaches Dann series: *Who Killed What's-Her-Name?* (1994), *Remember the Alibi* (1994), *Memory Can be Murder* (1995), *Whose Death is it Anyway?* (1997), *Is There a Dead Man in the House?* (1998), *Where There's a Will* (1999), *Forget About Murder* (2000).

Non-series: *Kill the Messenger* (1990).

Awards: Agatha, best short story (1996).
Website: <www.booktalk.com/edsquire/>
Similar stuff: Margaret MARON, Mary Monica PULVER (as Monica Ferris).
Final fact: EDS took the handprints and read the palms of Salvador Dali, Helen Hayes and Carl Sandburg.

Dana Stabenow (b. 1952) US

DS is an Alaskan who trained as a journalist but ended up doing a variety of jobs, including working on the Alaskan oil pipeline, until she settled down to write. Her first published books were science fiction, a series about the evacuation of Earth starting with *Second Star* (1991), but she had previously written a crime novel, which she had not sought to publish and, at the urging of her publisher, turned to writing mysteries. Her main series features Kate Shugak, an Aleut homesteader in the National Park and a former D.A. investigator. In the award-winning *A Cold Day for Murder* she goes in search of a missing Park Ranger assisted by Mutt, her half-wolf, half-husky canine friend. *A Fatal Thaw* poses an interesting problem – that one of the victims of a man who went on a killing spree was actually murdered by someone else. As the series develops, though, we find that these are not simply crime novels. They are stories of human endeavour and fortitude set against the dramatic scenery of Alaska, which is every bit as dominant a character as those of Kate and her lover and former D.A. boss, Jack Morgan. This is also true of DS's other series featuring disgraced state trooper Liam Campbell who is transferred to a small town in Alaska in *Fire and Ice*. Campbell has a tragic recent past and feels he has an uncertain future, which makes this another character-driven series amidst wild and uncompromising surroundings.

Novels

Kate Shugak series: *A Cold Day for Murder* (1992), *A Fatal Thaw* (1993), *Dead in the Water* (1993), *A Cold-Blooded Business* (1994), *Play With Fire* (1995), *Blood Will Tell* (1996), *Breakup* (1997), *Killing Grounds* (1998), *Hunter's Moon* (1999), *Midnight Come Again* (2000), *The Singing and the Dead* (2001), *A Fine and Bitter Snow* (2002).

Liam Campbell series: *Fire and Ice* (1998), *So Sure of Death* (1999), *Nothing Gold Can Stay* (2000), *Better to Rest* (2002).

Full name: Dana Helen Stabenow.
Where to start: *A Cold Day for Murder*.
Awards: Edgar, best paperback original (1993).
Website: <www.stabenow.com>

Similar stuff: Sue HENRY, Laurence GOUGH.
Final fact: VS's first novel had been written but left lying around in her grandfather's garage for three years before she submitted it to her publisher.

Susannah Stacey *pseudonym, see* Jill Staynes & Margaret Storey

Veronica Stallwood UK

Before becoming a full time writer VS was a librarian at the venerable Bodleian Library in Oxford and later at Lincoln College. Her first book, *Deathspell*, about a demanding husband and a disintegrating family that leads to murder, sold well and enticed her to full-time writing. She began a series about Oxford-resident novelist Kate Ivory. Ivory enjoys her early morning jog with the Fridesley Road running group and it's her involvement with them, in *Death and the Oxford Box*, that results in the whole group becoming suspects in a murder case. Kate tries to stay one step ahead of the police. *Oxford Exit* takes us into VS's world of academe as Ivory helps the OU discover who is stealing books. In *Oxford Knot* Ivory becomes the intended victim of a crime, though it's those about her who suffer more. In *Oxford Shadows*, while researching her next book, Ivory discovers some papers relating to the death of a child over 50 years ago and her investigations rebound on her. The series has a cozy feel without being overly traditional. Ivory and her circle of friends (despite their diminishing number) are richly drawn and Oxford, as always, is the ideal place for murder and mystery. VS has written one other non-series book to date, *The Rainbow Sign*, a psychological thriller also set in Oxford but where events started 30 years ago in the Levant now have dark repercussions.

Novels
Kate Ivory series: *Death and the Oxford Box* (1993), *Oxford Exit* (1994), *Oxford Mourning* (1995), *Oxford Fall* (1996), *Oxford Knot* (1998), *Oxford Blue* (1998), *Oxford Shift* (1999), *Oxford Shadows* (2000), *Oxford Double* (2001), *Oxford Proof* (2002).
Non-series: *Deathspell* (1992), *The Rainbow Sign* (1999).

Where to start: *Death and the Oxford Box*.
Similar stuff: Orania PAPAZOGLOU, Natasha COOPER's Willow King books, Joan SMITH.

Richard Stark *pseudonym, see* Donald E. Westlake

Jill Staynes (b. 1927) & Margaret Storey (b. 1926) UK

After having separately written several children's books, former teachers and longtime friends Staynes and Storey finally united to write crime novels and produced two surprisingly different series. The first was a traditional classic whodunnit featuring Superintendent Robert Bone. This series appeared in the US under the joint pseudonym Susannah Stacey. Bone was recently widowed when his wife was killed in a car accident, and he is left having to look after his injured teenage daughter alone which causes much friction and distress. It is some while before Bone is able to explore other romantic relationships but he does later remarry. The stories themselves are fine puzzles with plenty of suspects and red herrings. Bone is an intuitive detective and likes to analyse those he interviews, who are frequently strange or eccentric. The victims of the crimes are varied and interesting. A recently rich nanny in the first book, a transvestite in *Body of Opinion*, half the Clare family in *Grave Responsibility*, an English lord in *Bone Idle* and a TV star in *Quarry*. Their second series is set in Renaissance Italy in the 1490s and features Sigismondo, agent for the Duke of Rocca. In *Death of a Duchess*, Sigismondo's investigations are a race against time to stop feuds between rival families breaking out into open warfare when a young bride is kidnapped hours before her wedding and the Duke's wife murdered. The series is strong on atmosphere and period detail and has a wonderful array of Shakespearean characters.

Novels

Superintendent Bone series: *Goodbye, Nanny Gray* (1987), *A Knife at the Opera* (1988), *Body of Opinion* (1988), *Grave Responsibility* (1990), *The Late Lady* (1992), *Bone Idle* (1993), *Dead Serious* (1995), *Hunter's Quarry* (US 1997; as *Quarry*, UK 1999).

Sigismondo series as Elizabeth Eyre: *Death of a Duchess* (1991), *Curtains for the Cardinal* (1992), *Poison for the Prince* (1993), *Bravo for the Bride* (1994), *Axe for an Abbot* (1995), *Dirge for a Doge* (1996).

Pen-names: Elizabeth Eyre, Susannah Stacey (in US).
Where to start: Both series are best followed from the start.
Similar stuff: Ruth RENDELL's Wexford books for Bone; Iain PEARS and Derek WILSON for historical.
Final fact: The authors have found they've been able to do a lot of their research in books discovered at car boot sales.

Neville Steed UK

Like his main character, Peter Marklin, NS had a career in advertising where he created many television commercials. Settling back in his native Devon, NS began a series of books, also set in the West Country, about a collector of antique toys whose activities bring him into contact with all kinds of shenanigans. The first, *Tinplate*, where Marklin tries to recover his money or a stolen batch of toys, won the John Creasey Memorial Award. In later novels Marklin becomes involved with a faded Hollywood actress (*Die-Cast*), discovers a dead body in a vintage car (*Boxed-In*) and finds a killer has him in his sights when he discovers toys stolen from a murdered collector (*Wind-Up*). This enterprising series explores a corner of the collecting world generally overlooked by crime writers. As a change of venue, NS also wrote two books about raffish sleuth Johnny Black of the Black Eye Detective Agency set in England in the thirties. Both stories are an engaging blend of wit, atmosphere and nostalgia.

Novels

Peter Marklin series: *Tinplate* (1986), *Die-Cast* (1987), *Chipped* (1988), *Clockwork* (1989), *Wind Up* (1990), *Boxed In* (1991), *Dead Cold* (1992).
Johnny Black series: *Black Eye* (1989), *Black Mail* (1990).

Real name: Norman Sharam.
Pen-name: Neville Steed.
Where to start: *Tinplate*.
Awards: CWA John Creasey Memorial Award (1986).
Similar stuff: Jonathan GASH.
Final fact: NS is married to author Kate Sharam whose powerful contemporary novels include two with strong crime elements, *A Hard Place* (1997) and *Rough Exposure* (1998).

Richard Martin Stern (1915–2001) US

RMS will probably be best remembered as the author of *The Tower* (1973), one of the two books which formed the basis of the disaster film *The Towering Inferno* (1974). Its success caused him to write a number of other blockbuster disaster novels such as *Flood* (1979), *The Big Bridge* (1982) and *Wildfire* (1986). But he never neglected the crime fiction field. A former engineer, he turned full-time writer after WW2, selling mostly to the leading magazines before his first gangster novel, *The Bright Road to Fear*, which won an Edgar award. RMS's forte was in suspense, such as the race-against-time quest in *The Search for Tabitha Carr* or exploring the effects of a crime upon a small town, as in *Cry Havoc* and *These Unlucky Deeds*. RMS travelled extensively and produced several novels of espionage and intrigue set in Europe such as *The Kessler Legacy* and *Merry Go Round* in Austria and *I Hide, We Seek* in Scotland. *Manuscript for Murder* has a rather Buchanesque finale in Scotland as an American newspaperman follows the trail left by plans for a great train robbery. After RMS settled in Santa Fe in New Mexico he created the character of police lieutenant Johnny Ortiz, half-Apache, half-Chicano. The series is again strong on suspense. It has its share of races-against-time and searches (in *You Don't Need an Enemy* and *Missing Man*), but also deals with organized crime and drug dealing in *Death in the Snow* and computer crimes in *Tangled Murders*. The high desert lands around Santa Fe come alive in *You Don't Need an Enemy* and the first of the Ortiz novels, *Murder in the Walls*, where a dead body found in the desert provides a link to the murder of a young girl and a museum robbery. RMS's books are always full of action, local colour, suspense and variety.

Novels
Johnny Ortiz series: *Murder in the Walls* (1971), *You Don't Need an Enemy* (1971), *Death in the Snow* (1973), *Tangled Murders* (1989), *Missing Man* (1990), *Interloper* (1990).
Non-series: *The Bright Road to Fear* (1958), *The Search for Tabitha Carr* (1960), *These Unlucky Deeds* (1961; as *Quidnunc County*, UK 1961), *High Hazard* (1962), *Cry Havoc* (1963), *Right Hand Opposite* (1964), *I Hide, We Seek* (1965), *The Kessler Legacy* (1968), *The Merry Go Round* (1969), *Manuscript for Murder* (1970), *The Will* (1976).
Short Stories. *Suspense* (1959).

Where to start: *Murder in the Walls.*
Awards: Edgar, best first novel (1959).
Similar stuff: Michael ALLEGRETTO, Tony HILLERMAN.

Margaret Storey, *see* Jill Staynes & Margaret Storey

Carsten Stroud (b. 1946) Canada

CS is a former Toronto police officer who turned investigative journalist. His true-life books about life in the force, *The Blue Wall*, *Close Pursuit* (where he infiltrated the NYPD) and *Deadly Force*, are as action-packed and suspenseful as any novel. Indeed, *Deadly Force*, though a true account of several days in the life of a US Marshal in pursuit of a killer, is written like a novel. CS has written three novels, all of which draw upon his experiences. The first two both won awards from the Crime Writers of Canada. *Sniper's Moon* is a story of the NYPD's search for a killer where the trail leads them back to one of their own men. *Lizard Skin* is set in Montana where a Highway Patrol officer finds himself caught up in a feud between a truck-stop owner and a group of Dakota native Americans. *Black Water Transit* is a thriller of a man against the system when poor communications lead to an informer falling foul of the police.

Novels. *Sniper's Moon* (1990), *Lizard Skin* (1992), *Black Water Transit* (2001).
Non-fiction. *The Blue Wall* (1983), *Close Pursuit* (1987), *Contempt of Court* (1993), *Iron Bravo* (1995), *Deadly Force* (1996).

Where to start: *Sniper's Moon.*
Awards: Arthur Ellis, best first novel (1991), best novel (1993), National Magazine Awards, President's Medal (1998).
Similar stuff: James CRUMLEY for Montana setting; Paul BISHOP.
Final fact: *Iron Bravo*, about life in the US Army, is now a standard text at several American military academies.

Doug Swanson (b. 1953) US

An award-winning journalist, who has worked for the *Dallas Morning News* since 1982, DS became an award-winning author with his first book *Big Town*. This not only won the John Creasey Memorial Award from the CWA but was both an Edgar and an Anthony finalist. It introduced Jack

Flippo, a hot-shot in the Dallas D.A.'s office until a night of lust with a drug-dealer's wife found him out of a job and divorced. He becomes a lawyer's gumshoe but, as the series progresses, his cases, always laced with humour and cranky characters, become bigger and more violent. In *Dreamboat* it's an insurance scam. In *96 Tears* it's kidnapping, arson and stalking. And with *Umbrella Man* Flippo discovers the truth about the Kennedy assassination. An excellent series that remains exciting even when it doesn't always take itself seriously.

Novels

Jack Flippo series: *Big Town* (1994), *Dreamboat* (1995), *96 Tears* (1996), *Umbrella Man* (1999), *House of Corrections* (2000).

Awards: CWA, John Creasey Memorial Award (1994).
Website: <www.dougswanson.com>
Similar stuff: M.R.D. MEEK for another disbarred lawyer; Manuel Vázquez MONTALBÁN and Robert K. TANENBAUM for other Kennedy-related novels.

Julian Symons (1912–94) UK

JS's contribution to the genre is admirably patterned in the awards he received from the two premier organizations, the CWA and the MWA. Each gave him an award for his fiction, for his scholarship and for his life achievement. JS was as well known for his many critical studies of crime fiction as for his contributions to it, and he worked tirelessly in many capacities for the furtherance and appreciation of crime fiction for 50 years. It did not start that way. JS's early literary leanings were as a poet and he always demanded high standards. His first foray into crime fiction was really as a joke. *The Immaterial Murder Case* was written before WW2 and he gave no serious consideration to its publication until after the war. The whole novel is a satire of both pretentious artist movements and of the classic detective story. Even his detective is given the name Bland. Interestingly many years later JS wrote that his fascination with crime fiction came from the fact that such violence and evil could hide behind otherwise "bland" and respectable faces. Most of JS's fiction removes the masks from those faces to reveal the hidden truths as evident from the title of one of his last books, *Death's Darkest Face*, where a son tries to rebuild the past by clearing his father's name. JS began to use crime fiction seriously with *The Thirty-First of February*, where an innocent, inoffensive individual is hounded by the police. Three novels, *The Narrowing Circle*, *The Broken Penny* and *The End of Solomon Grundy* show how events can rapidly shatter an individual's life leading to crime. In some books, such as *The Man Who Killed Himself* and *The Man Whose Dreams Came True*, he charted how individuals may create alternative lives in the mistaken belief they will escape that decline. Key to these books are relationships between people, usually husbands and wives, but also parents/children, or old friends, which may have been harmonious for years until something pushes life out of synch – as in *The Criminal Comedy of the Contented Couple*, *Something Like a Love Affair* and *Playing Happy Families*.

Throughout these books you sense that JS is not really writing crime novels, but novels about people into whose life crime intrudes. It is a criticism of society's inability to control or police itself. JS often portrays people, victims as well as detectives, as less than bright. Elsewhere he considers how changes in society may provoke people into criminal activities. In *The Paper Chase* it's the growth in juvenile delinquency; in *The Progress of a Crime* it's motorbike gangs. JS even traced this ill-preparedness for change back to the 1890s in *The Detling Murders*. This was one of several novels JS wrote with a Victorian setting. Along with *Sweet Adelaide* and *The Blackheath Poisonings* they parody the Victorian literary style and worldview. JS used this same approach in rediscovering the great fictional detectives. Not only did he write several stories collected as *The Great Detectives*, which explored previously untold episodes in their lives, but he also wrote two quasi Sherlock Holmes pastiches. Both *A Three-Pipe Problem* and *The Kentish Manor Murders* feature Sheridan Haynes, an actor who portrays Holmes on the stage and who uses Holmes's methods to solve a crime. JS's crusade was for the psychological, not analytical, crime story, and his books are a remarkable set of variations on that theme. All of JS's studies of crime fiction are worth reading, especially *Bloody Murder*, which is a cornerstone volume for any reference shelf.

Novels

Inspector Bland series: *The Immaterial Murder Case* (1945), *A Man Called Jones* (1947), *Bland Beginning* (1949).

Inspector Crambo series: *The Narrowing Circle* (1954), *The Gigantic Shadow* (1958; as *The Pipe Dream*, US 1959).

Sheridan Haynes series: *A Three-Pipe Problem* (1975), *The Kentish Manor Murders* (1988).

Non-series: *The Thirty-First of February* (1950), *The Broken Penny* (1953), *The Paper Chase* (1956; as *Bogue's Fortune*, US 1957), *The Colour of Murder* (1957), *The Progress of a Crime* (1960), *The Killing of Francie Lake* (1962; as *The Plain Man*, US 1962), *The End of Solomon Grundy* (1964), *The Belting Inheritance* (1965), *The Man Who Killed Himself* (1967), *The Man Whose Dreams Came True* (1968), *The Man Who Lost His Wife* (1971), *The Players and the Game* (1972), *The Plot Against Roger Rider* (1973), *The Blackheath Poisonings* (1978), *Sweet Adelaide* (1980), *The Detling Murders* (1982; as *The Detling Secret*, US 1983), *The Name of Annabel Lee* (1983), *The Criminal Comedy of the Contented Couple* (1985; as *A Criminal Comedy*, US 1986), *Death's Darkest Face* (1990), *Something Like a Love Affair* (1992), *Playing Happy Families* (1994), *A Sort of Virtue* (1996).

Short Stories

Francis Quarles series: *Murder! Murder!* (1961), *Francis Quarles Investigates* (1965).

Non-series: *How to Trap a Crook* (1977), *The Great Detectives* (1981), *The Tigers of Subtopia* (1982), *The Man Who Hated Television* (1995).

Non-fiction. *The Detective Story in Britain* (1962), *Crime and Detection: An*

Illustrated History from 1840 (1966: as *A Pictorial History of Crime*, US 1966), *Bloody Murder* (1972, rev'd 1974; as *Mortal Consequences*, US 1972), *The Tell-Tale Heart: The Life and Works of Edgar Allan Poe* (1978), *Conan Doyle: Portrait of an Artist* (1979), *Crime and Detection Quiz* (1983), *Dashiell Hammett* (1985), *Criminal Practices: Symons on Crime Writing 60's to 90's* (1994).
Editor. *Verdict of Thirteen* (1979), *The Penguin Classic Crime Omnibus* (1984).

Full name: Julian Gustave Symons.
Where to start: *The Thirty-First of February*.
Awards: CWA, best novel (1957), CWA Special Merit (1966), Swedish Academy of Detection, Best Foreign (1971), CWA Diamond Dagger (1990); Edgar, best novel (1961), special Edgar (1973), Swedish Academy of Detection, Grand Master (1977); MWA Grand Master (1982).
Books about: Tribute anthology *The Man Who . . .* ed. H.R.F. Keating (1992); *Julian Symons, a Bibliography* by John J. Walsdorf (1996).
Similar stuff: For style Michael GILBERT, Ruth RENDELL (non-Wexford), Anne PERRY (historicals).

Robert K. Tanenbaum US

RKT writes almost manic legal thrillers drawn from his own experience as assistant District Attorney in New York. He served as Deputy Counsel on the House Select Committee's reinvestigation of the assassinations of John F. Kennedy and Martin Luther King, an experience he late fictionalized in *Corruption of Blood*. He has remained in private practice and has served a term as Mayor of Beverly Hills. He writes virtually full-time but his workload is such that he has a "ghost" collaborator, Michael Gruber. His novels almost trace his own career. They feature Roger "Butch" Karp, a former basketball player who, following an injury, turned to the law. Intensely competitive, Karp attacks his cases in the overworked D.A.'s office. In *No Lesser Plea*, set in the 1970s, Karp is still relatively young, and out to prove himself. Amongst the many cases he is dealing with is one involving a psychopath who believes he can beat his charge of first degree murder through a plea of insanity. *Depraved Indifference* deals with terrorists and an airline hijack. *Immoral Certainty*, which deals with a serial child murderer, also introduces a new D.A. who is ruthless and devious and antagonizes the other lawyers, thus adding to the tension. Also in the office is Marlene Ciampi, the only woman attorney who is attracted to Karp because they both like to challenge the system. RKT has also written two non-fiction dramatizations of true crime cases. Over seven million copies of RKT's books are in print. They are potent in-your-face books, which are at once exhausting and exhilarating but never disappointing.

Novels

"Butch" Karp series: *No Lesser Plea* (1987), *Depraved Indifference* (1989), *Immoral Certainty* (1991), *Reversible Error* (1992), *Material Witness* (1993), *Justice Denied* (1994), *Corruption of Blood* (1995), *Falsely Accused* (1996), *Irresistible Impulse*

(1997), *Reckless Endangerment* (1998), *Act of Revenge* (1999), *True Justice* (2000), *Enemy Within* (2001), *Absolute Rage* (2002).
Non-fiction. *Badge of the Assassin*, with Philip Rosenberg (1994), *The Piano Teacher*, with Peter S. Greenburg (1994).

Where to start: *No Lesser Plea.*
Similar stuff: John GRISHAM, Ed MCBAIN's Matthew Hope.
Final fact: When RKT worked at the D.A.'s office in New York he obtained an unbeatable record of never losing a murder case.

William G. Tapply (b. 1940) US

There's something of Brady Coyne in all of us. He is a Boston attorney but his work bores him. He perseveres because he is able to be selective and work with the rich and more interesting people and his fees allow him to indulge in his one true passion, fly-fishing. That is also the passion of Coyne's creator. WGT, a former high school teacher and housemaster, and a contributing editor to *Field and Stream*, has written several books on fishing and the outdoor life, including *A Fly-fishing Life* (1997). Because he's selective Coyne doesn't always do what you'd expect lawyers to do. He works more like a private detective – looking for a missing son in *The Vulgar Boatmen*, finding an estranged daughter in *Tight Lines*, delving into the truth behind an apparent suicide in *Death at Charity's Point*, or negotiating over a rare stamp in *The Dutch Blue Error*. Legal matters do sometimes arise. *Close to the Bone* explores legal ethics; *The Seventh Enemy*, in which Coyne is nearly killed, concerns gun control; and in *Client Privilege* he finds himself representing a judge. It's the variety and disregard for convention that's the appeal of this series and one that you know the author doesn't take entirely too seriously.

Novels

Brady Coyne series: *Death at Charity's Point* (1984), *The Dutch Blue Error* (1985), *Follow the Sharks* (1985), *The Marine Corpse* (1986; as *A Rodent of Doubt*, UK 1987), *Dead Meat* (1987), *The Vulgar Boatmen* (1987), *A Void in Hearts* (1988), *Dead Winter* (1989), *Client Privilege* (1990), *The Spotted Cats* (1991), *Tight Lines* (1992), *The Snake Eater* (1993), *The Seventh Enemy* (1995), *Close to the Bone* (1996), *Cutter's Run* (1998), *Muscle Memory* (1999), *Scar Tissue* (2000), *Past Tense* (2001).
Non-series: *Thicker Than Water*, with Linda Carlow (1995), *First Light*, with Phil Craig (2001).
Non-fiction. *The Elements of Mystery Fiction* (1995).

Full name: William George Tapply.
Where to start: *Close to the Bone.*
Awards: Scribner's Best First Mystery Award (1985).
Website: <www.williamgtapply.com>
Similar stuff: Terence FAHERTY for mood.
Final fact: WGT was once called upon to testify at a hearing on gun control and as a consequence he received threatening phone calls.

Andrew Taylor (b. 1951) UK

AT's first book won the John Creasey Memorial Award and he has justified that in subsequent years with a substantial body of work that has grown ever more challenging and daring. With AT's work you know you can expect the unexpected. In *Caroline Minuscule* we meet William Dougal, an unscrupulous postgrad history student who stumbles across the dead body of his hated tutor. He chooses not to report it, at which point he enters that shady territory on the edge of legality from where he continues to operate, kept only just in line by his long-term girlfriend Celia. As this book and its sequels progress we discover that Dougal is not averse to murder if it helps and he makes up the rules as he goes along. He becomes a private detective and is later employed by his one time adversary, the equally unscrupulous James Hanbury. It is to AT's credit that Dougal comes across as a likeable individual yet one whose comeuppance is anticipated in each book. The series is built upon secrets and lies. The third volume, *Our Fathers' Lies*, where Dougal and his father, a retired British intelligence officer, reopen a crime from the 1930s and a WW1 court martial, was a signpost of the direction AT's fiction would take. That book was nominated for the CWA Gold Dagger. Most of AT's later books explore relationships within families, across generations and within communities. He explores the ramifications of past actions and guilt on others and down through the years. This began with his trilogy featuring intelligence agent Eric Blaines, who had appeared in *Our Father's Lies* but now becomes a shadowy figure influencing events from the fifties to the nineties. AT then created a larger canvas with his Lydmouth series. Set in the decade after WW2 on the borders between England and Wales (roughly corresponding to where AT lives in the Forest of Dean) the books develop a small society which has its own communal conscience, secrets and mores but which is trying to come to terms with change. Although the books reflect multiple viewpoints and changing characters the main thread follows journalist Jill Francis and Inspector Thornhill. Neither are native to the area and both have their own emotional baggage, which steadily draws them together. The crimes they encounter form part of a tapestry of time rather than isolated incidents, creating a complex web of intrigue and one of the most fully realized sequences of crime novels. AT's most challenging work is the Roth trilogy. Conceived as a unified whole but delivered in three books, it works backwards in time from the 1990s to the 1950s (and earlier by implication), each book peeling back the layers to show the origins of the evil that confronts the two main families in the trilogy. The third volume, *The Office of the Dead*, won the Ellis Peters Historical Dagger Award. AT's books, which includes thrillers for children and other one-off psychological suspense novels, are amongst the best examples of novels where the crimes seep out of the bricks-and-mortar of life.

Novels

William Dougal series: *Caroline Minuscule* (1982), *Waiting for the End of the World* (1984), *Our Fathers' Lies* (1985), *An Old School Tie* (1986), *Freelance Death* (1987), *Blood Relation* (1990), *The Sleeping Policeman* (1992), *Odd Man Out* (1993).
Blaines Trilogy: *The Second Midnight* (1987), *Blacklist* (1988), *Toyshop* (1990).
Lydmouth Series: *An Air That Kills* (1994), *The Mortal Sickness* (1995), *The Lover of the Grave* (1997), *The Suffocating Night* (1998), *Where Roses Fade* (2000), *Death's Own Door* (2001).
Roth Trilogy: *The Four Last Things* (1997), *The Judgement of Strangers* (1998), *The Office of the Dead* (2000).
Bergerac series as Andrew Saville: *Bergerac is Back* (1985; as *Crimes of the Season* 1985), *Bergerac and the Fatal Weakness* (1988), *Bergerac and the Jersey Rose* (1988), *Bergerac and the Moving Fever* (1988), *Bergerac and the Traitor's Child* (1988).
Non-series: *The Raven on the Water* (1991), *The Barred Window* (1993).
Non-series books for older children: *Hairline Cracks* (1988), *Snapshot* (1989), *Double Exposure* (1990), *Negative Image* (1992), *The Invader* (1994).

Full name: Andrew John Robert Taylor.
Pen-names: Andrew Saville, John Robert Taylor.
Where to start: The Roth trilogy and *An Air That Kills*.
Awards: CWA, John Creasey Memorial Award (1982), Ellis Peters Historical Dagger (2001).
Website: <www.lydmouth.demon.co.uk>
Similar stuff: Robert BARNARD, Frances FYFIELD, Patricia HIGHSMITH.
Final fact: AT has developed RSI and now dictates much of his writing.

Domini Taylor *pseudonym, see* Roger Longrigg

Peter Temple (b. 1946) Australia

In a short space of time PT has established himself as one of Australia's leading writers of crime fiction. His first book, *Bad Debts*, which won the Ned Kelly award, introduced the character of Jack Irish, a lawyer and gambler turned debt collector and people finder. The books are set amongst the world of Australian football and the racetrack and Irish is never far from a pub – in fact in *Dead Point* he's looking for a missing barman. His cases lead him into the dark, violent and unsettling criminal underworld. All of PT's books are bleak, but the bleakest so far is *Shooting Star*, which also won a Ned Kelly award. This concerns a failed police-hostage negotiator who has turned freelance mediator and is dragged into a disturbing kidnapping case. PT's books depict the world of the loser trying to regain control.

Novels

Jack Irish series: *Bad Debts* (1996), *Black Tide* (1997), *Dead Point* (2000).
Non-series: *An Iron Rose* (1998), *Shooting Star* (1999), *In the Evil Day* (2002).

Where to start: *Bad Debts*.
Awards: Ned Kelly, best first novel (1997), best crime novel (2000, 2001).
Similar stuff: Peter CORRIS, Shane MALONEY.

Donald Thomas (b. 1934) UK

DT is an historian, criminologist and poet in addition to a writer of crime fiction. His historical studies include the much acclaimed biographies *Cardigan* (1975) and *Cochrane, Britain's Last Sea-King* (1980) and the literary biographies *Robert Browning* (1982), which was runner-up for the Whitbread Award, and *Lewis Carroll* (1996). His true crime books include studies of state trials, classic robberies and investigations into wrongful convictions and rough justice. These last include *Dead Giveaway, Hanged in Error?* and, under his Selwyn alias, *Gangland, the Case of Bentley and Craig* (1988). DT has a special fascination for the Victorian period and has written a detailed study, *The Victorian Underworld*. His first series of books, writing as Francis Selwyn, featured Sergeant William Verity, a strongly moralistic, almost prudish Victorian detective in the mid-19th century. DT contrasts Verity's righteous outlook with the real Victorian street-life. Verity has to use his brain, though, as most of the crimes are locked-room or impossible ones. For instance, in *Cracksman on Velvet*, which is based on a real great train robbery in 1857, gold bullion disappears from a locked, moving train. In *Verity and the Imperial Diamond*, set in India, it's the theft of a jewel from a casket under surveillance. Under his own name DT produced a similar series featuring Inspector Alfred Swain in the late 19th century. These also use real characters and historical events. *Belladonna* involves Lewis Carroll and the blackmailer Charles Augustus Howell. DT has recently returned to this period with several excellent Sherlock Holmes pastiches, all based on real crimes. Slightly out of period are DT's two novels about gangster Sonny Tarrant. *Dancing in the Dark* is set in the 1940s but *Red Flowers for Lady Blue* goes back to 1936. Of his non-series novels *Captain Wunder* is a wonderful turn-of-the-century romp rather like Anthony Hope meets George Macdonald Fraser.

Novels

Inspector Swain series: *Mad Hatter Summer* (US 1983; as *Belladonna*, UK 1984), *The Ripper's Apprentice* (1986), *Jekyll, Alias Hyde* (1988), *The Arrest of Scotland Yard* (1993).

Sonny Tarrant series: *Dancing in the Dark* (1992), *Red Flowers for Lady Blue* (2000).

Sergeant Verity series as Francis Selwyn: *Cracksman on Velvet* (1974; as *Sergeant Verity and the Cracksman*, 1975), *Sergeant Verity and the Imperial Diamond* (1975), *Sergeant Verity Presents His Compliments* (1977), *Sergeant Verity and the Blood Royal* (1979), *Sergeant Verity and the Swell Mob* (1980), *The Hangman's Child* (2000).

Non-series: *The Blindfold Game* (1981), *Captain Wunder* (1981), *The Day the Sun Rose Twice* (1985), *The Raising of Lizzie Meek* (1993).

Short Stories

Sherlock Holmes series: *The Secret Cases of Sherlock Holmes* (1997), *Sherlock Holmes and the Running Noose* (2001), *Sherlock Holmes and the Voice from the Crypt* (2002).

Non-fiction (selective). *State Trials 1 – Treason and Libel* (1972), *State Trials 2 – The Public Conscience* (1972), *Honour Among Thieves* (1991), *Dead Giveaway* (1993), *Hanged in Error?* (1994), *The Victorian Underworld* (1998).
as Francis Selwyn: *Hitler's Englishman: the Crime of Lord Haw-Haw* (1987), *Rotten to the Core? The Life and Death of Neville Heath* (1988), *Gangland: The Case of Bentley and Craig* (1988; as *Nothing but Revenge*, 1991).

Full name: Donald Serrell Thomas.
Pen-names: Francis Selwyn.
Where to start: *Belladonna*.
Awards: Eric Gregory Award for Poetry (1964).
Similar stuff: Peter LOVESEY, Julian SYMONS.

Paul Thomas (b. 1951) Australia/New Zealand

Born in Britain but raised in New Zealand, PT now lives in Sydney, Australia where he is a full-time writer and journalist. He has written several sports books but has more recently established a reputation for his tough yet amusing hard-boiled crime novels. He won the Ned Kelly award for *Inside Dope*, where an ex-cop discovers the whereabouts of a lost haul of cocaine and tries to get to it before an Asian drug syndicate. This was the second of three novels featuring maverick New Zealand cop Detective-Sergeant Tito Ihaka. All of PT's novels feature the innocent or not so innocent finding themselves out of their depth in a world of crime where matters get far worse before they get better. Tight plotting, wry observation and clever dialogue have made PT's books something special.

Novels
Tito Ihaka series: *Old School Tie* (1994), *Inside Dope* (1995), *Guerilla Season* (1996).
Non-series: *Dirty Laundry* (1994), *Final Cut* (1999).

Where to start: *Dirty Laundry*.
Awards: Ned Kelly, best novel (1996).
Similar stuff: Shane MALONEY.

Ross Thomas (1926–95) US

RT has been called "America's best storyteller". He was certainly a craftsman with fascinating characters, clever and witty dialogue and convoluted plots. Most of his works are classifiable as political thrillers. He was for many years in public relations and later became a political campaign consultant during President Lyndon Johnson's administration. This doubtless contributed to the healthy cynicism that permeates his books. His first book, *The Cold War Swap*, introduced two of his endearing characters, "Mac" McCorkle and Mike Padillo, who run a saloon in Bonn. Unknown to "Mac", Padillo is an undercover agent. This first book is a fairly traditional spy novel, but later books shuffle the pack considerably. In *Cast a Yellow Shadow*, for example, McCorkle's wife is kidnapped in order that Padillo will assassinate a South African prime minister. Along similar lines are the three books featuring Quincy Durant and the rather corpulent Asian-American Artie Wu who run an agency in Los Angeles and become involved in investigating major political scams. RT wrote a much underrated series under the alias Oliver Bleeck. These featured Philip St Ives, a professional go-between who acts as an intermediary between insurance companies and thieves or kidnappers and the victim's family. The third book, *The Procane Chronicle,* is unusual in that St Ives has to recover a burglar's stolen plans for a major heist. It was one of RT's few books to be filmed, as *St Ives* (1976). RT was also involved in the screenplay for *Hammett* (1983) and provided the story-lines for *Bound by Honour* (1993) and *Bad Company* (1995).

Most of RT's books are stand-alone novels, though many fall into a pattern of political intrigue in some Third World country. *The Seersucker Whipsaw* is often regarded as his best in this field, where a con-man succeeds in making a cannibal the president of a newly emerging African country. Of his other books four stand out. *The Fools in Town Are On Our Side* is a labyrinthine-plotted novel of an ex-agent's scheme to corrupt an entire town. *If You Can't Be Good* is a puzzler about a Washington senator who resigns but refuses to help police in finding his daughter's murderer. In *The Money Harvest*, P.I. Jake Pope has to discover what secret 92-year old political adviser Crawdad Gilmore took to his grave when he was murdered. Finally *Briarpatch*, which won RT his second Edgar, deal with an investigator's quest for truth into the murder of his sister, a homicide detective.

Novels

McCorkle & Padillo series: *The Cold War Swap* (1966; as *Spy in the Vodka*, UK 1967), *Cast a Yellow Shadow* (1967), *The Backup Men* (1971), *Twilight at Mac's Place* (1990).

Wu & Durant series: *Chinaman's Chance* (1978), *Out on the Rim* (1987), *Voodoo, Ltd.* (1992).

Philip St. Ives series as Oliver Bleeck: *The Brass Go-Between* (1969), *Protocol for a Kidnapping* (1971), *The Procane Chronicle* (1972; as *The Thief Who Painted Sunlight*, UK 1972; as *St Ives*, US 1976), *The Highbinders* (1974), *No Questions Asked* (1976).

Non-series: *The Seersucker Whipsaw* (1967), *The Singapore Wink* (1969), *The Fools in Town are on Our Side* (1970), *The Porkchoppers* (1972), *If You Can't Be Good* (1973), *The Money Harvest* (1975), *Yellow-Dog Contract* (1977), *The Eighth Dwarf* (1979), *The Mordida Man* (1981), *Missionary Stew* (1983), *Briarpatch* (1984), *The Fourth Durango* (1989), *Ah, Treachery!* (1994).

Full name: Ross Elmore Thomas.
Pen-name: Oliver Bleeck.
Where to start: *Briarpatch* or *The Brass Go-Between.*
Awards: Edgar, best first novel (1967), best novel (1985), Swedish Academy of Detection, Best Foreign (1990).

Similar stuff: Brian GARFIELD, E. Howard HUNT, Julian RATHBONE
Final fact: RT's first book was written in just six weeks between political campaigns. It sold first time out and went on to win an Edgar award.

Jim Thompson (1906–77) US

It took ten years or more after JT's death but eventually, as he predicted, his works – none of which was in print when he died – were rediscovered and he acquired both a cult and a literary status. JT had started writing for magazines in the 1920s but for the first half of his life he held a variety of jobs, struggling through the Depression and producing guidebooks of the state for the Federal Writers' Project in Oklahoma. His first novel, *Now and On Earth* (1942), owed more to Erskine Caldwell and John Steinbeck. Virtually all of his books appeared as ephemeral paperback originals, now highly collected, but at the time considered little more than pulp. So it was not the literary establishment but the honest worker who first discovered the dark power in *The Killer Inside Me* (filmed 1976), the book that started the word-of-mouth recommendations. Through the first person narrator, the seemingly dim-witted small-town deputy sheriff, we find ourselves in the mind of a cunning, relentless and violent killer, driven by "the sickness". This became JT's hallmark. In the fifties no one could get inside the mind of the psychopath better than Thompson and he paved the way for such classics as Davis Grubb's *The Night of the Hunter* (1953), Robert BLOCH's *Psycho* and even Thomas HARRIS's *Red Dragon*. Unfortunately JT was always in need of money – he drank most of it away – and wrote fast. Sometimes this adds power and passion to his works, even when he recycled ideas. He reworked *The Killer Inside Me* at least twice, though always with new ideas. As *Pop. 1280* (filmed 1981 as *Coup de Torchon*), it became a period piece injected with black humour, with a killer driven by religious zeal. In *After Dark, My Sweet* (filmed 1990) it's a genuine simple soul but this time with a conscience who is prepared to sacrifice himself. JT depicted victims of drink in *The Alcoholics* and *The Nothing Man* where alcoholism is just one further trigger into the world of JT's "sickness". JT's world is brutal, but not necessarily irredeemable. We see something of this in the last hours of the dying hit-man in *Savage Night*. Many of JT's books have been filmed. A later novel, *The Grifters* (filmed 1990), about the schooling of a con-man, was ideal material for Donald E. WESTLAKE whose screenplay won him an Edgar award. *The Getaway*, a Bonnie-and-Clyde style story of a bungled bank robbery, was filmed twice (1972, 1994). JT flirted with Hollywood himself, working with Stanley Kubrick on the caper film *The Killing* (1956) and *Paths of Glory* (1957). He even wrote scripts for the TV series *Dr Kildare* and *Convoy* and produced one novelization based on *Ironside*, none of which were the best channels for his special talent. Kubrick believed that JT had written "the most chilling and believable first-person story of a criminally warped mind" that he had ever read, and through JT we can experience the horrors almost first hand.

Novels. *Nothing More Than Murder* (1949), *The Killer Inside Me* (1952), *Cropper's Cabin* (1952), *Recoil* (1953), *The Alcoholics* (1953), *Bad Boy* (1953), *Savage Night* (1953), *The Criminal* (1953), *The Golden Gizmo* (1954), *Roughneck* (1954), *A Swell-Looking Babe* (1954), *A Hell of a Woman* (1954), *The Nothing Man* (1954), *After Dark, My Sweet* (1955), *The Kill-Off* (1957), *Wild Town* (1957), *The Getaway* (1959), *The Transgressors* (1961), *The Grifters* (1963), *Pop. 1280* (1964), *Texas by the Tail* (1965), *South of Heaven* (1967), *Ironside* (1967), *Child of Rage* (1972), *King Blood* (1973).
Omnibus/Compilations. *Hard Core* (1986), *More Hardcore* (1987; includes first publication of *The Rip-Off*), *Fireworks, The Lost Writings* (1988).

Full name: James Myers Thompson.
Where to start: *The Killer Inside Me.*
Books about: *Jim Thompson: The Killers Inside Him* by Max Allan Collins & Ed Gorman (1983), *Sleep With the Devil*, Michael McCauley (1991), *Difficult Lives: Jim Thompson–David Goodis–Chester Himes*, James Sallis (1993), *Savage Art*, Robert Polito (1995).
Website: A Jim Thompson Linksite is at <www.geocities.com/SoHo/Lofts/6437/intro.htm>
Similar stuff: James M. Cain, James Lee BURKE, Thomas HARRIS, Charles WILLEFORD.
Final fact: JT had a cameo appearance as Mr Grayle in the 1975 film adaptation of Chandler's *Farewell, My Lovely*.

June Thomson (b. 1930) UK

A former teacher, JT turned full-time writer in 1977, producing her long-running series featuring Detective Chief Inspector Finch – renamed Rudd for US publication. These are solidly reliable novels of detective work set in Essex where JT lives. They are traditional only in form and structure, not in plot or setting. They are puzzle novels, but all strongly character driven. Finch is a victim of his background, his upbringing and his lack of family – he lives with his sister. JT uses this quiet reserve in enabling Finch/Rudd to understand other personal relationships such as the violent relationship between mother and son in *Deadly Relations*. There is also plenty of scope for skeletons in the closet. In *To Make a Killing* an artist discovers that his young lover may be his daughter. In *The Unquiet Grave* a son discovers that his father, now dead, may have lead a double life. In addition to this excellent series JT has also written several worthy Sherlock Holmes pastiches as well as a "biography" of Holmes and Watson.

Novels
Inspector Finch series (renamed Inspector Rudd in US from book two): *Not One of Us* (1971), *Death Cap* (1973), *The Long Revenge* (1974), *Case Closed* (1977), *A Question of Identity* (1977), *Deadly Relations* (1979; as *The Habit of Loving*, US

1979), *Alibi in Time* (1980), *Shadow of a Doubt* (1981), *To Make a Killing* (1982; as *Portrait of Lilith*, US 1983), *Sound Evidence* (1984), *A Dying Fall* (1985), *The Dark Stream* (1986), *No Flowers, by Request* (1987), *Rosemary for Remembrance* (1988), *The Spoils of Time* (1989), *Past Reckoning* (1990), *Foul Play* (1991), *Burden of Innocence* (1996), *The Unquiet Grave* (2000).

Short Stories

Flowers for the Dead (1992).

Sherlock Holmes series: *The Secret Files of Sherlock Holmes* (1990), *The Secret Chronicles of Sherlock Holmes* (1992), *The Secret Journals of Sherlock Holmes* (1993), *The Secret Documents of Sherlock Holmes* (1997) and the "biography" *Holmes and Watson: A Study in Friendship* (1995).

Full name: June Valerie Thomson.
Where to start: *Not One of Us*.
Awards: Special Sherlock (2001).
Similar stuff: Patricia MOYES, Dorothy SIMPSON.
Final fact: Finch's name was changed to Rudd in the US because JT's American publisher already had a series featuring an Inspector Finch written by Margaret Erskine.

Ernest Tidyman (1928–84) US

ET is best known as the creator of the black P.I. John Shaft, a character who became internationally known through the film, *Shaft* (1971; remade 2000), starring Richard Roundtree, and the hit film theme by Isaac Hayes. In the books Shaft is a high-living, angry and vengeful New York P.I., living in Greenwich Village but invariably operating in his native Harlem. He tries to keep his own counsel, distrusting most whites but also avoiding black radicals or Mobsters. In *Shaft* he is hired to find the kidnapped daughter of a Harlem ganglord. The sequel, *Shaft Among the Jews* takes him into the diamond business. The third novel, *Shaft's Big Score*, where investigating the death of an old friend puts Shaft in the midst of two rival gangs, was also filmed (1972), but Tidyman was not involved with the third film, *Shaft in Africa* (1973). The TV series *Shaft* (1973–4), also starring Richard Roundtree, was less successful. Despite its title, *Goodbye, Mr. Shaft* was not the final novel, but we do see the end of him in *The Last Shaft*, which was only published in Britain. Shaft was the first major black P.I. in fiction, certainly the first who was cool, and a winner. Although ET was white, the National Association for the Advancement of Coloured People (NAACP) were so impressed by the portrayal and impact of Shaft that they gave ET the NAACP Image Award, one of the very few whites to receive it.

ET had been a journalist and reporter before he turned to writing full-time in 1966. His early books range from a look at the sexual freedom of the hippy movement in *Flower Power* (1968) to an account of one of the key battles of WW2 in which he was involved, *The Anzio Death Trap* (1968). He wrote two true-crime books: *Dummy* (filmed 1979), about two murder cases in Chicago in the sixties, and *Big Bucks*, about the Plymouth Mail Robbery. He also wrote *Line of Duty*, set in the Cleveland Police Department, with a sniper and a cop-turned-assassin. But apart from *Shaft* he is best known for his screenplays for *The French Connection* (1971), for which he received an Oscar and an Edgar award, and *High Plains Drifter* (1972), a remarkable supernatural western revenge story, which he later turned into a novel. ET worked mostly in TV and films from 1975, including *To Kill a Cop* (TV 1978), *Guyana Tragedy* (TV 1980) about cult leader Jim Jones, and *Alcatraz* (TV 1980).

Novels
Shaft series: *Shaft* (1970), *Shaft Among the Jews* (1972), *Shaft's Big Score* (1972), *Goodbye, Mr Shaft* (1973), *Shaft Has a Ball* (1973), *Shaft's Carnival of Killers* (1974), *The Last Shaft* (1975).
Non-series: *High Plains Drifter* (1973), *Line of Duty* (1974), *Table Stakes* (1978).
Non-fiction. *Dummy* (1974), *Big Bucks* (1982).

Where to start: *Shaft*.
Awards: Edgar, best screenplay (1972).
Similar stuff: See Ed LACY and Clarence COOPER, Jr. for other early perspectives on black detectives and criminals.
Final fact: ET had sold the idea of *Shaft* to his publisher but didn't have a name for his hero. According to his son, ET looked out of the publisher's window and saw a sign saying "Fire Shaft".

Mark Timlin (b. 1950) UK

MT is the author of the Nick Sharman P.I. books. Sharman is an ex-cop who was invalided out of the Met. just moments ahead of being thrown out for stealing drugs. Set up as a small-time investigator in South London Sharman soon enters a world of mega-violence. Sharman has been likened to SPILLANE's Mike Hammer, and certainly there's more violence than detection, but Sharman's more humorous, his world more credible, and his actions more probable. There is also a poignancy throughout the series as many of Sharman's friends (especially the females) meet violent ends. MT used to work in the music industry and this and the porn industry provide the background for most of the early novels. There's a change of pace with *Hearts of Stone*, where Sharman becomes a barman, but he regains his office in *Falls the Shadow*, one of the best of the series, where he acts more like a detective while on the trail of a gang of neo-Nazis. The world of Sharman bears some comparison to Derek RAYMOND's "Factory" series, and MT was a strong advocate of Raymond's work. Four books were adapted for TV, starting with *The Turnaround* (1995), in which Sharman becomes a prime suspect when a key witness is killed. A fifth TV episode, *Episode 4*, was specially written by Mick Ford. Amongst MT's other books, mostly pseudonymous, is *Champagne Sister* as by Johnny Angelo, about sexy female P.I. Marianne

Champagne, which includes links with the Sharman novel *Zip Gun Boogie*.

Novels

Nick Sharman series: *A Good Year for the Roses* (1988), *Romeo's Tune* (1990), *Gun Street Girl* (1990), *Take the A-Train* (1991), *The Turnaround* (1991), *Zip Gun Boogie* (1992), *Hearts of Stone* (1992), *Falls the Shadow* (1993), *Ashes by Now* (1993), *Pretend We're Dead* (1994), *Paint it Black* (1995), *Find My Way Home* (1996), *A Street That Rhymed with 3AM* (1997), *Dead Flowers* (1998), *Quick Before They Catch Us* (1999), *All the Empty Places* (2000).
as Johnny Angelo: *Champagne Sister* (1994).
as Jim Ballantyne: *The Torturer* (1995).
Short Stories. *Sharman and Other Filth* (1996).

Pen-names: April Amour, Johnny Angelo, Jim Ballantyne, Holly Delatour, Martin Milk, Tony Williams.
Where to start: Best start at the beginning but for a sample try either *Falls the Shadow* or the stories in *Sharman and Other Filth*.
Website: <www.nicksharman.co.uk/>
Similar stuff: Nicholas BLINCOE, Derek RAYMOND.
Final fact: MT reports that he always drives the same American cars as Sharman. When MT gets a new (old) one, so does Sharman. They also smoke the same cigarettes.

Charles Todd US

CT is the pen-name of an American mother-and-son writing team, Caroline and Charles, who became an instant hit with their first book, the Edgar-nominated *A Test of Wills*. Set in 1919, it features Inspector Ian Rutledge who had served in the Great War but has now returned to his job at Scotland Yard. He suffers from shell shock and is also haunted by the spirit of a soldier, Hamish, he had been forced to execute in the trenches. This powerful personification and guilt proves to be a significant driving force. The second novel, *Wings of Fire*, which delved into childhood secrets, was shortlisted for the Ellis Peters Historical Dagger award. The stories create a tangible brooding post-war atmosphere where so much of the Old World had been blown away by the loss of thousands of its sons. Rutledge takes on difficult cases all of them with secrets tucked away in the past, and all of them requiring much soul searching. It's a rewarding series and a strong reminder of lost innocence.

Novels

Ian Rutledge series: *A Test of Wills* (1996), *Wings of Fire* (1998), *Search the Dark* (1999), *Legacy of the Dead* (2000), *Watchers of Time* (2001), *A Fearsome Doubt* (2002).

Awards: Barry, best first novel (1997), Herodotus, best short story (2001).
Website: <www.charlestodd.com>
Similar stuff: Rennie AIRTH.
Final fact: Caroline and Charles commented that they never expected anyone to

publish the first novel and were unprepared for the nominations and enthusiasm that followed. They have grown fond of the solo "Charles Todd" alias and plan to leave him as the listed author rather than as a collaboration.

Marilyn Todd (b. 1958) UK

MT is the author of a series of bawdy Roman mystery novels, set in 13BC, featuring Claudia Seferius, dubbed by the *Sunday Express* "an arrogant superbitch". The books are almost what you might expect if Jackie Collins wrote Lindsey DAVIS. Claudia turns high-class prostitute in *I, Claudia*, in order to meet her gambling debts, but becomes the prime suspect when her clients turn up dead. Her husband is dead by *Virgin Territory* and Claudia has to earn a living. She is not a sleuth, but the jobs she takes on land her in trouble and she has to solve the problems, always with great flair and panache, and often with the help of Marcus Cornelius Orbilio, charismatic member of the Security Police. MT also writes short stories and ran her own secretarial agency before she turned full-time writer.

Novels

Claudia series: *I, Claudia* (1995), *Virgin Territory* (1996), *Man Eater* (1997), *Wolf Whistle* (1998), *Jail Bait* (1999), *Black Salamander* (2000), *Dream Boat* (2001), *Rogue Male* (2002).

Similar stuff: Lindsey DAVIS, Steven SAYLOR.

Final fact: MT's family tree is full of fascinating antecedents. Her grandfather used to fish suicides out of the Thames when a child but he got more if they were found on the Surrey side than the Middlesex so he used to drag them across. Her great-grandfather was Queen Victoria's cake-maker and became involved in the hunt for Jack the Ripper.

Masako Togawa (b. 1933) Japan

MT is one of Japan's leading writers of dark psychological mysteries. Only four of her books have been translated into English, but they are a good representation of her work. Her first novel, *The Master Key*, won the Edogawa Rampo award. It is a painstakingly cleverly constructed novel which reveals the causes behind a series of deaths through viewpoints of lonely elderly women living in an old apartment block. Her next book, *The Lady Killer*, which has been optioned for filming, was a best seller and established her name. It concerns a married man who haunts bars and nightclubs during the week looking for women. When some of his conquests turn up dead he becomes the prime suspect and it is down to his lawyer to find the evidence to prove him innocent. In *Slow Fuse* a student pleads guilty to a crime that has never happened and a psychiatrist tries to get to the bottom of the mystery. *A Kiss of Fire* concerns three men, once childhood friends who had played tragically with matches, and now, years later, two of them, a fireman and a detective, hunt the third, an arsonist. All of MT's books are complex studies of the human psyche and her work should be far better known outside Japan. She has been alikened to P.D. JAMES but the work of Minette WALTERS has a much closer affinity.

Novels. *The Master Key* (1957; UK 1984), *The Lady Killer* (1963; UK 1985), *Slow Fuse* (1967; US 1995), *A Kiss of Fire* (1985; US 1988).

Where to start: *The Lady Killer.*
Awards: Edogawa Rampo award (1979).
Similar stuff: Minette WALTERS.
Final fact: MT began her career as a nightclub singer and wrote her first book back stage between acts.

Rebecca Tope (b. 1948) UK

The adage "write about what you know" has worked admirably for RT. Her two series both reflect different careers during her life. Raised on farms in Cheshire and Devon and now living on a smallholding in rural Herefordshire, RT uses the farming milieu for her books featuring Constable (later Detective Constable) Den Cooper. RT also worked for seven years as an assistant undertaker and this gave her the expertise for her series featuring Drew Slocombe, an undertaker who never takes anything for granted. In both series RT looks at murders that could so easily be natural deaths. A farmer's body in his own slurry pit in *A Dirty Death* or an animal right's activist killed by a horse at a hunt protest in *Death of a Friend*, or the corpse that looked far too healthy in *Dark Undertakings.* Reviewers all agree that RT is an author to watch. By profession she is a milk recorder, monitoring milk quality, but she also runs her own small publishing company specializing in Victorian books but which has also published her own religious book *In Search of Life's Meaning*, written with Raymond Matley.

Novels
Den Cooper series: *A Dirty Death* (1999), *Death of a Friend* (2000), *A Death to Record* (2001).
Drew Slocombe series: *Dark Undertakings* (1999), *Grave Concerns* (2000).

Real name: Rebecca Smith.
Pen-names: Rebecca Tope.
Where to start: *Dark Undertakings.*
Website: <www.rebeccatope.com>
Similar stuff: Kate ELLIS, Margaret MARON.
Final fact: RT's experiences whilst working at the undertakers had some daunting moments. She recalls: "One of the most unforgettable jobs I ever had to do was photograph a young mother holding her dead baby. Her courage was enormous and far from unusual. Meeting families soon after a bereavement is guaranteed to increase respect for human beings – all ages, all situations behave with tremendous dignity."

Peter Tremayne (b. 1943) UK

Under his real name PT is a renowned Celtic scholar with over 30 non-fiction books to his credit, mostly meticulously researched volumes on Celtic life and history, starting with *Wales – a Nation Again* (1968). However, under his main pen-name, PT initially established a reputation as a writer of horror and fantasy fiction starting with *Hound of Frankenstein* (1977). Those books that were not recursive fantasies usually drew upon Celtic legend. He created a new persona, Peter MacAlan for adventure novels, most of them espionage and war thrillers. Tucked amongst those titles, however, was one, *Confession*, about an investigation into the purported suicide of a friar in the Vatican sanctuary, which was a more traditional crime novel and some indication of later books. It was not until 1993 that PT created the character of Sister Fidelma. Fidelma is a *dálaigh* or advocate of the Brehon Court of Ireland in the mid-7th century AD. In the first novel, *Absolution by Murder*, she is a representative at the all-important Synod of Whitby called by the Angle king of Northumbria in 663, where murder nearly disrupts the proceedings. PT is careful not to confine Fidelma solely to Ireland and in *Shroud for the Archbishop* she travels to Rome, *Act of Mercy* takes place at sea and *Smoke in the Wind* is in Wales. PT's knowledge of Celtic life and especially of Celtic law provides the twists and turns for this fascinating series which is one of a kind. When not deep in Celtic lore PT has also written several literary biographies.

Novels

Sister Fidelma series: *Absolution by Murder* (1994), *Shroud for the Archbishop* (1995), *Suffer Little Children* (1995), *The Subtle Serpent* (1996), *The Spider's Web* (1997), *Valley of the Shadow* (1998), *The Monk Who Vanished* (1999), *Act of Mercy* (1999), *Our Lady of Darkness* (2000), *Smoke in the Wind* (2001), *The Haunted Abbot* (2002).

Raffles series: *The Return of Raffles* (1981).

Non-series as Peter MacAlan: *The Judas Battalion* (1983), *The Confession* (1985), *Kitchener's Gold* (1986), *The Valkyrie Directive* (1987), *The Doomsday Decree* (1988), *Fireball* (1990), *The Windsor Protocol* (1993).

Short Stories

Sister Fidelma series: *Hemlock at Vespers* (2000).

Non-fiction. *H. Rider Haggard: A Voice from the Infinite* (1978), *By Jove, Biggles! The Life of Captain W.E. Johns* (1981; as *Biggles! The Life Story of Capt. W.E. Johns*, 1993), *The Last Adventurer: The Life of Talbot Mundy* (US 1984).

Real name: Peter John Philip Berresford Ellis.
Pen-names: Peter MacAlan, Peter Tremayne.
Where to start: *Absolution by Murder*.
Awards: *Irish Post* award for Irish historical studies (1988).
Website: <www.sisterfidelma.com>
Similar stuff: No one else has worked in PT's time period, but a similar atmosphere prevails in the Cadfael books of Ellis PETERS and the Dame Frevisse books by Margaret FRAZER.

Final fact: PT is one of the few people who can speak the Cornish language and is a Bard of the Cornish Gorsedd.

Miles Tripp (1923–2001) UK

MT served in the RAF Bomber Command during WW2 and his experiences, plus his later searches to find his former comrades twenty years later, form the basis for his fascinating book *The Eighth Passenger* (1969). MT qualified as a solicitor in 1950 and served for 30 years on the legal staff of the Charity Commission. His legal training came in useful in several of his novels, such as the courtroom drama *The Dimensions of Deceit*. He also used barristers in several books, including his series about adventurer Hugo Baron, a barrister turned espionage agent who works for DIECAST (Destruction of International Espionage and Counter Activities for Stability) – a rather typical sixties spy series. It took MT some years to become a regular writer. Despite his first novel in 1952 (*Faith is a Windsock* inspired by his wartime experiences), he did not really hit his stride until 1963 with *Kilo Forty*, a novel of murder and intrigue on the shores of the Red Sea. His books are characterized by the idiosyncratic. They are nearly all suspense novels where individuals (frequently vulnerable women) are threatened and taken to breaking point by someone known or unknown, either a con-man or a killer. *A Man Without Friends*, *Woman at Risk*, *Some Predators are Male*, *The Frightened Wife* all fit into that category. Sometimes the victim fights back – *Malice and the Maternal Instinct*, *Cruel Victim*, *Video Vengeance*, *A Woman of Conscience*. He also delighted in strange, quirky and obsessive people – a French doll manufacturer in *A Glass of Red Wine*, a con-man who reads handwriting in *A Man Without Friends*, a shoe fetishist in *High Heels*. Most of his later books featured English P.I. John Samson, though the pattern and formula of the books remained much the same.

Novels

John Samson series: *Obsession* (1973), *A Woman in Bed* (1976), *The Once a Year Man* (1977), *The Wife-Smuggler* (1978), *Cruel Victim* (1979), *High Heels* (1980), *One Lover Too Many* (1983), *Some Predators are Male* (1986), *Death of a Man-Tamer* (1987), *The Frightened Wife* (1987), *The Cords of Vanity* (1989), *Video Vengeance* (1990), *Samson and the Greek Delilah* (1995), *The Suitcase Killings* (1997), *Deadly Ordeal* (2000).

Hugo Baron series as [John] Michael Brett: *Diecast* (1963), *A Plague of Dragons* (1965), *A Cargo of Spent Evil* (1966).

Non-series: *The Image of Man* (1955), *A Glass of Red Wine* (1960), *Kilo Forty* (1963), *A Quartet of Three* (1965), *The Chicken* (1966; combined with *Zilla*, 1968), *One is One* (1968), *Malice and the Maternal Instinct* (1969), *A Man Without Friends* (1970), *Five Minutes With a Stranger* (1971), *The Claws of God* (1972), *Woman at Risk* (1974), *Going Solo* (1981), *A Charmed Death* (1984), *The Dimensions of Deceit* (1993), *A Woman of Conscience* (1994), *Extreme Provocation* (1995).

Full name: Miles Barton Tripp.

Pen-name: [John] Michael Brett.
Where to start: *Kilo Forty* if you can find it or *The Dimensions of Deceit.*
Similar stuff: Michael ALLEGRETTO, Robert RICHARDSON.

M. J. Trow (b. 1949) UK

Welsh author MJT studied history at King's College, London and became a teacher and lecturer. After his marriage he settled in the Isle of Wight and this became the setting for his first novel where he sort to rectify the balance in the attitude of Sherlock Holmes to Inspector Lestrade. This series is for all lovers of gaslight mysteries. MJT's Lestrade is a more astute, methodical and quick-thinking detective who solves a variety of weird and wonderful cases, mostly based on real historical events. They range from suffragettes to death in the royal household to Jack the Ripper. MJT's interest in Jack the Ripper lead to a further study of the case, *The Many Faces of Jack the Ripper.* MJT has revealed his skills as a criminologist, having written several books on notorious crimes or miscarriages of justice, starting with the infamous Derek Bentley case, *Let Him Have It, Chris.* More recently MJT has started a new series featuring Peter Maxwell, a teacher, whose attempts to solve the death of one of his students, ends up with him being suspended and under suspicion by the police. Thereafter he acquires the nickname "Mad Max" and becomes a smart amateur sleuth in later books, all of which are clever puzzles and slightly more light-hearted than the first.

Novels

Inspector Lestrade series: *The Adventures of Inspector Lestrade* (1985; as *The Supreme Adventure of Inspector Lestrade*, US 1985), *Brigade: the Further Adventures of Inspector Lestrade* (1986), *Lestrade and the Hallowed House* (1987), *Lestrade and the Leviathan* (1987), *Lestrade and the Brother of Death* (1988), *Lestrade and the Ripper* (1988), *Lestrade and the Guardian Angel* (1990), *Lestrade and the Deadly Game* (1990), *Lestrade and the Gift of the Prince* (1991), *Lestrade and the Magpie* (1991), *Lestrade and the Dead Man's Hand* (1992), *Lestrade and the Sign of Nine* (1992), *Lestrade and the Sawdust Ring* (1993), *Lestrade and the Mirror of Murder* (1993), *Lestrade and the Kiss of Horus* (1995), *Lestrade and the Devil's Own* (1996).

Peter Maxwell series: *Maxwell's House* (1994), *Maxwell's Flame* (1995), *Maxwell's Movie* (1998), *Maxwell's War* (1999), *Maxwell's Curse* (2000), *Maxwell's Ride* (2000), *Maxwell's Reunion* (2001).

Non-fiction. *Let Him Have it, Chris* (1990), *The Wigwam Murder* (1994), *The Many Faces of Jack the Ripper* (1997), *Hess: The British Conspiracy* (1999), *Who Killed Kit Marlowe?* (2001).

Full name: Meirion James Trow
Similar stuff: Anne PERRY, Donald THOMAS, June THOMSON.
Final fact: MJT is an expert on the British cavalry and collects military uniforms.

James Tucker, *see under pseudonym* Bill James

Peter Turnbull (b. 1950) UK

PT was a social worker for 23 years, most of that time in Glasgow. He turned to writing full-time in 1995, settling back in his native Yorkshire. He has used his knowledge of the inner-city social ills to good effect in his two main series, both of which are excellent examples of the police procedural. The first is set in "P" Division, a fictional police division in Glasgow under Inspector Fabian Donoghue. The novels develop many of the characters in the station without focusing on anyone in particular. The series is noted not only for its suspenseful atmosphere and realism but also for its tight plotting and portrayal of local colour. Although the first novel *Deep and Crisp and Even* has the inevitable serial killer plot, it remains one of his best books. Later novels are distinguished by a deviousness in their depiction of the victims. In *Dead Knock* an anonymous woman anounces her own impending murder which she seems to submit to without a struggle. In *Two Way Cut* the body is found mutilated but it's been washed and dressed. In *Condition Purple* it's a drug addict with a clue tattooed on her groin, while the title of *The Man With No Face* describes the condition of the latest victim. Despite the unrelenting darkness of these novels they are soft when compared to *Embracing Skeletons*, which deals with child abuse and a satanic cult. PT is unrestrained in his descriptions and the novel has a powerful impact. Since his move to Yorkshire PT has developed a new series featuring Detective Inspector Hennessey of the Vale of York Police, with his colleague Detective Sergeant Yellich. This is another no-holds-barred series and PT continues to produce complex plots and strong characters. PT has also written his own exposé about Jack the Ripper in *The Killer Who Never Was*.

Novels

"P" Division series: *Deep and Crisp and Even* (1981), *Dead Knock* (1982), *Fair Friday* (1983), *Big Money* (1984), *Two Way Cut* (1988), *Condition Purple* (1989), *And Did Murder Him* (1991), *Long Day Monday* (1993), *The Killing Floor* (1995), *The Man With No Face* (1998).
Carmen Pharaoh series: *Embracing Skeletons* (1996).
Chief Inspector Hennessey series: *Fear of Drowning* (2000), *Deathtrap* (2000), *Perils and Dangers* (2001), *The Return* (2001), *After the Flood* (2002).
Non-series: *The Claws of the Gryphon* (1986), *The Justice Game: The Lady from Rome* (1990).
Non-fiction. *The Killer Who Never Was* (1996).

Full name: Peter John Turnbull.
Where to start: *Deep and Crisp and Even* or *Fear of Drowning*. You need to work up to *Embracing Skeletons*.
Similar stuff: Quintin JARDINE, John HARVEY.

Scott Turow (b. 1949) US

When *Presumed Innocent* hit the bestseller lists ST established the legal thriller as a major marketing genre. Although he has written only five novels these have kept him as the most highly regarded of writers of legal dramas with over 20 million books in print worldwide. ST is still a practising attorney in Chicago. His experiences as a student at Harvard Law School provided the basis for his first book, the autobiographical *One L* (1977; as *What They Really Teach You at Harvard Law School*, UK 1988). It was 10 years before he achieved his goal and wrote his first novel. *Presumed Innocent* (filmed 1990) is a tense story about deputy prosecutor, Rusty Sabich, who is asked by his boss to investigate the rape and murder of one of his colleagues, Carolyn Polhernus, who had once been Rusty's lover. Rusty finds himself accused of her murder and it is the brilliant defence by attorney Sandy Stern that is the highlight of the novel. Stern returns in *The Burden of Proof* (filmed 1992) where his wife commits suicide and the emotionally racked Stern tries to get to the truth of her death. These novels remain two of the very best legal thrillers of the last 20 years. ST's books are set in Kindle County, a fictionalized version of Chicago. *Pleading Guilty* is a change of pace, dealing with an attorney and ex-cop who has to find a colleague who has vanished with over $5 million dollars, but he returned to the court room with *The Law of Our Fathers*. His latest, *Personal Injuries*, deals with the rising trend in personal injury claims. All of ST's books are packed with tense, emotional, compulsive plots.

Novels

Kindle County series: *Presumed Innocent* (1987), *The Burden of Proof* (1990), *Pleading Guilty* (1993), *The Law of Our Fathers* (1996), *Personal Injuries* (1999).

Editor. *Guilty as Charged* (1996).

Where to start: *Presumed Inocent*.

Awards: CWA Silver Dagger (1987), Swedish Academy of Detection, Best Foreign (1988).

Website: <www.scottturow.com>

Similar stuff: William BERNHARDT, John GRISHAM.

Final fact: ST represented one client, Alejandro Hernandez, who was eventually released in 1995 after being exonerated of a murder for which he had been sentenced to death.

Dorothy Uhnak (b. 1933) US

DU, born in the Bronx, was for fourteen years (1953–67) a New York Transit cop, rising to assistant to the Chief and receiving the Outstanding Police Duty Medal. In 1967, however, she felt forced to resign as a result of sex discrimination and her frustration poured out in her account of her experiences, *Policewoman: A Young Woman's Initiation into the Realities of Justice*, and into her first three novels. These featured Christie Opara, a Uhnak-like officer who braves sexism and discrimination in order to perform her job. The first book, *The Bait* (filmed TV 1973), where Christie acts as bait to catch a killer, won the Edgar for best first novel. *The Ledger*, where Christie goes undercover to infiltrate a drug ring, was the basis for the TV film and subsequent series *Get Christie Love!* (1974–75). Starting with *Law and Order* (filmed TV 1976), DU dropped the series character and concentrated on one-off novels and these are her best work. *Law and Order* and her latest novel, *Codes of Betrayal*, both explore changing attitudes and prejudices within the force and organized crime, over several generations. *The Investigation* draws upon the real-life Alice Crimmins case with an investigation into the abduction and murder of two young boys. It was adapted as an episode of *Kojak*, "The Price of Justice" (1987). Probably DU's most powerful book is *False Witness* (filmed TV 1989), in which a celebrity is raped and nearly killed and an ambitious female Assistant D.A. is determined to find the perpetrator. All of DU's novels are full of strong characters, vivid crime scenes and authentic police procedures (almost to overkill). Her work was an inspiration and encouragement to a new generation of women writers.

Novels
Christie Opara series: *The Bait* (1968), *The Witness* (1969), *The Ledger* (1970).
Non-series: *Law and Order* (1973), *The Investigation* (1977), *False Witness* (1981), *Victims* (1985), *The Ryer Avenue Story* (1993), *Codes of Betrayal* (1997).
Non-fiction. *Policewoman* (1964).

Where to start: *Law and Order*.
Awards: Edgar, best first novel (1969).
Similar stuff: Lillian O'DONNELL, Sandra SCOPPETTONE, Teri WHITE.

Michael Underwood (1916–92) UK

MU's writing career spanned 40 years and nearly 50 books. He was, by profession, a lawyer and barrister, having been called to the Bar in 1939. After the War he worked in the Public Prosecutions office for 30 years until his retirement. His books all show this thorough knowledge of the due process of law, in all its detail, following first the investigation of the trial, the gathering of evidence and then the presentation in court. They are thus usually combined police and legal procedurals. Most of his books fall into one of four main series, two of which overlap. His first character was Inspector (later Superintendent) Simon Manton who, in his first two books, finds he is investigating murders in court. In *Murder on Trial* a man accused of shooting a policeman is shot when he steps into the witness box, while in *Murder Made Absolute* a barrister dies of poison during a divorce trial. The Nick Atwell series starts in similar fashion with the deaths of and threats to several jurors in *The Juror*. Both Monk and Atwell are methodical policemen, though Atwell has the added bonus of help from his former policewoman wife, Clare. MU wrote two novels featuring lawyer Richard Monk, but his main legal series began with barrister Martin Ainsworth and then shifted to Rosa Epton. In *The Unprofessional Spy*, she appears briefly as a clerk in a solicitor's office and in later books becomes an efficient solicitor in her own series. These two series depict the change in the legal profession during this period. Ainsworth is a barrister of the old school and in his first novel he is recruited as a spy to rekindle an affair with a woman he knew in Germany before the War. *Reward for a Defector* also deals with a former agent and there is a strong Cold War feel about these novels. Rosa Epton, on the other hand, is a skilful and ambitious woman whose books represent the rise of feminism in the seventies and eighties. The Epton books are amongst MU's best with ingenious crimes painstakingly resolved. *Death In Camera*, in which a Judge meets his death, seemingly by accident, at the opening of a new Crown Court is generally regarded as the best of the series. Most of his non-series books are also legal procedurals and courtroom dramas, though *Victim of Circumstance*, in which a man who plots murder is himself murdered, is an unusual diversion. MU was an old-style craftsman whose work remained solid and reliable to the very end.

Novels

Simon Manton series: *Murder on Trial* (1954), *Murder Made Absolute* (1955), *Death on Remand* (1956), *False Witness* (1957), *Lawful Pursuit* (1958), *Arm of the Law* (1959), *Cause of Death* (1960), *Death by Misadventure* (1960), *Adam's Case* (1961), *The Case Against Phillip Quest* (1962), *Girl Found Dead* (1963), *The Crime of Colin Wise* (1964), *The Anxious Conspirator* (1965).

Martin Ainsworth series: *The Unprofessional Spy* (1964), *The Shadow Game* (1969), *A Trout in the Milk* (1971), *Reward for a Defector* (1973), *A Pinch of Snuff* (1974).

Richard Monk series: *The Man Who Died on Friday* (1967), *The Man Who Killed Too Soon* (1968).

Nick Atwell series: *The Juror* (1975), *Menaces, Menaces* (1976), *Murder With Malice* (1977), *The Fatal Trip* (1977), *Crooked Wood* (1978).

Rosa Epton series: *Crime Upon Crime* (1980), *Double Jeopardy* (1981), *Goddess of Death* (1982), *A Party to Murder* (1983), *Death in Camera* (1984), *The Hidden Man* (1985), *Death at Deepwood Grange* (1986), *The Uninvited Corpse* (1987), *The Injudicious Judge* (1987), *Dual Enigma* (1988), *A Compelling Case* (1989), *Rosa's Dilemma* (1990), *A Dangerous Business* (1990), *The Seeds of Murder* (1991), *Guilty Conscience* (1992). Also in Ainsworth novels *Unprofessional Spy* and *A Pinch of Snuff*.

Non-series: *A Crime Apart* (1966), *The Silent Liars* (1970), *Shem's Demise* (1970), *Anything But the Truth* (1978), *Smooth Justice* (1979), *Victim of Circumstances* (1979), *A Clear Case of Suicide* (1980), *The Hand of Fate* (1981).

Real name: John Michael Evelyn.
Pen-name: Michael Underwood.
Where to start: *Crime Upon Crime*.
Similar stuff: Michael GILBERT.

Andrew Vachss (b. 1942) US

AV's work is amongst the bleakest and most merciless in crime fiction and is most frightening because just a little too much of it is grounded in reality. AV is a criminal lawyer and a children's rights attorney, who began life as a social worker and director of a maximum security juvenile detention centre. He has seen more than his fair share of abused and neglected children and has written about this in *The Life-Style Violent Juvenile* (1979) and *The Child Abuse-Delinquency Connection* (1989). He has also fought against it with such vehemence in the courts that he broke his wrist. A national register of sex offenders has been developed in the US based on legislation that AV drafted. He seeks an outlet for all the tension created by these horrors through his fiction in the shape of the mononymic Burke, an ex-con turned soldier of fortune who, rather like Don PENDLETON's Executioner, tracks down and exacts retribution upon the deviants and molesters in society. Unlike Pendleton's Executioner, this is not mindless mayhem but well-plotted, reasoned, taut, edge-of-the-seat investigations. The set-up with Burke is perhaps the least likely aspect of the series. There's something of the pulp hero about him, like Doc Savage and Batman (about whom AV has also written a powerful novel). Burke lives in a special hideout and has a group of rather bizarre characters who help him in his crusade. Despite their sales, the Burke books have yet to win an award in America, though they have been recognized in France and Japan. They have been called the darkest of noir, and indeed AV was happily adopted by the devotees of horror fiction or dark suspense, a category almost invented for Vachss. AV has written just one non-series book to date, *Shella*, which includes a Burke-like character nicknamed Ghost, himself a victim of child abuse and now a contract killer. AV has produced several comic strips and graphic novels of which *Hard Looks* provides a good cross section. His stories, like red-hot splinters, are collected as *Born Bad*.

Novels

Burke series: *Flood* (1985), *Strega* (1987), *Blue Belle* (1988), *Hard Candy* (1989), *Blossom* (1990), *Sacrifice* (1991), *Down in the Zero* (1994), *Footsteps of the Hawk* (1995), *False Allegations* (1996), *Safe House* (1998), *Choice of Evil* (1999), *Dead & Gone* (2000), *Pain Management* (2001).

Non-series: *Shella* (1993), *Batman: The Ultimate Evil* (1995).

Short Stories. *Born Bad* (1994), *Everybody Pays* (1999).

Graphic Novels/Collections. *Hard Looks* (1992; exp. 1994), *Underground* (1993), *Predator: Race War* (1994), *Batman: The Ultimate Evil* (1995), *Cross* (1995).

Full name: Andrew Henry Vachss.
Where to start: *Flood.*
Awards: Grand Prix de Littérature Policière (1988), Japanese Maltese Falcon (1989).

Website: <www.vachss.com>
Similar stuff: Joe R. LANSDALE and Ed GORMAN for other dark suspense.
Final fact: AV wears an eyepatch over his right eye as a result of an accident in his childhood. He also suffers from malaria caught when he visited Biafra in 1969.

Jonathan Valin (b. 1948) US

JV is a former lecturer in English who became a freelance writer in 1979. His books are set in his home city of Cincinnati and feature Harry Stoner, a former Pinkerton agent and D.A. investigator before becoming a solo P.I. Big and strong (an ex-footballer) Stoner can well look after himself, and he needs to, because his cases frequently bring him into violent confrontations. He broods about the social decay of Cincinnati and the decline in family values where much of the conflict he encounters arises. In the first book, *The Lime Pit*, it's a young girl who has become involved with a snuff-movie maker. In *Final Notice* (filmed TV 1989) it's a psycho who mutilates pictures of women before moving on to the real thing. In *Day of Wrath* it's a missing teenager, while in *Missing* it's a girl's lover who disappears. Stoner's experiences bite into his soul and, as the series progresses, we find him becoming less moralistic and puritanical and more uncertain about the distinction between right and wrong. Different critics have their different favourites in the series, showing that is has something for everyone. *Extenuating Circumstances*, where a husband vanishes on Independence Day, won JV the Shamus award and *Second Chance*, where the daughter of a suicide mother vanishes, was also nominated for the award. After *Missing* JV felt a need to recharge his batteries and has since been editing film and music magazines.

Novels

Harry Stoner series: *The Lime Pit* (1980), *Final Notice* (1980), *Dead Letter* (1981), *Day of Wrath* (1982), *Natural Causes* (1984), *Life's Work* (1986), *Fire Lake* (1987), *Extenuating Circumstances* (1989), *Second Chance* (1991), *The Music Lovers* (1993), *Missing* (1995).

Full name: Jonathan Louis Valin.
Where to start: *The Lime Pit.*
Awards: Shamus, best hardcover novel (1990).
Similar stuff: James CRUMLEY (for attitude), Stephen GREENLEAF.
Final fact: JV's first novel, *The Celestial Railroad*, was written for fun and he's never sought to have it published. However he started on a second book when he was approached to ghost-write someone's autobiography, which fell through, but her agent learned of JV's work in progress, asked to see it, and JV finished the rest of the book in two weeks solid.

Janwillem van de Wetering (b. 1931) Netherlands

JvdW did not start writing until he was forty. Before then he had led a varied and much-travelled life. Born and raised in Holland, educated at Cambridge University and the University of London, he held various commercial posts in South Africa, Colombia, Peru and Australia before returning to Amsterdam as the director of a textiles company in 1965. At that time he was also a member of the Amsterdam Reserve Police. He still remained unsettled. For a year in 1958 he had been a lay Buddhist monk in Japan and in 1975 he settled in Maine, in the United States, in a Buddhist community. He has written of his Buddhist beliefs and experiences in a trilogy of books that almost constitute an autobiography, *The Empty Mirror* (1971), *A Glimpse of Nothingness* (1975) and *Afterzen* (1999). His experiences in the Amsterdam Reserve Police provided him with sufficient material to begin his much lauded Amsterdam Cop series. Its main characters are Adjutant Henk Grijpstra, a thickset and rather stolid officer, and the more attractive and romantic Sergeant Rinus de Gier. Though JvdW knows the police process in detail, and uses it where necessary in these books, they are not typical police procedurals. JvdW has long been a devotee of existentialism and primitivism in art, as well as something of an anarchist, and in these novels he loves to explore different perspectives of moral and ethical issues. Artists are frequent components of this slightly surreal jigsaw as is the author himself. He splits his personality between the Commissaris of Police, known only as Jan, and his near-twin cousin Willem, the "Napoleon of Crime", who appears in *Hard Rain*. JvdW takes his officers to other favourite parts of the globe, especially Japan and Maine, but also Papua-New Guinea. *The Maine Massacre* won JvdW the French Grand Prix de Littérature Policière. It is JvdW's philosophical worldview that makes these books fascinating and like nothing else in the annals of crime fiction.

JvdW has written a few non-series books. *The Butterfly Hunter* is more a treasure-hunt thriller, similar in some ways to his caper novel *Seesaw Millions*. He has written several stories featuring the Japanese police detective Saito collected as *Inspector Saito's Small Satori*. He has also written children's books and a biography of the Dutch author Robert VAN GULIK.

Novels

Grijpstra & de Gier series: *Outsider in Amsterdam* (1975), *Tumbleweed* (1976), *The Corpse on the Dike* (1976), *Death of a Hawker* (1977), *The Japanese Corpse* (1977), *The Blond Baboon* (1978), *The Maine Massacre* (1979), *The Mind-Murders* (1981), *The Streetbird* (1983), *The Rattle Rat* (1985), *Hard Rain* (1986), *Just a Corpse at Twilight* (1994), *The Hollow-Eyed Angel* (1996), *The Perfidious Parrot* (1997), *Shootout at Jackass Junction* (2001).

Non-series: *The Butterfly Hunter* (1982), *Murder by Remote Control* (1986), *Seesaw Millions* (1988)

Short Stories

Inspector Saito series: *Inspector Saito's Small Satori* (1985).

Grijpstra & de Gier series: *The Sergeant's Cat* (1987), *Judge Dee Plays His Lute* (1997), *The Amsterdam Cops* (1999).

Non-series: *Mangrove Mama* (1995).

Non-fiction. *Robert van Gulik: His Life, His Work* (1987).

Real name: Janwillem Lincoln van de Wetering.
Pen-name: Seiko Legru.
Where to start: *Outsider in Amsterdam.*
Awards: Grand Prix de Littérature Policière Best Foreign (1984).
Website: <www.dpbooks.com/vandewe.htm>
Similar stuff: A.C. BAANTJER, Nicolas FREELING.
Final fact: While living in South Africa in the early fifties, JvdW joined a motorbike gang.

Robert van Gulik (1910–1967) Netherlands

The translation of an 18th-century novel about the life of a 7th-century Chinese magistrate doesn't immediately suggest "modern" crime fiction, but it was RvG's rendition of *Wu-ze-tian-si-da-qi-an* as *Dee Goong An* in 1949 that introduced the Chinese detective story to readers in the West and became the real forerunner of the historical mystery. The fact that these are stories set in China, written in English by a Dutchman, several of which were first published in Malaya, simply adds to the uniqueness of the series. RvG was a Dutch diplomat, and later ambassador to Japan, who was raised in Java (then part of the Dutch East Indies where his father was a military doctor) and became fascinated with languages and Oriental studies. It was in 1940 that he discovered *Dee Goong An*, and his translation was privately published in 1949. These were stories about Dee Jen-djieh, rendered as Judge Dee, a magistrate and high-ranking minister who lived in Tang dynasty China. RvG became so fascinated with the character that he then began his own stories basing them on historical incidents and infusing them with traditional Chinese culture and a degree of eroticism. The stories are westernized versions of Chinese history, and are not classical Chinese stories, but nevertheless have an authentic feel. Publisher and bibliophile Everett Bleiler has called them "the finest ethnographic detective novels in English". *The Haunted Monastery* was adapted for TV by Nicholas Meyer as *Judge Dee and the Monastery Murders* (1974). RvG wrote one non-Dee novel, *The Given Day*, a philosophical thriller set in present-day Amsterdam, similar to the style of Janwillem VAN DER WETERING, who has written a biography of RvG.

Novels and novellas

Judge Dee series: *The Chinese Maze Murders* (1951; rev'd UK 1962), *The Chinese Bell Murders* (1951; rev'd UK 1958), *The Chinese Lake Murders* (1953; rev'd UK 1960), *The Chinese Gold Murders* (1959), *The Chinese Nail Murders* (1961), *The Emperor's Pearl* (1963), *The Haunted Monastery* (1961), *The Lacquer Screen* (1962), *The Red Pavilion* (1961), *The Monkey and the Tiger* (1965), *The Willow Pattern* (1965), *Murder in Canton* (1966), *The Phantom of the Temple* (1966), *Necklace and Calabash* (1967), *Poets and Murder* (1968; as *The Fox-Magic Murders*, UK 1973).
Non-series: *The Given Day* (1964).

Short Stories
Judge Dee series: *Dee Goong An* (1949; as *Celebrated Cases of Judge Dee*, US 1976), *Judge Dee at Work* (1967).

Full name: Robert Hans van Gulik.
Where to start: To read them in strict internal chronological order start with *The Chinese Gold Murders*.
Website: There is a Judge Dee site at <www.friesian.com/ross/dee.htm>
Books about: *Robert van Gulik: His Life and Work*, Janwillem van de Wetering (1987).
Similar stuff: Little set in ancient China but Laura Joh ROWLAND and Dale FURUTANI feature ancient Japan.

Per Wahlöö (1926–75) and Maj Sjöwall (b. 1935) Sweden

PW and MS met in 1961 while working as journalists for different magazines published by the same company. They married in 1962. Both ardent Marxists, they used fiction as a means of disseminating their views. PW initially wrote a series of political near-future thrillers with minimal crime content, but then MS, assisted by her husband, began a series of police procedural novels which ended up becoming world renowned. They featured police detective Martin Beck and his wise-cracking assistant Lennart Kollberg. The authors' plan was to show the dire effects of bourgeois capitalist authority on society, though this ended up playing second fiddle to the detective work. Beck does have to cope with increased pressure from a politically manipulated police force, and the crimes are inevitably committed by the rich or those who are leeches upon society. But in reality the authors became so immersed in their subject that the result was one of the best of all police procedural series. Tightly plotted and written in a fast-paced journalistic style, they are modelled, to some degree, on Ed MCBAIN's 87th Precinct novels, which PW and MS were translating into Swedish at the time. Beck and his colleagues are faced with a variety of major but complicated crimes that they have to solve quickly but through thorough police work. The first, *Roseanna* (filmed 1967), involves the discovery of an almost unidentifiable body of a woman in a canal and the search for her identity leads them to the USA. *The Man Who Went Up in Smoke* (filmed 1981) details the search for a missing journalist in Hungary. In *The Man on the Balcony* they have to find a serial rapist and murderer. *The Laughing Policeman* (filmed 1973), regarded by many as the best of the series, starts with the mass killing of passengers on a bus. It earned the Edgar award as best novel, rare for a book in translation. Despite its title *The Locked Room* (filmed 1992 as *Beck*) is not an especially good "impossible" crime. The best of the later books is *The Abominable Man* (filmed 1976 as *The Man on the Roof*) about a sniper and a rooftop siege. PW wrote two other crime novels on his own featuring

Chief Inspector Peter Jensen of which *Murder on the Thirty-First Floor*, where Jensen has to find a man threatening to blow up a publishing company, is closest to the Beck books in style. PW died tragically young in 1975 and thereafter MS wrote no further novels.

Novels
Martin Beck series: *Roseanna* (1965; US 1967), *The Man Who Went Up in Smoke* (1966; US 1968), *The Man on the Balcony* (1967; US 1968), *The Laughing Policeman* (1968; US 1970), *The Fire Engine That Disappeared* (1969; US 1971), *Murder at the Savoy* (1970; US 1971), *The Abominable Man* (1971; US 1972), *The Locked Room* (1972; US 1973), *Cop Killer* (1974; US 1975), *The Terrorists* (1975; US 1976).
Inspector Jensen series by Wahlöö alone: *Murder on the Thirty-First Floor* (1966; as *The Thirty-First Floor*, US 1967), *The Steel Spring* (1968; UK 1970).
Non-series by Wahlöö alone: *The Lorry* (1962; UK 1968; as *A Necessary Action*, US 1969), *The Assignment* (1963; UK 1965), *The Generals* (1965; UK 1974).

Where to start: *The Laughing Policeman.*
Awards: Swedish Sherlock award (1968), Edgar, best novel (1971).
Books about: *Polemical Pulps* by J. Kenneth Van Dover (1993).
Similar stuff: Ed McBain.

John Wainwright (b. 1921) UK

At first it may seem difficult to know where to start with JW's books. He wrote 80 novels over 30 years, at his peak producing four a year. They all draw upon his experiences as a police officer with the West Riding Constabulary in Yorkshire where he served for over 20 years (1947–69). Consequently all his books are authentic and at times extremely dramatic police procedurals set in his native Yorkshire. They are ensemble pieces with many of his characters reappearing in several novels but one usually takes the lead and goes it alone, regardless of advice or attempted input from others. This was clear from his first book, *Death in a Sleeping City*, where Superintendent Lewis pursues two Mafia killers despite advice to the contrary. JW's books cover just about every standard plot and story device, but he liked to take them a step further. There's a particularly nasty serial killer in *Who Goes Next?*. An ex-con seeks revenge against the copper who arrested him in *The Day of the Peppercorn Kill*. There are ramifications from the days of the Nazi concentration camps in *An Urge for Justice*. The murder of a policeman leads to a house under siege in *Sabbath Morn*. There's even an episode of a typical night at a police station in *All Through the Night* with a story-line reminiscent of an episode of *The Bill*. Of all of his books, though, the one latched on to by the movie people has been *Brainwash* (filmed 1981 as *The Inquisitor*, and 2000 as *Under Suspicion*), a powerful novel of the interrogation of a suspect lawyer. Like many of JW's books it has a surprise twist ending. JW wrote other non-series books, but even in these his cast of detectives often have peripheral rôles. His early books are now almost period pieces, but the overall body of work is probably the most substantial set of police procedurals in Britain.

Novels

Superintendent Lewis leads: *Death in a Sleeping City* (1965), *Talent for Murder* (1967), *Edge of Extinction* (1968), *The Take-Over Men* (1969).

Superintendent Sullivan leads: *Kill the Girls and Make Them Cry* (1974), *Coppers Don't Cry* (1975).

Superintendent Gilliant leads: *Ten Steps to the Gallows* (1965), *The Crystallised Carbon Pig* (1966), *Requiem for a Loser* (1972), *High-Class Kill* (1973), *A Ripple of Murders* (1978).

Superintendent Ripley leads: *Evil Intent* (1966), *The Worms Must Wait* (1967), *The Darkening Glass* (1968), *Freeze Thy Blood Less Coldly* (1970), *Night is a Time to Die* (1972), *A Touch of Malice* (1973), *The Hard Hit* (1974), *Death of a Big Man* (1975), *Portrait in Shadows* (1986).

Inspector/Superintendent Lennox leads: *The Evidence I Shall Give* (1974), *Square Dance* (1975), *Landscape With Violence* (1975), *Pool of Tears* (1977), *The Day of the Peppercorn Kill* (1977), *Take Murder...* (1979), *Spiral Staircase* (1983), *The Tenth Interview* (1986), *A Very Parochial Murder* (1988).

Inspector Lyle leads: *Brainwash* (1979), *Duty Elsewhere* (1979), *Dominoes* (1980), *The Man Who Wasn't There* (1989), *Hangman's Lane* (1992).

Superintendent Blayde leads: *All on a Summer's Day* (1981), *An Urge for Justice* (1981), *Blaÿde R.I.P.* (1982).

Superintendent Flensing leads: *Their Evil Ways* (1983), *The Ride* (1984).

Other Yorkshire C.I.D. characters: *Web of Silence* (1968).

Inspector Davis series as Jack Ripley: *Davis Doesn't Live Here Any More* (1971), *The Pig Got Up and Slowly Walked Away* (1971), *My Word You Should Have Seen Us* (1972), *My God How the Money Rolls In* (1972).

Non-series: *The Big Tickle* (1969), *Prynter's Devil* (1970), *The Last Buccaneer* (1971), *Dig the Grave and Let Him Die* (1971), *A Pride of Pigs* (1973), *The Devil You Don't* (1973), *Cause for a Killing* (1974), *Acquittal* (1976), *Walther P.38* (1976), *Who Goes Next?* (1976), *The Bastard* (1976), *A Nest of Rats* (1977). *Do Nothing "Till You Hear From Me* (1977), *The Jury People* (1978), *Thief of Time* (1978), *Death Certificate* (1978), *Tension* (1979), *The Reluctant Sleeper* (1979), *Home is the Hunter, and The Big Kayo* (1979), *The Venus Fly-Trap* (1980), *The Eye of the Beholder* (1980), *Man of Law* (1980), *A Kill of Small Consequence* (1980), *The Tainted Man* (1980), *Anatomy of a Riot* (1982), *The Distaff Factor* (1983), *Heroes No More* (1983), *Cul-de-Sac* (1984), *The Forest* (1984), *Clouds of Guilt* (1985), *All Through the Night* (1985), *The Forgotten Murders* (1987), *Blind Brag* (1988), *The Gauntley Incident* (1990), *Sabbath Morn* (1993), *Murder Story* (1994), *The Life and Times of Christopher Calvert... Assassin* (1995).

Non-fiction. *Wainwright's Beat* (1987).

Full name: John William Wainwright.
Pen-names: Jack Ripley.
Where to start: *Brainwash*.
Similar stuff: Pauline BELL, Peter ROBINSON, Peter N. Walker [Nicholas RHEA].

Mary Willis Walker (b. 1942) US

Former high-school teacher, Texas born and bred MWW hit all the right buttons with her first three books. *Zero at the Bone* was nominated for the Edgar and won the Agatha and Macavity for best first novel. *The Red Scream* was nominated for a Macavity and won the Edgar. Her third ran away with the Anthony, Macavity and Hammett. More than impressive. Three of the books feature true crime reporter Molly Cates and are compelling race-against-time novels which also deal with obsessives. In *The Red Scream* a serial killer is about to be executed and Molly's book about his crimes is just about to be published, but pressure is brought upon her to delete the final chapter. *Under the Beetle's Cellar*, inspired by the Waco tragedy, portrays a crazed cult leader holding a busload of schoolchildren hostage and only Molly knows how to get through to him. In *All the Dead Lie Down* Molly infiltrates the world of the homeless and learns a deadly secret. MWW's books tackle head on controversial issues such as gun control and the homeless. Like her first novel, *Zero at the Bone*, where a woman is investigating the death of her estranged father and unearths family secrets, MWW's books are emotionally charged and intense.

Novels
Molly Cates series: *The Red Scream* (1994), *Under the Beetle's Cellar* (1995), *All the Dead Lie Down* (1998).
Non-series: *Zero at the Bone* (1991).

Where to start: *The Red Scream.*
Awards: Agatha, first novel (1992), Macavity, first novel (1992), best novel (1996), Edgar, best novel (1995), Anthony, best novel (1996), Hammett Prize (1996), Swedish Martin Beck (1998).
Website: <www.twbooks.co.uk/authors/mwwalker.html>
Similar stuff: D.F. Mills, Karen KIJEWSKI.
Final fact: The serial killer in *The Red Scream* was based on a child who used to terrorize MWW at school, and MWW imagined what he might have become had he grown older.

Peter N. Walker, *see under* Nicholas Rhea

Marilyn Wallace (b. 1941) US

MW is the daughter of a New York City police officer, providing background to draw upon for her short series featuring California homicide detectives Jay Goldstein and Carlos Cruz. As usual the characters are opposites in many ways, providing the balance and tension to drive the series. Goldstein is a loner, introspective and philosophical, and totally immersed in his work while Cruz is a family man with too many commitments and a hang-up over his roots. In the first book, *A Case of Loyalties*, some of this gets in the way of the story, but MW's writing and plotting becomes tighter thereafter. Nevertheless the first book won a Macavity award and the other books in the series were nominated for Anthony awards. MW's best writing, though, has emerged in her one-off suspense novels. *So Shall Ye Reap* is an atmospheric novel of a woman's lost past coming alive along with events from deep in history. There's a stalker in *The Seduction*, which takes place in the same milieu as *So Shall Ye Reap*. *Lost Angel* deals with a kidnapping and murder. *Current Danger* deals with a series of revenge murders. In all these MW creates a powerful air of mystery derived from often long forgotten actions. MW also edited the *Sisters in Crime* series of anthologies, which contained many award-winning stories.

Novels

Goldstein & Cruz series: *A Case of Loyalties* (1986), *Primary Target* (1988), *A Single Stone* (1991).

Non-series: *So Shall You Reap* (1992), *The Seduction* (1993), *Lost Angel* (1996), *Current Danger* (1998).

Editor. *Sisters in Crimes* series (5 vols, 1989–92), *Best of Sisters in Crime* (1997; exp. 1998), *Deadly Allies*, with Robert J. Randisi (1992).

Full name: Marilyn Wallace (*née* Weiss).
Where to start: *So Shall You Reap*.
Awards: Macavity, best first novel (1987), American Mystery Award, best paperback original (1992).
Similar stuff: Susan DUNLAP, Mary Higgins CLARK.
Final fact: MW once worked as a pastry chef.

Minette Walters (b. 1949) UK

With her first three novels, every one an award-winner, MW established an enviable reputation as a major crime writer, a reputation she has sustained through her subsequent books. She was likened to all the major classic crime writers though in fact the only one she comes remotely near is Ruth RENDELL writing in her Barbara Vine guise. MW is very much her own master. For a start she has created no continuing series character and with each book she experiments with new techniques and perspectives. If there is any continuity between her novels it is her exploration of prejudice. She sucks her readers into the prejudices of her characters so that it blinds them to the truth, and thereby she can play tricks with the reader, especially in causing them to make assumptions. For instance in *The Ice House*, the investigating officers are entirely prejudiced against the prime suspect in a country mansion to the point where they assume her guilt and assume the identity of the victim. In *The Sculptress* the prejudice and assumptions come together in the character and crime of Olive Martin, whom everyone believes at the outset was guilty of the murder of her mother and sister. In *Scold's Bridle* the prejudice is against the village harpy whom no one likes. This approach continues through all her novels whether the issue is the homeless (*The Echo*), racism (*The Shape of Snakes*) or paedophilia (*Acid Row*). Broadly MW's books may be classified as psychological suspense, of which *The Dark Room*, about a victim's complete loss of memory, is the clearest in that vogue, but MW plays the field. *The Breaker*, about a small-town murder with minimal suspects, is a police procedural. *The Shape of Snakes* is reportorial and stretches across a period of 20 years. By not choosing a series character MW allows herself to remain creative and fresh with each novel, and each time she scores highly. After graduating from Durham University, MW was for many years an in-house editor at IPC magazines and wrote romance fiction under as yet unrevealed pseudonyms.

Novels. *The Ice House* (1992), *The Sculptress* (1993), *The Scold's Bride* (1994), *The Dark Room* (1995), *The Echo* (1997), *The Breaker* (1998), *Burning Point* (1999), *The Shape of Snakes* (2000), *Acid Row* (2001).

Full name: Minette Caroline Mary Walters (*née* Jebb).
Where to start: *The Ice House*.
Awards: CWA John Creasey Memorial award (1992), Edgar, best novel (1994), Macavity, best novel (1994), CWA Gold Dagger (1994), German Marlowe (1994).
Similar stuff: Ruth RENDELL as Barbara Vine, Margaret MILLAR, B.M. GILL.
Final fact: For several years MW was a prison visitor. Although this was not for the purpose of research, she nevertheless learned things that she would not have any other way.

Joseph Wambaugh (b. 1937) US

JW was one of the first serving policemen to write realistically about the psychological horrors and pressures of police work. He served in the LAPD from 1960–74 and his "acclimatization" to his work is told in the semi-autobiographical *The New Centurions* (filmed 1972, aka *Los Angeles Precinct 45*) about three rookie cops. All of JW's books are based on true events, and the distinction between his fiction and so-called "non-fiction" novels is often a thin line. His reputation was earned with *The Onion Field* (filmed 1979), a powerful and shocking novel about the mental disintegration of one policeman who is kidnapped by two petty thieves and forced to witness the death of a colleague. JW lightened the leaven slightly in *The Choirboys* (filmed 1978), another controversial novel where the irony was lost on many. It deals with the incompetence, prejudice and violence within the force, the latter often a safety valve to cope with the outside world, and how this influences officers' judgment. Having set the world alight, JW's subsequent novels are rather more traditional affairs of crime and detection, though always with a satirical edge and always with authentic detail. *The Black Marble* (filmed 1980) has a former homicide detective so psychologically drained by his work that he is assigned to burglary, but continues to operate as before. *The Glitter Dome* (filmed 1984) is JW's perspective of

Hollywood, where a movie mogul has been murdered. There is a poignancy about *The Secrets of Harry Bright*, written after JW's son was killed in a traffic accident, as it deals with the deaths of children. Of JW's other "non-fiction" novels, *The Blooding* is of interest because it's an early account of the use of genetic fingerprinting. Of his other novels, *Finnegan's Week*, dealing with the illegal dumping of toxic waste, is the most uncharacteristic in terms of subject matter but still has the powerful mixture of satire and cynicism that only comes from direct experience.

Novels. *The New Centurions* (1970), *The Blue Knight* (1972), *The Choirboys* (1975), *The Black Marble* (1978), *The Glitter Dome* (1981), *The Delta Star* (1983), *The Secrets of Harry Bright* (1985), *The Golden Orange* (1990), *Fugitive Nights* (1992), *Finnegan's Week* (1993), *Floaters* (1996), *The Fire Lover* (2002).
"Non-fiction" novels. *The Onion Field* (1973), *Lines and Shadows* (1983), *Echoes in the Darkness* (1987), *The Blooding* (1989).

Full name: Joseph Aloysius Wambaugh, Jr.
Where to start: *The Onion Field* or *The Choirboys.*
Awards: Special Edgar (1974), Edgar, best screenplay (1981), Rodolfo Walsh Prize, investigative journalism (1989).
Similar stuff: Paul BISHOP, Wendy HORNSBY.
Final fact: JW claims he never had to draw his pistol during his ten-year career with the LAPD.

Penny Warner (b. 1947) US

PW is best known for her many books for children, both fiction and non-fiction. She is a teacher for children with special needs, in particular the deaf, and teaches sign language and works with pre-school deaf children. When she decided to write a mystery series for adult readers she chose a deaf protagonist, Connor Westphal, a reporter who runs a newspaper in the one-horse town of Flat Skunk, California. These are typical small-town mysteries with the usual cast of eccentric characters and unusual events but with the added twist that Westphal, through her lip-reading and other skills, is a refreshingly different amateur sleuth. The series opener, *Dead Body Language*, was nominated for the Agatha award and won the Macavity for best first novel. Of the other books *Right to Remain Silent* is fascinating because not only is the sleuth deaf but also the prime murder suspect. PW has also started a series of mysteries for young teenagers involving a gang of four girl scouts starting with *Girls to the Rescue* (2000).

Novels
Connor Westphal series: *Dead Body Language* (1997), *Signs of Foul Play* (1998), *Right to Remain Silent* (1998), *Quiet Undertaking* (1999), *Blind Side* (2001).

Awards: Macavity, best first novel (1998).
Website: <http://pw2.netcom.com/~tpwarner/>
Similar stuff: Jan BURKE, Laura LIPPMAN.

Final fact: With her husband, Tom, PW writes and produces murder mystery events for libraries and other organizations in her area.

Colin Watson (1920–82) UK

CW was a journalist with a background in advertising and engineering who had strong views about the nature of British crime fiction. He elaborated on them in *Snobbery With Violence*, a delightful study of the genre showing the relationship between crime fiction and its readers, in which he coined the phrase "the Little World of Mayhem Parva" to describe the traditional cozy English village mystery. CW's fiction had reacted against this. His fictional town of Flaxborough, in East Anglia, was the complete opposite of all that was sentimental and romantic about country-house Britain. It was a town where, in the words of H.R.F. KEATING, "corruption was endemic" and where the police, usually in the form of the gentle Inspector Walter Purbright, just about cope. In the early novels, starting with *Coffin Scarcely Used*, where people believed the dead later reappeared, Purbright reveals his detective skills, but in later novels CW's delightful comic set-pieces take over and Purbright just becomes one of many trying to make head or tail of Flaxborough. CW parodies just about every crime plot device and creates some new ones – such as the villain who runs sideways in *The Flaxborough Crab*. *Hopjoy Was Here*, in which anonymous letters lead police on the trail of a wanted man, was shortlisted for the CWA Gold Dagger. One of the series was adapted for TV as *Murder Most English* (1977). CW wrote only one non-Flaxborough novel, *The Puritan*, where he demonstrated he could write serious material when he chose.

Novels
Flaxborough series: *Coffin, Scarcely Used* (1958), *Bump in the Night* (1960), *Hopjoy Was Here* (1962), *Lonelyheart 4122* (1967), *Charity Ends at Home* (1968), *The Flaxborough Crab* (1969; as *Just What the Doctor Ordered*, US 1969), *Broomsticks Over Flaxborough* (1972; as *Kissing Covens*, US 1972), *The Naked Nuns* (1975; as *Six Nuns and a Shotgun*, US 1975), *One Man's Meat* (1977; as *It Shouldn't Happen to a Dog*, US 1977), *Blue Murder* (1979), *Plaster Sinners* (1980), *Whatever's Been Going On in Mumblesby* (1982).
Non-series: *The Puritan* (1966).
Non-fiction. *Snobbery With Violence: Crime Stories and Their Audience* (1971; rev'd 1979).

Similar stuff: Peter GUTTRIDGE, Mike RIPLEY.

Noah Webster *pseudonym, see* Bill Knox

Donald E. Westlake (b. 1933) US

DEW is one of the most admired of all writers of crime fiction mostly because he can juggle between comic caper novels of tremendous fun and energy under his own name and dark, violent hard-boiled novels under his appropriately concocted alias Richard Stark. This rise to popularity happened steadily. He sold his first stories to the science fiction and mystery magazines in 1953. His writing was interrupted by military service in the USAF (1954–56) after which he continued his university education. His first book, *The Mercenaries*, was about a Mob hit-man torn between love and duty and marked him out as a new hard-boiled writer to watch. The next few books were all in that vein, dealing generally with young men forced into violence by local circumstances. *Killing Time* is about a small-town P.I. who keeps the peace because he knows everyone and takes care of anyone who steps out of line. *361* concerns a son who wreaks revenge on his father's killer. *Killy* is about the violence that erupts when unions try to infiltrate a closed shop. *Pity Him Afterwards*, about a madman who convincingly poses as someone sane, was a change towards more psychological suspense. By this time he had created his alter ego, Richard Stark and under that name DEW wrote books about a professional master thief called simply Parker. These are violent novels. At the start of *The Hunter* (filmed 1967 as *Point Blank*), Parker has been shot and left for dead and he plans revenge against his double-crossing wife and partner. A vulnerability remains with Parker in later books so that although we see him organize gangs and plan major heists, always seeking the perfect crime, he is still a loner and draws more into his shell as the "score" nears. The early Parker novels are rated as amongst the most accomplished of all hard-boiled books, especially *The Outfit* (filmed 1973; aka *Good Guys Always Win*) where Parker takes on organized crime. Most of these early books have been filmed, though in order that DEW can keep control of the name Parker, the character always has another name – Walker in *Point Blank*, McClain in *The Split* and so on. Parker mellows slightly as a character in later novels though the novels remain as hard-edged as ever. Parker's erstwhile partner, Alan Grofield, has a few, slightly less violent novels of his own. Grofield is an actor who turns to crime between jobs. Grofield and Parker come together again in what was to be a final adventure. *Butcher's Moon* is the last part of a sequence where Parker, as stubborn and unstoppable as ever, comes up against the Mafia. Many devotees regard this book as one of the all-time great crime novels. It took DEW over 20 years to think he could respond to it and eventually lure Parker out of retirement in *Comeback*, with a plot to steal half-a-million from a tele-evangelist.

At this time DEW had also created a new character called Mitch Tobin whom he wrote about under the alias Tucker Coe. Tobin is an ex-cop riddled with guilt. While Tobin was in bed with a woman his partner was killed answering a call. Tobin becomes a near recluse, gradually building a wall around himself, making himself an outsider and, as such, he steadily comes to terms with himself by helping other outsiders. The five books in the series find Tobin fighting crimes against gays, the mentally ill, and other outcasts until he's ready to face the world again.

While writing these powerful, dark novels DEW found relief in lightening the tone of the books under his own name. The first of his "comic" novels was *The Fugitive Pigeon*, in which a man finally decides to stand up for himself against his uncle, a Mafia don. But the fun really started with *The Busy Body* (filmed 1967), about a hunt for a missing corpse. In *The Spy in the Ointment* a misunderstanding results in a pacifist becoming a spy. In the Edgar-winning *God Save the Mark* a man is a sitting target for every con-artist which makes life chaotic when he inherits a fortune. *Help I Am Being Held Prisoner* has a prisoner escape and live a life outside of prison whilst still serving his prison sentence. *Two Much!* has a man who doubles up as a pretend twin brother in order to marry twins, but then creates further problems when he kills the twin off. Out of these delightful caper novels DEW established a new character, John Dortmunder, the complete antithesis of Parker. Dortmunder is also a criminal mastermind but no matter what he does everything always goes spectacularly wrong. The first adventure, *The Hot Rock* (filmed 1972; aka *How to Steal a Diamond in Four Uneasy Lessons*), was originally planned as a Parker novel (Grofield even appears in it) but ended up too funny. In *Jimmy the Kid*, Dortmunder plans a job based on one they read about in a Parker novel, *Child Heist*, and this book alternates between Parker's gang carrying off the crime and Dortmunder making a mess of it. Four of the books have been filmed, with a fifth planned. Although most of the later books under DEW's own name are comic capers he has recently turned serious. *The Ax* is an explosive novel about a downgraded corporate executive who wreaks revenge on his fellow workers. *The Hook* is a twist on HIGHSMITH's *Strangers on a Train*, where two authors, one with writer's block and an impending divorce, come to an agreement over murder though DEW, inevitably, takes it several stages further.

DEW has been so prolific throughout his writing career that it's impossible to cover all his work. He himself has called it "rather a mess", but if it is, then it's a highly creative and enjoyable "mess". With his third wife, Abby, DEW organizes murder-mystery weekends and two of their plots have been novelized as *Translyvania Station* and *High Jinx*. He has written short stories about New York cop Abe Levine collected as *Levine*, and a series about cop turned actor, Sam Holt. He has written a children's book, a comic war novel, political thrillers, soft-porn novels (as Alan Marshall and Edwin West), even a biography of Elizabeth Taylor (under the alias John B. Allan). He has also found time to write several screenplays, some adapted from his own books, but also *The Grifters* (1990), based on the novel by Jim THOMPSON, for which he won an Edgar and was nominated for an Oscar. In recognition for his work, DEW was made a Grand Master by the MWA in 1993 and received a lifetime achievement award from the Bouchercon committee in 1997.

Novels

Dortmunder series: *The Hot Rock* (1970), *Bank Shot* (1972), *Jimmy the Kid* (1974), *Nobody's Perfect* (1977), *Why Me?* (1983), *Good Behavior* (1985), *Drowned Hopes* (1990), *Don't Ask* (1993), *What's the Worst That Could Happen?* (1996), *Bad News* (2001).

Sara Joslyn series: *Trust Me On This* (1988), *Baby, Would I Lie?* (1994).

Non-series: *The Mercenaries* (1960; as *The Smashers*, 1962), *Killing Time* (1961; as *The Operator*, 1964), *361* (1962), *Killy* (1963), *Pity Him Afterwards* (1964), *The Fugitive Pigeon* (1965), *The Busy Body* (1966), *The Spy in the Ointment* (1966), *God Save the Mark* (1967), *Who Stole Sassi Manoon?* (1969), *Somebody Owes me Money* (1969), *I Gave at the Office* (1971), *Cops and Robbers* (1972), *Gangway!*, with Brian Garfield (1973), *Help I Am Being Held Prisoner* (1974), *Two Much!* (1975), *Brothers Keepers* (1975), *Dancing Aztecs* (1976; as *A New York Dance*, UK 1979), *Enough!* (1977), *Castle in the Air* (1980), *Kahawa* (1982), *High Adventure* (1985), *Sacred Monster* (1989), *Humans* (1992), *Smoke* (1995), *The Ax* (1997), *The Hook* (2000), *Put a Lid on It* (2002).

Mitchell Tobin series as Tucker Coe: *Kinds of Love, Kinds of Death* (1966), *Murder Among Children* (1968), *Wax Apple* (1970), *A Jade in Aries* (1970), *Don't Lie to Me* (1972).

Parker series as Richard Stark: *The Hunter* (1962; as *Point Blank*, UK 1967), *The Man With the Getaway Face* (1963; as *The Steel Hit*, UK 1971), *The Outfit* (1963), *The Mourner* (1963), *The Score* (1964; as *Killtown*, UK 1971), *The Jugger* (1965), *The Seventh* (1966; as *The Split*, UK 1969), *The Handle* (1966; as *Run Lethal*, UK 1972), *The Rare Coin Score* (1967), *The Green Eagle Score* (1967), *The Black Ice Score* (1968), *The Sour Lemon Score* (1969), *Deadly Edge* (1971), *Slayground* (1971), *Plunder Squad* (1972), *Butcher's Moon* (1974), *Comeback* (1997), *Backflash* (1998), *Payback* (1999), *Flashfire* (2000), *Firebreak* (2001).

Alan Grofield series as Richard Stark: *The Damsel* (1967), *The Dame* (1969), *The Blackbird* (1969), *Lemons Never Lie* (1971). Grofield is also in the Parker novels *The Score*, *The Handle*, *Butcher's Moon*.

as Timothy J. Culver: *Ex Officio* (1970; as *Power Play*, 1971).

as Samuel Holt: *I Know a Trick or Two* (1986), *One of Us is Wrong* (1986), *What I Tell You Three Times is False* (1987), *The Fourth Dimension is Death* (1989).

with Abby Westlake: *Transylvania Station* (1986), *High Jinx* (1986).

Short Stories

Abe Levine series: *Levine* (1984).

Non-series: *The Curious Facts Preceding My Execution* (1968), *Tomorrow's Crimes* (1989), *A Good Story* (1999).

Editor. *Once Against the Law*, with William Tenn (1968), *Murderous Schemes* (1996), *The Best American Mystery Stories 2000* (2000).

Real name: Donald Edwin Edmund Westlake.

Pen-names: John B. Allan, Curt Clark, Tucker Coe, Timothy J. Culver, J. Morgan Cunningham, Samuel Holt, Alan Marshall, Richard Stark, Edwin West.

Where to start: Try the first Parker and Dortmunder books or both at once in *Jimmy the Kid*.

Awards: Edgar, best novel (1968), best short story (1990), best screenplay (1991); MWA Grand Master (1993), Anthony, lifetime achievement (1997), French Trophée 813 (1999, 2000).

Website: <www.donaldwestlake.com>
Similar stuff: Lawrence BLOCK, Joe GORES.
Final fact: Always one for a joke, DEW wrote a spoof of Alex Haley's *Hotel* and *Airport* set in a toilet and called *Comfort Station*. It appeared under the alias J. Morgan Cunningham and DEW wrote a blurb on the cover saying, "I wish I had written this book."

Carolyn Wheat (b. 1946) US

CW was for 23 years a practising criminal lawyer, for most of that time a defence attorney with the Legal Aid Society in New York. She has also worked for the NYPD but changed careers entirely to become artist-in-residence at the University of Central Oklahoma. Her novels feature Brooklyn lawyer Cass Jameson who in the first novel, the Edgar-nominated *Dead Man's Thoughts*, is also with the Legal Aid Society. Cass turns detective to get to the truth behind the death of her lover. With *Where Nobody Dies*, Cass has set up in private practice. The novels are a well plotted combination of amateur sleuth and legal thriller. CW takes on a variety of challenging issues – the murky world of "grey-market" adoptions in *Fresh Kills*; defending a Mafia lawyer in *Mean Streak*, and having to defend her brother, a quadriplegic Vietnam vet charged with murder. This is a rewarding series that should be better known. CW has won several awards for her short stories, most of which are even more dark and provocative than her novels. *Tales Out of School* collects together most of these including the Cass Jameson story "Three Time Loser" and the award-winning "Accidents Will Happen", both of which concern justice for the elderly. CW was one of the founding members of Sisters in Crime and now lives in California where she teaches at the University of California at San Diego.

Novels
Cass Jameson series: *Dead Man's Thoughts* (1983), *Where Nobody Dies* (1986), *Fresh Kills* (1995), *Mean Streak* (1996), *Troubled Waters* (1997), *Sworn to Defend* (1998).
Short Stories. *Tales Out of School* (2000).
Non-fiction. *Funhouse and Roller Coaster: Creating the Reader's Experience in Mystery and Suspense Fiction* (2002).
Editor. *Murder on Route 66* (1999), *Women Before the Bench* (2001).

Awards: Agatha, best short story (1997), Anthony, best short story (1997), Macavity, best short story (1997), Shamus, best short story (1998).
Similar stuff: Julie SMITH, Dana STABENOW.
Final fact: CW has established a company called "Footprints Mystery Tours" to run a mystery tour of California from Sam Spade's San Francisco to Wade Miller's San Diego.

Teri White (b. 1946) US

TW's first novel, *Triangle*, which won an Edgar award, has been called by Ed Gorman "one of the best novels of its decade." It's about two Vietnam vets turned hit-men who kill an undercover cop by accident and are hunted by the cop's partner. It established the template for much of TW's fiction, which explores relationships between partners, usually men. She introduced two further Vietnam vets in the shape of LAPD detectives Spaceman Kowalski – the rough, tough, streetwise of the two, and Blue Maguire – rich, studious and haunted. The two books about them explore their developing relationship in the thick of violent crimes. In *Bleeding Hearts* it's gay murders, in *Tightrope* it's a diamond heist (again by Vietnam vets). In *Faultlines* the two ex-cons turned petty thieves are also gay who fall victim to a strong-willed woman. In all of TW's books the men never seem to have matured but are locked permanently in a juvenile game-playing rôle of either soldiers or cops-and-robbers, easily manipulated by women. In her hands the results are often chilling. Recently TW seems to have abandoned the crime fiction field for fantasy and science fiction, but it is hoped she will return.

Novels
Maguire & Kowalski novels: *Bleeding Hearts* (1984), *Tightrope* (1986).
Non-series: *Triangle* (1982), *Max Trueblood and the Jersey Desperado* (1987), *Fault Lines* (1988), *Thursday's Child* (1991).
as Stephen Lewis: *Cowboy Blues* (1985).
Short Stories. *Outlaw Blues*, one story (1992).

Full name: Teri Jean White (*née* Honohan).
Pen-name: Stephen Lewis.
Where to start: *Triangle*.
Awards: Edgar, best paperback original (1983).
Website: <www.comlink.ne.jp/~winkie.html>
Similar stuff: Joan SMITH, Dorothy UHNAK.

Collin Wilcox (1924–96) US

CW will best be remembered for his long-running series featuring Sergeant (later Lieutenant) Frank Hastings of the San Francisco Homicide Squad which blended the more personalized viewpoint of the hard-boiled P.I. novel with the police procedural. The Hastings series, starting with *The Lonely Hunter*, an apt description, grows out of the West Coast hippy scene of the late sixties and we follow Hastings through the whiplash effect of other social and cultural changes in California over the next quarter of a century. By *Calculated Risk* we're into gay-bashing and AIDS. With *Night Games*, CW switched the viewpoint from a first-person narrative to the third person, allowing greater freedom to explore the relationships that CW had developed amongst the police and within Hastings's own turbulent life. CW had been a partner in a furniture store and later ran his own lighting business before he turned full-time writer in 1970. His first two books featured San Francisco reporter Stephen Drake who is clairvoyant, making these borderline supernatural novels, though the emphasis is on traditional detection. Starting with *Bernhardt's Edge*, CW created a new character, Alan Bernhardt, an actor and playwright who fills in between engagements in a detective agency in San Francisco. It's the same world as Frank Hastings' – in fact Hastings puts in a cameo appearance in *Except for the Bones*. These novels are every bit as powerful, with *Silent Witness*, in which a young child, witness to a murder, is struck dumb, being amongst his best books. CW was able to create a considerable atmosphere of menace, which worked well in his non-series books *The Faceless Men*, where another child-witness to a murder is menaced by the killer, and *The Third Victim*. *Spellbinder* is also notable for being one of the earliest books to deal with television evangelists. CW wrote two spin-off novels from the *McCloud* TV series.

Novels

Stephen Drake series: *The Black Door* (1967), *The Third Figure* (1968).
Frank Hastings series: *The Lonely Hunter* (1969), *The Disappearance* (1970), *Dead Aim* (1971), *Hiding Place* (1973), *Long Way Down* (1974), *Aftershock* (1975), *Doctor, Lawyer . . .* (1977), *Power Plays* (1979), *Mankiller* (1980), *Stalking Horse* (1982), *Victims* (1985), *Night Games* (1986), *The Pariah* (1986), *A Death Before Dying* (1990), *Dead Center* (1992), *Switchback* (1993), *Calculated Risk* (1995).
McCloud series: *McCloud* (1973), *The New Mexico Connection* (1974).
Alan Bernhardt series: *Bernhardt's Edge* (1988), *Silent Witness* (1990), *Hire a Hangman* (1991), *Except for the Bones* (1991), *Find Her a Grave* (1993), *Full Circle* (1994).
Non-series: *The Third Victim* (1977), *The Watcher* (1978), *Twospot*, with Bill Pronzini (1978), *Spellbinder* (1981), *Swallow's Fall* (UK 1987).
as Carter Wick: *The Faceless Man* (1975), *Dark House, Dark Road* (1981).

Pen-name: Carter Wick.
Where to start: *The Lonely Hunter*.
Similar stuff: Bill PRONZINI, Roger L. SIMON.

Kate Wilhelm (b. 1928) US

KW is best known as a science-fiction writer. Her first story sales were science fiction and fantasy (in 1956) and she has won many awards in that field. However her first published novel, *More Bitter Than Death*, where a wife has to come to terms with her husband being a murder suspect, was a mystery, and KW's editor at that time, Clayton Rawson, advised she would be a best-seller if she stuck to mystery. However KW has too wide a range of interests and is also fascinated in the borderlands between genres so that whilst many like to pigeonhole her, she is really *suis generis*. After 25 years she returned to the mystery field. Starting with *The Hamlet Trap* she introduced retired arson investigator/police detective Charlie Meiklejohn and his wife, psychologist Constance Leidl. The first book is a fairly traditional theatrical murder mystery but later books show KW's delight for pushing boundaries and experimenting with genres. In *Smart House* they have to outwit a state-of-the-art high-tech house in the course of their murder investigation whilst *The Dark Door* involves the paranormal in the case of a serial arsonist. The novels, together with some shorter pieces, have been collected as *The Casebook of Constance and Charlie* in two volumes. Some people have alikened Constance and Charlie to KW and her author husband Damon Knight. KW has started a second series that has made her one of the top writers of legal suspense novels. This features defence attorney Barbara Holloway who operates in KW's hometown of Eugene, Oregon. *Death Qualified* is a challenging novel that introduces chaos theory into the courtroom drama where Holloway is defending a mental patient. A man with learning difficulties is the client in *Malice Prepense*, whilst in *Desperate Measures* her client is physically disabled. In *The Best Defense* Holloway defends a girl accused of killing her baby daughter. All of these novels create tense legal situations as a result of strong personal issues and family relationships, imbuing the series with powerful emotions as well as mystery and tension. KW has written a few non-series mystery novels that also have strong family issues. In *Justice for Some*, for example, a judge is asked to run for office following her husband's death but soon after her father dies and one of her children becomes a murder suspect.

Novels

Constance & Charlie series: *The Hamlet Trap* (1987), *The Dark Door* (1988), *Smart House* (1989), *Sweet, Sweet Poison* (1990), *Seven Kinds of Death* (1992).
Barbara Holloway series: *Death Qualified* (1991), *The Best Defense* (1994), *Malice Prepense* (1996; as *For the Defense*, 1997), *Defense for the Devil* (1999), *No Defense* (2000), *Desperate Measures* (2001).
Non-series: *More Bitter Than Death* (1963), *The Nevermore Affair* (1966), *Justice for Some* (1993), *Deepest Water* (2000), *Skeletons* (2002).

Short stories

Constance & Charlie series: *A Flush of Shadows* (1995).

Full name: Kate Gertrude Wilhelm Knight (*née* Meredith).
Where to start: *The Best Defense*.
Awards: Nebula, best short sf story (1969, 1988), best novelette (1987), Hugo award, best sf novel (1977), Jupiter, best sf novel (1977), Locus, best sf novel (1977), Prix Apollo, best sf novel (1981).
Similar stuff: Earl W. EMERSON for another former arson investigator; Lia MATERA, Lisa SCOTTOLINE for legal thrillers.
Final fact: KW recalls an uncle who said he was writing a thriller, and proceeded to tell her all about it: "Conspiracies, killings, skullduggery of all sorts, and no discernible plot. Then he said, 'So the hero/pilot has been shot and can't move, and the bad guy is dead, and the plane is out of control plummeting to earth. Now, Katie, how do we get out of this?' I'm afraid 'we' never finished his novel. But I learned something valuable. Start with the solution and work backwards. I've done it ever since."

Charles Willeford (1919–88) US

CW would have hated the 1990s. He was the arch-priest of the politically incorrect. CW wrote about the world as he saw it, full of villains, most of them psychotic, macho-men and with little, if any, justice. It was a world of despair that he had encountered at an early age, orphaned and on the road, which he later wrote about in *I Was Looking for a Street* (1988). He served for 20 years in the Army and Army Air Corps (1935–56), including right through the War. He fought at the Battle of the Bulge and was awarded two Purple Hearts, a Silver Star, a Bronze Star and the Luxembourg Croix-de-Guerre. By the end of his service he was being treated for depression. To keep himself sane he wrote poetry and his first book was *Proletarian Laughter* (1948), a mixture of prose and verse. He wrote about his post-war army experiences in *Something About a Soldier* (1986). His first novel was *High Priest of California*, which he started in 1949. It's about the ruthless, amoral and manipulative Russell Haxby who loves to score with married women. Throughout the fifties most of CW's work falls into the category of erotica all of which have crime elements although only *Pick-Up*, which has been called "probably the most depressing novel you will ever read' has a strong crime theme. Mix the nightmares of Cornell Woolrich, the noir of Jim THOMPSON, the violence of James CRUMLEY and the depressing reality of Edward BUNKER and you have some measure of CW. *The Woman Chaser* (filmed 1999) is almost a rewrite of *High Priest of California* but ends in an orgy of revenge. His most notorious novel of the sixties was *Cockfighter* (1962; filmed 1974). His output decreased in the later sixties when he taught English at the University of Miami. The best of his crime fiction began to appear in the seventies, starting with *The Burnt Orange Heresy*, a sinister portrayal of a murderer. It was during the seventies that he wrote *The Shark-Infested Custard*, an almost Tarantino-esque cavalcade of violence by four thugs who look out for each other. The book was regarded as too violent and depressing to publish at the time, although a self-contained extract did appear before CW's death as *Kiss Your Ass Good-Bye*. Amongst his non-fiction studies CW wrote an account of the Son of Sam case in *Off the Wall*. *Miami Blues* (filmed 1989) was the first of CW's Hoke Moseley novels. Moseley is a debauched homicide detective who spends as much time trying to sort out his crazy life as he does solving crimes. His work is always violent, nearly always involving psychopaths, yet the books have a humour and colourful perception that carries the reader along. CW may have been in his sixties when he created Moseley but there's nothing pensionable about him or his work. Like fine wine, CW just got better with age.

Novels

Hoke Moseley series: *Miami Blues* (1984), *New Hope for the Dead* (1985), *Sideswipe* (1987), *The Way We Die Now* (1988).

Non-series: *High Priest of California* (1953; reissued with *Wild Wives*, 1956), *Pick-*

Up (1955), *The Woman Chaser* (1960), *The Burnt Orange Heresy* (1971), *The Shark-Infested Custard* (1993; extract as *Kiss Your Ass Good-Bye*, 1987).
as Will Charles: *The Hombre from Sonora* (1971; as *The Difference* by CW, 1999).
Short Stories. *The Machine in Ward Eleven* (1963), *Everybody's Metamorphosis* (1988).
Non-fiction. *Off the Wall* (1980), *Writing and Other Blood Sports* (2000).

Full name: Charles Ray Willeford III.
Pen-name: Will Charles.
Where to start: *The Burnt Orange Heresy* or *Miami Blues.*
Awards: John D. MacDonald Award for Fiction (1999).
Books about: *Willeford* by Don Herron (1997).
Website: <www.twbooks.co.uk/authors/cwilleford.html>
Similar stuff: Jim THOMPSON, Edward BUNKER.
Final fact: CW played the part of a bartender in *Thunder and Lightning* (1977) for which he received a fee of $9.60 every time it was played on television.

David Williams (b. 1926) UK

DW was head of a major London advertising agency until a heart attack and a stroke forced him to retire when he was 50. Although he still keeps a hand in the business he turned to writing full time. His first long series of books featured London merchant banker Mark Treasure, who turns sleuth in *Unholy Writ* when murder and mystery follow the possible discovery of a Shakespearean manuscript. All of the Treasure series, which are marked by a sharp wit and a strong sense of the traditional whodunnit, require a key financial element to secure Treasure's involvement but that is often the lure for the crime. They have been highly praised as literate and intelligent mysteries. *Murder for Treasure*, involving a kidnapping, a death and a ransom demand, was nominated for the CWA Gold Dagger. After 17 books, though, DW wanted something on home territory. He was Welsh born and bred, even though he lives in Surrey, and bemoans the lack of Welsh detectives. He created Detective Chief Inspector Merlin Parry and Detective Sergeant Gomer Lloyd based in South Wales. Though the crimes are not necessarily rooted in the Welsh background, the stories nevertheless have the authentic touch. Ingenious problems, believable characters and solid detective work led the *Western Mail* (Wales's premier national newspaper) to refer to DW's "superbly crafted thriller writing." DW admits to seldom knowing "whodunit" until he reaches the final chapter, which invariably results in a surprise ending, but this adds to the books' appeal.

Novels

Mark Treasure series: *Unholy Writ* (1976), *Treasure by Degrees* (1977), *Treasure Up in Smoke* (1978), *Murder for Treasure* (1980), *Copper, Gold and Treasure* (1982), *Treasure Preserved* (1983), *Advertise for Treasure* (1984), *Wedding Treasure* (1985), *Murder in Advent* (1985), *Treasure in Roubles* (1987), *Divided Treasure* (1987), *Treasure in Oxford* (1988), *Holy Treasure!* (1989), *Prescription for Murder* (1990),

Treasure by Post (1991), *Planning on Murder* (1992), *Banking on Murder* (1993). Merlin Parry series: *Last Seen Breathing* (1994), *Death of a Prodigal* (1995), *Dead in the Market* (1996), *A Terminal Case* (1997), *Suicide Intended* (1998).
Short Stories. *Criminal Intentions* (2001).

Where to start: *Last Seen Breathing.*
Website: <www.twbooks.co.uk/authors/davidwilliams.html>
Similar stuff: Emma LATHEN, Arthur Maling, for financial-based thrillers; Roy LEWIS for Welsh settings.
Final fact: DW was at University (St John's College, Oxford) with Edmund Crispin and Kingsley Amis.

Gordon M. Williams (b. 1939) UK

The work of Scottish author and journalist GMW might not otherwise be remembered were it not for two particular books. He wrote *The Siege of Trencher's Farm*, which was adapted by Sam Peckinpah into the controversial film *Straw Dogs* (1971). It shows how a normally mild-mannered man can become violent when pushed beyond the limit, in this case the rape of his young wife. GMW's first book, *The Last Day of Lincoln Charles*, had also been about a man, in this case a black American soldier, losing control and going on a killing spree. GMW's other claim to fame was the creation of the character James Hazell in *The Bornless Keeper*. Hazell was one of the first true hard-boiled English P.I.s, operating in the south of London. He'd been invalided out of the police force because of an injured ankle (from a gang beating) and he turned to drink, losing his wife before he decided to make a comeback as a P.I. The stories were violent but also humorous and realistic. His former police boss did not like Hazell's independence and yearned to revoke his licence. GMW wrote the series with former footballer and manager of Crystal Palace F.C. Terry Venables (b. 1943), who helped on the London scene and cockney patter. The series transferred well to TV as *Hazell* (1978–80) but GMS only wrote a few of the early scripts. Surprisingly GMW did not follow up the success of this series with anything similar. He wrote a science-fiction/special agent series "Micronauts", starting with *The Micronauts* (1977), where agents are miniaturized, but his only other novel of note was an Edwardian mystery, *Pomeroy*. He also wrote the script for the film version of Ruth Rendell's *Tree of Hands* (filmed 1990; as *Innocent Victim*, US).

Novels

Hazell series with Terry Venables as P.B. Yuill: *The Bornless Keeper* (1974), *Hazell Plays Solomon* (1974), *Hazell and the Three Card Trick* (1975), *Hazell and the Menacing Jester* (1976).
Non-series: *The Last Day of Lincoln Charles* (1965), *From Scenes Like These* (1968), *The Siege of Trencher's Farm* (1969; as *Straw Dogs*, 1972), *Big Morning Blues* (1974), *Pomeroy* (1982).

Full name: Gordon Maclean Williams.

Pen-name: P.B. Yuill (with Terry Venables).
Where to start: *The Bornless Keeper.*
Similar stuff: James MITCHELL.

Timothy Williams (b. 1946) UK/France

Born in the UK, but a naturalized French citizen teaching in Guadeloupe, TW has chosen to set his series of police novels in Italy. They feature the ageing and moody Commissario Trotti and, like the novels of Magdalen NABB and Michael DIBDIN, explore violent and explosive crimes against a background of almost inpenetrable corruption and bureaucratic nightmare. In the first, *Converging Parallels*, Trotti becomes involved in a case of blackmail and kidnapping. The fourth book, *Black August*, where Trotti continues to investigate the murder of an old friend despite pressure to stop, won TW the CWA '92 Award for best work set in Europe. With *Big Italy*, Trotti is looking forward to retirement but still can't escape. TW's books are propelled along by rapid-fire dialogue, which feels authentically Continental.

Novels

Commissario Trotti series: *Converging Parallels* (1982; as *The Red Citroen*, US 1983), *The Puppeteer* (1985; as *The Metal Green Mercedes*, US 1985), *Persona Non Grata* (1987; as *The White Audi*, US 1987), *Black August* (1992), *Big Italy* (1996).

Awards: CWA '92 Award (1992).
Website: <www.twbooks.co.uk/authors/twilliams.html>
Similar stuff: Michael DIBDIN, Donna LEON, Magdalen NABB.

Derek Wilson (b. 1935) UK

DW is a noted historian and biographer. He has written books about the Rothschilds, the Astors and the Guinness families as well as studies of Henry VIII (*In the Lion's Court*), Charles I and Cromwell (*The King and the Gentleman*), Sir Francis Drake (*The World Encompassed*) and on exploration in *The Circumnavigators* (1989). He has a particular interest in Robert Dudley, the Earl of Leicester and not only wrote his biography in *Sweet Robin* (1981), but based two novels, *Feast in the Morning* (1975) and *A Time to Lose* (1976), on the Dudleys (under the alias Hugh Preston) and chronicled the life of Leicester's son in *The Bear's Whelp* (1978) and *Bear Rampant* (1979). Writing as Jonathan Kane, DW produced *Triple Take*, a novel about a con-artist in the world of international finance, and *Triptych*, a time-slip thriller set in Rome, before starting his series about Tim Lacy. Lacy is an ex-SAS officer who runs a security firm that specializes in recovering stolen art. Each of the books, starting from *The Triarchs*, where Lacy looks for a lost Raphael painting, is steeped in art history and culture and all are well constructed mysteries. Before becoming a full-time writer in 1971, DW worked by turns as an antiques dealer and schoolmaster, spending several years in Kenya (where he served as a radio broadcaster with the Voice of Kenya). He has brought together his passion for history and mystery in more recent books. *The Swarm of Heaven* is a wonderfully atmospheric Renaissance mystery featuring that great schemer Niccolo Machiavelli and his dealings with the Borgias. *Keene's Quest* launches a new series featuring George Keene whose death is faked so that he can become a spy in William Pitt's intelligence service at the time of the War with France in 1793. In *Tripletree* DW features another quirky crime buster, Dr Nathaniel Gye, a Cambridge don with an interest in the supernatural. He has also written radio plays and documentaries.

Novels

Tim Lacy series: *The Triarchs* (1994), *The Dresden Text* (1994), *The Hellfire Papers* (1995), *The Camargue Brotherhood* (1995), *The Borgia Chalice* (1996), *Cumberland's Cradle* (1996).

George Keene series: *Keene's Quest* (2000), *Keene's Terror* (2001) *Keene's Liberty* (2001).

Nathaniel Gye series: *Tripletree* (2002), *The Nature of Rare Things* (2003).

as Jonathan Kane: *Triple Take* (1990), *Triptych* (1991).

Non-series: *The Swarm of Heaven* (2001).

Real name: Derek Alan Wilson.

Pen-names: Jonathan Kane, Hugh Preston.

Website: <www.derekwilson.com> and <www.twbooks.co.uk/authors/dwilson.html>

Similar stuff: For Tim Lacy try also John MALCOLM and Iain PEARS; for Renaissance mysteries, Elizabeth EYRE.

Final fact: DW's latest enterprise is planning a mammoth history festival to be held in Cambridge in September 2003.

John Morgan Wilson (b. 1947) US

JMW is the author of the multi-award winning series featuring Benjamin Justice, a disgraced reporter whose career ended in scandal at the *Los Angeles Times* (where JMW was assistant editor in the 1980s). In *Simple Justice*, Benjamin is lured out of his alcoholic seclusion to investigate a teenager's confession to a gay murder that he may not have committed. This hard-edged, emotionally complex novel won the Edgar for best first mystery. Justice relies heavily on his journalist friend Alexandra Templeton and in future novels she is often the starting point for the investigations, which usually involve gay-related crimes, but with a mix of gay and straight characters. In *Justice at Risk* he has to cope with the possibility that he has contracted the HIV virus. JMW uses his own wealth of experience to provide different backgrounds to the books – newspapers, screenwriting, TV and celebrity profiling. Three of the books have been nominated for the Lambda award with two of them winning. Before he turned to novels, JMW scripted nearly a hundred TV documentaries and was the supervising writer on the series *Anatomy of Crime*. JMW is the author of *The Complete Guide to Magazine Article Writing* (1993) and *Inside Hollywood* (1998). In the fall of 2002 JMW introduces a new mystery series character, Philip Damon, in *Blue Moon*, set in the early sixties in the world of big band music. It is co-written with legendary American bandleader Peter Duchin, who serves as the inspiration for the lead character.

Novels

Benjamin Justice series: *Simple Justice* (1996), *Revision of Justice* (1997), *Justice at Risk* (1999), *The Limits of Justice* (2000).

Philip Damon series: *Blue Moon* (2002), *Good Morning, Heartache* (2003).

Awards: Edgar, best first novel (1997), Lambda, best gay men's mystery (2000, 2001).

Website: <www.johnmorganwilson.com/>

Similar stuff: R.D. Zimmerman for a gay news reporter; Joseph HANSEN, Mark ZUBRO.

Final fact: JMW notes that he originally intended to write *Simple Justice* as a light, slick, commercial page-turner but, from the first line, discovered a darker and more personal voice and the story took on a life of its own. He finished a rough draft in seven weeks. He says: "It was like intensive therapy. The reason, I believe, was that I was writing for the first time in the first person, which tapped all kinds of pent up stuff. It changed my writing life."

Robert Wilson (b. 1957) UK

RW is an inveterate traveller. After graduating from Oxford University he ran archaeological tours around Crete and subsequently worked in shipping, advertising and trading. He has travelled across the USA, driven to Nepal, cycled around Spain and Portugal and journeyed across Africa. The once Dark Continent inspired dark fiction and out of it came his series about Bruce Medway, a "fixer" for expat and African traders in Benin whose usefulness as a go-between means he sometimes gets employed as a P.I. His operations start above board but it doesn't take him long to be sucked into all kinds of corrupt and violent dealings. In *Instruments of Darkness* he's looking for a missing employee, in *The Big Killing* it's the porn trade, in *Blood is Dirt* it's Mafia money-laundering and toxic waste, while in *A Darkening Stain* it's a missing schoolgirl and Mafia revenge. RW was inspired to write crime fiction after discovering Raymond Chandler, and some of that knight errant mood clings to Medway, but his books read more like Elmore LEONARD out of Graham Greene. Medway is currently "resting" while RW has turned to a broader thriller canvas. His fascination with the Iberian Peninsula (he lives in an isolated farmhouse in Portugal) caused RW to write *A Small Death in Lisbon*, where the murder of a young girl causes police inspector Zé Coelho to investigate the past and find roots 50 years earlier during the Nazi occupation. The book won RW the CWA Gold Dagger. *The Company of Strangers* is an espionage thriller that also has its roots in wartime Portugal. RW has rapidly established himself as one of the more original voices of crime fiction in the 1990s.

Novels

Bruce Medway series: *Instruments of Darkness* (1995), *The Big Killing* (1996), *Blood is Dirt* (1997), *A Darkening Stain* (1998).
Non-series: *A Small Death in Lisbon* (1999), *The Company of Strangers* (2001).

Where to start: *Instruments of Darkness.*
Awards: CWA Gold Dagger (1999).
Website: <www.twbooks.co.uk/authors/rwilson.html>
Similar stuff: Walter SATTERTHWAIT for another African setting (albeit east Africa).
Final fact: Some of RW's travelling spirit may come from a maternal ancestor, "Walking Wathen", who apparently met Lord Byron on a trek through the Swiss Alps.

R. D. Wingfield UK

RDW used to work in the oil business but in 1970 his writing for radio took over. He still prefers radio work and finds writing novels and dealing with publishers frustrating, which is why there have only been five Frost novels to date, and that last one only arose because of pressure from his American publisher. The first Frost novel had been written in 1972 and took twelve years to find a publisher. Now the success of the *Frost* TV series has made the character a household name and the books highly popular. D.I. Jack Frost of Denton Police is an unorthodox, politically incorrect and insubordinate detective who annoys his fellow officers, yet is caring and compassionate to the victims of crime. He is not a great deductive detective but knows human nature and gets results. He often has more cases than he can handle, and they are frequently emotive. A missing child in *Frost at Christmas*, torture and suicide of a young girl in *Night Frost*, the murder of a young boy in *Hard Frost*, are just a few of the many testing cases Frost handles despite the ineptitude, in his view, of his colleagues. Little wonder he is so "frosty". Despite being cram-packed with events the books are written in a surprisingly uncomplicated, straightforward style.

Novels

Jack Frost series: *Frost at Christmas* (1984), *A Touch of Frost* (1987), *Night Frost* (1992), *Hard Frost* (1995), *Winter Frost* (1999).
Similar stuff: Jane ADAMS, Roger BUSBY, Anthea FRASER.
Final fact: The only Frost short story, "Just the Fax" (*Fresh Blood 2*, 1997), is really an exchange of faxes between Mike RIPLEY and RDW and the consequences of Ripley's persistence.

Mary Wings (b. 1949) US

MW is an artist and book designer who produced several lesbian comic strips, starting with *Come Out Comix* (1974), before turning her talents to writing mysteries. Her Emma Victor series of hard-boiled, witty, lesbian P.I. novels emerged while she was living in the Netherlands and suffering from what she called "language loneliness". In *She Came Too Late* Emma Victor is a helpline counsellor who follows up an anonymous call and finds a body. In the second book she has moved to San Francisco to help publicize a benefit concert and becomes involved in investigating a religious cult. MW suffered a writer's block on return to the US, which she attempted to overcome with a fairly traditional but still satisfying gothic thriller, *Divine Victim*, which won the Lambda Award. When she resurrected Victor in *She Came by the Book*, where she now has her P.I. licence, the writing is more forceful, the dialogue sharper and the character is ready to take on anything. The books have been likened to Raymond Chandler's – what hard-boiled P.I. books haven't? – but in many ways they are, though entirely from the lesbian-feminist perspective.

Novels

Emma Victor series: *She Came Too Late* (1987), *She Came in a Flash* (1988), *She Came by the Book* (1996), *She Came to the Castro* (1997), *She Came in Drag* (1999).
Non-series: *Divine Victim* (1993).

Real name: Born Mary Geller and changed name in 1972.
Awards: Lambda Literary Award (1994).
Website: <www.twbooks.co.uk/authors/mwings.html>
Similar stuff: Ellen HART, Val MCDERMID, Sandra SCOPPETTONE, Eve ZAREMBA.
Final fact: MW had to relocate the setting of *She Came Too Late* from San Francisco to Boston because someone guessed who the real person was that the murderer was based on and ME had to disguise them further.

Don Winslow (b. 1953) US

Set in the 1970s, DW's first novel, *A Cool Breeze on the Underground*, which was nominated for both the Edgar and Shamus awards, introduced the engaging character of Neal Carey. He was an orphaned street urchin taken in by Joe Graham after young Neal tried to pick Joe's pocket. Whilst Neal is receiving a solid education he also does special jobs for his adoptive father who runs a "Friends of the Family" bank which, with no questions asked, sorts out any other difficult problems for its clients. Whenever Neal's talents are required he is pressed into service. In the first book he has to find the runaway daughter of a politician. In *The Trail to Buddha's Mirror* the search for an absentee scholar takes Neal to China. The later books don't quite live up to the refreshing difference of the first, but the series scores highly on originality. DW created a more traditional

P.I. in Walter Withers, a former CIA agent who specialized in entrapment, but who has settled down in New York in the fifties as a P.I. In *Isle of Joy*, he is hoisted by his own petard when his former colleagues at the CIA seem determined to set him up as the prime suspect in the death of a woman he was trying to protect. Oddly the sequel, *A Winter Spy*, which reworked many of the same ploys, appeared under the alias MacDonald Lloyd. Of his non-series books, *The Death and Life of Bobby Z* is about a felon who is offered a deal to impersonate a drug lord in an exchange of prisoners. *California Fire and Life* draws on DW's own experience as an arson investigator. It's a fascinating study by an insurance investigator into a fire which he believes was arson to hide a murder. The book won DW the Shamus award. DW has been a cinema manager, and a film production assistant as well as working as a P.I. in New York.

Novels

Neal Carey series: *A Cool Breeze on the Underground* (1991), *The Trail to Buddha's Mirror* (1992), *Way Down on the High Lonely* (1993), *A Long Walk up the Water Slide* (1994), *While Drowning in the Desert* (1996).

Walter Withers series (second title as by MacDonald Lloyd): *Isle of Joy* (1996), *A Winter Spy* (1997).

Non-series: *The Death and Life of Bobby Z* (1997), *California Fire and Life* (1999).

Pen-name: MacDonald Lloyd.

Where to start: *A Cool Breeze on the Underground.*

Awards: Japanese Maltese Falcon (1994), Shamus, best PI hardcover (2000).

Website: <www.donwinslow.com>

Similar stuff: Earl EMERSON for arson investigation; Carol O'CONNELL.

Final fact: DW should not be confused with another Don Winslow who writes erotic novels or, for that matter, with the pulp and comic-book hero of the thirties and forties, Don Winslow of the Navy – though, curiously, DW's father was in the Navy.

Steven Womack (b. 1952) US

A former journalist, news photographer and partner in a property-tax management firm, SW has produced two crime series. The first featured Jack Lynch, a New Orleans PR man and troubleshooter who, because of his work for a power-hungry broker and banker, is dragged into political corruption. The series never really caught on, even though *Murphy's Fault* was included on the *New York Times's* list of top crime novels for that year. His next series, however, with another ex-reporter, Nashville-based P.I. Harry James Denton, has blazed a trail through the awards. Every book in the series has been nominated for the major awards, with the first winning the Edgar and the fifth winning the Shamus. It's difficult to put a finger on its appeal because unlike many P.I. novels it's not especially fast-paced or quick-witted. SW takes time to develop the plot and paint local colour. Most of the fun is the ride, finding what difficult situations Denton, who is still rather naïve and unskilled as P.I., ends up in. Some of these are based on real events in Nashville, such as the arsonist in *Torch Town Boogie* or the eruptions of a local fundamentalist cult in *Way Past Dead*. SW has also produced and co-written two TV films, *Proudheart* (1993) and *Volcano: Fire on the Mountain* (1996).

Novels

Jack Lynch series: *Murphy's Fault* (1990), *Smash Cut* (1991), *The Software Bomb* (1993).

Harry James Denton series: *Dead Folks' Blues* (1993), *Torch Town Boogie* (1993), *Way Past Dead* (1995), *Chain of Fools* (1996), *Murder Manual* (1998), *Dirty Money* (2000).

Full name: Steven James Womack.

Where to start: *Dead Folks' Blues.*

Awards: Edgar, best paperback original (1994), Shamus, best paperback original (1999).

Website: <www.womackbooks.com>

Similar stuff: Warren MURPHY's Trace/Digger series for another inexperienced P.I.

Final fact: For four years SW ran a writers' workshop in Tennessee State Penitentiary. He remarks that he "learned more from them than they ever learned from me."

Ted Wood (b. 1931) Canada

TW was born in England, at Shoreham, and was educated in Worcestershire. He originally worked as an insurance salesman but in 1954 emigrated to Canada where he had served in the RAF during the War. He became a police constable in Toronto for three years before entering the advertising business, retiring to become a full-time writer in 1974. TW's main series features Vietnam vet Reid Bennett, a Toronto cop who resigns from the force after killing two youths who were trying to rape a girl. When his wife also leaves him Bennett decides to abandon the city for a quiet life in the northern town of Murphy's Harbor, where he becomes the one-man police force, along with his trusty German shepherd dog, Sam. Life doesn't get any quieter. Bodies pile up in most of his cases, or float up in *Dead in the Water*, the first in the series which won the Scribner crime novel award. Bennett is often put to the test in these books – both physically, where he tries to find a kidnap victim in a blizzard – and mentally, when he tries to avoid a repetition of his earlier "crime" when a gang of bikers arrive. Bennett is a strong, forceful character set in a beautiful but also hazardous terrain and the combination works well. Under the alias Jack Barnao, TW has also written a series about ex-SAS counter-terrorist operative John Locke. Returning to Canada, Locke becomes a bodyguard and all-action hero.

Novels

Reid Bennett series: *Dead in the Water* (1983), *Murder on Ice* (1984; as *The Killing Cold*, UK 1984), *Live Bait* (1985; as *Dead Centre*, UK 1985), *Fool's Gold* (1986),

Corkscrew (1987), *When the Killing Starts* (1989), *On the Inside* (1990), *Flashback* (1992), *Snowjob* (1993), *A Clean Kill* (1995).
John Locke series as Jack Barnao: *Hammerlocke* (1987), *Lockestep* (1988), *TimeLocke* (1991).

Full name: Edward John Wood.
Pen-name: Jack Barnao.
Where to start: *Dead in the Water.*
Awards: Scribner Crime Novel award (1983), CWC Derrick Murdoch Award (1999).
Similar stuff: Doug ALLYN, Eric WRIGHT's Mel Pickett.

Daniel Woodrell (b. 1953) US

DW doesn't really write crime fiction. He thinks of his books as social realism and has christened them "Country noir". They are dark eruptions of the underlying current of violence that flows throughout society. DW was born in the Ozark mountain territory of Missouri, where he still lives. He served briefly in the Marines and after his military service returned to college and subsequently the Iowa Writers' School. *Under the Bright Lights*, set in the bayou country of Louisiana, introduced his no-nonsense Cajun cop and ex-prizefighter Rene Shade, who looks beyond the obvious in an apparent burglary that went wrong to find a trail of corruption and betrayal. Two further Shade novels followed, the last, *The Ones You Do*, bringing Shade head-on with his gambling father. These are taut, atmospheric novels reminiscent of James Lee BURKE. DW has also written a brutal novel set during the American Civil War, *Woe To Live On* (filmed 1999 as *Ride With the Devil*), the fatalistic *Give Us a Kiss* which, like *Tomato Red*, explores the dynamics when losers present a hope of escape to other losers. At the root of all of DW's work is the tension of family relationships embedded in small-town southern communities. He normally paints with dark, bold colours but he brings a finer palette to *The Death of Sweet Mister*, which explores the steady corruption of a young boy by his mother and her man.

Novels

Rene Shade series: *Under the Bright Lights* (1986), *Muscle for the Wing* (1988), *The Ones You Do* (1992).
Non-series: *Woe to Live On* (1987; as *Ride with the Devil*, 1998), *Give Us a Kiss* (1996), *Tomato Red* (1998), *The Death of Sweet Mister* (2001).

Where to start: *Under the Bright Lights.*
Website: <www.twbooks.co.uk/authors/dwoodrel.html>
Similar stuff: James Lee BURKE.

Stuart Woods (b. 1938) US

SW was born and raised in Georgia, the setting for many of his early books. His early career was in advertising until he got the sailing bug and took part in the 1976 *Observer* Single-handed Transatlantic Race which he wrote about in *Blue Water, Green Skipper* (1977). Although he had always wanted to write he kept evading finishing his first novel until a contract deadline forced him. The result, *Chiefs*, about the consequences of a murder in small-town Georgia spread down through the generations, became a bestseller in paperback and was made into a TV mini-series (1983). SW's nautical interests emerge in *Run before the Wind*, a quasi autobiographical novel about wealthy Will Lee who escapes his confining day job to travel and finds himself caught up in the terrorist troubles in Ireland. SW returned to Will Lee for two further political thrillers tracing his rise through the ranks to become a state senator of which *Grass Roots* was also filmed for TV (1992). *Deep Lie*, a Cold War espionage thriller is related to the series as it features Lee's future wife Katie Rule of the CIA. SW's best known character is Stone Barrington. In *New York Dead* he is a NYPD detective who becomes involved in the murder of a TV personality. When SW resurrected him in *Dirt* he had left the force and become an attorney and sometime investigator. The Barrington series takes place generally amongst the high life. It's the world of gossip columnists in *Dirt*, the rich and exclusive in the Caribbean in *Dead in the Water*, Hollywood in *Swimming to Catalina*. There's a change of scene but not of pace in *Worst Fears Realized* which takes Barrington back to his former cop colleagues looking for an ex-con who is now taking his revenge on the police. Several of SW's thrillers are about the vulnerable having to learn fast in difficult situations. This is the background to *Orchid Beach*, the first of the Holly Barker books. Barker is a US Army Major who is forced to retire early through a sexual harassment scandal and ends up as deputy chief of police in the eponymous small beach town in Florida. Unfortunately the police chief is killed in the line of duty and Barker finds herself catapulted into prominence and alone, except for her trusted Doberman Pinscher. All of SW's books are strong on suspense, high on atmosphere and fast paced. Amongst his best non-series novels are *Under the Lake* and *Imperfect Strangers*. The first is about the dark secrets of a north Georgia town and what lies hidden beneath the town reservoir, while the second, which won the French Grand Prix de Littérature Policière, develops the idea from Patricia HIGHSMITH's *Strangers on a Train* with two men on a flight from London to New York agreeing to help each other out, with dire consequences.

Novels

Stone Barrington series: *New York Dead* (1991), *Dirt* (1996), *Dead in the Water* (1997), *Swimming to Catalina* (1998), *Worst Fears Realized* (1999), *L.A. Dead* (2000), *Cold Paradise* (2001), *The Short Forever* (2002).

Will Lee series: *Run Before the Wind* (1983), *Grass Roots* (1989), *The Run* (2000).

Holly Barker series: *Orchid Beach* (1998), *Orchid Blues* (2001).

Non-series: *Chiefs* (1981), *Deep Lie* (1986), *Under the Lake* (1987), *White Cargo*

(1988), *Palindrome* (1990), *Santa Fe Rules* (1992), *L.A. Times* (1993), *Dead Eyes* (1994), *Heat* (1994), *Imperfect Strangers* (1995), *Choke* (1995).

Full name: Stuart Chevalier Woods.
Where to start: *Chiefs* or *Under the Lake*.
Awards: Edgar, best first novel (1982), Grand Prix de Littérature Policière Best Foreign (1997).
Website: <www.stuartwoods.com>
Similar stuff: For other cases mostly involving the rich see Carol Higgins CLARK, Susan MOODY, Lawrence SANDERS and William G. TAPPLY.
Final fact: SW's father was an ex-con who left the family when SW was just two to escape further charges for burglary. SW met him only twice afterwards.

Eric Wright (b. 1929) Canada

Born in England, EW emigrated to Canada in 1951 where he became a Professor of English at Ryerson University until his retirement in 1989. He wrote an appealing reminiscence of his youth in *Always Give a Penny to the Blind Man*, whilst his first forays into the Canadian world of academe lent more than a little to his comic novel *Moodie's Tale*. EW did not turn to his crime novels until he was in his fifties. *The Night the Gods Smiled*, which won the John Creasey and Arthur Ellis awards, introduced his main character, Inspector Charlie Salter of the Toronto police. These are traditional police procedurals with a heavy English flavour, despite their setting – though *Death in the Old Country*, another award-winner, is set in England. Salter is a family man, methodical, astute but not favoured by his superiors. He always solves his cases, which invariably concern the worlds of the professional (academia, films, the theatre, books, medicine) rather than the low-life, but doesn't necessarily hold them in high priority, thinking as much about his family and friends as the villains and victims. The series thus turns no new soil, but yields a satisfying crop nonetheless. EW has considered bringing the series to an end. In *Buried in Stone* he developed a new character, retired policeman Mel Pickett, who had helped Salter in *A Sensitive Case*, about the death of a masseur with influential connections. Pickett has retired to a cabin in northern Ontario but still involves himself in local cases particularly in *Death of a Hired Man* where he believes it was he who was the intended victim not the man who was killed. In *Death of a Sunday Writer* EW introduced Lucy Trimble Brenner, a small-town librarian who, like P.D. JAMES's Cordelia Gray, inherits her cousin's private detective agency and decides to continue it. *The Kidnapping of Rosie Dawn* introduced yet another character, English lecturer and occasional sleuth Joe Barley, who comes up against political correctness at his college when he goes in search of a missing exotic dancer. These books have a light humorous touch. EW seldom strolls far from familiar territory, but that just makes the books all the more homely.

Novels
Charlie Salter series: *The Night the Gods Smiled* (1983), *Smoke Detector* (1985), *Death in the Old Country* (1985), *The Man Who Changed His Name* (1986; as *A Single Death*, UK 1986), *A Body Surrounded by Water* (1987), *A Question of Murder* (1988), *A Sensitive Case* (1990), *Final Cut* (1991), *A Fine Italian Hand* (1992), *Death by Degrees* (1993), *The Last Hand* (2002).
Mel Pickett series: *Buried in Stone* (1996), *Death of a Hired Man* (2001).
Lucy Trimble series: *Death of a Sunday Writer* (1996), *Death on the Rocks* (1999).
Joe Barley series: *The Kidnapping of Rosie Dawn* (2000).
Non-fiction. *Always Give a Penny to the Blind Man* (1999).
Editor. *Criminal Shorts*, with Howard Engel (1992).

Where to start: *The Night the Gods Smiled.*
Awards: CWA John Creasey award (1983), Arthur Ellis, best novel (1984, 1986), best short story (1988, 1992), CWC Derrick Murdoch award (1998), Barry award (2001).
Similar stuff: Peter ROBINSON, Ted WOOD.
Final fact: EW writes all his books in longhand.

L. R. Wright (1939–2001) Canada

Former reporter for the *Calgary Herald* LRW, known as "Bunny", turned to writing novels when her husband changed jobs and they moved to Edmonton. She won the annual Search-for-a-new-Alberta-novelist competition with *Neighbours*, issued under the name Laurali Wright. Though published as a mainstream book, this has the hallmark of her later mysteries. Two neighbours become concerned at the declining mental state of a third neighbour, which seems to have its root in the distant past. The way that people close to each other can suddenly become alienated was the theme of her first crime novel, the award-winning *The Suspect*, which introduced Royal Canadian Mounted Policeman, Karl Alberg, who operates out of the small town of Sechelt on the coast of British Columbia. Alberg, who is himself lonely, divorced from his wife and separated from his daughters, and seeking a relationship with the town librarian, applies himself to the study of the prime suspect in a murder case where it is known that one old man murdered his old friend. The novel deals with Alberg's painstaking and methodical search for a reason. All of LRW's subsequent books have a similar approach, with Alberg delving into the psychology of the crime, usually something from long ago, and frequently involving friends or family. *Acts of Murder* introduced a new assistant, Edwina "Eddie" Henderson. LRW recalled that when she began the Alberg series there were no women staff sergeants in the RCMP and thus she had had to write about a man. Now things had changed and with *Kidnap* she moved Eddie Henderson centre stage. Alas LRW's death from cancer at the age of 61 meant she completed only one further book in the series and we will not know her plans to further develop Henderson and Alberg. Her death robbed the field of one of its most perceptive writers.

Novels
Sergeant Alberg series: *The Suspect* (1985), *Sleep While I Sing* (1986), *A Chill Rain in January* (1990), *Fall from Grace* (1991), *Prized Possessions* (1993), *A Touch of Panic* (1994), *Mother Love* (1995), *Strangers Among Us* (1996), *Acts of Murder* (1997).
Eddie Henderson series: *Kidnap* (2000), *Menace* (2001).
Non-series: *Neighbours* (1979).

Full name: Laurali Rose Wright (*née* Appleby).
Where to start: *The Suspect*.
Awards: Edgar, best novel (1986), Arthur Ellis, best novel (1991, 1996), CWC Derrick Murdoch award (2001).
Similar stuff: Charlotte MACLEOD as Alisa Craig for another RCMP series; Margaret YORKE.
Final fact: LRW would probably never have turned to writing fiction had she and her husband not moved yet, ironically, they divorced a few years later.

Margaret Yorke (b. 1924) UK

A former librarian, MY later won the CWA's Golden Handcuff's award for the author most popular in libraries. In a career of over 40 years she has written nearly 50 books. Early on she wrote a few traditional whodunnits featuring Oxford don and amateur sleuth Patrick Grant, but the rest of her novels are all stand-alones and are almost all variations on the theme of people or communities with hidden secrets. She is one of the most adept writers at exploring the undercurrent of tension and suspicion within village communities. This was the case in her very first novel, *Summer Flight*, which explores the consequences when a fugitive from justice seeks refuge in a small village, and it remains the case up to such recent novels as *False Pretences*, where the arrival of various people from the past in a small village upsets the status quo. The calendar changes in MY's novels, and the books all have a currency – with environmentalists in *False Pretences* and violent young thugs in *Act of Violence*, but beneath it all MY knows that people do not change. Her books are full of secrets and skeletons in the closet, people trying to lead different lives and escape their past. One of the most original twists on this is in *The Point of Murder*, where a spinster, trapped in a life of caring for her mother, takes on a new persona but faces a dilemma when, as that character, she witnesses a murder. Revenge is a deep motivation in several of MY's novels. It may be against an innocent ex-con (*Intimate Kill*), or against the man who is proven innocent but nevertheless becomes the victim of the aggrieved family (*A Question of Belief*), or a family seeking revenge upon the guilty (*Almost the Truth*). A murderer assumes a new life in *A Small Deceit* whilst a con-man is accused of a murder he didn't do in *The Smooth Face of Evil*. Nothing is ever what it seems in MY's novels which is why the *Daily Telegraph* dubbed her "the mistress of unease."

Novels

Patrick Grant series: *Dead in the Morning* (1970), *Silent Witness* (1972), *Grave Matters* (1973), *Mortal Remains* (1974), *Cast for Death* (1976).

Non-series: *Summer Flight* (1957), *Christopher* (1959), *The China Doll* (1961), *Once a Stranger* (1962), *The Birthday* (1963), *Full Circle* (1965), *No Medals for the Major* (1974), *The Small Hours of the Morning* (1975), *The Cost of Silence* (1977), *The Point of Murder* (1978; as *The Come-On*, US 1979), *Death on Account* (1979), *The Scent of Fear* (1980), *The Hand of Death* (1981), *Devil's Work* (1982), *Find Me a Villain* (1983), *The Smooth Face of Evil* (1984), *Intimate Kill* (1985), *Safely to the Grave* (1986), *Evidence to Destroy* (1987), *Speak for the Dead* (1988), *Crime in Question* (1989), *Admit to Murder* (1990), *A Small Deceit* (1991), *Criminal Damage* (1992), *Dangerous to Know* (1993), *Almost the Truth* (1994), *Serious Intent* (1995), *A Question of Belief* (1996), *Act of Violence* (1997), *False Pretences* (1998), *The Price of Guilt* (1999), *A Case to Answer* (2001), *Cause for Concern* (2001).

Short Stories. *Pieces of Justice* (1994).

Real name: Margaret Beda Nicholson (*née* Larminie).
Pen-name: Margaret Yorke.
Where to start: *The Point of Murder.*
Awards: Swedish Academy of Detection, Best Foreign (1982), CWA Golden Handcuffs (1993), Diamond Dagger (1999).
Website: <www.twbooks.co.uk/authors/margaretyorke.html>
Similar stuff: Sheila RADLEY, Ruth RENDELL, June THOMSON.
Final fact: MY was the first ever woman to work at Christ Church college library at Oxford in 1963.

P. B. Yuill *pseudonym, see under* Gordon M. Williams

Eve Zaremba (b. 1930) Canada

EZ was born in Poland and emigrated to Canada in 1952. She has worked as a librarian and for a while ran a bookshop, and was a founder of *Broadside, A Feminist Review*. Her first book, *Privilege of Sex, A Century of Canadian Women* appeared in 1972. She wrote six novels about lesbian P.I. Helen Keremos, a former intelligence operative who retains a network of contacts all over Canada. It's a highly radical in-your-face series where Keremos continues to act more like a special agent than a P.I. Her centre of operations is Vancouver but the action of the first two novels is mostly in Toronto. *The Butterfly Effect* takes her to Japan. EZ has stated that *White Noise*, in which Keremos agrees to help a former client from Hong Kong who is being pursued and flees to Vancouver, is the last in the series.

Novels

Helen Keremos series: *A Reason to Kill* (1978), *Work for a Million* (1986), *Beyond Hope* (1987), *Uneasy Lies* (1990), *The Butterfly Effect* (1994), *White Noise* (1997).

Similar stuff: Sandra SCOPPETTONE, Mary WINGS.

Mark Richard Zubro (b. 1948) US

MRZ is a high-school English teacher in Chicago. He is openly gay and has written and talked about the problems arising from being gay and a teacher. His first series features Tom Mason, who is also a gay high school teacher, and his lover Scott Carpenter, a professional baseball player. *A Simple Suburban Murder*, where Mason investigates the death of a student, won the Lambda award for best gay mystery novel. Too many deaths at one school rather stretch credulity so after the fourth novel MRZ takes his protagonists elsewhere. They're on the run in *An Echo of Death*, while in *Rust on the Razor*, they visit Scott's dying father in Georgia only for Scott to be arrested following the death of the local sheriff. MRZ's other series features gay Chicago cop Paul Turner who had previously been married and has two sons. In *Sorry Now?* Turner investigates the murder of a homophobic's tele-evangelist's daughter. This series is more realistic with a stronger sense of character, bolstered by Turner's relationship with his sons, and the gay themes are more central to the plot without being over-emphasized.

Novels

Tom Mason series: *A Simple Suburban Murder* (1989), *Why Isn't Becky Twitchell Dead?* (1990), *The Only Good Priest* (1991), *The Principal Cause of Death* (1992), *An Echo of Death* (1994), *Rust on the Razor* (1996), *Are You Nuts?* (1998), *One Dead Drag Queen* (2000), *Here Comes the Corpse* (2002).
Paul Turner series: *Sorry Now?* (1991), *Political Poison* (1993), *Another Dead Teenager* (1996), *The Truth Can Get You Killed* (1997), *Drop Dead* (1999), *Sex and Murder.com* (2001).

Where to start: *Sorry Now?*
Awards: Lambda (1990).
Similar stuff: Joseph HANSEN's Dave Brandstetter, Michael NAVA's Henry Rios.

Sharon Zukowski US

SZ is the senior publications editor at a New York financial services firm and this provides her with authentic background for some of the episodes in her series featuring female P.I. Blaine Stewart. Stewart's a former cop whose husband, another cop, is killed in the line of duty. Stewart resigns and turns to the bottle but is rescued by her attorney sister and becomes a partner in her agency. Blaine covers the investigative work and the sister the legal side. Many of their clients are corporate Wall Street firms meaning that Stewart is frequently involved with wealthy and therefore determined individuals. The first novel, *The Hour of the Knife*, where Stewart investigates the murder of an old college friend, is rather too cliché-ridden and contains everything but the kitchen sink, but with that out of SZ's system the later books take on challenging issues with considerable directness. The best are *Dancing in the Dark*, about animal-rights activists, and *Leap of Faith*, about a missing surrogate mother.

Novels

Blaine Stewart series: *The Hour of the Knife* (1991), *Dancing in the Dark* (1992), *Leap of Faith* (1994), *Prelude to Death* (1996), *Jungle Land* (1997).

Similar stuff: Jane DENTINGER, Sandra SCOPPETTONE.
Final fact: SZ is a seasoned traveller, having rafted down the Grand Canyon and explored Iceland in addition to traditional venues like France and Scotland.

Television Series and Major Films

This section provides entries on over 300 TV series and films. They are organized alphabetically by title. Following the film title is the year of release, the country of origin and the film's length in minutes. Films are assumed to be in colour, but monochrome films are identified by "b&w". After the TV series title is the country of origin, the dates the series began and ended and the number of episodes. Both list the producer(s) and director(s), the writers of the screenplay and the leading actors.

Entries have been selected based on their influence, popularity or originality. All relate to modern crime fiction or cases so films or series based on classic or golden age characters, such as Sherlock Holmes, Hercule Poirot or Perry Mason are not included.

A Bout de Souffle [*aka* Breathless]

(1960, French, 90 minutes, b&w)
Director: Jean-Luc Godard. **Producer:** Georges de Beauregard.
Screenplay: Jean-Luc Godard, based on a story by François Truffaut.
Starring: Jean-Paul Belmondo, Jean Seberg, Daniel Boulanger, Jean-Pierre Melville.
A classic cult film and one of the first of the French New Wave movies, influencing a generation. Filmed in casual *cinema verité* documentary style it is the story of a young car thief (Belmondo) who kills a policeman, falls in love with a literary woman (Seberg) and goes on the run until his inevitable death. The film was remade in the US by James McBride in 1983 as *Breathless*, starring Richard Gere and Valerie Kaprisky, set in Las Vegas, but this was a pale imitation and a simple excuse for sex and violence.

Adam 12

(US TV series, 1968–75, 150 episodes)
Creator: Jack Webb. **Producer:** Tom Williams.
Starring: Martin Milner, Kent McCord, William Boyett.
Half-hour police procedural series following the adventures of two officers of the LAPD on patrol-car duty, Pete Malloy and Jim Reed. "Adam 12" was their car identification. They encountered a variety of crimes and problems each week, many serious but some humorous. At the start Malloy (Milner) was the veteran officer, saddened by the death of his partner and thinking about quitting the force. He takes on a new rookie partner, Reed (McCord), and the two form a strong bond. Just as he had done with *Dragnet*, Webb's emphasis was on fast action, rapid dialogue and authenticity, with story-lines based on cases from the LAPD files and a real police dispatch reader speaking the show's "One Adam-12" signature. Over the seven seasons you followed the promotion of the officers and became more involved with their lives and events at the station. The series was resurrected as *The New Adam 12* (1989–90; 52 episodes) with new characters – officers Gus Grant (Peter Parros) and Matt Doyle (Ethan Wayne) but it showed no advancement and was dropped after one season.

Alfred Hitchcock Presents

(US TV series, 1955–62, b&w; 1962–5, 361 episodes; revived 1985–6, 80 episodes. Series retitled *The Alfred Hitchcock Hour* between 1962–5)
A half-hour anthology series (increased to an hour in 1962) that is still a by-word for quality and originality in crime-suspense production and scriptwriting. Hitchcock gave the series his own personal touch, providing a witty introduction to each episode plus a sardonic conclusion. At the start Hitchcock walked into a self-drawn caricature profile of himself on the screen, always on a bizarre set, accompanied by the theme tune adapted from Gounod's "Funeral March of a Marionette". Hitchcock directed only 20 episodes himself, and the series became a good vehicle for new directors, including Robert Altman, William Friedkin, Sydney Pollack, even William Shatner. Many episodes were derived from previously published short stories, including many classics. A typical Hitchcock story involved a husband or wife who planned on disposing of their partner, or pulling off some major heist. Often they would end up in some odd predicament but frequently they would get away with it, which is why Hitchcock would provide a winding up commentary that would explain how justice prevailed in order to meet broadcasting codes of ethics. This enabled Hitchcock to keep the story itself true to the original. Hitchcock loved stories with clever twists and surprise endings, and the more macabre the better. Few of them were police procedurals or stan-

dard whodunnits. A few were supernatural. Henry SLESAR wrote more scripts for the series than anyone else (about 50). Others whose stories were frequently adapted include Robert Arthur, Bill S. Ballinger, Robert BLOCH, Ray Bradbury, John Cheever, Roald Dahl, Avram Davidson, Stanley ELLIN, Edward HOCH and Gerald Kersh. The episode "An Unlocked Window" won an Edgar in 1966. Hitchcock died in 1980 but the series was resurrected in 1985 with his introductions reconstituted in colour but not necessarily matched to the story that followed. The new production qualities were not a patch on the original series.

All the President's Men

(1976, US, 138 minutes)
Director: Alan J. Pakula. **Producer:** Walter Coblenz.
Screenplay: William GOLDMAN.
Starring: Dustin Hoffman, Robert Redford, Jack Warden, Jason Robards, Martin Balsam.
William Goldman won an Oscar for his script for this tense, fast-paced portrayal of the discovery of the link between the White House and the Watergate affair by two reporters from the *Washington Post*. Pakula succeeds in sustaining the suspense in a detective-like investigation even though we know the outcome. Both Pakula and the film were also nominated for Academy Awards.

The American Friend

(1977, West German, 127 minutes)
Director: Wim Wenders. **Producer:** Robby Müller.
Screenplay: Wim Wenders from the book, *Ripley's Game*, by Patricia HIGHSMITH.
Starring: Dennis Hopper, Bruno Ganz, Lisa Kreuzer, Gérard Blain.
Moviemakers have been attracted to Highsmith's amoral, cynical but charismatic Mr Ripley. Dennis Hopper takes on the rôle in this co-West German/French production, which captures the atmosphere of the books and in particular Ripley's self-loathing that manifests in his constant gambling with death. Here Ripley becomes involved with the Mafia and is asked to find a non-professional hit-man. He sets his sights on an innocent family man in Hamburg (Ganz) whom he convinces has a fatal blood disease. See also *The Talented Mr Ripley*.

American Psycho

(2000, US, 101 minutes)
Director: Mary Harron. **Producers:** Edward R. Pressman, Chris Hanley, Christian Halsey Solomon.
Screenplay: Mary Harron and Guinevere Turner from the book by Bret Easton ELLIS.

Starring: Christian Bale, Willem Dafoe, Jared Leto, Josh Lucas, Samantha Mathis.

Ellis's original novel caused a furore when it was first published because of the relish it took on the depraved hobby of psychopath Patrick Bateman (Bale) a seemingly normal, likeable and witty character on the surface, but who enjoys torturing, murdering and dissecting women. It would have been too easy to adapt this book into just another gore-ridden slasher movie, but Harron's intelligent handling moves to the psychological heart of Bateman and his perception of the world. You perceive his vacuous, materialistic, yuppie world of the eighties, and his need to express himself in a way that only he can. The chilling aspect of the film is not what Bateman does, but that we find ourselves attracted to him, even when we know the horrors he performs. Moreover, because he is a product of the soulless materialism of our world with which we can all identify, we can even understand why he does it. Inevitably the success of the film has led to a sequel, *American Psycho II: All American Girl* (2002), directed by Morgan J. Freeman and set 15 years later where a survivor of Bateman's lure, Mila Kunis (played by Rachelle Newman) has herself become infected by the desire to kill.

Amsterdam Affair

(1968, UK, 100 minutes)

Director: Gerry O'Hara. **Producer:** Gerry Willoughby.

Screenplay: Edmund Ward from *Love in Amsterdam* by Nicolas FREELING.

Starring: Wolfgang Kieling, Catherine Schell, William Marlowe.

The first of the Van der Valk series to be adapted for the big screen and the only one to date filmed in English. It is a fairly faithful adaptation of the original novel where the Dutch detective investigates a writer who is believed to have murdered his mistress. Kieling is a convincing Van der Valk. There has also been a Dutch version of *Because of the Cats* filmed in 1973, with Bryan Marshall as the detective, and two German TV adaptations with Frank Finlay in the rôle, but the character will be best known through Barry Foster's interpretation in the long-running UK TV series *Van der Valk*.

Amy Prentiss

(US TV series, 1974–5; 3 episodes)

Producer: Cy Chermak. **Directors:** Lou Antonio, Boris Sagal, Gordon Hessler.

Starring: Jessica Walter, Art Metrano, Steve Sandor, Helen Hunt.

Jessica Walter (relatively fresh from her rôle as the spurned lover in Clint Eastwood's *Play Misty for Me*) played Amy Prentiss who becomes the first chief of detectives in the San Francisco police department when her boss dies suddenly. Prentiss is a 35-year-old widowed mother with all the complications that that entails. Her pre-teen daughter was played by 10-year-old Helen Hunt. Prentiss's problems are further aggravated by the male officers finding it difficult to report to a woman. Like Jane Tennison in *Prime Suspect*, 16 years later, Prentiss earns the respect of the force for her ability to crack difficult crimes. Apart from this ground-breaking departure this series was otherwise relatively straightforward and was overshadowed by its compatriots *Columbo*, *McCloud* and *McMillan and Wife* as one of the programmes in the *Sunday Mystery Movie* cycle.

Anatomy of a Murder

(1959, US, 161 minutes, b&w)
Director/Producer: Otto Preminger.
Screenplay: Wendell Mayes from the 1958 novel by Robert Traver (1903–91).
Starring: James Stewart, Ben Gazzara, George C. Scott, Lee Remick.
This courtroom drama, nominated for seven academy awards, is still powerful, though no longer as controversial as it was when first screened through the use of such "daring" descriptive words as "panties". It is a faithful adaptation of Traver's novel about a country lawyer (Stewart) who defends an army sergeant (Gazzara) on the charge of murdering the man who raped his wife (Remick). The film catapulted George C. Scott, who plays the prosecuting attorney, his first major rôle, into stardom. The authenticity of the film derives in some degree from the fact that not only was the book it was based on written pseudonymously by a retired judge, John D. Voelker, but the trial judge in the film was played by real-life judge Joseph N. Welch. He had established a reputation in 1954 when he defended the US Army against Senator Joseph McCarthy and helped precipitate the senator's downfall.

The Anderson Tapes

(1971, US, 99 minutes)
Director: Sidney Lumet. **Producer:** Robert M. Weitman.
Screenplay: Frank R. Pierson based on the novel by Lawrence SANDERS.
Starring: Sean Connery, Dyan Cannon, Martin Balsam, Alan King, Christopher Walken.
Sanders's novel, which was written in the form of reports and official documents did not lend itself to easy adaptation to the screen. The surprising element of the book, which is that a thief (Connery) plans to burgle an entire apartment block oblivious to the fact that he is being monitored by government surveillance equipment, becomes all too obvious in the film and thus loses its impact. The film has moments of slickness and tension but comes apart at the end in a violent and at times ludicrous climax.

Archer

(US TV series, 1975, 6 episodes)
Directors: Gary Nelson, Paul Stanley, Edward Abroms, John Llewellyn Moxey, Arnold Laven, Jack Arnold.
Writers: David P. Harmon, Jim Byrnes, Leigh Brackett, David Karp, Harold Livingston, Anthony Lawrence, Wallace Ware.
Starring: Brian Keith, John P. Ryan.
Following the TV pilot, *The Underground Man* (1974), with Peter Graves in the rôle of Ross MACDONALD's Lew Archer, Brian Keith took over the part for the hour-long series that ran during the winter of 1975. Although Keith played Archer straight down the line, albeit a stockier and less clean-cut image than Graves, the series did not catch on and ceased after six hour-long episodes. The character worked better on the big screen with Paul Newman – see *Harper* and *The Drowning Pool.*

Arrest and Trial

(US TV series, 1963–4, 30 episodes, b&w)
Producer: Frank P. Rosenberg. **Directors:** Jack Smight, Lewis Milestone.
Starring: Ben Gazzara, Chuck Connors, John Larch, John Kerr, Roger Perry, Noah Keen.
Advanced for its day, *A&T* tried a split format. The first half of each 90-minute episode followed Detective Sergeant Nick Anderson (Gazzara) as he tracked down and arrested the villain whilst in the second half defence attorney John Egan (Connors) did his best to find him innocent. The problem with this format meant that if the man was innocent then Anderson had failed and if he wasn't then Egan failed. This spoiled the show's credibility and it closed after one season. The series nevertheless had some good guest stars including Robert Duvall, Martin Sheen, Mickey Rooney, Peter Fonda, William Shatner and Telly Savalas. The format was reinvigorated to much better effect with *Law & Order* and *Trial and Retribution. Arrest & Trial* was also the name of a US series launched in 2000 which dramatized real-life cases from the investigation to the verdict. This series was hosted by Brian Dennehy.

The Avengers *see under* Police Surgeon

B. L. Stryker

(US TV series, 1989–90, 12 episodes)
Executive Producers: Burt Reynolds and Tom Selleck.
Directors: Burt Reynolds, Tony Wharmby and others.
Starring: Burt Reynolds, Ossie Davis, Michael O. Smith, Rita Moreno.
BLS rotated on a three-week cycle in a slot shared with the revived *Columbo* and *Gideon Oliver*. It was a relatively soft-boiled P.I. series star-

ring Burt Reynolds as retired cop B.L. (Buddy Lee) Stryker who moves back home from New Orleans to settle on an old houseboat moored off Palm Beach, Florida. His former wife, Kimberley Baskin (Moreno), who had subsequently married a millionaire but is now a widow, also lives in Palm Beach. The regular cast each week included Stryker's friend and former boxer Oz Jackson (Davis) and Head of Palm Beach Police Chief McGee (Smith). It is a rapist's attacks on young socialites that draws Stryker out of retirement in the first episode, "The Dancer's Touch". The series was a pleasing mix of clever whodunnits to stalkers and psychotics. Scriptwriters included Joe GORES, who contributed a particularly complex mystery, "Blind Chess", and Robert B. PARKER, with "Blues for Buder". This series was Burt Reynolds's third and most successful attempt at a regular TV crime series. He had previously starred in *Hawk* (1966; 17 episodes), where he played an Iroquois American Indian working in the D.A.'s homicide bureau, and *Dan August* (1970–1; 26 episodes) where he was a cop in his home town in California.

Badger

(UK TV series, 1999–2000, 13 episodes)
Producer: Murray Ferguson (series 1), Ann Tricklebank (series 2).
Director: Paul Harrison.
Writer: Kieran Prendiville.
Starring: Jerome Flynn, Kevin Doyle, Adrian Bower, Phillippa Wilson.
Jerome Flynn plays DC Tom McCabe, a Northumberland police wildlife liaison officer and former marine. With his sidekick Jim Cassidy (Doyle) the two monitor infringements of wildlife legislation, one of the fastest growing crimes in the UK, and other related environmental issues, such as pollution. The character was based on real-life officer Paul Henery.

Badlands

(1974, US, 94 minutes)
Producer/Director: Terrence Malick.
Screenplay: Terrence Malick.
Starring: Martin Sheen, Sissy Spacek, Warren Oates.
Malick's impressive debut film, in which a young garbage collector (Sheen) vents his anger by killing his girlfriend's father and then the two go on a murder spree across the Dakota Badlands, rapidly became a cult movie. The strength of the film is in Malick's exploration of the psyche of the two main characters – Sheen, the James Dean-like rebel without a cause, Spacek as a vapid, easily led girl wrapped up in a fantasy world through her reading of popular magazines. Thirty years on the film remains unsettling since so little has changed.

Banacek

(US TV series, 1972–4, 16 episodes plus pilot)
Creator: Anthony Wilson. **Producer:** Howie Horowitz
Directors: Herschel Daugherty, Andrew McLaglen, Jack Smight.
Executive Story Consultant: Robert van Scoyk.
Starring: George Peppard, Ralph Manza, Murray Matheson, Christine Belford (in second series).
Thomas Banacek (Peppard) was a freelance insurance investigator based in Boston who was called in by insurance companies when their own investigations drew a blank. That meant Banacek got the more baffling, "impossible" crimes. He was good at his job and lived a flash life, being chauffered about in his limousine, though this slick image plus endless girlfriends now dates the series, despite the fascination of the plots. He was assisted in his cases by rare book dealer Felix Mulholland (Matheson) and in the second series by insurance agent Carlie Kirkland (Belford) who also provided a romance angle. In the pilot film, "Detour to Nowhere", scripted by Anthony Wilson, Banacek has to solve how an armoured car full of gold bullion disappeared on a deserted stretch of highway. Regular writers for the series included Stanley Ralph Ross, Harold Livingston and Stephen Kandel. The first episode, "Let's Hear it for a Living Legend" by Del Reisman, in which a star football halfback vanishes in front of a full stadium, was novelized as *Banacek* by Deane Romano (1973).

Banyon

(US TV series, 1972–3, 15 episodes plus pilot)
Creator: Ed Adamson. **Producer:** Ed Adamson for Quinn Martin Productions.
Directors: Lawrence Dobkin, Charles S. Dubin, Marvin Chomsky, Daniel Petrie, Ralph Senensky.
Story Editor: Norman Katkov.
Starring: Robert Forster, Richard Jaeckel, Joan Blondell, James B. Sikking, Julie Gregg.
Miles Banyon (Forster) was an ex-cop turned P.I. in Los Angeles in 1937. He remains in contact with his former police partner Lieutenant Pete McNeil (Jaeckel) though frequently falls foul of plainclothes detective Andrews (Sikking). Many of Banyon's cases involved the Hollywood set, including radio stars and even pulp writers. The show had a strong thirties atmosphere and also cast several well-known period stars, including Pat O'Brien and Joan Blondell. It had all the conventions of the thirties hard-boiled P.I. but was out of tune for the seventies and survived only one season. The two-hour pilot episode, "Banyon" by Ed Adamson, which had aired in March 1971, was novelized as *Banyon* by William Johnston (1971).

Baretta

(US TV series, 1975–8, 80 episodes)
Creator: Stephen J. Cannell. **Producer:** Jo Swerling, Jr. (first season) then Ed Waters.
Directors: Russ Mayberry, Don Medford and others including Robert Blake.
Starring: Robert Blake, Dana Elcar/Edward Grover, Michael D. Roberts, Tom Ewell, Chino Williams.
This series was a reworking of *Toma* after that star's show declined a second season. The program was remoulded around the character of actor Robert Blake as Tony Baretta, a streetwise and unorthodox undercover city cop in California. Baretta is a loner and lives in a seedy hotel room with his pet cockatoo, Fred. The hotel is managed by alcoholic ex-cop Billy Truman (Ewell). Baretta had a rough childhood and knows the streets, as well as being a master of disguise, so is able to blend in with gangs and criminals. One of his informants is a fancy dude pimp called Rooster (Roberts). Needless to say Baretta does his own thing and doesn't fit in with his superior Inspector Shiller (Elcar) in the first season or Lieutenant Brubaker (Grover) thereafter. The series was action-orientated though Blake, who involved himself in the production, demanded that the violence be kept to a minimum. There were two Baretta spin-off books: *Beyond the Law*, Andrew Patrick and *Sweet Revenge*, Thom Racina (both 1977).

Barlow at Large *see under* Softly, Softly

Barnaby Jones

(US TV series, 1973–80, 175 episodes)
Producer: Adrian Samish and others for Quinn Martin productions.
Editorial Supervisor: Richard Brockway.
Story Consultant: Robert Blees, Norman Jolley.
Starring: Buddy Ebsen, Lee Meriwether, Mark Shera, Vince Howard/John Carter.
BJ was rushed into production to fill a gap in the schedules and went on to be one of TV's longest-running crime shows. In the first episode, "Requiem for a Son", written by Edward Hume from a story by Adrian Samish, Jones (Ebsen) has retired from his detective agency, now in the hands of his son, Hal; but when Hal is murdered Jones comes out of retirement and, with the help of Frank Cannon (see *Cannon*) solves the murder. Ebsen continues to run the agency with the help of his daughter-in-law Betty (Meriwether) and, from season five, his cousin Jedediah Jones (Shera). His regular contact at with the police is Lieutenant Joe Taylor (Howard), later Lieutenant Biddle (Carter). Jones was methodical and, due to his age, there was little heavy action, except when left to the youngsters, though there was no shortage of violent crimes and vicious

criminals. A feature of the series was Jones's own home laboratory where he analysed clues. With such a long-running series it was inevitable that plots became repetitious over time and Jones increasingly more unbelievable, but it was relatively harmless fun. A typical Quinn Martin production.

Bergerac

(UK TV series, 1981–91, 87 episodes)
Creator: Robert Banks Stewart.
Starring: John Nettles, Terence Alexander, Sean Arnold, Deborah Grant.
This popular series was set on the island of Jersey in the Channel Islands off the French coast, a tax haven for the super-rich and an ideal locale for smuggling. Sergeant Jim Bergerac (Nettles) of the Jersey police has fought back against alcoholism but is separated from his wife (Grant) though is regularly involved with her rich and influential father Charlie Hungerford (Alexander). The charm of the series was the beautiful island setting. The long run allowed for the development of several sub-plots such as Bergerac's pursuit of sharp-witted con-artiste Phillipa Vale (played by Liza Goddard). John Nettles would later return in the series *Midsomer Murders*. The series spawned several spin-off books. Michael Hardwick wrote *Bergerac* (1981) and then Andrew TAYLOR, writing as Andrew Saville, wrote *Bergerac is Back* (1985), *Crimes of the Season* (1985), *Bergerac and the Fatal Weakness* (1988), *Bergerac and the Jersey Rose* (1988), *Bergerac and the Moving Fever* (1988), *Bergerac and the Traitor's Child* (1988).

Best Seller

(1987, US, 95 minutes)
Director: John Flynn. **Producer:** Carter de Haven.
Screenplay: Larry Cohen.
Starring: James Woods, Brian Dennehy, Victoria Tennant.
Former hit-man Cleve (Woods), who is as amoral and manic as all the best villains, agrees to help LA Detective Meechum (Dennehy) write a book about an old unsolved case. Dennehy is burnt-out as a cop and, since his wife's death, dried-up as a novelist, but Cleve's offer gives him a new lease of life and gives Cleve a chance to appear a hero. The film's strength lies in the developing relationship between cop and killer. The film was nominated for an Edgar.

Beverly Hills Cop

(1984, US, 105 minutes)
Director: Martin Brest. **Producer:** Don Simpson, Jerry Bruckheimer.
Screenplay: Daniel Petrie, Jr.

Starring: Eddie Murphy, Judge Reinhold, John Ashton, Steven Berkoff. Although this rôle was originally planned for Sylvester Stallone the final product was written around Eddie Murphy giving him a chance to shine in all his fast-talking loud-mouthed glory. Murphy plays Detroit cop, Axel Foley, who ends up in Beverly Hills on the trail of his best friend's killer. The rest of the cast just play along. Nevertheless the film was one of the highest-grossing films that year. Petrie was nominated for an Oscar for his script and the film was shortlisted for an Academy Award. The success inevitably spawned two sequels, *Beverly Hills Cop II* (1987) and *III* (1994), though a phalanx of scriptwriters failed to produce anything but minor retreads. There is no novel of the original film, but Robert Tine penned *Beverly Hill Cops II* (1987).

The Big Easy

(1986, US, 101 minutes)
Director: Jim McBride. **Producer:** Stephen J. Friedman.
Screenplay: Jim McBride, Daniel Petrie, Jr. and Jack Baran based on the 1970 novel by James Conaway.
Starring: Dennis Quaid, Ellen Barkin, Ned Beatty, John Goodman.
Quaid plays the corruptible New Orleans homicide detective Lieutenant Remy McSwain who is persuaded by Assistant D.A. Ann Osborne (Barkin) to investigate corruption amongst his colleagues. McSwain is eccentric, cussed and smooth-talking, and it requires a heroin scam and a series of murders before he sits up and takes notice. Although the film doesn't offer anything new, it packages what it has very neatly. It was nominated for an Edgar and won the Anthony Award for the year's best movie. The film eventually spawned a TV series called *The Big Easy* (US, 1996–7, 35 episodes) with Tony Crane as McSwain and Susan Walters as Osborne. The series played on the contrast between McSwain always trying to cut corners and Osborne, the stickler for process and probity, and it lost its drive when actress Walters left at the end of the first series. She was replaced by Leslie Bibb as Detective Janine Rebbenack, but by then the series had lost its dynamics.

The Big Fix

(1978, US, 108 minutes)
Director: Jeremy Paul Kagan. **Producer:** Carl Borack, Richard Dreyfuss.
Screenplay: Roger L. SIMON from his own novel.
Starring: Richard Dreyfuss, Susan Anspach, John Lithgow, Bonnie Bedelia.
Between them Simon and Dreyfuss managed to capture admirably on the screen the subverted nostalgia of the book for an ersatz hippy golden age of the late sixties. Dreyfuss plays Moses Wine, an industrial investigator

turned quasi-private eye who drifts back into the California of his college years trying to unravel a case of political and ethnic corruption. At times the movie seems aimless but the threads all weave together at the end. The nature of the film means that it has now become even more of a nostalgia item and it hasn't really dated, only mulled.

The Big Heat

(1953, US, 90 minutes, b&w)
Director: Fritz Lang. **Producer:** Robert Arthur.
Screenplay: Sydney Boehm based on the 1952 novel by William P. McGivern.
Starring: Glenn Ford, Gloria Grahame, Jocelyn Brando, Lee Marvin, Alexander Scourby.
It may be 50 years old but at the time of its release this was considered a very violent and controversial film, and it unlocked the cage for new standards of realism in crime films. Police detective Dave Bannion (Ford) takes on big city organized crime when a bomb meant for him kills his wife (Brando). For its day it included a number of "shock" scenes (such as the suicide at the start and good-time girl Debby Marsh (Grahame) being scalded by hot coffee thrown in her face) which reviewers saw as arbitrary and "pointless" violence. The film remains effective and is regarded by many as one of the best of the "late noir" movies. It received an Edgar award in 1954 as the year's best film but was entirely overlooked for the Oscars.

The Bill

(UK TV series, 1984–*current*)
Creator: Geoff McQueen.
Producers: Many including Michael Chapman, Peter Cregeen (also original Director).
The Bill, set at the fictional Sun Hill police station in East London, is the longest-running (continuous) police series in the world. It started as a one-hour weekly programme. The first episode was broadcast on 16 October 1984, developed from a one-off play, "Woodentop", broadcast in the *Storyboard* series on 16 August 1983. That episode followed the daily patrol of two characters, P.C. Ackland (Trudie Goodwin) and P.C. Jim Carver (Mark Wingett), both of whom are still in the series. After 35 hourly episodes the series switched to two weekly half-hour episodes in 1988 increasing to three per week in 1993 before reverting to two weekly hour-long episodes in 1998. Many of the more recent series have been multi-part story arcs concentrating on the lives and problems of individual officers with less emphasis on the day-to-day police work of the original series. However the series has retained the friction that exists between C.I.D. operations and the uniformed force and is especially good

at exploring the tensions within the station. It is the most authentic TV police procedural series since *Z Cars* and frequently has weekly viewing figures of eight million or more. The series has had too many characters and too many story-lines to do more than scratch the surface. One of the most popular characters to emerge early in the series was bullish Detective Sergeant (later Inspector) Frank (originally called Tommy) Burnside (Chris Ellison) who was never averse to bending the rules especially when it came to roughing the thugs. His relationship with D.S. Roach (Tony Scannell), who was too fond of the bottle, brought sparks in the series' early years. More recently the series explored police corruption in considerable detail with bent detective Don Beech (Billy Murray). When his true colours were declared, following the accidental killing of a fellow officer, the whole of Sunhill C.I.D. were subject to scrutiny and heads rolled. Many officers have come and gone through the series, some more dramatically than others. The death of W.P.C. Martella (Nula Conwell), killed by a raider, shocked many as did the sudden shooting of W.P.C. Jo Morgan by a hit-man. An attempt to move into the drug squad sealed the fate of P.C. Eddie Santini in a dramatic story arc where he not only committed murder but was himself killed after his trial. Race riots in 2002 ended in the torching of Sun Hill and the deaths of six officers. The series also has its light moments, usually provided by stickler-for-detail P.C. Reg Hollis (Jeffrey Stewart). Burnside, who had moved on in 1993, returned briefly to the series in 1998 in a trouble-shooting rôle. His character later had his own spin-off series, *Burnside* (2000; 6 episodes) where he became head of a special unit within the National Crime Squad. Six novels based on *The Bill* episodes and characters were written by John F. Burke (1985–92) and there is a comprehensive book about the series, *The Bill: The Inside Story* by Rachel Silver (1999). Further details will be found on the show's website <www.thebill.com>.

The Bird With the Crystal Plumage

(1969, Italy, 98 minutes)
Director: Dario Argento. **Producer:** Salvatore Argento.
Screenplay: Dario Argento.
Starring: Tony Musante, Suzy Kendall, Eva Renzi, Umberto Raho.
Also known as *The Gallery Murders*, this joint Italian/German production, which originally went under the name *L'Uccello dalle Plume di Cristallo*, marked the directorial debut of Dario Argento, fresh from his work with Sergio Leone. It concerns an American writer (Musante) who witnesses a knife attack and turns paranoid that he will be the next victim. He becomes obsessed with tracking down a serial killer. Argento creates a strong atmosphere of suspense and suspicion with sudden moments of stark shock and an increasing sense of dread. The film was nominated for an Edgar award in 1971.

The Black Marble

(1980, US, 113 minutes)
Director: Harold Becker. **Producer:** Frank Capra, Jr.
Screenplay: Joseph WAMBAUGH, based on his own novel.
Starring: Robert Foxworth, Paula Prentiss, Harry Dean Stanton, Barbara Babcock.
Wambaugh teamed up again with Becker for this second film about the pressures and problems in the police force following the success of *The Onion Field*. Sergeant Valnikov is driven to drink through the stress of the job, particularly coping with child murders and animal torturing, but is brought back from the brink by his new policewoman partner, Sergeant Zimmerman (Prentiss). The film seems less potent today than it did 20 years ago, because the world has caught up with the horrors that the police force has to face, partly thanks to the crusading work of Wambaugh. The film won an Edgar award in 1981.

Black Rain

(1989, US, 125 minutes)
Director: Ridley Scott. **Producer:** Stanley R. Jaffe and Sherry Lansing.
Screenplay: Craig Bolotin and Warren Lewis.
Starring: Michael Douglas, Andy Garcia, Ken Takakura, Yusaku Matsuda, Kate Capshaw.
Nick Conklin (Douglas) is a corrupt and headstrong New York detective who finds himself in the middle of a gang war between members of the Japanese Mafia (the Yakuza). He and his partner, Charlie Vincent (Garcia) escort a Yakuza (Matsuda) back to Tokyo where he escapes. Conklin and Vincent have to team up with Japanese detective Matsumoto (Takakura) to track down the murderer. Ridley Scott took the opportunity to explore the cultural differences between Japan and the US, or more especially between Conklin's arrogant bullishness and Matsumoto's more traditional values. The film was accused of being racist and it certainly displays an unhealthy image of American chauvanism. There is plenty of high action, as you'd expect from Scott, but the film's strength is in its contrast and comparison of American and Japanese society. Bizarrely, because of production problems, the final scenes in Japan had to be filmed in New York. The book of the film is by Mike Cogan.

Blood Simple

(1983, US, 99 minutes)
Director: Joel Coen. **Producer:** Ethan Coen.
Screenplay: Joel & Ethan Coen.
Starring: John Getz, Frances McDormand, Dan Hedaya, M. Emmet Walsh.

The exhilarating debut film by the Coen Brothers. Dubbed "comic noir" by some, if that isn't a contradiction in terms, the film does swing from dark suspense, through grisly horror and violence to moments of genuine high farce. As a result it appeals to all the emotions. Moody Texas bar owner Marty (Hedaya) is enraged when his wife, Abby (McDormand), leaves him for Ray (Getz). Marty hires a private detective (Walsh) first to spy on Abby and Ray and then to kill them. Things rapidly go awry when the detective turns the tables on Marty with a rising crescendo of violence and unpredictability, with everyone out to kill everyone else. Joel Coen directed this while post-production was still being wrapped up on *The Evil Dead*, and some of the influence of Sam Raimi's work is evident in the visual techniques, especially the burial-alive scene. The film was short-listed for the Edgar award in 1986. The screenplay of the film was published separately in 1988.

The Blue Knight

(1973, US, 96 minutes from 8-hour mini-series)
Director: Robert Butler. **Producer:** Walter Coblenz.
Screenplay: E. Jack Neuman based on the novel by Joseph WAMBAUGH.
Starring: William Holden, Lee Remick, Joe Santos, Eileen Brennan, Sam Elliott.
Wambaugh's novel about the LAPD, and in particular the final days in the force of veteran cop Bumper Morgan (Holden) leading up to his retirement, formed the basis for both US TV's first ever mini-series (screened on four consecutive nights in November 1973 and severely edited for cinema release) and a regular series broadcast in 1975–6. The series, which ran for 13 60-minute episodes, starred George Kennedy in the lead rôle supported by Phillip Pine and Charles Siebert as his colleagues. The scripts were mostly by Del Reisman. Morgan was an old-fashioned cop who still pounded the beat, rather than have a patrol car, and upheld traditional values in a rapidly changing world. Morgan knew everyone and, no matter how rough the neighbourhood, there was a degree of respect and tolerance on both sides. In the US, the series was up against *Charlie's Angels* on ABC, and clearly the fast action, sex-appeal show edged out the last echoes of the good-old-days of policing. Nevertheless the series became a strong influence on future realism on TV police shows, especially *Police Story*, on which Wambaugh was a consultant.

The Bone Collector

(1999, US, 118 minutes)
Director: Phillip Noyce. **Producer:** Martin & Michael Bregman, Louis A. Stoller.
Screenplay: Jeremy Iacone based on the novel by Jeffery DEAVER.

Starring: Denzel Washington, Angelina Jolie, Queen Latifah, Michael Rooker.

Deaver's original novel about an injured cop, Lincoln Rhyme (Washington), who conducts an investigation into a serial killer from his bed, with the help of assistant Amelia Donaghy (Jolie), was remarkably effective, despite the unlikely set-up. Transferred to the visual medium, the scenario is less plausible and the set pieces more predictable, although it is still suspenseful. The most effective moments are the crime scenes, which are genuinely chilling.

Bonnie and Clyde

(1967, US, 111 minutes)

Director: Arthur Penn. **Producer:** Warren Beatty.

Screenplay: David Newman, Robert Benton.

Starring: Warren Beatty, Faye Dunaway, Michael J. Pollard.

The story of thirties' gangsters Clyde Barrow (Beatty) and Bonnie Parker (Dunaway) had been told twice before, in *Gun Crazy* (1949) and *The Bonnie Parker Story* (1958), but it was Penn's version, notorious in its day for its callous glorification of violence, that has become the classic. The film succeeds because of its intensity and the reckless inevitability of their fate. It emphasizes the senseless tragedy emerging from the underside of American rural life and desperation in the years during and after the Depression. Although the film follows the historical facts with reasonable accuracy, Penn was more concerned with establishing an American myth – "the crucial American film about love and death", critic David Thomson observed. And so the images live on, from their first introduction to driver C.W. Moss with "We rob banks" to the final apocalyptic ambush. The film was nominated in several categories for an Academy award, including best picture, and won the Oscar for best photography. It was also nominated for an Edgar.

Borsalino

(1970, French/Italian, 126 minutes)

Director: Jacques Deray. **Producer:** Alain Delon.

Screenplay: Jean-Claude Carrier, Claude Sautet, Jacques Deray, Jean Cau.

Starring: Jean-Paul Belmondo, Alain Delon, Michel Bouquet, Catherine Rouvel.

This film was an affectionate tribute to the gangster moves of the thirties though, at over two hours' duration, it almost overstays its welcome. It succeeds partly because of the excellent performances of the two main stars, especially Alain Delon, something of a heart-throb in his day and who had established a reputation for himself in French gangster movies since *Plein Soleil.* He and Belmondo play two gangsters, Siffredi (Delon) and Capella (Belmondo) in Marseilles who become friends and join forces to take control of the port's markets. The film was moderately successful and was even nominated for an Edgar. Delon went on to produce a sequel, *Borsalino & Co* (1974; 91 minutes), where Siffredi takes on a lone struggle after Capella's death but now faces the might of the Mafia. Alas, here the pastiche becomes paper-thin and the story-line too predictable.

The Boston Strangler

(1968, US, 120 minutes)
Director: Richard Fleischer. **Producer:** Robert Fryer.
Screenplay: Edward Anhalt based on the non-fiction book by Gerold Frank (1966).
Starring: Tony Curtis, Henry Fonda, George Kennedy, Mike Kellin, Sally Kellerman.
An innovative film at the time, using split-screen techniques to recreate the mystique and atmosphere of the murders that terrorized Boston in the early sixties. Many believed it was a brave move by Tony Curtis to play the strangler, Albert De Salvo, though in retrospect he over-humanizes the character. The first part of the film concentrates on the investigation into the baffling crimes, led by detectives Bottomley (Fonda) and DiNatale (Kennedy). It effectively establishes the near powerlessness of the police to get one step ahead of the Strangler as he progressively murders 11 women in their own apartments. The police unearth various likely suspects but nothing conclusive. The second half of the film shifts to follow De Salvo's routine and it is here that the film begins to fail, not through Curtis's own performance, but because the very revelation of the Strangler has removed the mystery. Nevertheless the film is still a watchable recreation of one of the first modern-day serial killers.

Breathless *see* A Bout de Souffle

Brooklyn South

(US TV series, 1997–8, 22 episodes)
Creator: Steven Bochco and David Milch.
Starring: John Tenney, Gary Basaraba, Michael DeLuise, Yancy Butler, James B. Sikking.
Another of Steven Bochco's realistic police procedurals, following *NYPD Blue*, though this one did not survive beyond the first season. Each episode explored the growing and often complicated relationships between the officers at the Brooklyn South station, along with a continuing thread from the pilot episode. There a gunman had shot and killed a police officer outside the station and then gone on a rampage. He is captured but dies in custody. There is an Internal Affairs investigation into his death that continues through the series. It is also revealed that Sergeant Donovan

(Tenney) had been recruited as an informant by the I.A.B. and this causes further tension and conflict. As with all Bochco's series the episodes are full of action and angst with strong characterization and excellent plots.

Budgie

(UK TV series, 1971–2, 26 episodes)
Producer: Verity Lambert.
Directors: James Goddard, Michael Lindsay-Hogg, Mike Newell.
Writers: mostly Keith Waterhouse and Willis Hall.
Starring: Adam Faith, Iain Cuthbertson, Georgina Hale, Lynn Dalby.
Budgie was an extremely popular series, and one of the first to feature a criminal as the lead character. "Budgie" Bird (Faith) was a young delinquent in London's Soho. Although ambitious and eternally optimistic, Budgie was really a loser whose grand ideas came to nothing. Budgie teams up with local villain Charlie Endell (Cuthbertson), whom Budgie thinks of as "Mr Big", but Endell is always one step ahead of him. The series remained light-hearted, with sub-plots involving Budgie's ex-wife (Hale), girlfriend (Dalby) and various members of his family. Budgie was almost a precursor to the character of Terry McCann in Leon Griffiths's *Minder* series ten years later.

Bugsy

(1991, US, 136 minutes)
Director: Barry Levinson. **Producers:** Mark Johnson, Warren Beatty, Barry Levinson.
Screenplay: James Toback.
Starring: Warren Beatty, Harvey Keitel, Annette Bening, Ben Kingsley, Elliott Gould.
A romanticized but nevertheless highly enjoyable account of the life and death of gangster Bugsy Siegel. Siegel is sent to run the Mob's business affairs in California and takes to the west coast life. He has an affair with Hollywood starlet Virginia Hill (Bening) and dreams of establishing a casino hotel in Las Vegas. Obsessive and given to outbursts of homicidal rage, Siegel's lifestyle and obsessions, especially with Mob money, eventually turn the Mob against him. Beautifully staged (the film won academy awards for its production design and costumes) the film, the director and the leading actors were all nominated for the Oscar, as was Ennio Morricone's soundtrack.

Bullitt

(1968, US, 113 minutes)
Director: Peter Yates. **Producer:** Philip D'Antoni.
Screenplay: Alan R. Trustman and Harry Kleiner from the novel *Mute Witness* by Robert L. Pike (Robert L. FISH).

Starring: Steve McQueen, Jacqueline Bisset, Robert Vaughn, Robert Duvall, Gon Gordon.
One scene in almost everyone's top ten is the car chase through San Francisco from *Bullitt*. Done for real it has been heavily copied ever since. The film concerns Detective Lieutenant Frank Bullitt (McQueen) of the SFPD who is assigned to protect an important witness in a Mafia case. The witness is killed early in the film but Bullitt decides to conceal the death while he pursues the killers. He also finds himself battling it out for supremacy with an ambitious politician, Walter Chalmers (Vaughn). The plot itself is fairly straightforward but the film scores hands-down on just about every front. As critic Hollis Alpert observed: "It has energy, drive, impact, and above all, style." It won an Academy Award for its editor, Frank Keller, and also won an Edgar.

Bulman *see under* Strangers

Bunny Lake is Missing

(1965, UK, 107 minutes)
Producer/Director: Otto Preminger.
Screenplay: Penelope & John MORTIMER from the book by Evelyn Piper (1957).
Starring: Laurence Olivier, Keir Dullea, Carol Lynley, Noel Coward.
This is a surprisingly underrated and overlooked film, which has improved with age. Anne Lake (Lynley) is recently settled in England and goes to collect her daughter, Bunny, from her first day at school. However the school has no record of the girl, and the police, led by Superintendent Newhouse (Olivier) can find no evidence of the girl's existence, a fact seemingly supported by Anne's brother Stephen (Dullea). Newhouse continues to search for the girl with the growing belief that the mother may be mentally disturbed and there is no child after all. Preminger's direction is masterful leading the audience steadily towards a most shocking and memorable climax. The film's merit was at least recognized by die-hard mystery fans as it received an Edgar nomination for best film in 1966.

Burke's Law

(US TV series, 1963–6, 81 episodes; revived 1994–5, 27 episodes)
Creator: Ivan Goff, Ben Roberts and Ernest Kinoy.
Producer: Aaron Spelling.
Directors: Many, including Lewis Allen, Stanley Z. Cherry, Murray Golden, Walter Graumann, Jerry Hopper, Don Weis.
Starring: Gene Barry, Gary Conway, Regis Toomey, Leon Lontec; in 1994 revival Peter Barton, Danny Kamekona and Dom DeLuise were also regulars.

Amos Burke (Barry) was the independently wealthy chief of detectives of the LAPD who travelled everywhere in his Rolls Royce chauffered by the everwise Henry (Lontoc/Kamekona) who doubled as his butler. He lived in a mansion, was an eligible bachelor, and somehow his cases only ever involved the rich and influential. He had two main sidekicks, the veteran cop Sergeant Les Hart (Toomey) and the younger whizkid Tim Tilson (Conway). If you accepted the otherwise unbelievable premise the cases themselves were interesting and well plotted – episode titles always began "Who Killed . . .?" – with many written by Richard Levinson and William Link. The series was given a high profile and became a showcase for many well known Hollywood stars, often with their last screen or TV appearances, including Buster Keaton, Jayne Mansfield and Zasu Pitts. Unfortunately the series changed radically in the third season (1965–6; 30 episodes) when it was retitled *Amos Burke – Secret Agent*. All the regular cast and format were dropped and the series became an imitation of *The Men From U.N.C.L.E.* Defying all laws of logic and decency, the series was revived in 1994, again with Barry, but otherwise with an all new cast and although the old format was restored it had already mummified, as had most of the cast. The new series included Burke's son, Peter (Barton) who was a detective with the LAPD, and somewhat more impulsive than his infuriatingly debonair and laidback father.

One of the final episodes of the original *Burke's Law*, "Who Killed the Jackpot?" (April 1965) introduced the character of Honey West, played by Anne Francis, who took over her father's P.I. agency on his death, and who outwitted Burke. The character was continued in a spin-off series, *Honey West* (1965–6; 30 episodes), and she even returned in the revived *Burke's Law*. The character of Honey West had been created by G.G. Fickling (Gloria & Forrest Fickling) in a series of books starting with *The Girl for Hire* in 1957. She was arguably the first independent female P.I. The character of Amos Burke had first appeared in *The Dick Powell Show* in 1961 where he was played by Powell. There were two novelizations based on episodes from the first series published in 1964: *Who Killed Beau Sparrow?* (UK *Burke's Law*) and *Who Killed Madcap Millicent* (UK *The Martini Murders*), both by Roger Fuller.

Cade's County

(US TV series, 1971–2, 24 episodes)
Creators: Rick Husky, Tony Wilson.
Executive Producer: David Gerber. **Producer:** Charles Larson.
Starring: Glenn Ford, Edgar Buchanan, Peter Ford, Taylor Lacher, Sandra Ego/Betty Ann Carr.

The 60-minute weekly series featured the present-day cases of Sam Cade (Ford), sheriff of Madrid County in California. He was assisted by an elderly, old-style deputy, J.J. Jackson (Buchanan) plus three younger deputies one of whom, Pete, was played by Glenn Ford's son. Although the series created no great stir, it was methodical and reliable and pleased enough people for at least one of the episodes, "Company Town" by Cliff Gould, to be nominated for an Edgar. Alfred Lawrence wrote a novelization of the series as *Cade's County* (1972).

Cadfael

(UK TV series, 1994–8, 13 episodes)
Producer: Stephen Smallwood.
Directors: Ken Grieve, Mary McMurray, Herbert Wise, Graham Theakston, Malcolm Mowbray, Richard Stroud.
Writers: Russell Lewis, Paul Pender, Ben Rostul, Christopher Russell, Richard Stoneman based on the books by Ellis PETERS.
Starring: Derek Jacobi, Michael Culver, Peter Copley, Julian Firth, Sean Pertwee/Eoin McCarthy/Anthony Green.
The Cadfael books were painstakingly recreated by the production team under Ted Childs (of *Inspector Morse* fame) and Stephen Smallwood. Filming was done in Hungary as a suitably "medieval" location and a mock-up was built of Shrewsbury Abbey and village, mostly out of wood and polystyrene, though it remained standing and weathered suitably for five years. Cadfael was portrayed by Derek Jacobi and, though he did not look like the Cadfael of the books, he captured the compassion, resilience and justice of the character. All of the characters were well portrayed, particularly Michael Culver as the haughty Prior Robert and Julian Firth as his obsequious toady, Brother Jerome. It is unfortunate that no one actor remained to portray Hugh Beringar throughout the series. The scripts were faithful to the books. Unfortunately the series was expensive to produce, despite its popularity around the world, and it was stopped after adapting 13 of the original 20 books.

Cagney and Lacey

(US TV series, 1982–8, 125 episodes)
Creators: Barney Rosenzweig, Barbara Corday and Barbara Avedon.
Executive Producer: Barney Rosenzweig. **Producers:** Peter Lefcourt, Shelley List, Richard M. Rosenbloom.
Directors: Primarily Sharron Miller and others including Ralph S. Singleton, James Frawley, Jackie Cooper and Georg Standford Brown.
Writers: Many, but primarily Barbara Avedon, Barbara Corday, Frank Abatemarco, Terry Louise Fisher, Michael Piller, Del Reisman and Aubrey Solomon.
Starring: Tyne Daly, Meg Foster/Sharon Gless, Al Waxman, Martin Kove, Carl Lumbly, John Karlen, Dick O'Neill.
Regarded by many as one of the best TV cop shows, *C&G* was the first such series where the two lead characters were female. They are detective

partners in a New York precinct. Mary Beth Lacey (Daly) is married and thus torn between her growing family and work. She has a devoted husband (Karlen), who is fearful for her in her job and feels frustrated at his own inadequacies. Christine Cagney (Foster in season 1; thereafter Gless) is single, though has many relationships with men, is forceful and determined to prove herself in a man's world. She doted on her father, a former policeman, but he became an alcoholic, and after his death from drink Cagney also turns to the bottle. The cases in which they were involved, which were many and varied and occasionally based on real events, emphasized both the duos' strengths and vulnerabilities. Other regulars in the series included the station boss the strict but caring Lieutenant Samuels (Waxman), the macho Detective Isbecki (Kove), whom Cagney loves to outshine, and the smart but pressurized black Detective Petrie (Lumbly). Others came and went, some more violently than others. The murders of Detectives Jonah Newman (Dan Shor) and Manny Esposito (Robert Hegyes) had ramifications through the squad. The series was not afraid to tackle significant issues – racism and sexism, drugs, date-rape, disabilities, Lacy's cancer scare, Cagney's alcoholism – all were treated fairly and sensibly. The series was regarded as a breakthrough for serious female roles and between them Daly and Gless won six consecutive Emmy Awards for Outstanding Lead Actress in a Drama series.

The show nevertheless had a chequered history. It was conceived by Barney Rosenzweig after he had worked on *Charlie's Angels* and wanted to do something more realistic. With feminists Barbara Corday and Barbara Avedon he developed an outline in 1974 that was turned down by all of the networks because no one believed a series about female cops would work. It was not until 1981 that a pilot film (with Loretta Swit as Cagney) was aired and its success led to a short-run series in 1982 (with Meg Foster as Cagney). Ratings were poor and the series cancelled but viewers' protests brought the series back. The strong feminist views were toned down slightly and Gless was brought in as more feminine, though the actress brought to the rôle considerable strength, feistiness and depth as well as beauty. The series ended in 1988 with both characters being offered a promotion to the Major Case Squad. Each actress went their separate ways (Gless to *The Trials of Rosie O'Neill*) but they were reunited six years later in *Cagney and Lacey: The Return* (1994), a one-off TV film. Lacey had retired from the force but her husband has a massive heart attack and can no longer work. She returns as a temporary assistant to Cagney, who is also now married, to a wealthy businessman. The temp soon became permanent and three further TV movies were made, *Together Again* (1995), *The View Through the Glass Ceiling* (1995), in which Cagney is divorced, and *True Convictions* (1996). There has been one novel based on the series, *Before the Fourteenth* (1985; as *Cagney & Lacey*, UK 1986) by Serita

Deborah Stevens, which looked at how the two came together, and an interesting study of the effect of the series on women in television, *Defining Women: Television and the Case of Cagney & Lacey* (1994) by Julie D'Acci.

Callan

(UK TV series, 1967–72, 43 episodes)
Creator: James MITCHELL. **Producer:** Lloyd Shirley (season 1), Reginald Collins.
Writers: Mostly James Mitchell but also Robert Banks Stewart, Ray Jenkins, Bill Craig and others.
Starring: Edward Woodward, Russell Hunter, Ronald Radd/Michael Goodliffe/Derek Bond/William Squire/Hugh Walters, Anthony Valentine.
Callan (Woodward) was created by James Mitchell in a one-off TV play, *A Magnum for Schneider*, broadcast in February 1967. He was a one-time government agent employed by a top-secret department and used as an assassin, if necessary, to silence enemies of the state. In the pilot Hunter, the head of the section, double crosses Callan, using another agent, Meres (Peter Bowles in the pilot; thereafter Valentine) in an attempt to frame him. The play was popular and Callan was brought back by public demand. One of the tensions of the series is that Meres is jealous of Callan and would do anything to have him discredited or destroyed. Moreover Callan has a conscience and will not carry out killings to order thereby leaving himself vulnerable. The appeal of the series was how Callan tried to outwit both Hunter (a title rather than name and thus played by a succession of actors) and Meres and achieve his objectives. A popular character in the series was Lonely (Hunter), a petty thief whom Callan had met in prison and who supplies Callan with "untraceable" guns. Lonely got his name because he was smelly. The original introductory play was later reworked as a film, *Callan* (1974; aka *The Neutralizer*). Nine years after the series finished the characters were brought back in a one-off special, *Wet Job* (1981), in which Callan had retired and lives under another name, but is once more tricked back into service.

Cannon

(US TV series, 1971–6, 121 episodes)
Producers: Anthony Spinner, Alan Armer, Harold Gast and Winston Miller for Quinn Martin Productions.
Directors: Many, including Marvin J. Chomsky, Richard Donner, Jimmy Sangster and Charles S. Dubin.
Writers: Many, including Bill S. Ballinger, Steve Fisher, Harold Gast, Jackson Gillis, Stephen Kandel, Del Reisman, Jimmy Sangster, Anthony Spinner, Phyllis White, Carey Wilber, Collier Young.
Starring: William Conrad.

Frank Cannon (Conrad) was a former cop who quit the force after the death of his wife and young son in an apparent accident (later revealed to be murder). Sombre and determined he puts all his energies into his job as a P.I. Unlike most other detectives, Cannon was on the large size and drove everywhere in his Lincoln Continental. He was methodical, thorough and suffered no fools. He was also a loner. Unusual amongst series Cannon had no regular sidekicks or supporting cast. It was just him. But the personality of William Conrad as an honest, no-nonsense, get-his-man gumshoe, carried the show for five seasons, plus a one-off TV film, *The Return of Frank Cannon* (1980), in which he comes out of retirement to investigate the apparent suicide of a former Army friend. In the final season the episode "The Deadly Conspiracy" introduced the character of Barnaby Jones (Buddy Ebsen) who rapidly developed into his own series (see *Barnaby Jones*), with Cannon making an occasional appearance. Conrad (1920–94) was a well-known voice on American radio having appeared in many drama series, including playing Matt Dillon in the long-running radio version of *Gunsmoke* (1952–61). He reappeared on TV in the series *Jake and the Fatman*. There were eight novels drawn from the Cannon series: *Murder by Gemini* and *The Stewardess Strangler* (both 1971) by Richard Gallagher, *The Deadly Chance* (1973), *The Golden Bullet* (1973), *I've Got You Covered* (1973) and *The Falling Blonde* (1975) all by Paul Denver, and *Farewell, Little Sister* (1978) and *Shoot-Out!* (1979) by Douglas Enefer.

Cape Fear

(1961, US, 105 minutes, b&w; remade 1991, 128 minutes)
Director: J. Lee Thompson (1961), Martin Scorsese (1991).
Producer: Sy Bartlett (1961), Barbara DeFina (1991).
Screenplay: James R. Webb (1961), Wesley Strick (1991), based on the novel *The Executioners* by John D. MacDonald.
Starring: 1961: Gregory Peck, Robert Mitchum, Polly Bergen, Lori Martin, Martin Balsam, Telly Savalas; 1991: Robert De Niro, Nick Nolte, Jessica Lange, Juliette Lewis, Joe Don Baker.
The story-line, extracted from MacDonald's novel, is simple. Max Cady (Mitchum/De Niro) was imprisoned for rape, but is now out and seeking revenge on his attorney, Sam Bowden (Peck/Nolte), whom he believes suppressed evidence that may have resulted in his being found innocent. Both film versions are strong on tension and nerve-racking suspense. Thompson's original version was severely edited at the time because the British censor considered it too nasty. It also polarizes the main protagonists too strongly. Peck is too upright and righteous as the attorney; Mitchum too sadistic in his demand for revenge. Scorsese's version blurs the edges. Nolte is seen as less honest, and though De Niro is manically vengeful and seemingly unstoppable, the audience feels some need for

justice. Both versions have their merits. Mitchum's performance is solid and relentless; De Niro's is the stuff of nightmare. Intriguingly Scorsese included Peck, Mitchum and Balsam in minor roles in his remake. Both De Niro and Juliette Lewis, who played Bowden's daughter, were nominated for Academy awards.

Cassie and Company *see* Police Woman

C.A.T.S. Eyes

(UK TV series, 1985–7, 31 episodes)
Creator: Terence Feely.
Producer: Dickie Bamber, Frank Cox (season 1), Raymond Menmuir (seasons 2-3).
Writers: Mostly Terence Feely, Ray Jenkins, Jeremy Burnham and Paul Wheeler.
Starring: Rosalyn Landor/Tracy-Louise Ward, Jill Gascoine, Leslie Ash, Don Warrington.
This was the British attempt at *Charlie's Angels*. C.A.T.S. stood for Covert Activities, Thames Section, a rather forced acronym to allow for a feline description of three female crimefighters Pru Standfast (Landor), Maggie Forbes (Gascoine) and Fred Smith (Ash). They operated from the Eyes Enquiry Agency but were in fact working undercover for a Special Home Office unit under the "Man from the Ministry" (Warrington). Their rôle was to track down anything likely to breach security from spies to illegal immigrants to extortionists. Although Standfast was the original leader of the trio, the main character (and leader from series 2) was Forbes, her rôle moving over from *The Gentle Touch*. In the second series Landor was replaced by Ward as Tessa Robinson. The series was popular in Britain, even though the basic premise was every bit as ridiculous as *Charlie's Angels*.

Chandler & Co.

(UK TV series, 1994–95, 11 episodes)
Creator: Paula Milne. **Producer:** Ann Skinner.
Writers: Paula Milne, Jacqueline Holborough, Bill Gallagher.
Starring: Catherine Russell, Barbara Flynn/Susan Fleetwood, Peter Capaldi/Adrian Lukis.
This series concentrated on domestic crimes and violence. Dee Tate (Flynn) convinces her sister-in-law, Elly Chandler (Russell) that they should set up a private investigation agency specializing in runaway children and battered wives. They are helped out by another enquiry agent, Larry Blakeston (Capaldi). The two soon discover the problems they have let themselves in for. Other commitments (including *Cracker*)

stopped Flynn doing more than one series so new lady Kate Phillips (Fleetwood), whom they had helped out, joined the organization as a rather cautious but nevertheless determined investigator. The series ended abruptly with Susan Fleetwood's tragic death from cancer. Its creator, Paula Milne, had earlier worked in *Juliet Bravo*.

Charlie's Angels

(US TV series, 1976–81, 109 episodes)
Creators: Aaron Spelling and Ivan Goff.
Executive Producers: Aaron Spelling and Leonard Goldberg.
Producers: Rick Huskey, David Levinson, Barney Rosenzweig.
Directors: Many, including Allen Baron, Dennis Donnelly, Don Chaffey, George Stanford Brown, Kim Manners, Paul Stanley.
Writers: Over 40, including Ronald Austin, John D.F. Black, Stephen Kandel, Edward J. Lakso, Laurie Lakso, B.W. Sandefur, Lee Sheldon.
Starring: Kate Jackson, Farrah Fawcett-Majors, Jaclyn Smith, Cheryl Ladd, Shelley Hack/Tanya Roberts, David Doyle, and the voice of John Forsythe.

One of the most popular TV shows of the seventies and one that proves beauty nearly always wins out over brain. The brainchild of Aaron Spelling (also responsible for *Burke's Law*, *Hart to Hart* and *Dynasty*) and Ivan Goff, the series told of three attractive girls who were brought fresh out of Police Academy to work for the Charles Townsend Detective Agency. You never saw Charlie but only ever heard his voice, usually over the phone. It was the voice of John Forsythe (Blake Carrington of *Dynasty*). The link man was John Bosley (Doyle). The "Angels" were Sabrina Duncan (Jackson), the "smart angel", Jill Munroe (Fawcett-Majors), the "athletic angel" and Kelly Garrett (Smith), the "streetwise angel". Their mission was as undercover agents but only ever in the world of the rich, famous, glamorous or sporty. The opening episode of the first series, "Hellrider", has them investigating the death of a female racing car driver. In "Night of the Strangler" it's amongst high fashion models. In "Angels at Sea" they're on a cruise ship whilst "Lady Killer", one of the most popular episodes in the first season, has Munroe posing as a play-mate centrefold to find who's killing the models. The series was accused of voyeurism but all the while it was top of the ratings, who bothered. Success went to Farrah Fawcett-Major's head and she opted out at the end of the first season and new girl Cheryl Ladd (as Munroe's sister, Kris) was introduced, to equal acclaim. Farrah Fawcett was contractually obliged to appear in a certain number of episodes in later seasons. Kate Jackson left after the third season resulting in new Angel Tiffany Welles (Hack) and in the final season, Julie Rogers (Roberts). The series wasn't all glamour. It did occasionally deal with more down-to-earth problems. Drug smuggling in "The Mexican Conection", the murder of army recruits in "Bullseye", witness protection in "The Killing Kind", but these became the exception as the series steadily became a parody of itself and the ratings fell. Nevertheless it has remained popular in many memories. There was an attempt to relaunch the series in 1988 with four "angels", all actresses who formed a detective agency when their series were dropped, but this series never made it to the screen. More recently Drew Barrymore, Cameron Diaz and Lucy Liu became the new Angels in the widescreen version, *Charlie's Angels* (2000). Jaclyn Smith later surfaced in the short-lived two-hour series *Christine Cromwell* (1989–90, 4 episodes) where she was a financial advisor to the rich and privileged and was drawn into their often criminous affairs. The original *Charlie's Angels* spawned a host of merchandise including five novels by Richard Deming writing as Max Franklin, based on different episodes: *Charlie's Angels* (1977), *Angels in Chains* (1977), *The Killing Kind* (1977), *Angels on a String* (1977) and *Angels on Ice* (1978).

The Chief

(UK TV series, 1990–7)
Creator: Jeffrey Caine. **Producers:** Ruth Boswell, John Davies.
Directors: Brian Farnham (series 1), Desmond Davis (series 2).
Starring: Tim Pigott-Smith/Martin Shaw, Karen Archer, Judy Loe, Eamon Boland, David Cardy.
John Stafford (Pigott-Smith) is the new no-nonsense Chief Constable in rural East Anglia who brings with him his former Head of C.I.D., Anne Stewart (Archer) as he Assistant Chief Constable and Head of Crime and Operations. Needless to say the existing incumbents (mostly men) don't like Stafford's regime of tough discipline or having a woman appointed over them. The series emphasized the political angle of the police force and how pressure can be brought to bear by the Home Office. Stafford finds himself is suspended and, from season 3, Martin Shaw took over as the new Chief Constable, Alan Cade. The series was produced at a time of high profile amongst the police force, with charges of corruption and prejudice being aimed at the highest levels. Every effort was made to make the series authentic, and the technical advisor was John Alderson, the former Chief Constable of Devon and Cornwall.

Chinatown

(1974, US, 131 minutes)
Director: Roman Polanski. **Producer:** Robert Evans.
Screenplay: Robert Towne.
Starring: Jack Nicholson, Faye Dunaway, John Huston, Perry Lopez, John Hillerman.
Polanski's *homage* to Raymond Chandler is regarded as one of his best films and the definitive gangster movie set in the thirties. J.J. Gittes

(Nicholson) is a small-time P.I. looking into an adultery case who stumbles across a major racket involving the water supply to Los Angeles masterminded by the robber baron Noah Cross (Huston). Gittes gets roughed up by Cross' cronies but he is persistent, not only in his investigation but in his ultimately futile attempt to save Cross' daughter Evelyn (Dunaway) whom Cross had himself raped. It's a despairing film, where your heart tells you that evil can prevail and there's not always light at the end of the tunnel. Sixteen years and much hassle later Nicholson directed the film's sequel, *The Two Jakes* (1990), again scripted by Towne. Set 11 years later, in late forties Los Angeles, it again involves a major con – this time oil rather than water. Gittes is equally persistent and equally futile against the new robber baron, real estate developer Jake Berman (Harvey Keitel). The sequel relies heavily on a knowledge of *Chinatown*, and the two work together remarkably well as bookends on the evolution of organized crime and conspiracy in America. Towne won an Oscar for his script for *Chinatown* (which was published in 1988) and the film, Polanski, Nicholson and Dunaway were all nominated. The film also won the Edgar award. See also the series *City of Angels*.

The Chinese Detective

(UK TV series, 1981, 14 episodes)
Creator: Ian Kennedy Martin. **Producer:** Terrence Williams.
Directors: Tom Clegg, Leonard Lewis, Brian Lighthill, Jeremy Summers, Ian Toynton.
Starring: David Yip, Derek Martin, Arthur Kelly.
This series received mixed reactions at the time, though it was a brave attempt to depict an ethnic policeman coping with prejudice and dealing with crimes amongst his fellow Chinese in the Limehouse region of London. Detective Sergeant Johnny Ho (Yip) is scruffy, unpredictable and short (in fact too short for the Metropolitan Police). He not only tackles difficult and violent cases but is also trying to clear the reputation of his father. He is teamed with Detective Sergeant Chegwyn (Kelly), a more traditional cop, who tries to refine Ho.

CHiPS

(US TV series, 1977–83, 138 episodes)
Creator: Rick Rosner.
Producers: Cy Chernak (executive), Paul Mason, Paul Rabwin, Rick Rosner.
Directors: Many, including Edward M. Abroms, Don Chaffey, Robert Pine, Larry Wilcox.
Head Writer: Joseph Gunn.
Starring: Erik Estrada, Larry Wilcox, Robert Pine, Paul Linke, Lou Wagner.

CHiPS stands for California Highway Patrol, and the series was really an excuse for the two handsome lead stars, Erik Estrada (Officer Frank Poncherello) and Larry Wilcox (Officer Jon Baker) to ride motorbikes and meet women. Each weekly hour-long episode consisted of a mixture of incidents, seldom violent (the men never carried guns) and occasionally humorous. Apparently many patrolmen used to watch it as it was entertaining if a rather romanticized view of the job. The main characters were reunited in a one-off two-hour TV movie, *CHiPS '99* (1998)

The Choirboys

(1977, US, 120 minutes)
Director: Robert Aldrich. **Producer:** Merv Adelson, Lee Rich.
Screenplay: Christopher Knopf based on the novel by Joseph WAMBAUGH.
Starring: Charles Durning, Lou Gossett, Perry King, Tim McIntire.
This film caused an outcry upon release and unfairly tarnished the reputation of the author, Joseph Wambaugh. Wambaugh's original book had looked at the pressures and demands placed upon the police and how officers would sometimes react in an eruption of violence and prejudice as a safety valve for their own sanity. Unfortunately the film just concentrated on their often sick and depraved antics without balancing it against the work and the result was a travesty.

City of Angels

(US TV series, 1976, 13 episodes)
Creators: Roy Huggins, Stephen J. CANNELL.
Producers: Jo Swerling, Jr. (executive), Roy Huggins.
Directors: Barry Shear, Douglas Heyes, Jerry London, Robert Douglas, Don Medford, Allen Reisner, Sigmund Neufield, Jr.
Writers: Stephen J. Cannell, John Thomas James, Gloryette Clark, Philip DeGuere, Mervyn Gerard, Douglas Heyes, Stephen & Elinor Karpf.
Starring: Wayne Rogers, Clifton James, Elaine Joyce, Philip Sterling.
This series took its cue from the film *Chinatown*. It was set in the 1930s and followed the exploits of freewheeling P.I. Jake Axminster (Rogers) through the corrupt mean streets of Los Angeles. Jake's your typical loner, not trusting anyone, not even his lawyer Michael Brimm (Sterling), who's forever getting Jake out of gaol. Jake's not averse to bending the rules when it suits but he's far less corrupt than the cops, especially Axminster's nemesis Lieutenant Quint (James), who has a rake-off from every deal going. On the surface the series had much in its favour, and the opening three-parter, "The November Plan", by Cannell, based on a real plot to overthrow Roosevelt, was well received. But the series had been a mid-term replacement and was always being prepared in haste with

scripts still being written as the episodes were being filmed. Wayne Rogers publicly declared his dissatisfaction with the series and apparently the public were not yet prepared to see Rogers (still fondly remembered from *M.A.S.H.*) in such a serious rôle. It was dropped at the end of the season, but is still regarded by many, including Max Allan COLLINS, as one of the best TV P.I. series.

Clean, Shaven

(1993, US, 80 minutes)
Producer/Director: Lodge Kerrigan.
Screenplay: Lodge Kerrigan.
Starring: Peter Greene, Molly Castelloe, Megan Owen, Robert Albert, Alice Levitt.

An intense, harrowing but remarkable film that has been surprisingly overlooked – perhaps because its imagery is so disturbing. It is an ingenious study of schizophrenia and paranoia, the effects achieved by clever editing, fragmented images and minimal dialogue. Peter Winter (Greene) is in extreme mental decline. His family have disowned him and he has not seen his missing daughter in a long time. He goes in search of her, pursued by a detective (Albert) who believes Winter may be a murderer. The film took over two years to make.

The Client

(1994, US, 121 minutes)
Director: Joel Schumacher. **Producers:** Arnon Milchan, Steven Reuther.
Screenplay: Robert Getchell, Akiva Goldsman from the novel by John GRISHAM.
Starring: Tommy Lee Jones, Susan Sarandon, Mary-Louise Parker, Anthony LaPaglia, Brad Renfro, David Speck.

One of the best of the adaptations of John Grisham's novels. A young streetwise kid, Mark Sway (Renfro), witnesses a suicide and learns from the dying man's words where a Mafia murder victim is buried. The boy becomes hounded by both the Mafia and the FBI, via prosecutor Roy Foltrigg (Jones) and he and his brother come under the protection of defence attorney Reggie Love (Sarandon). The strength of the book is amplified in the film especially in Mark's adult outlook and coming-of-age, as he makes choices that shame his elders. The popularity of the film led to a TV series, with the full title *John Grisham's The Client* (1995–96; 21 episodes). JoBeth Williams played Reggie Love and John Heard was Roy Foltrigg. The series concentrated on juveniles in trouble and posed some intriguing legal dilemmas raised by social problems.

Cobra

(1986, US, 87 minutes)
Director: George P. Cosmatos. **Producer:** Menahem Golan, Yoram Globus.
Screenplay: Sylvester Stallone from the novel *Fair Game* by Paula GOSLING.
Starring: Sylvester Stallone, Brigitte Nielsen, Reni Santoni, Andrew Robinson, Brian Thompson.
Still in the mode of Rambo from *First Blood* and *First Blood II*, Stallone created a different but in all other ways identical all-action cop hero, Lieutenant Marion Cobretti, who goes after the villains guns blazing. The film is all hokum, but you can't help getting wrapped up in the action, especially a remarkable car chase, and Stallone delivers his one-liners, like "You're the disease, I'm the cure," in a gravel-filled monotone that is wholly imitable. What little plot remains from Gosling's novel concerns Cobretti protecting a witness (Nielsen) from a psycho (Thompson). For a more faithful version of the novel see *Fair Game*. The TV series *Cobra* (1993–94; 22 episodes), where the mutilated and left-for-dead "Scandal" Jackson is rebuilt by the billionaire-run secret organization called Cobra to help victims of crime who have not received justice, is not related to the film or the book, though has a lot in common in its high-tech action.

Columbo

(US TV series, 1971–8, 43 episodes plus 2 pilots; 1989–91, 13 episodes; plus 10 specials to date)
Creators: Richard Levinson and William Link.
Producers: Many, but primarily Dean Hargrove, Everett Chambers, Edward K. Dodds and Richard Alan Simmons.
Directors: Many, including Steven Spielberg, Bernard Kowalski, Boris Sagal, Richard Quine, Ben Gazzara, Patrick McGoohan, Ted Post, Harvey Hart, James Frawley, Sam Wanamaker and Vincent McEveety.
Writers: Many, including Richard Levinson & William Link, Steven Bochco, Jackson Gillis, Peter S. Fischer, William Driskill, William R. Woodfield and Robert van Scoyk.
Starring: Peter Falk. Guest stars include Gene Barry, Robert Culp, John Cassavetes, Ray Milland, Richard Basehart, Anne Baxter, Leonard Nimoy, Laurence Harvey, Martin Landau, Patrick McGoohan, Jose Ferrer, Johnny Cash, Dick van Dyke, George Hamilton, Robert Vaughn, William Shatner, Louis Jordan.
One of the most popular of all TV detective shows and the classic example of an inverted detective story. Each episode began with the crime, usually impeccably planned, with the murderer known to viewers from the outset. The delight of the series is to watch Columbo (Falk) working on the prime suspect, usually much to his or her annoyance, and steadily

breaking down his alibi and discovering what the one vital clue was that the murderer overlooked. It was often something minor. Columbo is one of the great TV characters. Dressed in a shabby raincoat, whatever the weather, his car long overdue for the scrapheap, often stuck with his basset hound and never with a pencil or paper, he is a seemingly bumbling and ineffectual detective, always with one last question to ask, and always apologetic. But that is all a cover for a sharp, perceptive mind who wears down his man. The murderer, who is nearly always rich, influential and convinced he is smarter than Columbo, is always played by a leading guest star some of whom came back for more – Robert Culp, Jack Cassidy and Patrick McGoohan amongst them.

The character of Columbo was created by writers Richard Levinson (1934–87) and William Link (b. 1933) in an episode they wrote for *The Chevy Mystery Show* in 1961 called "Enough Rope" where the detective was played by Ben Freed. They adapted this episode for the stage as *Prescription: Murder*, which opened on 15 January 1962 in San Francisco. Veteran actor Thomas Mitchell played Columbo. It was not until the play was adapted for television as a one-off movie in February 1968 that Peter Falk played the part. He was not the first choice as he was considered too young for the part, but the initial preferences – Lee J. Cobb and Bing Crosby – were not available. *Prescription: Murder* had been a solo play with no intentions of a sequel and it was three years before NBC considered the character for a new format, a mystery "wheel" as it was called, where three different 90-minute programmes were run in a cycle. After a second pilot, "Ransom for a Dead Man", aired in March 1971, the series proper started in September 1971 with "Murder by the Book". That episode was produced by Link and Levinson, directed by Steven Spielberg and scripted by Steven Bochco, a formidable team. *Columbo* alternated in the "wheel" with *McCloud* and *McMillan and Wife*, but was by far the most popular. Falk, however, refused to star in a weekly series as he did not have the time for such a commitment and felt the show would suffer from the hectic schedule. It is almost certainly because of this that the series retained such a high quality. The show ran for seven seasons and Columbo hung up his raincoat in May 1978, but Falk agreed to resurrect Columbo in 1989 as *New Columbo*, and the programme continues to be made on an irregular basis, with Falk now having played the part for over 30 years. The episode "Murder Under Glass" won an Edgar in 1979.

One of the in-jokes in the series was Columbo's wife, whom we never see. After the original series finished the producers tried to continue the formula with a new series featuring his wife. *Mrs Columbo*, starring Kate Mulgrew, began in February 1979. Kate was a newspaper reporter and was drawn into investigating crimes that were solved in a similar manner. The gimmick, though, did not work. After five episodes Kate was hastily renamed Kate Callahan and any reference to Columbo was dropped. The new series was retitled variously *Kate the Detective* and *Kate Loves a Mystery* before folding after a total of 13 episodes in December 1979.

There have been the following Columbo novels: *Columbo* (1972) and *The Dean's Death* (1975), both by Alfred Lawrence; *Any Old Port in a Storm* (1975) and *By Dawn's Early Light* (1975), both by Henry Clement; *A Deadly State of Mind* (1976) and *Murder by the Book* (1976), both by Lee Hays; and *Columbo and the Samurai Sword* (1980) by Craig Schenk and Bill Magee. Most recently a new series of novels has been produced by William HARRINGTON. The complete dossier on Columbo will be found in *The Columbo Phile* (1988) by Mark Dawidziak, whilst the Columbo website is <www.columbo-site.freeuk.com>.

Coogan's Bluff

(1968, US, 94 minutes)
Producer/Director: Don Siegel.
Screenplay: Herman Miller, Howard Rodman, Dean Riesner.
Starring: Clint Eastwood, Lee J. Cobb, Don Stroud, Susan Clark, Tisha Sterling.

Eastwood plays an Arizona deputy, complete with stetson and boots, who arrives in New York city to escort a prisoner (Stroud) back home. The prisoner escapes and Coogan searches for him through New York, much to the amusement of the New York authorities. The idea of the cowboy in the city could simply have been played for laughs but under Siegel's direction it develops into a struggle between big city and rural western values and ideals with the film considering the significance of both. This seminal film not only paved the way for Eastwood's other cop films, especially *Dirty Harry*, but it was also the inspiration for the TV series *McCloud*.

Cookie's Fortune

(1998, US, 118 minutes)
Director: Robert Altman. **Producer:** Robert Altman, Etchie Stroh.
Screenplay: Anne Rapp.
Starring: Glenn Close, Julianne Moore, Liv Tyler, Charles S. Dutton, Patricia Neal, Ned Beatty, Donald Moffat.

Every now and again a film comes along that eschews existing trends towards brash violence and high-tech and settles for simple values, relationships and honest characterization. *Cookie's Fortune* is one such film. Camille (Close) is a social climber in Holly Springs, Mississippi, and is horrified to discover that her aunt, Cookie (Neal) has apparently killed herself. Such would be a disgrace, so Camille arranges it to look like murder. But the police (Beatty) and lawyer (Moffat) are not so sure, especially when the obvious perpetrator is their old fishing friend Willis

(Dutton). It takes a while to untangle the mess and that's the delight of the film, allowing excellent actors and colourful characters to shine in this black comedy-of-manners. The film was nominated for an Edgar award.

Cop

(1987, US, 110 minutes)
Director: James B. Harris. **Producer:** James B. Harris, James Woods.
Screenplay: James B. Harris from the novel *Blood on the Moon* by James Ellroy.
Starring: James Woods, Lesley Ann Warren, Charles Durning, Charles Haid.
Blood on the Moon was the first of Ellroy's dark and moody books to be filmed and signalled the way for a shift towards more cynical and deeply psychological films where the police are depicted as obsessed and psychotic as the villains. In this case the eponymous LAPD cop Lloyd Hopkins (Woods) is so obsessed with his job that it is all he can talk about and it drives his wife away with their young daughter. No one else he works with respects him either. He lives for the dark side of life. He is soon on the trail of a serial killer who mutilates and humiliates feminist-minded or free living women and the trail leads him to a feminist book-shop whose owner, Kathleen McCarthy (Warren) has links with Hopkins's own murky past. The film is slick but at times its message becomes blurred by its depressing and unredeeming bleakness.

Cops and Robbers

(1973, US, 89 minutes)
Director: Aram Avakian. **Producer:** Elliott Kastner.
Screenplay: Donald E. Westlake based on his own novel.
Starring: Cliff Gorman, Joseph Bologna, Dick Ward.
It's surprising there aren't more films with this title, but you know that in the hands of Donald E. Westlake it's going to be exactly the kind of spoof the title suggests. It's one of his clever caper stories. Two New York cops use their position as a cover to allow them to pull off a Wall Street securities heist. They then try and double-cross the Mafia contacts who were supposed to fence their ill-gotten gain resulting in the inevitable hide-and-seek. A good fun film.

The Cosby Mysteries

(US TV series, 1994–5, 18 episodes plus pilot)
Creators: David Black and William Link.
Producers: Lee Goldberg, Frank Cardea, George Schenk, William Rabkin.
Directors: Primarily Jerry London, Philip Sgriccia, E.W. Swackhamer, Alan J. Levi, Corey Allen, Lou Antonio.

Writers: Primarily David Black & William Link (pilot), Robert Van Scoyk, Charles Kipps, Siobhan Byrne, Lee Goldberg.
Starring: Bill Cosby, James Naughton, Rita Moreno, Lynn Whitfield, Robert Stanton.
In between his top ratings sitcoms *The Cosby Show* and *Cosby*, Bill Cosby turned to a more serious rôle as criminologist and forensics expert Guy Hanks, who retired when he won the lottery but missed the job so still helps the police when necessary. The show, though, never registered. Despite being a fine actor the viewers associated Cosby with comedy and were not sure how seriously to take the show. Characters drifted in and out disrupting the flow and despite good story-lines, including some by Columbo co-creator William Link, who gave Hanks a Columbo-like bumblingness, the series closed after one season and Cosby returned to the sitcom.

Cotton Comes to Harlem

(1970, US, 97 minutes)
Director: Ossie Davis. **Producer:** Samuel Goldwyn.
Screenplay: Arnold Perl and Ossie Davis based on the novel by Chester HIMES.
Starring: Godfrey Cambridge, Raymond St. Jacques, Calvin Lockhart, J.D. Cannon.
Toned down from Chester Himes' original novel, this film was still influential in its day, paving the way for *Shaft* and its successors. It brings to the screen Himes's two cynical and corrupt black cops Coffin Ed Johnson (St. Jacques) and Grave Digger Jones (Cambridge) who are pursuing a bogus preacher, Deke O'Malley (Lockhart) who is operating a rehabilitation scam. They are also trying to beat everyone else to a fortune stashed in a bale of cotton. The movie has some clever comic moments and was original in its day for its patter and jive-talk.

Cracker

(UK TV series, 1993–6, 24 episodes)
Creator: Jimmy McGovern.
Producers: Gub Neal (season 1), Paul Abbott (season 2), Hilary Bevan Jones (seasons 3–4).
Directors: Michael Winterbottom, Andy Wilson, Simon-Cellan Jones, Tim Fywell, Julian Jarrold, Jean Stewart, Roy Battersby, Charles MacDougall, Richard Standeven.
Writers: Jimmy McGovern, Ted Whitehead, Paul Abbott.
Starring: Robbie Coltrane, Geraldine Somerville, Barbara Flynn, Lorcan Cranitch, Christopher Eccleston, Ricky Tomlinson.
Edward Fitzgerald (Coltrane), or "Fitz" to everyone, is an unconventional criminal psychologist and profiler. His private life is in a mess, he

chain-smokes and he is trying to kick his compulsive gambling habit. As a gambler he enjoys taking risks and he brings this same attitude to his work, pushing suspects to the brink under his intense interrogations. He is always convinced he is right and this arrogance leads to conflict with the police who call him in, especially DCI Bilborough (Eccleston), with dire consequences. The series was dark, moody and unpredictable where lead characters were as likely to be murdered or raped or commit suicide as the victims. Each season consisted of two or three multi-episode stories, but always with an ongoing thread, such as Fitz's failing marriage and his relationship with DS Penhaligon (Sommerville). The series was immensely popular with viewing figures in excess of ten million. The episodes "To Say I Love You", (1985) and "Brotherly Love" (1997) won Edgars in 1985 and 1997 respectively.

The series was converted to US television (1997–9; 16 episodes) set in Los Angeles with Robert Pastorelli as Fitz. Unfortunately the dark edges were polished away and the characters dumbed down so that the series lost its impact. Several of the original UK episodes were adapted and new episodes written. Robbie Coltrane appeared in the final US episode, "Faustian Fitz", as a film producer involved in the murder of a little girl.

Books based on the series are *Cracker: To Say I Love You* (1994) by Molly Brown and *Cracker: The Mad Woman in the Attic* (1996) by Jim Mortimore, both based on individual episodes.

Cribb

(UK TV series, 1979 (pilot), 1980–1, 13 episodes plus pilot)

Creator: Peter LOVESEY.

Producers: Peter Eckersley (executive), June Wyndham Davies.

Directors: June Wyndham Davies, Julian Aymes, Alan Grint, Gordon Flemyng, Oliver Horsbrugh, Bill Gilmour, Brian Mills, George Spenton-Foster.

Writers: Peter and Jacqueline Lovesey, Pauline Macauley, Brian Thompson, Bill MacIlwraith, Alan Plater, Arden Winch

Starring: Alan Dobie, William Simons, David Waller.

This series was based on the character created by Peter Lovesey in his novels starting with *Wobble to Death*. They are set in London in the late Victorian period in the early days of the Criminal Investigation Department. Alan Dobie portrays Cribb as a very upright, no-nonsense, humourless detective determined to let criminals know that they stood no chance against the Law. His luckless assistant was Constable Thackeray (Simons) and his boss at Scotland Yard was Inspector Jowett (Waller). The series was a wonderful evocation of the Victorian period, so popular on British television at that time. The 90-minute pilot was based on Lovesey's novel *Waxwork*. An earlier Victorian police series was *Sergeant Cork*.

Crime Story

(US TV series, 1986–8, 43 episodes)
Creators: Chuck Adamson and Gustave Reininger.
Producers: Michael Mann, Stuart Cohen, Gail Morgan Hickman.
Directors: Many, including Michael Mann, Abel Ferrara, James Quinn, Mark Rosner, David Soul.
Writers: Many, including David J. Burke, Chuck Adamson, Peter Lance, Gustave Reininger.
Starring: Dennis Farina, Anthony Denison, Paul Butler, Bill Campbell, Johann Carlo.
While *Miami Vice* was still top of the ratings, producer Michael Mann tried a new, experimental crime show. On the surface it was a straightforward harkback to the old movie serials. There was one continuing underlying story with cliffhangers each episode. Set in 1963 it was the story of law enforcer Lieutenant Michael Torelli (Farina, himself an ex-cop) in charge of a Special Crimes Unit, and his quest to track down and nail the murderous but charismatic crime boss Ray Luca (Denison, a former professional gambler). Others in the series also had a colourful past. One of Luca's henchmen, Johnny Santuci, was played by Paul Taglia, a former criminal. The first series is set in Chicago and follows Luca's rose to power in the Mafia, despite Torelli's attempts to thwart his every move. In the second series Luca is sent to run Mob affairs in Las Vegas and Torelli's unit becomes part of the FBI to enable them to follow. The need for a cliff-hanger ending with each week trying to improve on the last meant that the series steadily moved into the realms of the incredible. At the end of the first season viewers were left believing that Luca had perished in a nuclear explosion, while the second series climaxed with near total destruction in a plane crash. Believable or not the series left its mark and will remain one of the cult series of the eighties. The series won the American Mystery Award in 1988.

Crimes and Misdemeanours

(1989, US, 104 minutes)
Director: Woody Allen.
Producer: Robert Greenhut.
Screenplay: Woody Allen.
Starring: Woody Allen, Martin Landau, Alan Alda, Claire Bloom, Mia Farrow, Anjelica Huston.
It's no surprise that Woody Allen's "crime" film is no traditional story but is deeply philosophical and moralistic. There are two plots that only come together at the end. Clifford Stern (Allen) is reluctantly making a documentary about his brother-in-law (Alda), a maker of sitcoms, mostly because Stern has fallen in love with the programme's producer (Farrow). Meanwhile ophthalmologist Judah Rosenthal (Landau) has

decided to be rid of his lover (Huston) before his wife (Bloom) finds out, but after his mistress's death is racked by guilt. Allen uses the film as a vehicle to explore ethics, justice and what constitutes good and evil. The film is as educational as it is entertaining. It clearly appealed to mystery fans as it was shortlisted for the Edgar award and won the Anthony in 1990.

The Criminal [US: The Concrete Jungle]

(1960, UK, 97 minutes, b&w)
Director: Joseph Losey. **Producer:** Jack Greenwood.
Screenplay: Alun Owen.
Starring: Stanley Baker, Sam Wanamaker, Patrick Magee, Margit Saad.
It may be over 40 years old but this film still has a punch. Johnny Bannion (Baker) has served fifteen years in prison for a racecourse hijack and has hidden his loot. A loner, Bannion has managed to build a defence around him against the machinations of the sadistic, power-crazed warder (Magee) but once out he becomes vulnerable and at the mercy of a power-crazed thug (Wanamaker) who plans to kill Bannion and take the money. It's a simple but relentlessly gripping film with a haunting but inevitable ending.

Crown Court

(UK TV series, 1972–84, 600+ episodes)
When British television switched to daytime schedules it needed plenty of material and one such series was the highly popular *Crown Court*. It broadcast three half-hour lunchtime episodes each week and the gimmick was that the jury was made up of real members of the public. Although some of the cases were the run-of-the-mill daily grind that allowed an opportunity to observe the rudiments of justice, many cases dealt with serious issues including rape, racism, nasty neighbours and wife battering. The series became renowned for developing new writers, directors and actors as well as many well-known names appearing including Caroline Blakiston, Connie Booth, Michael Gough, Vivien Merchant, Judy Parfitt, and Juliet Stevenson.

Cutter's Way [US: Cutter and Bone]

(1981, UK, 109 minutes)
Director: Ivan Passer. **Producer:** Paul R. Gurian.
Screenplay: Jeffrey Alan Fiskin based on the novel by Newton Thornburg (1976).
Starring: Jeff Bridges, John Heard, Lisa Eichhorn, Ann Dusenberry.
Alex Cutter (Heard) is a mutilated Vietnam war veteran feeling on the scrap heap. His friend, Bone (Bridges) witnesses a murder, and seeking the murderer, believed to be an oil tycoon, and exacting justice gives

Cutter a goal in life. Bone reluctantly helps him. The film soon moves beyond a simple quest for retribution by the underdog against the mighty, and becomes a complex metaphor exploring the changing values in society. The film was overlooked for an Academy Award but it won the Edgar in 1982.

Dalziel and Pascoe

(UK TV series, 1996–*current*, 22 episodes to season 6)
Producers: Eric Abraham, Chris Parr.
Directors: Ross Devonish, Maurice Phillips, Richard Standeven, Gareth Davies, Edward Bennett, David Wheatley, Suri Krishnamma, Stephen Whittaker, Matthew Evans, Paul Marcus.
Writers: Alan Plater, Malcolm Bradbury, Stephen Lowe, Michael Chaplin, Ed Whitmore, Timothy Prager, David Ashton, Michael Jenner, Matthew Hall.
Starring: Warren Clarke, Colin Buchanan, David Royle, Susannah Corbett, Jo-Anne Stockham.
Based on the characters created by Reginald HILL, plus original scripts by such major writers as Alan Plater and Malcolm Bradbury, this series of 90-minute programmes has firmly established itself amongst the nation's favourites. That's due in no small part to the strong persona of Warren Clarke as the coarse, grumpy, old-fashioned but caring Detective Superintendent Andy Dalziel (pronounced Dee-ell). At times one wonders why his sidekick, D.I. Peter Pascoe (Buchanan) puts up with him. Pascoe is the younger officer who tries to do things by the book. In the TV series his life is further fraught by the failure of his marriage with his wife (Corbett) having taken their daughter to the USA. Two other officers also have important roles, Detective Sergeant Edgar Wield (Royle) and Detective Constable Shirley "Ivor" Novello (Stockham), both of whom also serve as foils for Dalziel's temper but who remain loyal and thorough in their work. It's usually "Wieldy" and "Ivor" who do most of the hard-grind detective work while Dalziel and Pascoe go their own ways in resolving the crime, often crossing each other in the process. The series covers many sensitive subjects, sometimes involving the past of both main officers. The episode "On Beulah Height" (1999), involving the death of a young girl with links to a case 15 years before, received the Edgar Award.

Dance with a Stranger

(1984, UK, 102 minutes)
Director: Mike Newell. **Producer:** Roger Randall-Cutler.
Screenplay: Shelagh Delaney.
Starring: Miranda Richardson, Rupert Everett, Ian Holm, Joanne Whalley-Kilmer.

This film tells the tragic real-life story of Ruth Ellis (Richardson) the last woman to be hanged in Britain. She was so infatuated with her lover, David Blakely (Everett), a complete no-hoper, that she chose to kill him rather than lose him, and that sent her to the gallows. The film works at both the gut level of sympathy for Ellis, and at the recreation of the depressing Britain of the 1950s, and how that society could create the world in which Ellis loved and died.

Dangerfield

(UK TV series, 1995–9, 62 episodes)
Creator: Don Shaw.
Producers: Chris Parr (executive), Julian Murphy (executive), Adrian Bate, Beverley Dartnell.
Directors: Many, primarily Lawrence Gordon Clark, Graham Moore, Ken Hannam.
Writers: Many, primarily Peter J. Hammond, Amanda Coe, Barbara Cox, Don Shaw, Simon Tyrrell.
Starring: Nigel Le Vaillant/Nigel Havers, Amanda Redman, Lisa Faulkner/Tamzin Malleson, Sean Maguire/Tim Vincent, George Irving, Nicola Cowper, Lynsey Baxter.
This series was almost two separate programmes. It began as a vehicle for Nigel Le Vaillant, who had been a popular actor in the medical drama series *Casualty*. He played Dr Paul Dangerfield whose working life is torn between running a medical centre and operating as a police doctor. His home life is also in turmoil. Having lost his wife in a car accident he struggles to do the best for his two teenage children who are going through all the usual problems of adolescence. The first three seasons placed the emphasis on the medical practice. When Le Vaillant left he was replaced by Havers as Dr Jonathan Paige and the emphasis shifted to his work as a police doctor, eventually leaving the medical practice entirely. Paige became involved with the police investigations, often too deeply, and also found a romantic entanglement with DS Diamond (Cowper). The series was popular as much if not more for its characters than for its plots which sometimes seemed an after thought but at their best Paige did some interesting medical detective work. A novel derived from the first series is *Dangerfield* (1996) by Joanna Toye.

The Dark Wind

(1991, US, 111 minutes)
Director: Errol Morris. **Producer:** Robert Redford (executive), Patrick Markey.
Screenplay: Neal Jimenez, Mark Horowitz, Eric Bergren from the novel by Tony HILLERMAN.
Starring: Lou Diamond Phillips, Gary Farmer, Fred Ward, John Karlen.

This was planned as the first of a series of adaptations of the books by Tony Hillerman featuring his Navajo detective Jim Chee, but such a political wrangle erupted because the actor who played Chee, Lou Diamond Phillips, was not Navajo, that it left a sour taste with everyone. Yet everyone who worked on the film had considerable respect for Native American culture and the film itself, despite taking some liberties with Hillerman's work, is relatively competent. Alas Phillips's portrayal of Chee is not the same character as in the book and is rather lacklustre, and the film's strength lies in the Arizona landscape and the Navajo beliefs. Nevertheless it is one of the few films to depict an American Indian detective, in this instance investigating several cases, including drug-smuggling, which gradually merge together as one, and it is hoped further, more faithful attempts will be made.

Darker Than Amber

(1970, US, 97 minutes)
Director: Robert Clouse. **Producer:** Walter Seltzer, Jack Reeves.
Screenplay: Ed Waters from the novel by John D. MacDonald.
Starring: Rod Taylor, Suzy Kendall, Theodore Bikel, Jane Russell.
Surprisingly only one theatrical film has been made so far from the Travis McGee books of John D. MacDonald. *DTA* is a competent film with Rod Taylor as a rather more pleasant McGee than the books suggest, though he's vindictive enough here as he goes after the killers of a girl he'd tried to help. The film contains a well-choreographed fist-fight between McGee and one of the villains (William Smith). The film also marked the last cinema screen appearance of Jane Russell who played the Alabama Tigress.

Dead Silence

(1996, US, 95 minutes)
Director: Daniel Petrie, Jr.,
Screenplay: Donald Stewart from the novel *A Maiden's Grave* by Jeffery Deaver.
Starring: James Garner, Kim Coates, Marlee Matlin, Lolita Davidovitch, Charles Martin Smith.
A good adaptation, capturing the suspense and frustration in Deaver's novel. Three convicts, led by Theodore Handy (Coates) hijack a bus full of deaf students and their hearing-impaired teacher (Martin). Along comes FBI hostage negotiator John Potter (Garner) who plays the waiting game. Although straightforward the film is somewhat out of the ordinary and the strong performances from the cast make a very satisfying result.

Deathtrap

(1982, US, 116 minutes)
Director: Sidney Lumet. **Producer:** Burtt Harris.
Screenplay: Jay Presson Allen based on the stage play by Ira LEVIN.
Starring: Michael Caine, Christopher Reeve, Dyan Cannon, Irene Worth.
This film was adapted from Ira Levin's stageplay about a Broadway playwright (Caine) who has lost the touch but decides to kill one of his students (Reeve) who has produced a remarkable play and pass that play off as his own. It loses the direct empathy a theatre creates between audience and actors and some of the surprises that sustain the suspense on stage. Nevertheless Sidney Lumet has added other tricks, some of which work, to keep you guessing, though the film is carried more by the actors than the plot. The translation from stage to screen is less successful than with Shaffer's *Sleuth*, which also starred Caine, but is still a good example of its kind.

Death Wish

(1974, US, 94 minutes)
Director: Michael Winner. **Producers:** Hal Landers, Bobby Roberts, Michael Winner.
Screenplay: Wendell Mayes from the novel by Brian GARFIELD.
Starring: Charles Bronson, Hope Lange, Vincent Gardenia, Stuart Margolin.
Brian Garfield objected to this adaptation of his novel because it glorified violence and revenge. Bronson plays Paul Kersey, normally mild-mannered but who goes after the thugs who kill his wife and rape his daughter, and becomes a populist vigilante. Comparison between book and film is the stuff of academic theses, but Garfield sought to establish that revenge is not in itself a form of redemption and that you need to be positive otherwise you sink to the level of the oppressor. Winner ignored all of that for a glorified urban western. The film was nevertheless a success and no doubt the cheering of cinema audiences as Kersey takes his revenge must have seemed sufficient justification to Winner, though all this did is underscore the animal instinct in us all. Spot Jeff Goldblum in his first film rôle as the leader of the gang of thugs. The film not only spawned a host of imitations but four direct sequels. The first two, *Death Wish II* (1981) and *Death Wish 3* (1985) were also directed by Winner but *Death Wish 4: The Crackdown* (1987) was directed by J. Lee Thompson and *Death Wish 5: The Face of Death* (1994) by Allan Goldstein. Bronson starred in them all and was 74 by the fifth. It's difficult to find any redeeming features in any of them. Even worse was Winner's female equivalent, *Dirty Weekend* (1992), based on Helen Zahavi's violent 1991 novel, in which Bella (Lia

Williams) tires of being abused and goes on a crazed weekend of revenge killings.

The Debt Collector

(1999, UK, 110 minutes)
Director: Anthony Neilson. **Producers:** Graham Broadbent, Damian Jones.
Screenplay: Anthony Neilson.
Starring: Billy Connolly, Ken Stott, Francesca Annis, Iain Robertson, Annette Crosbie.
Nickie Dryden (Connolly) has served seventeen years for murder and during that time has reformed and become a respected writer and sculptor. However, his wish to settle down in society is thwarted by his former arresting officer Gary Keltie (Stott) who believes it's time that Dryden paid in full. The clash between the two has disturbing consequences. This compelling film is a fascinating exploration of what constitutes justice.

The Defenders

(US TV series, 1961–5, 132 episodes)
Creator: Reginald Rose.
Producers: Herbert Brodkin (executive), George Justin.
Directors: Many, including John Newland, Sydney Pollack, Daniel Petrie, Michael Powell, David Pressman, Boris Sagal, Jack Smight, Sam Wanamaker.
Writers: Many, including George BAXT, Max Ehrlich, Howard FAST, David Karp, David Rintels, Jerome Ross, Andrea Russo, Robert van Scoyk.
Starring: E.G. Marshall, Robert Reed.
This was one of the most popular and creative courtroom drama series on American TV. Unlike *Perry Mason*, which was designed to show Mason's brilliance in outwitting the villain, *The Defenders* took on key issues of the day, including abortions, euthanasia and civil rights, and explored their impact on individuals. One episode, "Blacklist" (1964), about political blacklisting, earned both writer Ernest Kinoy and actor Jack Klugman Emmy Awards. The series featured a father-and-son law firm, Preston & Preston. Lawrence Preston (Marshall) was the seasoned veteran whilst Kenneth Preston (Reed) was newly qualified and often learning the hard way. The series was given a Raven Award by the MWA for its overall quality and two episodes were nominated for Edgars. The series was based on a play by Reginald Rose that he had written for the TV series *Studio One* in 1957 starring Ralph Bellamy and William Shatner defending a young Steve McQueen. In 1997, aged 83, E.G. Marshall teamed up with Beau Bridges to make two TV movies reprising his rôle:

The Defenders: Payback and *The Defenders: Choice of Evils*. A novel based on the series is *The Defenders* (1961) by Edward S. Aarons.

The Defiant Ones

(1958, US, 96 minutes, b&w)
Producer/Director: Stanley Kramer.
Screenplay: Nedrick Young (as Nathan E. Douglas) and Harold Jacob Smith.
Starring: Tony Curtis, Sidney Poitier, Theodore Bikel, Charles McGraw, Lon Chaney.
This film is more a drama of racial equality than it is a crime film, for all that it features two convicts who have escaped from a chain gang. The problem is that Jackson (Curtis) is white and a bigot and he's still chained to black Noah Cullen. The film scores on all points especially the powerful interplay between Jackson and Cullen. It won an Oscar for best screenplay and an Edgar as best film. The 1986 remake with Robert Urich and Carl Weathers in the lead rôles lacks the impact of the original though it still has much to say about prejudice.

Dempsey and Makepeace

(UK TV series, 1985–6, 30 episodes)
Creator: Tony Wharmby. **Producers:** Nick Elliott (executive), Tony Wharmby.
Directors: Tony Wharmby, William Brayne, Christian Marnham, Gerry Mill, Victor Ritelis, Graham Theakston, Baz Taylor, Robert Tronson, John Hough, Roger Tucker, Christopher King, Michael Brandon.
Writers: Ranald Graham, Jesse Carr-Martindale, Dave Humphries, Jonathan Hales, Neil Rudyard, Murray Smith, Roger Marshall, Paul Wheeler, David Crane, Jeffrey Caine, David Wilks, John Field, Guy Meredith.
Starring: Michael Brandon, Glynis Barber, Ray Smith, Tony Osoba.
Jim Dempsey (Brandon) was a New York cop who stumbled across a case of police corruption that placed him in danger so for his safety he was transferred to England to work in an elite crime-fighting unit SI-10. There he was teamed with the attractive Sergeant Harriet "Harry" Makepeace (Barber) who was also a member of the aristocracy with influential friends. Their boss was the loudmouth Liverpudlian Chief Superintendent Gordon Spikings (Smith). It was a formulaic, high action, violent series with an impetuous trigger-happy Dempsey. The couple frequently tried to outdo each other at first. Initially frustrated with their partnership a sexual chemistry grew between them both on and off screen, which was the main appeal of the series. Brandon and Barber married in 1989. The episode "Make Peace, Not War", where the duo infiltrate a drug-smuggling ring, was dramatized by its author, Jesse Carr-Martindale under that title (1985).

Department S

(UK TV series, 1969–70, 28 episodes)

Creators: Monty Berman, Dennis Spooner. **Producer:** Monty Berman.

Directors: Cyril Frankel, Ray Austin, John Gilling, Roy Ward Baker, Paul Dickson, Gill Taylor, Leslie Norman.

Writers: Gerald Kelsey, Philip Broadley, Terry Nation, Donald James, Tony Williamson, Donald James, Leslie Darbon, Harry H. Junkin.

Starring: Peter Wyngarde, Joel Fabiani, Rosemary Nicols, Dennis Alaba Peters.

The original *Department S* was an interesting programme, if a little derivative of *The Avengers*. It dealt with the operations of a special unit of Interpol, based in Paris, that investigated bizarre crimes that had baffled everyone else, such as an airliner that disappears for six days or when a town's entire inhabitants are kidnapped. The head of the unit was black African Sir Curtis Seretse (Peters) but the principal investigator who stole the show was Jason King (Wyngarde). A womanizing dandy with a typical late-sixties outrageous dress sense, King was a writer of thrillers and approached each investigation as if it were a new case for his fictional detective Mark Caine. He was assisted by American agent Stewart Sullivan (Fabiani) and British computer whiz Annabelle Hurst (Nicols). The cases were always fascinating and a challenge to resolve. The success of the Jason King character led to a spin-off series, *Jason King* (1971–2; 26 episodes), from the same production team, but without the other characters. King was now independent, still writing his thrillers, and travelling to exotic locations where there were always plenty of women, but little crime fighting. The spin-off series led to two spin-off books, both by John F. Burke under the alias Robert Miall, *Jason King* (1972) and *Kill Jason King* (1972).

The Detective

(1968, US, 109 minutes)

Director: Gordon Douglas. **Producer:** Aaron Rosenberg.

Screenplay: Abby Mann from the novel *The Detective* (1966) by Roderick Thorp.

Starring: Frank Sinatra, Lee Remick, Ralph Meeker, Jack Klugman.

Frank Sinatra played a number of good cop rôles in the sixties. After *Tony Rome* he and Gordon Douglas teamed up again for this one-off film about cynical New York cop Joe Leland (Sinatra) facing political corruption within City Hall while he tries to investigate the murder of a gay man. For its day this film was controversially frank about homosexuality, and it's that which now dates the film. But it still packs a punch with good performances all round and a suitably sleazy atmosphere. It may seem hard to believe but the sequel to the original novel by Roderick Thorpe (1936–99) spawned the film *Die Hard*.

The Detectives

(US TV series, 1959–62, 97 episodes, b&w)
Producer: Arthur Gardner, Arnold Laven, Jules Levy.
Directors: Richard Carlson, Murray Golden, Arnold Laven, Don McDougall.
Starring: Robert Taylor, Tige Andrews, Lee Farr/Mark Goddard, Russell Thorson/Adam West, Ursula Theiss.
This series originally ran for 67 weekly half-hour episodes but when it switched from ABC to NBC in September 1961 it increased to a full hour and was renamed *Robert Taylor's Detectives*. Moving from the big to the small screen, film star Robert Taylor played Captain Matt Holbrook, a tough Elliott Ness-like police detective in a big, modern-day but unnamed city. He led a team of detectives including Lieutenant John Russo (Andrews) of Burglary, Lieutenant Jim Conway (Farr) of Homicide and Lieutenant Otto Lindstrom (Thorson) of the Bunco squad. The episodes would shift between the detectives each week and seldom did all four pursue one case. The second season included some romantic interest for widower Holbrook in the shape of reporter Lisa Bonay, played by Taylor's real-life wife, Ursula Theiss. A slight change of cast in the third season brought future TV Batman Adam West on board as Sergeant Steve Nelson.

Devil in a Blue Dress

(1995, US, 101 minutes)
Director: Carl Franklin. **Producer:** Gary Goetzman, Jesse Beaton.
Screenplay: Carl Franklin, based on the novel by Walter MOSLEY.
Starring: Denzel Washington, Tom Sizemore, Jennifer Beals, Don Cheadle.
The first of Mosley's novels about Easy Rawlins (Washington), set in the forties, makes a stylish and refreshingly intelligent thriller. Rawlins is hired by dubious Dewitt Allbright (Sizemore) to find a politician's girlfriend (Beals), but before long finds himself suspected of murder and being pursued both by the police and Allbright's henchmen. Rawlins seeks help, albeit reluctantly, from his psychopathic friend Mouse (Cheadle). The film is an excellent introduction to Mosley's work.

Diagnosis: Murder

(US TV series,1993–2001, 178 episodes)
Producers: Michael Gleason (executive), Dean Hargrove, Lee Goldberg & William Rabkin.
Directors: Many, including Lou Antonio, Tom Chehak, Jonathan Frakes, Bernard L. Kowalski, Michael Lange, Vincent McEveety, William Rabkin, and Michael Schultz.
Writers: Many, including Paul BISHOP, Jacquelyn Blain, Tom Chehak, Gerry Conway, Lee Goldberg, Ernest Kinoy, William Rabkin.

Starring: Dick Van Dyke, Barry Van Dyke, Victoria Rowell, Scott Baio/Charlie Schlatter.

DM was a relatively cozy mystery series that nevertheless had clever and often ingenious plots to baffle the police. Dick Van Dyke played Dr Mark Sloan, head of internal medicine (later teaching physician) at a General Hospital in Los Angeles. His real-life son, Barry, was his on-screen son Detective Steve Sloan of the LAPD, and the Doctor served as a special consultant to the police. Through that connection Dr Sloan frequently became involved in puzzling crimes. For the first two series he was assisted by interns Dr Jack Stewart (Baio) and Amanda Livingston (Rowell). From the third series Stewart was replaced by Dr Travis (Schlatter). The character of Dr Sloan had first appeared in an episode of *Jake and the Fatman* in 1991 and then in three special TV movies, *Diagnosis of Murder* (1992), *The House on Sycamore Street* (1992) and *A Twist of the Knife* (1993) and their popularity led to the long-running series. It reached its height of popularity around the fifth season under the creative production of Lee Goldberg and William Rabkin when they began to produce a number of recursive episodes using characters and images from other crime and thriller series. For instance, Joe Mannix turns up in "Little Girl Lost' (1997) and he and Sloan determine to solve a 25-year old murder case originally aired in a 1973 *Mannix* episode. By this time it seemed that half of Van Dyke's family were appearing in the show. *Diagnosis: Murder* knew how to entertain.

Dial 999

(UK TV series, 1958–9, 39 episodes, b&w)

Producer: Harry Alan Towers.

Starring: Robert Beatty, Duncan Lamont, John Witty.

The earliest British police-reality show, made in conjunction with the US company Ziv that produced *Highway Patrol.* Often filmed on location, in conjunction with Scotland Yard, the series featured Robert Beatty as Canadian policeman, Mike Maguire, who is sent to Scotland Yard to learn new crime-detection techniques. Beatty's tough-talking approach contrasted well with the traditional staid English style, portrayed by D.I. Winter (Lamont). Each week's half-hour episode began with lights flashing and the car chasing through the streets and always ended with a car chase, in the hope that this would appeal to US viewers.

Die Hard

(1988, US, 132 minutes)

Director: John McTiernan. **Producer:** Lawrence Gordon, Joel Silver.

Screenplay: Jeb Stuart, Steven E. De Souza from the novel *Nothing Lasts Forever* (1979) by Roderick Thorp.

Starring: Bruce Willis, Alan Rickman, Bonny Bedelia, Reginald Veljohnson, William Atherton.

There comes a point where crime fiction hands over to the all-action thriller, and this film, one of the great action films, is perhaps the best example. Renegade New York cop John McClane (Willis) has gone to a multi-storey office block where his estranged wife Holly (Bedelia) works only to find himself in the midst of a hijack by terrorist Hans Gruber (Rickman). Outside the police squabble and appear impotent though patrolman Sergeant Al Powell (Veljohnson) makes radio contact with McClane who uses whatever diversionary tactics he can to defeat Gruber and his gang. Surprisingly, the novel on which it is based by Roderick Thorp, is a sequel to *The Detective*, which means Willis is playing the character originally played by Frank Sinatra. The film's success inevitably led to two sequels, *Die Hard 2: Die Harder* (1990) and *Die Hard With a Vengeance* (1995). Though neither live up to the full-blown power of the first film, both are surprisingly good as sequels and the third adds a clever element of complicated puzzles to the race-against-time ploy.

Dirty Harry

(1971, US, 101 minutes)

Producer/Director: Don Siegel.

Screenplay: Harry Julian Fink, Rita M. Fink, Dean Riesner.

Starring: Clint Eastwood, Harry Guardino, Reni Santoni, John Vernon, Andy Robinson, John Mitchum.

The seminal cop-takes-law-into-own-hands film, which heralded a whole new generation of "dirty cop" and vigilante films. Renegade cop Harry Callahan (Eastwood) abhors all bureaucracy and when a sniper (Robinson) is released through lack of evidence, Callahan goes after him. Robinson is superb as the gibbering psychopathic killer and Eastwood is at his best as the relentless, definitive hard-boiled, no-nonsense "make my day" enforcer. The sequels fail to work as well because the character of Callahan becomes more moralistic, though each film has its individual merits. In *Magnum Force* (1973) he's out to get rookie cops who have embarked on a "Dirty Harry"-style wipe-out of "criminal scum". In *The Enforcer* (1976), which also features Tyne Daly, Callahan goes after a gang of revolutionary hoodlums. *Sudden Impact* (1983), the film in which Callahan first says, "Go ahead, make my day", has Callahan tracking down a woman (Sondra Locke) who's taking revenge on the men who raped her and her sister. Finally, in *The Dead Pool* (1988), the weakest of the series, Callahan deals with a fanatic killing off minor film celebrities. By this time the series and character were well past their sell-by date. The rôle of Harry Callahan had originally been offered to Frank Sinatra but he turned it down because he had injured his hand. Three of the films were novelized: *Dirty Harry* (1971) by Philip Rock, *Magnum Force* (1974) by Mel Valley and *Sudden Impact* (1983) by Joe Stinson. There was also a series issued between 1981 and 1983 under the house name Dane Hartman but which were written primarily by Richard S. Meyers and Leslie Alan Horvitz. Titles are *Death on the Docks*, *Duel for Cannons*, *The Long Death*, *Blood of the Strangers*, *City of Blood*, *Family Skeletons*, *Hatchet Men*, *Massacre at Russian River*, *The Mexican Kill*, *The Dealer in Death*, *Death in the Air* and *The Killing Conection*.

Dirty Weekend *see under* Death Wish

Diva

(1981, French, 117 minutes)
Director: Jean-Jacques Beineix. **Producer:** Irène Silberman.
Screenplay: Jean-Jacques Beineix and Jean van Hamme based on the novel by Daniel ODIER.
Starring: Frédéric Andrei, Richard Bohringer, Wilhelminia Wiggins Fernandez, Jacques Fabbri.
An instant cult film, heralding the experimental and stylistic French *cinéma du look*, *Diva* turns crime into art and fantasy. A postal worker, Jules (Andrei), secretly records an opera singer who refuses to make official recordings. Unfortunately his tape becomes switched with a surveillance tape and poor Jules finds himself being hunted down by two psychopathic thugs. The film uses some wonderfully surreal fairy-tale images that remove the film out of any simple genre identification. It's a perfect example of the visual medium achieving what the printed page cannot, and yet the story works superbly in both forms.

Dog Day Afternoon

(1975, US, 130 minutes)
Director: Sidney Lumet. **Producer:** Martin Bregman, Martin Elfand.
Screenplay: Frank R. Pierson from the book by Patrick Mann.
Starring: Al Pacino, John Cazale, Sully Boyar, Chris Sarandon, Charles Durning.
Based on a true story, this is the tale of a bank robbery that goes wrong. The bisexual Sonny (Pacino) had planned the robbery in order to get money to finance a sex-change operation for his lover Leon (Sarandon) and teams up with the equally inept Sal (Cazale). When it fails the heist turns into a siege directed by police chief Moretti (Durning). Crowds gather, and when the purpose of the robbery is revealed, gay supporters arrive, resulting in an explosive situation both inside and outside the bank. Although with moments of humour, it is also a poignant film with Lumet able to create audience empathy with all the main characters. A

considerable achievement, which was nominated for the Oscar for best picture and won Pierson an Oscar for best screenplay.

Dragnet

(US TV series,1952–9, b&w, 276 episodes; revived 1967–70, 98 episodes; revived 1989–90, 52 episodes)
Creator: Jack Webb.
Producers: 1952–70: Jack Webb (executive), Robert A. Cinader, William Stark.
Directors: 1952–70: mostly Jack Webb.
Writers: 1952–9: mostly Jack Webb, James E. Moser, John Robinson, Frank Burt; 1967–70 mostly Richard L. Breen, Robert C. Dennis, James Doherty, Henry Irving, Jerry D. Lewis, Sidney Morse, Burt Prelutsky, Robert Soderburg, David Vowell, Preston Wood.
Starring: 1952–9: Jack Webb, Barton Yarborough/Barney Phillips/Herb Ellis/Ben Alexander; 1967–70: Jack Webb, Harry Morgan; 1989–90: Jeff Osterhage, Bernard White, Thalmus Rasulala, Don Stroud.
The most influential of the early TV cop shows and the first American police drama to be shown on British TV. Jack Webb went for an accurate, no-frills, authentic recreation of police investigations, many of the cases drawn from the files of the LAPD. Webb's monotone narration, as Sergeant Joe Friday, under-dramatized the action and his phrases "Just the facts, ma'am" and "That's my job" passed into the language. The dramatic introductory music (by Walter Schumann) became a hit and the series was so well known that it was brilliantly lampooned by Stan Freberg with "St George and the Dragonet". The code of broadcasting ensured that in the series the police always triumphed, the main drawback being that this sometimes resulted in a holier-than-thou image of the police force. The series had started on radio and it was there that the famous opening lines, "The story you are about to hear is true. Only the names have been changed to protect the innocent," were first used. It ran on radio for six years (1949–1955; 318 episodes), jointly with the TV broadcasts, and with mostly the same performers. A film, *Dragnet*, scripted by Richard L. Breen and again directed by Jack Webb, was released in 1954, though padding out the half-hour format to ninety minutes diluted the effect. *Dragnet* was resurrected in colour first as a one-off TV movie, *Dragnet 1966* (not shown until 1969), and then as a regular half-hour series in 1967 as *Dragnet '67* (etc.). By now the format seemed dated against the faster action shows and the series shifted from the police procedural to demonstrating the social aspect of the work. Nevertheless the continued moralizing of the show, especially about the drug culture, did not endear it to young audiences. Jack Webb died in 1982 (flags were flown at half-mast from police stations throughout Los Angeles) but his legacy lives on. There was a new feature-length film, an affectionate if relentless parody, *Dragnet*, released

in 1987, starring Dan Aykroyd and Tom Hanks, and a new TV series, followed, called *The New Dragnet*, with Jeff Osterhage as Vic Daniels and Bernard White as Carl Molina. By now, though, the format was lost on the audiences and it ran for just one season. A biography of Jack Webb is *Just the Facts, Ma'am* (1999) by Daniel Moyer and Eugene Alvarex, whilst a detailed study of *Dragnet* and Webb's other TV series is *My Name's Friday* (2001) by Michael Hayde. James Reach wrote a stage play based on the series, *Dragnet* (1956), and Richard Deming compiled a collection of stories *Dragnet* (1957). There are also four tie-in novels: *Dragnet: Case No. 561* (1956) by David Knight, *Dragnet: The Case of the Courteous Killer* (1958) by Richard Deming (Richard S. Prather), *Dragnet: The Case of the Crime King* (1959) by Richard Deming and *Dragnet 1968* (1967) by David Vowell. Jack Webb (1920–82) should not be confused with the author Jack Webb (b. 1916) who wrote the Father Shanley and Sammy Golden series of novels, also set in Los Angeles, in the 1950s.

Due South

(US TV series,1994–8)
Creator: Paul Haggis.
Producers: Paul Haggis, Jeff King, Kathy Slevin, Paul Gross (all executive), Robert Wertheimer.
Directors: Many, including George Bloomfield, Steve DiMarco, Paul Haggis, Joseph L. Scanlon.
Writers: Primarily Paul Lynch.
Starring: Paul Gross, David Marciano, Beau Starr, Ramona Milano, Keith Rennie, Gordon Pinsent.
Paul Gross plays Constable Benton Fraser, a charmingly polite and politically correct Royal Canadian Mountie, who is assigned to the Canadian consulate in Chicago. Fraser had visited Chicago before searching for the murderer of his father (Pinsent) and had met Detective Ray Vecchio (Marciano). The two now team up, even though Fraser is not supposed to be involved in any investigative work. With a Dudley Do-Right personality and occasionally unbelievable dexterity, Fraser often outdoes streetwise wise-cracking Vecchio. Although the series was played for its humour, and spoofed most crime show conventions, it developed an aura of its own, especially in Fraser's relationship with the spirit of his dead father who acts like a conscience. In the final episode, when his father's murderer is apprehended, the old man can rest in peace at last. There was also a delightful relationship between Fraser and his deaf lip-reading pet wolf Diefenbaker. For the final season Vecchio goes undercover (though his cover is nearly blown by Fraser) and Fraser's new partner is the equally cynical Detective Kowalski (Rennie), who frequently bends the rules, much to Fraser's admonishment. An original and refreshingly bright series.

8 Million Ways to Die

(1986, US, 110 minutes)
Director: Hal Ashby.
Producer: Mark Damon (executive), Charles Mulvehill, Stephen J. Roth.
Screenplay: Oliver Stone, David Lee Henry, revised by Robert Towne, from the novel by Lawrence BLOCK.
Starring: Jeff Bridges, Rosanna Arquette, Andy Garcia, Lisa Sloan, Alexandra Paul.

Block's original book is regarded as one of the modern P.I. classics, but adapting it to the big screen was fraught with problems. Oliver Stone had to pull out due to financial problems and his script was rewritten by Robert Towne while replacement director Hal Ashby was fired towards the end of production and the film only just trickled out. Jeff Bridges gives a creditable performance as Matthew Scudder, the cop who is sinking into an alcoholic chasm and struggling to survive while being dragged back into a world of vice and corruption. Block's original story-line works because it's the climax of a long series, which was difficult to transform into a single film and though the end result lacks the power and haunting atmosphere of the book, it is an effectively morbid portrayal of the underside of Los Angeles.

87th Precinct

(US TV series,1961–2, 30 episodes, b&w)
Creator: Ed MCBAIN (based on his series of novels).
Producers: Hubbell Robinson Production.
Writers: Several, including Evan HUNTER, Donald E. WESTLAKE.
Starring: Robert Lansing, Ron Harper, Gregory Walcott, Norman Fell, Gena Rowlands.

Based in Manhattan's 87th police precinct this series was NBC's response to the success of ABC's *The Naked City*. Both were solid, high-action police procedurals which explored the lives of the detectives as much as their police work. Heading the team was Detective Steve Carella (Lansing), whose wife Teddy (Rowlands) was a deaf-mute, which provided some thoughtful moments. The series, though, was often stolen by Detective Meyer (Fell) the older, more cynical detective, who'd seen it all before. Although the TV series ceased, the books have continued and there have been several full-length film adaptations, both for TV and the cinema. The cinema adaptations began with *Cop Hater* (1958) and *The Mugger* (1958), both directed by William Berke from scripts by Henry Kane, neither of which lit fires. Of more interest was *The Pusher* (1960), scripted by Harold Robbins, and which introduced Lansing to the rôle of Carella. The success of this film launched the TV series. Ed McBain was not averse to parodying his own series in the light-hearted *Fuzz* (1972), with Burt Reynolds as Carella, which had some funny set pieces, but doesn't feel part of the series. It contrasts starkly with Philippe Labro's French treatment of the novel *Ten Plus One*, transferred to the Riviera as *Without Apparent Motive* (1972) with Jean-Louis Trintignant as a world-weary Carella trying to fathom a series of motiveless murders. This is the best cinematographic interpretation to date. Recent TV movies of the series, under the banner title *Ed McBain's 87th Precinct* have been *Lightning* (1995), *Ice* (1996) and *Heatwave* (1997).

Eischied [UK as Chief of Detectives]

(US TV series,1979–83, 13 episodes)
Creator: Robert Daley. **Producers:** David Gerber (executive), Matthew Rapf, Jay Daniel.
Directors: Several, including Larry Elikann, Gene Kearney, Leo Penn, Nicholas Sgarro, Jack Starrett.
Writers: Several, including Frank Abatemarco, Sean Baine, Stephen Downing, Gene Kearney, Irv Pearlberg.
Starring: Joe Don Baker, Alan Fudge, Alan Oppenheimer, Eddie Egan, Vincent Bufano.
The character of Chief Earl Eischied (pronounced Eye-shyed) first appeared in the novel *To Kill a Cop* (1976) by former NYPD Deputy Police Commissioner Robert Daley (b. 1930), who is also the author of *Year of the Dragon*. Eischied is a corrupt, cunning, but tired cop who has to save his own skin and those of his fellow officers when someone starts killing patrolmen. The book formed a three-part mini-series, *To Kill a Cop* (1978), adapted by *Shaft* author Ernest TIDYMAN, which introduced Joe Don Baker to the rôle of Eischied. The subsequent series was less successful because it was broadcast at the same time as *Dallas*. Baker reprised the rôle, which was made less corrupt, though he still bent the rules because of his focused dedication to the job. His methods bring conflict with the politically ambitious Deputy Commissioner Kimbrough (Fudge) but Eischied finds ways round that. Eischied was not married and his only companion outside work was his cat, P.C.

Electra Glide in Blue

(1976, US, 113 minutes)
Producer/Director: James William Guercio.
Screenplay: Robert Boris.
Starring: Robert Blake, Billy Green Bush, Mitchell Ryan.
More influenced by the success of *Easy Rider* than of the crime field, this one-off movie by former record producer Guercio became an instant cult classic. Motorcycle cop John Wintergreen (Blake), though diminutive,

believes he can change the world and follows his inner voice in his tough-guy pursuit of criminals, but he rapidly becomes disillusioned. The film was notorious in its day for its graphic violence.

The Empty Beach

(1985, Australian, 86 minutes)
Director: Chris Thomson.
Screenplay: Keith Dewhurst from the novel by Peter CORRIS.
Starring: Bryan Brown, Anna Maria Monticelli, Ray Barrett, John Wood.
A still rare example of an Australian hard-boiled P.I. film. It's a faithful adaptation of one of Peter Corris's Cliff Hardy novels in which Hardy (Brown) is hired by a wealthy widow (Monticelli) to solve her husband's disappearance. The film is fascinating for its portrayal of the dark side of Sydney, and for a change in P.I. lingo from the standard American to some original Australian.

The Enforcer *see under* Dirty Harry

The Equalizer

(US TV series,1985–9, 88 episodes)
Creator: Michael Sloan, Richard Lindheim.
Producers: James McAdams (executive), Alan Barnette, Daniel Lieberstein, Colman Luck, Alan Metzger, Peter A. Runfolo, Scott Shepherd.
Directors: Many, including Tobe Hooper, Russ Mayberry, Alan Metzger, Mark Sobel.
Writers: Many, including Robert CRAIS, Mark Frost, Victor Hsu, Scott Shepherd, Michael Sloan.
Starring: Edward Woodward, Robert Lansing, Keith Szarabajka, William Zabka.
Robert McCall (Woodward) had served as a secret agent, codename "The Equalizer", but in his retirement feels guilty about his past actions and decides to pay something back to society. He advertises: "Got a problem? Odds against you? Call the Equalizer." After weeding out the junk calls McCall helps out the others, sometimes as a bodyguard, but usually as an avenger, almost a vigilante, sorting out the muggers, rapists and other street-scum, often with the help of his guns. McCall was always immaculately dressed and drove around in a Jaguar, trying not to expend too much energy. He left the hard work to his assistant Mickey Kostmayer (Szarabajka), and sometimes liaised with his old Agency boss (Lansing, in his final appearance). The series was extremely popular if a little basic and was only dropped, after four years, in a price war between CBS and Universal. Three novels were

based on the series, all by David George Deutsch: *The Equalizer* (1986), *Blood and Wine* (1987) and *To Even the Odds* (1988). The episode "The Cup" won an Edgar in 1987.

Escape from Alcatraz

(1979, US, 112 minutes)
Producer/Director: Don Siegel.
Screenplay: Richard Tuggle.
Starring: Clint Eastwood, Patrick McGoohan, Jack Thibeau, Roberts Blossom, Fred Ward.
The ultimate non-action thriller. This is the story of the one presumed successful escape from the island fortress prison of Alcatraz. Clint Eastwood plays Frank Morris who has been driven to the limit by restrictive warden Patrick McGoohan and the violence of his cell mates. With fellow prisoners John and Clarence Anglin (Ward and Thibeau) they go for broke. Siegel directs with the hand of a master and creates more tension than an arsenal full of Stallones and Schwarzeneggers.

The Expert

(UK TV series,1968–71, 52 episodes; revived 1976, 10 episodes)
Creator: Gerard Glaister, N.J. Crisp. **Producers:** Gerard Glaister, Andrew Osborn.
Writers: Roger Parkes.
Starring: Marius Goring, Ann Morrish, Victor Winding, Sally Nesbitt.
Gerard Glaister based the character of Professor John Hardy (Goring) on his uncle, John Glaister, who was Professor of Forensic Medicine at Glasgow University. Hardy lives in Warwickshire with his wife, Jo (Morrish) who is a doctor. Between them they are able to provide expert forensic advice to their police friend DCI Fleming (Winding). The series was meticulously researched not only by Glaister but by Goring, who took his rôle seriously. Story-lines were also contributed by forensic pathologist and barrister Bernard Knight who wrote a novel based on the series, *The Expert* (1976) under the alias Bernard Picton.

The Face of Fear

(1971, US TV movie, 75 minutes)
Director: George McGowan. **Producer:** Quinn Martin (executive).
Screenplay: Edward Hume from the novel *Sally* by E.V. Cunningham (Howard FAST).
Starring: Elizabeth Ashley, Ricardo Montalban, Jack Warden.
One of the best of all TV suspense films. Sally Dillman (Ashley) believes she is dying of leukemia and rather than face an agonizing death she hires a hit-man to kill her at some unarranged time. She then discovers the

diagnosis is wrong, and it becomes a race against time for Sergeant Frank Ortega (Montalban) and Lieutenant George Coye (Warden) to find the killer.

Fair Game

(1995, US, 86 minutes)
Director: Andrew Sipes. **Producer:** Joel Silver.
Screenplay: Charles Fletcher based on the novel by Paula GOSLING.
Starring: William Baldwin, Cindy Crawford, Steven Berkoff, Christopher McDonald.
Hyped up at the time, because it was model Cindy Crawford's first film, this is a more accurate but admittedly less exciting adaptation of Paul Gosling's novel *Fair Game* which had also been the basis for Stallone's all-action thriller *Cobra*. Detective Max Kirkpatrick (Baldwin) is assigned to protect Miami lawyer Kate McQuean (Crawford) who is wanted by arch Russian villain Kazak (Berkoff), who believes McQuean knows something about their American spying operations (if she does, we don't discover). Thereafter it becomes a standard car-chase/shoot-out gimme-bang-bang thriller.

Falling Down

(1992, US, 115 minutes)
Director: Joel Schumacher. **Producers:** Arnold Kopelson, Herschel Weingrod, Timothy Harris.
Screenplay: Ebbe Roe Smith.
Starring: Michael Douglas, Robert Duvall, Barbara Hershey, Frederic Forrest, Tuesday Weld.
This movie had everyone talking. In the hands of a lesser director it might have sunk into just another psychotic vigilante shoot-out, but Schumacher creates more of a moral odyssey. "D-Fens" (Douglas), redundant from his job and separated from his wife and child, has a mental relapse while stuck in a traffic jam on the Los Angeles freeway. Abandoning his car he makes his way to the home of his former wife (Hershey) and en route his violence grows as he is confronted by the social morass of commercialized and corrupt California. The final conflict comes when he meets a rabid neo-Nazi storeowner (Forrest). Even without the violence this is a provocative study of urban America and social degradation, exploring what pushes people over the edge.

Family Plot

(1976, US, 115 minutes)
Producer/Director: Alfred Hitchcock.
Screenplay: Ernest Lehman based on the novel *The Rainbird Pattern* by Victor Canning.

Starring: Bruce Dern, Karen Black, Barbara Harris, William Devane, Ed Lauter, Katherine Helmond.
Hitchcock's last movie was a mischievous comedy thriller up there with his best. Blanche (Harris) is a fake medium who, with her partner Lumley (Dern), creates a fake heir in order to inherit some money. This sets them up against kidnappers Fran (Black) and Adamson (Devane). The film is full of misunderstandings, twists and turns which never fully resolve themselves but still result in a satisfyingly clever denouement. The film won an Edgar award in 1977.

Father Dowling Mysteries

(US TV series,1989–91, 43 episodes plus 2-part pilot)
Creator: Ralph McInerny; developed for TV by Dean Hargrove and Joel Steiger.
Producers: Dean Hargrove and Fred Silverman (executive); Robert Hamilton, Barry Steinberg.
Directors: Many, primarily Charles S. Dubin, Christopher Hibler, James Frawley.
Writers: Many, including Robert Hamilton, Doc Barnett, Joyce Burditt, Dean Hargrove.
Starring: Tom Bosley, Tracy Nelson, Mary Wickes, James Stephens.
Although the character of Father Dowling was drawn from the books by Ralph McInerny, the TV series took on a separate life. After a pilot movie, *Fatal Confession* in November 1987, the series was launched in January 1989 with Tom Bosley in the title rôle. Bosley portrays an amiable parish priest in Chicago, who is assisted in his investigations by Sister Steve (Nelson), a former street kid who still knows how to pick locks. The two use the cover of their cloth to delve where the police find it difficult to follow. The Bishop asks the rather bumbling Father Prestwick (Stephens) to keep an eye on them. This delightfully cozy series proved very popular, partly because of the easygoing and non-violent characters but also because of the often devious plots. The series was shown in the UK as *Father Dowling Investigates*.

The F.B.I.

(US TV series,1965–74, 239 episodes)
Producers: Charles Larson, Anthony Spinner, Philip Saltzman for Quinn Martin Productions.
Directors: Many, including Earl Bellamy, Richard Donner, Robert Douglas, Don Edford, Walter Grauman, Jesse Hibbs, Allen Reisner.
Writers: Many, including John D.F. Black, Richard Landau, Norman Lessing, Andy Lewis.
Starring: Efrem Zimbalist, Jr., Philip Abbott, Stephen Brooks/William Reynolds.

One of the US's longest running crime series, the programmes were based on actual FBI files and the series was endorsed by FBI Director J. Edgar Hoover. The series was even used by the FBI to make broadcasts at the end of each week's programme about their currently most wanted men. Lynch-pin of the series was the smartly dressed Inspector Lewis Erskine (Zimbalist) whose life was his work and who had little time for humour. In the first season his daughter appears (played by Lynn Loring) but the character was written out on the basis that FBI agents had no time for a private life. The daughter's boyfriend, Agent Rhodes (Brooks) only lasted a season further. Erskine's main colleague was Agent Colby (Reynolds) and his boss at the FBI was Arthur Ward (Abbott). The series covered the range of federal crimes from organized crime to communist spies. Appearing at an especially volatile period in American history, the series also reflected civil rights, anti-Vietnam protests and drugs. The series was briefly revived as *Today's F.B.I.* (1981–2) with Mike Connors in the Zimbalist rôle as Ben Slater, following the same clean-cut moralistic format. Ten years later ABC ran *F.B.I.: The Untold Stories* (1991–3) which was introduced by Pernell Roberts. This had no continuing characters and were dramatizations of real FBI cases.

The Fellows *see under* The Man in Room 17

A Few Good Men

(1992, US, 138 minutes)
Director: Rob Reiner. **Producers:** Andrew Scheinman, David Brown, Rob Reiner.
Screenplay: Aaron Sorkin based on his own stage play (1990).
Starring: Jack Nicholson, Tom Cruise, Demi Moore, Kevin Bacon, Kiefer Sutherland.
An excellent Hollywood cast spit fire into this otherwise old-style courtroom drama. Two naval lawyers, Lieutenants Kaffee (Cruise) and Galloway (Moore) defend two marines in a case of bullying that led to the death of a fellow marine. Nicholson steals the film as the marines' martinet colonel, whom Kaffee has to discredit, leading to an incandescent exchange. Both the film and Nicholson were nominated for Oscars and the film was also nominated for an Edgar.

The Firm

(1993, US, 148 minutes)
Director: Sydney Pollack. **Producers:** Scott Rudin, John Davis, Sydney Pollack.
Screenplay: David Rabe, Robert Towne, David Rayfiel from the novel by John GRISHAM.

Starring: Tom Cruise, Gene Hackman, Gary Busey, Holly Hunter, Ed Harris.

This was the film that established John Grisham's reputation for his legal thrillers. It simplifies the book somewhat, but what survives is enough for a solid film with strong performances from all the cast. Tom Cruise plays Mitch McDeere, a young, ambitious but still rather naïve lawyer who takes a job with a small Memphis law firm, rather than the big New York outfits, only to discover that it helps out the Mafia. Gene Hackman plays his jaded boss, Avery Tolar. McDeere has to make some rather difficult choices. As legal thrillers go, this is not necessarily the best (Pollack had directed his best with *Presumed Inocent*, three years earlier) but it is certainly one of the more original.

The First Deadly Sin

(1980, US, 112 minutes)

Director: Brian G. Hutton. **Producers:** George Pappas, Mark Shanker.

Screenplay: Mann Rubin, based on the novel by Lawrence SANDERS.

Starring: Frank Sinatra, Faye Dunaway, David Dukes, George Coe, Brenda Vaccaro.

A fairly routine police drama about Detective Edward Delany (Sinatra), coming up for retirement and concerned about his wife (Dunaway), who is in hospital following a kidney operation. Delany's last case involves a homicidal maniac and the drama of the film is as much from Delany's attempts to track down the murderer as it is with his wife's struggle for life. Overall it's a fairly depressing film but it animated fans enough to nominate it for an Edgar award.

48 Hrs

(1982, US, 89 minutes)

Director: Walter Hill. **Producer:** Lawrence Gordon, Joel Silver.

Screenplay: Roger Spottiswoode, Walter Hill, Larry Gross, Steven E. De Souza.

Starring: Eddie Murphy, Nick Nolte, Annette O'Toole, Frank McRae.

Two years before *Beverley Hills Cop*, Eddie Murphy is at his best here as Reggie Hammond, a convicted felon who is sprung from prison by cop Jack Cates (Nolte). Cates needs Hammond to help him track down the rest of the gang – all the more necessary because the gang have Cates' shooter. Nolte is the perfect foil for Murphy, though the "buddy" wise-cracks are held in check by the tension and pace of the film. This one gets the balance right. The *New Yorker* commented that this film was like *The French Connection*, *Dirty Harry* and *Butch Cassidy* in cartoon form. Eight years later the same team put together *Another 48 Hrs* (1990), but that was 48 hours too much. The original film was nominated for an Edgar.

Foul Play

(1978, US, 110 minutes)

Director: Colin Higgins. **Producers:** Thomas L. Miller, Edward K. Milkis.

Screenplay: Colin Higgins.

Starring: Goldie Hawn, Chevy Chase, Burgess Meredith, Rachel Roberts, Dudley Moore, Brian Dennehy.

All too often parodies of the crime genre fall over themselves trying to by funny and to do a true comedy homage you have to know your field. In this film Higgins just about makes it. He throws in almost every set piece and makes most of them work. The plot is simple. Gloria Mundy (Hawn) is a librarian who discovers a plot to kill the Pope. No one believes her, though detective Tony Carlson (Chase) goes along for the ride. The film was nominated for an Edgar. There was a short run TV spin-off series, *Foul Play* (1981; 10 episodes) though Gloria Mundy (played by Deborah Raffin) was the only linking character. She was now a talk-show host who teams up with violinist-turned-cop Tucker Pendleton (Barry Bostwick). The series failed as both a crime show and a comedy. The film was novelized as *Foul Play* (1978) by James Cass Rogers.

The Fraud Squad

(UK TV series, 1969–70, 26 episodes)

Creator: Ivor Jay. **Producer:** Nicolas Palmer.

Directors: Several, primarily Michael Currer Briggs, Paul Annett and John Sichel.

Writers: Several, including Robert Holmes, Joshua Adam, Jack Trevor Story, Basil Dawson, George Lancaster, Robert Banks Stewart, Stuart Douglas, Ivor Jay.

Starring: Patrick O'Connell, Joanna Van Gyseghem, Ralph Nossek, Elizabeth Weaver, Katherine O'Connell.

Patrick O'Connell played Detective Inspector Gamble of Scotland Yard's Fraud Squad who was helped in his investigations by D.S. Vicky Hicks (Van Gyseghem), British TV's first woman detective. The series explored not only financial fraud but con tricks and religious cults. For instance Jack Trevor Story's script, "Anybody Here Seen Kelly?" concerns a valuable painting believed destroyed in a fire but which turns up in Ireland, whilst Lewis Greifer's "Golden Island" deals with a fund raised to finance a treasure hunt. There were sufficient twists for two series before the interest declined.

The French Connection

(1971, US, 99 minutes)

Director: William Friedkin. **Producer:** Philip D'Antoni.

Screenplay: Ernest TIDYMAN from the novel by Robin Moore.

Starring: Gene Hackman, Fernando Rey, Roy Scheider, Tony Lo Bianco.

Gene Hackman plays New York cop Jimmy "Popeye" Doyle who was based on the real character of detective Eddie Egan, renowned for bending the rules to get results. Doyle and his colleague Buddy Russo (Scheider) discover a massive haul of drugs and try and break a narcotics ring headed by impeturbable Alain Charnier (Rey). The film became famous for its elevated railway car chase and its sheer frenetic action. The film won an Academy award as did Friedkin, Hackman and Tidyman. It also won the Edgar award. There was the inevitable sequel, *The French Connection II* (1978), directed by John Frankenheimer, where Hackman and Rey reprise their roles. It's pretty much more of the same but capably done and wraps up the loose ends of the original. Robin Moore tied up his loose ends by novelizing the sequel.

Frenzy

(1972, UK, 110 minutes)

Producer/Director: Alfred Hitchcock.

Screenplay: Anthony SHAFFER from the novel *Goodbye Piccadilly, Farewell Leicester Square* (1966) by Arthur La Bern.

Starring: Jon Finch, Alec McGowan, Vivien Merchant, Anna Massey, Barry Foster, Barbara Leigh-Hunt.

Critics have mixed views about this film but, like much of Hitchcock's later fare, it's a mixture of his extremes, blending shock tactics with black humour and irony. In other words it's Hitchcock unrestrained – he only pulled in the chains slightly for his final film, *Family Plot*. This film concerns the panic that arises when a serial killer, the "necktie murderer", is on loose in London. Richard Blaney (Finch) becomes the prime suspect but wrong man for the determined detective Chief Inspector Oxford (McGowan), whilst the audience knows the identity of the killer. Solid performances all round, with a tight script by Shaffer and some excellent set pieces, like the fight with a corpse in a lorry load of potatoes, some almost voyeuristic, yet the sum of the parts doesn't quite add up. That didn't stop mystery fans nominating it for an Edgar though it lost out, intriguingly, to Shaffer's own *Sleuth*.

The Friends of Eddie Coyle

(1973, US, 102 minutes)

Director: Peter Yates. **Producer:** Paul Monash.

Screenplay: Paul Monash from the novel by George V. HIGGINS.

Starring: Robert Mitchum, Peter Boyle, Richard Jordan, Alex Rocco.

Robert Mitchum may not be the character who immediately springs to mind when reading the novel of *The Friends of Eddie Coyle*, but he turns in here a bravura performance of the small-time gangster and loser,

"Fingers" Coyle, who decides to turn police informer to save his own skin after a bank heist turns to murder. His former "friends" decide to eliminate him and Dillon (Boyle), who had contributed to betraying the gang, is the hit-man. Yates, who showed he could turn on the action in *Bullitt*, used a more subtle approach in his exploration of character which he contrasts with a jagged portrayal of the criminal underworld that proves far more unsettling.

The Fugitive

(US TV series, 1963–7, 120 episodes, b&w, last 30 in colour; revived 2000—1, 22 episodes)
Creator: Roy Huggins.
Producers: original series: Alan A. Armer, Wilton Schiller and Frederick W. Ziv for Quinn Martin Productions.
Directors: original series: Many, primarily Robert Butler, Richard Donner, William A. Graham, Ida Lupino, Don Medford, James Sheldon, Alexander Singer.
Writers: original series: Many, including Alan A. Armer, John D.F. Black, Howard Browne, Robert C. Dennis, George Eckstein, Lawrence L. Goldman, Robert Hamner, Glen A. Larson, Richard Levinson & William Link and Man Rubin.
Starring: original series: David Janssen, Barry Morse, Bill Raisch.
The simplest ideas are always the best and though the idea of the innocent man on the run trying to find the real guilty party is one of the oldest it worked to perfection in this popular TV series. Dr. Richard Kimble (Janssen) is wrongly convicted for the murder of his wife. On his way to prison the train crashes and Kimble escapes. All he knows is that he had seen a one-armed man (Raisch) running away from his house and the rest of the series was how Kimble eluded the police, primarily Lieutenant Gerard (Morse) and found the one-armed man. The suspense was retained for four years until the series was brought to a final satisfying conclusion. The final two-part episode held the record at that time for the biggest viewing audience of a drama series. Janssen (1930–80) was excellent as Kimble, and it proved to be his most memorable performance, though he was also highly regarded in *Harry O*. The series received an Emmy Award and an Edgar in 1965. Thirty years after Kimble found the one-armed man, Warner Brothers decided to do it all again on the big screen in *The Fugitive* (1993), directed by Andrew Davis with a script by Robert Twohy. Harrison Ford played Kimble and Tommy Lee Jones put in an Oscar-winning performance as Deputy Marshal Gerard. The film inevitably lacked the plot development and cliff-hanger suspense of the series but it still captured the imagination and earned an Oscar and an Edgar nomination. The book-of-the-film is *The Fugitive* (1993) by J.M. Dillard. Most recently a new series has run in the

US with Tim Daly as Kimble, Mykelti Williamson as Gerard and Stephen Lang as the One-Armed Man.

Gangsters

(UK TV series, 1976–8, 12 episodes)
Producer: David Rose. **Director:** Alistair Reid.
Writer: Philip Martin.
Starring: Maurice Colbourne, Ahmed Khalil, Elizabeth Cassidy, Saeed Jaffrey, Philip Martin.
Gangsters began as a single one-off play broadcast in the *Play for Today* series in January 1975. Set in Birmingham, it was about a series of revenge killings in the Birmingham underworld as John Kline (Colbourne), released from prison for manslaughter, is hunted down by the dead man's brother, played by the play's author Philip Martin. The popularity of the play resulted in a six-part series that explored Kline's further fight for survival as a result of his connections with organized crime amongst the Asian community, under Aslam Rafiq (Jaffrey). The end of the first series wrapped up all the threads, but a second series was produced in 1978 that took Kline into the world of the Chinese Triads and took on increasingly surreal proportions. The second series was loved by some but tarnished the overall series' reputation for many, otherwise it might be better remembered for its realistic portrayal of the Birmingham underworld.

Garde à Vue [The Inquisitor] – *see under* Suspicion

The Gentle Touch

(UK TV series, 1980–4, 56 episodes)
Producers: Kim Mills, Jack Williams (seasons 1–2), Michael Verney-Elliott (seasons 2–5) under executive producer Tony Wharmby.
Directors: Many, including Tony Wharmby, Christopher Hodson, Paul Annett, David Askey, Nic Phillips, Christopher Baker and Gerry Mill.
Writers: Many, including Brian Finch, Roger Marshall, Terence Feely, Tony Parker, P.J. Hammond, Neil Rudyard and Guy James.
Starring: Jill Gascoine, William Marlowe, Paul Moriarty, Derek Thompson, Nigel Rathbone.
The character of Maggie Forbes (Gascoine) is usually regarded as British TV's first female detective, though that honour properly belongs to D.S. Vicky Hicks, played by Joanna Van Gyseghem, in *Fraud Squad*, ten years earlier. It is true though that Forbes was the first senior policewoman with the lead rôle in a series. Forbes was a Detective Inspector in the Metropolitan Police. In the opening episode her husband, a police constable, is killed and Forbes, after tracking down the killers, hands in her resignation. Lured back, the basis was now set for the series with Forbes trying to fulfil her duties whilst rearing her wayward son Steven

(Rathbone). The cases were standard fare though often violent, to which Forbes brought her gentle approach, hence the series title. After five seasons the character moved into the less realistic series *C.A.T.S. Eyes*.

Get Carter

(1971, UK, 112 minutes)
Director: Mike Hodges. **Producer:** Michael Klinger.
Screenplay: Mike Hodges based on the novel *Jack's Return Home* by Ted LEWIS.
Starring: Michael Caine, Britt Ekland, John Osborne, Ian Hendry, Geraldine Moffatt.
This film marked a turning point in the British gangster movie. It depicted the violent and seedy side of the British underworld. Nothing is black and white, all are shades of grey. Jack Carter (Caine) returns to Newcastle after the murder of his brother, and sets about avenging his death and dismantling a blue-movie ring, which has ensnared his brother's daughter. The film made the city of Newcastle part of the atmosphere, its unremitting bleakness adding to the sombre degeneration of society and morality. Playwright John Osborne makes one of his rare screen appearances as the vicious northern crime boss Cyril Kinnear. The film was plundered by US director George Armitage for a US blaxploitation film the following year, *Hit Man* (1972), and lost everything but the violence in the process. Recently Sylvester Stallone stepped into Michael Caine's shoes as the new Jack Carter in *Get Carter* (2000), returning to his home town of Seattle. The film loses the bleakness and stark reality of the original.

Get Christie Love

(US TV series, 1974–5, 22 episodes)
Producers: David L. Wolper (executive), Paul Mason.
Directors: Several, including Edward Abrams, Gene Nelson.
Writers: Several, including Detective Olga Ford.
Starring: Teresa Graves, Charles Cioffi/Jack Kelly, Andy Romano.
Dorothy UHNAK's novel *The Ledger* was the basis for the TV movie *Get Christie Love!* (1974), which in turn inspired this series. It was the first TV crime series to feature a black woman detective. Teresa Graves, of *Rowan and Martin's Laugh-In* fame, played Christie Love as an undercover cop in the LAPD. The series had plenty of action and Graves was good at breaking the rules. It also gave her an opportunity to show off her wardrobe and her figure, but it only scratched the surface of prejudice within the force. It was Graves's last acting rôle. After the series was cancelled she turned to religion.

Get Shorty

(1995, US, 100 minutes)
Director: Barry Sonnenfeld.
Producer: Danny DeVito, Michael Shamberg, Stacey Sher.
Screenplay: Scott Frank, from the novel by Elmore LEONARD.
Starring: John Travolta, Gene Hackman, Danny DeVito, Rene Russo, Delroy Lindo, Dennis Farina.

Post Tarantino, this is the first film that really gets under the skin of an Elmore Leonard novel and gets to the heart, depicting the delightful interplay between characters each sizing up the other and trying to move up one in the pecking order. Chili Palmer (Travolta) is a loan shark who travels from Florida to Hollywood to collect a bad debt but becomes enamoured by the sleazy film world of shlock movie-maker Harry Zimm (Hackman) and wants part of the action. Relationships hang together by the finest of threads but there's real menace behind every step.

Gloria

(1980, US, 121 minutes)
Director: John Cassavetes. **Producer:** Sam Shaw.
Screenplay: John Cassavetes.
Starring: Gena Rowlands, John Adames, Buck Henry.

Gloria (Rowlands) is a former chorus girl who was a girlfriend of one of the Mob gangsters who wiped out Jack Dawn (Henry) and his family. All that is except the six-year-old son Phil (Adames). Gloria ends up taking Phil under her wing and soon they're on the run. Phil's father had been the accountant for the Mob but had turned informer, and Phil still has his father's account book. Although the emphasis is on the chase and the action there is a powerful interplay between survivor Gloria and the innocent boy. Rowlands was nominated for an Oscar for her performance. The film was remade in 1998 by Sidney Lumet with Sharon Stone as Gloria and Jean-Luke Figueroa as the boy (this time called Nicky). Strong though this is it lacks the style and depth of Cassavetes' version. An alternate version is *Léon*, where the rôles are reversed.

The Godfather

(1972, US, 171 minutes)

The Godfather, Part II

(1974, US, 200 minutes)

The Godfather, Part III

(1990, US, 140 minutes)
Director: Francis Ford Coppola. **Producers:** Albert S. Ruddy; Francis Ford Coppola (II & III).
Screenplay: Mario PUZO.

Starring: Marlon Brando (I only), Al Pacino, James Caan, Richard Castellano, Robert Duvall, Diane Keaton, John Cazale, Robert De Niro (II only), Andy Garcia (III only).

The film that rewrote the public image of the gangster is also consistently voted everyone's number one crime movie. Parts I and II should be considered together, since they are both based on Mario Puzo's novel, and in 1977 Coppola re-edited the two films for TV as a continuous feature shown in four parts and running to 435 minutes, making it the third-longest feature film of all time. It was further restored for video as *The Godfather: The Complete Epic (1902–58)* (1981). Set in the decade after WW2 the film follows the final days of Mafia don Vito Corleone (Brando) and the rise to power of his favourite son, Michael (Pacino). Following the adage that "absolute power corrupts absolutely" Coppola parallels Michael's dominance and psychotic decline, with the American social structure seeming to disintegrate about him. *Part II* contrasts the America of opportunity in the early years of the 20th century when young Vito Corleone (De Niro) arrives in the country and establishes himself. In some ways the story parallels the rise and fall of the Augustan Caesars, a period of history that fascinated Coppola. The film's appeal is not its plot but its characters, their relationship with each other in the full meaning of "family", their codes and how they get things done. The final part of the trilogy, made 16 years later, purportedly to help Coppola finance a film about ancient Rome, is almost an afterthought and not crucial to the first two parts, though it continues the thread of decay and corruption. Now older but not wiser, Michael Corleone still suffers guilt over the death of his brother and believes he can redeem himself through a huge investment in a company that would in turn benefit the Church. The first two films both won Academy Awards for Best Picture and Oscars went to Brando, Coppola, Puzo, De Niro and others.

Goodfellas

(1990, US, 145 minutes)

Director: Martin Scorsese. **Producer:** Irwin Winkler.

Screenplay: Nicholas Pileggi and Martin Scorsese from Pileggi's book *Wiseguy* (1985).

Starring: Robert De Niro, Ray Liotta, Joe Pesci, Lorraine Bracco.

This film has been called the *real* Godfather. It tells the story of Henry Hill, a real-life Mobster who, after thirty years in organized crime, turned police informer. We see Hill (Liotta) punished as a child, becoming a street punk and admiring the gangsters he grows up with – the "good fellas". Scorsese uses the full arsenal of cinematic techniques to tell Hill's life and frequently contrasts moments of humour and fellowship with sudden outbursts of uncontrolled violence. It provides a complete insider's view of gangster life, as compulsive as it is unnerving.

The film was nominated for an Edgar and an Oscar, and Joe Pesci, as the psychotic hoodlum Tommy DeVito, won the Oscar for Best Supporting Actor.

Gorky Park

(1983, US, 128 minutes)
Director: Michael Apted. **Producer:** Gene Kirkwood, Howard W. Koch, Jr.
Screenplay: Dennis Potter from the novel by Martin Cruz SMITH.
Starring: William Hurt, Lee Marvin, Brian Dennehy, Ian Bannen, Joanna Pacula.
Although a comparatively faithful adaptation of Smith's novel, the film is only half successful, the complexity of the original plot becoming blurred in the bleak portrayal of Soviet intrigue. Renko (Hurt) is a Moscow policeman trying to solve the murder of three people whose faceless corpses are discovered in Gorky Park. The appearance of KGB man William Kirwill (Dennehy) suggests their deaths may be linked to espionage but the involvement of businessman Jack Osborne (Marvin) hints at more commercial motives. The film entertains without wholly satisfying. Nevertheless it won an Edgar award in 1984.

The Grifters

(1990, US, 105 minutes)
Director: Stephen Frears. **Producer:** Martin Scorsese, James Painten, Richard Harris.
Screenplay: Donald E. WESTLAKE based on the 1963 novel by Jim THOMPSON.
Starring: Anjelica Huston, John Cusack, Annette Bening, Pat Hingle.
Donald E. Westlake was the ideal author to adapt Jim Thompson's bleak novel of a family of confidence tricksters for the cinema because he was able to inject more pathos and colour into what is otherwise a depressing "iron maiden" of a story. Anjelica Huston delivers a stunning performance as Lilly Dillon, employed by the Mob to run a racetrack scam. Her boss, Bobo Justus (Hingle), keeps her in line with the occasional punch or cigarette burn, unaware that Dillon is working a double scam, skimming off Mob money for her own nest egg. Dillon is also looking out for her ambitious son, Roy (Cusack), whose girlfriend Myra (Bening) urges him on. Each double-crosses the other and it's a case of survival of the fittest. The film won an Edgar in 1991.

Gumshoe

(1971, UK, 84 minutes)
Director: Stephen Frears. **Producer:** Michael Medwin.
Screenplay: Neville Smith.

Starring: Albert Finney, Billie Whitelaw, Frank Finlay, Fulton Mackay, Caroline Seymour.

A loving pastiche of the hard-boiled crime novel held together by tight direction and a knowledgable cast of British reliables. Eddie Ginley (Finney) is a Liverpool bingo-caller who has dreams of writing the ultimate P.I. novel and starring in the ultimate P.I. film. Then he suddenly finds himself in a real murder mystery, and not a pleasant one at that, in the world of drugs and gunrunning and he tries to achieve his dream whilst keeping himself alive. Frears keeps a fine balance between humour and tragedy, and the final result is a highly original British film.

Hamish Macbeth

(UK TV series, 1995–7, 20 episodes)

Creator: M.C. BEATON. **Producers:** Andrea Calderwood (executive), Deidre Keir, Charles Salmon.

Directors: Several, including Patrick Lau, Nicholas Renton, Ian Knox, Sid Roberson.

Writers: Daniel Boyle, Bryan Elsley, Julian Spilsbury, Dominic Minghella, Julian Spilsbury.

Starring: Robert Carlyle, Ralph Riach, Jimmy Yuill, Valerie Gogan, Shirley Henderson.

A Scottish version of *Heartbeat* but with more bite. Macbeth (Carlyle) is a community policeman in the remote Scottish village of Lochdubh (pronounced "Lok-doo"). He turns a blind eye to minor infringements but is not the pushover he may seem if any real villains come along (usually outsiders). Filmed on location with colourful local characters the series had that good blend of light whimsy, poignancy and action that typifies many British series.

The Hanged Man *see under* The Main Chance

Hardcastle and McCormack

(US TV series, 1983–6, 65 episodes)

Creators: Patrick Hasburgh, Stephen J. CANNELL.

Producers: Stephen J. Cannell, Patrick Hasburgh, Jo Swerling, Jr., Lawrence Hertzog.

Directors: Jimmy Giritlian, Michael Hiatt, Daniel Hugh-Kelly, Kim Manners.

Writers: Alan Cassidy, Daniel Hugh-Kelly, Evan Lawrence, Steven L. Sears, Thomas E. Szollosi.

Starring: Brian Keith, Daniel Hugh-Kelly.

This series could as easily have been called *The Ones That Got Away*. Milton Hardcastle (Keith) was a retired judge who wanted to catch all those certain criminals who had somehow escaped conviction because of clever lawyers and legal loopholes. Being a bit old to go chasing criminals he recruited a petty criminal, "Skid" McCormack, who was also a hot-shot racing driver. They had a flashy experimental sports car with the licence plate "DE JUDGE" and the judge wore T-shirts with such slogans as "FIND 'EM AND HANG 'EM". It was played for fun, though there was always a serious underlying message.

Harper [aka The Moving Target]

(1966, US, 121 minutes)
Director: Jack Smight. **Producer:** Jerry Gershwin, Elliott Kastner.
Screenplay: William GOLDMAN, based on the novel by Ross MACDONALD.
Starring: Paul Newman, Lauren Bacall, Julie Harris, Janet Leigh.
Although it is clearly a product of the sixties, *Harper* is still a highly watchable movie and Paul Newman is a very credible Lew Harper – the name changed from Ross Macdonald's Lew Archer. It's helped by a sound script by William Goldman – his first solo product. Newman's no Bogart, but the casting of Lauren Bacall as Harper's client, asking for his help to find her husband, provides a pleasing association with *The Big Sleep*. Clearly mystery fans enjoyed it as it received an Edgar award in 1967. Nine years later Newman played Harper again in *The Drowning Pool* (1975), directed by Stuart Rosenberg. The locale shifts from California to New Orleans where Harper is asked by Iris Devereaux (Joanne Woodward) to investigate attempted blackmail against her. Newman remains strong, and though the sixties excesses are lost the film fails to conjure up sufficient atmosphere. It was still shortlisted for an Edgar.

Harry O

(US TV series, 1974–6, 45 episodes)
Creator: Howard Rodman.
Producers: Jerry Thorpe (executive), Robert E. Thompson, Robert Dozier, Buck Houghton, Alex Beaton.
Directors: Several, including Richard Bennett, Barry Crane, Richard Lang, Jerry London, Russ Mayberry, John Newland, Don Weiss.
Writers: Many, including Robert CAMPBELL, Robert C. Dennis, Herman Groves, Stephen Kandel, Howard Rodman, Michael Sloan.
Starring: David Janssen, Henry Darrow/Anthony Zerbe, Les Lannom, Farrah Fawcett-Majors.
Harry O is fondly remembered amongst fans of private detective series. Harry Orwell (Janssen) was a Los Angeles police officer who was shot in the back and the bullet lodged in the spine. Disabled but not crippled Harry is still able to get about, but with difficulty. He is invalided out of

the police force and becomes a P.I. – none too happily. His voice-over narration tells us a lot about his inner thoughts, an element that is well handled and unusual in TV P.I. shows though a common element of the books. Harry O lives in a beachfront cottage near San Diego but later in the season moves to Santa Monica which allows a change of cast and for Harry to meet some attractive girls – Farrah Fawcett-Majors and Loni Anderson amongst them – though Harry wasn't really one for such distractions. The change in locale also meant Harry O lost his former contact with the LAPD, Lieutenant Manny Quinlan (Darrow), and had to deal with the sarcastic Lieutenant Trench (Zerbe), which increased Harry's frustration. His car, which never seemed roadworthy, added to his problems, so he was forced to use public transport. The series had two pilot episodes, a one-hour "Such Dust as Dreams Are Made On" (1973) and "Smile Jenny, You're Dead" (1974) before the series began in September 1974. The first episode, "Gertrude", was nominated for an Edgar. Despite the popularity of the series, it lost out in ratings against *The Rockford Files*. There are two spin-off novels by Lee Hays: *Harry-O* (1975) and *Harry-O #2* (1976; as *The High Cost of Living*, UK 1978).

Hart to Hart

(US TV series, 1979–84, 110 episodes)
Creator: Sidney Sheldon.
Producers: Aaron Spelling, Leonard Goldberg (executives); David Levinson, Matt Crowley.
Directors: Many, including Earl Bellamy, Dennis Donnelly, Bruce Kessler, Tom Mankiewicz, Stuart Margolin, Leo Penn, Sam Wanamaker.
Writers: Many, including Earl Bellamy, Stephen Kandel, David Levinson, Tom Mankiewicz, Martin Roth, Sidney Sheldon.
Starring: Robert Wagner, Stefanie Powers, Lionel Stander.
Perhaps the ultimate in schlock, and always highly improbable, *Hart to Hart* was nevertheless an immensely popular series from the same stable as *Burke's Law*, which it resembled. The handsome couple were Jonathan Hart (Wagner), a self-made millionaire and his wife, Jennifer (Powers), an internationally known freelance journalist. Every week they would be amongst the rich and famous where inevitably someone would be murdered and only the Harts could fathom out the solution. When not flying everywhere in their private jet they were chauffered around by Max (Stander), who referred being with the Harts as "moider". Since the series finished in 1984 there have been eight occasional TV movies: *Hart to Hart Returns* (1993), *Home is Where the Hart is* (1994), *Crimes of the Hart* (1994), *Old Friends Never Die* (1994), *Secrets of the Hart* (1995), *Two Harts in Three-Quarters Time* (1995),

Till Death Do Us Hart (1996) and *Harts in High Season* (1996). Although author Sidney Sheldon created the characters he chose not to write about them. A collection of episodes from the second season were converted into stories and published as *Hart to Hart* (1981) by Roger Bowdler.

Hawaii Five-O

(US TV series, 1968–80, 278 episodes plus pilot)
Creator: Leonard Freeman.
Executive Producers: Leonard Freeman, Philip Leacock, Douglas Greene.
Directors: Many, including Edward M. Abroms, Corey Allen, Marvin J. Chomsky, Nicholas Colasanto, Dennis Donnelly, Charles S. Dubin, Harry Falk, Jack Lord, Bernard McEveety, John Newland, Leo Penn, Allen Resiner, Bob Sweeney, Don Weis.
Writers: Many, including Eric Bercovici, Larry Brody, Richard DeRoy, Robert C. Dennis, David Deutsch, Jackson Gillis, Robert Hamner, James L. Henderson, Stephen Kandel, Leonard B. Kaufman, Ed Lasko, Robert Lewin, Jerome Ross, Carey Wilber, Preston Wood.
Starring: Jack Lord, James MacArthur, Kam Fong, Zulu, Richard Denning, Khigh Dhiegh.

The longest-running cop show on US TV began with the pilot "Cocoon", which introduced all the major characters and elements that remained virtually unchanged throughout the series. Steve McGarrett (Lord) was head of an elite unit in Hawaii who were dealing with major crimes and could call upon Hawaii's other police forces as necessary. He was assisted by Danny Williams (MacArthur), immortalized each week by the command "Book him, Danno" when the villain was apprehended, and two Hawaiian detectives, Chin Ho Kelly (Kam Fong) and Kono Kalakaua (Zulu). McGarrett's arch enemy was Wo Fat (Dhiegh), a communist Chinese master criminal who had operations throughout the Pacific area. Wo Fat episodes are dotted throughout the series, but he was introduced in "Cocoon" and finally apprehended in the last episode "Woe to Wo Fat". Over such a long series it was inevitable that the plots would become repetitive and in fact the story-lines were often very thin and formulaic. The appeal of the series was the island itself. Even though its overall beauty was often downplayed for the seedier elements, it still held a magical aura unlike the usual venues of New York or Los Angeles, and the thundering opening theme music by Morton Stevens always heralded fast action and exotic climes. McGarrett was a no-nonsense, smart, determined, shackled-to-the-job officer responding to the island's governor (Denning) and with no home life or love interest. His team was loyal and instantly responsive. There was something fairy-talish about it all, but it was always enjoyable. Plans are afoot for a feature length film. There are six spin-off novels: *Hawaii Five-O* (1968) and *Terror in the Sun* (1969) both by Michael AVALLONE, *Top Secret* (1969) by Robert Sidney Bowen, *The Octopus Caper* (1971) by Leo R. Ellis and *The Angry Battalion* (1972) and *Serpents in Paradise* (1972) both by Herbert Harris.

Hazell

(UK TV series, 1978–80, 22 episodes)
Creators: Gordon WILLIAMS and Terry Venables.
Producers: June Roberts (season 1), Tim Aspinall (season 2).
Directors: Jim Goddard, Alistair Reid, Brian Farnham, Moira Armstrong, Don Leaver, Alan Grint, Colin Bucksey, Carol Wilkes, Baz Taylor, Mike Vardy, Gerry Mill, Marek Kanievska.
Writers: Gordon Williams, Richard Harris, Tony Hoare, Leon Griffiths, Willis Hall, Trevor Preston, P.J. Hammond, Jim Hawkins, Brian Glover.
Starring: Nicholas Ball, Roddy McMillan, Barbara Young, Desmond McNamara.
James Hazell (Ball), or more appropriately 'azell, was a Cockney ex-policeman invalided out of the force with a dodgy ankle, who turns P.I. A bit of a Jack-the-Lad, Hazell's bright but often ends up in trouble and needs help to get out, sometimes provided by his sparring partner in the police, C.I.D. officer "Choc" Minty (McMillan), a no-nonsense officer who would be far happier if Hazell was out of the way. Hazell's cases are usually at the bottom end of the food chain but he sometimes comes a crop with major operators, such as Dave Castle, played by future *Bill* bent copper Billy Murray. Big Dave employs Hazell to find his missing car and Hazell ends up in the midst of a gang feud. The series was sharply written with strong characters and a great series of one-liners.

Heartbeat

(UK TV series, 1992–*current*, 150+ episodes)
Creator: Peter Walker (as Nicholas RHEA).
Producers: Keith Richardson (executive), Stuart Doughty, Steve Lanning, Carol Wilks, Gerry Mill.
Directors: Several, including Brian Farnham, Ken Horn.
Writers: Many, including Johnny Byrne, Jonathan Critchley, Steve Trafford.
Starring: Nick Berry/Jason Durr, Derek Fowlds, Bill Maynard, Niamh Cusack, Tricia Penrose.
Set in the Yorkshire moors in the 1960s, *Heartbeat* is based on the fictionalized reminiscences of real-life policeman Peter Walker. It has become a popular TV series emulating for the police what James Herriott achieved for vets. Nick Rowan (Berry) is the village bobby in Aidensfield, reporting to the grumpy but fair Sergeant Blaketon (Fowlds). There's never much in the way of major crime, and most petty problems arise from the

shenanigans of local lovable rogue Claude Greengrass (Maynard). The series has achieved high viewing figures in the UK, up to 17 million, and none higher than with the death of Rowan's wife, Kate (Cusack) after giving birth to a daughter. When Nick Berry left the series (his character went to Canada to become a Mountie for which there was a special video episode, *Changing Places*), new constable Mike Bradley arrived. Blaketon had also retired by now and was running the local post office. Otherwise the series has continued business as usual. Peter Walker has adapted two books from the series, but his own reminiscences, as Nicholas Rhea, continue as separate books.

Heat

(1995, US, 171 minutes)
Producer/Director: Michael Mann. **Screenplay:** Michael Mann.
Starring: Robert De Niro, Al Pacino, Val Kilmer, Jon Voight, Amy Brenneman.
At nearly three hours, this film has virtually everything except the right ending. Vincent Hanna (Pacino) is an LA police detective whose dedication to his work is crumbling his third marriage. He is investigating a daring armed robbery masterminded by Neil McCauley (De Niro), head of a vicious gang of thieves but in reality a single-minded loner who lives by the creed that he could walk out of his life and start anew in thirty seconds. The film has time to explore depth of character, especially with De Niro and his gang, but there is still plenty of time for some of the best action scenes in any crime movie. The film was a slick remake of Mann's TV movie *LA Takedown* (1989).

Heavenly Creatures

(1994, New Zealand, 98 minutes)
Director: Peter Jackson.
Producer: Jim Booth.
Screenplay: Frances Walsh, Peter Jackson.
Starring: Melanie Lynskey, Kate Winslet, Clive Merrison, Sarah Peirse, Diana Kent.
This film is significant in a number of ways. It launched the career of Kate Winslet, it established Peter Jackson as a significant director (who has since gone on to make *Lord of the Rings*), and interest in the film led to the revelation that one of the girls in the real-life drama it portrayed was none other than present-day author Anne PERRY. The film retells a murder that happened in New Zealand in 1954 when two teenage girls, Pauline Parker (Lynsky) and Juliet Hulme (Winslet), murdered Pauline's mother (Peirse). Jackson succeeds in establishing the suffocatingly real world in which they lived as well as the bizarre, unreal world in which their relationship existed. It is also a frighteningly disturbing study of an avoidable motive for murder.

Heaven's Prisoners

(1996, US, 131 minutes)
Director: Philip Joanou.
Producer: Albert S. Ruddy, Andre E. Morgan, Leslie Greif.
Screenplay: Harley Peyton, Scott Frank from the novel by James Lee BURKE.
Starring: Alec Baldwin, Kelly Lynch, Mary Stuart Masterson, Eric Roberts, Teri Hatcher.

The first and, so far, only attempt to bring James Lee Burke's Dave Robicheaux to the screen is partly successful. *Heaven's Prisoners* is a crucial book in the series, since it involves Robicheaux rescuing a child, which he adopts, from a plane crash and sees the murder of his wife as a consequence of Robicheaux investigating drug smuggling and illegal immigrants. Robicheaux refuses to accept his wife's death and is haunted by her memory. Burke is brilliant at creating the atmosphere of the Louisiana swamps and of Robicheaux's deep angst and this is not wholly conveyed in the film. Baldwin is only half successful in his portrayal of Robicheaux, and Joanou drags the film on for far too long in the hope of creating an atmosphere when in fact the film starts to lose it. Burke's work is difficult to catch on the screen, and lessons will be learned from this first brave attempt.

Henry: Portrait of a Serial Killer

(1986, US, 77 minutes)
Producer/Director: John McNaughton.
Screenplay: Richard Fire, John McNaughton.
Starring: Michael Rooker, Tracy Arnold, Tom Towles.

Regarded by some as a violent exploitation movie, *Henry* is a darkly voyeuristic odyssey of a sociopath. Out of prison Henry (Rooker) travels from town to town indiscriminately murdering. Returning to Chicago he teams up with his old prison buddy Otis (Towles) and Otis's sister Becky (Arnold), and inducts Otis into his world of casual but grotesque murder. The imagery is at times unwatchable, the sound track of the victims' final moments unbearable, and the whole effect is torturing, but it is also profound. It is one of the most uncomfortably realistic films about the psychology of a cold-blooded killer. Ten years later director Charles Parello made an unnecessary and all too imitative sequel, *Henry: Portrait of a Serial Killer, Part II* (1996).

Hetty Wainthropp Investigates

(UK TV series, 1996–8, 27 episodes)
Creators: David Cook, in his novel *Missing Persons* (1986).
Producers: Carol Parks.
Directors: John Glenister, Roger Bamford, David Giles, Robert Tronson.

Writers: David Cook, John Bowen, Philip Martin, Jeremy Paul, Brian Finch.
Starring: Patricia Routledge, Derek Benfield, Dominic Monaghan, John Graham Davies.
Not to be taken too seriously, *HWI* featured bright and bossy Hetty Wainthropp (Routledge), a sprightly Lancashire pensioner, who sets up her own private detective agency, much to the horror of her husband. She recruits street kid Geoffrey Shawcross (Monaghan) to help her. She is suffered by, and secretly admired by, DCI Adams (Davies). Wainthropp was based on the author's own mother. Years before an elderly man had asked Mrs Cook to help him find his 50-year-old son. Hetty's cases soon move on from missing persons and minor misdemeanours until, by the third series, she's involved in black magic and other serious crimes, which she takes in her stride. Routledge plays the character with great gusto, often going undercover, but it's still like watching a Hyacinth Bucket version of *Barnaby Jones*.

Highway Patrol

(US TV series, 1955–9, 156 episodes, b&w)
Producers: Vernon E. Clark (executive), Jack Herzberg, Frederick W. Ziv.
Directors: Many, including Don Brinkley, William Conrad, Jack Herzberg and Herbert L. Strock.
Writers: Many, including Don Brinkley, George & Gertrude Fass, Bob Mitchell, Robert M. Fresco, Stuart Jerome, Norman Jolley, William L. Driskell, Jack Rock and Robert Shaw.
Starring: Broderick Crawford, William Boyett.
Broderick Crawford played Chief Dan Matthews, head of a Highway Patrol unit in some unnamed western US state. The series demonstrated the growing need for fast responses to crimes taking advantage of the vast highway network across America. The opening music and the aerial views sweeping along the Highway provided a dramatic curtain-raiser for each half-hour episode. Crawford's deep, monotone gravel voice was forever shouting codes into his intercom such as "Ten-Four" for "Message Received and Understood", which passed into the lingo. Each half-hour was packed with action, and included a wide variety of plots. Gene Levitt's story for the second episode in season 1 involves the theft of a giant computer!

Hill Street Blues

(US TV series, 1981–7, 145 episodes)
Creators: Steven Bochco, Michael Kozoll.
Producers: Gregory Hoblit, David Anspaugh, Anthony Yerkovich.
Directors: Many, including Corey Allen, Gabrielle Beaumont, Scott

Brazil, Thomas Carter, Gregory Hoblit, Christian Nyby, Arthur A. Seidelman, Rick Wallace.
Writers: Many, primarily Steven Bochco, Mark Frost, Jeffrey Lewis, David Milch, Michael Wagner, Robert CRAIS.
Starring: Daniel J. Travanti, Michael Conrad/Robert Prosky, Michael Warren, Bruce Weitz, Rene Enriquez, James B. Sikking, Robert Hirschfield, Veronica Hamel, Joe Spano, Taurean Blacque, Lisa Sutton, Betty Thomas, Dennis Franz.
Regarded by many as the best of all police procedural series *HSB* was the story of the daily life and personal stresses of the officers at a station in an unnamed big city not unlike Chicago. The show had a large cast, even among the primary actors. It was as much a weekly soap as a crime series, with emphasis on the officers' homes lives. Head of the station was Captain Frank Furillo (Travanti), a patient but firm commander whose personal life was in chaos. His second in command was Sergeant Phil Esterhaus (Conrad). Conrad died during the series and the character was written out as having had a heart attack while making love. He was replaced by Sergeant Jablonski (Prosky). The team included Mick Belker (Weitz), who went undercover on the streets as a tramp and was known to bite those he arrested after he had commanded them to sit down unless they would "prefer internal bleeding"; the community affairs officer and rabid anti-racist Henry Goldblume (Spano), the trigger-happy redneck Howard Hunter (Sikking), who was head of the SWAT team and his alcoholic partner Neal Washington (Blacque). There were representatives of most relevant ethnic origins, though only one female officer at the outset, Lucille Bates (Thomas). Many of the cast changed over the lifetime of the show and one important character introduced in the last three seasons, Lieutenant Buntz (Franz) was rewarded with his own series with Officer Leo Schnitz (Hirschfield), albeit a comedy series, *Beverly Hills Buntz* (1987–88), about two seedy P.I.s. Franz in a similar Buntz persona would resurface in *N.Y.P.D. Blue*.

As a day-in-the-life each episode had many threads in the air at once, as different officers became involved in various incidents that would continue on through future episodes. The precinct was located in a run-down, seedy area that attracted just about every kind of criminal. There were almost too many continuing story-lines, confusing the viewers and at the end of the first season ratings were low, even though critical acclaim was high. After its first season the series won eight Emmy awards and many episodes were nominated for the Edgar with the award going to the opener, "Hill Street Station". NBC supported the series but demanded changes. The story-lines became more contracted but less creative and more predictable. Nevertheless ratings increased and over time this allowed the show to be more experimental again. Eventually, though, the series settled into a rut and the characters at the station became too homogenized. Yet even at the end *Hill Street Blues* still had a charisma and believability lacking from most other cop shows. Steve Bochco achieved much kudos from the series and went on to create *L.A. Law* and *N.Y.P.D. Blue*.

The Hit

(1984, US, 93 minutes)
Director: Stephen Frears. **Producer:** Jeremy Thomas.
Screenplay: Peter Prince.
Starring: John Hurt, Tim Roth, Terence Stamp, Fernando Rey, Jim Broadbent.
This black comedy thriller shows how well strong characterization carries a simple plot. Willie Parker (Stamp) was a supergrass who had a new life in Spain but has been tracked down by Braddock and Myron (Hurt and Roth), who escort him back to Paris to be killed. Parker, though, is totally unconcerned about his fate and takes it all in his stride and his benign smiling attitude has a testing effect on Braddock and Myron, leading to a satisfying if not entirely surprising climax. At the time some critics regarded the film as self-indulgent, although mystery fans delighted in it and it was nominated for an Edgar. It has survived the test of time and is a lesson in simplicity.

Homicide

(1991, US, 102 minutes)
Director: David Mamet. **Producers:** Michael Hausman, Edward R. Pressman.
Screenplay: David Mamet.
Starring: Joe Mantegna, William H. Macy, Natalija Nogulich, Ving Rhames.
Without being overly didactic or preachy, this film explores racial prejudice both within the police force and beyond. Bob Gold (Mantegna) is a Jewish cop brought in (initially against his wishes) to help a Jewish family where the father, a pawnbroker, has been murdered. In the process he stumbles across not only a drug cartel but a strong anti-Semitic faction and a Jewish resistance. He is forced to consider his own background and the outcome of his actions lead to some surprising results. You continue to think about this film long afterwards.

Homicide: Life on the Street

(US TV series, 1993–9, 122 episodes)
Creator: Paul Attanasio, based on the book *Homicide: A Year on the Killing Streets* by David Simon.
Producers: Tom Fontana, Barry Levinson (executive), Anya Epstein, David Simon.

Directors: Many, including Kathy Bates, Steve Buscemi, Kenneth Fink, Barry Levinson, Barbara Kipple, Peter Medak, Alan Taylor, Peter Weller.
Writers: Many, including Paul Attanasio, Tom Fontana, Yaphet Kotto, Anya Epstein, David Simon, James Yoshimura.
Starring: Ned Beatty, Yaphet Kotto, Jon Polito, Richard Belzer, Kyle Secor, Clark Johnson.
NBC let *Homicide* do what it had stopped *Hill Street Blues* doing. This was a semi-documentary, reality series of the life on the mean streets of Baltimore, with episodes developing many open-ended cases, not all of which were resolved. It tried to be as true to life as possible, using a variety of direct filming techniques to depict the scene of crime from all angles. It confused some viewers but others were hooked, though its ratings were never high. It was also shocking in how many of the cast were blasted away as the series went on, and yet the series sustained its momentum despite a carousel of characters. The series was frequently manic but always watchable. In the last three seasons an almost entirely new cast had arrived with even more complex story-lines and not everything was resolved by the time the series came to an end. Some threads linked in to the companion series *Law and Order*, and there was also a follow-up film *Homicide: The Movie* (2000) which wrapped up most issues.

Honey West *see under* Burke's Law

The Hot Rock

(1972, US, 100 minutes)
Director: Peter Yates. **Producer:** Hal Landers, Bobby Roberts.
Screenplay: William GOLDMAN from the novel by Donald E. WESTLAKE.
Starring: Robert Redford, George Segal, Zero Mostel, Moses Gunn.
The combination of Goldman and Westlake is here irresistable, producing one of the best all-time caper films in which Redford and Segal thrive. They head a gang of four criminals who steal a diamond from the Brooklyn museum and just as quickly lose it again and spend the rest of the film trying to get it back. It would have been too easy to turn this into a predictable farce, but here it's an ever changing whirligig. It was short-listed for an Edgar award in 1973.

Hunter

(US TV series, 1984–91, 151 episodes plus pilot)
Creator: Frank Lupo. **Executive Producers:** Stephen J. CANNELL, Roy Huggins, Lawrence Kubik.
Directors: Many, including David Soul, Stephanie Kramer, Corey Allen, Don Chaffey, James Darren, Gary Winter.

Writers: Many, including Sidney Ellis, Roy Huggins, Robert Vincent O'Neil, Richard C. Okie.
Starring: Fred Dryer, Stephanie Kramer/Darlanne Fluegel, Charles Hallahan.
Detective Sergeant Rick Hunter of the LAPD, played by six-foot-six ex-football player Fred Dryer, was TV's answer to Clint Eastwood's Harry Callahan in *Dirty Harry*. He was slightly softened for TV and had a female partner, Detective Sergeant Dee Dee McCall (Kramer), but he was still the same near vigilante extreme right-wing redneck cop, with the same powerful Magnum handgun. His one-liners weren't quite so catchy – instead of "Make my day" he said "Works for me", and if any street-scum challenged him when he asked them to accompany him to the station and asked, "Who says?" he would thrust the gun into their faces and say "Simon says." Hunter had the usual problems with the bureaucracy back at City Hall where his police superiors didn't like the way he operated, not helped by Hunter coming from a family of gangsters and Mobsters. Otherwise each week saw the usual routine of Hunter blasting his way after villains. It palled after a while and, in the sixth season Hunter was transferred to the LAPD's elite Metro Division, giving him a wider range of cases. At that time his partner changed to Officer Molenski (Fluegel) but otherwise life was much the same.

In the Heat of the Night

(1967, US, 109 minutes)
Director: Norman Jewison. **Producer:** Walter Mirisch.
Screenplay: Stirling Silliphant from the novel by John BALL.
Starring: Sidney Poitier, Rod Steiger, Warren Oates, Quentin Dean, James Patterson.
Released at the height of the civil rights movement in the US, this film makes you wince today at its portrayal of bigotry. Black Philadelphia policeman Virgil Tibbs (Poitier) is wrongly arrested for murder in Mississippi while changing trains. Only later does bigoted local sheriff Bill Gillespie (Steiger) discover Tibbs's identity and then has to swallow pride and work with Tibbs in resolving the case. The film, which had to be shot in Illinois, admirably plays the race card whilst still being a good crime story. It won five Oscars, including best picture and best screenplay, and also won an Edgar award. There were two other Virgil Tibbs films, *They Call Me MISTER Tibbs!* (1970) and *The Organization* (1971), both starring Poitier. They miss the character interplay with Steiger, though the third film, in which Tibbs clashes with a drug syndicate and works with a group of youngsters who are against drugs, still has something to say. There was also a long-running US TV series called *In the Heat of the Night* (1988–94; 140 episodes), starring Howard Rollins as Tibbs and Carroll O'Connor as Gillespie. In these later years the racial

tension was not emphasized so strongly; rather it was the old gruff Southerner versus the bright black Chief of Detectives from the North. It worked well for a few seasons but soon became involved in local relationships and political infighting and the characters of Gillespie and Tibbs were virtually written out of the final season.

In the Line of Fire

(1993, US, 123 minutes)
Director: Wolfgang Petersen. **Producer:** Jeff Apple.
Screenplay: Jeff Maguire.
Starring: Clint Eastwood, John Malkovich, Rene Russo.
With Eastwood in his early sixties in this film and visibly ageing, we know it's not the hard-edged Clint of old but, even with a tear in his eye, he still has a lot to prove in the character of Frank Horrigan. And with a musical score by Ennio Morricone the film recaptures moments of the past. Horrigan is a secret service agent still riddled with guilt for not having prevented the assassination of Kennedy 30 years before. When he learns of a possible new attempt on the President he feels he can at last redeem himself and is soon on the trail of taunting sociopath Mitch Leary – for which Malkovich received an Oscar nomination. Strong performances and perceptive directing make this a satisfying story.

The Inquisitor *see under* Under Suspicion

Inspector Morse

(UK TV series 1987–2000, 33 episodes)
Creator: Colin DEXTER, and adapted for television by Kenny McBain.
Executive Producers: Ted Childs (executive), Kenny McBain (series 1–2), Chris Burt (series 3), David Lascelles (series 4–5), Deidre Keir (series 6).
Directors: Alastair Reid, Brian Parker, Peter Hammond, Edward Bennett, Peter Duffell, Herbert Wise, James Scott, Anthony Simmons, Jim Goddard, John Madden, Sandy Johnson, Danny Boyle, Roy Battersby, Colin Gregg, Adrian Shergold, Antonia Bird, Stuart Orme, Stephen Whittaker, Charles Beeson, Robert Knights, Jack Gold.
Writers: Anthony Minghella, Julian Mitchell, Thomas Ellice, Charles Wood, Michael Wilcox, Peter Buckman, Alma Cullen, Jeremy Burnham, Geoffrey Case, Peter Nichols, Daniel Boyle, John Brown, Russell Lewis, Malcolm Bradbury, Stephen Churchett.
Starring: John Thaw, Kevin Whately, James Grout, Peter Woodthorpe/Amanda Hillwood/Clare Holman.
The most successful of all British TV detective series, *IM* boasted amongst the highest viewing figures around the world, with audiences purported to total 750 million. Based upon the novels of Colin Dexter,

the series adapted the characters and added further episodes until it established its own firm persona. John Thaw played the ageing, irascible, lonely but dedicated Inspector Morse accompanied by his perceptive, long suffering but loyal sergeant Robert Lewis (Whately). Morse is frequently summoned by his superior, Chief Superintendent Strange (Grout), to explain himself, but he continues to plough his own furrow. The cases are set in and about Oxford, sometimes involving the University, but covering all aspects of life. Thwarted in love Morse sometimes becomes attracted to women involved in the case, though never succeeds in a permanent relationship. He sees the family life enjoyed by Lewis and perhaps yearns for it, but retreats to his own love of opera and classical music, and the demon drink, which claims him in the end. Rare amongst detective series, this follows Morse through to his death. Morse was portrayed as a moody but essentially lovelorn character, a poignancy echoed in the haunting theme music by Barrington Pheloung. Thanks to early producer Kenny McBain this series established two hours as the time slot for exploring plot, character and atmosphere in detail. In addition to the books by Dexter there is an overview of the series, *The Making of Inspector Morse* (1990) by Mark Sanderson. The series won an Anthony in 1990 and a Sherlock in 2001.

Investigation of a Citizen Above Suspicion

(1970, Italy, 112 minutes)
Director: Elio Petri. **Producer:** Daniele Senatore.
Screenplay: Elio Petri and Ugo Pirro.
Starring: Gian Maria Volonté, Florinda Bolkan, Gianni Santuccio, Orazio Orlando, Sergio Tramonti.
This film won both the Academy Award as the Best Foreign Film and the Edgar Award in its day, as well as being nominated for the Oscar for the screenplay, and yet it has not sustained its reputation, despite the protest that accompanied its release. It was a bold production that chose to face head on the fascist legacy in Italy and the corruption that pervaded the higher echelons of the police force. A police inspector (Volonté) murders his mistress but believing himself above suspicion taunts his detectives with clues. Viewed with hindsight Petrie lays on the symbolism too thickly, and the film looks more like a Kafkaesque nightmare than a true portrayal of Italian justice, but it still remains an important film in the development of the Italian crime film genre. It is sometimes shown under the UK title, *Investigation of a Private Citizen.*

Ironside [aka A Man Called Ironside]

(US TV series, 1967–75, 198 episodes plus pilot)
Creator: Collier Young.

Executive Producers: Joel Rogosin, Cy Chermak (executive), Albert Aley, Norman Jolley, Lou Morheim.
Directors: Many, including Charles S. Dubin, David Friedkin, Russ Mayberry, Christian I. Nyby II, Leo Penn, Daniel Petrie, Boris Sagal, Jimmy Sangster, Don Weis.
Writers: Many, including Albert Aley, Cy Chermak, Norman Jolley, Ken Kolb, Sy Salkowitz, Collier Young.
Starring: Raymond Burr, Don Galloway, Barbara Anderson/Elizabeth Baur, Don Mitchell, Gene Lyons.
Following his success in the long-running series *Perry Mason*, Raymond Burr returned to the small screen as San Francisco Chief of Detectives Robert T. Ironside. In the pilot, originally made as a one-off TV movie, Ironside is paralysed by a would-be assassin's bullet and is confined to a wheelchair. Still agile of mind, Ironside insists that he remains with the force as a consultant on difficult cases. He is given a specially adapted room and vehicle and a small team consisting of two former assistants, Sergeant Ed Brown (Galloway) and policewoman Eve Whitfield (Anderson). Also serving as his general aide and bodyguard was former street delinquent Mark Sanger (Mitchell). The pilot proved so successful that a series was commissioned which remained perennially popular, always in the top ratings and running for eight seasons. Suitably politically correct, Ironside showed that his disability did not restrict him. There seemed few places he couldn't go, and he was able to use his wheelchair to good effect in trapping villains on many an occasion. Although a solid, fairly old-fashioned show, the series glowed with the energy of Burr, always a commanding actor, and the restricted action meant that it relied on a lot more brainpower, making the shows more intellectually interesting. Following a contract dispute, Anderson left after the fourth season and was replaced by Elizabeth Baur as Fran Belding, but all the characters came back for a grand reunion in the later TV movie *The Return of Ironside* (1993), aired just five months before Burr's death. There were two spin-off books from the series: *Ironside* (1967) by no less than Jim THOMPSON and *The Picture Frame Frame-Up* (1969) by William Johnstone.

The Italian Job

(1969, UK/US, 95 minutes)
Director: Peter Collinson. **Producer:** Michael Deeley.
Screenplay: Troy Kennedy Martin.
Starring: Michael Caine, Noel Coward, Benny Hill, Robert Powell, Raf Vallone, Tony Beckley.
One of the great comedy crime caper films and a wonderful advert for the mini car. From his prison cell Mr Bridger (Coward) masterminds a bullion heist in Turin using as head of the operation Charlie Croker

(Caine). Croker gets together a motley crew of villains including computer expert Professor Peach (Hill). The highlight of the film is the remarkable chase and escape of the gang using the mini, but even that is upstaged by the literal cliff-hanger ending. The film was scripted by the creator of *Z Cars*, who also wrote the book-of-the-film, *The Italian Job* (1969), with Ken Wlaschin.

Jackie Brown

(1997, US, 154 minutes)
Director: Quentin Tarantino. **Producer:** Lawrence Bender.
Screenplay: Quentin Tarantino, based on Elmore LEONARD's novel *Rum Punch.*
Starring: Pam Grier, Samuel L. Jackson, Robert Forster, Michael Keaton, Bridget Fonda, Robert De Niro.
Elmore Leonard's work had long been an influence on Tarantino so his adaptation of *Rum Punch* was as much a labour of love as a homage to Leonard's work. Jackie Brown (Grier) is an air hostess caught for smuggling cash and drugs for Ordell Robbie (Jackson) and knowing Robbie will exact revenge if she informs, she sets up an entrapment scam. Grier puts in a remarkable performance as does Robert Forster in his Oscar-nominated rôle as the bail bondsman Max Cherry, in whom Grier confides. Tarantino goes more for character study than slam-bang violence and the result is a little gem.

Jagged Edge

(1985, US, 104 minutes)
Director: Richard Marquand. **Producer:** Martin Ransohoff.
Screenplay: Joe Eszterhas.
Starring: Glenn Close, Jeff Bridges, Peter Coyote, Lance Henriksen, Robert Loggia.
A highly effective if traditional suspense thriller of the "is he-isn't he?" variety. Jack Forrester (Bridges) is accused of murdering his wife. His defence attorney, Teddy Barnes (Close), becomes attracted to Forrester and they become lovers. But is Forrester guilty, and will Barnes be his next victim, or is he being stitched up by prosecuting attorney Thomas Crasny (Coyote)? Marquand keeps the question open till the very last frame.

Jake and the Fatman

(US TV series, 1987–92, 106 episodes)
Creator: Dean Hargrove, Joel Steiger.
Executive Producers: Fred Silverman, Dean Hargrove, Ed Waters.
Directors: Several, including Bernard Kowalski, Michael Lange, Christian I. Nyby, Russ Mayberry, David Moessinger, Leo Penn.

Writers: Many, including Doc Barnett, Gerry Conway, George Eckstein, Dean Hargrove, Bernard Kowalski, Ed Waters.
Starring: William Conrad, Joe Penny, Alan Campbell, Olga Russell.
Ten years after *Cannon* and a brief period as *Nero Wolfe*, William Conrad returned to TV for what would be his final series. Now in his mid-sixties, Conrad plays J.L. McCabe, known as the "Fatman", a tough Los Angeles D.A. and former cop who knows how to use the rules or bend them. His legman is Jake Styles (Penny) who frequently goes undercover to gather evidence. McCabe is inseparable from his bulldog, Max. For the second series the locale was transplanted to Hawaii where McCabe is now retired but working as an undercover agent for the Honolulu prosecuting attorney's office. With the third series, though, he was back in Los Angeles, taking on the present corrupt D.A. and subsequently returning to his old job. At times the rather slovenly McCabe resembled an Americanized Rumpole! Dr Mark Sloane of *Diagnosis Murder* first appeared in *Jake and the Fatman* in 1991.

Jason King *see under* Department S

Joe Forrester *see under* Police Story

Jonathan Creek

(UK TV series 1997–*current*, 19 episodes to date)
Creator/Writer: David Renwick.
Directors: Marcus Mortimer, Sandy Johnson, Keith Washington, Richard Holthouse.
Starring: Alan Davies, Caroline Quentin/Julia Sawalha.
Jonathan Creek (Davies) is a deviser of magic tricks for a stage magician and thus knows that things are not what they seem. He is a bit of a loner and lives in a converted windmill. He is befriended by journalist Madeline Magellan (Quentin) whose investigations always draw her to seemingly impossible crimes. The series is full of all the wonderful trappings of the impossible – locked room murders, people in two places at once, people returning from the dead – with the solutions re-enacted to show how it all worked. Renwick, who also created the irascible Victor Meldrew in *One Foot in the Grave*, has an eye for the eccentric and injects a quirky humour into the series, which remains endlessly fascinating. Ingenious puzzles and background to the series will be found in *The World of Jonathan Creek* (1999) by Steve Clark.

Johnny Staccato

(US TV series, 1959–60, 27 episodes, b&w)
Creator: John Cassavetes. **Producer:** William Frye (executive), Everett Chambers.

Directors: John Cassavetes, Boris Sagal, Gernard Girard, Robert Parrish.
Writers: Mostly John Cassavetes.
Starring: John Cassavetes, Eduardo Ciannelli.
Although this series ran for just one season of half-hour episodes before it was cancelled by NBC, it has remained memorable and improved with age. It was the pet of experimental director and actor John Cassavetes, who was ahead of his time. Right from its impressive opening music by Elmer Bernstein, through the smoke-filled jazz club in Greenwich Village where private-eye Staccato (Cassavetes) was a pianist, and where he saw his clients, this series was filled with atmosphere. It benefitted from being in black-and-white as Cassavetes used that for creating a *noir* mood. It remains one of the most perfectly presented P.I. series. A novel based on it was *Johnny Staccato* (1960) by Frank Boyd (alias of Frank Kane).

Judd, for the Defense

(US TV series, 1967–9, 50 episodes)
Executive Producers: Paul Monash (executive), Harold Gast, Charles Russell.
Directors: Several, including Harvey Hart, Seymour Robbie, Robert Butler, Boris Sagal, Leo Penn, William Hale, George McCowan, Charles S. Dubin.
Writers: Many, including Sheldon Stark, Paul Monash, William Kelley, Harold Gast, E. Arthur Kean.
Starring: Carl Betz, Stephen Young.
A legal drama series that was rooted in its period, raising many contemporary issues, but which has since been virtually forgotten. Clinton Judd (Betz) was a big-time lawyer who jetted all over the US with his assistant Ben Caldwell (Young) taking on any case that intrigued him. This meant it ranged from hippy draft dodgers to illegal immigrants, civil rights murders, labour activists, everything that was turbulent in the flower-power years. The final episode saw Tyne Daly in one of her first TV appearances. Lawrence Goldman wrote two books based on the series, *Judd, for the Defense* and *The Secret Listeners* (both 1968). The episode "Tempest in a Texas Town" won an Edgar in 1968.

Judge John Deed

(UK TV series, 2001–*current*, 4 episodes + pilot to date)
Creator/Producer: G.F. NEWMAN.
Director: Alrick Riley.
Writer: G.F. Newman.
Starring: Martin Shaw, Jenny Seagrove, Caroline Langrishe, Donald Sinden, Christopher Cazenove.
Deed (Shaw) is a zealous High Court judge whose attitude and actions

often place him at odds with the Lord Chancellor's Department as he seeks to ensure justice and fight corruption. Newman is renowned for his anti-bureaucratic and authoritarian views and uses the character of Deed to voice opinions about power in high places and how it influences the true delivery of justice.

Juliet Bravo

(UK TV series, 1980–5, 82 episodes)
Creator: Ian Kennedy Martin.
Executive Producers: Terence Williams, Jonathan Alwyn, Geraint Morris.
Directors: Several, including Jonathan Alwyn, Tristan De Vere Cole, Brian Finch, Derek Lister, Carol Wilks.
Writers: Many, primarily Ian Kennedy Martin, Wally K. Daly, Susan Pleat, Tony Charles.
Starring: Stephanie Turner/Anna Carteret, David Hargreaves, David Ellison, Noel Collins, James Grout, Gerard Kelly.
Although this series started just a few weeks after *The Gentle Touch*, it was a more realistic police procedural and the first such to feature a woman police inspector as the lead character. Stephanie Turner played Inspector Jean Darblay, who takes over as head of the fictional Hartley police station in Lancashire. Inevitably she faces prejudice from the other officers but also from the public, though she soon earned the respect of both parties. Her husband Tom (Hargreaves), a social worker, was also supportive. The series focused on local human drama and Turner brought a personal touch to her investigations, though her life was seldom unruffled. After three series, Turner was promoted and her rôle taken over by Inspector Kate Longton (Carteret). Mollie Hardwick reworked several of the story-lines into two novels and a collection, *Juliet Bravo #1* and *#2* (both 1980) and *Calling Juliet Bravo* (1981).

Justice

(UK TV series, 1971–4, 39 episodes)
Creators/Writers: James MITCHELL, Edward Ward.
Producer: Peter Willes (executive), James Ormerod, Jacky Stoller.
Directors: Tony Wharmby, John Frankau, Alan Bromly, Christopher Hodson, Brian Farmham.
Starring: Margaret Lockwood, Anthony Valentine, John Stone, Philip Stone.
Margaret Lockwood played determined lady barrister Harriet Peterson. During the first season her cases were mostly in northern England but with the second series she settled in London and tested her mettle against rival barrister James Eliot (Valentine). The series was strong on court procedure and Peterson did not always win her cases. In fact the best

episodes were those where the frustration of the system sometimes questioned the nature of justice.

Kate Loves a Mystery *see under* Columbo

Kavanagh Q.C.

(UK TV series, 1995–2001, 29 episodes)
Creator/Producer: Chris Kelly. **Executive Producer:** Ted Childs.
Directors: Charles Beeson, Jack Gold, Andrew Grieve, Paul Greengrass, Colin Gregg, Tristram Powell, Penny Rye, David Thacker.
Writers: Malcolm Bradbury, Stephen Churchett, Andy de la Tour, Russell Lewis, Charles Wood.
Starring: John Thaw, Lisa Harrow, Anna Chancellor, Oliver Ford Davies, Nicholas Jones, Daisy Bates, Tom Brodie.
Even while still filming the final specials of *Inspector Morse*, John Thaw donned the wig and a Manchester accent and became the determined and unswervable barrister James Kavanagh. The character was based to some degree on the well-known British barrister Michael Mansfield, Q.C. Both he and Kavanagh fought for the underdog against sometimes overwhelming odds imposed by the justice system. Kavanagh also took on especially difficult cases. One involved the rights of a Jehovah's Witness parent in a blood-transfusion case whilst in another a man is accused of murder but appears unable to speak because of the trauma suffered when a soldier in Bosnia. Kavanagh didn't always win, though you always felt right was on his side. However his home life was less than organized, struggling to keep two teenage children on the straight and narrow and also living with an ambitious wife, Lizzie (Harrow). With the fourth series Kavanagh's wife had died, allowing for more romantic entanglements with a rather more melancholic Kavanagh. The series also dwelt on happenings at Chambers, rather like in *Rumpole*, and Kavanagh was frequently crossing verbal swords with fellow barrister Jeremy Aldermarten (Jones), whilst also trying to help his junior, Julia Piper (Chancellor). Spin-off novels from the series are *Kavanagh Q.C.* (1995) and *Kavanagh Q.C. II* (1996), both by Tom McGregor and *Kavanagh Q.C.: Ties That Bind* (1998) by Wendy Holden. There is also *The Making of Kavanagh Q.C.* by Geoff Tibballs.

A Kiss Before Dying

(1956, US, 94 minutes)
Director: Gerd Oswald. **Producer:** Robert L. Jacks.
Screenplay: Lawrence Roman from the novel by Ira LEVIN.
Starring: Robert Wagner, Jeffrey Hunter, Joanne Woodward, Mary Astor, Virginia Leith.
Ira Levin's structurally ingenious novel did not easily lend itself to

adaptation, but Lawrence Roman's script and Gerd Oswald's stylish quasi-noir presentation makes it work, despite having to reveal the murderer at the outset. Oswald turns that to his advantage in following the cold-blooded Bud Dillon (Wagner) as he disposes of his first, pregnant wife (Woodward) and then works his way on to her sister (Leith). It is unusual to see Wagner cast as a villain, but he clearly relished the rôle and suggests he has been miscast too often since. The 1991 remake, directed by James Dearden from his own script is less effective simply because it has been updated to the corporate yuppified eighties and no longer seems shocking. Matt Dillon is a suitably menacing murderer, but the rest just follows the motions.

Kiss Me Deadly

(1955, US, 105 minutes)
Producer/Director: Robert Aldrich.
Screenplay: Al Bezzerides, from the novel by Mickey SPILLANE.
Starring: Ralph Meeker, Albert Dekker, Paul Stewart, Maxine Cooper, Cloris Leachman.
There are two classic examples of *film noir. The Killers* (1946) directed by Robert Siodmak and based on a 1927 short story by Ernest Hemingway belongs to the Golden Age, but *Kiss Me Deadly*, directed by Robert Aldrich from a Mike Hammer novel by Spillane is firmly at the dawn of modern crime fiction and sets the standard. At the start Hammer nearly runs over a desperate girl (Leachman), and though he rescues her she disappears after an accident. Hammer finds her too late and goes on an orgy of revenge. Although almost as brutal as Spillane's novel, Meeker gives the character of Hammer an honourable savage mentality when seen in the context of the paranoid Cold War/McCarthyite early fifties totalitarianism. The soundtrack and Aldrich's camera direction add to the film's disquiet.

Klute

(1971, US, 114 minutes)
Producer/Director: Alan J. Pakula.
Screenplay: Andy K. Lewis, Dave Lewis.
Starring: Jane Fonda, Donald Sutherland, Charles Cioffi, Roy Scheider.
John Klute (Sutherland) is a small-town cop who takes time off to travel to New York and look into the disappearance of a friend. He becomes involved with the man's friend Bree Daniels (Fonda), an actress and call girl, becoming increasingly obsessed with protecting her from a stalker and murderer. From here on the detective work is minimal and the film becomes a study in relationships and paranoia. Fonda dominates the film in what became an Oscar-winning performance. The film was also nominated for an Edgar in 1972 but lost out

to *The French Connection.* The book-of-the-film was *Klute* (1971) by William Johnston.

The Knock

(UK TV series, 1994–2001)
Creator: Paul Knight.
Executive Producer: Sally Head, Jo Wright, David Newcombe (executive); Paul Knight, Anita Bronson, Paul Leach.
Directors: Several, including James Hazeldine, Gerry Poulson, Frank Smith.
Writers: Several, including Geoffrey Case, Ian Kennedy Martin, Stephen Leather, Steve Trafford.
Starring: Malcolm Storry/Mark Lewis Jones, David Morrissey, Alex Kingston, Caroline Lee Johnson.
For once a series that moved away from the police and looked at the work of London's undercover Customs and Excise officers as the worked to trap international smugglers. The nature of the work meant that they were not always hanging around harbours or airports but also following the threads back to the sources in faraway places. It made the series exciting and different, almost a flashback to some of the adventure series of the sixties but with modern values and dramatic action. The series usually consisted of three- or four-part story-lines and involved major guest stars like Oliver Tobias, Cherie Lunghi and Anthony Valentine.

Kojak

(US TV series, 1973–78, 119 episodes, plus pilot and specials)
Creator: Abby Mann.
Producers: Matthew Rapf (executive), James McAdams, Jack Laird, Chester Krumholz.
Directors: Many, including Edward M. Abroms, Richard Donner, Charles S. Dubin, David Friedkin, Gene R. Kearney, Russ Mayberry, Christian Nyby, Leo Penn, Allen Reisner, Telly Savalas.
Writers: Many, including Robert C. Dennis, Jerrold Friedman, Joe GORES, Robert Hoskins, Gene R. Kearney, Jack Laird, William P. McGivern.
Starring: Telly Savalas, Dan Frazer, George Savalas, Kevin Dobson.
Theo Kojak was an unconventional New York cop, different in every way. Though tough, he called his villains "Pussycat" and sucked on a lollypop. Completely bald, he wore a trilby and fancy waistcoats and his catchphrase was "Who loves ya, baby". Like most TV cops he bent the rules, which annoyed his former partner, now his senior, Captain Frank McNeil (Frazer). Kojak was always calling to his Lieutenant Crocker (Dobson) but he saved most of his jokes for Detective Stavros, played by Savalas's brother George. It was Savalas who carried the show, mostly through his

own force of character but also because he was compassionate but uncompromising. Straight talking and cynical, Kojak knew his city and knew what made the people tick. The pilot, "The Marcus Nelson Murders" (1973), won an Emmy award. It was based on a real murder case (the Wylie-Hoffert murders) and saw Kojak help a young black kid who had been bullied into a confession for a crime he hadn't committed. The series was always high in the ratings, second only to *Hawaii Five-O* during its run. After the series finished Savalas returned for seven special Kojak TV movies, *The Belarus File* (1985), *The Price of Justice* (1987), *Ariana* (1989), *Fatal Flaw* (1989), *Flowers for Matty* (1990), *It's Always Something* (1990) and *None So Blind* (1990). Always stylish and only violent when necessary, *Kojak* showed the new face of the police. In addition to creator Abby Mann's novel of the show, *Kojak* (1974) and Thom Racina's *Kojak in San Francisco* (1976), there were nine books by Victor B. Miller based on individual episodes: *Siege* (1974), *Requiem for a Cop* (1974), *Girl in the River*, *Death is Not a Passing Grade*, *Therapy in Dynamite*, *A Very Deadly Game*, *Gun Business*, *Take-Over* and *The Trade-Off* (all 1975).

L. A. Confidential

(1997, US, 138 minutes)
Director: Curtis Hanson. **Producers:** Arnon Milchan, Curtis Hanson, Michael Nathanson.
Screenplay: Brian Helgeland, Curtis Hanson based on the novel by James ELLROY.
Starring: Kevin Spacey, Russell Crowe, Guy Pearce, James Cromwell, Kim Basinger, Danny DeVito.
After *Blood on the Moon*, this was only the second of James Ellroy's novels to be adapted for the screen. Their complex plots and wide range of mood do not lend themselves to an easy transition but Hanson and Helgeland worked marvels in reshaping the story. Set in the 1950s, a Mob murder in a diner brings together L.A. detectives Ed Exley (Pearce) and Bud White (Crowe). The two are total opposites – White the instinctive hard man using brawn before brain, Exley the ambitious new "golden boy". Exley despises White, all the more so when White is attracted to the mysterious Lynn Bracken (Basinger), who seems to be one of the keys to unlock the web of intrigue behind the murder. Into this web comes a third detective, Jack Vincennes (Spacey), the celebrity of the force, who advises TV on the wonderful work the LAPD do. Hanson keeps weaving the web, drawing in both the characters and the audience to a powerful climax. The film is regarded as one of the best films of the nineties and one of the most influential crime films since *Chinatown*. Kim Basinger won an Oscar for her performance as did Helgeland and Hanson for their screenplay but the film lost out to *Titanic*.

L. A. Law

(US TV series, 1986–94, 171 episodes)
Creator: Steven Bochco and Terry Louise Fisher.
Producers: Steven Bochco and David E. Kelley (executive); Gregory Hoblit, Rick Wallace.
Directors: Gregory Hoblit, Elodie Keene, Sharron Miller, Randy Roberts, Arthur Allan Seidelman, Brad Silberling, E.W. Swackhamer, Mark Tinker, Rick Wallace, Anson Williams.
Writers: Stephen Bochco, Alan Brennert, Jacob Epstein, Terry Louise Fisher, David E. Kelley, Paul Manning, Julie Martin, John Tinker.
Starring: Richard Dysart, Alan Rachins, Jill Eikenberry, Corbin Bernsen, Susan Dey, Michael Tucker, Jimmy Smits, Michele Greene, Harry Hamlin, Susan Ruttan, Larry Drake, Blair Underwood, Diana Muldaur.

Having established a strong ensemble police procedural series in *Hill Street Blues*, writer/producer Steven Bochco teamed with *Cagney and Lacey's* Terry Louise Fisher, herself an attorney, to create a similar ensemble legal procedural – as much soap opera as legal drama. *L.A. Law* follows the hectic private and working lives of the lawyers in the high-powered Los Angeles firm of McKenzie, Brackman, Chaney and Kuzak. The senior partner is Leland McKenzie (Dysart), a rather fatherly figure and the only survivor from the original firm. His partner was Chaney but he's found dead in his office at the start of the first episode. Brackman had died and his son, Douglas (Rachins), struggles to live up to his father's reputation and aggravates everyone in the process. Michael Kuzak (Hamlin) is the younger partner, bright, dependable and compassionate. Arnie Becker (Bernsen), whose name is later added to the practice's title, is the most insufferable of them all: a goading, womanizing divorce lawyer who likes to create discord to make a case more interesting and usually more profitable. There are plenty of others – the show has a huge cast – including the usual quota of ethnics, disabled and just plain eccentrics. There is plenty of office politics and scandal both within the firm and between the firm and the D.A.'s office where the deputy D.A., Grace Van Owen (Dey) has an affair with Kuzak, while the firm's tax attorney, Stuart Markowitz (Tucker), is passionately in love with, and later marries, Ann Kelsey (Eikenberry), the cool, idealistic lawyer. There are endless continuing stories and story arcs. The firm takes on a wide variety of cases, sometimes quite unusual, especially after David E. Kelley joined the series as co-producer and writer. He enjoyed spicing up the show with quirky legal cases, as he would later with his own *Ally McBeal* and *The Practice*. Over time the cast changed, perhaps the most dramatic being the introduction of new partner Rosalind Shays (Muldaur), a successful but unpopular attorney who clashes with the other partners, suing them for over two million dollars. However she met her fate by falling down the lift shaft. After seven seasons ratings dropped and it was eventually discontinued. Nevertheless the series won fifteen Emmy Awards and was named Outstanding Drama series on four occasions. It also won an American Mystery Award in 1991. Kelley received the prestigious Peabody Award for his work on the show. There were several spin-off books: six novels by Charles Butler, *The Partnership*, *A Fair Trial*, *Into the Dark* (all 1991) and *Cold Blood*, *Expert Witness* and *Out of Court* (all 1992) plus *A Woman Scorned* (1992) by Julie Robitaille.

The Last of Sheila

(1973, US, 123 minutes)
Producer/Director: Herbert Ross.
Screenplay: Anthony Perkins, Stephen Sondheim.
Starring: James Coburn, James Mason, Raquel Welch, Richard Benjamin, Ian McShane, Dyan Cannon.
A contrived and somewhat overlong piece of fun that hinges on one gimmick. Clinton (Coburn) invites a star cast of friends and colleagues onto his luxury yacht to play an elaborate mystery word-game, the result of which will reveal the murderer of his wife, who had been killed in a hit-and-run incident. The film came about because of Sondheim and Perkins's delight for wordplay, and this is really all it has going for it, yet it clearly appealed to mystery fans as it won an Edgar award in 1974 beating out *Serpico*, *Don't Look Now* and *The Sting*!

The Late Show

(1977, US, 89 minutes)
Director: Robert Benton. **Producer:** Robert Altman.
Screenplay: Robert Benton.
Starring: Art Carney, Lily Tomlin, Joanna Cassidy, Eugene Roche, Bill Macy.
An affectionate piece of retro-*noir*, which attempts to recreate the P.I. movies of the forties, but with tongue firmly in cheek. Nevertheless Art Carney as Ira Wells puts in a fine performance in an otherwise overly complicated plot that begins with him looking for a missing cat belonging to Margo (Tomlin) and ends up including a theft of postage stamps, blackmail and murder. Nevertheless it won an Edgar award in 1978.

The Laughing Policeman [aka An Investigation of Murder]

(1973, US, 111 minutes)
Producer/Director: Stuart Rosenberg.
Screenplay: Thomas Rickman, based on the novel by Per WAHLÖÖ.
Starring: Walter Matthau, Bruce Dern, Lou Gossett, Anthony Zerbe, Albert Paulsen.

Based on Per Wahlöö's novel, vocal images of Charles Penrose's classic song caused the title to be changed in Britain to the rather bland *An Investigation of Murder*, a blandness that alas is inherited from the film. Wahlöö's novel was intense and suspenseful, but Rosenberg's production, in an attempt to downplay the violence of recent cop movies, especially *Dirty Harry*, has Matthau as a methodical, traditional cop, Jake Martin, pursuing a machine-gun toting maniac who has already slaughtered a bus-load of people. Martin is also unconventional and at odds with his superiors, but despite the potential for action and some beautiful scenic photography – plus an inevitable bus climax down the San Francisco streets – the film fails to deliver the impact of the novel.

Law & Order

(US TV series, 1990–*current*, 270 + episodes)
Creator: Dick Wolf.
Producers: Many, primarily Dick Wolf (executive) and currently Barry Schindel, Jeffrey Hayes, Peter Jankowski; Gary Karr, William Fordes (supervising), Kati Johnston, Roz Weinman, Wendy Battles.
Directors: Many, including Richard Dobbs, James Frawley, Matthew Penn, John Patterson, James Quinn.
Writers: Many, including William M. Finkelstein, Joe Gannon, Charles Kipps, I.C. Rapoport, Craig Tepper, Dick Teresi, Dick Wolf, Ed Zuckerman.
Starring: George Dzundza/Paul Sorvino/Jerry Orbach, Christopher Noth/Jesse L. Martin, Dann Florek/S. Epetha Merkeson, Michael Moriarty/Sam Waterston, Richard Brooks/Jill Hennessy, Steven Hill.
L&O took the format used nearly thirty years earlier by the unsuccessful *Arrest and Trial* and made it work. In fact it works so well that it is the longest-running US TV drama series currently showing and with its contract renewed to 2005 it will overtake *Hawaii Five-O* for the record. The first half of the show has the NYPD investigate that week's crime whilst the second half follows the D.A.'s prosecution. Unlike *Arrest and Trial*, where the two halves were clear-cut, here the edges are blurred, the circumstances of the case not always clear, and the perpetrator is not always found guilty. The series emphasizes attempts to get justice despite the system. Many of the crimes are based on fictionalized real-life cases. The programme has had a regular turn over of actors during its run and the only original member still appearing is the D.A. himself, Adam Schiff (Steve Hill). The original investigating officer, Detective Sergeant Max Greevey (Dzundza), was killed on duty at the end of the first series. His rôle is now filled by Lennie Briscoe (Orbach) helped by Detective Ed Green (Martin). The main prosecuting attorney is currently Jack McCoy (Waterston). The series has been nominated for the Outstanding Drama series Emmy Award ten years in a row, and six episodes have won Edgar

awards. It has generated the spin-off series *Trial & Error* plus several one-off specials. There have also been three novels based on the series by Jack Gregory, *Black Out* (1993), *In Deep* (1993) and *Dead End* (1994).

Léon [aka The Professional]

(1994, French, 130 minutes, Director's cut)
Director/Producer/Screenplay: Luc Besson.
Starring: Jean Reno, Gary Oldman, Natalie Portman.
This is an emotionally taut and telling story of a skilled hit-man, Léon (Reno), who finds himself protecting and caring for Mathilde (Portman), the 12-year-old daughter of his neighbours in a New York apartment block, when her parents are killed in a savage drugs raid led by corrupt cop Stansfield (Oldman). Mathilde is bright and intelligent, compared to Léon's intellectual innocence. She seeks revenge and asks Léon to teach her in the art of killing. The film follows Léon's emotional collapse as the girl penetrates his defensive barriers. The film is a twist on *Gloria*, though goes deeper into the psyche, at least in the full European version. The US version was cut by 20 minutes to concentrate on the action.

Lethal Weapon

(1987, US, 112 minutes)
Producer/Director: Richard Donner.
Screenplay: Shane Black.
Starring: Mel Gibson, Danny Glover, Gary Busey, Mitchell Ryan, Tom Atkins.
Mel Gibson really is the lethal weapon in this fun all-action film. Gibson plays Martin Riggs, a Vietnam vet turned cop who has become utterly carefree of life since his wife's death. He is teamed up with Roger Murtaugh (Glover) a by-the-book family man cop who is outraged by Riggs' near-suicidal antics but becomes wrapped up in the action as the two go after a drugs ring. This film works on all levels, but mostly because of Mel Gibson's crazed exuberance. This spills over with enough energy to sustain three easily numbered sequels, all with the same team. Although the characters were created by Shane Black they bore sufficient resemblance to cops Razoni and Jackson in the series by Warren MURPHY that Murphy came in to help on the script of *Lethal Weapon 2* (1989), the least rewarding of the films. *Lethal Weapon 3* (1992), where Rene Russo plays equally crazed cop Lorna Cole, is as good as sequels get. The original film was novelized as *Lethal Weapon* (1987) by Joel Norst.

Lock, Stock and Two Smoking Barrels

(1998, UK, 102 minutes)
Director: Guy Ritchie. **Producer:** Matthew Vaughn.
Screenplay: Guy Ritchie.

Starring: Jason Flemyng, Dexter Fletcher, Nick Moran, Jason Statham, Vinnie Jones, P.H. Moriarty.

This is one of those films where you know that events are going to go from bad to worse and you find yourself hoping it will get better for the sake of the four East End street-foolish lads who end up in serious debt to Mobster Hatchet Harry (Moriarty). They devise a series of schemes to try and raise the money in a week, which feels rather like *Pulp Fiction* meets *The Lavender Hill Mob*. Guy Ritchie skilfully directs yet another film in the long line of British comic crime, but this time with a violent and nasty edge that has you wincing when you might otherwise be laughing. The film received the Edgar award in 2000. The success of the film led to a short TV series, *Lock Stock* (2000; 7 episodes), about the adventures of four dodgy "likely lads" in the East End, directed by David Thacker. The book of the film was *Lock, Stock & Two Smoking Barrels* (1999) by Andrew Donkin, whilst the scripts of the TV series was published as *Lock, Stock* (2000) by Guy Ritchie, Chris Baker, Andrew Day, Bernard Dempsey and Kevin McNally.

The Long Good Friday

(1979, UK, 114 minutes)

Director: John MacKenzie. **Producer:** Barry Hanson.

Screenplay: Barrie Keefe.

Starring: Bob Hoskins, Helen Mirren, Dave King, Bryan Marshall, Derek Thompson.

Cockney gangster Harold Shand (Hoskins) has dreams of building a new town in London's docklands with money raised from organized crime, but his opponents want none of that and one by one his gang is picked off by anonymous gunmen. Despite his efforts to benefit from the Thatcher years, crime does not pay for poor Harold, especially when he discovers his enemies are the IRA, whom one of his underlings double-crossed. It is still regarded, along with *Get Carter*, as one of Britain's best and most realistic gangster films. The book-of-the-film is *Long Good Friday* by Russell Claughton (1981). It won an Edgar in 1983.

Longstreet

(US TV series, 1971–2, 23 episodes)

Creator: Stirling Silliphant.

Producers: Stirling Silliphant (executive), Joel Rogosin.

Directors: Several, including Leslie H. Martinson, Lee Philips, Joseph Sargent, Don McDougall, David Lowell, Paul Krasny, Charles Dubin.

Writers: Several, including Stirling Silliphant, Lionel E. Siegel, Sandor Stern, Steven Lord, Stephen Kandel, Robert M. Young, Richard Landau, Jackson Gillis.

Starring: James Franciscus, Marilyn Mason, Peter Mark Richman.

Mike Longstreet (Franciscus) was an insurance investigator who, in the original TV movie *Longstreet* (1971), is blinded by the same bomb explosion that kills his wife. Longstreet fights back though. Trained in self defence by Li Tsung (Bruce Lee) and equipped with his German shepherd guide dog, Pax, and an electronic cane, he goes back on the trail of the baddies. Gimmicky at its worst, the series nevertheless had some good performances and interesting plots which play to Longstreet's other strengths.

Lovejoy

(UK TV series, 1986, 1991–4, 71 episodes)
Creator: Jonathan GASH; developed for TV by Ian La Frenais.
Producers: Robert Banks Stewart, Richard Everitt, Emma Hayter, Jo Wright, Colin Schindler.
Directors: Many, including David Reynolds, Roger Tucker, Baz Taylor, Ken Hannam, Roger Tucker, Don Leaver, John Woods, William Brayne, Bill Hays, Sarah Hellings, Peter Barber-Fleming.
Writers: Many, including Ian La Frenais, Terry Hodgkinson, David Brown, Francis Megahy, Murray Smith, T.R. Bowen, Alan Clews, Roger Marshall, Geoff Lowe, Jeremy Paul, Mike RIPLEY, Douglas Watkinson, Geoff McQueen.
Starring: Ian McShane, Dudley Sutton, Chris Jury/Diane Parish, Phyllis Logan, Caroline Langrishe, Pavel Douglas, Mel Martin.
Ian McShane played the lovable rogue Lovejoy, the wheeler-dealing "divvie" of the antiques trade, who ends up investigating dodgy goings on in East Anglia. Although developed from the books by Jonathan Gash, and adapting a number of them, the series developed along its own lines, particularly with Lovejoy's romantic entanglements with the likes of Lady Felsham (Logan) and later auctioneer Charlotte Cavendish (Langrishe), let alone his ex-wife and plenty of beautiful female clients. Lovejoy's two business companions were Tinker (Sutton) and Eric (Jury), the latter replaced by Beth (Parish) from series five. Like many adapted books, the TV series bears only superficial resemblance to the novels but both were excellent at portraying some of the shady dealings in the antiques business.

McCallum

(UK TV series, 1995, 1997–8, 9 episodes)
Producers: Murray Ferguson.
Directors: Richard Holthouse, Patrick Lau, David Tucker.
Starring: John Hannah/Nathaniel Parker, Gerard Murphy, Suzanna Hamilton, Zara Turner.
Before he became Rebus, John Hannah had appeared briefly as motorbike riding forensic pathologist Iain McCallum. McCallum worked at St Patrick's Mortuary in London and ended up becoming involved in the murder cases on which he was advising. Regular police contact was D.I.

Bracken (Murphy). The series was moody, with much lovelorn angst – particularly in the pilot episode when he has to perform an autopsy on the girl with whom he'd just had an affair. The individual cases were well handled with some intriguing deductions. After two short series Hannah, who did not want to become too typecast, chose not to continue. A one-off special was filmed under the *McCallum* title though with Nathaniel Parker as Dr Dan Gallagher in the same setting, but nothing more followed.

McCloud

(US TV series, 1970–7, 46 episodes)
Creator: Herman Miller, Glen A. Larson.
Producers: Glen A. Larson, Leslie Stevens, Richard Irving (executives); Michael Gleason, Dean Hargrove, Ron Satlof, Herbert Wright.
Directors: Many, including Lou Antonio, Richard A. Colla, Russ Mayberry, Boris Sagal, Jimmy Sangster, Ron Satlof, Barry Shear.
Writers: Many, including Richard Levinson & William Link, Lonne Elder III, Sy Salkowitz.
Starring: Dennis Weaver, J.D. Cannon, Diana Muldaur, Terry Carter, Ken Lynch.
McCloud was one of the series in the *NBC Mystery Movie* story-wheel that included *Columbo* and *McMillan and Wife*. In fact it had premiered the previous season and was supposedly inspired by Clint Eastwood's character Walt Coogan in *Coogan's Bluff*. Like Coogan, Deputy Marshal Sam McCloud (Weaver) comes to New York, from New Mexico, to recapture an escaped prisoner. This story formed the basis of the pilot, *Who Killed Miss U.S.A.?* (1970), which had been reworked by Columbo creators Richard Levinson and William Link from an earlier unsuccessful script. With its success McCloud stayed on in New York to learn big-city ways and hopefully tone down his countryfied strong-arm tactics. He never did, much to the annoyance of his superior, Chief Clifford (Cannon) and the frustration of his partner, Sergeant Broadhurst (Carter). McCloud continued to act like a cowboy, and the series at times felt like a modern-day western. His catchphrase, having learned the facts of the case, was "There you go". Although played light, Weaver was believable in his rôle, once you'd forgotten he'd been the gammy-legged Chester in *Gunsmoke*, and the stories were different than the rest of the TV fare. In fact the cycle of *McCloud* with *Columbo* and *McMillan and Wife* not only provided a pleasing variety but also some of the most sustained quality writing for TV crime series. Weaver has since become a strong environmentalist and only agreed to do one further turn as McCloud if it was built around that theme. In *The Return of Sam McCloud* (1989), he is now a senator fighting for environmental issues. Most of the old team returned. There have been six novelizations based on the series: two by Collin WILCOX, *McCloud* and *The New Mexico Connection* (both

1974) and four by David Wilson, *The Killing* and *The Corpse Maker* (both 1974) and *A Dangerous Place to Die* and *Park Avenue Executioner* (both 1975). The episode "The New Mexico Connection" won an Edgar in 1973.

McMillan and Wife

(US TV series, 1971–7, 40 episodes)
Creator/Executive Producer: Leonard B. Stern.
Producers: Jon Epstein, Paul Mason, Ted Rich.
Directors: Many, including Edward M. Abroms, Lou Antonio, John Astin, Harry Falk, Bob Finkel, Gary Nelson, Daniel Petrie, James Sheldon, E.W. Swackhamer.
Writers: Many, including Steven Bochco, Oliver Hailer, Robert Lewin, Don M. Mankiewicz, Leonard B. Stern.
Starring: Rock Hudson, Susan Saint James, John Schuck, John Astin, Nancy Walker/Martha Raye.
Stewart McMillan (Hudson) was the San Francisco Police Commissioner who, rather in the style of Nick and Nora Charles in the *Thin Man* series, was invariably drawn into murder cases by his scatty wife Sally (James). Their professional lifestyle meant that these crimes usually involved the rich and famous, and the series echoed the classic English country house murder, with some delightfully complex plots, including several locked room mysteries. The casting worked well and the banter between McMillan and his wife was always good fun, as were the acid observations by housekeeper Mildred (Walker). Unfortunately in 1976 Susan Saint James left through a contract dispute, and Nancy also left. The series continued simply as *McMillan*, with the pretence that Sally had been killed in a plane crash, but the central spark was lost and the series soon folded.

Madigan

(1968, US, 100 minutes)
Director: Don Siegel. **Producer:** Frank P. Rosenberg.
Screenplay: Henri Simoun, Abraham Polonsky from the 1963 novel *The Commissioner* by Richard Dougherty.
Starring: Richard Widmark, Henry Fonda, Inger Stevens, Harry Guardino, Steve Ihnat.
Madigan now has the look of a dated film, yet the feel of a modern one. It was the first of Don Siegel's big three cop films that culminated in *Dirty Harry* and saw the transition from the traditional to the new. In *Madigan* the settings and the clothing still have the look of the fifties, but the characters are rapidly catching up with the sixties. Richard Widmark plays Dan Madigan, a detective who's in trouble because a maniac has stolen his service revolver and has already killed someone. Madigan and his partner,

Rocco Bonaro (Guardino), have just 72 hours to find him. Both Widmark and Guardino are excellent as strong-arm no-nonsense cops coping with a changing world, but their action is diluted by the film's sub-plot of marital distress, both in Madigan's world and that of the Police Commissioner, Anthony Russell (Fonda), whose duplicity contrasts new values with the old. Despite the fate of Madigan's character in the film, it did not stop Universal reviving him for a TV series. *Madigan* (1972–3; 6 episodes) again starred Richard Widmark but unfortunately shifted him around the world, and the character lost his locus.

Magic

(1978, US, 107 minutes)
Director: Richard Attenborough.
Producer: Joseph E. Levine, Richard P. Levine.
Screenplay: William GOLDMAN, based on his own novel.
Starring: Anthony Hopkins, Ann-Margret, Burgess Meredith.
Pre Hannibal Lecter, Anthony Hopkins plays another psychotic, this time a ventriloquist with a guilty secret that his dummy is not allowed to hide. The dummy-takes-over-the-ventriloquist plot is an old one and was best exploited in *Dead of Night* (1945), but Hopkins, who did his own ventriloquism, is suitably sinister and the film has moments of real suspense. Mystery fans awarded it an Edgar in 1979.

Magnum, P.I.

(US TV series, 1980–8, 162 episodes)
Creator: Donald P. Bellisario.
Producers: Donald P. Bellisario, Glen A. Larson, Tom Selleck (executives).
Directors: Many, including Donald P. Bellisario, Georg Stanford Brown, Ivan Dixon, James Frawley, David Hemmings, Rick Kolbe, Bernard Kowalski, Stuart Margolin, Russ Mayberry, Roger E. Mosley, Leo Penn, Tony Wharmby.
Writers: Many, including Chris Abbott-Fish, Donald P. Bellisario, Bruce Cervi, Joe GORES, Jack Huguely, Glen A. Larson, Reuben Leder, Del Reisman, Tom Selleck, Jeri Taylor, Robert van Scoyk.
Starring: Tom Selleck, John Hillerman, Roger E. Mosley, Larry Manetti.
Tall, dark and handsome, moustachioed Tom Selleck was ideal for the part of bodyguard and security agent Thomas Magnum. Selleck had interested Universal TV when he briefly played the rôle of P.I. Lance White in *The Rockford Files* and they developed *Magnum* around him. Magnum was employed by Robin Masters, a rich writer whom you never saw (though his voice was spoken by Orson Welles) but who owned a palatial estate on Hawaii, which Magnum looked after.

Magnum didn't have it all his own way because Masters' manservant, Higgins (Hillerman), curbed his excesses and was as likely to let the dogs loose on him. Magnum was an ex-Vietnam vet and with him were former buddies (ex Navy SEALS) Theodore "TC" Calvin (Mosley) and Rick Wright (Manetti). TC ran a helicopter service between the islands and Wright owned an exclusive night club (later a beach club), both very convenient. The setting was ideal for linking Magnum to attractive women, the series serving as something of a transition between *Hawaii Five-O* and *Baywatch*. In fact the series used the same production facilities as *Hawaii Five-O*, and Magnum would sometimes refer to Steve McGarrett as if he was still operating. Although Magnum worked as a P.I. most of the time, the series took advantage of Selleck's penchant for humour and later episodes often contained no crime elements at all but interesting interplay between the main characters. Expecting the show to finish, the series took the unusual step of killing Magnum off in a surreal episode, "Limbo" (1987), partly written by Selleck, where Magnum is shot and, while in a coma, his spirit wanders over the island resolving outstanding matters before vanishing into the clouds. Then the series was renewed for one further season and they had to bring him back from the dead, explaining it all as a delirium. There were two novels based on the series, both called *Magnum P.I.*, the first by Roger Bowdler (1981), the other by Dan Zadra (1985). The episode "China Doll" won an Edgar in 1981.

The Main Chance

(UK TV series, 1969–75, 46 episodes)
Creator: Edmund Ward.
Producers: David Cunliffe (executive); John Frankau, Peter Willes.
Directors: Many, including Derek Bennett, Cyril Coke, Michael Ferguson, John Frankau, Chris Hodson, Marc Miller, Tony Wharmby.
Writers: Edmund Ward, Ray Jenkins, John Bett.
Starring: John Stride, John Wentworth, Kate O'Mara, Anna Palk.
A series about an ambitious and super-efficient solicitor, David Main (Stride), who was always looking for the big break – "the main chance". Although he went out of the way to find the best cases, so as to benefit both financially and enhance his reputation, he often found himself helping out the less fortunate. Sometimes he would survive just by the seat of his pants, relying on his extensive knowledge of the law to resolve complicated situations. His wife, Julia (O'Mara), appeared only in the first series, but his secretary, the little rich girl Sarah Courtenay (Palk), who became Lady Radchester, remained throughout. After the series finished creator Edmund Ward produced a novel about the character, *The Main Chance* (1977). Ward also wrote the thriller serial, *The Hanged Man* (1975; 8 episodes; book, 1976) about businessman Lew Burnett (Colin Blakely)

who, after three attempts on his life, pretends he was killed and goes undercover to find who want him dead.

Manhunter

(1986, US, 120 minutes)
Director: Michael Mann. **Producer:** Richard Roth.
Screenplay: Michael Mann based on the novel *Red Dragon* by Thomas HARRIS.
Starring: William Peterson, Kim Greist, Brian Cox, Tom Noonan, Dennis Farina, Stephen Lang.
Somewhat overshadowed by the success of *The Silence of the Lambs*, the earlier novel by Harris, which introduced the infamous Dr Hannibal Lecter, *Red Dragon*, was made into this powerful and, if anything, superior film. Will Graham (Petersen) is the FBI agent who had brought in Lecter. He has since retired, psychologically damaged from his confrontation with Lecter, but he is brought out of retirement as the only hope to track down a serial killer known as the "Tooth Fairy"' (Noonan). Graham has to work with Lecter in order to understand the killer's mentality. Lecter, not surprisingly, does his best to turn the tables on Graham. It's a frighteningly powerful film, one of the best thrillers of the late eighties, with an impressive performance by Brian Cox as Lecter.

A Man Called Hawk *see under* Spenser For Hire

The Man in Room 17

(UK TV series, 1965–6, 26 episodes, b&w); relaunched as THE FELLOWS (1967; 12 episodes, b&w)
Creator: Robin Chapman. **Producers:** Robin Chapman, Peter Plummer.
Directors: Richard Everitt, David Boisseau, David Cunliffe, Peter Plummer, Philip Casson, Claude Whatham, Peter Dews, Bob Hird, Gerard Dynevor.
Writers: Many, including Gerald Wilson, Patrick Thursfield, John Lucarotti, Ludovic Peters, N.J. Crisp, John Burke, Martin Woodhouse, Ian Stuart Black, Reed de Rouen, Michael GILBERT, David Weir, John Hawksworth, John Kruse, Michael Sullivan, Alan Grant.
Starring: Richard Vernon, Michael Aldridge/Denholm Elliott, Willoughby Goddard.
This was one of those wonderfully eccentric series that Granada Television loved to experiment with in the mid-sixties. The "Man" in Room 17 was Oldenshaw (Vernon), a long-serving government official with a remarkable mind who was instructed to establish a small unit to study the criminal mind and help the government with especially difficult crimes. Oldenshaw agreed to do it on a strict time basis and, as his assistant,

he recruited the like-minded Dimmock (Aldridge). The two never left their room. The only outside contact was their boss, Sir Geoffrey Norton (Goddard), who brought them their cases and to whom they relayed their proposals. The cases were anything complicated from industrial espionage to sudden disappearances to missing confidential reports to checking over intelligence agents and even devising security for foreign officials. The action outside Room 17 was directed and scripted separately to allow for complete detachment. For the second series Aldridge was indisposed and so new recruit Defraits (Elliott) was introduced. At the end of the second season Oldenshaw's prescribed term ended. A new series was launched called *The Fellows*. Oldenshaw was appointed to the Peel Research Fellowship at Cambridge University where he was reunited with Dimmock and the two carried on just as before studying the nature of crime within a social context. This time they were not so isolated and had a small team of helpers. *The Fellows* was more a serial than a series with several continuing story-lines overlapping from one episode to the next. One of these involved an operation against gangster Alec Spindoe (Ray McAnally). He was convicted and imprisoned but a further spin-off series, *Spindoe* (1968; 6 episodes) followed his release and his plans to regain his criminal empire. What was intriguing about this sequence of series, all devised by Robin Chapman (who later adapted several of P.D. JAMES's Dalgliesh novels for television, was how it showed similarities between the government thinktank and the criminal mastermind.

Mannix

(US TV series, 1967–75, 193 episodes)
Creator: William Link and Richard Levinson.
Producers: Bruce Geller (executive); Ben Roberts, Ivan Goff.
Directors: Many, including Corey Allen, Bill Bixby, Marvin J. Chomsky, Harvey Hart, Vincent McEveety, Lohn Llewellyn Moxey, Allen Reisner, David L. Rich.
Writers: Many, including Chester Krumholz, Richard Landau, Jackson Gillis, Stephen Kandel, Ed Adamson, Donn Mullally, John Meredyth Lucas, Edward J. Lakso, Mann Rubin, Howard Browne, Dan Ullman.
Starring: Mike Connors, Joseph Campanella/Gail Fisher, Robert Reed, Ward Wood.
When *Columbo* creators William Link and Richard Levinson first devised the *Mannix* series they had a specific set up. Joe Mannix (Connors), a Korean veteran who prefers the hard-and-fast way of solving crimes, was employed by a state-of-the-art Los Angeles detective agency called Intertect. Its head, Lou Wickersham (Campanella), was into computers and sophisticated charts and analyses and believed this was the way to catch criminals. Needless to say he and Mannix didn't see eye to eye and they fell out. The banter between them livened up the first series but it

soon ran its course. By series two Mannix had set up his own agency. He employed a secretary, Peggy Fair, who was the widow of a police officer killed in the line of duty. She was played by black actress Gail Fisher. Nothing was made of this, though she was one of the first black actresses to have a leading rôle in a major TV drama series, and she won the Golden Globe award twice for her performances. Thereafter Mannix settled down to playing a traditional fast-action sports-car driving P.I., a toned-down Mike Hammer with Gail (like Hammer's Velda) prone to being threatened or kidnapped. The series ran for eight years and was nominated twice for an Emmy award and four times for the Golden Globe (winning in 1972). Episodes were also nominated four times for an Edgar award with Mann Rubin's "A Step in Time" (1971) winning. There were five spin-off novels: *Mannix* (1968) by Michael AVALLONE and four under the house name J.T. MacCargo: *The Faces of Murder*, *A Fine Day for Dying*, *Round Trip to Nowhere* and *A Walk on the Blind Side* (all 1975).

Matlock

(US TV series, 1986–95, 195 episodes)
Creator: Dean Hargrove.
Producers: Dean Hargrove, Fred Silverman (executive); Ron Carr, Anne Collins, Jeff Peters, Robert Schlitt.
Directors: Many, including Charles S. Dubin, Christopher Hibler, Russ Mayberry, John L. Moxey, Christian I. Nyby II, Leo Penn, Nicholas Sgarro.
Writers: Many, including Robert Hamilton, Dean Hargrove, Michael Petryni.
Starring: Andy Griffith, Linda Purl/Nancy Stafford/Brynn Thayer, Kene Holliday/Clarence Gilyard, Jr./Daniel Roebuck.
Matlock was a straight imitation *Perry Mason*. Benjamin L. Matlock (Griffith) was a clever Harvard-educated southern attorney from Georgia, who looked unassuming but whose sharp mind managed to secure some last minute courtroom confession. He was initially assisted by his lawyer daughter, Charlene (Purl) and stock-market expert Tyler Hudson (Holliday), who did most of his investigative work, but the series had a regular turnover of cast. It was nevertheless popular, partly because Griffith had established a strong screen persona in his long running sitcom *The Andy Griffith Show*, and it ran for nine seasons. The pilot episode "Diary of a Perfect Murder" by Dean Hargrove was nominated for an Edgar award.

Matt Houston

(US TV series, 1982–5, 69 episodes)
Creator: Lawrence Gordon.
Producers: Aaron Spelling (executive); Michael Fisher.

Directors: Many, including Hy Averback, Corey Allen, Cliff Bole, Don Chaffey, Jerome Courtland, Peter Crane, Barbara Peters, Don Weis.
Writers: Many, including Robert C. Dennis, Larry Forrester, Tom Edwards, Daniel J. Pyne
Starring: Lee Horsley, Pamela Hensley, George Wyner.
Another featherlight fancy from the same stable as *Charlie's Angels* and *Hart to Hart*. Matt Houston (Horsley) was a rich man's son with little work to do, leaving that to his partner Murray Chase (Wyner) and so spent his time being a detective. Or at least, that was the idea. It was really an excuse to drive around in fast cars and be surrounded by beautiful women, including his assistant, lawyer C.J. Parsons (Hensley). This palled by the end of the first series so in the second he became a slightly more serious detective. His cases were always amongst the rich and famous and became increasingly eccentric, the only real appeal of the series, apart from its rota of guest stars which included Britt Ekland, Janet Leigh, David Cassidy, George Maharis, and Simon MacCorkindale. The first episode, "X-22", was nominated for an Edgar. Towards the end of the series the action slowed down a little as Houston's elderly uncle, Roy, a former detective, came out of retirement to help him. Roy was played by Buddy Ebsen, who had previously played Barnaby Jones.

Mean Streets

(1973, US, 110 minutes)
Director: Martin Scorsese. **Producer:** Jonathan Taplin.
Screenplay: Martin Scorsese, Mardik Martin.
Starring: Harvey Keitel, Robert De Niro, Amy Robinson, David Proval, David Carradine.
Despite the title this is not a private-eye film, but a story of street life, in some ways the world behind *West Side Story*, a modern *Asphalt Jungle*. Scorsese even integrated rock music into the film. It's the story of youths coping with life and their experiences on the fringes of organized crime. Charlie (Keitel) is the nephew of a Mafiosi and wants to advance within the Mob but is kept at arm's length. Unfortunately his involvement with his cousin, a street punk, Johnny Boy (De Niro), who is heavily in debt, leads to a grim conclusion. It was with this film that Scorsese became noticed.

Memento

(2000, US, 113 minutes)
Director: Christopher Nolan. **Producer:** Suzanne Todd, Jennifer Todd.
Screenplay: Christopher Nolan, from a story by Jonathan Nolan.
Starring: Guy Pearce, Carrie-Anne Moss, Joe Pantoliano, Stephen Tobolowsky.
A highly memorable film about memory. Leonard Shelby (Pearce) wants

to take revenge on whoever raped and killed his wife but he suffers from short-term memory loss and his recollection of events is always far back in time. The film follows these distant events with occasional flashes of the present that Shelby remembers briefly and tries to capture in photographs and notes. The film steadily works back in time to the beginning, allowing viewers some idea of Shelby's mental state. It becomes a torturous but instructive experiment in how and what we remember and leads to a surprising climax.

Messenger of Death

(1988, US, 92 minutes)
Director: J. Lee Thompson.
Screenplay: Paul Jarrico, based on the novel *The Avenging Angel* by Rex BURNS.
Starring: Charles Bronson, Trish Van Devere, Daniel Benzali.
Featuring Charles Bronson, who was still appearing in *Death Wish* sequels, the film might suggest another revenge flick. But it isn't. Quite the opposite. Bronson plays Garret Smith, a Denver crime reporter who is looking into a series of murders and his investigations uncover a renegade Mormon sect who are ritualistically re-enacting Old Testament murders. It's competently handled and makes for an intriguing and strangely effective little thriller.

Miami Blues

(1990, US, 92 minutes)
Director: George Armitage. **Producer:** Jonathan Demme, Gary Goetzman.
Screenplay: George Armitage from the novel by Charles WILLEFORD.
Starring: Fred Ward, Alec Baldwin, Jennifer Jason Leigh.
Charles Willeford's Hoke Moseley books are not as violent or disturbing as his early work but they are almost as crazy, and adapting them to film is a brave venture. Armitage succeeds better than you could hope, thanks to a superb performance by Alec Baldwin as the psychopath, Junior Frenger, who steals Moseley's gun, badge and (yes) false teeth while Moseley is in hospital recovering from his first encounter with Frenger. Moseley has to track him down. Armitage succeeds in conveying both the menace and the eccentricities of Willeford's world, even if he doesn't quite capture the deep-down madness.

Miami Vice

(US TV series, 1984–9, 111 episodes)
Creators: Michael Mann, Anthony Yerkovich.
Producers: Michael Mann, Anthony Yerkovich (executive); Richard Brams, John Nicollella.

Directors: Many, including George Stanford Brown, Paul Michael Glaser, Don Johnson, Michael Mann, Russ Mayberry, John Llewellyn Moxey, James Quinn, David Soul.
Writers: Many, including Chuck Adamson, Julia Cameron, Robert Crais, Thomas M. Disch, Maurice Hurley, John Mankiewicz, Miguel Pinero, Daniel Pyne, Alfonse Ruggiero, Jr., Joel Surnow, Dick Wolf.
Starring: Don Johnson, Philip Michael Thomas, Edward James Olmos, Saundra Santiago, Olivia Brown.
Asked to develop a police series that looked and sounded like an MTV video, Mann and Yerkovich came up with the ultimate in fast, snazzy, stylish and hip action drama. In the pilot episode, "Brother's Keepers", Sonny Crockett (Johnson) is an undercover cop for the Miami Vice department, operating as Sonny Burnett (an alter-ego which, in later episodes, he has trouble divorcing himself from). Crockett is separated from his wife and young son and lives on a yacht called *St Vitus Dance* with a pet alligator. Ricardo Tubbs (Thomas) is a New York cop who has come undercover to Miami under his own steam, to avenge the murder of his brother, another cop killed during a drugs deal with Colombian smuggler Calderone. Crockett discovers his own partner is leaking information and he teams up with Tubbs to capture Calderone. Thereafter Tubbs stays and the series follows the two around Miami, from the high life to the dregs, usually in Crockett's Ferrari Spider (later a Testarossa), sorting out the drugs, the porn and the sleaze. With Jan Hammer's pulsating theme music, Johnson's designer stubble and Versace outfits, the series was just what NBC wanted, and in its first season it was in the top ten ratings and received fifteen Emmy nominations. The opening episode was also nominated for an Edgar award. Later, the series was set against *Dallas*, and ratings fell. At its peak the series attracted such major stars and recording artists as Frank Zappa, Phil Collins, Little Richard, Iggy Pop, Bruce Willis, Eartha Kitt, Melanie Griffiths and Julia Roberts. Singer Sheena Easton appeared briefly and became Crockett's second wife before being gunned down. Some episodes were directed by *Starsky and Hutch* buddies David Soul and Paul Michael Glazer. Later episodes became a little weird – there was even a UFO experience scripted by Thomas M. Disch – but they were always high energy, if a little repetitious on plot. Between 1985 and 1987 David J. Schow wrote six novels based on the series under the alias Stephen Grave: *The Vengeance Game*, *The Florida Burn*, *China White*, *The Razor's Edge*, *Probing by Fire* and *Hellhole*.

Mickey Spillane's Mike Hammer

(US TV series, 1984–7, 46 episodes; last season called The New Mike Hammer); revived as Mike Hammer, Private Eye (1997–8, 26 episodes)

Creator: Mickey SPILLANE. **Producers:** Jay Bernstein (executive); Frank Abatemarco, Lew Gallo.
Directors: Many, including Ray Danton, James Frawley, Stacy Keach, Bernard Kowalski, Gary Nelson, Leo Penn, Michael Preece, Sy Salkowitz.
Writers: Many, including Larry Brody, Stephen Downing, Joe GORES, Larry Gross, Janis Hendler, Stephen Kandel, Chester Krumholz, James M. Miller, James Schmerer, Bill Stratton.
Starring: Stacy Keach, Lindsay Bloom, Don Stroud, Kent Williams, Lee Benton, Donna Denton.
Despite the prevailing wisdom that Spillane's Mike Hammer books are too violent and corrupting to be taken seriously they have lent themselves to frequent adaptation for the big and small screens, ever since the first movie adaptation, *I, the Jury* in 1953 (see entry *Kiss Me Deadly*). The first TV adaptation ran for 78 episodes during 1958–9 with Darren McGavin as Hammer. Decried as violent the series was nevertheless popular. The same attitude applied to the 1984 revival with Stacy Keach portraying the definitive screen Hammer, now a Vietnam vet. The series was preceded by two two-hour pilot movies, *Murder Me, Murder You* (1983), which won an Edgar award, and *More Than Murder* (1984) that had most of the same cast and crew. These included Lindsay Bloom as the loyal and beautiful Velda, Lee Benton as Hammer's sexy informant, Jenny the bartender, Don Stroud as his long suffering NYPD contact, Captain Pat Chambers and Kent Williams as the assistant D.A. with whom Hammer was always at odds. Each episode reflected the same near vigilante vengeance and brutality with Hammer either pounding the villains to pulp or filling them full of lead from his pistol, "Betsy". The early episodes were rather more sexy than the later ones, which were tamed down to attract more women viewers, though the violence increased. One continuing mystery in the series was a woman whom Hammer spotted in each episode but never got to speak to. She became known as "The Face" (Denton). A planned confrontation was delayed when Keach was arrested and jailed in Britain for possession of cocaine, but they finally got to meet in the last episode, "A Face in the Night" (1987). During Keach's imprisonment the series was curtailed, but a TV special was made, *The Return of Mickey Spillane's Mike Hammer* (1986), to test the waters before the final season was launched as *The New Mike Hammer*. There was a further TV movie, *Murder Takes All* (1989). After a break of nearly ten years Keach returned as Hammer in *Mike Hammer, Private Eye*, with only Kent Williams from the original cast, now Deputy Mayor. This series was still hard-boiled but a little more tired and conventional.

Midnight Caller

(US TV series, 1988–91, 61+ episodes)
Creator: Richard Diello. **Producers:** Robert Singer (executive); John F. Perry.
Directors: Many, including Thomas Carter, Larry Gross, Kevin Hooks, David Israel, Mimi Leder, Bradford May, James Quinn, Reynaldo Villalobos, Michael Zinberg, Randall Zisk.
Writers: Many, including Richard DiLello, David Israel, Julie Sayres, Robert Singer. Stephen Zito.
Starring: Gary Cole, Wendy Kilbourne/Lisa Eilbacher, Dennis Dun, Arthur Taxier, Peter Boyle.
A refreshingly different series, though the UK had seen something slightly similar in *Shoestring*. Jack Killian (Cole) was a former cop who accidentally killed his partner in a shoot-out. Horrified, and ostracized by most of his colleagues, he resigns and turns to drink but is pulled back from the pit by the stylish Devon King (Kilbourne) who owns a radio station. Killian hosts an all-night chat show, revealing an affinity with the minions of the night. His calls frequently involve people in trouble, sometimes from stalkers or killers, but often from a wider circle of social ills – child abuse, AIDS, lost children and so on. Killian's own childhood was unhappy from a broken home. His father, who had abandoned him as a child, reappears from time to time, trying to come to terms with his son. Sometimes the show went out of its way to be controversial. "The Execution of John Saringo" by Richard DiLello concerns the final hours of a prisoner on death row whilst "Blues for Mr Charlie" by Thania St John involves America's gun laws. A moody, atmospheric series, it was original and provocative.

Midsomer Murders

(UK TV series, 1997–*current*, 18 + episodes)
Creator: Caroline GRAHAM. **Producers:** Betty True-May, Betty Willingdale.
Directors: Several, including Moira Armstrong, Peter Cregeen, Jeremy Silbertson, Peter Smith, Baz Taylor.
Writers: Caroline Graham, Anthony Horowitz, Douglas Livingstone, Chris Russell, Douglas Watkinson, Hugh Whitmore.
Starring: John Nettles, Daniel Casey, Jane Wymark, Laura Howard.
A traditional English country-village mystery series, with frequently macabre murders and motives, based on Caroline Graham's novels and which took over the cozy nook left by the *Miss Marple* series. John Nettles, formerly of *Bergerac*, plays the easy-going family man D.C.I. Tom Barnaby, who lives in style and comfort in the Heart of England, but who has to cope with eccentric villagers and a constant undercurrent of menace. The series is light-hearted and excellent at what it purports to be.

Daniel Casey plays Barnaby's impetuous sergeant, Gavin Troy. The two-hour slot allows for lots of atmosphere plus an explanation with flashbacks at the end in case anyone dozed off.

Miller's Crossing

(1990, US, 115 minutes)
Director: Joel Coen. **Producer:** Ethan Coen.
Screenplay: Joel & Ethan Coen.
Starring: Gabriel Byrne, Jon Polito, Albert Finney, Marcia Gay Harden, John Turturro.
This is the Coen Brothers on top form. A tribute to the gangster movies of the Prohibition era, it both transcends its genre and epitomizes all that is representative of the field. Tom Reagan (Byrne) falls in love with Verna (Harden), the mistress of his boss, the politician Leo (Finney). This becomes a catalyst in the gang war that simmers and erupts between Leo and Mobster Casper (Polito) who wants Verna's brother Bernie (Turturro) dead. The plot's like a well-trained whirlwind with the action leading towards the inevitable and eponymous denouement.

Mind to Kill

(UK TV series, 1995–*current*, 13 + episodes)
Producer: Peter Edwards (executive), Mike Parker, Ed Thomas.
Writers: Several, including David Joss Buckley, D.T. Caballo
Starring: Philip Madoc, Gillian Elisa, Sharon Morgan, Ffion Wilkins.
Unusual for UK TV, this two-hourly series is produced in Wales and has been shown to international acclaim all over the world, but is hardly known in England, where it is broadcast on Channel 5 and Sky One. It stars Philip Madoc as the gritty but humorous DCI Noel Bain, whose bold and solid exterior is inwardly haunted by the death of his wife by a drunken driver. Bain endeavours to raise his daughter (Wilkins) who, in the latest series, has become a "rookie" constable. This series pulls no punches in its brutal portrayal of crime and its social roots, or in its realism in police detection. Bain does not always solve his cases easily, quite often with events taking over and Bain being swept along striving to stay in control, but he remains methodical and determined.

Moonlighting

(US TV series, 1985–89, 67 episodes)
Creator: Glenn Gordon Caron. **Producers:** Glenn Gordon Caron (executive); Jay Daniel.
Directors: Many, including Allan Arkush, Robert Butler, Dennis Dugan, Kevin Connor, Paul Krasny, Paul Lynch, Christian I. Nyby II, Chris Welch, Peter Werner.

Writers: Many, including Glenn Gordon Caron, Roger Director, Joe Gannon, James Kramer, Peter Silverman, Bruce Franklin Singer.
Starring: Cybill Shepherd, Bruce Willis, Allyce Beasley, Curtis Armstrong.
Maddie Hayes (Shepherd) is a model who, through the mismanagement of her accountant, has gone bust. She closes down various operations the accountant had set up but finds that one of them is a detective agency run by the quirky David Addison (Willis) and his eccentric receptionist Agnes (Beasley). Instead of closing it down Maddie decides to keep it going and, renamed the Blue Moon Detective Agency, it becomes a going concern. The appeal of the series was the will-they-won't-they relationship between Maddie and Addison, which not only ignited a sexual chemistry but led to some wonderful verbal exchanges. He lusted after her; she resisted – at least for two seasons. Their cases were all a bit odd. A client's secret designs being stolen by a psychic. Another woman claims to be a leprechaun and asks their help in finding a pot of gold. One night they each separately dream the solution to an unsolved 40-year-old murder case. Even Agnes sets out to solve the mystery of a haunted house to impress Bert Viola (Armstrong), their gofer. *Moonlighting* was definitely one of those oddball series that was fun while it lasted.

Murder Bag *see under* No Hiding Place

Murder Call

(Australian TV series, 1997–2000, 56 episodes)
Creator: Jennifer ROWE.
Producers: Hal McElroy, Kris Noble, Errol Sullivan.
Directors: Many, including Richard Jasek, Richard Sarell, Geoffrey Cawthorn, Ian Watson, Grant Brown, Ray Quint, Chris Martin-Jones.
Writers: Jennifer Rowe wrote most of the story-lines.
Starring: Lucy Bell, Peter Mochrie, Gary Day, Jennifer Kent, Glenda Linscott, Geoff Morell.
Australia's most successful police procedural series featuring homicide detectives Tessa Vance (Bell) and Steve Hayden (Mochrie). Initially antagonistic, the two gradually complement each other in which becomes a taut, dramatic series which takes full advantage of Australia's beautiful scenery and lifestyle. The story-lines were all highly original – a man found dead on a beach buried up to his neck in the sand, a man found dead in a zoo in a gorilla suit, and plenty of apparent but suspicious suicides. The show was cancelled after 48 episodes in August 1999 and the final eight were shown as a short series the following year. Rowe adapted two episodes into novels, *Deadline* (1997) and *Something Wicked* (1998).

Murder One

(US TV series, 1995–97, 31 episodes)
Creator: Steven Bochco, Charles H. Eglee, Channing Gibson.
Producers: Steven Bochco, Charles H. Eglee, Michael Fresco (executive); Marc Buckland, Ann Donahue, Joe Ann Fogle, Geoffrey Neigher.
Directors: Several, including Charles Haid, Michael Fresco, Adam Nimoy, Elodie Keene, Nancy Savoca.
Writers: Several, including Steven Bochco, Channing Gibson, Charles H. Eglee, Charles D. Holland, David Milch, Doug Palau.
Starring: Daniel Benzali, Michael Hayden, J.C. Mackenzie, Mary McCormack, Barbara Bosson, Gregory Itzin.
A bold experiment devised by TV genius Steven Bochco, the idea behind *Murder One* was to follow through one trial for an entire season, building on the public fascination for major real-life trials such as the O.J. Simpson case. The set up was the firm of Hoffman & Co. led by shaven-headed Theodore Hoffman (Benzali) and his team of young ambitious lawyers. The first case involved the defence of a selfish young film star accused of killing a young woman. It was complex, with many twists and turns and a surprise ending. Ratings, however, were not high, but a second series was attempted with a change of cast and dealing with three cases rather than one. Ratings did not recover, despite the critical acclaim of the series and it was eventually dropped, with the final case being run as a three-part mini-series, *Diary of a Serial Killer* (1997).

Murder 101

(1991, US, 100 minutes)
Director: Bill Condon.
Screenplay: Bill Condon, Roy Johanson.
Starring: Pierce Brosnan, Dey Young, Antoni Corone, Raphal Sbarge.
This TV movie stars a pre-Bond Pierce Brosnan as Charles Lattimore, an English professor who challenges his college pupils to write the perfect crime story and then finds himself as the intended victim. It may sound corny but the film is superbly directed with considerable suspense and packs quite a punch. Mystery fans voted it an Edgar award in 1992.

Murder, She Wrote

(US TV series, 1984–96, 261 episodes + 3 TV films)
Creators: Peter S. Fischer, Richard Levinson, William Link.
Producers: Peter S. Fischer, Richard Levinson (executive), Douglas Benton, Todd London, Angela Lansbury, Robert Van Scoyk.
Directors: Many, including John Astin, Chuck Bowman, Kevin Corcoran, Peter Crane, Walter Grauman, David Hemmings, Jerry Jameson, Michael J. Lynch, John Llewellyn Moxey.
Writers: Many, including Peter S. Fischer, Philip Gerson, Robert

Hamner, Bruce Lansbury, Donald Ross, Paul Savage, Tom Sawyer, Robert Van Scoyck, J. Michael Straczynski, Robert E. Swanson.
Starring: Angela Lansbury, Tom Bosley/Ron Masak, Michael Horton, William Windom, Richard Paul.
The consummate cozy, *Murder, She Wrote* oozed the inspiration of Agatha Christie, particularly the Miss Marple stories, with a dash of Ellery Queen. Jessica Fletcher (Lansbury) is a late middle-aged widow and best-selling writer of detective stories who lives in Cabot Cove, Maine. She has a wide circle of friends and contacts and invariably stumbles across a murder that only her astute mind can solve. The plots, as one would expect from the creators of *Columbo*, are often convoluted and constructed like puzzles and the fascination with the series is to try and solve the crime before Jessica. She is the only one continuing character in the series though there are frequent regulars, especially Dr Hazlitt (Windom), with whom she plays chess, her nephew Grady (Horton), the town's hopeless sheriff (Bosley/Masak) and the mayor, Sam Booth (Paul). In one episode, "Novel Connection" (1986), she even helped out Magnum (Tom Selleck). A few episodes included a scruffy but sharp Boston P.I., Harry McGraw (Jerry Orbach), and he earned a short-lived series of his own, *The Law and Harry McGraw* (1987–8). Since Cabot Cove could cope with only so many murders, after seven seasons Jessica moved to New York, where she taught criminology at university, returning to Cabot Cover at weekends. Since the series finished in 1996 Lansbury has played Fletcher in three TV specials, *South by Southwest* (1997), *A Story to Die For* (2000) and *The Last Free Man* (2001). The series won an American Mystery Award in 1989, an Anthony in 1986 and the "Deadly Lady" won an Edgar in 1985. The series encouraged several spin-off books. James ANDERSON wrote three novels: *The Murder of Sherlock Holmes* (1985), *Hooray for Homicide* (1985), *Lovers and Other Killers* (1986). David Deutsch wrote *Murder in Two Acts* (UK 1986). Donald Bain, writing under the name Jessica Fletcher, wrote *Gin and Daggers* (1989; rev'd 2000), *Manhattans and Murder* (1994), *Rum and Razors* (1995), *Brandy and Bullets* (1995), *Martinis and Murder* (1995), *A Deadly Judgment* (1996), *A Palette for Murder* (1996), *The Highland Fling Murders* (1997), *Murder on the QEII* (1997), *Murder in Moscow* (1998), *A Little Yuletide Murder* (1998), *Murder at the Powderhorn Ranch* (1999), *Knock 'em Dead* (1999), *Trick or Treachery* (2000), *Blood on the Vine* (2001), *Murder in a Minor Key* (2001). There is a complete guide to the series, *The Unofficial Murder, She Wrote Casebook* (1997) by James Robert, three anthologies of stories inspired by the series, *Murder, They Wrote* (1997), *Murder, They Wrote II* (1998) and *More Murder, They Wrote* (1999) all edited by Elizabeth Foxwell and Martin H. Greenberg and there's even *The Murder, She Wrote Cookbook* by Tom Culver and Nancy Goodman Iland. What more could anyone ask for!

The Naked City

(US TV series, 1958–63, 138 episodes, b&w)

Creators: Characters Malvin Wald; developed for TV by Mark Hellinger and Stirling Silliphant.

Producers: Herbert B. Leonard (executive); Charles Russell.

Directors: Many, including William Beaudine, Leo Benedek, John Brahm, William Conrad, Walter Grauman, Buzz Kulik, Stuart Rosenberg, Jack Smight.

Writers: Many, including W.R. Burnett, Howard Rodman, Gene Roddenberry, Stirling Silliphant.

Starring: John McIntire/Horace McMahon, James Franciscus/Paul Burke, Harry Bellaver.

The original 1948 film *The Naked City* popularized the documentary approach to filming, with emphasis on location shooting, natural police dialogue and character-driven immediacy. The film, directed by Jules Dassin from a screenplay by Albert Maltz and Malvin Wald, followed police Lieutenant Dan Muldoon (Barry Fitzgerald) and detective Jimmy Halloran (Don Taylor) on their search for the murderer of a woman in a bathtub. The tag-line, "There are eight million stories in the naked city. This has been one of them," spilled over into the TV series where it was used to end every episode. The first season of half-hour episodes also had detectives Muldoon (McIntire) and Halloran (Franciscus) undertaking investigations in authentic police procedural style until the dramatic death of Muldoon in a car chase. The second season (now extended to hourly episodes) introduced new characters Lieutenant Mike Parker (McMahon) and detective Adam Flint (Burke) who, with Sergeant Frank Arcaro (Bellaver), originally a patrolman in the first series, were the mainstays thereafter. Like *Dragnet*, the series developed a strong affinity between the viewers and the police action on the street, especially with the determined no-nonsense drive of Parker. A collection of stories based on episodes from the series is *The Naked City* (1959) by Charles Einstein, whilst the original film screenplay by Wald and Maltz was published by Southern Illinois University Press in 1979.

The Name of the Rose

(1986, West German/Italian/French, 131 minutes)

Director: Jean-Jacques Annaud. **Producer:** Bernd Eichinger.

Screenplay: Andrew Birkin, Gerard Brach, Howard Franklin, Alain Godard from the novel by Umberto Eco.

Starring: Sean Connery, Christian Slater, F. Murray Abraham, Michael Lonsdale, Elya Baskin.

A wonderful brooding and atmospheric adaptation of Eco's superb novel about an investigation into a series of murders in a remote 14th-century monastery. Sean Connery plays the Holmes-like character of William of

Baskerville unravelling the labyrinthine and literary clues. What it lacks in the depth and complexity of the novel it more than makes up for in the grotesquerie and mood of the setting and characters.

Nash Bridges

(US TV series, 1996–*current*, 122 + episodes)
Creators: Don Johnson, Hunter S. Thompson.
Producers: Carlton Cuse, John Wirth (executives); Don Johnson, Jed Seidel.
Directors: Many, including Chuck Bowman, Colin Bucksey, David Carson, Jim Charleston, Tucker Gates, Robert Mandel, Adam Nimoy.
Writers: Many, including Carlton Cuse, Glenn Mazzara, Michael Norell, Alan Ormsby, Shawn Ryan, Reed Steiner, John Wirth.
Starring: Don Johnson, Richard Marin, Jaime P. Gomez, Jeff Perry, Daniel Roebuck.
Nash Bridges offers little that is new to the police detective drama, though its production is good and the characters are eminently watchable. Don Johnson plays Nash Bridges who, after the first season, is head of a Special Investigations Unit of the SFPD. Their headquarters from the second series is based on a boat moored off the Hyde Street pier. As usual with so many of these series Bridges is a dedicated cop with a disastrous home life – two failed marriages, a headstrong daughter, a lesbian sister and a hard-drinking, interfering father who is becoming senile. None of this stops Bridges having relationships with further women. His working life, as if it is not complicated enough going undercover (most of the time) trying to capture the city's low-life, also involves a former police partner, Joe Dominguez (Marin) who had left the force to become a P.I., but rejoins, though continuing to run his detective agency. As the series develops Bridges joins Dominguez in trying to build up a partnership in an agency. All this makes for a hectic, flash action series, a kind of *Miami Vice* meets *The Streets of San Francisco* – typical of the nineties.

Natural Born Killers

(1994, US, 119 minutes)
Director: Oliver Stone. **Producer:** Jane Hamsher, Don Murphy, Clayton Townsend.
Screenplay: David Veloz, Richard Rutowski, Oliver Stone from an original story by Quentin Tarantino.
Starring: Woody Harrelson, Juliette Lewis, Robert Downey Jr., Tommy Lee Jones, Tom Sizemore.
This excessively violent film, based to some degree on the notorious Starkweather murders in Nebraska in 1958, follows the murderous rampage of Mickey (Harrelson) and Mallory Knox (Lewis), who blast away anyone who gets in their way. Talk-show host Wayne Gale

(Downey) becomes so fascinated in their lives that his broadcasts turn them into folk heroes, hindering the efforts of Detective Jack Scagnetti (Sizemore) to capture them. The film, which was criticized by Quentin Tarantino because it had been taken beyond his original intentions, is an attack on the media for glorifying violence and carries its message with overpowering effect. Tarantino's original screenplay is available as *Natural Born Killers* (1996) as is the book-of-the-film by Jane Hamsher and John August (1994).

New Scotland Yard

(UK TV series, 1972–4, 45 episodes)
Producers: Jack Williams (executive), Rex Firkin.
Directors: Many, including Paul Annett, Bill Bain, Cyril Coke, David Cunliffe, Christopher Hodson, Oliver Horsbrugh, Bryan Izzard, James Oremerod, John Reardon, Bill Turner, Tony Wharmby.
Writers: Many, including Stuart Douglas, P.J. Hammond, Richard Harris, Tony Hoare, Don Houghton, John Lucarotti, Philip Martin, Robert Banks Stewart.
Starring: John Woodvine, John Carlisle, Michael Harris, Michael Turner, Clive Francis.
Building on the success of *Z-Cars* and *Softly, Softly*, London Weekend Television produced this one hour tough, realistic series portraying the investigations and difficult lives of the detectives in New Scotland Yard's CID. The series focused on two policemen, the po-faced but reasonable Detective Chief Superintendent John Kingdom (Woodvine) and Detective Inspector Alan Ward (Carlisle), the more ruthless, act-now-think-later member of the team. Ward's actions often get him into trouble. In one episode, "Nothing to Live For", he is demoted to uniformed sergeant on charges of misconduct, whilst in "Hoax" someone who has a vendetta against him seeks revenge. There was good interplay between the characters and the plots were inventive and original for their day. In the final series they were joined by two further detectives, Detective Chief Superintendent Clay (Turner) and Detective Sergeant Dexter (Francis) to allow for more rotation of characters.

New York Undercover

(US TV series, 1994–8, 89 episodes)
Producers: Dick Wolf, Andre Harrell, Don Kurt (executives); Kevin Arkadie, Arthur Forney, Peter McIntosh.
Directors: Many, including Jace Alexander, Norberto Barba, Oscar L. Costo, Frederick King Keller, Don Kurt, Michael Lange, Melanie Mayron, Timothy Van Patten, Anson Williams.
Writers: Many, including Kevin Arkadie, Gar Anthony HAYWOOD, Angel Dean Lopez, Shane Salerno.

Starring: Malik Yoba, Michael DeLorenzo, Patti D'Arbanville-Quinn, Jonathan LaPaglia, Fatima Faloye, Michael Michele, Lauren Velez.
A hard-hitting cop series with a strong ethnic mix. Set on the streets of Harlem it featured black detective J.C. Williams (Yoba) and his partner, Puerto Rican Eddie Torres (De Lorenzo). Their boss was the tough Lieutenant Cooper (D'Arbanville-Quinn). A white detective, Tommy McNamara (LaPaglia) joined in the third season. As the title suggests most of the operations were undercover dealing primarily with murder, drugs and vice. Much of the drive of the series were the characters private lives, especially the problems of J.C. who has a son by a former girlfriend, Chantal (Faloye), and is expecting another child by new girlfriend Sandra Gill (Michele). Tragically Gill is murdered at the end of the first season leaving J.C. emotionally disturbed. In the second season Eddie becomes romantically involved with new cop Nina Moreno (Velez) who is also shot but survives, though paralyzed. Add to this issues about AIDS and drugs and you have a series which is fraut with angst and high emotions. Unfortunately major changes in the fourth season, including locale and cast, neutered the series and it soon folded. At its height, though, *NYU* was an especially powerful and unsettling series.

Night Heat

(US/Canadian TV series, 1985–9, 96 episodes)
Producers: Robert Lantis (executive); Larry Gross, Sonny Jacobson, Andras Hamori, Jeff King.
Directors: Many, including Mario Azzopardi, George Kaczender, George Mendeluk, Jorge Mentesi, Gilbert M. Shilton.
Starring: Scott Hylands, Allan Royal, Jeff Wincott, Susan Hogan, Stephen Mendel, Eugene Clark.
"Night Heat" was the title of a newspaper column written by reporter Tom Kirkwood (Royal) who followed the activities of the graveyard shift cops in a large metropolitan city. The series was filmed in Toronto though the intention was that the setting should be some unnamed US conurbation. Unfortunately the Toronto sanitation department were too efficient at keeping the streets clean so it looks more Canadian than American. The series was certainly unusual for Canadian TV in that it tried to replicate the hard-hitting American style but whilst remaining a more routine, softer approach, in trying to follow more authentic police procedure. The two main cops were the experienced veteran Kevin O'Brien (Hylands) and his younger partner, the temperamental womanizer Frank Giambone (Wincott). The series was produced at a fast rate, running three episodes a night by the fourth season, and production value suffered and the series stopped soon after. Nevertheless it's a good example of an offbeat, unconventional series that tried to be upbeat and traditional.

Night Moves

(1975, US, 99 minutes)
Director: Arthur Penn. **Producer:** Robert M. Sherman.
Screenplay: Alan Sharp.
Starring: Gene Hackman, Jennifer Warren, Susan Clark, Edward Binns, James Woods, Melanie Griffith.
This is one of those films where the plot is deceptively simple but the world behind it so complex that one viewing is not enough to plumb the depths and understand the full implications. Harry Moseby (Hackman) is a tired and inexperienced P.I. with the inevitably tortured private life. He is hired by aging Hollywood actress Paula (Warren) to find her missing stepdaughter, played by Melanie Griffith in her first screen role. This he achieves relatively easily but soon events spiral out of control and Moseby finds himself way out of his depth and struggling to survive. Moseby's world collapses around him heading towards a climax that will leave you wondering and thinking about the film for a long time. Penn, who also directed *Bonnie & Clyde*, here pays tribute to the film *noir* of the forties.

Night of the Hunter

(1955, US, 92 minutes)
Director: Charles Laughton. **Producer:** Paul Gregory.
Screenplay: James Agee from the novel by Davis Grubb.
Starring: Robert Mitchum, Shelley Winters, Lillian Gish, Billy Chapin, James Gleason, Peter Graves.
Charles Laughton's only film as a director is an American classic and a masterpiece of the cinema thanks, primarily, to the astonishing screen presence of Robert Mitchum. Set in the 1930s, Harry Powell (Mitchum) is a crazed killer in prison on a minor charge who learns from condemned fellow prisoner (Graves) of the rough whereabouts of the loot from a robbery. When Powell is released he tracks down the prisoner's widow (Winters), pretending to be a preacher, but intent on finding the money. His true identity is given away by the tattooes of LOVE and HATE on his knuckles. In his frustration Powell kills Winters and pursues her children, who know where the money is hidden. Mitchum's menace in the lonely and vulnerable backwater home is tangible and the film is unforgettable. It was remade in 1991, directed by David Greene from a script by Edmond Stevens, but even with Richard Chamberlain as the preacher, this version is best forgotten.

No Hiding Place

(UK TV series, 1959–67, 236 episodes, b&w)
Creator: character, Glyn Davies.
Producers: Ray Dicks, Richard Matthews, Johnny Goodman, Peter Wiles, Geoffrey Nugus.

Directors: Many, including Jonathan Alwyn, Cyril Coke, Richard Doubleday, Ian Fordyce, Christopher Hodson, James Ormerod.
Writers: Many, including Terence Feely, Leon Griffiths, Roger Marshall, Terry Nation, Dennis Spooner.
Starring: Raymond Francis, Eric Lander, Johnny Briggs, Sean Caffrey.
No Hiding Place was the end result of two earlier series that had featured the character of Superintendent Lockhart of New Scotland Yard, played with efficient authority by Raymond Francis. The first series was *Murder Bag* (1957–9; 55 episodes), an early attempt at exploring forensic science. Each week Lockhart was assigned a case and took with him his well-equipped murder bag with which he gathered the evidence and undertook detailed analysis. After two seasons the series was revamped as *Crime Sheet* (1959; 17 episodes), another half-hourly series. Lockhart had been promoted to Chief Superintendent and his remit broadened to cover all kinds of major crime. The success of this series caused Associated Rediffusion Television to develop the character further and the hour-long *No Hiding Place* was born. Lockhart had various assistants, best known amongst them being Sergeant Harry Baxter (Lander), a clever and aspiring young detective who played an excellent foil against Lockhart's hard-nosed experience. Baxter was later given a fairly mundane series of his own, *Echo Four-Two* (1961), which ran for ten episodes before being curtailed by an actors' strike, with no great desire to revive it. *No Hiding Place*, on the other hand, was so popular that when it was dropped in 1965 the public protest was such that it was restored for another two seasons. By the end of it Francis had played Lockhart for ten years and 307 episodes, the longest-running in the world at that time, and still amongst the top ten. The main drawback of the series, which covered a wide range of crimes, was that it was broadcast live, and the stresses of a weekly schedule led to frequent pauses due to forgotten lines, but this was usually forgiven by the viewer for the fascination with each week's story-line.

No Way to Treat a Lady

(1968, US, 108 minutes)
Director: Jack Smight. **Producer:** Sol C. Siegel.
Screenplay: John Gay from the novel by William GOLDMAN.
Starring: Rod Steiger, Lee Remick, George Segal, Eileen Heckart.
One of the few examples of a crime spoof that works, thanks to clever direction, a good script from Goldman's early novel, and a vehicle where Steiger's OTT form of acting works to a treat. Steiger plays Christopher Gill, a serial strangler who takes on various disguises as he works his way through his victims, causing total confusion for hen-pecked detective "Mo" Brummel (Segal).

North by Northwest

(1959, US, 136 minutes)
Producer/Director: Alfred Hitchcock.
Screenplay: Ernest Lehman.
Starring: Cary Grant, Eva Marie Saint, James Mason, Leo G. Carroll.
One of the great chase suspense thrillers. Roger Thornhill (Grant) is a businessman who is mistaken as a spy and pursued across America by enemy agents culminating in the classic scene on Mount Rushmore. Hitchcock uses all his tricks of the trade and puts them to good use in a film longer than usual for him and which does start to pall. Nevertheless the film won an Edgar award in 1960 and Ernest Lehman was nominated for an Oscar for his screenplay.

N.Y.P.D. Blue

(US TV series, 1993–*current*, 182 + episodes)
Creator: Steven Bochco, David Milch, Gregory Hoblit.
Producers: Steven Bochco, David Milch, Burton Armus, Robert J. Doherty, Ted Mann, David Mills.
Directors: Many, including Paris Barclay, Kathy Bates, Donna Deitch, Elodie Keene, Adam Nimoy, Randall Zisk.
Writers: Many, including Ann Biderman, Steven Bochco, Rosemary Breslin, Bill Clark, Larry Cohen, Channing Gibson, Charles H. Eglee, David Milch.
Starring: Dennis Franz, David Caruso/Jimmy Smits, James McDaniel, Nicholas Turturro, Sharon Lawrence.
Regarded by many as the premier TV cop series, *N. Y.P.D. Blue* was really the first to explore adult issues within an ensemble production already developed in programmes like *Hill Street Blues*, bringing to it the emotion and drama developed in such non-crime sophisticated soap series as *thirtysomething*. Set in New York's 15th Precinct, *N. Y.P.D. Blue* follows the lives, loves, careers and fates of a wide cross-section of cops. Developed by Steven Bochco and David Milch, both from *Hill Street Blues*, ensured the series had strong characters with many continuing story-threads to attract the "soap" audience, and consequently introducing many romantic elements, but also interlaced tense dramatic content. It was a formula Bochco had used in many preceding series, and this time the selection of characters and actors brought it to a finely tuned bludgeon. The chief character is Detective Andy Sipowicz (Franz) originally partnered by John Kelly (Caruso) but, in the second season, when Caruso left under a cloud, by Bobby Simone (Smits). All have tortured lives. Sipowicz, trying to cope with the work, had turned to drink and women and was trying to regain control. Simone's first wife had died. He has a relationship with an alcoholic, then his reputation becomes tarnished as a bent cop, and finally he has heart failure. *N. Y.P.D. Blue* is

a series which is probably better known for its adult sex content than for its crime elements – after all it is still a fairly standard police procedural, with undercover cops, drug busts, murders, sieges and the usual fare of city law enforcement. But *N.Y.P.D. Blue* became headline news for its nude scenes, its gay relationships, its approach to drugs, alcoholism and racist issues. With high production values and a strong cast the series won six Emmy awards in its first season (out of a record-breaking 26 nominations). Episodes also won Edgar awards in 1994, 1995 and 1996. Books based on the series include *NYPD Blue: Blue Beginning* (1995) and *NYPD Blue: Blue Blood* (1997), both by Max Allan COLLINS. There is also a book about the series, *True Blue: The Real Stories Behind N.Y.P.D. Blue* (1995) by David Milch and Bill Clark.

The Onion Field

(1979, US, 126 minutes)
Director: Harold Becker. **Producer:** Walter Coblenz.
Screenplay: Joseph WAMBAUGH.
Starring: John Savage, James Woods, Franklyn Seales, Ted Danson, Christopher Lloyd.
Joseph Wambaugh kept a tighter leash on this film after his disappointment with *The Choirboys*. The result swings the other way and though it is more authentic it remains an equally depressing film about the psychological hell of police work. It is based on a true incident in 1963. Officer Karl Hettinger (Savage) and his partner Ian Campbell (Danson) are kidnapped by two hijackers (Woods and Seales) they had tried to arrest. Campbell is murdered and the story follows Hettinger's anguish and mental decline. It's a powerful film that clearly states its message, but without any remitting balance it becomes an exercise in violence.

Out of Sight

(1998, US, 117 minutes)
Director: Steven Soderbergh. **Producer:** Danny DeVito, Michael Shamberg, Stacey Sher.
Screenplay: Scott Frank from the novel by Elmore LEONARD.
Starring: George Clooney, Jennifer Lopez, Dennis Farina, Ving Rhames, Michael Keaton, Samuel L. Jackson, Don Cheadle.
A greater sophistication in acting, directing and cinema audiences means that romantic crime capers which, in the seventies, were fun but a little twee, are now more exciting and suspenseful, blending the two genres seamlessly. Bank robber Jack Foley (Clooney) holds Federal Marshal Karen Sisco (Lopez) hostage when he escapes from prison. Their relationship develops, Sisco determined to recapture Foley, but Foley is assured he will escape. The sexual tension between them would fry eggs but this adds to rather than detracts from the overall atmosphere of the

film. The film won the Edgar award in 1999 and even picked up an Oscar nomination for its sharp editing.

The Outfit

(1973, US, 103 minutes)
Director: John Flynn. **Producer:** Carter De Haven Jr.
Screenplay: John Flynn from the novel by Donald E. WESTLAKE.
Starring: Robert Duvall, Joe Don Baker, Karen Black, Robert Ryan, Joanna Cassidy.
An excellent adaptation of one of Donald Westlake's early Parker novels though, as in *Point Blank*, his name is changed to protect the copyright. Here he's Earl Macklin (Duvall) who, after being released from prison for bank robbery, sets out to take revenge on whoever murdered his brother. He had not known at the time that the bank he'd robbed was owned by the Mob. With the help of his friend, Cody (Baker), the trail leads to ageing and insecure Mob leader Mailer, portrayed with cruel menace by Robert Ryan. The film is played straight, its tension carried by the depth of and relationship between the characters. All the villains are villains, including the brutal and demanding Macklin, yet the audience's sympathies are drawn to the individual versus the organization. For most of the film you watch the irresistable versus the immovable and if the final moments don't quite live up to the start it still packs a powerful punch. It should not be confused with the 1993 film of the same name, which is a weak effort about an undercover operation against the Mob.

Owen Marshall, Counselor at Law

(US TV series, 1971–4, 70 episodes)
Creators: David Victor, Jerry McNeely. **Producer:** David Victor (executive).
Directors: Several, including Harry Falk, Steven Spielberg.
Writers: Several, including Richard Bluel, Jerry McNeely, David Victor, Shimon Wincelberg.
Starring: Arthur Hill, Lee Majors, Christine Matchett, David Soul.
Owen Marshall (Hill) was an ageing and always compassionate defence attorney working in a small town in souther California. This popular series strove for accuracy and authenticity in its portrayal of a wide variety of cases, and even won several public service awards. Marshall's main junior partner was Jess Brandon played by Lee Majors just at the time he was also appearing in *The Six Million Dollar Man*. The series also saw early appearances from David Soul and Sharon Gless, plus an early piece of directing from Steven Spielberg on the fourth episode, "Eulogy for a Wide Receiver." The series was made by the same team as produced the medical drama *Marcus Welby* and on two occasions episodes were linked. The episode "Victim in Shadow" (1972) was nominated for an Edgar.

Peeping Tom

(1960, UK, 109 minutes)
Producer/Director: Michael Powell. **Screenplay:** Leo Marks.
Starring: Carl Boehm, Anna Massey, Maxine Audley, Moira Shearer, Shirley Ann Field.
At the time this film seemed to cost Michael Powell, one of Britain's most innovative and courageous directors, his career and reputation, as he tried to push British film-making into the present day. Now it is regarded as one of Britain's most daring and certainly most notorious films. It is the story of Mark Lewis (Boehm), a film technician whose psyche has been scarred by his father's experiments, and who becomes the ultimate voyeur, filming the final agonies of his murder victims. Believed excessive at the time the film is, in fact, remarkably restrained, Powell leaving far more to the imagination, but because the viewer is drawn into Lewis's voyeuristic pleasure the film shocks and disturbs. Released before *Psycho*, it was one of the first to explore the mind and origins of the psychopath.

The Persuaders

(UK TV series, 1971–2, 24 episodes)
Creator: Robert S. Baker. **Producers:** Robert S. Baker, Terry Nation, Johnny Goodman.
Directors: Roy Ward Baker, Basil Dearden, David Greene, Val Guest, Sidney Hayers, James Hill, Gerald Mayer, Roger Moore, Leslie Norman.
Writers: Tony Barwick, Walter Black, Brian Clemens, Val Guest, Terence Feely, Milton S. Gelman, Donald James, Harry H. Junkin, John Kruse, Terry Nation, Michael Pertwee, Tony Williamson, Peter Yeldham.
Starring: Roger Moore, Tony Curtis, Laurence Naismith.
This slick, stylish and utterly vacuous series was designed to sell to the United States, but the US could not see its appeal – its approach being too British – and as a result the series was cancelled. It featured Roger Moore as the rich aristocrat Lord Brett Sinclair and Tony Curtis as the Brooklyn street-kid who became a self-made millionaire, Danny Wilde. The two are playboys, brought together by Judge Fulton (Naismith), who employs them to solve crimes around the glamour spots of Europe. The crimes are always facile, the main joy of the series being the interplay between Curtis and Moore which, at times, was genuinely funny. Otherwise the series relied on the eye-candy of its attractive female stars who included Susan George, Anna Palk, Catherine Schell, Kate O'Mara, Joan Collins and Suzy Kendall.

Peter Gunn

(US TV series, 1958–61, 114 episodes, b&w)
Creator/Producer: Blake Edwards.
Directors: Several, including Robert Altman, Alan Crosland Jr., Blake Edwards, Lamont Johnson, Gene Reynolds, Boris Sagal.
Writers: Several, including Tony & Steffi Barrett, Blake Edwards, George & Gertrude Fass, Vicki Knight, Lewis Reed.
Starring: Craig Stevens, Lola Albright, Herschel Bernardi, Hope Emerson/Minerva Urecal.
Laid back and cool, Peter Gunn (Stevens) was one of the new breed of hip, sophisticated P.I.s that began to proliferate on TV in the jazz-pop-beatnik era of the late fifties. *Johnny Staccato* was another, largely modelled on Gunn. Gunn had offices in fashionable uptown Los Angeles though spent a lot of his time at a jazz club run by Mother (Emerson; later Urecal) where Gunn had a passion for singer Edie Hart (Albright). His friend on the force was Lieutenant Jacoby (Bernardi). Shows were quick and stylish, action punctuated by jazz themes by Henry Mancini who also provided the hit theme music. Blake Edwards (of *Pink Panther* fame) used the success of the series as his stepping stone to the big screen and he later made a movie of the character, *Gunn* (1967), which he scripted with William Peter Blatty, with Stevens again playing Gunn. Edwards returned to the character twenty years later with a TV pilot, *Peter Gunn* (1989), with Peter Strauss as an even cooler and squeaky-clean P.I. The hoped-for new series did not follow. A novel based on the original series was *Peter Gunn* (1960) by Henry Kane.

Petrocelli

(US TV series, 1974–6, 45 episodes plus pilot)
Creators: Sidney J. Furie, Harold Buchman, E. Jack Newman.
Producers: Thomas L. Miller, Edward J. Milkis (executives), Ralph Riskin (associate), Leonard Katzman, Lou Morheim.
Directors: Several, including Richard Donner, Leonard Katzman, Russ Mayberry, Vincent McEveety, Allen Resiner, Don Weis.
Writers: Several, including Harold Buchman, Robert C. Dennis, Sidney J. Furie, Leonard Katzman, Edward J. Lasko, Thomas L. Miller, Mann Rubin.
Starring: Barry Newman, Susan Howard, Albert Salmi, David Huddleston.
The character of Tony Petrocelli first appeared in the film *The Lawyer* (1968), where he is a hot shot big-city defence attorney who takes on the case of an uncooperative client accused of murdering his wife. It was based on the notorious Dr Sam Sheppard trial in 1954. For the series, director Sidney J. Furie transplanted Petrocelli and his wife from New

York to the southwest fictional town of San Remo, which is not used to his big-city ways. Petrocelli lives in a camper and is building his own house though never seems to get beyond the main wall. One of the intriguing gimmicks of the series was rerunning scenes from the viewpoint of various witnesses showing how memories varied. Petrocelli was a likeable character, always congratulating people on their work. After a successful ninety-minute pilot the series ran for a popular first season (especially in Britain) but was curtailed before the end of the second season with the final few episodes not being shown.

Plein Soleil *see under* The Talented Mr Ripley

Picket Fences

(US TV series, 1992–6, 89 episodes)
Creators: David E. Kelley, Michael Pressman.
Producers: David E. Kelley (executive), Mark B. Perry, Tracy Fetterolf, Alice West.
Directors: Several, including James Frawley, Michael Lange, Joe Napolitano, Tom Skerritt.
Writers: Primarily David E. Kelley with Mark B. Perry.
Starring: Tom Skerritt, Kathy Baker, Holly Marie Combs, Justin Shenkarow, Lauren Holly, Ray Walston.
Fresh from *L.A. Law*, *Picket Fences* was David E. Kelley's first series as writer-producer and it allowed him full rein for his quirky and often surreal imagination. On the surface the small town of Rome, Wisconsin, is quaint, picturesque and normal – typified by the pattern of picket fences around all the houses. But below the surface the town is like no other this side of Twin Peaks. The oddest things happen. There is the serial bather who creeps into people's homes and takes a bath. There's the student who brings a severed hand into class, or the small-time actor who is killed by a lethal injection of nicotine. As he would later develop to extremes in *Ally McBeal*, Kelley revels in the eccentric and bizarre, the foibles of the human condition, and always the just possible. Somehow local sheriff Jimmy Brock has to investigate all these oddities (not helped by his equally quirky family) and Judge Bone (Walston) will make his judgement each episode. It's a fascinating series where Kelley uses the absurd to heighten awareness of deep-down real human issues. The public weren't quite ready for it and although the series was a critical success, winning the Emmy award for Outstanding Drama in 1993 and 1994, it seldom rose high in the ratings and was dropped.

Point Blank

(1967, US, 92 minutes)
Director: John Boorman. **Producer:** Judd Bernard, Robert Chartoff.

Screenplay: Alexander Jacobs, David & Rafe Newhouse from the novel *The Hunter* by Richard Stark (Donald E. WESTLAKE).
Starring: Lee Marvin, Angie Dickinson, Keenan Wynn, Carroll O'Connor, Lloyd Bochner, John Vernon, Sharon Acker.
One of the crucial turning points in modern cinema, *Point Blank* signalled a change also being developed by Don Siegel, for more realistic, violent, gritty films peopled with strong, vengeful characters. *Point Blank* was adapted from the first of Donald E. Westlake's Parker novels. In the film the character has become Walker (Marvin) who, after he and his partner Mal (Vernon) rob a Mob shipment, is double-crossed, shot and left for dead in the deserted Alcatraz prison. But Walker survives and the film follows his relentless quest for revenge. The film benefits from direction by a Briton in America, as it uses the American cityscape in an almost alienist, futuristic sense as would later become Ridley Scott's trademark. Walker is representative of a fifties gangster being reborn into the modern world and it was through this rebirth that Boorman helped create the modern thriller.

Police Story

(US TV series, 1973–7, 84 episodes)
Creator: Joseph WAMBAUGH.
Producers: Stanley Kallis, David Gerber (executives), Liam O'Brien, Christopher Morgan, Hugh Benson, Larry Broder.
Directors: Many, including Edward M. Abroms, Corey Allen, Marvin J. Chomsky, Vince Edwards, David Friedkin, Tony Lo Bianco, Don Medford, John Llewellyn Moxey, Leo Penn, Seymour Robbie.
Writers: Many, including Eric Bercovici, Larry Brody, Morton S. Fine, David Friedkin, Michael Mann, E. Jack Neuman, Sy Salkowitz, Joseph Wambaugh.
Police Story was an anthology series with no regular recurring characters. It was created by Joseph Wambaugh to depict a more realistic portrayal of police life rather than the more glamorous series of the sixties, and it presented it in all its forms, from the mundane to the tragic, in a semi-documentary style. The series emphasized the pressure on the police and the effect on the individual's psychology. It also considered racial prejudice within the force. The series spawned two further series of their own. *Policewoman* (see entry) arose from the episode "The Gamble", whilst "The Return of Joe Forrester", with Lloyd Bridges, gave rise to *Joe Forrester* (1975–6; 13 episodes). This last was about an old-style friendly big-city cop who had developed good neighbourhood relationships, an idea close to Wambaugh's heart. Bizarrely the series was short-lived because it was competing against Wambaugh's other TV series, *The Blue Knight*. Two years in a row, episodes from *Police Story* won the Edgar award, and it was nominated for the Emmy during each year of its run.

There were occasional *Police Story* specials, ninety- or a hundred-minute episodes instead of the usual hour. In 1987 the title was revived for a series of occasional TV movies, reworking original scripts, usually from these longer episodes. These titles included *The Freeway Killings* (1987), *The Watch Commander* (1988), *Burnout* (1988), *Cop Killer* (1988), *Gladiator School* (1988) and *Monster Manor* (1988).

Police Surgeon

(UK TV series, 1960, 12 episodes)
Producers: Julian Bond, Leonard White.
Directors: Primarily Don Leaver, also Robert Hartford-Davis, John Knight, James Ormerod, Guy Verney.
Writers: Primarily Julian Bond, also Bill MacIllwraithe, W.F. Woodlands, Richard Harris.
Starring: Ian Hendry, John Warwick, Ingrid Hafner.
This short series featured Ian Hendry in his first TV rôle as Geoffrey Brent, a young police surgeon assigned to the Bayswater police division. Inevitably (as in his distant spiritual successor, *Dangerfield*), Brent became more deeply involved in the crimes, turning investigator himself at times, though other episodes concentrated purely on the medical side. The series failed to capture an audience and after twelve weeks it was dropped and entirely revamped as *The Avengers* (1961–9; 161 episodes). The first season of *The Avengers* was not the eccentric espionage series for which it became renowned but a more straightforward crime series. Ian Hendry was now recast as Dr David Keel, a doctor whose fiancée, Peggy (Catherine Woodville), is gunned down in the street. Keel teams up with suave and sophisticated undercover agent John Steed (Patrick MacNee) in their search for the gang. That story-line however was soon taken over by Steed's other rôle as a spy-smasher and even before the end of the first series some of the episodes, especially those by Brian Clemens, Terence Feely and Dennis Spooner, indicated the direction the series would take into the bizarre and unusual. With season two (in September 1962) the character of Dr Keel was dropped and amongst Steed's new assistants was Cathy Gale (Honor Blackman). From hereon the series evolved into the eccentric adventure field, often bordering on science fiction rather than crime, and became a legend.

Police Woman

(US TV series, 1974–8, 92 episodes)
Creator: Robert E. Collins.
Producers: David Gerber (executives), Edward DeBlasio, Abram S. Ginnes, George Lehr, Douglas Benton.
Directors: Many, including Corey Allen, Douglas Benton, Charles S. Dubin, Michael Mann, John Newland, Robert Vaughn.

Writers: Many, including Douglas Benton, Larry Brody, Jack M. Casey, Robert E. Collins, Jackson Gillis, Chester Krumholz, Dan Ullman.
Starring: Angie Dickinson, Earl Holliman, Ed Bernard, Charles Dierkop.
Sergeant Suzanne "Pepper" Anderson (Dickinson) had first appeared as policewoman Lisa Beaumont in "The Gamble" episode of *Police Story*, broadcast in March 1974. This featured all the same characters who would reappear in *Policewoman* except Lieutenant Bill Crowley (Holliman), Anderson's boss. Anderson was an undercover agent in the criminal conspiracy unit of the LAPD. This frequently required her posing as a hooker, or a gangster's moll or even a stripper – anything to take advantage of her looks. The series concentrated on action rather than the psychological aspects of its parent series, but Dickinson brought more than glamour to the rôle, depicting a strong, determined, intelligent woman every bit the equal of her male colleagues. The series paved the way for *Cagney & Lacey*. Unfortunately Dickinson's follow-up series, *Cassie & Company* (1982; 13 episodes), in which she played a P.I. who had taken over the business from a retired partner, was less successful.

The Practice

(US TV series, 1997–*current*, 110 + episodes)
Creator/Producer: David E. Kelley.
Directors: Many, including Allan Arkush, James Frawley, Elodie Keen, Robert Mandel, Joe Napolitano, Adam Nimoy, Michael Pressman, Rick Rosenthal, Oz Scott, Michael Shultz, Michael Zinberg.
Writers: Many, including David E. Kelley, Adam Armus, Jill Goldsmith, Alfonso Moreno, Catherine Stribling, Frank Renzulli, Kay Forster, Samantha Howard Corbin, Marc Guggenheim.
Starring: Dylan McDermott, Steve Harris, Lisa Gay Hamilton, Michael Badalucco, Kelli Williams, Camryn Manheim, Lara Flynn Boyle.
This series flies by heckle-power. There's never a moment's peace and seldom a moment when someone isn't shouting or struggling to be heard. The enterprising and endlessly challenging David E. Kelley, who had worked on *L.A. Law*, turned the format round and instead of a prestigious, rich firm looked at a small, on-the-edge, struggling-to-learn firm who takes on any business to pay the bills. Head of the firm is the handsome, chisel-jawed Bobby Donnell (McDermott) who is forever trying to do deals with the D.A. (Boyle) to reduce sentences for offenders. Frequently they find themselves defending the guilty and questioning the ethics. Other times they struggle to help the innocent where everything is stacked against them. Kelley, who was himself a practising attorney, ducks and dives through legal loopholes and where he can't find any creates ones of his own. Always inventive, Kelley holds the law up to scrutiny and fires as many holes through it as an hourly episode can take.

Their work leaves little time for private lives, yet these are glimpsed through the whirlwind of legal chaos. The series and the actors have won several Emmy Awards and has become firmly established as one of the best of all legal dramas.

Presumed Innocent

(1990, US, 127 minutes)
Director: Alan J. Pakula. **Producer:** Sydney Pollack, Mark Rosenberg.
Screenplay: Alan J. Pakula and Frank R. Pierson from the novel by Scott TUROW.
Starring: Harrison Ford, Brian Dennehy, Raul Julia, Bonnie Bedelia, Greta Scacchi.
Although *Presumed Innocent* is a first-class legal drama, it shows the problems of adapting a complex, highly focused novel to the screen, and it is worthwhile reading the book and watching the film to see the different perspectives. Rusty Sabich (Ford) is an attorney who becomes a murder suspect when a colleague (Scacchi) with whom he had had an affair, is raped and murdered. Whereas the novel is able to explore, through Sabich, the psychological stress and nightmare of the situation, the film is forced to concentrate on the investigation to clear (or convict) Sabich. Both are equally fascinating, and you pays-your-money and takes-your-choice. The film won an American Mystery Award and an Anthony in 1991.

Prime Suspect

(UK TV series, 1991–96, 11 episodes)
Creator: Lynda LA PLANTE.
Producers: Sally Head (executive); Don Leaver, Paul Marcus, Brian Park, Lynn Horsford.
Directors: Christopher Menaul, John Strickland, David Drury, Sara Pia, John Madden, Philip David.
Writers: Lynda La Plante, Allan Cubitt, Paul Billing, Eric Deacon, Guy Hibbert, Guy Andrews.
Starring: Helen Mirren, John Benfield, Tom Bell, Jack Ellis, Richard Hawley.
Winner of three Emmy awards and two BAFTAs for outstanding mini-series, *Prime Suspect* took television by storm. Helen Mirren plays the determined, obsessive but vulnerable DCI (later Superintendent) Jane Tennison who overcomes prejudice within the force, especially from such oldtimers as DS Bill Otley (Bell), to prove her abilities in a series of difficult cases. Initially in the Met, and subsequently transferred to the Soho vice squad and later to Manchester, Tennison wrestles with her own uncertainties and weaknesses through a variety of high profile crimes ending in a case of police corruption. A combination of excellent scripts, brilliant acting and the forceful character of Mirren herself (who also won

an Emmy and three BAFTAs for her performances), made this one of the major crime series of the 1990s. The series also won two Edgars, an Anthony award and an American Mystery Award

Prince of the City

(1981, US, 167 minutes)
Director: Sidney Lumet. **Producer:** Burtt Harris.
Screenplay: Jay Presson Allen and Sidney Lumet from a book by Robert Daley.
Starring: Treat Williams, Jerry Orbach, Richard Foronjy, Kenny Marino.
If this film had been an hour shorter it might have shifted from being great to superb. There is a lot to tell, but the story unravels slowly and the tension is lost until the final part. What makes this true story complex is the constant uncertainty. Daniel Ciello (Williams) is a New York cop who turns informer about police corruption provided he does not have to betray his partners. He soon finds matters getting way over his head and the film's length is used to explore the labyrinthine connections between the police and the underworld. Lumet won the New York Film Critics Circle award for his direction and the film was nominated for an Edgar award.

Prizzi's Honor

(1985, US, 129 minutes)
Director: John Huston. **Producer:** John Foreman.
Screenplay: Richard Condon, Janet Roach, from the novel by Richard Condon.
Starring: Jack Nicholson, Kathleen Turner, Anjelica Huston, Robert Loggia, John Randolph, William Hickey.
A black comedy that presses all the right buttons. Charley Partanna (Nicholson), a grandson of the Godfather, is a none-too-bright hit-man for the Mob. Although engaged to Maerose Prizzi (Huston) he breaks that off when he falls in love with Irene Walker (Turner), a freelance assassin. The fun comes from each being commissioned to murder the other. John Huston just manages to stop a humorous pastiche tripping into parody and the witty dialogue, especially between Partanna and Prizzi, is golden. The film was nominated for an Oscar in several categories and Anjelica Huston won for Best Supporting Actress.

The Professionals

(UK TV series, 1977–83, 57 episodes)
Creator: Brian Clemens.
Producers: Brian Clemens, Albert Fennell (executive); Sidney Hayers, Raymond Menmuir.

Directors: Many, including Douglas Camfield, Charles Crichton, Martin Campbell, Tom Clegg, Chris Burt, David Wickes, Raymond Menmuir, Dennis Abey, Francis Megahy.
Writers: Many, including Brian Clemens, Dennis Spooner, Roger Marshall, Tony Barwick.
Starring: Lewis Collins, Martin Shaw, Gordon Jackson, Steve Alder, Bridget Brice.
From the same stable as *The Avengers*, with many of the same writers working for *The Sweeney*, this series tried to combine a hard, fast action crime series with the mystique of covert operations but didn't quite score on all counts. William Bodie (Collins) and Ray Doyle (Shaw) work for George Cowley (Jackson) of CI5 – specializing in "Criminal Intelligence". Their purpose is to forestall crimes before they happen, especially terrorism. The strength of the series rested solely on the shoulders of the two leads. Bodie is a former SAS hero whilst Doyle is an ex-policeman. The two worked well together but the series had little "intelligence" content, shifting from one high-action scene to the next and frequently being criticized for its level of violence. One strong anti-racist episode, "The Klansman", was not broadcast. Although the series is fondly remembered it is more for Doyle and Bodie than for plots of any significance. Even so Brian Clemens saw fit to revive it as *CI5: The New Professionals* (1999; 13 episodes) with Edward Woodward in the Gordon Jackson rôle as Harry Malone. It had nothing new. The original series led to 16 spin-off novels written mostly by Kenneth Bulmer but with a few (marked RH) by Robert Holdstock, all under the alias of Ken Blake: *Hunter Hunted*, *Long Shot*, *Stake Out* and *Where the Jungle Ends* [RH] (all 1978), *Blind Run*, *Fall Girl* (both 1979), *Dead Reckoning*, *Hiding to Nothing* (both 1980), *Cry Wolf* [RH], *No Stone*, *Spy Probe* (all 1981), *Assassin!*, *Foxhole*, *Operation Susie* [RH], *The Untouchables* [RH] and *You'll Be All Right* [RH] (all 1982).

The Protectors

(UK TV series, 1972–4, 52 episodes)
Creator: Lew Grade. **Producers:** Gerry Anderson, Reg Hill.
Directors: Many, including Don Chaffey, Roy Ward Baker, John Hough, Michael Lindsay-Hogg, David Tomblin, Charles Crichton, Don Leaver, Robert Vaughn.
Writers: Many, including Terence Feely, Brian Clemens, Donald James, Tony Barwick, Sylvia Anderson, Dennis Spooner, Terry Nation, Robert Banks Stewart.
Starring: Robert Vaughn, Nyree Dawn Porter, Tony Anholt, Yasuko Nagazami, Anthony Chinn.
The Protectors wasn't so much a programme as a package. It was yet another attempt by Lew Grade to produce an identikit series that would

suit the American market. Having failed with *The Persuaders* this version was more successful, although that has little to do with the quality of the series or the adequate but scarcely original plots by Britain's factory of adventure scriptwriters. The Protectors were an independent crime-fighting team who jetted around Europe offering their services to whatever government needed them. They were Harry Rule (Vaughn), the cool, sophisticated American who operated from a high-tech London office, and had a martial-arts expert (Nagazami) as his au pair; Contessa di Contini (Porter), an English widow who lived in Rome; and Paul Buchet (Anholt) a stereotypical Frenchman. The series was all gloss and no undercoat, but like so many productions of its period, seemed adequate for the time.

Psycho

(1960, US, 108 minutes)
Producer/Director: Alfred Hitchcock.
Screenplay: Joseph Stefano from the novel by Robert BLOCH.
Starring: Anthony Perkins, Janet Leigh, Vera Miles, Martin Balsam, John Gavin.
Arguably everyone's classic shock movie and one where Hitchcock defies the rules and conventions. Audiences forget that the story begins with Marion Crane (Leigh) absconding with money and driving to meet her lover Sam (Gavin). Driving through the night in appalling weather she stops at a motel and meets Norman Bates (Perkins). A few moments later Crane is killed in the memorable shower scene, one of the most famous scenes in all movie history. Her car, complete with the stolen money, is pushed into a lake. Soon after the investigator who is pursuing her, Milton Arbogast (Balsam) is also murdered. In both cases it is suggested that Bates's maniacal mother is the murderer. It is only through the persistence of Crane's sister, Lila (Miles), that the crimes are solved and Bates's true madness emerges. Frequently parodied, and with an utterly pointless scene-by-scene remake in 1998, the original remains the seminal study of a mother-dominated psychopath, with a definitive performance by Perkins. Both Hitchcock and Janet Leigh were nominated for Oscars and the film won an Edgar award. The film eventually spawned three sequels. As sequels go they each have a certain merit, especially *Psycho II* (1983) which follows Bates's release from prison and his attempt to return to a normal life, but alas "Mother" refuses to lie down. Both Perkins and Miles reprise their roles and the film was nominated for an Edgar award. *Psycho III* (1986), directed by Perkins, is a pointless addition in which we find Bates falling in love with a suicidal nun. Perkins is still up to the rôle but the film falls into unoriginal pastiche. Finally *Psycho IV; the Beginning* (1990), scripted by Joseph Stefano, showed some originality in having Bates (still played by Perkins) recounting his childhood, with the young

Bates played by Henry Thomas, and exploring the relationship with his mother, played by Olivia Hussey. If *Psycho III* is ignored, the others make a satisfying trilogy. Best ignored is the TV movie *Bates Motel* (1987) directed by Richard Rothstein and intended as a pilot for a series that was thankfully never made.

Public Eye

(UK TV series, 1965–75, 87 episodes, first 28 b&w)
Creator: Roger Marshall, Anthony Marriott.
Producers: Lloyd Shirley, Robert Love (executives); Don Leaver, Richard Bates, John Bryce, Michael Chapman, Kim Mills.
Directors: Many, including Jonathan Alwyn, Laurence Bourne, Bill Bain, Piers Haggard, Don Leaver.
Writers: Many, including Julian Bond, Michael Chapman, Roger Marshall, Anthony Skene, Robert Banks Stewart, Jack Trevor Story, David Whittaker.
Starring: Alfred Burke, Ray Smith, Peter Childs.
Frank Marker (Burke) was a down-at-heel, rather sad, slightly seedy private enquiry agent who worked out of a shabby back-room in London (later he shifted to Birmingham and finally Brighton). His work, often for those far richer than he, brought him up against clients who lacked all moral fibre and frequently did the dirty on him. Marker even ended up in prison at one point for handling stolen jewellery even though he was only a go-between with an insurance company. Nevertheless Marker persevered because he felt the work he did meant something. The character was superbly betrayed by the melancholic Alfred Burke and it showed a far more realistic side to crime and the underside of life than the glitzy glamour of most US series then prevailing on TV.

Pulp Fiction

(1994, US, 154 minutes)
Director: Quentin Tarantino. **Producer:** Lawrence Bender.
Screenplay: Quentin Tarantino and Roger Avary.
Starring: John Travolta, Samuel L. Jackson, Uma Thurman, Bruce Willis, Harvey Keitel, Rosanna Arquette, Eric Stoltz, Christopher Walken, Tim Roth, Amanda Plummer.
This is one of those films that rewrites the rule-book, even more so than Tarantino's earlier *Reservoir Dogs*. Here the casual violence is packaged within a series of meaningful vignettes and sharp-witted dialogue that provide a moral depth and allow you to understand, if not necessarily accept, the action. The film is a tribute to the hard-boiled pulp stories of the thirties – Tarantino was originally going to call the film *Black Mask*, after the pulp magazine – but the intention is to showcase those stories within a modern-day pop culture. Tarantino weaves together three basic

story threads. In the first a Mobster, Vincent Vega (Travolta) has to look after his boss's irresponsible wife (Thurman), with inevitable consequences. In the second Butch Coolidge (Willis), a washed-up boxer tries to outwit the Mob by winning rather than throwing a fight. In the third two hit-men, Vega and Jules Winnfield (Jackson), find an assignment becomes messy and they call in a "cleaner" known as The Wolf (Keitel). The stories are shown out of real-time, so that the death of Vega in the middle episode comes as a major shock. The overall effect is exhilarating and turns hard-boiled into hard-core action. The film won both the Edgar and Anthony awards. Tarantino's screenplay, for which he won an Oscar, was published as *Pulp Fiction* (1994).

Purple Noon *see under* The Talented Mr Ripley

Quincy, M.E.

(US TV series, 1976–83, 148 episodes)
Creator: Glen Larson, Lou Shaw.
Producers: Glen Larson (executive); Robert F. O'Neil, Lou Shaw, Michael Star, Peter Thompson.
Directors: Many, including Georg Fenady, Alvin Ganzer, Rod Holcomb, Paul Krasny, Leslie H. Martinson, Ron Satlof, Daniel Petrie, E.W. Swackhamer.
Writers: Many, including Michael Braverman, Robert CRAIS, Sam Egan, Steve Greenberg, Jack Klugman, Mann Rubin, Michael Sloan, Jeri Taylor.
Starring: Jack Klugman, Robert Ito, Garry Walberg, Val Bisoglio, John S. Ragin, Joseph Roman.

Quincy (Klugman) – we never learn his first name though sharp-eyed viewers will know his initial is R. – is a medical examiner with the Los Angeles County Coroner's Office. His forensic expertise usually allows him to detect foul play when the police believe accidental death and his enthusiasm for determining the truth runs away with him. Each week he and his assistant, Sam Fujiyama (Ito) go looking for evidence to support their theories and inevitably treading on the toes of the police, especially Lieutenant Monahan (Walberg), much to the frustration of Quincy's boss, Dr Astin (Ragin). Within that standard format, however, and despite frequent histrionics, the story-lines had some well-considered detail and hard-hitting circumstances that allowed for both clever plot resolutions and a strong public message. In one episode bite marks are used to identify a criminal and a nurse, who had seen this episode, photographed a rape victim's bite marks which helped solve the case. Another episode about orphan drugs helped contribute to a change in the law. An early episode, "The Thigh Bone's Connected to the Knee Bone", about the discovery of a single bone on a building site, won an Edgar award and two later episodes were nominated for the Edgar. Two novels were written around the series, both by Thom Racina, *Quincy M.E.* (1977) and *Quincy M.E. 2* (1977) – the latter being the "Thigh Bone" episode.

The Rainmaker

(1997, US, 135 minutes)
Director: Francis Ford Coppola. **Producers:** Michael Douglas, Steven Reuther, Fredric S. Fuchs.
Screenplay: Francis Ford Coppola from the novel by John GRISHAM.
Starring: Matt Damon, Claire Danes, Jon Voight, Mickey Rourke, Danny DeVito, Dean Stockwell, Johnny Whitworth.
This is by far the best of the film adaptations of Grisham's novels. It takes the essence of the book – that of an inexperienced young lawyer (Damon) up against corporate power in the form of an insurance company that refuses to meet its obligations for a victim (Whitworth) dying of leukemia – and uses this to flavour a range of other subplots all of which coalesce into a legal blockbuster. There are superb character portrayals by the other cast, especially Jon Voight as the slimy, sold-out lawyer Leo Drummond, and Mickey Rourke as his corrupt employer, Bruiser Stone. The end result is even more convincing than the book.

Raising Arizona

(1987, US, 94 minutes)
Director: Joel Coen. **Producer:** Ethan Coen.
Screenplay: Joel & Ethan Coen.
Starring: Nicolas Cage, Holly Hunter, John Goodman, Trey Wilson, William Forsythe.
A textbook example of how to make a simple plot into a complex and extremely funny film. Hi McDonough (Cage) is a no-hoper who becomes spliced with prison officer Edwina (Hunter). Unable to have children, the two decide to kidnap one of the well-known quintuplets of the Arizona family, on the basis that no one's going to miss one of them. However, Nathan Arizona (Wilson) hires the biker from Hell to track down the missing infant at the same time as McDonough and Edwina are visited by two of his former prison inmates now on the run (Goodman and Forsythe). The result is a wonderful maelstrom that reflects the chaos and absurdities of life more accurately than most thrillers.

Remington Steele

(US TV series, 1982–7, 91 episodes)
Creator: Michael Gleason, Robert Butler.
Producers: Michael Gleason (executive); Glenn Gordon Caron, Gareth Davies, Lee Zlotoff.

Directors: Many, including Gabrielle Beaumont, Burt Brinckerhoff, Robert Butler, Sidney Hayers, Christopher Hibler, Rocky Lang, Will Mackenzie, Peter Medak, Leo Penn, Seymour Robbie, Don Weis.
Writers: Many, including Glenn Caron, Brian Clemens, Michael Gleason, Joe GORES, Jeff Melvoin, John Wirth, Lee Zlotoff.
Starring: Pierce Brosnan, Stephanie Zimbalist, Doris Roberts.
LA private eye Laura Holt (Zimbalist) finds it difficult to attract clients because she's female so she invents a male boss, Remington Steele, and then finds herself scuppered when clients keep asking to see him. When a mysterious stranger (Brosnan), whose real identity we never learn, turns up he takes on this fictitious rôle. With no knowledge of how to be a P.I., Steele plays it as if in the movies, and there are frequent quotes and scenes set up from classic films. Though the series was light-hearted, with the emphasis on the romantic potential between Steele and Holt, the storylines were cleverly plotted. Joel Steiger's script for "In the Steele of the Night" (1982), involving a murder at a reunion of Laura's former colleagues, won the Edgar award. As the series developed Caron increased the romantic element and then reworked it for a new set-up which became *Moonlighting*.

Renegade

(US TV series, 1992–97, 110 episodes)
Creator: Stephen J. CANNELL.
Producers: Richard C. Okie, Stu Segall (executives); Ray Harting, Perry Husman, Lorenzo Lamas.
Directors: Many, including B.J. Davis, Ron Garcia, Ralph Hemecker, Bruce Kessler, Terence O'Hara, Michael Levine, Charles Siebert. Adam Winkler.
Writers: Many, including Stephen J. Cannell, Nick Corea, Charles Grant Craig, Robert Hamner, Marvin Herbert, Larry Molin, Bill Nuss, Richard C. Okie.
Starring: Lorenzo Lamas, Branscombe Richmond, Stephen J. Cannell.
An all-action chase film which used a variant of *The Fugitive* theme but never quite mastered the cult status. Reno Raines (Lamas) is a young cop in Bay City, California who is framed for a murder by corrupt cop Dutch Dixon (Cannell), the real murderer. Raines escapes, takes on a new identity as Vince Black, and becomes a bounty hunter for his old friend Bobby Sixkiller (Richmond). For the next two seasons Raines/Black is both hunter and hunted as Dixon tries to track him down. He is eventually caught, brought to trial and convicted but escapes again and the set up continues as before until the inevitable showdown between Raines and Dixon.

Reservoir Dogs

(1991, US, 99 minutes)
Director: Quentin Tarantino. **Producer:** Lawrence Bender.
Screenplay: Quentin Tarantino.
Starring: Harvey Keitel, Tim Roth, Chris Penn, Eddie Bunker, Michael Madsen, Steve Buscemi, Lawrence Tierney.
Although a simple heist-gone-wrong film – a gang with colour-coded names hole up in a warehouse after a bungled jewel robbery – Tarantino fills the screen with verbal pyrotechnics and unrelenting violence. This, along with Tarantino's follow-up, *Pulp Fiction*, not only rewrote the rule-book for gangster fiction but it raised the stakes considerably, bringing a realism and humour into its world of bleak and savage hopelessness. A film where the real world deafens and defies you.

Richie Brockleman, Private Eye *see under* The Rockford Files

The Rockford Files

(US TV series, 1974–80, 123 episodes + pilot + 8 TV movies)
Creators: Roy Huggins, Stephen J. CANNELL.
Producers: Stephen J. Cannell, Meta Rosenberg (executives); Juanita Bartlett, David Chase, Charles Floyd Johnson, Lane Slate.
Directors: Many, including William Wiard, Lawrence Doheny, Ivan Dixon, Reza Badiyi.
Writers: Many, including Stephen J. Cannell, Juanita Bartlett, David Chase, Roy Huggins (as John Thomas James), Gordon Dawson.
Starring: James Garner, Noah Beery, Jr., Joe Santos, Stuart Margolin, Gretchen Corbett, John Cooper, Bo Hopkins.
James Garner is the ideal persona for a determined, tough but compassionate P.I. He played James Rockford, who had once served time for a crime he did not commit and now operates out of a beachfront house trailer in downtown Los Angeles. Rockford is not especially enamoured of the police though maintains contact with Sergeant (later Lieutenant) Becker (Santos). His speciality is in hopeless cases that the police have never solved and he charges his clients dearly for his services, though doesn't always collect. He dislikes guns (keeping his revolver in a biscuit barrel) but still gets beaten up most episodes. He also keeps bad company. Former cell-mate Angel Martin (Margolin) is always in need of help because of the company he keeps, whilst John Cooper (Hopkins) is a disbarred lawyer. Rockford relies heavily on his girlfriend, attorney Beth Davenport (Corbett), to get him out of trouble. Both Garner and Margolin won Emmy awards for their roles. Two episodes were nominated for Edgar awards: "The Oracle Wore a Cashmere Suit" (1976), where a psychic claims that Rockford knows more about a double

disappearance than he's prepared to admit, and "The Deadly Maze" (1977), where a less-than-eager client pays Rockford handsomely to find his missing wife. Garner eventually quit the series because of injury arising from his own stuntwork, but has to date done eight special TV movies, *I Still love L.A.* (1994), *A Blessing in Disguise* (1995), *If the Frame Fits*, *Godfather Knows Best*, *Friends and Foul Play*, *Crime and Punishment* (all 1996), *Murder and Misdemeanours* (1997) and *If it Bleeds, it Leads* (1999). The series produced one short-lived spin-off series, *Richie Brockelman, Private Eye* (1978; 5 episodes) starring Dennis Dugan as Brockelman, an all-too-young-looking P.I. with a glib line in patter. Tom Selleck also appeared in the final season of *Rockford Files* and so impressed the producers that they gave him his own series, *Magnum, P.I.* There were two novels based on the series, both by Mike JAHN, *The Unfortunate Replacement* (1975) and *The Deadliest Game* (1976).

Rosetti and Ryan

(US TV series, 1977, 8 episodes)
Producers: Leonard B. Stern (executives); Jerry Davis.
Directors: John Astin.
Writers: Don Mankiewicz, Gordon Cotler, Sam Rolfe.
Starring: Tony Roberts, Squire Fridell, Jane Elliot, Dick O'Neill, William Marshall.
A short-lived series about two attorneys, Joseph Rosetti (Roberts), a smooth, arrogant, rich egotist and Frank Ryan (Fridell), a former cop who was modest but determined. The two were as chalk and cheese and made an interesting combination in this powerful legal series that nevertheless failed to make a hit with the public and was soon dropped. The pilot episode, however, "Men Who Love Women", where the duo defend a rich heiress accused of murdering her husband, won an Edgar award.

Rumpole of the Bailey

(UK TV series, 1978–92, 42 episodes)
Creator: John MORTIMER.
Producers: Lloyd Shirley (executives); Irene Shubik, Jacqueline Davis.
Directors: Many, including Roger Bamford, Derek Bennett, Rodney Bennett, Jim Goddard, Peter Hammond, Bill Hays, Robert Knights, Donald McWhinnie.
Writer: John Mortimer.
Starring: Leo McKern, Julian Curry, Patricia Hodge, Peter Bowles, Peggy Thorpe-Bates/Marion Mathie, Samantha Bond/Abigail McKern, David Yelland, Bill Fraser, Robin Bailey.
Rumpole first appeared in a one-off play broadcast by the BBC in its *Play for Today* series in 1975, but when the BBC failed to take up the option for a series it transferred to ITV where it ran successfully, if intermittently,

for 14 years. Leo McKern was superb as the grumpy, idiosyncratic, old-fashioned, poetry-spouting ageing barrister, Horace Rumpole, whose wife, Hilda (Thorpe-Bates/Mathie), usually referred to as "She-Who-Must-Be-Obeyed", was always disappointed that he had not risen to High Court Judge or even Head of Chambers as had her father. Rumpole was a stickler for justice and the saviour of the underdog, though he seldom endeared himself to the bullish and equally eccentric judges. He almost always defended, never prosecuted, and always took on the losers in life rather than go for the rich briefs. Other barristers in chambers were wonderfully lampooned, especially the snooty Phyllida Trant (Hodge) and her future Wagner-loving husband Claude Erskine-Brown (Curry). Mortimer has continued to write stories featuring Rumpole including the occasional radio play.

Ruth Rendell Mysteries

(UK occasional TV series, 1988–*current*, 31 + episodes)
Created for television: John Davies.
Producers: Graham Benson (executives); John Davies, Neil Zeiger.
Directors: John Davies, Matthew Evans, Jim Goddard, John Gorrie, Alan Grint, Piers Haggard, Bill Hays, Sarah Hellings, Sandy Johnson, James Cellan Jones, Don Leaver, Bruce MacDonald, Mary McMurray, Gavin Millar, Jan Sargent, Mike Vardy, Herbert Wise.
Writers: George Baker, Ken Blakeson, Julian Bond, Clive Exton, John Harvey, Matthew Jacobs, Douglas Livingstone, Roger Marshall, Guy Meredith, Alan Plater, Trevor Preston, Peter Ransley, Christopher Russell, Ted Whitehead.
Starring (for Wexford series only): George Baker, Christopher Ravenscroft, Louie Ramsay, Sean Pertwee, Deborah Poplett.
The title was originally used to cover adaptations of Ruth RENDELL's Chief Inspector Wexford stories, starting with *Shake Hands Forever* (1988). Wexford was played by George Baker and his sidekick, the morose Inspector Mike Burden, by Christopher Ravenscroft. The series were straight adaptations of Rendell's novels, either as two-or-three part serials or as two-hour specials. Set in Kingsmarkham (and filmed in the town of Romsey in Hampshire), the series has a relaxed countrified atmosphere and Wexford (played by Baker with a strong Hampshire/Somerset burr) is a methodical, plodding detective who is a compassionate family man (Baker's real wife, Louie Ramsay, plays his on-screen wife). In 1992 TVS lost its franchise when only 12 of the 15 novels had been adapted. The new production company acquired rights only to new Wexford novels as they were published, starting with *Simisola* (1995), so that from 1992 the title *The Ruth Rendell Mysteries* became an umbrella for adapting other Rendell novels and stories, again either as short mini-series or two-hour specials. These began with *Talking to Strange Men* (1992) and have

included Rendell's novels *Master of the Moor*, *Vanity Dies Hard*, *The Secret House of Death*, *Heartstones*, *Going Wrong*, *The Lake of Darkness* as well as several short stories.

Séance on a Wet Afternoon

(1964, UK, 116 minutes, b&w)
Director: Bryan Forbes. **Producer:** Richard Attenborough, Bryan Forbes.
Screenplay: Bryan Forbes based on the novel by Mark McShane.
Starring: Kim Stanley, Richard Attenborough, Mark Eden, Nanette Newman, Patrick Magee, Judith Donner.
Superb character acting by Stanley and Attenborough and masterful direction by Forbes turns what would otherwise be a routine thriller into a compelling and suspenseful drama. Myra Savage (Stanley) is a medium who browbeats her husband (Attenborough) into kidnapping a young girl (Donner) so that she can prove her powers by identifying where the child is hidden. Kim Stanley, better known as a stage actress, was nominated for an Oscar for her rôle and the film won an Edgar award.

Sea of Love

(1989, US, 113 minutes)
Director: Harold Becker. **Producer:** Martin Bregman, Louis A. Stroller.
Screenplay: Richard Price.
Starring: Al Pacino, Ellen Barkin, John Goodman, William Hickey.
Compelling performances by Pacino and Barkin overcome the plot faults in this suspense thriller. Frank Keller (Pacino) is a New York cop investigating a series of brutal murders of men who have advertized in the lonely-hearts column. Chief suspect is Helen (Barkin) and Keller breaks rule number one by becoming rather more than romantically involved with her, despite advice from his kindly sidekick Touhey (Goodman). The sexual tension sizzles and blinds Keller to the truth, leading to the predictable but still suspenseful climax. The film was nominated for an Edgar award.

Sergeant Cork

(UK TV series, 1963–8, 65 episodes, b&w)
Creator: Ted Willis. **Producers:** Jack Williams.
Directors: Phil Dale, Josephine Douglas, Ian Fordyce, Quentin Lawrence, Bill Stewart, Dennis Vance.
Writers: Julian Bond, Bill Craig, Richard Harris, Malcolm Hulke, Bill McIlwraithe, Michael Pertwee, Alan Prior, Bruce Stewart, Ted Willis.
Starring: John Barrie, William Gaunt, Arnold Diamond/Charles Morgan, John Richmond.

Long before Peter LOVESEY's Sergeant Cribb and even longer before Anne PERRY's Inspector Pitt, Ted Willis created the formidable character of Sergeant Cork (Barrie). Cork was in the fledgling CID and his thinking was way ahead of his time, being more into the forensic detection of Sherlock Holmes than the hue and cry of his forebears. Sometime's Cork's efforts were thwarted by his antideluvian boss, Detective Bird (Diamond), but later Bird was transferred and the new Superintendent Rodway (Morgan) was intrigued by Cork's methods. Cork's ever-resourceful young assistant was Sergeant Bob Marriott (Gaunt). Six episodes were adapted into short stories by Arthur Swinson and collected as *Sergeant Cork's Casebook* (1965) and *Sergeant Cork's Second Casebook* (1966).

Serpico

(1973, US, 130 minutes)
Director: Sidney Lumet. **Producer:** Martin Bregman.
Screenplay: Waldo Salt, Norman Wexler from the 1973 book by Peter Maas.
Starring: Al Pacino, John Randolph, Jack Kehoe, Tony Roberts, Biff McGuire.
The definitive, though slightly dated, film of a cop who blows the whistle on his corrupt colleagues, based on a true story. Pacino plays Frank Serpico, an idealistic cop who could not abide the corruption and bribery in the NYPD but finds his actions cost him dearly. Considering his later gangster roles, Pacino comes across as a sincere and genuine cop. The film is played straight, unlike Lumet's later more convoluted *Prince of the City*, so while it lacks the suspense of the later film, the end result is more realistic. Both the writers and Pacino were nominated for an Oscar and the film was nominated for an Edgar. The film inspired a short-lived TV series (1976–7; 15 episodes) with David Birney as the loner New York cop. In the series Serpico was more into undercover work and less involved in rooting out corruption.

77 Sunset Strip

(US TV series, 1958–64, 205 episodes, b&w)
Creator: Roy Huggins.
Producers: William T. Orr, Jack Webb (esexutives); William Conrad, Fenton Earnshaw, Howie Horwitz, Joel Rogosin, Harry Tatelman.
Directors: Many, including Budd Boetticher, William Conrad, Lawrence Dobkin, Robert Douglas, Douglas Heyes, Leslie H. Martinson, Leo Penn, Richard Sarafian.
Writers: Many, including Howard Browne, Marion Hargrove, Douglas Heyes, Roy Huggins, Leonard Lee, Charles Sinclair, Roger Smith.
Starring: Efrem Zimbalist, Jr., Roger Smith, Edd Byrnes, Louis Quinn, Jacqueline Beer.

A top-ten TV series in its heyday, *77 Sunset Strip* was the first of the glamorous P.I. series that would influence the next generation of TV shows. The title was the Hollywood address of an agency run by former undercover agents Stu Bailey (Zimbalist) and Jeff Spencer (Smith), and each week would see them driving or jetting to various glamour spots to resolve some unmemorable crime. Sometimes both stars would be involved in a case but usually each week alternated between Bailey and Spencer. Both men were judo experts; Bailey was an expert in languages whilst Spencer was a qualified lawyer. You can see the roots of such series as *The Man from U.N.C.L.E.* and *Burke's Law*, amongst others. The series was one of the first to become more important for its stars than for its plots. The hit of the show was Edd Byrnes who played the hip-talking "Kookie" Kookson, who looked after the adjoining parking lot and was forever combing his hair. He made a hit record, "Kookie, Kookie, Lend Me Your Comb" (1959) and the catchy theme tune by Mack David and Jerry Livingston was also a hit. Byrnes's popularity led to him wanting a more important rôle and he was promoted to a partner after briefly walking out on the show. When ratings finally dropped the show was completely revamped and the cast dropped except for Zimbalist who became a globe-trotting agent. The character of Stuart Bailey had been created by veteran writer Roy Huggins in the novel *The Double Take* (1946), where Bailey becomes the pawn of a wealthy businessman. The book was subsequently filmed as *I Love Trouble* (1948), starring Franchot Tone as the detective. In that novel and later stories Bailey is portrayed as a Chandleresque world-weary P.I. and the character was totally revamped for TV. The short story "Death and the Skylark" (1952) formed the basis for the first TV adaptation in the anthology series *Conflict* in 1957. That story, with two others, was collected in *77 Sunset Strip* (1959). Huggins (1914–2002), who had created the TV series *Cheyenne* and *Maverick* (in fact several *Maverick* scripts were rewritten for *Sunset Strip*) went on to create *The Fugitive* and *The Rockford Files*. The PWA recognized Huggins' contribution to the genre with a Lifetime Achievement award in 1991.

Shadow Squad

(UK TV series, 1957–9, 175 episodes, b&w)
Producer: Barry Baker.
Directors: Bill Hitchcock, Jean Hamilton, David Main, James Ormerod, Michael Scott, Robert Tronson, Herbert Wise.
Writers: Barry Baker, Geoffrey Bellman, Julian Bond, H.V. Kershaw, Tony Warren, John Whitney, Peter Yeldham.
Starring: Rex Garner/Peter Williams, George Moon, Kathleen Boutall.
This early evening series proved incredibly popular in Britain at the end of the fifties, offering something different to the glossy US P.I. shows. Vic Steele (Garner) was a former Flying Squad policeman who disliked the

restraints of the force so left to become a P.I. He was assisted by streetwise Cockney Ginger Smart, played by former variety actor George Moon. Also helping out at their offices was cleaning lady Mrs Moggs. Stories ran in two half-hourly linked episodes each week. After three months, and with no explanation, Steele was written out of the series and a new character, Don Carter (Williams) appeared. A former Scotland Yard detective, Carter was more reliable than Steele and less shifty, appealing to the British viewers and the series soared in popularity.

Shaft

(1971, US, 100 minutes)
Director: Gordon Parks. **Producer:** Joel Freeman.
Screenplay: Ernest TIDYMAN, John D.F. Black.
Starring: Richard Roundtree, Moses Gunn, Charles Cioffi, Gwenn Mitchell, Lawrence Pressman.
This was the film attributed with launching the blaxploitation movies of the seventies. With its funky Oscar-winning theme music by Isaac Hayes, and a real cool dude, John Shaft (Roundtree) as cinema's first major black P.I., the film, in retrospect, isn't actually anything special, but at the time it seemed to remove barriers and change perceptions overnight. Roundtree is excellent as the well-to-do black New York P.I. who is investigating a racketeer's activities whilst also looking for his kidnapped daughter. The near unnecessary new *Shaft* (2000) scores because of Samuel L. Jackson's slick portrayal. The success of the first film spawned two sequels, the Bondesque *Shaft's Big Score* (1972) and *Shaft in Africa* (1973). There was also a brief and far less successful TV series, *Shaft* (1973–4, 7 episodes) which failed because the character was too toned down for TV audiences. Nevertheless, Roundtree conducts himself superbly throughout all these sequels.

Shannon's Deal

(US TV series, 1990–1, 14 episodes + pilot)
Creator: John Sayles. **Producer:** James Margellos.
Directors: Lewis Teague (pilot), Allan Arkush, Aaron Lipstadt, John Sayles.
Writers: John Sayles.
Starring: Jamey Sheridan, Elizabeth Pena, Jenny Lewis, Richard Edson.
Jack Shannon (Sheridan) was a major attorney in a leading Philadelphia law firm who quit because he became disillusioned after years of working on behalf of corrupt corporate clients. He wanted to get back to the real world and turned P.I., scraping a living from small clients, and occasionally undertaking minor litigation. Unfortunately he also built up major debts and was at the mercy of debt collector Wilmer Slade (Edson). This gritty

series received much critical acclaim but was not around long enough to score with the public. The pilot film, aired in June 1989, where Shannon takes on an international drug smuggling ring, won an Edgar award in 1990.

The Shawshank Redemption

(1994, US, 142 minutes)
Director: Frank Darabont. **Producer:** Niki Marvin.
Screenplay: Frank Darabont from the story "Rita Hayworth and the Shawshank Redemption" by Stephen King.
Starring: Tim Robbins, Morgan Freeman, Bob Gunton, Gil Bellows, Clancy Brown, James Whitmore.
Once in a while there is a film that takes a long time to get seemingly nowhere but the pleasure of the trip is in itself transcendent. Andy Dufresne (Robbins) has been wrongly sentenced to double-life for the murder of his wife and her lover. Incarcerated in Shawshank State Prison Dufresne draws into himself to cope with the brutal prison regime until he gets to know fellow lifer Red Redding (Freeman) and together they learn how to cope and seek redemption. The mood of the film is almost cathartic, which accounts for its popularity. It was nominated for the Oscar in several categories including best picture.

Shoestring

(UK TV series, 1979–80, 21 episodes)
Creator/Producer: Robert Banks Stewart.
Directors: Several, including Douglas Camfield, Paul Ciapessoni, Mike Vardy.
Writers: Several, including Terence Feely, William Hood, Peter King, John Kruse, Robert Banks Stewart.
Starring: Trevor Eve, Michael Medwin, Doran Godwin.
Recovering from a nervous breakdown, former computer expert turned P.I., Eddie Shoestring (Eve), secures work as a phone-in host on a West-country radio station, Radio West. The idea is that people ring in with cases for him to investigate and his results are fed back on the programme. He's nicknamed the "Private Ear". Most of the calls are frivolous but occasionally special cases come along, such as a girl involved with a bizarre cult, or an old woman who believes she's witnessed a murder. Shoestring was unkempt and unconventional, which is what made him and the series popular. He was sometimes helped or advised in his investigations by his girlfriend and landlady, who was also a lawyer, Erica Bayliss (Godwin). After two series Eve decided to return to the stage, and creator Stewart converted the remaining story-lines into a new series about another unkempt, alcoholic detective, Jim Bergerac. There were two novels based on the series, *Shoestring* (1979) and *Shoestring's Finest Hour* (1980), both by Paul Ableman.

The Silence of the Lambs

(1991, US, 118 minutes)
Director: Jonathan Demme. **Producer:** Edward Saxon, Kenneth Utt, Ron Bozman.
Screenplay: Ted Tally from the novel by Thomas HARRIS.
Starring: Jodie Foster, Anthony Hopkins, Scott Glenn, Ted Levine.
Although almost a reworking of *Red Dragon*, which had been filmed as *Manhunter*, with Brian Cox as Hannibal Lecter, it was this film, with Anthony Hopkins's masterfully haunting performance as Lecter, that captured everyone's imagination. FBI trainee Clarice Starling (Foster) becomes closely involved with mass murderer and incarcerated cannibal, Lecter, whose help she seeks in her hunt for the serial killer, "Buffalo Bill" (Levine). The plot is almost immaterial; it is the interplay between Lecter and Clarice along with Hopkins's portrayal of a maniac that makes this film so watchable. The film walked away with the Oscars including best film and awards for Hopkins and Foster for their performances and for Demme and Tally. It also won an Edgar award and an American Mystery Award.

Silent Witness

(UK TV series, 1996–*current*, 18 + episodes)
Creator: Nigel McCrery.
Producer: Caroline Oulton (executive), Tony Dennis, Alison Lumb, Anne Pivcevic, Lars Macfarlane, Diana Kyle.
Directors: Many, including Harry Hook, Mike Barker, Noella Smith, Ben Bolt, Julian Jarrold, Nick Laughland, Richard Signy, Jonas Grimas, Alex Pillai, Bill Anderson.
Writers: Many, including Nigel McCrery, Kevin Hood, Ashley Pharaoh, John Milne, Gillian Richmond, Peter Lloyd, Tony McHale, Gwyneth Hughes, Niall Leonard.
Starring: Amanda Burton, Ruth McCabe, Richard Huw, William Armstrong.
At the outset this series was set in Cambridge (though filmed mostly around Ely) but since the fourth series has shifted to London. Dr Samantha Ryan (Burton) is a forensic pathologist who has set up her own practice with friend Trevor Stewart (Armstrong). Her work involves her in the most gruesome and despairing of cases ranging from child abuse to industrial negligence and throughout Ryan applies herself assiduously, almost obsessively, not prepared to give a quick solution if she believes there is more to the case than the quick answer the police want. Ryan has plenty of personal troubles. From an Irish background, she had regularly argued with her father who was killed by terrorists. Her mother is suffering from Alzheimer's, she is at odds with her sister, and all of this fuels the angst that drives Ryan into her work. With the fourth series Ryan

has become Professor of Forensic Pathology at a London teaching hospital and her reputation is such that she is now in demand across the country. Though most of the continuing characters no longer appear she has not left her past behind her. The strength of the series lies not only in its convoluted plots and a strong sense of believability but in the performance of Amanda Burton herself as a strong, determined, resilient but inwardly turbulent character. The episode "Blood, Sweat and Tears" (1997) won an Edgar award and a further nomination went to "Fallen Idol" (1998). The series was based on the book *Silent Witness* (1996) by Nigel McCrery (b. 1953), a former policeman who now works for the BBC. Subsequent books include *Strange Screams of Death* (1997), *The Spider's Web* (1998) and *Faceless Strangers* (2000).

Silk Stalkings

(US TV series, 1991–9, 176 episodes)
Creator: Stephen J. Cannell.
Producer: David Peckinpah (executive); Stu Segall.
Directors: Many, including Ron Ames, Stephen J. Cannell, Alan Cassidy, James Darren, Don Edmonds, Peter Ellis, Rob Estes, Ron Garcia, Tucker Gates, Ralph Hemecker, Perry Husman, Maria Lease, Terrence O'Hara, David Schmoeller, Charles Siebert, Brian Trenchard-Smith, Carl Weathers.
Writers: Many, including David Abramowitz, Simon Ayer, Jerry P. Brown, Erica Byrne, Stephen J. Cannell, Liz & Lou Comici, Gordon Dawson, Stephen G. Geyer, Sam Glickson, David Kemper, David Peckinpah, Garner Simmons, Todd Trotter, David Tynan.
Starring: Rob Estes/Nick Kokotakis/Chris Potter, Mitzi Kapture/Tyler Layton/Janet Gunn, Ben Vereen/Charlie Brill, Mitzi McCall.
Originally set up as a jointly financed production between CBS and the cable network USA, CBS dropped the series after two seasons and thereafter it ran on cable alone, becoming the longest-running cable crime series. Set in Palm Beach, California, amongst the rich and the glamorous, the series featured the investigations of Sergeant Chris Lorenzo (Estes) and his partner the sexy Sergeant Rita Lance (Kapture) into various crimes of passion or other sordid dealings. Sex was a major ingredient in this series, at least as a motive for crime, but not between the two officers, where the "will-they-won't-they" card was played for several seasons. Nevertheless the attraction between them was evident and eventually warmed up in season five when they married, though not until after Lorenzo had been shot. A few episodes later he was shot again, and this time killed, and Rita decides she must leave and consider the future with her as yet unborn child. Another team took over briefly, Michael Price (Kokotakis) and Holly Rawlins (Layton) before, in the final three seasons the team became Tom Ryan (Potter) and Cassy St John (Gunn), a

divorced couple where electricity still sparked between them. The series reached a cliff-hanging conclusion with the Internal Affairs officers moving in for the kill with signs of corruption which was never resolved.

Simon & Simon

(US TV series, 1981–8, 156 episodes + 2 films)
Creator: Philip De Guere.
Producer: Philip De Guere (executive); Chas Floyd Johnson, John Stephens.
Directors: Many, including Corey Allen, Bruce Bilson, Roy Campanella, Dennis Donelly, Alan J. Levi, Vincent McEveety, David Moessinger, Christian I. Nyby II, Bob Sweeney.
Writers: Many, including Howard Browne, Roy Campanella, Don M. Mankiewicz, David Moessinger, Thomas Perry, Ross THOMAS.
Starring: Jameson Parker, Gerald McRaney, Mary Carver, Tim Reid/Joan McMurtrey, Eddie Barth, Mary Carver.
This was a series of mixed quality and rather stereotypical characters following formula action. It featured two brothers. Rick (McRaney), the eldest, was cynical, eccentric, scarred from his days in Vietnam, easily caught in a fight and tended to scruffiness. Andrew or "A.J." (Parker) was the ambitious one, squeaky clean, refined, dedicated. Clearly they didn't get on with each other but they still ran the eponymous private detective agency. The series was often played for laughs, following the Magnum formula (in fact there was a cross-over episode with *Magnum*). Many episodes were superficial, like "The Bare Facts" (1983), where they go "undercover" in a nudist colony, or "The Apple Doesn't Fall Far From the Tree" (1986), an end-of-season barrel-scraper where they play various ancestors in their family tree. But at times they were thought-provoking and clever. They include a 1982 adaptation of Howard Browne's novel *Thin Air*, plus "Reunion at Alcatraz" (1985), where an author hires them to help him solve what happened to the only prisoner to escape from the island prison. Four episodes were nominated for Edgar awards, "Simon Eyes"' (1981), "Ashes to Ashes, and None Too Soon" (1982), "Grand Illusion" (1983), an ingenious plot involving conjuring tricks, and "May the Road Rise Up" (1988), a particularly poignant one where the brothers investigate the circumstances around their father's death. There were two follow-up TV movies, *Precious Cargo* (1994) and *In Trouble Again* (1995).

A Simple Plan

(1998, US/UK/Japan/German/French, 121 minutes)
Director: Sam Raimi. **Producer:** James Jacks, Adam Schroeder.
Screenplay: Scott B. Smith from his 1993 novel.
Starring: Bill Paxton, Billy Bob Thornton, Brent Briscoe, Bridget Fonda, Gary Cole.

Simple plans and simple plots often produce the best stories and that's true in this modern-day fable. Three previously decent men discover that a crashed light aircraft in a remote part of Minnesota contains over $4 million in cash. They work out how to share the money between them without telling anyone except Hank (Paxton)'s wife Sarah (Fonda) but needless to say once corruption has laid a hold sod's law soon follows and everything starts to deteriorate, leading to a disturbing but compelling conclusion. Thornton received an Oscar nomination for his wonderful portrayal of Hank's slow-witted brother Jacob and the film was nominated for an Edgar.

Sleuth

(1972, UK, 139 minutes)
Director: Joseph L. Mankiewicz. **Producer:** Morton Gottlieb.
Screenplay: Anthony SHAFFER based on his own stage play.
Starring: Laurence Olivier, Michael Caine.
Sometimes over-the-top acting and direction works, because people do go OTT now and again, especially author Andrew Wyke (Olivier) who flips his lid when he discovers his wife is having an affair with Milo Tindle (Caine) and plots to kill him. The interplay between these two characters – Caine at his whining but devious best and Olivier at his most sinister – within a labyrinthine plot that keeps you spellbound, makes for a compelling film. Both Olivier and Caine received Oscar nominations and the film won an Edgar award (as had the stage play).

Sling Blade

(1995, US, 126 minutes)
Director: Billy Bob Thornton. **Producer:** Brandon Rosser, David L. Bushell.
Screenplay: Billy Bob Thornton.
Starring: Billy Bob Thornton, Dwight Yoakum, J.T. Walsh, John Ritter, Lucas Black, Natalie Canerday.
A tender but suspenseful character study that keeps you on edge. Karl Childers (Thornton), is a mentally disturbed man who has been released after serving 25 years in a psychiatric unit after murdering his mother and her lover when a child. Now working as a handyman he befriends a lonely young boy, Frank (Black), but friction starts between Childers and Doyle (Yoakum), the violent boyfriend of Frank's mother. Is history about to repeat itself? An exceptional film all round. Thornton's screenplay won an Oscar and he was nominated for his performance. The film also won an Edgar.

Softly, Softly

(UK TV series, 1966–76, 200 episodes) and BARLOW AT LARGE (1971–75, 30 episodes)

Creator: Elwyn Jones. **Producer:** David E. Rose, Leonard Lewis, Geraint Morris.
Directors: Many, including Philip Dudley, Vere Lorrimer.
Writers: Many, including Elwyn Jones, Robert Jones, Alan Plater.
Starring: Stratford Johns, Frank Windsor.

Softly, Softly was a spin-off series from *Z Cars*, building on the success of the character of Detective Chief Superintendent Charlie Barlow. Played by Stratford Johns, Barlow was a bullish, no-nonsense detective who worked in a bad-guy/good-guy relationship with his Chief Inspector John Watt (Windsor). For this series they were moved to a new location at Wyvern constabulary (= Bristol). Though working with other officers, mostly notably the morose dog-handler, PC Snow (Rigby), the key to the series was the relationship between Barlow and Watt and particularly the forcefulness of Barlow in getting results, almost regardless of consequences. The team stayed together when moved to Thamesford Constabulary in 1969 when the series name changed slightly to *Softly, Softly Task Force*. (The title, incidentally, comes from the old adage "Softly, softly, catchee monkey", the very thing Barlow was not!) Unaccountably the BBC fractured this well-tested formula in 1971 when Barlow was promoted to work at the Police Research Services Branch in Whitehall in *Barlow at Large*. This unit looked at especially difficult cases across the country, helping out local forces. Barlow had a supercilious boss, A.G. Fenton (Neil Stacy) and though he had a new colleague, Detective Sergeant David Rees (Norman Comer), Barlow seemed lost without John Watt to take the brunt of his vehemence. Retitled *Barlow* for its final season in 1974–5, this series had played with the formula once too often. *Softly, Softly* continued without Barlow, and indeed outlived its successor, but despite the quality of the scripts, and a constant testing edge to the plots, it too felt like a galleon no longer at full sail. Following a successful one-off in which Barlow and Watt reopened the Jack the Ripper files, the BBC reunited the duo one last time in a non-fiction series, *Second Verdict* (1976; 6 episodes), where they reinvestigated classic unsolved mysteries, such as Lizzie Borden. Episodes from the *Softly, Softly* series were reworked by Arnold Yarrow as short stories in *Softly, Softly Casebook* and *Softly, Softly Murder Casebook* (both 1973) and by Elwyn Jones in *Softly, Softly* (1976). Elwyn Jones also developed the character of Barlow in four novels, *Barlow in Charge* (1973), *Barlow Comes to Judgement* (1974), *Barlow Exposed* (1976) and *Barlow Down Under* (1977), plus the collection, with John Lloyd, *The Barlow Casebook* (1975). Jones and Lloyd also compiled *The Ripper File* (1975) with Barlow and Watt.

A Soldier's Story

(1984, US, 101 minutes)
Director: Norman Jewison. **Producer:** Norman Jewison, Ronald L. Schwary, Patrick Palmer.
Screenplay: Charles Fuller based on his 1982 stage play.
Starring: Howard E. Rollins, Jr., Adolph Caesar, Art Evans, David Alan Grier, David Harris, Dennis Lipscomb, Denzel Washington.
The quality of this film is attested by the fact that the play upon which it is based won a Pulitzer prize, the film was nominated for an Oscar, as was Fuller's screenplay and Adolph Caesar for his performance, and the film also won an Edgar. It is a gripping and highly emotive whodunnit. Set in 1944, US Army Captain Davenport (Rollins) goes to a military base deep in the southern states of the USA to investigate the murder of a black sergeant. Whilst the racial element is strong the emphasis is on what it is to be a black soldier and, through Davenport's intense investigation, and powerful performances by the whole cast, the film brings to life the nature of murder and the turbulent currents that feed the motives.

Something Wild

(1986, US, 114 minutes)
Director: Jonathan Demme. **Producers:** Jonathan Demme, Kenneth Utt.
Screenplay: E. Max Frye.
Starring: Jeff Daniels, Melanie Griffith, Ray Liotta.
This film shows how easily and suddenly humour can be turned through nervous laughter into cold fear. Demme develops this emotional cocktail through a simple plot of a fun weekend that turns all too serious. Charlie Driggs (Daniels), a decent and normally upright businessman, fails to pay for his meal at a diner and is noticed by *femme fatale* Lulu Hankel (Griffith), who lures him away for a weekend of debauchery. But then Lulu's paranoid ex-con husband Ray Sinclair (Liotta) turns up and decides to use the couple of his own vengeful purposes. What was dangerously naughty now becomes fearfully dangerous as Demme unexpectedly tightens the screw and Lulu and Charlie are soon on the run for their lives. The tension is increased by an excellent rock soundtrack by John Cale and Laurie Anderson. The film won the Edgar award in 1987.

The Sopranos

(US TV series, 1999–*current*, projected 65 episodes)
Creator: David Chase.
Producers: David Chase, Brad Grey, Mitchell Burgess, Robin L. Green, Frank Renzulli (executives); Ilene S. Landress.
Directors: Many, including Daniel Attias, Steve Buscemi, David Chase,

Allen Coulter, Nick Gomez, John Patterson, Matthew Penn, Lorraine Senna Ferrara, Lee Tamahori, Alan Taylor, Timothy Van Patten, Andy Wolk.

Writers: Many, including David Chase, Jason Cahill, Michael Imperoli, Todd A. Kessler, James Manos Jr., Terence Winter.

Starring: James Gandolfini, Lorraine Bracco, Edie Falco, Michael Imperioli, Dominic Chianese, Tony Sirico, Steve Van Zandt.

This ground-breaking TV series is one of the hugest hits on cable television and has been re-dubbed, removing many of the profanities, to allow its syndication on network TV. Even so the violence and realism of life in and around a high-ranking Mob family makes this one of the most exciting and original series around and it has garnered a bewildering number of Emmy nominations and awards. The series centres on Tony Soprano (Gandolfini), head of the local Mob outfit, and how he controls (or tries to control) the lives of his family – particularly his hot-headed nephew Chris (Imperioli) – and of his rivals. In the pilot episode, made two years before the series was commissioned, pressure has got to him so much that he had to visit a psychiatrist, itself a life-threatening action. Tony also has a fear that the days of the Mob are over and that he is a failure when compared to his predecessors. The series follows these tensions and concentrates as much if not more on the character interplay and personal lives than on the violence and action. David Chase, the creator and executive producer of the series, had established his reputation with work on *The Rockford Files* and *Northern Exposure*, but had planned to hand the series over to others when he was made an offer he could not refuse. He plans to wrap the whole story-line up over five seasons. A book about the characters is *The Sopranos: a Family History* (2000) by Allen Rucker, whilst *Bright Lights, Baked Ziti* (2001) by David Bishop is the unofficial guide to the series.

Special Branch

(UK TV series, 1969–74, 53 episodes)

Producers: Lloyd Shirley, George Taylor (executive); Reginald Collin, Robert Love, Geoffrey Gilbert, Ted Childs.

Directors: Many, including Jonathan Alwyn, William Brayne, Douglas Camfield, Tom Clegg, Peter Duiguid, James Goddard, Don Leaver, William G. Stewart, Dennis Vance, Mike Vardy, Guy Verney.

Writers: Many, including David Butler, Michael Chapman, P.J. Hammond, Ray Jenkins, George Markstein, Roger Marshall, Ian Kennedy Martin, Trevor Preston, Anthony Skene, Robert Banks Stewart, Tony Williamson.

Starring: Derren Nesbitt/George Sewell, Wensley Pithey/Fulton Mackay/Patrick Mower, Frederick Jaeger, Paul Eddington.

The first of the British TV series to look at the new-style undercover police who were as heavily into guns and violence as they were fashion and wisecracks. The series caused a public outcry early on because it seemed to glorify violence and did not represent the true British bobby, but the series soon became very popular and paved the way for *The Sweeney*. It underwent much revamping. The original leads were the trendy D.I. Jordan (Nesbitt) who, with his boss Superintendent Eden (Pithey) – and later Superintendent Inman (Mackay) – worked for Scotland Yard's Special Branch which dealt with national security, and was predominantly an anti-espionage unit. After two seasons the characters were completely changed and in came the even trendier DCI Alan Craven (Sewell) and DCI Tom Haggerty (Mower) and their remit, whilst still dealing with security, extended to terrorists, hippies, fraudsters, muggers and kidnapping. A book based on the series was the belated *Special Branch: In at the Kill* (1976) by John Eyers.

Spenser For Hire

(US TV series, 1985–8, 64 episodes + pilot)

Creator: developed for TV by John Wilder from the books by Robert B. Parker.

Producers: John Wilder (executive); William Robert Yates, Dick Gallegy, Robert Hamilton.

Directors: Many, including Robert Colla, Harvey Hart, Winrich Kolbe, Virgil Vogel, David M. Whorf, William Wiard, John Wilder.

Writers: Many, including Juanita Bartlett, Bob Bielak, David Carren, Michael Fisher, Daniel Freudenberger, Alex Gansa, Lee Goldberg, Howard Gordon, Robert Hamilton, Stephen Hattman, Robert B. Parker & Joan H. Parker, William Rabkin, John Wilder, William Robert Yates.

Starring: Robert Urich, Avery Brooks, Ron McLarty, Barbara Stock.

Drawing upon Robert Parker's books about his Boston-based P.I., Spenser, and with Parker as story consultant, this series nevertheless remained fairly run-of-the-mill. Urich, a capable enough actor, was ill-cast as Spenser, albeit he endeavoured to capture the smugness of the character. The series lacked the wit and style of the books, which it endeavoured to mask in endless violence and chases. Spenser's black sidekick, Hawk (Brooks), proved popular enough to have his own spin-off series, *A Man Called Hawk* (1989), and though not as psychotic as Parker's original, Brooks brought more power and thrust to the character. After the original series was cancelled Spenser returned in a series of TV movies. Urich again played the rôle in *Ceremony* (1993), *Pale King and Princes* (1993), *The Judas Goat* (1994) and *A Savage Place* (1995). Joe Mantegna took over in *Small Vices* (1999), *Thin Air* (2000) and *Walking Shadow* (2001). These are adapted more directly from Parker's books and have a more authentic feel, especially with Mantegna as a sharper, more responsible Spenser.

Spindoe *see under* The Man in Room 17

Stakeout

(1987, US, 117 minutes)
Director: John Badham. **Producers:** Jim Kouf, Cathleen Summers.
Screenplay: Jim Kouf.
Starring: Richard Dreyfuss, Emilio Estevez, Madeleine Stowe, Aidan Quinn.

This attempt to heighten the comedy and retain the violent action of the *Lethal Weapon* movies doesn't quite come off. Richard Dreyfuss and Emilio Estevez, as two ill-matched Seattle detectives on a stakeout to capture the crazed escaped con "Stick" Montgomery (Quinn), don't quite gel in their roles. The film might have been better played straight since the suspense certainly builds as it leads to the climactic encounter between Quinn and the cops. Even so the film won an Edgar award and was a box office hit leading to a sequel, *Another Stakeout* (1993), which whilst not adding anything new did seem to work better over all.

Starsky and Hutch

(US TV series, 1975–9, 92 episodes + pilot)
Creator: William Blinn.
Producers: Aaron Spelling, Leonard Goldberg (executive); Joseph T. Naar.
Directors: Many, including Reza Badiyi, Earl Bellamy, Georg Stanford Brown, Nicholas Colasanto, Ivan Dixon, Paul Michael Glaser, Ivan Nagy, Leo Penn, Nicholas Sgarro, David Soul, Don Weis.
Writers: Many, including William Blinn, Michael Fisher, Steve Fisher, David P. Harmon, Edward J. Lasko, Michael Mann, Mann Rubin.
Starring: Paul Michael Glaser, David Soul, Bernie Hamilton, Antonio Fargas.

One of the best-loved cop shows of the seventies – almost representative of the era: brash, stylish, strong on violence, action quick patter and buddyism but low on plot and anything beyond formula stories. The series focused on two cops, the impulsive and streetwise Dave Starsky (Glaser) and the cooler, soft-spoken Ken Hutchinson (Soul) who blazed around the big city (very much like Los Angeles) in a red Ford Gran Torino with white speed stripes. Their informant was black jive-talking pimp Huggy Bear (Fargas) and their long-suffering but rather ineffectual boss was Captain Dobey (Hamilton). The fun of the series was the interplay between the two leads where there was a definite chemistry, making it one of TV's best buddy series. Their names remain synonymous for "high action but low on detection" cops. Richard Deming wrote eight novels based on the series under the alias Max Franklin: *Starsky and Hutch*, *Death Ride*, *Kill Huggy Bear* (all 1976), *Bounty Hunter*, *The*

Psychic, *Terror on the Docks* (all 1977), *Murder on Playboy Island* and *The Set-Up* (both 1978).

Still of the Night

(1982, US, 91 minutes)
Director: Robert Benton. **Producer:** Arlene Donovan.
Screenplay: Robert Benton from a story by David Newman and Robert Benton.
Starring: Roy Scheider, Meryl Streep, Jessica Tandy.
A semi-successful if fairly traditional film that fails to break new ground but is effective nonetheless. Brooke Reynolds (Streep) is a mysterious woman who may have murdered one of the patients of psychiatrist Sam Rice (Scheider). Predictably Rice falls in love with Reynolds and we watch the theme played out. The idea was handled better in *Jagged Edge* but this film was nevertheless nominated for an Edgar award.

The Sting

(1973, US, 129 minutes)
Director: George Roy Hill. **Producers:** Tony Bill, Michael & Julia Phillips.
Screenplay: David S. Ward.
Starring: Paul Newman, Robert Redford, Robert Shaw, Charles Durning, Ray Walston.
Regarded by many as the classic scam movie, which garnered seven Oscar nominations and won four, including best picture. It was also nominated for an Edgar. The ever reliable team of Redford and Newman play two con-men who, in revenge for the death of an old friend, play an exceedingly complex con-trick on Mobster Doyle Lonnegan (Shaw) in order to sting him for a fortune. Set in the 1930s with period music by Scott Joplin, the film is full of atmosphere. Unfortunately Hollywood can never leave well enough alone and they tried it all again with *The Sting II* (1983), this time with Jackie Gleason and Mac Davis as the con-men and Oliver Reed as the Mobster. It fails on all the points on which the original scored. The book of the original film is *The Sting* (1973) by Robert Weverka.

Straight Time

(1978, US, 114 minutes)
Director: Ulu Grosbard. **Producers:** Stanley Beck, Tim Zinneman.
Screenplay: Alvin Sargent, Jeffrey Boam, Edward BUNKER from Bunker's book *No Beast So Fierce*.
Starring: Dustin Hoffman, Theresa Russell, Gary Busey, Harry Dean Stanton, M. Emmet Walsh.
A sharp little nugget of a movie, overlooked and underrated in its time, but part of the transition towards more realistic gangster movies. Max

Dembo (Hoffman) is an ex-con on parole who, surrounded by all the low life of Los Angeles, finds it near impossible to go straight. Based on Bunker's semi-autobiographical novel, the story emphasizes how little the system supports people trying to go straight and how easy it is to sink back into old ways. Hoffman had originally planned to direct this movie but found it too much acting in it as well.

The Strange Report

(UK TV series, 1969–70, 17 episodes, b&w)
Creator: Norman Felton.
Producers: Norman Felton (executive); Robert Berger.
Directors: Several including Charles Crichton, Daniel Petrie, Peter Duffell and Brian Smedley-Ashton.
Writers: Several, including Don Brinkley, Roger Parkes, John Kruse and Edward de Blasio.
Starring: Anthony Quayle, Kaz Garas, Anneke Wills, Gerald Sim, Charles Lloyd Pack.
Adam Strange (Quayle) was a retired Home Office criminologist who was still consulted by his former colleagues, especially Chief Superintendent Cavanagh (Sim) whenever a case baffled them. Strange's flat had a state-of-the-art forensic laboratory but he also consulted Professor Marks (Lloyd Pack – the father of Trigger in *Only Fools and Horses)*. He was also helped by his American friend Hamlyn Gynt (Garas) and his girl friend Evelyn McLean (Wills). The cases, which always had report numbers and a file reference such as "Report 5055: Cult" and "Report 2642: Hostage", were complex and intriguing. For instance, "Report 0649: Skeleton" was about the discovery of a wartime skeleton in a basement and "Report 1021: Shrapnel" tried to unravel whether a laboratory explosion was an accident or murder. The series was frequently topical with episodes on illegal immigrants, heart transplants and strange religious sects. There were plans to develop the series in the US but they fell through when Quayle and Wills decided not to continue. The book of the series was *Strange Report* (1970) by John F. Burke.

Strangers

(UK TV series, 1978–82, 32 episodes) followed by BULMAN (1985–87, 20 episodes)
Creator: Murray Smith, Richard Everitt. **Producer:** Richard Everitt.
Directors: Several, including Ben Bolt, William Brayne, Tristan DeVere Cole, Ken Grieves, Laurence Moody, Charles Sturridge, Baz Taylor, Jonathan Wright-Miller.
Writers: Several, including Edward Boyd, Murray Smith.
Starring: Don Henderson, Dennis Blanch, John Ronane, Frances Tomelty, Marc McManus, Thorley Walters.

The character of DS George Bulman (Henderson) first appeared in the three-part TV serial *The XYY Man* (1976), which itself spawned a short TV series (1977; 10 episodes). It was based on the first of the Spider Scott novels by Kenneth Royce (1920–97) and the title alluded to the fact that Scott (Stephen Yardley) had been born with an extra Y chromosome which gave him the urge to steal and turned him into an excellent cat burglar. Scott's talents were useful to British intelligence and he was recruited to break into a foreign embassy. The subsequent series had Scott still working occasionally for the secret service but, on his days off, continuing to commit crime and Bulman, along with DC Derek Willis (Blanch) were the Scotland Yard detectives on his trail. When *The XYY Man* series came to an end Bulman was resurrected in *Strangers*, along with Willis, but now relocated to Manchester, on the basis that local villains would not recognize these "strangers". This series allowed Henderson to develop Bulman's oddities – his preference for wearing fingerless gloves, sniffing inhalers, quoting Shakespeare and talking in a harsh whisper. After two series Bulman and his team were transferred back to London as part of an "Inner City Squad" which could be despatched anywhere in England. New members to the team included Mark McManus as Chief Superintendent Lambie, a tough, no-nonsense officer in what became a preamble for Taggart. Although the series ended in 1982 Bulman was given one further outing in *Bulman*. Now retired and running a clock and watch repair shop he is consulted by his former colleagues Lambie and Blanch and in effect becomes a P.I., egged on by Lucy McGinty (Siobhan Redmond) the daughter of an old friend. Bulman frequently went undercover but his identity is discovered and a contract placed on him and he has to leave the country. In the second series there was a continuing thread involving his former boss, William Dugdale (Walters) which reached a climax in the final episode. There were three spin-off Bulman novels, two by Robert Holdstock, *Bulman Returns* and *One of Our Pigeons is Missing* (both 1984) and *Thin Ice* (1987) by John Brosnan writing as John Raymond.

Straw Dogs

(1971, UK, 118 minutes)

Director: Sam Peckinpah. **Producer:** Daniel Melnick.

Screenplay: David Zelag Goodman, Sam Peckinpah based on the novel *The Siege of Trencher's Farm* by Gordon M. WILLIAMS.

Starring: Dustin Hoffman, Susan George, Peter Vaughan, Colin Welland, T.P. McKenna.

A seminal film in the early seventies which tested the acceptability of screen violence. David (Hoffman) is a harmless American maths teacher who settles in a Cornish village where his new young wife was raised. He soon finds himself in conflict with the locals and his pacifism is put to the test when his wife is raped. Even thirty years on the film is uncompromising and shocking.

Street Legal

(Canadian TV series, 1986–94, 124 episodes)
Creator: William DEVERELL.
Directors: Many, including Milan Cheylov, Stacey Curtis, Allan Harmon, Bruce Pittman.
Writers: Many, including James Nadler, William Deverell.
Starring: Sonja Smits, C. David Johnson, Eric Peterson, Cynthia Dale.
The longest-running Canadian legal drama, developed by Deverell from his script for the TV movie *Shellgame* (1985). It was set in a small but growing Toronto law firm with a strong and contrasting cast of characters who each took their leads in an otherwise ensemble performance. The show was inevitably compared to *L.A. Law*, and initially *Street Legal* was preferred by Canadian audiences as more human and more realistic, but over time they welcomed its mutation into a hectic *L.A. Law* clone with a whirlwind cast of characters. Despite its long success the series was curtailed suddenly with a final TV movie where Novak (Dale) is charged with assisting a suicide. Deverell adapted his pilot as the book *The Betrayal* (1995).

The Streets of San Francisco

(US TV series, 1972–7, 120 episodes)
Creator: Quinn Martin.
Producers: Quinn Martin (executive), John Wilder, William Yates, Cliff Gould.
Directors: Many, including Corey Allen, Barry Crane, Richard Donner, Michael Douglas, Harry Falk, Walter Grauman, William Hale, Bernard Kowalski, Arthur Nadel, Michael Preece, Seymour Robbie, Barry Shear.
Writers: Many, including Rod Maker, Walter Black, Rick Husky, Del Reisman.
Starring: Karl Malden, Michael Douglas.
Karl Malden was excellent as streetwise experienced cop Lieutenant Mike Stone who is teamed with smart, young college-educated detective Steve Keller (Douglas). Stone's avuncular feelings towards Keller were genuine, as Malden had known Douglas since his childhood. The series was developed from Carolyn Weston's novel *Poor, Poor Ophelia* (1972), but with a twist. In the novel, where the detectives are called Al Krug and Casey Kellog, the young detective is the empathic one with new ideas, but in the TV series, it is the older detective who understands the ways of the young and the new detective who has much to learn. Weston wrote two more Krug and Kellog novels, *Susannah Screaming* (1975) and *Rouse the Demon* (1976),

but by then the TV series had developed its own persona and they were not adapted. The strength of the series lay not only in the strong bond between Stone and Keller but in the adaptability of the characters, especially Stone, who was able to blend new police methods into his years of experience. When Douglas moved on to big-time films he was replaced by Richard Hatch as Inspector Dan Robbins, but the chemistry was gone and the series was wrapped up the following year. A one-off TV movie, *Back to the Streets of San Francisco* (1992), saw Malden reprise his rôle. The episode "Requiem for Murder" won an Edgar in 1977.

The Sweeney

(UK TV series, 1975–82, 53 episodes + pilot)

Creator: Ian Kennedy Martin.

Producers: Lloyd Shirley, George Taylor (executives); Ted Childs.

Directors: Many, including William Brayne, Douglas Camfield, Ted Childs, Tom Clegg, Jim Goddard, Terry Green, Mike Vardy, David Wickes.

Writers: Many, including Ranald Graham, Martin Hall, Tony Hoare, Tony Marsh, Roger Marshall, Troy Kennedy Martin, Trevor Preston, Alan Prior, Robert Banks Stewart.

Starring: John Thaw, Dennis Waterman, Garfield Morgan.

The same team that produced *Special Branch*, and developed the basis for hard-hitting, relentless TV cops, cranked the rack up a notch with *The Sweeney* – the title based on Cockney rhyming slang for the Flying Squad – Sweeney Todd. John Thaw played Inspector Jack Regan, a streetwise, 24-hour a day cop, who had no time for villains and just wanted to be out there sorting them out, even if that meant a punch up or two. Much to the frustration of his boss, Chief Inspector Haskins (Morgan), Regan would use whatever strong-arm tactics were necessary and cared little for the rules. His partner was Sergeant George Carter (Waterman) who, had it not been for some wise teaching, would have run the streets himself. Instead he joined in with Regan, and also consorted with villains, but did not always agree with Regan's tactics, and part of the fun of the series was the bickering between them. The series originally raised eyebrows for its swearing, vulgarisms and violence, but no one could deny its appeal. It was really little more than a modern-day rough-and-tumble cops-and-robbers chase series, culminating in Regan nabbing the villain with a triumphant "Yer nicked." The series appeal was mostly due to the performances of Thaw and Waterman but also because it had a tight team of experienced writers and directors. The pilot episode was to be called *The Outcasts*, but was changed to *Regan* (1974). There were also two spin-off feature films, *Sweeney!* (1976) and *Sweeney 2* (1978) which took the language and violence to extra depths. The creator, Ian Kennedy Martin, wrote three novels based on the series: *Regan* (1975; as *The Sweeney*,

1975), *Regan and the Manhattan File* (1975) and *Regan and the Deal of the Century* (1977). Seven more novels appeared under the alias Joe Balham: *Regan and the Lebanese Shipment*, *Regan and the Human Pipeline*, *Regan and the Snout Who Cried Wolf*, *Regan and the Bent Stripper* (all 1977), *Regan and the Venetian Virgin* and *Regan and the High Rollers* (both 1978). There was also the book of the second film, *Sweeney 2: The Blag* (1978).

Taggart

(UK TV series, 1983–*current*, 50 + episodes)
Creator: Glenn Chandler. **Producers:** Robert Love, Murray Ferguson, Graeme Gordon.
Directors: Many, including Laurence Moody, Haldane Duncan, Danny Hiller, Alan Macmillan, Ian Madden, Marcus White.
Writers: Many, including Glenn Chandler, Eric Coulter, Mark Greig, Steve Griffiths, Danny McMahon, John Milne, Julian Jones, Stuart Hepburn.
Starring: Mark McManus/Alex Norton, Neil Duncan, James MacPherson, Blythe Duff, Colin McCredie, Robert Robertson, John Michie, Iain Anders, Harriet Buchan.
After *The Bill*, *Taggart* is the world's second longest-running TV crime drama series. It first aired as a one-off three-part serial called *Killer*, in which Chief Inspector Jim Taggart (McManus) and graduate policeman, DS Peter Livingstone (Duncan), find a straightforward murder is not so simple after all and they have a serial strangler in their midst. The author of that serial, Glenn Chandler, thereafter developed the series around McManus as the tough, cynical, determined Scottish detective at Glasgow C.I.D. who finds himself involved in especially gruesome or violent crimes. Taggart has seen hard times and his life continues to be difficult – his wife Jean (Buchan) is confined to a wheelchair – and with the pressure of the job he is frequently angry, frustrated and bitter even when trying to remain fair, calm and professional. Unlike other TV series *Taggart* did not appear in groups of six or twelve weekly episodes, but as one-off short serials. However, from 1987 it did switch to a weekly hourly (and more recently two-hourly) format, but it has always remained occasional. One consequence of this is that more time is spent on each series and the quality shows. Throughout its long life it has been remained original, consistent and of high quality. A new colleague, DC Mike Jardine (MacPherson), joined in the sixth episode, "The Killing Philosophy", which involved a burglar who threatened housewives with a crossbow. Jardine, a thorough but principled teetotaller with a strong ethical code, soon replaced Livingstone and, as the series progressed, worked his way up through the ranks. After McManus's sudden death in 1994, when the series might have ceased, it continued with Jardine in charge, but became more of an ensemble piece with Jardine's colleagues

DC Jackie Reid (Duff), who had joined in 1990, DC Stuart Fraser (McCredie), who joined in 1994, and finally DI Robbie Ross (Michie) who joined in 1998 with Jardine's promotion to DCI. This has allowed episodes to play to individuals' strength and also to develop tensions and relationships between them, especially with the maverick Ross. Most recently, however, Jardine was murdered by a vengeful ex-con, and new boss DCI Matt Burke (Norton) has taken over, returning to the hard edge of Taggart. Glenn Chandler produced a novel based on his pilot episode, *Killer* (1983). Five other episodes have been novelized by Peter Cave: *Murder in Season* (1985), *Gingerbread* (1993), *Nest of Vipers* (1993), *Fatal Inheritance* (1994) and *Forbidden Fruit* (1994).

The Taking of Pelham One Two Three

(1974, US, 104 minutes)
Director: Joseph Sargent. **Producers:** Gabriel Katzka, Edgar J. Sherick.
Screenplay: Peter Stone, based on the novel by John GODEY.
Starring: Robert Shaw, Walter Matthau, Martin Balsam, Dick O'Neill, James Broderick.
One of the seminal films of the seventies for the tense high-action hostage film, which was again updated for the nineties with Jan De Bont's *Speed* (1994). Here mega-thug Robert Shaw, known only by the code-name "Blue", along with his colour-coded henchmen, hijack a New York subway train and threaten to kill the hostages unless they are paid a ransom of $1 million. Transport cop Lieutenant Garber (Matthau) has to keep Shaw talking and look like progress is being made while planning how to thwart the hijackers. The direction, editing and pace sustain the tension and keep this film eminently watchable.

The Talented Mr Ripley

(1999, US, 139 minutes)
Director: Anthony Minghella. **Producer:** William Horberg, Tom Sternberg.
Screenplay: Anthony Minghella based on the novel by Patricia HIGHSMITH.
Starring: Matt Damon, Gwyneth Paltrow, Jude Law, Cate Blanchett, James Rebhorn.
Patricia Highsmith's amoral Mr Ripley is much liked by film-makers and has appeared in several films. The novel on which this film was based was previously made into the film *Plein Soleil* (1960; aka *Purple Noon, Broad Daylight* and *Lust for Evil*) by French director René Clément. Both versions are excellent and follow the book fairly faithfully. Ripley (Damon) is mistaken by rich businessman Greenleaf (Rebhorn) to be a friend of his son Dickie (Law), and Ripley finds

himself invited to visit the Greenleaf villa in France. Ripley succeeds in winning over Dickie and his wife Marge (Paltrow) and having tasted the high life Ripley will do whatever is necessary to keep it. In Clément's version (with Alain Delon as Ripley and Maurice Ronet changed to Philippe rather than Dickie), Ripley remains charismatic but is more devious and the cinematography contrasts his corruptive influence against the beautiful world around him. The vanity of Philippe almost excuses Ripley's actions. Minghella does much the same except that in his version Ripley's charisma comes from his cruelty and his totally selfish attitude. He is more of an anti-hero than Delon, and it is doubtless a sign of the times that his true villainy can take on an acceptability. Highsmith's work is always disturbing and probing and both these adaptations develop different perspectives each to considerable effect.

Target

(UK TV series, 1977–8, 17 episodes)
Producer: Philip Hinchcliffe.
Directors: Many, including Den Bolt, Gordon Flemyng, Mike Vardy, David Wickes.
Writers: Many, including David Agnew, Ken Follett, P.J. Hammond, Philip Hinchcliffe, Tony Hoare, David Wickes.
Starring: Patrick Mower, Philip Madoc, Vivien Heilbron, Brendan Price.

Target was BBC's answer to *The Sweeney*. Even though *The Sweeney* had evoked its share of public outcry, the BBC's viewers were even more vocal and there was much hostility to the show's violence and thuggish portrayal of the police. It was set in Hampshire's regional crime squad with activity around an unnamed major port (not a million miles from Southampton). Despite the attraction of Patrick Mower as the trendy DS Steve Hackett and the stolid resourcefulness of his boss, DCS Tate (Madoc) the series lacked the appeal of *The Sweeney*, primarily because it lacked the humour and relationship between its main characters. The violence was toned down for the second series, but it never made it to a third.

Taxi Driver

(1976, US, 114 minutes)
Director: Martin Scorsese. **Producer:** Michael & Julia Phillips.
Screenplay: Paul Schrader.
Starring: Robert De Niro, Jodie Foster, Cybill Shepherd, Harvey Keitel, Peter Boyle.

A film that left its influence on other movies and on pop culture. De Niro plays Travis Bickle, a deeply disturbed Vietnam veteran who is now a

New York taxi driver, but he haunts and reckies the streets as if the enemy was around every corner and behind every sign. In this world Bickle is either the hunter or the hunted. When he is rejected by his girlfriend Betsy (Shepherd), Bickle transfers his affections to a young prostitute, Iris (Foster), whom he determines to rescue from the vile world about her. His attack on her pimp, Sport (Keitel), and his gang lets loose a new warfare in which Bickle becomes a crazed one-man crusader. Its muted photography, ominous musical score (by Bernard Herrmann) and sinister portrayal of New York makes this film a stark example of seventies *noir*, and Bickle's descent into punk also reflects the anarchy of that movement. The film, along with De Niro, Foster and Herrmann, were all nominated for Oscars.

T.J. Hooker

(US TV series, 1982–6, 92 episodes)
Creator: Rick Husky.
Producers: Aaron Spelling, Leonard Goldberg (executives); Chuck Bowman, Stephen Downing, Jack V. Fogarty, Don Ingalls, Jeffrey M. Hayes, Rick Husky, Kenneth R. Koch, Bernie Kukoff, Simon Muntner, Ed Waters.
Directors: Many, including Don Chaffey, James Darren, Vincent McEveety, Leonard Nimoy, William Shatner.
Writers: Many, including Joe GORES, Allison Hock, Stephen Kandel.
Starring: William Shatner, Heather Locklear, James Darren, Adrian Zmed, Richard Herd.
T.J. Hooker was a clean-cut, honest cop, which resulted in a relatively trivial series that seemed out of place and out of time. After he had boldly gone from *Star Trek*, Shatner became the dedicated and upright law enforcer T.J. Hooker, a former detective with the "L.C.P.D." who gave up his shield and declined promotion in order to be out there on the streets. Hooker was somewhat tested by life – he was divorced and his former working partner had been killed. He gave the benefit of his experience in the Police Academy and worked frequently with trainees and rookies. Unfortunately Shatner made Hooker almost a parody of himself and the character and series generally lacked credibility. *T.J. Hooker* might have worked as a young adults' series, but for adult audiences it was a dinosaur. Nevertheless it attracted several star names including Sharon Stone and Leonard Nimoy, who also directed some episodes.

Toma

(US TV series, 1973–4, 23 episodes)
Creator: Edward Hume.
Producer: Roy Huggins, Jo Swerling (executives); Stephen J. CANNELL.

Directors: Richard Bennett, Nicholas Colasanto, Marc Daniels, Charles S. Dubin, Daniel Haller.
Writers: Many, including Stephen J. Cannell, Edward Hume, Roy Huggins, Dave Toma, Tony Musante.
Starring: Tony Musante, Simon Oakland, Susan Strasberg.
The character of Toma was based on a real cop, Detective David Toma of the Newark, New Jersey, police department. He preferred operating alone and did things his own way, frustrating his boss, Inspector Spooner (Oakland). Toma was adept at disguise so was an ideal undercover agent and frequently served as a decoy. In real life this is what won Toma fame – his true story is told in *Toma: The Compassionate Cop* (1973) by Michael Brett and David Toma, which formed the basis for the series. When the show was renewed for a second season Musante stunned everyone by leaving, maintaining that he had only ever intended to stay for one season. The producers brought in new actor Robert Blake but Blake wanted to change the character and in the end the show was relaunched as *Baretta*. One of Cannell's rejected scripts for the *Toma* series became the basis for *The Rockford Files*. Toma lent his name to two novels, based on the series, by Jack Pearl, *The Airport Affair* (1975) and *The Affair of the Unhappy Hooker* (1976).

Topkapi

(1964, US, 120 minutes)
Producer/Director: Jules Dassin.
Screenplay: Monja Danischewsky, based on the novel *The Light of Day* by Eric Ambler.
Starring: Peter Ustinov, Merlina Mercouri, Maxmilian Schell, Robert Morley, Akim Tamiroff.
Dassin returned to the success of his hit heist movie, *Rififi* (1955), but this time with a light-hearted touch and, as a result, established the comic crime caper as a rightful sub-genre. Elizabeth Lipp (Mercouri) and William Walter (Schell) mastermind a daring jewel robbery from an Istanbul museum and hire a gang of misfits, led by Arthur Simpson (Ustinov) to carry it out. The film mixes humour with suspense in just the right doseage. Ustinov received an Oscar for his performance. The film was itself lampooned by Blake Edwards' *The Pink Panther*, which ushered in the hilarious career of Inspector Clouseau.

A Touch of Frost

(UK TV series, 1992–*current*, 28 episodes)
Creator: R.D. Wingfield.
Producer: Richard Bates, Philip Burley, David Jason, Vernon Lawrence (executives); Martyn Auty, Don Leaver, Simon Lewis, Lars Macfarlane.
Directors: Many, including Roger Bamford, Roy Battersby, Ross

Devenish, John Glenister, Robert Knights, Don Leaver, Adrian Shergold, Anthony Simmons, Graham Theakston, Herbert Wise,
Writers: Many, including Malcolm Bradbury, David Gilman, Richard Harris, Christopher Russell, Michael Russell.
Starring: David Jason, Bruce Alexander, Neil Phillips, Matt Bardock.
David Jason, Britain's favourite comic actor, showed he could play it straight as the irascible, old-style detective, Jack Frost, who refuses to conform. Frost is always at odds with his modernist, bureaucratic, but out-of-touch boss, Superintendent Mullett (Alexander) but because Frost was something of a local hero (he had been shot when on duty and was awarded the George Cross) and knows his patch inside out, Mullett lets Frost have so much rope. Frost suffers no fools and is forever chiding his young assistants. Audience sympathy, however, is always with Frost, not just because in the first series his wife is terminally ill, but because Frost has a true compassion for the victims of crime and does his best to help them. Each episode is a two-hour special, following in the wake of *Inspector Morse* (indeed, Frost similarly passed into the nation's affections), allowing for considerable plot and character development. Frost usually tries to solve two or three unconnected crimes at once and seems to survive on very little sleep, bacon sandwiches and stealing other people's mugs of tea. After the death of a colleague Frost resigned but was eventually lured back for a further series and one-off specials.

Traffik

(1989, UK TV, 360 minutes)
Director: Alistair Reid. **Producer:** Brian Eastman.
Screenplay: Simon Moore.
Starring: Bill Paterson, Lindsay Duncan, Jamal Shah, Talal Hussain, George Kukura, Julia Ormond.
Traffik was broadcast as a five-part serial on UK's Channel 4 in June/July 1989 and was released on video/DVD in 2001. It was an in-depth study of the drug trade seen from three perspectives. Firstly there is an English MP, Jack Lithgow (Paterson), who has been appointed the drug supremo with the remit of getting some control over the huge problem. Unbenknown to him his daughter Caroline (Ormond) is an addict. Secondly there is Helen, the wife (Duncan) of a rich German drug dealer, Karl (Kukura), whose husband has been caught dealing and she takes over his operation. Finally there is a farmer (Shah) in Pakistan who struggles to make a living by growing the poppies and has to kowtow to drug overlord Tariq Butt (Hussain). The film follows the whole process, rather like a car assembly line (as Moore perceived it), exploring the social circumstances that encourage the process and the corruption that pervades government and police operations in allowing

the trade to flourish. This fascinating serial formed the basis for the Oscar and Edgar-winning film, *Traffic* (2000). Moore's script was adapted by Stephen Gaghan and the film was directed by Steven Soderbergh. The action was translated to the Americas with Michael Douglas as the drug tsar, Steven Bauer as the wealthy drug dealer and Catherine Zeta Jones as his wife. Mexico replaces Pakistan where Benicia Del Toro gives a riveting performance as a cop investigating the drug trade and torn between his duty and temptation.

Trial and Retribution

(UK TV series, 1997–*current*, 4 2-part episodes)
Creator/Producer: Lynda LA PLANTE.
Directors: Aisling Walsh, Jo Johnson, Michael Whyte.
Writer: Lynda La Plante.
Starring: David Hayman, Kate Buffery.
This occasional series is presented in two two-hour parts. The first part looks at the investigations by Detective Superintendent Walker (Hayman) and D.I. North (Buffery) and the second part involves the trial or culmination of the case. The crimes are always violent. The first episode involved a child murder, the second a serial killer, the third (with an especially fine performance by Richard E. Grant) involves a missing child and the fourth reopens a case in which Walker had been involved eight years before. The relationship between Walker and North is often tense, especially when they become an item. Walker is single-minded, stubborn and irascible whilst North tries to be calm and positive. The series makes good use of split screen techniques.

12 Angry Men

(1957, US, 95 minutes, b&w)
Director: Sidney Lumet. **Producer:** Henry Fonda, Reginald Rose.
Screenplay: Reginald Rose, based on his TV play.
Starring: Henry Fonda, Lee J. Cobb, Ed Begley, E.G. Marshall, Jack Warden, Martin Balsam, John Fiedler, Jack Klugman, Edward Binns, Joseph Sweeney, George Voskovec, Robert Webber.
This classic jury-room drama was originally broadcast as an episode in the TV series *Studio One* on 20 September 1954. That went on to win an Emmy award for the author, Reginald Rose, the director (Frank Schaffner) and for actor Bob Cummings who played the one member of a jury who is convinced that the defendant is innocent. In the film version Henry Fonda takes that rôle. (Only two actors, Joseph Sweeney and George Voskovec, were in both the TV and film versions.) The entire film was shot in a real New York jury room yet Lumet, in his directorial debut, along with the cinematographic art of Boris Kaufman, was able to use a multitude of camera angles and shots to create a suspenseful atmosphere.

The film superbly captures the drama of a jury room and explores how prejudices play a part in individual's judgements, regardless of the evidence. The film was nominated for an Oscar, as were Rose and Lumet, and the film won the Edgar award. Rose's original teleplay was published in 1955. He updated it a further time for a cable TV movie version, as *Twelve Angry Men* (2000), directed by William Friedkin, with Jack Lemmon as the sole juror who believes in the defendant's innocence.

Under Suspicion

(1999, US, 99 minutes)
Director: Stephen Hopkins. **Producer:** Lori McCreary, Anne Marie Gillen, Stephen Hopkins.
Screenplay: Tom Provost, W. Peter Iliff from the script for *Garde à Vue* [aka *The Inquisitor*] by Claude Miller, Jean Herman and Michel Audiard, based on the novel *Brainwashed* by John WAINWRIGHT.
Starring: Morgan Freeman, Gene Hackman, Thomas Jane, Monica Bellucci.
John Wainwright's tense novel, *Brainwashed*, has twice lent itself to cinema adaptation. In 1981 Claude Miller directed *Garde à Vue*, which was set in France, while the latest version has moved to Puerto Rico. Both are set on the evening of celebrations (New Year's Eve in the latest case) and both films follow the plot almost identically. Two young girls have been raped and murdered and police captain Victor Benezet (Freeman) has some queries over the statement made by attorney Henry Hearst (Hackman), who discovered the second body. He calls him in to clarify a few points and the questioning steadily shifts from a casual chat to a taut interrogation on both sides. Both versions build on every ounce of psychological suspense but English audiences lose much in *Garde à Vue* through sub-titles, so an English-speaking version is welcomed.

An Unsuitable Job for a Woman

(1981, UK, 94 minutes)
Director: Christopher Petit. **Producers:** Michael Relph, Peter McKay.
Screenplay: Elizabeth McKay, Brian Scobie and Christopher Petit from the novel by P.D. JAMES.
Starring: Billie Whitelaw, Pippa Guard, Paul Freeman, David Horovich.
Pippa Guard plays Cordelia Gray, a partner in a detective agency who takes over the business when her partner commits suicide. Guard is excellent in her portrayal of a determined but uncertain detective in what was one of the earliest female P.I. films. She is hired by Elizabeth Leaming (Whitelaw) to discover the truth behind a purported suicide by a rich businessman's son in a rented country cottage. The film is faithful to the novel without recourse to explanatory flashbacks and includes some

classic moments such as Gray struggling to get herself out of a well. The novel was adapted for TV as a three-part serial in 1997 with Helen Baxendale as Cordelia Gray and Annette Crosbie as her well-meaning elderly assistant, Edith Sparshott. This proved to be the pilot for an occasional series of specials which have numbered three to date: "A Last Embrace" (1998) by William Humble, "Living on Risk" (1999) by Christopher Russell and "Playing God" (2001) by Barbara Machin. P.D. James was apparently dissatisfied with these later productions and has vowed not to write another Cordelia Gray novel. Baxendale, however, portrays a determined and wholly realistic female P.I.

The Untouchables

(US TV series, 1959–63, 118 episodes, b&w; revived 1992–4, 44 episodes)

Producer: First series: Alan A. Armer, Leonard Freeman, Quinn Martin, Jerry Thorpe (executives), Alvin Cooperman, Roger Kay, Norman Retchin, Stuart Rosenberg, Charles Russell. Second series: Tim Iacofano, Richard Brams.

Directors: Many, including (first series) Robert Gist, Walter Grauman, Howard W. Koch, Ida Lupino, Bernard McEveety, Vincent McEveety, Don Medford, Allen Reisner, Stuart Rosenberg; (second series) Tucker Gates.

Writers: Many, including (first series) Theodore Apstein, George Bellak, Robert C. Dennis, George Eckstein, David Zelag Goodman, David P. Harmon, David Karp, Ernest Kinoy, E. Jack Neuman, Jerome Ross, Sy Salkowitz; (second series) Morgan Gendel, Tim Iacofano, Andrew Mirisch, Dan Peterson.

Starring: First series: Robert Stack, Jerry Paris, Abel Fernandez, Nick Georgiade, Bruce Gordon, Neville Brand; Second series: Tom Amandes, John Rhys-Davies, David James Elliott, William Forsythe, Paul Regina.

The Untouchables was inspired by the book of that title by Eliot Ness and Oscar Fraley which revealed the work of Ness, a Treasury Man, and his team of incorruptible cops in Chicago in the 1930s and how they eventually caught Al Capone and other gangsters. The book was the source of a two-part TV film, *The Scarface Mob*, broadcast in the *Desilu Playhouse* series in April 1959, which starred Robert Stack as Ness. The success of that production led to a series, which began in October 1959. These weekly black-and-white episodes caught the atmosphere of the thirties. Filmed in semi-documentary style, with voice over narration by Walter Winchell, the series gave a strong impression that they were all based on true cases. In fact, apart from the constant battle between Ness and Capone's second-in-command Frank Nitti (Gordon), they soon moved away from Ness's book and covered investigations into many renowned criminals of the thirties including Ma Barker, Bugs Moran, Vincent Coll and Dutch Schultz.

Increasingly the series became fictional, bringing criticism from Italian Americans that they were always being shown as gangsters. The series was also criticized for its unrelenting violence, which was toned down in later episodes. Nevertheless the series remained perenially popular and ran for four seasons. Over 20 years after the series ceased Brian De Palma returned to the original book for the feature film *The Untouchables* (1987) with Kevin Costner as Ness, Sean Connery as reliable cop Jim Malone and Robert De Niro as Al Capone. This led in turn to Robert Stack reprising his rôle in the TV movie *The Return of Eliot Ness* (1991) and finally to a revival of the series in 1993. Since Stack was now in his seventies, Tom Amandes played Ness, John Rhys-Davies was Agent Malone and William Forsythe was Capone. This series ran as a serial rather than a series of episodes and spent more time on the private lives of Ness and his team. The book of the 1987 film is *The Untouchables* by Marvin H. Albert. There were no books arising from either series, but Max Allan COLLINS has written four books featuring Eliot Ness: *The Dark City* (1987), *Butcher's Dozen* (1988), *Bullet Proof* (1989), *Murder by the Numbers* (1993).

The Usual Suspects

(1995, US, 108 minutes)

Director: Bryan Singer. **Producer:** Bryan Singer, Michael McDonnell.

Screenplay: Christopher McQuarrie.

Starring: Gabriel Byrne, Kevin Spacey, Stephen Baldwin, Pete Postlethwaite, Chazz Palminteri, Dan Hedaya.

Once in a while a fairly traditional, if complicated, story, told with nineties bravura, will capture the imagination. Such was *The Usual Suspects*. The story is revealed almost entirely in flashback by Kint (Spacey) the sole survivor of a gang which had been brought together in a police line-up as being "the usual suspects". One of them, McManus (Baldwin) suggests they join forces on what proves to be a successful robbery, but when they subsequently try to launder the money they find themselves trapped in a gameplan by master criminal Keyzer Soze. Soze, who you never see and who acts through his lawyer Kobayashi (Postlethwaite), forces the gang to steal a drugs consignment from a ship and from that point on the gang's fortunes are doomed. The convoluted plot is pieced together by customs officer Dave Kujan (Palminteri), who is trying to find the identity of Soze whom he suspects does not exist. The film, which is fascinating in its twists and turns, holds its ace card till the final moment. Clever and ingenious, it's the type of film that restores your faith in the ability of the cinema. It received both the Edgar and Anthony awards as the year's best crime film. McQuarrie's screenplay was published along with an interview as *The Usual Suspects* (1996).

Van der Valk

(UK TV series, 1972–3, 1977, 1991–2, 32 episodes)
Creator: Nicolas FREELING.
Producers: Lloyd Shirley, George Taylor, Brian Walcroft (executives); Michael Chapman, Robert Love, Geoffrey Gilbert, Chris Burt.
Directors: Several, including Ben Bolt, William Brayne, Douglas Camfield, Ted Childs, Tom Clegg, Peter Duguid, Graham Evans, James Goddard, Don Leaver, Mark Miller, Anthony Simmons, Dennis Vance, Mike Vardy.
Writers: Several, including Philip Broadley, Michael Chapman, Geoffrey Gilbert, Roger Marshall, Arden Winch.
Starring: Barry Foster, Susan Travers/Joanna Dunham/Meg Davies, Nigel Stock/Ronald Hines, Michael Latimer.
Although Barry Foster is often seen playing villains he adapted well to portraying the frequently morose and moody Dutch police inspector and, indeed, Foster's screen persona gave Van der Valk a renegade edge which suited the character. As in the novels Van der Valk is portrayed as having a strong family life with his wife, Arlette, frequently offering her views on cases. The series took full advantage of filming around Amsterdam and developed plots with more relevance to Holland and the surrounding territory. In the 1977 season the series was being produced by the same team as *The Sweeney* and the violence quota increased. The series fitted itself around Foster's screen commitments so was never regular, with seasons running in 1972, 1973 and 1977 before a long hiatus and a brief revival for two-hour episodes in 1991 and 1992. The series was popular, especially in its early run, when its theme music, "Eye Level" by Jack Trombey, became a UK number-one hit.

Vega$

(US TV series, 1978–81, 66 episodes + pilot)
Creator: Michael Mann.
Producer: Aaron Spelling, Douglas S. Cramer (executives); Alan Godfrey.
Directors: Many, including Cliff Bole, Don Chaffey, Mark Daniels, Larry Dobkin, Harry Falk, Bob Kelljan, Richard Lang, Bernard McEveety, Sutton Roley,
Writers: Many, including Larry Alexander, Dennis Donnelly, Larry Forrester, David Harmon, Bill Stratton, Robert Swanson.
Starring: Robert Urich, Tony Curtis, Phyllis Davis, Bart Braverman.
Vega$ was a typical Aaron Spelling (he of *Dynasty*, *Charlie's Angels*, *Matt Houston*, *Hart to Hart*) glitz-and-glamour series – all puffery and very little substance. Dan Tanna (Urich) is a P.I. in Las Vegas with an office at the Desert Inn Casino owned by Philip Roth (Curtis). Tanna makes it known he won't do divorces or serve as a bodyguard and so most of his

cases, for the rich and fabulous at the casinos, are looking for little rich-girls. He drives around in a flash red Thunderbird sports car, so he clearly doesn't do undercover work, and he has sexy, glamorous assistants. In fact there was so much glitz in this series, and so many well-known film stars in cameo roles, that the stories suffered near white-out from the glare. After this the P.I. series had nowhere else to go so Michael Mann converted the idea into an all action-police series, *Miami Vice*. There was one novel based on Mann's script for the pilot, called *Vega$* (1978) by Max Franklin.

V.I. Warshawski

(1991, US, 89 minutes)
Director: Jeff Kanew. **Producer:** Jeffrey R.Lurie.
Screenplay: David Aaron Cohen, Edward Taylor, Nick Thiel.
Starring: Kathleen Turner, Jao O. Sanders, Charles Durning, Angela Goethals, Nancy Paul.
Sara PARETSKY's strong-minded feminist P.I. Victoria Warshawski should have adapted well to the screen, especially played by Kathleen Turner, who seems tailor-made for the part. Unfortunately Kanew chose to have a special script written rather than adapt one of the novels and this weak story, about a young teenager who hires Warshawski to find the truth about her father's death, fails to deliver. Turner and others, especially Charles Durning as the compassionate cop Lieutenant Mallory, do their best but they belong on another set. A quality adaptation of the Warshawski series has yet to happen.

The Way of the Gun

(2000, US, 119 minutes)
Director: Christopher McQuarrie. **Producer:** Kenneth Kokin.
Screenplay: Christopher McQuarrie.
Starring: Ryan Phillippe, Benicio Del Toro, Juliette Lewis, Taye Diggs, James Caan.
McQuarrie followed the success of *The Usual Suspects* with his directorial debut of this far less convoluted but considerably more violent flashback to the Peckinpah-style gangster movies of the seventies. Two petty hoodlums, Parker (Phillippe) and Longbaugh (Del Toro) get way out of their depth when they kidnap a surrogate mother (Lewis) in the hope of getting a ransom from the wealthy parents-to-be. Little do they know that the father has underworld connections and he soon has hit-man Sarno (Caan) on their trail. Strong performances and McQuarrie's versatile script produce what might otherwise have been a fairly basic film and, once again, he delivers a gripping finale.

Wiseguy

(US TV series, 1987–90, 75 episodes)
Creator: Stephen J. CANNELL, Frank Lupo.
Producer: Stephen J. Cannell (executive).
Directors: Many, including Charles Correll, Lyndon Chubbuck, Bill Corcoran, Dennis Dugan, William A. Fraker, Rod Holcomb, Robert Iscove, Aaron Lipstadt, Larry Shaw.
Writers: Many, including David J. Burke, Stephen J. Cannell, David J. Burke, Stephen Kronish, Frank Lupo, Alfonse Ruggerio.
Starring: Ken Wahl, Jonathan Banks, Jim Byrnes, Gerald Anthony, Steven Bauer.

A "wiseguy" is an undercover agent and one such is Vinnie Terranova (Wahl) who works for the Organized Crime Bureau (OCB). In a series of extremely well-executed story-lines, Terranova infiltrates a crime syndicate and establishes himself until he is able to gather enough evidence to reel the crime boss in. Terranova's cover has to be complete – even his friends think he's become a crook. His only link to his OCB boss, Frank McPike (Banks), is a man known as "Lifeguard" (Byrnes), who must also maintain the utmost secrecy to keep Terranova safe. Each undercover assignment was complicated and stories could not be wrapped up in a single hourly episode so they were stretched over story arcs of up to ten episodes. There were ten such story arcs through the series. Ken Wahl left because of a dispute after the third series but Cannell used that to his advantage, making the final season an investigation into Terranova's disappearance (perhaps kidnapped by a Salvadoran death squad) and new wiseguy, disbarred US prosecutor Michael Santana (Bauer), is assigned to track him down. Six years after the series finished Terranova did return with all the old cast in a one off TV movie of *Wiseguy* (1996) in which he becomes involved in organized high-tech information brokering. *Wiseguy* was inspired to some degree by Nicholas Pileggi's book *Wiseguy* (1985) which also inspired the film *Goodfellas*. Two episodes of *Wiseguy* were shortlisted for the Edgar award with "White Noise" (1990) winning; the series also won the American Mystery Award in 1990.

Witness

(1985, US, 112 minutes)
Director: Peter Weir. **Producer:** Edward S. Feldman.
Screenplay: Earl W. Wallace and William Kelley.
Starring: Harrison Ford, Kelly McGillis, Josef Sommer, Jan Rubes, Lukas Haas.

Although this film won both the Edgar and Anthony awards as the year's best crime movie, the crime element is only the springboard for what is really a romance and an exploration of cultural attitudes. A young Amish boy (Haas) witnesses a murder and cop John Book (Ford) has to go undercover in the Amish community in order to protect him. Book is attracted to the boy's mother, Rachel (McGillis), which causes friction within the community in addition to Book's own attitudes to violence. It comes to a head when the villains (including corrupt cops) come to get the boy and Book and the Amish community have to decide how to deal with the problem. The end result, though inevitable, is in some ways disappointing, but the overall film is a delight. It won Oscars for its editing and screenplay and was also nominated as best picture.

Wycliffe

(UK TV series, 1993–8, 38 episodes)
Creator: W.J. BURLEY.
Producers: Jenny Reeks, Steve Matthews (executive); Pennant Roberts (pilot), Geraint Morris, Michael Bartley.
Directors: Several, including Roger Bamford, Graeme Harper, David Innes, Martyn Friend, Patrick Lau, Michael Owen Morris, A.J. Quinn, Pennant Roberts, Jack Shepherd.
Writers: Several, including Isabelle Grey, P.J. Hammond, Rob Heyland, Andrew Holden, Russell Lewis, Jonathan Rich, Steve Trafford.
Starring: Jack Shepherd, Lynn Farleigh, Helen Masters, Jimmy Yuill.
Set in Cornwall this was a rather low-key police drama series featuring the investigations of Detective Superintendent Charles Wycliffe (Shepherd). Wycliffe has a team of sharp and intelligent officers, especially D.I.s Lane (Masters) and Kersey (Yuill), who do most of the groundwork, whilst Wycliffe does the thinking and absorbs the atmosphere. Not Cornish himself, Wycliffe remains detached from the locals and studies them objectively, concentrating on the lives of the victims of crime to see what emerges. Though it was a well-scripted series and Wycliffe was every bit as smart as, say, Morse or Frost, it lacked the chemistry of those series probably because Shepherd played his part with an air of detachment, apart from occasional outbursts of temper. He had a family life, though this was kept mostly off screen till the final series. At the end of the fourth series Wycliffe is shot and severely injured and though determined to return to work his character became even more lost in his thoughts. Many of Burley's books were adapted for the series with several original episodes being written.

The XYY Man *see under* Strangers

The Yakuza [aka The Brotherhood of the Yakuza]

(1974, US, 112 minutes)
Director: Sydney Pollack. **Producer:** Sydney Pollack, Michael Hamilburg.

Screenplay: Paul Schrader, Robert Towne, from a story-line by Leonard Schrader.
Starring: Robert Mitchum, Ken Takakura, Brian Keith, Keiko Kishi, Eiji Okada.
A Yakuza is a member of a major Japanese crime syndicate, in effect a Mobster, but one shaped by Japanese tradition and society, which colours it with images of the Samurai, making a Yakuza an outlaw, but one that in the movies (rather than historically) operates by strict codes. There has been a sub-genre of Yakuza films in Japan since the 1940s with imitations in Hong Kong cinema (especially the films of John Woo starting with *A Better Tomorrow* [1986] and peaking with *The Killer* [1989]) and occasionally in Hollywood. The best westernized film is, undoubtedly, *The Yakuza*, even though it stumbles a bit in its attempts to fuse the two cultural traditions. Harry Kilmer (Mitchum) is a P.I. who is sent to Japan by George Tanner (Keith) to rescue Tanner's daughter who has been kidnapped by the Yakuza. In order to penetrate the Yakuza, Kilmer has to team up with ex-Yakuza Ken Tanaka (Takakura), who has his own strong code of honour. It's an uneasy alliance and inevitably, through western eyes, Mitchum's persona holds the screen against the incomprehensibility of another culture, whilst the film probably has the same dichotomy to eastern audiences. Nevertheless it is a bravura performance by Mitchum in a fascinating if slightly flawed film. For another example see Ridley Scott's *Black Rain*. The book of the film is *The Yakuza* (1975) by Leonard Schrader.

Year of the Dragon

(1985, US, 134 minutes)
Director: Michael Cimino. **Producer:** Dino De Laurentiis.
Screenplay: Oliver Stone, Michael Cimino.
Starring: Mickey Rourke, John Lone, Ariane, Leonard Termo.
A film which, through the portrayal of the central character, NYPD's Captain Stanley White (Rourke), sails dangerously close to being racist, and certainly anti-Oriental. White, a highly decorated but almost stereotypical renegade cop, is given the assignment of sorting out the street gangs in New York's Chinatown (though the sets were entirely rebuilt in North Carolina). White, going beyond his remit and ultimately upsetting everyone he knows, takes on the Chinese underworld and it becomes a one-man vendetta against anyone remotely Oriental. There are some well-filmed action scenes, but in between White's relentless campaign becomes distasteful. If anyone is redeemed in this film it is the character of Joey Tai (Lone), a young crime-lord who is trying to get his own house in order, despite being the main target of the vengeful White. The book of the film is *Year of the Dragon* (1981) by Robert Daley.

The Young Savages

(1961, US, 103 minutes, b&w)

Director: John Frankenheimer. **Producer:** Pat Duggan.

Screenplay: Edward Anhalt, J.P. Miller from the novel, *A Matter of Conviction*, by Evan Hunter [Ed McBain].

Starring: Burt Lancaster, Shelley Winters, John Davis Chandler, Telly Savalas.

A compelling film of justice and the root causes of crime. Hank Bell (Lancaster) is an honourable assistant DA who is prosecuting three young delinquents for the murder of a blind Puerto Rican boy. Bell recalls his own youth in the New York slums and feels some affinity with the hooligans, and through this understanding he begins to suspect that at least one of them is not guilty, but is tied by his bond with the gang. This is the type of film that seems all-too ordinary today but was significant in its day in its attempts to understand youth culture.

Z

(1968, French/Algerian, 125 minutes)

Director: Costa-Gavras. **Producer:** Jacques Perrin.

Screenplay: Costa-Gavras, Jorge Semprun based on the novel by Vassilis Vassilikos.

Starring: Yves-Montand, Jean-Louis Trintignant, Irene Papas, Jacques Perrin.

A French film with English subtitles, this is a political thriller based on the real-life Lambrakis affair in Greece in 1963. A leading opposition politician (Montand) is killed at a political rally and the police are keen to cover it up as an accident, but the relentless examination by the investigating magistrate (Trintignant) uncovers a web of police and government corruption. The film was banned in Greece until the overthrow of the military government in 1974. It won both an Oscar and Edgar as best foreign film.

Z Cars

(UK TV series, 1962–78, 695 episodes)

Creator: Troy Kennedy Martin.

Producers: David E. Rose, Colin Morris, Ronald Travers, Richard Beynon, Roderick Graham, Ron Craddock.

Directors: Many, including Christopher Barry, Alan Bromly, Terence Dudley, Michael Hayes, Richard Harding, Ken Loach, John McGrath, Paddy Russell, Shaun Sutton.

Writers: Many, including Robert Barr, Keith Dewhurst, John Hopkins, Elwyn Jones, Troy Kennedy Martin, John McGrath, Alan Plater, Allan Prior.

Starring: Stratford Johns/John Barrie, Frank Windsor/John Slater, James Ellis, Brian Blessed, Joseph Brady, Jeremy Kemp/Colin Welland.

Until superseded by *The Bill*, *Z Cars* was Britain's longest-running TV crime series and it was the first to reflect accurately the lives of everyday policemen. It was originally broadcast live, in black and white. It was set in Liverpool in the fictional area of Newtown and Seaport. A new team was established under the overall control of Detective Inspector Barlow (Johns) and D.S. Watt (Windsor). There were two patrol cars, Z Victor 1 and Z Victor 2. In the first car was burly northerner "Fancy" Smith (Blessed) and Scot Jock Weir (Brady) whilst the other car had Irishman Bert Lynch (Ellis) and the irascible Bob Steele (Kemp). Over the years the teams would change. Colin Welland, for instance, came in as Lynch's new partner, PC David Graham. The character of Lynch remained throughout the series. The team of Barlow and Watt were the first to establish themselves: Barlow as the bullish, arrogant, strong-minded head of the unit and Watt as the cooler, more thoughtful, more approachable individual. This team proved so strong that they had their own spin-off series, *Softly, Softly*, and with their departure at the end of 1965 it was planned to stop *Z Cars* but it returned in 1967 with new lead detectives Sam Hudson (Barrie) and Tom Stone (Slater). Originally with a weekly 50-minute episode it briefly switched to twice-weekly half-hour episodes during 1971/72, by which time it was in glorious colour. The public drew many of the characters to their hearts, and audience figures exceeded 14 million during the first season. It was headline news when young P.C. Sweet (Terence Edmond) died during an heroic rescue. The series tackled all of the major crime issues of the day and was amongst the first to show domestic violence and the rise of drugs. In time, though, *Z Cars* was overtaken by such high action American influenced series as *The Sweeney* which though less realistic had more energy. Later series, such as *Juliet Bravo* and especially *The Bill*, have managed to recapture and update the formula of *Z Cars* and adapt it for a new audience. There were three novels drawn from the series: *Z Cars* (1962) by Troy Kennedy Martin, *Z Cars Again* (1963) by Allan Prior and *Z Cars: Barlow on Trial* (1965) by Ian Kennedy Martin.

Appendix 1
Award Winners

The two most prestigious awards in the crime fiction field are the Edgars, presented by the Mystery Writers of America (starting in 1946) and the Daggers, presented by the Crime Writers' Association in Great Britain (starting in 1953). Also highly coveted is the French Grand Prix de Littérature Policière, first presented in 1948. Since 1979 a host of new and specialist awards have been created. These include the Anthony Award (named after Anthony Boucher) presented at the World Mystery Convention, the Macavity Award sponsored by Mystery Readers International, the Shamus Award presented by the Private Eye Writers of America, and the Canadian Arthur Ellis Award, presented by the Crime Writers of Canada Association. There are also awards presented in Germany, Sweden and Japan for Best Foreign Novel in translation which frequently goes to British or American books.

The following lists all awards presented by these and other bodies in alphabetical order of the award's name. Unless stated otherwise the year cited is the year the award was presented, for items published in the previous year.

Agatha Award

Presented annually since 1989 at the Malice Domestic convention held in Washington D.C. each May. The award, in the form of a teapot, celebrates the traditional mystery, typified by the works of Agatha Christie.

1989.
Best Novel: *Something Wicked*, Carolyn G. Hart.
Best First Mystery Novel: *A Great Deliverance*, Elizabeth George.
Best Short Story: "More Final Than Divorce", Robert Barnard (*EQMM*, October 1988).

1990.
Best Novel: *Naked Once More*, Elizabeth Peters.
Best First Mystery Novel: *Grime and Punishment*, Jill Churchill.
Best Short Story: "A Wee Doch and Doris", Sharyn McCrumb (*Mistletoe Mysteries*, ed. Charlotte MacLeod).
Lifetime Achievement: Phyllis A. Whitney.

1991.
Best Novel: *Bum Steer*, Nancy Pickard.
Best First Mystery Novel: *The Body in the Belfry*, Katherine Hall Page.

Best Short Story: "Too Much to Bare", Joan Hess (*Sisters in Crime 2*, ed. Marilyn Wallace).

1992:
Best Novel: *I.O.U.*, Nancy Pickard.
Best First Mystery Novel: *Zero at the Bone*, Mary Willis Walker.
Best Short Story: "Deborah's Judgment", Margaret Maron (*A Woman's Eye*, ed. Sara Paretsky).

1993.
Best Novel: *Bootlegger's Daughter*, Margaret Maron.
Best First Mystery Novel: *Blanche on the Lam*, Barbara Neely.
Best Short Story: "Nice Gorilla', Aaron & Charlotte Elkins (*Malice Domestic 1*, ed. Elizabeth Peters).

1994.
Best Novel: *Dead Man's Island*, Carolyn G. Hart.
Best First Mystery Novel: *Track of the Cat*, Nevada Barr.
Best Short Story: "Kim's Game", M.D. Lake (*Malice Domestic 2*, ed. Mary Higgins Clark).
Best Non-fiction: *The Doctor, The Murder, The Mystery*, Barbara D'Amato.
Lifetime Achievement: Mignon G. Eberhart.

1995.
Best Novel: *She Walks These Hills*, Sharyn McCrumb.
Best First Mystery Novel: *Do Unto Others*, Jeff Abbott.
Best Short Story: "The Family Jewels", Dorothy Cannell (*Malice Domestic 3*, ed. Nancy Pickard).
Best Non-fiction: *By a Woman's Hand*, Jean Swanson & Dean James.

1996.
Best Novel: *If I'd Killed Him When I Met Him*, Sharyn McCrumb.
Best First Mystery Novel: *The Body in the Transept*, Jeanne M. Dams.
Best Short Story: "The Dog Who Remembered Too Much", Elizabeth Daniels Squire (*Malice Domestic 4*, ed. Carolyn G. Hart).
Best Non-fiction: *Mystery Readers Walking Guide – Chicago*, Alzina Stone Dale.

1997.
Best Novel: *Up Jumps the Devil*, Margaret Maron.
Best First Mystery Novel: *Murder on a Girl's Night Out*, Anne George.
Best Short Story: "Accidents Will Happen", Carolyn Wheat (*Malice Domestic 5*, ed. Phyllis A. Whitney).
Best Non-fiction: *Detecting Women 2*, Willetta Heising.
Lifetime Achievement: Emma Lathen.

1998.
Best Novel: *The Devil in Music*, Kate Ross.
Best First Mystery Novel: *The Salaryman's Wife*, Sujata Massey.

Best Short Story: "Tea for Two", M.D. Lake (*Funnybones*, ed. Joan Hess).
Best Non-fiction: *Detecting Men*, Willeta Heising.
Lifetime Achievement: Charlotte MacLeod.

1999.
Best Novel: *Butcher's Hill*, Laura Lippman.
Best First Mystery Novel: *The Doctor Digs a Grave*, Robin Hathaway.
Best Short Story: "Of Course You Know That Chocolate is a Vegetable", Barbara D'Amato (*EQMM*, November 1998).
Best Non-fiction: *Mystery Reader's Walking Guide to Washington D.C.*, Alzina Stone Dale.
Lifetime Achievement: Patricia Moyes.

2000.
Best Novel: *Mariner's Compass*, Earlene Fowler.
Best First Mystery Novel: *Murder with Peacocks*, Donna Andrews.
Best Short Story: "Out of Africa", Nancy Pickard (*Mom, Apple Pie, and Murder*, ed. Nancy Pickard).
Best Non-fiction: *Teller of Tales: The Life of Arthur Conan Doyle*, Daniel Stashower.
Lifetime Achievement: Dick Francis.

2001.
Best Novel: *Storm Track*, Margaret Maron.
Best First Mystery Novel: *Death on a Silver Tray*, Rosemary Stevens.
Best Short Story: "The Man in the Civil Suit", Jan Burke (*Malice Domestic 9*, ed. Joan Hess).
Best Non-fiction: *100 Favorite Mysteries of the Century*, Jim Huang.
Lifetime Achievement: Mildred Wirt Benson.

American Mystery Award

Established in 1988 by *Mystery Scene* magazine with a view to establishing a more defined categorization of mystery fiction. The award was voted for by readers of *Mystery Scene*, with a final adjudication by the magazine's publishers. It was presented each summer and consisted of a plaque. It was dropped after 1993 because of insufficient votes.

1988.
Best Traditional Mystery: *The Corpse in Oozak's Pond*, Charlotte MacLeod.
Best Private Eye Novel: *A Trouble of Fools*, Linda Barnes.
Best Crime Novel: *Bandits*, Elmore Leonard.
Best Espionage Novel: *Siege*, Richard Hoyt.
Best Police Procedural: *Tricks*, Ed McBain.
Best Paperback Original: *Wild Night*, L.J. Washburn.
Best Romantic Suspense: *Trojan Gold*, Elizabeth Peters.
Best Short Story: "Soft Monkey", Harlan Ellison (*Mystery Scene Reader #1*, ed. Ed Gorman).

Best Scholarly Work: *Crime & Mystery: The Best 100 Books*, H.R.F. Keating.
Best Book Editor: Michael Seidman (Tor Books).
Best Movie: *Fatal Attraction*.
Best TV series: *Crime Story*.

1989.
Best Traditional Mystery: *The Silver Ghost*, Charlotte MacLeod.
Best Private Eye Novel: *Down River*, Loren D. Estleman.
Best Crime Novel: *Silence of the Lambs*, Thomas Harris.
Best Espionage Novel: *Thai Horse*, William Diehl.
Best Police Procedural: *D.O.A.*, Dave Pednau.
Best Paperback Original: *The Grub-and-Stakes Pinch a Poke*, Alisa Craig [Charlotte MacLeod].
Best Romantic Suspense: *Smoke & Mirrors*, Barbara Michaels.
Best Scholarly Work: *Silk Stockings*, Victoria Nichols and Susan Thompson.
Best Book Editor: Mary Ann Eckels, Chris Cox, Joe Blades (Ballantine Books).
Best Fan Publication: *Mystery and Detective Monthly*.
Best Movie: *Mississippi Burning*.
Best TV series: *Murder She Wrote*.
Best TV Show: *The Billionaire Boys Club*.

1990.
Best Traditional Mystery: *Diet to Die For*, Joan Hess.
Best Private Eye Novel: *The Shape of Dread*, Marcia Muller.
Best Crime Novel: *Killshot*, Elmore Leonard.
Best Espionage Novel: *A Season in Hell*, Jack Higgins.
Best Police Procedural: *A Good Night Kill*, Lillian O'Donnell.
Best Paperback Original: *Trouble in the Brasses*, Charlotte MacLeod.
Best Romantic Suspense: *Naked Once More*, Elizabeth Peters.
Best Short Story: "Afraid all the Time", Nancy Pickard (*Sisters in Crime*, ed. Marilyn Wallace).
Best Scholarly Work: *A Catalogue of Crime*, Jacques Barzun and Wendell Hertig Taylor.
Best Critic: Jon L. Breen.
Best Fan Publication: *The Drood Review*.
Best Editor: Kate Miciak (Bantam Books).
Best Movie: *Heathers*.
Best TV Show: *Wiseguy*.

1991.
Best Traditional Mystery: *The Gladstone Bag*, Charlotte MacLeod.
Best Private Eye Novel: *Jackpot*, Bill Pronzini.
Best Crime Novel: *Whiskey River*, Loren Estleman.
Best Thriller/Espionage Novel: *Countdown*, David Hagberg.
Best Police Procedural: *Vespers*, Ed McBain.
Best Paperback Original: *The Man Who Would Be F. Scott Fitzgerald*, David Handler.
Best Romantic Suspense: *Goodnight, Mr. Holmes*, Carole Nelson Douglas.

Best Short Story: "A Poison That Leaves No Trace", Sue Grafton (*Sisters in Crime 2*, ed. Marilyn Wallace).
Best Scholarly Work: *John Dickson Carr: A Critical Study*, S.T. Joshi.
Best Fan Publication: *The Armchair Detective*.
Best Editor: Kate Miciak (Bantam Books).
Best Movie: *Presumed Innocent*.
Best TV Show: *L.A. Law*.

1992.
Best Traditional Mystery: *The Last Camel Died at Noon*, Elizabeth Peters.
Best Private Eye Novel: *"H" is for Homicide*, Sue Grafton.
Best Crime Novel: *Rough Justice*, Ken Gross.
Best Espionage Novel: *Crossfire*, David Hagberg.
Best Police Procedural: *Widows*, Ed McBain.
Best Paperback Original: *Sisters in Crime 4*, ed. Marilyn Wallace.
Best Romantic Suspense: *Woman Without a Past*, Phyllis A. Whitney.
Best Short Story: "Nine Sons", Wendy Hornsby (*Sisters in Crime 4*, ed. Marilyn Wallace).
Best Scholarly Work: *Edgar A. Poe: Mournful and Never-Ending Remembrance*, Kenneth Silverman.
Best True Crime Book: *Predator*, Jack Olsen.
Best Fan Publication: *The Drood Review*.
Best Book Editor: Jane Chelius (Pocket Books).
Best Movie: *Silence of the Lambs*.
Best TV Series: *Mystery*.

1993.
Best Traditional Mystery: *Defend & Betray*, Anne Perry.
Best Private Eye Novel: *"I" is for Innocent*, Sue Grafton.
Best Crime Novel: *Without Due Process*, J.A. Jance.
Best Espionage Novel: *Critical Mass*, David Hagberg.
Best Police Procedural: *Kiss*, Ed McBain.
Best Paperback Original: *Poisoned Ivy*, M.D. Lake.
Best Romantic Suspense: *All Around the Town*, Mary Higgins Clark.
Best Short Story: "Candles in the Rain', Doug Allyn (*EQMM*, November 1992).
Best Scholarly Work: *Alias S.S. Van Dine*, John Loughery.
Best True Crime Book: *Swift Justice*, Harry Farrel.
Best Fan Publication: *The Armchair Detective*.
Best Book Editor: Susanne Kirk (Scribner's).
Best Movie: *The Player*.
Best TV Show: *Prime Suspect*.

Anthony Award

Presented each autumn since 1986 at the World Mystery Convention, known as Bouchercon. The award, which has been variably a plaque and a sculpture, is named after Anthony Boucher and is voted upon by members of Bouchercon.

1986.

Best Novel: *"B" is for Burglar*, Sue Grafton.
Best First Novel: *When the Bough Breaks*, Jonathan Kellerman.
Best Paperback Original: *Say No to Murder*, Nancy Pickard.
Best Short Story: "Lucky Penny", Linda Barnes (*New Black Mask Quarterly #3*, ed. Matthew Bruccoli & Richard Laymon).
Best TV Series: *Murder, She Wrote*.
Best Movie: *Witness* (director Peter Weir).
Grand Master: Barbara Mertz (aka Elizabeth Peters and Barbara Michaels).

1987.

Best Novel: *"C" is for Corpse*, Sue Grafton.
Best First Novel: *Too Late to Die*, Bill Crider.
Best Paperback Original: *The Junkyard Dog*, Robert Campbell.
Best Short Story: "The Parker Shot Gun", Sue Grafton (*Mean Streets*, ed. Robert J. Randisi).

1988.

Best Novel: *Skinwalkers*, Tony Hillerman.
Best First Novel: *Caught Dead in Philadelphia*, Gillian Roberts.
Best Paperback Original: *The Monkey's Raincoat*, Robert Crais.
Best Short Story: "Breakfast Television", Robert Barnard (*EQMM*, January 1987).
Best TV Series: *Mystery!*
Best Movie: *The Big Easy* (director Jim McBride).

1989.

Best Novel: *The Silence of the Lambs*, Thomas Harris.
Best First Novel: *A Great Deliverance*, Elizabeth George.
Best Paperback Original: *Something Wicked*, Carolyn G. Hart.
Lifetime Achievement: Dorothy Salisbury Davis.
Distinguished Contribution: Joan Kahn.

1990.

Best Novel: *The Sirens Sang of Murder*, Sarah Caudwell.
Best First Novel: *Katwalk*, Karen Kijewski.
Best Paperback Original: *Honeymoon With Murder*, Carolyn Hart.
Best Short Story: "Afraid All the Time", Nancy Pickard (*Sisters in Crime*, ed. Marilyn Wallace).
Best TV Series: *Inspector Morse*.
Best Movie: *Crimes and Misdemeanors* (director Woody Allen)
Lifetime Achievement: Michael Gilbert.

1991.

Best Novel: *"G" is for Gumshoe*, Sue Grafton.
Best First Novel: *Postmortem*, Patricia Cornwell.
Best Paperback Original: (tie) *Grave Undertaking*, James McCahery; *Where's Mommy Now?*, Rochelle Krich.

Best Short Story: "The Celestial Buffet", Susan Dunlap (*Sisters in Crime 2*, ed. Marilyn Wallace).
Best Critical Work: *Synod of Sleuths*, ed. Jon L. Breen & Martin H. Greenberg.
Best TV Series: *Mystery!*
Best Motion Picture: *Presumed Innocent* (director Alan J. Pakula, based on novel by Scott Turow).
Lifetime Achievement: William Campbell Gault.

1992.
Best Novel: *The Last Detective*, Peter Lovesey.
Best First Novel: *Murder on the Iditarod Trail*, Sue Henry.
Best True Crime: *Homicide: A Year on the Killing Streets*, David Simon.
Best Short Story: "Lucky Dip", Liza Cody (*A Woman's Eye*, ed. Sara Paretsky).
Best Anthology: *A Woman's Eye*, ed. Sara Paretsky.
Best Critical/Biographical Work: *100 Great Detectives*, Maxim Jakubowski.
Booksellers' Award: *Native Tongue*, Carl Hiaasen.
Lifetime Achievement: Charlotte MacLeod.

1993.
Best Novel: *Bootlegger's Daughter*, Margaret Maron.
Best First Novel: *Blanche on the Lam*, Barbara Neely.
Best True Crime: *The Doctor, the Murder, the Mystery*, Barbara D'Amato.
Best Critical Work: *Doubleday Crime Club Compendium*, Ellen Nehr.
Best Short Story: "Cold Turkey", Diane Mott Davidson (*Sisters in Crime 5*, ed. Marilyn Wallace).
Best Motion Picture: *The Crying Game* (director Neil Jordan).
Lifetime Achievement: (joint) Hammond Innes, Ralph McInerny.

1994.
Best Novel: *Wolf in the Shadows*, Marcia Muller.
Best First Novel: *Track of the Cat*, Nevada Barr.
Best Critical Work: *The Fine Art of Murder*, ed. Ed Gorman, Martin H. Greenberg, Larry Segriff & Jon L. Breen.
Best True Crime: *A Rose for Her Grave*, Ann Rule.
Best Short Story: "Checkout", Susan Dunlap (*Malice Domestic 2*, ed. Mary Higgins Clark).
Best Short Story Anthology: *Malice Domestic 2*, ed. Mary Higgins Clark.
Lifetime Achievement: Tony Hillerman.

1995.
Best Novel: *She Walks These Hills*, Sharyn McCrumb.
Best First Novel: *The Alienist*, Caleb Carr.
Best Short Story: "The Monster of Glamis", Sharyn McCrumb (*Royal Crimes*, ed. Maxim Jakubowski & Martin H. Greenberg).
Best Critical Work: *Crime Fiction* (2nd edition), ed. B.A. Pike & J. Cooper.
Best Anthology/Short Story Collection: *The Mysterious West*, ed. Tony Hillerman.

Best True Crime: *Criminal Shadows*, David Canter.
Best TV Series: *Prime Suspect* (Lynda La Plante).
Best Movie: *Pulp Fiction* (director Quentin Tarantino).

1996.
Best Novel: *Under the Beetle's Collar*, Mary Willis Walker.
Best First Novel: *Death in Bloodhound Red*, Virginia Lanier.
Best Paperback Original: *Deal Breaker*, Harlan Coben.
Best Short Story: "And Pray Nobody Sees You", Gar Anthony Haywood (*Spooks, Spies, and Private Eyes*, ed. Paula L. Woods).
Best Short Story Collection: *The McCone Files*, Marcia Muller.
Best True Crime: *Dead by Sunset*, Ann Rule.
Best Critical Work: *The Armchair Detective Book of Lists* (2nd edition), Kate Stine.
Best TV Show: *The X-Files.*
Best Movie: *The Usual Suspects* (director Bryan Singer).
Best Magazine/Digest/Review Publication: *The Armchair Detective.*
Best Editor: Sara Ann Freed (Mysterious Press).
Best Publisher: St Martin's Press.
Best Cover Art: for *The Body in the Transept* by Jeanne Dams (Walker Books).

1997.
Best Novel: *The Poet*, Michael Connelly.
Best First Novel: (tie) *Death in Little Tokyo*, Dale Furutani; *Somebody Else's Child*, Terris McMahan Grimes.
Best Paperback Original: *Somebody Else's Child*, Terris McMahan Grimes.
Best Short Story: "Accidents Will Happen", Carolyn Wheat (*Malice Domestic 5*, ed. Phyllis A. Whitney).
Best Critical/Biographical Work: *Detecting Women 2*, Willetta Heising.
Best Fanzine: *The Armchair Detective.*
Lifetime Achievement: Donald Westlake.

1998.
Best Novel: *No Colder Place*, S.J. Rozan.
Best First Novel: *Killing Floor*, Lee Child.
Best Paperback Original: *Big Red Tequila*, Rick Riordan.
Best Short Story: (tie) "A Front Row Seats", Jan Grape (*Vengeance is Hers*, ed. Mickey Spillane & Max Allan Collins); "One Bag of Coconuts", Edward D. Hoch (*EQMM*, November 1997).
Best Cover Art: Michael Kellner for *Night Dogs* by Kent Anderson (Dennis McMillan).
Distinguished Contribution: Ruth Cavin.

1999.
Best Novel: *Blood Work*, Michael Connelly.
Best First Novel: *Iron Lake*, William Kent Krueger.
Best Paperback Original: *Butcher's Hill*, Laura Lippman.
Best Short Story: "Of Course You Know That Chocolate is a Vegetable", Barbara D'Amato (*EQMM*, November 1998).

Best Critical Non-fiction: *Deadly Pleasures* magazine, ed. George Easter.
Lifetime Achievement: Len & June Moffatt.

2000.
Best Novel: *In a Dry Season*, Peter Robinson.
Best First Novel: *Murder With Peacocks*, Donna Andrews.
Best Paperback Original: *In Big Trouble*, Laura Lippman.
Best Short Story: "Noir Lite", Margaret Chittenden (*EQMM*, January 1999).
Best Critical Non-Fiction: *Detecting Women 3*, Willetta Heising.
Best Series of the Century: Agatha Christie's Hercule Poirot.
Best Writer of the Century: Agatha Christie.
Best Novel of the Century: *Rebecca*, Daphne DuMaurier (published 1938).
Lifetime Achievement: Jane Langton.

2001.
Best Novel: *A Place of Execution*, Val McDermid.
Best First Novel: *Death of a Red Heroine*, Qiu Xiaoling.
Best Paperback Original: *Death Dances to a Reggae Beat*, Kate Grilley.
Best Short Story: "The Problem of the Potting Shed", Edward D. Hoch (*EQMM*, July 2000).
Best Critical Non-Fiction: *100 Favorite Mysteries of the Century*, edited Jim Huang.
Best Anthology/Story Collection: *Master's Choice II*, edited Lawrence Block.
Best Fan Publication: *Mystery News*.
Lifetime Achievement: Edward D. Hoch.

Arthur Ellis Award

Presented annually (each May) since 1984 by the Crime Writers of Canada (CWC) at their Annual Dinner. They are named after Canada's chief hangman in the 1920s whose name has now become synonymous for the hangman. The award is limited to Canadian writers. The CWC also presents the Derrick Murdoch Award for outstanding contribution to the genre of crime writing in Canada. Originally called the Chairman's Award it is named after its first recipient.

1984.
Best Novel: *The Night the Gods Smiled*, Eric Wright.
Chairman's Award: Derrick Murdoch.

1985.
Best Novel: *Murder Sees the Light*, Howard Engel.
Best True Crime: *The Trials of Israel Lipsky*, Martin Friedland.
Derrick Murdoch Award: Tony Aspler.

1986.
Best Novel: *Death in the Old Country*, Eric Wright.
Best True Crime: *A Canadian Tragedy*, Maggie Siggins.
Derrick Murdoch Award: Margaret Millar.

1987.
Best Novel: *Buried on Sunday*, Edward O. Phillips.
Best First Novel: *Murder on the Run*, Medora Sale.
Best True Crime: *Hunting Humans*, Elliott Leyton.
Derrick Murdoch Award: The CBC Drama Department.

1988.
Best Novel: *Swann: A Mystery*, Carol Shields.
Best First Novel: *The Goldfish Bowl*, Laurence Gough.
Best Short Story: "Looking for an Honest Man", Eric Wright (*Cold Blood*, ed. Peter Sellers).
Best True Crime: *Stung: The Incredible Obsession of Brian Moloney*, Gary Ross.
Derrick Murdoch Award: J.D. Singh & Jim Reicker.

1989.
Best Novel: *Jack*, Chris Scott.
Best First Novel: *A Stone of the Heart*, John Brady.
Best Short Story: "Killer in the House", Jas. R. Petrin (*AHMM*, mid-December 1988).
Best True Crime: *Conspiracy of Brothers*, Mick Lowe.

1990.
Best Novel: *Hot Shots*, Laurence Gough.
Best First Novel: *The Man Who Murdered God*, John Lawrence Reynolds.
Best Short Story: "Humbug", Josef Škvorecký (in *The End of Lieutenant Boruvka*).
Best True Crime: *Conspiracy of Silence*, Lisa Priest.
Derrick Murdoch Award: Eric Wilson.

1991.
Best Novel: *A Chill Rain in January*, L.R. Wright.
Best First Novel: *Sniper's Moon*, Carsten Stroud.
Best Short Story: "Innocence", Peter Robinson (*Cold Blood III*, ed. Peter Sellers).
Best True Crime: *Ginger: The Life and Death of Albert Goodwin*, Susan Mayse.
Best Genre Criticism/Reference: *Sherlock Holmes Among the Pirates*, Donald A. Redmond.

1992.
Best Novel: *Past Reason Hated*, Peter Robinson.
Best First Novel: *Flesh Wound*, Paul Grescoe.
Best Short Story: "Two in the Bush", Eric Wright (*Christmas Stalkings*, ed. Charlotte MacLeod).
Best True Crime: *Arms and the Man: Dr. Gerald Bull, Iraq and the Supergun*, William Lowther.
Best Genre Criticism/Reference: *Spy Fiction, Spy Films and Real Intelligence*, Wesley A. Wark.
Derrick Murdoch Award: William Bankier, James Powell & Peter Sellers.

1993.
Best Novel: *Lizardskin*, Carsten Stroud.
Best First Novel: *Passion Play*, Sean Stewart.
Best Short Story: "Mantrap", Nancy Kilpatrick (in *Murder, Mayhem and the Macabre*).
Best True Crime: *Redrum the Innocent*, Kirk Makin.

1994.
Best Novel: *Gypsy Sins*, John Lawrence Reynolds.
Best First Novel: *Memory Trace*, Gavin Scott.
Best Short Story: "Just Like Old Times", Robert J. Sawyer (*On Spec*, Summer 1993).
Best True Crime: *With Malice Aforethought*, David R. Williams.
Best Juvenile: *Abalone Summer*, John Dowd.
Best Play: *The Stillborn Lover*, Timothy Findley.

1995.
Best Novel: *A Colder Kind of Death*, Gail Bowen.
Best First Novel: *What's a Girl Gotta Do?*, Sparkle Hayter.
Best Short Story: "The Midnight Boat Toronto Palermo", Rosemary Aubert (*Cold Blood V*, ed. Peter Sellers).
Best True Crime: *The Prodigal Husband*, Michael Harris.
Derrick Murdoch Award: Jim & Margaret McBride.
Best Juvenile: *Torn Away*, James Heneghan.

1996.
Best Novel: *Mother Love*, L.R. Wright.
Best First Novel: (tie) *The Last Castrato*, John Spencer Hill; *Moonlit Days and Nights*, D.H. Toole.
Best Short Story: "Cotton Armour", Mary Jane Maffini (*The Ladies Killing Circle*, ed. Victoria Cameron & Audrey Jessup).
Best True Crime: *The Secret Lives of Sgt. John Wilson*, Lois Simmie.
Best Juvenile: *Mistaken Identity*, Norah McClintock.

1997.
Best Novel: *Innocent Graves*, Peter Robinson.
Best First Novel: *Death at Buckingham Palace,* C.C. Benison.
Best Short Story: "Dead Run", Richard J. Bercuson (*Storyteller*, Winter 1996/7).
Best True Crime: *The Cassock and the Crown*, Jean Monet.
Best Juvenile: *How Can a Frozen Detective Stay Hot on the Trail*, Linda Bailey.

1998.
Best Novel: *Trial of Passion,* William Deverell.
Best First Novel: *Deja Dead*, Kathy Reichs.
Best Short Story: "Widow's Weeds", Sue Pike (*Cottage Country Killers*, ed. Vicki Cameron & Linda Wiken).
Best True Crime: *When She Was Bad: Violent Women and the Myth of Innocence*, Patricia Pearson.

Best Juvenile: *The Body in the Basement*, Norah McClintock.
Derrick Murdoch Award: Howard Engel & Eric Wright.

1999.
Best Novel: *Old Wounds*, Nora Kelly.
Best First Novel: *Sudden Blow*, Liz Brady.
Best Short Story: "Last Inning", Scott MacKay (*EQMM*, February 1998).
Best True Crime: *No Claim to Mercy*, Derek Finkle.
Best Juvenile: *Sins of the Father*, Norah McClintock.
Derrick Murdoch Award: Ted Wood.

2000.
Best Novel: *The Feast of Stephen*, Rosemary Aubert.
Best First Novel: *Lost Girls*, Andrew Pyper.
Best Short Story: "One More Kill", Matt Hughes (*Blue Murder* e-zine).
Best True Crime: *Cowboys and Indians*, Gordon Sinclair, Jr.
Best Juvenile: *How Can a Brilliant Detective Shine in the Dark*, Linda Bailey.
Best Crime Writing in French: *Louna*, Lionel Noel.

2001.
Best Novel: *Cold is the Grave*, Peter Robinson.
Best First Novel: *Hands Like Coulds*, Mark Zuehlke.
Best Short Story: "Murder in Utopia", Peter Robinson (*Crime Through Time III*, ed. Sharan Newman).
Best True Crime: *The Spinster and the Prophet*, A.B. McKillip.
Best Original Crime Book in French: *Le Roman Policier en Amerique Française*, Norbert Spencer.
Derrick Murdoch Award: L.R. Wright.

Barry Award

Presented annually since 1997 by *Deadly Pleasures* magazine. They are named after the book reviewer and mystery fiction fan Barry Gardner (1939-1996). The recommended titles are short-listed by the editorial staff and then voted upon by readers.

1997.
Best Novel: *Bloodhounds*, Peter Lovesey.
Best First Novel: *Test of Wills*, Charles Todd.
Best Paperback Original: *Walking Rain*, Susan Wade.
Best Non-fiction: *Detecting Women 2*, Willetta L. Heising.

1998.
Best Novel: *Trunk Music*, Michael Connelly.
Best First Novel: *Killing Floor*, Lee Child.
Best Paperback Original: *Backspin*, Harlan Coben.

1999.

Best Novel: (tie) *On Beulah Height*, Reginald Hill; *Gone, Baby Gone*, Dennis Lehane.
Best First Novel: *Iron Lake*, William Kent Krueger.

2000.
Best Novel: *In a Dry Season*, Peter Robinson.
Best First Novel: *Murder With Peacocks*, Donna Andrews.
Best British Crime Novel: *A Place of Execution*, Val McDermid.
Best Paperback Original: (tie) *Every Move She Makes*, Robin Burcell; *An Antidote for Avarice*, Caroline Roe.

2001.
Best Novel: *Deep South*, Nevada Barr.
Best First Novel: *A Conspiracy of Paper*, David Liss.
Best British Crime Novel: *Black Dog*, Stephen Booth.
Best Paperback Original: *The Kidnapping of Rosie Dawn*, Eric Wright.
Don Sandstrom Memorial Award for Lifetime Achievement in Mystery Fandom: Marv Lachman.

Chester Himes Award

Presented annually to an Afro-American writer at the Chester Himes Mystery Conference in Oakland, California each May.

1996. Gar Anthony Haywood.
1997. Terris McMahon Grimes.
1998. Robert Greer.
1999. Walter Mosley.
2000. Eleanor Taylor Bland.
2001. Alice Holman.

Crime Writers' Association Awards

Presented annually since 1956 by the British Crime Writers' Association. Originally called the Crossed Red Herrings for the year's best crime fiction novel published in Britain, they became the Gold Dagger Award in 1960. In 1969 a Silver Dagger Award was introduced for the runner-up. Non-fiction was included from 1978. The Gold Dagger is now sponsored by The Macallan distillers so is officially called the Macallan Gold Dagger and Silver Dagger. The Diamond Dagger is sponsored by Cartier and is awarded to the author for outstanding contribution to the genre. The John Creasey Award is presented to the best first crime novel. The short-lived *Police Review* Award was for the novel that best represented police work. The CWA '92 Award was sponsored by Hazel Wynn Jones to run for three years and recognize novels set wholly or partly on the European continent. Since 1990 the *New Law Journal* has sponsored an occasional Rumpole Award for novels with a British legal setting. There is also the Last Laugh Award (formerly the *Punch* Award) for the most humorous crime book of the year, the CWA/Macallan Short Story Award, the Dagger in the Library (previously the Golden Handcuffs Award) for the author most popular with library readers, and the Ellis Peters Historical Dagger Award. A few other awards have been presented over the years as detailed below.

1955.
Best Novel: *The Little Walls*, Winston Graham.

1956.
Best Novel: *The Second Man*, Edward Grierson.

1957.
Best Novel: *The Colour of Murder*, Julian Symons.

1958.
Best Novel: *Someone from the Past*, Margot Bennet.

1959.
Best Novel: *Passage of Arms*, Eric Ambler.
Special Merit Awards: Roy Vickers for his contributions to crime fiction; Janet Green for her screenplay for *Sapphire*.

1960.
Gold Dagger: *The Night of Wenceslas*, Lionel Davidson.

1961.
Gold Dagger: *The Spoilt Kill*, Mary Kelly.
Special Merit Award: Berkley Mather for the quality of his television crime plays.

1962.
Gold Dagger: *When I Grow Rich*, Joan Fleming.

1963.
Gold Dagger: *The Spy Who Came in from the Cold*, John le Carré.
Special Merit Award: Allan Prior for his outstanding television crime plays.

1964.
Gold Dagger: *The Perfect Murder*, H.R.F. Keating.
Best Foreign: *The Two Faces of January*, Patricia Highsmith.
Special Merit Award: Herbert Harris for his valuable services in editing *Red Herrings* (the CWA Newsletter).

1965.
Gold Dagger: *The Far Side of the Dollar*, Ross Macdonald.
Best British: *Midnight Plus One*, Gavin Lyall.

1966.
Gold Dagger: *A Long Way to Shiloh*, Lionel Davidson.
Best Foreign: *In the Heat of the Night*, John Ball.
Special Merit Award: Julian Symons for *Crime and Detection: An Illustrated*

History from 1840.

1967.
Gold Dagger: *Murder Against the Grain*, Emma Lathen.
Best British: *Dirty Story*, Eric Ambler.
Special Award: Charles Franklin for his work as editor of the *Crime Writer*.

1968.
Gold Dagger: *Skin Deep*, Peter Dickinson.
Best Foreign: *The Lady in the Car with Glasses and a Gun*, Sebastian Japrisot.

1969.
Gold Dagger: *A Pride of Heroes*, Peter Dickinson.
Silver Dagger: *Another Way of Dying*, Francis Clifford.
Best Foreign: *The Father Hunter*, Rex Stout.

1970.
Gold Dagger: *Young Man, I Think You're Dying*, Joan Fleming.
Silver Dagger: *The Labyrinth Makers*, Anthony Price.
Special Award: Gavin Lyall for his work in editing the *Crime Background* pamphlets.

1971.
Gold Dagger: *The Steam Pig*, James McClure.
Silver Dagger: *Shroud for a Nightingale*, P.D. James.

1972.
Gold Dagger: *The Levanter*, Eric Ambler.
Silver Dagger: *The Rainbird Pattern*, Victoria Canning.

1973.
Gold Dagger: *The Defection of A.J. Lewinter*, Robert Littell.
Silver Dagger: *A Coffin for Pandora*, Gwendoline Butler.
John Creasey Memorial Award: *Don't Point That Thing at Me*, Kyril Bonfiglioli.

1974.
Gold Dagger: *Other Paths to Glory*, Anthony Price.
Silver Dagger: *The Grosvenor Square Goodbye*, Francis Clifford.
John Creasey Memorial Award: *The Big Fix*, Roger L. Simon.

1975.
Gold Dagger: *The Seven Per Cent Solution*, Nicholas Meyer.
Silver Dagger: *The Black Tower*, P.D. James.
John Creasey Memorial Award: *Acid Drop*, Sara George.
Special Awards: Gladys Mitchell in honour of 50 outstanding books; Anne Britton for ten years of editing *Red Herrings*; Jean Bosden & Penelope Wallace for their work in connection with the first Crime Writers' International Congress.

1976.
Gold Dagger: *A Demon in my View*, Ruth Rendell.
Silver Dagger: *Rogue Eagle*, James McClure.
John Creasey Memorial Award: *Death of a Thick-Skinned Animal*, Patrick Alexander.

1977.
Gold Dagger: *The Honourable Schoolboy*, John le Carré.
Silver Dagger: *Laidlaw*, William McIlvanney.
John Creasey Memorial Award: *The Judas Pair*, Jonathan Gash.

1978.
Gold Dagger: *The Chelsea Murders*, Lionel Davidson.
Silver Dagger: *Waxwork*, Peter Lovesey.
John Creasey Memorial Award: *A Running Duck*, Paula Gosling.
Gold Dagger, Non-fiction: *The Mystery of the Princes*, Audrey Williamson.
Silver Dagger, Non-fiction: *The Capture of the Black Panther*, Harry Hawkes.
Red Herrings Special Awards: Alberto Tedeschi of Mondadori Publishers, Italy; Frederic Dannay & Nigel Morland "for services to crime fiction".

1979.
Gold Dagger: *Whip Hand*, Dick Francis.
Silver Dagger: *Service of all the Dead*, Colin Dexter.
John Creasey Memorial Award: *Saturday of Glory*, David Serafin.
Gold Dagger, Non-fiction: *Rachman*, Shirley Green.
Silver Dagger, Non-fiction: *Fraud*, Jon Connell & Douglas Sutherland.
Red Herrings Special Award: Madelaine Duke & Frank Arthur "for services to the Association".

1980.
Gold Dagger: *The Murder of the Maharajah*, H.R.F. Keating.
Silver Dagger: *Monk's Hood*, Ellis Peters.
John Creasey Memorial Award: *Dupe*, Liza Cody.
Gold Dagger, Non-fiction: *Conspiracy*, Anthony Summers.
Special Silver Dagger: Elizabeth Ferrars in recognition of her 50 outstanding books.

1981.
Gold Dagger: *Gorky Park*, Martin Cruz Smith.
Silver Dagger: *The Dead of Jericho*, Colin Dexter.
John Creasey Memorial Award: *The Ludi Victor*, James Leigh.
Gold Dagger, Non-fiction: *Prisoner Without a Name, Cell Without a Number*, Jacobo Timerman.

1982.
Gold Dagger: *The False Inspector Dew*, Peter Lovesey.
Silver Dagger: *Ritual Murder*, S.T. Haymon.

John Creasey Memorial Award: *Caroline Minuscule*, Andrew Taylor.
Gold Dagger, Non-fiction: *Earth to Earth*, John Cornwell.

1983.
Gold Dagger: *Accidental Crimes*, John Hutton.
Silver Dagger: *The Papers of Tony Veitch*, William McIlvanney.
John Creasey Memorial Award: (tie) *The Ariadne Clue*, Carol Clemeau; *The Night the Gods Smiled*, Eric Wright.
Gold Dagger, Non-fiction: *Double Dealer*, Peter Watson.
Red Herrings Special Award: F.E. Pardoe for 25 years' service on the Fiction Panel.

1984.
Gold Dagger: *The Twelfth Juror*, B.M. Gill.
Silver Dagger: *The Tree of Hands*, Ruth Rendell.
John Creasey Memorial Award: *A Very Private Enterprise*, Elizabeth Ironside.
Gold Dagger, Non-fiction: *In God's Name*, David Yallop.

1985.
Gold Dagger: *Monkey Puzzle*, Paula Gosling.
Silver Dagger: *Last Seen Alive*, Dorothy Simpson.
John Creasey Memorial Award: *The Latimer Mercy*, Robert Richardson.
Gold Dagger, Non-fiction: *Killing for Company*, Brian Masters.
Police Review Award: *After the Holiday*, Andrew Arncliffe [Nicholas Rhea].
Red Herrings Special Award: Marian Babson for "Ten years of magnificent secretaryship".

1986.
Diamond Dagger: Eric Ambler.
Gold Dagger: *Live Flesh*, Ruth Rendell.
Silver Dagger: *A Taste for Death*, P.D. James.
John Creasey Memorial Award: *Tinplate*, Neville Steed.
Gold Dagger, Non-fiction: *Evil Angels*, John Bryson.
Police Review Award: *The Crossfire Killings*, Bill Knox.

1987.
Diamond Dagger: P.D. James.
Gold Dagger: *A Fatal Inversion*, Barbara Vine [Ruth Rendell].
Silver Dagger: *Presumed Innocent*, Scott Turow.
John Creasey Memorial Award: *Dark Apostle*, Denis Kilcommons.
Gold Dagger, Non-fiction: *Perfect Murder*, Bernard Taylor & Stephen Knight.
Police Review Award: *Snowman*, Roger Busby.

1988.
Diamond Dagger: John le Carré.
Gold Dagger: *Ratking*, Michael Dibdin.
Silver Dagger: *Toxic Shock*, Sara Paretsky.
John Creasey Memorial Award: *Death's Bright Angel*, Janet Neel.

Gold Dagger, Non-fiction: *The Secret Lives of Trebitsch Lincoln*, Bernard Wasserstein.
Punch Prize (funniest crime novel): *Death in a Distant Land*, Nancy Livingston.

1989.
Diamond Dagger: Dick Francis.
Gold Dagger: *The Wench is Dead*, Colin Dexter.
Silver Dagger: *The Shadow Run*, Desmond Lowden.
John Creasey Memorial Award: *A Real Shot in the Arm*, Annette Roome.
Gold Dagger, Non-fiction: *A Gathering of Saints*, Robert Lindsey.
Last Laugh Award (funniest crime novel): *Angel Touch*, Mike Ripley.
Red Herrings Special Award: Glyn Hardwicke & John Kennedy Melling for editing *The Crime Writers' Practical Handbook*.

1990.
Diamond Dagger: Julian Symons.
Gold Dagger: *Bones and Silence*, Reginald Hill.
Silver Dagger: *The Late Candidate*, Mike Phillips.
John Creasey Memorial Award: *Postmortem*, Patricia Cornwell.
Gold Dagger, Non-fiction: *The Passing of Starr*, Jonathan Goodman.
Last Laugh Dagger: *Killer Cinderella*, Simon Shaw.
CWA '92 Award: *Vendetta*, Michael Dibdin.
Rumpole Award: *Trial by Fire*, Frances Fyfield.

1991.
Diamond Dagger: Ruth Rendell.
Gold Dagger: *King Solomon's Carpet*, Barbara Vine [Ruth Rendell].
Silver Dagger: *Deep Sleep*, Frances Fyfield.
John Creasey Memorial Award: *Devil in a Blue Dress*, Walter Mosley.
Gold Dagger, Non-fiction: *Giordano Bruno and the Embassy Affair*, John Bossy.
Last Laugh Dagger: *Angels in Arms*, Mike Ripley.
CWA '92 Award: *Gaudi Collective*, Barbara Wilson.

1992.
Diamond Dagger: Leslie Charteris.
Gold Dagger: *The Way Through the Woods*, Colin Dexter.
Silver Dagger: *Bucket Nut*, Liza Cody.
John Creasey Memorial Award: *The Ice House*, Minette Walters.
Gold Dagger, Non-fiction: *The Reckoning: the Murder of Christopher Marlowe*, Charles Nicholl.
Last Laugh Dagger: *Native Tongue*, Carl Hiaasen.
CWA '92 Award: *Black August*, Timothy Williams.
Golden Handcuffs Award (author most popular with library users); Catherine Aird.

1993.
Diamond Dagger: Ellis Peters.
Gold Dagger: *Cruel and Unusual*, Patricia Cornwell.

Silver Dagger: *Fatlands*, Sarah Dunant.
John Creasey Memorial Award: no award.
Short Story Dagger: "Some Sunny Day", Julian Rathbone (*Constable New Crimes 2*, ed. Maxim Jakubowski).
Gold Dagger, Non-fiction: *Murder in the Heart*, Alexandra Artley.
Last Laugh Dagger: *Mamur Zapt and the Spoils of Egypt*, Michael Pearce.
Golden Handcuffs: Margaret Yorke.

1994.
Diamond Dagger: Michael Gilbert.
Gold Dagger: *The Scold's Bride*, Minette Walters.
Silver Dagger: *Miss Smilla's Feeling for Snow*, Peter Høeg.
John Creasey Memorial Award: *Big Town*, Doug J. Swanson.
Gold Dagger, Non-fiction: *Criminal Shadows*, David Canter.
Last Laugh Dagger: *The Villain of the Earth*, Simon Shaw.
Golden Handcuffs: Robert Barnard.

1995.
Diamond Dagger: Reginald Hill.
Gold Dagger: *The Mermaids Singing*, Val McDermid.
Silver Dagger: *The Summons*, Peter Lovesey.
John Creasey Memorial Award: *One for the Money*, Janet Evanovich.
Short Story Dagger: "Funny Story", Larry Beinhart (*No Alibi*, ed. Maxim Jakubowski).
Gold Dagger, Non-fiction: *The Prodigal Husband*, Michael Harris.
Last Laugh Dagger: *Sunburn*, Laurence Shames.
Dagger in the Library (formerly Golden Handcuffs): Lindsey Davis.

1996.
Diamond Dagger: H.R.F. Keating.
Gold Dagger: *Popcorn*, Ben Elton.
Silver Dagger: *Bloodhounds*, Peter Lovesey.
John Creasey Memorial Award: no award but there was a non-CWA First Blood Award for Best First Crime Novel, *Quite Ugly One Morning*, Christopher Brookmyre.
Short Story Dagger: "Herbert in Motion", Ian Rankin (*Perfectly Criminal*, ed. Martin Edwards).
Gold Dagger, Non-fiction: *The Gunpowder Plot: Terror and Faith in 1605*, Antonia Fraser.
Last Laugh Dagger: *Two for the Dough*, Janet Evanovich.
Dagger in the Library: Marian Babson.
Rusty Dagger (unofficial award for Best Crime Novel of the 1930s): *The Nine Tailors*, Dorothy L. Sayers.

1997.
Diamond Dagger: Colin Dexter.
Gold Dagger: *Black & Blue*, Ian Rankin.
Silver Dagger: *Three to Get Deadly*, Janet Evanovich.

John Creasey Memorial Award: *Body Politic*, Paul Johnston.
Short Story Dagger: "On the Psychiatrist's Couch", Reginald Hill (*Whydunit*, ed. Martin Edwards).
Gold Dagger, Non-fiction: *The Jigsaw Man*, Paul Britton.

1998.
Diamond Dagger: Ed McBain.
Gold Dagger: *Sunset Limited*, James Lee Burke.
Silver Dagger: *Manchester Slingback*, Nicholas Blincoe.
John Creasey Memorial Award: *Garnethill*, Denise Mina.
Short Story Dagger: "Roots", Jerry Sykes (*Mean Time*, ed. Jerry Sykes).
New Writing Competition: *Stone Baby*, Julie Denby.
Gold Dagger, Non-fiction: *Cries Unheard: the Story of Mary Bell*, Gitta Sereny.

1999.
Diamond Dagger: Margaret Yorke.
Gold Dagger: *A Small Death in Lisbon*, Robert Wilson.
Silver Dagger: *Vienna Blood*, Adrian Mathews.
John Creasey Memorial Award: *Lie in the Dark*, Dan Fesperman.
Short Story Dagger: "Taking Care of Frank", Antony Mann (*Crimewave* #2, June 1999).
Ellis Peters Historical Dagger: *Two for the Lions*, Lindsey Davis.
Gold Dagger, Non-fiction: *The Case of Stephen Lawrence*, Brian Cathcart.

2000.
Diamond Dagger: Peter Lovesey.
Gold Dagger: *Motherless Brooklyn*, Jonathan Lethem.
Silver Dagger: *Friends in High Places*, Donna Leon.
John Creasey Memorial Award: *God is a Bullet*, Boston Teran.
Short Story Dagger: "Helena and the Babies", Denise Mina (*Fresh Blood 3*, ed. Mike Ripley & Maxim Jakubowski).
Ellis Peters Historical Dagger: *Absent Friends*, Gillian Linscott.
Gold Dagger, Non-fiction: *Mr. Blue: Memoirs of a Renegade*, Edward Bunker.

2001.
Diamond Dagger: Lionel Davidson.
Gold Dagger: *Sidetracked*, Henning Mankell.
Silver Dagger: *Forty Words for Sorrow*, Giles Blunt.
John Creasey Memorial Award: *The Earthquake Bird*, Susanna Jones.
Short Story Dagger: "Prussian Snowdrops", Marion Arnott (*Crimewave* #4, 2000).
Ellis Peters Historical Dagger: *The Office of the Dead*, Andrew Taylor.
Debut Dagger, for unpublished writers: *Clea's Moon*, Edward Wright.
Gold Dagger, Non-fiction: *The Infiltrators*, Philip Etienne and Martin Maynard with Tony Thompson.

2002.
Diamond Dagger: Sara Paretsky.

Derrick Murdoch Award ***see under*** **Arthur Ellis Award**

Derringer Award

Presented annually since 1998 by the Short Mystery Fiction Society for excellence in the field of short stories. The name derives from the palm-sized handgun, the "derringer", chosen because the crime short story may also be "small, but dangerous". The award is dated in line with the year of publication.

1997.

Best Short Story: (tie) "The Adventurers', Barbara White-Rayczek; "L.A. Justice", Kris Neri (*Murder by Justice*, ed. Priscilla English, Lisa Seidman & Mae Woods).
Best Short-Short Story: "Guavaberry Christmas", Kate Grilley (*Murderous Intent*, Fall 1997).
Best Flash: "Curiosity Kills", Michael Mallory (*Murderous Intent*, Fall 1997).
Best First Short Mystery: "Back Stairs", Eileen Brosnan (*Murderous Intent*, Fall 1997).
Best Novella: "Image of Conspiracy", Margo Power (booklet).

1998.

Best Short Story: "Capital Justice", Kris Neri (*Blue Murder* e-zine, #1)
Best Flash: "Pretty Kitty", Joyce Holland (*Murderous Intent*, Winter 1998).
Golden Derringer for Lifetime Achievement: Edward D. Hoch.
Reader Award for Significant Contribution: Kate Derie.

1999.

Best Short Story: "The Way to a Man's Heart", Elizabeth Dearl (The Case.com, February 1999).
Best Short-Short Story: (tie) "When in Rome", Dorothy Francis (*Murderous Intent*, December 1999/January 2000); "Just a Man on the Sidewalk", Carol Kilgore (The Case.com, 12-18 March, 1999).
Best First Short Story: "Death in Full Bloom", Ray Wonderly (*Futures*, August 1999)
Best Novella: "Saint Bobby", Doug Allyn (*EQMM*, April 1999).
Golden Derringer for Lifetime Achievement: Henry Slesar.
Reader Award for Significant Contribution: (joint) Robert Foster; Jiro Kimura.

2000.

Best Short Story: "Erie's Last Day", Steve Hockensmith (*AHMM*, May 2000).
Best Flash Mystery: (tie). "Polls Don't Lie", Earl McGill (*Blue Murder*); "The New Lawyer", Mike Wiecek (*Crimestalker Casebook*, Spring 2000).
Best Puzzle Story: "The Cabin Killer", Henry Slesar (*EQMM*, July 2000).
Best Novella: "Lilacs and Lace", Lynda Douglas (*Futures*, June 2000).
Golden Derringer for Lifetime Achievement: John Lutz.
Reader Award for Significant Contribution: Babs Lakey.

Dilys Award

Presented annually since 1992 by the Independent Mystery Booksellers Association for the book that "we most enjoyed selling."

1992. *Native Tongue*, Carl Hiaasen.
1993. *Booked to Die*, John Dunning.
1994. *Smilla's Sense of Snow*, Peter Høeg.
1995. *One for the Money*, Janet Evanovich.
1996. *The Last Coyote*, Michael Connelly.
1997. *The Poet*, Michael Connelly.
1998. *Three to Get Deadly*, Janet Evanovich.
1999. *Gone, Baby, Gone*, Dennis Lehane.
2000. *L.A. Requiem*, Robert Crais.
2001. *A Place of Execution*, Val McDermid.
2002. *Mystic River*, Dennis Lehane.

Edgar Awards

Presented annually since 1946 by the Mystery Writers of America (MWA) in recognition of the best mystery fiction and non-fiction published in the previous year or adapted for the radio or the screen. The award is named after Edgar Allan Poe and is the mystery world's equivalent of the Oscar. The MWA also administers the Ellery Queen Award for outstanding contributions to the genre, the Robert L. Fish Award for the best short story arising from the MWA's new writers' training programme, the Raven Award for non-writers who are highly supportive of the genre and, most recently, the Mary Higgins Clark Award for the book most closely in the tradition of that author.

1946.

Best First Novel: *Watchful at Night*, Julius Fast.
Outstanding Mystery Criticism: Anthony Boucher.
Best Radio Drama: *The Adventures of Ellery Queen*, Frederic Dannay & Manfred B. Lee.
Best Motion Picture: *Murder My Sweet*, screenplay by John Paxton based on *Farewell My Lovely*, Raymond Chandler (1940).

1947.

Best First Novel: *The Horizontal Man*, Helen Eustis.
Outstanding Mystery Criticism: William Weber (in *Saturday Review of Literature*).
Best Radio Drama: *The Adventures of Sam Spade*, Bob Tallman & Jason James; William Spier (director).
Best Motion Picture: *The Killers*, screenplay by Anthony Veiller based on "The Killers", Ernest Hemingway (*Scribner's*, March 1927).

1948.

Best First Novel: *The Fabulous Clipjoint*, Fredric Brown.
Short Story Award: Ellery Queen (for anthology and magazine editing).
Outstanding Mystery Criticism: Howard Haycraft (in *EQMM*).
Best Fact Crime: *Twelve Against the Law*, Edward D. Radin.
Best Radio Drama: *Suspense*, William Spier (producer/director).

Best Motion Picture: *Crossfire*, screenplay by John Paxton based on *The Brick Fox-Hole*, Richard Brooks (1945)

1949.

Best First Novel: *The Room Upstairs*, Mildred Davis.

Short Story Award: William Irish [Cornell Woolrich] (for sustained excellence in short story writing and collections *Deadman Blues* and *The Blue Ribbon*).

Outstanding Mystery Criticism: James Sandoe (in *Chicago Sun-Times*).

Best Fact Crime: Regional Murder series, ed. Marie Rodell.

Best Radio Drama: *Inner Sanctum*, John Roeburt (principal writer) & Himan Brown (producer/ director).

Best Motion Picture: *Call Northside 777*, screenplay by Quentin Reynolds, Leonard Hoffman, Jay Dratler, Jerome Cady based on articles by James P. McQuire.

Best Foreign Film: *Jenny Lamour*.

Special Edgar: (joint) Clayton Rawson for *Clue* magazine; Arthur A. Stoughton, custodian of Poe Cottage; Peter W. Williams for creating the Edgar bust.

1950.

Best First Novel: *What a Body*, Alan Green.

Short Story Award: Ellery Queen (for ten years service through *EQMM*).

Outstanding Mystery Criticism: Anthony Boucher (in *EQMM* and *New York Times*).

Special Edgar (Best Biographical Work): *The Life of Sir Arthur Conan Doyle*, John Dickson Carr.

Best Fact Crime: *Bad Company*, Joseph Henry Jackson.

Best Radio Drama: *Murder by Experts*, Robert Arthur & Dovan Kogan (producers).

Best Motion Picture: *The Window*, screenplay by Mel Dinelli based on "Fire Escape" [orig. "The Boy Cried Murder"] by Cornell Woolrich (*Mystery Book Magazine*, March 1947).

Best Play: *Detective Story*, Sidney Kingsley.

1951.

Best First Novel: *Nightmare in Manhattan*, Thomas Walsh.

Short Story Award: *Diagnosis: Homicide* by Lawrence G. Blochman.

Outstanding Mystery Criticism: Dorothy B. Hughes (in *Albuquerque Times*).

Best Fact Crime: *Twelve Against Crime*, Edward D. Radin.

Best Radio Drama: *Dragnet*, James Moser & Jack Webb.

Best Motion Picture: *The Asphalt Jungle*, screenplay by Ben Maddow based on the book by W.R. Burnett (1949).

Special Award (Best Television series); Franklin Heller, producer-director of *The Web*.

1952.

Best First Novel: *Strangle Hold*, Mary McMullen.

Short Story Award: *Fancies and Goodnights*, John Collier.

Outstanding Mystery Criticism: Lenore Glen Offord (in *San Francisco Chronicle*).

Best Fact Crime: *True Tales from the Annals of Crime and Rascality*, St. Clair McKelway.
Best Radio Drama: *Dragnet*, James Moser & Jack Webb.
Best Motion Picture: *Detective Story*, screenplay by Philip Yordan & Robert Wyler based on book and stageplay by Sidney Kingsley (1949).
Best Television Series/Segment: *The Web*.
Special Edgar: Ellery Queen for *Queen's Quorum*.

1953.
Best First Novel: *Don't Cry for Me*, William Campbell Gault.
Short Story Award: *Something to Hide*, Philip MacDonald.
Outstanding Mystery Criticism: Anthony Boucher (in *New York Times* & *EQMM*).
Best Fact Crime: *Court of Last Resort*, Erle Stanley Gardner.
Best Radio Drama: *The Mysterious Traveler*, Robert Arthur & David Kogan.
Best Motion Picture: *Five Fingers*, screenplay by Michael Wilson & Otto Lang based on *Operation Cicero*, L. C. Moyzisch (1950).
Best Television Series/Segment: *Dragnet*.
Best Play: *Dial M for Murder*, Frederick Knott.
Raven Award: E.T. Guymon, Jr. for his outstanding library of mystery literature.

1954.
Best Novel: *Beat Not the Bones*, Charlotte Jay.
Best First Novel: *A Kiss Before Dying*, Ira Levin.
Short Story Award: *Someone Like You*, Roald Dahl.
Outstanding Mystery Criticism: Brett Halliday & Helen McCloy.
Best Fact Crime: *Why Did They Kill?*, John Bartlow Martin.
Best Radio Drama: "The Shot" episode of *Suspense*, E. Jack Neuman.
Best Motion Picture: *The Big Heat*, screenplay by Sidney Boehm based on novel by William P. McGivern (1952).
Best Television Series/Segment: "Crime at Blossoms" episode in *Studio One*, Jerome Ross.
Raven: (joint) Dr. Thomas A. Gonzales, retiring Chief Medical Examiner, NYC; Dr. Harrison Martland, retiring Chief Medical Examiner, Essex Co. NJ; Tom Lehrer for his mystery parodies.
Special Edgar: Mary Roberts Rinehart for *The Frightened Wife and Other Murder Stories*.

1955.
Grand Master: Agatha Christie.
Best Novel: *The Long Good-Bye*, Raymond Chandler.
Best First Novel: *Go, Lovely Rose*, Jean Potts.
Best Short Story: "The House Party", Stanley Ellin (*EQMM*, May 1954).
Best Radio Drama: "The Tree" episode of *21st Precinct*, Stanley Niss.
Outstanding Mystery Criticism: Drexel Drake (in *Chicago Tribune*).
Best Fact Crime: *The Girl With the Scarlet Brand*, Charles Boswell & Lewis Thompson.

Best Motion Picture: *Rear Window*, screenplay by John Michael Hayes based on story "It Had to be Murder", Cornell Woolrich (*Dime Detective*, February 1942).

Best Television Series/Segment: "Smoke" episode of *Suspense*, Gore Vidal.

Best Play: *Witness for the Prosecution*, Agatha Christie.

Raven Award for Best Book Jacket illustration: Dell Books.

Special Edgar: Berton Roueche for his stories of medical detection, *Eleven Blue Men*.

1956.

Best Novel: *Beast in View*, Margaret Millar.

Best First Novel: *The Perfectionist*, Lane Kauffman.

Best Short Story: "Dream No More", Philip MacDonald (*EQMM*, November 1955).

Best Fact Crime: *Dead and Gone*, Manly Wade Wellman.

Best Motion Picture: *The Desperate Hours*, screenplay by Joseph Hayes based on his own book (1954).

Best Television Series/Segment: "A Taste of Honey" episode of *The Elgin Hour*, Alvin Sapinsley.

Raven Award (for Best Hardcover Jacket illustration): Charles Scribner's Sons.

Special Edgar: Henri-Georges Clouzot for writing and directing *Les Diaboliques*.

1957.

Best Novel: *A Dram of Poison*, Charlotte Armstrong.

Best First Novel: *Rebecca's Pride*, Donald McNutt Douglas.

Best Short Story: "The Blessington Method", Stanley Ellin (*EQMM*, June 1956).

Outstanding Mystery Criticism: Curtis Casewit (in *Denver Post*).

Best Fact Crime: *Night Fell on Georgia*, Charles & Louise Samuels.

Best Motion Picture: no award.

Best Television Series/Segment: (joint) "The Fine Art of Murder" episode of *Omnibus*, Sidney Carroll; *Playhouse 90* series.

Raven Award (Best Hardcover Book Jacket illustration): Tony Palladino for *Inspector Maigret and the Burglar's Wife* (Doubleday Crime Club).

Special Edgars: Meyer Levin for *Compulsion*; Miss Dorothy Kilgallen as "Reader of the Year".

1958.

Grand Master: Vincent Starrett.

Best Novel: *Room to Swing*, Ed Lacy.

Best First Novel: *Knock and Wait a While*, William Rawle Weeks.

Best Short Story: "The Secret of the Bottle", Gerald Kersh (*Saturday Evening Post*, 7 December 1957).

Best Fact Crime: *The D.A.'s Man*, Harold R. Danforth & James D. Horan.

Best Radio Drama: *The Galindez-Murphy Case*, Jay McMullen.

Best Motion Picture: *Twelve Angry Men*, screenplay by Reginald Rose based on his own stageplay (1955).

Best Television Series/Segment: *Mechanical Manhunt*, Harold Swanton.

Raven Award (Best Book Jacket illustration): Harper Brothers for general excellence.

Raven Scroll: Dell, for their Great Mystery Series book jackets.

1959.

Grand Master: Rex Stout.

Best Novel: *The Eighth Circle*, Stanley Ellin.

Best First Novel: *The Bright Road to Fear*, Richard Martin Stern.

Best Short Story: "Over There, Darkness", William O'Farrell (*Sleuth*, October 1958).

Best Fact Crime: *They Died in the Chair*, Wenzell Brown.

Best Radio Drama: *Suspense*, William Robson.

Best Motion Picture: *The Defiant Ones*, original screenplay by Nathan E. Douglas & Harold Jacob Smith.

Best Foreign Film: *Inspector Maigret* [France], screenplay by R.M. Arlaud, Michel Audiard & Jean Delanoy based on *Maigret Tend un Piege* [*Maigret Sets a Trap*], Georges Simenon (1955).

Best Television Series/Segment: (joint) "Edge of Truth" episode of *Studio One*, Adrian Spies; "Capital Punishment" episode of *Omnibus*, James Lee.

Raven Awards: Lawrence G. Blochman for long and distinguished service to MWA and editorship of *The Third Degree*; Frederick G. Melcher on his retirement after 35 years with *Publisher's Weekly*; Franklin D. Roosevelt (posthumous) as "Reader of the Year"; Western Printing & Lithography Co. for general excellence in production of Dell book jackets.

Special Edgar: Alice Woolley Burt for *American Murder Ballads*.

1960.

Best Novel: *The Hours Before Dawn*, Celia Fremlin.

Best First Novel: *The Grey Flannel Shroud*, Henry Slesar.

Best Short Story: "The Landlady", Roald Dahl (*The New Yorker*, November 1959).

Best Fact Crime: *Fire at Sea*, Thomas Gallager.

Best Motion Picture: *North by Northwest*, original screenplay by Ernest Lehman.

Best Foreign Film: *Sapphire* [UK], original screenplay by Janet Green & Lukas Heller.

Best Television Series/Segment: *The Empty Chair*, David Karp.

Raven Awards: Ray Brennan for crime reporting; Lucille Fletcher radio play *Sorry, Wrong Number*; Gail Jackson, producer of *Perry Mason* TV series; David C. Cooke for editing *Best Detective Stories of the Year*; Alfred Hitchcock for his contribution to the field; Phyllis McGinley as "Mystery Fan of the Year"; Simon & Schuster for best hardcover book jacket illustration.

1961.

Grand Master: Ellery Queen (Frederic Dannay & Manfred B. Lee).

Best Novel: *The Progress of a Crime*, Julian Symons.

Best First Novel: *The Man in the Cage*, John Holbrooke Vance.

Best Short Story: "Tiger", John Durham (*Cosmopolitan*, February 1960).

Best Juvenile: *The Mystery of the Haunted Pool*, Phyllis A. Whitney.

Outstanding Mystery Criticism: James Sandoe (in *New York Herald-Tribune*).
Best Fact Crime: *The Overbury Affair*, Miriam Allen deFord.
Best Motion Picture: *Psycho*, screenplay by Joseph Stefano based on the novel by Robert Bloch (1959).
Best Television Series/Segment: (joint) *The Case of the Burning Court*, Kelly Roos; *The Day of the Bullet*, Bill Ballinger.
Raven Awards: Charles Addams for his macabre cartoons; Philip Wittenberg, legal counsel; Charles Scribner's Sons for best hardcover book jacket illustration, *A Mark of Displeasure*; Dell Books for best paperback book cover illustration, *The Three Coffins*; Ilka Chase as "Reader of the Year".
Special Edgar: Elizabeth Daly, grand dame of women mystery writers.

1962.
Grand Master: Erle Stanley Gardner.
Best Novel: *Gideon's Fire*, J.J. Marric (John Creasey).
Best First Novel: *The Green Stone*, Suzanne Blanc.
Best Short Story: "Affair at Lahore Cantonment", Avram Davidson (*EQMM*, June 1961).
Best Juvenile: *The Phantom of the Walkaway Hill*, Edward Fenton.
Best Fact Crime: *Death and the Supreme Court*, Barrett Prettyman, Jr.
Best Motion Picture: *The Innocents*, screenplay by Truman Capote & William Archibald based on *The Turn of the Screw*, Henry James (1898).
Best Foreign Film: *Plein Soleil* [aka *Broad Daylight*; *Purple Noon*; *Lust for Evil*] [France], screenplay by Paul Degauff and Rene Clement based on *The Talented Mr. Ripley*, Patricia Highsmith (1955).
Best Television Series/Segment: *Witness in the Dark*, Leigh Vance & John Lemont.
Best Play: *Write Me a Murder*, Frederick Knott.
Raven Awards: Herbert Brodkin (producer) for the TV series *The Defenders*.
Special Edgar: Thomas McDade for *The Annals of Murder*.

1963.
Grand Master: John Dickson Carr.
Best Novel: *Death and the Joyful Woman*, Ellis Peters.
Best First Novel: *The Fugitive*, Robert L. Fish.
Best Short Story: "The Sailing Club", David Ely (*Cosmopolitan*, October 1962).
Best Juvenile: *Cutlass Island*, Scott Corbett.
Best Fact Crime: *Tragedy in Dedham*, Francis Russell.
Best Motion Picture: no award.
Best Television Series/Segment: *The Problem of Cell 13*, teleplay by A.A. Roberts based on the story by Jacques Futrelle.
Raven Awards: Doubleday for best hardcover book jacket illustration; Collier Books for best paperback book cover illustration.
Special Edgars: Patrick Quentin for his collection *The Ordeal of Mrs. Snow*; Philip Reisman for TV series *Cops and Robbers*; E. Spencer Shew for reference work *Companion to Murder*; Frances & Richard Lockridge for their fiftieth thriller, *The Ticking Clock*.

1964.

Grand Master: George Harmon Coxe.

Best Novel: *The Light of Day*, Eric Ambler.

Best First Novel: *Florentine Finish*, Cornelius Hirschberg.

Best Short Story: "Man Gehorcht", Leslie Ann Browning (*Story*, January/February 1963).

Best Juvenile: *Mystery of the Hidden Hand*, Phyllis A. Whitney.

Outstanding Mystery Criticism: Hans Stefan Santesson (in *The Saint Mystery Magazine*).

Best Fact Crime: *The Deed*, Gerold Frank.

Best Motion Picture: *Charade*, screenplay by Peter Stone based on his story "The Unsuspecting Wife".

Best Television Series/Segment: "End of the World Baby" episode of *Kraft Suspense Theater*, Luther Davis.

Raven Awards: Random House for best hardcover book jacket illustration; Bantam Books for best paperback book cover illustration.

Special Edgars: Philip Durham for *Down These Mean Streets*.

1965.

Best Novel: *The Spy Who Came In From the Cold*, John le Carré.

Best First Novel: *Friday the Rabbi Slept Late*, Harry Kemelman.

Best Short Story: "H as in Homicide", Lawrence Treat (*EQMM*, March 1964).

Best Juvenile: *Mystery at Crane's Landing*, Marcella Thum.

Best Fact Crime: *Gideon's Trumpet*, Anthony Lewis.

Best Motion Picture: *Hush, Hush, Sweet Charlotte*, original screenplay by Henry Farrell & Lukas Heller.

Best Foreign Film: *Séance on a Wet Afternoon* [UK], screenplay by Bryan Forbes based on the novel by Mark McShane (1961).

Best Television Series/Segment: *The Fugitive* series, Alan Armer.

Raven Awards: Doubleday for best hardcover book jacket illustration; Bantam Books for best paperback book cover illustrations.

Special Edgar: Dr. Milton Helpern for his work in forensic medicine.

1966.

Grand Master: Georges Simenon.

Best Novel: *The Quiller Memorandum*, Adam Hall.

Best First Novel: *In the Heat of the Night*, John Ball.

Best Short Story: "The Possibility of Evil", Shirley Jackson (*Saturday Evening Post*, 18 December 1965).

Best Juvenile: *The Mystery at 22 East*, Leon Ware.

Best Fact Crime: *In Cold Blood*, Truman Capote.

Best Motion Picture: *The Spy Who Came in from the Cold*, screenplay by Paul Dehn & Guy Trosper based on the novel by John Le Carré (1963).

Best Foreign Film: *The Ipcress File* [UK], screenplay by Bill Canaway & James Doran based on the novel by Len Deighton (1962).

Best Television Series/Segment: "An Unlocked Window" episode of *Alfred Hitchcock Hour*, James Bridges.

Raven Awards: Random House for best hardcover book jacket illustration (*Girl on the Run*); Bantam Books for best paperback book cover illustration (*Knock and Wait a While*).

Special Edgar: Rev. O.C. Edwards for "The Gospel According to 007" in *The Living Church*.

1967.

Grand Master: Baynard Kendrick.

Best Novel: *The King of the Rainy Country*, Nicolas Freeling.

Best First Novel: *The Cold War Swap*, Ross Thomas.

Best Short Story: "The Chosen One", Rhys Davies (*The New Yorker*, 4 June 1966).

Best Juvenile: *Sinbad and Me*, Kin Platt.

Outstanding Mystery Criticism: John T. Winterich (in *Saturday Review*).

Best Fact Crime: *The Boston Strangler*, Gerold Frank.

Best Motion Picture: *Harper*, screenplay by William Goldman based on *The Moving Target*, Ross MacDonald (1949).

Best Television Series/Segment: "Operation Rogesh" episode of *Mission Impossible*, Jerome Ross.

Raven Awards: *EQMM* on its 26th anniversary; William Morrow for best hardcover book jacket illustration (*Let Sleeping Girls Lie*); Collier Books for best paperback book cover illustration (*I Am the Cat*).

Special Award: Richard Watts, Jr. "Reader of the Year".

Special Edgar: Clayton Rawson for decades of service to the MWA.

1968.

Best Novel: *God Save the Mark*, Donald E. Westlake.

Best First Novel: *Act of Fear*, Michael Collins.

Best Short Story: "The Oblong Room", Edward D. Hoch (*The Saint*, July 1967).

Best Juvenile: *Signpost to Terror*, Gretchen Sprague.

Best Fact Crime: *A Private Disgrace*, Victoria Lincoln.

Best Motion Picture: *In the Heat of the Night*, screenplay by Stirling Silliphant based on the novel by John Ball (1965).

Best Television Series/Segment: "Tempest in a Texas Town" episode of *Judd, for the Defense*, Harold Gast & Leon Tokatyan.

Raven Awards: Doubleday for best hardcover book jacket illustration; Ballantine Books for best paperback book cover illustration (*Johnny Underground*).

Special Blunt Instrument Award: Joey Adams as "Reader of the Year."

1969.

Grand Master: John Creasey.

Best Novel: *A Case of Need*, Jeffery Hudson [Michael Crichton].

Best First Novel: (tie) *Silver Street*, E. Richard Johnson; *The Bait*, Dorothy Uhnak.

Best Short Story: "The Man Who Fooled the World", Warner Law (*Saturday Evening Post*, 24 August 1968).

Best Juvenile: *The House of Dies Drear*, Virginia Hamilton.

Best Fact Crime: *Poe, the Detective*, John Walsh.

Best Motion Picture: *Bullitt*, screenplay by Alan Trustman & Harry Kleiner based on *Mute Witness*, Robert L. Fish (1963).

Best Television Series/Segment: *The Strange Case of Dr. Jekyll and Mr. Hyde*, teleplay by Ian Hunter based on the novel by Robert Louis Stevenson.

Raven Awards: Scribner's for best hardcover book jacket illustration (*God Speed the Night*); Ballantine for best paperback book cover illustration (*The Dresden Green*).

Special Edgar: Ellery Queen on the 40th anniversary of *The Roman Hat Mystery*.

1970.

Grand Master: James M. Cain.

Best Novel: *Forfeit*, Dick Francis.

Best First Novel: *A Time for Predators*, Joe Gores.

Best Paperback Original: *The Dragon's Eye*, Scott C.S. Stone.

Best Short Story: "Goodbye, Pops", Joe Gores (*EQMM*, December 1969).

Best Juvenile: *Danger at Black Dyke*, Winifred Finlay.

Best Fact Crime: *The Case That Will Not Die*, Herbert B. Ehrmann.

Best Motion Picture: *Z*, screenplay by Jorge Semprun & Costa Gavras based on the novel by Vassili Vassilikos (1968).

Best Television Series/Segment: *Daughter of the Mind*, Luther Davis.

Raven Awards: E.P. Dutton for best hardcover book jacket illustration (*The Spanish Prisoner*); Avon Books for best paperback book cover illustration in their Classic Crime collection.

Special Edgar: John Dickson Carr for forty years as a mystery writer.

1971.

Grand Master: Mignon G. Eberhart.

Best Novel: *The Laughing Policeman*, Maj Sjowall & Per Wahlöö.

Best First Novel: *The Anderson Tapes*, Lawrence Sanders.

Best Paperback Original: *Flashpoint*, Dan J. Marlowe.

Best Short Story: "In the Forests of Riga the Beasts are Very Wild Indeed", Margery Finn Brown (*McCall's*, July 1970).

Best Juvenile: *The Intruder*, John Rowe Townsend.

Best Fact Crime: *A Great Fall*, Mildred Savage.

Best Motion Picture: *Investigation of a Citizen Above Suspicion*, original screenplay by Elio Petri & Ugo Pirro.

Best Television Series/Segment: *Berlin Affair*, Richard Alan Simmons.

Best Play: *Sleuth*, Anthony Shaffer.

Raven Awards: Doubleday for best hardcover book jacket illustration (*If Laurel Shot Hardy the World Would End*); Popular Library for best paperback book cover illustration (*Picture Miss Seeton*).

1972.

Grand Master: John D. MacDonald.

Best Novel: *The Day of the Jackal*, Frederick Forsyth.

Best First Novel: (posthumous) *Finding Maubee*, A.H.Z. Carr.

Best Paperback Original: *For Murder I Charge More*, Frank McAuliffe.

Best Short Story: "Moonlight Gardener", Robert L. Fish (*Argosy*, December 1971).
Best Juvenile: *Nightfall*, Joan Aiken.
Best Fact Crime: *Beyond a Reasonable Doubt*, Sandor Frankel.
Best Motion Picture: *The French Connection*, screenplay by Ernest Tidyman based on the novel by Robin Moore (1969).
Best Television Feature: *Thief*, John D.F. Black.
Best Television Series/Segment: "A Step in Time" episode of *Mannix*, Mann Rubin.
Raven Awards: G.P. Putnam's for best hardcover book jacket illustration (*If You Want to See Your Wife Again*).
Special Edgar: Jacques Barzun & Wendell Hertig Taylor for *A Catalog of Crime*.

1973.
Grand Master: (joint) Judson Philips & Alfred Hitchcock.
Best Novel: *The Lingala Code*, Warren Kiefer.
Best First Novel: *Squaw Point*, R.H. Shimer.
Best Paperback Original: *The Invader*, Richard Wormser.
Best Short Story: "The Purple Shroud", Joyce Harrington (*EQMM*, September 1972).
Best Juvenile: *Deathwatch*, Robb White.
Best Fact Crime: *Hoax*, Stephen Fay, Lewis Chester & Magnus Linkletter.
Best Motion Picture: *Sleuth*, screenplay by Anthony Shaffer based on his own play (1970).
Best Television Feature: *The Night Stalker*, Richard Matheson.
Best Television Series/Segment: "The New Mexico Connection" episode of *McCloud*, Glenn A. Larson.
Raven Awards: Random House for best hardcover book jacket illustration (*Dead Skip*); Ace Books for best paperback book cover illustration (*Fetish Murders*).
Special Edgars: Julian Symons for *Mortal Consequences: A History from the Detective Story to the Crime Novel*; Jeanine Larmoth & Charlotte Turgeon for *Murder on the Menu*.

1974.
Grand Master: Ross Macdonald.
Best Novel: *Dance Hall of the Dead*, Tony Hillerman.
Best First Novel: *The Billion Dollar Sure Thing*, Paul E. Erdman.
Best Paperback Original: *Death of an Informer*, Will Perry
Best Short Story: "The Whimper of Whipped Dogs", Harlan Ellison (*Bad Moon Rising*, ed. Thomas M. Disch).
Best Juvenile: *The Long Black Coat*, Jay Bennett.
Best Fact Crime: *Legacy of Violence*, Barbara Levy.
Best Motion Picture: *The Last of Sheila*, original screenplay by Anthony Perkins & Stephen Sondheim.
Best Television Feature: *Isn't it Shocking*, Lane Slate.
Best Television Series/Segment: "Requiem for an Informer" episode of *Police Story*, Sy Salkiwitz.

Raven Awards: Simon & Schuster for best hardcover book jacket illustration (*The Cold Ones*).
Special Edgar: Joseph Wambaugh for *The Onion Field*.

1975.
Best Novel: *Peter's Pence*, Jon Cleary.
Best First Novel: *Fletch*, Gregory Mcdonald.
Best Paperback Original: *The Corpse That Walked*, Roy Winsor.
Best Short Story: "The Fallen Curtain", Ruth Rendell (*EQMM*, August 1974).
Best Juvenile: *The Dangling Witness*, Jay Bennett.
Best Fact Crime: *Helter Skelter*, Vincent Bugliosi & Curt Gentry.
Best Motion Picture: *Chinatown*, original screenplay by Robert Towne.
Best Television Feature: *The Law*, Joel Oliansky.
Best Television Series/Segment: "Requiem for C.Z. Smith" episode of *Police Story*, Robert Collins.
Raven Awards: The Royal Shakespeare Company for its revival of the play *Sherlock Holmes*; CBS's *Radio Mystery Theatre* for the nightly Himan Brown series; ABC-TV for the *Wide World of Mystery* series.
Special Edgars: Howard Haycraft for his distinguished contribution to mystery criticism and scholarship; Francis M. Nevins, Jr. for *Royal Bloodline: Ellery Queen, Author and Detective*.

1976.
Grand Master: Eric Ambler.
Best Novel: *Hopscotch*, Brian Garfield.
Best First Novel: *The Alvarez Journal*, Rex Burns.
Best Paperback Original: *Autopsy*, John R. Feegel.
Best Short Story: "The Fail", Jesse Hill Ford (*Playboy*, March 1975).
Best Juvenile: *Z for Zachariah*, Robert C. O'Brien.
Best Fact Crime: *A Time to Die*, Tom Wicker.
Best Motion Picture: *Three Days of the Condor*, screenplay by Lorenzo Semple, Jr. & David Rayfiel based on the novel by James Grady (1974).
Best Television Feature: *The Legend of Lizzie Borden*, William Baxt.
Best Television Series/Segment: "No Immunity for Murder" episode of *Kojak*, Joe Gores.
Raven Award: Leo Margulies as editor of *Mike Shayne Mystery Magazine*; Eddie Lawrence, "Reader of the Year".
Special Edgars: Jorge Luis Borges for distinguished contribution to the genre; Donald J. Sobol for the Encyclopedia Brown series of juvenile mysteries.

1977.
Grand Master: Graham Greene.
Best Novel: *Promised Land*, Robert B. Parker.
Best First Novel: *The Thomas Berryman Number*, James Patterson.
Best Paperback Original: *Confess, Fletch*, Gregory Mcdonald.
Best Short Story: "Like a Terrible Scream", Etta Revesz (*EQMM*, May 1976).
Best Juvenile: *Are You in the House Alone?*, Richard Peck.

Best Critical/Biographical Work: *Encyclopedia of Mystery and Detection*, Chris Steinbrunner, Otto Penzler, Marvin Lachman & Charles Shibuk.
Best Fact Crime: *Blood and Money*, Thomas Thompson.
Best Motion Picture: *Family Plot*, screenplay by Ernest Lehman based on *The Rainbird Pattern*, Victor Canning (1972).
Best Television Feature: *Helter Skelter*, J.P. Miller.
Best Television Series/Segment: "Requiem for Murder" episode of *The Streets of San Francisco*, James J. Sweeney.
Raven Award: *The Edge of Night* TV production.

1978.
Grand Master: (joint) Daphne du Maurier, Dorothy B. Hughes, Ngaio Marsh.
Best Novel: *Catch Me: Kill Me*, William H. Hallahan.
Best First Novel: *A French Finish*, Robert Ross.
Best Paperback Original: *The Quark Maneuver*, Mike Jahn.
Best Short Story: "Chance After Chance", Thomas Walsh (*EQMM*, November 1977).
Best Juvenile: *A Really Weird Summer*, Eloise Jarvis McGaw.
Best Critical/Biographical Work: *Rex Stout*, John McAleer.
Best Fact Crime: *By Person Unknown*, George Jonas & Barbara Amiel.
Best Motion Picture: *The Late Show*, original screenplay by Robert Benton.
Best Television Feature: *Men Who Love Women* (pilot for *Rosetti and Ryan* series), Gordon Cotler & Don M. Mankiewicz.
Best Television Series/Segment: "The Thigh Bone Connected to the Knee Bone" episode of *Quincy*, Tony Lawrence & Lou Shaw.
Raven Award: Edward Gorey for his set designs for the Broadway production of *Dracula*.
Special Awards: Danny Arnold, executive producer of *Barney Miller* TV series; Richard N. Hughes, executive producer of *I Am My Brother's Keeper* series; Lawrence Treat as editor of *The Mystery Writer's Handbook*.
Special Edgars: Allen J. Hubin for a decade of *The Armchair Detective*; Dilys Winn for *Murder Ink*.

1979.
Grand Master: Aaron Marc Stein.
Best Novel: *The Eye of the Needle*, Ken Follett.
Best First Novel: *Killed in the Ratings*, William L. DeAndrea.
Best Paperback Original: *Deceit and Deadly Lies*, Frank Bandy.
Best Short Story: "The Cloud Beneath the Eaves", Barbara Owens (*EQMM*, January 1978).
Best Juvenile: *Alone in Wolf Hollow*, Dana Brookins.
Best Critical/Biographical Work: *The Mystery of Agatha Christie*, Gwen Robins.
Best Fact Crime: *Til Death Do Us Part*, Vincent Bugliosi & Ken Hurwitz.
Best Motion Picture: *Magic*, screenplay by William Goldman based on his own novel (1976).
Best Television Feature: *Dashiell Hammett's The Dain Curse*, Robert Lenski.
Best Television Series/Segment: "Murder Under Glass" episode of *Columbo*, Robert van Scyok.

Raven Award: Alberto Tedeschi of Mondadori, publisher of the most successful Italian series of mysteries.

Special Award: Mignon C. Eberhart & Frederic Dannay on celebrating the 50th anniversary of both their first novels; Richard Levinson & William Link (producers) for the TV series *Columbo* and *Ellery Queen*.

1980.

Grand Master: W.R. Burnett.

Best Novel: *The Rheingold Route*, Arthur Maling.

Best First Novel: *The Lasko Tangent*, Richard North Patterson.

Best Paperback Original: *The HOG Murders*, William L. DeAndrea.

Best Short Story: "Armed and Dangerous", Geoffrey Norman (*Esquire*, March 1979).

Best Juvenile: *The Kidnapping of Christa Lattimore*, Joan Lowery Nixon.

Best Critical/Biographical Work: *Dorothy L. Sayers, A Literary Biography*, Ralph E. Hone.

Best Fact Crime: *The Falcon and the Snowman*, Robert Lindsey.

Best Motion Picture: *The Great Train Robbery*, screenplay by Michael Crichton based on his novel (1975).

Best Television Feature: *Murder by Natural Causes*, Richard Levinson & William Link.

Best Television Series/Segment: "Skin", *Roald Dahl's Tales of the Unexpected*, Robin Chapman & Roald Dahl.

Best Play: *Death Trap*, Ira Levin.

Raven Award: "Muppet Murders" episode of *The Muppet Show*.

Special Edgars: Chester Gould, creator of Dick Tracy; J.H.H. Gaute & Robin Odell for *The Murderer's Who's Who*; Allan J. Hubin for *The Bibliography of Crime Fiction, 1749-1975*.

1981.

Grand Master: Stanley Ellin.

Best Novel: *Whip Hand*, Dick Francis.

Best First Novel: *The Watcher*, K. Nolte Smith.

Best Paperback Original: *Public Murders*, Bill Granger.

Best Short Story: "Horn Man", Clark Howard (*EQMM*, July 1980).

Best Juvenile: *The Séance*, Joan Lowery Nixon.

Best Critical/Biographical Work: *Twentieth Century Crime and Mystery Writers*, John Reilly.

Best Fact Crime: *A True Deliverance*, Fred Harwell.

Best Motion Picture: *The Black Marble*, screen play by Joseph Wambaugh based on his own novel (1978).

Best Television Feature: *City in Fear*, Albert Rubin.

Best Television Series/Segment: "China Doll" episode of *Magnum, P.I.*, Donald Bellisario and Glen A. Larson.

Best Play: *Ricochet*, Paul Nathan.

Special Edgars: Joan Evans of PBS *Mystery!* series for the best international mystery programming; *The Edge of Night* TV series, celebrating its 25th anniversary; Lawrence Spivak, founding publisher of *EQMM* 40 years ago.

1982.

Grand Master: Julian Symons.

Best Novel: *Peregrine*, William Bayer.

Best First Novel: *Chiefs*, Stuart Woods.

Best Paperback Original: *The Old Dick*, L.A. Morse.

Best Short Story: "The Absence of Family", Jack Ritchie (*EQMM*, January 1981).

Best Juvenile: *Taking Terri Mueller*, Norma Fox Mazer.

Best Critical/Biographical Work: *What About Murder?*, John L. Breen.

Best Fact Crime: *The Sting Man*, Robert W. Greene.

Best Motion Picture: *Cutter's Way*, screenplay by Jeffrey Alan Fiskin based on the novel by Newton Thornburg (1976).

Best Television Feature: *Killjoy*, Sam H. Rolfe.

Best Television Series/Segment: "Hill Street Station" episode of *Hill Street Blues*, Steven Bochco & Michael Kozoll.

Best Play: *A Talent for Murder*, Jerome Chodorov & Norman Panama.

Special Award: William Vivian Butler for *The Young Detective's Handbook*.

Special Edgar: HBO for its special production of the William Gillette play, *Sherlock Holmes*.

1983.

Grand Master: Margaret Millar.

Best Novel: *Billingsgate Shoal*, Rick Boyer.

Best First Novel: *The Butcher's Boy*, Thomas Perry.

Best Paperback Original: *Triangle*, Teri White.

Best Short Story: "There Are No Snakes in Ireland", Frederick Forsyth (from *No Comebacks*).

Best Juvenile: *The Murder of Hound Dog Bates*, Robbie Branscum.

Best Critical/Biographical Work: *Cain*, Roy Hoopes.

Best Fact Crime: *The Vatican Conection*, Richard Hammer.

Best Motion Picture: *The Long Good Friday*, original screenplay by Barrie Keeffe.

Best Television Feature: *Rehearsal for Murder*, Richard Levinson & William Link.

Best Television Series/Segment: "In the Steele of the Night" episode of *Remington Steele*, Joel Steiger.

Raven Award: Isaac Bashevis Singer "Reader of the Year".

Ellery Queen Award: Emma Lathen.

Special Edgar: Stephen Talbot (writer) for PBS documentary *The Case of Dashiell Hammett*.

1984.

Grand Master: John le Carré.

Best Novel: *La Brava*, Elmore Leonard.

Best First Novel: *The Bay Psalm Book Murder*, Will Harriss.

Best Paperback Original: *Mrs. White*, Margaret Tracy.

Best Short Story: "The New Girlfriend", Ruth Rendell (*EQMM*, August 1983).

Best Juvenile: *The Callender Papers*, Cynthia Voigt.

Best Critical/Biographical Work: *The Dark Side of Genius: The Life of Alfred Hitchcock*, Donald Spoto.

Best Fact Crime: *Very Much a Lady*, Shana Alexander.

Best Motion Picture: *Gorky Park*, screenplay by Dennis Potter based on the novel by Martin Cruz Smith (1981).

Best Television Feature: *Mickey Spillane's Murder Me, Murder You*, Bill Stratton.

Best Television Series/Segment: "The Pencil" episode of *Philip Marlowe*, Jo Eisinger.

Raven Award: Sylvia Porter, "Reader of the Year".

Robert L. Fish Award: "Locked Doors", Lilly Carlson (*EQMM*, October 1983)

Special Edgar: Richard Lancelyn Green & John Michael Gibson for *A Bibliography of A. Conan Doyle*.

1985.

Grand Master: Dorothy Salisbury Davis.

Best Novel: *Briarpatch*, Ross Thomas.

Best First Novel: *Strike Three, You're Dead*, R.D. Rosen.

Best Paperback Original: *Grandmaster*, Warren Murphy & Molly Cochran.

Best Short Story: "By Dawn's Early Light", Lawrence Block (*Playboy*, August 1984).

Best Juvenile: *Night Cry*, Phyllis Reynolds Naylor.

Best Critical/Biographical Work: *Novel Verdicts: A Guide to Courtroom Fiction*, Jon L. Breen.

Best Fact Crime: *Double Play: The San Francisco City Hall Killings*, Mike Weiss.

Best Motion Picture: *A Soldier's Story*, screenplay by Charles Fuller based on his play *A Soldier's Play* (1982).

Best Television Feature: *The Glitter Dome*, Stanley Kallis.

Best Television Series/Segment: "Deadly Lady" episode of *Murder, She Wrote*, Peter S. Fischer.

Raven Award: Eudora Welty, "Reader of the Year".

Ellery Queen Award: Joan Kahn.

Robert L. Fish Award: "Poor, Dumb Mouths", Bill Crenshaw (*AHMM*, May 1984).

Special Edgar: Mark Nykanen for "The Silent Shame", NBC news report on child abuse crimes.

1986.

Grand Master: Ed McBain.

Best Novel: *The Suspect*, L.R. Wright.

Best First Novel: *When the Bough Breaks*, Jonathan Kellerman.

Best Paperback Original: *Pigs Get Fat*, Warren Murphy.

Best Short Story: "Ride the Lightning", John Lutz (*AHMM*, January 1985).

Best Juvenile: *The Sandman's Eyes*, Patricia Windsor.

Best Critical/Biographical Work: *John Le Carré*, Peter Lewis.

Best Fact Crime: *Savage Grace*, Natalie Robins & Steven M.L. Aronson.

Best Motion Picture: *Witness*, original screenplay by Earl W. Wallace & William Kelley.

Best Television Feature: *Guilty Conscience*, Richard Levinson & William Link.

Best Television Series/Segment: "The Amazing Falsworth" episode of *Amazing Stories*, Mick Garris.

Best Play: *The Mystery of Edwin Drood*, Rupert Holmes based on the novel by Charles Dickens.
Raven Award: Suzi Oppenheimer, "Reader of the Year".
Robert L. Fish Award: "Final Rites", Doug Allyn (*AHMM*, December 1985).
Special Edgar: Walter Albert for *Detective and Mystery Fiction: An International Bibliography of Secondary Sources.*

1987.
Grand Master: Michael Gilbert.
Best Novel: *A Dark-Adapted Eye*, Barbara Vine (Ruth Rendell).
Best First Novel: *No One Rides for Free*, Larry Beinhart.
Best Paperback Original: *The Junkyard Dog*, Robert Campbell.
Best Short Story: "Rain in Pinton County", Robert Sampson (*New Black Mask*, May 1986).
Best Juvenile: *The Other Side of Dark*, Joan Lowery Nixon.
Best Critical/Biographical Work: *Here Lies: An Autobiography*, Eric Ambler.
Best Fact Crime: *Careless Whispers*, Carlton Stowers.
Best Motion Picture: *Something Wild*, screenplay by E. Max Frye.
Best Television Feature: *When the Bough Breaks*, Phil Penningroth.
Best Television Series/Segment: "The Cup" episode of *The Equalizer*, David Jackson & Carleton Eastlake.
Ellery Queen Award: Eleanor Sullivan, editor of *EQMM*.
Robert L. Fish Award: "Father to the Man", Mary Kittredge (*AHMM*, November 1986).

1988.
Grand Master: Phyllis A. Whitney.
Best Novel: *Old Bones*, Aaron Elkins.
Best First Novel: *Death Among Strangers*, Deidre S. Laiken.
Best Paperback Original: *Bimbos of the Death Sun*, Sharyn McCrumb.
Best Short Story: "Soft Monkey", Harlan Ellison (*Mystery Scene Reader #1*, ed. Ed Gorman).
Best Juvenile: *Lucy Forever and Miss Rosetree, Shrinks*, Susan Shreve.
Best Critical/Biographical Work: *Introduction to the Detective Story*, Leroy Lad Panek.
Best Fact Crime: *CBS Murders*, Richard Hammer.
Best Motion Picture: *Stakeout*, screenplay by Jim Kouf.
Best Television Feature: *Nutcracker: Money, Murder and Madness*, William Hanley.
Best Television Series/Segment: "The Musgrave Ritual" episode of *The Return of Sherlock Holmes*, teleplay by Jeremy Paul based on the story by Arthur Conan Doyle.
Raven Award: Angela Lanbsury & Vincent Price.
Ellery Queen Award: Ruth Cavin.
Robert L. Fish Award: "Roger, Mr. Whilkie!", Eric M. Heideman (*AHMM*, July 1987).

1989.

Grand Master: Hillary Waugh.

Best Novel: *A Cold Red Sunrise*, Stuart M. Kaminsky.

Best First Novel: *Carolina Skeletons*, David Stout.

Best Paperback Original: *The Telling of Lies*, Timothy Findley.

Best Short Story: "Flicks", Bill Crenshaw (*AHMM*, August 1988).

Best Young Adult: *Incident at Loring Groves*, Sonia Levitin.

Best Juvenile: *Megan's Island*, Willo Davis Roberts.

Best Critical/Biographical Work: *Cornell Woolrich: First You Dream, Then You Die*, Francis M. Nevins, Jr.

Best Fact Crime: *In Broad Daylight*, Harry N. MacLean.

Best Motion Picture: *The Thin Blue Line*, screenplay by Errol Morris.

Best Television Feature: *Man Against the Mob*, David J. Kinghorn.

Best Television Series/Segment: "The Devil's Foot" episode of *Mystery! The Return of Sherlock Holmes*, teleplay by Gary Hopkins based on the story by Arthur Conan Doyle.

Raven Awards: Bouchercon Annual World Mystery Convention for its contribution to the mystery field (presented to Anthony Boucher's widow, Phyllis White); Marilyn Abrams & Bruce Jordan for *Shear Madness*, the longest-running off-Broadway play.

Ellery Queen Award: Richard Levinson & William Link for their writing and TV collaborations.

Robert L. Fish Award: "Different Drummers", Linda O. Johnston (*EQMM*, July 1988).

Special Edgar: Joan Kahn for lifetime achievement on her retirement after fifty years in mystery publishing.

1990.

Grand Master: Helen McCloy.

Best Novel: *Black Cherry Blues*, James Lee Burke.

Best First Novel: *The Last Billable Hour*, Susan Wolfe.

Best Paperback Original: *The Rain*, Keith Peterson.

Best Short Story: "Too Many Crooks", Donald E. Westlake (*Playboy*, August 1989).

Best Young Adult: *Show Me the Evidence*, Alane Ferguson.

Best Juvenile: no award.

Best Critical/Biographical Work: *The Life of Graham Greene, Volume I: 1904-1939*, Norman Sherry.

Best Fact Crime: *Doc: The Rape of the Town of Lovell*, Jack Olsen.

Best Motion Picture: *Heathers*, screenplay by Daniel Waters.

Best Television Feature/Mini-series: *Shannon's Deal*, John Sayles.

Best Television Episode: "White Noise" episode of *Wiseguy*, David J. Burke & Alfonse Ruggiero, Jr.

Best Play: *City of Angels*, David Zippel (lyrics) & Cy Coleman (music) based on the book by Larry Gelbart.

Ellery Queen Award: Joel Davis, publisher of *EQMM* and *AHMM*.

Robert L. Fish Award: "Hawks", Connie Colt (*AHMM*, June 1989).

1991.

Grand Master: Tony Hillerman.

Best Novel: *New Orleans Mourning*, Julie Smith.

Best First Novel: *Post Mortem*, Patricia Cornwell.

Best Paperback Original: *The Man Who Would Be F. Scott Fitzgerald*, David Handler.

Best Short Story: "Elvis Lives", Lynne Barrett (*EQMM*, September 1990).

Best Young Adult: *Mote*, Chap Reaver.

Best Juvenile: *Stonewords*, Pam Conrad.

Best Critical/Biographical Work: *Trouble Is Their Business: Private Eyes in Fiction, Film, and Television, 1927-1988*, John Conquest.

Best Fact Crime: *In a Child's Name*, Peter Maas.

Best Motion Picture: *The Grifters*, screenplay by Donald E. Westlake based on the novel by Jim Thompson (1963).

Best Television Feature/Mini-series: *Killing in a Small Town*, Cynthia Cidre.

Best Television Episode: "Goodnight, Dear Heart" episode of *Quantum Leap*, Paul Brown.

Best Play: *Accomplice*, Rupert Holmes.

Raven Awards: Sarah Booth Conroy, "Reader of the Year"; Carol Brener for her skill in selling books to the public.

Robert L. Fish Award: "Willie's Story", Jerry F. Skarky (*AHMM*, June 1990).

Special Edgars: Jay Robert Nash for *The Encyclopedia of World Crime, Criminal Justice, Criminology and Law Enforcement*.

1992.

Grand Master: Elmore Leonard.

Best Novel: *A Dance at the Slaughterhouse*, Lawrence Block.

Best First Novel: *Slow Motion Riot*, Peter Blauner.

Best Paperback Original: *Dark Maze*, Thomas Adcock.

Best Short Story: "Nine Sons", Wendy Hornsby (*Sisters in Crime 4*, ed. Marilyn Wallace).

Best Young Adult: *The Weirdo*, Theodore Taylor.

Best Juvenile: *Wanted ... Mud Blossom*, Betsy Byars.

Best Critical/Biographical Work: *Edgar A. Poe: Mournful and Never-ending Remembrance*, Kenneth Silverman.

Best Fact Crime: *Homicide: A Year on the Killing Streets*, David Simon.

Best Motion Picture: *Silence of the Lambs*, screenplay by Ted Tally based on the novel by Thomas Harris (1988).

Best Television Feature/Mini-series: *Murder 101*, Bill Condon & Roy Johansen.

Best Television Episode: "Poirot: The Lost Mine" episode of *Mystery!*, Michael Baker & David Renwick.

Raven Award: Harold Q. Masur for his years of service as general counsel to the MWA.

Ellery Queen Award: Margaret Norton.

Robert L. Fish Award: no award.

1993.

Grand Master: Donald E. Westlake.
Best Novel: *Bootlegger's Daughter*, Margaret Maron.
Best First Novel: *The Black Echo*, Michael Connelly.
Best Paperback Original: *A Cold Day for Murder*, Dana Stabenow.
Best Short Story: "Mary, Mary, Shut the Door", Benjamin M. Schutz (*Deadly Allies* ed. Robert J. Randisi & Marilyn Wallace).
Best Young Adult: *A Little Bit Dead*, Chap Reaver.
Best Juvenile: *Coffin on a Case!*, Eve Buntings.
Best Critical/Biographical Work: *Alias S.S. Van Dine*, John Loughery.
Best Fact Crime: *Swift Justice*, Harry Farrell.
Best Motion Picture: *The Player*, screenplay by Michael Tolkin based on his own novel (1988).
Best Television Feature/Mini-series: *Prime Suspect*, Lynda La Plante.
Best Television Episode: "Conspiracy" episode of *Law & Order*, Michael S. Chernuchin & Rene Balcer.
Raven Award: President Bill Clinton, "Reader of the Year".
Robert L. Fish Award: "A Will is a Way", Steven Saylor (*EQMM*, March 1992).

1994.

Grand Master: Lawrence Block.
Best Novel: *The Sculptress*, Minette Walters.
Best First Novel: *A Grave Talent*, Laurie R. King.
Best Paperback Original: *Dead Folk's Blues*, Steven Womack.
Best Short Story: "Keller's Therapy", Lawrence Block (*Playboy*, May 1993).
Best Young Adult: *The Name of the Game was Murder*, Joan Lowery Nixon.
Best Juvenile: *The Twin in the Tavern*, Barbara Brooks Wallace.
Best Critical/Biographical Work: *The Saint: A Complete History*, Burl Barer.
Best Fact Crime: *Until the Twelve of Never*, Bella Stumbo.
Best Motion Picture: *Falling Down*, screenplay by Ebbe Roe Smith.
Best Television Feature/Mini-series: *Prime Suspect 2*, Allan Cubitt.
Best Television Episode: "4B or Not 4B" episode of *NYPD Blue*, David Milch.
Ellery Queen Award: Otto Penzler.
Robert L. Fish Award: "Wicked Twist", D.A. McGuire (*AHMM*, October 1993).

1995.

Grand Master: Mickey Spillane.
Best Novel: *The Red Scream*, Mary Willis Walker.
Best First Novel: *The Caveman's Valentine*, George Dawes Green.
Best Paperback Original: *Final Appeal*, Lisa Scottoline.
Best Short Story: "The Dancing Bear", Doug Allyn (*AHMM*, March 1994).
Best Young Adult: *Toughing It*, Nancy Springer.
Best Juvenile: *The Absolutely True Story … How I Visited Yellowstone Park with the Terrible Rubes*, Willo Davis Roberts.
Best Critical/Biographical Work: *Encyclopedia Mysteriosa*, William L. DeAndrea.
Best Fact Crime: *To Protect and to Serve*, Joe Domanick.

Best Motion Picture: *Pulp Fiction*, screenplay by Quentin Tarantino based on storyline by him and Roger Avary.
Best Television Feature/Mini-series: *Cracker: To Say I Love You*, Jimmy McGovern.
Best Television Episode: "Simone Says" episode of *NYPD Blue*, Steven Bochco, Walen Green, David Milch.
Raven Award: Dr. Paul LeClerc, President of the New York Public Library.
Robert L. Fish Award: "Me and Mr. Harry", Batya Swift Yasgur (*EQMM*, mid-December 1994).

1996.
Grand Master: Dick Francis.
Best Novel: *Come to Grief*, Dick Francis.
Best First Novel: *Penance*, David Housewright.
Best Paperback Original: *Tarnished Blue*, William Heffernan.
Best Short Story: "The Judge's Boy", Jean B. Cooper (*EQMM*, August 1995)
Best Young Adult: *Prophecy Rock*, Rob MacGregor.
Best Juvenile: *Looking for Jamie Bridger*, Nancy Springer.
Best Critical/Biographical Work: *Savage Art: A Biography of Jim Thompson*, Robert Polito.
Best Fact Crime: *Circumstantial Evidence*, Pete Earley.
Best Motion Picture: *The Usual Suspects*, screenplay by Christopher McQuarrie.
Best Television Feature/Mini-series: *Citizen X*, Chris Gerolmo.
Best Television Episode: "Torah! Torah! Torah!" episode of *NYPD Blue*, Theresa Rebeck.
Raven Award: The Library of America for *The Collected Writings of Raymond Chandler*.
Ellery Queen Award: Jacques Barzun.
Robert L. Fish Memorial Award: "The Word for Breaking August Sky", James Sarafin (*AHMM*, July 1995).

1997.
Grand Master: Ruth Rendell.
Best Novel: *The Chatham School Affair*, Thomas H. Cook.
Best First Novel: *Simple Justice*, John Morgan Wilson.
Best Paperback Original: *Fade Away*, Harlan Coben.
Best Short Story: "Red Clay", Michael Malone (*Murdered for Love*, ed. Otto Penzler).
Best Young Adult: *Twisted Summer*, Willo Davis Roberts.
Best Juvenile: *The Clearing*, Dorothy Reynolds Miller.
Best Critical/Biographical Work: *The Secret Marriage of Sherlock Holmes*, Michael Atkinson.
Best Fact Crime: *Power to Hurt*, Darcy O'Brien.
Best Motion Picture: *Sling Blade*, original screenplay by Billy Bob Thornton.
Best Television Feature/Mini-series: "Brotherly Love" from *Cracker*, Jimmy McGovern.
Best Television Episode: "Deadbeat" episode of *Law & Order*, Ed Zuckerman & I.C. Rappaport.

Raven Award: Marvin Lachman.
Ellery Queen Award: Francois Guerif.
Robert L. Fish Memorial Award: "The Prosecutor of Duprey", David Vaughn (*EQMM*, January 1996).

1998.
Grand Master: Barbara Mertz (aka Elizabeth Peters, Barbara Michaels).
Best Novel: *Cimarron Rose*, James Lee Burke.
Best First Novel: *Los Alamos*, Joseph Kanon.
Best Paperback Original: *Charm City*, Laura Lippman.
Best Short Story: "Keller on the Spot", Lawrence Block (*Playboy*, November 1997).
Best Young Adult: *Ghost Canoe*, Will Hobbs.
Best Juvenile: *Sparrows in the Scullery*, Barbara Brooks Wallace.
Best Critical/Biographical Work: *"G" is for Grafton: The World of Kinsey Millhone*, Natalie Hevener Kaufman & Carol McGinnis Kay.
Best Fact Crime: *The Death of Innocents*, Richard Firstman & Jamie Talan.
Best Motion Picture: *L.A. Confidential*, screenplay by Curtis Hanson & Brian Helgeland based on the novel by James Ellroy (1990).
Best Television Feature/Mini-series: "Blood, Sweat, and Tears" from *Silent Witness*, John Milne.
Best Television Episode: "Double Down" episode of *Law & Order*, story by Richard Sweren & Shimon Wincelberg; teleplay by Ed Zuckerman & Shimon Wincelberg.
Best Play: *A Read Death*, adapted by David Barr.
Raven Award: Sylvia K. Burack (editor of *The Writer* magazine).
Ellery Queen Award: Hiroshi Hayakawa (President of Hayakawa Publishing).
Robert L. Fish Memorial Award: "If Thine Eye Offend Thee", Rosalind Roland (*Murder* × *13*, ed Priscilla English, Lisa Seidman & Mae Woods).

1999.
Grand Master: P.D. James.
Best Novel: *Mr. White's Confession*, Robert Clark.
Best First Novel: *A Cold Day in Paradise*, Steve Hamilton.
Best Paperback Original: *The Widower's Two-Step*, Rick Riordan.
Best Short Story: "Poachers", Tom Franklin (*The Texas Review*, Fall/Winter 1998).
Best Young Adult: *The Killer's Cousin*, Nancy Werlin.
Best Children's: *Sammy Keyes and the Hotel Thief*, Wendelin Van Draanen.
Best Critical/Biographical Work: *Mystery and Suspense Writers*, ed. Robin Winks.
Best Fact Crime: *To the Last Breath*, Carlton Stowers.
Best Motion Picture: *Out of Sight*, screenplay by Scott Frank based on the novel by Elmore Leonard (1996).
Best Television Feature/Mini-series: *Law & Order: Exiled*, Charles Kipps.
Best Television Episode: "Bad Girl" episode of *Law & Order*, Rene Balcer & Richard Sweren.
Best Play: *Voices in the Dark*, John Pielmeier.
Raven Award: Steven Bochco.

Ellery Queen Award: Sara Ann Freed.
Robert L. Fish Memorial Award: "Clarity", Bryn Bonner (*EQMM*, May 1998).

2000.
Grand Master: Mary Higgins Clark.
Best Novel: *Bones*, Jan Burke.
Best First Novel: *The Skull Mantra*, Eliot Pattison.
Best Paperback Original: *Fulton County Blues*, Ruth Birmingham.
Best Short Story: "Heroes", Anne Perry (*Murder and Obsession*, ed. Otto Penzler).
Best Young Adult: *Never Trust a Dead Man*, Vivian Vande Velde.
Best Critical/Biographical Work: *Teller of Tales: The Life of Arthur Conan Doyle*, Daniel Stashower.
Best Fact Crime: *Blind Eye*, James B. Stewart.
Best Juvenile: *The Night Flyers*, Elizabeth McDavid Jones.
Best Motion Picture: *Lock, Stock and Two Smoking Barrels*, screenplay by Guy Ritchie.
Best Television Feature/Mini-series: *A Slight Case of Murder*, Steven Schachter & William H. Macy, based on the novel by Donald E. Westlake.
Best Television Episode: "Refuge, Part 2" episode of *Law and Order*, Rene Balcer.
Best Play: *The Art of Murder*, Joe Di Pietro.
Raven Award: The Mercantile Library, director Harold Augenbraum.
Ellery Queen Award: Susanne Kirk (editor, Simon & Schuster).
Robert L. Fish Memorial Award: "Cro-Magnon, P.I.", Mike Reiss (*AHMM*, July/August 1999).

2001.
Grand Master: Edward D. Hoch.
Best Novel: *The Bottoms*, Joe R. Lansdale.
Best First Novel: *A Conspiracy of Paper*, David Liss.
Best Paperback Original: *The Black Maria*, Mark Graham.
Best Short Story: "Missing in Action", Peter Robinson (*EQMM*, November 2000).
Best Young Adult: *Counterfeit Son*, Elaine Marie Alphin.
Best Children's: *Dovey Coe*, Frances O'Roark Dowell.
Best Critical/Biographical Work: *England, Dorothy L. Sayers, and Lord Peter: Conundrums for the Long Weekend*, Robert Kuhn MacGregor & Ethan Lewis.
Best Fact Crime: *Black Mass: The Irish Mob, the FBI, and a Devil's Deal*, Dick Lehr & Gerard O'Neill.
Best Motion Picture: *Traffic*, screenplay by Stephen Gaghan based on the original TV mini-series, *Traffik* by Simon Moore.
Best TV Episode: "Limitations" episode of *Law & Order*, Michael Perry.
Best TV Feature/Miniseries: *Dalziel & Pascoe: On Beulah Height*, Michael Chaplin (based on the novel by Reginald Hill).
Raven Award: Barbara Peters of The Poisoned Pen; Tom & Enid Schantz of The Rue Morgue.
Ellery Queen Award: Douglas Greene for Crippen & Landru.
Robert L. Fish Memorial Award: "The Witch and the Relic Thief", M.J. Jones (*AHMM*, October 2000).

Mary Higgins Clark Award: *Authorized Personnel Only*, Barbara D'Amato.
Special Award: Mildred Wirt Benson.

Ellery Queen Award *see under* Edgar Award

Grand Prix de Littérature Policière

Presented annually by French crime fiction devotee Maurice Endrèbe since 1948 in recognition of the best French crime novel of the year and the best foreign novel translated into French. The latter are invariably UK or US titles. The following lists the Best Foreign winner only, giving the English title as appropriate.

1948. *The Bellamy Trial*, Frances Noyes Hart.
1949. *Puzzle for Pilgrims*, Patrick Quentin.
1950. *After Midnight*, Marta Albrand.
1951. *The Red Right Hand*, Joel Townsley Rogers.
1952. *Follow as the Night*, Patricia MacGerr.
1953. (tie) *The End is Known*, Geoffrey Holiday Hall; *Horns for the Devils*, Louis Malley.
1954. *The Body in Grant's Tomb*, William Irish [Cornell Woolrich].
1955. *Death in Captivity*, Michael Gilbert.
1956. *The Desperate Hours*, Joseph Hayes.
1957. *Nothing in Her Way*, Charles Williams.
1958. *The Talented Mr. Ripley*, Patricia Highsmith.
1959. *La reine des pommes* [*For Love of Imabelle*, aka *A Rage in Harlem*], Chester Himes.
1960. *Orders to Kill*, Donald Downes.
1961. *The Evil of the Day* [aka *Murder in Venice*], Thomas Sterling.
1962. *The Green Stone*, Suzanne Blanc.
1963. *The Ballad of the Running Man*, Shelley Smith.
1964. *A Key to the Suite*, John D. MacDonald.
1965. *Gun Before Butter*, Nicolas Freeling.
1966. *Berlin Memorandum*, Adam Hall.
1967. *I Start Counting*, Audrey Erskine Lindop.
1968. *Traditori di tutti* [*Duca and the Milan Murders*], Giorgio Scerbanenco.
1969. (tie) *Fire, Burn*, John Dickson Carr; *The Daughter of Time*, Josephine Tey.
1970. *To Lathos*, Antonis Samarkis.
1971. *Hændeligt Uheld* [*One Down* (US) or *Hit and Run, Run, Run* (UK)], Anders Bodelsen.
1972. *The Children Are Watching*, Laird Koenig & Peter L. Dixon.
1973. *Millie*, E.V. Cunningham [Howard Fast].
1974. *Mirror, Mirror on the Wall*, Stanley Ellin.
1975. *The Dark Number*, Edward Boyd & Roger Parkes.
1976. *Doctor Frigo*, Eric Ambler.
1977. *City of the Dead*, Herbert Lieberman.
1978. *And on the Eighth Day…*, Ellery Queen.
1979. *Katar* [*The Chain of Chance*], Stanislaw Lem.

1980. *A Stranger is Watching*, Mary Higgins Clark.
1981. *Los Mares del Sur* [*Southern Seas*], Manuel Vázquez Montalbán.
1982. *Party of the Year*, John Crosby.
1983. *No Comebacks*, Frederick Forsyth.
1984. *The Maine Massacre*, Janwillem van de Wetering.
1985. *Swing, Swing Together*, Peter Lovesey.
1986. *City Primeval*, Elmore Leonard.
1987. *Dance Hall of the Dead*, Tony Hillerman.
1988. (tie) *A Taste for Death*, P.D. James; *Strega*, Andrew Vachss.
1989. *Snowbound*, Bill Pronzini.
1990. *A Great Deliverance*, Elizabeth George.
1991. *The Silence of the Lambs*, Thomas Harris.
1992. *Black Cherry Blues*, James Lee Burke.
1993. *La Table de Flandes* [*The Flanders Panel*], Arturo Pérez-Reverte.
1994. *Cabal*, Michael Dibdin.
1995. *Degree of Guilt*, Richard North Patterson.
1996. *The Alienist*, Caleb Carr.
1997. *Imperfect Strangers*, Stuart Woods.
1998. *A Clear Conscience*, Frances Fyfield.
1999. *Blood Work*, Michael Connelly.
2000. *River of Darkness*, Rennie Airth.
2001. *In a Dry Season*, Peter Robinson.

The Hammett Prize

Presented annually since 1992 by the North American Branch of the International Association of Crime Writers for the best work (fiction or non-fiction) of literary excellence in crime writing by a U.S. or Canadian author. The winner is selected by a panel of three judges and receives a bronze sculpture in the form of a falcon-headed "Thin Man". The works do not have to be "hard-boiled" crime fiction. It is presented at the Bouchercon. There are other Hammett Prizes awarded in other countries for the best work in other languages.

1992. *Maximum Bob*, Elmore Leonard.
1993. *Turtle Moon*, Alice Hoffman.
1994. *Mexican Tree Duck*, James Crumley.
1995. *Dixie City Jam*, James Lee Burke.
1996. *Under the Beetle's Cellar*, Mary Willis Walker.
1997. *Rose*, Martin Cruz Smith.
1998. *Trial of Passion*, William Deverell.
1999. *Tidewater Blood*, William Hoffman.
2000. *Havana Bay*, Martin Cruz Smith.
2001. *The Blind Assassin*, Margaret Atwood.

Herodotus Award

Presented annually (September) since 1999 by the Historical Mystery Appreciation Society for works of excellence in the fields of historical mystery and detective fiction. The award is of a bust of Herodotus in clear plexiglass lightly tinted green, about 10 inches high.

1999.
Best Short Story: "Fatherhood" by Thomas Cook (*Murder for Revenge*, ed. Otto Penzler).
Best First US Historical Mystery: *The Last Kabbalist of Lisbon*, Richard Zimler.
Best International Historical Mystery: *Ex-Libris*, Ross King.
Best US Historical Mystery: *Cursed in the Blood*, Sharan Newman.
Lifetime Achievement: Anne Perry.

2000.
Best Short Story: "Neither Pity, Love nor Fear" by Margaret Frazer (*Royal Whodunnits*, ed. Mike Ashley).
Best First International Historical Mystery: *Guilty Knowledge*, Clare Curzon.
Best First US Historical Mystery: *Faded Coat of Blue*, Owen Parry.
Best International Historical Mystery: *Absent Friends*, Gillian Linscott.
Best US Historical Mystery: *Rubicon*, Steven Saylor.
Lifetime Achievement: Paul Doherty.

2001.
Best Short Story: "The Man Who Never Was" by Charles Todd (*Malice Demistic 9*, ed. Joan Hess).
Best First International Historical Mystery: *Bone House*, Betsy Tobin.
Best First US Historical Mystery: *The Bottoms,* Joe R. Lansdale.
Best International Historical Mystery: *The Company*, Arabella Edge.
Best US Historical First Mystery: *A Dangerous Road*, Kris Nelscott.
Lifetime Achievement: Lindsey Davis.

Lambda Literary Award

Presented annually by the Lamda Literary Foundation, a non-profit organization supporting gay, lesbian, bisexual and transgender literature in the US. There are awards in several categories of which two recognize excellence in gay and lesbian mystery fiction.

1989.
Lesbian Mystery: *Skiptrace*, Antoinette Azolatov.
Gay Men's Mystery: *Golden Boy*, Michael Nava.

1990.
Lesbian Mystery: *The Beverly Malibu*, Katherine V. Forrest.
Gay Men's Mystery: *A Simple Suburban Murder*, Mark Zubro.

1991.
Lesbian Mystery: *Gaudi Afternoon*, Barbara Wilson.
Gay Men's Mystery: *How Town*, Michael Nava.

1992.
Lesbian Mystery: *Murder by Tradition*, Katherine V. Forrest.
Gay Men's Mystery: *Country of Old Men*, Joseph Hansen.

1993.
Lesbian Mystery: (tie) *The Two Bir Tango*, Elizabeth Pincus; *Crazy for Loving*, Jaye Maiman.
Gay Men's Mystery: *The Hidden Law*, Michael Nava.

1994.
Lesbian Mystery: *Divine Victim*, Mary Wings.
Gay Men's Mystery: *Catalina's Riddle*, Steven Saylor.

1995.
Lesbian Mystery: No award.
Gay Men's Mystery: No award.

1996.
Lesbian Mystery: *Intersection of Law and Desire*, J.M. Reddmann.
Gay Men's Mystery: *Closet*, R.D. Zimmerman.

1997.
Lesbian Mystery: *Robber's Wine*, Ellen Hart.
Gay Men's Mystery: *Death of Friends*, Michael Nava.

1998.
Lesbian Mystery: *Father Forgive Me*, Randye Lordon.
Gay Men's Mystery: *The Magician's Tale*, David Hunt.

1999.
Lesbian Mystery: *The Blue Place*, Nicola Griffith.
Gay Men's Mystery: *Outburst*, R.D. Zimmerman.

2000.
Lesbian Mystery: *Hunting the Witch*, Ellen Hart.
Gay Men's Mystery: *Justice at Risk*, John Morgan Wilson.

2001.
Lesbian Mystery: *Mommy Deadest*, Jean Marcy.
Gay Men's Mystery: *The Limits of Justice*, John Morgan Wilson.

Lefty Award

Presented each Spring by the Left Coast Crime convention in California for the most humorous mystery novel published in the previous year.

1996. *The Fat Innkeeper*, Alan Russell.
1997. no award.

1998. *Four to Score*, Janet Evanovich.
1999. *High Five*, Janet Evanovich.
2000. *Murder With Peacocks*, Donna Andrews.
2001. no award.
2002. (tie) *Revenge of the Wrought-iron Flamingos*, Donna Andrews; *Fender Benders*, Bill Fitzhugh.

Macavity Award

Presented annually since 1987 (each autumn at Bouchercon) by Mystery Readers International based on votes by members for their favourite mysteries. The award, a certificate, is named after T.S. Eliot's "mystery cat" in *Old Possum's Book of Practical Cats*.

1987.
Best Novel: *A Taste for Death*, P.D. James.
Best First Novel: (tie) *A Ritual Bath*, Faye Kellerman; *A Case of Loyalties*, Marilyn Wallace.
Best Critical/Biographical: *1001 Midnights*, Marcia Muller & Bill Pronzini.
Best Short Story: "The Parker Shotgun", Sue Grafton (*Mean Streets*, ed. Robert J. Randisi).

1988.
Best Novel: *Marriage is Murder*, Nancy Pickard.
Best First Novel: *The Monkey's Raincoat*, Robert Crais.
Best Critical/Biographical: *Son of Gun in Cheek*, Bill Pronzini.
Best Short Story: "The Woman in the Wardrobe", Robert Barnard (*EQMM*, December 1987).

1989.
Best Novel: *A Thief of Time*, Tony Hillerman.
Best First Novel: *The Killings at Badger's Drift*, Caroline Graham.
Best Critical/Biographical: *Silk Stalkings*, Victoria Nichols & Susan Thompson.
Best Short Story: "Déjà vu", Doug Allyn (*AHMM*, June 1988).

1990.
Best Novel: *A Little Class on Murder*, Carolyn G. Hart.
Best First Novel: *Grime and Punishment*, Jill Churchill.
Best Critical/Biographical: *The Bedside Companion to Crime*, H.R.F. Keating.
Best Short Story: "Afraid All the Time", Nancy Pickard (*Sisters in Crime*, ed. Marilyn Wallace).

1991.
Best Novel: *If Ever I return Pretty Peggy-O*, Sharyn McCrumb.
Best First Novel: *Postmortem*, Patricia Cornwell.
Best Critical/Biographical: *Agatha Christie: The Woman and Her Mysteries*, Gillian Gill.

Best Short Story: "Too Much to Bare", Joan Hess (*Sisters in Crime 2*, ed. Marilyn Wallace).

1992.

Best Novel: *I.O.U.*, Nancy Pickard

Best First Novel: (tie) *Murder on the Iditarod Trail*, Sue Henry; *Zero at the Bone*, Mary Willis Walker.

Best Critical/Biographical: *Talking Mysteries: A Conversation with Tony Hillerman*, Tony Hillerman & Ernie Bulow.

Best Short Story: "Deborah's Judgement", Margaret Maron (*A Woman's Eye*, ed. Sara Paretsky).

1993.

Best Novel: *Bootlegger's Daughter*, Margaret Maron.

Best First Novel: *Blanche on the Lam*, Barbara Neely.

Best Critical/Biographical: *Doubleday Crime Club Companion*, Ellen Nehr.

Best Short Story: "Henrie O's Holiday", Carolyn Hart (*Malice Domestic 1*, ed. Elizabeth Peters).

1994.

Best Novel: *The Sculptress*, Minette Walters.

Best First Novel: *Death Comes as Epiphany*, Sharan Newman.

Best Critical/Biographical: *The Fine Art of Murder*, ed. Ed Gorman, Martin H. Greenberg, Larry Segriff & Jon L. Breen.

Best Short Story: "Checkout", Susan Dunlap (*Malice Domestic 2*, ed. Mary Higgins Clark).

1995.

Best Novel: *She Walks These Hills*, Sharyn McCrumb.

Best First Novel: *Do Unto Others*, Jeff Abbott

Best Critical/Biographical: *By a Woman's Hand*, Dean James & Jean Swanson.

Best Short Story: (tie) "Cast Your Fate to the Wind", Deborah Adams (*Malice Domestic 3*, ed. Nancy Pickard); "Unharmed", Jan Burke (*EQMM*, mid-Dec 1994).

1996.

Best Novel: *Under the Beetle's Cellar*, Mary Willis Walker.

Best First Novel: *The Strange Files of Fremont Jones*, Dianne Day.

Best Critical/Biographical: *Detecting Women*, Willetta L. Heising.

Best Short Story: "Evans Tries an O-Level", Colin Dexter (*Morse's Greatest Mystery and Other Stories*, though first published in *Winter's Crimes 9*, ed. George Hardinge, 1977).

1997.

Best Novel: *Bloodhounds*, Peter Lovesey.

Best First Novel: *Death in Little Tokyo*, Dale Furutani.

Best Non-Fiction: *Detecting Women 2*, Willetta Heising.

Best Short Story: "Cruel and Unusual", Carolyn Wheat (*Guilty as Charged*, ed. Scott Turlow).

1998.
Best Novel: *Dreaming of the Bones*, Deborah Crombie.
Best First Novel: *Dead Body Language*, Penny Warner.
Best Non-Fiction: *Deadly Women*, Jan Grape, Dean James & Ellen Nehr.
Best Short Story: "The Two Ladies of Rose Cottage", Peter Robinson (*Malice Domestic 6*, ed. Anne Perry).

1999.
Best Novel: *Blood Work*, Michael Connelly.
Best First Novel: *Sympathy for the Devil*, Jerrilyn Farmer.
Best Critical/Biographical: *Killer Books*, Jean Swanson & Dean James.
Best Short Story: "Of Course You Know That Chocolate is a Vegetable", Barbara D'Amato (*EQMM*, November 1998).

2000.
Best Novel: *The Flower Master*, Sujata Massey.
Best First Novel: *Inner City Blues*, Paula L. Woods.
Best Non-fiction: *Ross Macdonald*, Tom Nolan.
Best Short Story: "Maubi and the Jumbies", Kate Grilley (*Murderous Intent*, Fall 1999).

2001.
Best Novel: *A Place of Execution*, Val McDermid.
Best First Novel: *A Conspiracy of Paper*, David Liss.
Best Critical/Biographical: *The American Regional Mystery*, Marvin Lachman.
Best Short Story: "A Candle for Christmas", Reginald Hill (*EQMM*, January 2000).

Maltese Falcon Award

Presented annually since 1983 by the Japanese Maltese Falcon Society for the best hard-boiled mystery published in Japan (either original or, more often, in translation).

1983. *Early Autumn*, Robert B. Parker.
1984. *The Old Dick*, L.A. Morse
1985. *The Wrong Case*, James Crumley.
1986. *Hammett*, Joe Gores.
1987. *When the Sacred Ginmill Closes*, Lawrence Block.
1988. *Hard Line*, Michael Z. Lewin.
1989. *Strega*, Andrew Vachss.
1990. *The Girl I Killed*, Ryo Hara.
1991. *"F" is for Fugitive*, Sue Grafton.
1992. *A Ticket to the Boneyard*, Lawrence Block.
1993. *Book Case*, Stephen Greenleaf.

1994. *A Cool Breeze on the Underground*, Don Winslow.
1995. *The Black Ice*, Michael Connelly.
1996. no award.
1997. *White Jazz*, James Ellroy.
1998. no award.
1999. *The Big Blowdown*, George P. Pelecanos.
2000. no award.

[Philip] Marlowe Award

Issued annually by the Raymond Chandler Society at the Department of Language & Literature at the University of Ulm. The society was founded in 1991 and holds a symposium every July where it presents two awards – the best German language crime novel and the best International crime novel. A third award for best German language short story was added in 1996. The following lists the International winners.

1992. *Called by a Panther*, Michael Z. Lewin
1993. *Guardian Angel*, Sara Paretsky.
1994. *The Sculptress*, Minette Walters.
1995. *The Burglar Who Traded Ted Williams*, Lawrence Block.
1996. *Animals,* Simon Beckett.
1997. *The Poet*, Michael Connolly.
1998. *Musclebound*, Liza Cody.
1999. *The Sweet Forever*, George Pelecanos.
2000. no award.
2001. *Tracking Time*, Leslie Glass.

Martin Beck Award *see* Swedish Academy of Detection

Mary Higgins Clark Award *see under* Edgar Award

Ned Kelly Award

Presented annually since 1996 (no award 1998) by the Crime Writers Association of Australia for the best crime works by Australian writers. They are named after Australia's most famous outlaw.

1996.
Best Australian Crime Novel: (tie) *The Malcontenta*, Barry Maitland; *Inside Dope*, Paul Thomas.
Best First Australian Crime Novel: *Dark Angel*, John Dale.
Lifelong Contribution: Jon Cleary.

1997.
Best Australian Crime Novel: *Brush Off*, Shane Maloney.

Best First Australian Crime Novel: (tie) *Bad Debts*, Peter Temple; *Get Rich Quick*, Peter Doyle.
Best Non-fiction: *How to Write Crime*, Marele Day.
Lifelong Contribution: Peter Yates (Carter Brown).

1999.
Best Australian Crime Novel: *Amaze Your Friends*, Peter Doyle.
Best First Australian Crime Novel: *The Last Days*, Andrew Masterson.
Lifelong Contribution: Peter Corris.

2000.
Best Australian Crime Novel: *Shooting Star*, Peter Temple.
Best First Australian Crime Novel: *The Wooden Leg of Inspector Anders*, Marshall Browne.
Best True Crime: (tie) *Huckstepp: A Dangerous Life*, John Dale; *Underbelly 3*, John Silvester & Andrew Rule.
Lifelong Contribution:

2001.
Best Australian Crime Novel: (tie) *Dead Point*, Peter Temple; *The Second Coming*, Andrew Masterson.
Best First Australian Crime Novel: *Last Drinks*, Andrew McGahn.
Best True Crime: *Broken Lives*, Estelle Blackburn.
Crime Factory Magazine Readers' Vote: *Bleeding Hearts*, Lindy Cameron.
Lifetime Achievement: Stephen Knight.

Nero Wolfe Award

Presented annually since 1979 at their annual dinner, the Black Orchid Banquet, each December by the Wolfe Pack, devotees of the work of Rex Stout, for the book that best represents the spirit of the Nero Wolfe novels.

1979. *The Burglar Who Liked to Quote Kipling*, Lawrence Block.
1980. *Burn This*, Helen McCloy.
1981. *Death in a Tenured Position*, Amanda Cross.
1982. *Past, Present and Murder*, Hugh Pentecost.
1983. *The Anodyne Necklace*, Martha Grimes.
1984. *Emily Dickinson is Dead*, Jane Langton.
1985. *Sleeping Dog*, Dick Lochte.
1986. *Murder in E Minor*, Robert Goldsborough.
1987. *The Corpse in Oozak's Pond*, Charlotte MacLeod.
1988-90. no award.
1991. *Coyote Waits*, Tony Hillerman.
1992. *A Scandal in Belgravia*, Robert Barnard.
1993. *Booked to Die*, John Dunning.
1994. *Old Scores*, Aaron Elkins.
1995. *She Walks These Hills*, Sharyn McCrumb.
1996. *A Monstrous Regiment of Women*, Laurie R. King.

1997. *The Poet*, Michael Connelly.
1998. *Sacred*, Dennis Lehane.
1999. *Coffin Dancer*, Jeffery Deaver.
2000. *Coyote Revenge*, Fred Harris.
2001. *The Sugar House*, Laura Lippman.

Raven Award *see under* Edgar Award

Robert L. Fish Award *see under* Edgar Award

Swedish Academy of Detection

Since 1971 this Academy has presented a range of awards for crime fiction including one for Best Foreign Novel. In 1996 this was renamed the Martin Beck Award (after Per Wahlöö's detective). The awards are given by a jury formed by members of the Academy and takes the form of a diploma. There are also awards for the best Swedish crime novel, first novel, children and young adult, TV, films, editors and occasionally for non-fiction. There is also a Grand Master award. The following lists just the Best Foreign novel and the Grand Master winners only.

1971. Best Foreign: *The 31st of February*, Julian Symons.
1972. Best Foreign: *The Day of the Jackal*, Frederick Forsyth.
Grand Master: Agatha Christie, Ellery Queen.
1973. Best Foreign: *The Walter Syndrome*, Richard Neely
Grand Master: John Dickson Carr, Rex Stout.
1974. Best Foreign: *Malice Aforethought*, Francis Iles.
Grand Master: Eric Ambler, Georges Simenon.
1975. Best Foreign: *Rendezvous in Black*, Cornell Woolrich.
Grand Master: Michael Innes, Vic Suneson.
1976. Best Foreign: *The Last of Philip Banter/Devil Take the Blue-Tail Fly*, John Franklin Bardin.
Grand Master: Ross Macdonald, Ed McBain.
1977. Best Foreign: *Dangerous Davies*, Leslie Thomas.
Grand Master: Julian Symons.
1978. Best Foreign: *Other Paths to Glory*, Anthony Price.
Grand Master: Graham Greene.
1979. Best Foreign: *Recoil*, Brian Garfield.
Grand Master: Patricia Highsmith.
1980. Best Foreign: *Make Death Love Me*, Ruth Rendell.
Grand Master: W.R. Burnett, Geoffrey Household.
1981. Best Foreign: *L'été meurtrier* [*One Deadly Summer*], Sebastien Japrisot.
Grand Master: Bernard Borge, Michael Gilbert, Christianna Brand, Hillary Waugh, Dorothy B. Hughes.
1982. Best Foreign: *The Scent of Fear*, Margaret Yorke.
Grand Master: Jan Broberg.

1983. Best Foreign: *Le commissaire dans la truffière*, Pierre Magnan [France].
Grand Master: no award.
1984. Best Foreign: *Berlin Game*, Len Deighton.
Grand Master: no award.
1985. Best Foreign: *LaBrava*, Elmore Leonard.
Grand Master: no award.
1986. Best Foreign: *A Perfect Spy*, John Le Carré.
Grand Master: Allen J. Hubin.
1987. Best Foreign: *Harjunpää ja kiusantekijät* [*Harjunpää and the Stone Murders*], Matti Joensuu [Finland]
Grand Master: no award.
1988. Best Foreign: *Presumed Innocent*, Scott Turow.
Grand Master: Hammond Innes.
1989. Best Foreign: *Mørklægning* ["Blackout"], Anders Bodelsen [Denmark]
Grand Master: John Le Carré.
1990. Best Foreign: *Chinaman's Chance*, Ross Thomas.
Grand Master: no award.
1991. Best Foreign: *Weinschröter, du musst hängen* [*How Many Miles to Babylon?*], Doris Gercke [Germany]
Grand Master: no award.
1992. Best Foreign: *Los mares del Sur* [*Southern Seas*], Manuel Vázquez Montalbán [Spain]
Grand Master: no award.
1993. Best Foreign: *Het gouden ei* [*The Vanishing*], Tim Krabbé [Netherlands]
Grand Master: Tony Hillerman.
1994. Best Foreign: *Het woeden der gehele wereld* ["The Rage of the Whole World"], Maarten 't Hart [Netherlands]
Grand Master: no award.
1995. Best Foreign: *A Simple Plan*, Scott Smith
Grand Master: no award.
1996. Martin Beck award: *Snow Falling on Cedars*, David Guterson.
Grand Master: P.D. James, Ruth Rendell.
1997. Martin Beck award: *Morality Play*, Barry Unsworth.
Grand Master: Jan Ekström.
1998. Martin Beck award: *Under the Beetle's Cellar*, Mary Willis Walker.
Grand Master: no award.
1999. Martin Beck award: *An Instance of the Fingerpost*, Iain Pears.
Grand Master: no award.
2000. Martin Beck award: *The Chatham School Affair*, Thomas H. Cook.
Grand Master: Colin Dexter.
2001. Martin Beck award: *In a Dry Season*, Peter Robinson.
Grand Master: no award.

Shamus Award

A plaque presented annually since 1982 at Bouchercon by the Private Eye Writers of America (PWA) to honor work of excellence in the Private Eye genre. Winners are chosen by a committee of members of the PWA. The award for Lifetime Achievement is called "the Eye". The joint St. Martin's Press/PWA Best First Novel contest is for *unpublished* works.

1982.
Best P.I. Hardcover: *Hoodwink*, Bill Pronzini.
Best Original P.I. Paperback: *California Thriller*, Max Byrd.
Lifetime Achievement: Ross Macdonald.

1983.
Best P.I. Hardcover: *Eight Million Ways to Die*, Lawrence Block.
Best Original P.I. Paperback: *The Cana Diversion*, William Campbell Gault.
Best P.I. Short Story: "What You Don't Know Can't Hurt You", John Lutz (*AHMM*, November 1982).
Lifetime Achievement: Mickey Spillane.

1984.
Best P.I. Hardcover: *True Detective*, Max Allan Collins.
Best Original P.I. Paperback: *Dead in Centerfield*, Paul Engelman.
Best P.I. Short Story: "Cat's Paw", Bill Pronzini (chapbook).
Lifetime Achievement: William Campbell Gault.

1985.
Best P.I. Hardcover: *Sugartown*, Loren D. Estleman.
Best Original P.I. Paperback: *Ceiling of Hell*, Warren Murphy.
Best First P.I. Novel: *A Creative Kind of Killer*, Jack Early.
Best P.I. Short Story: "By the Dawn's Early Light", Lawrence Block (*Playboy*, August 1984).
Lifetime Achievement: Howard Browne.

1986.
Best P.I. Hardcover: *"B" is for Burglar*, Sue Grafton.
Best Original P.I. Paperback: *Poverty Bay*, Earl Emerson.
Best First P.I. Novel: *Hardcover*, Wayne Warga.
St. Martins' Press/PWA Best First P.I. Novel: "An Infinite Number of Monkeys", Les Roberts.
Best P.I. Short Story: "Eight Mile and Dequindre", Loren D. Estleman (*AHMM*, May 1985).
Lifetime Achievement: Richard S. Prather.

1987.
Best P.I. Hardcover: *The Staked Goat*, Jeremiah Healy.
Best Original P.I. Paperback: *The Back Door Man*, Rob Kantner.
Best First P.I. Novel: *Jersey Tomatoes*, J.W. Rider.
St. Martins' Press/PWA Best First P.I. Novel: "Fear of the Dark", Gar Anthony Haywood.
Best P.I. Short Story: "Fly Away Home", Rob Kantner (*Mean Streets*, ed. Robert J. Randisi).
Lifetime Achievement: Bill Pronzini.

1988.

Best P.I. Hardcover: *A Tax in Blood*, Benjamin Schutz.

Best Original P.I. Paperback: *Wild Night*, L.J. Washburn.

Best First P.I. Novel: *Death on the Rocks*, Michael Allegretto.

St. Martins' Press/PWA Best First P.I. Novel: "Katwalk", Karen Kijewski.

Best P.I. Short Story: "Turn Away", Ed Gorman (*Black Lizard Anthology of Crime Fiction*, ed. Ed Gorman).

Lifetime Achievement: (joint) Dennis Lynds; Wade Miller (Robert Wade & Bob Miller).

1989.

Best P.I. Hardcover: *Kiss*, John Lutz

Best Original P.I. Paperback: *Dirty Work*, Rob Kantner.

Best First P.I. Novel: *Fear of the Dark*, Gar Anthony Haywood.

St. Martins' Press/PWA Best First P.I. Novel: "Kindred Crimes", Janet Dawson.

Best P.I. Short Story: "The Crooked Way", Loren D. Estleman (*A Matter of Crime, volume 3*, ed. Matthew J. Bruccoli & Richard Layman).

1990.

Best P.I. Hardcover: *Extenuating Circumstances*, Jonathan Valin.

Best Original P.I. Paperback: *Hell's Only Half Full*, Rob Kantner.

Best First P.I. Novel: *Katwalk*, Karen Kijewski.

St. Martins' Press/PWA Best First P.I. Novel: "The Loud Adios", Ken Kuhlken.

Best P.I. Short Story: "The Killing Man", Mickey Spillane (*Playboy*, December 1989).

1991.

Best P.I. Hardcover: *"G" is for Gumshoe*, Sue Grafton.

Best Original P.I. Paperback: *Rafferty: Fatal Sisters*, W. Glenn Duncan.

Best First P.I. Novel: *Devil in a Blue Dress*, Walter Mosley.

St. Martins' Press/PWA Best First P.I. Novel: "A Sudden Death at the Norfolk Cafe", Winona Sullivan.

Best P.I. Short Story: "Final Resting Place", Marcia Muller (*Justice for Hire*, ed. Robert J. Randisi).

Lifetime Achievement: Roy Huggins.

1992.

Best P.I. Hardcover: *Stolen Away*, Max Allan Collins.

Best Original P.I. Paperback: *Cool Blue Tomb*, Paul Kemprecos.

Best First P.I. Novel: *Suffer Little Children*, Thomas Davis.

St. Martins' Press/PWA Best First P.I. Novel: "Storm Warning", A.C. Ayres (published as *Hour of the Manatee*).

Best P.I. Short Story: "Dust Devil", Nancy Pickard (*The Armchair Detective*, Winter 1991).

Lifetime Achievement: Joseph Hansen.

1993.
Best P.I. Hardcover: *The Man Who Was Taller Than God*, Harold Adams.
Best Original P.I. Paperback: *The Last Tango of Delores Delgado*, Marele Day.
Best First P.I. Novel: *The Woman Who Married a Bear*, John Straley.
St. Martins' Press/PWA Best First P.I. Novel: "The Harry Chronicles", Allan Pedrazas.
Best P.I. Short Story: "Mary, Mary, Shut the Door", Benjamin Schutz (*Deadly Allies*, ed. Robert J. Randisi & Marilyn Wallace).
Lifetime Achievement: Marcia Muller.

1994.
Best P.I. Novel: *The Devil Knows You're Dead*, Lawrence Block.
Best Original P.I. Paperback: *Brothers and Sinners*, Rodman Philbrick.
Best First P.I. Novel: *Satan's Lambs*, Lynn Hightower.
St. Martins' Press/PWA Best First P.I. Novel: "The Heaven Stone", David Daniel.
Best P.I. Short Story: "The Merciful Angel of Death", Lawrence Block (*New Mystery*, ed. Jerome Charyn).
Lifetime Achievement: Stephen J. Cannell.

1995.
Best P.I. Novel: *"K" is for Killer*, Sue Grafton.
Best Original P.I. Paperback: *Served Cold*, Ed Goldberg.
Best First P.I. Novel: *A Drink Before the War*, Dennis Lehane.
St. Martins' Press/PWA Best First P.I. Novel: "Diamond Head", Charles Knief.
Best P.I. Short Story: "Necessary Brother", Brendan DuBois (*EQMM*, May 1994).
Lifetime Achievement: (joint) John Lutz & Robert B. Parker.

1996.
Best P.I. Novel: *Concourse*, S.J. Rozan.
Best Original P.I. Paperback: *Native Angels*, William Jaspersohn.
Best First P.I. Novel: *The Innocents*, Richard Barre.
St. Martins' Press/PWA Best First P.I. Novel: no award.
Best P.I. Short Story: "And Pray Nobody Sees You", Gar Anthony Haywood (*Spooks, Spies, and Private Eyes*, ed. Paula L. Woods).

1997.
Best P.I. Novel: *Sunset Express*, Robert Crais.
Best Original P.I. Paperback: *Fade Away*, Harlan Coben.
Best First P.I. Novel: *This Dog for Hire*, Carol Lea Benjamin.
St. Martins' Press/PWA Best First P.I. Novel: "A Cold Day in Paradise", Steve Hamilton..
Best P.I. Short Story: "Dead Drunk", Lia Matera (*Guilty as Charged*, ed. Scott Turlow).
Lifetime Achievement: Stephen Marlowe.

1998.
Best P.I. Novel: *Come Back Dead*, Terence Faherty.
Best Original P.I. Paperback: *Charm City*, Laura Lippman.
Best First P.I. Novel: *Big Red Tequilla,* Rick Riordan.
St. Martins' Press/PWA Best First P.I. Novel: "The Losers' Club", Lise S. Baker.
Best P.I. Short Story: "Love Me for my Yellow Hair Alone", Carolyn Wheat (*Marilyn: Shades of Blonde*, ed. Carole Nelson Douglas).

1999.
Best P.I. Hardcover: *Boobytrap*, Bill Pronzini.
Best Original P.I. Paperback: *Murder Manual*, Steve Womack.
Best First P.I. Novel: *A Cold Day in Paradise*, Steve Hamilton.
St. Martins' Press/PWA Best First P.I. Novel: "Street Legal", Robert Truluck.
Best P.I. Short Story: "Another Day, Another Dollar", Warren Murphy (*Murder on the Run*, ed. Adams Round Table).
Lifetime Achievement: Maxine O'Callaghan.

2000.
Best P.I. Hardcover: *California Fire and Life*, Don Winslow.
Best Original P.I. Paperback: *In Big Trouble*, Laura Lippman.
Best First P.I. Novel: *Every Dead Thing*, John Connolly.
Best P.I. Short Story: "Akitada's First Case", I.J. Parker (*AHMM*, July/August 1999).
Lifetime Achievement: Edward D. Hoch.

2001.
Best P.I. Hardcover: *Havana Heat*, Carolina Garcia-Aguilera.
Best Original P.I. Paperback: *Death in the Steel City*, Thomas Lipinski.
Best First P.I. Novel: *Street Level*, Bob Truluck.
Best P.I. Short Story: "The Road's End" Brendan DuBois (*EQMM*, April 2000).
Lifetime Achievement: no award.

Sherlock Award

Presented annually by *Sherlock Holmes: The Detective Magazine* for the best detective appearing in a crime novel, split into three categories.

1999.
Best British Detective: John Harvey's Charlie Resnick in *Last Rites*.
Best Detective Created by an American: Robert B. Parker's Spenser.
Best Comic Detective: Sparkle Hayter's Robin Hudson.
Special Sherlock for Holmesian research: Leslie S. Klinger for his annotated edition of *The Adventures of Sherlock Holmes*.

2000.
Best British Detective: Colin Dexter's Inspector Morse.
Best Detective Created by an American: Patricia Cornwell's Kay Scarpetta.

Best Comic Detective: Lindsey Davis's Marcus Didius Falco.
Special Sherlock for Holmesian research: Michael Cox for *A Study in Celluloid*.

2001.
Best British Detective: Ian Rankin's Inspector Rebus.
Best Detective Created by an American: Michael Connelly's Detective Sergeant Harry Bosch.
Best Comic Detective: Christopher Brookmyre's Jack Parlabane.
Special Sherlock: June Thompson for her "biography" of Holmes and Watson.
Best TV Detective: *Inspector Morse*.

Trophy 813 Award

Presented annually since 1981 by the French Sociète 813, the French professional crime writer's association. The award is named after the novel, *813* by Maurice Leblanc, featuring the adventures of Arsène Lupin, published in 1910. There are categories for Best Novel, short story/collection, graphic novel, film, TV series, critical work and best reprint. The categories are open to works in translation as well as French works. In 1994 the best novel category was split specifically to include a Best Foreign Novel and these are listed below.

1994. *Cosa Facil*, Paco Ignacio Taïbo II (Cuban)
1995. *Not Till the Red Fog Rises*, Robin Cook
1996. *From Potter's Field*, Patricia Cornwell.
1997. *Raphaël*, Gregory McDonald.
1998. *Burning Angel*, James Lee Burke.
1999. *The Ax*, Donald E. Westlake.
2000. *Smoke*, Donald E. Westlake.
2001. *The Cold Six Thousand*, James Ellroy.

Appendix 2
Current Magazines and Websites

Magazines

Once upon a time there was a proliferation of crime and mystery fiction magazines, of which the best known and most influential was *Black Mask*, which ran for 340 issues from 1920 to 1951. It ended with the death of the pulp magazines, which also marked the transition from the old world to the new. The fifties saw plenty of digest magazines, of which the most influential was *Manhunt* (1953-67; 113 issues) but these in turn faded away in the sixties and now only a handful of crime-fiction magazines survive. The following lists all current fiction magazines plus a selection of useful non-fiction reference and review magazines.

Alfred Hitchcock's Mystery Magazine [US]
Published since 1956. Current publisher: Dell Magazines. Current editor: Linda Landrigan. Monthly, but combined July/August issue. Subscription address: P.O. Box 54011, Boulder, Colorado 80322-4011.
Website: <www.themysteryplace.com>.
Originally an independent publication but now a sister title to *Ellery Queen's Mystery Magazine*. In honour of its eponymous patron, the magazine specializes in clever, unusual and often macabre stories, usually with a twist ending. The emphasis is on detective stories, with a lot of P.I. fiction, and its contents are slightly more hard-boiled than its companion. Regular *Alfred Hitchcock* anthologies have been compiled from its contents over the years.

Ellery Queen's Mystery Magazine [US]
Published since 1941. Current publisher: Dell Magazines. Current editor: Janet Hutchings. Monthly, but combined September/October issue. Subscription address: P.O. Box 54052, Boulder, Colorado 80322-4052. Website: <www.themysteryplace.com>.
The oldest surviving crime and mystery magazine with over 700 issues published. For many years it was edited by Frederick Dannay, one half of the Ellery Queen writing team. It has always favoured the more traditional form of crime fiction, with a fair share of mystery stories. It publishes a lot of puzzle stories, but not too many "cozies". Edward D. HOCH holds an astonishing record of having appeared in every issue since May 1973. It encourages new writers and has run a "Department of First Stories" for many years. Stories from the magazine frequently win awards, and many anthologies have been derived from the contents. Both *EQMM* and *AHMM* have readers' forums at their website.

Crime Factory [Australia]
Published since February 2001. Publisher: Shiv Publishing. Editor: David

Honeybone. Quarterly. Editorial/Subscription address: C/- Preston P.O., 3 Gilbert Road, Preston, Victoria 3072. Website: <www.crimefactory.net>.
Since the end of *Mean Streets* in 1999, *Crime Factory* is now Australia's only magazine of crime fiction. It concentrates mostly on homegrown fiction, plus interviews, features, film, comics, true crime and reviews. International appeal with an Australian slant.

Crimewave [UK]
Published since 1999. Publisher: TTA Press. Editor: Andy Cox. Twice yearly. Editorial/Subscription address: 5 Martins Lane, Witcham, Ely, CB6 2LB.Website: <www.tta-press.freewire.co.uk>.
The only British all-fiction crime magazine. In its short life it has already garnered much praise and published award-winning stories. Its contents lean towards dark suspense and noir with a modern cutting edge.

Hardboiled [US]
Published since 1988. Publisher: Gryphon Books. Editor: Gary Lovisi. A double-issue per year. Editorial/Subscription address: PO Box 280-209, Brooklyn, New York 1228-0209. Website: <www.gryphonbooks.com>.
More like an annual anthology these days. It began life as an amateur publication called *Detective Story Magazine*, but later took over the title of another amateur magazine, *Hardboiled*. As the title says, it runs mostly hard-boiled crime and P.I. fiction, with some news and feature columns.

Shots [UK]
Published since 1994. Publisher: Shots Collective. Editor: Mike Stotter. Three issues a year. Subscription address: 56 Alfred St., Ripley, Derbyshire, DE5 3LD.Website: <www.shotsmag.co.uk>.
Began as an amateur magazine called *Shots in the Dark* but has steadily evolved into a substantial glossy magazine. It publishes mostly articles and interviews, though tries to squeeze one or two stories into each issue. Since issue #11 it has become an on-line web magazine.

The Strand Magazine [US]
Published since 1998. Publisher: The Strand Magazine. Editor: Andrew F. Gulli. Twice yearly. Editorial/Subscription address: P.O. Box 1418, Birmingham, Michigan 48012-1418.Website: <www.strandmag.com>.
Although it has taken on the name of the venerable British magazine of popular fiction (which ran from 1891–1950) this new incarnation concentrates solely on crime and mystery fiction. It draws its inspiration from the original *Strand* as being the publisher of the Sherlock Holmes stories and other gaslight detectives and this magazine follows in those same footsteps with the emphasis on traditional crime fiction. It publishes four or five stories per issue plus interviews, articles and features.

Clues: A Journal of Detection [US]
Published since 1980. Publisher: Popular Press. Current editor: Pat Browne. Twice yearly. Subscription address: Bowling Green State University, Bowling

Green, Ohio 43403. Website: <www.bgsu.edu/offices/press/pp0017.html>
More of an academic publication with scholarly articles on the history, development and contribution of crime and mystery fiction to the popular culture.

Crime Time [UK]
Published since 1995. Publisher: Crime Time/Oldcastle Books. Current editor: Barry Forshaw. Five to six issues per year. Subscription address: 18 Coleswood Road, Harpenden, Herts. AL5 1EQ. Website: <www.crimetime.co.uk>
Primarily a magazine of news, reviews, interviews and informative articles. Publishes occasional fiction, mostly extracts from forthcoming novels. A substantial publication in paperback format it provides the most comprehensive coverage of crime fiction available in Britain. It covers the entire field but the emphasis is on hard-boiled and cutting-edge fiction. Recently issues have been theme based. It has an excellent website full of features and many useful hotlinks.

Deadly Pleasures [US]
Published since 1993. Publisher: Refunding Makes Cents, Inc. Publisher/Editor: George Easter. Quarterly. Subscription address: 1718 S. Ridge Point Drive, Bountiful, Utah 84010. Website: <www.deadlypleasures.com>
Primarily a review magazine though also publishes author interviews and feature articles on specific themes. It received the Anthony Award in 1999 as the Best Critical publication. Since 1997 it has presented the Barry Award for the best fiction of the year. It provides all-round coverage with no particular bias to any category.

The Drood Review [US]
Published since 1982. Publisher: Drood Review. Current editor: Jim Huang. Bimonthly. Subscription address: 484 East Carmel Drive #378, Carmel, Indiana 46032. Website: <www.droodreview.com>
As the title says this is wholly a review of crime and mystery fiction plus listings of forthcoming titles. It reviews around 150 books a year plus feature articles on the field and occasional specialist supplements.

Mystery Readers Journal [US]
Published since 1985. Publisher: Mystery Readers Journal. Editor: Janet A. Rudolph. Quarterly. Subscription address: PO Box 8116, Berkeley, California 94707. Website: <www.mysteryreaders.org>
The official publication of Mystery Readers International, the world's largest mystery fan organization. The magazine is devoted to articles and studies on specific authors and themes plus substantial reviews. Members of the organization vote annually to nominate and select the winners of the Macavity Award.

Mystery Scene [US]
Published since 1985. Publisher: Mystery Enterprises. Editor: Ed GORMAN. Bimonthly. Subscription address: 3601 Skylark Lane SE, Cedar Rapids, Iowa 52403. Website: <www.mysteryscene.cjb.net>
The main news magazine of the crime fiction field, providing a complete round-up of current and forthcoming events. Also runs extensive articles, interviews and

reviews. Usually has a featured author or authors each issue. Commissions no fiction but sometimes runs first chapters from novels.

Sherlock: The Detective Magazine [UK]
Published since 1991. Publisher: PMH Publications. Editor: David Stuart Davies. Bi-monthly. Subscription address: PO Box 100, Chichester, West Sussex.
Began as *The Sherlock Holmes Gazette* and was initially a slim magazine dedicated to Sherlock Holmes. It has since diversified and though the emphasis remains on matters Holmesian it provides a broader coverage of detective fiction, with a bias towards the traditional field, both old and new. Primarily non-fiction, with articles and reviews, it publishes one or two stories per issue. Since 1999 it has sponsored the Sherlock Award for the best fictional detective.

Websites

There is a mass of information on the Internet about crime fiction. There are also a number of web-based e-zines, though many of these are ephemeral and not of a high quality. The best webzine, *Blue Murder Magazine* (www.bluemurder.com) recently went into hiatus. Other recent webzines worth checking are *HandHeldCrime* (www.handheldcrime.com) and *Nefarious Tales of Mystery* (www.thewindjammer.com/nefarious/). The following does not attempt to list current webzines but does list a selection of useful sites that provide a lot of information available nowhere else and plenty of links to other sites and on-line publications. From the following you will be able to find almost everything relevant on the Web.

ClueLass
Website: <www.cluelass.com>. Run by Kate Derie.
An extensive site of reviews, news, awards, and a directory of shops and on-line sources. This site has now taken over the *Mysterious Home Page*, the first website for mystery fans founded by Jan B. Steffenson in 1994. That site provides a comprehensive guide and links to sites of interest on the web.

The Gumshoe Site
Website: <www.nsknet.or.jp/~jkimura>. Run by Jiro Kimura.
A Japanese site but in English. It is mostly a news site with immediate up-to-date details on events and developments, especially awards, forthcoming books, and author features. Although its title suggests an emphasis on private-eye fiction it covers news on the whole field.

Magical Mystery Tour
Website: <http://members.home.net/monkshould>. Run by Sue Feder.
Essentially a book review site (around 1000), predominantly mystery fiction, but also occasional feature articles on specific writers. There are also links to Sue's Historical Mystery Appreciation Society.

The Mysterious Home Page see under *ClueLass*

Mysterious Readers
Website: <www.mysteriousreaders.com>. Run by Angie Dixon.
A fan site providing reviews, a discussion forum, an e-zine (*Mysterious Happenings*), interviews, games, quizzes and reading groups. A much more informal way to share information on mystery fiction, it also has an impressive page of links to other sites.

The Mystery Reader
Website: <www.themysteryreader.com>. Run by D.N. Anderson.
Primarily an extensive book review site but also with a growing number of other features including author spotlights, guides to specialist small press publishers and thematic sites such as "police/detective", "suspense", "historical".

Mystery Vault
Website: <www.mysteryvault.net>.
This is a link page and archive to an extensive array of fan sites, forums, discussion groups and newsletters. It includes the long-running "DorothyL Mystery Literature Forum", which has been running since 1995, the "Sisters-in-Crime Internet Chapter", the "Gaslight Digest" and publishers' newsletters.

Stop, You're Killing Me!
Website: <www.stopyourekillingme.com/index.html>. Run by Bonnie Brown.
This site lists the books of several hundred writers organized by series and non-series and with hotlinks to book ordering sites. It is also developing a number of thematic sites. A handy quick reference to help track down your favourite author's latest books.

Tangled Web
Website: <www.twbooks.co.uk>.
A site dedicated to crime, mystery and fantastic fiction. It has over 400 author profiles and bibliographies, extensive reviews and coverage of books since the site was established in 1996, special features and interviews and a discussion forum.

The Thrilling Detective
Website: <www.thrillingdetective.com>. Run by Kevin Burton Smith.
One of the most impressive and thorough sites on the internet. It is devoted to private-eye fiction, though generously spills over into related fiction if applicable. In addition to pages for hundreds of fictional detectives it also has essays on key authors, extensive bibliographies and pages on awards and magazines.

The Ultimate Mystery/Detective Web Guide
Website: <www.magicdragon.com/UltimateMystery/index.html>.
For once the title means what it says. This extremely ambitious site covers a wide variety of genre-based fiction, and the mystery section has details on almost 2,500 authors (over 700 of them with hotlinks), plus coverage of television series, films, magazines, bookstores and games. The site is still developing but it is already very impressive.

Index to Key Characters and Series

This provides a quick handy reference to all of the major key characters or series with an index to their author included in 'Books and Authors' or the relevant film/TV series in 'TV and Films'.

Cade, Chief Constable Alan – see TV series *The Chief*
Cade, Sam – see TV series *Cade's County*
Cadfael, Brother – Ellis Peters
Cagney, Chris – see TV series *Cagney & Lacey*
Cain series – Peter Corris as Sean A. Key
Cain, Jenny – Nancy Pickard
Calder & Behrends – Michael Gilbert
Callahan, Harry – see film *Dirty Harry* and sequels
Callan, David – James Mitchell
Campbell, Liam – Dana Stabenow
Canaletto – Janet Laurence
Cannon, Frank – see TV series *Cannon*
Canterbury Tales – Paul C. Doherty
Cardoza, Cheryl – Elizabeth Peters as Barbara Michaels
Carella, Steve (87th Precinct) – Ed McBain
Carey, Neal – Don Winslow
Carey, Robert – Patricia Finney as P.F. Chisholm
Carlyle, Carlotta – Linda Barnes
Carmody – Bill Pronzini as Alex Saxon
Carnaby-King, Det Sgt – Nicholas Rhea as Peter N. Walker
Carpenter & Quincannon – Bill Pronzini
Carrick, Webb – Bill Knox
Carter, Don – see TV series *Shadow Squad*
Carter, Sgt George – see TV series *The Sweeney*
Carter, Jack – Ted Lewis
Carter, Nick – created by John R. Coryell for the *Nick Carter* dime novels in 1886 and continued in magazines through to 1936. The character was resurrected for a series of monthly paperbacks in 1964 running to 1990. Early writers of this series were Valerie Moolman and Michael Avallone. Others included in this encyclopedia are Thomas Chastain, Michael Collins, Bill Crider, Michael Jahn, Robert J. Randisi and Martin Cruz Smith.
Caruso, Enrico – Barbara Paul
Carvalho, Pepe – Manuel Vázquez Montalbán
Carver, Fred – John Lutz
Casella, Tony – Larry Beinhart
Castang, Henri – Nicolas Freeling
Castlemere series (Inspector Liz Graham & D.C.I. Frank Shapiro) – Jo Bannister
Cates, Molly – Mary Willis Walker
Celebrity Murder series – George Baxt
Cervantes, Chico – Bruce Cook
Chalice, Henry – Donald MacKenzie
Chamberlain, Lindsay – Beverly Connor
Champion, Kyle – Harold Adams
Chandler, Elly – see TV series *Chandler & Co.*
Chee, Jim – Tony Hillerman
Childs, Sunny – Walter Sorrells as Ruth Birmingham
Chin, Lydia – S.J. Rozan
Christopher, Bob – Robert R. Irvine

Hill, Dr Tony – Val McDermid
Hiscock, Inspector – Jeremy Potter
Ho, Johnny – see TV series *The Chinese Detective*
Hockaday, Neil – Thomas Adcock
Hoggett, Ron – James Mitchell
Holbrook, Matt – see TV series *The Detectives*
Holden, Sidney – Jerome Charyn
Holland, Billy Bob – James Lee Burke
Holland, Rosie – Jo Bannister
Holloway, Barbara – Kate Wilhelm
Holmes, Sherlock – created by Arthur Conan Doyle in 1887. Even before Doyle's death there were pastiches and parodies and in the last thirty years it has become an industry. Authors covered in this encyclopedia include Michael Dibdin, Carole Nelson Douglas, Loren Estleman, H.R.F. Keating, Laurie R. King, Michael Kurland, Robert Richardson, Donald Thomas, June Thomson and M.J. Trow. See also the Schlock Homes stories by Robert L. Fish, the Sheridan Haynes novels by Julian Symons and the novel about Conan Doyle and Dr Joseph Bell by Howard Engel.
Homes, Schlock – Robert L. Fish
Hooker, T.J. – see TV series *T.J. Hooker*.
Hope, Matthew – Ed McBain
Hopkins, Lloyd – James Ellroy
Hopkins, Marty – P.M. Carlson
Houston, Matt – see TV series *Matt Houston*
Howard, Jeri – Janet Dawson
Howe, Emma – Gillian Roberts
Hoyland, Tamara – Jessica Mann
Hudson, Robin – Sparkle Hayter
Hunt, Gil & Claire – Robert J. Randisi
Hunter, Leah – Kay Mitchell as Sarah Lacey
Hunter, Rick – see TV series *Hunter*
Hutchinson, Ken – see TV series *Starsky & Hutch*
Huuygens, Kek – Robert L. Fish
Ichiro, Sano – Laura Joh Rowland
Ihaka, Tito – Paul Thomas
Imanishi, Inspector – Seichō Matsumoto
Inquisitor, The – Martin Cruz Smith as Simon Quinn
Iris House series – Jean Hager
Irish, Jack – Peter Temple
Ironside, Robert T. – see TV series *Ironside*
Isaac the Physician – Caroline Roe
Ivory, Kate – Veronica Stallwood
Jackson, Kane – Michael Collins as William Arden
Jackson, Ken – Anthea Fraser
Jacoby, Miles 'Kid' – Robert J. Randisi
Jacovich, Milan – Les Roberts
James, Det Sgt Gemma & Kincaid, Supt Duncan – Deborah Crombie
Jameson, Cass – Carolyn Wheat

Marklin, Peter – Neville Steed
Marks series – Dorothy Salisbury Davis
Marsala, Cat – Barbara D'Amato
Marshall, Owen – see TV series *Owen Marshall, Counselor-at-Law*
Martin, Saz – Stella Duffy
Martinelli, Kate – Laurie R. King
Martins, DCI Harriet – H.R.F. Keating
Marx, Groucho – real character in novels by Ron Goulart
Marz, Stella – Richard North Patterson
Mason, Perry – created by Erle Stanley Gardner in 1933. Series was continued briefly by Thomas Chastain. See also Steve Winslow novels by Parnell Hall.
Mason, Tom – Mark R. Zubro
Masters, Caroline – Richard North Patterson
Masters, Superintendent George & Green, Inspector Bill – Douglas Clark
Masuto, Masao – Howard Fast as E.V. Cunningham
Matlock, Benjamin L. – see TV series *Matlock*
Matthews, Chief Dan – see TV series *Highway Patrol*
Matthews, Daphne – Ridley Pearson
Mavity, H.J. & Spanner, Ben – Ron Goulart
Maxwell, Peter – M.J. Trow
Maybridge, Tom – B.M. Gill
M'butu, Sergeant – Walter Satterthwait
Mearns & Denny – Butler, Gwendoline
Medway, Bruce – Robert Wilson
Meehan, Alvirah – Mary Higgins Clark
Meiklejohn, Charlie – Kate Wilhelm
Mendoza, Lieut Luis – Elizabeth Linington as Dell Shannon
Menlo, Anne – Maxine O'Callaghan
Mensing, Loren – Francis Nevins
Middleton-Brown, David & Kingsley, Lucy (Book of Psalms series) – Kate Charles
Midnight Louie & Barr, Temple – Carole Nelson Douglas
Milano, Johnny – Stanley Ellin
Millhone, Kinsey – Sue Grafton
Milodragovitch, Milo – James Crumley
Milton, DCS James – Ruth Dudley Edwards
Minogue, Sgt/Inspector Matt – John Brady
Mitchell, DC Benny – Pauline Bell
Mitchell, Meredith & Markby, Alan – Ann Granger
Mitchell, Michelle "Mitch" – Allyn, Doug
Mitchell, Scott – John Harvey
Monaghan, Tess – Laura Lippman
Monk, Osbert & Dittany – Charlotte MacLeod as Alisa Craig
Monk, Richard – Michael Underwood
Monk, William – Anne Perry
Montero, Britt – Edna Buchanan
Mooney, Bridget – P. M. Carlson
Moore, Toussaint – Ed Lacy

Thackeray, Michael & Ackroyd, Laura – Patricia Hall
Thane, DCI Colin & Moss, Inspector Phil – Bill Knox
Thanet, Inspector Luke – Dorothy Simpson
Thatcher, John Putnam – Emma Lathen
Thomson, Barney – Douglas Lindsay
Thorn – James W. Hall
Thornhill, Inspector – Andrew Taylor
Tibbett, Henry & Emma – Patricia Moyes
Tibbs, Virgil – John Ball
Tillman, Virgil – William Marshall
Tobin – Ed Gorman
Tobin, Mitchell – Donald E. Westlake as Tucker Coe
Tonneman family – Annette & Martin Meyers
Torelli, Lieut Michael – see TV series *Crime Story*
Tracy, Dick – created by Chester Gould in 1931 in a comic strip for the *Chicago Tribune*. Character continued in novels and comic strips by Max Allan Collins
Tracy, "Trace" – Warren Murphy
Treasure, Mark – David Williams
Trethowan, DI Perry – Robert Barnard
Trewley & Stone – Sarah J. Mason
Trimble, Lucy – Eric Wright
Trotti, Commissario – Timothy Williams
Turner, Jane & Beaumont, Philip – Walter Satterthwait
Turner, Milo – Francis Nevins
Turner, Paul – Mark R. Zubro
Underwood, Toni – Diane Mott Davidson
Underworld USA series – James Ellroy
Unwin, Harriet – H.R.F. Keating
Valentine, Claudia – Marele Day
Van der Valk, Piet – Nicolas Freeling
Van Larsen, Max & Plotkin, Sylvia – George Baxt
Vance, Tessa – Jennifer Rowe
Varaday, Fran – Ann Granger
Varallo, Vic – Elizabeth Linington as Lesley Egan
Vecchio, Ray – see TV series *Due South*
Velvet, Nick – Edward D. Hoch
Verity, Mr/Fathom, Mr – Anthony & Peter Shaffer
Verity, Sgt William – Donald Thomas as Francis Selwyn
Victor, Emma – Mary Wings
Wager, Gabe – Rex Burns
Wainthropp, Hetty – see TV series *Hetty Wainthropp Investigates*
Walker, Amos – Loren D. Estleman
Walker, Calico Jack – Paul Bishop
Walker, Diana – J.A. Jance
Walker, Superintendent Mike – Lynda La Plante
Wallis, Talba – Julie Smith
Walsh, Jack – Ed Gorman

Bibliography

This encyclopedia required considerable research. In addition to my own collection of books and magazines I have made extensive use of authors' own websites and other internet sites and magazines listed in Appendix 2. I have also consulted all of the following books and acknowledge here my indebtedness to the authors.

Bourgeau, Art, *The Mystery Lover's Companion*, New York: Crown, 1986.

Challen, Paul, *Get Dutch! A Biography of Elmore Leonard*, Toronto: ECW Press, 2000.

Cooper, John & Pike, B.A., *Detective Fiction: The Collector's Guide*, Aldershot: Scolar Press, 1994.

DeAndrea, William L., *Encyclopedia Mysteriosa*, New York: Prentice Hall, 1994.

Gorman, Ed & Greenberg, Martin H. (editors), *Speaking of Murder*, New York: Berkley, 1998; and *Speaking of Murder, Volume II*, New York: Berkley, 1999.

Goulart, Ron, *The Dime Detectives*, New York: The Mysterious Press, 1988.

Grape, Jan, James, Dean & Nehr, Ellen (editors), *Deadly Women*, New York: Carroll & Graf, 1998.

Hardy, Phil, *The BFI Companion to Crime*, London: Cassell, 1997.

Heising, Willetta L., *Detecting Men*, Dearborn: Purple Moon Press, 1998.

Heising, Willetta L., *Detecting Women*, Dearborn: Purple Moon Press, 2000 (3rd edition).

Herbert, Rosemary (editor), *The Oxford Companion to Crime & Mystery Writing*, New York: Oxford University Press, 1999.

Hubin, Allen J. (editor), *The Armchair Detective*, 1967–1997 (30 volumes)

Hubin, Allen J., *Crime Fiction III, A Comprehensive Bibliography 1749–1995* (CD-ROM version), Oakland: Locus Press, 1999.

Jakubowski, Maxim (editor), *100 Great Detectives*, London: Xanadu, 1991.

Keating, H.R.F., *The Bedside Companion to Crime*, London: Michael O'Mara, 1989.

Keating, H.R.F., *Crime & Mystery: The 100 Best Books*, New York: Carroll & Graf, 1987.

Keating, H.R.F., *Whodunit? A Guide to Crime, Suspense & Spy Fiction*, London: Windward, 1982.

Levinson, Richard & Link, William, *Stay Tuned, An Inside Look at the Making of Prime-Time Television*, New York: St. Martin's Press, 1981.

Lewis, Jon E. & Stempel, Penny, *Cult TV: The Detectives*, London: Pavilion Books, 1999.

Loder, John, *Australian Crime Fiction*, Port Melbourne: D.W. Thorpe, 1994.

McBride, Jim, *In Cold Blood*, Toronto: Crime Writers of Canada, 1997 (4th edition).

McCormick, Donald, *Who's Who in Spy Fiction*, London: Elm Tree Books, 1977.

McLeish, Kenneth & Valerie, *Bloomsbury Good Reading Guide to Murder, Crime Fiction & Thrillers*, London: Bloomsbury, 1990.

Moody, Susan, *The Hatchards Crime Companion*, London: Hatchards, 1990.

Mottram, James, *Public Enemies: The Gangster Movie A-Z*, London: Batsford, 1998.

Nichols, Victoria & Thompson, Susan, *Silk Stalkings*, Lanham, MD: Scarecrow Press, 1998.

Oleksiw, Susan, *A Reader's Guide to the Classic British Mystery*, London: Blandford Press, 1989.

Ousby, Ian, *The Crime and Mystery Book*, London: Thomas and Hudson, 1997.

Pederson, Jay P. (editor), *St. James Guide to Crime & Mystery Writers*, Detroit: St. James Press, 1996 (4th edition).

Penzler, Otto, Steinbrunner, Chris & Lachman, Marvin, *Detectionary*, Woodstock, NY: Overlook Press, 1977.

Penzler, Otto & Friedman, Mickey, *The Crown Crime Companion: The Top 100 Mystery Novels of All Time*, New York: Crown, 1995.

Pronzini, Bill & Muller, Marcia, *1001 Midnights*, New York: Arbor House, 1986.

Rennison, Nick & Shephard, Richard, *Waterstone's Guide to Crime Fiction*, Brentford: Waterstone's, 1997.

Rogers, Dave, *The ITV Encyclopedia of Adventure*, London: Boxtree, 1988.

Rowland, Susan, *From Agatha Christie to Ruth Rendell*, Basingstoke: Palgrave, 2001.

Skene-Melvin, David, *Canadian Crime Fiction*, Shelburne, Ontario: The Battered Silicon Dispatch Box, 1996.

Steinbrunner, Chris & Penzler, Otto, *Encyclopedia of Mystery & Detection*, New York: McGraw-Hill, 1976.

Stine, Kate, *The Armchair Detective Book of Lists*, New York: Otto Penzler Books, 1995.

Swanson, Jean & James, Dean, *By a Woman's Hand*, New York: Berkley, 1996 (2nd edition).

Swanson, Jean & James, Dean, *Killer Books*, New York: Berkley, 1998.

Symons, Julian, *Bloody Murder: From the Detective Story to the Crime Novel*, London: Faber, 1972, plus revisions.

Symons, Julian, *Criminal Practices*, London: Macmillan, 1994.

Other titles available from Robinson

The Mammoth Encyclopedia of Science Fiction Ed. George Mann **£9.99** ☐
This new encylopedia offers the most up-to-date guide to the world of Science Fiction. Arranged in an A–Z format, and featuring a comprehensive index and cross-referencing system, *The Mammoth Encyclopedia of Science Fiction* is the most accessible and easy to use encyclopedia of its kind currently available. Compiled by expert SF editor and author George Mann, this is a concise, informative and entertaining reference.

The Mammoth Book of Science Fiction Ed. Mike Ashley **£6.99** ☐
This anthology contains some of the best science fiction produced over the last 50 years. Twenty leading authors of the genre ask the question "What if . . .?" and give their own fascinating versions of the changes that will happen in the centuries to come, making this one of the most entertaining and thought-provoking anthologies in light years.

The Mammoth Book of How It Happened: The Titanic Ed. Geoff Tibballs **£7.99** ☐
Nothing could be as graphic or revealing as the recorded accounts of the eye-witnesses, those who were actually there. This book strips away the Hollywood gloss and tells the real story of the ship they called "unsinkable" stage by stage from her glorious launch in Belfast to the sombre burial at sea of those who had perished on her first and only voyage.

Robinson books are available from all good bookshops or can be ordered direct from the Publisher. Just tick the title you want and fill in the form below.

TBS Direct
Colchester Road, Frating Green, Colchester, Essex CO7 7DW
Tel: +44 (0) 1206 255777
Fax: +44 (0) 1206 255914
Email: sales@tbs-ltd.co.uk

UK/BFPO customers please allow £1.00 for p&p for the first book, plus 50p for the second, plus 30p for each additional book up to a maximum charge of £3.00. Overseas customers (inc. Ireland), please allow £2.00 for the first book, plus £1.00 for the second, plus 50p for each additional book.

Please send me the titles ticked above.

NAME (block letters) ....

ADDRESS ....

....

POSTCODE ....

I enclose a cheque/PO (payable to TBS Direct) for ....
I wish to pay by Switch/Credit card

Number ....

Card Expiry Date ....

Switch Issue Number ....